THE CRADLE WILL FALL

MARY HIGGINS CLARK grew up in New York with two burning ambitions – to travel and to write. Quickly she achieved both, first with an advertising agency and later when she became a stewardess with Pan Am.

She achieved remarkable success with short stories published in all the major American magazines and many in England, and when her husband died tragically, leaving her with five children to support, she turned to radio script writing, covering travel, history, food, fashion and current affairs.

Both *Where Are the Children?* and *A Stranger is Watching*, her second novel, were huge successes in America and elsewhere. *The Cradle Will Fall* is her latest novel.

MARY HIGGINS CLARK

The Cradle Will Fall

FONTANA/Collins

First published in 1980 by William Collins Sons & Co. Ltd.
First issued in Fontana Books 1981

© 1980 by Mary Higgins Clark

Made and printed in Great Britain by
William Collins Sons & Co Ltd Glasgow

Grow old along with me!
The best is yet to be,
The last of life, for which the first was made.

Robert Browning

*For some patients, though conscious that
their condition is perilous,
recover their health simply through
their contentment with the goodness of the physician.*

Hippocrates

CHAPTER ONE

If her mind had not been on the case she had won, Katie might not have taken the curve so fast, but the intense satisfaction of the guilty verdict was still absorbing her. It had been a close one. Roy O'Connor was one of the top defence attorneys in New Jersey. The defendant's confession had been suppressed by the court, a major blow for the prosecution. But still she had managed to convince the jury that Teddy Copeland was the man who had viciously murdered eighty-year-old Abigail Rawlings during a robbery.

Miss Rawlings's sister, Margaret, was in court to hear the verdict and afterwards had come up to Katie. 'You were wonderful, Mrs DeMaio,' she'd said. 'You look like a young college girl. I never would have thought you could, but when you talked, you *proved* every point; you made them *feel* what he did to Abby. What will happen now?'

'With his record, let's hope the judge decides to send him to prison for the rest of his life,' Katie answered.

'Thank God,' Margaret Rawlings had said. Her eyes, already moist and faded with age, filled with tears. Quietly she brushed them away as she said, 'I miss Abby so. There was just the two of us left. And I keep thinking how frightened she must have been. It would have been awful if he'd gotten away with it.'

'*He didn't get away with it!*' The memory of that reassurance distracted Katie now, made her press her foot harder on the accelerator. The sudden increase in speed as she rounded the curve made the car fishtail on the sleet-covered road.

'Oh . . . no!' She gripped the wheel frantically. The county road was dark. The car raced across the divider and spun around. From the distance she saw headlights approaching.

. She turned the wheel into the skid but could not control the car. It careened on to the shoulder of the road, but the shoulder too was a sheet of ice. Like a skier about to jump, the car poised for an instant at the edge of the shoulder, its wheels lifting as it slammed down the steep embankment into the wooded fields.

A dark shape loomed ahead: a tree. Katie felt the sickening crunch as metal tore into bark. The car shuddered. Her body was flung forward against the wheel, then slammed backward. She raised her arms in front of her face, trying to protect it from the splinters of flying glass that exploded from the windshield. Sharp, biting pain attacked her wrists and knees. The headlights and panel lights went out. Dark, velvety blackness was closing over her as from somewhere off in the distance she heard a siren.

The sound of the car door opening; a blast of cold air. 'My God, it's Katie DeMaio!'

A voice she knew. Tom Coughlin, that nice young cop. He testified at a trial last week.

'She's unconscious.'

She tried to protest, but her lips wouldn't form words. She couldn't open her eyes.

'The blood's coming from her arm. Looks like she's cut an artery.'

Her arm was being held; something tight was pressing against it.

A different voice: 'She may have internal injuries, Tom. Westlake's right down the road. I'll call for an ambulance. You stay with her.'

Floating. Floating. I'm all right. It's just that I can't reach you.

Hands lifting her on to a stretcher; she felt a blanket covering her, sleet pelting her face.

She was being carried. A car was moving. No, it was an ambulance. Doors opening and closing. If only she could make them understand. I can hear you. I'm not unconscious.

Tom was giving her name. 'Kathleen DeMaio, lives in Abbington. She's an assistant prosecutor. No, she's not married. She's a widow. Judge DeMaio's widow.'

John's widow. A terrible sense of aloneness. The blackness was starting to recede. A light was shining in her eyes. 'She's coming around. How old are you, Mrs DeMaio?'

The question, so practical, so easy to answer. At last she could speak. 'Twenty-eight.'

The tourniquet Tom had wrapped around her arm was being

removed. Her arm was being stitched. She tried not to wince at the needles of pain.

X-rays. The emergency-room doctor. 'You're quite fortunate, Mrs DeMaio. Some pretty severe bruises. No fractures. I've ordered a transfusion. Your blood count is pretty low. Don't be frightened. You'll be all right.'

'It's just . . .' She bit her lip. She was coming back into focus and managed to stop herself before she blurted out that terrible, unreasoning, childish fear of hospitals.

Tom asking, 'Do you want us to call your sister? They're going to keep you here overnight.

'No. Molly's just over the flu. They've all had it.' Her voice sounded so weak. Tom had to bend over to hear her.

'All right, Katie. Don't worry about anything. I'll have your car hauled out.'

She was wheeled into a curtained-off section of the emergency room. Blood began dripping through a tube inserted into her right arm. Her head was clearing now.

Her left arm and knees hurt so much. Everything hurt. She was in a hospital. She was alone.

A nurse was smoothing her hair back from her forehead. 'You're going to be fine, Mrs DeMaio. Why are you crying?'

'I'm *not* crying.' But she was.

She was wheeled into a room. The nurse handed her a paper cup of water and a pill. 'This will help you rest, Mrs DeMaio.'

Katie was sure this must be a sleeping pill. She didn't want it. It would give her nightmares. But it was so much easier not to argue.

The nurse turned off the light. Her footsteps made soft padding sounds as she left the room. The room was cold. The sheets were cold and coarse. Did hospital sheets always feel like this? Katie slid into sleep knowing the nightmare was inevitable.

But this time it took a different form. She was on a roller coaster. It kept climbing higher and higher, steeper and steeper, and she couldn't get control of it. She was trying to get control. Then it went around a curve and off the tracks and it was falling. She woke up trembling just before it hit the ground.

Sleet rapped on the window. She pulled herself up unsteadily. The window was open a crack and making the shade rattle. That was why the room was so draughty. She'd close the window and raise the shade and then maybe she'd be able to sleep. In the morning she could go home. She hated hospitals.

Unsteadily she walked over to the window. The hospital gown they'd given her barely came to her knees. Her legs were cold. And that sleet. It was mixed with more rain now. She leaned against the windowsill, looked out.

The parking lot was turning into streams of gushing water.

Katie gripped the shade and stared down into the lot two storeys below.

The trunk lid of a car was going up slowly. She was so dizzy now. She swayed, let go of the shade, and it snapped up. She grabbed the windowsill. She stared down into the trunk. Was something white floating down into it? A blanket? A large bundle?

She must be dreaming this, she thought, then Katie pushed her hand over her mouth to muffle the shriek that tore at her throat. She was staring down into the trunk of the car. The trunk light was on. Through the waves of sleet-filled rain that slapped against the window, she watched the white substance part. As the trunk closed she saw a face – the face of a woman grotesque in the uncaring abandon of death.

CHAPTER TWO

The alarm woke him promptly at two o'clock. Long years of learning to awake to urgency made him instantly alert. Getting up, he went over to the examining-room sink, splashed cold water on his face, pulled his tie into a smooth knot, combed his hair. His socks were still wet. They felt cold and clammy when he took them off the barely warm radiator. Grimacing, he pulled them on and slipped his feet into his shoes.

He reached for his overcoat, touched it and winced. It was still soaked through. Hanging it near the radiator had been useless. He'd end up with pneumonia if he wore it. Beyond that, the white fibres of the blanket might cling to the dark blue. That would be something to explain.

The old Burberry he kept in the closet. He'd wear that, leave the wet coat here, drop it off at the cleaner's tomorrow. The raincoat was unlined. He'd freeze, but it was the only thing to do. Besides, it was so ordinary – a drab olive green, outsized now that he'd lost weight. If anyone saw the car, saw him *in* the car, there was less chance of being recognized.

He hurried to the clothes closet, pulled the raincoat from the wire hanger where it was unevenly draped and hung the heavy wet Chesterfield in the back of the closet. The raincoat smelled unused – a dusty, irritating smell that assailed his nostrils. Frowning with distaste, he pulled it on and buttoned it.

He went over to the window and pulled the shade back an inch. There were still enough cars in the parking lot so that the presence or absence of his would hardly be noticed. He bit his lip as he realized that the broken light that always made the far section of the lot satisfactorily dark had been replaced. The back of his car was silhouetted by it. He would have to walk in the shadows of the other cars and get the body into the trunk as quickly as possible.

It was time.

Opening the medical supply closet, he bent down. With expert hands he felt the contours of the body under the blanket. Grunting slightly, he slipped a hand under the neck, the other under the knees, and picked up the body. In life she had weighed somewhere around one hundred and ten pounds, but she had gained weight during her pregnancy. His muscles felt every ounce of that weight as he carried her to the examining table. There, working only from the light of the small flashlight propped on the table, he wrapped the blanket around her.

He studied the floor of the medical supply closet carefully and relocked it. Noiselessly opening the door to the parking lot, he grasped the trunk key of the car in two fingers. Quietly he moved to the examining table and picked up the dead woman. Now for the twenty seconds that could destroy him.

Eighteen seconds later he was at the car. Sleet pelted his cheek; the blanket-covered burden strained his arms. Shifting the weight so that most of it rested on one arm, he tried to insert the key into the trunk lock. Sleet had glazed over the lock.

Impatiently he scraped it off. An instant later the key was in the lock and the trunk door rose slowly. He glanced up at the hospital windows. From the centre room on the second floor a shade snapped up. Was anyone looking out? His impatience to lay the blanketed figure in the trunk, to have it out of his arms, made him move too quickly. The instant his left hand let go of the blanket, the wind blew it apart, revealing her face. Wincing, he dropped the body and slammed the trunk closed.

The light had been on the face. Had anyone seen? He looked up again at the window where the shade had been raised. Was someone there? He couldn't be sure. How much could be seen from that window? Later he would find out who was in that room.

He was at the driver's door, turning the key in the car. He drove swiftly from the lot without turning on the headlights until he was well along the county road.

Incredible that this was his second trip to Chapin River tonight. Suppose he hadn't been leaving the hospital when she burst out of Fukhito's office and hailed him.

Vangie had been close to hysteria, favouring her right leg as she limped down the covered portico to him. 'Doctor, I can't make an appointment with you this week. I'm going to Minneapolis tomorrow. I'm going to see the doctor I used to have, Dr Salem. Maybe I'll even stay there and let him deliver the baby.'

If he had missed her, everything would have been ruined.

Instead he persuaded her to come into the office with him, talked to her, calmed her down, offered her a glass of water. At the last minute she'd suspected, tried to brush past him. That beautiful, petulant face had filled with fear.

And then the horror of knowing that even though he'd managed to silence her, the chance of discovery was still so great. He locked her body in the medical supply closet and tried to think.

Her bright red car had been the immediate danger. It was vital to get it out of the hospital parking lot. It would surely have been noticed there after visiting hours ended – top-of-the-line Lincoln Continental with its aggressive chrome front, every arrogant line demanding attention.

He knew exactly where she lived in Chapin River. She'd told

him that her husband, a United Airlines pilot, wasn't due home until tomorrow. He decided to get the car on to her property, to leave her handbag in the house, make it seem as though she'd come home.

It had been unexpectedly easy. There was so little traffic because of the vile weather. The zoning ordinance in Chapin River called for home-sites with a minimum of two acres. The houses were placed far back from the road and reached by winding driveways. He opened her garage door with the automatic device on the dashboard of the Lincoln and parked the car in the garage.

He found the door key on the ring with the car keys, but did not need it; the interior door from the garage to the den was unlocked. There were lamps on throughout the house, probably on a timing device. He'd hurried through the den down the hall into the bedroom wing, looking for the master bedroom. It was the last one on the right and no mistaking it. There were two other bedrooms, one fitted as a nursery, with colourful elves and lambs smiling out from freshly applied wallpaper and an obviously new crib and chest.

That was when he realized he might be able to make her death look like a suicide. If she'd begun to furnish the nursery three months before the baby was expected, the threatened loss of that baby was a powerful motive for suicide.

He'd gone into the master bedroom. The king-sized bed was carelessly made, with the heavy white chenille bedspread thrown unevenly over the blankets. Her nightgown and robe were on a chaise longue near it. If only he could get her body back here, put it on top of her own bed! It was dangerous, but not as dangerous as dumping her body in the woods somewhere. That would have meant an intensive police investigation.

He left her handbag on the chaise longue. With the car in the garage and the handbag here, at least it would look as though she'd returned home from the hospital.

Then he walked the four miles back to the hospital. It had been dangerous – suppose a police car had come down the road of that expensive area and stopped him? He had absolutely no excuse for being there. But he'd made the trip in less than an hour, skirted the main entrance to the hospital and let himself into the office through the back door that led from the parking lot. It was just ten o'clock when he got back.

His coat and shoes and socks were soaked. He was shivering. He realized it would be too dangerous to try to carry the body out until there was a minimal chance of encountering anyone. The late nursing shift came on at midnight. He decided to wait until well after midnight before going out again. The emergency entrance was on the east side of the hospital. At least he didn't have to worry about being observed by emergency patients or a police car rushing a patient in.

He'd set the alarm for two o'clock and lain down on the examining table. He managed to sleep until the alarm went off.

Now he was turning off the wooden bridge on to Winding Brook Lane. Her house was on the right.

Turn off the headlights; turn into the driveway; circle behind the house; back the car against the garage door; pull off driving gloves; put on surgical gloves; open the garage door; open the trunk; carry the wrapped form past the storage shelves to the inside door. He stepped into the den. The house was silent. In a few minutes he'd be safe.

He hurried down the hall to the master bedroom, straining under the weight of the body. He laid the body on the bed, pulling the blanket free.

In the bathroom off the bedroom he shook crystals of cyanide into the flowered blue tumbler, added water and poured most of the contents down the sink. He rinsed the sink carefully and returned to the bedroom. Placing the glass next to the dead woman's hand, he allowed the last drops of the mixture to spill on the spread. Her fingerprints were sure to be on the glass. Rigor mortis was setting in. The hands were cold. He folded the white blanket carefully.

The body was sprawled face up on the bed, eyes staring, lips contorted, the expression an agony of protest. That was all right. Most suicides changed their minds when it was too late.

Had he missed anything? No. Her handbag with the keys was on the chaise; there was a residue of the cyanide in the glass. Coat on or off? He'd leave it on. The less he handled her the better.

Shoes off or on? Would she have kicked them off?

He lifted the long caftan she was wearing and felt the blood

14

drain from his face. The swollen right foot wore a battered moccasin. Her left foot was covered only by her stocking.

The other moccasin must have fallen off. Where? In the parking lot, the office, this house? He ran from the bedroom, searching, retracing his steps to the garage. The shoe was not in the house or garage. Frantic at the waste of time, he ran out to the car and looked in the trunk. The shoe was not there.

It had probably come off when he was carrying her in the parking lot. He'd have heard it fall in the office, and it wasn't in the medicine closet. He was positive of that.

Because of that swollen foot she'd been wearing those moccasins constantly. He'd heard the receptionist joke with her about them.

He would have to go back, search the parking lot, find that shoe. Suppose someone picked it up who had seen her wearing it? There would be talk about her death when her body was discovered. Suppose someone said, 'Why, I saw the moccasin she was wearing lying in the parking lot. She must have lost it on her way home Monday night'? But if she had walked even a few feet in the parking lot without a shoe, the sole of her stocking would be badly soiled. The police would notice that. He had to go back to the parking lot and find that shoe.

But now, rushing back to the bedroom, he opened the door of the walk-in closet. A jumble of women's shoes were scattered on the floor. Most of them had impossibly high heels. Ridiculous that anyone would believe she had been wearing them in her condition and in this weather. There were three or four pairs of boots, but he'd never be able to zip a boot over that swollen leg.

Then he saw them. A pair of low-heeled shoes, sensible-looking, the kind most pregnant women wore. They looked fairly new, but had been worn at least once. Relieved, he grabbed them. Hurrying back to the bed, he pulled the one shoe from the dead woman's foot and slipped her feet into the shoes he had just taken from the closet. The right one was tight, but he managed to lace it. Jamming the moccasin she had been wearing into the wide loose pocket of his raincoat, he reached for the white blanket. With it under his arm he strode from the room, down the hall, through the den and out into the night.

By the time he drove into the hospital parking lot the sleet and rain had stopped falling but it was windy and very cold. Driving to the farthermost corner of the area, he parked the car. If the security guard happened to come by and spoke to him, he'd simply say that he'd received a call to meet one of his patients here; that she was in labour. If for any reason that story was checked, he'd act outraged, say it was obviously a crank call.

But it would be much safer not to be seen. Keeping in the shadow of the shrubbery that outlined the divider island of the lot, he hurried to retrace his steps from the space where he'd kept the car to the door of the office. Logically the shoe might have fallen off when he'd shifted the body to open the trunk. Crouching, he searched the ground. Quietly he worked his way closer to the hospital. All the patients' rooms in this wing were dark now. He glanced up to the centre window on the second floor. The shade was securely down. Someone had adjusted it. Bending forward, he slowly made his way across the macadam, If anyone saw him! Rage and frustration made him unaware of the bitter cold. Where was that shoe? He had to find it.

Headlights came around the bend into the parking lot. A car screeched to a halt. The driver, probably heading for the emergency room, must have realized he'd taken the wrong turn. He made a U-turn and raced out of the lot.

He had to get out of here. It was no use. He fell forward as he tried to straighten up. His hand slid across the slippery macadam. And then he felt it: the leather under his fingers. He grabbed it, held it up. Even in the dim light he could still be sure. It was the moccasin. He had found it.

Fifteen minutes later, he was turning the key in the lock of his home. Peeling off the raincoat, he hung it in the foyer closet. The full-length mirror on the door reflected his image. Shocked, he realized that his trouser knees were wet and dirty. His hair was badly dishevelled. His hands were soiled. His cheeks were flushed, and his eyes, always prominent, were bulging and wide-lensed. He looked like a man in emotional shock, a caricature of himself.

Rushing upstairs, he disrobed, sorted his clothing into the hamper and cleaning bag, bathed and got into pyjamas and a robe. He was far too keyed up to sleep, and besides, he was savagely hungry.

The housekeeper had left slices of lamb on a plate. There was a fresh wedge of Brie on the cheese board on the kitchen table. Crisp, tart apples were in the fruit bin of the refrigerator. Carefully he prepared a tray and carried it into the library. From the bar he poured a generous whiskey and sat at his desk. As he ate, he reviewed the happenings of the night. If he had not stopped to check his calendar he would have missed her. She would have been gone and it would have been too late to stop her.

Unlocking his desk, he opened the large centre drawer and slid back the false bottom where he always kept his current special file. A single manila expansion file was there. He reached for a fresh sheet of paper and made a final entry:

February 15
At 8.40 p.m. this physician was locking the rear door of his office. Subject patient had just left Fukhito. Subject patient came over to this physician and said that she was going home to Minneapolis and would have her former doctor, Emmet Salem, deliver her baby. Patient was hysterical and was persuaded to come inside. Obviously patient could not be allowed to leave. Regretting the necessity, this physician prepared to eliminate patient. Under the excuse of getting her a glass of water, this physician dissolved cyanide crystals into the glass and forced patient to swallow the poison. Patient expired at precisely 8.51 p.m. The foetus was 26 weeks old. It is the opinion of this physician that had it been born it might have been viable. The full and accurate medical records are in this file and should replace and nullify the records at the Westlake Hospital office.

Sighing, he laid down the pen, slipped the final entry into the manila envelope and sealed the file. Getting up, he walked over to the last panel on the bookcase. Reaching behind a book, he touched a button, and the panel swung open on hinges, revealing a wall safe. Quickly he opened the safe and inserted the file, subconsciously noting the growing number of envelopes. He could have recited the names of them by heart: Elizabeth Berkeley, Anna Horan, Maureen Crowley, Linda Evans – over six dozen of them: the successes and failures of his medical genius.

He closed the safe and snapped the bookcase back into place, then went upstairs slowly. He took off his bathrobe, got into the massive four-poster bed and closed his eyes.

Now that he was finished with it, he felt exhausted to the point of sickness. Had he overlooked anything, forgotten anything? He'd put the vial of cyanide in the safe. The moccasins. He'd get rid of them somewhere tomorrow night. The events of the last hours whirled furiously through his mind. When he had been doing what must be done, he'd been calm. Now that it was over, like the other times, his nervous system was screaming in protest.

He'd drop his own cleaning off on the way to the hospital tomorrow morning. Hilda was an unimaginative housekeeper, but she'd notice the mud and dampness of his trouser knees. He'd find out what patient was in the centre room on the second floor of the east wing, what the patient could have seen. Don't think about it now. Now he must sleep. Leaning on one elbow, he opened the drawer of his night table and took out a small pillbox. The mild sedative was what he needed. With it he'd be able to sleep for two hours.

His fingers groped for and closed over a small capsule. Swallowing it without water, he leaned back and closed his eyes. While he waited for it to take effect, he tried to reassure himself that he was safe. But no matter how hard he tried, he could not push back the thought that the most damning proof of his guilt was inaccessible to him.

CHAPTER THREE

'If you don't mind, we'd like you to leave through the back entrance,' the nurse said. 'The front driveway froze over terribly, and the workmen are trying to clear it. The cab will be waiting there.'

'I don't care if I climb out the window, just as long as I can get home,' Katie said fervently. 'And the misery is that I have to come back here Friday. I'm having minor surgery on Saturday.'

'Oh.' The nurse looked at her chart. 'What's wrong?'

'I seem to have inherited a problem my mother used to have. I practically haemorrhage every month during my period.'

'That must have been why your blood count was so low when you came in. Don't worry about it. A D-and-C is no big deal. Who's your doctor?'

'Dr Highley.'

'Oh, he's the best. But you'll be over in the west wing. All his patients go there. It's like a luxury hotel. He's top man in this place, you know.' She was still looking at Katie's chart. 'You didn't sleep much, did you?'

'Not really.' Katie wrinkled her nose with distaste as she buttoned her blouse. It was spattered with blood, and she let the left sleeve hang loosely over her bandaged arm. The nurse helped her with her coat.

The morning was cloudy and bitterly cold. Katie decided that February was getting to be her least-favourite month. She shivered as she stepped out into the parking lot, remembering her nightmare. This was the area she had been looking at from her room. The cab pulled up. Gratefully she walked over to it, wincing at the pain in her knees. The nurse helped her in, said good-bye and closed the door. The cab-driver pressed his foot on the accelerator. 'Where to, lady?'

From the window of the second-floor room that Katie had just left, a man was observing her departure. The chart the nurse had left on the desk was in his hand. *Kathleen N. DeMaio, 10 Woodfield Way, Abbington. Place of Business: Prosecutor's office, Valley County.*

He felt a thrill of fear go through him. *Katie DeMaio.*

The chart showed she had been given a strong sleeping pill.

According to her medical history, she took no medication regularly, including sleeping pills or tranquillizers. So she'd have no tolerance for them and would have been pretty groggy from what they'd given her last night.

There was a note on the chart that the night nurse had found her sitting on the edge of the bed at 2.08 a.m. in an agitated state and complaining about nightmares.

The shade in the room had snapped up. She must have been at the window. How much had she seen? If she'd observed anything, even if she thought she'd been having a nightmare, her professional training would nag at her. She was a risk, an unacceptable one.

CHAPTER FOUR

Shoulders touching, they sat in the end booth of the Eighty-seventh Street drugstore. Uneaten English muffins had been pushed away, and sombrely they sipped coffee. The arm of her teal-blue uniform jacket rested on the gold braid on his sleeve. The fingers of his right hand were entwined with those of her left hand.

'I've missed you,' he said carefully.

'I've missed you too, Chris. That's why I'm sorry you met me this morning. It just makes it worse.'

'Joan, give me a little time. I swear to God we'll work this out. We've got to.'

She shook her head. He turned to her and with a wrench noticed how unhappy she looked. Her hazel eyes were cloudy. Her light brown hair, pulled back this morning in a chignon, revealed the paleness of her usually smooth, clear skin.

For the thousandth time he asked himself why he hadn't made the clean break with Vangie when he was transferred to New York last year. Why had he responded to her plea to try just a little longer to make a go of their marriage when ten years of trying hadn't done it? And now a baby coming. He thought of the ugly quarrel he'd had with Vangie before he left. Should he tell Joan about that? No, it wouldn't do any good.

'How did you like China?' he asked.

She brightened. 'Fascinating, completely fascinating.' She was a flight attendant with Pan American. They'd met six months ago in Hawaii when one of the other United captains, Jack Lane, threw a party.

Joan was based in New York and shared an apartment in Manhattan with two other Pan Am attendants.

Crazy, incredible how right some people are together from the first minute. He'd told her he was married, but also was able to say honestly that when he transferred from the Minneapolis base to New York he had wanted to break with Vangie. The last-ditch attempt to save the marriage wasn't working. No one's fault. The marriage was something that never should have happened in the first place.

And then Vangie had told him about the baby.

Joan was saying, 'You got in last night.'

'Yes. We had engine trouble in Chicago and the rest of the flight was cancelled. We deadheaded back. Got in around six and I checked into the Holiday Inn on Fifty-seventh Street.'

Why didn't you go home?'

'Because I haven't seen you for two weeks and I wanted to see you, *had* to see you. Vangie doesn't expect me till about eleven. So don't worry.'

'Chris, I told you I put in an application to transfer to the Latin American Division. It's been approved. I'll be moving to Miami next week.'

'Joan, no!'

'It's the only way. Look, Chris, I'm sorry, but it's not my nature to be an available lady for a married man. I'm not a home wrecker.'

'Our relationship has been totally innocent.'

'In today's world who would ever believe that? The very fact that in an hour you'll be lying to your wife about when you got in says a lot, doesn't it? And don't forget, I'm the daughter of a Presbyterian minister. I can just see Dad's reaction if I tell him that I'm in love with a man who not only is married but whose wife is finally expecting the baby she's prayed for for ten years. He'd be real proud of me, let me tell you.'

She finished the coffee. 'And no matter what you say, Chris, I still feel that if I'm not around, there's the chance that you and your wife will grow closer. I'm occupying your thoughts when you should be concerned about her. And you'll be amazed how a baby has a way of creating a bond between people.'

Gently she withdrew her fingers from his. 'I'd better get

home, Chris. It was a long flight and I'm tired. You'd better get home too.'

They looked directly at each other. She touched his face, wanting to smooth away the deep, unhappy creases in his forehead. 'We really could have been awfully good together.' Then she added, 'You look terribly tired, Chris.'

'I didn't sleep very much last night.' He tried to smile. 'I'm not giving up, Joan. I swear to you that I'm coming to Miami for you, and when I get there I'll be free.'

CHAPTER FIVE

The cab dropped Katie off. She hurried painfully up the porch steps, thrust her key into the lock, opened the door and murmured, 'Thank God to be home.' She felt that she'd been away weeks rather than overnight and with fresh eyes appreciated the soothing, restful earth tones of the foyer and living-room, the hanging plants that had caught her eye when she'd visited this house for the first time.

She picked up the bowl of African violets and inhaled the pungent perfume of their leaves. The odours of antiseptics and medicines were trapped in her nostrils. Her body was aching and stiff, even more now than it had been when she got out of bed this morning.

But at least she was home.

John. If he were alive, if he had been here to call last night . . .

Katie hung up her coat and sank down on the apricot velvet couch in the living-room. She looked up at John's portrait over the mantel. John Anthony DeMaio, the youngest judge in Essex County. She could remember so clearly the first time she'd seen him. He'd come to lecture to her Torts class at Seton Hall Law School.

When the class ended, the students clustered around him. 'Judge DeMaio, I hope the Supreme Court turns down the appeal on the *Collins* case.'

'Judge DeMaio, I agree with your decision on *Reicher versus Reicher*.'

And then it had been Katie's turn. 'Judge, I have to tell you I don't agree with your decision in the *Kipling* case.'

John had smiled. 'That obviously is your privilege, Miss . . .'

'Katie . . . Kathleen Callahan.'

She never understood why at that moment she'd dragged up the Kathleen. But he'd always called her that, Kathleen Noel.

That day they'd gone out for coffee. The next night he'd taken her to the Monsignor II restaurant in New York for dinner. When the violinists came to their table, he'd asked them to play 'Vienna, City of My Dreams'. He'd sung it softly with them: '*Wien, Wien nur Du allein* . . .' When they finished he asked, 'Have you ever been to Vienna, Kathleen?'

'I've never been out of the country except for the school trip to Bermuda. It rained for four days.'

'I'd like to take you abroad some day. But I'd show you Italy first. Now, there's a beautiful country.'

When he dropped her off that night he'd said, 'You have the loveliest blue eyes I've ever had the pleasure of looking into. I don't think a twelve-year age difference is too much, do you, Kathleen?'

Three months later, when she was graduated from law school, they married.

This house. John had been raised in it, had inherited it from his parents.

'I'm pretty attached to it, Kathleen, but be sure you are. Maybe you want something smaller.'

'John, I was raised in a three-room apartment in Queens. I slept on a daybed in the living-room. "Privacy" was a word I had to look up in the dictionary. I *love* this house.'

'I'm glad, Kathleen.'

They loved each other so much – but besides that, they were such good friends. She'd told him about the nightmare. 'I warn you that every once in a while I'll wake up screaming like a banshee. It started when I was eight years old after my father died. He'd been in the hospital recovering from a heart attack and then he had a second attack. Apparently the old man in the room with him kept pressing the buzzer for the nurse, but no one came. By the time someone got around to answering the buzzer, it was too late.'

'And then you started having nightmares.'

'I guess I heard the story so much it made an awful impression on me. In the nightmare I'm in a hospital going from bed to bed, looking for Daddy. I keep seeing faces of people I know in the beds. They're all asleep. Sometimes it would be girls from school, or cousins – or just anybody. But I'd be trying to find Daddy. I knew he needed me. Finally I see a nurse and run up to her and ask her where he is. And she smiles and says, "Oh, he's dead. All these people are dead. You're going to die in here too." '

'You poor kid.'

'Oh, John, intellectually I know it's nonsense not to get over it. But I swear to you I'm scared silly at the thought of ever being a patient in a hospital.'

'I'll help you get over that.'

She'd been able to tell him how it really was after her father died. 'I missed him so much, John. I was always such a daddy's girl. Molly was sixteen and already going around with Bill, so I don't think it hit her as hard. But all through school, I kept thinking what fun it would be if he were at the plays and the graduations. I used to dread the Father and Daughter Dinner every spring.

'Didn't you have an uncle or someone who could have gone with you?'

'Just one. It would have taken too long to sober him up.'

'Oh, Kathleen!' The two of them laughing. John saying, 'Well, darling, I'm going to uproot that core of sadness in you.'

'You already have, Judge.'

They'd spent their honeymoon travelling through Italy. The pain had begun on that trip. They'd come back in time for the opening of court. John presided on the bench in Essex County. She'd been hired to clerk for a criminal judge in Valley County.

John went for a checkup a month after they got home. The overnight stay at Mt Sinai stretched into three days of additional tests. Then one evening he'd been waiting for her at the elevator, impeccably elegant in the dark red velour robe, a wan smile on his face. She'd run over to him, aware as always of the glances the other elevator passengers threw at him, thinking

24

how even in pyjamas and a robe, John looked impressive. She'd been about to tell him that when he said, 'We've got trouble, darling.'

Even then, just the way he said, '*We've* got trouble.' In those few short months, in every way, they had become one. Back in his room he'd told her. 'It's a malignant tumour. Both lungs, apparently. And for God's sake, Kathleen, I don't even smoke.'

Incredulously they had laughed together in a paroxysm of grief and irony. John Anthony DeMaio, Superior Court Judge of Essex County, Past President of the New Jersey Bar Association, not thirty-eight years old, had been condemned to an indeterminate sentence of Six Months to Life. For him there would be no parole board, no appeal.

He'd gone back on the bench. 'Die with your robes on – why not?' he'd shrugged.

'Promise me you'll remarry, Kathleen.'

'Some day, but you'll be a hard act to follow.'

'I'm glad you think so. We'll make every minute we have count.'

Even in the midst of it, knowing their time was slipping away, they'd had fun.

One day he came home from court and said, 'I think that's about it for the bench.'

The cancer had spread. The pain got steadily worse. At first he'd go to the hospital for a few days at a time for chemotherapy. Her nightmare began again; it came regularly. But John would come home and they'd have more time. She resigned her clerkship. She wanted every minute with him.

Towards the end, he asked, 'Would you want to have your mother come up from Florida and live with you?'

'Good Lord, no. Mama's great, but we lived together until I went to college. That was enough. But anyhow, she loves Florida.'

'Well, I'm glad Molly and Bill live near by. They'll look out for you. And you enjoy the children.'

They'd both been silent then. Bill Kennedy was an orthopaedic surgeon. He and Molly had six kids and lived two towns away in Chapin River. The day Katie and John were married, they'd bragged to Bill and Molly that they were going to beat their record. 'We'll have seven offspring,' John had declared.

The last time he went in for chemotherapy, he didn't come back. He was so weak they had him stay overnight. He was talking to her when he slipped into the coma. They'd both hoped that the end would come at home, but he died in the hospital that night.

The next week Katie applied to the Prosecutor's office for a job and was accepted. It was a good decision. The office was chronically shorthanded, and she always had more cases than she could reasonably handle. There wasn't any time for introspection. All day, every day, even on many week-ends, she'd had to concentrate on her case load.

And in another way it was good therapy. That anger which had accompanied the grief, the sense of being cheated, the fury that John had been cheated of so much of life, she directed into the cases she tried. When she prosecuted a serious crime, she felt as though she were tangibly fighting at least one kind of evil that destroyed lives.

She'd kept the house. John had willed her all of his very considerable assets, but even so, she knew it was silly for a twenty-eight-year-old woman on a twenty-two-thousand-dollar salary to live in a home worth a quarter of a million dollars with five acres surrounding it.

Molly and Bill were always urging her to sell it.

'You'll never put your life with John behind you until you do,' Bill had told her.

He was probably right. Now Katie shook herself and got up from the couch. She was getting downright maudlin. She'd better call Molly. If Molly had tried to get her last night and not received an answer she'd have been delighted. She was always making a novena that Katie would 'meet someone'. But she didn't want Molly to try to reach her at the office and find out that way that she'd been in an accident.

Maybe Molly would come over and they'd have lunch together. She had salad makings and Bloody Mary ingredients. Molly was perpetually on a diet, but would not give up her lunchtime Bloody Mary. 'For God's sake, Kate, how could anyone with six kids *not* have a belt at lunch?' Molly's cheerful presence would quickly dispel the sense of isolation and sadness.

Katie became aware of the bloodstained blouse she was wearing. After she'd talked to Molly, while she was waiting for her to come over, she'd bathe and change.

Glancing into the mirror over the couch, she saw that the bruise under her right eye was assuming a brilliant purple colour. Her naturally olive complexion, which Mama called the 'Black Irish' look from her father's side, was a sickly yellow. Her collar-length dark brown hair, which usually bounced full and luxuriant in a natural wave, was matted against her face and neck.

'You should see the other guy,' she murmured ruefully.

The doctor had told her not to get her arm wet. She'd wrap the bandage in a Baggie and keep it dry. Before she could pick up the phone, it began to ring. Molly, she thought. I swear she's a witch.

But it was Richard Carroll, the Medical Examiner. 'Katie, how are you? Just heard that you'd been in some kind of accident.'

'Nothing much. I took a little detour off the road. The trouble is there was a tree in the way.'

'When did it happen?'

'About ten last night. I was on my way home from the office. I'd worked late to catch up on some files. Spent the night in the hospital and just got home. I look a mess, but I'm really okay.'

'Who picked you up? Molly?'

'No. She doesn't know yet. I called a cab.'

'Always the Lone Ranger, aren't you?' Richard asked. 'Why the blazes didn't you call *me*?'

Katie laughed. The concern in Richard's voice was both flattering and threatening. Richard and Molly's husband were good friends. Several times in the last six months Molly had pointedly invited Katie and Richard to small dinner parties. But Richard was so blunt and cynical. She always felt somewhat unsettled around him. Anyhow, she simply wasn't looking to get involved with anyone, and especially anyone she worked with so frequently. 'Next time I run into a tree I'll remember,' she said.

'You're going to take a couple of days off, aren't you?'

'Oh, no,' she said. 'I'm going to see if Molly's free for a quick lunch; then I'll get in to the office. I've got at least ten files to work on, and I'm trying an important case on Friday.'

'There's no use telling you you're crazy. Okay. Gotta go. My other phone's ringing. I'll poke my head in your office around five-thirty and catch you for a drink.' He hung up before she could reply.

Katie dialled Molly's number. When her sister answered, her voice was shaken. 'Katie, I guess you've heard about it.'

'Heard about what?'

'People from your office are just getting there.'

'Getting where?'

'Next door. The Lewises. That couple who moved in last summer. Katie, that poor man; he just came home from an overnight flight and found her – his wife, Vangie. She's killed herself. Katie, she was six months pregnant!'

The Lewises. *The Lewises*. Katie had met them at Molly and Bill's New Year's Day open house. Vangie a very pretty blonde. Chris an airline pilot.

Numbly she heard Molly's shocked voice: 'Katie, why would a girl who wanted a baby so desperately kill herself?'

The question hung in the air. Cold chills washed over Katie. That long blonde hair spilling over shoulders. Her nightmare. Crazy the tricks the mind plays. As soon as Molly said the name, last night's nightmare had come back. The face she'd glimpsed through the hospital window was Vangie Lewis's.

CHAPTER SIX

Richard Carroll parked his car within the police lines on Winding Brook Lane. He was shocked to realize that the Lewises lived next door to Bill and Molly Kennedy. Bill had been a resident when Richard interned at St Vincent's. Later he'd specialized in forensic medicine and Bill in orthopaedics. They'd been pleasantly surprised to bump into each other in the Valley County courthouse when Bill was appearing as an expert witness in a malpractice trial. The friendship that had been casual in the St Vincent's days had become close. Now he and Bill golfed together frequently, and Richard often stopped back to their house for a drink after the game.

He'd met Molly's sister, Katie DeMaio, in the Prosecutor's office and had been immediately attracted to the dedicated young attorney. She was a throwback to the days when the Spanish invaded Ireland and left a legacy of descendants with olive skin and dark hair to contrast with the intense blue of Celtic eyes. But Katie had subtly discouraged him when he'd suggested getting together, and he'd philosophically dismissed her from his thoughts. There were plenty of mighty attractive ladies who enjoyed his company well enough.

But hearing Molly and Bill and their kids talk about Katie, what fun she could be, how chopped up she was over her husband's death, had rekindled his interest. Then in the past few months he'd been at a couple of parties at Bill and Molly's and found to his chagrin that he was far more intrigued by Katie DeMaio than he wanted to be.

Richard shrugged. He was here on police business. A thirty-year-old woman had committed suicide. It was his job to look for any medical signs which might indicate that Vangie Lewis had not taken her own life. Later today he'd perform an autopsy. His jaw tightened as he thought of the foetus she was carrying. Never had a chance. How was that for motherly love? Cordially, objectively, he already disliked the late Vangie Lewis.

A young cop from Chapin River let him in. The living-room was to the left of the foyer. A guy in an airline captain's uniform was sitting on the couch, hunched forward, clasping and unclasping his hands. He was a lot paler than many of the deceased Richard dealt with and was trembling violently. Richard felt a brief twinge of sympathy. The husband. Some brutal kick to come home and find your wife a suicide. He decided to talk with him later. 'Which way?' he asked the cop.

'Back here.' He nodded his head to the rear of the house. 'Kitchen straight ahead, bedrooms to the right. She's in the master bedroom.'

Richard walked quickly, absorbing as he did the feel of the house. Expensive, but carelessly furnished, without flair or even interest. The glimpse of the living-room had shown him the typical no-imagination interior-designer look you see in so many Main Street decorator shops in small towns. Richard had an acute sense of colour. Privately he thought it helped him considerably in his work. But clashing shades registered on his consciousness like the sound of discordant notes.

Charley Nugent, the detective in charge of the Homicide Squad, was in the kitchen. The two men exchanged brief nods. 'How does it look?' Richard asked.

'Let's talk after you see her.'

In death Vangie Lewis was not a pretty sight. The long blonde hair seemed a muddy brown now; her face was contorted; her legs and arms, stiff with the onslaught of rigor mortis, had the appearance of being stretched on wires. Her coat was buttoned and, because of her pregnancy, hiked over her knees. The soles of her shoes were barely showing under a long flowered caftan.

Richard pulled the caftan up past her ankles. Her legs, obviously swollen, had stretched the panty hose. The sides of her right shoe bit into the flesh.

Expertly he picked up one arm, held it for an instant, let it drop. He studied the mottled discoloration around her mouth where the poison had burned it.

Charley was beside him. 'How long you figure?'

'Anywhere from twelve to fifteen hours, I'd guess. She's pretty rigid.' Richard's voice was noncommittal, but his sense of harmony was disturbed. The coat on. Shoes on. Had she just come home, or had she been planning to go out? What had suddenly made her take her own life? The tumbler was beside her on the bed. Bending down, he sniffed it. The unmistakable bitter-almond scent of cyanide entered his nostrils. Incredible how many suicides took cyanide ever since that Jones-cult mess in Guyana. He straightened up. 'Did she leave a note?'

Charley shook his head. Richard thought that Charley was in the right job. He always looked mournful; his lids drooped sadly over his eyes. He seemed to have a perpetual dandruff problem. 'No letters; no nothing. Been married ten years to the pilot; he's the guy in the living-room. Seems pretty broken up. They're from Minneapolis; just moved east less than a year ago. She

30

always wanted to have a baby. Finally got pregnant and was in heaven. Starts decorating a nursery; talks baby morning, noon and night.'

'*Then she kills it and herself?*'

'According to her husband, she'd been nervous lately. Some days she had some sort of fixation that she was going to lose the baby. Other times she'd act scared about giving birth. Apparently knew she was showing some signs of a toxic pregnancy.'

'And rather than give birth or face losing the baby, she kills herself?' Richard's tone was sceptical. He could tell Charley wasn't buying it either. 'Is Phil with you?' he asked. Phil was the other senior member of the Homicide team from the Prosecutor's office.

'He's out around the neighbourhood talking to people.'

'Who found her?'

'The husband. He just got in from a flight. Called for an ambulance. Called the local cops.'

Richard stared at the burn marks around Vangie Lewis's mouth. 'She must have really splashed that in,' he said meditatively, 'or maybe tried to spit it out but it was too late. Can we talk to the husband, bring him in here?'

'Sure.' Charley nodded to the young cop, who turned and scampered down the long hallway.

When Christopher Lewis came into the bedroom, he looked as though he were on the verge of getting sick. His complexion was now a sickly green. Perspiration, cold and clammy, beaded on his forehead. He had pulled open his shirt and tie. His hands were shoved into his pockets.

Richard studied him appraisingly. Lewis looked distraught, sick, nervous. But there was something missing. He did not look like a man whose life has been shattered.

Richard had seen death countless times. He'd witnessed some next of kin grieving in dumbstruck silence. Others shrieked hysterically, screamed, wept, threw themselves on the deceased. Some touched the dead hand, trying to understand. He thought of the young husband whose wife had been caught in a shoot-out while they were getting out of their car to do the grocery shopping. When Richard got there, he was holding the body, bewildered, talking to her, trying to get through to her.

That was grief.

Whatever emotion Christopher Lewis was experiencing now, Richard would stake his life on the fact that he was not a heartbroken husband.

Charley was questioning him. 'Captain Lewis, this is tough for you, but it will make it easier all around if we can ask you some questions.'

'Here?' It was a protest.

'You'll see why. We won't be long. When was the last time you saw your wife?'

'Two nights ago. I was on a run to the Coast.'

'And you arrived home at what time?'

'About an hour ago.'

'Did you speak with your wife in those two days?'

'No.'

'What was your wife's mental state when you left?'

'I told you.'

'If you'd just tell Dr Carroll.'

'Vangie was worried. She'd become quite apprehensive that she might miscarry.'

'Were you alarmed about that possibility?'

'She'd become quite heavy, looked like she was retaining fluid, but she had pills for that and I understand it's quite a common condition.'

'Did you call her obstetrician to discuss this with him, to reassure yourself?'

'No.'

'All right. Captain Lewis, will you look around this room and see if you notice anything amiss. It isn't easy, but will you study your wife's body carefully and see if there's anything that in some way is different. For example, that glass. Are you sure it's the one from your bathroom?'

Chris obeyed. His face going progressively whiter, he carefully looked at every detail of his dead wife's appearance.

Through narrowed eyes, Charley and Richard watched him.

'No,' he whispered finally. 'Nothing.'

Charley's manner became brisk. 'Okay, sir. As soon as we

take some pictures, we'll remove your wife's body for an autopsy. Can we help you get in touch with anyone?'

'I have some calls to make. Vangie's father and mother. They'll be heartbroken. I'll go into the study and phone them now.'

After he'd left, Richard and Charley exchanged glances.

'He saw something we missed,' Charley said flatly.

Richard nodded. 'I know.' Grimly the two men stared at the crumpled body.

CHAPTER SEVEN

Before she'd hung up, Katie had told Molly about the accident and suggested lunch. But Molly's twelve-year-old Jennifer and her six-year-old twin boys were home from school recovering from flu. 'Jennifer's okay, but I don't like to leave those boys alone long enough to empty the garbage,' Molly had said, and they'd arranged that she would pick Katie up and bring her back to her own house.

While she waited, Katie bathed quickly, managing to wash and blow-dry her hair using only her right hand. She put on a thick wool sweater and well-tailored tweed slacks. The red sweater gave some hint of colour to her face, and her hair curled loosely just below her collar. As she bathed and dressed, she tried to rationalize last night's hallucination.

Had she even *been* at the window? Or was that part of the dream? Maybe the shade had snapped up by itself, pulling her out of a nightmare. She closed her eyes as once more the scene floated into her consciousness. It had seemed so real: the trunk light had shone directly into the trunk on the staring eyes, the long hair, the high-arched eyebrows. For one instant it had seemed so clear. That was what frightened her: the clarity of the image. The face had been familiar even in the dream.

Would she talk to Molly about that? Of course not. Molly had been worried about her lately. 'Katie, you're too pale. You work too hard. You're getting too quiet.' Molly had bullied her into the scheduled operation. 'You can't let that condition go on indefinitely. That haemorrhaging can be dangerous if you let it go.' And then she'd added, 'Katie, you've got to realize you're a young woman. You should take a real vacation, relax, go away.'

From outside, a horn blew loudly as Molly pulled up in her battered station wagon. Katie struggled into a warm beaver jacket, turning the collar up around her ears, and hurried out as fast as her swollen knees would allow. Molly pushed open the door for her and leaned over to kiss her. She eyed her critically. 'You're not exactly blooming. How badly *were* you hurt?'

'It could have been a lot worse.' The car smelled vaguely of peanut butter and bubble gum. It was a comforting, familiar smell, and Katie felt her spirits begin to lift. But the mood was broken instantly when Molly said, 'Our block is some mess. Your people have the Lewis place blocked off, and some detective from your office is going around asking questions. He caught me just as I was leaving. I told him I was your sister and we did the number on how wonderful you are.'

Katie said, 'It was probably Phil Cunningham or Charley Nugent.'

'Big guy. Beefy face. Nice.'

'Phil Cunningham. He's a good man. What kind of questions were they asking?'

'Pretty routine. Had we noticed what time she left or got back – that kind of thing.'

'And did you?'

'When the twins are sick and cranky, I wouldn't notice if Robert Redford moved in next door. Anyhow, we can barely see the Lewises' house on a sunny day, never mind at night in a storm.'

They were driving over the wooden bridge just before the turn to Winding Brook Lane. Katie bit her lip. 'Molly, drop me off at the Lewis house, won't you?'

Molly turned to her, astonished. 'Why?'

Katie tried to smile. 'Well, I'm an assistant prosecutor, and for what it's worth, I'm also adviser to the Chapin River Police Department. I wouldn't normally have to go, but as long as I'm right here, I think I should.'

The hearse from the Medical Examiner's office was just backing into the driveway of the Lewis home. Richard was in the doorway watching. He came over to the car when Molly pulled up. Quickly Molly explained: 'Katie's having lunch with me and thought she should stop by here. Why don't you come over with her, if you can?

He agreed and helped Katie out of the car. 'I'm glad you're here,' he said. 'There's something about this setup I don't like.'

Now that she was about to see the dead woman, Katie felt her mouth go dry. She remembered the image of the face in her dream. 'The husband is in the den,' Richard said.

'I've met him. You must have too. At Molly's New Year's Day party. No. You came late. They'd left before you arrived.'

Richard said, 'All right. We'd better talk about it later. Here's the room.'

She forced herself to look at the familiar face, and recognized it instantly. She shuddered and closed her eyes. Was she going crazy?

'You all right, Katie?' Richard asked sharply.

What kind of fool was she? 'I'm perfectly all right,' she said, and to her own ears her voice sounded normal enough. 'I'd like to talk to Captain Lewis.'

When they got to the den, the door was closed. Without knocking, Richard opened it quietly. Chris Lewis was on the phone, his back to them. His voice was low but distinct. 'I know it's incredible, but I swear to you, Joan, she didn't know about us.'

Richard closed the door noiselessly. He and Katie stared at each other. Katie said, 'I'll tell Charley to stay here. I'm going to recommend to Scott that we launch a full investigation.' Scott Myerson was the Prosecutor.

'I'll do the autopsy myself as soon as they bring her in,' Richard said. 'The minute we're positive it was the cyanide that killed her, we'd better start finding out where she got it. Come on; let's make the stop at Molly's a quick one.'

Molly's house, like her car, was a haven of normality. Katie often stopped there for a glass of wine or dinner on her way home from work. The smell of good food cooking; the kids' feet clattering on the stairs; the blare of the television set; the noisy young voices, shouting and battling. For her it was re-entry into the real world after a day of dealing with murderers, kidnappers, muggers, vandals, deviates, arsonists and penny-ante crooks. And dearly as she loved the Kennedys, the visit made her appreciate the serene peace of her own home. Except, of course, for the times that she would feel the emptiness of her house and try to imagine what it would be like if John were still alive and their children had started to arrive.

'Katie! Dr Carroll!' The twins came whooping up to greet them. 'Did you see all the cop cars, Katie? Something happened next door!' Peter, older than his twin by ten minutes, was always the spokesman.

'Right next door!' John chimed in. Molly called them 'Pete and Repeat'. 'Get lost, you two,' she ordered now. 'And leave us alone while we eat.'

'Where are the other kids?' Katie asked.

'Billy, Dina and Moira went back to school this morning, thank God,' Molly said. 'Jennifer's in bed. I just looked in and she's dozed off again. Poor kid still feels lousy.'

They settled at the kitchen table. The kitchen was large and cheerfully warm. Molly produced Reubens from the oven, offered drinks, which they refused, and poured coffee. Molly had a way with food, Katie thought. Everything she fixed tasted good. But when Katie tried to eat, she found her throat was closed. She glanced at Richard. He had piled hot mustard on to the corned beef and was eating with obvious pleasure. She envied him his detachment. On one level he could enjoy a good sandwich. On the other, she was sure that he was concentrating on the Lewis case. His forehead was knitted; his thatch of brown hair looked ruffled; his blue-grey eyes were thoughtful; his rangy shoulders hunched forward as with two fingers he lightly drummed the table. She'd have bet that they were both pondering the same question: Who had been on the phone with Chris Lewis?

She remembered the only conversation she'd had with Chris. It had been at the New Year's party, and they'd discussed hijacking. He'd been interesting, intelligent, pleasant. With his rugged good looks, he was a very appealing man. And she remembered that he and Vangie had been at opposite ends of the crowded room and he'd been unenthused when she, Katie, congratulated him on the coming baby.

'Molly, what was your impression of the Lewises — I mean their relationship to each other?' she asked.

Molly looked troubled. 'Candidly, I think it was on the rocks. She was so hung up with being pregnant that whenever they were here she kept yanking the conversation back to babies, and he obviously was upset about it. And since I had a hand in the pregnancy, it was a real worry for me.'

Richard stopped drumming his fingers and straightened up. 'You had *what*?'

'I mean, well, you know me, Katie. The day they moved in, last summer, I went rushing over and invited them to dinner. They came, and right away Vangie told me how much she hoped to have a baby and how upset she was about her best childbearing years being over because she'd turned thirty.'

Molly took a gulp of her Bloody Mary and eyed the empty glass regretfully. 'I told her about Liz Berkeley. She never was able to conceive until she went to a gynaecologist who's something of a fertility expert. Liz had just given birth to a little girl and of course was ecstatic. Anyhow, I told Vangie about Dr Highley. She went to him and a few months later conceived. But since then I've been sorry I didn't keep out of it.'

'Dr Highley?' Katie looked startled.

Molly nodded. 'Yes, the one who's going to . . .'

Katie shook her head, and Molly's voice trailed off.

CHAPTER EIGHT

Edna Burns liked her job. She was bookkeeper-receptionist for the two doctors who staffed and ran the Westlake Maternity Concept team. 'Dr Highley's the big shot,' she confided to her friends. 'You know, he was married to Winifred Westlake and she left him everything. He runs the whole show.'

Dr Highley was a gynaecologist/obstetrician, and as Edna explained, 'It's a riot to see the way his patients act when they finally get pregnant; so happy you'd think they invented kids.

He charges them an arm and a leg, but he's practically a miracle worker.

'On the other hand,' she'd explain, 'Highley is also the right person to see if you've got an internal problem that you *don't* want to grow. If you know what I mean,' she'd add with a wink.

Dr Fukhito was a psychiatrist. The Westlake Maternity Concept was one of holistic medicine: that mind and body must be in harmony to achieve a successful pregnancy and that many women could not conceive because they were emotionally charged with fear and anxiety. All gynaecology patients consulted Dr Fukhito at least once, but pregnant patients were required to schedule regular visits.

Edna enjoyed telling her friends that the Westlake Concept had been dreamed up by old Dr Westlake, who had died before he acted on it. Then, eight years ago, his daughter Winifred had married Dr Highley, bought the River Falls Clinic when it went into bankruptcy, renamed it for her father and set up her husband there. 'She and the doctor were crazy about each other,' Edna would sigh. 'I mean she was ten years older than he and nothing to look at, but they were real lovers. He'd have me send her flowers a couple of times a week, and busy as he is, he'd go shopping with her for her clothes. Let me tell you, it was some shock when she died. No one ever knew her heart was that bad.

'But,' she'd add philosophically, 'he keeps busy. I've seen women who never were able to conceive become pregnant two and three times. Of course, a lot of them don't carry the babies to term, but at least they know there's a chance. And you should see the kind of care they get. I've seen Dr Highley bring women in and put them to bed in the hospital for two months before a birth. Costs a fortune, of course, but buh-lieve me, when you want a baby and can afford it, you'll pay anything to get one. But you can read about it yourself, pretty soon,' she'd add. '*Newsmaker* magazine just did an article about him and about the Westlake Maternity Concept. It's coming out Thursday. They came last week and photographed him in his office standing next to the pictures of all those babies he's delivered. Real nice. And if you think we're busy now, wait till that comes out. The phone'll never be on the hook.'

Edna was a born bookkeeper. Her records were marvels of accuracy. She loved receipts and took a sensual pride in making frequent and healthy bank deposits in her employer's account. A neat but prominent sign on her desk let it be known that all payments must be made in cash; no monthly bills would be rendered; retainer fees and payment schedules would be explained by Miss Burns.

Edna had been told by Dr Highley that unless specifically instructed otherwise, she was to be sure to make follow-up appointments with people as they left; that if for any reason a patient did not keep the next appointment, Edna should phone that patient at home and firmly make a new one. It was a sound arrangement and, as Edna gleefully noted, a financial bonanza.

Dr Highley always complimented Edna on the excellent records she maintained and her ability to keep the appointments book full. The only time Dr Highley really gave her the rough side of his tongue was when she was overheard talking to one patient about another's problems. She had to admit that had been foolish, but she'd allowed herself a couple of Manhattans for lunch that day and that had lowered her guard.

The doctor had finished up his lecture by saying, 'Any more talking and you're through.'

She knew he meant it.

Edna sighed. She was tired. Last night both doctors had had evening hours, and it had been hectic. Then she'd worked on the books for a while. She couldn't wait to go home this evening, and wild horses wouldn't drag her out again. She'd put on a robe and mix herself a nice batch of Manhattans. She had a canned ham in the refrigerator, so she'd make that do for supper and watch television.

It was nearly two o'clock. Three more hours and she could clear out. While it was quiet she had to check yesterday's calendar to make sure she'd made all the necessary future appointments. Frowning nearsightedly, she leaned her broad, freckled face on a thick hand. Her hair felt messy today. She hadn't had time to set it last night. She'd been kind of tired after she had a few drinks.

She was an overweight woman of forty-four who looked ten years older. Her unleavened youth had been spent taking care of ageing parents. When Edna saw pictures of herself from Drake Secretarial School she was vaguely surprised at the pretty girl she'd been a quarter of a century ago. Always a mite too heavy, but pretty nevertheless.

Her mind was only half on the page she was reading, but then something triggered her full attention. She paused. The eight-o'clock appointment last night for Vangie Lewis.

Last night Vangie had come in early and sat talking with Edna. She was sure upset. Well, Vangie was kind of a complainer, but so pretty Edna enjoyed just looking at her. Vangie had put on a lot of weight during the pregnancy and, to Edna's practised eye, was retaining a lot of fluid. Edna prayed that Vangie would deliver that baby safely. She wanted it so much.

So she didn't blame Vangie for being moody. She really wasn't well. Last month Vangie had started wearing those moccasins because her other shoes didn't fit any more. She'd shown them to Edna. 'Look at this. My right foot is so bad, I can only wear these clodhoppers my cleaning woman left behind. The other one is always falling off.'

Edna had tried to kid her. 'Well, with those glass slippers I'll just have to start calling you Cinderella. And we'll call your husband Prince Charming.' She knew Vangie was nuts about her husband.

But Vangie had just pouted and said impatiently, 'Oh, Edna, Prince Charming was Sleeping Beauty's boy-friend, not Cinderella's. Everybody knows that.'

Edna had just laughed. 'Mama must have been mixed up. When she told me about Cinderella she said Prince Charming came around with the glass slipper. But never mind — before you know it, you'll have your baby and be back in pretty shoes again.'

Last night Vangie had pulled up that long caftan she'd started wearing to hide her swollen leg. 'Edna,' she'd said, 'I can hardly even get this clodhopper on. And for what? God Almighty, for what?' She'd been almost crying.

'Oh, you're just getting down in the dumps, honey,' Edna had said. 'It's a good thing you came in to talk to Dr Fukhito. He'll relax you.'

Just then Dr Fukhito had buzzed and said to send Mrs Lewis in. Vangie started down the corridor to his office. Just as she left the reception area, she stumbled. She'd walked right out of that loose left shoe.

'Oh, to hell with it!' she cried, and just kept going. Edna picked up the moccasin, figuring Vangie would come back for it when she finished with Dr Fukhito.

Edna always stayed late Monday nights to work on the books. But when she was ready to go home around nine o'clock, Vangie still hadn't come back. Edna decided to take a chance and ring Dr Fukhito and just tell him that she'd leave the shoe outside the office door in the corridor.

But there was no answer in Dr Fukhito's office. That meant that Vangie must have walked out the door that led directly to the parking lot. That was crazy. She'd catch her death of cold getting her foot wet.

Irresolutely Edna had held the shoe in her hand and locked up. She went out to the parking lot towards her own car just in time to see Vangie's big red Lincoln Continental with Dr Highley at the wheel pull out. She'd tried to run a few steps to wave to him, but it was no use. So she'd just gone home.

Maybe Dr Highley had already made a new appointment with Vangie, but Edna would phone her just to be sure. Quickly she dialled the Lewis number. The phone rang once, twice.

A man's voice answered: 'Lewises' residence.'

'Mrs Lewis, please.' Edna assumed her Drake Secretarial School business voice, crisp but friendly. She wondered if she was talking to Captain Lewis.

'Who's calling?'

'Dr Highley's office. We want to set up Mrs Lewis's next appointment.'

'Hold on.'

She could tell the transmitter was being covered. Muffled voices were talking. What could be going on? Maybe Vangie had been taken sick. If so, Dr Highley should be told at once.

The voice at the other end began to speak. 'This is Detective Cunningham of the Valley County Prosecutor's office. I'm sorry, but Mrs Lewis has died suddenly. You can tell her doctor that he'll be contacted tomorrow morning by someone on our staff.'

41

'*Mrs Lewis died!*' Edna's voice was a howl of dismay. 'Oh, what happened?'

There was a pause. 'It seems she took her own life.' The connection was broken.

Slowly Edna lowered the receiver. It wasn't possible. It just wasn't possible.

The two-o'clock appointments arrived together: Mrs Volmer for Dr Highley, Mrs Lashley for Dr Fukhito. Mechanically Edna greeted them.

'Are you all right, Edna?' Mrs Volmer asked curiously. 'You look upset or something.'

She knew that Mrs Volmer had talked to Vangie in the waiting-room sometimes. It was on the tip of her tongue to tell her that Vangie was dead. But some instinct warned her to tell Dr Highley first.

His one-thirty appointment came out. He was on the intercom. 'Send Mrs Volmer in, Edna.' Edna glanced at the women. There was no way she could talk on the intercom without their hearing her.

'Doctor, may I step in for a moment, please? I'd like to have a word with you.' That sounded so efficient. She was pleased at her own control.

'Certainly.' He didn't sound very happy about it. Highley was a bit scary; still, he could be nice. She'd seen that last night.

She moved down the hall as fast as her overweight body would allow. She was panting when she knocked at his office door. He said, 'Come in, Edna.' His voice was edged with irritation.

Timidly she opened the door and stepped inside his office.

'Doctor,' she began hurriedly, 'you'll want to know. I just phoned Mrs Lewis, Vangie Lewis, to make an appointment. You told me you want to see her every week now.'

'Yes, yes. And for heaven's sake, Edna, close that door. Your voice can be heard through the hospital.'

Quickly she obeyed. Trying to keep her voice low, she said, 'Doctor, when I phoned her house, a detective answered. He said she killed herself and that they're coming to see you tomorrow.'

'Mrs Lewis what?' He sounded shocked.

Now that she could talk about it, Edna's words crowded in her mouth, tumbling out in a torrent. 'She was so upset last night, wasn't she, Doctor? I mean we both could see it. The way she talked to me and the way she acted like she didn't care about anything. But you must know that; I thought it was the nicest thing when I saw you drive her home last night. I tried to wave to you, but you didn't see me. So I guess of all people you know how bad she was.'

'Edna, how many people have you discussed this with?'

There was something in his tone that made her very nervous. Flustered, she avoided his eyes. 'Why, nobody, sir. I just heard this minute.'

'You did not discuss Mrs Lewis's death with Mrs Volmer or anyone else in the reception area?'

'No . . . no, sir.'

'And not with the detective on the phone?'

'No, sir.'

'Edna, tomorrow when the police come, you and I will tell them everthing we know about Mrs Lewis's frame of mind. But listen to me now.' He pointed his finger at her and leaned forward. Unconsciously, she stepped back. 'I don't want Mrs Lewis's name mentioned by you to anyone – *anyone*, do you hear? Mrs Lewis was an extremely neurotic and unstable woman. But the fact is that her suicide reflects very badly on our hospital. How do you think it's going to look in the papers if it comes out that she was a patient of mine? And I certainly won't have you gossiping in the reception room with the other patients, some of whom have very tenuous holds on the foetuses they are carrying. Do you understand me?'

'Yes, sir,' Edna quavered. She should have known he'd think she'd gossip about this.

'Edna, you like your job?'

'Yes, sir.'

'Edna, do not discuss with anyone – *anyone*, mind you – *one word* about the Lewis case. If I hear you have so much as mentioned it, you're finished here. Tomorrow we'll talk with the police, but no one else. Mrs Lewis's state of mind is confidential. Is that clear?'

'Yes, sir.'

'Are you going out with friends tonight? You know how you get when you drink.'

Edna was close to tears. 'I'm going home. I'm not feeling well, Doctor. I want to have my wits about me tomorrow when the police talk to me. Poor little Cinderella.' She gulped as easy tears came to her eyes. But then she saw the expression on his face. Angry. Disgusted.

Edna straightened up, dabbed at her eyes. 'I'll send Mrs Volmer in, Doctor. And you don't have to worry,' she added with dignity. 'I value our hospital. I know how much your work means to you and to our patients. I'm not going to say one single word.'

The rest of the afternoon was busy. She managed to push the thought of Vangie to the back of her mind as she talked with patients, made future appointments, collected money, reminded patients if they were falling behind in their payments.

Finally, at five o'clock she could leave. Warmly wrapped in a leopard-spotted fake-fur coat and matching hat, she drove home to her garden apartment in Edgeriver, six miles away.

CHAPTER NINE

In the clinically impersonal autopsy room of the Valley County Morgue, Richard Carroll gently removed the foetus from the corpse of Vangie Lewis. His long, sensitive fingers lifted the small body, noting that the amniotic fluid had begun to leak. Vangie Lewis could not have carried this baby much longer. He judged that it weighed about two and a half pounds. It was a boy.

The firstborn son. He shook his head at the waste as he laid it on an adjacent slab. Vangie had been in an advanced state of toxaemia. It was incredible that any doctor had allowed her to progress so far in this condition. He'd be interested to know what her white-cell count had been. Probably terrifically high.

He'd already sent fluid samples to the laboratory. He had no doubt that the cyanide killed the woman. Her throat and mouth were badly burned. She'd swallowed a huge gulp of it, God help her.

The burns on the outside of her mouth? Carefully Richard examined them. He tried to visualize the moment she'd drunk the poison. She'd started to swallow, felt the burning, changed her mind, tried to spit it out. It had run over her lips and chin.

To him it didn't wash.

There were fine white fibres clinging to her coat. They looked as though they'd come from a blanket. He was having them analysed. It seemed to him that she had been lying on a chenille spread. He wanted to compare fibres from the spread with those taken from the coat. Of course, the coat was pretty tired-looking, and they might have been picked up at any time.

Her body had become so bloated that it looked as though Vangie had just put on whatever clothes she could find that would cover her.

Except for the shoes. That was another incongruous note. The shoes were well cut and expensive. More than that, they looked quite new. It was unlikely Vangie could have been outdoors on Monday in those and have them in such mint condition. There were no water spots or snow marks on them, even though the ankles of her panty hose had spatters of dirty snow. Didn't that suggest that she must have been out, come in, decided to leave again, changed her shoes and then committed suicide?

That didn't wash either.

Another thing. Those shoes were awfully tight. Particularly the right foot. She could barely lace the shoe, and the vamp was narrow. It would have been like putting on a vice. Considering the rest of the way she was dressed, why bother to put on shoes that will kill you?

Shoes that will kill you . . .

The phrase stuck in Richard's mind. He straightened up. He was just about finished here. As soon as they had a lab report he could tell Scott Myerson what he had found.

Once more he turned to study the foetus. The cyanide had entered its bloodstream. Like its mother, it must have died in agony. Carefully Richard examined it. The miracle of life never

45

ceased to awe him; if anything, it grew with every experience he had with death. He marvelled at the exquisite balance of the body: the harmony of its parts, muscles and fibres, bones and sinews, veins and arteries; the profound complexity of the nervous system, the ability of the body to heal its own wounds, its elaborate attempt to protect its unborn.

Suddenly he bent over the foetus. Swiftly he freed it from the placenta and studied it under the strong light. Was it possible?

It was a hunch, a hunch he had to check out. Dave Broad was the man for him. Dave was in charge of prenatal research at Mt Sinai. He'd send this foetus to him and ask for an opinion.

If what he believed was true, there was a damn good reason why Captain Chris Lewis would have been upset about his wife's pregnancy.

Maybe even upset enough to kill her!

CHAPTER TEN

Scott Myerson, the Valley County Prosecutor, scheduled a five o'clock meeting in his office for Katie, Richard and the two Homicide Squad detectives assigned to the Lewis suicide. Scott's office did not fit the television world's image of a prosecutor's private chambers. It was small. The walls were painted a sickly yellow. The furniture was battered; the ancient files were battleship grey. The windows looked out on the county jail.

Katie arrived first. Gingerly she eased into the one reasonably comfortable extra chair. Scott looked at her with a hint of a smile. He was a small man with a surprisingly deep voice. Large rimmed glasses, a dark, neat moustache and meticulously tailored conservative suit made him look more like a banker than a law enforcer. He had been in court all day on a case he was personally trying and had spoken to Katie only by phone. Now he observed her bandaged arm and the bruise under her eye and the wince of pain that came over her face as she moved her body.

'Thanks for coming in, Katie,' he said. 'I know how overloaded you are and do appreciate it. But you'd better take tomorrow off.'

Katie shook her head. 'No. I'm okay, and this soreness will probably be a lot better in the morning.'

'All right, but remember, if you start feeling rotten, just go home.' He became businesslike. 'The Lewis case. What have we got on it?'

Richard and the detectives came in while she was talking. Silently they settled in the three folding chairs remaining.

Scott tapped a pencil on his desk as he listened. He turned to the detectives. 'What did you come up with?'

Phil Cunningham pulled out his notebook. 'That place was no honeymoon cottage. The Lewises went to some neighbourhood gatherings.' He looked at Katie. 'Guess your sister tried to have them included. Everyone liked Chris Lewis. They thought Vangie was a pain in the neck – obviously jealous of him; not interested in getting involved with any activities in the community; not interested in *anything*. At the parties she was always hanging on him; got real upset if he talked more than five minutes to another woman. He was very patient with her. One of the neighbours said her husband told her after one of those parties that if he were married to Vangie, he'd kill her with his bare hands. Then when she got pregnant she was really insufferable. Talked baby all the time.'

Charley had opened his notebook. 'Her obstetrician's office called to set up an appointment. I said we'd be in to talk to her doctor tomorrow.'

Richard spoke quietly. 'There are a few questions I'd like to ask that doctor about Vangie Lewis's condition.'

Scott looked at Richard. 'You've finished the autopsy?'

'Yes. It was definitely cyanide. She died instantly. The mouth and throat were badly burned. Which leads to the crucial point.'

There were a water pitcher and paper cups on top of the file. Walking over to the file, Richard poured a generous amount of water into a paper cup. 'Okay,' he said, 'this is filled with dissolved cyanide. I am about to kill myself. I take a large gulp.' Quickly he swallowed. The paper cup was still nearly half full. The others watched him intently.

He held up the paper cup. 'In my judgement, Vangie Lewis

47

must have drunk at least the approximately three ounces I just swallowed in order to have the amount of cyanide we found in her system. So far it checks out. But here's the problem. The outside of her lips and chin and even neck were burned. The only way that could have happened would have been if she spat some of the stuff out . . . quite a lot of it out. But if she swallowed as much as she did in one gulp, it means her mouth was empty. Did she then take another mouthful and spit it out? No way. The reaction is instantaneous.'

'She couldn't have swallowed half of the mouthful and spat out the rest?' Scott asked.

Richard shrugged. 'There was too much both in her system and on her face to suggest a split dose. Yet the amount spilled on the spread was negligible, and there were just a few drops at the bottom of the glass. So if she was holding a full tumbler, she'd have had to splash some of it all over her lips and chin, then drink the rest of it to justify the amount expended. It *could* have happened that way, but I don't believe it. The other problem is the shoes she had on.'

Quickly he explained his belief that Vangie Lewis could not have walked comfortably in the shoes that had been laced to her feet. While she listened, Katie visualized Vangie's face. The dead face she had seen in the dream and the dead face she'd seen on the bed slid back and forth in her mind. She forced her attention back to the room and realized Charley was talking to Scott. '. . . Richard and I both feel the husband noticed something about the body that he didn't tell us.'

'I think it was the shoes,' Richard said.

Katie turned to him. 'The phone call Chris Lewis made. I told you about that before, Scott.'

'You did.' Scott leaned back in his chair. 'All right. You two –' he pointed to Charley and Phil – 'find out everything you can about Captain Lewis. See who this Joan is. Find out what time his plane came in this morning. Check on phone calls Vangie Lewis made the last few days. Have Reta see Mrs Lewis's doctor and get his opinion of her mental and physical condition.'

'I can tell you about her physical condition,' Richard said. 'If she hadn't delivered that baby soon, she could have saved her cyanide.'

'There's another thing,' Scott said. 'Where did she get the cyanide?'

'No trace of it in the house,' Charley reported. 'Not a drop. But she was something of a gardener. Maybe she had some stashed away from last summer.'

'Just in case she decided to kill herself?' Scott's voice was humourless. 'Is there anything else?'

Richard hesitated. 'There may be,' he said slowly. 'But it's so far out . . . and in light of what I've just heard, I think I'm barking up the wrong tree. So give me another twenty-four hours. Then I may have something else to throw on the table.'

Scott nodded. 'Get back to me.' He stood up. 'I believe we all agree. We're not closing this as a suicide.' He looked at Richard. 'One more question. Is there any chance that she died somewhere else and was put back in her bed?'

Richard frowned. 'Possible . . . but the way the blood congealed in her body tells me she was lying in the position in which we found her from the minute she drank that cyanide.'

'All right,' Scott said. 'Just a thought. Let's wrap it up for tonight.'

Katie started to get up. 'I know it's insane. But . . .' She felt Richard's arm steadying her.

'You sure look stiff,' he interrupted.

For an instant she'd been about to tell them about the crazy dream she'd had in the hospital. His voice snapped her back to reality. What a fool she'd have appeared to them. Gratefully she smiled at Richard. 'Stiff in the head mostly, I think,' she commented.

CHAPTER ELEVEN

He could not let Edna destroy everything he'd worked for. His hands gripped the wheel. He could feel the trembling in them. He had to calm down.

The exquisite irony that she of all people had seen him drive the Lincoln out of the parking lot. Obviously she'd assumed that Vangie was with him in the car. But the minute she told her story to the police, everything would be over. He could hear the questions: 'You drove Mrs Lewis home, Doctor. What did you do when you left her? Did you call a cab? What time was that, Doctor? Miss Burns tells us that you left the parking lot shortly after nine p.m.'

The autopsy would certainly prove that Vangie had died around that time. What would they think if he told them he'd walked back to the hospital in that storm?

Edna had to be silenced. His medical bag was on the seat next to him. The only thing in it was the paperweight from his office desk. He didn't usually bother to carry a bag with him any more, but he'd taken it out this morning planning to put the moccasins in it. He'd intended to drive into New York for dinner and leave the shoes in separate litter cans to be collected in the morning.

But this morning Hilda had come in early. She'd stood in the foyer talking to him while he put on his grey tweed overcoat. She'd handed him his hat and the bag. It was impossible to transfer the moccasins from the Burberry to the bag in front of her. What would she have thought? But no matter. The Burberry was to the back of the closet. She had no reason to go near it, and tonight when he finished with Edna he would go home. He'd get rid of the shoes tomorrow night.

It was a stroke of luck that Edna lived so near the hospital. That was why he knew her apartment. Several times he'd dropped off work for her when she was laid up with sciatica. He'd just had to check the apartment number to be sure. He'd have to make it look like a murder committed during a felony. Katie DeMaio's office would be involved, but would certainly never connect the homicide of an obscure bookkeeper with either her employer or Vangie Lewis.

He'd take her wallet, grab any bits of jewellery she had. Racking his brain, he remembered that she owned a butterfly-shaped pin with a minuscule ruby and an engagement ring with a dot of a diamond in it. She'd shown them to him when he'd left some work at her place a few months ago.

'This was my mother's ring, Doctor,' she'd said proudly. 'Dad and she fell in love on their first date and he brought it to her on their second date. Would you believe they were both in their early forties then? Dad gave it to me when Mom died. That was three years ago, and you know he didn't live but two months without her. Of course, Mom had smaller fingers; that's why I wear it on my pinkie. And he gave her the pin on their tenth anniversary.'

He'd chafed through the tiresome recital, but now realized that like everything else, it was potentially useful. He'd been sitting by her bed. She kept her cheap plastic jewellery box in the night-table drawer. That ring, the pin and the wallet from her handbag would be easy to carry and would clearly establish a robbery-connected murder.

Then he'd get rid of them and the shoes and that would be the end.

Except for Katie DeMaio.

He rubbed the underside of his lower lip over his upper lip. His mouth was dry.

He had to think about Edna's apartment. How would he get in? Did he dare ring the bell, let her admit him? Suppose she wasn't alone?

But she would be alone. He was sure of it. She was going home to drink. He could tell from the nervous, eager movements she made while he watched her from the corridor. She'd been excited, agitated, obviously filled with the stories she wanted to tell to the police tomorrow.

Freezing perspiration drenched him at the thought that she might have decided to talk to the patients in the reception room before she talked to him about Vangie. The Ednas of this world want an audience. Listen to me. Notice me. I exist!

Not for long, Edna, not for long.

He was driving into her apartment area. Last time he'd left the car behind her apartment in one of the visitor stalls. Did he dare drive right there now? It was cold, windy, dark. Few people would be standing around. Anyone who was coming in would be hurrying, not noticing a perfectly ordinary dark, medium-priced car. Last time he'd walked around the end of her apartment-building unit. She lived on the ground floor of the last apartment. Thick bushes tried to hide a rusting chain-link fence that separated the complex from a steep ravine which dropped down a dozen feet and terminated in railroad tracks, a spur of the main line.

Edna's bedroom window backed on to the parking lot. There were high, untrimmed bushes under her window. The window was ground level – quite low, if he remembered correctly. Suppose that window was unlocked? By now, if he had any judgement, Edna would be very drunk. He could go in and out by the window. That would lend credence to the burglary. Otherwise, he'd ring the bell, go in, kill her and then leave. Even if he were found out, were seen, he'd simply say that he'd stopped by to drop off papers, then decided not to leave them because she was drinking. Some intruder must have come in later. No one in his right mind would accuse a wealthy doctor of robbing a penniless bookkeeper.

Satisfied, he slowed down as he approached the apartment complex. The double units, all exactly the same, looked stark and forlorn in the cold February night.

The parking area had a half-dozen cars in it. He drove between a camper and a stationwagon. His car disappeared into the cavelike space the larger vehicles provided. He pulled on his surgical gloves and put the paperweight in his coat pocket. Sliding cautiously out, he closed the door noiselessly and disappeared into the deep shadows cast by the building. Silently he thanked the gods that Edna lived in the very last apartment. Absolutely no chance of his mistaking where to go.

Her bedroom shade was pulled down most of the way, but she had a plant in the window. The shade rested on the top of the plant, and he could see in clearly. The room was lighted by a foyer fixture. The window was open a crack. She must be in the living-room or dining area. He could hear the faint sound of a television programme. He would go in through the window.

Glancing rapidly about, he once again assured himself that the area was deserted. With steely-strong gloved fingers he raised the window, noiselessly pulled up the shade, quietly lifted the plant out on to the ground. Later it would be clear proof of the method of entry. He hoisted himself on to the windowsill. For a big man he was surprisingly agile.

He was in the bedroom. In the dim light he absorbed the virginal tidiness, the candlewick bedspread, the crucifix over the bed, the framed photos of an elderly couple, the lace runner on the scarred top of the mahogany-veneer dresser.

Now for the necessary part, the part he detested. He felt for the paperweight in his pocket. He had decided to bludgeon her. Once he had read that a doctor had been proved guilty of murder because of the flawlessly accurate stabbing. He could not risk having his medical knowledge reveal him. It was his medical knowledge that had brought him to this place.

He began to tiptoe down the short foyer. Bathroom to the right. Living-room six feet ahead to the left. Cautiously he peered into it. The television set was on, but the room was empty. He could hear the sound of a chair creaking. She must be at the dinette table. With infinite care he moved into the living-room. This was the moment. If she saw him and screamed . . .

But her back was to him. Wrapped in a woolly blue robe, she was slumped in a chair at the head of the table. One hand was next to an outsized cocktail glass, the other folded in her lap. A tall pitcher in front of her was almost empty. Her head was on her chest. Faint, even breathing told him she was asleep. She smelled heavily of alcohol.

Quickly he appraised the situation. His eye fell on the hissing radiator to the right of the table. It was the old-fashioned kind with sharp, exposed pipes. Was it possible he didn't need the paperweight after all? Maybe . . .

'Edna,' he whispered softly.

'Wha . . . oh . . .' She looked up at him with bleary eyes. Confused, she began to rise, twisting awkwardly in her chair. 'Doctor . . .'

A mighty shove sent her smashing backwards. Her head cracked against the radiator. Blinding lights exploded in her brain. Oh, the pain! Oh, God, the pain! Edna sighed. The soothing warmth of her gushing blood floated her into darkness. The pain spread, intensified, peaked, receded, ended.

He jumped back, careful to stay clear of the spattered blood, then bent over her carefully. As he watched, the pulse in her throat flickered and stopped. He held his face close to hers. She had stopped breathing. He slipped the paperweight into his pocket. He wouldn't need it now. He wouldn't have to bother robbing her. It would look as though she'd fallen. He was lucky.

He was meant to be safe.

Quickly retracing his steps, he went back into the bedroom. Scanning to assure himself that the parking area was still empty, he stepped out the window, remembered to replace the plant, pulled down the shade and closed the window to the exact place where Edna had had it.

As he did, he heard the persistent chiming of a doorbell – *her doorbell!* Frantically he looked around. The ground, hard and dry, offered no evidence of his footprints. The windowsill was meticulously clean. No disturbed dust there. He'd stepped over it, so no sign of his shoes marred the white surface.

He ran back to his car. Quietly the engine started. Without turning on his headlights he drove out of the apartment complex. As he approached Route 4, he turned on the lights.

Who was standing on Edna's doorstep? Would that person try to get in? Edna was dead. She couldn't gossip about him now. But it had been so close, so terribly close.

Adrenaline pounded through his veins. Now there was only one possible threat left: Katie DeMaio.

He would begin to remove that threat now. Her accident had given him the excuse he needed to start medication.

It was a matter of hospital record that her blood count was low. She had received a transfusion in the emergency room.

He would order another transfusion for her on the pretence of building her up for the operation.

He would give cumadin pills to her. They would short-circuit her clotting apparatus and negate the benefits of the transfusion. By Friday when she came into the hospital she'd be on the verge of haemorrhaging.

It might be possible to perform emergency surgery without administering further anticoagulants. But if necessary he would inject her with heparin. There would be a total depletion of the coagulation precursors. She would not survive that surgery.

The initial low blood count, the cumadin and the heparin would be as effective on Katie DeMaio as the cyanide had been on Vangie Lewis.

CHAPTER TWELVE

Richard and Katie left Scott's office together. She had known he'd be annoyed if she suggested calling a cab to take her home. But when they got into his car, he said, 'Dinner first. A steak and a bottle of wine will set your juices running.'

'What juices?' she asked cautiously.

'Saliva. Stomach. Whatever.'

He chose a cabin-type restaurant that perched precariously on the Palisades. The small dining-room was warmed by a blazing fire and lit by candles.

'Oh, this is nice,' she said.

The proprietor obviously knew Richard well. 'Dr Carroll, a pleasure,' he said as he guided them to the table in front of the fireplace and pulled out a chair for Katie.

She grinned as she sat down, thinking that either Richard rated or she must look as chilled and woebegone as she felt.

Richard ordered a bottle of St Emilion; a waiter produced hot garlic bread. They sat in companionable silence, sipping and nibbling. Katie realized it was the first time she had been with him like this, across a small table, separated from everyone else in the room, looking at each other.

Richard was a big man with a wholesome, thoroughly healthy look that was manifested in his thick crop of dark brown hair, his strong, even features and broad, rangy shoulders. When he's old, he'll have a leonine quality, she thought.

'You just smiled,' Richard said. 'The usual penny for your thoughts.'

She told him.

'Leonine.' He considered the word thoughtfully. 'A lion in winter. I'd settle for that. Are you interested in what I'm thinking?'

'Sure.'

'When your face is in repose, your eyes are very sad, Katie.'

'Sorry. I don't mean them to be. I don't think of myself as being sad.'

'Do you know I've been wanting to ask you out for the last six months but it took an accident that might have killed you to make it happen?'

'You never asked me out,' she said evasively.

'You never *wanted* to be asked out. There's a definite signal you release. "Do Not Disturb." Why?'

'I don't believe in going out with anyone I work with,' she said. 'Just on general principles.'

'I can understand that. But that's not what we're talking about. We enjoy each other's company. We both know it. But you're having none of it. Here's the menu.'

His manner changed, became brisk. '*L'entrecote* ánd the steak *au poivre* are the specialties here,' he told her. When she hesitated, he suggested, 'Try the *poivre*. It's fantastic. Rare,' he added hopefully.

'Well done,' Katie said.

At his look of horror she laughed out loud. 'Of course rare.'

His face cleared. He ordered salads with house dressing and baked potatoes, then leaned back and studied her.

'Are you having none of it, Katie?'

'The salad? The steak?'

'No. Don't keep weaving and dancing. All right, I'm not being fair. I'm trying to pin you down and you're a captive audience. But tell me what you do when you're not at the office or the Kennedys'. I know you ski.'

'Yes. I have a college friend who's divorced. The winter after John died, she dragged me up to Vermont with her. Now she and I and two couples rent a condominium in Stowe during the ski season. I go weekends as often as I can. I'm not a great skier, but I enjoy it.'

'I used to ski,' Richard said. 'Had to give it up because of a twisted knee. I should try it again. Maybe you'll invite me up some time with you.' He did not wait for an answer. 'Sailing is my sport. I took my boat to the Caribbean last spring and went from island to island . . . "brilliance of cloudless days with broad bellying sails, they glide to the wind tossing green water . . ." Here's your steak,' he finished lightly.

'And you also quote William Carlos Williams,' she murmured.

She had secretly expected him to be impressed that she knew the quotation, but he didn't seem surprised. 'Yes, I do,' he said. 'The house dressing is good, isn't it?'

They lingered over coffee. By then Richard had told her about himself. 'I was engaged during med school to the girl next door. I think you know I grew up in San Francisco.'

'What happened?' Katie asked.

'We kept postponing the wedding. Eventually she married my best friend, whoever he is.' Richard smiled. 'I'm joking, of course. Jean was a very nice girl. But there was something missing. One night when for the fourth or fifth time we were discussing getting married, she said, "Richard, we love each other, but we both know there's something more." She was right.'

'No regrets; no second thoughts?' Katie asked.

'Not really. That was seven years ago. I'm a little surprised that the "something more" didn't happen along before now.'

He did not seem to expect her to comment. Instead he began to talk about the Lewis case. 'It makes me so angry; any waste of life affects me like that. Vangie Lewis was a young woman. She should have had a lot of years ahead of her.'

'You're convinced it wasn't a suicide?'

'I'm not *convinced* of anything. I'll need to have much more information before I pass judgement.'

'I don't see Chris Lewis as a murderer. It's too easy to get a divorce today if you want to be free.'

'There's another angle to that.' Richard pressed his lips together. 'Let's hold off talking about it.

It was nearly ten-thirty when they turned into Katie's driveway. Richard looked quizzically at the handsome fieldstone house. 'How big is this place?' he asked. 'I mean how many rooms have you got?'

'Twelve,' Katie said reluctantly. 'It was John's house.'

'I didn't think you bought it on an assistant prosecutor's salary,' Richard commented.

She started to open the car door. 'Hold it,' he said. 'I'll come around. It may still be slippery.'

She had not planned to invite him in, but he did not give her the chance to say good-night at the door. Taking the key from her hand, he put it in the lock, turned it, opened the door and followed her in. 'I'm not going to stay,' he said, 'but I do admit to an overwhelming curiosity as to where you keep yourself.'

She turned on the light and watched somewhat resentfully as he looked over the foyer and then the living-room. He whistled. 'Very, very nice.' He walked over to John's portrait and studied it. 'From what I heard, he was quite a guy.'

'Yes, he was.' Uncomfortably, Katie realized that on nearly every table there was a picture of herself and John. Richard went from one to the next. 'A trip abroad?'

'Our honeymoon.' Her lips were stiff.

'How long were you married, Katie?'

'One year.'

He watched as a look of pain flickered over her face; it was more than that: an expression of surprise too, as though she were still puzzled about what had happened. 'When did you find out that he was sick? It was cancer, I understand.'

'Shortly after we got back from our honeymoon.'

'So you never really had more than that trip, did you? After that it was a deathwatch. Sorry, Katie; my job makes me blunt – too blunt for my own good, I guess. I'll take off now.' He hesitated. 'Don't you believe in drawing these drapes when you're alone here?'

She shrugged. 'Why? No one's going to come barging in on me.'

'You, of all people, should be aware of the number of home burglaries. And in this location you'd be a prime target, especially if anyone knew you're alone here. Do you mind?'

Without waiting for an answer he went over to the window and pulled the draperies shut. 'I'll be on my way. See you tomorrow. How are you going to get to work? Will your car be ready?'

'No, but the service people are going to lend me one. They'll drop it off in the morning.'

'Okay.' For a moment he stood with his hand on the knob, then in a highly credible brogue said, 'I'll be leavin' ye, Katie Scarlett. Lock your door, now. I wouldn't want anyone tryin' to break into Tara.' He bent down, kissed her cheek and was gone.

Smiling, Katie closed the door. A memory raced through her mind. She was five years old, joyously playing in the muddy backyard in her Easter dress. Her mother's outraged cry. Her father's amused voice doing his Gerald O'Hara imitation: 'It's the land, Katie Scarlett' – then, in a wheedling voice, to her mother: 'Don't get mad at her. All good Micks love the land.'

The clock chimed musically. After Richard's bear-warm presence, the room seemed hollow. Quickly she turned out the light and went upstairs.

The phone rang just as she got into bed. Molly has probably been trying to get me, she thought as she lifted the receiver. But it was a man's voice who responded when she said hello.

'Mrs DeMaio?'

'Yes.'

'This is Dr Highley. I hope I'm not calling too late, but I've tried several times to reach you this evening. The fact that you were in an accident and were in our hospital overnight has come to my attention. How are you feeling?'

'Quite well, Doctor. How nice of you to call.'

'How is the bleeding problem? According to your records you had a transfusion here last night.'

'I'm afraid it's about the same. I thought I was over my period, but it started again yesterday. I honestly think I may have been a bit light-headed when I lost control of the car.'

'Well, as you know, you should have taken care of this condition at least a year ago. Never mind. It will all be behind you by this time next week. But I do want you to have another transfusion to build you up for the surgery, and I also want you to start in on some pills. Can you come to the hospital tomorrow afternoon?'

'Yes. As a matter of fact, there was a chance I was coming anyhow. You've heard about Mrs Lewis?'

'I have A terrible and sad situation. Well, then, I'll see you tomorrow. Call in the morning and we'll arrange a definite time.'

'Yes, Doctor. Thank you, Doctor.'

Katie hung up. As she turned out the light, she reflected that Dr Highley hadn't really appealed to her on her first visit. Was it because of his reserved, even aloof attitude?

It shows how you can misjudge people, she decided. It's very nice of him to personally keep trying to get in touch with me tonight.

CHAPTER THIRTEEN

Bill Kennedy rang the bell of the Lewis house. An orthopaedic surgeon at Lenox Hill Hospital, he had been operating all day and did not hear about Vangie Lewis's death until he returned home. Tall, prematurely white, scholarly and somewhat shy in his professional life, Bill became a different person when he entered the warm haven of the home Molly created for him.

Her bustling presence made it possible for him to leave behind the problems of his patients and relax. But tonight the atmosphere had been different. Molly had already fed the children and given them strict orders to stay out of the way. Briefly she told him about Vangie. 'I called and asked Chris to come to dinner and to sleep in the den tonight rather than be alone over there. He doesn't want to, but you go drag him here. I'm sure he'll at least come to dinner.'

As he walked between the houses, Bill considered the shock it would be to come home and find he had lost Molly. But it wouldn't be the same for Chris Lewis. No one in his right mind could think that that marriage had been anything like his and Molly's. Bill had never told Molly that one morning when he was having coffee at a drugstore near the hospital he'd seen Chris in a booth with a very pretty girl in her early twenties. It was written all over the two of them that they were involved with each other.

Had Vangie known about the girl? Was that why she'd committed suicide? But so violently! His mind flashed back to the summer. Vangie and Bill had been over for a barbecue. Vangie had started to roast a marshmallow and gotten her hand too near the heat. Her finger had blistered and she'd carried on as though she'd been covered with third-degree burns. She'd gone shrieking to Chris, who had tried to calm her down. Embarrassed for her, Chris had explained, 'Vangie has a low pain tolerance.' By the time Bill got salve and applied it, the blister was practically non-existent.

Where would a person of Vangie's emotional make-up get the courage to take cyanide? Anyone who'd read anything about that poison would know that even though death was almost instantaneous, one died in agony.

No. Bill would have sworn that Vangie Lewis committing suicide would have swallowed sleeping pills and fallen asleep. Showed how little anyone knew about the human mind . . . even someone like himself who was supposed to be a pretty good judge of people.

Chris Lewis opened the door. Ever since he'd spotted him with the girl, Bill had been somewhat reserved with Chris. He just didn't cotton to men who ran around when their wives were pregnant. But now the sight of Chris's drawn face and the genuine sadness in his eyes called up Bill's compassion. He gripped the younger man's arms. 'I'm terribly sorry.'

Chris nodded woodenly. It seemed to him that like an onion peeling layer by layer, the meaning of the day was sinking in on him. Vangie was dead. Had their quarrel driven her to kill herself? He couldn't believe it, and yet he felt lonely, frightened and guilty. He allowed Bill to persuade him to come to dinner. He had to get out of the house – he couldn't think clearly there. Molly and Bill were good people. Could he trust them with what he knew? Could he trust *anyone*? Numbly reaching for a jacket, he followed Bill down the street.

Bill poured a double scotch for him. Chris gulped it. When the glass was half-empty he forced himself to slow down. The whisky burned his throat and chest, making a passage through the tension. Calm down, he thought, calm down. Be careful.

The Kennedy kids came into the den to say good-night. Well-behaved kids, all of them. Good-looking too. The oldest boy, Billy, resembled his father. Jennifer was a dark-haired beauty. The younger girls, Dina and Moira, were fair like Molly. The twins. Chris almost smiled. The twins looked like each other. Chris had always wanted children. Now his unborn child had died with Vangie. Another guilt. He had resented her pregnancy. His child, and he hadn't wanted it, not for one single second. And Vangie had known it. What had, *who* had driven her to kill herself? Who? That was the question. Because Vangie hadn't been alone last night.

He hadn't told the police. It would be opening up a can of worms, *begging* them to start an investigation. And where would that lead? To Joan. The other woman. To him.

The clerk had seen him leave the motel last night. He'd started to come home, to have it out with Vangie. He'd even jotted down figures to discuss with her. She could have the house. He'd give her twenty thousand a year, at least until the baby was eighteen. He'd carry a large insurance policy on his life for her. He'd educate the baby. She could keep on going to that Japanese psychiatrist she was so crazy about. Only let me go, Vangie. Please let me go. I can't spend any more of my life with you. It's destroying both of us . . .

He'd gotten as far as the house. Somewhere around midnight he'd arrived. He'd driven in and the minute the garage door opened, knew something was up. Because he'd almost rammed the Lincoln. She'd parked in his space. No, someone else parked her car in *his* space. Because no way would Vangie ever try to drive that wide car into the area between the posts and the right wall. The garage was an oversized one. One side could hold two cars. That was the side Vangie always used. And she needed every inch. She was a lousy driver, and her peripheral vision probably wasn't that great either. She simply couldn't judge space well. Chris always parked his Corvette in the narrower side. But last night the Lincoln had been expertly parked there.

He'd gone in and found the house empty. Vangie's handbag was on the chaise in their room. He'd been puzzled but not alarmed. Obviously she'd gone off with someone to stay overnight. He'd even been pleased that maybe she had a girl-friend to confide in. He'd always tried to make her develop friends. And Vangie could be secretive. He wondered if she'd forgotten her handbag. Vangie was forgetful, or maybe she'd packed an overnight bag and didn't want to bother with the heavy purse.

The house depressed Chris. He decided to go back to the motel. He hadn't told Joan about coming home. He was careful to say as little as possible to Joan about Vangie. To Joan, any mention of Vangie was a continuing reminder of what she saw to be her own position as an interloper. If he'd told Joan this morning that he and Vangie had quarrelled and Vangie had obviously been so upset she'd gone to stay with someone rather than be alone, Joan would have been heartsick.

But then this morning he'd found Vangie dead. Somebody had parked the car for her before midnight. Somebody had driven her home after midnight. And those shoes. The one day she'd worn them she'd complained endlessly about them. That was around Christmas when he'd taken her to New York, trying to give her some fun. Fun! God, what a miserable day. She hadn't liked the play. The restaurant didn't serve veal piccata and she'd set her heart on it. And she'd talked incessantly about how the shoe dug into her right ankle.

For weeks now she'd worn nothing but those dirty moccasins. He'd asked her to please get some decent shoes, but she'd said these were the only comfortable ones. Where were they? Chris had searched the house thoroughly. Whoever drove her home might know.

He hadn't told the police any of this. He hadn't wanted to involve Joan. 'I checked into a motel because my wife and I had quarrelled. I wanted a divorce. I decided to come home and try to reason with her. She wasn't here and I left.' It hadn't seemed necessary to drag all this in. Even the shoes really weren't that important. Vangie might have wanted to be fully dressed when she was found. That swollen leg embarrassed her. She was vain.

But he should have told the cops about his being here, about the way the car was parked.

'Chris, come into the dining-room. You'll feel better if you eat something.' Molly's voice was gentle.

Wearily, Chris looked up. The soft hallway light silhouetted Molly's face, and for the first time he could see a family resemblance between her and Katie DeMaio.

Katie DeMaio. Her *sister*. He couldn't discuss this with Bill and Molly. It would put Molly in the middle. How could she honestly advise him whether or not to keep quiet about his coming home last night when her own sister was in the Prosecutor's office? No. He'd have to decide this on his own.

He brushed a hand over burning eyes. 'I would like to have something, Molly,' he said. 'Whatever it is, sure smells good. But I'll have to leave pretty quickly. The funeral director is coming to the house for Vangie's clothes. Her mother and father want to be able to see her before the interment.'

'Where will it be?' Bill asked.

'The coffin will be flown to Minneapolis tomorrow afternoon. I'll be on that plane too. The service will be the next day. The Medical Examiner released her body late this afternoon.' The words hammered in his ears . . . Coffin . . . Body . . . Funeral . . . Oh, God, he thought, this had to be a nightmare. I wanted to be free of you, Vangie, but I didn't want you to die. I drove you to suicide. Joan's right. I should have stood by you.

At eight he went back to his house. At eight-thirty, when the funeral director came, he had a suitcase with underwear and the flowing caftan Vangie's parents had sent her for Christmas.

The funeral director, Paul Halsey, was quietly sympathetic. He requested the necessary information quickly. Born April 15. He jotted down the year. Died February 15 – just two months short of her thirty-first birthday, he commented.

Chris rubbed the ache between his eyes. Something was wrong. Even in this unreal situation where *everything* was wrong, there was something specific. 'No,' he said, 'today's the *sixteenth*, not the *fifteenth*.'

'The death certificate clearly states that Mrs Lewis died between eight and ten p.m. last night, February fifteenth,' Halsey said. 'You're thinking the sixteenth because you *found* her this morning. But the examiner who performed the autopsy can pinpoint the time of death accurately.'

Chris stared at him. Waves of shock dissolved his sense of exhaustion and unreality. He had been home at midnight and the car and Vangie's purse had been here. He'd waited around for about half an hour before he drove back to the motel in New York. When he'd come home this morning, he'd assumed that Vangie had come in some time after he left and killed herself.

But at midnight she'd already been dead three or four hours. That meant that some time after midnight, after he left, someone had brought her body here, put it on her bed and laid the empty glass beside her.

Someone had wanted to make it seem that Vangie had committed suicide.

Had she killed herself somewhere else? Had someone brought her back who simply didn't want to be involved? Of course not. Vangie had never inflicted the pain of cyanide poisoning on herself. Her murderer had staged the suicide.

'Oh, Christ,' Chris whispered. 'Oh, Christ.' Vangie's face filled his vision. The wide, thickly lashed, petulant eyes; the short, straight nose; the honey-coloured hair that fell over her forehead; the small, perfectly formed lips. At the last moment she must have known. Someone had held her, forced that poison into her, viciously killed her and the baby she was carrying. She must have been so frightened. A tearing wrench of pity brought tears to his eyes. No one, no *husband*, could be silent and let those deaths go unpunished.

But if he told the police; if he started an investigation, there was one person they would inevitably accuse. As the funeral director stared at him, Chris said aloud, 'I have to tell them, and they're going to blame it on me.'

CHAPTER FOURTEEN

He hung up the phone slowly. Katie DeMaio suspected nothing. Even when she mentioned Vangie Lewis's name there hadn't been any hint that her office wanted anything more than to discuss Vangie's emotional state with him.

But Katie's accident had happened barely twenty-four hours ago. She was probably still experiencing a certain amount of shock reaction.

Her blood count was already low. Tomorrow when the cumadin was introduced into her system, the clotting mechanism would begin to collapse, and with the further haemorrhaging she'd begin to feel disoriented, light-headed. Certainly she would not be analytical enough to separate a supposed nightmare from an actual event.

Unless, of course, there were too many questions about the

suicide. Unless the possibility of Vangie's body's having been moved was introduced and discussed in her office.

The danger was still so great.

He was in the library of the Westlake home – his home now. The house was a manorlike Tudor. It had archways and built-in bookcases and marble fireplaces and hand-blocked antique wallpaper and Tiffany stained-glass windows: the kind of home impossible to duplicate today at any price. The craftsmanship wasn't available.

The Westlake House. The Westlake Hospital. The Westlake Maternity Concept. The name had served him well, given him immediate entrée, socially and professionally. He was the distinguished obstetrician who had met Winifred Westlake on a transatlantic sailing, married her and relocated in America to carry on her father's work.

The perfect excuse for having left England. No one, including Winifred, knew about the years before Liverpool at Christ Hospital in Devon.

Towards the end she had started to ask questions.

It was nearly eleven o'clock and he hadn't had dinner yet. Knowing what he was going to do to Edna had robbed him of the desire to eat.

But now that it was over, the release had come. Now the need for food had become a craving. He went into the kitchen. Hilda had left dinner for him in the microwave oven: a small Cornish hen with wild rice. He just needed to heat it up for a few minutes. When he had time he preferred to cook his own meals. Hilda's food was without imagination, even though it was well enough prepared.

She was a good housekeeper, too. He liked coming home to the elegant orderliness of this place, to sip a drink, to eat when he chose, to spend hours working on his notes in the library, unthreatened by the possibility of someone's dropping in, as occasionally happened at his hospital laboratory.

He needed the freedom of the house. He'd gotten rid of the live-in housekeeper Winifred and her father had had. Hostile bitch, looking at him with sour, sullen eyes, swollen with weeping. 'Miss Winifred was almost never sick until . . .'

He'd stared at her and she hadn't finished. What she was

66

going to say was 'until she married you.'

Winifred's cousin resented him bitterly, had tried to make trouble after Winifred's death. But he couldn't prove anything. There hadn't been one shred of tangible evidence. They'd dismissed the cousin as a disgruntled ex-heir.

Of course, there hadn't been that much money at all. Winifred had sunk so much into purchasing the hospital. Now his research was taking staggering amounts, and most of it had to come directly from the practice. He couldn't apply for a grant, of course. But even so, he could manage. Women were willing to pay anything to conceive.

Hilda had set the table for him in the small dining-room off the pantry – the morning room it used to be called. He would not eat any meal in the kitchen, but the twenty-by-thirty-foot dining-room was ostentatious and ridiculous for a solitary diner. This room with its round pedestal table, Queen Anne cabinet and view of the tree-filled side lawn was far more appealing.

Selecting a chilled bottle of Pouilly-Fuissé from the refrigerator, he sat down to eat.

He finished dinner thoughtfully, his mind running over the exact dosage he would give Katie DeMaio. The cumadin would not be suspected in her bloodstream after death. Failure of coagulation would be attributed to the transfusions. If he had to administer the heparin, traces of it and the cumadin might show if there was a thorough autopsy. But he had an idea of what he could do to circumvent that.

Before going to bed, he went out to the foyer closet. He'd get those moccasins safely in his bag now, not risk a recurrence of this morning's annoyance. Reaching back into the closet, he put his hand in one pocket of the Burberry and pulled out a misshapen shoe. Expectantly he put his free hand in the other pocket – first matter-of-factly, then urgently. Finally he grabbed the coat and rummaged frantically all over it. Then he sank to his knees and pawed through the overshoes neatly stacked on the closet floor.

Finally he stood up, staring at the battered moccasin he was holding. Again he saw himself tugging the shoe off Vangie's right foot.

67

The *right* shoe.

The shoe he was holding.

Hysterically he began to laugh – noisy, rattling sounds wrenched from the frustrated fury of his being. After all the danger, after the ignominious crawling around the parking lot like a dog sniffing to pick up a scent, he had botched it.

Somehow in the dark, probably that time he'd shrunk against the shrubbery when the car roared into the parking lot, the shoe had fallen out of his pocket. The shoe he'd *found* was the one he'd already *had*.

And somewhere, the battered, shabby, ugly left moccasin that Vangie Lewis had been wearing was waiting to be found; waiting to trace her footsteps back to him.

CHAPTER FIFTEEN

Katie had set the clock radio for six a.m., but was wide awake long before the determinedly cheery voice of the CBS anchorman wished her a bright morning. Her sleep had been troubled; several times she'd almost started to jump up, frightened by a vague, troubling dream.

She always turned the thermostat low at night. Shivering, she ran to adjust it, then quickly made coffee and brought a cup back upstairs to bed.

Propped against the pillows, the thick comforter wrapped around her, she eagerly sipped as the heat of the cup began to warm her fingers. 'That's better,' she murmured. 'And now, what's the matter with me?'

The antique Williamsburg dresser with its oval centre mirror was directly opposite the bed. She glanced into it. Her hair was tousled, a dark brown smudge against the ivory eyelet-edged pillowcases. The bruise under her eye was now purple tinged with yellow. Her eyes were swollen with sleep. Deep crescents accentuated the thinness of her face. As Mama would say, I look like something the cat dragged in, she reflected.

But it was more than the way she looked. It was even more

than the overall achiness from the accident. It was a heavy feeling of apprehension. Had she started to dream that queer, frightening nightmare again last night? She couldn't be sure.

Vangie Lewis. A line from John's funeral service came to her: 'We who are saddened at the certainty of death . . .' Death was certain, of course. But not like that. It was bad enough to think of Vangie taking her own life, but it seemed impossible that anyone would choose to kill her by forcing cyanide down her throat. She simply didn't believe Chris Lewis was capable of that kind of violence.

She thought of Dr Highley's call. That damn operation. Oh, there were thousands of D-and-Cs performed every year on women of every age. It wasn't the operation itself. It was the reason for it. Suppose the D-and-C didn't clear up the haemorrhaging? Dr Highley had hinted that eventually it might be necessary to consider a hysterectomy.

If only she had become pregnant during the year with John. But she hadn't.

Suppose she did remarry some day. Wouldn't it be a bitter, miserable trick if by then she couldn't have children? Knock it off, she warned herself. Remember that line from *Faust*? We weep for what we may never lose.

Well, at least she was getting the operation over with. Check in Friday night. Operation Saturday, home Sunday. At work Monday. No big deal.

Molly had called her after she got to the office yesterday. She'd said, 'Katie, I could tell you didn't want me to talk in front of Richard, but don't you think it would be better to postpone going to the hospital till next month? You got a pretty good shaking up.'

She'd been vehement. 'No way. I want to be through with this; and besides, Molly, I wouldn't be surprised if this darn business contributed to the accident. I felt light-headed a couple of times Monday.'

Molly had been distressed. 'Why didn't you tell me?'

'Oh, come on,' Katie had said. 'You and I both hate complainers. When it's really bad, I swear I'll yell for you.'

'I hope so,' Molly said. 'I guess you might as well get it over with.' Then she'd asked, 'Are you going to tell Richard?'

Katie had tried not to sound exasperated. 'No, and I'm not going to tell the elevator operator or the street-crossing guard or Dial-a-Friend. Just you and Bill. And that's where we leave it. Okay?'

'Okay. And don't be a smart-ass.' Molly had hung up decisively, her tone a combination of affection and authoritativeness, the warning-signal voice she used when one of the kids was getting out of line.

I'm not your child, Molly, girl, Katie thought now. I love you, but I'm not your child. But as she sipped the coffee she wondered if she was leaning too much on Molly and Bill, drawing emotional support from them. Was she indeed coasting on their coat-tails out of the mainstream of life?

Oh, John. She glanced instinctively at his picture. This morning it was just that, a picture. A handsome, grave-looking man with gentle, penetrating eyes. Once during that first year after his death she'd picked up that picture, stared at it, then slammed it face down on the dresser crying, 'How could you have left me?'

The next morning she'd been back on balance, ashamed of herself, and had made a resolution never to have three glasses of wine when she was feeling low. When she'd straightened the picture, she'd found a gouge in the lovely old dresser top which had been caused by the embossed silver frame. She'd tried to explain to the picture. 'It isn't just self-pity, Judge. I'm angry for *you*. I wanted you to have another forty years. You knew how to enjoy life; how to do something worthwhile with life.'

For who hath known the mind of the Lord? or who hath been His counsellor? That phrase from the Bible had flitted across her mind that day.

Remembering, Katie thought, I'd better think along those lines now.

Stripping off her pale green nightgown, she went into the bathroom and turned on the shower. The nightgown trailed over the bench at her dressing table. In college she'd favoured striped drop-seat p.j.'s. But John had bought her exquisite gowns and peignoirs in Italy. It still seemed appropriate to wear them here in this house, in his bedroom.

Maybe Richard was right. Maybe she was keeping a deathwatch. John would be the first one to blast her for that.

The hot shower helped to pick up her spirits. She had a plea-bargaining session scheduled for nine, a sentencing at ten and two new cases to begin preparing for trial for next week. And she had plenty of work to do on this Friday's trial. It's Wednesday already, she thought with dismay. I'd better get a move on.

She dressed quickly, selecting a soft brown wool skirt and a new turquoise silk shirt with full sleeves that covered the bandage on her arm.

The loan car from the service station arrived as she finished a second coffee. She dropped the driver back at the station, whistled as she saw the extensive damage to the front of her car, counted her blessings that she hadn't been seriously injured and drove to the office.

It had been a busy night in the county. A fourteen-year-old girl had been raped. People were talking about a drunken-driving accident that had resulted in four deaths. A local police chief had called requesting that the Prosecutor help set up a line-up for the victim to view suspects who had been picked up after an armed robbery.

Scott was just coming out of his office. 'Lovely night,' Katie observed.

He nodded. 'Son of a bitch – that jerk who rammed into the car with all those kids was so blotto he couldn't stand up straight. All four kids were killed. They were seniors at Pascal Hills on the way to a prom-committee meeting. Incidentally, I was planning to send Reta over to talk to the doctors at Westlake Hospital, but she's covering the rape case. I'm especially interested in the psychiatrist Vangie Lewis was going to. I'd like his opinion as to her mental state. I can send Charley or Phil, but I think a woman would be less noticeable over there, might be able to drift around a bit and see if Mrs Lewis talked to the nurses or became friendly with other patients. But it'll have to wait until tomorrow. Reta's been up all night, and now she's driving around with that kid who was raped to see if she can spot her attacker. We're pretty sure he lives near her.'

Katie hesitated. She had not planned to tell Scott that she was

Dr Highley's patient or that she'd be checking into Westlake Friday night. But it would be unthinkable to have someone from the office report that to him. She temporized. 'Maybe I can help out. Dr Highley is my gynaecologist. I actually have an appointment with him today.' She pressed her lips together, deciding there was no need to go into a tiresome recital about her scheduled operation.

Scott's eyebrows shot up. As always when he was surprised, his voice became deeper. 'What are your impressions of him? Richard made some crack yesterday about Vangie's condition; seemed to think that Highley was taking chances with her.'

Katie shook her head. 'I don't agree with Richard. Dr Highley's specialty is difficult pregnancies. He's practically considered a miracle man. That's the very point. He tries to bring to viable term the babies other doctors lose.' She thought of his phone call to her. 'I can vouch for the fact that he's a very concerned doctor.'

Scott's frown made deep crease lines in his forehead and around his eyes. 'That's your gut-level reaction to him? How long have you known him?'

Trying to be objective, Katie thought about the doctor. 'I don't know him long or well. The gynaecologist I used to go to retired and moved a couple of years ago, and I'd just not bothered about another one. Then when I started having trouble – well, anyhow, my sister Molly knew about Dr Highley because her friend raves about him. Molly goes to someone in New York, and I didn't want to bother with that. So I made an appointment last month. He's very knowledgeable.' She remembered her examination. He had been gentle but thorough. 'You're quite right to have come,' he'd said. 'In fact, I must suggest that you should not have ignored this condition for over a year. I think of the womb as a cradle that must always be kept in good repair.'

The one thing that had surprised her was that he did not have a nurse in attendance. Her other gynaecologist had always called the nurse in before he began an examination; but then, he'd been from another generation. She judged Dr Highley to be in his mid-forties.

'What's your schedule today?' Scott asked.

'Busy morning, but this afternoon is adjustable.'

'All right. You go see Highley, and talk to the shrink too. Get a feeling of whether or not they think she was capable of suicide. Find out when she was over there last. See if she talked about the husband. Charley and Phil are checking on Chris Lewis now. I was awake half the night and kept thinking that Richard is right. Something about that suicide stinks. Talk to the nurses too.'

'Not the nurses,' Katie smiled. 'The receptionist, Edna. She knows everbody's business. I wasn't in the waiting room two minutes last month before I found myself giving her my life history. In fact, maybe you ought to hire her to interrogate witnesses.'

'I ought to hire a lot of people,' Scott commented drily. 'Talk to the Board of Freeholders. All right, I'll see you later.'

Katie went into her own office, grabbed her files and rushed to her appointment with a defence attorney about an indicted defendant. She agreed to drop a heroin charge from 'Possession with intent to distribute' to simple 'possession'. From there she hurried to a second-floor courtroom where she reflectively listened as a twenty-year-old youth she had prosecuted was sentenced to seven-years in prison. He could have received twenty years for the armed robbery and atrocious assault. Of the seven years, he'd probably serve one-third the term and be back on the streets. She knew his record by heart. Forget rehabilitation with this bird, she thought.

In the sheaf of messages waiting for her, there were two phone calls from Dr Carroll. One had come in at nine fifteen, the other at nine forty. She called back, but Richard was out on a case. Her feeling of slight pressure at the two calls was replaced by a sensation of disappointment when she couldn't reach him.

She phoned Dr Highley's office fully expecting to hear the nasal warmth of Edna's voice. But whoever answered was a stranger, a crisp, low-spoken woman. 'Doctors' offices.'

'Oh!' Katie thought swiftly and decided to ask for Edna. 'Is Miss Burns there?'

There was a fraction of a minute's pause before the answer came. 'Miss Burns won't be in today. She called in sick. I'm Mrs Fitzgerald.'

Katie realized how much she was counting on talking to

Edna. 'I'm sorry Miss Burns is not well.' Briefly she explained that Dr Highley expected her call and that she'd also like to see Dr Fukhito. Mrs Fitzgerald put her on hold and a few minutes later came back on the line.

'They'll both see you, of course. Dr Fukhito is free fifteen minutes before the hour any time between two and five, and Dr Highley would prefer three o'clock if it is also convenient for you.'

'Three o'clock with Dr Highley is fine,' Katie said, 'and then please confirm three forty-five with Dr Fukhito.' Lowering the phone, she turned to the work on her desk.

At lunchtime, Maureen Crowley, one of the office secretaries, popped her head in and offered to bring a sandwich to Katie. Deep in preparation for Friday's trial, Katie nodded affirmatively.

'Ham on rye with mustard and lettuce and dark coffee,' Maureen said.

Katie looked up, surprised. 'Am I really that predictable?'

The girl was about nineteen, with a mane of red-gold hair, emerald-green eyes and the lovely pale complexion of the true redhead. 'Katie, I have to tell you, about food you're in a rut.' The door closed behind her.

'You look peaked.' 'You're on a deathwatch.' 'You're in a rut.'

Katie swallowed over a hard lump in her throat and was astonished to realize she was close to tears. I *must* be sick if I'm getting this thin-skinned, she thought.

When the sandwich and coffee arrived, she ate and sipped, only vaguely aware of what she was having. The case on which she was trying to concentrate was a total blur. Vangie Lewis's face was constantly before her. But why had she seen it in a nightmare?

CHAPTER SIXTEEN

Richard Carroll had had a rough night. The phone rang at eleven o'clock, a few minutes after he got home from Katie's house, to inform him that four kids were in the morgue.

He replaced the receiver slowly. He lived on the seventeenth floor of a high-rise north of the George Washington Bridge. For moments he stared out the wall-length picture window at the New York skyline, at the cars darting swiftly down the Henry Hudson Parkway, at the blue-green lights that revealed and silhouetted the graceful lines of the George Washington Bridge.

Right now phones were ringing to tell the parents of those youngsters that their children wouldn't be coming home.

Richard looked around his living-room. It was comfortably furnished with an oversized sofa, roomy armchairs, an Oriental rug in tones of blue and brown, a wall bookcase and sturdy oak tables that had once graced the parlour of a New England ancestor's farmhouse. Original watercolours with sailing themes were scattered tastefully on the walls. Richard sighed. His deep leather reclining chair was next to the bookcase. He'd planned to fix a nightcap, read for an hour and turn in. Instead he decided to go to the morgue to be there when the parents came to identify those youngsters. God knew there was precious little anyone could do for those people, but he knew he'd feel better for trying.

It was four a.m. before he got back to the apartment. As he undressed he wondered if he was getting too saddened by this job. Those kids were so messed up; the crash impact had been terrific. Yet you could see how attractive they'd all been in life. One girl particularly got under his skin. She had dark hair, a slim, straight nose, and even in death she was graceful.

She reminded him of Katie.

The thought that Katie had been in an automobile accident Monday night jolted Richard anew. It seemed to him that they'd progressed light-years in their relationship in the couple of hours they'd spent together at dinner.

What was she afraid of, poor kid? Why couldn't she let go of John DeMaio? Why couldn't she say 'Thanks for the memory' and move on?

As he got into bed he felt bleakly grateful that he'd been able to help the parents a little. He'd been able to assure them that the youngsters had died instantly, that they probably never knew or felt anything.

He slept restlessly for two hours and was in the office by seven. A few minutes later a summons came that an old lady had hanged herself in a deteriorating section of Chester, a small town at the north end of the county. He went to the death scene. The dead woman was eighty-one years old, frail and birdlike. A note was pinned to her dress: *There's nobody left. I'm so sick and tired. I want to be with Sam. Please forgive me for causing trouble.*

The note brought into focus something that had been nagging Richard. From everything he'd heard about Vangie Lewis, it seemed in character that if she'd taken her life, she'd have left a note to explain or to blame her action on her husband.

Most women left notes.

When he got back to the office Richard tried phoning Katie twice, hoping to catch her between court sessions. He wanted to hear the sound of her voice. For some reason he'd felt edgy about leaving her alone in that big house last night. But he was unable to reach her.

Why did he have a hunch that she had something on her mind that was troubling her?

He went back to the lab and worked straight through until four thirty. Returning to his office, he picked up his messages and was absurdly pleased to see that Katie had returned his calls. Why wouldn't she? he asked himself cynically. An assistant prosecutor wouldn't ignore calls from the Medical Examiner. Quickly he phoned her. The switchboard operator in the Prosecutor's section said that Katie had left and wouldn't be back today. The operator didn't know where she was going.

Damn.

That meant he wouldn't get to talk to her today. He was having dinner in New York with Clovis Simmons, an actress on

76

one of the soaps. Clovis was fun; he always enjoyed himself with her, but the signs were that she was getting serious.

Richard made a resolve. This was the last time he'd take Clovis out. It wasn't fair to her. Refusing to consider the reason for that sudden decision, he leaned back in his chair and scowled. A mental alarm was sending out a beeping signal. It reminded him of travelling in the Midwest when the radio station would suddenly announce a tornado watch in effect. A *warning* was the sure thing. A *watch* suggested potential trouble.

He had not been exaggerating when he'd told Scott that if Vangie Lewis had not delivered that baby soon she wouldn't have needed the cyanide. How many women got into that same kind of condition under the Westlake Maternity Concept? Molly raved about the obstetrician because one of her friends had had a successful pregnancy. But what about the failures over there? How many of *them* had there been? Had there been anything unusual about the ratio of deaths among Westlake's patients? Richard switched on the intercom and asked his secretary to come in.

Marge was in her mid-fifties. Her greying hair was carefully bubbled in the style made popular by Jacqueline Kennedy in the early sixties. Her skirt was an inch over her plump knees. She looked like a suburban housewife on a television game show. She was in fact an excellent secretary who thoroughly enjoyed the constant drama of the department.

'Marge,' he said, 'I'm playing a hunch. I want to do some unofficial investigating of Westlake Hospital – just the maternity section. That maternity concept has been in operation for about eight years. I'd like to know how many patients died either in childbirth or from complications of pregnancy and what the ratio is between death and the number of patients treated there. I don't want to let it out that I'm interested. That's why I don't want to ask Scott to have the records subpoenaed. Do you know anybody over there who might look at the hospital records for you on the quiet?'

Marge frowned. Her nose, not unlike a small, sharp canary's beak, wrinkled. 'Let me work on it.'

'Good. And something else. Check into any malpractice suits that have been filed against either of the doctors over at

Westlake Maternity. I don't care whether the suits were dropped or not. I want to know the reason for them, if any exist at all.'

Satisfied at getting the investigation under way, Richard dashed home to shower and change. Seconds after he left his office, a call came for him from Dr David Broad of the prenatal laboratory at Mt Sinai Hospital. The message Marge took asked that Richard contact Dr Broad in the morning. The matter was urgent.

CHAPTER SEVENTEEN

Katie left for the hospital at quarter to three. The weather had settled into a tenacious, sombre, cloudy cold spell. But at least the warmth of the cars had melted most of the sleet from the roads. She deliberately slowed down as she rounded the curve that had been the starting point of her accident.

She was a few minutes early for her appointment, but could have saved her time. The receptionist, Mrs Fitzgerald, was coolly pleasant, but when Katie asked if she filled in for Edna very often, Mrs Fitzgerald replied stiffly, 'Miss Burns is almost never absent, so there's very little need to substitute for her.'

It seemed to Katie that the answer was unduly defensive. Intrigued, she decided to pursue the issue. 'I was so sorry to hear that Miss Burns is ill today,' she added. 'Nothing serious, I hope?'

'No.' The woman was distinctly nervous. 'Just a virus sort of thing. She'll be in tomorrow, I'm sure.'

There were several expectant mothers sitting in the reception area, but they were deep in magazines. There was no way Katie could feasibly strike up a conversation with them. A pregnant woman, her face puffy, her movements slow and deliberate, came from the corridor that led to the doctors' offices. A buzzer sounded at the desk. The receptionist picked up the phone.

'Mrs DeMaio, Dr Highley will see you now,' she said. She sounded relieved.

Katie walked quickly down the corridor. Dr Highley's office was the first one, she remembered. Following the printed instructions to knock and enter, she opened the door and stepped into the medium-sized office. It had the air of a comfortable study. Bookshelves lined one wall. Pictures of mothers with babies nearly covered a second wall. A club chair was placed near the doctor's elaborately carved desk. Katie remembered that the examining room, a lavatory and a combination kitchen/instrument-sterilizing area completed the suite. The doctor was behind his desk. He stood up to greet her. 'Mrs DeMaio.' His tone was courteous; the faint British accent, barely perceptible. He was a medium-tall man, about five feet eleven inches. His face, smooth-skinned with rounded cheeks, terminated in a plump oval chin. His body gave the impression of solid strength, carefully controlled. He looked as though he could easily put on weight. Thinning sandy hair, streaked with grey, was carefully combed in a side part. Eyebrows and lashes, the same sandy shade, accentuated protruding steel-grey eyes. Feature by feature he was not an attractive man, but his overall appearance was imposing and authoritative.

Katie flushed, realizing that he was aware of her scrutiny and not pleased by it. She sat down quickly and to establish rapport thanked him for the phone call.

He dismissed her gratitude. 'I wish you had something to thank me for. If you had told the emergency-room doctor that you were my patient, he would have given you a room in the west wing. Far more comfortable, I assure you. But just about the same view,' he added.

Katie had started to fish in her shoulder bag for a pad and paper. She looked up quickly. 'View. Anything would be better than the one I thought I had the other night. Why . . .' She stopped. The pad in her hand reminded her that she was here on official business. What would he think of her talking about nightmares? Unconsciously she tried to straighten up in the too-low, too-soft chair.

'Doctor, if you don't mind, let's talk about Vangie Lewis first.' She smiled. 'I guess our roles are reversed at least for a few minutes. I get to ask the questions.'

His expression became sombre. 'I only wish there were a

79

happier reason for our roles to be reversed. That poor girl. I've thought of little else since I heard the news.'

Katie nodded. 'I knew Vangie slightly, and I must say I've had the same reaction. Now, it's purely routine, of course, but in the absence of a note, my office does like to have some understanding of the mental state of a suicide victim.' She paused, then asked, 'When was the last time you saw Vangie Lewis?'

He leaned back in the chair. His fingers interlocked under his chin, revealing immaculately clean nails. He spoke slowly. 'It was last Thursday evening. I've been having Mrs Lewis come in at least weekly since she completed the halfway point of her pregnancy. I have her chart here.'

He indicated the manila file on his desk. It was tabbed LEWIS,VANGIE. It was an impersonal item, Katie decided, a reminder that exactly one week ago Vangie Lewis had lain in the examining room adjoining this office having her blood pressure checked, the heartbeat of her foetus confirmed.

'How was Mrs Lewis,' she asked, 'physically and emotionally?'

'Let me answer as to her physical condition first. It was a worry, of course. There was danger of toxic pregnancy, which I was watching very closely. But you see, every additional day she carried increased the baby's chance of survival.'

'Could she have carried the baby to full term?'

'Impossible. In fact, last Thursday I warned Mrs Lewis that it was highly likely that we would have to bring her in within the next two weeks and induce labour.'

'How did she respond to that news?'

He frowned. 'I expected Mrs Lewis to have a very valid concern for the baby's life. But the fact is that the closer she came to the potential birth, the more it seemed to me that she feared the birth process. The thought even crossed my mind that she was not unlike a little girl who wanted to play house, but would have been terrified if her doll turned into a real baby.'

'I see.' Katie doodled reflectively on the pad she was holding. 'But did Vangie show any specific depression?'

Dr Highley shook his head. 'I did not see it. However, I think that answer should come from Dr Fukhito. He saw her on

Monday night, and he's better trained than I to recognize that symptom if it's being masked. My overall impression was that she was getting morbidly fearful of giving birth.'

'A last question,' Katie asked. 'Your office is right next to Dr Fukhito's. Did you at any time Monday night see Mrs Lewis?'

'I did not.'

'Thank you, Doctor. You've been very helpful.' She slipped her pad back into her shoulder bag. 'Now it's your turn to ask questions.'

'I don't have too many. You answered them last night. When you've finished talking with Dr Fukhito, please go to room one-o-one on the other side of the hospital. You'll be given a transfusion. Wait about a half-hour before driving after you've received it.'

'I thought that was for people who gave blood,' Katie said.

'Just to make sure there's no reaction. Also . . .' He reached into the deep side drawer of his desk. Katie caught a glimpse of small bottles in exquisite order in the drawer. He selected one containing about nine or ten pills. 'Take the first one of these tonight,' he said. 'Then one every four hours tomorrow; the same on Friday. Take four pills in all tomorrow and Friday. You have just enough here. I must stress that it's very important you don't neglect this. As you know, if this operation does not cure your problem, we must consider more radical surgery.'

'I'll take the pills,' Katie said.

'Good. You'll be checking in around six o'clock Friday evening.'

Katie nodded.

'Fine. I'll be making my late rounds and will look in on you. You're not worried, I trust?'

She had admitted her fear of hospitals to him on the first appointment. 'No,' she said, 'not really.'

He opened the door for her. 'Till Friday, then, Mrs DeMaio,' he said softly.

CHAPTER EIGHTEEN

The investigative team of Phil Cunningham and Charley
Nugent returned to the Prosecutor's office at four p.m. exuding
the strained excitement of hounds who have treed their quarry.
Rushing into Scott Myerson's office, they proceeded to lay their
findings before him.

'The husband's a liar,' Phil said crisply. 'He wasn't due back
till yesterday morning, but his plane developed engine trouble.
The passengers were off-loaded in Chicago, and he and the crew
deadheaded back to New York. He got in Monday evening.'

'Monday evening!' Scott exploded.

'Yeah. And checked into the Holiday Inn on West Fifty-
seventh Street.'

'How did you get that?'

'We got a list of his crew on the Monday flight and talked to
all of them. The purser lives in New York. Lewis gave him a ride
into Manhattan and then ended up having dinner with him.
Lewis told some cock-and-bull story about his wife being away
and he was going to stay in the city overnight and take in a
show.'

'He told the purser that?'

'Yeah. He parked the car at the Holiday Inn, checked in; then
they went to dinner. The purser left him at seven twenty. After
that Lewis got his car, and the garage records show he had it for
over two hours. Brought it back at ten. And get this. He took off
again at midnight and came back at two.'

Scott whistled. 'He lied to us about his flight. He lied to the
purser about his wife. He was somewhere in his car between
eight and ten and between midnight and two a.m. What time did
Richard say Vangie Lewis died?'

'Between eight and ten p.m.,' Ed said.

Charley Nugent had been silent. 'There's more,' he said.
'Lewis has a girl-friend, a Pan Am stewardess. Name's Joan
Moore. Lives at two-o-one East Eighty-seventh Street in New

82

York. The doorman there told us Captain Lewis drove her home from the airport yesterday morning. She left her bag with him and they went for coffee in the drugstore across the street.

Scott tapped his pencil on the desk, a sure sign that he was about to issue orders. His assistants waited, notebooks in hand.

'It's four o'clock,' Scott said crisply. 'The judges will be leaving soon. Get one of them on the phone and ask him to wait around for fifteen minutes. Tell him we're having a search warrant sworn out.'

Phil sprinted from his chair and reached for the telephone.

'You' – Scott pointed to Charley – 'find out what funeral director picked up Vangie Lewis's body in Minneapolis. Get to him. The body is not to be interred, and make damn sure Chris Lewis doesn't decide to cremate it. We may want to do more work on it. Did Lewis say when he was coming back?'

Charley nodded. 'He told us he'd return tomorrow immediately after the services and interment.'

Scott grunted. 'Find out what plane he's coming in on and be waiting for him. Invite him here for questioning.'

'You don't think he'll try to skip?' Charley asked.

'No, I don't. He'll try to brazen it through. If he has any brains he'll know that we have nothing specific on him. And I want to talk to the girl-friend. What do you know about her?'

'She shares an apartment with two other stewardesses. She's planning to switch to Pan Am's Latin American Division and fly out of Miami. She's down in Fort Lauderdale right now signing a lease on an apartment. She'll be back late Friday afternoon.'

'Meet her plane too,' Scott said. 'Invite her here for a few questions. Where was she Monday night?'

'In flight on her way to New York. We're absolutely certain.'

'All right.' He paused. 'Something else. I want the phone records from the Lewis house, particularly from the last week, and when you do the search see if there isn't some kind of answering machine on one of the phones. He's an airline captain. It would make sense to have one.'

Phil Cunningham was hanging up the phone. 'Judge Haywood will wait.'

Scott reached for the phone, swiftly dialled Richard's office, asked for him and softly muttered, 'Damn. The one day he

83

leaves early has to be today!'

'Do you need him right now?' Charley's tone was curious.

'I want to know what he meant by saying there was something else that didn't jibe. Remember that remark? It might be important to know what it is. All right, let's get busy. And when you search that house, search it with a fine-tooth comb. And look for cyanide. We've got to find out fast where Vangie Lewis got the cyanide that killed her.

'Or where Captain Lewis got it,' he added quietly.

CHAPTER NINETEEN

By contrast with Dr Highley's office, Dr Fukhito's seemed more spacious and brighter. The writing table with long, slender lines occupied less space than Dr Highley's massive English desk. Graceful cane-backed chairs with upholstered seats and arms and a matching chaise substituted for the clubby leather chairs in the other office. Instead of the wall with framed pictures of mothers and babies, Dr Fukhito had a series of exquisite reproductions of Ukiyo-e woodcuts.

Dr Fukhito was tall for a Japanese. Unless, Katie thought, his posture was so upright that he seemed even taller than he probably was. No, she judged him to be about five feet ten.

Like his associate, Dr Fukhito was expensively and conservatively dressed. His pin-striped suit was accentuated by a light blue shirt and silk tie in muted tones of blue. His hair and small, neat moustache complemented pale gold skin and brown eyes more oval than almond-shaped. By either Oriental or Occidental standards he was a strikingly handsome man.

And probably a very good psychiatrist, Katie thought as she reached for her notebook, deliberately giving herself time to absorb impressions.

Last month her visit with Dr Fukhito had been brief and informal. Smiling, he'd explained, 'The womb is a fascinating part of the anatomy. Sometimes, irregular or inordinate flowing may indicate an emotional problem.'

'I doubt it,' Katie had told him. 'My mother had the same problem for years, and I do understand it's hereditary, or can be.'

He'd queried her about her personal life. 'And suppose a hysterectomy becomes necessary some day? What would you feel about that?'

'I would feel terrible,' Katie had replied. 'I've always wanted a family.'

'Then have you any plans to be married? Have you a relationship with someone?'

'No.'

'Why not?'

'Because right now I'm more interested in my job.' She had terminated the interview abruptly. 'Doctor, you're very kind, but I don't have any big emotional hang-ups, I can assure you. I'm looking forward very much to being relieved of this problem, but I assure you it's a purely physical one.'

He had acceded gracefully, standing up at once and holding out his hand. 'Well, if you're to become Dr Highley's patient, please remember I'm right here. And if a time comes when you'd like to talk things out with someone, you might want to try me.'

Several times in the past month it had fleetingly crossed Katie's mind that it might not be a bad idea to talk with him to get a professional and objective view of where she was at emotionally. Or, she wondered, had that thought sprung into being much more recently – for instance, since last night's dinner with Richard?

Pushing that thought away, she straightened in the chair and held up her pen. Her sleeve fell back, revealing her bandaged arm. To her relief, he did not question her about it.

'Doctor, as you know, a patient of yours and Dr Highley's, Vangie Lewis, died some time Monday evening.'

She noticed that his eyebrows rose slightly. Was it because he was expecting her to positively state that Vangie committed suicide?

She continued, 'Doctor, you saw Vangie at about eight o'clock that night. Isn't that true?'

He nodded. 'I saw her at precisely eight o'clock.'

'How long did she stay?'

'About forty minutes. She phoned Monday afternoon and asked for an appointment. I usually work until eight on Monday night and was completely booked. I told her so and suggested she come in Tuesday morning.'

'How did she respond?'

'She began to cry over the phone. She acted quite distressed, and of course I told her to come in, that I could see her at eight.'

'Why was she so distressed, Doctor?'

He spoke slowly, choosing his words carefully. 'She had quarrelled with her husband. She was convinced he did not love her or want the baby. Physically, the strain of the pregnancy was beginning to tell on her. She was quite immature, really – an only child who had been inordinately spoiled and fussed over. The physical discomfort was appalling to her, and the prospect of the birth had suddenly become frightening.'

Unconsciously, his eyes shifted to the chair at the right of his desk. She had sat in it Monday evening, that long caftan folding around her. Much as she had claimed to want a baby, Vangie had hated maternity clothes, hated losing her figure. In the last month she'd tried to conceal her outsized body and swollen leg by wearing floor-length dresses. It was a miracle she hadn't tripped and fallen the way they flapped around her feet.

Katie stared at him curiously. This man was nervous. What advice had he given Vangie that had sent her rushing home to kill herself? Or had sent her to a killer, if Richard's hunch was right? The quarrel. Chris Lewis had not admitted that he and Vangie had quarrelled.

Leaning forward quickly, Katie asked, 'Doctor, I realize that you want to protect the confidentiality of Mrs Lewis's discussions with you, but this is an official matter. We do need to know whatever you can tell us about the quarrel Vangie Lewis had with her husband.'

It seemed to him that Katie's voice came from far off. He was seeing Vangie's eyes terrified and staring at him. With a fierce effort he cleared his thoughts and looked directly at Katie. 'Mrs Lewis told me that she believed her husband was in love with someone else; that she'd accused him of that. She told me she had warned him that when she found out who the woman was she'd make her life hell. She was angry, agitated, bitter and frightened.'

'What did you tell her?'

'I promised her that before and during the birth she would be given everything necessary to make her comfortable. I told her that we hoped she would have the baby she's always wanted and that it might be the instrument to give her marriage more time.'

'How did she react to that?'

'She began to calm down. But then I felt it necessary to warn her that after the baby was born, if her marriage relationship did not improve, she should consider the possibility of terminating it.'

'And then?'

'She became furious. She swore that she would never let her husband leave her, that I was like everyone else, on his side. She got up and grabbed her coat.'

'What did you do, Doctor?'

'It was clearly time for me to do nothing. I told her to go home, get a good night's sleep and to call me in the morning. I realized it was far too early for her to deal with the seemingly irrevocable fact that Captain Lewis wanted a divorce.'

'And she left?'

'Yes. Her car was parked in the rear parking area. Occasionally she'd ask if she could use my private entrance in order to go out the back way. Monday night she didn't ask. She simply walked out through that door.'

'And you never heard from her again?'

'No.'

'I see.' Katie got up and walked over to the panelled wall with the pictures. She wanted to keep Dr Fukhito talking. He was holding something back. He was nervous.

'I was a patient here myself Monday night, Doctor,' she said. 'I had a minor automobile accident and was brought here.'

'I'm glad it was minor.'

'Yes.' Katie stood in front of one of the pictures, *A Small Road at Yabu Koji Atagoshita*. 'That's lovely,' she said. 'It's from the *Hundred Views of Yedo* series, isn't it?'

'Yes. You're very knowledgeable about Japanese art.'

'Not really. My husband was the expert and taught me a little about it, and I have other reproductions from the series, but this one is beautiful. Interesting, isn't it, the concept of one hundred views of the same place?'

He became watchful. Katie's back was to him and she did not see that he pressed his lips into a rigid line.

Katie turned around. 'Doctor, I was brought in here around ten o'clock Monday night. Can you tell me, is there any chance that Vangie Lewis did not leave at eight o'clock; that she was still around the hospital; that at ten o'clock, when I was brought in, semiconscious, I might have seen her?'

Dr Fukhito stared at Katie, feeling clammy wet fear crawl across his skin. He forced himself to smile. 'I don't see how,' he said. But Katie noticed that his knuckles were clenched and white, as if he were forcing himself to sit in his chair, not to run away, and something – was it fury or fear? – flashed in his eyes.

CHAPTER TWENTY

At five o'clock Gertrude Fitzgerald turned the phone over to the answering service and locked the reception desk. Nervously she phoned Edna's number. Again there was no answer. There was no doubt. Edna had been drinking more and more lately. But she was such a cheerful, good person. Really loved everybody. Gertrude and Edna often had lunch together, usually in the hospital cafeteria. Sometimes Edna would say, 'Let's go out and get something decent.' That meant she wanted to go to the pub near the hospital where she could get a Manhattan. Those days Gertrude always tried to make her keep it down to one drink. She'd kid her along. 'You can have a couple tonight, honey,' she'd say.

Gertrude understood Edna's need to drink. She didn't drink herself, but she understood that hollow, burning feeling when all you do is go to work every day and then go home and stare at four walls. She and Edna laughed sometimes about all the articles that told you to take up yoga or tennis or join a bird-watching club or take a course. And Edna would say, 'I couldn't get these fat legs in the cross-leg position; there's no way I'll ever touch the ground without bending my knees; I'm allergic to birds and at the end of the day I'm too tired to worry about the history of ancient Greece. I just wish that somewhere along the way I'd meet a nice guy who wanted to come home to me at night, and buh-lieve me, I wouldn't care if he snored.'

Gertrude was a widow of seven years, but at least she had the children and grandchildren; people who cared about her, called her up, sometimes borrowed a few hundred bucks; people who needed her. She had her own lonely times, God knew, but it wasn't the same as it was for Edna. She'd *lived*. She was sixty-two years old, in good health, and she had something to look back on.

She could swear Dr Highley had known she was lying when she said Edna had called in sick. But Edna had admitted that Dr Highley had warned her about the drinking. And Edna needed the job. Those old parents of hers had cost her a mint before they died. Not that Edna ever complained. Sad thing was, she wished they were still around; she missed them.

Suppose Edna *hadn't* been drinking? Suppose she was sick or something? The thought made Gertrude catch her breath sharply. No two ways about it. She'd have to check up on Edna. She'd drive over to her house right now. If she was drinking, she'd make her stop and sober her up. If she was sick, she'd take care of her.

Her mind settled, Gertrude got up from the desk briskly. Something else. That Mrs DeMaio from the Prosecutor's office. She'd been very nice, but you could tell she'd been anxious to talk to Edna. She'd probably phone Edna tomorrow. What could she want of her? Whatever would Edna be able to tell her about Mrs Lewis?

It was an intriguing problem, one that kept Gertrude occupied as she drove the six miles to Edna's apartment. But she was still unable to come up with an answer by the time she drove into the visitors' parking area behind Edna's apartment and walked around to the front door.

The lights were on. Even though the shiny, self-lined drapery was drawn, Gertrude could tell that there were lights coming from the living-room and dinette. As she neared the door, she heard the faint sound of voices. The television set, of course.

A momentary irritation flashed through her. She might just get really annoyed if Edna was sitting all nice and comfortable in her recliner and hadn't even bothered to answer the phone. She, Gertrude, had covered her work for her, covered her absence and now driven miles out of her way to make sure she wasn't in need.

Gertrude rang the bell. It pealed in a clanging double chime. She waited. Even though she listened hard, there was no sound of hurrying feet approaching the door, or a familiar voice calling, 'Right with you.' Maybe Edna was rinsing her mouth with Scope. She was always afraid that one of the doctors might drop in with emergency work to do. That had happened a few times on days Edna was out. That was how Dr Highley had first noticed Edna's problem.

But there was no reassuring sound of voice or footsteps. Gertrude shivered as she firmly pushed the bell again. Maybe Edna was sleeping it off. It was so terribly cold. She wanted to get home herself.

By the time she'd rung the bell four times, the annoyance had passed and Gertrude was thoroughly alarmed. There was no use fooling around; something was wrong and she had to get into the apartment. The superintendent, Mr Krupshak, lived directly across the court. Hurrying over, Gertrude told her story. The super was eating dinner and looked annoyed, but his wife, Gana, reached for the wide key ring on a nail over the sink. 'I'll go with you,' she said.

The two women hurried across the courtyard together. 'Edna's a real friend,' Gana Krupshak volunteered. 'Sometimes in the evening I pop in on her and we visit and have a drink together. My husband doesn't approve of liquor, even wine. Just last night I stopped over at about eight. I had a Manhattan with her, and she told me that one of her favourite patients had killed herself. Well, here we are.'

The women were on the small porch leading to Edna's apartment. The superintendent's wife fumbled with the keys. 'It's this one,' she murmured. She inserted the key into the lock, twisted it. 'This lock has a funny little thing – you have to kind of jiggle it.'

The lock turned and she pushed open the door as she spoke.

The two women saw Edna at exactly the same moment: lying on the floor, her legs crumpled under her, her blue robe open, revealing a flannel nightgown, her greying hair plastered around her face, her eyes staring, crusted blood making a crimson crown on the top of her head.

'No. No.' Gertrude felt her voice rise, high, shrill, an entity she could not control. She pressed her knuckles to her mouth.

In a dazed voice Gana Krupshak said, 'It's just last night I was sitting here with her. And – ' the woman's voice broke – 'she was pretty under the weather – you know what I mean, the way Edna could get – and she was talking about a patient who killed herself. And then she phoned that patient's husband.' Gana began to sob – noisy, racking sounds. 'And now poor Edna is dead too!'

CHAPTER TWENTY-ONE

Chris Lewis stood next to Vangie's parents to the right of the coffin, numbly acknowledging the sympathetic utterances of friends. When he'd phoned them about her death, they had agreed that they would view her body privately, have a memorial service tomorrow morning followed by a private interment.

Instead, when he'd arrived in Minneapolis this afternoon, he found that they had arranged for public viewing tonight and that after the chapel service tomorrow morning a cortège would follow Vangie's body to the cemetery.

'So many friends will want to say good-bye to our little girl. To think that two days ago she was alive, and now she's gone,' her mother sobbed.

Was it only Wednesday? It seemed to Chris that weeks had passed since he'd walked into that nightmare scene in the bedroom yesterday morning. *Yesterday morning.*

'Doesn't our baby look lovely?' her mother was asking the visitor who had just approached the coffin.

Our little girl. Our baby. If only you had let her grow up,

Chris thought, it might all have been so different. Their hostility to him was controlled, but lurked below the surface ready to spring out. 'A happy girl does not take her own life,' her mother had said accusingly.

They looked old and tired and shattered with grief – plain, hard-working people who had denied themselves everything to surround their unexpectedly beautiful child with luxury, who had brought her up to believe her wish was law.

Would it be easier for them when the truth was revealed that someone had taken Vangie's life? Or did he owe it to them to say nothing, to keep that final horror from them? Her mother was already trying to find comfort, to frame a version she could live with: 'Chris was on a trip and we're so far away, and my baby was feeling so sick and she took a sip of something and went to sleep.'

Oh, God, Chris thought, how people twist truth, twist life. He wanted to talk to Joan. She'd been so upset when she heard about Vangie that she'd hardly been able to talk. 'Did she know about us?' He'd finally had to admit to her that Vangie suspected that he was interested in someone else.

Joan would be back from Florida Friday evening. He was going to return to New Jersey tomorrow afternoon right after the funeral. He would say nothing to the police until he'd had a chance to talk to Joan, to warn her that she might be dragged into this. The police would be looking for a motive for him to kill Vangie. In their eyes, Joan would be the motive.

Should he leave well enough alone? *Did* he have the right to drag Joan into this, to unearth something that would hurt Vangie's parents even more?

Had there been someone else in Vangie's life? Chris glanced over at the coffin, at Vangie's now-peaceful face, the quietly folded hands. He and Vangie had scarcely lived as man and wife in the past few years. They'd lain side by side like two strangers; he emotionally drained from the endless quarrelling, she wanting to be cajoled, babied. He'd even suggested separate rooms, but she'd become hysterical.

She became pregnant two months after they moved to New Jersey. When he'd agreed to one more final try at the marriage, he had made a genuine effort to make it work. But the summer had been miserable. By August he and Vangie had barely been speaking. Only once, around the middle of the month, had they slept together. He had thought it an irony of fate that after ten years she had become pregnant just as he met someone else.

A suspicion that Chris realized had been sitting somewhere in his subconscious sprang full-blown to life. Was it possible that Vangie had become involved with another man, a man who did not want to take responsibility for her and a baby? Had she confronted that other man? Vangie had threatened that if she knew whom Chris was seeing, she'd make her wish she were dead. Suppose she had been having some kind of affair with a married man. Suppose she'd hurled hysterical threats at *him*?

Chris realized that he had been shaking hands, murmuring thanks, looking into familiar faces and not really seeing them: neighbours from the condominium where he and Vangie had lived before the move to New Jersey; airline friends; friends of Vangie's parents. His own parents were retired in North Carolina. Neither was well. He had told them not to make the trip to Minneapolis in the bitterly cold weather.

'I'm very sorry.' The man who was clasping his hand was in his mid-sixties. He was a slightly-built man, but sturdily attractive, with winter-grey hair and bushy brows over keen, penetrating eyes. 'I'm Dr Salem,' he said, 'Emmet Salem. I delivered Vangie and was her first gynaecologist. She was one of the prettiest things I ever brought into this world, and she never changed. I only wish I hadn't been away when she phoned my office Monday.'

Chris stared at him. 'Vangie phoned you Monday?'

'Yes. My nurse said she was quite upset. Wanted to see me immediately. I was teaching a seminar in Detroit, but the nurse made an appointment with me for her for today. She was planning to fly out yesterday, from what I understand. Maybe I could have helped her.'

Why had Vangie called this man? Why? It seemed to Chris that it was impossible to think. What would make her go back to a doctor she hadn't seen in years? She wasn't well, but if she wanted a consultation, why a doctor thirteen hundred miles away?

'Had Vangie been ill?' Dr Salem was looking at him curiously, waiting for an answer.

'No, not ill,' Chris said. 'As you probably know, she was expecting a baby. It was a difficult pregnancy from the beginning.'

'*Vangie was what?*' The doctor's voice rose. He stared at Chris in astonishment.

'I know. She had just about given up hope. But in New Jersey she started the Westlake Maternity Concept. You may have heard of it, or of Dr Highley – Dr Edgar Highley.'

'Captain Lewis, may I speak with you?' The funeral director had a hand under his arm, was propelling him towards the private office across the foyer from the viewing room.

'Excuse me,' Chris said to the doctor. Nonplussed by the director's agitation, he allowed himself to be guided into the office.

The funeral director closed the door and looked at Chris. 'I've just received a call from the Prosecutor's office in Valley County, New Jersey,' he said. 'Written confirmation is on the way. We are forbidden to inter your wife's body. Your wife's body is to be flown back to the Medical Examiner's office in Valley County immediately after the service tomorrow.'

They know it wasn't a suicide, Chris thought. They already know that. There was nothing he could do to hide it. Once he had a chance to talk to Joan Friday night, he'd tell the Prosecutor's office everything he knew or suspected.

Without answering the funeral director, he turned and left the office. He wanted to speak to Dr Salem, find out what Vangie had said to the nurse on the phone.

But when he went back to the other room, Dr Salem was already gone. He had left without speaking to Vangie's parents. Vangie's mother rubbed swollen eyes with a damp crumpled handkerchief. 'What did you say to Dr Salem that made him leave like that?' she asked. 'Why did you upset him so terribly?'

CHAPTER TWENTY-TWO

Wednesday evening he arrived home at six o'clock. Hilda was just leaving. Her plain, stolid face was guarded. He was always aloof with her. He knew she liked and wanted this job. Why not? A house that stayed neat; no mistress to constantly give orders; no children to clutter it.

No children. He went into the library, poured a scotch and broodingly watched from the window as Hilda's broad body disappeared down the street towards the bus line two blocks away.

He had gone into medicine because his own mother had died in childbirth. His birth. The accumulated stories of the years, listened to from the time he could understand, told by the timid, self-effacing man who had been his father. 'Your mother wanted you so much. She knew she was risking her life, but she didn't care.'

Sitting in the chemist's shop in Brighton, watching his father prepare prescriptions, asking questions: 'What is that?' 'What will that pill do?' 'Why do you put caution labels on those bottles?' He'd been fascinated, drinking in the information his father so willingly shared with him – the one topic his father could talk about; the only world his father knew.

He'd gone to medical school, finished in the top ten per cent of his class; internships were offered in leading hospitals in London and Glasgow. Instead he chose Christ Hospital in Devon, with its magnificently equipped research laboratory – the opportunity it gave for both research and practice. He'd become staff; his reputation as an obstetrician had grown rapidly.

And his project had been held back, retarded, cursed by his inability to test it.

At twenty-seven he'd married Claire, a distant cousin of the Earl of Sussex – infinitely superior to him in social background, but his reputation, the expectation of future prominence had been the leveller.

And the incredible ignominy. He who dealt in birth and fertility had married a barren woman. He whose walls were covered with pictures of babies who never should have been carried to term had no hope of becoming a father himself.

When had he started to hate Claire? It took a long time – seven years.

It was when he finally realized that she didn't care; had never cared; that her disappointment was faked; that she'd *known* before she married him that she could not conceive.

Impatiently he turned from the window. It would be another cold, wind-filled night. Why did February, the shortest month of the year, always seem to be the longest one? When all this was over he'd take a vacation. He was getting edgy, losing grip on his nerves.

He had nearly given himself away this morning when Gertrude told him that Edna had phoned in sick. He'd grasped the desk, watched his knuckles whiten. Then he'd remembered. The fluttering pulse that had stopped beating, the unfocused eyes, the muscles relaxing in extremis. Gertrude was covering for her friend. *Gertrude was lying.*

He'd frowned at Gertrude. When he spoke he'd made his voice icy. 'It is most inconvenient that Edna is absent today. I hope and expect that she will be here tomorrow.'

It had worked. He could tell from the nervous licking of the lips, from Getrude's averted eyes. She believed that he was furious at Edna's absence. She probably knew that he'd spoken sharply to Edna about her drinking.

Gertrude might prove to be an ally.

POLICE: And how did the doctor respond when you told him Miss Burns was absent?

GERTRUDE: He was quite angry. He's very methodical. He doesn't like anything that upsets the routine.

The missing shoe. This morning he'd gone to the hospital soon after dawn and once again searched the parking lot and the office. Had Vangie been wearing it when she came into his office Monday night? He realized that he couldn't be sure. She'd been wearing that long caftan, her winter coat buttoned awkwardly over it. The caftan was too large; the coat strained at the abdomen. She lifted the caftan to show him her swollen right leg. He'd seen the moccasin on that foot, but he'd never noticed the other shoe. Had she been wearing it? He simply didn't know.

If it had fallen off in the parking lot when he carried her body to the car, someone had picked it up. Maybe a maintenance man had seen it; discarded it. Often patients who were checking out had overflowing shopping bags, stuffed with cards or plants and last-minute personal items that didn't fit in the suitcase, and lost things between the hospital room and the parking lot. He'd inquired at the lost-and-found desk, but they had no footwear. It might simply have been thrown into the rubbish bag.

He thought about lifting Vangie out of the trunk of the car, carrying her past the shelves in her garage. They had been filled with garden tools. Was it possible that the looser shoe had perhaps brushed against something protruding? If it was found on a shelf in the garage, questions would be asked.

If Vangie did *not* have the shoe on when she left Fukhito's office, her stocking sole would have become soiled. But the portico between the offices was sheltered. If her left foot was badly soiled, he'd have noticed it when he laid her out on the bed.

The horror of finding that he was carrying the *right* shoe, the shoe that he had struggled to pull off Vangie's foot, had unnerved him. The more fool he. After the terrible, terrible risk.

The right shoe was in his bag in the trunk of the car. He wasn't sure whether to dispose of it – not until he was positive the other one wouldn't still show up.

Even if the police started an intensive investigation into the suicide, there was nothing that constituted evidence against him. Her file in the office could bear intensive professional scrutiny. Her true records, all the true records of the special cases, were in the wall safe here. He defied anyone to locate that safe. It wasn't even in the original plans of the house. Dr Westlake had installed it personally. Only Winifred had known about it.

No one had any reason to suspect him – no one except Katie DeMaio. She'd been on the verge of telling him something when he'd mentioned the view from the hospital room, but she had changed her mind abruptly

Fukhito had come in to him just as he was locking up tonight. Fukhito was nervous. He'd said, 'Mrs DeMaio was asking a lot of questions. Is it possible that they don't believe Mrs Lewis committed suicide?'

'I really don't know.' He'd enjoyed Fukhito's nervousness; understood the reason for it.

'That interview you gave to *Newsmaker* magazine; that's going to come out tomorrow, isn't it?'

He'd looked at Fukhito disdainfully. 'Yes. But I assure you I gave the distinct impression I use a number of psychiatric consultants. Your name will not appear in the article.'

Fukhito was not relieved. 'Still, it's going to put the spotlight on this hospital; on us,' he complained.

'On *yourself* – isn't that what you're saying, Doctor?'

He'd almost laughed aloud at the troubled, guilty look on Fukhito's face.

Now, finishing his scotch, he realized that he had been overlooking another avenue of escape. If the police came to the conclusion that Vangie had been murdered; if they *did* investigate Westlake; it would be an easy matter to reluctantly suggest that they interrogate Dr Fukhito. Especially in view of his past.

After all, Dr Fukhito was the last person known to have seen Vangie Lewis alive.

CHAPTER TWENTY-THREE

After leaving Dr Fukhito, Katie went to the east wing of the hospital for the transfusion. It was given to her in a curtained-off area near the emergency room. As she lay on top of a bed, her sleeve rolled back, the needle strapped in her arm, she tried to reconstruct her arrival at the hospital Monday night.

She thought she remembered being in this room, but she wasn't sure. The doctor who had sewed the cut in her arm looked in. 'Hi. I thought I saw you at the desk. I see Dr Highley ordered another transfusion. I hope you're looking into that low blood count.'

'Yes. I'm under Dr Highley's care.'

'Fine. Let's take a look at that arm.' He rebandaged it as she lay there. 'Good job. Have to admit it myself. You won't have a scar to show your grandchildern.'

'If I have any,' Katie said. 'Doctor, tell me, was I on this bed Monday night?'

'Yes, we had you in here after the X-rays. You don't remember?'

'It's all such a blur.'

'You lost a lot of blood. You were in a pretty good state of shock.'

'I see.'

When the transfusion was finished, she remembered that Dr Highley had told her not to drive for about half an hour. She decided to go to the admitting office and fill out the necessary forms for an inpatient stay. Then she wouldn't have to bother with them Friday evening.

When she left the hospital it was nearly six o'clock. She found herself automatically turning the car in the direction of Chapin River. Nonsense, she thought. You're having dinner with Molly and Bill tomorrow night. Forget about dropping in tonight.

The decision settled, she made a U-turn and drove to Palisades Parkway. She was getting hungry, and the thought of going home did not appeal to her. Who was the poet who had written on the joys of solitude and then had finished the poem with the lines 'But do not go home alone after five/Let someone be waiting there'?

Well, she had learned to cope with loneliness, had taught herself to genuinely enjoy a quiet evening of reading with the stereo playing.

The feeling of emptiness that came over her lately was something new.

She passed the restaurant where she and Richard had eaten the night before and on impulse swung into the parking area. Tonight she'd try the other specialty, the *entrecôte*. Maybe in the warm, intimate, quiet restaurant she'd be able to think.

The proprietor recognized her and beamed with pleasure. 'Good evening, Madam. Dr Carroll did not make a reservation, but I have a table near the fireplace. He is parking the car?'

She shook her head. 'Just me tonight, I'm afraid.'

For an instant the man looked embarrassed, but recovered quickly. 'Then I suspect we have made a new and beautiful friend.' He led her to a table near the one she had shared with Richard.

Nodding at the suggestion of a glass of Burgundy, Katie leaned back and felt the same sense of unwinding she'd experienced the night before. Now if she could just collect her thoughts, sort out the impressions that she'd received talking to Dr Highley and Dr Fukhito about Vangie Lewis.

Taking out her pad, she began to scan what she had jotted down during the interviews. Dr Highley. She'd expected him to explain or defend the fact that Vangie Lewis was obviously in serious trouble with her pregnancy. He had done exactly that, and what he told her was completely reasonable. He was going day by day to buy the baby time. The remarks he'd made about Vangie's reaction to the impending birth rang true. She'd heard from Molly the story of Vangie's hysterical reaction to a blister on the finger.

What then? What more did she want of Dr Highley? She thought of Dr Wainwright, the cancer specialist in New York, who had taken care of John. After John died, he'd spoken to her, his face and voice filled with pain. 'I want you to know, Mrs DeMaio, we tried everything possible to save him. Nothing was left undone. But sometimes God takes it out of our hands.'

Dr Highley had expressed regret over Vangie's death, but certainly not sorrow. But of course, he had to stay objective. She'd heard Bill and Richard discussing the need to stay objective when you practise medicine. Otherwise you'd constantly be torn in two and end up useless.

Richard. Inadvertently her eyes slid over to the table where she'd been with him. He'd said, 'We both know we could enjoy each other.' He was right. She did know it. Maybe that was why she usually felt unsettled with him, as though things could be taken out of her hands. Is it possible that it could happen twice in a lifetime? From the very beginning you *know* something is right, someone is right.

When she and Richard were leaving Molly's after that quick lunch yesterday, Molly had asked them both to dinner Thursday night – tomorrow. Molly said, 'Liz and Jim Berkeley are coming over. She's the one who thinks Dr Highley is God. You two might be interested in talking with her.'

Katie realized how much she was looking forward to that dinner.

Again she looked down at her notes. Dr Fukhito. Something was wrong there. It seemed to her that he'd deliberately weighed every word he said when he'd discussed Vangie's Monday-night visit. It had been like watching someone walk step by step through a mined field. What was he afraid of? Even allowing for the reasonable concern of protecting the doctor-patient relationship, he'd been afraid he would say something that she would pounce on.

Then he'd been openly hostile when she asked if by any chance Vangie might still have been in the hospital at ten o'clock when she, Katie, was brought in.

Suppose she *had* glimpsed Vangie? Suppose Vangie had been just leaving Dr Fukhito's office; had been walking somewhere in the parking lot? That would explain seeing her face in that crazy nightmare.

Dr Fukhito said that Vangie left by his private entrance.

No one had seen her go.

Suppose she *hadn't* left? Suppose she'd stayed with the doctor. Suppose he'd left with her or followed her home. Suppose he'd realized that she was suicidal, that he was responsible in some way . . .

Enough to make him nervous.

The waiter arrived to take her order. Before she put away the pad, Katie made one final note: *Investigate Dr Fukhito's background*.

CHAPTER TWENTY-FOUR

Even before he crossed the George Washington Bridge and drove down the Harlem River and FDR Drive Wednesday evening, Richard knew that he should have cancelled the date with Clovis. He was preoccupied about Vangie Lewis's death;

his subconscious was suggesting that he had missed something in the autopsy. There had been something he'd intended to examine more closely. What was it?

And he was worried about Katie. She had looked so thin last night. She'd been extremely pale. It wasn't until she'd had a couple of glasses of wine that some colour had come into her face.

Katie wasn't well. That was it. He was a doctor and should have spotted it sooner.

That accident. How carefully had she been examined? Was it possible that she'd been hurt more than anyone realized? The thought haunted Richard as he turned on to the Fifty-third Street exit from the FDR Drive and headed for Clovis's apartment one block away.

Clovis had a pitcher of very dry martinis waiting to be poured and a plate of hot crabmeat-filled puffs fresh from the oven. With her flawless skin, tall, slender body and Viking colouring, she reminded Richard of a young Ingrid Bergman. Until recently he'd toyed with the idea that they might end up together. Clovis was intelligent, interesting and good-tempered.

But as he returned her kiss with honest affection, he was acutely aware that he'd never worry about Clovis the way he now found himself worrying about Katie DeMaio.

He realized Clovis was talking to him. '. . . and I'm not home ten minutes. The rehearsal ran over. There was a lot of rewriting. So I fixed the drinks and nibbles and figured you could relax while I get dressed. Hey, are you listening to me?'

Richard accepted the drink and smiled apologetically. 'I'm sorry. I'm on a case that won't let go. Do you mind if I make a couple of calls while you're getting ready?'

'Of course I don't mind,' Clovis said. 'Go ahead and dial away.' She picked up her glass and started towards the foyer that led into the bedroom and bath.

Richard took his credit card from his wallet and dialled the operator. There was no way he was going to put a call to one woman on another woman's phone bill. Quickly he gave his account number to the operator. When the connection went through, he allowed the phone to ring a dozen times before he finally gave up. Katie wasn't home.

Next he tried Molly's house. Probably Katie had stopped there. But Molly had not spoken to her at all today.

'I don't really expect her,' Molly said. 'You're both coming tomorrow night. Don't forget that. She'll probably call me later. But I wish she'd gone home by now. She could stand taking it easy.'

It was the opening he needed. 'Molly, what's the matter with Katie?' he asked. 'There is something wrong physically, isn't there? Besides the accident, I mean?'

Molly hesitated. 'I think you'd better talk to Katie about that.'

Certainty. Cold fear washed over him.

'Molly, I want to know. *What's the matter with her?*'

'Oh, not much,' Molly said hastily. 'I promise you that. But it's nothing she wanted to discuss. And now I've probably said more than I should. See you tomorrow.'

The connection broke. Richard frowned into the dead receiver. He started to replace it on the cradle, then on impulse put through a call to his office. He spoke to the assistant on the evening shift. 'Anything unusual going on?' he asked.

'We just got a call for the wagon. A body was found in an apartment in Edgeriver. Probably an accident, but the local police thought we'd better take a look. Scott's people are heading over there.'

'Switch me to Scott's office,' Richard said.

Scott did not waste time on preliminaries. 'Where are you?' he demanded.

'In New York. Do you need me?'

'Yes. This woman who was found in Edgeriver is the receptionist Katie wanted to talk to today at Westlake. Name's Edna Burns. Supposedly she phoned in sick today, but there's no question she's been dead a good twenty-four hours. Body was found by a co-worker from Westlake. I'm trying to get Katie. I'd like her to go over there.'

'Give me the address,' Richard said.

He wrote it quickly and hung up the phone. Katie had wanted to question this Edna Burns about Vangie Lewis, and now Edna Burns was dead. He knocked on Clovis's bedroom door. She opened it, wrapped in a terry-cloth robe. 'Hey, what's the hurry?' she asked, smiling. 'I just got out of the shower.'

'Clo, I'm sorry.' Quickly he explained. Now he was frantic to get away.

She was clearly disappointed. 'Oh, of course I understand, but I was counting on seeing you. It's been a couple of weeks – you do know that. All right. Go, but let's have dinner tomorrow night. Promise?'

Richard temporized. 'Well, very soon.' He started to leave, but she caught him by the arm and pulled his face down for a kiss.

'Tomorrow night,' she told him firmly.

CHAPTER TWENTY-FIVE

On the way home from the restaurant, Katie turned over in her mind the conversation she'd had with Edna Burns on her first visit to Dr Highley. Edna was a born listener. Katie was not given to discussing her personal affairs, but when Edna took the preliminary information, she had clucked sympathetically. Not quite believing her own ears, Katie had heard herself telling Edna all about John.

How much had *Vangie* told Edna? She'd been going to Westlake since last summer. How much did Edna know about Dr Fukhito? There was something oddly intimidating about his nervousness. Why should he be nervous?

Katie pulled up in front of her house and decided not to put the car away yet. It was Wednesday and Mrs Hodges had been here. The house smelled faintly of lemon wax. The mirror over the antique marble table in the hall was shining. Katie knew her bed had been made with fresh linen; the ceramic kitchen tile would be gleaming; the furniture and rugs had been vacuumed; her laundry would be back in the drawers or closet.

Mrs Hodges had worked full time when John was alive. Now pensioned off, she'd begged for the chance to come in one day a week and take care of 'my house'.

It wouldn't last much longer. It couldn't. Mrs Hodges was past seventy now.

Whom would she get when Mrs Hodges no longer came in? Who would exercise the same care with the valuable bric-à-brac, the antiques, the English furniture, the lovely old Orientals?

'It's time to sell,' Katie thought. 'I know it.'

Taking off her coat, she tossed it on a chair. It was only a quarter of eight. The night loomed long ahead of her. Edna had told her that she lived in Edgeriver. That was less than twenty minutes' drive away. Suppose she phoned Edna now? Suppose she suggested driving down to see her? Mrs Fitzgerald had said that Edna was expected at work tomorrow, so she couldn't be too sick. If Katie was any judge, Edna would love a chance to gossip about Vangie Lewis.

Mrs Hodges always left a freshly baked cake or pie or muffins in the bread box for Katie. She'd take whatever was there now down to Edna and have a cup of tea with her. A lot of gossip could be exchanged over a teapot.

Edna was listed in the telephone book. Quickly Katie dialled her number. It rang once and the receiver was picked up. She formed the words 'Hello, Miss Burns,' but never got to speak them.

A man's voice said, 'Yes?' The short word was delivered in a clipped, not-unfamiliar voice.

'Is Miss Burns there?' Katie asked. 'This is Mrs DeMaio from the Prosecutor's office.'

'Katie!'

Now she recognized the voice. It was Charley Nugent, and he was saying, 'Glad Scott got in touch with you. Can you come right down?'

'Come down?' Afraid of what she'd hear, Katie asked the question: 'What are you doing at Edna Burns's apartment?'

'Don't you know? She's dead, Katie. Fell — or was pushed — into the radiator. Split her head open.' His voice lowered. 'Get this, Katie. She was last seen alive around eight o'clock last night. A neighbour was with her.' His voice became a whisper. 'The neighbour heard her on the phone with Vangie Lewis's husband. Edna Burns told Chris Lewis that she was going to talk to the police about Vangie's death.'

CHAPTER TWENTY-SIX

After he finished the second scotch he went into the kitchen and opened the refrigerator. He had told Hilda not to prepare anything for him tonight, but had given her a long shopping list. He nodded in approval at the new items in the meat drawer: the boneless breasts of chicken, the filet mignon; the double loin lamb chops. Fresh asparagus, tomatoes and watercress were in the vegetable bin. Brie and Jarlsberg were in the cheesebox. Tonight he'd have the lamb chops, asparagus and a watercress salad.

Emotional exhaustion always compelled him to eat. The night Claire died, he'd left the hospital, to all outward appearances a husband benumbed with grief, and had gone to a quiet restaurant a dozen blocks away and eaten heavily. Then he'd trudged home masking an acute sense of wellbeing with the weary posture of the grief-stricken. The friends who were gathered waiting to greet him, to commiserate with him had been deceived.

'Where were you, Edgar? We were worried about you.'

'I don't know. I don't remember. I've just been walking.'

It had been the same after Winifred's death. He'd left her relatives and friends at the grave site, refused invitations to join them for dinner. 'No. No. I need to be alone.' He'd come back to the house, waited long enough to answer a few phone calls, then contacted the answering service. 'If anyone phones, please explain that I'm resting and that I'll return all calls later.'

Then he'd gotten into the car and driven to the Carlyle in New York. There he had requested a quiet table and ordered dinner. Halfway through the meal he looked up and saw Winifred's cousin, Glenn Nickerson, across the room – Glenn, the high school athletics coach who had been Winifred's heir until he came along. Glenn was dressed in the dark blue suit and black tie he'd worn to the funeral, a bargain-priced, ill-fitting suit obviously bought specially for the occasion. His normal garb was a sports jacket, slacks and loafers.

Nickerson was obviously watching him. He'd lifted his glass in a toast, a mocking smile on his face. He might as well have shouted his thoughts: 'To the grieving widower.'

He'd done what was necessary: walked over to him without the slightest sign of distress and spoken pleasantly. 'Glenn, why didn't you join me when you saw I was here? I didn't realize you came to the Carlyle. This was a favourite dining spot of ours. We became engaged here – or did Winifred ever tell you that? I'm not Jewish, but I think that one of the most beautiful customs in this bewildering world is that of the Jewish faith, where after a death the family eats eggs to symbolize the continuity of life. I am here to quietly celebrate the continuity of love.'

Glenn had stared at him, his expression stony. Then he'd stood up and signalled for his check. 'I admire your ability to philosophize, Edgar,' he said. 'No. I don't consider the Carlyle one of my regular eating spots. I simply followed you here because I had decided to visit you and reached your block just as your car pulled out. I had the feeling it might be interesting to keep an eye on you. How right I was.'

He'd turned his back on Glenn, walked with dignity back to his own table and not glanced in his direction again. A few minutes later he'd seen Glenn at the door of the dining room on his way out.

The next week, Alan Levine, the doctor who'd treated Winifred, indignantly told him that Glenn had asked to see Winifred's medical records.

'I threw him out of my office,' Alan said heatedly. 'I told him that Winifred had developed classic angina symptoms and that he would do himself a favour if he studied the current statistics on women in their early fifties having heart attacks. Even so, he had the gall to speak to the police. I had a call from the Prosecutor's office asking in so many words if a heart ailment could be induced. I told them that being alive today was enough to induce heart trouble. They backed off immediately, said it was obviously a disinherited relative trying to cause trouble.'

But you *can* induce heart trouble, Dr Levine. You can prepare intimate little dinners for your dear wife. You can use her susceptibility to gastroenteritis to bring on attacks so strong that they register as heart seizures on her cardiogram. After enough of these the lady apparently has a fatal seizure. She dies in the presence of her own physician, who arrives to find the physician husband applying mouth-to-mouth resuscitation. No one suggests an autopsy. And even if someone had, there would have been little risk.

The only risk would have occurred of they had thought to delve into Claire's death.

The chops were nearly cooked. He expertly seasoned the watercress, removed the asparagus from the steamer and took a half-bottle of Beaujolais from the wine rack in the pantry.

He had just begun to eat when the phone rang. He debated ignoring it, then decided that at this time it was dangerous to miss any calls. Slapping his napkin on the table, he hurried to the extension in the kitchen. 'Dr Highley,' he said curtly.

A sob sounded over the phone. 'Doctor – oh, Dr Highley. It's Gertrude, Gertrude Fitzgerald. Doctor, I decided to go see Edna on my way home.'

He tightened his grip on the receiver.

'Doctor, Edna is dead. The police are here. She fell. Doctor, could you come here right away? They're talking about performing an autopsy. She always hated autopsies. She used to say how terrible it was to cut up dead people. Doctor, you know how Edna was when she drank. I told them that you've been here in her apartment; that you've caught her drinking. Doctor, come here and tell them how you would find her sometimes. Oh, please come here and convince them that she fell and that they don't have to cut her up.'

CHAPTER TWENTY-SEVEN

Before she left the house, Katie made a cup of tea and carried it to the car. Driving with one hand, she held the bubbling liquid to her lips with the other. She'd planned to bring cake down to Edna and have tea with her. And now Edna was dead.

How could a person she'd met only once have made such an

impression on her? Was it simply that Edna was such a good person, so truly concerned with the patients? So many people were so indifferent, so non-caring. In that one conversation with Edna last month, it had been so easy to talk about John.

And Edna had understood. She'd said, 'I know what it is to watch someone die. On the one hand, you want the misery to be over for them. On the other hand you don't want to let them go.' She'd shared the aftermath of loss. 'When both Mom and Dad died, all my friends said, "Now you're free, Edna." And I said, "Free for what?" And I bet you felt that way too.'

Edna reassured her about Dr Highley. 'You couldn't find a better doctor for any GYN problem. That's why it makes me so mad when I hear him criticized. And all those people who file malpractice suits! Let me tell you, I could shoot them myself. That's the trouble when people think you're God. They think you can do the impossible. I tell you when a doctor loses a patient today, he has to worry. And I don't just mean obstetricians. I mean geriatric doctors too. I guess nobody's supposed to die any more.'

What had Charley meant by telling her that Edna had phoned Chris Lewis last night? In practically the same breath Charley had suggested the possibility of foul play.

'I don't believe it,' Katie said aloud as she turned off Route 4 on to Edgeriver. It would be like Edna to call Chris Lewis to express her sympathy. Was Charley suggesting Edna might have in some way *threatened* Chris Lewis?

She had a vague idea of where the apartment development was and was able to find it easily. She mused that as garden apartments went, this one was getting somewhat rundown. When she sold the house she'd probably move into a high-rise for a while. There were some buildings overlooking the Hudson that had lovely apartments with terraces. And it would be interesting to be near New York. She'd be more likely to go to the theatre and museums. *When* I sell the house, she thought. At what point did *if* become *when*?

Charley had told her that Edna's apartment was the last one in units 41 through 60. He'd said to drive behind that row and park. She slowed down, realizing that a car had entered the development from another road and was pulling into that same area ahead of her. It was a black medium-sized car. For a moment the driver hesitated, then chose the first parking spot available on the right. Katie pulled around him. If Edna's apartment was the end one on the left, she'd try to get closer to it. She found a spot directly behind that building and parked. She got out of the car, realizing that she must be looking at the back window of Edna's apartment. The window was raised an inch. The shade was pulled down to the top of a plant. A faint light could be seen from inside the apartment.

Katie thought of the view from her bedroom windows. They looked over the little pond in the woods behind the house. Edna had gazed out at a parking area and a rusting chain-link fence. Yet she had told Katie how much she enjoyed her apartment, how cosy it was.

Katie heard footsteps behind her and turned quickly. In the lonely parking area, any sound seemed menacing. A figure loomed near her, a silhouette accentuated by the dim light from the solitary lamp post. A sense of familiarity struck her.

'Excuse me. I hope I didn't startle you.' The cultured voice had a faint English accent.

'Dr Highley!'

'Mrs DeMaio. We didn't expect to see each other so soon and under such tragic circumstances.'

'Then you've heard. Did my office call you, Doctor?'

'It's chilly. Here. Let's take this footpath around the building.' Barely touching her elbow with his hand, he followed her on the path. 'Mrs Fitzgerald called me. She substituted for Miss Burns today and evidently she was the one to find her. She sounded terribly upset and begged me to come. I don't have any details of what happened as yet.'

'Neither do I,' Katie replied. They were turning the corner to the front of the building when she heard rapid footsteps behind them.

'Katie.'

She felt the pressure of the doctor's fingers on her elbow tighten and then release as she looked back. Richard was there. She turned, absurdly glad to see him. He grasped both her shoulders. In a gesture that ended even as it began, he pulled her to him. Then his hands dropped. 'Scott reached you?'

'No. I happened to call Edna myself. Oh, Richard, this is Dr Edgar Highley.' Quickly she introduced the two men, and they shook hands.

Katie thought, how absurd this is. I am making introductions and a few feet inside that door a woman is lying dead.

Charley let them in. He looked relieved to see them. 'Your people should be here in a couple of minutes,' he told Richard. 'We've got pictures, but I'd like you to have a look too.'

Katie was used to death. In the course of her job, she constantly held up vivid and gory pictures of crime victims. She was usually able to separate herself from the emotional aspect and concentrate on the legal ramifications of wrongful death.

But it was a different matter to see Edna crumpled against the radiator in the kind of flannel nightgown her own mother considered indispensable; to see the blue terry-cloth robe so like the ones her mother used to pick up on sale at Macy's; to see the solid evidence of loneliness – the slices of canned ham, the empty cocktail glass.

Edna had been such a cheery person, who found some small measure of happiness in this shabbily furnished apartment, and even the apartment had betrayed her. It had become the scene of her violent death.

Gertrude Fitzgerald was sitting on the old-fashioned velour couch at the opposite end of the L-shaped room, out of sight of the body. She was sobbing softly. Richard went directly into the dinette to examine the dead woman. Katie walked over to Mrs Fitzgerald and sat beside her on the couch. Dr Highley followed her and pulled up a straight-backed chair.

Gertrude tried to talk to them. 'Oh, Dr Highley, Mrs DeMaio, isn't this terrible, just terrible?' The words brought a fresh burst of sobs. Katie gently put a hand on the trembling shoulders. 'I'm so sorry, Mrs Fitzgerald. I know you were fond of Miss Burns.'

'She was always so nice. Such fun. She always made me laugh. And maybe she had that little weakness. Everybody has a little weakness, and she never bothered anyone with it. Oh, Dr Highley, you'll miss her too.'

Katie watched as the doctor bent over Gertrude, his face grave. 'I surely will, Mrs Fitzgerald. Edna was a marvellously

efficient person. She took so much pride in her work. Dr
Fukhito and I used to joke that she had our patients so relaxed by
the time we saw them that she could have put Dr Fukhito out of
his job.'

'Doctor,' Gertrude blurted out, 'I told them you've been
here. I told them that. You knew Edna's little problem. It's just
silly to say she didn't fall. Why would anyone want to hurt her?'

Dr Highley looked at Katie. 'Edna suffered from sciatica, and
when she was laid up I occasionally dropped off work for her to
do at home. Certainly not more than three or four times. On one
occasion when she was supposed to be ill, I came here
unexpectedly and it was then I realized that she had a serious
drinking problem.'

Katie looked past him and realized that Richard had
completed examining the body. She got up, walked over to him
and looked at Edna. Silently she prayed:

*Eternal rest grant unto her, O Lord. May legions of angels greet her.
May she be conducted to a place of refreshment, light and peace.*

Swallowing over the sudden lump in her throat, she quietly
asked Richard what he had found.

He shrugged. 'Until I have had a chance to see how bad the
fracture is, I'd say it could go either way. Certainly it was a hell of
a smash, but if she was drunk – and it's obvious she was -- she
might have stumbled when she tried to get up. She was a pretty
heavy woman. On the other hand, there's a big difference
between being run over by a a car and by a train. And that's the
kind of difference we have to evaluate.'

'Any sign of forced entry?' Katie asked Charley.

'None. But these locks are the kind you could spring with a
credit card. And if she was as drunk as we think she was, anyone
could have walked in on her.'

'Why would anyone walk in on her? What were you telling
me about Captain Lewis?'

'The superintendent's wife – name's Gana Krupshak – was a
buddy of Edna Burns. Fact is, she was with Mrs Fitzgerald when
the body was found. We let her go to her own apartment just
before you came. She's shook up bad. Anyhow, last night she

came over here around eight o'clock. She said Edna already had a bag on. She stayed till eight thirty, then decided to put out the ham, hoping Edna would eat something and start to sober up. Edna told her about Vangie's suicide.'

'Exactly *what* did she tell her?' Katie asked.

'Nothing much. Just mentioned Vangie's name and how pretty she'd been. Then Mrs Krupshak went into the kitchen and she heard Edna dialling the phone. Mrs Krupshak could hear most of the conversation. She swears Edna called whoever she was talking to "Captain Lewis" and told him she had to talk to the police tomorrow. And get this. Krupshak swears she heard Edna give Lewis directions for driving here and then Edna said something about Prince Charming.'

'Prince Charming!'

Charley shrugged. 'Your guess is as good as mine. But the witness is positive.'

Richard said, 'Obviously we'll treat this as a potential homicide. I'm beginning to agree with Scott's hunch about Chris Lewis.' He glanced into the living-room. 'Mrs Fitzgerald looks pretty washed out. Are you through talking to her, Katie?'

'Yes. She's in no condition to question now.'

'I'll get one of the squad cars to drive her home,' Charley volunteered. 'One of the other guys can follow in her car.'

Katie thought, I do not believe Chris Lewis could have done this to Edna; I don't believe he killed his wife. She looked around. 'Are you *sure* there's nothing valuable missing?'

Charley shrugged. 'This whole place would go for about forty bucks in a garage sale. Her wallet's in her pocketbook; eighteen dollars there. Credit cards. The usual. No sign of anything being disturbed, let alone ransacked.'

'All right.' Katie returned to Dr Highley and Gertrude. 'We're going to have you driven home, Mrs Fitzgerald,' she said gently.

'What are they going to do to Edna?'

'They must investigate the extent of her head injuries. I don't think they'll probe beyond that. But if there is even the faintest chance that someone did this to Edna, we have to know it. Think of it as a way of showing we valued her life.'

The woman sniffled. 'I guess you're right.' She looked at the doctor. 'Dr Highley, I had an awful nerve asking you to come here. I'm sorry.'

'Not at all.' He was reaching into his pocket. 'I brought these sedatives along in case you needed them. As long as you're being driven home, take one right now.'

'I'll get a glass of water,' Katie said. She went to the sink in the bathroom. The bathroom and bedroom were off a rear foyer. As she let the water run cold, she realized that she hated the idea that Chris Lewis was emerging as a prime suspect in two deaths.

Taking the water glass back to Gertrude, she again sat beside her. 'Mrs Fitzgerald, just to satisfy ourselves, we want to be positive there's no possibility of Edna's having been robbed. Do you know if she kept any valuables – any jewellery, perhaps?'

'Oh, she had a ring and a pin she was so proud of. She only wore them on special occasions. I wouldn't know where she kept them. This is the first time I've been here, you see. Oh, wait a minute. Doctor. I remember that Edna said she showed you her ring and pin. In fact, she told me she showed you her hiding place for them when you were here. Perhaps you can help Mrs DeMaio.'

Katie looked into the cold grey eyes. He hates this, she thought. He's really angry to be here. He doesn't want to be part of this.

Had Edna had a crush on the doctor? she wondered suddenly. Had she exaggerated the number of times he might have dropped off work, maybe even hinted to Gertrude that he was a little interested in her? Maybe without even meaning to shade the truth, she'd invented a little romance, fantasized a possible relationship with him. If so, it was no wonder Mrs Fitzgerald had rushed to summon him, no wonder he looked acutely embarrassed and uncomfortable now.

'I really don't know of hiding places,' he said, his voice stiff with an undercurrent of sarcasm. 'One time Edna did show me a pin and ring that were in a box in her night-table drawer. I hardly consider that a hiding place.'

'Would you show me, Doctor?' Katie asked.

Together they walked down the short foyer into the bedroom. Katie switched on the lamp, a cheap ginger-jar base with a pleated paper shade.

'It was in there,' Dr Highley told her, pointing to the drawer in the night table on the right side of the bed.

Using only the very tips of her fingers, Katie opened the drawer. She knew that there'd probably be a complete search for evidence and the fingerprint experts would be called in.

The drawer was unexpectedly deep. Reaching into it, Katie pulled out a blue plastic jewellery case. When she raised the lid, the bell-like tinkle of a music box intruded on the sombre silence. A small brooch and a thin old diamond ring were nestled against cotton velvet.

'Those are the treasures, I guess,' Katie said, 'and that, I would imagine, eliminates the robbery theory. We'll keep this in the office until we know who the next of kin is.' She started to close the drawer, then stopped and looked down into it.

'Oh, Doctor, look.' Hastily she set the jewellery box on the bed and reached into the drawer.

'My mother used to keep her mother's old battered black hat for sentimental reasons,' she said. 'Edna must have done the same thing.'

She was tugging at an object, pulling it out, holding it up for him to see.

It was a brown moccasin, heavily scuffed, badly worn, battered and shabby. It was shaped for the left foot.

As Dr Edgar Highley stared at the shoe, Katie said, 'This was probably her mother's and she considered it such a treasure she kept it with that pathetic jewellery. Oh, Doctor, if memorabilia could talk, we'd have a lot of stories to hear, wouldn't we?'

CHAPTER TWENTY-EIGHT

At precisely eight a.m. Thursday morning, the Investigative Squad of the Homicide Division of Valley County pulled up to the Lewis home. The six-man team was headed by Phil Cunningham and Charley Nugent. The detectives in charge of fingerprinting were told to concentrate on the bedroom, master bath and kitchen.

It was admittedly a slim possibility that they would find

significant fingerprints that did not belong to either Chris or Vangie Lewis. But the lab report had raised another question. Vangie's fingerprints were on the tumbler that had been lying next to her, but there was some question about the positioning of those prints. Vangie had been right-handed. When she poured the cyanide crystals into the glass, it would have been natural for her to hold the glass with her left hand and pour with her right. But only her right prints were on the tumbler. It was an inconclusive, troublesome fact that further discredited the apparent suicide.

The medicine chests in both bathrooms and the guest powder room had already been searched after the body was found. Once again they were examined in minute detail. Every bottle was opened, sniffed. But the bitter-almond scent they were looking for was not to be found.

Charley said, 'She must have kept the cyanide in *something*.'

'Unless she was carrying just the amount she used in the glass and then flushed the envelopes or capsule she had it in down the john?' Phil suggested.

The bedroom was carefully vacuumed in the hope of finding human hair that did not come from the head of either Vangie or Chris. As Phil put it: 'Any house can have hairs from delivery people, neighbours, anybody. We're all shedding hair all the time. But most people don't bring even good friends into the bedroom. So it you find human hair that doesn't belong to the people who sleep in the bedroom, you just might have something.'

Particular attention was given to the shelves in the garage. The usual half-empty cans of paint, turpentine, some garden tools, hoses, insecticides, rose powder and weed killer were there in abundance. Phil grunted in annoyance as the prong of a hand spade pulled at his jacket. That prong had been protruding over the edge of the shelf, its handle wedged into place between the end of the shelf and a heavy paint can. Bending to free his sleeve, he noticed a sliver of printed cotton hooked on the prong.

That print. He'd seen it recently. It was that faded Indian stuff; madras. The dress Vangie Lewis was wearing when she died.

He called the police photographer out to the garage. 'Get a picture of that,' he said, pointing to the tool. 'I want a close-up of that material.' When the picture was taken, he carefully removed the piece of material from the prong and sealed it in an envelope.

In the house, Charley was going through the desk in the living-room. Funny, he thought. You can get a real slant on people from the way they keep their records. Chris Lewis obviously had taken care of all the book-keeping in the family. The chequebook stubs were precisely written, the balances accurate to the penny. Bills were apparently paid in full as they came in. The large bottom drawer held upright files. They were alphabetically arranged: AMERICAN EXPRESS; BANK AMERICARD; FEDERATED ANSWERING SERVICE; INSURANCE; PERSONAL LETTERS.

Charley reached for the personal-letter file. Quickly he leafed through it. Chris Lewis maintained a regular correspondence with his mother. *Many thanks for the cheque, Chris. You shouldn't be so generous.* That was written only two weeks ago. A January letter began: *Got Dad the TV for the bedroom and he's enjoying it so much.* One from last July: *The new air conditioner is such a blessing.*

If Charley was disappointed at not finding more significant personal data, he did admit grudgingly that Christopher Lewis was a concerned and generous son to ageing parents. He reread the mother's letters, hoping for clues to Vangie and Chris's relationship. The recent letters all ended the same way: *Sorry Vangie isn't feeling well* or *Women do sometimes have difficult pregnancies* or *Tell Vangie we're rooting for her.*

At noon, Charley and Phil decided to leave the rest of the team to complete the search and return to the office themselves. They were scheduled to meet Chris Lewis's plane at six o'clock. They had ruled out forced entry. There was no trace of cyanide in the house or garage. The contents of Vangie's stomach revealed that she'd eaten lightly on Monday; that she had probably had toast and tea about five hours before she died. A new loaf of bread in the bread box had two slices missing. The soiled dishes in the dishwasher told their own story: a single dinner plate, cup and saucer, salad dish, probably from Sunday night; a juice glass and cup, Monday's breakfast; a cup, saucer and plate with toast crumbs from the Monday supper.

Vangie had apparently dined alone Sunday night; no one had eaten with her Monday night. The coffee mug in the sink had not been there Tuesday morning. Undoubtedly Chris Lewis had made himself instant coffee some time after the body was found.

The driveway and grounds were being searched with minute care and so far revealed nothing unusual.

'They'll be at this all day, but we haven't missed anything,' Charley said flatly. 'And other than the fact that she tore her dress on that prong on the garage shelf, we've come up with a big zero. Wait a minute. We still haven't checked the answering service for messages.'

He got the Federated Answering Service number from the file in the desk, dialled and identified himself. 'Give me any messages left for either Captain or Mrs Lewis starting with Monday,' he ordered.

Taking out his pen, he began to write. Phil looked over his shoulder: *Monday, February 15, 4.00 p.m. Northwest Orient Reservations phoned. Mrs Lewis is confirmed on Flight 235 at 4.10 p.m. from LaGuardia Airport to the Twin Cities of Minneapolis§t Paul on Tuesday, February 16.*

Phil whistled silently. Charley asked, 'Did Mrs Lewis receive that message?'

He held the phone slightly away from his ear so that Phil could hear. 'Oh, yes,' the operator said. 'I was on the board myself Monday evening and gave it to her at about seven thirty.' The operator's voice was emphatic. 'She sounded very relieved. In fact, she said, "Oh, thank God."'

'All right,' Charley said. 'What else have you got?'

'Monday, February fifteenth, nine thirty p.m. Dr Fukhito left word for Mrs Lewis to call him at home as soon as she got in. He said she had his home number.'

Charley raised one eyebrow. 'Is that it?'

'Just one more,' the operator replied. 'A Miss Edna Burns called Mrs Lewis at ten p.m. Monday. She wanted Mrs Lewis to be sure and phone her no matter how late it was.'

Charley doodled triangles on the pad as the operator told him that there were no further messages on the service for either Tuesday or Wednesday, but that she knew a call had come through Tuesday evening and had been picked up by Captain Lewis. 'I was just starting to answer when he came on,' she explained. 'I got right off.' In reply to Charley's question, she affirmed that Mrs Lewis had not learned about either Dr Fukhito's or Miss Burns's call. Mrs Lewis had not contacted the service after seven thirty on Monday night.

'Thank you,' Charley said. 'You've been very helpful. We'll probably want a complete file of messages you've taken for the Lewises going back some time, but we'll be in touch about that later on.'

He hung up the receiver and looked at Phil. 'Let's go. Scott's going to want to hear all about this.'

'How do you read it?' Phil asked.

Charley snorted. 'How else can I read it? As of seven thirty Monday evening Vangie Lewis was planning to go to Minneapolis. A couple of hours later she's dead. As of ten o'clock Monday night, Edna Burns had an important message for Vangie. The next night Edna's dead and the last person who saw her alive heard her talking to Chris Lewis telling him she had information for the police.'

'What about that Japanese shrink who called Vangie Monday night?' Phil asked.

Charley shrugged. 'Katie talked to him yesterday. She may have some answers for us.'

CHAPTER TWENTY-NINE

For Katie, Wednesday night seemed endless. She'd gone to bed as soon as she returned from Edna's apartment, remembering first to take one of the pills Dr Highley had given her.

She'd slept fitfully, her subconscious restless with images of Vangie's face floating through a dream. Before she woke up, that dream dissolved into a new one: Edna's face as it had looked in death; Dr Highley and Richard bending over her.

She'd awakened with vague, troubling questions that eluded her, refusing to come into focus. Her grandmother's battered old black hat. Why was she thinking about that hat? Of course. Because of that shabby old shoe Edna obviously prized; the one she had kept with her jewellery. That was it. But why just *one* shoe?

Grimacing as she got out of bed, she decided that the soreness throughout her body had intensified during the night. Her knees, bruised from slamming into the dashboard, felt stiffer now than they had right after the accident. I'm glad the Boston Marathon isn't being run today, she thought wryly. I'd never win.

Hoping that a hot bath might soak some of the achiness away, she went into the bathroom, leaned down and turned on the taps in the tub. A wave of dizziness made her sway, and she grabbed the side of the tub to keep from falling. After a few moments the sensation receded, and she turned slowly, afraid that she might still faint. The bathroom mirror revealed the deathly pallor of her skin, the faint beads of perspiration on her forehead. It's this damn bleeding, she thought. If I weren't going into the hospital tomorrow night, I'd probably end up being carried in.

The bath did reduce some of the stiffness. Beige foundation make-up minimized the paleness. A new outfit – a shirred skirt and matching jacket in heather tweed and a crew-neck sweater – completed the attempt at camouflage. At least now I don't look as though I'm about to fall on my face, she decided, even if I am.

With her orange juice she swallowed another of Dr Highley's pills and thought about the still-incredible fact of Edna's death. After they left Edna's apartment, she and Richard had gone to a diner for coffee. Richard ordered a hamburger, explaining that he'd planned to have dinner in New York. He'd been taking someone out. She was sure of it. And why not? Richard was an attractive man. He certainly didn't spend all his evenings sitting in his own apartment or in family situations at Molly and Bill's. Richard had been surprised and pleased when she told him that she'd gone back to the Palisades restaurant. Then he'd become preoccupied, almost absent-minded. Several times he'd seemed to be on the verge of asking her a question, then apparently changed his mind. Even though she protested, he'd insisted on following her home, going into the house with her, checking that doors and windows were locked.

'I don't know why I feel uncomfortable about you alone in this place,' he'd told her.

She'd shrugged. 'Edna was in a garden apartment with thin walls. No one realized she was hurt and needed help.'

'She didn't,' Richard said shortly. 'She died almost instantly. Katie, that Dr Highley. You know him?'

'I questioned him about Vangie this afternoon,' she'd hedged.

Richard's frown had lightened. 'Of course. All right. See you tomorrow. I imagine Scott will call a meeting about Edna Burns.'

'I'm sure he will.'

Richard had looked at her, his expression troubled. 'Bolt the door,' he'd said. There had been no lighthearted good-bye kiss on the cheek.

Katie put her orange-juice glass in the dishwasher. Hurriedly she grabbed a coat and her handbag and went out to the car.

Charley and Phil were beginning the search of the Lewis house this morning. Scott was consciously drawing a web around Chris Lewis – a circumstantial web, but a strong one. If only she could prove that there was another avenue to explore before Chris was indicted. The trouble with being arrested on a homicide charge is that even if you prove your innocence, you never lose the notoriety. In years to come people would be saying, 'Oh, that's Captain Lewis. He was involved in his wife's death. Some smart lawyer got him off, but he's guilty as sin.'

She arrived at the office just before seven thirty and wasn't surprised to find Maureen Crowley already there. Maureen was the most conscientious secretary they had. Beyond that, she had a naturally keen mind and could handle assignments without constantly asking for direction. Katie stopped at her desk. 'Maureen, I've got a job. Could you come in when you have a minute?'

The girl got up quickly. She had a narrow-waisted, graceful young body. The green sweater she was wearing accentuated the vivid green of her eyes. 'How about now, Katie? Want coffee?'

'Great,' Katie replied, then added, 'but no ham on rye – at least, not yet.'

Maureen looked embarrassed. 'I'm sorry I said that yesterday.

You, of all people, are not in a rut.'

'I'm not sure about that.' Katie went into her office, hung up her coat and settled down with the pad she'd used at Westlake Hospital.

Maureen brought in the coffee, pulled up a chair and waited silently, her steno book on her lap.

'Here's the problem,' Katie said slowly. 'We're not satisfied that the Vangie Lewis death is a suicide. Yesterday I talked with her doctors, Dr Highley and Dr Fukhito, at Westlake Hospital.'

She heard a sharp intake of breath and looked up quickly. The girl's face had gone dead white. As Katie watched, two bright spots darkened her cheekbones.

'Maureen, is anything the matter?'

'No. No. I'm sorry.'

'Did I say anything to startle you?'

'No. Really.'

'All right.' Unconvinced, Katie looked back at her pad. 'As far as we know, Dr Fukhito, the psychiatrist at Westlake, was the last person to see Vangie Lewis alive. I want to find out as much as I can about him as fast as possible. Check the Valley County Medical Society and the AMA. I've heard he does volunteer work at Valley Pines Hospital. Maybe you can learn something there. Emphasize the confidentiality, but find out where he came from, where he went to school, other hospitals he's been connected with, his personal background: whatever you can get.'

'You don't want me to talk to anyone at Westlake Hospital?'

'Good heavens, no. I don't want anyone there to have any idea we're checking on Dr Fukhito.'

For some reason the younger woman seemed relieved. 'I'll get right on it, Katie.'

'It's not really fair to have you come in early to do other work and then throw a job at you. Good old Valley County isn't into overtime. We both know that.'

Maureen shrugged. 'That doesn't matter. The more I do in this office, the more I like it. Who knows? I may go for a law degree myself, but that means four years of college and three years of law school.'

'You'd be a good lawyer,' Katie said, meaning it. 'I'm

surprised you didn't go to college.'

'I was insane enough to get engaged the summer I finished high school. My folks persuaded me to take the secretarial course before I got married so at least I'd have some kind of skill. How right they were. The engagement didn't stand the wait.'

'Why didn't you start college last September instead of coming to work?' Katie asked.

The girl's face became brooding. Katie thought how unhappy she looked and decided that Maureen must have been pretty hurt about the breakup.

Not quite looking at Katie, Maureen said, 'I was feeling restless and didn't want to settle down to being a schoolgirl. It was a good decision.'

She went out of the room. The telephone rang. It was Richard. His voice was guarded. 'Katie, I've just been talking to Dave Broad, the head of prenatal research at Mt Sinai. On a hunch, I sent the foetus Vangie Lewis was carrying over to him. Katie, my hunch was right. Vangie *was not pregnant with Chris Lewis's child. The baby I took from her womb has distinctly Oriental characteristics!*'

CHAPTER THIRTY

Edgar Highley stared at Katie DeMaio as she stood with that shoe in her hand, holding it out to him. Was she mocking him? No. She believed what she was saying, that the shoe had had some sentimental memory for Edna.

He *had* to have that shoe. If only she didn't talk about it to the Medical Examiner or the detectives. Suppose she decided to show it to them? Gertrude Fitzgerald might recognize it. She'd been at the desk many times when Vangie came in. He'd heard Edna joke with her about Vangie's glass slippers.

Katie put the shoe back, closed the drawer and walked out of the bedroom, the jewellery box tucked under her arm. He followed her, desperate to hear what she would say. But she simply handed the jewellery box to the detective. 'The ring and pin are here, Charley,' she said. 'I guess that shoots any possibility of burglary. I didn't go through the bureau or closet.'

'It doesn't matter. If Richard suspects wrongful death, we'll search this place with a fine-tooth comb in the morning.'

There was a staccato rap at the door, and Katie opened it to admit two men carrying a stretcher.

Edgar Highley walked back to Gertrude. She had drunk the water in the glass Katie had given her. 'I'll get you more water, Mrs Fitzgerald,' he said quietly. He glanced over his shoulder. The others all had their backs to him, as they watched the attendants prepare to lift the body. It was his chance. He had to risk taking the shoe. As long as Katie hadn't mentioned it immediately, it was unlikely she'd bring it up now.

He walked rapidly to the bathroom, turned on the tap and slipped across the hall to the bedroom. Using his handkerchief to avoid fingerprints, he opened the night-table drawer. He was just reaching for the shoe when he heard footsteps coming down the hall. Quickly he pushed the drawer shut, stuffed his handkerchief into his pocket and was standing at the door of the bedroom when the footsteps stopped.

Willing himself to appear calm, he turned. Richard Carroll, the Medical Examiner, was standing in the foyer between the bedroom and the bathroom. His eyes were questioning. 'Doctor,' he said, 'I'd like to ask you a few questions about Edna Burns.' His voice was cold.

'Certainly.' Then, in what he hoped was a casual tone, he added, 'I have just been standing here thinking of Miss Burns. What a shame her life was so wasted.'

'Wasted?' Richard's voice was sharply questioning.

'Yes. She actually had a good mathematical mind. In this computer age Edna might have used that talent to make something of herself. Instead, she became an overweight, gossiping alcoholic. If that seems harsh, I say it with real regret. I was fond of Edna, and quite frankly I shall miss her. Excuse me. I'm letting the water run. I want to give Mrs Fitzgerald a glass of cold water. Poor woman, she's terribly distressed.'

Dr Carroll stood aside to let him pass. Had his criticism of Edna distracted the Medical Examiner from wondering what he was doing in Edna's room?

He rinsed the glass, filled it and brought it to Gertrude. The attendants had left with the body, and Katie DeMaio was not in the room.

'Has Mrs DeMaio left?' he asked the detective.

'No. She's talking to the super's wife. She'll be right back.'

He did not want to leave himself until he was sure that Katie did not talk about the shoe in front of Gertrude. But when she came back a few minutes later, she did not mention it.

They left the apartment together. The local police would keep it under surveillance until the official search was completed.

Deliberately he walked with Katie to her car, but then the Medical Examiner joined them. 'Let's have coffee, Katie,' he said. 'You know where the Golden Valley diner is, don't you?'

The Medical Examiner waited until she was in the car and had started to pull out before he said, 'Good night, Dr Highley' and abruptly left.

As he drove home, Edgar Highley decided there was a personal relationship of some sort between Katie DeMaio and Richard Carroll. When Katie bled to death, Richard Carroll would be both professionally and emotionally interested in the cause of death. He would have to be very, very careful.

There was hostility in Carroll's attitude towards him. But Carroll had no reason to be hostile to him. Should he have gone over to Edna's body? But what would have been the point? He should not have pushed her so hard. Should he have robbed her? That had been his original intention. If he had, he would have found the shoe last night.

But Edna had talked. Edna had told Gertrude that he'd been at her apartment. Edna might even have made it sound more frequent, more important. Gertrude had told Katie that he knew where the pitiful jewellery was kept. If they decided Edna had been murdered, would they tie the murder to Edna's job at the hospital? What else had Edna told people?

The thought haunted him as he drove home.

Katie was the key. Katie DeMaio. With her safely out of the way there was no evidence to tie him to Vangie's death – or Edna's. The office files were in perfect order. The current patients could bear the most minute scrutiny.

He turned into his driveway, drove into the garage, entered

the house. The lamb chops were on the plate, cold and edged with grease; the asparagus had wilted; the salad was limp and warm. He would reheat the food in the microwave oven, prepare a fresh salad. In a few minutes the table would look as it had before the phone call.

As he once again prepared the food, he found himslf becoming calm. He was so near to being safe. And soon it would be possible to share his genius with the world. He already had his success. He could prove it beyond doubt. Some day he would be able to proclaim it. Not yet, but some day. And he wouldn't be like that braggart who claimed to have successfully cloned but refused to offer even a shred of proof. He had accurate records, scientific documentation, pictures, X-rays, the step-by-step, day-by-day accounts of all the problems that had arisen and how he had dealt with them. All in the files in his secret safe.

When the proper time came he would burn the files about the failures and claim the recognition that was due him. By then there would surely be more triumphs.

Nothing must stand in his way. Vangie had nearly spoiled everything. Suppose he had not met her just as she came out of Fukhito's office? Suppose she hadn't told him about her decision to consult Emmet Salem?

Happenstance. Luck. Call it what you will.

But it had also been happenstance that sent Katie DeMaio to the window just as he left with Vangie's body. And exquisite irony that Katie had come to him in the first place.

Once again he sat down at the table. With intense satisfaction he saw that the dinner looked as appetizing, as delicious as when he'd first prepared it. The watercress was crisp and fresh; the chops bubbling; the asparagus piping hot under a delicate hollandaise. He poured wine into a thin goblet, admiring the delicate satiny feel of the crystal as he picked it up. The wine had the hearty Burgundy flavour he'd been anticipating.

He ate slowly. As always, food restored his sense of well-being. He would do what he must, and then he'd be safe.

Tomorrow was Thursday. The *Newsmaker* article would be on the stands. It would enhance his social as well as his medical prestige.

The fact that he was a widower lent him a specific appeal. He knew how his patients talked. 'Dr Highley is so brilliant. He's so distinguished. He has a beautiful home in Parkwood.'

After Winifred's death, he had allowed his connections with her friends to lapse. There was too much hostility there. That cousin of hers kept making insinuations. He knew it. That was why these three years he hadn't bothered with another woman. Not that he found solitude a sacrifice. His work was all-absorbing, all-satisfying. The time dedicated to it had been rewarded. His worst professional critics admitted that he was a good doctor, that the hospital was magnificently equipped, that the Westlake Maternity Concept was being copied by other physicians.

'My patients are not allowed to drink or smoke during their pregnancies,' he had told the *Newsmaker* interviewer. 'They are required to follow a specific diet. Many so-called barren women would have the babies they want if they would show the same dedication as athletes in training. Many of the long-range health problems suffered today would have been prevented entirely if mothers had not been eating the wrong food, taking the wrong medication. We have had the visible example of what Thalidomide did to scores of unfortunate victims. We recognize that a mother on drugs may produce an infant addict; an alcoholic mother will often be delivered of a retarded, undersized, emotionally disturbed child. But what of the many problems that we consider simply the lot of man . . . Bronchitis, dyslexia, hyperactivity, asthma, hearing and sight impairment? I believe that the place to eliminate these is not in the laboratory, but in the womb. I will not accept a patient who will not co-operate with my methods. I can show you dozens of women I have treated with a history of several miscarriages who now have children. Many more could experience that same joy, *if* they were willing to change their habits, particularly their eating and drinking habits. Many others would conceive and bear a child if their emotions were not so disturbed that in effect they are wearing mental contraceptives far more efficient than any device for sale in the drugstore. This is the reason, the basis of the Westlake Maternity Concept.'

The *Newsmaker* reporter had been impressed. But her next

question was a loaded one. 'Doctor, isn't it a fact that you have been criticized for the exorbitant fees you charge?'

'Exorbitant is *your* word. My fees, aside from rather spartan living expenses, are spent to develop the hospital and to pursue prenatal study.'

'Doctor, isn't it a fact that a large percentage of your cases have been women who miscarried several times under your care, even *after* following your schedule rigidly – and paying you ten thousand dollars, plus all hospital and lab expenses?'

'It would be insanity for me to claim that I could bring every difficult pregnancy to term. Yes. There have been cases where the desired pregnancy was begun, but spontaneously aborted. After several of these occurrences, I suggest that my patient adopt a child and help to arrange a suitable adoption.'

'For a fee.'

'Young woman, I assume you are being paid to interview me. Why don't *you* use your time for volunteer work?'

It had been foolish to attack the reporter like that. Foolish to risk animosity, foolish to give her any reason to discredit him, to delve too deeply into his background. He'd told her that he'd been obstetrical chief in Liverpool before his marriage to Winifred. But of course he hadn't discussed Christ Hospital in Devon.

The interviewer's next question had been meant to entrap him.

'Doctor, you perform abortions, do you not?'

'Yes, I do.'

'Isn't that incongruous for an obstetrician? To try to save one foetus and to eliminate another?'

'I refer to the womb as a cradle. I despise abortion. And I deplore the grief I witness when women come to me who have no hope of conceiving because they have had abortions and their wombs have been pierced by stupid, blundering, careless doctors. I think everyone – and I include my colleagues – would be astounded to learn how many women have denied themselves any hope of motherhood because they decided to defer that motherhood by abortion. It is my wish that all women carry their babies to healthy term. For those who do not want to, at least I can make sure that when they eventually want a child, they will still be able to have one.'

That point had been well received. The reporter's attitude had changed.

He finished eating. Now he leaned back in the chair and poured more wine into his glass. He was feeling expansive, comfortable. The laws were changing. In a few years he'd be able to announce his genius without fear of prosecution. Vangie Lewis, Edna Burns, Winifred, Claire . . . they'd be unrelated statistics. The trail would be cold.

He studied the wine as he drank, refilled his glass and drank again. He was tired. Tomorrow morning he had a caesarean section scheduled – another difficult case that would add to his reputation. It had been a difficult pregnancy, but the foetus had a strong heartbeat; it should be delivered safely. The mother was a member of the socially prominent Payne family. The father, Delano Aldrich, was an officer of the Rockefeller Foundation. This was the sort of family whose championship would make the difference if the Devon scandal were ever to surface again.

Only one obstacle left. He had brought Katie DeMaio's file home from the office. He would begin now to prepare the substitute file that he would show to the police after her death.

Instead of the history she'd given him of prolonged periods of bleeding over the past year, he would write, 'Patient complains of frequent and spontaneous haemorrhaging, unrelated to monthly cycles.' Instead of sponginess of uterine walls, probably familial, a condition that would be remedied indefinitely by a simple D-and-C, he would note findings of vascular breakdown. Instead of a slightly low haemoglobin he would indicate that the haemoglobin was chronically in the danger zone.

He went into the library. The file marked KATHLEEN DeMAIO which he had taken from the office was on top of his desk. From the drawer he extracted a new file and put Katie's name on it. For half an hour he worked steadily, consulting the office file for information on her previous medical history. Finally he was finished. He would bring the revised file with him to the hospital. He added several paragraphs to the file he had taken from the office, the one he would put in the wall safe when completed.

Patient was in minor automobile accident on Monday night, February 15. At 2.00 a.m. patient, in sedated condition, observed from the window of her room the transferral of the remains of Vangie Lewis by this physician. Patient still does not understand that what she observed was a true event rather than an hallucination. Patient is slightly traumatized by accident, and persistent haemorrhaging. Inevitably she will be able to achieve clear recollection of what she observed and for this reason cannot be permitted to remain as a threat to this physician.

Patient received blood transfusion on Monday night in emergency room of hospital. This physician prescribed second transfusion on pretence of preparation for Saturday surgery. This physician also administered anticoagulant medication, cumadin pills to be taken on regular basis until Friday night.

Pursing his lips, he laid down the pen. It was easy to imagine how he would complete this report.

Patient entered the hospital at 6.00 p.m. Friday, February 19, complaining of dizziness and general weakness. At 9.00 p.m. this physician, accompanied by Nurse Renge, found the patient haemorrhaging. Blood pressure was falling rapidly. With whole blood hanging, emergency surgery was performed at 9.45 p.m.

The patient, Kathleen Noel DeMaio, expired at 10.00 p.m.

He smiled in anticipation of completing this troublesome case. Every detail was perfectly planned, even to assigning Nurse Renge to floor duty Friday night. She was young, inexperienced and terrified of him.

After putting the file in the temporary hiding place in the top desk drawer, he went upstairs to bed and slept soundly until six in the morning.

Three hours later he delivered a healthy baby boy by caesarean section to Mrs Delano Aldrich and accepted as his due the tearful gratitude of the patient and her husband.

CHAPTER THIRTY-ONE

The funeral service for Vangie was held on Thursday morning at ten o'clock in the chapel of a Minneapolis funeral home. His heart aching with pity for Vangie's parents, Chris stood beside them, their muffled sobs assaulting him like hammer blows. Could he have done things differently? If he had not at first tried to placate Vangie, would she be lying here now? If he'd insisted that she go with him to a marriage counsellor years ago would it have helped their marriage? He had suggested that to her. But she had refused. 'I don't need any counselling,' she'd said. 'And don't you suggest any time I get upset about anything that there's something the matter with me. It's the other way around. You never get upset about anything; you don't care about anything or anybody. You're the problem, not me.'

Oh, Vangie. Vangie. Was truth somewhere in the middle? He had stopped caring very early in their marriage.

Her parents had been outraged to hear that Vangie could not be buried, that her body was to be shipped back east. 'Why?'

'I simply don't know.' There was no use in answering beyond that – not now.

'Amazing grace, how sweet the sound.' The soloist's soprano voice filled the chapel. 'I once was lost but now am found.'

Months ago, last summer, he'd felt life was bleak and hopeless. Then he'd gone to that party in Hawaii. And Joan had been there. He could remember the precise moment he'd seen her. She was on the terrace in a group of people. Whatever she'd said made them all laugh, and she'd laughed too, her eyes crinkling, her lips parting, her head tilting back. He'd gotten a drink and joined that group. And he hadn't left Joan's side again that evening.

'. . . was blind and now I see.' The Medical Examiner would not have released Vangie's body Tuesday night if he'd suspected foul play. What had happened to change his mind?

He thought of Edna's call. How much talking had she done to

other people? Could she throw some light on Vangie's death? Before he left Minneapolis, he had to call Dr Salem. He had to find out what he knew about Vangie that had made him react with such shock last night. Why had Vangie made an appointment to see him?

There had been someone else in Vangie's life. He was sure of it now. Suppose Vangie had killed herself in front of someone and that person brought her home? God knew she'd have had plenty of opportunity to be involved with another man. He was away from home at least half the month. Maybe she had met someone after they moved to New Jersey.

But would Vangie have caused herself pain?

Never!

The minister was saying the final prayer '. . . when every tear shall be dried . . .' Chris led Vangie's parents into the anteroom and accepted the expressions of sympathy from the friends who had attended the service. Vangie's parents were going to stay with relatives. They had agreed that the body should be cremated in New Jersey and the urn returned to be buried in the family plot.

Finally Chris was able to get away. It was just after eleven o'clock when he arrived at the Athletic Club in downtown Minneapolis and took the elevator to the fourteenth floor. There in the solarium he ordered a Bloody Mary and took it to a phone.

When he reached Dr Salem's office, he said, 'This is Vangie Lewis's husband. It's urgent I speak with the doctor immediately.'

'I'm sorry,' the nurse told him. 'Dr Salem left a short time ago for the American Medical Association convention in New York. He will not be back until next week.'

'New York.' Chris digested the information. 'Can you tell me where he's staying, please? It may be necessary for me to contact him there.'

The nurse hesitated. 'I suppose it's all right to tell you that. I'm sure Dr Salem intends to get in touch with you. He asked me to look up your New Jersey phone number, and I know he took your wife's medical records with him. But just in case he misses you, you can reach him at the Essex House on Central Park South in New York City. His extension there is three-two-one-nine.'

Chris had pulled out the small notebook that he kept in a compartment of his wallet. Repeating the information, he wrote it down quickly.

The top of the page was already filled. On it were Edna Burns's address and the directions to her apartment in Edgeriver.

CHAPTER THIRTY-TWO

Scott called a noon meeting in his office with the same four people who had been present at the meeting a day and a half earlier to discuss Vangie Lewis's death.

This meeting was different. Katie could feel the heightened atmosphere as she went into the office. Scott had Maureen waiting with a pen and paper.

'We're bringing sandwiches in here,' he said. 'I'm due in court again at one thirty and we've got to move fast on Captain Lewis.'

It was as she'd expected, Katie thought. Scott is zeroing in on Chris. She looked at Maureen. The girl had an aura of nervousness around her that was almost visible. It started when I gave her that assignment this morning, Katie thought.

Maureen caught her glance and half-smiled. Katie nodded. 'Uh-huh. The usual.' Then added, 'Did you have any luck with the phoning?'

Maureen looked at Scott, but he was scanning a file and ignoring them. 'So far not much. Dr Fukhito's not a member of the AMA or the Valley County Medical Society. He donates a lot of his time to disturbed children at Valley Pines Psychiatric Clinic. I have a call in to the University of Massachusetts. He attended medical school there.'

'Who told you that?' Katie asked.

Maureen hesitated. 'I remember hearing it somewhere.'

Katie had a feeling of evasiveness in the answer, but before she could probe further, Richard, Charley and Phil came into the office together. Quickly they gave their lunch choices to

Maureen, and Richard pulled a chair next to Katie's. He tossed his arm over her chair and touched the back of her head. His fingers were warm and strong as for an instant he massaged her neck muscles. 'Boy, are you tense,' he said.

Scott looked up, grunted, and began to speak. 'All right, by now you all know that the baby Vangie Lewis was carrying had Oriental characteristics. So that opens two possiblities. One: with the birth imminent it's possible she panicked and killed herself. She must have been frantic knowing she could never pass the baby off as her husband's. The second possibility is that Christopher Lewis found out that his wife had been having an affair and killed her. Let's try this. Suppose he went home unexpectedly Monday evening. They quarrelled. Why was she rushing home to Minneapolis? Was it because she was afraid of him? Don't forget, he never admitted she was going home and she expected to be gone before he returned from his trip. From what Katie tells us, the psychiatrist claims she ran out of his office nearly hysterical.'

'The *Japanese* psychiatrist,' Katie said. 'I have Maureen checking on him right now.'

Scott looked at her. 'Are you suggesting that you think there was something between him and Vangie?'

'I'm not suggesting anything yet,' Katie replied. 'The fact that he's Oriental certainly doesn't say that Vangie didn't know another Oriental man. But I can tell you this. He was nervous when I spoke with him yesterday, and he was carefully choosing every word he said to me. I certainly did not get the whole truth from him.'

'Which brings us to Edna Burns,' Scott said. 'What about it, Richard? Did she fall or was she pushed?'

Richard shrugged. 'It is not impossible that she fell. The alcohol level in her blood was point two five. She was blotto. She was heavy.'

'What about that business of drunks and babies being able to fall without getting hurt?' Katie asked.

Richard shook his head. 'That may be true about breaking bones, but not when your skull cracks into a sharp metal object. I would say that unless someone admits killing Edna, we'll never be able to prove it.'

'But it is possible she was murdered?' Scott persisted.

He shrugged. 'Absolutely.'

'And Edna was heard talking to Chris Lewis about Prince Charming.' Katie spoke slowly. She thought of the handsome psychiatrist. Would someone like Edna refer to *him* as Prince Charming? Would she have called Chris after Vangie's death to tell him she suspected an affair? 'I don't believe that,' she said.

The men looked at her curiously. 'What don't you believe?' Scott asked.

'I don't believe that Edna was vicious. I know she wasn't. I don't think she ever would have called Chris Lewis after Vangie died to hurt him by telling him about an affair Vangie was having.'

'She may have felt sorry enough for him that she didn't want him to consider himself a bereaved husband,' Richard said.

'Or she may have been looking for a few bucks,' Charley suggested. 'Maybe Vangie told her something Monday night. Maybe she knew Chris and Vangie had quarrelled and why they'd quarrelled. She had nothing. Apparently she was still paying off medical bills for her parents, and they've been dead a couple of years. Maybe she didn't think there was any harm in putting the arm on Lewis. She did threaten to go to the police.'

'She said she had something to tell the police,' Katie objected. 'That's the way the super's wife put it.'

'All right,' Scott said. 'What about the Lewis house? What did you turn up?'

Charley shrugged. 'So far, not much. There's a phone number with a six-one-two area code scribbled on the pad beside the kitchen phone. It's not Vangie's parents' number, we know that. We thought we'd call it from here. Maybe Vangie was talking to a friend, gave some of her plans. The other thing is that she tore that dress she was wearing on a prong sticking out from the shelf in the garage.'

'What do you mean the dress she was wearing?' Scott demanded.

'The dress she was found in. You couldn't miss it. It was a long job with one of those madras print designs.'

'Where are the clothes she was wearing?' Scott asked Richard.

'The lab probably still has them,' Richard said. 'We were

going over them on a routine check.'

Scott picked up the message pad Charley had handed him and tossed it to Katie. 'Why don't you dial this now? If it's a woman, you might get more out of her.'

Katie dialled the number. There was a pause and then a phone began ringing. 'Dr Salem's office.'

'It's a doctor's office,' she whispered, her hand over the phone. To the person on the other end she said, 'Perhaps you can help me. I'm Kathleen DeMaio from the Valley County, New Jersey, Prosecutor's office. We're conducting a routine inquiry into the death of Mrs Vangie Lewis last Monday, and she had the doctor's phone number on her pad.'

She was interrupted: 'Oh, that is a coincidence. I just hung up with Captain Lewis. He's trying to reach the doctor too. As I explained to him, Dr Salem is on his way to New York right now to the AMA convention. You can reach him later in the day at the Essex House Hotel on Central Park South.'

'Fine. We'll do that.' On a chance, Katie added, 'Do you know anything about Mrs Lewis's call? Did she speak with the doctor?'

'No. She did not. She spoke to me. She called Monday and was so disappointed that he wasn't going to be back in his office till Wednesday. I made an emergency appointment for her on Wednesday because he was going right out again. She said she had to see him.'

'One last question,' Katie said: 'What kind of doctor is Dr Salem?'

The woman's tone became proud, 'Oh, he's a prominent obstetrician and gynaecologist.'

'I see. Thank you. You've been very helpful.' Katie hung up the phone and reported the conversation to the others.

'And Chris Lewis knew about the appointment,' Scott said, 'and he wants to talk to the doctor now. I can't wait to get at him tonight. We'll have a lot of questions for him.'

There was a knock at the door and Maureen came in without waiting for a response. She was carrying a cardboard tray with inserts for coffee cups and a bag of sandwiches. 'Katie,' she said, 'that call from Boston about Dr Fukhito is just coming in. Do you want to take it?'

Katie nodded. Richard reached over and picked up the phone, holding it out to her. As she waited for the call to be switched, Katie became aware of a slow, persistent headache. That rap against the steering wheel hadn't been hard enough for a concussion, but she realized that her head had been bothering her the last few days. I just am not operating on all cylinders, she thought. So many things were teasing her mind. What was she trying to recall? Something. Some impression.

When she explained her credentials, she was quickly switched to the head of personnel at the University of Massachusetts Medical School. The man's voice was guarded. 'Yes, Dr Fukhito graduated from U Mass in the first third of his class. He interned at Massachusetts General and later became affiliated with the hospital and also had a private practice. He left the hospital seven years ago.'

'Why did he leave?' Katie asked. 'You must understand this is a police investigation. All information will be kept confidential, but we must know if there are any factors in Dr Fukhito's past that we should be aware of.'

There was a pause; then the informant said, 'Dr Fukhito was asked to resign seven years ago, and his Massachusetts licence was suspended for a period of one year. He was found guilty of unethical behaviour after he unsuccessfully defended a malpractice suit.'

'What was the cause of the suit?' Katie asked.

'A former patient sued Dr Fukhito for inducing her to have a personal relationship with him when she was under psychiatric treatment. She had recently been divorced and was in great emotional difficulty. As a result of that relationship she bore Dr Fukhito's child.'

CHAPTER THIRTY-THREE

Molly bustled around her kitchen rejoicing in the fact that all the children were back in school. Even twelve-year-old Jennifer had been well enough to go this morning; in fact, had pleaded to go. 'You're just like Katie,' Molly had scolded, 'when you set your head to anything. Well, all right, but you can't walk. It's too cold. I'll drive you.'

Bill was not going into New York until the afternoon. He was planning to attend one of the seminars at the AMA convention. They were enjoying a rare chance to chat in peace as Bill sat at the table sipping coffee and Molly sliced vegetables. 'I'm sure Katie and Richard and the Berkeleys will enjoy each other,' Molly was saying. 'Jim Berkeley is bright and he's a lot of fun. Why is it that most people in advertising really *are* so interesting?'

'Because their stock in trade is words,' Bill suggested. 'Although I must say I've met some that I wouldn't spend time looking up again.'

'Oh, sure,' Molly agreed absently. 'Now, if Liz just doesn't spend the whole evening talking about the baby . . . Although I must say she's getting better about that. When I phoned to invite her the other day she only spent the first twenty minutes on Maryanne's latest trick . . . which, incidentally, is to blow her oatmeal all over the place as she's being fed. Isn't that cute?'

'It is if it's your first baby and you waited fifteen years to have one,' Bill commented. 'I seem to remember every time Jennifer blinked you recorded it in her baby book.'

Molly began slicing celery. 'Remember your aunt gave me a baby book to keep for the twins. I don't think I ever got the wrapping paper off it . . . Anyhow, it should be fun. And even if Liz does rave about the baby, maybe a little of it will sink in on Katie and Richard.'

Bill's eyebrows rose. 'Molly, you're about as subtle as a sledgehammer. You'd better watch out or they'll start avoiding each other completely.'

'Nonsense. Don't you see the way they look at each other? There's something smouldering – better than smouldering – there. My God, Richard called me last night to see if Katie was here and then wanted to know if there was something the matter with her. You should have heard how worried he sounded. I tell you he's crazy about her, but is just smart enough not to show it and scare her off.'

'Did you tell him about the operation?'

'No. Katie gave me hell the other morning when I asked if she had told him. Honest to God, the way most people let everything hang out these days . . . Look, why can't she just say to Richard, "I've got this problem, it's a nuisance, Mother had it and had to have a D-and-C every couple of years, and it looks like I'm built like her"? Instead, the poor guy is obviously worried that it's something serious. I don't think it's fair to him.'

Bill got up, walked over to the sink, rinsed out his cup and saucer and put them in the dishwasher. 'I don't think you have ever realized that Katie has been desperately hurt by losing the two men she loved and counted on . . . your father when she was eight, and then John when she was twenty-four. She reminds me of the last scene in *Gone with the Wind* when Rhett says to Scarlett, "I gave my heart to you and you broke it. Then I gave it to Bonnie and she broke it. I'll not risk it a third time." That's something of Katie's problem. But frankly, I think she's got to work it out herself. Your hovering over her like a mother hawk isn't helping her. I'd like nothing better than to see her get together with Richard Carroll. He'd be good for her.'

'And he plays golf with you,' Molly interjected.

Bill nodded. 'That too.' He picked up a stalk of celery and nibbled on it. 'A word of advice. If Katie doesn't want to tell Richard about this operation, don't fill him in. That's not fair to her. If he's persistent in being concerned about her, it has to make some sort of statement to her. You've gotten them together. Now – '

'Now bug off,' Molly sighed.

'Something like that. And tomorrow night when Katie goes into the hospital, you and I are going to the Met. I got tickets for *Otello* months ago and I don't plan to change them. You be there when she comes out of the recovery room Saturday morning, but it won't hurt her any to wish she had someone with her. Friday evening maybe she'll do a little thinking.'

'Go into the hospital by herself?' Molly protested.

'By herself,' Bill said firmly. 'She's a big girl.'

The telephone rang. 'Pray it isn't the school nurse saying one of the kids started with the virus again,' Molly muttered. Her 'Hello' was guarded. Then her tone became concerned. 'Liz, hi. Now, don't tell me you're going to cancel on me tonight.'

She listened. 'Oh, for heaven's sake, bring her along. You

have the folding carriage . . Sure, we'll put her up in our room and she'll be fine . . . Of course I don't mind. So if she wakes up we'll bring her down and let her join the party. It'll be like old times around here . . . Great. See you at seven. Bye.'

She hung up. 'Liz Berkeley's regular baby-sitter had to cancel and she's afraid to leave her with someone she doesn't know, so she's bringing the baby along.'

'Fine.' Bill looked at the kitchen clock. 'I'd better get out of here. It's getting late.' He kissed Molly's cheek. 'Will you quit worrying about your little sister?'

Molly bit her lip. 'I can't. I've got this creepy feeling about Katie, like something might happen to her.'

CHAPTER THIRTY-FOUR

When Richard returned to his office, he stood for a long time staring out the window. His view was somewhat more appealing than the one from Scott's office. Besides the northeast corner of the county jail, a distinct section of the pocket-sized park in front of the courthouse was visible to him. Only half aware of what he was seeing, he watched as a flurry of sleet-weighted snow pelted the already-slick frozen grass.

Wonderful weather, he thought. He glanced up at the sky. Heavy snow clouds were forming. Vangie Lewis's body was being flown into Newark from Minneapolis on a two-thirty flight. It would be picked up at seven and brought to the morgue. Tomorrow morning he'd re-examine it. Not that he expected to find anything more than he already knew. There were absolutely no bruise marks on it. He was sure of that. But there was something about her left foot or leg that he had noticed and dismissed as irrelevant.

He pushed that thought aside. It was useless to speculate until he could re-examine the body. Vangie had obviously been highly emotional. Could she have been induced to suicide by Fukhito? If Vangie was carrying Fukhito's child, he must have been panicked. He'd be finished as a doctor if he were found to be involved with a patient again.

But Chris Lewis had a girl-friend – a good reason for wanting his wife out of the way. Suppose he had learned of the affair? Apparently even Vangie's parents hadn't known she was planning to come home to Minneapolis. Was it possible Vangie hoped to be delivered of the baby by the Minnesota obstetrician and keep quiet about it? Maybe she'd say she'd lost it. If she wanted to preserve her marriage, she might have been driven to that. Or if she realized a divorce was inevitable, the absolute proof of her infidelity might have weighed in the settlement.

None of it rang true.

Sighing, Richard reached over, snapped on the intercom and asked Marge to come in. She had been at lunch when he returned from Scott's office and he had not collected his messages.

She hurried in with a sheaf of slips in her hand. 'None of these are too important,' she informed him. 'Oh, yes, there was one right after you went to Mr Myerson's office. A Dr Salem. He didn't ask for you by name; he wanted the Medical Examiner. Then he asked if we had performed the autopsy on Vangie Lewis. I said you were the ME and that you'd performed it personally. He was catching a plane from Minneapolis, but asked if you'd call him at the Essex House in New York around five o'clock. He sounded anxious to talk to you.'

Richard pursed his lips in a soundless whistle. 'I'm anxious to talk to *him*,' he said.

'Oh, and I got the statistics on the Westlake obstetrical patients,' Marge said. 'In the eight years of the Westlake Maternity Concept, sixteen patients have died either in childbirth or of toxic pregnancies.'

'*Sixteen?*'

'*Sixteen*,' Marge repeated with emphasis. 'However, the practice is huge. Dr Highley is considered an excellent doctor. Some of the babies he's brought to term are near miracles, and the women who died had all been warned by other doctors that they were high pregnancy risks.'

'I'll want to study all the fatalities,' Richard said. 'But if we ask Scott to subpoena the files from the hospital, we'll alert them, and I don't want to do that yet. Have you got anything else?'

'Maybe. In these eight years two people filed malpractice suits against Dr Highley. Both suits were dismissed. And a cousin of his wife's came in and claimed that he didn't believe she'd died of a heart attack. The Prosecutor's office contacted her personal physician and he said the cousin was crazy. The cousin had been the sole heir before Winifred Westlake married Dr Highley, so that may be why he wanted to start trouble.'

'Who was Winifred Westlake's personal physician?'

'Dr Alan Levine.'

'He's a top internist,' Richard said. 'I'll have a talk with him.'

'How about the people who filed the malpractice suits? Do you want to know who they are?'

'Yes, I do.'

'I figured that. Here.'

Richard looked down at the two names on the sheet of paper Marge handed him. *Anthony Caldwell, Old Country Lane, Peapack, N.J.*, and *Anna Horan, 415 Walnut Street, Ridgefield Park, N.J.*

'You do nice work, Marge,' he said

She nodded. 'I know.' Her tone was satisfied.

'Scott is in court by now. Will you leave word for him to call me when he gets back to his office? Oh, and tell the lab I want Vangie Lewis's clothes available to put on her first thing tomorrow morning. All tests have to be finished on the clothing by this afternoon.'

Marge left, and Richard turned to the work on his desk.

It was after four before Scott returned the call. He listened to Richard's decision to interview the complainants against Dr Highley and was clearly not impressed. 'Look, today there isn't any doctor, no matter who he is, who isn't hit by malpractice suits. If Dr Schweitzer were still alive, so help me, he'd be defending himself against them in the jungle. But go ahead on your own if you want to. We'll subpoena the hospital records when you're ready for them. I am concerned about the high number of obstetrical deaths of mothers, but even that may be explainable. He does deal in high-risk pregnancies.'

Scott's voice deepened. 'What I'm most interested in is what this Dr Salem has to say. You talk with him and get back to me and then I'll get in on the act. Between you and me, Richard, I think we're going to pull a tight-enough circumstantial case around Captain Chris Lewis that we may force him to come clean. We know that his movements are unaccounted for on Monday night, when his wife died. We know Edna Burns called him Tuesday night. We now know that the funeral director left him before nine on Tuesday night. After that he was alone and could easily have gone out. Suppose he did go down and see her? He's handy. Charley tells me he's got sophisticated tools in his garage. Edna was almost blind drunk when she called him. The neighbour told us that. Suppose he drove there, slipped the lock, got into the apartment and shoved that poor dame before she knew what hit her? Frankly, that's the way my gut sees it, and we'll have him here tonight to tell us all about it.'

'You may be right,' Richard said. 'But I'm still going to check these people out.'

He caught Dr Alan Levine just as he was leaving his office. 'Buy you a drink,' Richard suggested. 'I'll only take fifteen minutes.'

They agreed to meet at the Parkwood Country Club. A midway point for both of them, it had the virtue of being quiet on weekdays. They'd be able to talk in the bar without worry about being overheard or having people drop over to say hello.

Alan Levine was a Jimmy Stewart-at-fifty-five look-alike – a fact that endeared him to his older patients. They enjoyed the easy cordiality of professionals who respected each other, enjoyed a drink together if their paths crossed, waved to each other on the golf links.

Richard came directly to the point. 'For various reasons we're interested in Westlake Hospital. Winifred Westlake was your patient. Her cousin tried to insinuate that she did not die of a heart attack. What can you tell me about it?'

Alan Levine looked directly at Richard, sipped his martini, glanced out the picture window at the snow-covered fairway and pursed his lips. 'I have to answer that question on a couple of levels,' he said slowly. 'First: Yes, Winifred was my patient. For years she'd had a near-ulcer. Specifically, she had all the classic symptoms of a duodenal ulcer, but it never showed up on X-ray. When she'd periodically experience pain, I'd have the usual X-rays done, get negative results, prescribe an ulcer diet, and she experienced relief almost immediately. No great problem.

'Then the year before she met and married Highley she had a severe attack of gastroenteritis which actually altered her cardiogram. I put her in the hospital for a suspected heart attack. But after two days in the hospital the cardiogram was well within the normal range.'

'So there might or might not have been a problem with her heart?' Richard asked.

'I didn't think there was. It never showed up in the standard tests. But her mother died of a heart attack at fifty-eight. And Winifred was nearly fifty-two when she died. She was older than Highley by some ten years, you know. Several years after her marriage she began to come to me more frequently, constantly complaining of chest pains. The tests produced nothing significant. I told her to watch her diet.'

'And then she had a fatal attack?' Richard asked.

The other doctor nodded. 'One evening, during dinner, she had a seizure. Edgar Highley phoned his service immediately. Gave them my number, the hospital's number, told them to call the police. From what I was told, Winifred keeled over at the dining-room table.'

'You were there when she died?' Richard queried.

'Yes. Highley was still trying to revive her. But it was hopeless. She died a few minutes after I arrived.'

'And you're satisfied it was heart failure?' Richard asked.

Again there was the hint of hesitation. 'She'd been having chest pains over a period of years. Not all heart trouble shows up on cardiograms. In the couple of years before she died she was suffering periodically from high blood pressure. There's no question that heart trouble tends to run in families. Yes. I was satisfied at the time.'

'*At the time.*' Richard underscored the words.

'I suppose the cousin's absolute conviction that something was wrong about her death has troubled me these three years. I practically threw him out of my office when he came in and as much as accused me of falsifying records. Figured he was a disgruntled relative who hated the guy who took his place in the will. But Glenn Nickerson is a good man. He's coach at Parkwood High, and my kids go there now. They're all crazy about him. He's a family man, active in his church, on the town council; certainly not the kind of man who would go off half-cocked at being disinherited. And certainly he must have known that Winifred would leave her estate to her husband. She was crazy about Highley. Why, I never could see. He's a cold fish if ever I met one.'

'I gather you don't like him.'

Alan Levine finished his drink. 'I don't like him at all. And have you caught the article about him in *Newsmaker*? Just came out today. Makes a little tin god of him. He'll be even more insufferable, I suppose. But I've got to hand it to him. He's an excellent doctor.'

'Excellent enough to have chemically induced a heart attack in his wife?'

Dr Levine looked directly at Richard. 'Frankly, I've often wished I'd insisted on an autopsy.'

Richard signalled for the check. 'You've been a great help, Alan.'

The other man shrugged. 'I don't see how. What possible use is any of this to you?'

'For the present, it gives me insight when I talk to some people. After that, who knows?'

They parted at the entrance to the bar. Richard fished in his pocket for change, went over to the public telephone and phoned the Essex House Hotel in New York. 'Dr Emmet Salem, please.'

There was the jabbing sound of a hotel phone ringing. Three, four, five, six times. The operator broke in. 'I'm sorry, but there's no answer there.'

'Are you sure Dr Salem has checked in?' Richard asked.

'Yes, sir, I am. He called specifically to say that he was expecting an important phone call and he wanted to be sure to get it. That was only twenty minutes ago. But I guess he changed his mind or something. Because we are definitely ringing his room and there's no answer.'

CHAPTER THIRTY-FIVE

When she left Scott's office, Katie called in Rita Castile and together they went over the material Katie would need for upcoming trials. 'That armed robbery on the twenty-eighth,' Katie said, 'where the defendant had his hair cut the morning after the crime. We'll need the barber to testify. It's no wonder the witnesses couldn't make a positive identification. Even though we made him wear a wig in the line-up, he didn't look the same.'

'Got it.' Rita jotted down the barber's address. 'It's too bad you can't let the jury know that Benton has a long juvenile record.'

'That's the law,' Katie sighed. 'I sure hope that some day it stops bending backward to protect criminals. That's about all I have for you now, but I won't be coming in over the weekend, so next week will really be a mess. Be prepared.'

'You won't be coming in?' Rita raised her eyebrows. 'Well, it's about time. You haven't given yourself a full weekend off in a couple of months. I hope you're planning to go some place and have fun.'

Katie grinned. 'I don't know how much fun it will be. Oh, Rita, I have a hunch that Maureen is upset about something today. Without being nosy, is there anything wrong that you know about? Is she still down about the breakup with her fiance?'

Rita shook her head. 'No, not at all. That was just kid stuff, and she knew it. The usual going-steady-from-the-time-they-were-fifteen, an engagement ring the night of the prom. They both realized by last summer that they weren't ready to get married. He's in college now, so that's no problem.'

'Then why is she so unhappy?' Katie asked.

'Regret,' Rita said simply. 'Just about the time they broke up she realized she was pregnant and had an abortion. She's weighted down with guilt about it. She told me that she keeps dreaming about the baby, that she hears a baby crying and is trying to find it. Said she'd do anything to have had the baby, even though she would have given it out for adoption.'

Katie remembered how much she had hoped to conceive John's child, how furious she'd been when after his death someone commented that she was lucky not to be stuck with a baby. 'Life is so crazy,' she said. 'The wrong people get pregnant, and then it's so easy to make a mistake you have to live with for the rest of your life. But that does explain it. Thanks for telling me. I was afraid I'd said something to hurt her.'

'You didn't,' Rita said. She gathered up the files Katie had assigned her. 'All right. I'll serve these subpoenas and hunt for the barber.'

After Rita left, Katie leaned back in her chair. She wanted to talk again with Gertrude Fitzgerald and Gana Krupshak. Mrs Fitzgerald and Edna had been good friends; they'd often lunched together. Mrs Krupshak had frequently dropped into Edna's apartment at night. Maybe Edna had said something to one of them about Dr Fukhito and Vangie Lewis. It was worth a try.

She called Westlake Hospital and was told that Mrs Fitzgerald was home ill; requested and got her home phone number. When the woman answered she was obviously still distraught. Her voice was weak and shaking. 'I have one of my migraines, Mrs DeMaio,' she said, 'and no wonder. Every time I think of how Edna looked, poor dear . . .'

'I was going to suggest that we get together either here or at your home,' Katie said. 'But I'll be in court all day tomorrow, so I guess it will have to wait until Monday. There's just one thing I would like to ask you, Mrs Fitzgerald. Did Edna ever call either of the doctors she worked for "Prince Charming"?'

'*Prince Charming?*' Gertrude Fitzgerald's voice was astonished. 'Prince Charming? My goodness. Dr Highley or Dr Fukhito? Why would anyone call either of them Prince Charming? My heavens, no.'

'All right. It was just a thought.' Katie said good-bye and dialled Mrs Krupshak. The superintendent answered. His wife was out, he explained. She'd be back around five.

Katie glanced at the clock. It was four thirty. 'Do you think she'd mind if on my way home I stopped to talk to her for a few minutes? I promise I won't be long.'

'Suit yourself,' the man answered shortly, then added, 'What's going on with the Burns apartment? How long before it gets cleared out?'

'That apartment is not to be entered or touched until this office releases it,' Katie said sharply. She hung up, packed some files in her briefcase and got her coat. She'd have just enough time to talk to Mrs Krupshak, then go home and change. She wouldn't stay late at Molly's tonight. She wanted one decent night's sleep before the operation. She knew she wouldn't sleep well in the hospital.

She was just ahead of the evening traffic, and Mrs Krupshak was home when she rang her bell. 'Now, isn't that timing?' she exclaimed to Katie. The shock of discovering Edna's body had begun to wear off for this woman, and clearly she was beginning to enjoy the excitement of the police investigation.

'This is my bingo afternoon,' she explained. 'When I told my friends what happened they could hardly keep their cards straight.'

Poor Edna, Katie thought, then realized that Edna would have been delighted to be the centre of an active discussion.

Mrs Krupshak ushered her into an L-shaped living-room, a mirror image of the unit Edna had lived in. Edna's living-room had been furnished with an old-fashioned velour couch, matching straight-backed fireside chairs, a fading Oriental rug. Like Edna, the apartment had had its own innate dignity.

The superintendent's wife had an imitation-leather couch and club chair, an oversized cocktail table topped by an exactly centred plastic flower arrangement and an orange-toned autumnal print over the couch that picked up the wildly vivid shade of the carpeting. Katie sat down. This place is ordinary, she reflected. It's unimaginative, yet it's clean and comfortable and you get the feeling that even if her husband is brusque and unsociable, Gana Krupshak is a happy woman. Then Katie wondered why she was suddenly so concerned with defining happiness.

With a mental shrug she turned to the questions she wanted to ask. 'Mrs Krupshak,' she said, 'we talked last night, but of course, you were so shocked. Now I wonder if you would go over with me very carefully what happened on Tuesday night: how long were you with Edna; what did you talk about; did you get the impression that when she spoke to Captain Lewis she made an appointment with him.'

Gana Krupshak leaned back in her chair, looked past Katie, half-closed her eyes and bit her lip.

'Now, let's see. I went over to Edna's right at eight o'clock, because Gus started to watch the basketball game and I thought, To hell with the basketball game, I'll pop over to Edna's and have a beer with her.'

'And you went over there,' Katie encouraged.

'I did. The only thing is, Edna had made a pitcher of Manhattans and they were about half gone and she was feeling pretty rocky. You know, like, sometimes she'd get in moods, kind of *down*, if you know what I mean, and I thought she was in one of those. Like, last Thursday was her mother's birthday and I stopped in then and she was crying about how much she missed her mother. Now, I don't mean she'd take it out on you, no way, but when I popped over there Thursday she was sitting with her folks' picture in her hands and the jewellery box on her lap and tears rolling down her cheeks. I gave her a big hug and said, "Edna, I'm going to pour you a nice Manhattan and we'll toast your maw and if she was here she'd be joining us." So if you know what I mean, I kind of kidded her out of the blues and she was fine, but when I went over Tuesday night and saw her under the weather I figured she really wasn't over the lonesome spell.'

'Did she tell you she was still depressed Tuesday night?' Katie asked.

'No. No. That's it. She was kind of excited. She talked in a sort of rambly way about this patient who had died, how beautiful she'd been, like a doll, and how sick she'd been getting and how she – Edna, I mean – could tell the cops a lot about her.'

'Then what happened?' Katie asked.

'Well, I had a Manhattan, or two, with her and then figured I'd better get home because Gus gets in a snit if I'm still out when he goes to bed. But I hated to see Edna drink much more, because I knew she'd be feeling real bad in the morning, so I got out that nice canned ham and opened it and cut off a few slices for her.'

'And that was when she made the call?'

'Just like I told you last night.'

'And she talked to Captain Lewis about Prince Charming?'

'As God is my witness.'

'All right, but one last thing, Mrs Krupshak: do you know if Edna kept any articles of clothing of her mother's as a sentimental keepsake?'

'Clothing? No. She did have a lovely diamond pin and ring.'

'Yes, yes, we found those last night. But – well, for example, my mother used to keep her mother's old black felt hat in her closet for sentimental reasons. I noticed an old moccasin in Edna's jewellery drawer. It was quite shabby. Did she ever show it to you or mention it?'

Gana Krupshak looked directly at Katie. 'Absolutely not,' she said flatly.

CHAPTER THIRTY-SIX

The *Newsmaker* article was on the stands Thursday morning. The phone calls began as soon as he went to his office after delivering the Aldrich baby. He instructed the switchboard to ring through directly to him. He wanted to hear the comments. They were beyond his expectations. 'Doctor, when can I have an appointment? My husband and I have longed for a baby. I can fly to New Jersey at your convenience. God bless you for your work.' The Dartmouth Medical School phoned. Would he consider a guest lecture? An article writer for *Ladies' Home Journal* wanted to interview him. Would Dr Highley and Dr Fukhito appear together on *Eyewitness News*?

That request troubled him. He'd been careful to give the *Newsmaker* reporter the impression that he worked with a number of psychiatrists, in the same sense a family lawyer might have his clients consult with any one of a dozen counsellors. He had clearly suggested that the programme was entirely under his control, not a joint effort. But the reporter had picked up

Fukhito's name from a number of the safe patients he'd given her to interview. Now the reporter credited Fukhito as the psychiatrist who seemed to be primarily involved with Dr Edgar Highley in the Westlake Maternity Concept.

Fukhito would be desperately troubled by the publicity. That was why he'd been chosen. Fukhito had to keep his mouth shut even if he ever started to get suspicious. He was in no position to allow a breath of scandal to hit Westlake. He'd be permanently ruined if that happened.

Fukhito was becoming a distinct liability. It would be easy enough to get rid of him now. He was giving a lot of time on a voluntary basis to the clinic at Valley Pines. He could undoubtedly become staff there now. Probably Fukhito would be glad to scramble for cover. Then he could start to rotate psychiatrists; he knew enough of them by now who weren't competent to counsel anyone. They'd be easy enough to dupe.

Fukhito would have to go.

The decision made, he signalled for his first patient to come in. She was new, as were the two scheduled after her. The third patient was an interesting case: a womb so tipped that she'd never be able to conceive without intervention.

She would be his next Vangie.

The phone call came at noon just as he was leaving for lunch. The nurse covering the reception desk was apologetic. 'Doctor, it's a long-distance call from a Dr Emmet Salem in Minneapolis. He's in a phone booth at the airport now and insists on speaking with you at once.'

Emmet Salem! He picked up the phone. 'Edgar Highley here.'

'Doctor Highley.' The voice was icy cold. 'Dr Highley from Christ Hospital in Devon?'

'Yes.' A chill, sickening fear made his tongue heavy, his lips rubbery.

'Dr Highley, I learned last night that you treated my former patient, Mrs Vangie Lewis. I'm leaving for New York immediately. I'll be at the Essex House Hotel in New York. I must tell you that I am planning to consult with the Medical Examiner in New Jersey about Mrs Lewis's death. I have her medical records with me. In fairness to you I suggest we discuss her case before I level accusations.'

'Doctor, I'm troubled by your tone and insinuations.' Now he could talk. Now his own voice hardened into chips of granite.

'My plane is boarding. I'll be checking into room three-two-one-nine of the Essex House Hotel shortly before five o'clock. You can call me there.' The connection was broken.

He was waiting in the Essex House when Emmet Salem emerged from the cab. Swiftly he disappeared into an elevator to the thirty-second floor, walked past room 3219 until the corridor turned in a right angle. Another elevator stopped at the floor. He listened as a key clicked, a bellman said, 'Here we are, Doctor.' A minute later the bellman emerged again. 'Thank you, sir.'

He waited until he heard the elevator stop at the floor for the bellman. The corridors were silent. But that wouldn't last long. Many of the delegates to the AMA convention were probably staying here. There was always the danger of running into someone he knew. But he had to take the chance. He had to silence Salem.

Swiftly he opened his leather bag and brought out the paperweight that only forty-eight hours ago he had intended to use to silence Edna. Incongruous, impossible – that he, the healer, the doctor, was repeatedly forced to kill.

He slipped the paperweight into his coat pocket, put on his gloves, grasped the bag firmly in his left hand and knocked on the door.

Emmet Salem pulled the door open. He'd just removed his suit jacket. 'Forgot something?' His voice trailed off. Obviously he'd expected the bellman had come back.

'Dr Salem!' He reached for Salem's hand, walking forward, backing the older man into the room, slipping the door closed behind him. 'I'm Edgar Highley. It's good to see you again. You got off the phone so abruptly that I couldn't tell you I was having dinner with several colleagues who are attending the convention. I have only a very few minutes, but I'm sure we can clear up any questions.'

He was still walking forward, forcing the other man to retreat. The window behind Salem was wide open. He'd probably had the bellman open it. The room was very hot. The window was low. His eyes narrowed. 'I tried to phone you, but your extension is out of order.'

'Impossible. I just spoke to the operator.' Dr Salem stiffened, his face suddenly cautious.

'Then I do apologize. But no problem. I'm so anxious to go over the Lewis file with you. I have it in my case here.' He reached for the paperweight in his pocket, then cried, 'Doctor, behind you, watch out!'

The other man spun around. Holding the paperweight in his fist, he crashed it on Salem's skull. The blow sent Emmet Salem staggering. He slumped against the windowsill.

Jamming the paperweight back into his pocket, Edgar Highley cupped his palms around Emmet Salem's foot and shoved up and out.

'No. No. Christ, please!' The half-conscious man slid out the window.

He watched dispassionately as Salem landed on the roof of the extension some fifteen floors below.

The body made a muffled thud.

Had it been seen? He had to hurry. From Salem's suit coat on the bed, he pulled out a key ring. The smallest key fitted the attaché case on the luggage rack.

The Vangie Lewis file was on top. Grabbing it, he shoved it into his own briefcase, relocked Salem's bag, returned the keys to the suit-coat pocket. He took the paperweight from his pocket and placed it in his own bag with the file. The wound had not spurted blood, but the paperweight was sticky.

He closed his own bag and glanced around. The room was in perfect order. There was no trace of blood on the windowsill. It had taken less than two minutes.

He opened the door cautiously and looked out. The corridor was empty. He stepped out. As he closed the door, the phone in Salem's room began to ring.

He did not dare be seen getting on the elevator on this floor. His picture was in the *Newsmaker* article. Later people might be questioned. He might be recognized.

The fire-exit stairway was at the end of the corridor. He descended four levels to the twenty-eighth floor. There he re-entered the carpeted corridor. An elevator was just stopping. He got on it, his eyes scanning the faces of the passengers. Several women, a couple of teenagers, an elderly couple. No doctors. He was sure of that.

At the lobby he walked rapidly to the Fifty-eighth Street exit of the hotel, turned west and then south. Ten minutes later he reclaimed his car from the park-and-lock garage on West Fifty-fourth Street, tossed his bag into the trunk and drove away.

CHAPTER THIRTY-SEVEN

Chris arrived at the Twin Cities airport at ten minutes of one. He had an hour to wait before his plane left for Newark. Vangie's body would be on that plane. Yesterday, coming out here, he'd thought of nothing except that coffin in the hold of the plane. He'd held on to some semblance of normality by reassuring himself that soon it would be over.

He had to see Dr Salem. Why had Dr Salem been so upset? Tonight when he got off the plane at Newark, the Medical Examiner's office would be waiting for Vangie's body.

And the Prosecutor's office would be waiting for him. The certainty haunted Chris. Of course. If they were suspicious in any way about Vangie's death, they were going to look to him for answers. They'd be waiting to bring him in for questioning. They might even arrest him. If they'd investigated at all, they knew by now that he'd returned to the New Jersey area Monday night. He had to see Dr Salem. If he was detained for questioning he might not be able to talk to him. He did not want to talk to the Prosecutor's office *about* Dr Salem.

Once again he thought of Molly and Bill Kennedy. So what if Molly was Katie DeMaio's sister? They were good people, honest people. He should have trusted them, talked to them. He had to talk to someone.

He had to talk to Joan.

His need for her was a hunger. The minute he started to tell the truth, Joan became involved.

Joan, who in this sleazy world still held such inviolate

principles, was about to be dragged through the mud.

He had the phone number of the stewardess with whom she was staying in Florida. Not knowing what he would say, he went to the phone, automatically gave his credit-card number, heard the ring.

Kay Corrigan answered. 'Kay, is Joan there? It's Chris.'

Kay knew about him and Joan. Kay's voice was concerned. 'Chris, Joan has been trying to phone you. Tina called from the New York apartment. The Valley County Prosecutor's office has been around asking all kinds of questions about you two. Joan is frantic!'

'When will she be back?'

'She's over at the new apartment now. It doesn't have a phone. From there she has to go to the company personnel office in Miami. She won't be here till about eight tonight.'

'Tell her to stay in and wait till I call her,' Chris said. 'Tell her I've got to talk to her. Tell her . . .' He broke the connection, leaned against the phone and pushed back a dry sob. Oh, God, it was too much, it was all too much. He couldn't think. He didn't know what to do. And in a few hours he'd be in custody, suspected of killing Vangie . . . maybe *charged* with killing Vangie.

No. There was another way. He'd get the flight into LaGuardia. He could still make it. Then he'd be in Manhattan and able to see Dr Salem at almost the same time he reached the hotel. The Prosecutor's office wouldn't realize he wasn't on the Newark flight until six o'clock. Maybe Dr Salem could help him somehow.

He barely made the LaGuardia flight. The coach section was full, but he bought a first-class ticket and was able to get on the plane. He didn't worry about his luggage, which was checked through to Newark.

On the plane he accepted a drink from the stewardess, waved away the food and listlessly thumbed through *Newsmaker* magazine. The page opened to Science and Medicine. His eye caught the headline: 'Westlake Maternity Concept Offers New Hope to Childless Couples.' *Westlake*. He read the first paragraph. 'For the past eight years, a small privately owned clinic in New Jersey has been operating a programme called the

Westake Maternity Concept which has made it possible for childless women to become pregnant. Named after a prominent New Jersey obstetrician, the programme is carried on by Dr Edgar Highley, obstetrician-gynaecologist, who was the son-in-law of Dr Franklin Westlake . . .'

Dr Edgar Highley. Vangie's doctor. Funny she never talked very much about him. It was always the psychiatrist. 'Dr Fukhito and I talked about Mama and Daddy today . . . he said it was obvious I was an only child . . . Dr Fukhito asked me to draw a picture of Mama and Daddy as I visualized them; it was fascinating. I mean it really was interesting to see how I visualized them. Dr Fukhito was asking about you, Chris.'

'And what did you say, Vangie?'

'That you worshipped me. You do, don't you, Chris? I mean underneath that put-downy way you have with me, aren't I your little girl?'

'I'd rather you thought of yourself as my wife, Vangie.'

'See, I can't talk with you about anything. You always get nasty . . .'

He wondered if the police had talked to either of Vangie's doctors.

This last month she had looked so ill. He had suggested that she have a consultation. The company doctor would have recommended someone. Or Bill Kennedy would surely have been able to suggest someone from Lenox Hill. But of course, Vangie had refused to have a consultation.

Then on her own she'd made an appointment with Dr Salem.

The plane landed at four thirty. Chris hurried through the terminal and hailed a cab. One of the few breaks of this rotten day was that he'd be ahead of the five-o'clock rush.

'The Essex House, please,' he told the driver.

It was just two minutes of five when he reached the hotel. He headed for a lobby telephone. 'Dr Emmet Salem, please.'

'Thank you, sir.'

There was a pause. 'That line is busy, sir.'

He hung up. At least Dr Salem was here. At least he'd have a chance to talk to him. He remembered he'd written Dr Salem's extension in his notebook, opened it and dialled '3219'. The phone rang . . . again . . . again. After six rings he broke the connection and dialled the operator. Explaining that the line had been busy only a few minutes before, he asked the operator to try it for him.

The operator hesitated, spoke to someone, then came back. 'Sir, I just gave this message to another party. Dr Salem checked in, contacted me to say that he expected an important call and be sure to reach him and then apparently stepped out. Why don't you try again in a few minutes?'

'I'll do that. Thank you.' Irresolutely Chris hung up the phone, walked over to a lobby chair facing the south elevator bank and sat down. The elevators opened and dislodged passengers, filled again, disappeared in a streak of ascending panel lights.

One elevator caught his attention. There was something vaguely familiar about someone on it. Dr Salem? Quickly he scanned the passengers. Three women, some teenagers, an elderly couple, a middle-aged man with a turned-up coat collar. No. Not Dr Salem.

At five thirty Chris tried again. And at quarter of six. At five past six he heard the whispers that ran through the lobby like a flash fire. 'Someone jumped from a window. The body spotted on the roof of the extension.' From somewhere along Central Park South the wail of an ambulance and the yip-yap of police cars were frantic explosions of increasing sound.

With the certainty of despair, Chris went to the bell captain's desk. 'Who was it?' he asked. His tone was crisp, authoritative; suggested he had a right to know.

'Dr Emmet Salem. He was a big shot in the AMA. Room three-two-one-nine.'

Walking with the measured gait of an automaton, Chris pushed through the revolving door at the Fifty-eighth Street entrance. A cab was cruising from west to east. He hailed it, got in and leaned back in the seat closing his eyes. 'LaGuardia, please,' he said; 'the National Airlines terminal.'

There was a seven-o'clock flight to Miami. He could just make it.

In three hours he'd be with Joan.

He had to get to Joan, try to make her understand before he was arrested.

CHAPTER THIRTY-EIGHT

Twelve-year-old Jennifer threw open the door as Katie came up the walk. 'Katie, hi.' Her voice was joyous, her hug sturdy. The two smiled at each other. With her intense blue eyes, dark hair and olive skin, Jennifer was a younger version of Katie.

'Hi, Jennie. How do you feel?'

'Okay. But how about you? I was so worried when Mom told me about your accident. You sure you're okay now?'

'Let's put it this way: by next week I'll be in great shape.' She changed the subject. 'Anybody here yet?'

'Everybody. Dr Richard is here too . . . You know what his first question was?'

'No.'

'"Is Katie here yet?" I swear he's got a case on you, Katie. Mom and Dad think so too. I heard them talking about it. How about you? Have you got a case on him?'

'Jennifer!' Half laughing, half irritated, Katie started up the short staircase towards the den in the back of the house, then looked back over her shoulder. 'Where are the other kids?'

'Mom shipped them off with a baby-sitter to eat at McDonald's and then to a movie. She said the Berkeley baby would never sleep if the twins were around.'

'Good thinking,' Katie murmured. She started down the foyer to the den. After leaving Gana Krupshak, she'd gone home, showered and changed. She'd left the house at quarter of seven thinking, Very soon Chris Lewis will be in Scott's office being questioned . . . What explanation could he give for not admitting that he was in the New Jersey area Monday night? Why hadn't he volunteered that immediately?

She wondered if Richard had spoken to the Minnesota doctor yet. He might have cleared up a lot of questions. She'd try to get Richard aside and ask him.

Driving over, she had resolved to put the case out of her mind for the rest of the evening. Maybe *not* thinking about it for a while would help her to follow up the elusive threads that kept escaping her –

She reached the den. Liz and Jim Berkeley were seated on the couch, their backs to her. Molly was passing hors d'oeuvre. Bill and Richard were standing by the window talking. Katie studied Richard. He was wearing a navy blue pin-striped suit that she'd never seen before. His dark-brown hair had touches of grey she'd never noticed. His fingers on the stem of the glass he was holding were long and finely shaped. Funny how this past year she'd seen him as a composite, never noticing details. It seemed to her that she was like a camera that had been locked into one position and was just beginning to focus again. Richard looked serious. His forehead was creased. She wondered if he was telling Bill about the Lewis foetus. No, he wouldn't discuss that even with Bill.

At that moment Richard turned his head and saw her. 'Katie.' His smile matched the pleased tone in his voice. He came hurrying over to her. 'I've been listening for the doorbell.'

So often in these three years she'd entered a room where she was the outsider, the loner, amidst couples. Now here tonight, Richard had been waiting for her, listening for her.

Before she had time to consider her feelings, Molly and Bill were saying hello, Jim Berkeley had stood up and the usual confusion of greetings was taking place.

On the way to the dining room she did manage to ask Richard if he'd reached Dr Salem. 'No. Apparently I just missed him at five,' Richard explained. 'Then I tried again from my place at six, but there was no answer. I left this number with the hotel operator and with my answering service. I'm very anxious to hear what that man has to say.'

By tacit agreement, none of them brought up the Lewis suicide until dinner was almost over. And then it came about because Liz Berkeley said, 'What luck. I have to admit I've been holding my breath that Maryanne wouldn't wake up and be fussy. Poor kid, her gums are so swollen she's in misery.'

Jim Berkeley laughed. He was darkly handsome with high cheekbones, charcoal-brown eyes and thick black eyebrows. 'When Maryanne was born, Liz used to wake her up every fifteen minutes to make sure she was still breathing. But since she's teething, Liz has become like every other mother.' He imitated her voice, 'Quiet, dummy, don't wake up the baby.'

Liz, a Carol Burnett type, with sinewy slenderness, an open, pleasant face and flashing brown eyes, made a face at her husband. 'You have to admit I'm calming down to being normal. But she *is* a miracle to us. I'd just about given up hope and then we tried to adopt, but now there just aren't babies. Especially with the two of us in our late thirties, they told us to forget it. And then Dr Highley. He's a miracle maker, that man.'

Katie watched as Richard's eyes narrowed. 'You genuinely think that?' Richard queried.

'Positively. I mean, Dr Highley isn't the warmest person on earth —' Liz began.

'What you mean is that he's an egocentric son of a bitch and as cold a fish as ever I've met,' her husband interrupted. 'But who gives a damn about that? What matters is that he knows his business, and I have to say he took excellent care of Liz. Put her to bed in the hospital almost two months before the delivery and personally checked on her three or four times a day.'

'He does that with all his difficult pregnancies,' Liz said. 'Not just me. Listen, I pray for that man every night. The difference that baby has made in our lives, I can't even begin to tell you! And don't let this one fool you' – she nodded in the direction of her husband: 'he's up ten times a night to make sure that Maryanne is covered and that there's no draught on her. Tell the truth.' She looked at him. 'When you went up to the john before, didn't you look in on her?'

He laughed. 'Sure I did.'

Molly said what Katie was thinking. 'That's the way Vangie Lewis would have felt about her child.'

Richard looked at Katie questioningly and she shook her head. She knew he was wondering if she'd told Molly and Bill that the Lewis baby was Oriental. Deliberately Richard pulled the conversation from Vangie. 'I understand that you used to live in San Francisco,' he said to Jim. 'I grew up there. In fact, my father still practises at San Francisco General . . .'

'One of my favourite towns,' Jim replied. 'We'd go back there in a minute, wouldn't we, Liz?'

As the others chatted, Katie listened with half a mind,

contributing enough to the conversation that her silence wasn't noticeable. She had so much thinking to do. These few days in the hospital would give her time for that too. She was feeling light-headed and fatigued, but did not want to make a move too soon for fear of breaking up the party.

Her chance came as they left the table to go into the living-room for a nightcap. 'I'm going to say good night,' Katie said. 'I have to admit I haven't slept well this week and I'm really bushed.'

Molly looked at her knowingly and did not protest. Richard said, 'I'll walk you to the car.'

'Fine.'

The night air was cold, and she shivered as they started down the walk. Richard noticed immediately and said, 'Katie, I'm worried about you. I know you're not feeling up to par. You don't seem to want to talk about it, but at least let's have dinner tomorrow night. With the way the Lewis case is breaking, the office will be a zoo tomorrow.'

'Richard, I'm sorry. I can't. I'm going away this weekend.' Katie realized her tone was apologetic.

'You're *what*? With all that's happening at the office? Does Scott know that?'

'I . . . I'm committed.' What a lame, stupid thing to say, Katie thought. This is ridiculous. I'm going to tell Richard that I'll be in the hospital. The driveway lights were on his face, and his expression of mingled disappointment and disapproval was unmistakable.

'Richard, it's not something I've talked up, but . . .'

The front door was thrown open. 'Richard, Richard!' Jennifer's shout was rushed and excited. 'Clovis Simmons is on the phone.'

'Clovis Simmons!' Katie said. 'Isn't she the actress on that soap opera?'

'Yes. Oh, hell, I was supposd to call her and forgot. Hold on, Katie. I'll be right back.'

'No. I'll see you in the morning. You go ahead.' Katie got into the car and pulled the door closed. She fished for the ignition key in her handbag, found it and inserted it into the lock. Richard looked irresolute for an instant, then hurried into the house, listening as Katie's car drove away. Hell, he thought, of all the times. His 'Hello, Clovis,' was brusque.

'Well, Doctor, it's a shame I have to track you down, but we did discuss dinner, didn't we?'

'Clovis, I'm *sorry*.' No, Clovis, he thought, *you* discussed dinner. *I* didn't.

'Well, obviously it's too late now.' Her tone was cool. 'Actually, I just got in from the taping and wanted to apologize in case you'd kept the evening. I should have known better.'

Richard glanced at Jennifer, who was standing at his elbow.

'Clovis, look, let me call you tomorrow. I can't talk very well now.'

There was a sharp click in his ear. Richard hung up the phone slowly. Clovis was angry, but more than that, she was hurt. How much we take people for granted, he thought. Just because I wasn't serious about her, I didn't bother to think about her feelings. Tomorrow he could only call and apologize and be honest enough to tell her that there was someone else.

Katie. Where was she going this weekend? Was there someone else for her? She'd looked so troubled, so worried. Was it that he'd been misreading her all along? He'd put her reticence, her lack of interest in him to the probability that she was living in the past. Maybe there was someone else in her life. Was he being as much a fool about her feelings as in a different way he'd been with Clovis?

The possibility sheared away the pleasure of the evening. He'd make his excuses and go home. It still wouldn't be too late to try Dr Salem again.

He went into the living-room. Molly, Bill and the Berkeleys were there. And swathed in blankets, sitting straight up on Liz's lap, was a baby girl.

'Maryanne decided to join the party,' Liz said. 'What do you think of her?' Her smile was proud as she turned the baby to face him.

Richard looked into solemn green eyes set in a heart-shaped face. Jim Berkeley was sitting next to his wife, and Maryanne reached over and grabbed his thumb.

Richard stared at the family. They might have posed for a magazine cover: the smiling parents, the beautiful offspring.

The parents handsome, olive-skinned, brown-eyed, square-featured; the baby fair-complexioned, red-blonde, with brilliant green eyes.

Who the hell do they think they're kidding? Richard thought. That child has to be adopted.

CHAPTER THIRTY-NINE

Phil Cunningham and Charley Nugent watched in disgust as the final stragglers filed through the waiting-room at Newark Airport's Gate 11. Charley's perpetually mournful expression deepened.

'That's it.' He shrugged. 'Lewis must have figured we'd be waiting for him. Let's go.'

He headed for the nearest pay phone and dialled Scott. 'You can go home, boss,' he said. 'The Captain didn't feel like flying tonight.'

'He wasn't on board? How about the coffin?'

'That came in. Richard's guys are picking it up. Want us to hang around? There are a couple of indirect flights he might be on.'

'Forget it. If he doesn't contact us tomorrow, I'm issuing a pickup order for him as a material witness. And first thing in the morning, I want you two to go through Edna Burns's apartment with a fine-tooth comb.'

Charley hung up the phone. He turned to Phil. 'If I know the boss, I'd say that by tomorrow night at this time there'll be a warrant out for Lewis's arrest.'

Phil nodded. 'And after we get Lewis, I hope we can hang something on that shrink if he was the one who made that poor gal pregnant.'

The two men wearily started down the stairs to the exit. They passed the baggage area, ignoring the people clustered around the carousels waiting for their luggage. A few minutes later the area was deserted. Only one unclaimed bag circled forlornly on the ramp: a large black carryall, properly tagged, in accordance with airline regulations, CAPT. CHRISTOPHER LEWIS, NO. 4, WINDING BROOK LANE, CHAPIN RIVER, N.J. Inside the bag, placed there at the last minute, was the picture Vangie's parents had pressed on Chris.

It was a nightclub photo of a youthful couple. The inscription read, *Remembrance of my first date with Vangie, the girl who will change my life. Love, Chris.*

CHAPTER FORTY

Richard phoned the Essex House Hotel as soon as he reached his apartment after leaving the Kennedys'. But once again there was no answer on Dr Salem's number. When the operator came back on the line, he said, 'Operator, did Dr Salem receive my message to phone me? I'm Dr Carroll.'

The woman's voice was oddly hesitant. 'I'll check, sir.'

While he was waiting, Richard reached over and flipped on the television set. *Eyewitness News* had just begun. The camera was focusing on Central Park South. Richard watched as the marquee of the Essex House Hotel was featured on the screen. Even as the telephone operator said, 'I'm connecting you with our supervisor,' Richard heard reporter Gloria Rojas say, 'This evening in the prestigious Essex House Hotel, headquarters for the American Medical Association convention, a prominent obstetrician-gynaecologist, Dr Emmet Salem of Minneapolis, Minnesota, fell or jumped to his death.'

CHAPTER FORTY-ONE

Joan Moore sat distractedly by the telephone. 'Kay, what time did he say he'd phone?' she asked. Her voice trembled, and she bit her lip.

The other young woman looked at her with concern. 'I told

you, Joan. He called about eleven thirty this morning. He said he'd be in touch with you tonight and that you should wait in for his call. He sounded upset.'

The doorbell rang insistently, making them both jump from their chairs. Kay said, 'I don't expect anybody.' Some instinct made Joan run to the door and yank it open.

'Chris – oh, my God, Chris!' She threw her arms around him. He was ghastly white, his eyes were bloodshot, he swayed as she held him. 'Chris, what is it?'

'Joan, Joan.' His voice was nearly a sob. Hungrily he pulled her to him. 'I don't know what's happening. There's something wrong about Vangie's death, and now the only man who might have told us about it is dead too.'

CHAPTER FORTY-TWO

He had planned to go directly home from the Essex House, but after he drove out of the parking lot and started up the West Side Highway in the heavy traffic, he changed his mind. He was so terribly hungry. His stomach had been empty all day. He never ate before operating, and this morning the call from Salem had come just before he would have left for lunch.

He didn't want to take the time to prepare food tonight. He'd go to the Carlyle. Then if the question ever arose as to his whereabouts tonight, he could truthfully admit he had been in New York. The maître d' would emphatically reassure the police that Dr Edgar Highley was a valued and frequent patron.

He would have smoked salmon, vichyssoise, a rack of lamb . . . His mouth salivated in anticipation. The sudden, terrible depletion of energy now that it was over needed to be corrected. There was still tomorrow. Inevitably there'd be a thorough investigation when Kathleen DeMaio died. But her former gynaecologist had retired and moved away. No one would loom from the past with old medical records to challenge him.

And then he'd be safe. Right now, all over the AMA convention, doctors were probably discussing the *Newsmaker* article and the Westlake Maternity Concept. Their remarks would be tinged with jealousy, of course. But even so, there would be offers for him to speak at future AMA seminars. He was now on the path to public fame. And Salem, who might have stopped him, was finished. He was anxious to go through Vangie's medical history in the file he'd taken from Salem. He'd incorporate it with his own records. That history would be invaluable in his future research.

The last new patient this morning. She would be next. He parked on the street in front of the Carlyle. It was nearly six thirty. Parking would be legal at seven. He'd just wait in the car until then. It would give him a chance to calm himself down.

His bag was locked in the trunk. Vangie's file, the paperweight and the shoe were in it. How should he dispose of the shoe and the paperweight? Where should he dispose of them? Any one of the overflowing trash baskets in this city would do. No one would fish them out. They'd be collected in the morning together with the tons of garbage that accumulated every twenty-four hours in this city of eight million, lost in the smell of decaying food and discarded newspapers . . .

He'd do it on the way home, under cover of darkness, never noticed.

A sense of buoyancy at the anticipation of how well it was going made him suddenly straighten up in his seat. He leaned over and looked into the rearview mirror. His skin was glistening, as if with perspiration about to burst through the pores. His eyelids and the skin under his eyes were accumulating fatty tissue. His hairline still showed no sign of receding, but the dark sandy hair was shot with silver now . . . He was starting to age. The subtle change that began in the mid-forties was happening to him. He was forty-five now. Young enough, but also time to become aware of the swift passage of years. Did he want to remarry? Did he want to father children of his own? He'd wanted, expected them from Claire. When they hadn't come he'd checked his own sperm count, found it surprisingly low, secretly blamed himself all those years for Claire's inability to conceive. Until he learned that she'd made a fool of him.

He would not have minded having a child by Winifred. But she was virtually past childbearing years when they married.

After she became suspicious of him, he didn't bother to touch her. When you are planning to eliminate someone, she is already dead to you, and sex is for the living.

But now. A younger woman, a woman unlike Claire and Winifred. Claire, haughtily demeaning him with her sneering comments about his father's apothecary; Winifred the do-gooder, with her causes and charities. Now he needed a wife who would not only be socially at ease, but also like to entertain, to travel, to mingle.

He hated those things. He knew his contempt showed. He needed someone who would take care of all that for him, soften his image.

One day he would be able to carry out his work publicly. One day he would have the fame he deserved. One day the fools who said his work was impossible would be forced to acknowledge his genius.

It was seven o'clock. He got out of the car and carefully locked it. He walked to the entrance of the Carlyle, his dark blue suit covered by a blue cashmere coat, his shoes shined to a soft lustre, his silver-tipped hair unruffled by the biting night draughts.

The doorman held the door open for him. 'Good evening, Dr Highley. Pretty bad weather, isn't it, sir?'

He nodded without answering and went into the dining room. The corner table he preferred was reserved, but the maître d' quickly switched the expected diners to another table and led him to it.

Wine warmed and soothed him. The dinner gave him the strength he was anticipating. The demitasse and brandy restored him to total balance. His mind was clear and brittle. He reviewed each step of the procedure that would lead Katie DeMaio to death by haemorrhage.

There would be no mistakes.

He was just signing his check when the maître d' came to his table, his footsteps uncharacteristically hurried, his manner agitated. 'Dr Highley, I'm afraid there's a problem.'

His fingers gripped the pen. He looked up.

'It's just, sir, that a young man was observed prying at the trunk of your car. The doorman saw him just as he got it open.

167

Before he could be stopped, he had stolen a bag from the trunk. The police are outside. They believe it was a drug addict who chose your car because of the MD licence plates.'

His lips were rubbery. It was hard to form words. Like an X-ray machine he mentally examined the contents of the bag: the bloodstained paperweight; the medical file with both Vangie and Salem's names on it; Vangie's moccasin.

When he spoke, his voice was surprisingly steady. 'Do the police believe that my bag will be recovered?'

'I asked that question, sir. I'm afraid they just don't know. It might be discarded a few blocks from here after he's taken what he wants from it, or it might never show up again. Only time will tell.'

CHAPTER FORTY-THREE

Before she went to bed, Katie packed an overnight bag for her stay in the hospital. The hospital was halfway between the house and the office, and it would have been an unnecessary waste of time to return home for the bag tomorrow.

She realized that she was packing with a sense of urgency. She'd be so glad to get this over with. The heavy sense of being physically out of tune was wearing her down mentally and emotionally. Tonight she'd felt almost buoyant setting out for Molly's. Now she felt depleted, exhausted, depressed. It was all physical, wasn't it?

Or was the nagging thought that maybe Richard was involved with someone contributing to the feeling of depression?

Maybe when this wasn't hanging over her, she'd be able to think more clearly. It felt as though her mind were being plagued by half-completed thoughts like swarms of mosquitoes, landing, biting, but gone before she could reach them. Why did she have the sensation of missing threads, of not asking the right questions, of misreading signals?

By Monday she'd be feeling better, thinking straight.

Wearily, she showered, brushed her teeth and hair and got

into bed. A minute later she pulled herself up on one elbow, reached for her handbag and fished out the small bottle Dr Highley had given her.

Almost forgot to take this, she thought as she swallowed the pill with a gulp from the water glass on her night table. Turning off the light, she closed her eyes.

CHAPTER FORTY-FOUR

Gertrude Fitzgerald wearily let the water run cold in the bathroom tap and opened the prescription bottle. The migraine was beginning to let up. If it didn't start in on the other side of her head, she'd be all right by the morning. This last pill should do it.

Something was bothering her . . . something over and beyond Edna's death. It had to do with Mrs DeMaio's call. It was so silly, asking if Edna had ever called Dr Fukhito or Dr Highley Prince Charming. Perfect nonsense.

But *Prince Charming*.

Edna *had* talked about him. Not in relation to the doctors, but somehow in the last couple of weeks. If she could only remember. If Mrs DeMaio had asked if Edna had ever mentioned him, it might have helped her remember right away. Now it was eluding her, the exact circumstance.

Or was she imagining it? Power of suggestion.

When this headache was finished, she'd be able to think. Really think. And maybe remember.

She swallowed the pill and got into bed. She closed her eyes. Edna's voice sounded in her ears. 'And I said that Prince Charming won't . . .'

She couldn't remember the rest.

CHAPTER FORTY-FIVE

At four a.m. Richard gave up trying to sleep, got out of bed and made coffee. He had phoned Scott at home about Emmet Salem's death, and Scott had immediately alerted the New York police that his office wanted to co-operate in the investigation. More than that it had been impossible to accomplish. Mrs Salem was not at home in Minneapolis. The doctor's answering service could only supply the emergency number of the doctor covering the practice and did not know how to reach his nurse.

Richard began writing notes. 1. *Why did Dr Salem phone our office?* 2. *Why did Vangie make an appointment with him?* 3. *The Berkeley baby.*

The Berkeley baby was the key. Was the Westlake Maternity Concept as successful as had been touted? Or was it a cover-up for private adoptions for women who either couldn't conceive or could not carry babies to term? Was the fact that they were being put to bed in the hospital two months before the supposed delivery nothing but a cover-up for what would become an obvious non-pregnant condition?

Babies were hard to adopt. Liz Berkeley had openly admitted that she and her husband had tried that route. Suppose Edgar Highley had said to them, 'You'll never have your own child. I can get you a child. It will cost you money and it will have to be absolutely confidential.'

They'd have gone along with it. He'd stake his life on that.

But Vangie Lewis had been pregnant. So she didn't fit into the adoptive pattern. Granted she was desperate to have a child . . . but how the hell did she expect to pass off an Oriental baby on her husband? Was there any chance that there was Oriental blood in either family? He'd never considered that.

The malpractice suits. He had to find out the reason those people sued Highley. And Emmet Salem had been Vangie's doctor. His office would have her medical records. That would be a place to start.

Vangie's body had come back on the plane that Chris Lewis did not take. It was in the lab now. First thing in the morning he'd review the autopsy findings. He'd go over the body again. There was something . . . It had seemed unimportant at the time. He'd brushed over it. He'd been too involved with the foetus and the cyanide burns.

Could Vangie have simply spilled the cyanide on herself? Maybe she'd been frantically nervous. But the glass would have had more prints. She'd have picked it up, refilled it; there'd be something – an envelope, a vial – that she'd have used to hold more cyanide.

It hadn't happened like that.

At five thirty Richard turned out the light. He set the alarm for seven. At last sleep came. And he dreamed of Katie. She was standing behind Edna Burns's apartment looking in the window, and Dr Edgar Highley was watching her.

CHAPTER FORTY-SIX

As befits a book-keeper, Edna had kept meticulous records. When the search team headed by Phil Cunningham and Charley Nugent descended on her apartment on Friday morning, they found a simple statement in the old-fashioned breakfront:

Since my one blood relative never bothered to inquire about or send a card to my dear parents in their illness, I have decided to leave my worldly goods to my friends, Mrs Gertrude Fitzgerald and Mrs Gana Krupshak. Mrs Fitzgerald is to receive my diamond ring and whatever household possessions she cares to have. Mrs Krupshak is to receive my diamond pin, my imitation fur coat and whatever household possessions Mrs Fitzgerald does not wish to have. I have discussed my funeral with the establishment that handled my parents' arrangements so beautifully. My $10,000 insurance policy less funeral expenses is assigned to the nursing home which took such fine care of my parents and to whom I am still financially indebted.

171

Methodically the team dusted for fingerprints, vacuumed for hair and fibres, searched for signs of forced entry. A smear of dirt on the bottom of the windowsill plant in the bedroom caused the crinkles around Phil's eyes and forehead to settle into a deep frown. He went around the back of the apartment building, thoughtfully scraped a sample of frozen dirt into an envelope and with his fingertips pushed up the bedroom window. For an average-sized person, it was low enough to step over.

'Possible,' he said to Charley. 'Someone could have come in here and sneaked up on her. But with the ground so frozen, you'd probably never be able to prove it.'

As the final step, they rang the doorbells of all the neighbours in the courtyard. The question was simple: had anyone noticed any strangers in the vicinity on Tuesday night?

They had not really expected success. Tuesday night had been dark and cold. The untrimmed shrubbery would have made it possible for anyone who did not want to be seen to stay in the shadows of the building.

But at the last apartment they had unexpected success. An eleven-year-old boy had just come home from school for lunch. He heard the question asked of his mother.

'Oh, I told a man which apartment Miss Burns lived in,' he reported. 'You remember, Ma, when you made me walk Porgy just before I went to bed, right after *Happy Days* . . .'

'That would be at nine thirty,' the boy's mother said. 'You didn't tell me you spoke to anyone,' she said accusingly to her son.

The boy shrugged. 'It was no big deal. A man parked at the curb just when I was coming back down the block. He asked me if I knew which apartment Miss Burns was in. I pointed it out. That's all.'

'What did he look like?' Charley asked.

The boy frowned. 'Oh, he was nice-looking. He had sort of dark hair and he was tall and *his car was neat*. It was a 'Vette.'

Charley and Phil looked at each other. 'Chris Lewis,' Charley said flatly.

CHAPTER FORTY-SEVEN

On Friday morning, Katie got into the office by seven o'clock and began a final review of the case she was trying. The defendants were eighteen- and seventeen-year-old brothers accused of vandalizing two schools by setting fires in twelve classrooms.

Maureen came in at eight thirty carrying a steaming coffee-pot. Katie looked up. 'Boy, I'm going all out to nail those two,' she said. 'They did it for kicks – *for kicks*. When you see the way people are struggling to pay taxes to keep up the schools their kids go to, it's sickening; it's more than a crime.'

Maureen reached for Katie's coffee cup and filled it. 'One of those schools is in my town, and the children next door go there. The ten-year-old had just finished a project for the science fair. It was fantastic – a solar heating unit. Poor little kid worked on it for months. It got burned in the fire. There was just nothing left of it.'

Katie jotted a note on the side of her opening statement. 'That gives me some extra ammunition. Thanks.'

'Katie . . .' Maureen's voice was hesitant.

Katie looked up into troubled green eyes. 'Yes?'

'Rita told me that she told you about . . . about the baby.'

'Yes, she did. I'm terribly sorry, Maureen.'

'The thing is I can't seem to get over it. And now this Vangie Lewis case . . . all the talk about that . . . only brings it back. I've been trying to forget . . .'

Katie nodded. 'Maureen, I'd have given anything to have had a baby when John died. That year I prayed I'd get pregnant so I'd have something of him. When I think of all the friends I have who elect never to have children or who have an abortion as casually as they have their hair set, I wonder about the way life works out. I just pray God that some day I will have children of my own. You will too, of course, and we'll both appreciate them because of not having the ones we wanted before.'

Maureen's eyes were filled with tears. 'I hope so. But the thing about the Vangie Lewis case is –'

The telephone rang. Katie reached for it. It was Scott. 'Glad you're in, Katie. Can you run over here for a minute?'

'Of course.' Katie got up. 'Scott wants me now. We'll talk later, Maureen.' Impulsively she hugged the girl.

Scott was standing by the window staring out. Katie was sure he was not seeing the barred windows of the county jail. He turned when she came in.

'You're in trial today – the Odendall brothers?'

'Yes. We have a good case.'

'How long will it take?'

'Most of the day, I'm sure. They're bringing character witnesses from their kindergarten teacher on up, but we'll get them.'

'You usually do, Katie. Have you heard about Dr Salem yet?'

'You mean the doctor from Minneapolis who called Richard? No, I haven't spoken to anyone this morning. I went straight to my office.'

'He fell – or was pushed – out of a window in the Essex House last night a few minutes after he checked into the hotel. We're working with the New York police on it. And incidentally, Vangie Lewis's body arrived from Minneapolis last night, but Lewis wasn't on the flight.'

Katie stared at Scott. 'What are you saying?'

'I'm saying that he probably took the flight that went into LaGuardia. It would have gotten him into New York about the time Salem checked in. I'm saying that if we find he was anywhere in the vicinity of that hotel, we may be able to wrap this case up. I don't like the Lewis suicide, I don't like the Edna Burns accidental death and I don't like the idea that Salem fell from a window.'

'I don't believe Chris Lewis is a murderer,' Katie said flatly. 'Where do you think he is now?'

Scott shrugged. 'Hiding out in New York, probably. My guess is that when we talk to his girl-friend she'll lead us to him, and she's due in from Florida tonight. Can you hang around this evening?'

Katie hesitated. 'This is the one weekend I have to be away. It's something I can't change. But I'll be honest, Scott. I feel so absolutely lousy that I'm not even thinking straight. I'll get through this trial . . . I'm well prepared; but then I will leave.'

Scott studied her. 'I've told you all week that you shouldn't have come in,' he said, 'and right now you look paler than you did Tuesday morning. All right, get the trial over with and clear out of here. There'll be plenty of work on this case next week. We'll go over everything Monday. You think you'll be in?'

'Positively.'

'You should have a complete check-up.'

'I'm going to see a doctor this weekend.'

'Good.'

Scott looked down at his desk, a signal that the meeting was over. Katie went back to her own office. It was nearly nine, and she was due in the courtroom. Mentally she reviewed the schedule of the pills Dr Highley had given her. She'd taken one last night, one at six o'clock this morning. She was supposed to take one every three hours today. She'd better swallow one now before going down to court. She washed it down with the last sip of coffee from the cup on her desk, then gathered her file. The sharp edge of the top page of the brief slit her finger. She gasped at the quick thrust of pain and popping a tissue from her top drawer wrapped it around the finger and hurried from the room.

Half an hour later as, with the rest of the people in the courtroom, she rose to acknowledge the entrance of the judge, the tissue was still wet with blood.

CHAPTER FORTY-EIGHT

Edna Burns was buried on Friday morning after an eleven-o'clock Mass of the Resurrection at St Francis Xavier Church. Gana Krupshak and Gertrude Fitzgerald followed the coffin to the nearby cemetery and, holding hands tightly, watched Edna placed in the grave with her parents. The priest, Father Durkin, conducted the final ceremony, sprinkled holy water over the coffin and escorted them back to Gertrude's car.

'Will you ladies join me for a cup of coffee?' he asked.

Gertrude dabbed at her eyes and shook her head. 'I really have to get to work,' she said. 'I'm taking Edna's place until they find a new receptionist, and the doctors both have office hours this afternoon.'

Mrs Krupshak also declined. 'But Father, if you're on your way back to the rectory, would you drop me off? Then I won't take Gertrude out of her way.'

'Of course.'

Gana turned to Gertrude. Impulsively she said, 'Why don't you come by for dinner with us tonight? I have a nice pot roast I'm cooking.'

The thought of going back to her own solitary apartment had been upsetting Gertrude, and she quickly accepted the offer. It would be good to talk about Edna tonight with the other person who'd been her friend. She wanted to express to Gana what a crying shame it was that neither of the doctors had come to the Mass, although at least Dr Fukhito had sent flowers. Maybe talking it out with Gana would help her to think clearly and she'd be able to get a handle on that thought which kept buzzing around inside her head – about something that Edna had said to her.

She said good-bye to Gana and Father Durkin, got into her car, turned on the ignition and released the brake. Dr Highley's face loomed in her mind: those big, fishlike, cold eyes. Oh, he'd been nice enough to her Tuesday night, giving her the pill to calm her down and what-have-you. But there was something funny about him that night. Like when he went to get her a drink of water, she'd started to follow him. She didn't want him waiting on her. He'd turned on the water tap, then gone into the bedroom. From the hall she'd seen him take out his handkerchief and start to open Edna's night-table drawer.

Then that nice Dr Carroll had started to walk down the hall and Dr Highley had closed the drawer, stuffed the handkerchief in his pocket and backed up so it looked like he was just standing in the bedroom doorway.

Gertrude had let Dr Carroll pass her, then slipped back into the living-room. She didn't want them to think she was trying to overhear what they were saying. But if Dr Highley wanted something from that drawer, why didn't he just say so and get it?

And why on earth would he open the drawer holding a handkerchief over his fingers? Certainly he didn't think Edna's apartment was too dirty for him to touch. Why, it was immaculate!

Dr Highley always was a strange man. Truth to tell, like Edna, she'd always been a little afraid of him. No way would she agree to take over Edna's job if it was offered to her. Her mind decided on that point, Gertrude steered the car off the cemetery road and on to Forest Avenue.

CHAPTER FORTY-NINE

The lifeless body of Vangie Lewis was placed on the slab in the autopsy room of the Valley County Medical Examiner. His face impassive, Richard watched as his assistant removed the silk caftan that was to have been Vangie's burial robe. What had seemed soft and natural in the gentle light of the funeral parlour now resembled a department-store mannequin, features with a total absence of life.

Vangie's blonde hair had been carefully coiffed to flow loose on her shoulders. Now the hair spray had begun to harden, separating the hairs into thin, straw-like groups. Fleetingly, Richard remembered that St Francis Borgia had given up a life at court and entered a monastery after viewing the decaying body of a once-beautiful queen.

Sharply, he pulled his mind to the medical problem at hand. He had missed something about Vangie's body on Tuesday afternoon. He was sure of that. It had something to do with her legs or feet. He would concentrate his attention there.

Fifteen minutes later he found what he was seeking: a two-inch scratch on Vangie's left foot. He had dismissed it because he'd been so involved with the cyanide burns and the foetus.

That scratch was fresh. There was no sign of healing skin. That was what had bothered him. Vangie's foot had been scratched shortly before her death, and Charley had found a piece of the cloth from the dress she was wearing when she died protruding from a sharp implement in the garage.

Richard turned to his assistant. 'The lab is supposed to be finished with the clothes Mrs Lewis was wearing when we brought her in. Will you please get them and dress her in them again. Call me when she's ready.'

Back in his office, he scribbled on a pad: *Shoes Vangie was wearing when found. Sensible walking shoes, cut fairly high on sides. Could not have been wearing them when foot was scratched.*

He began to examine the notes he'd made during the night. The Berkeley baby. He was going to talk to Jim Berkeley, get him to admit that the baby was adopted.

But what would that prove?

Nothing of itself, but it would begin the investigation. Once that admission was made, the whole Westlake Maternity Concept would be exposed as a gigantic fraud.

Would anyone kill to prevent that fraud from being exposed?

He needed to see Dr Salem's medical records on Vangie Lewis. By now, Scott must have reached Dr Salem's office. Quickly, he dialled Scott. 'Have you spoken to Salem's nurse?'

'Yes, and also to his wife. They're both terribly broken up. Both swear he had no history of high blood pressure or dizziness. No personal problems, no money problems, a full schedule of lecturing for the next six months. So I say, forget both the suicide and the accidental-fall angles.'

'How about Vangie Lewis? What did the nurse know?'

'Dr Salem asked her to get out Vangie's file yesterday morning in his office. Then, just before he left for his plane, he made a long-distance phone call.'

'That might have been the one to me.'

'Possibly. But the nurse said that he told her he had other long-distance calls to make, but he'd use his credit card from the airport after he checked in for his flight. Apparently he had a thing about getting to the airport with a lot of time to spare.'

'Is she sending Vangie's file to us? I want to see it.'

'No, she's not.' Scott's voice hardened. 'Dr Salem took it with him. She saw him put it in his attaché case. That case was found in his room. But the Lewis file wasn't in it. And get this: After Dr Salem left, Chris Lewis phoned his office. Said he had to talk to Salem. The nurse told him where Dr Salem would be staying in New York, even to giving him the room number. I'll tell you something, Richard: by end of the day I expect to be swearing out a warrant for Lewis's arrest.'

'You mean you think there was something in that file that Chris Lewis would kill to get? I find that hard to believe.'

'Someone wanted that file,' Scott said. 'That's pretty obvious, isn't it?'

Richard hung up the phone. *Someone* wanted the file. The medical file. Who would know what was in it that might be threatening?

A doctor.

Was Katie right in her suspicions about the psychiatrist? What about Edgar Highley? He'd come to Valley County with the imprimatur of the Westlake name, a name respected in New Jersey medical circles.

Impatiently, Richard searched on his desk for the slip of paper Marge had given him with the names of the two patients who had filed malpractice suits against Edgar Highley.

Anthony Caldwell, Old Country Lane, Peapack.
Anna Horan, 415 Walnut Street, Ridgefield Park.

Turning on the intercom, he asked Marge to try to phone both people.

Marge came in a few minutes later. 'Anthony Caldwell is no longer at that address. He moved to Michigan last year. I got a neighbour on the phone. She told me that his wife died of a tubal pregnancy and that he filed suit against the doctor, but it was dismissed. She was anxious to talk about it. Said Mrs Caldwell had been told by two other doctors that she'd never conceive, but that as soon as she started the Westlake Maternity Concept programme she became pregnant. But she was terribly sick all the time and finally died in her fourth month.'

'That gives me enough information for the moment,' Richard said. 'We're going to subpoena all the hospital records. What about Mrs Horan?'

'I caught her husband home. He's a law student at Rutgers. Says she's working as a computer programmer. Gave me her phone number at the job. Shall I get her for you now?'

'Yes, please.'

Marge picked up Richard's phone, dialled and asked for Mrs

Anna Horan. A moment later, she said, 'Mrs Horan, one moment please. Dr Carroll is calling.'

Richard took the phone. 'Mrs Horan.'

'Yes.' There was a lilting inflection in her voice, an accent he could not place.

'Mrs Horan, you filed a malpractice suit last year against Dr Edgar Highley. I wonder if I might ask you some questions about that case. Are you free to talk?'

The voice on the other phone became agitated. 'No . . . not here.'

'I understand. But it's urgent. Would it be possible for you to stop by my office after work today and talk with me?'

'Yes . . . all right.' Clearly, the woman wanted to get off the phone.

Richard gave the office address and offered directions, but was interrupted.

'I know how to get to you . . I'll be there by five thirty.'

The connection was broken. Richard looked at Marge and shrugged. 'She's not happy about it, but she's coming in.'

It was nearly noon. Richard decided to go to the courtroom where Katie was trying the Odendall case and see if she'd have lunch with him. He wanted to ventilate his thoughts about Edgar Highley. Katie had interviewed him. What had her reaction been? Would she agree that maybe there was something wrong about the Westlake Maternity Concept – either a baby ring or a doctor who took criminal chances with his patients' lives?

When he got to the courtroom, it was deserted except for Katie, who was still at the prosecutor's table.

Preoccupied with her notes, she barely looked up when he came over to her. At his suggestion of lunch she shook her head.

'Richard, I'm up to my eyes in this. Those skunks have retracted their confession. Now they're trying to say someone else set the fires, and they're such convincing liars I swear the jury is falling for it. I've got to work on the cross-examination.' Her eyes went back to her notes.

Richard studied her. Her usually olive skin was deadly pale. Her eyes when she'd looked up at him had been heavy and clouded. He noticed the tissue wrapped around her finger.

Gently, he reached over and unwound it.

Katie looked up. 'What . . . oh, that darn thing. It must be deep. It's been bleeding off and on all morning. I needed that.'

Richard studied the cut. Released from the tissue, it began to flow rapidly. Pressing the tissue over the cut, he reached for a rubber band and wound it above the cut. 'Leave this on for about twenty minutes. That should stop it. Have you been having any clotting problems, Katie?'

'Yes, some. But oh, Richard, I can't talk about it now. This case is running away from me and I feel so lousy.' Her voice broke.

The courtroom was empty except for the two of them. Richard reached down and put his arms around her. He hugged her head against his chest and put his lips on her hair. 'Katie, I'm going to clear out now. But wherever you go this weekend, do some thinking. Because I'm throwing my hat in the ring. I want you. I want to take care of you. If there's someone you're seeing now, tell him he's got stiff competition, because whoever he is, he's not watching out for you. If it's the past that's holding you, I'm going to try to break that hold.'

He straightened up. 'Now go ahead and win your case. You can do it. And for God's sake, take it easy this weekend. Monday, I'm going to need your input on an angle I see developing in the Lewis case.'

All morning she'd felt so cold – so desperately, icy cold. Even the long-sleeved wool dress hadn't helped. Now, so close to Richard, the warmth of his body communicated itself to her. As he turned to leave, she impulsively grasped his hand and held it against her face. 'Monday,' she said.

'Monday,' he agreed, and left the courtroom.

CHAPTER FIFTY

Before they left the garden apartment complex where Edna had lived, Charley and Phil rang the Krupshaks's doorbell. Gana had just returned from the funeral.

'We're finished with our investigation in the apartment,' Charley told her. 'You're free to enter it.' He showed her the note Edna had left. 'I have to check on whether this constitutes a will, but all that stuff isn't worth a thousand dollars, so my guess is that we'll return that jewellery to you, and you and Mrs Fitzgerald can divide it and the furniture. At least, you can look it over and decide it between yourselves; but don't remove anything yet.'

The two investigators returned to the office and went directly to the lab, where they turned in the contents of the vacuum bag, the plant that had been on the windowsill and the traces of earth they had removed from the ground. 'Run these through right away,' Phil directed. 'This stuff gets top priority.'

Scott was waiting for them in his office. At the news that Chris had been in the vicinity of Edna's apartment on Tuesday night, he grunted with satisfaction. 'Lewis seems to have been all over the map this week,' he said, 'and wherever he's been someone has died. I sent Rita over to New York this morning with a picture of Chris Lewis. Two bellmen positively identify him as being in the lobby of the Essex House around five o'clock. I'm putting out an APB for him and swearing out a warrant for his arrest.'

The phone rang. Impatiently, he reached for it and identified himself. Then his hand over the speaker, he said, 'Chris Lewis's girl-friend is calling from Florida . . . Hello, yes, this is the Prosecutor.' He paused. 'Yes, we are looking for Captain Lewis. Do you know where he is?'

Charley and Phil exchanged glances. Scott's forehead furrowed as he listened. 'Very well. He'll be on the plane with you arriving in Newark at seven p.m. I'm very glad to know that he's surrendering voluntarily. If he wishes to consult with a lawyer, he may want to have one here. Thank you.'

He hung up the phone. 'Lewis is coming in,' he said. 'We'll crack this case open tonight.'

CHAPTER FIFTY-ONE

Through the long, sleepless night, Edgar Highley rationalized the problem of the stolen bag. It might never show up. If it had been abandoned after the thief went through it, the odds were he'd never see it again. Few people would take the trouble to try to return it. More than likely they'd simply keep the bag and throw out the contents.

Suppose the bag were recovered intact by the New York police? His name and the address of the hospital were inside it. If the police phoned him, they'd probably ask for a list of the contents. He'd simply mention some standard drugs, a few instruments and several patients' files. A medical file with the name VANGIE LEWIS on the tab would mean nothing to them. They probably wouldn't bother to study it. They'd just assume it was his. If they asked about the shoe and the bloodstained paperweight, he would deny any knowledge of them; he'd point out that obviously, the thief must have put them there.

It would be all right. And tonight the last risk would be removed. At five a.m. he gave up trying to sleep; showered, standing under the hot needle spray nearly ten minutes until the bathroom was filled with steam; wrapped himself in a heavy ankle-length robe and went down to the kitchen. He was not going in to the office until noon, and he'd make his hospital rounds just before that. Until then, he'd go over his research notes. Yesterday's patient would be his new experiment. But he hadn't yet chosen the donor.

CHAPTER FIFTY-TWO

At four o'clock, Richard, Scott, Charley and Phil studied the body of Vangie Lewis, now dressed in the clothes in which she had died. The scrap of flowered material that had been found on the prong in the garage exactly fitted the tear near the hem of her dress. The panty hose on her left foot showed a two-inch slash directly over the fresh cut.

'No trace of blood on the hosiery,' Richard said. 'She was already dead when her foot caught on the prong.'

'How high was the shelf that prong was on?' Scott asked.

Phil shrugged. 'About two feet from the floor.'

'Which means that someone carried Vangie Lewis in through the garage, laid her on her bed and tried to give the appearance of a suicide,' Scott said.

'Without question,' Richard agreed. But he was frowning. 'How tall is Chris Lewis?' he asked.

Scott shrugged. 'He's a big one. Maybe six feet four. Why?'

'Let's try something. Wait a minute.' Richard left the room, returning with a ruler. Carefully, he marked the wall at heights of two, three and four feet from the floor. 'If we assume Chris Lewis was the one who carried Vangie in, I suggest that she would not have been scratched by that prong.' He turned to Phil. 'You're sure the shelf was two feet off the ground?'

Phil shrugged. 'Within an inch.' Charley nodded in agreement.

'All right. I'm six feet two.' Gently, Richard put one arm under the dead woman's neck, the other under her knees. Picking her up, he walked over to the wall. 'Look where her foot touches. She was small. It wouldn't have been grazed by any object lower than three feet on the shelf *if* she was carried by a tall man. On the other hand . . .' He walked over to Phil. 'How tall are you . . . About five feet ten?'

'Just about.'

'All right. Chris Lewis has over six inches on you. Take her and see where her foot falls when you hold her.'

Gingerly, Phil accepted the body and walked by the wall. Vangie's foot trailed against the first mark Richard had made. Quickly, Phil laid her back on the slab.

Scott shook his head. 'Inconclusive. Impossible to figure. Maybe he was bending over, trying to hold her away from him.' He turned to the attendant. 'We'll want those clothes as evidence. Take good care of them. Get some photos of the cut, the stocking and the dress.'

He walked with Richard back to his office. 'You're still thinking about the psychiatrist, aren't you?' he asked. 'He's about five ten.'

Richard hesitated and decided not to say anything until he had spoken with Jim Berkeley and the woman patient who had pressed the malpractice suit. He changed the subject. 'How's Katie doing?'

Scott shook his head. 'Hard to say. Those bums are blaming the vandalism on one of their friends who was killed on his motorcycle last November. Their new story is they took the rap for him because they felt sorry for his folks, but now their minister has persuaded them for the sake of their own family they have to tell the truth.'

Richard snorted. 'The jury isn't falling for that, is it?'

Scott said, 'It's out now. Listen, no matter how hard you try to pick your jury, there's always one bleeding-heart on it who will fall for a sob story. Katie's done a great job, but it could go either way. Okay. I'll see you later.'

At four thirty, Jim Berkeley returned Richard's call. 'I understand you've been trying to reach me.' His voice was guarded.

'Yes.' Richard matched the other man's impersonal tone. 'It's important that I speak with you. Can you stop in my office on your way home?'

'Yes, I can.' Now Jim's voice became resigned. 'And I think I know what you want to talk about.'

CHAPTER FIFTY-THREE

Edgar Highley turned from the girl on the examining table. 'You may get dressed now.'

She had claimed to be twenty, but he was sure she wasn't more than sixteen or seventeen. 'Am I . . .'

'Yes, my dear. You are very definitely pregnant. About five weeks, I should think. I want you to return tomorrow morning and we will terminate the pregnancy.'

'I was wondering: do you think I should maybe have the baby and have it adopted?'

'Have you told your parents about this?'

'No. They'd be so upset.'

'Then I suggest you postpone motherhood for several years at least. Ten o'clock tomorrow.'

He left the room, went into his office and looked up the phone number of the new patient he had chosen yesterday. 'Mrs Englehart, this is Dr Highley. I want to begin your treatment. Kindly come to the hospital tomorrow morning at eight thirty and prepare to spend the night.'

CHAPTER FIFTY-FOUR

While the jury was deliberating, Katie went into the courthouse cafeteria. She carefully chose a small table at the end of the room and sat with her back to the other tables. She did not want anyone to either join or notice her. The light-headed feeling was persistent now; she felt fatigued and weak, but not hungry. Just a cup of tea, she thought. Mama always thought that a cup of tea would cure all the ills of the world. She remembered coming back to the house from John's funeral, her mother's voice concerned, gentle: 'I'll make you a nice hot cup of tea, Katie.'

Richard. Mama would love Richard. She always liked big

men. 'Your dad was a skinny little one, but oh, Katie, didn't he seem like a big man?'

Yes, he did.

Mama was coming up for Easter. That was just six weeks from now. Mama would be so delighted if she and Richard got together.

I do want that, don't I? Katie thought as she sipped the tea. It's not just because I'm so aware of loneliness this week.

It was more that. Much more. But this weekend in the hospital, she'd be able to sort things through, to think quietly.

She sat for nearly an hour absently sipping the tea, reviewing every step of her summation. Had she convinced the jury that the Odendall boys were lying? The minister. She'd scored there. He'd agreed that neither boy was a churchgoer; that neither boy had ever consulted him for any reason before. Was it possible that he was being used by them to bolster their story? 'Yes,' he agreed. 'It is possible.' She had made that point. She was sure of it.

At five o'clock she returned to the courtroom. As she entered the jury sent word to the judge tht it had reached a verdict.

Five minutes later, the foreman announced the verdict: 'Robert Odendall, not guilty on all counts. Jonathan Odendall, not guilty on all counts.'

'I don't believe it.' Katie wasn't sure if she had spoken aloud. The judge's face hardened into angry lines. He dismissed the jury curtly and told the defendants to stand up

'You are very lucky,' he snapped, 'luckier than I hope you'll ever be again in either of your lives. Now clear out of my courtroom, and if you're smart you'll never appear before me again.'

Katie stood up. No matter if the judge clearly felt the verdict was erroneous, she had lost the case. She should have done more. She felt rather than saw the victorious smile the defence attorney shot at her. A thick, hard lump burned in her throat, making it impossible to swallow. She was within inches of tears. Those two criminals were about to be released on the streets after flouting justice. A dead boy had been labelled a criminal.

She stuffed her notes into her briefcase. Maybe if she hadn't felt so lousy all week she'd have conducted a better case. Maybe if she'd had this haemorrhaging problem taken care of a year ago instead of delaying and putting it off with this crazy, childish fear of hospitals, she wouldn't have had the accident Monday night.

'Will the State please approach the bench?'

She looked up. The judge was beckoning to her. She walked over to him. The spectators were filing out. She could hear delighted squeals as the Odendalls embraced their gum-chewing, bra-less girl-friends.

'Your Honour.' Katie managed to keep her voice steady.

The judge leaned over and whispered to her: 'Don't let it get you down, Katie. You proved that case. Those little bastards will be back here in two months on other charges. We both know it, and next time you'll nail them.'

Katie tried to smile. 'That's just what I'm afraid of, that they will be back. God knows how much damage they'll be doing before we can nail them. But thanks, Judge.'

She left the courtroom and went back to her office. Maureen looked up hopefully. Katie shook her head and watched the expression change to sympathy. She shrugged. 'What can you do, huh?'

Maureen followed her into her office. 'Mr Meyerson and Dr Carroll are in a meeting. They don't want to be disturbed. But of course, you can go in.'

'No. I'm sure it's the Lewis case, and I'd be of no use to them or anyone else right now. I'll catch up on Monday.'

'All right. Katie, I'm sorry about the Odendall verdict, but try not to take it so hard. You really look sick. Are you all right to drive? You're not dizzy or anything?'

'No, really, and I'm not going far. I'll be driving just fifteen minutes and then I won't budge till Sunday.'

As she walked to the car, Katie shuddered. The temperature had gotten up to about forty degrees in the afternoon, but was dropping rapidly again. The wet, damp air penetrated the loose sleeves of her red wool wraparound coat and pierced her nylon hose. She thought longingly of her own room, her own bed. How great it would be to be able to go there now, to just go to bed with a hot toddy and sleep the weekend away.

*

At the hospital, the admitting office had her completed forms waiting. The clerk was briskly bright.

'My goodness, Mrs DeMaio, you certainly rate. Dr Highley has given you the bedroom of Suite One on the third floor. That's like going on a vacation. You'll never dream you're in a hospital.'

'He said something about that,' Katie murmured. She was not about to confide her fear of hospitals to this woman.

'You may be a bit lonesome up there. There are just three suites on that floor, and the other two are empty. And Dr Highley is having the living-room of your suite redecorated. Why, I don't know. It was done less than a year ago. But anyhow, you won't need it. You'll only be here till Sunday. If you want anything, all you have to do is press the buzzer. The second-floor nursing station takes care of both the second- and third-floor patients. They're all Dr Highley's patients anyhow. Now, here's your wheelchair. If you'll just get into it, we'll whisk you upstairs.'

Katie stared in consternation. 'You don't mean I have to use a wheelchair now?'

'Hospital regulations,' the admitting clerk said firmly.

John in a wheelchair going up for chemotherapy. John's body shrinking as she watched him die. John's voice weakening, his wry, tired humour as the wheelchair was brought to his bed: 'Swing low, sweet chariot, coming for to carry me home.' The antiseptic hospital smell.

Katie sat down in the chair and closed her eyes. There was no turning back. The attendant, a middle-aged, solidly plump volunteer, pushed the chair down the corridor to the elevator.

'You're lucky to have Dr Highley,' she informed Katie. 'His patients get the best care in the hospital. You push that buzzer for someone and you'll have a nurse at your beck and call in thirty seconds. Dr Highley is strict. The whole staff trembles when he's around, but he's good.'

They were at the elevator. The attendant pushed the button. 'This place is so different from most hospitals. Most places don't want to see you until you're ready to deliver, and then they shove you out when the baby is a couple of days old. Not Dr Highley. I've seen him put pregnant women to bed here for two months just as a precaution. That's why he has suites, so people can have a homelike atmosphere. Mrs Aldrich is in the one on the second floor. She delivered by caesarean yesterday-and hasn't stopped crying. She's that happy. Her husband's just as bad. He slept on the sofa in the living-room of her suite last night. Dr Highley encourages that. Well, here's the elevator.'

Several other people got on the elevator with them. They glanced at Katie curiously. Observing the magazines and flowers they were carrying, she decided they were obviously visitors. She felt oddly removed from them. The minute you become a patient you lose your identity, she thought. You become a case.

They got off at the third floor. The corridor was carpeted in a soft green shade. Excellent reproductions of Monet and Matisse paintings enhanced by recessed framing were scattered along the walls.

In spite of herself, Katie was reassured. The volunteer wheeled her down the corridor and turned right. 'You're in the end suite,' she exclaimed. 'It's kind of far off. I don't think there's even any other patients on this floor today.'

'That's all right with me,' Katie murmured. She thought of John's room. The two of them wanting to absorb each other, to stockpile against the separation. Ambulatory patients coming to the door, looking in. 'How's it going today, Judge? He looks better, doesn't he, Mrs DeMaio?'

And she, lying, 'Indeed he does.' Go away, go away. We have so little time.

'I don't mind being alone on the floor,' she repeated.

She was wheeled into a bedroom. The walls were ivory; the carpet, the same soft green as the corridor. The furniture was antique white. Printed draperies in shades of ivory and green matched the bedspread. 'Oh, this is nice,' Katie exclaimed.

The attendant looked pleased. 'I thought you'd like it. The nurse will be in in a few minutes. Why don't you just put your things away and make yourself comfortable?'

She was gone. Somewhat uncertainly, Katie undressed, put on a nightgown and warm robe. She put her toilet articles on the vanity in the bathroom and hung her clothes in the closet. What in God's name would she do for the long, dreary evening that stretched before her? Last night at this time she'd been dressing to go to Molly's dinner party. And when she'd arrived, Richard had been waiting for her.

She realized she was swaying. Instinctively, she reached for the dresser and held on to it. The light-headed feeling passed. It was probably just the rushing, and the aftermath of the trial and – Let's face it, she thought: apprehension.

She was in a hospital. No matter how she tried to push away the thought, she was in a hospital. Incredible, childish, that she could not overcome her fear. Daddy. John. The two people she'd loved best in the world had gone into the hospital and died. No matter how she tried to intellectualize, rationalize, she could not lose that terrible feeling of panic. Well, maybe this stay would get her over it. Monday night hadn't been that bad.

There were four doors in the room. The closet door, the bathroom door, the one leading to the corridor. The other one must go into the living-room. She opened it and glanced in. As the admitting clerk had told her, it was pulled apart. The furniture was in the middle of the room and covered with painter's drop cloths. She flicked on the light. Dr Highley surely was a perfectionist. There was nothing the matter with the walls that she could see. No wonder hospital costs were so outrageous.

Shrugging, she turned off the light, closed the door and walked over to the window. The hospital was U-shaped, the two wings parallel to each other at right angles behind the main section.

She'd been on the other side Monday night, exactly opposite where she was now. Visitors' cars were beginning to fill the lot. Where was the parking stall she'd dreamed about? Oh, of course – that one, over to the side, directly under the last light post. There was a car parked there now, a black car. In her dream it had been a black car. Those wired spokes; the way they glinted in the light.

'How are you feeling, Mrs DeMaio?'

She spun around. Dr Highley was standing in the room. A young nurse was hovering at his elbow.

'Oh, you startled me. I'm fine, Doctor.'

'I knocked, but you didn't hear me.' His voice was gently

reproving. He came over to the window and drew the drapery. 'No matter what we do, these windows are draughty,' he commented. 'We don't want you catching cold. Suppose you sit on the bed and let me check your pressure. We'll want to take some blood samples too.'

The nurse followed him. Katie noticed that the girl's hands were trembling. She was obviously in awe of Dr Highley.

The doctor wrapped the pressure cuff around her arm. A wave of dizziness made Katie feel as though the walls of the room were receding. She clutched at the mattress.

'Is there anything wrong, Mrs DeMaio?' The doctor's voice was gentle.

'No, not really. I'm just a touch faint.'

He began to pump the bulb. 'Nurse Renge, kindly get a cold cloth for Mrs DeMaio's forehead,' he instructed.

The nurse obediently rushed into the bathroom. The doctor was studying the pressure gauge. 'You're a bit low. Any problems?'

'Yes.' Her voice sounded as though it belonged to someone else, or maybe as though she were in an echo chamber. 'My period started again. It's been dreadfully heavy since Wednesday.'

'I'm not surprised. Frankly, if you hadn't scheduled this operation, I'm quite sure you'd have been forced to have it on an emergency basis.'

The nurse came out of the bathroom with a neatly folded cloth. She was biting her lower lip to keep it from quivering. Katie felt a rush of sympathy for her. She neither wanted nor needed a cold compress on her forehead, but leaned back against the pillow. The nurse put it on her head. The cloth was soaking, and she felt freezing water run down her hairline. She resisted the impulse to brush it away. The doctor would notice, and she didn't want the nurse to be reprimanded.

A flash of humour raised her spirits. She could just see herself telling Richard, 'And this poor, scared kid practically drowned me. I'll probably have bursitis of the eyebrows from now on.'

Richard. She should have told him she was coming here. She wanted him with her now.

Dr Highley was holding a needle. She closed her eyes as he

drew blood from a vein in her right arm. She watched him put the blood-filled vacu-tubes on the tray the nurse held out to him.

'I want these run through immediately,' he said brusquely.

'Yes, Doctor.' The nurse scurried out, obviously delighted to get away.

Dr Highley sighed. 'I'm afraid that timid young woman is on desk duty tonight. But you won't require anything special, I'm sure. Did you complete taking the pills I gave you?'

Katie realized that she had not taken the three o'clock pill and it was now after six.

'I'm afraid I skipped at three o'clock,' she apologized. 'I was in court and everything but the trial went out of my mind, and I guess I'm overdue for the last one.'

'Do you have the pills with you?'

'Yes, in my handbag.' She glanced at the dresser.

'Don't get up. I'll hand it to you.'

When she took the bag from him, she unzipped it, fished inside and brought out the small bottle. There were just two pills in it. The night table held a tray with a carafe of ice water and a glass. Dr Highley poured water into the glass and gave it to her. 'Finish these,' he said.

'Both of them?'

'Yes. Yes. They're very mild, and I did want you to have them by six.' He handed her the glass and dropped the empty jar into his pocket.

Obediently, she swallowed the pills, feeling his eyes on her. His steel-rimmed glasses glinted under the overhead light. The glint. The spokes of the car glinting.

There was a blur of red on the glass as she laid it down. He noticed it, reached for her hand and examined her finger. The tissue had become damp again.

'What's this?' he asked.

'Oh, nothing. Just a paper cut, but it must be deep. It keeps bleeding.'

'I see.' He stood up. 'I've ordered a sleeping pill for you. Please take it as soon as the nurse brings it.'

'I really prefer not to take sleeping pills, Doctor. They seem to cause an overreaction in me.' She wanted to sound vehement.

Instead, her voice had a lazy, weak quality.

'I'm afraid I insist on the pill, Mrs DeMaio, particularly for someone like yourself who is likely to spend the night in sleepless anxiety without it. I want you well rested in the morning. Oh, here's your dinner now.'

Katie watched as a thin, sixtyish woman carrying a tray came into the room and glanced nervously at the doctor. They're all petrified of him, she thought. Unlike the usual plastic or metal hospital tray, this one was made of white wicker and had a side basket that held the evening newspaper. The china was delicate, the silverware gracefully carved. A single red rose stood in a slender vase. Double loin lamb chops were kept hot by a silver dome over the dinner plate. An arugula salad, julienne string beans, small hot biscuits, tea and sherbet completed the meal. The attendant turned to go.

'Wait,' Dr Highley commanded. He said to Katie, 'As you will see, all my patients are served fare that compares favourably with the food in a first-class restaunt. I think one of the abiding wastes in hospitals is the tons of institutional food that are thrown out daily while patients' families bring in CARE packages from home.' He frowned. 'However, I think I would prefer if you did not eat dinner tonight. I've come to believe that the longer a patient fasts before surgery, the less likelihood she will experience discomfort after it.'

'I'm not at all hungry,' Katie said.

'Fine.' He nodded to the attendant. She picked up up the tray and hurried out.

'I'll leave you now,' Dr Highley told Katie. 'You *will* take the sleeping pill.'

Her nod was noncommittal.

At the door he paused. 'Oh, I regret, your phone apparently isn't working. The repairmen will take care of it in the morning. Is there anyone you expect to call you here tonight? Or perhaps you'll be having a visitor?'

'No. No calls or visitors. My sister is the only one who knows I'm here, and she's at the opera tonight.'

He smiled. 'I see. Well, good night, Mrs DeMaio, and please relax. You can trust me to take care of you.'

'I'm sure I can.'

194

He was gone. She leaned back on the pillow, closing her eyes. She was floating somewhere; her body was drifting, drifting like . . .

'Mrs DeMaio.' A young voice was apologetic. Katie opened her eyes. 'What . . . oh, I must have dozed.' It was Nurse Renge. She was carrying a tray with a pill in a small paper cup. 'You're to take this now. It's the sleeping pill Dr Highley ordered. He said I was to stay and be sure you took it.' Even with Dr Highley gone, the girl seemed nervous. 'It always makes patients mad when we have to wake them up to give them a sleeping pill, but that's the way it works in the hospital.'

'Oh.' Katie reached for the pill, put it in her mouth, gulped down water from her carafe.

'Would you like to get settled in bed now? I'll turn down your covers for you.'

Katie realized she'd been sleeping on top of the spread. She nodded, pulled herself up and went into the bathroom. There she removed the sleeping pill from under her tongue. Some of it had already dissolved, but she managed to spit out most of it. No way, she thought. I'd rather be awake than have nightmares. She splashed water on her face, brushed her teeth and returned to the bedroom. She felt so weak, so vague.

The nurse helped her into bed. 'You really are tired, aren't you? Well, I'll tuck you in, and I'm sure you'll have a good night's sleep. Just push the buzzer if you need me for anything.'

'Thank you.' Her head was so heavy. Her eyes felt glued together.

Nurse Renge went over and pulled down the shade. 'It's started to snow again, but it's going to change to rain. It's a wicked night, a good night to be in bed.'

'Open the drapes and raise the window just about an inch, won't you?' Katie murmured. 'I always like fresh air in my bedroom.'

'Certainly. Shall I turn off the light now, Mrs DeMaio?'

'Please.' She didn't want to do anything except sleep.

'Good night, Mrs DeMaio.'

'Good night. Oh, what time is it, please?'

'Just eight o'clock.'

'Thank you.'

The nurse left. Katie closed her eyes. Minutes passed. Her breathing became even. At eight thirty, she was not aware of the faint sound that was caused when the handle on the door from the living-room of the suite began to turn.

CHAPTER FIFTY-FIVE

Gertrude and the Krupshaks lingered over Gana's pot-roast dinner. Gratefully, Gertrude acceded to Gana's urgings to have seconds, to have a generous slice of home-made chocolate cake.

'I don't usually eat this much,' she apologized, 'but I haven't swallowed a morsel since we found poor Edna.'

Gana nodded soberly. Her husband picked up his coffee cup and dessert plate. 'The Knicks are playing,' he announced. 'I'm gonna watch.' His blunt tone was not ungracious. He settled himself in the living-room and switched on the dial.

Gana sighed. 'The Knicks . . . the Mets . . . the Giants . . . One season after the other. But on the other hand, he's *here*. I can look across the room and there he is. Or if I come home from bingo, I know I'm not going into an empty place, like poor Edna always had to.'

'I know.' Gertrude thought of her own solitary home, then reflected on her oldest granddaughter. 'Gran, why not come to dinner?' or 'Gran, are you going to be home Sunday? We thought we'd drop in to say hello.' She could have it a lot worse.

'Maybe we should go in and take a look at Edna's place,' Gana said. 'I don't want to rush you . . . I mean, have more coffee, or another piece of cake . . .'

'No. Oh, no. we should go in. You kind of hate to do it, but it's something you can't avoid.'

'I'll get the key.'

They hurried across the courtyard. While they were at the table, the wet, cold combination of snow and rain had once again begun to fall. Gana dug her chin into her coat collar. She thought of Edna's lovely imitation-leopard coat. Maybe she could take it home tonight. It was hers.

Inside the apartment, they became quiet. The fingerprinting powder the detectives had used was still visible on the tabletops and door handles. Inadvertently, they both stared at the spot where Edna's crumpled body had lain.

'There's still blood in the radiator,' Gana muttered. 'Gus'll probably repaint it.'

'Yes.' Gertrude shook herself. Get this over with. She knew her granddaughter's taste. Besides the velour couch, Nan would love those matching chairs, the tall-backed ones with mahogany arms and legs. One was a rocker, the other a straight chair. She remembered Edna's telling her that when she was a child, they'd been covered in blue velvet with a delicate leaf pattern. She'd had them redone inexpensively and always sighed, 'They never looked the same.'

If Nan had them re-covered in velvet **again**, they'd be beautiful. And that piecrust table. Altman's had copies of that in the reproduction gallery. Cost a fortune, too. Of course, this one was pretty nicked, but Nan's husband could refinish anything. Oh, Edna, Gertrude thought. You were smarter than most of us. You knew the value of things.

Gana was at the closet removing the leopard coat. 'Edna loaned me this last year,' she said. 'I was going to a social with Gus. I love it.'

It did not take them long to finish sharing the contents of the apartment. Gana had little interest in the furniture; what Gertrude did not want she was giving to the Salvation Army; but she was delighted when Gertrude suggested she take the silver plate and good china. They agreed that Edna's wardrobe would also go to the Salvation army. She had been shorter and heavier than either of them.

'I guess that's it,' Gana sighed. 'Except for the jewellery, and the police will give that back to us pretty soon. You get the ring, and she left the pin to me.'

The jewellery. Edna had kept it in the night-table drawer. Gertrude thought of Tuesday night. That was the drawer Dr Highley had started to open.

'That reminds me,' she said: 'We never did look there. Let's make sure we didn't forget anything.' She pulled it open. She knew that the police had removed the jewellery box. But the deep drawer was not empty. A scuffed moccasin lay at the bottom of it.

'Well, as I live and breathe,' Gana sighed. 'Now, can you tell me why Edna would save that thing?' She picked it up and held it to the light. It was out of shape; the heel was run down; white stains on the sides suggested it had been exposed to salted snow.

'That's it!' Gertrude cried. 'That's what had me mixed up.'

At Gana's mystified expression, she tried to explain. 'Mrs DeMaio asked me if Edna called one of the doctors Prince Charming. And that's what confused me. Of course she didn't. But Edna did tell me how Mrs Lewis wore terrible old moccasins for her appointments. Why, she pointed them out to me only a couple of weeks ago when Mrs Lewis was leaving. Edna said that she always kidded Mrs Lewis. The left shoe was too loose, and Mrs Lewis was always walking out of it. Edna used to tease Mrs Lewis that she must be expecting Prince Charming to pick up her glass slipper.'

'But Prince Charming wasn't Cinderella's boyfriend,' Gana protested. 'He was in the "Sleeping Beauty" fairy tale.'

'That's what I mean. I told Edna that she had it mixed up. She just laughed and said that Mrs Lewis told her the same thing, but that her mother told her the story that way and it was good enough for her.'

Gertrude reflected. 'Mrs DeMaio was so anxious when she asked about that Prince Charming talk. And Wednesday night – I wonder: could Mrs Lewis's shoe be what Dr Highley wanted from this drawer? Is that possible? You know, I've half a mind to go to Mrs DeMaio's office and talk to her, or at least leave a message for her. Somehow I just feel I shouldn't wait till Monday.'

Gana thought of Gus, who wouldn't have his cycs off the set until nearly midnight. Her acquisitive desire for excitement surged. She'd never been in the Prosecutor's office. 'Mrs DeMaio asked me whether Edna kept her mother's old shoe for sentimental reasons,' she said. 'I'll bet she was talking about this moccasin. Tell you what: I'll drive over there with you. Gus'll never know I'm gone.'

CHAPTER FIFTY-SIX

Jim Berkeley parked his car in the courthouse lot and went into the main lobby. The directory showed that the medical examiner's office was on the second floor in the old wing of the building. He had seen the expression on Richard Carroll's face last night when he'd looked at the baby. Anger and resentment had made him want to say, 'So the baby doesn't look like us. So what?' But it would have been stupid to do that. Worse, it would have been useless.

After several wrong turns in the labyrinth of the building, he found Richard's office. The secretarial desk was empty, but Richard's door was open, and he came out immediately when he heard the reception-area door snap shut. 'Jim, it's good of you to come.' Obviously, he was trying to be friendly, Jim thought. He was trying to make this seem a casual meeting. His own greeting was reserved and cautious. They went inside. Richard eyed him, Jim stared back impassively. There was none of the easy humour of last night's dinner.

Obviously, Richard got the message. His manner became businesslike. Jim stiffened.

'Jim, we're investigating Vangie Lewis's death. She was a patient at Westlake Maternity Clinic. That's where your wife had the baby.'

Jim nodded.

Richard was obviously picking his words carefully. 'We are disturbed at some problems that we see coming out of our investigation. Now, I want to ask you some questions – and I swear to you that your answers will remain in this room. But you can be of tremendous help to us, if – '

'*If* I tell you that Maryanne is adopted. Is that it?'

'Yes.'

The anger drained from Jim. He thought of Maryanne. Whatever the cost, she was worth having. 'No, she is not adopted. I was at her birth. I filmed it. She has a small birthmark on her left thumb. It shows in those pictures.'

'It is quite unlikely for two brown-eyed parents to have a green-eyed child,' Richard said flatly. Then he stopped. 'Are you the baby's father?' he asked quietly.

Jim stared down at his hands. 'If you mean would Liz have had an affair with another man? No. I'd stake my life and my soul on that.'

'How about artificial insemination?' Richard asked. 'Dr Highley is a fertility expert.'

'Liz and I discussed that possibility,' Jim said. 'We both rejected it years ago.'

'Might Liz have changed her mind and not told you? It's not that unusual any more. There are some fifteen thousand babies born every year in the United States by that means.'

Jim reached into his pocket and pulled out his wallet. Flipping it open, he showed Richard two pictures of Liz, himself and the baby. In the first one, Maryanne was an infant; her eyes were almost shut. The second was a recent Kodachróme. The contrast between the skin tone and eye colour of the parents and the baby was unmistakable.

Jim said, 'The year before Liz became pregnant, we learned that it was almost impossible for us to adopt. Liz and I discussed artificial insemination. We both decided against it, but I was more emphatic than she. Maryanne had light brown hair when she was born, and blue eyes. A lot of babies start out having blue eyes and then they turn the parents' colour. So it's just the last few months that it's become obvious that something is wrong. Not that I care. That baby is everything to us.' He looked at Richard. 'My wife won't even tell a social lie. She's the most honest person I've ever known in my life. Last month I decided to make it easy for her. I said that I'd been wrong about artificial insemination, that I could see why people went ahead with it.'

'What did she say?' Richard asked.

'She knew what I meant, of course. She said that if I thought she could make a decision like that and not tell me, I didn't understand our relationship.

'I apologized to her, swore I didn't mean that; went through hell trying to reassure her. Finally, she believed me.' He stared at the picture. 'But of course, I know she was lying,' he blurted out.

'Or else she wasn't aware of what Highley did to her,' Richard said flatly.

CHAPTER FIFTY-SEVEN

Dannyboy Duke zigzagged across Third Avenue, racing towards Fifty-fifth and Second, where he had the car parked. The woman had missed her wallet just as he got on the escalator. He'd heard her scream, 'That man, the dark-haired one – he just robbed me.'

He'd managed to slide through the wall of women on Alexander's main floor, but that bitch came rushing down the escalator after him, shouting and pointing as he went out the door. The security guard would probably chase him.

If he could just get to the car. He couldn't ditch the wallet. It was stuffed with hundred-dollar bills. He'd seen them, and he needed a fix.

It had been a good idea to go into Alexander's fur department. Women brought cash to Alexander's. It took too long to get a cheque or credit card cleared. He'd found that out when he worked as a stock boy there while he was still in high school.

Tonight he'd worn a coat that made him look like a stock boy. Nobody had paid any attention to him. The woman had one of those big, open pocketbooks; she'd held it by one strap as she rummaged through the coat rack. It had been easy to grab her wallet.

Was he being followed? He didn't dare look back. He'd call too much attention to himself. Better to stay against the sides of the buildings. Everyone was hurrying. It was so lousy cold. He could afford a fix; plenty of fixes now.

And in a minute he'd be in the car. He wouldn't be a man running in the street. He'd drive away, over the Fifty-ninth Street Bridge, and be home in Jackson Heights. He'd get his fix.

He looked back. No one running. No cops. Last night had

been so lousy. The doorman had almost grabbed him when he broke into that doctor's car. And what did he get for his risk? No drugs in the bag. A medical file, a messy paperweight and an old shoe, for Christ sake.

The pocketbook he'd grabbed later from the old lady. Ten lousy bucks. He'd barely been able to get enough stuff to tide him over today. The pocketbook and bag were in the back seat of the car. He'd have to get rid of them.

He was at the car. He opened it, slipped in. Never, never, no matter how bad off he was, would he get rid of the car. Cops don't expect you to drive away. If you're spotted, they check the subway stations.

He put the key into the ignition, turned on the engine. Even before he saw the flashing dome light, he heard the siren of the police car as it raced the wrong way up the block. He tried to pull out, but the squad car cut him off. A cop, his hand on the butt of his pistol, jumped out. The headlights were blinding Danny.

The cop yanked open his door, looked in and removed the ignition key. 'Well, Dannyboy,' he said. 'You're still at it, right? Don't you never learn any new tricks? Now get the hell out, keep your goddamned hands where I can see them and brace so I can read you the goddamned *Miranda*. You're what – a three-time loser? I figure you got ten to fifteen coming, we get lucky with a judge.'

CHAPTER FIFTY-EIGHT

The plane circled over Newark. The descent was bumpy. Chris glanced at Joan. She was holding his hand tightly, but he knew it had nothing to do with flying. Joan was absolutely fearless in a plane. He'd heard her argue the point with people who hated to fly. 'Statistically, you're much safer in a plane than in a car, a train, a motorcycle or your bathtub,' she'd say.

Her face was composed. She'd insisted they have a drink when cocktails were served. Neither one of them had wanted dinner, but they'd both had coffee. Her expression was serious but composed. 'Chris,' she'd said, 'I can bear anything except thinking that because of me Vangie committed suicide. Don't worry about dragging me into this. You tell the truth when you're questioned and don't hold anything back.'

Joan. If they ever got through this, they'd have a good life together. She was a woman. He still had so much to learn about her. He hadn't even realized he could trust her with the simple truth. Maybe he'd gotten so used to shielding Vangie, from trying to avoid arguments. He had so much to learn about himself, let alone Joan.

The landing was rough. Several passengers exclaimed as the plane bounced down. Chris knew the pilot had done a good job. There was a hell of a downwind. If it kept up, they'd probably close the airport.

Joan grinned at him.

'The stewardess must have brought us in.' It was an old airline gag.

'Or at least was doing a little lap time.'

They were silent as the plane taxied over to the gate. People meeting passengers had to wait past the security gate. But Chris was not surprised to see the two detectives who had been at the house after he found Vangie waiting for him.

'Captain Lewis. Miss Moore.'

'Yes.'

'Please come with us.' Ed's voice was formal. 'It is my duty to inform you that you are a suspect in the death of your wife, Vangie Lewis, as well as in several other possible homicides. Anything you say may be used against you. You are not required to answer questions. It is your right to call a lawyer.'

Joan answered for him. 'He doesn't need a lawyer. And he'll tell you everything he knows.'

CHAPTER FIFTY-NINE

Molly settled back as the orchestra began the few bars of music that signalled the beginning of *Otello*. Bill *loved* opera. She *liked* it. Maybe that was part of the reason she couldn't relax. Bill was already totally absorbed, his expression serene and thoughtful. She glanced around. The Met was packed as usual. Their seats were excellent. They should be. Bill had paid seventy dollars for the pair. Overhead the chandeliers twinkled, glistened and then began to fade into silvery darkness.

She should have insisted on going to see Katie in the hospital tonight. Bill didn't, *couldn't* understand Katie's dread of hospitals. No wonder. Katie was ashamed to talk about it. The awful part was that there was a basis for her fear. Daddy *hadn't* gotten help in time. The old man who was in the room with him had told them that. Even Bill admitted that a lot of mistakes were made in hospitals.

With a start she heard applause as Placido Domingo descended from the ship. She'd heard nothing of the opera so far. Bill glanced over at her, and she tried to look as though she were enjoying herself. After the first act, she'd phone Katie. That would help to reassure her. Just hearing Katie's voice that she was all right. And by God, she'd be at that hospital early in the morning before the operation and make sure Katie wasn't too nervous.

The first act seemed interminable. She had never realized it was so long. Finally, intermission came. Impatiently refusing Bill's suggestion of a glass of champagne from the lobby bar, she hurried to a phone. Quickly, she dialled and jammed in the necessary coins.

A few minutes later, white-lipped, she rushed to Bill. Half sobbing, she grabbed his arm. 'Something's wrong, something's wrong . . . I called the hospital. They wouldn't put the call through to Katie's room. They said the doctor forbade calls.

I got the desk and insisted the nurse check on Katie. She just came back. She's a kid, she's hysterical. Katie's not in her room. Katie's missing.'

CHAPTER SIXTY

He left Katie's room and a smile of satisfaction flitted across his face. It was going very well. The pills were working. She was begining to haemorrhage. The finger proved that her blood was no longer clotting.

He went down to the second floor and stopped in to see Mrs Aldrich. The baby was in a crib by her bed. Her husband was with her. He smiled aloofly at the parents, then bent over the child. 'A handsome specimen indeed,' he proclaimed. 'I don't think we'll trade him in.'

He knew his attempts at humour were heavy-handed, but sometimes it was necessary. These people were important, very important. Delano Aldrich could direct thousands of dollars of research funds to Westlake. More research. He could work in the laboratory with animals, report his successes. Then, when he publicly began work with women, all the experimentation of these years would make immediate success inevitable. Fame deferred is not necessarily fame denied.

Delano Aldrich was staring at his son, his face a study in awe and admiration. 'Doctor, we still can't believe it. Everyone else was obviously wrong.' It was her anxiety that had been the main problem. Fukhito had spotted that. Muscular dystrophy in her father's family. She knew she might be a carrier. That and some fibroid cysts in her womb. He'd taken care of the cysts and she'd become pregnant. Then he'd done an early test of the amniotic fluid and had been able to reassure her on the dystrophy question.

Still, she was a highly emotional, almost hyperactive personality. She'd had two early miscarriages over ten years ago. He'd put her to bed two months before the birth. And it had worked.

'I'll stop in in the morning.' These people would be fervent witnesses for him if there was any question that Katie DeMaio's death was suspicious.

But there shouldn't be any question. The dropping blood pressure was a matter of hospital record. The emergency operation would take place in the presence of the top nurses on the staff. He'd even send for the emergency-room surgeon to assist. Molloy was on tonight. He was a good man, the best. Molloy would be able to tell the family and Katie's office that it had been impossible to stop the haemorrhaging, that Dr Highley had headed a team working frantically.

Leaving the Aldriches, he went to Nurse Renge's desk. He had carefully manipulated the schedule so that she was on. A more experienced nurse would check on Katie every ten minutes. Renge wasn't that bright.

'Nurse Renge.'

'Doctor.' She stood up quickly, her hands fluttering nervously.

'I am quite concerned about Mrs DeMaio. Her blood pressure is in the low normal limit, but I suspect the vaginal bleeding has been heavier than she realizes. I'm going out for dinner, then will come back. I want the lab report on her blood count ready. I did not want to distress her – she has a lifelong fear of hospitals – but I should not be surprised if we have to operate tonight. I'll make that judgement when I come back in about an hour. I persuaded her not to eat dinner, and if she requests any solid food, do not give it to her.'

'Yes, Doctor.'

'Give Mrs DeMaio the sleeping pill, and do not in any way intimate to her that emergency surgery may be necessary. Is that clear?'

'Yes, Doctor.'

'Very well.'

He made a point of speaking to several people in the main lobby. He'd decided to have dinner at the restaurant adjacent to the hospital grounds. It wasn't bad. One could get a quite decent steak, and he wanted to be able later to present the image of a conscientious doctor.

I was concerned about Mrs DeMaio. Instead of going home, I had dinner next door and went directly back to the hospital to check on her. Thank God I did. At least we *tried*.

And another important point. Even on a dismal night like this, it would not be unusual to walk over to the restaurant. That way no one would be quite sure how long he'd been gone.

Because while he was waiting for coffee to be served, he'd take the last necessary step. He had left Katie at five past seven. At quarter of eight he was in the restaurant. Katie was going to be given the sleeping pill at eight o'clock. It was a strong one. Thanks to her weakened condition, it would knock her out immediately.

By eight thirty it would be safe for him to go up the back stairs to the third floor, go into the living-room of the suite, make sure Katie was asleep and give her the shot of heparin, the powerful anticoagulant drug which, combined with the pills, would send her blood pressure and blood count plummeting.

He'd come back here and finish coffee, pay his bill and then return to the hospital. He'd take Nurse Renge up with him to check on Katie. Ten minutes later Katie would be in surgery.

She had made it so easy by not having visitors tonight. Of course, he'd been prepared for that possibility. He'd have slipped the heparin into the transfusion she'd be receiving during the operation. That would have been just as effective, but riskier.

The steak was adequate. Odd how hungry he became at times like this. He would have preferred waiting until after it was over to eat, but that would be almost impossible. By the time Katie's sister was reached it would be well after midnight, since she was at the opera. He'd wait at the hospital for her, to console her. She'd remember how kind he'd been. He wouldn't get home until two or three. He couldn't fast that long.

He permitted himself one glass of wine. He'd have preferred his usual half-bottle, but that was impossible tonight. Nevertheless, the one glass warmed him, made him more alert, helped his mind to rove over the possibilities, to anticipate the unexpected.

This would be the end of the danger. His bag had not shown up. It probably never would. The Salem threat had been eliminated. The papers reported his death as 'fell or jumped'. Edna was buried this morning. Vangie Lewis had been interred yesterday. The moccasin in Edna's drawer would mean nothing to the people who disposed of her shabby belongings.

A terrible week. And so unnecessary. He should be allowed to openly pursue his work. A generation ago artificial insemination was considered outrageous. Now thousands of babies were born that way every year.

Go back hundreds of years. The Arabs used to destroy their enemies by infiltrating their camps and impregnating their mares with cotton soaked with the semen of inferior stallions. Remarkable genius to have planned that.

The doctors who had performed the first successful in vitro fertilization were geniuses.

But his genius surpassed them all. And nothing would stand in the way of his reaping the rewards due him.

The Nobel Prize. Some day he would receive it. For contributions to medicine not imagined possible.

He had single-handedly solved the abortion problem, the sterility problem.

And the tragedy was that if it were known, like Copernicus he would be considered a criminal.

'Did you enjoy your dinner, Doctor?' The waitress was familiar. Oh, yes, he had delivered her some years ago. A boy.

'Very much indeed. And how is your son?'

'Fine, sir. Simply fine.'

'Wonderful.' Incredible this woman and her husband had met his fee, giving him the money saved for a down payment for a home. Well, she'd got what she wanted.

'I'd like cappuccino, please.'

'Certainly, Doctor, but that will take about ten minutes.'

'While you're getting it, I'll make some phone calls.' He'd be gone less than ten minutes. Now the waitress wouldn't miss him.

Through the window he noticed that the snow had stopped. He couldn't, of course, take his coat from the checkroom. Slipping out the side door near the hallway with the telephones and rest rooms, he hurried back across the path. The cold bit at his face, but he scarcely noticed it. He was planning every step.

It was easy to keep in the shadows. He had his key to the fire exit in the rear of the maternity wing. No one ever used those stairs. He let himself into the building.

The stairway was brightly lighted. He turned off the switch. He could find his way through this hospital blindfolded. At the third floor he opened the door cautiously, listened. There was no sound. Noiselessly he stepped into the hall. An instant later he was inside the living-room of Katie's suite.

That had been another problem he'd considered. Suppose someone accompanied her to the hospital: her sister, a friend? Suppose that person asked to stay overnight on the sofa bed in the living-room? The Westlake Clinic openly encouraged sleeping-in if the patient desired it. By ordering this living-room repainted, he'd effectively blocked that possibility.

Planning. Planning. It was everything, as useful and necessary in life as in the laboratory.

This afternoon he had left the needle with the heparin in a drawer of an end table under the painter's drop cloth. The light from the parking lot filtered through the window, giving him enough visibility to find the table at once. He reached for the needle.

Now for the most important moment of all. If Katie woke up and saw him, he'd be exposed to danger. Granted, she would probably fall back asleep immediately. Certainly she'd never question the injection. But when he returned with Nurse Renge later, if she was by some chance still conscious, if she said anything about the shot, it would be a risk. Oh, it would be easy enough to explain: she was confused; she meant when I took the blood samples. Even so. Better if she didn't wake up now.

He was in the room, bending over her. He reached for her arm. The drapery was partly open. Faint light was coming into the room. He could see her profile. Her face was turned from him. Her breathing was uneven. She was talking in her sleep. He could not catch the words. She must be dreaming.

He slipped the needle into her arm, squeezed. She winced and sighed. Her eyes, cloudy with sleep, opened as she turned her head. In the dim light he could see the enlarged pupils. She looked up at him puzzled. 'Dr Highley,' she murmured, 'why did you kill Vangie Lewis?'

CHAPTER SIXTY-ONE

Scott Myerson was more tired than angry. Since Vangie Lewis's body had been found Tuesday morning, two other people had died. Two very decent people – a hard-working receptionist who deserved a few years' freedom after supporting and caring for aged parents and a doctor who was making a real contribution to medicine.

They had died because he had not moved fast enough. Chris Lewis was a murderer. Scott was sure of that. The web drawing around Lewis was unbreakable. If only they had realized immediately that Vangie Lewis's death was a homicide. He'd have brought Lewis in for questioning immediately. They might have cracked him. And if they had, Edna Burns and Emmet Salem would be alive now.

Scott couldn't wait for the chance to get to Lewis. Any man who could murder his pregnant wife was capable of any cold-blooded murder. Lewis proved that. He was the worst kind of criminal. The one who didn't look or sound the part. The one you trusted and turned your back on.

Lewis and his girl-friend were landing at seven. They should be here by eight. Lewis was cool, all right. Knew better than to run. Thought he could brazen it out. Knows it's all circumstantial. But circumstantial evidence can be a lot better than eye-witness testimony when properly presented in court. Scott would try the case himself. It would be his pleasure.

At seven fifty, Richard walked into Scott's office. He did not waste time on preliminaries. 'I think we've uncovered a cesspool,' he said, 'and it's called the Westlake Maternity Concept.'

'If you're saying that the shrink was probably playing around with Vangie Lewis, I agree,' Scott said. 'But I thought we decided that this afternoon. Anyhow, it's going to be easy enough to find out. Get blood samples from the foetus and we'll bring Fukhito in. He can't refuse to have his blood tested. If he does, it's an open admission of guilt, and he'd be finished with medicine if another paternity case was proved.'

'That's not what I'm talking about,' Richard broke in impatiently. 'It's Highley I'm after. I think he's experimenting with his patients. I just spoke to the husband of one of them. There's no way he's the baby's father, but he was present at the birth. He's been thinking that his wife agreed to artificial insemination without his permission. I think it goes beyond that. I think Highley is performing artificial insemination without his patients' *knowledge*. That's why they're able to produce miracle babies under his care.'

Scott snorted. 'You mean to say you think Highley would inject Vangie Lewis with the semen of an Oriental father and expect to get away with it? Come on, Richard.'

'Maybe he didn't know the donor was Oriental. Maybe he made a mistake.'

'Doctors don't make mistakes like that. Even allowing your theory to be true . . . and frankly, I don't buy it . . . that doesn't make him Vangie's murderer.'

'There's something wrong with Highley,' Richard insisted. 'I've felt it from the first minute I laid eyes on him.'

'Look, we'll investigate Westlake Maternity. That's no problem. If there's any kind of violation there, we'll find it and prosecute it. If you're right and he's inseminating women without their consent, we'll get him. That's a direct violation of the Offence Against the Person Act. But let's worry about that later. Right now Chris Lewis is my first order of business.'

'Do this,' Richard persisted. 'Go back further with the check on Highley. I'm already looking into the malpractice suits against him. Some woman, a Mrs Horan, will be here shortly to tell why she pressed a suit. But the *Newsmaker* article says he was in Liverpool, in England, before he came here. Let's phone there and see if we can find any trace of impropriety. They'll give you that information.'

Scott shrugged. 'Sure, go ahead.'

The buzzer on his desk sounded. He switched on the intercom. 'Bring him in,' he said. Leaning back on his chair, he looked at Richard.

'The bereaved widower, Captain Lewis, is here with his paramour,' he said.

CHAPTER SIXTY-TWO

Dannyboy Duke sat in the precinct house hunched miserably forward in a chair. He was perspiring; his nerves were on edge. His arms were trembling. It was hard to see. In another thirty seconds he'd have been away. He'd be in his apartment now, the blissful release of the fix soaring through his body. Instead, this steamy, sweaty hell.

'Give me a break,' he whispered.

The cops weren't impressed. 'You give *us* a break, Danny. There's blood on this paperweight, Danny. Who'd you hit with it? Come on, Danny. We know it wasn't the old lady whose pocketbook you grabbed last night. You pushed her down. She's got a broken hip. That's pretty lousy when you're seventy-five, Danny. Odds are she'll wind up with pneumonia. Maybe die. That makes it murder two, Dannyboy. You help us, we'll see what we can do for you, you know?'

'I don't know what you're talking about,' Danny whispered.

'Sure you do. The doctor's bag was in your car. So was the pocketbook. The wallet you just grabbed in Alexander's was in your pocket. We know you stole the bag last night. We've got the call right here. The doorman saw you do it in front of the Carlyle Hotel. He can identify you. But who'd you hit with that paperweight, Danny? Tell us about it. And what about that shoe, Danny? Since when do you save beat-up shoes? Tell us about that.'

'It was in the bag,' Danny whispered.

The two detectives looked at each other. One of them shrugged and turned to the newspaper on the desk behind him. The other dropped the file he had been examining back into the bag. 'All right, Danny. We're calling Dr Salem to find out just what he had in this bag. That'll settle it. It could go easier if you'd co-operate. You've been around long enough to figure that out.'

The other detective looked up from the paper. 'Dr Salem?'

His voice was startled.

'Yeah. That's the name on the file. Oh, I see. The nameplate says Dr Edgar Highley. Guess he had a patient's file from some other doctor.'

The younger detective came over to the table carrying the morning *Daily News*. He opened the file and examined the sheaf of papers with the name EMMET SALEM, MD printed across the top. He pointed to page three of the *News*. 'Salem's the doctor who was found on the roof of the Essex House extension last night. The Valley County Prosecutor is working with our people on that case.'

The police officers looked at Dannyboy with renewed interest and narrowed, suspicious eyes.

CHAPTER SIXTY-THREE

He watched as Katie's eyes closed and her breathing became even. She'd fallen asleep again. The question about Vangie had come from somewhere in her subconscious, triggered perhaps by a duplication of her mental state of Monday night. She might not even remember asking the question, but he couldn't take the chance. Suppose she talked about it again in front of Nurse Renge or the other doctors in the operating room before they anaesthetized her? His mind groped for a solution. Her presence at the window last Monday night could still destroy him.

He had to kill her before Nurse Renge made her check, in less than an hour. The heparin shot would act to anticoagulate her blood immediately, but it would take several hours to complete the procedure. That was what he had planned. Now he couldn't wait. He had to give her a second shot, immediately.

He had heparin in his office. He didn't dare go near the hospital dispensary. He'd have to go down the fire stairs to the parking lot, use the private door to his office, refill the hypodermic needle and come back up here. It would take at least five minutes. The waitress would start to question his absence from the table, but there was no help for that. Satisfied that Katie was asleep, he hurried from the room.

CHAPTER SIXTY-FOUR

The technician in the Valley County Forensic Lab worked overtime on Friday evening. Dr Carroll had asked him to compare all microscopic samples from the home of the presumed suicide Vangie Lewis with all microscopic samples from the home of the presumed accident victim Edna Burns. Carefully he had sifted the vacuum-bag contents of the Lewis home and the Burns apartment and painstakingly searched for substances that might be out of the ordinary.

The technician knew he had a superb instinct for microscopic evidence, a hunch factor that rarely failed him. He was always particularly interested in loose hair, and he was fond of saying, 'We are like fur-bearing animals. It's astonishing how much hair we are constantly shedding, including people who are virtually bald.'

In the exhibits from the Lewis home he found an abundance of strands of the ash-blonde hair of the victim. He'd also found medium-brown hair, a fair quantity of it, in the bedroom. Undoubtedly the husband's, since those same hairs were in the den and living-room.

But there were also a number of silverish-sandy hairs in the victim's bedroom. That was unusual. In the kitchen or living-room, strands of hair could easily come from a visitor or deliveryman, but the bedroom? Even in this day, there were few non-family members who were invited to enter the bedroom. Shafts found there assumed special significance. The hair had come from a man's head. The length suggested that automatically. Some of the same strands were on the coat the victim had been wearing.

And then the technician found the connection Richard Carroll had been seeking. Several sandy hairs with silver roots were clinging to the faded blue bathrobe of Edna Burns.

He placed the samples of hair under powerful microscopes and painstakingly went through the sixteen points of comparison check.

There was absolutely no doubt. One person had been close to both dead women; close enough to have held a head near to Edna Burns's chest and to have brushed a head on Vangie Lewis's shoulder.

The technician reached for the phone to call Dr Carroll.

CHAPTER SIXTY-FIVE

She tried to wake up. There was a click: a door had closed. Someone had just been here. Her arm hurt. Dr Highley. She dropped off . . . What had she said to Dr Highley? Katie woke up a few minutes later and remembered. Remembered the black car and the shiny spokes and the light on his glasses. She'd seen that Monday night. Dr Highley had carried Vangie Lewis to his car Monday night. Dr Highley had killed Vangie.

Richard had suspected something. Richard had tried to tell her. But she wouldn't listen.

Dr Highley knew she knew about him. Why had she asked him that question? She had to get out of here. He was going to kill her too. She'd always had nightmares about hospitals. Because somehow she'd known that she would die in a hospital.

Where had Dr Highley gone? He'd be back. She knew that. Back to kill her. Help. She needed help. Why was she so weak? Her finger was bleeding. The pills he had given her. Since she'd been taking them she'd been so sick. The pills. They were making her bleed.

Oh God, help me, please. The phone. The phone! Katie fumbled for it. Her hand, weak and unsteady, knocked it over. Shaking her head, forcing her eyes to stay open, she pulled it up by the cord. Finally she had the receiver at her ear. The line was dead. Frantically she jiggled the cradle, tried dialling the operator.

Dr Highley had said the phone was being repaired. She pushed the bell for the nurse. The nurse would help her. But the click that should have turned on the light outside her door did not happen. She was sure the signal wasn't lighting the nurse's panel either.

She had to get out of here before Dr Highley came back. Waves of dizziness nauseated her as she stood up.

She had to. Vangie Lewis. The long blonde hair, the petulant, little-girl eagerness for a child. Dr Highley had killed Vangie. Killed her baby. Had there been others?

She made her way from the bed, holding on to the footrail. The elevator. She'd go down in the elevator to the second floor. There were people there – other patients, nurses.

From nearby a door closed. He was coming back. *He was coming back.* Frantically Katie looked at the open door to the corridor. He'd see her if she went out there. The bathroom door had no lock. The closet. He'd find her there. Through sheer willpower she managed to stumble to the door leading to the living-room, open it, go inside, close it before he came into the bedroom.

Where could she go? He'd look for her immediately. She couldn't stay here. If she tried to go out into the foyer, she'd pass the open door of the bedroom. He'd see her. She had to go down the foyer and turn left, then down the long hall to the elevator. She was no match for him. Where could she go? She heard a door open inside. He was in the bedroom looking for her. Should she try to hide under the drop cloth? No. No. She'd be trapped there. He'd find her, drag her out. She bit her lip as dizziness clawed at the space behind her eyes. Her legs were rubbery, her mouth and skin spongy.

She stumbled to the door of the living-room, the one that led to the hall. There was another door there, the fire exit. She'd seen it when she was wheeled in. She'd go down that to the second floor. She'd get help. She was in the hall. In a minute he'd be behind her.

The door to the fire stairs was heavy. She tugged at it . . . tugged again. Reluctantly it gave way. She opened it, stepped inside. It closed so slowly. Would he see it closing? The stairs. It was so dark here, terribly dark. But she couldn't turn on a light. He'd see it. Maybe he was running down the corridor towards the elevator. If he did that, she'd have an extra minute. She needed that minute. Help me. Help me. She grabbed on to the banister. The stairs were steep. Her bare feet were silent. How many stairs in a flight? Thirteen. No, that was a house. There was a landing here after eight steps. Then another flight. Eight more steps, then she'd be safe. Seven . . . five . . . one. She was at the door, tried to turn the handle. It was locked. It opened only from the other side.

From upstairs she heard the third-floor door open and heavy footsteps coming down the stairs.

CHAPTER SIXTY-SIX

Chris refused to call a lawyer. He sat opposite the Prosecutor. He had been so worried about this encounter, so afraid they wouldn't believe him. But Joan believed him; Joan had said, 'It just makes sense that they'll be suspicious of you, Chris. Tell every single thing you know. Remember that quote from the Bible, "The truth shall make you free."' Chris looked from the Prosecutor to the two detectives who had met him at the airport. 'I have nothing to hide,' he said.

Scott was unimpressed. A bookish-looking young man carrying a stenographer's pad came into the room, sat down, opened the pad and took out a pen. Scott looked directly at Chris. 'Captain Lewis, it is my duty to inform you that you are a suspect in the deaths of Vangie Lewis, Edna Burns and Dr Emmet Salem. You may remain silent. You are not required to answer any questions. At any point you may refuse to continue answering questions. You are entitled to the services of a lawyer. Any statement that you make can be used against you. Is that perfectly clear.'

'Yes,'

'Can you read?'

Chris stared at Scott. Was he being sarcastic? No, the man was deadly serious.

'Yes.'

Scott shoved a paper across the desk. 'This is a copy of the *Miranda* warning you have just heard. Please read it carefully. Be sure you understand it and then, if you are so disposed, sign it.'

Chris read the statement swiftly, signed it and handed it back.

'Very well.' Scott pushed the paper to one side. His manner changed, became somehow more intense. Chris realized the formal questioning was about to begin.

Funny, he thought, every night of your life, if you wanted to, you could watch some form of cops-and-robbers or courtroom drama show and you never expect to get involved in one yourself. The Prosecutor obviously believed that he had killed Vangie. Was he crazy not to have legal counsel? No.

The Prosecutor was talking. 'Captain Lewis, have you been in any way ill-treated or abused?'

'I have not.'

'Would you care for coffee or food?'

Chris rubbed his hand over his forehead. 'I would like coffee, please. But I am ready to answer your questions fully.'

Even so, he was not prepared for Scott's question. 'Did you murder your wife, Vangie Lewis?'

Chris looked directly at him. 'I did not murder my wife. I do not know if she was murdered. But I do know this. If she died before midnight Monday night, she did not kill herself in our home.'

Scott, Charley, Phil and the stenographer were startled into unprofessional astonishment as Chris calmly said, 'I was there just before midnight Monday. Vangie was not home. I returned to New York. At eleven the next morning I found her in bed. It wasn't until the funeral director came to the house for clothes to dress my wife for burial and told me the time of death that I realized that her dead body must have been returned to our house. But even before that I knew something was wrong. My wife would never have worn or even tried to put on the shoes she was wearing when she was found. For six weeks before her death the only shoes she could wear were a pair of battered moccasins a cleaning woman had left. Her right leg and foot were badly swollen. She even used those moccasins as bedroom slippers . . .'

It was easier than he had expected. He heard the questions coming at him: 'You left the hotel at eight p.m. Monday night and returned at ten. Where did you go?'

'To a movie in Greenwich Village. After I got back to the

motel, I couldn't sleep. I decided to drive home and talk to Vangie. That was shortly after midnight.'

'Why didn't you stay and wait for your wife?' And then the one that was a hammer-blow to his stomach: 'Did you know your wife was carrying a Japanese foetus?'

'Oh, my God!' Horror somehow mingled with a sense of release flooded Chris's being. *It hadn't been his baby.* A Japanese foetus. That psychiatrist. Was he louse enough to do that to her? She'd trusted him so. Oh, God, the poor kid. No wonder she was getting so frightened to give birth. That must have been why she called Dr Salem. She wanted to hide. Oh, God, she was such a child.

The questions came: 'You were not aware your wife was involved with another man?'

'No. No.'

'Why did you go to Edna Burns's apartment Tuesday night?'

The coffee came. He tried to answer. 'Wait, please – can we take this just the way it happened?' He began to sip the coffee. It helped. 'It was Tuesday night, just after I realized that Vangie had died before she was brought home, that that woman, Edna Burns, called. She was almost incoherent. She rambled on about Cinderella and Prince Charming, said she had something for me, something I'd want to have, and she had a story for the police. I thought she might know who Vangie had been with. I thought if she told me, I might not have to admit that I'd been home Monday night. I wanted to keep Joan out of this.'

He set down the coffee cup, remembering Tuesday night. It seemed so long ago. Everything was so out of proportion. 'I drove to Miss Burns's housing development. Some kid was walking his dog and pointed out her apartment to me. I rang the bell and knocked on the door. The television was on, the light was on, but she didn't answer. I figured she'd passed out and there was no use trying to talk to her, that maybe she was just a crank. I went home.'

'You never went in?'

'No.'

'What time was that?'

'About nine thirty.'

'All right. What did you do then?'

The questions, one after another; he drank more coffee. Truth. The simple truth. It was so much easier than evasion. Keep the future in mind. If they believed him, he and Joan would have a life together. He thought of the way she'd looked at him, thrown her arms around him last night in her apartment. For the first time in his entire life, he'd known there was someone he could go to in trouble; someone who would want to share it with him. Everyone else – Vangie, even his parents – had always leaned on him.

For better, for worse.

It would be *better* for them. Joan, my darling, he thought. He took a deep breath. They were asking about Dr Salem.

CHAPTER SIXTY-SEVEN

Richard sat at Katie's desk as he waited for the staff director of Christ Hospital, Devon, to answer his phone. Only by emphasizing the urgency of his need to talk to someone in authority who had been at the hospital more than ten years had he been given the man's private number.

While he waited, he looked around. The table behind Katie's desk was filled with files she was working on. It was no wonder she hadn't taken any time off after her accident. But no matter how busy, she should have stayed home. This afternoon she'd looked lousy. And losing that case today must have upset her terribly. He wished he'd seen her before she left.

The phone continued to jab. The guy must be out or asleep. Maybe it could wait till morning. No. He wanted to find out *now*.

There were snapshots in a frame on Katie's desk. Katie with an older woman, probably her mother. He knew the mother lived in Florida somewhere. Katie with Jennifer, Molly's eldest. Katie looked like Jen's big sister. Katie with a group of people in ski outfits. These must be the friends she stayed with in Vermont.

No picture of John DeMaio. But Katie wasn't the kind to subtly remind people at work that she was the widow of a prominent judge. And there certainly were plenty of pictures of him around that house.

The phone continued to ring. He'd give it another minute.

Richard realized he was pleased to note that there were no pictures of any other guy either. He'd been analysing his reaction to Katie's announcement that she'd be away for the weekend. He'd tried to make it look as though he were surprised that she wouldn't be available with a big case breaking. Hell. That had nothing to do with it. He was worried that she was with some other guy.

'Yes.' An angry, sleepy voice had answered the phone.

Richard straightened up, tightened his grip on the receiver. 'Mr Reeves? Mr Alexander Reeves?'

'Yes.'

Richard went directly to the point. 'Sir, I apologize profusely for calling you at this hour, but the matter is vital. This is a transatlantic call. I'm Dr Richard Carroll, the Medical Examiner of Valley County, New Jersey. I must have information about Dr Edgar Highley.'

The sleepiness vanished from the other man's voice. It became intense and wary. 'What do you want to know?'

'I have just spoken with Queen Mary Clinic in Liverpool and was surprised to learn that Dr Highley had been on staff there a relatively short time. We had been led to believe otherwise. However, I was told that Dr Highley was a member of the Christ Hospital staff for at least nine years. Is that accurate?'

'Edgar Highley interned with us after his graduation from Cambridge. He is a brilliant doctor and was invited to become staff, specializing in obstetrics and gynaecology.'

'Why did he leave?'

'After his wife's death he relocated in Liverpool. Then we heard he had emigrated to the United States. That's not uncommon, of course. Many of our physicians and surgeons will not tolerate the relatively low pay structure of our socialized medicine system.'

'There was no other reason for Dr Highley's resignation?'

'I don't understand your question.'

Richard took a chance. 'I think you do, Mr Reeves. This is, of course, totally confidential, but I can't waste time being discreet.

I believe that Dr Highley may be experimenting with his pregnant patients, perhaps even with their lives. Is there any justification that you can offer to support that possibility?'

There was a long pause. The words that came next were slow and deliberately enunciated. 'While he was with us, Dr Highley was not only a practising physician, but was deeply involved in prenatal research. He did quite brilliant experiments on embryos of frogs and mammals. Then a fellow doctor began to suspect that he was experimenting with aborted human foetuses – which is, of course, illegal.'

'What was done about it?'

'It was kept very quiet, of course, but he was being watched very carefully. Then a tragedy occured. Dr Highley's wife died suddenly. There was no way we could prove anything, but the suspicion existed that he had implanted her with an aborted foetus. Dr Highley was asked to resign. This is, of course, absolutely confidential. In no way is there a shred of proof, and I must expect that you treat this conversation as inviolable.'

Richard absorbed what he had heard. His hunch had been right. How many women had Highley killed experimenting on them? A question came into his mind – a wild, long-shot possibility.

'Mr Reeves,' he asked, 'do you by any chance know a Dr Emmet Salem?'

The voice warmed immediately. 'Of course I do. A good friend. Why, Dr Salem was visiting staff here at the time of the Highley scandal.'

CHAPTER SIXTY-EIGHT

Silently Katie ran down the stairs to the main floor. Desperately she grasped the knob, tried to open the door. But it would not give. It was locked. Upstairs, the footsteps had paused. He was trying the second-floor knob, making sure that she had not escaped him. The footsteps started again. He was coming down. No one would hear her if she screamed. These heavy doors were fireproof. No hospital sounds could be heard here. On the other side of the door, there were people: visitors, patients, nurses. Less than six inches away. But they could not hear her.

He was coming. He would reach her, kill her. She felt heavy, dull pain in her pelvic area. She was flowing heavily. Whatever he had given her had started the haemorrhaging. She was dizzy. But she had to get away. He had made Vangie's death look like suicide. He still might get away with that. Wildly she began rushing down the staircase. There was one more flight. It probably led to the basement of the hospital. He'd have to explain how and why she'd gotten there. The farther she got, the more questions would be asked. She stumbled on the last stair. Don't fall. Don't make it look like an accident. Edna had fallen. Or had she?

Had he killed Edna too?

But she'd be trapped here. Another door. This one would be locked too. Helplessly she turned the knob. He was on the mid landing. Dark as it was, she could see movement, a presence rushing down at her.

The door opened. The corridor was dimly lit. She was in the basement. She saw rooms ahead. Quiet. It was so quiet. The door snapped closed behind her. Could she hide somewhere? Help me. Help me. There was a switch on the wall. She pressed her hand on it. Her finger smeared it with blood. The corridor disappeared into blackness as a few feet behind her the door from the stairwell burst open.

CHAPTER SIXTY-NINE

Highley was suspected of causing his first wife's death. Winifred Westlake's cousin believed he had caused Winifred's death. Highley was a brilliant researcher. Highley may have been experimenting on some of the women who were his patients. Highley may have injected Vangie Lewis with the semen of an Oriental male. But why? Did he hope to get away with it? Undoubtedly he knew Fukhito's background. Would he try to accuse him? Why? Had it been an accident? Had he used the wrong semen? Or had Vangie been involved with Fukhito? Was Dr Highley's possible experimentation only incidental to Vangie's pregnancy?

Richard could not find the answer. He sat at Katie's desk twirling her Mark Cross pen. She always carried this. She must have rushed out of here this evening and forgotten to pick it up. But of course, she'd been upset. Losing that case must have rattled her badly. Katie would take that hard. Katie took a lot of things hard. He wished he knew where she was. He wanted to talk to her. The way her finger bled. He'd have to ask Molly if she knew whether or not Katie had a low platelet count. That could be a real problem.

A chill made Richard's fingers stiffen. That could be a sign of leukaemia. Oh, God. Monday, he'd drag Katie to a doctor if he had to tie her up to do it.

There was a soft knock on the door and Maureen looked in. Her eyes were emerald green, large and oval. Beautiful eyes. Beautiful kid.

'Dr Carroll.'

'Maureen, I'm sorry I asked you to stay. I thought Mrs Horan would be here long ago.'

'It's all right. She did phone. She's on her way. Something came up at work and they needed her. But there are two women here. They're friends of the Miss Burns who died. They wanted to see Katie. I told them she was gone, and one of them mentioned your name. She met you the other night when you were at the Burns apartment; a Mrs Fitzgerald.'

'Fitzgerald? . . . Sure. Mrs Fitzgerald is a part-time receptionist at Westlake Hospital.' As Richard said 'Westlake', he stood up. 'Tell them to come on in. Maybe you'd better call Scott.'

'Mr Myerson is absolutely not to be disturbed. He and Charley and Phil are still questioning Captain Lewis.'

'All right. I'll talk to them. Then if it's anything much, we'll make them wait.'

They came in together, Gana's eyes snapping with excitement. She had regretfully decided not to wear Edna's leopard coat. It just seemed too soon. But she had her story ready to tell.

Gertrude was carrying the moccasin in a paper bag. Her neat

grey hair was every inch in place. Her scarf was knotted at her throat. The good dinner had faded into memory, and now more than anything she wanted to get home and to bed. But she was glad to talk to Dr Carroll. She was going to tell him that the other night in poor Edna's apartment, Dr Highley had been pulling open the night-table drawer. There was nothing in that drawer except the shoe. Did Dr Carroll think that Dr Highley wanted to get that shoe for any reason?

Mrs DeMaio had been so interested in that Prince Charming business. Dr Carroll might want to know about that too. He could tell Mrs DeMaio when she came in Monday. Dr Carroll was looking at them expectantly.

Gertrude leaned forward, shook the bag, and the shabby moccasin fell on to Katie's desk. Primly she began to explain, 'That shoe is the reason we are here.'

CHAPTER SEVENTY

She zigzagged down the corridor. Would he know where the light switch was? Would he dare to turn it on? Suppose there was someone down here? Should she try to scream?

He knew this hospital. Where would she go? There had been a door at the end of the hall. The farthest door. Maybe he'd try the others first. Maybe she could lock herself in somewhere. She might miss the doors on the side. But if she ran straight, she'd have to touch that far wall. The door was in the middle. Her finger was bleeding. She'd try to smear blood on the door. When the nurse made her rounds, they'd start to search for her. Maybe they'd notice the bloodstains.

He was standing still. He was listening for her. Would he see a shadow when the door opened? Her outstretched hand touched a cold wall. Oh, God, let me find the door. Her hand ran down the wall. She touched a doorframe. Behind her she heard a faint squeaking sound. He had opened that first door. But now he wouldn't bother to look in that room. He'd realize he hadn't heard that squeak, that she hadn't tried that door. Her hand found a knob. She turned it deliberately, grinding her cut finger against it. A heavy formaldehyde smell filled her nostrils. From behind her she heard rushing feet. Too late. Too late. She tried to push the door closed, but it was shoved open. She stumbled and fell. She was so dizzy, so dizzy. She reached out. Her hand touched a pants leg.

'It's all over, Katie,' Dr Highley said.

CHAPTER SEVENTY-ONE

'Are you sure this is your wife's shoe?' Scott demanded. Wearily Chris nodded. 'I am absolutely certain. This is the one that was so loose on her . . . the left one.'

'When Edna Burns phoned you, did she tell you she had this shoe?'

'No. She said she had something to tell the police and that she wanted to talk to me.'

'Did you get an impression of blackmail . . . of threat?'

'No, drunken garrulousness. I knew she was from Westlake Hospital. I didn't realize then that she was the receptionist Vangie used to talk about. She said Edna was always kidding her about her glass slippers.'

'All right. Your statement will be typed immediately. Read it carefully, sign it if you find it accurate and then you can go home. We'll want to talk with you again tomorrow morning.'

For the first time Chris felt as though the Prosecutor had begun to believe him. He got up to go. 'Where is Joan?'

'She's completed a statement. She can go with you. Oh, one thing: what impression do you have of Dr Highley?'

'I never met him.'

'Did you read this article about him?' Scott held up *Newsmaker* magazine.

Chris looked at the article, at the picture of Dr Highley. 'I saw this yesterday on the plane into New York.'

Memory jogged.

'That's it,' he said. 'That's what I couldn't place.'

'What are you talking about?' Scott asked.

'That was the man who came down in the elevator at the Essex House last night when I was trying to reach Dr Salem.'

CHAPTER SEVENTY-TWO

He switched on a light. Through the haze she could see his full-cheeked face, his eyes protruding as he stared down at her, his skin glistening with perspiration, his sandy hair falling untidily on his forehead.

She managed to stumble to her feet. She was in a small area like a waiting room. It was so cold. A thick steel door was behind her. She shrank back against the door.

'You've made it so easy for me, Mrs DeMaio.' Now he was smiling at her. 'Everyone close to you knows about your fear of hospitals. When Nurse Renge and I make rounds in a few minutes, we'll assume you left the hospital. We'll call your sister, but she won't be home for several hours, will she? We won't start looking for you *in* the hospital until much later. Certainly no one will dream of looking for you here.

'An old man died in the emergency room tonight. He's in one of those vaults. Tomorrow morning when the undertaker comes for his body, you'll be found. It will be obvious what happened to you. You were haemorrhaging; you became disoriented, almost comatose. Tragically, you wandered down here and bled to death.'

'No.' His face was blurring. She was so dizzy. She was swaying.

He reached past her and opened the steel door. He pushed her through it, held her as she slid down. She had fainted. Kneeling beside her, he injected the last shot of heparin. She probably wouldn't recover consciousness again. Even if she did, she couldn't get out. From this side the door was locked. He looked at her thoughtfully, then got to his feet and brushed the smudge of dust from his trousers. At last he was finished with Katie DeMaio.

He closed the steel door that separated the vaults from the receiving area of the morgue and turned out the light. Cautiously he opened the door into the corridor and hurried down it, letting himself out into the parking lot of the hospital by the same door through which he'd come in fifteen minutes before.

A few minutes later, he was drinking lukewarm cappuccino, waving away the offer of the waitress to bring him a hot cup. 'My calls took a bit longer than I expected,' he explained. 'And now I must hurry back to the hospital. There's a patient there about whom I'm quite concerned.'

CHAPTER SEVENTY-THREE

'Good night, Dr Fukhito. I feel much better. Thank you.' The boyish face managed a smile.

'I'm glad. Sleep well tonight, Tom.' Jiro Fukhito got up slowly. This young man would make it. He'd been in deep depression for weeks, nearly suicidal. He'd been doing eighty miles an hour in a car that crashed. His younger brother was killed in the accident. Regret. Guilt. Overwhelming, more than the boy could handle.

Jiro Fukhito knew he had helped him through the worst of it. His work could be so satisfying, he reflected as he walked slowly down the corridor of Valley Pines Hospital. The work he did here, the volunteer work – this was where he wanted to practise.

Oh, he'd done enough for many of the patients at Westlake. But there were others he hadn't helped, hadn't been *allowed* to help.

'Good night, Doctor.' A number of the patients in the psychiatric ward greeted him as he walked towards the elevator. He'd been asked to come full time on staff here. He wanted to accept that offer.

Should he start the investigation that would inevitably destroy him?

Edgar Highley wouldn't hesitate to reveal the Massachusetts

case if he suspected that his associate had discussed his patient with the police.

But Mrs DeMaio already suspected something. She'd recognized his nervousness when she questioned him the other day.

He got into his car, sat in it irresolutely. Vangie Lewis did not commit suicide. She absolutely did not commit suicide by drinking cyanide. She had gotten on the subject of the Jones cult during one of their sessions when she was talking about religion.

He could see her sitting in his office, her earnest, shallow explanation of her religious beliefs. 'I'm not one for going to church, Doctor. I mean I believe in God. But in my own way. I think about God sometimes. That's better than rushing off to a service you don't pay attention to anyhow, don't you think? And as for those cults. They're all crazy. I don't see how people get involved in them. Why, remember all those people who killed themselves because they were told to? Did you hear the tape of them screaming after they drank that stuff? I had nightmares about it. And they looked so *ugly*.'

Pain. Ugliness. Vangie Lewis? Never!

Jiro Fukhito sighed. He knew what he had to do. Once again his professional life would pay for the terrible mistake of ten years ago.

But he had to tell the police what he knew. Vangie had run out of his office into the parking lot. But when he left, fifteen minutes later, her Lincoln Continental was still in the lot.

There was no longer any doubt in Jiro Fukhito's mind that Vangie had gone into Edgar Highley's office.

He drove out of the hospital parking lot and turned in the direction of the Valley County Prosecutor's office.

CHAPTER SEVENTY-FOUR

Scott held the moccasin. Richard, Charley and Phil sat around his desk.

'Let's try to put this together,' Scott said. 'Vangie Lewis did not die at home. She was taken there some time between midnight and eleven a.m. The last known place she visited was Dr Fukhito's office at the hospital. Vangie was wearing the moccasins Monday night. Somewhere in the hospital she lost one of them, and Edna Burns found it. Whoever brought her home put other shoes on her to try to cover up for the missing ones. Edna Burns found the shoe and was talking about it. And Edna Burns died.

'Emmet Salem wanted to reach you, Richard. He wanted to talk to you about Vangie's death. He came into New York and fell or was pushed to his death a few minutes later, and the file he was carrying on Vangie Lewis disappeared.'

'And Chris Lewis swears that he saw Edgar Highley in the Essex House,' Richard interjected.

'Which may or may not be true,' Scott reminded him.

'But Dr Salem knew about the scandal in Christ Hospital,' Richard said. 'Highley wouldn't want that to come out just when he's getting national publicity.'

'That's no motive to kill,' Scott said.

'How about Highley trying to get that shoe out of Edna's drawer?' Charley asked.

'We don't *know* that. That woman from the hospital claimed he was opening the drawer. He didn't touch anything.' Scott frowned. 'Nothing hangs together. We're dealing with a prominent doctor. We can't go off half-cocked because he was involved ten years ago in a hushed-up scandal. The big problem is motive. Highley had no motive to kill Vangie Lewis.'

The intercom buzzed. Scott switched it on. 'Mrs Horan is here,' Maureen said.

'All right, bring her in, and I want you to take down her

statement,' Scott directed.

Richard leaned forward. This was the woman who had filed the malpractice suit against Edgar Highley.

The door opened and a young woman preceded Maureen into the room. She was a Japanese girl in her early twenties. Her hair fell loosely on her shoulders. Bright red lipstick was an incongruous note against her tawny skin. Her delicate, graceful carriage gave a floating effect even to the inexpensive pantsuit she was wearing.

Scott stood up. 'Mrs Horan, we appreciate your coming. We'll try not to keep you too long. Won't you sit down?'

She nodded. Clearly nervous, she wet her lips and deliberately folded her hands in her lap. Maureen unobtrusively sat behind her and opened her steno book.

'Will you state your name and address?' Scott asked.

'I am Anna Horan. I live at four-one-five Walnut Street in Ridgefield Park.'

'You are or were Dr Edgar Highley's patient?'

Richard turned quickly as he heard Maureen gasp. But the girl quickly recovered herself and, bending her head, resumed taking notes.

Anna Horan's face hardened. 'Yes, I was that murderer's patient.'

'*That murderer?*' Scott said.

Now her words came in a torrent. 'I went to him five months ago. I was pregnant. My husband is a second-year law student. We live on my salary. I decided I had to have an abortion. I didn't want to, but I thought I had to.'

Scott sighed. 'And Dr Highley performed the procedure at your request and now you're blaming him?'

'No. That's not true. He told me to come back the next day. And I did. He took me to an operating room in the hospital. He left me, and I knew – I *knew* – that no matter how we managed, I wanted my baby. Dr Highley came back; I was sitting up. I told him I'd changed my mind.'

'And he probably told you that one out of two women say the same thing at that moment.'

'He said, "Lie down." He pushed me down on the table.'

'Was anyone else in the room? The nurse?'

231

'No. Just the doctor and me. And I said, "I know what I'm saying." And – '

'And you allowed him to persuade you?'

'No. No. I don't know what happened. He jabbed me with a needle while I was trying to get up. When I woke up, I was lying on a stretcher. The nurse said it was all over. She said I should rest for a while.'

'You don't remember the procedure?'

'Nothing. Nothing. The last I remember is trying to get away.' Her mouth worked convulsively. 'Trying to save my baby. I wanted my baby. Dr Highley took my baby from me.'

A harsh, pained cry echoed Anna Horan's heartbroken sobs. Maureen's face was contorted, her voice a wail. 'That's exactly what he did to me.'

Richard stared at the weeping young women: the Japanese girl; Maureen with her red-gold hair and emerald-green eyes. And with absolute certainty he knew where he had seen those eyes before.

CHAPTER SEVENTY-FIVE

He got off at the second floor of the hospital and instantly felt the tension in the air. Frightened-looking nurses were scurrying in the hall. A man and woman in evening dress were standing by Nurse Renge's desk.

Quickly he walked over to the desk. His voice was disapproving and brittle as he asked, 'Nurse Renge, is there something wrong?'

'Doctor, it's Mrs DeMaio. *She's missing.*'

The woman was in her mid-thirties and looked familiar. Of course! She was Katie DeMaio's sister. What had made her come to the hospital?

'I'm Dr Highley,' he said to her. 'What does this mean?'

Molly found it hard to talk. Something had happened to Katie. She knew it. She'd never forgive herself. 'Katie . . .' Her voice broke.

The man with her interrupted. 'I'm Dr Kennedy,' he said. 'My wife is Mrs DeMaio's sister. When did you see her, Doctor, and what was her condition?'

This was not a man to be easily deceived. 'I saw Mrs DeMaio a little more than an hour ago. Her condition is not good. As you probably know, she's had two units of whole blood this week. The laboratory is analysing her blood now. I expect it to be low. As Nurse Renge will tell you, I expect to perform a D-and-C tonight rather than wait for the morning. I think Mrs DeMaio has been concealing the extent of her haemorrhaging from everyone.'

'Oh, God, then where is she?' Molly cried.

He looked at her. She'd be easier to convince. 'Your sister has an almost pathological fear of hospitals. Is it possible that she would simply leave?'

'Her clothes are in the closet, Doctor,' Nurse Renge said.

'*Some* clothes may be in the closet,' he corrected. 'Did you unpack Mrs DeMaio's bag?'

'No.'

'Then you don't know what other articles of apparel she had with her?'

'It's possible,' Bill said slowly. He turned to Molly. 'Honey, you know it's possible.'

'We should have been here,' Molly told him. 'How bad is she, Doctor?'

'We must find her and get her back here. Would she be likely to go to her own home or to yours?'

'Doctor – ' Nurse Renge's timid voice had a tremor – 'that sleeping pill should have made Mrs DeMaio fall asleep. It was the strongest one you ever ordered.'

He glowered at her. 'I ordered it for the very reason that I understood Mrs DeMaio's anxiety. You were told to see that she swallowed it. She did not want the pill. Did you watch her take it?'

'I saw her put it in her mouth.'

'Did you watch her swallow it?'

'No . . . not really.'

He turned his back on the nurse in a gesture of contempt. He spoke to Molly and Bill, his voice reflective, concerned. 'I hardly think Mrs DeMaio is wandering around the hospital. Do you agree that she might have left of her own volition? She could simply have gotten on the elevator, gone to the lobby and walked out with the visitors who are coming and going all evening. Do you agree that's possible?'

'Yes. Yes. I do.' Molly prayed, Please let it be that way.

'Then let's hope and expect that Mrs DeMaio will be home very shortly.'

'I want to see if her car is in the parking lot,' Bill said.

The car. He hadn't thought about her car. If they started looking for her in the hospital now . . .

Bill frowned. 'Oh, hell, she's still got that loan car. Molly, what make is it? I don't think I've seen it.'

I . . . I don't know,' Molly said.

Edgar Highley sighed. 'I think even if you could identify her car, you'd be wasting your time looking in the parking lot. I would suggest that you phone her home. If she's not there, go and wait to see if she comes in. She's scarcely been gone an hour now. When you do contact her, please insist she return to the hospital. You can stay with her, Mrs Kennedy. Doctor, if you feel it will comfort Mrs DeMaio, I would be glad to have you with me in the operating room. But we must not allow that haemorrhaging to continue. Mrs DeMaio is a very sick girl.'

Molly bit her lip. 'I see. Thank you, Doctor. You're very kind. Bill, let's just go to Katie's house. Maybe she's there now and not answering the phone.'

They turned from him. They believed him. They would not suggest searching the hospital for several hours at least. And that was all he needed.

He turned to the nurse. In her own stupid, blundering way she had been an asset. Of course Katie had never swallowed that sleeping pill. Of course he was justified in having ordered it.

'I am sure that we'll be hearing from Mrs DeMaio shortly,' he said. 'Call me immediately when you do. I'll be at my home.' He smiled. 'I have some records to complete.'

CHAPTER SEVENTY-SIX

'We must seize Dr Highley's records before he has a chance to destroy them. To the best of your knowledge, does he keep all his records in his office?'

Jiro Fukhito stared at Richard. He had gone to the Prosecutor's office prepared to make a statement. They had listened to him almost impatiently, and then Dr Carroll had outlined his incredible theory.

Was it possible? Jiro Fukhito reviewed the times when suspicions had formed in his mind, then were calmed by Highley's obstetrical genius. *It was possible.*

Records. They had asked him about records. 'Edgar Highley would never keep records that suggest malfeasance in his office at the hospital,' he said slowly. 'There is always the danger of a malpractice subpoena. However, he frequently takes files to his home. I never could understand why he did that.'

'Have search warrants sworn out immediately,' Scott told Charley. 'We'll hit the office and his home simultaneously. I'll take the squad to the house. Richard, you come with me. Charley, you and Phil take the office. We'll pick up Highley as a material witness. If he's not there, I want a stakeout on the house and we'll nab him as soon as he gets home.'

'What worries me is that there may be someone he's experimenting on now,' Richard said. 'I'll lay odds that the hair shafts the lab found on Edna and Vangie's bodies came from Highley.' He looked at his watch. It was nine thirty. 'We'll wrap this up tonight,' he predicted.

He wished Katie were here. She'd be relieved to know that Chris Lewis was about to be eliminated as a suspect. Her hunch about Lewis had been right. But his own hunch about Highley had been right too.

Dr Fukhito stood up. 'Do you need me any longer?'

'Not right now, Doctor,' Scott said. 'We'll be in touch with you. If by any chance you happen to hear from Dr Highley before we arrest him, please do not discuss this investigation with him. You understand that?'

Jiro Fukhito smiled wearily. 'Edgar Highley and I are not friends. He would have no reason to call me at home. He hired me because he knew he would have a hold over me. How right he was. Tonight I shall analyse my own conduct and determine how many times I have forced back suspicions that should have been explored. I dread the conclusion I shall reach.'

He left the room. As he walked down the corridor, he saw a nameplate on a door: MRS K. DEMAIO. Katie DeMaio. Wasn't she supposed to have gone into the hospital tonight? But of course, she never would go through with her operation while Edgar Highley was under investigation.

Jiro Fukhito went home.

CHAPTER SEVENTY-SEVEN

She was drifting down a dark corridor. Way at the very end there was a light. It would be warm when she got there. Warm and safe. But something was holding her back. There was something she had to do before she died. She had to make them know what Dr Highley was. Her finger was dripping blood now. She could feel it. She was lying on the floor. It was so cold. All these years she'd had nightmares that she'd die in the hospital. But it wasn't so bad after all. She'd been so afraid of being alone. Alone without Daddy, then alone without John. So afraid of risking pain. We are all alike. We're born alone and die alone. There's really nothing to be afraid of. Couldn't she possibly smear Dr Highley's name on the floor with her finger? He was insane. He had to be stopped. Slowly, painfully, Katie moved her finger. Down, across, down again. H . . .

CHAPTER SEVENTY-EIGHT

He got home at quarter past nine. The gratifying sense of having at last eliminated the final threat gave him a sense of total buoyancy. He had finished eating less than an hour ago, but somehow could not even remember the meal. Perhaps Hilda had left something for a snack.

It was better than he had hoped. Fondue. Hilda made remarkably good fondue. It was perhaps her best culinary accomplishment. He lit the Sterno can under the pot, adjusted it to a low flame. A crisp loaf of French bread was in a basket, covered by a damask napkin. He'd make a salad; there was sure to be arugula. He'd instructed Hilda to buy some today.

While the fondue heated, he would complete Katie DeMaio's file. He was anxious to be finished with it. He wanted to think about the two patients tomorrow: the donor and the recipient. He was confident that he could duplicate his success.

But was that enough? Wouldn't it be more interesting if the recipient were given twins to carry? Two alien foetuses from separate donors

The immuno-reactive theory he'd perfected might break down. Almost certainly it would. But how long would it take? What specific problems would develop?

He went into the library, opened the desk drawer and withdrew Katie DeMaio's file from the hidden compartment. On the last page he made a final entry:

Patient entered hospital at approximately 6.00 p.m. with blood pressure 100/60, haemoglobin no more than 10 grams. This physician administered the final two cumadin pills at 7.00 p.m. At 8.30 this physician returned to Mrs DeMaio's room and administered 5 ml. heparin by injection. Mrs DeMaio awakened briefly. In a near-comatose state she asked this physician, 'Why did you kill Vangie Lewis?'

This physician left Mrs DeMaio to obtain more heparin. Obviously it was impossible to allow Mrs DeMaio to repeat that question before witnesses. When this physician returned, patient had

left room. Probably realizing what she had said, she tried to escape. Patient was apprehended and another 5 ml of heparin was administered. Patient will haemorrhage to death tonight in Westlake Hospital.

This file is now closed.

He put down his pen, stretched, walked over to the wall safe and opened it. Bathed in light from the crystal sconces, the buff-coloured files took on an almost golden sheen.

They *were* golden: the records of his genius at his fingertips. Expansively he lifted them all out, laid them on his desk. Like a Midas savouring his treasure, he ran his fingers over the name tabs. His great successes. Berkeley and Lewis. His fingers stopped and his face darkened. Appleton, Carey, Drake, Elliot . . . failures. Over eighty of them. But not really failures. He had learned so much. They had all contributed. Those who had died, those who had aborted. They were part of the history.

Lewis. An addendum was necessary. To Vangie's file he added an account of his meeting with Emmet Salem.

The fondue must be ready. Irresolutely he looked at the files. Should he put them away now or give himself the pleasure of reading some of them? Perhaps he should study them. This week had been so difficult. He needed to refresh himself concerning some of the drug combinations he would want to use in the new case.

From somewhere in the distance a sound was beginning to penetrate the library: the wailing shriek of police sirens carried by the bone-chilling wind. The sound crescendoed into the room, then abruptly ceased. He hurried to the window, snatched back the drapery and glanced out. A police car had pulled into the driveway. The police were here!

Had Katie been found? Had she been able to talk? With lightning movements he ran to the desk, stacked the files, replaced them in the still-open safe, closed it and slid back the panel.

Calm. He must be calm. His skin felt clammy. His lips and knees were rubbery. He must control himself. There was one last desperate card in the deck that he could always play.

If Katie had talked, it was all over.

238

But if the police were here for another reason, he might still be able to outwit them. Maybe Katie was already dead and her body had been found. Remember the questions and accusations when Claire died. They'd come to nothing. There had been absolutely no proof.

All the possibilities and consequences were exploding in his mind at once. It was exactly the same as during an operation or a delivery when something abruptly went wrong and he had to make an irrevocable decision.

And then it came. The icy, deliberate calm, the sense of power, the godlike omniscience that never failed him during difficult surgery. He felt it flowing through his body and brain.

There was a sharp, authoritative rap at the door. Slowly, deliberately, he smoothed his hair. His fingers, now miraculously dry and warm, tightened the knot in his tie. He walked to the front door and opened it.

CHAPTER SEVENTY-NINE

As the squad car raced towards Edgar Highley's home, Scott methodically reviewed the statements he'd heard in the past few hours from Chris Lewis, Gertrude Fitzgerald, Gana Krupshak, Jiro Fukhito, Anna Horan and Maureen Crowley.

Seemingly they pointed in one direction: to Dr Edgar Highley, placing him under grave suspicion of malpractice, malfeasance and murder.

Not three hours ago, most of this same circumstantial evidence had pointed to Chris Lewis.

Scott thought of Pick Up Sticks, the game he'd played as a kid. You had to remove the sticks from the pile, one by one, without disturbing the rest of them. If you so much as jiggled another stick, you lost. It was a game Scott had played skilfully. But the trouble was that almost always, no matter how much care he took, the pile would collapse.

Circumstantial evidence was like that. Piled up, it looks impressive. Take it apart piece by piece and it caves in.

Richard was sitting beside him on the back seat of the squad car. It was because of Richard's insistence on slanting all the evidence against Edgar Highley that they were here now rushing through Parkwood with sirens screeching. Richard had heated this investigation to fever pitch by arguing that Highley might destroy evidence if he knew he was under suspicion.

Edgar Highley was a prominent physician, an excellent obstetrician. A lot of important people were fervently indebted to him because of the babies he had delivered in their families. If this turned out to be a witch-hunt, the Prosecutor's office would be under attack from the press and the public.

'This stinks.' Scott did not realize he'd spoken aloud.

Richard, deep in thought, turned to him frowning. 'What stinks?'

'This whole business: this search, this assumption that Highley is a combination of genius and murderer. Richard, what proof have we got? Gertrude Fitzgerald *thinks* Highley was going into the night-table drawer for the shoe. Chris Lewis *thinks* he caught a glimpse of Highley in the Essex House. You *think* Highley has performed medical miracles.

'Look, even if the grand jury returns an indictment, which I doubt it will, a good lawyer could have this whole mess dismissed maybe without a trial. I've half a mind to turn around right now.'

'Don't!' Richard grasped Scott's arm. 'For God's sake, we've got to seize his records.'

Scott hunched back in the seat, pulling his arm free.

'Scott,' Richard urged, 'forget everything except the number of maternity deaths at Westlake. That alone is sufficient reason for an investigation.'

The squad car swerved around a corner. They were in the elegant west section of Parkwood. 'All right,' Scott snapped. 'But remember, Richard, by tomorrow morning the two of us may be regretting this excursion.'

'I doubt it,' Richard said shortly. He wished he could overcome the growing worry that was grinding the pit of his stomach. It had nothing to do with this moment, this case.

It was Katie. He was desperately, irrationally worried about Katie. Why?

The car pulled into a driveway. 'Well, this is it,' Scott said sourly. The two detectives who were in the front seat jumped out of the car. As Richard started to get out, he noticed the movement of drapery in a window at the far right of the house.

They had parked behind a black car with MD plates. Scott touched the hood. 'It's still warm. He can't have been here long.'

The younger detective who had driven the car rapped sharply on the front door. They waited. Scott stamped his feet impatiently, trying to warm them. 'Why don't you ring the doorbell?' he asked irritably. 'That's what it's there for.'

'We were seen,' Richard said. 'He knows we're here.'

The young investigator had just raised his finger to the bell when the door opened. Edgar Highley was standing in the foyer. Scott spoke first. 'Dr Highley?'

'Yes?' The tone was cold and questioning.

'Dr Highley, I'm Scott Myerson, the Valley County Prosecutor. We have a search warrant for these premises, and it is my duty to inform you that you have become a suspect in the wrongful deaths of Vangie Lewis, Edna Burns and Dr Emmet Salem. You have the right to consult a lawyer. You can refuse to answer questions. Anything you say may be used against you.'

Suspect. They weren't sure. They hadn't found Katie. Every shred of evidence had to be circumstantial. He stepped aside, opening the door wider to allow them to enter. His voice was brittle with controlled fury as he said, 'I cannot understand the reason for this intrusion, but come in, gentlemen. I will answer any questions you have; you are welcome to search my home. However, I must warn you, when I consult a lawyer it will be to bring suit against Valley County and against each one of you personally.'

When he'd left Christ Hospital in Devon, he'd threatened to sue if any word of the investigation was leaked. And for the most part it had been kept quiet. He'd managed to see his file in the Queen Mary Clinic in Liverpool and there was no reference to it.

Deliberately he led them into the library. He knew he made an imposing figure sitting behind the massive Jacobean desk. It was vital that he unnerve them, make them afraid to question too closely.

With a gesture that barely escaped being contemptuous, he waved them to the leather couch and chairs. The Prosecutor and Dr Carroll sat down; the other two men did not. Scott handed him the printed *Miranda* warning. Scornfully he signed it.

'We'll proceed with the search,' the older detective said politely. 'Where do you keep your medical records, Dr Highley?'

'At my office of course,' he snapped. 'However, please satisfy yourselves. I'm sure you will. There is a file drawer in this desk with personal papers.' He stood up, walked over to the bar and poured Chivas Regal into a crystal tumbler. Deliberately he added ice and a splash of water. He did not go through the ritual of offering a drink to the others. If they'd come even minutes sooner he would still have had Katie's file in the desk drawer. They were trained investigators. They might notice the false bottom in that drawer. But they would never discover the safe – not unless they tore the house apart.

He sat down in the high-backed striped velvet chair near the fireplace, sipped the scotch and eyed them coldly. When he'd come into the library he'd been so preoccupied that he hadn't noticed the fire Hilda had laid for him. It was burning splendidly. Later he'd have the fondue and wine here.

The questions began. When had he last seen Vangie Lewis?

'As I told Mrs DeMaio . . .'

'You are sure, Doctor, that Mrs Lewis did not enter your office Monday night after leaving Dr Fukhito?'

'As I told Mrs DeMaio . . .' They had no proof. Absolutely no proof.

'Where were you Monday night, Doctor?'

'Home. Right where you see me now. I came home directly after my office hours.'

'Did you receive any phone calls?'

'None that I recall.' The answering service had taken no messages Monday night. He'd checked.

'Were you in Edna Burns's apartment on Tuesday night?'

His smile, contemptuous. 'Hardly.'

'We'll want some hair samples from you.'

Hair samples. Had some been found on Edna or in that apartment? How about Vangie? But he'd been in Edna's apartment with the police on Wednesday night. Vangie always wore that black coat to the office. Even if strands of his hair had been found near the dead women, they could be explained.

'Were you in the Essex House Hotel last night after five p.m.?'

'Absolutely not.'

'We have a witness who is prepared to swear that he saw you get off the elevator there at approximately five thirty.'

Who had seen him? He had glanced around the lobby as he got off the elevator. He was certain that no one he knew well was there. Maybe they were bluffing. Anyhow, eyewitness identification was notoriously unreliable.

'I was *not* in the Essex House last night. I was in New York at the Carlyle! I dine there frequently; in fact to my dismay my medical bag was stolen while I was dining there.'

He'd give gratuitous information; make it seem as though he were becoming co-operative. It had been a mistake to mention Katie DeMaio's name. Would it be natural to tell these people that she was missing from the hospital? Obviously they didn't know she was a patient there. The sister had not yet contacted them. No. Say nothing about it. Doctor-patient confidentiality. Later he'd explain, 'I would have told you, but of course assumed that Mrs DeMaio had fled the hospital in nervous anxiety. I thought she would be troubled to have that fact a matter of record on her job.'

But it was foolish to have mentioned the theft.

'What was in your bag?' The Prosecutor's interest seemed perfunctory.

'A basic emergency kit, a few drugs. Hardly worth the thief's effort.' Should he mention that it contained files? No.

The Prosecutor was hardly listening. He beckoned to the younger investigator. 'Get that package out of the car.'

What package? Edgar Highley's fingers gripped the glass. Was this a trick?

They sat in silence, waiting. The detective returned and handed a small parcel fastened with a rubber band to Scott. Scott yanked the rubber band and pulled off the wrapping paper, revealing a battered shoe. 'Do you recognize this moccasin, Doctor?'

He licked his lips. Careful. Careful. Which foot would it fit?

Everthing depended on that. He leaned over, examined it. The *left* shoe, the one that had been in Edna's apartment. *They had not found his bag.*

'Certainly not. Should I recognize this shoe?'

'Vangie Lewis, your patient, wore it continually for several months. She saw you several times a week. And you didn't ever notice?'

'Mrs Lewis wore a pair of rather shabby shoes. I certainly do not address my attention to specifically recognizing one particular shoe when it's placed before me.'

'Did you ever hear of a Dr Emmet Salem?'

He pursed his lips. 'Possibly. The name seems familiar. I'd have to go through my records.'

'Wasn't he on staff with you at Christ Hospital in Devon?'

'Of course. Yes. He was visiting staff. Indeed, I do remember him.' How much did they know about Christ Hospital?

'Did you visit Dr Salem last night at the Essex House?'

'I believe that question has already been answered.'

'Were you aware that Vangie Lewis was carrying an Oriental baby?'

So that was it. Smoothly he explained: 'Mrs Lewis was becoming terrified at the prospect of giving birth. That explains it, does it not? She knew that she could never make anyone believe her husband was the father.'

Now they were asking about Anna Horan and Maureen Crowley. They were coming close; too close; like dogs baying as they closed in on their quarry.

'Those two young women are typical of many who demand abortions and then blame the physician when they experience emotional reactions. It's not uncommon, you know. Check with any of my colleagues.'

Richard listened as Scott persisted in his questioning. Scott was right, he thought bleakly. Together everything added up. Separately everything was refutable, explainable. Unless they could prove wrongful death in the maternity cases, it would be impossible to charge Edgar Highley with anything and make it stick.

Highley was so composed, so sure. Richard tried to think how his father, a neurologist, would react if he were questioned about the wrongful death of one of his patients. How would Bill Kennedy react? How would he, Richard, react both as a person and as a doctor? Not like this man – not with this sarcasm, this scorn.

It was an act. Richard was sure of it. Edgar Highley was acting. But how could they prove it? With sickening certainty he knew they'd never find anything incriminating in Highley's records. He was far too clever for that.

Scott was asking about the Berkeley baby. 'Doctor, you are aware that Mrs Elizabeth Berkeley gave birth to a baby who has green eyes. Isn't that a medical impossibility when both parents and all four grandparents have brown eyes?'

'I would say so, but clearly Mr Berkeley is not the father of that baby.'

Neither Scott nor Richard had expected the admission. 'That doesn't mean I know who the father is,' Edgar Highley said smoothly, 'but I seriously doubt that it is the obstetrician's business to delve into matters such as that. If my patient wishes to tell me that her husband is her baby's father, then so be it.'

A shame, he thought. He would have to defer fame a little longer. He'd never be able to admit the success of the Berkeley baby now. But there would be others.

Scott looked at Richard, sighed and stood up. 'Dr Highley, when you go to your office tomorrow you will learn that we have seized all your hospital and office records. We are deeply concerned at the number of maternity deaths at Westlake Hospital, and that matter is under intensive investigation.'

He was on safe ground. 'I invite the most minute scrutiny of all my patients' records. I can assure you that the Westlake maternity death ratio is remarkably low in consideration of the cases we handle.'

The smell of the fondue was filling the house. He wanted to eat it. He was so hungry. Unless it was stirred, it would surely burn. Just a few minutes more.

The phone rang. 'I'll let my service take it,' he said, then knew he could not. Undoubtedly it would be the hospital saying that Mrs DeMaio had not yet returned home and her sister was frantic. It might be the perfect opportunity to let the Prosecutor and Dr Carroll know about Katie's disappearance. He picked up the phone. 'Dr Highley here.'

'Doctor, this is Lieutenant Weingarden of the Seventeenth Precinct in New York. We've just arrested a man who answers the description of the person who stole a bag from the trunk of your car last night.'

The bag.

'Has it been recovered?' Something in his voice was giving him away. The Prosecutor and Dr Carroll were watching him curiously. The Prosecutor stalked over to the desk and openly reached for the other extension.

'Yes, we have recovered your bag, Doctor. That's exactly the point. Several of the items in it may lead to far more serious charges than theft. Doctor, will you describe the contents of your bag?'

'Some medicine – a few basic drugs; an emergency kit.'

'What about a patient's file from the office of a Dr Emmet Salem, a bloodstained paperweight and an old shoe?'

He could feel the hard, suspicious stare of the Prosecutor. He closed his eyes. When he spoke, his voice was remarkably controlled. 'Are you joking?'

'I thought you'd say that, sir. We're co-operating with the Valley County Prosecutor's office concerning the suspicious death of Dr Emmet Salem last night. I'll call the Prosecutor now. It looks as though the suspect might have killed Dr Salem in the process of a theft. Thank you, sir.'

He heard Scott Myerson's order to the New York policeman: 'Don't hang up!'

Slowly he replaced the receiver he was holding on the cradle. It was all over. Now that they had the bag, it was all over. Whatever chance he had had of bluffing his way through the investigation was finished.

The paperweight sticky with Emmet Salem's blood. The medical file on Vangie Lewis that contradicted the information in his office records. The shoe, that miserable filthy object.

If the shoe fits . . .

He stared down at his feet, objectively contemplating the patina of his handsome English cordovans.

They'd never stop searching now until they found the true files.

If the shoe fits wear it.

The moccasins had never fitted Vangie Lewis. The supreme irony was that they fitted *him*. As clearly as though he had walked in them, they tied him to the deaths of Vangie Lewis, Edna Burns, Emmet Salem.

Hysterical laughter rumbled inside him, shaking his stolid frame. The Prosecutor had completed the call. 'Dr Highley,' Scott Myerson's voice was formal, 'you are under arrest for the murder of Dr Emmet Salem.'

Edgar Highley watched as the detectives sitting at the desk stood up quickly. He hadn't realized the man had been taking notes. He watched as the detective pulled handcuffs from his pocket.

Handcuffs. Jail. A trial. Blobs of humanity passing judgement on *him*. He who had conquered the primary act of life, the birth process, a common prisoner.

He drew himself up. The indomitable strength was returning. He had performed an operation. Despite his brilliance the operation had failed. The patient was clinically dead. There was nothing left to do except turn off the life-sustaining apparatus.

Dr Carroll was looking at him curiously. From the moment of their Wednesday night meeting, Carroll had been hostile. Somehow Edgar Highley was sure that Richard Carroll was the man who had become suspicious of him. But he had his revenge. Katie DeMaio's death was his revenge on Richard Carroll.

The detective was approaching him. The handcuffs caught the glint of the fire.

He smiled politely at him. 'I have just remembered that I do have some medical records that might interest you,' he said. He walked over to the wall, released the spring that held the panel in place. The panel slid back. Mechanically he opened the wall safe.

He could gather up the records, make a dash for the fireplace. The fire Hilda had laid was fairly brisk now. Before they could stop him, he could get rid of the most important files.

No. Let them know his genius. Let them mourn it.

He lifted the files out of the safe, stacked them on the desk. They were all staring at him now. Carroll walked over to the desk. The Prosecutor still had his hand on the phone. One detective was waiting with the handcuffs. The other detective had just come back into the room. Probably he'd been going through the house snooping into his possessions. Dogs hounding their quarry.

'Oh, there is another case you'll want to have.'

He walked over to the table by the fireplace chair and reached for his scotch. Carrying it to the safe, he sipped it casually. The vial was there, right in the back of the safe. He'd put it away Monday night for possible future use. The future was now. He'd never expected it to end this way. But he was still in control of life and death. The supreme decision was his alone to make. A burning smell was permeating the room. Regretfully he realized it was the fondue.

At the safe he moved quickly. He flipped the vial open and dumped the crystals of cyanide into his glass. As understanding swept over Richard's face, he held up the glass in a mocking toast.

'Don't!' Richard shouted, throwing himself across the room as Edgar Highley raised the glass to his lips and gulped down the contents. Richard knocked the glass away as Highley fell, but knew it was too late. The four men watched futilely, helplessly, as Highley's screams and groans died into writhing silence.

'Oh, God!' the younger detective said. He bolted from the room, his face green.

'Why'd he do it?' the other detective asked. 'What a lousy way to die.'

Richard bent over the body. Edgar Highley's face was convulsed; foaming bubbles were blistering his lips. The protruding grey eyes were open and staring. He could have done so much good, Richard thought. Instead, he was an egocentric genius who used his God-given skill to experiment with lives.

'Once I got on the line with the New York police, he knew he couldn't lie or murder his way out any more,' Scott said. 'You were right about him, Richard.'

Straightening up, Richard went over to the desk and scanned the names on the files. BERKELEY. LEWIS. 'These are the records we're looking for.' He opened the Berkeley file. The first page began:

Elizabeth Berkeley, age 39, became my patient today. She will never conceive her own child. I have decided that she will be the next extraordinary patient.

'There's medical history here,' he said quietly.

Scott was standing over the body. 'And when you think that this nut was Katie's doctor,' he muttered.

Richard looked up from reading Liz Berkeley's file. 'What did you say?' he demanded. 'Are you suggesting that Highley was treating Katie?'

'She had an appointment with him Wednesday,' Scott replied.

'She had a *what*?'

'She happened to mention it when –' The phone interrupted him. Scott picked it up. 'Yes,' then said, 'I'm sorry, this is not Dr Highley. Who is calling, please?' His expression changed. Molly Kennedy. 'Molly!'

Richard stared. Apprehension strangled his neck muscles. 'No,' Scott said. 'I can't put Dr Highley on. What's the matter?'

He listened, then covered the mouthpiece with his hand. 'Oh, Jesus,' he said, 'Highley admitted Katie to Westlake tonight and she's missing.'

Richard yanked the phone from him. 'Molly, what's happened? Why was Katie there? What do you mean she's missing?'

He listened. 'Come on, Molly. Katie would never walk out of a hospital. You should know that. Wait.'

Dropping the phone, he frantically scattered the files on the desk. Near the bottom of the pile he found the one he dreaded to see. DeMAIO, KATHLEEN. Opening it, he raced through it, his face paling as he read. He came to the last paragraph.

With the calm of desperation, he picked up the phone 'Molly, put Bill on,' he ordered. As Scott and the detectives listened, he said, 'Bill, Katie is haemorrhaging somewhere in Westlake Hospital. Call the lab at Westlake. We'll need to hang a bottle of O negative the minute we find her. Have them ready to take a blood sample and analyse for haemoglobin, haematocrit and type and cross-match for four units of whole blood. Tell them to have an operating room ready. I'll meet you there.' He broke the connection.

Incredible, he thought. You can still function knowing that

already it may be too late. He turned to the detective at the desk. 'Call the hospital. Pull the search team from Highley's office and have them start looking for Katie. Tell them to look everywhere – every room, every closet. Get all the hospital personnel to help. Every second counts.'

Without waiting for instructions, the younger investigator ran to start up the car. 'Come on, Richard,' Scott snapped.

Richard grabbed Katie's file. 'We have to know what-all he's done to her.' For an instant he looked at Edgar Highley's body. They'd been seconds too late preventing his death. Would they be too late for Katie?

With Scott he hunched in the back of the squad car as it raced through the night. Highley had given Katie the heparin over an hour ago. It was fast-acting.

Katie, he thought, why didn't you tell me? Katie, why do you feel you have to go it alone? Nobody can. Katie, we could be so good together. Oh, Katie, we could have what Molly and Bill have. It's there waiting for us to reach out for it. Katie, you felt it too. You've been fighting it. Why? Why? If you'd only trusted me, *told* me you were seeing Highley. I'd never have let you go near him. Why didn't I see that you were sick? Why didn't I *make* you tell me? Katie, I want you. Don't die, Katie. Wait. Let me find you. Katie, *hang on* . . .

They were at the hospital. Squad cars were roaring into the parking lot. They ran up the stairs into the lobby. Phil, his face drawn into deep lines, was commanding the search.

Bill and Molly came running into the lobby. Molly was sobbing. Bill was deadly calm. 'John Pierce is on his way over. He's the best haematologist in New Jersey. They've got a reasonable supply of whole blood on hand here, and we can get more from the blood bank. Have you found her?'

'Not yet.'

The door to the fire stairs, partly ajar, burst open. A young policeman ran out. 'She's on the floor in the morgue. I think she's gone.'

Seconds later, Richard was cradling her in his arms. Her skin and lips were ashen. He could not get a pulse. 'Katie. Katie.'

Bill's hand gripped his shoulder. 'Let's get her upstairs. We'll have to work fast if there's any chance at all.'

CHAPTER EIGHTY

She was in a tunnel. At the end there was a light. It was warm at the end of the tunnel. It would be so easy to drift there.

But someone was keeping her from going. Someone was holding her. A voice. Richard's voice. 'Hang on, Katie, hang on.'

She wanted so not to turn back. It was so hard, so dark. It would be so much easier to slip away.

'Hang on, Katie.'

Sighing, she turned and began to make her way back.

CHAPTER EIGHTY-ONE

On Monday evening Richard tiptoed into Katie's room, a dozen roses in his hand. She'd been out of danger since Sunday morning, but hadn't stayed awake long enough to say more than a word or two.

He looked down at her. Her eyes were closed. He decided to go out and ask the nurse for a vase.

'Just lay them across my chest.'

He spun around. 'Katie.' He pulled up a chair. 'How do you feel?'

She opened her eyes and grimaced at the transfusion apparatus. 'I hear the vampires are picketing. I'm putting them out of business.'

'You're better.' He hoped the sudden moisture in his eyes wasn't noticeable.

She had noticed. With her free hand she gently reached up and brushed a finger across his eyelids. 'Before I fall asleep again, please tell me what happened. Otherwise I'll wake up about three in the morning and try to put it together. Why did Edgar

Highley kill Vangie?'

'He was experimenting on his patients, Katie. You know about the test-tube baby in England, of course.

'Highley was far more ambitious than to simply produce in vitro babies for their natural parents. What he set out to do was take foetuses from women who had abortions and implant those foetuses in the wombs of sterile women. And he did it! In these past eight years he learned how to immunize a host mother from rejecting an alien foetus.

'He had one complete success. I've shown his records to the fertility research lab in Mt Sinai Hospital, and they tell me that Edgar Highley made a quantum leap in blastocyst and embryonic research.

'But after that success, he wanted to break new ground. Anna Horan, a woman he aborted, claims that she changed her mind about the abortion, but that he knocked her out and took her foetus when she was unconscious. She was right. He had Vangie Lewis in the next room waiting for the implant. Vangie thought she was simply having some treatment to help her become pregnant with her own child. Highley never expected Vangie to retain the Oriental foetus so long, although his system had become perfected to such a degree that the race issue was really not a consideration.

'When Vangie didn't abort spontaneously, he couldn't bear to destroy the foetus. He decided to bring it to term, and then who would blame him if Vangie had a partly-Oriental child? The natural mother, Anna Horan, is married to a Caucasian.'

'He was able to suppress the immune system?' Katie remembered the elaborate charts in college science courses.

'Yes, and without harm to the child. The danger to the mother was much greater. He's killed sixteen women in the last eight years. Vangie was getting terribly sick. Unfortunately for her, she ran into Highley last Monday evening just as she left Fukhito. She told him she was going to consult her former doctor in Minneapolis. That would have been a risk, because a natural pregnancy for Vangie was a million-to-one shot, and any gynaecologist who had treated her would have known that.

'But it was when she mentioned Emmet Salem's name that she was finished. Highley knew that Salem would guess what had happened when Vangie produced a half-Oriental child, then swore that she'd never been involved with an Oriental man. Salem was in England when Highley's first wife died. He knew about the scandal.

'And now,' Richard said, 'that's enough of that. All the rest can wait. Your eyes are closing again.'

'No . . . You said that Highley had *one* success. Did he actually transfer a foetus and have it brought to term?'

'Yes. And if you had stayed five minutes longer at Molly's last Thursday night and seen the Berkeley baby, you could guess now who the natural mother is. Liz Berkeley carried Maureen Crowley's baby to term in her womb.'

'Maureen Crowley's baby.' Katie's eyes flew open, all sleepiness gone. She tried to pull herself up.

'Easy. Come on, you'll pull that needle out.' Gently he touched her shoulder, holding her until she leaned back. 'Highley kept complete case histories of what he did from the moment he aborted Maureen and implanted Liz. He listed every medication, every symptom, every problem until the actual delivery.'

'Does Maureen know?'

'It was only right to tell her and the Berkeleys and let the Berkeleys examine the records. Jim Berkeley has been living with the belief that his wife lied to him about artificial insemination. You know how Maureen felt about that abortion. It's been destroying her. She went to see her baby. She's one happy girl, Katie. She would have given it out for adoption if she had delivered it naturally. Now that she's seen Maryanne, sees how crazy the Berkeleys are about her, she's in seventh heaven. But I think you're going to lose a good secretary. Maureen's going back to college next fall.'

'What about the mother of Vangie's baby?'

'Anna Horan is heartbroken enough about the abortion. We saw no point in having her realize that her baby would have been born if Highley hadn't murdered Vangie last week. She'll have other children.'

Katie bit her lip. The question she'd been afraid to ask. She had to know. 'Richard, please tell me the truth. When they found me, I was haemorrhaging. How far did they have to go to stop the bleeding?'

'You're okay. They did the D-and-C. I'm sure they told you that.'

'But that's all?'

'That's all, Katie. You can still have a dozen kids if you want them.'

His hand reached over to cover hers. That hand had been there, had pulled her back when she was so near to death. That voice had made her want to come back.

For a long, quiet moment she looked up at Richard. Oh, how I love you, she thought. How very much I love you.

His troubled, questioning expression changed suddenly into a broad smile. Obviously he was satisfied at what he saw in her face.

Katie grinned back at him. 'Pretty sure of yourself, aren't you, Doctor?' she asked him crisply.

Helen MacInnes

Born in Scotland, Helen MacInnes has lived in the United States since 1937. Her first book, *Above Suspicion*, was an immediate success and launched her on a spectacular writing career that has made her an international favourite.

'She is the queen of spy-writers.' *Sunday Express*

'She can hang up her cloak and dagger right there with Eric Ambler and Graham Greene.' *Newsweek*

AGENT IN PLACE £1.35
THE SNARE OF THE HUNTER £1.25
THE UNCONQUERABLE £1.50
HORIZON £1.00
ABOVE SUSPICION £1.00
ASSIGNMENT IN BRITTANY £1.25
THE DOUBLE IMAGE £1.00
PRAY FOR A BRAVE HEART £1.00
PRELUDE TO TERROR £1.25
NORTH FROM ROME £1.35

Fontana Paperbacks

Fontana Paperbacks

Fontana is a leading paperback publisher of fiction and non-fiction, with authors ranging from Alistair MacLean, Agatha Christie and Desmond Bagley to Solzhenitsyn and Pasternak, from Gerald Durrell and Joy Adamson to the famous Modern Masters series.

In addition to a wide-ranging collection of internationally popular writers of fiction, Fontana also has an outstanding reputation for history, natural history, military history, psychology, psychiatry, politics, economics, religion and the social sciences.

All Fontana books are available at your bookshop or newsagent; or can be ordered direct. Just fill in the form and list the titles you want.

FONTANA BOOKS, Cash Sales Department, G.P.O. Box 29, Douglas, Isle of Man, British Isles. Please send purchase price, plus 8p per book. Customers outside the U.K. send purchase price, plus 10p per book. Cheque, postal or money order. No currency.

NAME (Block letters)

ADDRESS

乱序版

GRE

词汇精选

俞敏洪 ● 著

群言出版社
QUNYAN PRESS
· 北 京 ·

音频

图书在版编目(CIP)数据

GRE词汇精选：乱序版 / 俞敏洪编著. —北京：
群言出版社，2013（2020.11重印）
ISBN 978-7-80256-468-8

Ⅰ.①G… Ⅱ.①俞… Ⅲ.①GRE—词汇—自学参考资
料 Ⅳ.①H313

中国版本图书馆CIP数据核字（2013）第180386号

责任编辑：张 茜
封面设计：大愚设计

出版发行：群言出版社
地　　址：北京市东城区东厂胡同北巷1号（100006）
网　　址：www.qypublish.com（官网书城）
电子信箱：dywh@xdf.cn　qunyancbs@126.com
联系电话：010-62418641　65267783　65263836
经　　销：全国新华书店

印　　刷：三河市良远印务有限公司
版　　次：2013年10月第1版　2020年11月第20次印刷
开　　本：720mm×960mm　1/16
印　　张：32
字　　数：700千字
书　　号：ISBN 978-7-80256-468-8
定　　价：59.80元

美丽的鞭策（代序）

我做任何事情都不太容易抢占先机，因为天性有点与世无争，反映到学习和追求上就是不够上进，或者说没有进取心。1985年大学毕业后被留在北大当了老师，不是因为成绩优秀，而是因为当时北大公共英语迅速发展，严重缺老师，结果把我这个中英文水平都残缺不全的人留了下来。尽管当时我的教学水平不怎么样，但是却很喜欢北大宁静的生活，准备把一辈子托付给北大，在北大分给我的一间八平米的地下室里自得其乐，天天在见不到一丝阳光的房间里读着马尔克斯的《百年孤独》。整个楼房的下水管刚好从我房间旁边通过，二十四小时的哗哗水声传进耳朵，我把它听成美丽的瀑布而不去想象里面的内容。后来北大可怜我，把我从地下室拯救出来，搬到了北大十六楼同样八平米的宿舍里。每天早上打开窗户就能见到阳光，我感激得涕泗横流，决定把一辈子献给北大。

我是一个对周围事情的发展很不敏感的人。到今天为止，我对国内国际的政治形势和变化依然反应迟钝，认为这是大人物的事情，和我这样的草民没有太多关系。我对周围的人在做些什么反应也很迟钝，认为这是人家的私事，我没有知道的权利。在这种迟钝中，我周围的世界和人物都在悄悄地发生变化。中国已经向世界开放，出国的热潮在中国悄然兴起。我周围的朋友们都是奔走在风口浪尖上的人物，迅速嗅到了从遥远的国度飘过来的鱼腥味，偷偷地顺着味道飘来的方向前进（当时大家联系出国都不会让单位知道，甚至不愿意让朋友知道）。过了一段时间，我发现周围的朋友们都失踪了，最后收到他们从海外发来的明信片，才知道他们已经登上了北美大陆。

我依然没有生出太多的羡慕。我能从农村到北大就已经登天了，出国留学对于我来说是一件奢侈得不敢想的事情，还是顺手拿本《三国演义》读一读更加轻松。但不幸的是，我这时候已经结了婚，我不和别人比，我老婆会把我和别人比。她能嫁给我就够为难她的了，几乎是一朵鲜花插在了牛粪上，如果我太落后，这脸面往哪里搁呀？突然有一天我听到一声大吼：如果你不走出国门，就永远别进家门！我一哆嗦后立刻明白我的命运将从此改变。后来我发现，一个女人结婚以后最大的能力是自己不再进步，却能把一个男人弄得很进步或很失败。

老婆的一声吼远远超过了马克思主义的力量。从1988年开始我被迫为了出国而努力。每次我挑灯夜战TOEFL和GRE的时候，她就高兴地为我煮汤倒水；每次看到我夜读三国，她就杏眼圆睁，把我一脚从床上踹下。我化压力为动力，终于考过了TOEFL，又战胜了GRE，尽管分数不算很高，但毕竟可以联系美国大学了。于是开始选专业。但我的学习虽然是涉猎甚广，却对任何专业都没有真正的爱好和研究。病急乱投医，我几乎把美国所有的大学都联系了个遍。美国教授一个个鹰眼犀利，一下就看出来我是个滥竽充数的草包，连在太平洋一个小小岛屿上的夏威夷大学都对我不屑一顾。挣扎了三年，倾家荡产以后，我出国读书的梦想终于彻底破灭。

出国不成，活下去变成了我的第一选择，于是每天晚上出去授课赚取生活费用。三年多联系出国的经历，使我对出国考试有了很深的了解。而此时的中国已经进入了九十年代，大家已经开始明目张胆地为出国而拼命。北京的TOEFL、GRE班遍地开花。北大里面有TOEFL、GRE班，北大外面有很多培训机构也有TOEFL、GRE班。北大里面的班轮不到我去教，老资格的人把职位全占了，于是我就只能到外面去教，结果就影响了北大的生源，就得罪了北大，就被不明不白地给了一个行政记过处分。偷鸡不成反蚀一把米，出国没弄成，教书没挣到钱，反而连北大都待不下去了。我尽管不好胜，但也要脸，不像今天已经练就了死皮赖脸的本领，被处分了还怎么在学生面前露面啊？只能一狠心从北大辞了职。

于是就一心一意地搞英语培训。先是为别人教书，后来就发现自己干能挣更多的钱，就承包了一个民办学校的外语培训中心，先是搞TOEFL培训，后来又发现开GRE班比开TOEFL班更受欢迎，于是就开始搞GRE班。招来了几十个学生才发现没有任何老师能够教GRE的词汇，只能自己日夜备课，拼命翻各种英语大辞典，每天备课达十个小时，但上课时依然捉襟见肘，常常被学生的问题难倒，弄得张口结舌。为维护自己的尊严，我只能收起懒散的性情，开始拼命背英语词汇，家里的每一个角落都贴满了英语单词，最后居然弄破两本《朗文现代英汉双解词典》。男子汉不发奋则已，一发奋则几万单词尽入麾下。结果我老婆从此对我敬畏恩爱，如滔滔江水，绵绵不绝。

后来呢？后来就有了新东方学校，就有了《GRE词汇精选》这本书。最早写这本书时，中国还没有普及电脑，我就用一张卡片写一个单词和解释，在写完几千张卡片以后，再按照字母顺序整理出来送到出版社，结果出版社不收卡片，我只能又把几千张卡片抱回家，我老婆就在家里把一张张卡片上的内容抄在稿子上，每天都到深夜不辍。书终于出版了，由于用了红色封面被学生戏称为"红宝书"。后来为了不断跟上时代，又几经改版。由于有了电脑，修改起来也变得容易，不再需要任何人伏案抄写。但对我来说，这本书唯一的意义，就是直到永远都留在我感动中的——我老婆在灯光下帮我抄写手稿时的美丽背影。

俞敏洪

新东方教育科技集团董事长

1993年初版序言

GRE考生最头疼的事情就是背单词。要在两三个月内熟记大量的GRE词汇，并且还要了解这些单词的精确含义，真让人恨不得生出三头六臂来。本书的目的就是为了减轻考生背单词的负担，加快背单词的速度，让考生将更多的时间用在考题本身的学习上。下面我先谈一下本书的特色：

一、本书收词量是目前GRE词汇书中最多的一本，所选单词几乎全部来自GRE真题，并且对一些将来可能会考到的新单词进行了预测。所以只要背完本书，考试中的词汇量问题就能基本解决。

二、本书对大部分单词的记忆方法进行了说明，使考生记单词的速度至少提高一倍，有些单词甚至可以做到过目不忘。同时，部分单词配有例句或词组，使考生对单词的使用方法一目了然。

下面我再谈一下本书所提到的记忆方法。

一、词根词缀记忆法　　大部分英语单词都可以分成几个部分来记，它们通常的形式是：前缀+词根+后缀，如auto（自己）＋ bio（生命）＋ graph（写）＋ y（后缀），autobiography（写自己的生命→自传），这样就可以避免一个字母一个字母地死记硬背。英语中的基本词根、词缀不超过500个，只要了解了它们，就可以通过它们轻而易举地记上几千个单词。本书对反复出现的词根进行了详细解释和说明，并列举同根词进行参考，使记单词达到举一反三的效果。

二、分割联想记忆法　　对于没有词根的单词或词根难以记住的单词，本书采用了分割联想记忆法。所谓分割联想记忆法就是把一个单词分割成几个单词或几个部分，并用联想的方法记住。如：charisma（领导人的超凡魅力）可以这样记：cha看作China，ris看作rise，ma看作Mao，连起来为China rises Mao（中国升起了毛泽东）→超凡魅力。再如：adamant（坚定的）可以看作两个单词的组合：adam（亚当）＋ ant（蚂蚁），亚当和蚂蚁是坚定的人和动物。这样，"坚定的"一词就能记住了。有一点需要说明的是，这种方法是极不科学的，甚至是荒谬的，但为了记住单词，可以用尽一切手段。

三、寻根探源记忆法　　有些英文单词是外来词或因为某个人、物或社会事件所产生的单词，对于这一类的单词，只要了解其来源，一下子就能记住。如chauvinism（极度爱国主义），即来自一剧中主角Chauvin，他是拿破仑的士兵，狂热崇拜拿破仑及鼓吹以武力征服其他民族。再如，tantalize（惹弄，逗引）即来自希腊神话人物Tantalus，他因泄露天机，被罚立在齐下巴深的水中，头上有果树。口渴欲饮时，水即流失，腹饥欲食时，果子就被风吹去。本书对这一类单词的来源都作了说明，使大家一看到该单词即过目不忘。

四、比较记忆法　　有些英文单词拼写极为相似，这类单词如果并列在一起，就可以进行比较，并加强记忆。如：minnow（鲦鱼）和winnow（吹去杂质）；taunt（嘲弄）和daunt（恐吓）。如果将这些单词以比较的方式呈现，考生就能够一次记几个单词。本书把词形相同的单词都放到一起，使大家可以达到一箭数雕的目的。

五、单词举例记忆法　　对有些很短的单词和用法很特殊的单词，本书把它们放入具体的例句或词组中，使大家对于这些单词的用法十分清楚，以增强记忆，如shoal（浅滩；一群），例：strike on a shoal（搁浅）/ a shoal of tourists（大批游客），两组短语便把shoal的两个含义清楚地表达了出来。又如table一词，GRE中考的意义为"搁置，不加考虑"（table a suggestion），是所谓熟悉的单词不熟悉的意义，本书对这一类单词都进行了强调，并附例句说明。通过阅读本书，GRE中的常考多义词便能全部掌握。

本书的记忆方法讲完了，我还想再谈一下记GRE单词要注意的几个问题。

一、记GRE单词讲究的是迅速，只要你眼睛看到英文单词，能想起其中文意思，这个单词就算记住了，所以是"认"单词而不是"背单词"。如看到dilettante知道是"外行，业余爱好者"，看到emancipation知道是"解放"，这就够了，至于这些单词怎么拼写可以先不管，以后再说。本书把英文单词和释义部分分开，目的就是为了让你能够单独思考单词的含义。你在背完一页单词后，可以盖住右边的解释，再看一遍单词，边看边想这些单词的含义，能想起来就算过了关。

二、记单词讲究反复性。不管运用了什么样的记忆方法，说到底反复记忆是最好的方法，比如你今天背了100个单词用了30分钟，明天复习一下只要5分钟，再过几天复习一下仍只要5分钟，再过一星期复习一下还是5分钟，复习的间隔时间不断延长，记得就会越来越牢固。如果你记了100个单词10天都不看，一定会全部忘光，还得从头来，这就不合算了。请记住：学而时习之，不亦乐乎？

三、每天要给自己规定一定的任务量，或100个单词，或200个单词，不背完绝不罢休。可以采取自我奖惩的方式，如果完成了任务，就奖励一下自己，或美餐一顿，或看一场电影，或交朋会友。如果完不成则惩罚自己一下，惩罚方式当然由自己选择。另外，也可以采取互相监督的方式，找一个GRE的考伴，一起背单词，看谁能把规定的任务先完成，事实证明这种方法能激发起很高的积极性。

总之，记GRE单词不是件轻松的事情。本书只不过希望起到抛砖引玉的作用。如果你有更好的记忆方法，请主动运用到记单词中去，也希望你能告诉我，以进一步提高本书的质量。由于本书写作时间很短，所以中间一定会有大量的错误和不到之处，甚至会有很可笑的地方，希望得到大家的谅解和批评指正。对于在本书写作过程中给予我极大鼓励和帮助的各位朋友，以及给予我督促和动力的广大GRE学员，我在此表示衷心的感谢。

俞敏洪谨识

1993年12月15日深夜两点，于北京

本书特点

特点〈1〉《GRE词汇精选》被广大G族亲切地称为"红宝书",自1993年首版以来一直深受广大考生青睐,迄今为止已改版九次,是一本久经考验的GRE词汇精品书。本书影响了几十万的GRE考生,凡是认真背过本书的学生,都在GRE考试中取得了优异的成绩。

特点〈2〉《GRE词汇精选:乱序版》是《GRE词汇精选》的姊妹篇,收录词汇数量及内容相同,不同之处在于单词的排列方式。《GRE词汇精选》将所有单词按照字母顺序排列,而"乱序版"则采取乱序编排,没有任何规律。两种排列方式各有千秋,以满足考生学习单词的多样化需求,考生可以根据个人学习习惯进行自由选择。

特点〈3〉本书内容与以往版本相比有了重大的调整:单词数量有所减少。凡是在考试中出现的单词都一一收录,删去了在历年考试中从未出现过的单词。为顺应GRE考试改革的需要,这次改版对选词又进行了一次大幅度的筛选和调整。大致步骤如下:(1)对真题词汇进行计算机、词频及题型建模统计,以此为改版依据。(2)筛选出核心词汇(填空词和阅读词)、拓展词汇和数学词汇。分为计算机和人工两次加工完成,确保单词筛选的权威性和完整性。(3)考虑到核心词汇的重要性,根据韦氏词典给出英文释义进行人工筛选,同时根据真题给出单词短语和例句。(4)针对GRE改革后考试填空同义词题型特点,根据韦氏词典对核心词汇给出同义词,并对其进行加工筛选。

特点〈4〉改版后本书分为两个部分:第一部分的"核心词汇"收录了所有重要单词;第二部分的"拓展词汇"则根据对历年试题及GRE考试形势的分析给出。改版后的分类编排使本书成为迄今为止唯一一本涵盖此前GRE考试中出现的所有重点词汇并具有前瞻性的词汇宝典。

特点〈5〉本书为每一个重要单词配出了贴切、精炼的记忆方法,正文中以"记"标出。其中包括:词根词缀记忆法、分割联想记忆法和发音记忆法等。本书所倡导的记忆方法已经成为中国学生记忆单词的主流方法,其中联想记忆和发音记忆均是本书的独创。这些方法使英语单词记忆由枯燥的劳役变成了生动的游戏，可以帮助考生克服背单词的恐惧心理，增强记忆单词的趣味性，提高学习效率。此次改版对书中的记忆方法做出了一定程度的调整，修改后的记忆方法更加贴切、接近生活。此外，本书还在每页的底部设置了"返记菜单"，考生在结束每页的学习后可以及时进行复习和自测，有助于巩固对单词的掌握。

特点〈6〉本书给大量的重要单词配上了同根词"同"等，扩大横向词汇量，起到了记单词举一反三的效果，使记单词的自然重复率达到三倍以上。

特点〈7〉本书给单词配上了简单明了的英文注解。英文注解所使用的参考词典为ETS出题常用的Webster's Merriam-Webster、New World Thesaurus等词典，有助于考生更准确地理解单词释义。

特点〈8〉本书给部分单词配以常考搭配或经典实用的例句，便于考生了解单词用法，并在具体语境中加深对单词的理解。

特点〈9〉为了增加学习的趣味性，加深对单词的记忆，本书为一些单词配上了生动有趣的漫画插图。这使得记单词由枯燥的劳役变成了生动的游戏，极大地克服了学生对背单词的恐惧心理，提高了学习效率。

特点〈10〉本书提供600分钟的录音，对书中所有英文单词（美式发音）及其中文释义进行了朗读。考生可以登录封面上的网址下载本书音频，或通过扫描书中二维码收听及下载相关音频，在听单词发音的同时可以更有效地提高对单词的理解和记忆。

祝每位在备考中的考生都能痛并快乐着，在考试中超越自我，取得理想的成绩，做到"无愧我心"！

如何使用本书

本书对反复出现的词根进行了解释和说明，使记单词达到举一反三的效果。

英文注解简单明了，帮助考生精确了解词义。同时，英文注解后也加上了常考的同义词，达到了单词联合记忆的目的。

institution [ˌɪnstɪˈtuːʃn]	*n.* 机构(an established organization or corporation); 制度 记 来自 institute(*v.* 设立，创立；制定) 例 During the 1960's assessments of the family shifted remarkably, from general endorsement of it as a worthwhile, stable *institution* to wide spread censure of it as an oppressive and bankrupt one whose dissolution was both imminent and welcome.
warrantable [ˈwɔːrəntəbl]	*adj.* 可保证的，可承认的(capable of being warranted)
resonant [ˈrezənənt]	*adj.* (声音)洪亮的(enriched by resonance); 回响的，共鸣的(echoing) 记 词根记忆：re(反) + son(声音) + ant → 回声 → 回响的
crash [kræʃ]	*v.* 猛撞 (to break violently and noisily); 猛冲直闯 (to enter or attend without invitation or paying); 撞碎 (to break or go to pieces with or as if with violence and noise) 记 象声词：破裂声 → 撞碎
trauma [ˈtrɔːmə]	*n.* 创伤，外伤(an injury to living tissue caused by an extrinsic agent) 例 Because of the *trauma* they have experienced, survivors of a major catastrophe are likely to exhibit aberrations of behavior and may require the aid of competent therapists.
sophomoric [ˌsɑːfəˈmɔːrɪk]	*adj.* 一知半解的(conceited and overconfident of knowledge but poorly informed and immature)
formation [fɔːrˈmeɪʃn]	*n.* 组成，形成(thing that is formed); 编队，排列(an arrangement of a group of persons in some prescribed manner or for a particular purpose) 记 词根记忆：form(形状) + ation → 形成形状 → 形成
talented [ˈtæləntɪd]	*adj.* 天才的(showing a natural aptitude for sth.) 例 Gaddis is a formidably *talented* writer whose work has been, unhappily, more likely to intimidate or repel his readers than to lure them into his fictional world.
pilgrim [ˈpɪlɡrɪm]	*n.* 朝圣者(one who travels to a shrine as a devotee); (在国外的)旅行者 同 wayfarer
reverential [ˌrevəˈrenʃl]	*adj.* 表示尊敬的，恭敬的(expressing or having a quality of reverence) 例 The columnist was almost *reverential* when he mentioned his friends, but he was unpleasant and even acrimonious when he discussed people who irritated him.
unreserved [ˌʌnrɪˈzɜːrvd]	*adj.* 无限制的(without limit); 未被预订的(not reserved) 记 联想记忆：un(不) + reserved(预订的) → 未被预订的
captious [ˈkæpʃəs]	*adj.* 吹毛求疵的(quick to find fault; carping) 记 联想记忆：capt(拿) + ious → 拿(别人的缺点) → 吹毛求疵的
sordid [ˈsɔːrdɪd]	*adj.* 卑鄙的；肮脏的(dirty, filthy) 同 foul, mean, seedy
negotiable [nɪˈɡoʊʃiəbl]	*adj.* 可协商的(capable of being negotiated); 可通行的 同 navigable, passable

□ institution	□ warrantable	□ resonant	□ crash	□ trauma	□ sophomoric
□ formation	□ talented	□ pilgrim	□ reverential	□ unreserved	□ captious
□ sordid	□ negotiable				

联想记忆通过单词的分拆、谐音和词与词之间的联系将难词化简，轻松高效地记忆单词。

本书为重要单词提供了同义词等，扩大了横向词汇量。

每页底部设有返记菜单，考生结束每页的学习后可以及时进行复习和自测，有助于巩固对单词的掌握。

单词配以常考搭配或经典例句，便于考生了解单词用法，并在具体语境中加深对单词的理解。

幽默有趣的插图在解释单词含义、帮助考生记忆的同时，增加了学习的趣味性。

monumental [ˌmɑːnjuˈmentl]	*adj.* 极大的（massive；impressively large）；纪念碑的（built as a monument） 记 来自 monument（*n.* 纪念碑）
awe [ɔː]	*n./v.* 敬畏（to cause a mixed feeling of reverence and fear） 记 发音记忆：发音像 "噢" → 表示敬畏的声音 → 敬畏 搭 be in awe of... 对…望而生畏；对…感到害怕
cryptic [ˈkrɪptɪk]	*adj.* 秘密的，神秘的（mysterious；baffling） 记 词根记忆：crypt（秘密）+ ic → 秘密的
intransigent [ɪnˈtrænzɪdʒənt]	*adj.* 不妥协的（uncompromising） 记 联想记忆：in（不）+ transigent（妥协的）→ 不妥协的 例 Always circumspect, she was reluctant to make judgments, but once arriving at a conclusion, she was *intransigent* in its defense. 同 incompliant, intractable, obstinate, pertinacious

monumental

纪念碑

Genius only means hard-working all one's life.
天才只意味着终身不懈地努力。

——俄国化学家 门捷列夫（Mendeleyev, Russian chemist）

□ monumental　　□ awe　　　□ cryptic　　　□ intransigent

收录的名人名言在激励考生奋发向上的同时，还能成为 GRE 写作中的引用素材。笔记区可供考生记录学习过程中的心得。

配有 600 分钟录音，对所有英文单词及其中文释义进行了朗读。

目　录

美丽的鞭策（代序）
1993 年初版序言
本书特点
如何使用本书

核心词汇

拓展词汇

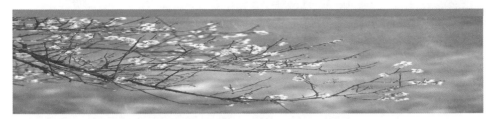

unidimensional [ˌjuːnɪdaɪˈmenʃənl]	*adj.* 一维的(one-dimensional) 记 词根记忆：uni(单一) + dimensional(空间的) → 一维的
agility [əˈdʒɪləti]	*n.* 敏捷(the quality or state of being agile) 记 来自 agile(*adj.* 灵活的，敏捷的)
retentive [rɪˈtentɪv]	*adj.* 有记性的，记忆力强的(capable of keeping the memory of)
flabby [ˈflæbi]	*adj.* (肌肉等)不结实的，松弛的(limp and soft; flaccid)；意志薄弱的(lacking force; weak) 参 flaggy(*adj.* 枯萎的), floppy(*adj.* 松软的)
overwhelm [ˌoʊvərˈwelm]	*v.* 战胜，征服，压倒(to overcome by superior force or numbers; crush; overpower)；淹没，席卷(to surge over and submerge; engulf) 记 组合词：over(在…上) + whelm(淹没) → 压倒；淹没
infamous [ˈɪnfəməs]	*adj.* 臭名昭著的(having a reputation of the worst kind) 同 notorious
fickleness [ˈfɪklnəs]	*n.* 浮躁；变化无常 同 inconstancy
unscrupulous [ʌnˈskruːpjələs]	*adj.* 肆无忌惮的(unprincipled) 记 联想记忆：un(不) + scrupulous(小心的) → 肆无忌惮的 例 The value of Davis' sociological research is compromised by his *unscrupulous* tendency to use materials selectively in order to substantiate his own claims, while disregarding information that points to other possible conclusions.
adopt [əˈdɑːpt]	*v.* 采纳，采用(to take up and practice or use)；正式接受，通过(to accept formally and put into effect) 记 词根记忆：ad + opt(选择) → 通过选择 → 采纳，采用 好！就用你 的方案吧！ adopt
chancy [ˈtʃænsi]	*adj.* 不确定的，不安的(uncertain in outcome or prospect, occurring by chance)

alienation [ˌeɪlɪəˈneɪʃn]	*n.* 疏远，离间（a withdrawing or separation of a person） 搭 alienation from 与…疏远
prestigious [preˈstɪdʒəs]	*adj.* 有名望的，有威望的（having prestige; honored） 记 来自 prestige（声望，威望）; pre（预先）+ stig（捆绑）+ e → 事先把人捆住 → 声望，威望 例 Many of the early Hollywood moguls sought to aggrandize themselves and enhance their celluloid empires by snaring *prestigious* writers and intellectuals as screenwriters. 同 distinguished, eminent, notable, prominent, renowned
contrition [kənˈtrɪʃn]	*n.* 悔罪，痛悔（remorse for having done wrong） 记 来自 contrite（*adj.* 痛悔的）
deplore [dɪˈplɔːr]	*v.* 悲悼，哀叹（to express or feel grief for）; 谴责（to condemn） 记 词根记忆：de（向下）+ plor（喊）+ e → 哀叹 同 bemoan, bewail, grieve, lament, moan
repetitive [rɪˈpetətɪv]	*adj.* 重复的（repetitious）; 反复性的（containing repetition） 记 词根记忆：re（再次）+ pet（寻找）+ itive → 再次寻找 → 重复的
congenital [kənˈdʒenɪtl]	*adj.* 先天的，天生的（existing as such at birth; innate） 记 词根记忆：con + gen（产生）+ ital → 与生俱来的 → 天生的
accredit [əˈkredɪt]	*v.* 授权（to give official authorization to or approval of） 搭 accredit sb. to 委任、委派
spartan [ˈspɑːrtn]	*adj.* 简朴的（of simplicity or frugality）; 刻苦的（strict self-discipline or self-denial） 记 来自 Sparta（斯巴达），希腊城邦，该地区的人以简朴刻苦著称
nonthreatening [nɑːn ˈθretnɪŋ]	*adj.* 不构成威胁的 记 联想记忆：non（不）+ threatening（威胁的）→ 不构成威胁的
irradiate [ɪˈreɪdieɪt]	*v.* 照射（to cast rays of light upon）; 照耀，照亮（to shine; light up） 记 词根记忆：ir（在里面）+ rad（光线）+ iate → 使在光线里面 → 照射; 照耀
opulent [ˈɑːpjələnt]	*adj.* 富裕的（very wealthy）; 充足的（profuse; luxuriant） 记 词根记忆：opul（财富）+ ent → 富裕的
cardiac [ˈkɑːrdiæk]	*adj.* 心脏的（of, relating to, situated near, or acting on the heart） 记 词根记忆：card（心）+ iac → 心脏的
self-doubt [ˌself ˈdaʊt]	*n.* 自我怀疑（a lack of faith or confidence in oneself）
estimable [ˈestɪməbl]	*adj.* 值得尊敬的（worthy of great respect）; 可估计的（capable of being estimated） 记 来自 estimate（*v.* 估计; 评价）
platitudinous [ˌplætɪˈtuːdənəs]	*adj.* 陈腐的（having the characteristics of a platitude） 搭 platitudinous remarks 陈腐的言论

piety	*n.* 孝顺，孝敬（fidelity to natural obligations（as to parents））；虔诚（religious devotion and reverence to God; devoutness）
['paɪəti]	例 Their *piety* was expressed in quotidian behavior: they worshipped regularly, according to all the regenerative processes of nature respect, and even awe.
excise	*v.* 切除，删去（to remove by cutting out or away）
['eksaɪz]	记 词根记忆：ex + cis(切) + e → 切出去 → 切除
solo	*adj.* 单独的（without companion）*n.* 独唱
['soʊloʊ]	记 词根记忆：sol(独自) + o → 单独的
stiffen	*v.* 使硬，使僵硬（to make stiff or stiffer）
['stɪfn]	同 congeal, harden, solidify
comic	*adj.* 可笑的；喜剧的（using comedy）*n.* 喜剧演员（comedian）
['kɑːmɪk]	搭 an inventive comic actor 一位有创造力的喜剧演员
refractory	*adj.* 倔强的，难管理的（stubborn; unmanageable）；（病）难治的（resistant to treatment or cure）
[rɪ'fræktəri]	记 词根记忆：re + fract(断裂) + ory → 宁折不弯 → 倔强的
automotive	*adj.* 汽车的，自动的（of, relating to, or concerned with self-propelled vehicles or machines）
[ˌɔːtə'moʊtɪv]	
ridge	*n.* 脊(如屋脊、山脊等)；隆起物
[rɪdʒ]	同 crest
talent	*n.* 天赋（the natural endowments of a person）；天才（a special often creative or artistic aptitude）
['tælənt]	记 联想记忆：tal(l)(高) + ent(人) → 高人 → 天才
	同 aptness, faculty, flair, genius
buckle	*n.* 皮带扣环 *v.* 扣紧（to fasten or join with a buckle）
['bʌkl]	搭 buckle up 扣紧安全带
inhibition	*n.* 阻止；抑制（the act of inhibiting）；抑制物（sth. that forbids, debars, or restricts）
[ˌɪn(h)ɪ'bɪʃn]	例 William James lacked the usual awe of death; writing to his dying father, he spoke without *inhibition* about the old man's impending death.
dividend	*n.* 红利，股利（bonus）
['dɪvɪdend]	记 词根记忆：di(分开) + vid(看) + end → 往不同方向看 → 红利
fanatic	*adj.* 狂热的，盲信的（marked by excessive enthusiasm and often intense uncritical devotion）*n.* 狂热者（a person marked or motivated by an extreme, unreasoning enthusiasm）
[fə'nætɪk]	记 来自 fan(*n.* 入迷者)
clemency	*n.* 温和（mildness, esp. of weather）；仁慈，宽厚（mercy）
['klemənsi]	记 和 cement(水泥)一起记
	同 caritas, charity, lenity
ideology	*n.* 思想体系，思想意识（a systematic body of concepts）
[ˌaɪdi'ɑːlədʒi]	记 联想记忆：ide(看作 idea，思想) + ology(学科) → 思想体系

□ piety	□ excise	□ solo	□ stiffen	□ comic	□ refractory
□ automotive	□ ridge	□ talent	□ buckle	□ inhibition	□ dividend
□ fanatic	□ clemency	□ ideology			

defamation	*n.* 诽谤，中伤(the act of defaming another)
[ˌdefəˈmeɪʃn]	同 aspersion, calumniation, denigration, vilification
disillusion	*v.* 使梦想破灭，使醒悟(to cause to lose naive faith and trust)
[ˌdɪsɪˈluːʒn]	记 联想记忆：dis(不) + illusion(幻想) → 不再有幻想 → 使梦想破灭，使醒悟
anterior	*adj.* 较早的，以前的(previous；earlier)
[ænˈtɪriər]	
encumber	*v.* 妨碍，阻碍(to impede or hamper)
[ɪnˈkʌmbər]	记 联想记忆：en + cumber(妨碍) → 妨碍
conformity	*n.* 一致；遵从，顺从(action in accordance with some specified standard or authority)
[kənˈfɔːrməti]	
vitriolic	*adj.* 刻薄的(virulent of feeling or of speech)
[ˌvɪtriˈɑːlɪk]	记 词根记忆：vitri(玻璃，引申为"刻薄") + olic → 刻薄的
	例 Although a few delegates gave the opposition's suggestions a *vitriolic* response, most greeted the statement of a counterposition with civility.
anticlimactic	*adj.* 突减的(of, relating to, or marked by anticlimax)
[ˌæntɪklaɪˈmæktɪk]	记 词根记忆：anti(相反) + climac(=climax 顶点) + tic → 与顶点相反 → 突减的
respiratory	*adj.* 呼吸的
[ˈrespərətɔːri]	例 Artificial light enhances the *respiratory* activity of some microorganisms in the winter but not in the summer, in part because in the summer their respiration is already at its peak and thus cannot be increased.
proclivity	*n.* 倾向(an inclination or predisposition toward sth.)
[prəˈklɪvəti]	同 leaning
constrict	*v.* 约束(to inhibit)；收缩(to make sth. tighter, smaller or narrower)
[kənˈstrɪkt]	记 词根记忆：con + strict(拉紧) → 拉到一起 → 收缩
connive	*v.* 默许；纵容(to feign ignorance of another's wrongdoing)；共谋(to conspire)
[kəˈnaɪv]	记 词根记忆：con + nive(眨眼睛) → 互相眨眼睛 → 共谋
resume	*v.* 重新开始，继续(to begin again after interruption)
[rɪˈzuːm]	记 词根记忆：re + sum(拿起) + e → 重新拿起 → 重新开始
controversial	*adj.* 引起或可能引起争论的(causing controversy)
[ˌkɑːntrəˈvɜːrʃl]	记 词根记忆：contro(相反) + vers(转) + ial → 反着转 → 引起或可能引起争论的
corroboration	*n.* 证实，支持(the act of corroborating)
[kəˌrɑːbəˈreɪʃn]	记 来自 corroborate (*v.* 支持；强化)
undecipherable	*adj.* 难破译的(not easily deciphered)
[ˌʌndɪˈsaɪfrəbl]	
haughty	*adj.* 傲慢的，自大的(blatantly and disdainfully proud)
[ˈhɔːti]	记 词根记忆：haught(=haut 高的) + y → 自视甚高的 → 傲慢的

rubbery [ˈrʌbəri]	*adj.* 橡胶似的，有弹性的（resembling rubber（as in elasticity, consistency, or texture））
supplant [səˈplænt]	*v.* 排挤，取代（to supersede by force or treachery） 记 词根记忆：sup(下面) + plant(种植) → 在下面种植 → 排挤，取代 例 When railroads first began to *supplant* rivers and canals as highways of commerce, they were regarded as blessings and their promoters were looked upon as benefactors.
institutionalize [ˌɪnstɪˈtuːʃənəlaɪz]	*v.* 使制度化（to make into an institution） 派 institutionalization(*n.* 制度化)
presuppose [ˌpriːsəˈpoʊz]	*vt.* 预先假定（to suppose beforehand）；以…为先决条件（to require as an antecedent in logic or fact）
succinct [səkˈsɪŋkt]	*adj.* 简明的，简洁的（marked by compact, precise expression） 记 词根记忆：suc(下面) + cinct(=gird 束起) → 原指把下面的衣服束起来方便干活 → 简洁的 例 You should delete this paragraph in order to make your essay more *succinct*. 同 concise, compendiary, compendious, curt, laconic
recede [rɪˈsiːd]	*v.* 后退，撤回（to move back; withdraw） 记 词根记忆：re(反) + ced(走) + e → 走回去 → 后退
derelict [ˈderəlɪkt]	*adj.* 荒废的（deserted by the owner; abandoned）；玩忽职守的（neglectful of duty; remiss）；疏忽的（negligent）*n.* 被遗弃的人（sb. abandoned by family and society） 记 词根记忆：de + re(向后) + lict(=linqu 留下) → 完全置后 → 被遗弃的人
hysteria [hɪˈstɪriə]	*n.* 歇斯底里症（a psychoneurosis marked by emotional excitability）；过度兴奋（behavior exhibiting emotional excess） 记 联想记忆：hyster(=hystero，子宫；癔症) + ia → 像患了癔症一样 → 歇斯底里症 例 During the Battle of Trafalgar, Admiral Nelson remained imperturbable and in full command of the situation in spite of the *hysteria* and panic all around him.
pollinate [ˈpɑːləneɪt]	*v.* 对…授粉（to carry out the transfer of pollen）
crater [ˈkreɪtər]	*n.* 火山口（a bowl-shaped cavity at the mouth of a volcano）；弹坑（a pit made by an exploding bomb）
indigenous [ɪnˈdɪdʒənəs]	*adj.* 土产的，本地的（native）；生来的，固有的（innate） 记 词根记忆：indi(内部) + gen(产生) + ous → 产生于内部的 → 本地的
immature [ˌɪməˈtʃʊr]	*adj.* 未充分成长的，未完全发展的（lacking complete growth, differentiation, or development）；（行为等）不成熟的（exhibiting less than an expected degree of maturity） 记 联想记忆：im(不) + mature(成熟的) → 不成熟的

□ rubbery □ supplant □ institutionalize □ presuppose □ succinct □ recede
□ derelict □ hysteria □ pollinate □ crater □ indigenous □ immature

5

provoke [prə'vouk]	*v.* 激怒(to incite to anger); 引起(to evoke); 驱使(to stir up purposely) 记 词根记忆: pro(在前) + vok (呼喊) + e → 在前面呼喊 → 激怒; 引起 例 For many young people during the Roaring Twenties, a disgust with the excesses of American culture combined with a wanderlust to *provoke* an exodus abroad.
skinflint ['skɪnflɪnt]	*n.* 吝啬鬼(miser; niggard) 记 参考词组: skin a flint(爱财如命)
inverse [ˌɪn'vɜːrs]	*adj.* 相反的(directly opposite); 倒转的(inverted) 记 词根记忆: in(反) + vers(转) + e → 反转 → 相反的; 倒转的
scourge [skɜːrdʒ]	*n.* 鞭笞(whip); 磨难(a cause of great affliction) *v.* 鞭笞; 磨难 记 和 courage(*n.* 勇气)一起记 例 One of the great killers until barely 50 years ago, tuberculosis ("consumption" as it was then named) seemed a *scourge* or plague rather than the long-term chronic illness it was.
dutiful ['duːtɪfl]	*adj.* 尽职的(filled with a sense of duty) 记 来自 duty(*n.* 责任)
boon [buːn]	*n.* 恩惠, 天赐福利(a timely blessing or benefit) 记 联想记忆: 从月亮(moon)得到恩惠(boon) → 天赐福利 搭 be a boon to 对…来说大有裨益
mural ['mjʊrəl]	*adj.* 墙壁的(of a wall) *n.* 壁画 记 词根记忆: mur(墙) + al → 墙壁的
transcend [træn'send]	*v.* 超出, 超越, 胜过(to rise above or go beyond the limit) 记 词根记忆: trans(超过) + (s)cend(爬) → 爬过 → 超越

mural

punishment ['pʌnɪʃmənt]	*n.* 惩罚, 刑罚(suffering, pain, or loss that serves as retribution); 虐待(severe, rough, or disastrous treatment) 例 A sense of fairness dictates that the *punishment* should fit the crime; yet, in actual practice, judicial decisions vary greatly for the same type of criminal offense.
unworldly [ʌn'wɜːrldli]	*adj.* 非世俗的(not swayed by mundane considerations); 精神上的(spiritual) 记 联想记忆: un(不) + world(世界, 尘世) + ly → 非世俗的 例 Without seeming *unworldly*, William James appeared wholly removed from the commonplaces of society, the conventionality of academy.
retaliate [rɪ'tælieɪt]	*v.* 报复, 反击(to get revenge) 记 词根记忆: re + tali(邪恶) + ate → 把邪恶还回去 → 报复
disgruntled [dɪs'grʌntld]	*adj.* 不悦的, 不满意的(annoyed or disappointed) 记 联想记忆: dis(不) + gruntle(使高兴) + d → 使不高兴 → 不悦的

□ provoke	□ skinflint	□ inverse	□ scourge	□ dutiful	□ boon
□ mural	□ transcend	□ punishment	□ unworldly	□ retaliate	□ disgruntled

rigid [ˈrɪdʒɪd]	*adj.* 严格的；僵硬的，刚硬的（stiff; not flexible or pliant） 记 词根记忆：rig(=rog 要求) + id → 不断要求 → 严格的 例 He was regarded by his followers, as something of a martinet, not only because of his insistence on strict discipline, but also because of his *rigid* adherence to formal details. 同 incompliant, inflexible, unpliable, unyielding
specialize [ˈspeʃəlaɪz]	*v.* 专门研究（to limit to a particular activity or subject） 记 来自 special(*adj.* 特殊的)
sumptuous [ˈsʌmptʃuəs]	*adj.* 豪华的，奢侈的（extremely costly, luxurious, or magnificent） 记 词根记忆：sumpt(拿，取) + uous → (把钱)拿出去 → 奢侈的 例 The *sumptuous* costumes of Renaissance Italy, with their gold and silver embroidery and figured brocades, were the antithesis of Spanish sobriety, with its dark muted colors, plain short capes, and high collars edged with small ruffs. 同 deluxe, palatial
deviant [ˈdiːviənt]	*adj.* 越出常规的（deviating especially from an accepted norm） 记 词根记忆：de(偏离) + vi(路) + ant → 偏离道路 → 越轨 → 越出常规的
complacence [kəmˈpleɪsns]	*n.* 自满（satisfaction with oneself）
mortality [mɔːrˈtæləti]	*n.* 死亡率（the rate of deaths） 记 词根记忆：mort(死亡) + ality(表性质) → 死亡率
underground [ˌʌndəˈɡraʊnd]	*adv.* 在地下；秘密地（in or into hiding or secret operation）*adj.* 地下的；秘密的 例 Just as astrology was for centuries an *underground* faith, countering the strength of established churches, so today believing in astrology is an act of defiance against the professional sciences. 同 subterranean, subterrestrial, underearth, underfoot
insight [ˈɪnsaɪt]	*n.* 洞察力（the power or act of seeing into a situation）；洞悉 记 联想记忆：in(进入) + sight(眼光) → 眼光深入 → 洞察力 例 Marison was a scientist of unusual *insight* and imagination who had startling success in discerning new and fundamental principles well in advance of their general recognition. 同 discernment, intuition, penetration, perception
towering [ˈtaʊərɪŋ]	*adj.* 高耸的（reaching a high point of intensity）；杰出的 记 联想记忆：tower(塔) + ing → 像塔一样的 → 高耸的
sobriety [səˈbraɪəti]	*n.* 节制（moderation）；庄重（gravity） 例 The sumptuous costumes of Renaissance Italy, with their gold and silver embroidery and figured brocades, were the antithesis of Spanish *sobriety*, with its dark muted colors, plain short capes, and high collars edged with small ruffs.

□ rigid	□ specialize	□ sumptuous	□ deviant	□ complacence	□ mortality
□ underground	□ insight	□ towering	□ sobriety		

accidental [ˌæksɪˈdentl]	*adj.* 偶然发生的（occurring unexpectedly or by chance） 记 来自 accident（*n.* 事故，意外）
accelerate [əkˈseləreɪt]	*v.* 加速（to increase the speed）；促进（to develop more quickly） 记 词根记忆：ac(加强) + celer(速度) + ate → 加速
abreast [əˈbrest]	*adv.* 并列，并排（side by side） 记 联想记忆：a + breast(胸) → 胸和胸并排 → 并排 搭 abreast of 与…并排
sultry [ˈsʌltri]	*adj.* 闷热的（very hot and humid; sweltering）；(人)风骚的（capable of exciting strong sexual desires）
understated [ˌʌndərˈsteɪtɪd]	*adj.* 轻描淡写的，低调的（avoiding obvious emphasis or embellishment） 同 unostentatious, unpretentious
rival [ˈraɪvl]	*n.* 竞争者，对手（one striving for competitive advantage）*v.* 竞争，与…匹敌（to attempt to equal or surpass） 记 联想记忆：对手(rival)隔河(river)相望，分外眼红 同 compete, contend, vie
resuscitate [rɪˈsʌsɪteɪt]	*v.* 使复活，使苏醒（to restore life or consciousness） 记 词根记忆：re + sus(在下面) + cit(引起) + ate → 再次从下面唤起来 → 使复活
obstinacy [ˈɑːbstɪnəsi]	*n.* 固执，倔强，顽固（the state of being obstinate; stubbornness） 记 词根记忆：ob(反) + stin(=stand 站) + acy → 反着站 → 固执，倔强
partiality [ˌpɑːrʃiˈæləti]	*n.* 偏袒，偏心（the state of being partial; bias） 记 来自 partial(*adj.* 有偏见的) 例 Although the revelation that one of the contestants was a friend left the judge open to charges of lack of disinterestedness, the judge remained adamant in her assertion that acquaintance did not necessarily imply *partiality*. 同 prejudice, proclivity, propensity, tendency
devoid [dɪˈvɔɪd]	*adj.* 空的，全无的（empty or destitute of） 记 词根记忆：de + void(空的) → 空的 搭 be devoid of... 缺乏…
notch [nɑːtʃ]	*n.* V 字形切口，刻痕；等级，档次 搭 top notch 大腕
reaffirmation [ˌriːˌæfərˈmeɪʃn]	*n.* 再肯定（renewed affirmation）
spiritedness [ˈspɪrɪtɪdnəs]	*n.* 有精神，活泼 同 liveliness, vivaciousness
overbalance [ˌoʊvərˈbæləns]	*v.* 使失去平衡（to cause to lose balance）
affectionate [əˈfekʃənət]	*adj.* 亲爱的，挚爱的（having affection or warm regard） 例 He is very *affectionate* towards his children.

□ accidental	□ accelerate	□ abreast	□ sultry	□ understated	□ rival
□ resuscitate	□ obstinacy	□ partiality	□ devoid	□ notch	□ reaffirmation
□ spiritedness	□ overbalance	□ affectionate			

slipshod [ˈslɪpʃɑːd]	*adj.* 马虎的，草率的（not exact or thorough） 同 careless, slovenly
perilous [ˈperələs]	*adj.* 危险的，冒险的（full of peril; hazardous） 记 来自 peril（ *n.* 危险）
engrave [ɪnˈɡreɪv]	*v.* 雕刻，铭刻（to cut or carve words or designs on a hard surface）；牢记，铭记（to impress sth. deeply on the memory or mind）
wrongheaded [ˌrɔːŋˈhedɪd]	*adj.* 坚持错误的，固执的（stubborn in adherence to wrong opinions or principles）
repudiate [rɪˈpjuːdieɪt]	*v.* 拒绝接受，回绝，抛弃（to refuse to accept） 记 词根记忆：re + pudi(=put 想) + ate → 重新思考 → 拒绝接受 例 Fashion is partly a search for a new language to discredit the old, a way in which each generation can *repudiate* its immediate predecessor and distinguish itself. 同 dismiss, reprobate, spurn
zealot [ˈzelət]	*n.* 狂热者（a zealous person） 同 bigot, enthusiast, fanatic
implausible [ɪmˈplɔːzəbl]	*adj.* 难以置信的（not plausible） 记 联想记忆：im(不) + plausible(可信的) → 难以置信的
modest [ˈmɑːdɪst]	*adj.* 谦虚的，谦逊的（humble; unassuming）；适度的（not large in quantity or size） 记 词根记忆：mod(方式；风度) + est → 做事有风度 → 谦虚的；适度的 例 The corporation expects only *modest* increases in sales next year despite a yearlong effort to revive its retailing business.
jeopardize [ˈdʒepərdaɪz]	*v.* 危及，危害（to endanger） 记 发音记忆："皆怕打死" → 当危及到自身安全时，谁都怕死 → 危及 同 compromise, hazard, imperil, jeopard
unqualified [ˌʌnˈkwɑːlɪfaɪd]	*adj.* 无资格的，不合格的（not having suitable qualifications）；无限制的，绝对的（not limited）
possessed [pəˈzest]	*adj.* 着迷的，入迷的（influenced or controlled by sth.） 记 来自 possess(*v.* 拥有；迷住)
dumbbell-like [ˈdʌmbelˌlaɪk]	*adj.* 哑铃状的 记 组合词：dumbbell(哑铃) + like(像) → 哑铃状的
nonchalance [ˌnɑːnʃəˈlɑːns]	*n.* 冷漠，冷淡（the quality or state of being nonchalant; casual lack of concern） 记 词根记忆：non(不) + chal(关心) + ance → 不关心 → 无动于衷 → 冷漠 例 Despite an affected *nonchalance* which convinced casual observers that he was indifferent about his painting and enjoyed only frivolity, Warhol cared deeply about his art and labored at it diligently.

过奖…

modest

□ slipshod	□ perilous	□ engrave	□ wrongheaded	□ repudiate	□ zealot
□ implausible	□ modest	□ jeopardize	□ unqualified	□ possessed	□ dumbbell-like
□ nonchalance					

9

collusive [kə'luːsɪv]	*adj.* 共谋的(having secret agreement or cooperation) 记 词根记忆：col(共同) + lus(大笑，玩) + ive → 一起玩 → 共谋的
outmoded [ˌaʊt'məʊdɪd]	*adj.* 过时的(no longer in fashion; obsolete) 记 联想记忆：out(出) + mode(时尚) + d → 不再时尚的 → 过时的
inherent [ɪn'hɪrənt]	*adj.* 固有的，内在的(involved in the constitution or essential character of sth.; belonging by nature or habit) 记 词根记忆：in(在里面) + her(黏附) + ent → 黏附在内的 → 固有的，内在的 搭 be inherent in 为…所固有
eradicate [ɪ'rædɪkeɪt]	*v.* 根除(to tear out by the roots; uproot)；扑灭(to exterminate) 记 词根记忆：e(出) + radic(根) + ate → 根除 同 abolish, annihilate, extirpate
suffrage ['sʌfrɪdʒ]	*n.* 选举权，投票权(the right of voting) 记 词根记忆：suf(=sub 下面) + frag(表示拥护的喧闹声) + e → 选举权
elaborate	[ɪ'læbərət] *adj.* 精致的，复杂的(marked by complexity, fullness of detail, or ornateness) [ɪ'læbəreɪt] *v.* 详尽地说明，阐明(to describe in detail) 记 联想记忆：e(出) + labor(劳动) + ate(使) → 辛苦劳动做出来的 → 精心制作的 → 精致的
molten ['məʊltən]	*adj.* 熔融的，熔化的(melted) 记 来自 melt(*v.* 融化，熔化)
hypothesis [haɪ'pɒθəsɪs]	*n.* 假设，假说(an unproved theory) 记 词根记忆：hypo(在…下面) + thesis(论点) → 下面的论点 → 假说
postoperative [ˌpəʊst'ɒpərətɪv]	*adj.* 手术后的(following a surgical operation) 搭 postoperative care 术后护理
premeditate [ˌpriː'medɪteɪt]	*v.* 预谋，预先考虑或安排(to plan, arrange, or plot in advance) 记 词根记忆：pre(预先) + med(注意) + itate → 事先就加以注意 → 预谋
frigid ['frɪdʒɪd]	*adj.* 寒冷的(very cold)；冷漠的，冷淡的(lacking in warmth and life) 记 词根记忆：frig(冷) + id(…的) → 寒冷的
vex [veks]	*v.* 使烦恼，使恼怒(to bring agitation to) 同 annoy, bother, fret, irk
stumble ['stʌmbl]	*v.* 绊倒(to strike one's foot against sth. and almost fall) 同 lurch, stagger, trip
contemptible [kən'temptəbl]	*adj.* 令人轻视的(despicable) 记 来自 contempt(*n.* 蔑视，轻视)
commentary ['kɒmənteri]	*n.* 实况报道(spoken description of an event as it happens)；(对书等的)集注(set of explanatory notes on a book) 记 词根记忆：comment(评论) + ary → 集注

hypothesis

哥德巴赫
1+1≠2

你不是一个人在战斗！

commentary

scrappy [ˈskræpi]	*adj.* 碎片的(made of disconnected pieces)；好斗的(liking to fight)；坚毅的(determined; gutsy)
territorial [ˌterəˈtɔːriəl]	*adj.* 领土的(of or relating to a territory)；地方的(nearby; local) 例 territorial economy 地方经济
galvanize [ˈgælvənaɪz]	*v.* 刺激，激起 (to stimulate)；电镀 (to plate metal with zinc, originally by galvanic action)；通电(to apply an electric current to) 记 来自 galvanic(*adj.* 电流的)
finicky [ˈfɪnɪki]	*adj.* 苛求的，过分讲究的(too particular or exacting; fussy) 记 单词 finical 的变体；fin(fine，精细的) + ical → 精细的 → 过分讲究的 同 dainty, fastidious, finicking
transferable [trænsˈfɜːrəbl]	*adj.* 可转移的(that can be moved from one place, person or use to another)
acquiescent [ˌækwiˈesnt]	*adj.* 默认的(inclined to acquiesce)
palatable [ˈpælətəbl]	*adj.* 美味的(agreeable to the palate or taste) 同 appetizing, savory, tasty
touchy [ˈtʌtʃi]	*adj.* 敏感的，易怒的 (acutely sensitive or irritable) 记 联想记忆：touch(触摸) + y → 一触即发的 → 敏感的，易怒的
chaotic [keɪˈɑːtɪk]	*adj.* 混乱的(in a state of complete disorder and confusion) 例 The traffic in the city is *chaotic* in the rush hour.
oligarch [ˈɑːləgɑːrk]	*n.* 寡头政治(a member of a form of government in which a small group of people hold all the power)；寡头统治集团 (a member of a small governing faction) 记 词根记忆：olig(少数) + arch(统治) → 由少数人来统治 → 寡头政治
agoraphobic [ˌægərəˈfoʊbɪk]	*n./adj.* 患旷野恐惧症的(人)
insipid [ɪnˈsɪpɪd]	*adj.* 乏味的，枯燥的(banal; dull; vapid) 记 词根记忆：in(不) + sip(有味道) + id → 没味道的 → 乏味的 例 Just as an *insipid* dish lacks flavor, an inane remark lacks sense. 同 distasteful, savorless, unappetizing, unpalatable, unsavory
sedate [sɪˈdeɪt]	*adj.* 镇静的(keeping a quiet steady attitude or pace; unruffled) 记 词根记忆：sed(=sid 坐下) + ate → 坐下来的 → 镇静的 同 sober, staid
trademark [ˈtreɪdmɑːrk]	*n.* 特征(a distinguishing characteristic or feature firmly associated with a person or thing)；商标 *v.* 保证商标权(to secure trademark rights)
evenhanded [ˌiːvnˈhændɪd]	*adj.* 公平的，不偏不倚的(fair and impartial) 记 组合词：even(平的) + hand(手) + ed → 两手放得一样平 → 公平的

palatable

□ scrappy	□ territorial	□ galvanize	□ finicky	□ transferable	□ acquiescent
□ palatable	□ touchy	□ chaotic	□ oligarch	□ agoraphobic	□ insipid
□ sedate	□ trademark	□ evenhanded			

cursory [ˈkɜːrsəri]	*adj.* 粗略的(superficial); 草率的(hasty) 记 词根记忆: curs(跑) + ory → 匆忙地跑过去 → 草率的 例 A *cursory* glance pays little attention to details.
shell [ʃel]	*n.* 贝壳; 炮弹 *v.* 剥去…的壳(to take out of a natural enclosing cover) 搭 shell fish 水生贝壳类动物

The supreme happiness of life is the conviction that we are loved.
生活中最大的幸福是坚信有人爱我们。

——法国小说家 雨果(Victor Hugo, French novelist)

evergreen [ˈevərgriːn]	*adj.* 常绿的（having foliage that remains green and functional through more than one growing season）
cozy [ˈkoʊzi]	*adj.* 舒适的，惬意的（marked by or providing contentment or comfort）；亲切友好的（friendly）
alienate [ˈeɪliəneɪt]	*v.* 使疏远，离间（to estrange; cause to become unfriendly or indifferent） 记 词根记忆：alien（外国的）+ ate → 把别人当外国人 → 使疏远 同 alien, disaffect
serial [ˈsɪriəl]	*adj.* 连续的，一系列的（arranged in a series of things） 搭 serial killings 系列杀人
indicate [ˈɪndɪkeɪt]	*v.* 指示，指出（to show sth.）；象征，显示（to be a sign of） 记 词根记忆：in + dic（说）+ ate → 指示，指出 例 These sporadic raids seem to *indicate* that the enemy is waging a war of attrition rather than attacking us directly. 同 attest, bespeak, betoken, signify
avoid [əˈvɔɪd]	*v.* 避开，躲避（to keep oneself away from） 记 词根记忆：a + void（空）→ 使落空 → 避开 搭 avoid (doing) sth. 避开（做）某事 同 elude, eschew, evade, shun
demotic [dɪˈmɑːtɪk]	*adj.* 民众的，通俗的（of or pertaining to the people） 记 词根记忆：demo（人民）+ tic（…的）→ 民众的
unecological [ˌʌniːkəˈlɑːdʒɪkl]	*adj.* 非生态的
resemble [rɪˈzembl]	*v.* 与…相似，像（to be like or similar to） 记 词根记忆：re + sembl（类似）+ e → 与…相似，像

| □ evergreen | □ cozy | □ alienate | □ serial | □ indicate | □ avoid |
| □ demotic | □ unecological | □ resemble | | | |

scruple [ˈskruːpl]	*n.* 顾忌，迟疑（an ethical consideration or principle that inhibits action） *v.* 顾忌（to hesitate） 同 boggle, stickle
sanitary [ˈsænəteri]	*adj.* （有关）卫生的，清洁的（of or relating to health） 记 词根记忆：sanit（=sanat 健康）+ ary → 卫生的，清洁的
resilient [rɪˈzɪliənt]	*adj.* 有弹性的；能恢复活力的，适应力强的（tending to recover from or adjust easily to misfortune or change）
authoritative [əˈθɑːrəteɪtɪv]	*adj.* 权威的，官方的（having or proceeding from authority）；专断的（dictatorial）
circumlocution [ˌsɜːrkəmləˈkjuːʃn]	*n.* 迂回累赘的陈述（a roundabout, lengthy way of expressing sth.） 记 词根记忆：circum（绕圈）+ locu（说话）+ tion → 说话绕圈子 → 迂回累赘的陈述
hereditary [həˈrediteri]	*adj.* 祖传的，世袭的（passed on from one generation to following generations）；遗传的 记 词根记忆：her（=heir，继承人）+ editary → 祖传的 例 Natural selection tends to eliminate genes that cause inherited diseases, acting most strongly against the most severe diseases; consequently, *hereditary* diseases that are lethal would be expected to be very rare, but, surprisingly, they are not.
judicious [dʒuˈdɪʃəs]	*adj.* 有判断力的（having or showing sound judgment）；审慎的（wise and careful） 记 词根记忆：jud（判断）+ icious → 有判断力的 同 judgmatic, prudent, sane, sapient, sensible
revelation [ˌrevəˈleɪʃn]	*n.* 显示（an act of making sth. known or seen）；揭露的事实（sth. revealed） 记 来自 reveal（*v.* 揭露；显示） 例 Although the *revelation* that one of the contestants was a friend left the judge open to charges of lack of disinterestedness, the judge remained adamant in her assertion that acquaintance did not necessarily imply partiality.
witty [ˈwɪti]	*adj.* 机智的（having good intellectual capacity）；风趣的（marked by or full of wit）
sparing [ˈsperɪŋ]	*adj.* 节俭的（frugal, thrifty） 记 来自 spare（*v.* 节约）；注意不要和 sparring（*n.* 拳击）相混
initial [ɪˈnɪʃl]	*adj.* 开始的，最初的（at the very beginning） *n.* （姓名的）首字母（the first letter of a name） 记 词根记忆：in（朝内）+ it（走）+ ial → 朝内走 → 开始的，最初的 例 Many of the earliest colonial houses that are still standing have been so modified and enlarged that the *initial* design is no longer discernible. 同 inceptive, incipient, initiative, initiatory, nascent

14

□ scruple   □ sanitary   □ resilient   □ authoritative   □ circumlocution   □ hereditary
□ judicious   □ revelation   □ witty   □ sparing   □ initial

intimation	*n.* 暗示
[ˌɪntɪˈmeɪʃn]	同 clue, cue, hint, suggestion
civil	*adj.* 国内的（relating to the state）；公民的（relating to the citizens of a
[ˈsɪvl]	country）；文明的（adequate in courtesy and politeness）
remunerative	*adj.* 报酬高的，有利润的（providing payment；profitable）
[rɪˈmjuːnərətɪv]	同 gainful, lucrative
verified	*adj.* 已查清的，已证实的
[ˈverɪfaɪd]	例 A hypothesis must not only account for what we already know, but it must also be *verified* by continued observation.
amend	*v.* 改正，修正（to put right）；改善（to change or modify for the better）
[əˈmend]	记 词根记忆：a(加强) + mend(修理) → 修正
wavy	*adj.* 波状的，多浪的（rising or swelling in waves）；波动起伏的（marked by undulation）
[ˈweɪvi]	
regenerate	*v.* 改造，改进（to change radically and for the better）；使再生，新生（to generate or produce anew）
[rɪˈdʒenəreɪt]	
fluffy	*adj.* 有绒毛的（covered with fluff）；无聊的，琐碎的（light or frivolous）
[ˈflʌfi]	记 来自 fluff(*n.* 绒毛)
profligacy	*n.* 放荡；肆意挥霍（the quality or state of being profligate）
[ˈprɑːflɪɡəsi]	
reassure	*v.* 使恢复信心（to restore to confidence）；使确信（to reinsure）
[ˌriːəˈʃʊr]	记 词根记忆：re(再次) + as + sure(确信) → 一再地确信 → 使恢复信心
barrier	*n.* 路障，障碍（obstruction as of a fence；obstacle）
[ˈbæriər]	记 联想记忆：bar(栅栏) + rier → 路障；障碍
	同 bar, barricade, block, blockade
instinctive	*adj.* 本能的（prompted by natural instinct）
[ɪnˈstɪŋktɪv]	记 来自 instinct(*n.* 本能)
	例 Ethologists are convinced that many animals survive through learning—but learning that is dictated by their genetic programming, learning as thoroughly stereotyped as the most *instinctive* of behavioral responses.
adulation	*n.* 奉承，谄媚（excessive or slavish admiration or flattery）
[ˌædʒəˈleɪʃn]	
correlate	*v.* 使相互关联；使相互影响（to establish a mutual or reciprocal relation）
[ˈkɔːrəleɪt]	搭 correlate...with... 使…与…相互关联
hardheaded	*adj.* （尤指做生意时）讲究实际的，冷静的，精明的 （shrewd and unsentimental；practical）
[ˌhɑːrdˈhedɪd]	记 组合词：hard(硬的) + head(头) + ed → 头脑坚硬的 → 冷静的
deficiency	*n.* 缺陷（absence of sth. essential；incompleteness）；不足（shortage）
[dɪˈfɪʃnsi]	记 词根记忆：de + fic(做) + iency → 没做好 → 缺陷

□ intimation	□ civil	□ remunerative	□ verified	□ amend	□ wavy
□ regenerate	□ fluffy	□ profligacy	□ reassure	□ barrier	□ instinctive
□ adulation	□ correlate	□ hardheaded	□ deficiency		

15

deprive [dɪˈpraɪv]	*v.* 剥夺，使丧失(to take sth. away from) 记 词根记忆：de(去掉) + priv(单个) + e → 从个人身边拿走 → 剥夺 同 denude, dismantle, divest, strip
utilitarian [ˌjuːtɪlɪˈteriən]	*adj.* 功利的，实利的(exhibiting or preferring mere utility)
allusion [əˈluːʒn]	*n.* 暗指，间接提到(an implied or indirect reference esp. in literature) 记 来自 allude(*v.* 暗指，间接提到)
allegory [ˈæləgɔːri]	*n.* 寓言(fable) 记 联想记忆：all + ego(自己) + ry → 全部关于自己的寓言 → 寓言
vestigial [veˈstɪdʒiəl]	*adj.* 退化的(degraded) 同 rudimentary
harmonic [hɑːrˈmɑːnɪk]	*adj.* 和声的；和谐的(pleasing to the ear) 记 来自 harmony(*n.* 和声，和谐)
prolong [prəˈlɑːŋ]	*v.* 延长，拉长(to lengthen) 记 词根记忆：pro(向前) + long(长) → 延长，拉长 例 In their determination to discover ways to *prolong* human life, doctors fail to take into account that longer lives are not always happier ones. 同 elongate, extend, prolongate, protract
defiant [dɪˈfaɪənt]	*adj.* 反抗的，挑衅的(bold, impudent) 搭 a defiant teenager 一个具有反叛性格的少年
explanatory [ɪkˈsplænətɔːri]	*adj.* 说明的，解释的(serving to explain)
stimulate [ˈstɪmjuleɪt]	*v.* 激励(to animate)；激发(to arouse) 记 词根记忆：stimul(刺，刺激) + ate → 激励；激发 例 In retrospect, Gordon's students appreciated her enigmatic assignments, realizing that such assignments were specifically designed to *stimulate* original thought rather than to review the content of her course. 同 excite, galvanize, motivate, provoke
ingratiating [ɪnˈgreɪʃieɪtɪŋ]	*adj.* 讨人喜欢的，迷人的(capable of winning favor)；讨好的，献媚的(calculated to please or win favor)
echo [ˈekoʊ]	*n.* 回声(the repetition of a sound caused by reflection of sound waves)；反响(reflection, repercussion, result, response)；共鸣(a sympathetic response) *v.* 回响，回荡(to resound with echoes)；重复，模仿(to repeat; imitate) 搭 an echo of... 对…共鸣 同 reverberate
evil [ˈiːvl]	*adj.* 邪恶的，罪恶的(sinful; wicked) *n.* 坏事，恶行(sth. that brings sorrow, distress, or calamity) 记 联想记忆：live → evil，位置颠倒 → 黑白颠倒，罪恶丛生 → 邪恶的 同 atrocious, foul, malicious, vile

□ deprive	□ utilitarian	□ allusion	□ allegory	□ vestigial	□ harmonic
□ prolong	□ defiant	□ explanatory	□ stimulate	□ ingratiating	□ echo
□ evil					

undirected	*adj.* 未受指导的(not planned or guided)
[ˌʌndaɪˈrektɪd]	记 联想记忆：un(不) + direct(指导) + ed → 未受指导的
stash	*v.* 藏匿(to store in a usually secret place for future use)
[stæʃ]	记 联想记忆：st(看作 stay, 待) + ash(灰) → 待在灰里 → 藏匿
deciduous	*adj.* 非永久的；短暂的(not lasting; ephemeral)；脱落的(falling off or
[dɪˈsɪdʒuəs]	out)；落叶的(shedding leaves annually)
	记 词根记忆：de + cid(落下) + uous → 脱落的
shifting	*adj.* 变动的；运动的
[ˈʃɪftɪŋ]	同 changing, moving
murky	*adj.* 黑暗的, 昏暗的(dark; gloomy)；朦胧的(vague)
[ˈmɜːrki]	记 来自 murk(*n.* 黑暗, 昏暗)
admonish	*v.* 训诫(to reprove mildly)；警告(to warn; advise)
[ədˈmɑːnɪʃ]	记 词根记忆：ad(一再) + mon(警告) + ish → 训诫；警告
glamorous	*adj.* 迷人的, 富有魅力的(full of glamour; fascinating; alluring)
[ˈglæmərəs]	记 来自苏格兰语 glamour(魔法), 因作家司各特常用 cast the glamour(施
	魔法)这一习语而成为人所共知的单词
disabuse	*v.* 打消(某人的)错误念头, 使醒悟(to rid of false ideas; undeceive)
[ˌdɪsəˈbjuːz]	记 联想记忆：dis(分离) + abuse(滥用, 误用) → 解除错误 → 使醒悟
	例 Although he attempted repeatedly to *disabuse* her of her conviction of
	his insincerity, he was not successful; she remained adamant in her
	judgment.
deferential	*adj.* 顺从的, 恭顺的(showing deference)
[ˌdefəˈrenʃl]	同 duteous, dutiful
denigrate	*v.* 污蔑, 诽谤 (to disparage the character or reputation of; defame;
[ˈdenɪgreɪt]	blacken)
	记 词根记忆：de + nigr(黑色的) + ate → 弄黑 → 诽谤
gratify	*v.* 使高兴, 使满足(to give pleasure or satisfaction)
[ˈgrætɪfaɪ]	记 词根记忆：grat(高兴) + ify → 使高兴
	同 arride, delectate, gladden, happify
fickle	*adj.* （尤指在感情方面）易变的, 变化无常的, 不坚定的(changeable or
[ˈfɪkl]	unstable especially in affection; inconstant)
	记 和 tickle(*v.* 呵痒)一起记
	例 Though dealers insist that professional art dealers can make money in
	the art market, even an insider's knowledge is not enough: the art world
	is so *fickle* that stock-market prices are predictable by comparison.
combustible	*adj.* 易燃的(flammable)；易激动的(easily aroused)
[kəmˈbʌstəbl]	记 词根记忆：com + bust(燃烧) + ible → 易燃的
tractable	*adj.* 易处理的, 驯良的(capable of being easily taught or controlled;
[ˈtræktəbl]	docile)
	记 词根记忆：tract(拉) + able → 拉得动的 → 易处理的

□ undirected	□ stash	□ deciduous	□ shifting	□ murky	□ admonish
□ glamorous	□ disabuse	□ deferential	□ denigrate	□ gratify	□ fickle
□ combustible	□ tractable				

relish [ˈrelɪʃ]	*n.* 美味，风味(pleasing flavor)；喜好，兴趣(a strong liking) *v.* 喜好，享受(to be gratified by) 记 联想记忆：rel(看作 real，真正的) + ish(看作 fish，鱼) → 真正的鱼 → 美味 例 Although I have always been confused by our transit system, I *relish* traveling on the subways occasionally.
investor [ɪnˈvestər]	*n.* 投资者 记 来自 invest(*v.* 投资)
reminiscent [ˌremɪˈnɪsnt]	*adj.* 回忆的(marked by or given to reminiscence)；使人联想的(tending to remind) 搭 reminiscent of sb./sth. 使回忆起某人或某事
bumper [ˈbʌmpər]	*adj.* 特大的(unusually large) *n.* 保险杠(a device for absorbing shock or preventing damage)
illusory [ɪˈluːsəri]	*adj.* 虚幻的(deceptive; unreal; illusive) 例 The trick for Michael was to conjure for his son an *illusory* orderliness；only alone at night, when the boy was asleep, could Michael acknowledge the chaos he kept hidden from his son. 同 chimerical, fanciful, fictive, imaginary
claim [kleɪm]	*v.* 要求或索要(to request sth.) *n.* 声称拥有的权利 记 本身为词根，意为"大叫" → 要求或索要 搭 claim against 对…要求赔偿；claim that… 要求… 同 argue, assert, contend, justify, maintain
complacent [kəmˈpleɪsnt]	*adj.* 自满的，得意的(self-satisfied; smug) 记 注意不要和 complaisant(*adj.* 随和的)相混
overconfident [ˌoʊvərˈkɑːnfɪdənt]	*adj.* 过于自信的，自负的
construe [kənˈstruː]	*v.* 解释(to explain or interpret)；翻译(to translate orally) 记 词根记忆：con + strue(=struct 结构) → 弄清结构 → 解释
undisturbed [ˌʌndɪˈstɜːrbd]	*adj.* 未受干扰的，安静的(not disturbed; calm) 同 unmolested
grind [graɪnd]	*v.* 磨碎，碾碎(to crush into bits or fine particles) *n.* 苦差事(long, difficult, tedious task) 记 联想记忆：将一块大(grand)石头磨碎(grind)
proximity [prɑːkˈsɪməti]	*n.* 接近，临近(the quality or state of being proximate) 记 词根记忆：prox(接近) + imity → 接近，临近
rebroadcast [rɪˈbrɔːdkæst]	*v.* 重播(to broadcast again)
energize [ˈenərdʒaɪz]	*v.* 给予…精力、能量(to make energetic, vigorous, or active) 同 activize, invigorate, reinforce, vitalize

□ relish	□ investor	□ reminiscent	□ bumper	□ illusory	□ claim
□ complacent	□ overconfident	□ construe	□ undisturbed	□ grind	□ proximity
□ rebroadcast	□ energize				

clinical	*adj.* 临床的（of, relating to, or conducted in or as if in a clinic）；冷静客观
[ˈklɪnɪkl]	的（coldly objective）
	记 词根记忆：clinic（医疗诊所）+ al → 临床的
	搭 clinical practice 临床实践
regimental	*adj.* 团的，团队的（of or relating to a regiment）
[ˌredʒɪˈmentl]	记 来自 regiment（*n.* 团；大量）
advocacy	*n.* 拥护，支持（the act or process of advocating）
[ˈædvəkəsi]	记 来自 advocate（*v.* 拥护，支持）
consult	*v.* 请教，咨询，商量（to consider; ask the advice or opinion of; refer to;
[kənˈsʌlt]	confer）*n.* 咨询（consultation）
	记 联想记忆：不顾侮辱（insult），不耻请教（consult）
transmute	*v.* 变化（to change or alter）
[trænzˈmjuːt]	记 词根记忆：trans（改变）+ mute（变化）→ 变化
prophesy	*v.* 预言（to predict with assurance or on the basis of mystic knowledge）
[ˈprɑːfəsɪ]	同 adumbrate, augur, portend, presage, prognosticate
upstart	*n.* 突然升官的人，暴发户（one that has risen suddenly; parvenu）
[ˈʌpstɑːrt]	记 联想记忆：up（向上）+ start（开始）→ 开始向上 → 暴发户
toady	*n.* 谄媚者，马屁精（one who flatters）
[ˈtoʊdi]	记 联想记忆：toad（癞蛤蟆）+ y → 像蛤蟆一样趴在地上的人 → 马屁精
	例 Just as sloth is the mark of the idler, obsequiousness is the mark of
	the *toady*.
	同 bootlicker, brownnoser, cringer, fawner
distinct	*adj.* 清楚的，明显的（definite; evident）
[dɪˈstɪŋkt]	记 词根记忆：di（分开）+ stinct（刺）→ 把刺分开 → 与众不同的 → 明显的
patronage	*n.* 资助，赞助（the support, especially financial, that is given to a person
[ˈpætrənɪdʒ]	or an organization by a patron）；惠顾（the trade given to a commercial
	establishment by its customers）
	记 来自 patron（*n.* 赞助人）
	例 Queen Elizabeth I has quite correctly been called a friend of the arts,
	because many young artists received her *patronage*.
realistic	*adj.* 现实主义的（representing what is real）
[ˌriːəˈlɪstɪk]	例 The documentary film about high school life was so *realistic* and
	evocative that feelings of nostalgia flooded over the college-age
	audience.
therapeutic	*adj.* 治疗的（of the treatment of diseases）
[ˌθerəˈpjuːtɪk]	记 词根记忆：therap（照看，治疗）+ eutic → 治疗的
	例 For centuries animals have been used as surrogates for people in
	experiments to assess the effects of *therapeutic* and other agents that
	might later be used in humans.
accomplice	*n.* 共犯，同谋（associate; partner in a crime）
[əˈkɑːmplɪs]	记 词根记忆：ac + com（共同）+ plic（重叠）+ e → 重叠一起干 → 同谋

□ clinical	□ regimental	□ advocacy	□ consult	□ transmute	□ prophesy
□ upstart	□ toady	□ distinct	□ patronage	□ realistic	□ therapeutic
□ accomplice					

palpable ['pælpəbl]	*adj.* 可触知的，可察觉的；明显的（tangible；perceptible；noticeable） 记 词根记忆：palp(摸) + able → 摸得到的 → 可触知的；明显的
defer [dɪˈfɜːr]	*v.* 遵从，听从（to yield with courtesy）；延期（to put off to a future time；delay）
stasis [ˈsteɪsɪs]	*n.* 停滞（motionlessness） 记 联想记忆：sta(stay) + sis(cease) → 保持停止状态 → 停滞 例 Some paleontologists debate whether the diversity of species has increased since the Cambrian period, or whether imperfections in the fossil record only suggest greater diversity today, while in actuality there has been either *stasis* or decreased diversity.
drollery [ˈdroʊləri]	*n.* 滑稽（quaint or wry humor） 记 来自 droll(*adj.* 滑稽的)
nutritious [nuˈtrɪʃəs]	*adj.* 有营养的，滋养的（nourishing） 同 alimentary, nutrient, nutritive
stint [stɪnt]	*v.* 节制，限量，节省（to restrict or limit, as in amount or number） 搭 stint on sth. 吝惜…
transcription [trænˈskrɪpʃn]	*n.* 誊写，抄写（an act, process, or instance of transcribing）；抄本，副本（copy, transcript）
astronomical [ˌæstrəˈnɑːmɪkl]	*adj.* 极大的（enormously or inconceivably large or great）；天文学的（of astronomy） 记 词根记忆：astro(星星) + nomical → 星星的，星体的 → 极大的 搭 systematic astronomical and weather observations 系统的天文气象观察
ambiguity [ˌæmbɪˈɡjuːəti]	*n.* 模棱两可的话（an ambiguous word or expression）；不明确（uncertainty） 同 amphibology, equivocality, equivocation, equivoque, tergiversation
fragile [ˈfrædʒl]	*adj.* 易碎的，易损坏的（brittle；crisp；friable） 记 词根记忆：frag(=fract 断裂) + ile(易…的) → 易碎的 同 breakable, delicate, frail, frangible, shatterable
perspicuous [pɜːrˈspɪkjuəs]	*adj.* 明晰的，明了的（clearly expressed or presented）
proprietary [prəˈpraɪəˌteri]	*adj.* 私有的（privately owned and managed）
seclusion [sɪˈkluːʒn]	*n.* 隔离（the act of secluding）；隔离地（a secluded or isolated place） 搭 be in seclusion 处于被隔离状态
repellent [rɪˈpelənt]	*adj.* 令人厌恶的（arousing disgust；repulsive） 同 loathsome, odious, repugnant, revolting
intrusively [ɪnˈtruːsɪvli]	*adv.* 入侵地 记 来自 intrusive(*adj.* 入侵的，打扰的)
sweep [swiːp]	*v.* 席卷，扫过（to clean with or as if with a broom or brush） 搭 sweep the board（在比赛中）囊括所有奖项

seclusion

□ palpable	□ defer	□ stasis	□ drollery	□ nutritious	□ stint
□ transcription	□ astronomical	□ ambiguity	□ fragile	□ perspicuous	□ proprietary
□ seclusion	□ repellent	□ intrusively	□ sweep		

argumentative [ˌɑːrɡjuˈmentətɪv]	*adj.* 好争辩的，好争吵的(characterized by argument) 记 来自 argument(*n.* 争论，争辩)
occupation [ˌɑːkjuˈpeɪʃn]	*n.* 工作，职业(a job; employment)；占有，占领(the act or process of taking possession of a place or area) 记 来自 occupy(*v.* 占有，占领；忙于)
flake [fleɪk]	*v.* 使成薄片(to form or break into flakes) 记 联想记忆：f(看作 fly，飞) + lake(湖) → 飞向湖中的薄片 → 使成薄片
uncompromising [ʌnˈkɑːmprəmaɪzɪŋ]	*adj.* 不妥协的(not making or accepting a compromise) 例 Despite her compassionate nature, the new nominee to the Supreme Court was single-minded and *uncompromising* in her strict adherence to the letter of the law.
trite [traɪt]	*adj.* 陈腐的，陈词滥调的(hackneyed or boring) 例 The plot of this story is so *trite* that I can predict the outcome. 同 bathetic, commonplace
empirically [ɪmˈpɪrɪkli]	*adv.* 凭经验地(in an empirical manner) 记 词根记忆：em(在里面) + pir(实验) + ical + ly → 在内部进行严密的实验 → 凭经验地
insubstantial [ˌɪnsəbˈstænʃl]	*adj.* 无实体的(immaterial)；脆弱的(frail) 记 联想记忆：in(不) + substantial(实体的；坚固的) → 无实体的；脆弱的
requisite [ˈrekwɪzɪt]	*n.* 必需物(sth. that is needed or necessary) *adj.* 必要的，必不可少的(required) 记 联想记忆：requi(看作 require，要求) + site → 要求的 → 必要的 例 Biography is a literary genre whose primary *requisite* is an ability to reconstruct imaginatively the inner life of a subject on the basis of all the knowable external evidence.
insatiably [ɪnˈseɪʃəbli]	*adv.* 不知足地，贪得无厌地(to an insatiable degree; with persistence but without satisfaction) 例 Most people are shameless voyeurs where the very rich are concerned, *insatiably* curious about how they get their money and how they spend it.
deign [deɪn]	*v.* 惠允(做某事)(to condescend to do sth.; stoop)；施惠于人(to condescend to give or grant) 记 参考：condescend(*v.* 屈尊)
tendentious [tenˈdenʃəs]	*adj.* 有偏见的(marked by a tendency in favor of a particular point of view) 记 词根记忆：tend(倾向) + ent(存在) + ious → 有倾向的 → 有偏见的
tint [tɪnt]	*n.* 色泽(slight degree of a color) *v.* 给…淡淡地着色(to give a slight color to)；染
vehicle [ˈviːəkl]	*n.* 交通工具；传播媒介(an agent of transmission) 记 词根记忆：veh(带来) + icle(东西) → 带人的东西 → 交通工具
extant [ekˈstænt]	*adj.* 现存的，现有的(currently or actually existing) 记 联想记忆：ex + tant(看作 stand，站) → 站出来 → 现存的

□ argumentative	□ occupation	□ flake	□ uncompromising	□ trite	□ empirically
□ insubstantial	□ requisite	□ insatiably	□ deign	□ tendentious	□ tint
□ vehicle	□ extant				

conjecture [kənˈdʒektʃər]	*v./n.* 推测，臆测 记 词根记忆：con + ject(推，扔) + ure → 全部是推出来的 → 臆测 同 presume, suppose, surmise
deprave [dɪˈpreɪv]	*v.* 使堕落，使恶化(to make bad) 记 词根记忆：de(向下) + prav(弯曲的) + e → 使弯曲 → 使堕落
infect [ɪnˈfekt]	*v.* 传染 (to contaminate with a disease-producing substance or agent)；使感染，侵染 (to communicate a pathogen or a disease)；污染 (to contaminate) 例 No computer system is immune to a virus, a particularly malicious program that is designed to *infect* and electronically damage the disks on which data are stored.
urbanize [ˈɜːrbənaɪz]	*v.* 使都市化，使文雅(to cause to take on urban characteristics)
provision [prəˈvɪʒn]	*n.* 供应 (a stock of needed materials or supplies)；(法律等)条款 (stipulation)
incorporate [ɪnˈkɔːrpəreɪt]	*v.* 合并，并入(to combine or join with sth. already formed; embody) 记 词根记忆：in(进入) + corp(身体) + orate → 进入体内 → 合并 搭 incorporate...into... 使并入，将…包括在内 同 assimilate, imbibe, inhaust, insorb, integrate
default [dɪˈfɔːlt]	*n.* 违约 (failure to perform a task or fulfill an obligation)；未履行的责任 (failure to do sth. required by duty or law)；拖欠 (a failure to pay financial debts) *v.* 不履行(to fail to fulfill a contract, agreement, or duty) 记 联想记忆：de + fault(错误) → 错下去 → 不履行
uncharitable [ʌnˈtʃærɪtəbl]	*adj.* 无慈悲心的(lacking in charity) 例 Being cynical, he was reluctant to credit the unselfishness of any kind act until he had ruled out all possible secret, *uncharitable* motives.
acquiescence [ˌækwiˈesns]	*n.* 默许(the act of acquiescing) 记 来自 acquiesce(*v.* 默认，默许)
regretfully [rɪˈgretfəli]	*adv.* 懊悔地(with regret) 记 来自 regret(*v.* 懊悔，惋惜)
repetitious [ˌrepəˈtɪʃəs]	*adj.* 重复的(characterized or marked by repetition)
ingenious [ɪnˈdʒiːniəs]	*adj.* 聪明的(clever)；善于创造发明的，心灵手巧的(original; inventive) 记 词根记忆：in(在里面) + gen(产生) + ious → 聪明产生于内 → 聪明的；注意不要和 ingenuous(*adj.* 纯真的，纯朴的；坦率的)相混
propel [prəˈpel]	*v.* 推进，促进(to drive forward or onward; push) 记 词根记忆：pro(向前) + pel(推) → 推进，促进
imponderable [ɪmˈpɑːndərəbl]	*adj.* (重量等)无法衡量的(incapable of being weighed or measured) 记 联想记忆：im(不) + ponder(仔细考量) + able → 无法衡量的 同 impalpable, imperceptible, indiscernible, insensible, unmeasurable

□ conjecture	□ deprave	□ infect	□ urbanize	□ provision	□ incorporate
□ default	□ uncharitable	□ acquiescence	□ regretfully	□ repetitious	□ ingenious
□ propel	□ imponderable				

roseate [ˈrouziət]	*adj.* 玫瑰色的(resembling a rose especially in color)；过分乐观的(overly optimistic)
intricate [ˈɪntrɪkət]	*adj.* 错综复杂的(having many complexly arranged elements; elaborate)；难懂的(complex; hard to follow or understand) 记 词根记忆：in(在里面) + tric(小障碍物) + ate → 在里面放入很多小障碍物 → 错综复杂的 例 Although the minuet appeared simple, its *intricate* steps had to be studied very carefully before they could be gracefully executed in public. 同 complicated, knotty, labyrinthine, sophisticated
heterogeneous [ˌhetərəˈdʒiːniəs]	*adj.* 异类的，多样化的(dissimilar; incongruous; foreign) 记 词根记忆：hetero(其他的；相异的) + gene(产生，基因) + ous → 异类的
instrumental [ˌɪnstrəˈmentl]	*adj.* 作为手段的，有帮助的(serving as a crucial means, agent, or tool; helpful in bringing sth. about)；器械的(of, relating to, or accomplished with an instrument or a tool) 记 来自 instrument(*n.* 器械；手段)
allot [əˈlɑːt]	*v.* 分配(to assign as a share or portion)；拨出(to distribute by or as if by lot)
subterranean [ˌsʌbtəˈreɪniən]	*adj.* 地下的，地表下的(being under the surface of the earth) 记 词根记忆：sub(下面) + terr(地) + anean → 地下的
stratify [ˈstrætɪfaɪ]	*v.* (使)层化(to divide or arrange into classes, castes, or social strata) 记 词根记忆：strat(层次) + ify → (使)层化
dismal [ˈdɪzməl]	*adj.* 沮丧的，阴沉的(showing sadness) 记 来自拉丁文 dies mail，意为"不吉利的日子"，后转变为"沮丧的，阴沉的"的意思 例 Despite a string of *dismal* earnings reports, the two-year-old strategy to return the company to profitability is beginning to work.
fluctuate [ˈflʌktʃueɪt]	*v.* 波动(to undulate as waves)；变动(to be continually changing) 记 词根记忆：fluct(=flu, 流动) + uate → 波动；变动
hormone [ˈhɔːrmoun]	*n.* 荷尔蒙，激素 记 发音记忆："荷尔蒙"
exterminate [ɪkˈstɜːrmɪneɪt]	*v.* 消灭，灭绝(to wipe out; eradicate) 记 词根记忆：ex + termin(范围；结束) + ate → 从范围中消除 → 消灭 同 abolish, annihilate, extirpate
cordiality [ˌkɔːrˈdʒæləti]	*n.* 诚恳，热诚(sincere affection and kindness) 同 heartiness, geniality, warmth
engender [ɪnˈdʒendər]	*v.* 产生，引起(to produce; beget) 记 词根记忆：en + gen(出生) + der → 使出生 → 产生，引起 同 cause, generate, induce, provoke
avarice [ˈævərɪs]	*n.* 贪财，贪婪(too great a desire to have wealth; cupidity) 记 发音记忆："爱不释手" → 贪婪

□ roseate	□ intricate	□ heterogeneous	□ instrumental	□ allot	□ subterranean
□ stratify	□ dismal	□ fluctuate	□ hormone	□ exterminate	□ cordiality
□ engender	□ avarice				

querulous [ˈkwerələs]	*adj.* 抱怨的，爱发牢骚的(habitually complaining; fretful) 记 联想记忆：que(看作 question，质疑) + rul(看作 rule，规则) + ous(…的) → 质疑规则 → 抱怨的 例 Satire as a political commentator is patently *querulous*; he writes biased editorials about every action the government takes.
obscurity [əbˈskjʊrəti]	*n.* 费解(the quality of being obscure)；不出名 例 The civil rights movement did not emerge from *obscurity* into national prominence overnight; on the contrary, it captured the public's imagination only gradually.

Every day I remind myself that my inner and outer life are based on the labors of other men, living and dead, and that I must exert myself in order to give in the same measure as I have received and am still receiving.

每天我都提醒着自己：我的精神生活和物质生活都是以别人的劳动为基础的，我必须尽力以同样的分量来报偿我所获得的和至今仍在接受着的东西。

————美国科学家 爱因斯坦(Albert Einstein, American scientist)

音频

misalliance [ˌmɪsə'laɪəns]	*n.* 不适当的结合(an improper alliance) 记 联想记忆: mis(坏) + alliance(结盟, 联盟) → 坏的联盟 → 不适当的结合
ultimate ['ʌltɪmət]	*adj.* 最后的(being or happening at the end of a process or course of action) 记 词根记忆: ultim(最后) + ate(…的) → 最后的 例 This project is the first step in a long-range plan of research whose *ultimate* goal, still many years off, is the creation of a new prototype.
plainspoken [ˌpleɪn'spoʊkən]	*adj.* 直言不讳的 同 candid, frank
miserable ['mɪzrəbl]	*adj.* 痛苦的, 悲惨的(being in a pitiable state of distress or unhappiness); 少得可怜的(wretchedly inadequate or meager) 记 来自 misery(*n.* 痛苦; 悲惨的境遇) 例 Hoping for a rave review of his new show, the playwright was *miserable* when the critics panned it unanimously. 同 afflicted, doleful, dolorous, woeful
undiscovered [ˌʌndɪs'kʌvərd]	*adj.* 未被发现的(not noticed or known about) 同 unexplored
insightful ['ɪnsaɪtfʊl]	*adj.* 富有洞察力的, 有深刻见解的(exhibiting or characterized by insight) 例 Although in his seventies at the time of the interview, Picasso proved alert and *insightful*, his faculties intact despite the inevitable toll of the years. 同 discerning, perceptive, sagacious, sage, sophic
corruption [kə'rʌpʃn]	*n.* 腐败, 堕落(impairment of integrity, virtue or moral principle) 记 来自 corrupt(*v.* 使腐化)
anecdotal [ˌænɪk'doʊtl]	*adj.* 轶事的, 趣闻的(of, relating to, or consisting of anecdotes) 记 来自 anecdote(*n.* 逸事, 趣闻)
commercialize [kə'mɜːrʃlaɪz]	*v.* 使商业化, 使商品化(to manage on a business basis for profit)
counteract [ˌkaʊntər'ækt]	*v.* 消除, 抵消(to act directly against; neutralize, or undo the effect of opposing action) 记 词根记忆: counter(反) + act(动作) → 做相反的动作 → 消除, 抵消

□ misalliance □ ultimate □ plainspoken □ miserable □ undiscovered □ insightful
□ corruption □ anecdotal □ commercialize □ counteract

25

supplement [ˈsʌplɪmənt]	*n.* 增补，补充（sth. that completes or makes an addition）*v.* 增补（to add or serve as a supplement to）
	记 联想记忆：supple（=supply 提供）+ ment → 提供补充 → 增补，补充
	例 Supporters of the proposed waterway argue that it will *supplement* rather than threaten railroad facilities, since the waterway will be icebound during the only months when the railroads can absorb much traffic.
	同 appendix, addendum, codicil, complement
attest [əˈtest]	*v.* 证明，证实（to declare to be true or genuine）
	记 词根记忆：at + test（证明）→ 证明
	搭 attest to 证实，证明
	同 certify, testify, witness
termite [ˈtɜːrmaɪt]	*n.* 白蚁
trickle [ˈtrɪkl]	*v.* 细细地流（to flow in a thin gentle stream）*n.* 细流
	同 dribble, drip, filter
anticipatory [ænˈtɪsəpətɔːri]	*adj.* 预想的，预期的（characterized by anticipation）
	记 来自 anticipate（*v.* 预测，预料）
incontrovertible [ˌɪnkɑːntrəˈvɜːrtəbl]	*adj.* 无可辩驳的（incapable of being disputed），不容置疑的
	记 联想记忆：in（不）+ controvertible（可辩论的）→ 无可辩驳的
pompous [ˈpɑːmpəs]	*adj.* 自大的（having or exhibiting self-importance）
	同 arrogant
enamored [ɪˈnæmərd]	*adj.* 倾心的，被迷住（inflamed with love; fascinated）
	记 词根记忆：en + amor（爱）+ ed → 珍爱的 → 倾心的
	搭 be enamored of... 珍爱…，喜爱…
	同 bewitched, captivated, charmed, enchanted, infatuated
configuration [kənˌfɪɡjəˈreɪʃn]	*n.* 结构，配置（arrangement of parts; form）；轮廓（contour; outline）
	记 来自 configure（*v.* 配置，使成型）
coherence [koʊˈhɪrəns]	*n.* 条理性，连贯性（the quality or state of cohering）
	同 adherence, adhesion, bond, cohesion
overlook [ˌoʊvərˈlʊk]	*v.* 俯视（to have a view from above）；忽视（not to notice）
	记 组合词：over（在…上）+ look（看）→ 在上面看 → 俯视；引申为"忽视"
repertoire [ˈrepərtwɑːr]	*n.*（剧团等）常备剧目（the complete list or supply of dramas, operas, or musical works）
	记 联想记忆：和 report（汇报）一起记，汇报演出需要常备节目
patronizing [ˈpeɪtrənaɪzɪŋ]	*adj.* 以恩惠态度对待的，要人领情的
	例 To take a *patronizing* attitude, looking down on others as one's inferiors, often is to eliminate any chance of favorable relations with them.
inure [ɪˈnjʊr]	*v.* 使习惯于（to accustom to accept something undesirable）；生效（to become of advantage）

rigorous	*adj.* 严格的，严峻的(manifesting, exercising, or favoring rigor)
[ˈrɪgərəs]	同 austere, rigid, severe, stern

diverse	*adj.* 不同的(different；dissimilar)；多样的
[daɪˈvɜːrs]	(diversified)
	记 词根记忆：di(离开) + vers(转) + e → 转开 → 不同的
	同 disparate, distant, divergent

diverse

rehabilitate	*v.* 使恢复(健康、能力、地位等)(to restore to a
[ˌriːəˈbɪlɪteɪt]	former health, capacity, rank, etc.)
	记 词根记忆：re + hab(拥有) + ilit + ate → 使重新拥有 → 使恢复

entrenched	*adj.* (权利、传统)确立的，牢固的(strongly established and not likely to
[ɪnˈtrentʃt]	change)

peripheral	*adj.* 周边的，外围的(of a periphery or surface part)
[pəˈrɪfərəl]	记 词根记忆：peri(周围) + pher(带) + al → 带到周围 → 周边的，外围的
	例 One virus strain that may help gene therapists cure genetic brain
	diseases can enter the *peripheral* nervous system and travel to the brain,
	obviating the need to inject the therapeutic virus directly into the brain.

incredulity	*n.* 怀疑，不相信(disbelief)
[ˌɪnkrəˈduːləti]	记 词根记忆：in(不) + cred(信任) + ulity → 怀疑，不相信

inconvenient	*adj.* 不便的，打扰的，造成麻烦的(not convenient especially in giving
[ˌɪnkənˈviːniənt]	trouble or annoyance)

endear	*v.* 使受喜爱(to cause to become beloved or admired)
[ɪnˈdɪr]	记 联想记忆：en(使) + dear(珍爱的) → 使受喜爱

discrete	*adj.* 个别的，分离的(individual；separate)；不连续的(made up of distinct
[dɪˈskriːt]	parts；discontinuous)
	记 词根记忆：dis(分离) + cre(生产) + te → 个别的，分离的
	同 different, diverse, several, various

excite	*v.* 激发 (to call to activity)；使动感情，使激动 (to rouse to an emotional
[ɪkˈsaɪt]	response)；使增加能量(to energize)
	同 galvanize, innervate, innerve, motivate, provoke

pollen	*n.* 花粉(a mass of microspores in a seed plant)
[ˈpɑːlən]	

nutritional	*adj.* 营养的，滋养的
[nuˈtrɪʃnl]	同 alimentary, nutritive

weightless	*adj.* 无重力的，失重的(having little weight; lacking apparent gravitational
[ˈweɪtləs]	pull)

anaerobic	*adj.* 厌氧的 (of, relating to, or being activity in which the body incurs an
[ˌæneˈroʊbɪk]	oxygen debt) *n.* 厌氧微生物
	记 词根记忆：an(不，无) + aero(空气) + bic → 不要空气的 → 厌氧的

indigent	*adj.* 贫穷的，贫困的(deficient；impoverished)
[ˈɪndɪdʒənt]	记 联想记忆：in(无) + dig(挖) + ent → 挖不出东西 → 贫穷的

□ rigorous	□ diverse	□ rehabilitate	□ entrenched	□ peripheral	□ incredulity
□ inconvenient	□ endear	□ discrete	□ excite	□ pollen	□ nutritional
□ weightless	□ anaerobic	□ indigent			

homespun	*adj.* 朴素的(simple)；家织的(spun or made at home)
[ˈhoʊmspʌn]	同 homely
asunder	*adj./adv.* 分离的(地)(apart or separate)；化为碎片的(地)(into pieces)
[əˈsʌndər]	记 分拆记忆：as + under → 好像在下面 → 分离的
mournful	*adj.* 悲伤的(feeling or expressing sorrow or grief)
[ˈmɔːrnfl]	同 doleful, dolorous, plaintive, woeful
collaborative	*adj.* 协作的(characterized or accomplished by collaboration)
[kəˈlæbəreɪtɪv]	
duplicate	[ˈduːplɪkət] *adj.* 复制的，两重的(consisting of or existing in two corresponding or identical parts or examples)
	[ˈduːplɪkeɪt] *v.* 复制(to make double) *n.* 复制品，副本(an additional copy of sth. already in a collection; counterpart)
	同 reduplicate, replicate, reproduce
preserve	*v.* 保护(to keep safe from injury, harm, or destruction; protect)；保存(to keep alive, intact, or free from decay; maintain)
[prɪˈzɜːrv]	记 联想记忆：pre(在前面) + serve(服务) → 提前提供服务 → 保护；保存
	例 The discovery by George Poinar and Roberta Hess that amber could *preserve* intact tissue from million-year-old insects raised the possibility, since proved correct, that it also could *preserve* intact DNA.
	同 conserve, reserve
typify	*v.* 代表，是…的典型(to represent in typical fashion)
[ˈtɪpɪfaɪ]	同 epitomize, symbolize
bask	*v.* 晒太阳，取暖(to warm oneself pleasantly in the sunlight)
[bæsk]	记 联想记忆：把 basket 去掉 et, 就是 bask → 拎着篮子晒太阳 → 取暖
distasteful	*adj.* (令人)不愉快的，讨厌的(unpleasant; disagreeable)
[dɪsˈteɪstfl]	记 联想记忆：dis(不) + tasteful(好吃的) → 不好吃的 → 讨厌的
incidental	*adj.* 作为自然结果的，伴随而来的(being likely to ensue as a chance or minor consequence)；偶然发生的(occurring merely by chance)
[ˌɪnsɪˈdentl]	例 Because we have completed our analysis of the major components of the proposed project, we are free to devote the remainder of this session to a study of the project's *incidental* details.
inalienable	*adj.* 不能转让的；不可剥夺的 (not transferable to another or capable of being repudiated)
[ɪnˈeɪliənəbl]	记 联想记忆：in(不) + alien(转让) + able → 不能转让的
officious	*adj.* 过于殷勤的，多管闲事的 (too ready or willing to give orders or advice; meddlesome)；非官方的(informal; unofficial)
[əˈfɪʃəs]	
photosensitive	*adj.* 感光性的(sensitive or sensitized to the action of radiant energy)
[ˌfoʊtoʊˈsensətɪv]	
ruminant	*adj.* (动物)反刍的；沉思的(meditative; thoughtful)
[ˈruːmɪnənt]	记 词根记忆：rumin(=rumen 反刍动物的第一胃，"瘤胃") + ant → 反刍的

□ homespun	□ asunder	□ mournful	□ collaborative	□ duplicate	□ preserve
□ typify	□ bask	□ distasteful	□ incidental	□ inalienable	□ officious
□ photosensitive	□ ruminant				

28

original	*adj.* 最初的，最早的(first or earliest)；有创意的，有创造性的(able to produce new ideas; creative)
[əˈrɪdʒənl]	记 来自 origin(*n.* 起源，由来)
	例 We find it difficult to translate a foreign text literally because we cannot capture the connotations of the *original* passage exactly.
entice	*v.* 诱使，引诱(to attract artfully or adroitly; lure)
[ɪnˈtaɪs]	记 联想记忆：ent(看作 enter，进入) + ice(冰) → 引诱人进入冰中 → 引诱
primal	*adj.* 原始的，最初的(original; primitive)；首要的(being first in importance)
[ˈpraɪml]	搭 primal chaos 原始的混沌状态
pine	*n.* 松树 *v.* (因疾病等)憔悴(to lose vigor; anguish)；渴望(to yearn intensely and persistently especially for sth. unattainable)
[paɪn]	记 联想记忆：松树(pine)的叶尖尖细细的，就像针(pin)
	同 crave, dream, hanker, thirst
fragment	*n.* 碎片(small part or piece)；片段(an incomplete or isolated portion)
[ˈfrægmənt]	记 词根记忆：frag(打碎) + ment(表名词) → 碎片
	同 scrap, shred
dogmatist	*n.* 独断家，独断论者(one who dogmatizes)
[ˈdɔːgmətɪst]	记 来自 dogma(*n.* 教条，信条)
egalitarian	*adj.* 主张人人平等的(advocating the belief that all people should have equal rights)
[iˌgælɪˈteriən]	记 词根记忆：egalit(平等的) + arian → 主张人人平等的；该词等同于 equalitarian(*adj.* 平等主义的)
submerged	*adj.* 在水中的，淹没的(covered with water)
[səbˈmɜːrdʒd]	同 dipped, immersed, sunken
vicissitude	*n.* 变迁，兴衰(natural change or mutation visible in nature or in human affairs)
[vɪˈsɪsɪtuːd]	
shiny	*adj.* 有光泽的(having a smooth glossy surface)；发光的(filled with light)
[ˈʃaɪni]	同 bright, gleaming, glistening
phonetic	*adj.* 语音的(about the sounds of human speech)
[fəˈnetɪk]	记 词根记忆：phon(声音) + etic → 语音的
pending	*adj.* 即将发生的(imminent; impending)；未决的(not yet decided)
[ˈpendɪŋ]	记 词根记忆：pend(挂) + ing → 挂着的 → 未决的
grandeur	*n.* 壮丽，宏伟(splendor; magnificence)
[ˈgrændʒər]	记 来自 grand(*adj.* 宏伟的，壮丽的)
favorable	*adj.* 有利的(helpful)；赞成的(showing approval)
[ˈfeɪvərəbl]	记 来自 favor(*n.* 好意，喜爱)
amorphous	*adj.* 无固定形状的(without definite form; shapeless)
[əˈmɔːrfəs]	记 词根记忆：a + morph(形状) + ous → 无固定形状的

□ original	□ entice	□ primal	□ pine	□ fragment	□ dogmatist
□ egalitarian	□ submerged	□ vicissitude	□ shiny	□ phonetic	□ pending
□ grandeur	□ favorable	□ amorphous			

density	*n.* 密集，稠密（the quality or state of being dense）
[ˈdensəti]	搭 population density 人口密度
restrict	*v.* 限制，约束（to confine within bounds）
[rɪˈstrɪkt]	记 联想记忆：re（一再）+ strict（严格的）→ 一再对其严格 → 限制，约束
	例 Getting into street brawls is no minor matter for professional boxers, who are required by law to *restrict* their aggressive impulses to the ring.
	同 circumscribe, confine, delimit, prelimit
distinguish	*v.* 成为…的特征，使有别于（to mark as separate or different）；把…分类（to separate into kinds, classes, or categories）；区别，辨别（to discern）
[dɪˈstɪŋgwɪʃ]	记 词根记忆：di（分开）+ sting（刺）+ uish → 将刺挑出来 → 区别，辨别
withhold	*v.* 抑制（to hold back from action）；扣留，保留（to keep on purpose）
[wɪðˈhoʊld]	记 联想记忆：with（附带着）+ hold（拿住）→ 保留
	同 bridle, constrain, inhibit, restrain
repeal	*v.* 废除（法律）（to annul by authoritative act）
[rɪˈpiːl]	记 词根记忆：re（反）+ peal（=call 叫）→ 叫回 → 废除
relegate	*v.* 使降级，贬谪（to send to exile; assign to oblivion）；交付，托付（to refer or assign for decision or action）
[ˈrelɪgeɪt]	记 词根记忆：re + leg（选择）+ ate → 重新选择职位 → 使降级
gaudy	*adj.* 俗丽的（bright and showy）
[ˈgɔːdi]	记 发音记忆："高低" → 花衣服穿得高高低低 → 俗丽的
sane	*adj.* 神志清楚的（having a normal, healthy mind）；明智的（sensible）
[seɪn]	同 rational
undifferentiated	*adj.* 无差别的，一致的
[ˌʌndɪfəˈrenʃieɪtɪd]	同 uniform
fallow	*n.* 休耕地（cultivated land that is allowed to lie idle during the growing season）*adj.* 休耕的（left uncultivated or unplanted）
[ˈfæloʊ]	记 和 fellow（*n.* 伙伴，同伙）一起记
unsubstantiated	*adj.* 未经证实的，无事实根据的（not proved to be true by evidence）
[ˌʌnsəbˈstænʃieɪtɪd]	同 uncorroborated
exonerate	*v.* 免除责任（to relieve from an obligation）；确定无罪（to clear from guilt; absolve）
[ɪgˈzɑːnəreɪt]	记 词根记忆：ex + oner（负担）+ ate → 走出负担 → 免除责任
stagger	*v.* 蹒跚，摇晃（to move on unsteadily）
[ˈstægər]	同 lurch, reel, sway, waver, wobble
agitation	*n.* 焦虑，不安（anxiety）；公开辩论，鼓动宣传（public argument or action for social or political change）
[ˌædʒɪˈteɪʃn]	
reexamination	*n.* 重考；复试；再检查
[ˌriːɪgˌzæmɪˈneɪʃn]	
artistry	*n.* 艺术技巧（skill of an artist）
[ˈɑːrtɪstri]	记 词根记忆：artist（艺术家）+ ry → 艺术技巧

□ density	□ restrict	□ distinguish	□ withhold	□ repeal	□ relegate
□ gaudy	□ sane	□ undifferentiated	□ fallow	□ unsubstantiated	□ exonerate
□ stagger	□ agitation	□ reexamination	□ artistry		

unerringly [ʌnˈɜːrɪŋlɪ]	*adv.* 无过失地
charter [ˈtʃɑːrtər]	*n.* 特权或豁免权(special privilege or immunity)
debate [dɪˈbeɪt]	*n.* 正式的辩论，讨论(formal argument of a question) *v.* 讨论，辩论 记 词根记忆：de(加强) + bat(打，击) + e → 加强打击 → 正式的辩论
quagmire [ˈkwægmaɪər]	*n.* 沼泽地(soft miry land)；困境(predicament) 记 组合词：quag(沼泽) + mire(泥潭) → quagmire(沼泽地) 同 dilemma, plight, scrape
infuse [ɪnˈfjuːz]	*v.* 注入，灌输(to instill; impart)；鼓励(to inspire) 记 词根记忆：in(进入) + fus(流) + e → 流进去 → 注入，灌输
articulate [ɑːrˈtɪkjuleɪt]	*v.* 清楚地说话(to express clearly)；（用关节）连接(to put together by joints) 记 词根记忆：articul(接合) + ate → 连接 同 enunciate
preclude [prɪˈkluːd]	*v.* 预防，排除(to rule out in advance; prevent)；阻止(to exclude or prevent (sb.) from a given condition or activity) 记 词根记忆：pre(预先) + clud(关闭) + e → 预先关闭 → 预防，排除 同 deter, forestall, forfend, obviate, ward
sensory [ˈsensəri]	*adj.* 感觉的，感官的(of or relating to sensation or to the senses) 记 词根记忆：sens(感觉) + ory → 感觉的
raucous [ˈrɔːkəs]	*adj.* 刺耳的，沙哑的(disagreeably harsh; hoarse)；喧嚣的(boisterously disorderly) 记 词根记忆：rauc(=hoarse 沙哑的) + ous → 沙哑的
frisky [ˈfrɪski]	*adj.* 活泼的，快活的(playful; frolicsome; merry) 同 impish, mischievous, sportive, waggish
stagnant [ˈstægnənt]	*adj.* 停滞的(not advancing or developing) 记 词根记忆：stagn(=stand 站住) + ant → 停滞的
effective [ɪˈfektɪv]	*adj.* 有效的，生效的(producing a decided, decisive, or desired effect)；给人印象深刻的(impressive; striking) 记 来自 effect(*n.* 影响，效果)
strength [streŋθ]	*n.* 体力(the quality or state of being strong)；强度(power of resisting attack)；力量(legal, logical, or moral force) 例 While Parker is very outspoken on issues she cares about, she is not fanatical; she concedes the ***strength*** of opposing arguments when they expose weaknesses inherent in her own.
disputable [dɪˈspjuːtəbl]	*adj.* 有争议的(not definitely true or right, arguable) 同 debatable
accessible [əkˈsesəbl]	*adj.* 易接近的(easy to approach)；易受影响的(open to the influence of) 搭 accessible to 达到 同 employable, operative, practicable, unrestricted, usable

□ unerringly	□ charter	□ debate	□ quagmire	□ infuse	□ articulate
□ preclude	□ sensory	□ raucous	□ frisky	□ stagnant	□ effective
□ strength	□ disputable	□ accessible			

autobiography [ˌɔːtəbaɪˈɑːgrəfi]	*n.* 自传 (story of a person's life written by that person) 记 词根记忆：auto(自己) + bio(生命) + graphy(写) → 写自己的一生 → 自传
generalize [ˈdʒenrəlaɪz]	*v.* 概括，归纳 (to draw a general conclusion from particular examples) 记 联想记忆：general(概括的) + ize → 概括，归纳
self-effacement [ˌselfɪˈfesmənt]	*n.* 自谦 例 His submissiveness of manner and general air of *self-effacement* made it unlikely he would be selected to take command of the firm.
aromatic [ˌærəˈmætɪk]	*adj.* 芬芳的，芳香的 (having a strong pleasant smell) 记 词根记忆：aroma(芳香，香味) + tic → 芳香的
serene [səˈriːn]	*adj.* 平静的，安详的 (marked by or suggestive of utter calm and unruffled repose or quietude)；清澈的；晴朗的 例 The paradoxical aspect of the myths about Demeter, when we consider the predominant image of her as a tranquil and *serene* goddess, is her agitated search for her daughter.
composure [kəmˈpoʊʒər]	*n.* 镇静，沉着；自若 (tranquillity；equanimity) 记 词根记忆：com + pos(放) + ure(状态) → 放在一起的状态 → 沉着 同 calmness, coolness, phlegm, sangfroid, self-possession
overblown [ˌoʊvərˈbloʊn]	*adj.* 盛期已过的，残败的 (past the prime of bloom)；夸张的 (inflated)
wring [rɪŋ]	*v.* 绞，拧，扭 (to squeeze or twist) 同 contort, deform, distort
pristine [ˈprɪstiːn]	*adj.* 原始的 (belonging to the earliest period or state)；质朴的，纯洁的 (not spoiled or corrupted by civilization；pure)；新鲜的，干净的 (fresh and clean) 记 词根记忆：pri(=prim 第一，首先) + st(站) + ine → 站在首位的 → 原始的 例 Scientists' *pristine* reputation as devotees of the disinterested pursuit of truth has been compromised by recent evidence that some scientists have deliberately fabricated experimental results to further their own careers.
voyeur [vwaɪˈɜːr]	*n.* 窥淫癖者 (one who habitually seeks sexual stimulation by visual means)
synthesize [ˈsɪnθəsaɪz]	*v.* 综合；合成 (to combine or produce by synthesis) 记 词根记忆：syn(共同，相同) + thes(放) + ize → 放到一起 → 合成
impecunious [ˌɪmpɪˈkjuːniəs]	*adj.* 不名一文的，没钱的 (having very little or no money) 记 词根记忆：im(无) + pecun(钱) + ious → 没钱的
proficient [prəˈfɪʃnt]	*adj.* 熟练的，精通的 (skillful；expert) 记 词根记忆：pro(在前) + fic(做) + ient → 做在别人前面的 → 熟练的 例 Experienced and *proficient*, Susan is a good, reliable trumpeter; her music is often more satisfying than Carol's brilliant but erratic playing.

□ autobiography	□ generalize	□ self-effacement	□ aromatic	□ serene	□ composure
□ overblown	□ wring	□ pristine	□ voyeur	□ synthesize	□ impecunious
□ proficient					

disproportionate [ˌdɪsprə'pɔːrʃənət]	*adj.* 不成比例的(being out of proportion) 记 联想记忆：dis(不) + proportion(比例) + ate → 不成比例的
diminution [ˌdɪmɪ'nuːʃn]	*n.* 减少，缩减(a case or the state of diminishing or being diminished) 记 词根记忆：di + minu(变小，减少) + tion → 减少，缩减
prefabricated [ˌpriː'fæbrɪkeɪtɪd]	*adj.* 预制构件的 记 来自 prefabricate(*v.* 预制)
consign [kən'saɪn]	*v.* 托运；托人看管(to give over to another's care) 记 词根记忆：con + sign(签名) → 签完名后交托运 → 托运
seductive [sɪ'dʌktɪv]	*adj.* 诱人的(tending to seduce) 同 attractive, captivating
bias ['baɪəs]	*n.* 偏见(bent, tendency, prejudice) *v.* 使有偏见(to give a settled and often prejudiced outlook to) 记 联想记忆：bi(两) + as → 两者只取其一 → 偏见 搭 bias toward... 对…有偏见 同 leaning, disposition, partiality, penchant
systematic [ˌsɪstə'mætɪk]	*adj.* 系统的，体系的(relating to or consisting of a system) 例 It has been argued that politics as a practice, whatever its transcendental claims, has always been the *systematic* organization of common hatreds.
conspiracy [kən'spɪrəsi]	*n.* 共谋，阴谋(plan made by conspiring) 搭 conspiracy against 共谋反对
commend [kə'mend]	*v.* 推荐；举荐(to recommend as worthy of confidence or notice)；表扬；称赞(to praise) 同 acclaim, applaud, compliment, praise, recommend
upscale [ˌʌp'skeɪl]	*v.* 升高级，升档(to raise to a higher level)
naturalistic [ˌnætʃrə'lɪstɪk]	*adj.* 自然主义的(of, characterized by, or according with naturalism) 同 natural, realistic, true, truthful
unprecedented [ʌn'presɪdentɪd]	*adj.* 前所未有的(never having happened before) 记 联想记忆：un(不) + precedent(先例) + ed → 没有先例的 → 前所未有的
epitome [ɪ'pɪtəmi]	*n.* 典型(sb./sth. showing all the typical qualities of sth.)；梗概(abstract; summary; abridgment) 记 词根记忆：epi(在…上) + tom(切) + e → 切下来放在最上面 → 梗概；单词 tome 意为"卷，册"
confine [kən'faɪn]	*v.* 限制，禁闭(to keep a person or an animal in a restricted space; restrain) 记 词根记忆：con(全部) + fin(限制) + e → 全限制 → 禁闭 同 circumscribe, delimit

□ disproportionate	□ diminution	□ prefabricated	□ consign	□ seductive	□ bias
□ systematic	□ conspiracy	□ commend	□ upscale	□ naturalistic	□ unprecedented
□ epitome	□ confine				

universality [ˌjuːnɪvɜːrˈsæləti]	*n.* 普遍性（the quality or state of being universal）；广泛性（universal comprehensiveness in range）
disparage [dɪˈspærɪdʒ]	*v.* 贬低，轻蔑（to speak slightingly of; depreciate; decry） 记 词根记忆：dis(除去) + par(平等) + age → 剥夺平等 → 贬低 同 belittle, derogate
pitiful [ˈpɪtɪfl]	*adj.* 值得同情的，可怜的（deserving pity） 记 来自 pity(*n.* 同情)
obsolescent [ˌɑːbsəˈlesnt]	*adj.* 逐渐荒废的（in the process of becoming obsolete） 派 obsolescence(*n.* 废弃，陈旧)
referent [ˈrefərənt]	*n.* 指示对象（one that refers or is referred to）
immodest [ɪˈmɑːdɪst]	*adj.* 不谦虚的（not modest）；不正派的 搭 immodest behavior 不雅的举动
dissent [dɪˈsent]	*n.* 异议（difference of opinion）*v.* 不同意，持异议（to differ in belief or opinion; disagree） 记 词根记忆：dis(分开) + sent(感觉) → 感觉不同 → 不同意 例 Even though political editorializing was not forbidden under the new regime, journalists still experienced discreet, though perceptible, governmental pressure to limit *dissent*.
tributary [ˈtrɪbjəteri]	*n.* 支流；进贡国 *adj.* 支流的；辅助的；进贡的（making additions or yielding supplies; contributory）
eulogize [ˈjuːlədʒaɪz]	*v.* 称赞，颂扬（to praise highly in speech or writing） 记 词根记忆：eu(好的) + log(说) + ize → 说好话 → 称赞
tawdry [ˈtɔːdri]	*adj.* 华而不实的，俗丽的（cheap but showy） 搭 tawdry clothing 廉价而花哨的衣服
overwrought [ˌoʊvərˈrɔːt]	*adj.* 紧张过度的，兴奋过度的（very nervous or excited）
welter [ˈweltər]	*n.* 混乱，杂乱无章（a disordered mixture） 记 联想记忆：像一个大熔炉(melter)一样一片混乱(welter)
recipient [rɪˈsɪpiənt]	*n.* 接受者，收受者（a person who receives） 记 词根记忆：re + cip(拿) + ient → 拿东西的人 → 接受者，收受者
modestly [ˈmɑːdɪstli]	*adv.* 谦虚地，谦逊地；适度地 记 来自 modest(*adj.* 谦虚的，谦逊的；适度的)
opacity [oʊˈpæsəti]	*n.* 不透明性（the quality of being opaque）；晦涩（obscurity of sense） 例 The semantic *opacity* of ancient documents is not unique; even in our own time, many documents are difficult to decipher.
susceptible [səˈseptəbl]	*adj.* 易受影响的，敏感的（unresistant to some stimulus, influence, or agency） 例 Because it has no distinct and recognizable typographical form and few recurring narrative conventions, the novel is, of all literary genres, the least *susceptible* to definition.

□ universality	□ disparage	□ pitiful	□ obsolescent	□ referent	□ immodest
□ dissent	□ tributary	□ eulogize	□ tawdry	□ overwrought	□ welter
□ recipient	□ modestly	□ opacity	□ susceptible		

desirable [dɪˈzaɪərəbl]	*adj.* 值得要的（advisable；worthwhile；beneficial） 记 来自 desire（*v./n.* 渴望）
gluttonous [ˈɡlʌtənəs]	*adj.* 贪吃的，暴食的（very greedy for food） 同 edacious, hoggish, ravenous, voracious
cometary [ˈkɒmɪtəri]	*adj.* 彗星的，彗星似的 记 来自 comet（*n.* 彗星）
compound	[ˈkɑːmpaʊnd] *n.* 复合物（sth. formed by a union of elements or parts especially）[kəmˈpaʊnd] *v.* 掺和（to mix sth. together） 记 词根记忆：com + pound（放）→ 放到一起 → 掺和
sophisticated [səˈfɪstɪkeɪtɪd]	*adj.* 老于世故的；（仪器）精密的（highly complicated） 记 联想记忆：sophist（诡辩家）+ icated → 诡辩家都是老于世故的 → 老于世故的 例 Totem craftsmanship reached its apex in the 19th century, when the introduction of metal tools enabled carvers to execute more *sophisticated* designs.
abet [əˈbet]	*v.* 教唆；鼓励，帮助（to incite, encourage, urge and help on） 记 联想记忆：a + bet（赌博）→ 教唆赌博 → 教唆

A man is not old as long as he is seeking something. A man is not old until regrets take the place of dreams.

只要一个人还有所追求，他就没有老。直到后悔取代了梦想，一个人才算老。

——美国演员 巴里穆尔（J. Barrymore, American actor）

Word List 4

音频

aesthetic [es'θetɪk]	*adj.* 美学的，审美的(relating to aesthetics or the beautiful) 记 词根记忆：a + esthe(感觉) + tic(…的) → 美学的；审美的
nonflammable [ˌnɑːn'flæməbl]	*adj.* 不易燃的(not flammable) 记 联想记忆：non（不）+ flammable（易燃的）→ 不易燃的；注意不要和 inflammable(*adj.* 易燃的)相混
penchant ['pentʃənt]	*n.* 爱好，嗜好(liking) 记 词根记忆：pench(=pend 挂) + ant → 对…挂着一颗心 → 爱好 例 Although retiring, almost self-effacing in his private life, he displays in his plays and essays a strong *penchant* for publicity and controversy.
egoistic(al) [ˌegoʊ'ɪstɪk(l)]	*adj.* 自我中心的，自私自利的(of or relating to the self) 同 egocentric, egomaniacal, self-centered, selfish
excessive [ɪk'sesɪv]	*adj.* 过度的，过分的(exceeding what is usual, proper, necessary, or normal) 例 Unfortunately, *excessive* care in choosing one's words often results in a loss of spontaneity. 同 exorbitant, extravagant, extreme, immoderate, inordinate
absent [æb'sent]	*v.* 缺席，不参加(to keep (oneself) away) *adj.* 缺席的 记 联想记忆：ab + sent(送走) → 把某人送走 → 缺席 例 Although Irish literature continued to flourish after the sixteenth century, a comparable tradition is *absent* in the visual arts: we think about Irish culture in terms of the word, not in terms of pictorial images.
clumsy ['klʌmzi]	*adj.* 笨拙的（lacking grace; awkward）；拙劣的（ill-constructed） 记 联想记忆：c + lum（亮度）+ sy → 没有亮光，不灵光 → 笨拙的 同 gawky, lumbering, lumpish
surly ['sɜːrli]	*adj.* 脾气暴躁的(bad tempered)；阴沉的(sullen) 记 联想记忆：sur（=sir 先生）+ ly → 像高高在上的先生一般 → 脾气暴躁的

clumsy

□ aesthetic	□ nonflammable	□ penchant	□ egoistic(al)	□ excessive	□ absent
□ clumsy	□ surly				

shed [ʃed]	*v.* 流出(眼泪等)(to pour forth in drops); 脱落, 蜕, 落(to lose by natural process) 搭 shed tears 流泪
briny [ˈbraɪni]	*adj.* 盐水的, 咸的(of, relating to, or resembling brine or the sea; salty) 记 来自 brine(*n.* 盐水)
calamity [kəˈlæməti]	*n.* 大灾祸, 不幸之事(any extreme misfortune) 记 词根记忆: calam(=destruction 破坏) + ity → 大灾祸
geomagnetic [ˌdʒiːoʊmæɡˈnetɪk]	*adj.* 地磁的(of or relating to terrestrial magnetism) 记 和 geomagnetism(*n.* 地磁学)一起记
hypothetical [ˌhaɪpəˈθetɪkl]	*adj.* 假设的(based on a hypothesis) 同 conjectural
incarnate [ɪnˈkɑːrnət]	*adj.* 具有人体的(given a bodily form); 化身的, 拟人化的(personified) 记 词根记忆: in(进入) + carn(肉体) + ate → 变成肉体的 → 具有人体的
moralistic [ˌmɔːrəˈlɪstɪk]	*adj.* 道学的, 说教的(concerned with morals) 记 来自 moral(*n.* 道德)
foreknowledge [fɔːrˈnɑːlɪdʒ]	*n.* 预知, 先见之明(knowledge of sth. before it happens or exists) 记 组合词: fore(预先) + knowledge(知道) → 预知
repetition [ˌrepəˈtɪʃn]	*n.* 重复(the act or an instance of repeating or being repeated); 背诵(recital) 记 来自 repeat(*v.* 重复)
torpid [ˈtɔːrpɪd]	*adj.* 懒散的; 迟钝的(lacking in energy or vigor; dull) 同 lethargic, sluggish, stupid
daunt [dɔːnt]	*v.* 使胆怯, 使畏缩(to dishearten; dismay) 记 联想记忆: d(看作 devil, 魔鬼) + aunt(姑姑) → 像鬼一样的姑姑 → 使胆怯
frustrate [ˈfrʌstreɪt]	*v.* 挫败, 使沮丧(to baffle; defeat) 记 联想记忆: frust(一部分) + rate(费用) → 买东西只带了一部分钱, 买不成 → 挫败 同 foil, thwart
syllable [ˈsɪləbl]	*n.* 音节 *v.* 分成音节(to give a number or arrangement of syllables to (a word or verse)) 记 联想记忆: syll(音似: say) + able → 可以说出来的 → 音节
slovenly [ˈslʌvnli]	*adj.* 不整洁的, 邋遢的(untidy especially in personal appearance) 同 dirty
ingenuous [ɪnˈdʒenjuəs]	*adj.* 纯真的, 纯朴的(simple; artless); 坦率的(frank) 同 natural, unsophisticated
flag [flæɡ]	*v.* 减弱, 衰退(to lose strength); 枯萎(to droop) 记 flag "旗, 国旗"之意众所周知 同 deteriorate, languish, wilt

4

□ shed	□ briny	□ calamity	□ geomagnetic	□ hypothetical	□ incarnate
□ moralistic	□ foreknowledge	□ repetition	□ torpid	□ daunt	□ frustrate
□ syllable	□ slovenly	□ ingenuous	□ flag		

sluggish [ˈslʌgɪʃ]	*adj.* 缓慢的，行动迟缓的（markedly slow in movement, flow, or growth）；反应慢的（slow to respond） 例 Species with relatively *sluggish* metabolic rates, including hibernators, generally live longer than those whose metabolic rates are more rapid. 同 torpid
retract [rɪˈtrækt]	*v.* 撤回，取消（to take back or withdraw）；缩回，拉回（to draw or pull back） 记 词根记忆：re(反) + tract(拉) → 拉回去 → 拉回
obliging [əˈblaɪdʒɪŋ]	*adj.* 乐于助人的（helpful; accommodating） 记 来自 oblige(*v.* 施恩惠于，帮助)
surmount [sərˈmaʊnt]	*v.* 克服，战胜（to prevail over; overcome）；登上（to get to the top of） 记 词根记忆：sur(在…下) + mount(山) → 将山踩在脚下 → 克服，战胜
ingrained [ɪnˈgreɪnd]	*adj.* 根深蒂固的（firmed, fixed or established） 搭 ingrained prejudices 很深的成见
psychological [ˌsaɪkəˈlɑːdʒɪkl]	*adj.* 心理学的（of or relating to psychology）；心理的，精神的（directed toward the will or the mind specifically in its conative function） 记 词根记忆：psycho(心灵，精神) + log(说) + ical(…的) → 心理的，精神的 例 In a nation where the economic reversals of the past few years have taken a *psychological* as well as a financial toll on many regions, what most distinguishes the South may be the degree of optimism throughout the region.
autograph [ˈɔːtəgræf]	*n.* 亲笔稿，手迹（something written or made with one's own hand）*v.* 在…上亲笔签名（to write one's signature in or on）*adj.* 亲笔的（being in the writer's own handwriting）
erudition [ˌeruˈdɪʃn]	*n.* 博学（extensive knowledge acquired chiefly from books） 同 eruditeness, scholarship
appease [əˈpiːz]	*v.* 使平静，安抚（to pacify or quiet） 记 词根记忆：ap + pease(和平) → 使平静 同 assuage, conciliate, mollify, pacify, propitiate
choppy [ˈtʃɑːpi]	*adj.* 波浪起伏的（rough with small waves）；（风）不断改变方向的（changeable; variable）
relinquish [rɪˈlɪŋkwɪʃ]	*v.* 放弃，让出（to give up; withdraw or retreat from） 记 词根记忆：re + linqu(=leave, 离开) + ish → 放弃，让出
celestial [səˈlestʃl]	*adj.* 天体的，天上的（of or in the sky or universe） 记 词根记忆：celest(天空) + ial → 天上的
procedure [prəˈsiːdʒər]	*n.* 程序，手续（a particular way of accomplishing sth. or of acting） 记 来自 proceed(*v.* 前进) 例 Despite the apparently bewildering complexity of this *procedure*, the underlying principle is quite elementary.

□ sluggish	□ retract	□ obliging	□ surmount	□ ingrained	□ psychological
□ autograph	□ erudition	□ appease	□ choppy	□ relinquish	□ celestial
□ procedure					

uncommitted [ˌʌnkəˈmɪtɪd]	*adj.* 不受约束的，不承担责任的（not pledged to a particular belief or allegiance） 记 联想记忆：un(不) + committed(有责任的) → 不承担责任的
boredom [ˈbɔːrdəm]	*n.* 厌烦（the state of being weary）；令人厌烦的事物（sth. boring） 记 词根记忆：bore(厌烦) + dom(表名词，参考 kingdom) → 厌烦
jest [dʒest]	*n.* 笑话，俏皮话（joke）*v.* 说笑，开玩笑（to joke; be playful in speech and actions） 同 fleer, flout, gibe, jeer, scoff
tantalize [ˈtæntəlaɪz]	*v.* 挑惹，挑逗（to tease or torment by a sight of sth. that is desired but cannot be reached） 记 来自希腊神话人物 Tantalus（坦塔洛斯），他因泄露天机而被罚立在近下巴深的水中，口渴欲饮时水即流失；头上有果树，腹饥欲食时果子即消失
prolific [prəˈlɪfɪk]	*adj.* 多产的，多果实的（fruitful; fertile） 记 联想记忆：pro(许多) + lif(看作 life，生命) + ic(…的) → 产生许多生命的 → 多产的 例 Having written 140 books to date, he may well be considered one of the most *prolific* novelists of the century. 同 fecund, productive
depreciate [dɪˈpriːʃieɪt]	*v.* 轻视（to make seem less important; belittle; disparage）；贬值（to reduce or drop in value or price） 记 词根记忆：de(低) + prec(价值) + iate → 贬值
tout [taʊt]	*v.* 招徕顾客；极力赞扬（to praise or publicize loudly） 例 In recent decades the idea that Cezanne influenced Cubism has been caught in the crossfire between art historians who credit Braque with its invention and those who *tout* Picasso.
betray [bɪˈtreɪ]	*v.* 背叛（to deliver to an enemy by treachery）；暴露（to reveal） 记 词根记忆：be + tray(背叛) → 背叛；联想记忆：bet(打赌) + ray(光线) → 打赌打到了光线下 → 暴露 同 disclose, divulge, uncover, unveil
redundant [rɪˈdʌndənt]	*adj.* 累赘的，多余的（exceeding what is necessary or normal; superfluous） 记 词根记忆：red(=re) + und(波动) + ant → 反复波动 → 反复出现的 → 累赘的，多余的 同 diffuse, prolix, verbose, wordy
zenith [ˈzenɪθ]	*n.* 天顶（the highest point of the celestial sphere）；极点（the highest point） 例 Her novel published to universal acclaim, her literary gifts acknowledged by the chief figures of the Harlem Renaissance, her reputation as yet untarnished by envious slights, Hurston clearly was at the *zenith* of her career. 同 acme, apex, culmination, meridian, pinnacle
beneficent [bɪˈnefɪsnt]	*adj.* 慈善的，仁爱的（doing or producing good）；有益的（beneficial） 记 词根记忆：bene(好) + fic(做) + ent(…的) → 做好事的 → 慈善的

4

□ uncommitted	□ boredom	□ jest	□ tantalize	□ prolific	□ depreciate
□ tout	□ betray	□ redundant	□ zenith	□ beneficent	

rhetoric	*n.* 修辞，修辞学；浮夸的言辞（insincere or grandiloquent language）
[ˈretərɪk]	记 来自 Rhetor（古希腊的修辞学教师、演说家）
commitment	*n.* 承诺，许诺（an agreement or pledge to do sth. in the future）
[kəˈmɪtmənt]	
inefficient	*adj.* 无效率的（not efficient）；无能的，不称职的（incapable; incompetent）
[ˌɪnɪˈfɪʃnt]	搭 an inefficient heating system 效率不佳的暖气系统
virtuous	*adj.* 有美德的（showing virtue）
[ˈvɜːrtʃuəs]	记 来自 virtue（*n.* 美德）
determinant	*n.* 决定因素（sth. that determines or decides how sth. happens）*adj.* 决定
[dɪˈtɜːrmɪnənt]	性的（decisive）
	记 来自 determine（*v.* 决定，下决心）
iridescent	*adj.* 色彩斑斓的（producing a display of lustrous, rainbowlike colors）
[ˌɪrɪˈdesnt]	记 词根记忆：irid（=iris 彩虹）+ escent（开始…的）→ 闪着彩虹般的光的 →
	色彩斑斓的
plaintive	*adj.* 哀伤的，悲伤的（expressive of woe; melancholy）
[ˈpleɪntɪv]	记 来自 plaint（*n.* 哀诉）
impressed	*adj.* 被打动的，被感动的
[ɪmˈprest]	搭 be impressed by（对…）钦佩，有深刻的好印象
insular	*adj.* 岛屿的；心胸狭窄的（illiberal; narrow-minded）
[ˈɪnsələr]	记 词根记忆：insul（岛）+ ar → 岛屿的
characterize	*v.* 表现…的特色，刻画…的性格（to describe the character or quality of）
[ˈkærəktəraɪz]	记 来自 character（*n.* 人或事物的特点、特征）
frugal	*adj.* 节约的，节俭的（careful and thrifty）
[ˈfruːɡl]	记 发音记忆："腐乳过日" → 吃腐乳过日子 → 节约的
rivalry	*n.* 竞争，对抗（the state of being a rival）
[ˈraɪvlri]	同 competition, contention, contest
overturn	*v.* 翻倒（to (cause to) turn over or capsize）；推翻，倾覆（to cause the ruin
[ˌouvərˈtɜːrn]	or destruction of; overthrow）
penitent	*adj.* 悔过的，忏悔的（expressing regretful pain; repentant）
[ˈpenɪtənt]	记 词根记忆：pen（处罚）+ it + ent → 受了处罚所以后悔 → 悔过的
benign	*adj.* （病）良性的（of a mild type or character that does not threaten health
[bɪˈnaɪn]	or life）；亲切和蔼的（showing kindness and gentleness）；慈祥的（good
	natured; kindly）
	记 词根记忆：ben（好）+ ign（形容词后缀）→ 好的 → 亲切和蔼的
hyperbole	*n.* 夸张法（extravagant exaggeration）
[haɪˈpɜːrbəli]	记 词根记忆：hyper（过度）+ bole（扔）→ 扔得过度 → 夸张法
	例 Rhetoric often seems to triumph over reason in a heated debate, with
	both sides engaging in *hyperbole*.
	同 overstatement

fantasy [ˈfæntəsi]	*n.* 想象，幻想(imagination or fancy) 记 发音记忆："范特西" → 听着周杰伦的范特西，陷入无限的想象 → 想象，幻想
unedited [ʌnˈedɪtɪd]	*adj.* 未编辑的(not yet edited)
ingenuously [ɪnˈdʒenjuəsli]	*adv.* 纯真地；坦率地
arable [ˈærəbl]	*adj.* 适于耕种的(suitable for plowing and planting) 记 联想记忆：ar(看作 are) + able → 是能够耕种的 → 适于耕种的 搭 arable field 可耕地
perpetrate [ˈpɜːrpətreɪt]	*v.* 犯罪(to commit)；负责(to be responsible for)
arcane [ɑːrˈkeɪn]	*adj.* 神秘的，秘密的(mysterious; hidden or secret) 记 词根记忆：arcan(秘密) + e → 神秘的 同 cabalistic, impenetrable, inscrutable, mystic
peerless [ˈpɪrləs]	*adj.* 出类拔萃的，无可匹敌的(matchless; incomparable) 记 联想记忆：peer(同等的人) + less(无) → 无可匹敌的
proofread [ˈpruːfriːd]	*v.* 校正，校对(to read and mark corrections) 记 组合词：proof(校对) + read(读) → 校正，校对
self-adulation [ˌselfædʒəˈleɪʃn]	*n.* 自我吹捧(the act of praising or flattering excessively by oneself) 例 It is ironic that a critic of such overwhelming vanity now suffers from a measure of the oblivion to which he was forever consigning others; in the end, all his *self-adulation* has only worked against him.
amenable [əˈmiːnəbl]	*adj.* 顺从的；愿接受的(willing; submissive) 记 联想记忆：a + men(人) + able(能…的) → 一个顺从的人 → 顺从的 搭 be amenable to 服从
impound [ɪmˈpaʊnd]	*v.* 限制(to confine)；依法没收，扣押(to seize and hold in the custody of the law; take possession of)
forested [ˈfɔːrɪstɪd]	*adj.* 树木丛生的(wooded) 记 来自 forest(*n.* 森林)
succor [ˈsʌkər]	*v.* 救助，援助(to go to the aid of) 记 词根记忆：suc(下面) + cor(跑) → 跑到下面来 → 救助
cavil [ˈkævl]	*v.* 挑毛病，吹毛求疵(to object when there is little reason to do so; quibble) 搭 cavil at 在…方面挑毛病
fault [fɔːlt]	*n.* 错误(mistake)；【地质】断层(a fracture in the crust of a planet) 同 deficiency, demerit, foible, imperfection
adept [əˈdept]	*adj.* 熟练的，擅长的(highly skilled; expert) 记 词根记忆：ad + ept(能力) → 有能力 → 熟练的，擅长的 搭 be adept at 擅长

4

□ fantasy	□ unedited	□ ingenuously	□ arable	□ perpetrate	□ arcane
□ peerless	□ proofread	□ self-adulation	□ amenable	□ impound	□ forested
□ succor	□ cavil	□ fault	□ adept		

compliment [ˈkɑːmplɪmənt]	*n./v.* 恭维，称赞（praise；flattery） 同 congratulate, felicitate, laud	**compliment**
catastrophe [kəˈtæstrəfi]	*n.* 突如其来的大灾难（sudden great disaster） 记 词根记忆：cata（向下）+ strophe（转）→ 天地向下转 → 突如其来的大灾难 搭 a major catastrophe 一次严重的灾难	
cautionary [ˈkɔːʃəneri]	*adj.* 劝人谨慎的，警戒的（giving advice or a warning） 记 词根记忆：caution（小心，谨慎）+ ary → 劝人谨慎的，警戒的 同 admonishing, admonitory, cautioning, monitory	
humane [hjuːˈmeɪn]	*adj.* 人道的，慈悲的（marked by compassion, sympathy, or consideration for humans or animals）；人文主义的（humanistic） 搭 humane treatment 人道的待遇	
torpor [ˈtɔːrpər]	*n.* 死气沉沉（extreme sluggishness of function） 同 dullness, languor, lassitude, lethargy	
superannuate [ˌsuːpərˈænjueɪt]	*v.* 使退休领养老金（to retire and pension because of age or infirmity）	
artisan [ˈɑːrtəzn]	*n.* 技工（skilled workman or craftsman） 记 词根记忆：arti（技术）+ san（人）→ 技工	
predetermine [ˌpriːdɪˈtɜːrmɪn]	*v.* 预先注定（to foreordain; predestine）；预先决定（to determine beforehand） 记 联想记忆：pre（在前面）+ determine（决定）→ 预先决定	
unstable [ʌnˈsteɪbl]	*adj.* 不稳定的（not stable） 记 联想记忆：un（不）+ stable（稳定的）→ 不稳定的	
interruption [ˌɪntəˈrʌpʃn]	*n.* 中断，打断 同 break, disruption, pause, suspension	
untimely [ʌnˈtaɪmli]	*adj.* 过早的（occurring or done before the due, natural, or proper time）；不合时宜的（inopportune, unseasonable） 记 联想记忆：un（不）+ timely（及时的，适时的）→ 不合时宜的	
readable [ˈriːdəbl]	*adj.* 易读的（able to be read easily）	
valorous [ˈvælərəs]	*adj.* 勇敢的（brave） 记 联想记忆：val（强大）+ orous → 勇敢使人强大 → 勇敢的	
threaten [ˈθretn]	*v.* 威胁（to utter threats against） 同 browbeat, bully, intimidate, menace	
aberrant [æˈberənt]	*adj.* 越轨的（turning away from what is right）；异常的（deviating from what is normal） 记 词根记忆：ab + err（错误）+ ant → 走向错误 → 越轨的	
piercing [ˈpɪrsɪŋ]	*adj.* 冷得刺骨的（penetratingly cold）；敏锐的（perceptive） 同 shrill	

□ compliment	□ catastrophe	□ cautionary	□ humane	□ torpor	□ superannuate
□ artisan	□ predetermine	□ unstable	□ interruption	□ untimely	□ readable
□ valorous	□ threaten	□ aberrant	□ piercing		

42

rave [reɪv]	*n.* 热切赞扬（an extravagantly favorable remark）*v.* 胡言乱语，说疯话（to talk irrationally in or as if in delirium）
hazardous [ˈhæzərdəs]	*adj.* 危险的，冒险的（marked by danger; perilous; risky） 例 Given the inconclusive state of the published evidence, we do not argue here that exposure to low-level microwave energy is either *hazardous* or safe.
divert [daɪˈvɜːrt]	*v.* 转移，（使）转向（to turn from one course to another）；使娱乐（to entertain） 记 词根记忆：di(离开) + vert(转) → (使)转向
violate [ˈvaɪəleɪt]	*v.* 违反，侵犯（to disregard or act against） 记 发音记忆："why late" → 违反制度迟到了 → 违反，侵犯 例 Scientists who are on the cutting edge of research must often *violate* common sense and make seemingly absurd assumptions because existing theories simply do not explain newly observed phenomena. 同 breach, contravene, infract, infringe, transgress
embryological [ˌembriəˈlɑːdʒɪkl]	*adj.* 胚胎学的 记 联想记忆：embryo(胚胎) + olog(y)(…学) + ical → 胚胎学的
engage [ɪnˈgeɪdʒ]	*v.* 从事，参加（to involve）；雇用，聘用（to hire）；使参与（to induce to participate; participate）；引起…的注意（to hold the attention of） 记 联想记忆：en(使…) + gage(挑战) → 使接受挑战 → 从事
comparison [kəmˈpærɪsn]	*n.* 比较，对照（act of comparing）；比喻 记 来自compare(*v.* 比较) 搭 by comparison 通过比较；in comparison with/to 与…比较
flaunty [ˈflɔːnti]	*adj.* 炫耀的，虚华的（ostentatious） 记 来自flaunt(*v.* 炫耀，夸耀)
procurement [prəˈkjʊrmənt]	*n.* 取得，获得（the obtaining by effort or careful attention）；采购 记 来自动词procure(*v.* 取得，获得) 例 Remelting old metal cans rather than making primary aluminum from bauxite ore shipped from overseas saves producers millions of dollars in *procurement* and production costs.
arduous [ˈɑːrdʒuəs]	*adj.* 费力的，艰难的（marked by great labor or effort） 搭 arduous march 艰难行军
idyllic [aɪˈdɪlɪk]	*adj.* 田园诗的（of, relating to, or being an idyll） 搭 an idyllic vacation 田园诗般的假日
sinuous [ˈsɪnjuəs]	*adj.* 蜿蜒的，迂回的（characterized by many curves and twists; winding） 记 词根记忆：sinu(弯曲) + ous → 弯曲的 → 蜿蜒的
sprawling [ˈsprɔːlɪŋ]	*adj.* 植物蔓生的，(城市)无计划地扩展的（spreading out ungracefully） 搭 sprawling handwriting 潦草的笔迹
exasperate [ɪgˈzæspəreɪt]	*v.* 激怒，使恼怒（to make angry; vex） 记 词根记忆：ex + asper(粗鲁的) + ate → 显出粗鲁 → 激怒 同 huff, irritate, peeve, pique, rile, roil

4

□ rave	□ hazardous	□ divert	□ violate	□ embryological	□ engage
□ comparison	□ flaunty	□ procurement	□ arduous	□ idyllic	□ sinuous
□ sprawling	□ exasperate				

43

archetypally [ˌɑːrki ˈtaɪpəli]	*adv.* 典型地 记 来自 archetype(*n.* 典型)
domesticated [də ˈmestɪkeɪtɪd]	*adj.* 驯养的，家养的 记 词根记忆：dom(家) + esticated → 家养的
captivating [ˈkæptɪveɪtɪŋ]	*adj.* 吸引人的 (very attractive and interesting, in a way that holds your attention)
vacillate [ˈvæsəleɪt]	*v.* 游移不定，踌躇 (to waver in mind, will or feeling) 记 词根记忆：vacill(摇摆) + ate → 游移不定
polarize [ˈpoʊləraɪz]	*v.* (使人、观点等)两极化，(使)截然对立 (to divide into groups based on two completely opposite principles or political opinions) 记 来自 polar(*adj.* 两极的)
graft [ɡræft]	*v.* 嫁接（ to cause a scion to unite with a stock ），结合（ to be or become joined ）；贪污（ to get by graft ）*n.* 嫁接，结合；贪污 记 联想记忆：g(看作 go) + raft(木筏) → 用木筏运送嫁接的树苗 → 嫁接
parasitic [ˌpærə ˈsɪtɪk]	*adj.* 寄生的 例 The tapeworm is an example of a *parasitic* organism, one that lives within or on another creature, deriving some or all of its nutriment from its host.
benevolent [bə ˈnevələnt]	*adj.* 善心的，仁心的 (kindly; charitable) 记 词根记忆：bene(好) + vol(意志) + ent → 好意的 → 善心的，仁心的 同 altruistic, humane, philanthropic
fireproof [ˈfaɪərpruːf]	*adj.* 耐火的，防火的 (proof against or resistant to fire)
castigate [ˈkæstɪɡeɪt]	*v.* 惩治，严责 (to punish or rebuke severely) 记 联想记忆：cast(扔) + i(我) + gate(门) → 向我的门扔东西 → 惩治，严责 同 chasten, chastise, discipline
relieved [rɪ ˈliːvd]	*adj.* 宽慰的，如释重负的 (experiencing or showing relief especially from anxiety or pent-up emotions) 例 Sponsors of the bill were *relieved* because there was no opposition to it within the legislature until after the measure had been signed into law.
custodian [kʌ ˈstoʊdiən]	*n.* 管理员，监护人 (a person who has the custody or care of sth.; caretaker) 记 发音记忆："卡死偷电" → 管理比较严，卡死偷电的 → 管理员
juncture [ˈdʒʌŋktʃər]	*n.* 关键时刻，危急关头 (a critical point)；结合处，接合点 (a joining point) 例 The TV news magazine sits precisely at the *juncture* of information and entertainment, for while it is not a silly sitcom, it is not a documentary either.
untouched [ʌn ˈtʌtʃt]	*adj.* 未触动过的，未改变的 (not changed in any way) 同 uninfluenced, unswayed
hierarchy [ˈhaɪərɑːrki]	*n.* 阶层；等级制度 (a system of ranks) 记 词根记忆：hier(神圣的) + archy(统治) → 神圣的统治 → 等级制度

□ archetypally	□ domesticated	□ captivating	□ vacillate	□ polarize	□ graft
□ parasitic	□ benevolent	□ fireproof	□ castigate	□ relieved	□ custodian
□ juncture	□ untouched	□ hierarchy			

controversy [ˈkɑːntrəvɜːrsi]	*n.* 公开辩论, 论战(dispute; quarrel; strife) 记 词根记忆: contro (相反) + vers (转) + y → 意见转向相反的方向 → 论战 同 altercation, bickering, contention, hurrah
hatch [hætʃ]	*n.* 船舱盖(a covering for a ship's hatchway) *v.* 孵化(to produce young by incubation); 策划(to bring into being; originate) 搭 hatch a plot 策划阴谋
precedent [ˈpresɪdənt]	*adj.* 在先的, 在前的(prior in time, order, arrangement, or significance) *n.* 先例(an earlier occurrence of sth. similar); 判例(a judicial decision that may be used as a standard in subsequent similar cases) 例 In failing to see that the justice's pronouncement merely qualified previous decisions rather than actually establishing a *precedent*, the novice law clerk overemphasized the scope of the justice's judgment.
portend [pɔːrˈtend]	*v.* 预兆, 预示(to give an omen) 记 联想记忆: port(港口) + end(尽头) → 港口到了尽头, 预示着临近海洋 → 预示
promote [prəˈmoʊt]	*v.* 提升(to give sb. a higher position or rank); 促进(to help in the growth or development) 记 词根记忆: pro(向前) + mot(动) + e → 向前动 → 促进 例 Some activists believe that because the health-care system has become increasingly unresponsive to those it serves, individuals must circumvent bureaucratic impediments in order to develop and *promote* new therapies.
diffident [ˈdɪfɪdənt]	*adj.* 缺乏自信的(not showing much belief in one's own abilities) 同 bashful, coy, demure, modest, self-effacing
rustic [ˈrʌstɪk]	*adj.* 乡村的, 乡土气的(of, relating to, or suitable for the country) 记 词根记忆: rust(乡村) + ic → 乡村的
veracity [vəˈræsəti]	*n.* 真实(devotion to the truth); 诚实(truthfulness) 记 词根记忆: ver(真实的) + acity → 真实 例 Trying to prove Hill a liar, Senator Specter repeatedly questioned her *veracity*.
combine [kəmˈbaɪn]	*v.* (使)联合, 结合(to merge, intermix, blend; possess in combination); 协力(to act together) 记 词根记忆: com(共同) + bi(两个) + ne → 使两个在一起 → (使)联合 同 associate, bracket, coalesce, conjoin
tenacious [təˈneɪʃəs]	*adj.* 坚韧的, 顽强的(persistent in maintaining or adhering to sth. valued or habitual) 记 词根记忆: ten(拿住) + acious(有…性质的) → 拿住不放 → 坚韧的
renewal [rɪˈnuːəl]	*n.* 更新(the act or process of renewing, the quality or state of being renewed); 复兴, 振兴
facetious [fəˈsiːʃəs]	*adj.* 滑稽的, 好开玩笑的(joking or jesting often inappropriately) 记 联想记忆: face(脸) + tious → 做鬼脸 → 好开玩笑的

4

□ controversy	□ hatch	□ precedent	□ portend	□ promote	□ diffident
□ rustic	□ veracity	□ combine	□ tenacious	□ renewal	□ facetious

context [ˈkɑːntekst]	*n.* (语句等的)上下文(words that come before and after a word, phrase, or statement) 记 词根记忆：con(共同) + text(编织) → 共同编织在一起的 → 上下文
surreptitious [ˌsɜːrəpˈtɪʃəs]	*adj.* 鬼鬼祟祟的(acting or doing sth. clandestinely) 记 词根记忆：sur (在…下) + rep (=rap 拿，抓住) + titious → 偷偷拿 → 鬼鬼祟祟的 例 The Turner Network's new production is an absorbing *Heart of Darkness*, watchful, *surreptitious*, almost predatory as it waits to pounce on our emotions.
bulky [ˈbʌlki]	*adj.* 庞大的(large of its kind)；笨重的(corpulent) 记 来自 bulk(*n.* 巨大的体重(或重量、形状、身体等))
relentless [rɪˈlentləs]	*adj.* 无情的，残酷的(cruel) 同 merciless, pitiless, ruthless
topple [ˈtɑːpl]	*v.* 倾覆，推倒(to overthrow) 记 联想记忆：top(顶) + ple → 使顶向下 → 倾覆，推倒
perishable [ˈperɪʃəbl]	*adj.* 易腐烂的，易变质的(likely to decay or go bad quickly) *n.* 易腐烂的东西(stuff subject to decay) 记 来自 perish(*v.* 毁灭；腐烂) 例 Given the *perishable* nature of wood, the oldest totem poles of the Northwest Coast Indians eventually fell to decay; only a few still stand today.
dismiss [dɪsˈmɪs]	*v.* 解散(to permit or cause to leave)；解雇(to remove from position or service) 记 词根记忆：dis(分开) + miss(送，放出) → 解散
symbolic [sɪmˈbɑːlɪk]	*adj.* 符号的(using, employing, or exhibiting a symbol)；象征的(consisting of or proceeding by means of symbols) 例 Once Renaissance painters discovered how to render volume and depth, they were able to replace the medieval convention of *symbolic*, two-dimensional space with the more realistic illusion of actual space.
cessation [seˈseɪʃn]	*n.* 中止，(短暂的)停止(a short pause or a stop) 记 词根记忆：cess(走) + ation → 不走的状态 → 中止
contagious [kənˈteɪdʒəs]	*adj.* 传染的，有感染力的(easily passed from person to person; communicable) 记 词根记忆：con + tag(接触) + ious → 接触(疾病的) → 传染的
prodigious [prəˈdɪdʒəs]	*adj.* 巨大的(extraordinary in bulk, quantity, or degree)；惊人的，奇异的 记 来自 prodigy(*n.* 惊人的事物；奇观) 例 Although Barbara Tuchman never earned a graduate degree, she nonetheless pursued a scholarly career as a historian noted for her vivid style and *prodigious* erudition. 同 colossal, gigantic, immense, marvelous, stupendous

□ context   □ surreptitious   □ bulky   □ relentless   □ topple   □ perishable
□ dismiss   □ symbolic   □ cessation   □ contagious   □ prodigious

abstruse [əb'struːs]	*adj.* 难懂的，深奥的(hard to understand；recondite) 记 词根记忆：abs + trus(走，推) + e → 走不进去 → 难懂的
oval ['oʊvl]	*adj.* 卵形的，椭圆形的(having the shape of an egg) 记 联想记忆：o(音似：喔) + val(音似：哇哦) → 发"哇哦"这些音时嘴要张成椭圆形 → 椭圆形的

4

If you would go up high, then use your own legs! Do not let yourselves carried aloft; do not seat yourselves on other people's backs and heads.

如果你想要走到高处，就要使用自己的两条腿！不要让别人把你抬到高处；不要坐在别人的背上和头上。

——德国哲学家 尼采(F. W. Nietzsche, German philosopher)

wanderlust [ˈwɑːndərlʌst]	*n.* 漫游癖，旅游癖(strong longing for or impulse toward wandering) 记 组合词: wander(漫游) + lust(欲望) → 漫游癖 例 For many young people during the Roaring Twenties, a disgust with the excesses of American culture combined with a *wanderlust* to provoke an exodus abroad.
suspicious [səˈspɪʃəs]	*adj.* 怀疑的 (expressing or indicative of suspicion) 搭 be suspicious of/about... 对…怀疑的 同 doubtful, dubious, problematic
imply [ɪmˈplaɪ]	*v.* 暗示，暗指(to express indirectly) 记 词根记忆: im(进入) + ply(重叠) → 重叠表达 → 暗示 例 Although the revelation that one of the contestants was a friend left the judge open to charges of lack of disinterestedness, the judge remained adamant in her assertion that acquaintance did not necessarily *imply* partiality. 同 connote, indicate, insinuate, intimate
sectarianism [sekˈteriənɪzəm]	*n.* 宗派主义；教派意识
inform [ɪnˈfɔːrm]	*v.* 对…有影响(to have an influence on sth.)；使活跃，使有生气(to animate)；告诉，通知(to impart information or knowledge) 记 词根记忆: in(进入) + form(形成) → 形成文字，进行通知 → 通知 例 Just as the authors' book on eels is often a key text for courses in marine vertebrate zoology, their ideas on animal development and phylogeny *inform* teaching in this area. 同 acquaint, apprise
scant [skænt]	*adj.* 不足的，缺乏的(barely or scarcely) 搭 scant attention/consideration 缺乏注意/考虑
reverberate [rɪˈvɜːrbəreɪt]	*v.* 发出回声，回响(to resound, echo) 记 词根记忆: re + verber(打，振动) + ate → 振动回来 → 发出回声

□ wanderlust	□ suspicious	□ imply	□ sectarianism	□ inform	□ scant
□ reverberate					

innocence	*n.* 无辜，清白（the quality of being innocent）
[ˈɪnəsns]	记 词根记忆: in(无) + noc(伤害) + ence → 无辜，清白
	例 Melodramas, which presented stark oppositions between *innocence* and criminality, virtue and corruption, good and evil, were popular precisely because they offered the audience a world devoid of neutrality.
inquisitive	*adj.* 好奇的，好问的（inclined to ask questions; prying）; 爱打听的
[ɪnˈkwɪzətɪv]	记 词根记忆: in(进入) + quis(询问) + itive → 进入询问 → 好奇的，好问的
	例 Excited and unafraid, the *inquisitive* child examined the stranger with bright-eyed curiosity.
hibernate	*v.* 冬眠（to spend the winter in a dormant or torpid state）
[ˈhaɪbərneɪt]	记 词根记忆: hibern(冬天) + ate → 冬眠
unify	*v.* 统一，使成一体; 使相同（to make all the same）
[ˈjuːnɪfaɪ]	记 词根记忆: uni(单一) + fy(动词后缀) → 统一
	例 The text brims with details, but there are no overarching theses to *unify* them.
hypnotic	*adj.* 催眠的（tending to produce sleep） *n.* 催眠药（a sleep-inducing agent）
[hɪpˈnɑːtɪk]	
gallant	*adj.* 勇敢的，英勇的（brave and noble）; （对女人）献殷勤的（polite and attentive to women）
[ˈɡælənt]	记 词根记忆: gall(胆) + ant → 有胆量的 → 勇敢的，英勇的
disarray	*n.* 混乱，无秩序（an untidy condition; disorder; confusion）
[ˌdɪsəˈreɪ]	记 联想记忆: dis(离开) + array(排列) → 没有进行排列 → 无秩序
	例 Because of their frequent *disarray*, confusion, and loss of memory, those hit by lightning while alone are sometimes mistaken for victims of assault.
synonymous	*adj.* 同义的（having the same connotations, implications, or reference）
[sɪˈnɑːnɪməs]	记 来自 synonym(*n.* 同义词)
phobia	*n.* 恐惧症（an exaggerated illogical fear）
[ˈfoʊbiə]	记 词根记忆: phob(恐惧) + ia(表病) → 恐惧症
valiant	*adj.* 勇敢的，英勇的（courageous）
[ˈvæliənt]	同 valorous
bilingual	*adj.* （说）两种语言的（of two languages）
[ˌbaɪˈlɪŋɡwəl]	记 词根记忆: bi(两个) + lingu(语言) + al → （说）两种语言的
hurl	*v.* 用力投掷（to throw with force）; 大声叫骂（to shout out violently）
[hɜːrl]	同 fling, yell
constraint	*n.* 强制，强迫; 对感情的压抑（sth. that limits one's freedom of action or feelings）
[kənˈstreɪnt]	
conventionalize	*v.* 使按惯例，使习俗化（to make conventional）
[kənˈvenʃənəlaɪz]	记 词根记忆: convention(*n.* 习俗) + alize(使…) → 使习俗化

5

□ innocence	□ inquisitive	□ hibernate	□ unify	□ hypnotic	□ gallant
□ disarray	□ synonymous	□ phobia	□ valiant	□ bilingual	□ hurl
□ constraint	□ conventionalize				

astounding [ə'staʊndɪŋ]	*adj.* 令人震惊的(causing astonishment or amazement)
chromatic [krə'mætɪk]	*adj.* 彩色的，五彩的(having color or colors) 记 词根记忆：chrom(颜色) + atic → 彩色的
vigilant ['vɪdʒɪlənt]	*adj.* 机警的，警惕的(alertly watchful to avoid danger)
alternate	['ɔːltərnət] *adj.* 轮流的，交替的(occurring or succeeding by turns) ['ɔːltərneɪt] *v.* 轮流，交替(to perform by turns or in succession) ['ɔːltərnət] *n.* 候选人，代替者(one that substitutes for or alternates with another) 记 词根记忆：alter(改变) + nate → 来回改变 → 轮流的，交替的 同 alternative, backup, surrogate
inborn [ˌɪn'bɔːrn]	*adj.* 天生的，先天的(naturally present at birth; innate) 记 联想记忆：in(内) + born(出生) → 与生俱来的 → 天生的
inhabit [ɪn'hæbɪt]	*v.* 居住于(to live in; occupy)；占据 记 词根记忆：in(进入) + hab(拥有) + it → 在里面拥有 → 居住于；占据 例 With the evolution of wings, insects were able to disperse to the far ecological corners, across deserts and bodies of water, to reach new food sources and *inhabit* a wider variety of promising environmental niches.
feminist ['femənɪst]	*n.* 女权运动者(a person who supports and promotes women's rights) 记 词根记忆：femin(女人) + ist → 女权运动者
replete [rɪ'pliːt]	*adj.* 充满的，供应充足的(fully or abundantly provided or filled) 记 词根记忆：re + plet(满) + e → 充满的
conceptual [kən'septʃuəl]	*adj.* 概念上的(of, relating to, or consisting of concepts) 记 词根记忆：concept(*n.* 概念) + ual → 概念上的
precursor [priː'kɜːrsər]	*n.* 先驱，先兆(one that precedes and indicates the approach of another) 记 词根记忆：pre(在前面) + curs(跑) + or → 跑在前面的人 → 先驱 同 forerunner, harbinger, herald, outrider
hoard [hɔːrd]	*v.* 贮藏，秘藏(to accumulate and hide or keep in reserve) *n.* 贮藏，秘藏 记 把东西藏(hoard)在木板(board)后
scale [skeɪl]	*n.* 鱼鳞；音阶(a graduated series of musical tones)
impending [ɪm'pendɪŋ]	*adj.* 即将发生的，逼近的(imminent) 记 词根记忆：im(进入) + pend(挂) + ing → 挂到眼前 → 即将发生的，逼近的 例 William James lacked the usual awe of death; writing to his dying father, he spoke without inhibition about the old man's *impending* death.
interplay ['ɪntərpleɪ]	*v.* 相互影响(to interact) *n.* 相互影响(interaction) 记 联想记忆：inter (在…之间) + play (扮演角色) → 在两者中间扮演角色 → 相互影响

□ astounding	□ chromatic	□ vigilant	□ alternate	□ inborn	□ inhabit
□ feminist	□ replete	□ conceptual	□ precursor	□ hoard	□ scale
□ impending	□ interplay				

outburst [ˈaʊtbɜːrst]	*n.* 爆发，迸发(a violent expression of feeling；eruption)；激增(a surge of activity or growth) 例 He was habitually so docile and accommodating that his friends could not understand his sudden *outburst* against his employers. 同 burst, explosion, gust, sally
motley [ˈmɑːtli]	*adj.* 混杂的(heterogeneous)；多色的，杂色的(of many colors) 记 词根记忆：mot(=mote 微粒) + ley → 各种微粒混合 → 混杂的
posthumously [ˈpɑːstʃəməsli]	*adv.* 死后地(after death) 例 Like many other pioneers, Dr. Elizabeth Blackwell, founder of the New York Infirmary, the first American hospital staffed entirely by women, faced ridicule from her contemporaries but has received great honor *posthumously.*
predictable [prɪˈdɪktəbl]	*adj.* 可预知的 例 Though dealers insist that professional art dealers can make money in the art market, even an insider's knowledge is not enough: the art world is so fickle that stock-market prices are *predictable* by comparison.
blameworthy [ˈbleɪmwɜːrði]	*adj.* 该责备的，有过失的(deserving blame) 同 blamable, blameful, censurable, culpable, reprehensible
illegitimate [ˌɪləˈdʒɪtəmət]	*adj.* 不合法的(illegal；unlawful)；私生的(born of parents not married) 记 联想记忆：il(不) + legitimate(合法的) → 不合法的 例 An example of an *illegitimate* method of argument is to lump dissimilar cases together deliberately under the pretense that the same principles apply to each.
scorn [skɔːrn]	*n.* 轻蔑(disrespect or derision mixed with indignation) *v.* 轻蔑，瞧不起(to show disdain or derision) 同 contemn, despise
reigning [ˈreɪnɪŋ]	*adj.* 统治的，起支配作用的
discouraging [dɪsˈkɜːrɪdʒɪŋ]	*adj.* 令人气馁的(making sb. lose the confidence or determination)
cohesive [koʊˈhiːsɪv]	*adj.* 凝聚的(sticking together) 记 词根记忆：co + hes(粘着) + ive → 有粘合力的 → 凝聚的
disenfranchise [ˌdɪsɪnˈfræntʃaɪz]	*v.* 剥夺…的权利(to deprive of a franchise, of a legal right, or of some privilege or immunity)
disrupt [dɪsˈrʌpt]	*v.* 使混乱(to cause disorder in sth.)；使中断(to break apart) 记 词根记忆：dis(分开) + rupt(断) → 使断裂开 → 使中断
petroleum [pəˈtroʊliəm]	*n.* 石油
humiliate [hjuːˈmɪlieɪt]	*v.* 羞辱，使丢脸(to hurt the pride or dignity；mortify；degrade) 记 词根记忆：hum(地) + iliate(使…) → 使人靠近地面 → 羞辱

□ outburst	□ motley	□ posthumously	□ predictable	□ blameworthy	□ illegitimate
□ scorn	□ reigning	□ discouraging	□ cohesive	□ disenfranchise	□ disrupt
□ petroleum	□ humiliate				

51

uniform [ˈjuːnɪfɔːrm]	*n.* 制服 *adj.* 相同的，一致的(consistent) 记 词根记忆：uni(单一) + form(形式) → 一致的 例 Not all the indicators necessary to convey the effect of depth in a picture work simultaneously; the picture's illusion of *uniform* three-dimensional appearance must therefore result from the viewer's integration of various indicators perceived successively.
antecedent [ˌæntɪˈsiːdnt]	*n.* 前事(a preceding event, condition or cause)；祖先(a person's ancestors or family and social background) *adj.* 先行的(preceding in time and order)
inflexible [ɪnˈfleksəbl]	*adj.* 坚定的，不屈不挠的(rigidly firm in will or purpose)
hearten [ˈhɑːrtn]	*v.* 鼓励，激励(to make sb. feel cheerful and encouraged) 记 联想记忆：heart(心) + en → 鼓励别人的心 → 鼓励
circulate [ˈsɜːrkjəleɪt]	*v.* 循环；流通(to move around)；发行(to distribute) 记 词根记忆：circ(圆，环) + ulate → 绕圈走 → 循环
charismatic [ˌkærɪzˈmætɪk]	*adj.* 有魅力的(having, exhibiting, or based on charisma or charism) 搭 characterize...as... 将…的特点描述成…
negligent [ˈneglɪdʒənt]	*adj.* 疏忽的，粗心大意的(marked by or given to neglect especially habitually or culpably) 例 Because of his *negligent* driving, the other car was forced to turn off the road or be hit. 同 neglectful, regardless, remiss, slack
expository [ɪkˈspɑːzətɔːri]	*adj.* 说明的(explanatory; serving to explain) 记 来自 exposit(*v.* 解释，说明)
colorful [ˈkʌlərfl]	*adj.* 富有色彩的(having striking colors)；有趣的(full of variety or interest)
tenet [ˈtenɪt]	*n.* 信条(a principle, belief, or doctrine generally held to be true)；教义 记 词根记忆：ten(握住) + et → 紧抓不放的东西 → 信条 例 "The show must go on" is the oldest *tenet* of show business; every true performer lives by that creed.
treacherous [ˈtretʃərəs]	*adj.* 背叛的，叛逆的(showing great disloyalty and deceit) 记 词根记忆：treach(=trick 诡计)+erous → 背叛的
believable [bɪˈliːvəbl]	*adj.* 可信的(capable of being believed especially as within the range of known possibility or probability)
humanistic [ˌhjuːməˈnɪstɪk]	*adj.* 人性的；人文主义的 例 Even after safeguards against the excesses of popular sovereignty were included, major figures in the *humanistic* disciplines remained skeptical about the proposal to extend suffrage to the masses.
centralization [ˌsentrələˈzeɪʃn]	*n.* 集中；集权化(concentration) 记 来自 centralize(*v.* 集中)

□ uniform	□ antecedent	□ inflexible	□ hearten	□ circulate	□ charismatic
□ negligent	□ expository	□ colorful	□ tenet	□ treacherous	□ believable
□ humanistic	□ centralization				

involve [ɪnˈvɑːlv]	*v.* 包含，含有(to contain as a part; include)；参与(to engage as a participant)；牵涉，牵连(to oblige to take part) 记 词根记忆：in(使⋯) + volv(卷) + e → 使卷入 → 牵涉，牵连 例 When you learn archaeology solely from lectures, you get only an abstract sense of the concepts presented, but when you hold a five-thousand-year-old artifact in your hands, you have a chance to *involve* your senses, not just your intellect.
injurious [ɪnˈdʒʊriəs]	*adj.* 有害的(harmful) 记 来自injury(*n.* 伤害)
placid [ˈplæsɪd]	*adj.* 安静的，平和的(serenely free of interruption) 记 词根记忆：plac(平静的) + id → 平和的，安静的
tussle [ˈtʌsl]	*n.* 扭打，争斗(a physical contest or struggle)；争辩(an intense argument; controversy) *v.* 扭打，争斗(to struggle roughly) 记 联想记忆：tuss (看作fuss，忙乱) + le → 为什么忙乱，因为有人扭打搏斗 → 扭打，争斗
opposite [ˈɑːpəzət]	*adj.* 相反的，对立的(contrary to one another or to a thing specified) 记 词根记忆：op(反) + pos(放) + ite(表形容词) → 放在反面的 → 相反的，对立的
dappled [ˈdæpld]	*adj.* 有斑点的，斑驳的(covered with spots of a different color) 记 联想记忆：d + apple + d → 苹果上有斑点 → 有斑点的
adversary [ˈædvərseri]	*n.* 对手，敌手 (one that contends with, opposes, or resists) *adj.* 对手的，敌对的(having or involving antagonistic parties or opposing interests)
erudite [ˈerudaɪt]	*adj.* 博学的，饱学的(learned; scholarly) 记 词根记忆：e(出) + rud(原始的，无知的) + ite → 走出无知 → 博学的
realm [relm]	*n.* 王国(a country ruled over by a king or queen)；领域，范围(an area of activity, study, etc.)
enigma [ɪˈnɪgmə]	*n.* 谜一样的人或事物(sth. hard to understand or explain; an inscrutable or mysterious person) 例 To astronomers, the moon has long been an *enigma*, its origin escaping simple solution.
heartfelt [ˈhɑːrtfelt]	*adj.* 衷心的，诚挚的(deeply felt) 记 组合词：heart(心) + felt(感觉到的) → 能感觉到心意的 → 衷心的，诚挚的
obtainable [əbˈteɪnəbl]	*adj.* 能得到的(capable of being obtained) 记 来自obtain(*v.* 得到) 同 attainable, available, procurable, securable
evince [ɪˈvɪns]	*v.* 表明，表示(to show plainly; indicate; make manifest) 记 词根记忆：e + vinc(展示) + e → 向外展示 → 表明
bemuse [bɪˈmjuːz]	*v.* 使昏头昏脑，使迷惑(to puzzle, distract, absorb) 同 bedaze, daze, paralyze, petrify, stun

5

□ involve	□ injurious	□ placid	□ tussle	□ opposite	□ dappled
□ adversary	□ erudite	□ realm	□ enigma	□ heartfelt	□ obtainable
□ evince	□ bemuse				

superficial [ˌsuːpərˈfɪʃl]	*adj.* 表面的，肤浅的(shallow) 记 词根记忆：super(在…上面) + fic(做) + ial → 在上面做 → 表面的 例 He continually describes what superhuman labor it has cost him to compose his poems and intimates that, in comparison with his own work, the poetry of other poets is *superficial*.
scrutinize [ˈskruːtənaɪz]	*v.* 仔细检查(to examine closely and minutely) 搭 scrutinize balloting 监票
inexcusable [ˌɪnɪkˈskjuːzəbl]	*adj.* 不可原谅的，不可宽恕的(impossible to excuse or justify)
insidious [ɪnˈsɪdiəs]	*adj.* 暗中危害的，阴险的(working or spreading harmfully in a subtle or stealthy manner) 记 词根记忆：in(在里面) + sid(坐) + ious → (祸害)坐在里面的 → 暗中危害的
colossal [kəˈlɑːsl]	*adj.* 巨大的，庞大的(like a colossus in size; huge; gigantic) 记 词根记忆：coloss(大) + al → 巨大的
polish [ˈpoʊlɪʃ]	*v.* 磨光，擦亮(to make smooth and glossy) *n.* 上光剂(a preparation that is used to polish sth.)；优雅(freedom from rudeness or coarseness) 记 联想记忆：波兰(Polish)产的擦光剂(polish) 同 burnish, furbish, gloss, refine
connotation [ˌkɑːnəˈteɪʃn]	*n.* 言外之意，内涵(idea or notion suggested in addition to its explicit meaning or denotation) 记 词根记忆：con + not(注意) + ation → 全部注意到的内容 → 言外之意
vivid [ˈvɪvɪd]	*adj.* 鲜艳的；生动的；逼真的 记 词根记忆：viv(生命) + id → 有生命力的 → 生动的 例 She writes across generational lines, making the past so *vivid* that our belief that the present is the true locus of experience is undermined.
gripping [ˈɡrɪpɪŋ]	*adj.* 吸引注意力的，扣人心弦的(holding the interest strongly) 例 Telling *gripping* tales about a central character engaged in a mighty struggle with events, modern biographies satisfy the American appetite for epic narratives.
self-righteousness [ˌselfˈraɪtʃəsnəs]	*n.* 自以为是 例 The action and characters in a melodrama can be so immediately classified that all observers can hiss the villain with an air of smug but enjoyable *self-righteousness*.
factorable [ˈfæktərəbl]	*adj.* 能分解成因子的(capable of being factored) 记 联想记忆：factor(因素) + able(能…的) → 能分解成因素 → 能分解成因子的
stark [stɑːrk]	*adj.* 光秃秃的；荒凉的 (barren; desolate)；(外表)僵硬的 (rigid as if in death)；完全的(utter; sheer) 例 Melodramas, which presented *stark* oppositions between innocence and criminality, virtue and corruption, good and evil, were popular precisely because they offered the audience a world devoid of neutrality.

□ superficial	□ scrutinize	□ inexcusable	□ insidious	□ colossal	□ polish
□ connotation	□ vivid	□ gripping	□ self-righteousness	□ factorable	□ stark

deterrent [dɪˈtɜːrənt]	*adj.* 威慑的，制止的(serving to deter) 记 来自 deter(*v.* 威慑，吓住)
influence [ˈɪnfluəns]	*n.* 影响 *v.* 影响(to affect or alter by indirect or intangible means) 记 联想记忆：in(进入) + flu(流感) + ence → 患上流感容易影响别人 → 影响 搭 influence on 对…产生影响
efface [ɪˈfeɪs]	*v.* 擦掉，抹去(to wipe out; erase) 记 词根记忆：ef + fac(脸，表面) + e → 从表面去掉 → 擦掉
dilettante [ˌdɪləˈtænti]	*n.* 一知半解者，业余爱好者(dabbler; amateur) 记 词根记忆：di + let(=delect 引诱) + tante → 受到了诱惑 → 业余爱好者
interpolate [ɪnˈtɜːrpəleɪt]	*v.* 插入(to insert between or among others)；(通过插入新语句)篡改(to alter by putting in new words) 记 词根记忆：inter + pol(修饰) + ate → 通过在中间放入某物来修饰 → 插入；篡改
camaraderie [ˌkɑːməˈrɑːdəri]	*n.* 同志之情，友情(a spirit of friendly good-fellowship)
evaluation [ɪˌvæljuˈeɪʃn]	*n.* 评价，评估(the determined or fixed value of) 记 来自 evaluate(*v.* 评价，评估)
ill-prepared [ˌɪlprɪˈperd]	*adj.* 准备不足的(not ready for sth.) 例 As former Supreme Court Justice Warren Burger was fond of pointing out, many lawyers are not legal hotshots; they often come to court *illprepared* and lacking professional skills.
effete [ɪˈfiːt]	*adj.* 无生产力的(spent and sterile)；虚弱的(lacking vigor) 记 词根记忆：ef(没有) + fet(生产性的) + e → 无生产力的
improvident [ɪmˈprɑːvɪdənt]	*adj.* 无远见的，不节俭的(lacking foresight or thrift) 记 联想记忆：im(不) + provident(有远见的；节俭的) → 无远见的，不节俭的 例 Left to endure a penniless old age, the *improvident* man lived to regret his prodigal youth.
streak [striːk]	*n.* 条纹(a line or mark of a different color or texture from the ground) *v.* 加线条(to have a streak) 例 People who don't outgrow their colleges often don't grow in other ways; there remained in Forster's life and imagination a *streak* of the undergraduate, clever but immature.
unrecognized [ʌnˈrekəgnaɪzd]	*adj.* 未被承认的，未被认出的
feckless [ˈfekləs]	*adj.* 无效的，效率低的(inefficient)；不负责任的(irresponsible) 记 联想记忆：feck(效果) + less(无…的) → 没有效果 → 无效的；注意不要和 reckless(*adj.* 轻率的)相混
reclusive [rɪˈkluːsɪv]	*adj.* 隐遁的，隐居的(seeking or preferring seclusion or isolation)

□ deterrent	□ influence	□ efface	□ dilettante	□ interpolate	□ camaraderie
□ evaluation	□ ill-prepared	□ effete	□ improvident	□ streak	□ unrecognized
□ feckless	□ reclusive				

ordinary [ˈɔːrdneri]	*adj.* 普通的，平常的（routine；usual）；拙劣的，质量差的（deficient in quality；of poor or inferior quality）*n.* 惯例，寻常情况（the regular or customary condition or course of things） 同 commonplace, quotidian, unremarkable
obscure [əbˈskjʊr]	*adj.* 难以理解的，含糊的（cryptic；ambiguous）；不清楚的，模糊的（not clear or distinct）*v.* 使变模糊（to make less conspicuous）；隐藏（to conceal） 记 词根记忆：ob(在…之上) + scur(覆盖) + e → 盖上一层东西 → 使变模糊；隐藏 例 The *New Yorker* short stories often include esoteric allusions to *obscure* people and events: the implication is, if you are in the in-crowd, you'll get the reference; if you come from Cleveland, you won't. 同 dislimn, haze, obfuscate, overcast
exotic [ɪɡˈzɑːtɪk]	*adj.* 异国的，外来的（not native；foreign）；奇异的，珍奇的（strikingly unusual） 记 词根记忆：exo(外面) + tic → 外来的 例 Surprisingly enough, it is more difficult to write about the commonplace than about the *exotic* and strange.
ritual [ˈrɪtʃuəl]	*n.* 仪式，惯例（ceremonial act or action） 记 来自 rite(*n.* 仪式)
orbital [ˈɔːrbɪtl]	*adj.* 轨道的 记 来自 orbit(*n.* 轨道 *v.* 绕轨道运行)
stained [steɪnd]	*adj.* 污染的，玷污的 同 blemished, discolored, marked, spotted, tarnished
inducible [ɪnˈduːsəbl]	*adj.* 可诱导的（capable of being induced）
codify [ˈkɑːdɪfaɪ]	*v.* 编成法典，编辑成书 记 来自 code(*n.* 法典)
habituate [həˈbɪtʃueɪt]	*v.* 使习惯于（to make used to；accustom） 记 词根记忆：habit(住；习惯) + uate → 使习惯于
constrain [kənˈstreɪn]	*v.* 束缚，强迫(to make sb. do sth. by strong moral persuasion or force)；限制(to inhibit) 记 词根记忆：con + strain(拉紧) → 拉到一起 → 束缚，强迫 同 bridle, check, curb, withhold
distortion [dɪˈstɔːrʃn]	*n.* 扭曲（the act of distorting）；曲解（a statement that twists fact；misrepresentation）
intangible [ɪnˈtændʒəbl]	*adj.* 触摸不到的（not tangible；impalpable）；无形的（incorporeal） 记 词根记忆：in(不) + tang(触摸) + ible → 触摸不到的 同 imperceptible, indiscernible, untouchable

titular	*adj.* 有名无实的，名义上的(existing in title only)
[ˈtɪtʃələr]	记 来自 title(*n.* 头衔)
temperate	*adj.* (气候等)温和的(marked by moderation)；(欲望、饮食等)适度的，有
[ˈtempərət]	节制的
predestine	*v.* 预先注定(to destine or determine beforehand)
[ˌpriːˈdestɪn]	记 联想记忆：pre(在前面) + destine(注定) → 预先注定
	同 foreordain, predetermine, preordain
forlorn	*adj.* 孤独的(abandoned or deserted)；凄凉的(wretched; miserable)
[fərˈlɔːrn]	记 词根记忆：for(出去) + lorn(被弃的) → 抛弃 → 孤独的
sun-bronzed	*adj.* 被太阳晒成古铜色的
[ˈsʌnbrɑːnzd]	
rampant	*adj.* 猖獗的，蔓生的(marked by a menacing wildness or absence of restraint)
[ˈræmpənt]	记 联想记忆：ram(羊) + pant(喘气) → 因为草生长猖獗，所以羊高兴得直喘气 → 猖獗的，蔓生的
quarantine	*n.* 隔离检疫期，隔离(enforced isolation to prevent the spread of disease)
[ˈkwɔːrəntiːn]	记 联想记忆：quarant(40) + ine → 隔开 40 天 → 隔离
factual	*adj.* 事实的，实际的(restricted to or based on fact)
[ˈfæktʃuəl]	记 来自 fact(*n.* 事实)
trepidation	*n.* 恐惧，惶恐(timorousness; uncertainty; agitation)
[ˌtrepɪˈdeɪʃn]	记 词根记忆：trep(害怕) + id + ation → 恐惧，惶恐
	例 Salazar's presence in the group was so reassuring to the others that they lost most of their earlier *trepidation*; failure, for them, became all but unthinkable.
endure	*v.* 忍受，忍耐(to suffer sth. painful or uncomfortable patiently)
[ɪnˈdʊr]	记 联想记忆：end(结束) + ure → 坚持到结束 → 忍受，忍耐
	同 abide, bear, brook, swallow
verse	*n.* 诗歌(a line of metrical writing, poems)
[vɜːrs]	记 词根记忆：vers(转) + e → 诗歌的音节百转千回 → 诗歌
suspense	*n.* 悬念(pleasant excitement as to a decision or outcome)；挂念(anxiety)
[səˈspens]	同 apprehension, uncertainty
indulge	*v.* 放纵，纵容(to allow to have whatever one likes or wants)；满足(to satisfy a perhaps unwarranted desire)
[ɪnˈdʌldʒ]	同 cosset, pamper, spoil
brook	*n.* 小河(a small stream)
[brʊk]	
tranquil	*adj.* 平静的(free from agitation of mind or spirit)
[ˈtræŋkwɪl]	例 Their married life was not *tranquil* since it was fraught with bitter fighting and arguments.

5

endure

□ titular	□ temperate	□ predestine	□ forlorn	□ sun-bronzed	□ rampant
□ quarantine	□ factual	□ trepidation	□ endure	□ verse	□ suspense
□ indulge	□ brook	□ tranquil			

propensity	*n.* 嗜好，习性（an often intense natural inclination or preference）
[prə'pensəti]	记 词根记忆：pro(提前) + pens(挂) + ity → 总是喜欢预先挂好 → 嗜好，习性
	例 The poet W. H. Auden believed that the greatest poets of his age were almost necessarily irresponsible, that the possession of great gifts engenders the *propensity* to abuse them.
	同 bent, leaning, tendency, penchant, proclivity

rescue	*v.* 解救（to save or set free from harm, danger, or loss）；把…从法律监管下强行夺回（to take from legal custody by force）*n.* 解救（the act of rescuing）
['reskjuː]	记 联想记忆：res(看作 rest，休息) + cue(线索) → 放弃休息紧追线索，进行营救 → 解救

rescue

HELP!

hiatus	*n.* 空隙，裂缝（a gap or interruption in space, time, or continuity; break）
[haɪ'eɪtəs]	记 联想记忆：hi(音似："嗨") + at + us → 对我们喊"嗨"，我们能听到，说明有空隙 → 空隙

ubiquitous	*adj.* 无处不在的（existing or being everywhere at the same time）
[juː'bɪkwɪtəs]	记 联想记忆：ubi(=where) + qu(=any) + itous → anywhere → 无处不在的

respect	*v.* 尊敬（to consider worthy of high regard）*n.* 尊敬（high or special regard）
[rɪ'spekt]	记 词根记忆：re + spect(看) → 一再地看望 → 尊敬

obese	*adj.* 极胖的（very fat; corpulent）
[oʊ'biːs]	记 发音记忆："O 必死" → 对怕胖的女人来说，O 形身材必死无疑 → 极胖的

visionary	*adj.* 有远见的；幻想的 *n.* 空想家（one who is given to impractical or speculative ideas）
['vɪʒəneri]	例 Although the architect's concept at first sounded too *visionary* to be practicable, his careful analysis of every aspect of the project convinced the panel that the proposed building was indeed, structurally feasible.
	同 dreamy, idealistic, utopian

conceive	*v.* 想象，构想（to imagine）；怀孕（to become pregnant）
[kən'siːv]	记 词根记忆：con(共同) + ceiv(抓) + e → 一起抓(思想) → 构想

elicit	*v.* 得出，引出（to draw forth or bring out）
[i'lɪsɪt]	记 词根记忆：e(出) + licit(引导) → 引出

uncommunicative	*adj.* 不爱说话的，拘谨的（not disposed to talk or impart information）
[ˌʌnkə'mjuːnɪkətɪv]	记 与 incommunicative(*adj.* 不爱交际的，沉默寡言的)一起记

boost	*v.* 增加，提高（to make higher）；促进（to promote the cause or interests）；往上推（to raise by a push）
[buːst]	记 联想记忆：boo(看作 boot，靴子) + st → 穿上靴子往高处走 → 提高

□ propensity	□ rescue	□ hiatus	□ ubiquitous	□ respect	□ obese
□ visionary	□ conceive	□ elicit	□ uncommunicative	□ boost	

exempt [ɪgˈzempt]	*adj.* 被免除的，被豁免的(not subject to a rule or obligation) *v.* 免除，豁免 (to free from a rule or obligation) 记 词根记忆：ex + empt(拿；买) → 拿出去 → 被免除的
downplay [ˌdaʊnˈpleɪ]	*v.* 贬低，不予重视(to belittle) 记 组合词：down(向下) + play(玩) → 玩下去 → 不予重视
genus [ˈdʒiːnəs]	*n.* (动植物的)属，类(division of animals or plants, below a family and above a species)
remoteness [rɪˈmoʊtnəs]	*n.* 遥远；偏僻
discomfited [dɪsˈkʌmfɪtɪd]	*adj.* 困惑的，尴尬的(frustrated; embarrassed) 例 While not completely nonplussed by the unusually caustic responses from members of the audience, the speaker was nonetheless visibly *discomfited* by their lively criticism.
preliminary [prɪˈlɪmɪneri]	*adj.* 预备的，初步的，开始的(coming before a more important action or event; preparatory) 记 词根记忆：pre(预先) + limin(门槛；起点) + ary → 预先跨入 → 预备的
pivotal [ˈpɪvətl]	*adj.* 中枢的，枢轴的(of, relating to, or constituting a pivot)；极其重要的，关键的(vitally important)
humble [ˈhʌmbl]	*adj.* 卑微的(ranking low in a hierarchy or scale)；谦虚的(not proud or haughty) *v.* 使谦卑(to make humble) 记 词根记忆：hum(地面) + ble → 接近地面的 → 低下的 → 卑微的
erratically [ɪˈrætɪkli]	*adv.* 不规律地，不定地(in an erratic and unpredictable manner) 记 来自 erratic(*adj.* 无规律的)

| □ exempt | □ downplay | □ genus | □ remoteness | □ discomfited | □ preliminary |
| □ pivotal | □ humble | □ erratically | | | |

59

Word List 6

音频

atheist [ˈeɪθiːɪst]	*n.* 无神论者 (one who believes that there is no deity)
unspotted [ˌʌnˈspɑːtɪd]	*adj.* 清白的, 无污点的 (without spot; flawless) 记 联想记忆: un(不) + spot(污点) + ted → 无污点的
acknowledge [əkˈnɑːlɪdʒ]	*v.* 承认 (to recognize as genuine or valid); 致谢 (to express gratitude) 记 联想记忆: ac + knowledge (知识, 知道) → 大家都知道了, 所以不得不承认 → 承认 同 admit, avow, concede, confess
aspiring [əˈspaɪərɪŋ]	*adj.* 有抱负的, 有理想的 记 来自 aspire (*v.* 渴望成就…, 有志成于…)
textured [ˈtekstʃərd]	*adj.* 手摸时有感觉的; 有织纹的 记 来自 texture (*n.* 质地; 结构)
paltry [ˈpɔːltri]	*adj.* 无价值的, 微不足道的 (trashy; trivial; petty) 记 联想记忆: pal(=pale 苍白的) + try(努力) → 白努力 → 无价值的
ill-repute [ˌɪlrɪˈpjuːt]	*n.* 名誉败坏 (bad fame) 同 notoriousness
theoretical [ˌθiːəˈretɪkl]	*adj.* 假设的 (existing only in theory); 理论(上)的 (relating to or having the character of theory) 记 来自 theory (*n.* 理论)
substitute [ˈsʌbstɪtuːt]	*n.* 代替品 (a person or thing that takes the place or function of another) *v.* 代替 (to replace) 记 词根记忆: sub(下面) + stit(站) + ute → 站在下面的 → 代替品 例 Many welfare reformers would *substitute* a single, federally financed income support system for the existing welter of overlapping programs.
forbear [fɔːrˈber]	*v.* 克制 (to hold oneself back from especially with an effort); 忍耐 (to control oneself when provoked)
tentatively [ˈtentətɪvli]	*adv.* 试验性地 同 experimentally
reprisal [rɪˈpraɪzl]	*n.* 报复, 报复行动 (practice in retaliation for damage or loss suffered) 记 词根记忆: re(回) + pris(=price 代价) + al → 还给对方代价 → 报复

□ atheist　　□ unspotted　　□ acknowledge　　□ aspiring　　□ textured　　□ paltry
□ ill-repute　　□ theoretical　　□ substitute　　□ forbear　　□ tentatively　　□ reprisal

commission [kə'mɪʃn]	*n.* 委托（piece of work given to sb. to do）；佣金（payment to sb. for selling goods） 记 词根记忆：com + miss（送，放出）+ ion → 共同送出 → 委托
surrender [sə'rendər]	*v.* 投降（to give in to the power）；放弃（to give up possession or control）；归还（to give back） 记 词根记忆：sur（在…下）+ render（给予）→ 把（枪）交出来，放在地上 → 投降
shrug [ʃrʌg]	*v.* 耸肩（表示怀疑等）（to raise in the shoulders to express aloofness, indifference, or uncertainty） 记 联想记忆：shru（看作拼音 shu，舒）+ g（音似：胳）→ 舒展舒展胳膊 → 耸肩 搭 shrug sth. off/aside 不把…当回事；对…满不在乎
compassionate [kəm'pæʃənət]	*adj.* 有同情心的（sympathetic） 搭 compassionate nature 怜悯的性格
culinary ['kʌlɪneri]	*adj.* 厨房的（of the kitchen）；烹调的（of cooking） 搭 culinary skills 烹饪技巧
incomplete [ˌɪnkəm'pliːt]	*adj.* 不完全的，不完整的（not complete）
sagacious [sə'geɪʃəs]	*adj.* 聪明的，睿智的（showing keen perception and foresight） 记 来自 sage（*n.* 智者）
inordinate [ɪn'ɔːrdɪnət]	*adj.* 过度的，过分的（immoderate; excessive） 记 词根记忆：in（不）+ ordin（次序）+ ate → 无序的 → 不正常的 → 过度的，过分的 例 In the absence of native predators to stop their spread, imported deer thrived to such an *inordinate* degree that they overgrazed the countryside and threatened the native vegetation.
grain [greɪn]	*n.* 谷物（small hard seeds of food plants）；小的硬粒（tiny hard bit）
treatise ['triːtɪs]	*n.* 论文（a long written work dealing systematically with one subject） 记 联想记忆：treat（对待）+ ise → 对待问题 → 论文
gravitational [ˌgrævɪ'teɪʃnl]	*adj.* 万有引力的，重力的（of or relating to gravitational force） 记 来自 gravitation（*n.* 引力；倾向） 例 Clearly refuting sceptic, researchers have demonstrated not only that *gravitational* radiation exists but that it also does exactly what theory predicted it should do.
vainglorious [ˌveɪn'glɔːriəs]	*adj.* 自负的（marked by vainglory; boastful）
congenial [kən'dʒiːniəl]	*adj.* 意气相投的，趣味相投的（having the same tastes and temperament; companionable）；性情好的（amiable）；适意的（agreeable） 记 词根记忆：con + geni（=genius 才能）+ al → 有共同才能的 → 意气相投的，趣味相投的

6

□ commission	□ surrender	□ shrug	□ compassionate	□ culinary	□ incomplete
□ sagacious	□ inordinate	□ grain	□ treatise	□ gravitational	□ vainglorious
□ congenial					

61

flatter [ˈflætər]	*v.* 恭维，奉承（to praise sb. too much） 同 adulate, blandish, honey, slaver
eminence [ˈemɪnəns]	*n.* 卓越，显赫，杰出（a position of prominence or superiority） 同 distinction, illustriousness, preeminence
participation [pɑːrˌtɪsɪˈpeɪʃn]	*n.* 参加，参与（the act of taking part or sharing in something） 例 Because medieval women's public *participation* in spiritual life was not welcomed by the male establishment, a compensating involvement with religious writings, inoffensive to the members of the establishment because of its privacy, became important for many women.
cleave [kliːv]	*v.* 劈开（to divide with an axe）；分裂（to split; separate） 记 联想记忆：c + leave(分开) → 把 c 分开 → 劈开
submission [səbˈmɪʃn]	*n.* 从属，服从（an act of submitting to the authority or control of another） 记 词根记忆：sub(下面) + miss(放) + ion → 放在下面 → 从属，服从 例 The losing animal in a struggle saves itself from destruction by an act of *submission*, an act usually recognized and accepted by the winner.
irreversible [ˌɪrɪˈvɜːrsəbl]	*adj.* 不能撤回的，不能取消的（not reversible） 同 irrevocable, unalterable
unconvinced [ˌʌnkənˈvɪnst]	*adj.* 不信服的（not certain that sth. is true or right） 例 Many of her followers remain loyal to her, and even those who have rejected her leadership are *unconvinced* of the wisdom of replacing her during the current turmoil.
far-reaching [ˌfɑːˈriːtʃɪŋ]	*adj.* 影响深远的（having a wide influence） 记 组合词：far(远的) + reaching(到达) → 影响到达很远的地方 → 影响深远的
collaborate [kəˈlæbəreɪt]	*v.* 合作，协作（to work together with sb.）；通敌（to help enemy occupying one's country） 记 词根记忆：col(共同) + labor(劳动) + ate → 共同劳动 → 合作
bewilder [bɪˈwɪldər]	*v.* 使迷惑，混乱（to confuse） 记 词根记忆：be（使…成为） + wilder（迷惑） → 使迷惑 同 befog, confound, perplex
ineptitude [ɪˈneptɪtuːd]	*n.* 无能；不适当（the quality or state of being inept）
variability [ˌveriəˈbɪləti]	*n.* 变化性（the quality, state, or degree of being variable or changeable） 同 unevenness, variableness, variance
graphic [ˈɡræfɪk]	*adj.* 图表的（of graphs）；生动的（vivid） 记 来自 graph(*n.* 图表，图解) 同 pictorial
empathy [ˈempəθi]	*n.* 同感，移情（作用）（the mental ability of sharing other people's ideas and feelings）；全神贯注 记 词根记忆：em + path(感情) + y → 感情移入 → 移情

喵喵

bewilder

□ flatter	□ eminence	□ participation	□ cleave	□ submission	□ irreversible
□ unconvinced	□ far-reaching	□ collaborate	□ bewilder	□ ineptitude	□ variability
□ graphic	□ empathy				

salvation [sæl'veɪʃn]	*n.* 拯救(deliverance from the power and effects of sin); 救助(deliverance from danger or difficulty)
affluent ['æfluənt]	*adj.* 富有的，丰富的(rich) 搭 affluent western countries 富裕的西方国家
burst [bɜːrst]	*v.* 爆炸；爆裂(to break open, apart, or into pieces); 突然发生(to emerge or spring suddenly)
muddle ['mʌdl]	*n.* 迷惑，困惑(a confused or disordered state); 混乱(mess) 记 联想记忆：mud(泥浆) + dle → 混入泥浆 → 混乱
romance ['roʊmæns]	*n.* 传奇故事；虚构(something that lacks basis in fact); 浪漫氛围；风流韵事(love affair) *v.* 虚构(to exaggerate or invent detail or incident)
self-analysis [ˌselfə'næləsɪs]	*n.* 自我分析
touched [tʌtʃt]	*adj.* 被感动的(emotionally stirred) 同 affected, inspired, moved
scour ['skaʊər]	*v.* 冲刷(to clear, dig, or remove by or as if by a powerful current of water); 擦掉(to rub hard); 四处搜索(to go through or range over in a search)
movement ['muːvmənt]	*n.* 乐章(a principal division or section of a sonata or symphony)
molecular [mə'lekjələr]	*adj.* 分子的(of, relating to, consisting of, or produced by molecules) 记 来自 molecule(*n.* 分子)
impolitic [ɪm'pɑːlətɪk]	*adj.* 不明智的，失策的(unwise; injudicious) 记 联想记忆：im(不) + politic(有手腕的，有策略的)，失策的 例 Although Tom was aware that it would be *impolitic* to display annoyance publicly at the sales conference, he could not hide his irritation with the client's unreasonable demands. 同 imprudent, indiscreet
imitate ['ɪmɪteɪt]	*v.* 模仿(to mimic, counterfeit) 记 联想记忆：im + it(它) + ate(eat 的过去式，吃) → 它照着别人的样子吃 → 模仿 同 ape, burlesque
perfunctory [pər'fʌŋktəri]	*adj.* 例行公事般的，敷衍的(characterized by routine or superficiality) 例 Her first concert appearance was disappointingly *perfunctory* and derivative, rather than the inspired performance in the innovative style we had anticipated.
spatial ['speɪʃl]	*adj.* 有关空间的，在空间的(of, relating to, involving, or having the nature of space)
stride [straɪd]	*v.* 大步行走(to move with or as if with long steps) 记 联想记忆：st + ride(骑自行车) → 走得像骑自行车一样快 → 大步行走 stride

□ salvation	□ affluent	□ burst	□ muddle	□ romance	□ self-analysis
□ touched	□ scour	□ movement	□ molecular	□ impolitic	□ imitate
□ perfunctory	□ spatial	□ stride			

63

ephemeral	*adj.* 朝生暮死的（lasting only for a day）；生命短暂的（transitory；transient）
[ɪ'femərəl]	记 词根记忆：e + phem(出现) + eral → 一出现就消失 → 生命短暂的
	同 evanescent, fleeting, fugacious, momentary
restoration	*n.* 恢复，复原（an act of restoring or the condition of being restored）
[ˌrestə'reɪʃn]	例 Despite careful *restoration* and cleaning of the murals in the 1960s, the colors slowly but steadily deteriorated.
vehement	*adj.* 猛烈的，热烈的（marked by forceful energy）
['viːəmənt]	同 exquisite, fierce, furious, intense, violent
promulgate	*v.* 颁布(法令)（to put a law into action or force）；宣传，传播（to spread the news）
['prɑːmlɡeɪt]	记 词根记忆：pro(前面) + mulg(人民) + ate → 放到人民前面 → 宣传，传播
	同 announce, annunciate, declare, disseminate, proclaim
dose	*n.* 剂量，(一)剂（an exact amount of a medicine）
[doʊs]	记 词根记忆：dos(给予) + e → 给予力量 → 剂量
dearth	*n.* 缺乏，短缺（scarcity）
[dɜːrθ]	记 联想记忆：dear(珍贵的) + th → 物以稀为贵 → 缺乏，短缺
idiosyncratic	*adj.* 特殊物质的，特殊的，异质的（peculiar to the individual）
[ˌɪdiəsɪŋ'krætɪk]	例 To have true disciples, a thinker must not be too *idiosyncratic*: any effective intellectual leader depends on the ability of other people to reenact thought processes that did not originate with them.
	同 characteristic, distinctive
interpretation	*n.* 解释，说明（the act or the result of interpreting）；演绎（a particular adaptation or version of a work, method, or style）
[ɪnˌtɜːrprɪ'teɪʃn]	例 Fossils may be set in stone, but their *interpretation* is not; a new find may necessitate the revision of a traditional theory.
tarnish	*v.* 失去光泽，晦暗（to dull or destroy the luster by air, dust, or dirt）*n.* 晦暗，无光泽
['tɑːrnɪʃ]	记 词根记忆：tarn(隐藏) + ish → 隐藏光泽 → 失去光泽，晦暗
individualism	*n.* 个人主义（a doctrine that the interests of the individual are or ought to be ethically paramount）
[ˌɪndɪ'vɪdʒuəlɪzəm]	
tardy	*adj.* 迟延，迟到的（delayed beyond the expected or proper time）；缓慢的、迟钝的（slow to act; sluggish）
['tɑːrdi]	记 词根记忆：tard(迟缓) + y → 缓慢的，迟钝的
juvenile	*adj.* 青少年的（of or like young people）；孩子气的，幼稚的（marked by immaturity; childish）
['dʒuːvənl]	记 词根记忆：juven(年轻的) + ile → 青少年的
transitional	*adj.* 转变的，变迁的（of, relating to, or characterized by transition）
[træn'zɪʃənl]	例 Current data suggest that, although *transitional* states between fear and aggression exist, fear and aggression are as distinct physiologically as they are psychologically.

□ ephemeral	□ restoration	□ vehement	□ promulgate	□ dose	□ dearth
□ idiosyncratic	□ interpretation	□ tarnish	□ individualism	□ tardy	□ juvenile
□ transitional					

routine [ruːˈtiːn]	*n.* 常规(a reiterated speech or formula) *adj.* 平常的(ordinary); 常规的(of, relating to, or being in accordance with established procedure) 记 联想记忆：例行公事(routine)就是按常规路线(route)走 例 He felt that the uninspiring *routine* of office work was too prosaic for someone of his talent and creativity. 同 accustomed, customary, quotidian, unremarkable
exodus [ˈeksədəs]	*n.* 大批离去，成群外出(a mass departure or emigration) 记 词根记忆：ex(外面) + od(=hod 路) + us → 走上外出的道路 → 成群外出 例 For many young people during the Roaring Twenties, a disgust with the excesses of American culture combined with a wanderlust to provoke an *exodus* abroad.
infuriate [ɪnˈfjʊrieɪt]	*v.* 使恼怒，激怒(to enrage) 记 词根记忆：in(进入) + furi(=fury 狂怒) + ate → 进入狂怒 → 使恼怒，激怒
irate [aɪˈreɪt]	*adj.* 发怒的(angry; incensed) 记 联想记忆：i(我) + rate(责骂) → 我被责骂了 → 发怒的
sequential [sɪˈkwenʃl]	*adj.* 连续的，一连串的(serial) 记 词根记忆：sequ(跟随) + ent + ial → 连续的，一连串的
unleash [ʌnˈliːʃ]	*v.* 发泄，释放(to set feelings and forces free from control) 记 联想记忆：un(不) + leash(控制，约束) → 不去控制 → 发泄
underestimated [ˌʌndərˈestɪmeɪtɪd]	*adj.* 低估的 记 来自 underestimate(*v.* 低估)
clannish [ˈklænɪʃ]	*adj.* 排他的，门户之见的(tending to associate closely with one's own group and to avoid others) 记 词根记忆：clan(宗派，家族) + nish → 门户之见的
stilted [ˈstɪltɪd]	*adj.* (文章、谈话)不自然的；夸张的(pompous) 记 来自 stilt(*n.* 高跷)
diminish [dɪˈmɪnɪʃ]	*v.* (使)减少，缩小(to make less or cause to appear less, belittle, dwindle) 记 词根记忆：di + mini(小) + sh → 缩小
crossfire [ˈkrɔːsfaɪər]	*n.* 交叉火力(the firing of guns from two or more directions at the same time, so that the bullets cross) 记 组合词：cross(交叉) + fire(火) → 交叉火力
suppliant [ˈsʌpliənt]	*adj.* 恳求的，哀求的(humbly imploring) *n.* 恳求者，哀求者(one who supplicates) 同 beggar, prayer, suitor, supplicant
bygone [ˈbaɪɡɔːn]	*adj.* 过去的(gone by) 搭 a bygone age 过去的年代
allusive [əˈluːsɪv]	*adj.* 暗指的，间接提到的(containing allusions) 记 词根记忆：allu(=allude 暗指) + sive → 暗指的

□ routine	□ exodus	□ infuriate	□ irate	□ sequential	□ unleash
□ underestimated	□ clannish	□ stilted	□ diminish	□ crossfire	□ suppliant
□ bygone	□ allusive				

awe-struck [ˈɔːstrʌk]	*adj.* 充满敬畏的(filled with awe) 记 组合词：awe(敬畏) + struck(打动) → 充满敬畏的
canny [ˈkæni]	*adj.* 精明仔细的(shrewd and careful) 记 联想记忆：can(能) + ny → 能干的 → 精明仔细的
remorse [rɪˈmɔːrs]	*n.* 懊悔，悔恨(a gnawing distress; self-reproach) 记 词根记忆：re(反) + mors(咬) + e → 反过去咬自己 → 悔恨 例 Although *remorse* is usually thought to spring from regret for having done something wrong, it may be that its origin is the realization that one's own nature is irremediably flawed. 同 compunction, contriteness, contrition, penance, penitence
conifer [ˈkɑːnɪfər]	*n.* 针叶树(a tree that has leaves like needles) 记 联想记忆：con(=cone 圆锥，松果) + i + fer(带来) → 带来松果的树 → 针叶树
egocentric [ˌiːɡoʊˈsentrɪk]	*adj.* 利己的(self-centered) 记 词根记忆：ego(我) + centr(中心) + ic → 以自我为中心的 → 利己的
unwonted [ʌnˈwoʊntɪd]	*adj.* 不寻常的，不习惯的(unusual; unaccustomed)
reiterate [riˈɪtəreɪt]	*v.* 重申，反复地说(to state over again or repeatedly) 记 词根记忆：re(反复) + iter (重申) + ate → 重申，反复地说 同 ingeminate, iterate
scavenge [ˈskævɪndʒ]	*v.* 清除(to cleanse)；从废物中提取有用物质(to salvage from discarded or refuse material)
disavowal [ˌdɪsəˈvaʊəl]	*n.* 否认(repudiation) 记 词根记忆：dis(不) + a(=ad 向) + vow(=voc 叫喊) + al → 向人们大喊说不是 → 否认
transmit [trænsˈmɪt]	*v.* 传送，传播(to send or convey from one person or place to another) 记 词根记忆：trans (横过) + mit (送) → 送过去 → 传送 transmit
pregnant [ˈpreɡnənt]	*adj.* 怀孕的(gravid)；充满的(full; teeming) 记 词根记忆：pre(在前面) + gn(出生) + ant → 尚未出生的 → 怀孕的
aristocratic [əˌrɪstəˈkrætɪk]	*adj.* 贵族（化）的(belonging to, having the qualities of, or favoring aristocracy)
rebuke [rɪˈbjuːk]	*v.* 指责，谴责(to criticize sharply; reprimand) 记 词根记忆：re(再次) + buk(=beat 打) +e → 反复打 → 指责 同 admonish, chide, reproach
gloom [ɡluːm]	*n.* 昏暗 (darkness; dimness; obscurity)；忧郁 (deep sadness or hopelessness) 例 Our mood swings about the economy grow more extreme: when things go well, we become euphoric; when things go poorly, *gloom* descends.

□ awe-struck	□ canny	□ remorse	□ conifer	□ egocentric	□ unwonted
□ reiterate	□ scavenge	□ disavowal	□ transmit	□ pregnant	□ aristocratic
□ rebuke	□ gloom				

insurgent [ɪnˈsɜːrdʒənt]	*adj.* 叛乱的，起义的（rebellious）*n.* 叛乱分子（a person engaged in insurgent activity） 记 联想记忆：in(内部) + surge(浪涛；升起) + nt → 内部起浪潮 → 叛乱的
innate [ɪˈneɪt]	*adj.* 天生的，固有的(inborn; inbred) 记 词根记忆：in(在内) + nat(出生) + e → 出生时带来的 → 天生的 例 Unlike Sartre, who was born into a cultivated environment, receiving culture in his feeding bottle, so to speak, the child Camus had to fight to acquire a culture that was not *innate*. 同 connate, connatural, indigenous
septic [ˈseptɪk]	*adj.* 腐败的(of, relating to, or causing putrefaction)；脓毒性的(relating to, involving, caused by, or affected with sepsis) 记 词根记忆：sept(细菌；腐烂) + ic → 腐败的
soundproof [ˈsaʊndpruːf]	*v.* 使隔音(to insulate so as to obstruct the passage of sound) *adj.* 隔音的 搭 soundproof door 隔音门
warrant [ˈwɔːrənt]	*n.* 正当理由(justification)；许可证(a commission or document giving authority) *v.* 保证；批准 例 Dr. Smith cautioned that the data so far are not sufficiently unequivocal to *warrant* dogmatic assertions by either side in the debate. 同 certify, guarantee, vindicate
enrage [ɪnˈreɪdʒ]	*v.* 激怒，触怒(to make sb. very angry) 记 联想记忆：en(进入) + rage(狂怒) → 进入狂怒 → 激怒
potent [ˈpoʊtnt]	*adj.* 强有力的，有影响力的，有权力的(having or wielding force, authority, or influence)；有效力的，有效能的(exerting or capable of exerting strong physiological or chemical effects)
unseemly [ʌnˈsiːmli]	*adj.* 不适宜的，不得体的(not according with established standards of good form or taste) 记 联想记忆：un(不) + seemly(适宜的) → 不适宜的
falsify [ˈfɔːlsɪfaɪ]	*v.* 篡改(to alter a record, etc. fraudulently)；说谎(to tell falsehoods; lie) 记 词根记忆：fals(假的) + ify → 造假 → 篡改
thorny [ˈθɔːrni]	*adj.* 有刺的，多刺的(full of thorns)；多障碍的，引起争议的(full of difficulties or controversial points) 记 来自 thorn(*n.* 刺)
exuberant [ɪgˈzuːbərənt]	*adj.* (人)充满活力的(very lively and cheerful)；(植物)茂盛的((of plant) produced in extreme abundance)) 记 词根记忆：ex(出) + uber(=udder 乳房，引申为"果实") + ant → 出果实的 → 充满活力的；茂盛的
interconnected [ˌɪntərkəˈnektɪd]	*adj.* 相互连接的(mutually joined or related) 记 联想记忆：inter(在…中间) + connect(连接) + ed → 在中间连接 → 相互连接的
spinning [ˈspɪnɪŋ]	*adj.* 旋转的 同 revolving, rotating, turning, twirling, wheeling, whirling

□ insurgent	□ innate	□ septic	□ soundproof	□ warrant	□ enrage
□ potent	□ unseemly	□ falsify	□ thorny	□ exuberant	□ interconnected
□ spinning					

67

incense	[ˈɪnsens] *n.* 香味(any pleasant fragrance)
	[ɪnˈsens] *v.* 激怒(to arouse the wrath of)
	记 词根记忆：in (进入) + cens (=cand 发光) + e → 焚烧 → 点燃怒气 → 激怒
	同 enrage, infuriate, madden
overdraw [ˌoʊvərˈdrɔː]	*v.* 透支(to draw checks on (a bank account) for more than the balance; make an overdraft); 夸大(to exaggerate)
distent [dɪsˈtent]	*adj.* 膨胀的(swollen); 扩张的(expanded)
	记 词根记忆：dis(分开) + tent(延伸) → 向外延伸的 → 扩张的
complementary [ˌkɑːmplɪˈmentri]	*adj.* 互补的(combining well to form a whole)
	记 来自complement(*n.* 补充物)
	搭 be complementary to 与…互补
grateful [ˈɡreɪtfl]	*adj.* 感激的，感谢的(expressing gratitude; appreciative)
	记 不要和grate(*v.* 磨碎)相混
quantifiable [ˈkwɑːntɪfaɪəbl]	*adj.* 可以计量的; 可量化的
	记 词根记忆：quant(数量) + ifi + able(可…的) → 可以计量的
expertise [ˌekspɜːrˈtiːz]	*n.* 专门技术，专业知识(the skill, knowledge, judgment of an expert)
	记 来自expert(*n.* 专家)
rancor [ˈræŋkər]	*n.* 深仇，怨恨(bitter deep-seated ill will; enmity)
	例 For someone suffering from stress, a holiday can act as a tonic, dispelling *rancor*, transforming indecision, and renewing the spirit.
pounce [paʊns]	*n.* (猛禽的)爪(the claw of a bird of prey); 猛扑(the act of pouncing)
	v. 猛扑(to swoop upon and seize sth. with or as if with talons); 突然袭击(to make a sudden assault or approach)
	搭 pounce on 突然袭击
opponent [əˈpoʊnənt]	*n.* 对手，敌手(one that opposes another or others in a battle, contest, controversy, or debate)
	记 词根记忆：op(反) + pon(放) + ent → 处于对立位置 → 对手
	同 adversary, antagonist
agitate [ˈædʒɪteɪt]	*v.* 鼓动，煽动(to argue publicly or campaign for/against sth.); 使不安，使焦虑(to cause anxiety)
	记 词根记忆：ag (做) + itate (表示不断的动作) → 使不断地做 → 鼓动，煽动
doctrinaire [ˌdɑːktrəˈner]	*n.* 教条主义者(one who attempts to put into effect an abstract doctrine) *adj.* 教条的，迂腐的(stubbornly adhering to a doctrine)
	记 来自doctrine(*n.* 教条)
	同 authoritarian, authoritative, dictatorial, dogmatic
flagrant [ˈfleɪɡrənt]	*adj.* 罪恶昭彰的; 公然的(conspicuously offensive)
	记 不要和fragrant(*adj.* 芳香的)相混

agitate

快跳呀! 快跳呀!

□ incense	□ overdraw	□ distent	□ complementary	□ grateful	□ quantifiable
□ expertise	□ rancor	□ pounce	□ opponent	□ agitate	□ doctrinaire
□ flagrant					

hypocrisy [hɪˈpɑːkrəsi]	*n.* 伪善，虚伪（a feigning to be what one is not or to believe what one does not） 同 cant, pecksniff, sanctimony, sham
brassy [ˈbræsi]	*adj.* 厚脸皮的，无礼的（brazen; insolent） 记 联想记忆：brass（黄铜）+ y → 脸皮像黄铜一样厚 → 厚脸皮的
titanic [taɪˈtænɪk]	*adj.* 巨人的，力大无比的（colossal） 记 来自希腊神话中的巨神 Titan；也可以联想电影 *Titanic*（《泰坦尼克号》）
abolition [ˌæbəˈlɪʃn]	*n.* 废除，废止（the state of being abolished; prohibition） 记 来自 abolish（*v.* 废除，废止）
impassive [ɪmˈpæsɪv]	*adj.* 无动于衷的，冷漠的（stolid; phlegmatic） 记 词根记忆：im（没有）+ passi（感情）+ ve → 没有感情的；注意不要和 impassioned（*adj.* 充满激情的）相混
waxy [ˈwæksi]	*adj.* 像蜡的，苍白的，光滑的（looking or feeling like wax）
accede [əkˈsiːd]	*v.* 同意（to give assent; consent） 记 词根记忆：ac + cede（走）→ 走到一起 → 同意 搭 accede to 答应
timeliness [ˈtaɪmlinəs]	*n.* 及时，适时 记 来自 timely（*adj.* 及时的，适时的）
optimum [ˈɑːptɪməm]	*adj.* 最有利的，最理想的（most favorable or desirable） 记 词根记忆：optim（最好的）+ um → 最有利的
nonconformist [ˌnɑːnkənˈfɔːrmɪst]	*adj.* 不墨守成规的 *n.* 不墨守成规的人 记 联想记忆：non（不）+ conform（遵守）+ ist → 不墨守成规的人
ethnic [ˈeθnɪk]	*adj.* 民族的，种族的（of a national, racial or tribal group that has a common culture tradition） 记 词根记忆：ethn（民族，种族）+ ic → 民族的，种族的
repugnant [rɪˈpʌgnənt]	*adj.* 令人厌恶的（strong distaste or aversion） 记 词根记忆：re + pugn（打斗）+ ant → 总是打斗 → 令人厌恶的 搭 be repugnant to sb. 使某人嫌恶，使某人反感
notorious [noʊˈtɔːriəs]	*adj.* 臭名昭著的（widely and unfavorably known） 记 词根记忆：not（知道）+ orious → 人所共知的 → 臭名昭著的
accuse [əˈkjuːz]	*v.* 谴责，指责（to blame） 记 词根记忆：ac + cuse（理由）→ 有理由说别人 → 指责 同 arraign, charge, criminate, incriminate, inculpate
remarkable [rɪˈmɑːrkəbl]	*adj.* 值得注意的，显著的（worthy of being or likely to be noticed） 例 As delicate and fragile as insect bodies are, it is *remarkable* that over the ages enough of them have survived, preserved in amber, for scientists to trace insect evolution. 同 extraordinary, singular

□ hypocrisy	□ brassy	□ titanic	□ abolition	□ impassive	□ waxy
□ accede	□ timeliness	□ optimum	□ nonconformist	□ ethnic	□ repugnant
□ notorious	□ accuse	□ remarkable			

69

epidemic [ˌepɪˈdemɪk]	*adj.* 传染性的，流行性的（prevalent and spreading rapidly in a community） 记 词根记忆：epi(在…中) + dem(人民) + ic → 在一群人之中 → 流行性的
claustrophobic [ˌklɔːstrəˈfoʊbɪk]	*adj.* (患)幽闭恐怖症的，导致幽闭恐怖症的（affected with or inclined to claustrophobia）
unmitigated [ʌnˈmɪtɪɡeɪtɪd]	*adj.* 未缓和的，未减轻的（not lessoned or excused in any way） 记 词根记忆：un(不) + mitigate(缓和的) + d → 未缓和的
tread [tred]	*v.* 踏，践踏（to press beneath the feet; trample）；行走 *n.* 步态；车轮胎面 同 step
diligent [ˈdɪlɪdʒənt]	*adj.* 勤奋的，勤勉的（characterized by steady, earnest, and energetic effort）
cosmic [ˈkɑːzmɪk]	*adj.* 宇宙的（of or relating to the cosmos） 记 词根记忆：cosm(宇宙) + ic → 宇宙的
trilogy [ˈtrɪlədʒi]	*n.* 三部曲（a group of three related books） 记 词根记忆：tri(三) + logy(说话，作品) → 三部曲
subservient [səbˈsɜːrviənt]	*adj.* 次要的，从属的（useful in an inferior capacity）；恭顺的（obsequiously submissive）
solvent [ˈsɑːlvənt]	*adj.* 有偿债能力的（capable of meeting financial obligations）*n.* 溶剂 记 来自solve(*v.* 解决；溶化)
austere [ɔːˈstɪr]	*adj.* 朴素的（very plain; lacking ornament） 记 词根记忆：au + stere(冷) → 冷面孔 → 朴素的
refrigerate [rɪˈfrɪdʒəreɪt]	*v.* 使冷却，冷藏（to make or keep cold or cool）
capture [ˈkæptʃər]	*v.* 俘获（to take as a prisoner）；夺取或赢得（to take or win）*n.* 战利品 记 词根记忆：capt(抓) + ure → 抓住的状态 → 俘获
philosophic [ˌfɪləˈsɑːfɪk]	*adj.* 哲学(家)的（of or relating to philosophers or philosophy） 记 来自philosophy(*n.* 哲学)
abstain [əbˈsteɪn]	*v.* 禁绝，放弃（to refrain deliberately and often with an effort of self-denial from an action or practice） 记 词根记忆：abs(不) + tain(拿住) → 不拿住 → 放弃

□ epidemic	□ claustrophobic	□ unmitigated	□ tread	□ diligent	□ cosmic
□ trilogy	□ subservient	□ solvent	□ austere	□ refrigerate	□ capture
□ philosophic	□ abstain				

sporadic [spəˈrædɪk]	*adj.* 不定时发生的（occurring occasionally） 例 These *sporadic* raids seem to indicate that the enemy is waging a war of attrition rather than attacking us directly.
personally [ˈpɜːrsənəli]	*adv.* 亲自（in person）; 作为个人（as a person） 例 Despite the daunting size of her undergraduate class, the professor made a point of getting to know as many as possible of the more than 700 students *personally*.
wilt [wɪlt]	*v.* 凋谢，枯萎（to lose vigor from lack of water） 同 mummify, shrivel, wither
impart [ɪmˈpɑːrt]	*v.* 传授，赋予（bestow）; 传递（transmit）; 告知，透露（to make known） 记 词根记忆：im（进入）+ part（部分）→ 使成为一部分 → 告知
operable [ˈɑːpərəbl]	*adj.* 可操作的，可使用的（fit, possible, or desirable to use）; 可手术治疗的（likely to result in a favorable outcome upon surgical treatment）
antipathy [ænˈtɪpəθi]	*n.* 反感，厌恶（strong dislike） 记 词根记忆：anti + pathy（感情）→ 反感 同 animosity, animus, antagonism, enmity, hostility
carnivorous [kɑːrˈnɪvərəs]	*adj.* 肉食动物的（flesh-eating） 记 词根记忆：carn（肉）+ i + vor（吃）+ ous → 肉食动物的
acoustic [əˈkuːstɪk]	*adj.* 听觉的，声音的（having to do with hearing or sound）
monochromatic [ˌmɑːnəkroʊˈmætɪk]	*adj.* 单色的（having only one color） 记 词根记忆：mono（单一）+ chrom（颜色）+ atic → 单色的 例 Most people who are color-blind actually can distinguish several colors; some, however, have a truly *monochromatic* view of a world all in shades of gray.
prehistoric [ˌpriːhɪˈstɔːrɪk]	*adj.* 史前的（of a time before recorded history） 记 联想记忆：pre（在前面）+ historic（历史的）→ 史前的

□ sporadic	□ personally	□ wilt	□ impart	□ operable	□ antipathy
□ carnivorous	□ acoustic	□ monochromatic	□ prehistoric		

71

ultimatum [ˌʌltɪˈmeɪtəm]	*n.* 最后通牒（a final proposition, condition, or demand） 记 联想记忆：ultim（最后的）+ a + tum（看作 term，期限）→ 最后的期限 → 最后通牒
diverge [daɪˈvɜːrdʒ]	*v.* 分歧，分开（to go or move in different directions; deviate） 记 词根记忆：di（离开）+ verg（转向）+ e → 转开 → 分歧
escalate [ˈeskəleɪt]	*v.* （战争等）升级（to make a conflict more serious）；扩大，上升，增强（to grow or increase rapidly） 例 The mayor and school superintendent let their dispute over budget cuts *escalate* to ugly and destructive proportions.
interrogation [ɪnˌterəˈgeɪʃn]	*n.* 审问，质问；疑问句 同 inquiry, query, question
advertise [ˈædvərtaɪz]	*v.* 做广告（to call public attention to arouse a desire to buy or patronize）；通知（to make publicly and generally known）
sarcastic [sɑːrˈkæstɪk]	*adj.* 讽刺的（sneering; caustic; ironic） 搭 sarcastic comments 讽刺的评论
apportion [əˈpɔːrʃn]	*v.* （按比例或计划）分配（to divide and share out according to a plan） 搭 apportion sth. among/between/to sb. 分配，分发
aesthetically [esˈθetɪkli]	*adv.* 审美地（according to aesthetics or its principles）；美学观点上地（in an aesthetic manner）
ignorance [ˈɪgnərəns]	*n.* 无知，愚昧（lack of knowledge, education, or awareness） 记 词根记忆：ig（不）+（g）nor（知道）+ ance → 什么都不知道 → 无知，愚昧 同 benightedness, illiteracy, unacquaintance
tedium [ˈtiːdiəm]	*n.* 冗长乏味（boredom） 记 联想记忆：媒体（medium）的节目都很乏味（tedium）
infectious [ɪnˈfekʃəs]	*adj.* 传染的，有传染性的（capable of causing infection; communicable by infection）
stringent [ˈstrɪndʒənt]	*adj.* （规定）严格的，苛刻的（severe）；缺钱的（marked by scarcity of money, credit restrictions, or other financial strain） 记 联想记忆：string（线，绳）+ ent → 像用绳限制住一样 → 严格的 例 These regulations are so *stringent* that we feel we have lost all our privileges. 同 draconian, rigorous
idiomatic [ˌɪdiəˈmætɪk]	*adj.* 符合语言习惯的（of, relating to, or conforming to idiom）；惯用的（peculiar to a particular group, individual, or style）

最后三天
ultimatum

别喝，我有肝炎
infectious

accustom [əˈkʌstəm]	*v.* 使习惯（to make familiar with something through use or experience） 记 词根记忆：ac(一再) + custom(习惯) → 使习惯
hypochondriac [ˌhaɪpəˈkɑːndriæk]	*n.* 忧郁症患者（a person affected with hypochondria）*adj.* 忧郁症的（relating to or affected with hypochondria）
investigate [ɪnˈvestɪɡeɪt]	*v.* 调查（to examine in order to obtain the truth） 记 联想记忆：in + vest(背心) + i + gate(大门) → 穿上背心出大门去调查 → 调查
subtractive [səbˈtræktɪv]	*adj.* 减法的（tending to subtract）；负的
elite [eɪˈliːt]	*n.* 精英；主力，中坚（the group regarded as the best and most powerful） 记 词根记忆：e + lit (=lig 选择) + e → 选出来的 → 精英
inconclusive [ˌɪnkənˈkluːsɪv]	*adj.* 非决定性的；无定论的（leading to no conclusion or definite result） 例 Given the *inconclusive* state of the published evidence, we do not argue here that exposure to low-level microwave energy is either hazardous or safe.
proclamation [ˌprɑːkləˈmeɪʃn]	*n.* 宣布，公布（an official public statement） 记 词根记忆：pro(在前面) + clam(=claim 叫喊) + ation → 在前面喊 → 宣布，公布
giddy [ˈɡɪdi]	*adj.* 轻浮的，轻率的（not serious; frivolous） 同 flighty, frothy
diagnostic [ˌdaɪəɡˈnɑːstɪk]	*adj.* 诊断的（of, relating to, or used in diagnosis）*n.* 诊断（the art or practice of diagnosis）
disingenuous [ˌdɪsɪnˈdʒenjuəs]	*adj.* 不坦率的（lacking in candor） 记 词根记忆：dis(不) + in + gen(出生) + uous → 失去刚出生时的状态 → 不坦率的
iconographic [aɪˌkɔnəˈɡræfik]	*adj.* 肖像的，肖像学的；图解的（representing something by pictures or diagrams）
ablaze [əˈbleɪz]	*adj.* 着火的，燃烧的（being on fire）；闪耀的（radiant with light or emotion） 搭 ablaze with sth. 闪耀、发光
elucidate [iˈluːsɪdeɪt]	*v.* 阐明，说明（to give a clarifying explanation） 记 词根记忆：e + luc(清晰的) + id + ate → 弄清晰 → 阐明
boisterous [ˈbɔɪstərəs]	*adj.* 喧闹的（noisy and unruly）；猛烈的（violent） 记 词根记忆：boister(喧闹) + ous → 喧闹的 同 disorderly, rambunctious, tumultuous, turbulent
critical [ˈkrɪtɪkl]	*adj.* 挑毛病的（looking for faults）；关键的；危急的（of or at a crisis） 搭 be critical of... 对…挑毛病
untrustworthy [ʌnˈtrʌstwɜːrði]	*adj.* 不能信赖的，靠不住的（not capable of being trusted or depended on） 记 和 untrusty(*adj.* 不可靠的)一起记

麻烦您填个调查问卷！

investigate

7

elegiac [ˌelɪˈdʒaɪək]	*adj.* 哀歌的，挽歌的(of, relating to, or involving elegy or mourning or expressing sorrow for that which is irrecoverably past) *n.* 哀歌，挽歌(elegy)
frivolous [ˈfrɪvələs]	*adj.* 轻薄的，轻佻的(marked by unbecoming levity) 记 词根记忆：friv(愚蠢) + olous → 愚蠢的 → 轻佻的
consciousness [ˈkɑːnʃəsnəs]	*n.* 意识，观念(awareness; mind)；清醒状态；知觉(the normal state of conscious life) 同 concern, heed, heedfulness, regard
overemphasize [ˌoʊvərˈemfəsaɪz]	*v.* 过分强调(to give something more importance than it deserves or than is suitable) 同 magnify, overplay
adorn [əˈdɔːrn]	*v.* 装饰(to decorate; beautify) 记 词根记忆：ad + orn(装饰) → 装饰
didactic [daɪˈdæktɪk]	*adj.* 教诲的(morally instructive)；说教的(boringly pedantic or moralistic) 记 联想记忆：did(做) + act(行动) + ic → 教人如何做或行动 → 教诲的
equivalent [ɪˈkwɪvələnt]	*adj.* 相等的，等值的(equal in quantity, value, meaning, etc.) 记 词根记忆：equi(平等的) + val(力量) + ent → 力量平等的 → 相等的 搭 be equivalent to... 与…相等或等值
navigate [ˈnævɪgeɪt]	*v.* 驾驶(to direct the course of a ship or plane)；航行(to follow a planned course on, across, or through)；使通过 记 词根记忆：nav(船) + ig(走) + ate → 坐船走 → 航行 例 As more people try to *navigate* the legal system by themselves, representing themselves in court and drawing up their own wills and contracts, the question arises whether they will be able to avoid judicial quagmires without lawyers to guide them.
celibate [ˈselɪbət]	*n.* 独身者(an unmarried person) *adj.* 不结婚的 记 词根记忆：celib(独身) + ate → 独身者
separate	[ˈsepəreɪt] *v.* 使分开(to set or keep apart) [ˈseprət] *adj.* 不同的(not the same)；独自的(not shared with another)
breed [briːd]	*v.* 繁殖(to produce offspring by hatching or gestation)；教养(to bring up) *n.* 品种，种类(class; kind)
also-ran [ˈɔːlsoʊ ræn]	*n.* 落选者(a contestant that does not win)；不重要的参与者(one that is of little importance)
fraud [frɔːd]	*n.* 欺诈，欺骗(deceit; trickery)；骗子(impostor; cheat) 记 frau 是德语"妻子，太太"之意；如果妻子(frau) 欺骗丈夫，那就是欺骗(fraud) 例 Paradoxically, while it is relatively easy to prov art is a *fraud*, it is often virtually impossible to prov is genuine.

现在投资就有100倍回报！

fraud

deviation [ˌdiːviˈeɪʃn]	*n.* 背离（noticeable or marked departure from accepted norms of behavior） 同 aberration, deflection, divergence, diversion
offstage [ɔːfˈsteɪdʒ]	*adj.* 台后的，幕后的（not on the open stage） 记 组合词：off(离开…) + stage(舞台) → 离开舞台 → 台后的
voluble [ˈvɑːljəbl]	*adj.* 健谈的（talkative）；易旋转的（rotating）
reprimand [ˈreprɪmænd]	*n.* 训诫，谴责（a severe or formal reproof） *v.* 训诫，谴责（to reprove sharply or censure formally） 记 联想记忆：re(重新) + prim(首要) + (m)and(命令) → 再次给以严厉的命令 → 谴责
apex [ˈeɪpeks]	*n.* 顶点，最高点（peak；vertex） 搭 reach the apex 达到顶点 同 acme, climax, crest, crown, fastigium
grope [ɡroʊp]	*v.* 摸索，探索（to feel or search about blindly） 记 联想记忆：g(看作 grasp，抓住) + rope(绳子) → 抓住绳子 → 摸索，探索
bluff [blʌf]	*n.* 虚张声势（pretense of strength）；悬崖峭壁（high cliff） 记 联想记忆：和 buffalo(美洲野牛)一起记，buffalo bluffs(野牛虚张声势)
climate [ˈklaɪmət]	*n.* 气候；风气（the prevailing set of conditions） 同 atmosphere, clime
postwar [ˈpoʊstwɔːr]	*adj.* 战后的（occurring or existing after a war） 记 组合词：post(在…之后) + war(战争) → 战后的
pantomime [ˈpæntəmaɪm]	*n.* 哑剧（a performance done using gestures and postures instead of words） 记 词根记忆：panto(=pan 全部) + mim(模仿) + e → 模仿他人进行的表演 → 哑剧
soporific [ˌsɑːpəˈrɪfɪk]	*adj.* 催眠的（tending to cause sleep） *n.* 安眠药 记 词根记忆：sopor(昏睡) + ific → 催眠的
forthright [ˈfɔːrθraɪt]	*adj.* 直率的（clear and honest in manner and speech） 同 candid, frank, straightforward
salvage [ˈsælvɪdʒ]	*v.* （从灾难中）抢救，海上救助（to save sth. from loss, fire, wreck, etc.） *n.* 海上救助 记 词根记忆：salv(救) + age → 抢救 例 Many industries are so beleaguered by the impact of government sanctions, equipment failure, and foreign competition that they are beginning to rely on industrial psychologists to *salvage* what remains of employee morale.
transitory [ˈtrænsətɔːri]	*adj.* 短暂的（transient） 记 词根记忆：trans(改变) + (s)it(坐) + ory → 坐一下就改变了 → 短暂的
propriety [prəˈpraɪəti]	*n.* 礼节（decorum）；适当，得体（appropriateness） 记 词根记忆：propr(拥有) + iety → 拥有得体的行为 → 礼节；得体

7

□ deviation	□ offstage	□ voluble	□ reprimand	□ apex	□ grope
□ bluff	□ climate	□ postwar	□ pantomime	□ soporific	□ forthright
□ salvage	□ transitory	□ propriety			

flimsy ['flɪmzi]	*adj.* 轻而薄的（thin and easily broken or damaged）；易损坏的（poorly made and fragile） 记 联想记忆：flim（看作 film, 胶卷）+ sy → 像胶卷一样的东西 → 易损坏的
sacred ['seɪkrɪd]	*adj.* 神圣的，庄严的（holy; inviolable） 同 divine
indecipherable [ˌɪndɪ'saɪfrəbl]	*adj.* 无法破译的（incapable of being deciphered） 记 联想记忆：in（不）+ decipher（破解，破译）+ able → 无法破译的
precise [prɪ'saɪs]	*adj.* 精确的，准确的，确切的（exactly or sharply defined or stated） 记 词根记忆：pre（表加强）+ cis（切）+ e → 细心地切下 → 精确的 例 One of photography's most basic and powerful traits is its ability to give substance to history, to present *precise* visual details of a time gone by.
ceremonious [ˌserə'mounɪəs]	*adj.* 仪式隆重的（very formal） 记 来自 ceremony（*n.* 典礼，仪式）
akin [ə'kɪn]	*adj.* 同族的（related by blood）；类似的（essentially similar, related, or compatible）
eminent ['emɪnənt]	*adj.* 显赫的，杰出的（prominent; conspicuous） 记 词根记忆：e + min（突出）+ ent → 突出来 → 显赫的 例 The *eminent* ambassador was but an indifferent linguist; yet he insisted on speaking to foreign dignitaries in their own tongues without resorting to a translator's aid.
assorted [ə'sɔːrtəd]	*adj.* 各式各样的（consisting of various kinds）；混杂的（mixed） 记 词根记忆：as + sort（种类）+ ed → 把各种东西放到一起 → 混杂的
incompetent [ɪn'kɑːmpɪtənt]	*adj.* 无能力的，不胜任的（lacking the qualities needed for effective action） 记 联想记忆：in（不）+ competent（有能力的）→ 无能力的
craft [kræft]	*n.* 行业；手艺（occupation, especially one that needs skill） 搭 arts and crafts 手工艺
bashfulness ['bæʃflnəs]	*n.* 羞怯（shyness, timidity） 记 来自 bashful（*adj.* 羞怯的，忸怩的）
halting ['hɔːltɪŋ]	*adj.* 踌躇的，迟疑不决的（marked by hesitation or uncertainty） 记 来自 halt（*v.* 停住，停顿）
surpass [sər'pæs]	*v.* 超过（to go beyond in amount, quality, or degree） 记 词根记忆：sur（超过，在上面）+ pass（通过）→ 在上面通过 → 超过 例 No real life hero of ancient or modern days can *surpass* James Bond with his nonchalant disregard of death and the fortitude with which he bears torture. 同 exceed, excel, outshine, outstrip

precise

□ flimsy	□ sacred	□ indecipherable	□ precise	□ ceremonious	□ akin
□ eminent	□ assorted	□ incompetent	□ craft	□ bashfulness	□ halting
□ surpass					

conquer [ˈkɑːŋkər]	*v.* 以武力征服 (to take possession of sth. by force) 记 词根记忆：con(全部) + quer(寻求；询问) → 全部寻求到 → 以武力征服
world-beater [ˈwɜːrldbiːtər]	*n.* 举世无双的人 (a person or thing that is better than all others)
substantive [səbˈstæntɪv]	*adj.* 根本的 (dealing with essentials)；独立存在的 (being a totally independent entity)
short-sightedness [ˌʃɔːrt ˈsaɪtɪdnəs]	*n.* 目光短浅；近视 (the state of being able to see things clearly only if they are very close to you) 例 Many elderly people are capable of working, but they are kept from gainful employment by the *short-sightedness* of those employers who mistakenly believe that young people alone can give them adequate service.
vagueness [ˈveɪɡnəs]	*n.* 含糊 (unclearness by virtue of being vague) 例 Wincing at the *vagueness* of the interviewer's wording, the scholar was as sensitive to words and phrases as a sectarian is to creeds.
irresolute [ɪˈrezəluːt]	*adj.* 未决定的 (uncertain how to act or proceed)；犹豫不决的 (lacking in resolution; indecisive)
irreverent [ɪˈrevərənt]	*adj.* 不尊敬的 (lacking proper respect or seriousness) 同 disrespectful
pedant [ˈpednt]	*n.* 迂腐之人，学究 (one who unduly emphasizes minutiae in the use of knowledge) 记 词根记忆：ped(教育) + ant → 与儿童教育相关的人 → 学究
interchangeable [ˌɪntərˈtʃeɪndʒəbl]	*adj.* 可互换的 (incapable of being interchanged) 记 来自 interchange(*v.* 互换)
unexceptionable [ˌʌnɪkˈsepʃənəbl]	*adj.* 无可挑剔的 (incapable of being disapproved of) 记 联想记忆：un(不) + exceptionable(可反对的) → 无可挑剔的 例 Although some of her fellow scientists decried the unorthodox laboratory methodology that others found innovative, unanimous praise greeted her experimental results: at once pioneering and *unexceptionable*.
foliage [ˈfoʊliɪdʒ]	*n.* 叶子 (mass of leaves; leafage) 记 词根记忆：foli(树叶) + age → 叶子
corroborate [kəˈrɑːbəreɪt]	*v.* 支持或证实 (to bolster; make more certain)；强化 (to strengthen) 记 词根记忆：cor + robor(力量) + ate → 加强力量 → 强化
apathetic [ˌæpəˈθetɪk]	*adj.* 无感情的 (having or showing little or no feeling or emotion)；无兴趣的 (having little or no interest or concern) 搭 be apathetic about 对…冷淡

irreverent

□ conquer □ world-beater □ substantive □ short-sightedness □ vagueness □ irresolute
□ irreverent □ pedant □ interchangeable □ unexceptionable □ foliage □ corroborate
□ apathetic

77

mutable [ˈmjuːtəbl]	*adj.* 可变的(capable of change or of being changed);易变的(capable of or liable to mutation) 同 changeable, fluid, mobile, protean
chorale [kəˈræl]	*n.* 赞美诗(a hymn or psalm sung to a traditional or composed melody in church);合唱队(chorus; choir)
unpromising [ʌnˈprɑːmɪsɪŋ]	*adj.* 无前途的, 没有希望的(not promising) 记 不要和 uncompromising(*adj.* 不妥协的)相混
willful [ˈwɪlfl]	*adj.* 任性的(perversely self-willed);故意的(intentional) 同 deliberate, knowing, wilful
overcast [ˌoʊvərˈkæst]	*adj.* 阴天的, 阴暗的 同 bleak, cloudy, gloomy, somber
infer [ɪnˈfɜːr]	*v.* 推断, 推论, 推理(to reach an opinion from reasoning) 记 词根记忆: in(进入) + fer(带来) → 带进(意义) → 推断
comprehensible [ˌkɑːmprɪˈhensəbl]	*adj.* 可理解的, 易于理解的(that can be understood) 记 词根记忆: comprehen(=comprehend 理解) + sible(能够) → 能够理解的 → 可理解的
time-consuming [ˈtaɪmkənsuːmɪŋ]	*adj.* 费时间的(using or taking up a great deal of time) 搭 a time-consuming job 一项费时的工作
prophetic [prəˈfetɪk]	*adj.* 先知的, 预言的, 预示的(correctly telling of things that will happen in the future) 记 词根记忆: pro(提前) + phe(说) + tic → 提前说出来 → 先知的, 预言的
subsist [səbˈsɪst]	*v.* 生存下去, 继续存在(to exist);维持生活 记 词根记忆: sub(下面) + sist(站) → 站下去, 活下去 → 生存下去
iniquitous [ɪˈnɪkwɪtəs]	*adj.* 邪恶的, 不公正的(wicked; unjust) 记 词根记忆: in(不) + iqu(公正的) + itous → 不公正的
journalistic [ˌdʒɜːrnəˈlɪstɪk]	*adj.* 新闻业的, 新闻工作者的(of, relating to, or characteristic of journalism or journalists)
grieve [griːv]	*v.* 使某人极为悲伤(to cause great sorrow to sb.) 搭 grieve over 因为…而悲伤 同 aggrieve, bemoan, deplore, distress, mourn
prevail [prɪˈveɪl]	*v.* 战胜(to gain ascendancy through strength or superiority);流行, 盛行(to be frequent) 记 词根记忆: pre(在前面) + vail(=val 力量) → 在力量上胜过他人 → 战胜 同 conquer, master, predominate, triumph
hallow [ˈhæloʊ]	*v.* 把…视为神圣(to make or set apart as holy);尊敬, 敬畏(to respect or honor greatly; revere) 记 注意不要和 hollow(*adj.* 空洞的)相混
unbiased [ʌnˈbaɪəst]	*adj.* 没有偏见的(free from all prejudice and favoritism) 例 The fact that a theory is plausible does not necessarily ensure its scientific truth, which must be established by *unbiased* controlled studies.

□ mutable	□ chorale	□ unpromising	□ willful	□ overcast	□ infer
□ comprehensible	□ time-consuming	□ prophetic	□ subsist	□ iniquitous	□ journalistic
□ grieve	□ prevail	□ hallow	□ unbiased		

hazard [ˈhæzərd]	*n.* 危险(risk; peril; danger) 搭 at hazard 在危急关头
repute [rɪˈpjuːt]	*v.* 认为，以为 *n.* 名声，名誉(reputation) 记 词根记忆：re + put(想) + e → 认为，以为
unmoved [ˌʌnˈmuːvd]	*adj.* 无动于衷的，冷漠的(not affected by feelings of pity, sympathy) 记 联想记忆：un(不) + moved(感动的) → 无动于衷的
adhesive [ədˈhiːsɪv]	*adj.* 黏着的，带黏性的(tending to adhere or cause adherence) *n.* 黏合剂(an adhesive substance) 记 联想记忆：ad + hes(=stick 粘住) + ive → 带粘性的；粘合剂
stagnation [stæɡˈneɪʃn]	*n.* 停滞 搭 blood stagnation 瘀血
insatiable [ɪnˈseɪʃəbl]	*adj.* 不知足的，贪得无厌的(very greedy) 记 词根记忆：in(不) + sati(填满) + able → 填不满的 → 不知足的
entangle [ɪnˈtæŋɡl]	*v.* 使卷入(to involve in a perplexing or troublesome situation) 记 联想记忆：en + tangle(纠缠，混乱) → 使卷入
contrite [kənˈtraɪt]	*adj.* 悔罪的，痛悔的(feeling contrition; repentant) 记 词根记忆：con + trit(摩擦) + e → (心灵)摩擦 → 痛悔的
self-deprecation [ˌselfdeprəˈkeɪʃn]	*n.* 自嘲(self-mockery) 例 Comparatively few rock musicians are willing to laugh at themselves, although a hint of *self-deprecation* can boost sales of video clips very nicely.
prominence [ˈprɑːmɪnəns]	*n.* 突出物(something prominent)；突出，显著(the quality, state, or fact of being prominent or conspicuous) 例 Despite the growing *prominence* of Hispanic actors in the American theater, many Hispanic experts feel that the Spanish speaking population is underrepresented on the stage. 同 eminence, kudos, preeminence, prestige
autobiographical [ˌɔːtəˌbaɪəˈɡræfɪkl]	*adj.* 自传的，自传体的 记 词根记忆：auto(自己的) + biography(传记) + ical → 自传的
compromise [ˈkɑːmprəmaɪz]	*v.* 妥协(to settle by concessions)；危害(to lay open to danger or disrepute) 记 词根记忆：com(共同) + promise(保证) → 相互保证 → 妥协
indiscriminately [ˌɪndɪˈskrɪmɪnətli]	*adv.* 随意地，任意地(in a random manner; promiscuously) 例 Although most worthwhile criticism concentrates on the positive, one should not *indiscriminately* praise everything. 同 arbitrarily
deteriorate [dɪˈtɪriəreɪt]	*v.* (使)变坏，恶化(to make inferior in quality or value) 记 词根记忆：de(向下) + ter(=terr 地) + iorate → 向着地面下降 → (使)变化，恶化 同 degenerate, descend, languish, weaken
equation [ɪˈkweɪʒn]	*n.* 等式(two expressions connected by the sign "=")；等同，相等(action of making equal)

□ hazard　　　　□ repute　　　　□ unmoved　　　　□ adhesive　　　　□ stagnation　　　　□ insatiable
□ entangle　　　　□ contrite　　　　□ self-deprecation　□ prominence　　　□ autobiographical　□ compromise
□ indiscriminately □ deteriorate　　□ equation

79

ornamental [ˌɔːrnəˈmentl]	*adj.* 装饰性的(of, relating to, or serving as ornament) 记 词根记忆：orn(装饰) + amental → 装饰性的
conjure [ˈkʌndʒər]	*v.* 召唤，想起(to call or bring to mind; evoke)；变魔术，变戏法(to practise magic or legerdemain) 搭 conjure for 召唤
unimpressed [ˌʌnɪmˈprest]	*adj.* 没有印象的
trenchant [ˈtrentʃənt]	*adj.* 犀利的，尖锐的(sharply perceptive; penetrating) 记 联想记忆：trench(沟) + ant → 说话像挖沟，入木三分 → 犀利的
spineless [ˈspaɪnləs]	*adj.* 没骨气的，懦弱的(lacking courage or willpower) 记 联想记忆：spine(脊椎，刺) + less → 无脊椎的 → 没骨气的 例 Are we to turn into *spineless* equivocators, afraid to take a forthright stand, unable to answer a question without pussyfooting?
converse	[kənˈvɜːrs] *v.* 谈话，交谈(to exchange thoughts and opinions in speech) [ˈkɑːnvɜːrs] *adj.* 逆向的(opposite) *n.* 相反的事物(an opposite) 记 词根记忆：con + vers(转) + e → 全部转换方向 → 逆向的
electromagnetic [ɪˌlektroʊmæɡˈnetɪk]	*adj.* 电磁的(of, relating to, or produced by electromagnetism) 记 词根记忆：electr(电) + o + magnetic(磁的) → 电磁的
down [daʊn]	*n.* 绒毛(a covering of soft fluffy feathers)；软毛(fine soft hair)
numerous [ˈnuːmərəs]	*adj.* 许多的，很多的 记 词根记忆：numer(计数) + ous → 不计其数的 → 许多的，很多的 例 Known for his commitment to *numerous* worthy causes, the philanthropist deserved credit for his altruism. 同 abundant, multitudinous, myriad, various
code [koʊd]	*n.* 密码；法典 *v.* 将某事物编写成密码(to put in or into the form or symbols of a code)
fleeting [ˈfliːtɪŋ]	*adj.* 短暂的；飞逝的(transient; passing swiftly) 记 来自 fleet(*v.* 疾飞，掠过)
overinflated [ˌoʊvərɪnˈfleɪtɪd]	*adj.* 过度充气的(filled with too much air) 例 Like a balloon that is *overinflated*, aneurysms sometimes enlarge so much that they burst.
shopworn [ˈʃɑːpwɔːrn]	*adj.* 在商店中陈列久了的(ruined or damaged from being on display in a store)；陈旧的，磨损的
retain [rɪˈteɪn]	*v.* 保留，保持(to keep possession of)；留住，止住(to hold in place) 记 词根记忆：re + tain(拿) → 拿住 → 保留，保持
awkward [ˈɔːkwərd]	*adj.* 笨拙的 (ungainly)；难用的 (difficult to use)；不便的 (causing inconvenience) 记 发音记忆："拗口的" → 笨拙的；难用的 同 clumsy, gawky, lumbering, lumpish

□ ornamental	□ conjure	□ unimpressed	□ trenchant	□ spineless	□ converse
□ electromagnetic	□ down	□ numerous	□ code	□ fleeting	□ overinflated
□ shopworn	□ retain	□ awkward			

80

guilt [gɪlt]	*n.* 罪行(crime; sin); 内疚(a painful feeling of self-reproach) 搭 be free of guilt 无罪的
vertebrate ['vɜːrtɪbrət]	*n./adj.* 脊椎动物(的)(an animal that has a spine) 记 来自 vertebra(*n.* 脊椎骨) 例 Just as the authors' book on eels is often a key text for courses in marine *vertebrate* zoology, their ideas on animal development and phylogeny inform teaching in this area.
derogatory [dɪ'rɑːgətɔːri]	*adj.* 不敬的, 贬损的(disparaging; belittling) 记 词根记忆: de (向下) + rog (询问) + at + ory → 为贬低某人而询问 → 贬损的
extract [ɪk'strækt]	*v.* 拔出(to take sth. out with effort or by force); 强索(to forcefully obtain money or information) 记 词根记忆: ex(出) + tract(拉) → 拉出 → 拔出
cold-blooded [ˌkoʊld'blʌdɪd]	*adj.* 冷血的; 残酷的(without pity)
crumple ['krʌmpl]	*v.* 把…弄皱; 起皱(to crush together into creases or wrinkles); 破裂(to fall apart)
demur [dɪ'mɜːr]	*v.* 表示异议, 反对(to object) 记 词根记忆: de(加强) + mur(延迟) → 一再拖延 → 反对
oppressive [ə'presɪv]	*adj.* 高压的, 压制性的(unreasonably burdensome or severe); 压抑的(overwhelming or depressing to the spirit or senses) 例 During the 1960's assessments of the family shifted remarkably, from general endorsement of it as a worthwhile, stable institution to wide spread censure of it as an *oppressive* and bankrupt one whose dissolution was both imminent and welcome.
damped [dæmpt]	*adj.* 潮湿的; 减震的, 压低(声音)的
solitary ['sɑːləteri]	*adj.* 孤独的(without companions) *n.* 隐士(recluse) 记 词根记忆: solit(单独) + ary → 孤独的 例 There are no *solitary*, free-living creatures; every form of life is dependent on other forms. 同 forsaken, lonesome, lorn
adumbrate ['ædəmbreɪt]	*v.* 预示(to foreshadow in a vague way) 记 词根记忆: ad + umbr(影子) + ate → 影子提前来到 → 预示

7

□ guilt   □ vertebrate   □ derogatory   □ extract   □ cold-blooded   □ crumple
□ demur   □ oppressive   □ damped   □ solitary   □ adumbrate

81

Word List 8

音频

gratuitous [grəˈtuːɪtəs]	*adj.* 无缘无故的(without cause or justification); 免费的(free) 记 来自 gratuity(*n.* 小费); 付小费严格说不是义务, 所以有"无缘无故"之意
histrionic [ˌhɪstriˈɑːnɪk]	*adj.* 做作的(deliberately affected); 戏剧的(of or relating to actors, acting, or the theater) 记 词根记忆: histrion(演员) + ic → 戏剧的; 注意不要和 historic(*adj.* 历史的)相混 同 theatrical; dramatic
coincidentally [koʊˌɪnsɪˈdentəli]	*adv.* 巧合地(by coincidence) 记 来自 coincident(*adj.* 巧合的)
anachronistic [əˌnækrəˈnɪstɪk]	*adj.* 时代错误的(an error in chronology) 记 词根记忆: ana(错) + chron(时间) + istic → 时代错误的
infrequently [ɪnˈfriːkwəntli]	*adv.* 稀少地, 罕见地 同 rarely, seldom
solicitous [səˈlɪsɪtəs]	*adj.* 热切的(full of desire; eager); 挂念的(expressing care or concern) 搭 be solicitous of/for/about... 为…操心
ancestral [ænˈsestrəl]	*adj.* 祖先的, 祖传的(of, relating to, or inherited from an ancestor) 记 词根记忆: ances(原始的) + tral → 祖先的
demagnetize [diːˈmæɡnətaɪz]	*v.* 消磁, 使退磁(to deprive of magnetic properties)
dehumanize [ˌdiːˈhjuːmənaɪz]	*v.* 使失掉人性(to deprive of human qualities, personality, or spirit) 记 分拆记忆: de + humanize(使人性化) → 使失掉人性
disseminate [dɪˈsemɪneɪt]	*v.* 传播, 宣传(to spread abroad; promulgate widely) 记 词根记忆: dis(分开) + semin(种子) + ate → 散布(种子) → 传播
imperious [ɪmˈpɪriəs]	*adj.* 傲慢的, 专横的(overbearing; arrogant) 记 词根记忆: imper(命令) + ious → 命令的 → 专横的 搭 imperious manner 专横的态度 同 magisterial, peremptory

□ gratuitous □ histrionic □ coincidentally □ anachronistic □ infrequently □ solicitous
□ ancestral □ demagnetize □ dehumanize □ disseminate □ imperious

fascinating [ˈfæsɪneɪtɪŋ]	*adj.* 迷人的，醉人的(extremely interesting or charming) 例 Walpole's art collection was huge and *fascinating*, and his novel *The Castle of Otranto* was never out of print; none of this mattered to the Victorians, who dismissed him as, at best, insignificant.
uncharted [ˌʌnˈtʃɑːrtɪd]	*adj.* 图上未标明的(not marked on a map or chart) 同 chartless, unmapped
brute [bruːt]	*n./adj.* 野兽(的)(beast)；残忍的(人)((a person who is) brutal) 同 bestial, beastly
trivial [ˈtrɪviəl]	*adj.* 琐碎的；没有价值的(concerned with or involving trivia; of little worth) 记 词根记忆：tri(三) + via(路) + l → 三条路的会合点 → 没有价值的；古罗马妇女喜欢停在十字路口同人闲聊些无关紧要或琐碎的事情，故 trivial 有 "琐碎的；没有价值的"的意思 同 paltry, picayune, picayunish, trifling
irresponsible [ˌɪrɪˈspɑːnsəbl]	*adj.* 不对更高一级负责的(not answerable to higher authority)；不承担责任的(said or done with no sense of responsibility)；无责任感的(lacking a sense of responsibility)；无负责能力的(unable especially mentally or financially to bear responsibility) *n.* 不负责任的人，无责任感的人(a person who is irresponsible) 例 It is *irresponsible* for a government to fail to do whatever it can to eliminate a totally preventable disease.
override [ˌoʊvərˈraɪd]	*v.* 驳回(to disregard；overrule)；蹂躏，践踏(to ride over or across；trample) 记 组合词：over(在…上) + ride(骑) → 骑在…之上 → 蹂躏
colony [ˈkɑːləni]	*n.* 菌群(a group of the same kind of one-celled organisms living or growing together)；殖民地
patronize [ˈpeɪtrənaɪz]	*v.* 屈尊俯就(to behave towards sb. as if one were better or more important than him)；光顾，惠顾(to be a frequent or regular customer or client of) 记 来自 patron(*n.* 赞助人)
prescribe [prɪˈskraɪb]	*v.* 开处方(to say what treatment a sick person should have)；规定(to lay down a rule) 记 词根记忆：pre(预先) + scrib(写) + e → 预先写好 → 规定
volatile [ˈvɑːlətl]	*adj.* 反复无常的(subject to rapid or unexpected change)；易挥发的(readily vaporizable) 记 词根记忆：volat(飞) + ile → 飞走的 → 易挥发的 例 Despite the mixture's *volatile* nature, we found that by lowering its temperature in the laboratory we could dramatically reduce its tendency to vaporize. 同 capricious, fickle, inconstant, mercurial

illiterate [ɪˈlɪtərət]	*adj.* 文盲的(ignorant; uneducated)
	记 联想记忆: il(不) + literate(识字的) → 不识字的 → 文盲的
ferocity [fəˈrɑːsəti]	*n.* 凶猛, 残暴(the quality or state of being ferocious)
	同 fierceness, furiousness, vehemence, wildness
denounce [dɪˈnaʊns]	*v.* 指责(to accuse publicly)
	记 词根记忆: de + nounc(报告) + e → 坏报告 → 指责
	例 Although it is unusual to *denounce* museum-goers for not painting, it is quite common, even for those, who are unenthusiastic about sports, to criticize spectators for athletic inactivity.
suspend [səˈspend]	*v.* 暂停, 中止(to stop to be inactive or ineffective for a period of time); 吊, 悬(to hang from above)
	记 词根记忆: sus + pend(挂) → 挂在下面 → 吊, 悬
garble [ˈgɑːbl]	*v.* 曲解, 窜改(to alter or distort as to create a wrong impression or change the meaning)
	记 联想记忆: 美国女影星嘉宝(Garbo)
generosity [ˌdʒenəˈrɑːsəti]	*n.* 慷慨, 大方(willingness to share; unselfishness)
	例 Although ordinarily skeptical about the purity of Robinson's motives, in this instance Jenkins did not consider Robinson's *generosity* to be alloyed with consideration of personal gain.
euphemism [ˈjuːfəmɪzəm]	*n.* 婉言, 委婉的说法(the act or example of substituting a mild, indirect, or vague term for one considered harsh, blunt, or offensive)
	记 词根记忆: eu(好的) + phem(出现) + ism → 以好的语言出现 → 委婉的说法
allude [əˈluːd]	*v.* 暗指, 影射, 间接提到(to refer in an indirect way)
	记 词根记忆: al + lud(嬉笑) + e → 在嬉笑中说 → 暗指, 影射
serendipity [ˌserənˈdɪpəti]	*n.* 意外发现新奇事物的才能或现象(the faculty or phenomenon of finding valuable or agreeable things not sought for)
	记 出自 18 世纪英国作家 Horace(荷拉斯)的童话故事 The Three Princes of Serendip, 书中主人公具有随处发现珍宝的本领
	例 Many scientific discoveries are a matter of *serendipity*: Newton was not sitting there thinking about gravity when the apple dropped on his head.
snobbery [ˈsnɑːbəri]	*n.* 势利(snobbish conduct or character)
venial [ˈviːniəl]	*adj.* (错误等)轻微的, 可原谅的(forgivable; pardonable)
	记 联想记忆: ven(=venus 维纳斯) + ial → 出于爱而原谅的 → 可原谅的
	例 In view of the fact that there are mitigating circumstances, we must consider this a *venial* offense.
	同 excusable, remittable

84

□ illiterate　□ ferocity　□ denounce　□ suspend　□ garble　□ generosity
□ euphemism　□ allude　□ serendipity　□ snobbery　□ venial

gravity [ˈɡrævəti]	*n.* 严肃，庄重(solemnity or sedateness; seriousness) 记 词根记忆：grav(重) + ity → 庄重 例 At first, I found her *gravity* rather intimidating; but, as I saw more of her, I found that laughter was very near the surface.
detect [dɪˈtekt]	*v.* 洞察(to discover the true character of)；查明，探测(to discover or determine the existence) 记 词根记忆：de(去掉) + tect(=cover 遮盖) → 去除遮盖 → 查明
halfhearted [ˌhæfˈhɑːrtɪd]	*adj.* 不认真的，不热心的(showing little interest, enthusiasm, or heart) 记 组合词：half(半) + heart(心) + ed → 只花一半心思的 → 不认真的
neutron [ˈnuːtrɑːn]	*n.* 中子(a particle carrying no electric charge)
bilateral [ˌbaɪˈlætərəl]	*adj.* 两边的(having two sides)；双边的(affecting reciprocally two nations or parties)
elusive [iˈluːsɪv]	*adj.* 难懂的，难以描述的(hard to comprehend or define)；不易被抓获的(tending to evade grasp or pursuit) 记 词根记忆：e(出) + lus(光) + ive → 没有灵光出来的 → 难懂的 例 The guerrillas were so *elusive* that the general had to develop various strategies to trap them.
flout [flaʊt]	*v.* 蔑视(to mock or scoff at; show scorn or contempt for)；违抗 记 联想记忆：fl(=fly，飞) + out(出去) → 飞出去 → 不再服从命令 → 违抗 同 fleer, gibe, jeer, jest, sneer
cavity [ˈkævəti]	*n.* (牙齿等的)洞，腔(a hollow place in a tooth)
nutrient [ˈnuːtriənt]	*n.* 营养品，滋养物(substance serving as or providing nourishment) 记 词根记忆：nutri(滋养) + ent(表物) → 滋养物 例 Biologists categorize many of the world's environments as deserts: regions where the limited availability of some key factor, such as water, sunlight, or an essential *nutrient*, places sharp constraints on the existence of living things.
unscented [ʌnˈsentɪd]	*adj.* 无气味的(without scent) 记 联想记忆：un(不) + scented(有气味的) → 无气味的
quixotic [kwɪkˈsɑːtɪk]	*adj.* 不切实际的，空想的(foolishly impractical) 记 来自 *Don Quixote*《堂·吉诃德》；亦作 quixotical
opalescent [ˌoʊpəˈlesnt]	*adj.* 发乳白色光的(reflecting an iridescent light)
warp [wɔːrp]	*v.* 弯曲，变歪(to turn or twist out of or as if out of shape) *n.* 弯曲，歪斜(a twist or curve that has developed in something flat or straight) 记 发音记忆："卧铺" → 卧铺太窄，只有弯曲身体才能睡下 → 弯曲

8

□ gravity	□ detect	□ halfhearted	□ neutron	□ bilateral	□ elusive
□ flout	□ cavity	□ nutrient	□ unscented	□ quixotic	□ opalescent
□ warp					

affinity [əˈfɪnəti]	*n.* 相互吸引(a mutual attraction between a man and a woman); 密切关系(close relationship) 记 词根记忆: af + fin(范围) + ity → 在范围内 → 密切关系
fallible [ˈfæləbl]	*adj.* 易犯错的(liable to be erroneous) 例 For those who admire realism, Louis Malle's recent film succeeds because it consciously shuns the stuff of legend and tells an unembellished story as it might actually unfold with *fallible* people in earthly time.
garrulous [ˈgærələs]	*adj.* 唠叨的, 多话的(loquacious; talkative) 同 chatty, conversational, voluble
technique [tekˈniːk]	*n.* 技能, 方法, 手段(the manner in which technical details are treated or basic physical movements are used) 记 词根记忆: techn(技艺) + ique(…术) → 技能 例 Dr. Charles Drew's *technique* for preserving and storing blood plasma for emergency use proved so effective that it became the model for the present blood bank system used by the American Red Cross.
preferably [ˈprefrəbli]	*adv.* 更可取地, 更好地, 宁可 记 来自 prefer(*v.* 宁可, 更喜欢)
substantiate [səbˈstænʃieɪt]	*v.* 证实, 确证(to establish by proof or competent evidence, verify) 例 The value of Davis' sociological research is compromised by his unscrupulous tendency to use materials selectively in order to *substantiate* his own claims, while disregarding information that points to other possible conclusions. 同 embody, externalize, incarnate, materialize
obstruct [əbˈstrʌkt]	*v.* 阻塞(道路、通道等)(to block or close up by an obstacle); 妨碍, 阻挠(to hinder from passage, action, or operation) 记 词根记忆: ob(反) + struct(建造) → 反着建 → 阻塞
paradigm [ˈpærədaɪm]	*n.* 范例, 示范(a typical example or archetype) 记 词根记忆: para(旁边) + digm(显示) → 在一旁显示 → 范例, 示范
antithetical [ˌæntɪˈθetɪkl]	*adj.* 相反的(constituting or marked by antithesis); 对立的(opposite) 同 contradictory, contrary, converse, counter, reverse
intrepid [ɪnˈtrepɪd]	*adj.* 勇敢的, 刚毅的(characterized by fearless-ness and fortitude) 记 词根记忆: in(不) + trep(害怕) + id → 不害怕 → 勇敢的
descend [dɪˈsend]	*v.* 下降(to pass from a higher place or level to a lower one); 降格, 屈尊(to lower oneself in status or dignity) 记 词根记忆: de(向下) + scend(爬) → 向下爬 → 下降 例 The critics were distressed that an essayist of such glowing promise could *descend* to writing such dull, uninteresting prose. 同 decline, degenerate, deteriorate, sink

intrepid

□ affinity	□ fallible	□ garrulous	□ technique	□ preferably	□ substantiate
□ obstruct	□ paradigm	□ antithetical	□ intrepid	□ descend	

activate [ˈæktɪveɪt]	*v.* 刺激，使活动(to make active or more active) 例 The burglar alarm is *activated* by movement.
glaze [gleɪz]	*v.* 上釉于(to apply a glaze to)；使光滑(to give a smooth glossy surface to) *n.* 釉
usable [ˈjuːzəbl]	*adj.* 可用的(capable of being used)；好用的(convenient and practicable for use)
extremity [ɪkˈstreməti]	*n.* 极度(the utmost degree)；绝境，险境，临终(a moment marked by imminent destruction or death)
successively [səkˈsesɪvli]	*adv.* 接连地，继续地(in proper order or sequence) 例 Not all the indicators necessary to convey the effect of depth in a picture work simultaneously; the picture's illusion of uniform three-dimensional appearance must therefore result from the viewer's integration of various indicators perceived *successively*. 同 consecutively, continuously, uninterruptedly
inhibit [ɪnˈhɪbɪt]	*v.* 阻止(to prohibit from doing something)；抑制(to hold in check) 记 词根记忆：in(不) + hib(拿) + it → 不许拿 → 阻止；抑制 同 bridle, constrain, withhold
stimulus [ˈstɪmjələs]	*n.* 刺激物，激励 同 incentive
serrated [səˈreɪtɪd]	*adj.* 锯齿状的(saw-toothed) 搭 serrated knife/edge 锯齿状刀子/边缘
barbarous [ˈbɑːrbərəs]	*adj.* 野蛮的(uncultured; crude)；残暴的(cruel; brutal) 记 发音记忆："把爸勒死" → 残暴的
obfuscate [ˈɑːbfʌskeɪt]	*v.* 使困惑，使迷惑(to muddle; confuse; bewilder) 记 词根记忆：ob(在…之上) + fusc(黑暗的) + ate → 使变成全黑 → 使困惑，使迷惑
extinct [ɪkˈstɪŋkt]	*adj.* 绝种的，不存在的(no longer in existence) 记 词根记忆：ex + tinct(刺) → 用针刺使…失去 → 绝种的 例 Given the ability of modern technology to destroy the environment, it is clear that if we are not careful, the human race may soon be as *extinct* as the dinosaur.
rocky [ˈrɑːki]	*adj.* 多岩石的(abounding in or consisting of rocks)；坚若磐石的(firmly held)
compensatory [kəmˈpensətɔːri]	*adj.* 补偿性的，报酬的(compensating) 例 He received a *compensatory* payment of £20,000.
exquisite [ɪkˈskwɪzɪt]	*adj.* 精致的(elaborately made; delicate)；近乎完美的(consummate; perfected) 记 词根记忆：ex + quis(要求，寻求) + ite → 按要求做出的 → 精致的
dilapidated [dɪˈlæpɪdeɪtɪd]	*adj.* 破旧的，毁坏的(broken down; shabby and neglected) 记 词根记忆：di (=dis 分离) + lapid (石头) + ated → 石头裂或碎片的 → 毁坏的

8

□ activate	□ glaze	□ usable	□ extremity	□ successively	□ inhibit
□ stimulus	□ serrated	□ barbarous	□ obfuscate	□ extinct	□ rocky
□ compensatory	□ exquisite	□ dilapidated			

condense [kənˈdens]	*v.* 浓缩(to cause sth. to become thicker) 记 词根记忆：con + dense(浓密) → 浓缩 同 compress, constrict
touch [tʌtʃ]	*v.* 涉及(to relate to or have an influence on)；触动(to hurt the feelings of)；接触(to be in contact) *n.* 触摸(a light stroke, tap, or push) 例 Although Henry was not in general a sentimental man, occasionally he would feel a *touch* of nostalgia for the old days and would contemplate making a brief excursion to Boston to revisit his childhood friends. 同 feel, finger
equator [ɪˈkweɪtər]	*n.* 赤道(the imaginary line around the earth at an equal distance from the North and South poles) 记 词根记忆：equ(相等的) + ator → 使(地球)平分 → 赤道
gorgeous [ˈɡɔːrdʒəs]	*adj.* 华丽的；极好的(brilliantly showy; splendid) 记 联想记忆：gorge(峡谷) + ous → 峡谷是美丽的 → 华丽的
concurrent [kənˈkɜːrənt]	*adj.* 并发的(operating or occurring at the same time)；协作的，一致的(acting in conjunction)
eventful [ɪˈventfl]	*adj.* 多事的(full of or rich in events)；重要的(momentous) 记 来自 event(*n.* 事件)
moratorium [ˌmɔːrəˈtɔːriəm]	*n.* 延缓偿付(a legal authorization to delay payment of money)；活动中止(a suspension of activity) 记 词根记忆：mor(推迟) + at + orium → 延缓偿付 例 The breathing spell provided by the *moratorium* on arms shipments should give all the combatants a chance to reevaluate their positions.
constructive [kənˈstrʌktɪv]	*adj.* 建设性的(promoting improvement or development) 搭 constructive suggestions 建设性的提议
unparalleled [ʌnˈpærəleld]	*adj.* 无比的，空前的(having no parallel or equal) 同 unique, unequaled
sensitize [ˈsensətaɪz]	*v.* 使某人或某事物敏感(to make sb./sth. sensitive) 记 词根记忆：sens(感觉) + itize → 使某人或某事物敏感
aseptic [ˌeɪˈseptɪk]	*adj.* 净化的(not contaminated)；无菌的(not septic) 记 词根记忆：a(无) + sept(菌) + ic → 无菌的
delimit [diˈlɪmɪt]	*v.* 定界，划界(to fix the limits of) 记 联想记忆：de + limit(界限) → 划界
solder [ˈsɑːdər]	*v.* 焊接，焊在一起，焊合(to bring into firm union) 记 和 soldier(*n.* 战士)一起记
impersonate [ɪmˈpɜːrsəneɪt]	*v.* 模仿(to mimic)；扮演(to act the part of) 记 联想记忆：im(进入) + person(人，角色) + ate → 进入角色 → 扮演

□ condense	□ touch	□ equator	□ gorgeous	□ concurrent	□ eventful
□ moratorium	□ constructive	□ unparalleled	□ sensitize	□ aseptic	□ delimit
□ solder	□ impersonate				

augment [ɔːɡˈment]	*v.* 提高，增加(to become greater; increase) 记 词根记忆：aug(提高) + ment → 提高 同 enlarge, expand, heighten, mount, wax
self-confident [ˌselfˈkɑːnfɪdənt]	*adj.* 自信的(confident in oneself and in one's powers and abilities)
pottery [ˈpɑːtəri]	*n.* 制陶(the manufacture of clayware)；制陶工艺(the art or craft of the potter)；陶器(earthenware)
avid [ˈævɪd]	*adj.* 渴望的(having an intense craving)；热心的(eager) 搭 be avid for 渴望
concentrate [ˈkɑːnsntreɪt]	*v.* 聚集，浓缩(to bring into one main body) 记 词根记忆：con(加强) + centr(中心) + ate(做) → 重点放在一个中心 → 聚集 同 compress, condense, converge, concenter
embed [ɪmˈbed]	*v.* 牢牢插入，使嵌入(to set or fix firmly in a surrounding mass; wedge) 记 联想记忆：em(进入) + bed(床) → 深深进入内部 → 牢牢插入
abstract [ˈæbstrækt]	*n.* 摘要(summary) *adj.* 抽象的(disassociated from any specific instance) 记 词根记忆：abs + tract(拉) → 从文章中拉出 → 摘要 搭 an abstract sense of the concept 对于概念抽象的理解
spined [spaɪnd]	*adj.* 有背骨的，有脊柱的
fervent [ˈfɜːrvənt]	*adj.* 炙热的(very hot)；热情的(exhibiting or marked by great intensity of feeling)
adaptability [əˌdæptəˈbɪləti]	*n.* 适应性(capable of being or becoming adapted) 记 来自 adapt(*v.* 适应)
improper [ɪmˈprɑːpər]	*adj.* 不合适的，不适当的(incorrect; not regularly or normally formed) 同 indecorous, malapropos, undue, unfitting, unseasonable
domination [ˌdɑːmɪˈneɪʃn]	*n.* 控制，支配，管辖(exercise of mastery or ruling power) 记 词根记忆：domin(支配) + ation → 控制，支配，管辖
unquestioning [ʌnˈkwestʃənɪŋ]	*adj.* 无异议的，不犹豫的(not questioning) 同 implicit
discount [ˈdɪskaʊnt]	*n.* 折扣(amount of money taken off the cost of sth.) 记 词根记忆：dis(除去) + count(数量) → 除去一定的数 → 打折 → 折扣
execute [ˈeksɪkjuːt]	*v.* 执行，履行(to carry out)；将(某人)处死(to kill sb. as a legal punishment) 记 联想记忆：exe(电脑中的可执行文件) + cute → 执行，履行 例 Totem craftsmanship reached its apex in the 19th century, when the introduction of metal tools enabled carvers to *execute* more sophisticated designs. 同 administer, administrate, implement, perform

nostalgia	*n.* 思乡（the state of being homesick）；怀旧之情（a sentimental yearning for return to or of some past period）
[nəˈstældʒə]	记 词根记忆：nost(家) + alg(痛) + ia → 想家想到心痛 → 思乡
	例 The documentary film about high school life was so realistic and evocative that feelings of *nostalgia* flooded over the college-age audience.
pseudonym	*n.* 假名，笔名（a fictitious name, especially penname）
[ˈsuːdənɪm]	记 词根记忆：pseudo(假) + nym(名字) → 假名
intimidate	*v.* 恐吓（to make timid）；胁迫（to compel by or as if by threats）
[ɪnˈtɪmɪdeɪt]	记 词根记忆：in(使…) + timid(害怕) + ate → 使害怕 → 恐吓
	例 Gaddis is a formidably talented writer whose work has been, unhappily, more likely to *intimidate* or repel his readers than to lure them into his fictional world.
competing	*adj.* 有竞争性的（rivalrous）；不相上下的
[kəmˈpiːtɪŋ]	记 来自 compete(*v.* 竞争，对抗)
dissident	*n.* 唱反调者（a person who disagrees; dissenter）
[ˈdɪsɪdənt]	记 词根记忆：dis(分开) + sid(坐) + ent → 分开坐的人 → 唱反调者
apprehensive	*adj.* 害怕的（anxious or fearful that sth. bad or unpleasant will happen）；敏悟的（capable of apprehending or quick to do so）
[ˌæprɪˈhensɪv]	记 联想记忆：ap + prehen（看作 prehend，抓住） + sive → 抓住不放 → (因为)害怕的
seminal	*adj.* 有创意的（creative）
[ˈsemɪnl]	记 词根记忆：semin(种) + al → 种子的 → 有创意的
decorous	*adj.* 合宜的，高雅的（marked by propriety and good taste）
[ˈdekərəs]	记 词根记忆：decor(*n.* 装饰布局) + ous → 经过装饰的 → 合宜的，高雅的
stalk	*v.* 隐伏跟踪(猎物)（to pursue quarry or prey stealthily）
[stɔːk]	记 stalk 作为"茎，秆"之意大家都熟悉
nibble	*v.* 一点点地咬，慢慢啃（to bite off small bits）
[ˈnɪbl]	记 联想记忆：nib（笔尖） + ble → 每次只咬笔尖那么多 → 一点点地咬；注意不要和 nipple(*n.* 乳头)相混
perfervid	*adj.* 过于热心的（excessively fervent）
[pəˈfɜːrvɪd]	记 词根记忆：per(十分，完全) + ferv(热的) + id → 十分热的 → 过于热心的
truculent	*adj.* 残暴的，凶狠的（feeling or displaying ferocity; cruel）
[ˈtrʌkjələnt]	记 词根记忆：truc(凶猛) + ulent → 残暴的，凶狠的
transit	*n.* 通过（passage）；改变（change; transition）；运输（conveyance） *v.* 通过（to pass over or through）
[ˈtrænzɪt]	记 词根记忆：trans(改变) + it → 改变它的地点 → 运输
	例 Although I have always been confused by our *transit* system, I relish traveling on the subways occasionally.

□ nostalgia	□ pseudonym	□ intimidate	□ competing	□ dissident	□ apprehensive
□ seminal	□ decorous	□ stalk	□ nibble	□ perfervid	□ truculent
□ transit					

truculence [ˈtrʌkjələns]	*n.* 野蛮，残酷(the quality or state of being truculent) 同 truculency
deter [dɪˈtɜːr]	*v.* 威慑，吓住(to discourage)；阻止(to inhibit) 记 词根记忆：de + ter(=terr 吓唬) → 威慑，吓住 例 A major goal of law, to *deter* potential criminals by punishing wrongdoers, is not served when the penalty is so seldom invoked that it ceases to be a credible threat.
moisten [ˈmɔɪsn]	*v.* 弄湿，使湿润(to make moist) 记 来自 moist(*adj.* 潮湿的)
enumerate [ɪˈnuːməreɪt]	*v.* 列举，枚举(to name one by one) 记 词根记忆：e + numer(数字) + ate → 用数字表示出来 → 列举
typographical [taɪˈpɑːɡrəfikl]	*adj.* 印刷上的(of typography) 记 来自 typography(*n.* 印刷术) 例 Because it has no distinct and recognizable *typographical* form and few recurring narrative conventions, the novel is, of all literary genres, the least susceptible to definition.
mythic [ˈmɪθɪk]	*adj.* 神话的；虚构的 同 legendary, mythical, mythological
ignore [ɪɡˈnɔːr]	*v.* 不顾，不理，忽视(to refuse to take notice of) 记 联想记忆：ig+nore(看作 nose, 鼻子) → 翘起鼻子不理睬 → 不理 例 Johnson never scrupled to *ignore* the standards of decent conduct mandated by company policy if literal compliance with instructions from his superiors enabled him to do so, whatever the effects on his subordinates.
control [kənˈtroʊl]	*n.* (科学实验的)对照标准，对照物(sth. used as a standard against which the results of a study can be measured) 记 control 的基本意思是"控制"
contradict [ˌkɑːntrəˈdɪkt]	*v.* 反驳，驳斥(to affirm the contrary of a statement, etc.) 记 词根记忆：contra(反) + dict(说话，断言) → 反说 → 反驳
glucose [ˈɡluːkoʊs]	*n.* 葡萄糖(a form of sugar)
herald [ˈherəld]	*v.* 宣布…的消息(to give notice of)；预示…的来临(to signal the approach of) *n.* 传令官；信使；先驱(forerunner) 记 联想记忆：her(她) + ald(看作 old, 老的) → 她带来老人的告诫 → 信使
sociable [ˈsoʊʃəbl]	*adj.* 好交际的，合群的(fond of the company of other people)；友善的(friendly) 记 词根记忆：soci(结交) + able → 好交际的
incommensurate [ˌɪnkəˈmenʃərət]	*adj.* 不成比例的，不相称的(not proportionate; not adequate) 记 联想记忆：in(不) + commensurate(成比例的，相称的) → 不成比例的，不相称的

8

□ truculence	□ deter	□ moisten	□ enumerate	□ typographical	□ mythic
□ ignore	□ control	□ contradict	□ glucose	□ herald	□ sociable
□ incommensurate					

91

impromptu [ɪmˈprɒmptuː]	*adj.* 即席的，即兴的(without preparation; offhand)
	记 联想记忆：im(不) + prompt(按时的) + u → 不按照时间来的 → 即席的
summary [ˈsʌməri]	*n.* 摘要，概要(an abstract; abridgment) *adj.* 摘要的，简略的(converting the main points succinctly)
	记 词根记忆：sum(总和) + mary → 摘要，概要
	例 No *summary* of the behavior of animals toward reflected images is given, but not much else that is relevant seems missing from this comprehensive yet compact study of mirrors and mankind.
	同 epitome, recapitulation
penal [ˈpiːnl]	*adj.* 惩罚的，刑罚的(of, relating to, or involving punishment, penalties, or punitive institutions)
sycophant [ˈsɪkəfænt]	*n.* 马屁精(a servile self-seeking flatterer)
	记 词根记忆：syco(无花果) + phan(显现) + t → 献上无花果 → 马屁精
bowlegged [ˌboʊˈlegɪd]	*adj.* 弯脚的，弓形腿的
contemporary [kənˈtempəreri]	*adj.* 同时代的(simultaneous)；当代的；现代的(modern; current)
	记 词根记忆：con(共同) + tempor(时间) + ary(人) → 同时代的人 → 同时代的
	搭 contemporary art 现代艺术
founder [ˈfaʊndər]	*v.* (船)沉没(to sink)；(计划)失败(to collapse; fail)
	记 founder "创建者"之意众所周知
predominant [prɪˈdɑːmɪnənt]	*adj.* 支配的，占优势的，主导的(having superior strength, influence, or authority; prevailing)
	记 联想记忆：pre(在前面) + dominant(统治的) → 在前面统治的 → 支配的，占优势的
rugged [ˈrʌgɪd]	*adj.* 高低不平的；崎岖的(having a rough uneven surface)
	同 bumpy, craggy
generation [ˌdʒenəˈreɪʃn]	*n.* 一代人(a group of individuals born and living at about the same time)；(产品类型的)代(single stage in the development of a type of product)；产生，发生(production)
affront [əˈfrʌnt]	*v.* 侮辱，冒犯(to offend)
	记 词根记忆：af + front(前面，脸面) → 冲着别人的脸 → 冒犯
	同 confront, encounter
organism [ˈɔːrgənɪzəm]	*n.* 生物，有机体(an individual form of life; a body made up of organs, organelles, or other parts that work together to carry on the various processes of life)
	记 词根记忆：organ(器官) + ism → 生物，有机体
survive [sərˈvaɪv]	*v.* 幸存(to continue to exist or live after)
	记 词根记忆：sur(在…下) + viv(存活) + e → 在(事故)下面活下来 → 幸存
	例 If a species of parasite is to *survive*, the host organisms must live long enough for the parasite to reproduce; if the host species becomes extinct, so do its parasites.

pragmatic [præg'mætɪk]	*adj.* 实际的(relating to matters of fact or practical affairs often to the exclusion of intellectual or artistic matters); 务实的, 注重实效的(practical as opposed to idealistic); 实用主义的(of or relating to pragmatism) 记 词根记忆: prag(做) + matic → 付诸行动的 → 务实的, 注重实效的 例 Although skeptics say financial problems will probably prevent our establishing a base on the Moon, supporters of the project remain enthusiastic, saying that human curiosity should overcome such *pragmatic* constraints.
decline [dɪ'klaɪn]	*v.* 拒绝; 变弱, 变小(to become smaller, weaker, fewer) *n.* 消减(gradual and continuous loss of strength, power or numbers) 记 词根记忆: de(向下) + clin(倾斜, 斜坡) + e → 向下斜 → 消减
prone [proʊn]	*adj.* 俯卧的(lying flat or prostrate); 倾向于…的(being likely) 搭 prone to sth./do sth. 易于…; 有做…的倾向
assuming [ə'suːmɪŋ]	*adj.* 傲慢的, 自负的(pretentious; presumptuous)
righteousness ['raɪtʃəsnəs]	*n.* 正当, 正义, 正直
drowsy ['draʊzi]	*adj.* 昏昏欲睡的(ready to fall asleep) 记 来自 drowse(*v.* 打瞌睡)
critique [krɪ'tiːk]	*n.* 批评性的分析(critical analysis) 例 The book provides a radical *critique* of modern workplace structure.
speculate ['spekjuleɪt]	*v.* 沉思, 思索(to meditate on or ponder); 投机(to assume a business risk in hope of gain) 记 词根记忆: spec(看) + ulate(做) → 看得多想得也多 → 思索

8

□ pragmatic	□ decline	□ prone	□ assuming	□ righteousness	□ drowsy
□ critique	□ speculate				

93

Word List 9

音频

notate	v. 以符号表示 (to put into notation)
[ˈnoʊtɪt]	记 词根记忆：not (标示) + ate → (用符号) 标示 → 以符号表示
folklore	n. 民间传说；民俗学
[ˈfoʊklɔːr]	记 组合词：folk (乡民) + lore (传说，学问) → 民间传说
blighted	adj. 枯萎的 (withered)
[ˈblaɪtɪd]	记 来自 blight (v. 使枯萎)
banal	adj. 乏味的，陈腐的 (dull or stale; commonplace; insipid)
[bəˈnɑːl]	记 联想记忆：ban (禁止) + al → 应该禁止的 → 陈腐的
	同 bland, flat, sapless, vapid
estranged	adj. 疏远的，不和的 (alienated)
[ɪˈstreɪndʒd]	记 联想记忆：e + strange (陌生的) + d → 使⋯陌生的 → 疏远的
	例 In attempting to reconcile *estranged* spouses, counselors try to foster a spirit of compromise rather than one of stubborn implacability.
confrontation	n. 对抗 (the clashing of forces or ideas)
[ˌkɑːnfrənˈteɪʃn]	记 来自 confront (v. 面临，对抗)
forestall	v. 预先阻止，先发制人 (to hinder by doing sth. ahead of time; prevent)
[fɔːrˈstɔːl]	记 组合词：fore (前面) + stall (停止) → 预先阻止
	同 deter, forfend, obviate, preclude
dexterous	adj. 灵巧的，熟练的 (adroit; handy)
[ˈdekstrəs]	记 词根记忆：dexter (右手) + ous → 如右手般灵活 → 灵巧的
decisiveness	n. 坚决，果断
[dɪˈsaɪsɪvnəs]	记 来自 decisive (adj. 坚决的，果断的)
glutinous	adj. 黏的，胶状的 (gluey; sticky)
[ˈɡluːtənəs]	记 来自 glue (n. 胶，胶水)
contemplate	v. 深思 (to think about intently)；凝视
[ˈkɑːntəmpleɪt]	记 词根记忆：con + templ (看作 temple, 庙) + ate → 像庙中人一样 → 深思
	搭 contemplate doing sth. 考虑做某事
	同 excogitate, perpend, ponder, view, gaze
impassable	adj. 不能通行的，无法通过的 (incapable of being passed, traveled, crossed, or surmounted)
[ɪmˈpæsəbl]	

☐ notate	☐ folklore	☐ blighted	☐ banal	☐ estranged	☐ confrontation
☐ forestall	☐ dexterous	☐ decisiveness	☐ glutinous	☐ contemplate	☐ impassable

inimical [ɪˈnɪmɪkl]	*adj.* 敌意的，不友善的（hostile; unfriendly） 记 词根记忆：in(不) + im(爱) + ical → 不爱的 → 敌意的，不友善的
apposite [ˈæpəzɪt]	*adj.* 适当的，贴切的（appropriate; apt; relevant） 记 词根记忆：ap + pos（放）+ ite → 放在一起 → 适当的；注意不要和 opposite(*adj.* 相反的)相混淆
underplay [ˌʌndərˈpleɪ]	*v.* 弱化…的重要性（to make sth. appear less important than it really is）；表演不充分（to underact） 记 联想记忆：under(不足，少于) + play(玩) → 没玩够 → 表演不充分 例 Those who fear the influence of television deliberately *underplay* its persuasive power, hoping that they might keep knowledge of its potential to effect social change from being widely disseminated.
innocuous [ɪˈnɑːkjuəs]	*adj.* (行为、言论等)无害的（harmless） 记 词根记忆：in(无) + noc(伤害) + uous → 无害的 例 The articles that he wrote ran the gamut from the serious to the lighthearted, from objective to the argumentative, from the *innocuous* to the hostile. 同 innocent, innoxious, inoffensive, unoffensive
illicit [ɪˈlɪsɪt]	*adj.* 违法的（unlawful; prohibited） 记 词根记忆：il(不) + licit(合法的) → 违法的
swampy [swɑːmpɪ]	*adj.* 沼泽的，湿地的（marshy） 搭 swampy lake 沼泽湖泊
persevere [ˌpɜːrsəˈvɪr]	*v.* 坚持不懈（to persist in a state, enterprise, or undertaking in spite of counterinfluences, opposition, or discouragement）
inquiry [ˈɪnkwərɪ]	*n.* 询问（a request for help or information） 同 interrogation, query, question
mystic [ˈmɪstɪk]	*adj.* 神秘的（having a spiritual meaning or reality that is neither apparent to the senses nor obvious to the intelligence）；谜样的，难解的（enigmatic; obscure）*n.* 神秘主义者
fortitude [ˈfɔːrtətuːd]	*n.* 坚毅，坚忍不拔（strength of mind that enables a person to encounter danger or bear pain） 记 词根记忆：fort(强) + itude(状态) → 坚毅
homogenize [həˈmɑːdʒənaɪz]	*v.* 使均匀（to reduce to small particles of uniform size and distribute evenly usually in a liquid）
resentful [rɪˈzentfl]	*adj.* 忿恨的，怨恨的（full of resentment） 同 indignant
stately [ˈsteɪtli]	*adj.* 庄严的，堂皇的；宏伟的（marked by lofty or imposing dignity） 同 august, dignified, majestic
tenuous [ˈtenjuəs]	*adj.* 纤细的；稀薄的（not dense; rare）；脆弱的，无力的（flimsy; weak） 记 词根记忆：tenu(薄，细) + ous → 纤细的；稀薄的

9

□ inimical	□ apposite	□ underplay	□ innocuous	□ illicit	□ swampy
□ persevere	□ inquiry	□ mystic	□ fortitude	□ homogenize	□ resentful
□ stately	□ tenuous				

95

attenuation	*n.* 变瘦；减少；减弱（the act of attenuating or the state of being attenuated）
[əˌtenjʊˈeɪʃn]	
perquisite	*n.* 额外收入，津贴（a payment or profit received in addition to a regular wage or salary）；小费（a tip）
[ˈpɜːrkwɪzɪt]	记 词根记忆：per(全部) + quis(要求) + ite → 要求全部得到 → 额外收入，津贴
	同 cumshaw, lagniappe, largess
accomplish	*v.* 完成，做成功（to succeed in doing sth.）
[əˈkɑːmplɪʃ]	记 词根记忆：ac + compl(满) + ish → 圆满 → 完成
	同 achieve, attain, gain, realize
haggle	*v.* 讨价还价（to bargain, as over the price of sth.）
[ˈhægl]	同 dicker, wrangle
falter	*v.* 蹒跚（to walk unsteadily；stumble）；支吾地说（to stammer）
[ˈfɔːltər]	同 flounder, stagger, tumble
postdate	*v.* 填迟…的日期（to put a date on (a check, for example) that is later than the actual date）
[ˈpɑːstdeɪt]	
affable	*adj.* 和蔼的（gentle；amiable）；友善的（pleasant and easy to approach or talk to）
[ˈæfəbl]	记 词根记忆：af + fable(说，讲) → 可以说话的 → 易于交谈的 → 友善的
solemn	*adj.* 严肃的；庄严的，隆重的（made with great seriousness）；黑色的
[ˈsɑːləm]	记 词根记忆：sol(太阳)+emn → 古代把太阳看作是神圣的 → 庄严的
flustered	*adj.* 慌张的，激动不安的（nervous or upset）
[ˈflʌstərd]	同 perturbed, rattled
adore	*v.* 崇拜（to worship as divine）；爱慕（to love greatly；revere）
[əˈdɔːr]	记 词根记忆：ad + ore(讲话) → 不断想对某人讲话 → 爱慕(某人)
peripatetic	*adj.* 巡游的，流动的（travelling from place to place；itinerant）
[ˌperipəˈtetɪk]	记 词根记忆：peri(周围) + pat(走) + et + ic → 巡游的，流动的
whimsy	*n.* 古怪，异想天开（whim；a fanciful creation）
[ˈwɪmzi]	例 It is to the novelist's credit that all of the episodes in her novel are presented realistically, without any *whimsy* or playful supernatural tricks.
	同 boutade, caprice, crotchet, freak
indigence	*n.* 贫穷，贫困（poverty；lacking money and goods）
[ˈɪndɪdʒəns]	记 联想记忆：in(无) + dig(挖) + ence → 挖不出东西 → 贫穷
	例 Micawber's habit of spending more than he earned left him in a state of perpetual *indigence*, but he persevered in hoping to see a more affluent day.
	同 destitution, impecuniousness, impoverishment, penury, privation
composed	*adj.* 镇定的，沉着的（tranquil；self-possessed）；由…组成的（be made or formed from several parts）
[kəmˈpoʊzd]	搭 be composed of sth. 由…组成的

preoccupation [pri͵ɑːkjuˈpeɪʃn]	*n.* 全神贯注，专注 (the state of being preoccupied)；使人专注的东西 (sth. that takes up one's attention) 例 Certainly Murray's *preoccupation* with the task of editing the *Oxford English Dictionary* begot a kind of monomania, but it must be regarded as a beneficent or at least an innocuous one.
allure [əˈlʊr]	*v.* 引诱，诱惑 (to entice by charm or attraction)
contradictory [͵kɑːntrəˈdɪktəri]	*adj.* 反驳的，反对的，抗辩的 (involving, causing, or constituting a contradiction)
apparition [͵æpəˈrɪʃn]	*n.* 幽灵 (a strange figure appearing suddenly and thought to be a ghost)；特异景象 (an unusual or unexpected sight) 记 词根记忆：appar(出现) + ition → 出现的幽灵 → 幽灵；和 appearance (*n.* 出现；外貌)来自同一词源 同 phantasm, phantom, revenant, specter
xenophobic [͵zenəˈfoʊbik]	*adj.* 恐外的，恐惧外国人的 (having abnormal fear or hatred of the strange or foreign)
flip [flɪp]	*v.* 用指轻弹 (to strike quickly or lightly)；蹦蹦跳跳 (to move with a small quick motion) *adj.* 无礼的；冒失的；轻率的 (rude; glib; flippant)
qualified [ˈkwɑːlɪfaɪd]	*adj.* 合格的 (having complied with the specific requirements or precedent conditions)；有限制的 (limited) 记 来自动词 qualify(*v.* 具有资格；限制) 例 Even though the general's carefully *qualified* public statement could hardly be faulted, some people took exception to it.
emulate [ˈemjuleɪt]	*v.* 与…竞争，努力赶上 (to strive to equal or excel) 记 词根记忆：em(模仿) + ulate → 与…竞争
hot-tempered [͵hɑt ˈtempərd]	*adj.* 性急的，易怒的，暴躁的 (tending to become very angry easily) 同 irascible
isolate [ˈaɪsəleɪt]	*v.* 孤立 (to set apart from others) 记 词根记忆：isol(岛) + ate → 使成为孤岛 → 孤立 例 Some biologists argue that each specifically human trait must have arisen gradually and erratically, and that it is therefore difficult to *isolate* definite milestones in the evolution of the species. 同 enisle, insulate, segregate
collusion [kəˈluːʒn]	*n.* 共谋，勾结 (secret agreement or cooperation) 搭 collusion with 与…勾结
panacea [͵pænəˈsiːə]	*n.* 万灵药 (a remedy for all ills or difficulties) 记 词根记忆：pan(全部) + acea(治疗) → 包治百病 → 万灵药 例 Although the discovery of antibiotics led to great advances in clinical practice, it did not represent a *panacea* for bacterial illness, for there are some bacteria that cannot be effectively treated with antibiotics.

□ preoccupation	□ allure	□ contradictory	□ apparition	□ xenophobic	□ flip
□ qualified	□ emulate	□ hot-tempered	□ isolate	□ collusion	□ panacea

97

smug [smʌg]	*adj.* 自满的，自命不凡的（highly self-satisfied） 记 联想记忆：s + mug（杯子）→ 杯子满了 → 自满的 例 The action and characters in a melodrama can be so immediately classified that all observers can hiss the villain with an air of *smug* but enjoyable self-righteousness.
peevish ['piːvɪʃ]	*adj.* 不满的，抱怨的（discontented; querulous）；暴躁的，坏脾气的，易怒的（fractious; fretful） 记 来自 peeve（*v.* 使气恼，使焦躁） 例 Safire as a political commentator is patently never satisfied; he writes *peevish* editorials about every action the government takes. 同 huffy, irritable, pettish
demystify [ˌdiːˈmɪstɪfaɪ]	*v.* 减少…的神秘性（to make sth. less mysterious） 记 联想记忆：de（去掉）+ mystify（使迷惑）→ 去掉迷惑 → 减少…的神秘性
indistinguishable [ˌɪndɪˈstɪŋgwɪʃəbl]	*adj.* 无法区分的，难以分辨的（not distinguishable） 搭 be indistinguishable from 无法从…中区分
cater ['keɪtər]	*v.* 迎合；提供饮食及服务（to provide food and services） 记 联想记忆：毛毛虫 caterpillar 的前半部分为 cater，原意为"猫"，引申为"迎合" 搭 cater to 迎合
imbue [ɪmˈbjuː]	*v.* 浸染，浸透（to permeate or influence as if by dyeing）；使充满，灌输，激发（to endow）
astray [əˈstreɪ]	*adj.* 迷路的，误入歧途的（off the right path or way） 记 联想记忆：a + stray（走离）→ 走离正道 → 误入歧途的
cumbersome ['kʌmbərsəm]	*adj.* 笨重的，难处理的（hard to handle or deal with; clumsy） 记 联想记忆：cumber（阻碍）+ some → 受到阻碍的 → 笨重的
impassioned [ɪmˈpæʃnd]	*adj.* 充满激情的，慷慨激昂的（filled with passion or zeal） 记 联想记忆：im（进入）+ passion（激情）+ ed → 投入激情的 → 慷慨激昂的
restive ['restɪv]	*adj.* 不安静的，不安宁的（marked by impatience） 记 注意不要看作"休息的"的意思；restive=restless 例 Waiting impatiently in line to see Santa Claus, even the best-behaved children grow *restive* and start to fidget.
fictitious [fɪkˈtɪʃəs]	*adj.* 假的（not real; false）；虚构的（imaginary; fabulous） 记 词根记忆：fict（做）+ itious → 做出来的 → 假的
overcrowd [ˌoʊvərˈkraʊd]	*v.* （使）过度拥挤（to cause to be too crowded; crowd together too much）
gainsay [ˌɡeɪnˈseɪ]	*v.* 否认（to deny） 记 联想记忆：gain（=against 反）+ say（说）→ 反着说 → 否认 同 contradict, disaffirm, negate
financial [faɪˈnænʃl]	*adj.* 财政的，金融的（relating to finance or financiers） 搭 financial scandal 金融丑闻

□ smug	□ peevish	□ demystify	□ indistinguishable	□ cater	□ imbue
□ astray	□ cumbersome	□ impassioned	□ restive	□ fictitious	□ overcrowd
□ gainsay	□ financial				

brazen [ˈbreɪzn]	*adj.* 厚脸皮的(showing no shame; impudent) 记 词根记忆：braz(=brass 黄铜) + en → 像黄铜一样 → 厚脸皮的
abbreviate [əˈbriːvieɪt]	*v.* 缩短(to make shorter); 缩写(to shorten a word or phrase) 记 词根记忆：ab(加强) + brev(短) + iate → 缩短
utopian [juːˈtoʊpiən]	*adj.* 乌托邦的，空想的(impossibly ideal; visionary) 例 The impracticability of such *utopian* notions is reflected by the quick disintegration of the idealistic community at Brooke Farm.
impractical [ɪmˈpræktɪkl]	*adj.* 不切实际的(not wise to put into or keep in practice or effect) 例 Though one cannot say that Michelangelo was an *impractical* designer, he was, of all nonprofessional architects known, the most adventurous in that he was the least constrained by tradition or precedent.
frantic [ˈfræntɪk]	*adj.* 疯狂的，狂乱的(wild with anger; frenzied) 记 联想记忆：fr(看作 fry，炸) + ant(蚂蚁) + ic(看作 ice，冰) → 在冰上炸蚂蚁吃 → 疯狂的
adoration [ˌædəˈreɪʃn]	*n.* 崇拜，爱慕(the act of adoring) 记 来自 adore(*v.* 崇拜)
hydrate [ˈhaɪdreɪt]	*n.* 水合物 *v.* (使)水合(to cause to take up or combine with water) 记 词根记忆：hydr(水) + ate → 水合
synergic [ˈsɪnərdʒɪk]	*adj.* 协同作用的(of combined action or cooperation) 记 来自 synergy(*n.* 协同作用)
operative [ˈɑːpərətɪv]	*adj.* (计划等)实施中的，运行着的(operating); 生效的(effective) 记 词根记忆：oper(做) + ative → 在做的 → 实施中的
subdued [səbˈduːd]	*adj.* (光和声)柔和的，缓和的；(人)温和的(unnaturally or unusually quiet in behavior)
constitution [ˌkɑːnstəˈtuːʃn]	*n.* 宪法(system of laws and principles according to which a state is governed); 体质(physical makeup of a person) 记 词根记忆：con + stitut(建立，放) + ion → 国无法不立 → 宪法
recessive [rɪˈsesɪv]	*adj.* 隐性遗传的；后退的(tending to recede; withdrawn)
reconnaissance [rɪˈkɑːnɪsns]	*n.* 侦察，预先勘测(a preliminary survey to gain information) 记 注意不要和 renaissance(*n.* 复兴；复活)相混
institute [ˈɪnstɪtuːt]	*v.* 设立，创立(社团等); 制定(政策等)(to set up; establish) *n.* 学院，学会，协会 记 词根记忆：in(进入) + stit(站) + ute → 站进去 → 设立，创立 例 Doreen justifiably felt she deserved recognition for the fact that the research *institute* had been returned to a position of preeminence, since it was she who had directed the transformation. 同 constitute, inaugurate, initiate, launch
abridge [əˈbrɪdʒ]	*v.* 删减(to reduce in scope or extent); 缩短(to condense) 记 联想记忆：a + bridge(桥) → 一座桥把路缩短了 → 缩短

9

fraught [frɔːt]	*adj.* 充满的(filled; charged; loaded) 记 和 freight(*n.* 货物)一起记 例 Their married life was not tranquil since it was *fraught* with bitter fighting and arguments.
tangible [ˈtændʒəbl]	*adj.* 可触摸的(touchable; palpable) 例 Her remarkable speed, which first became apparent when she repeatedly defeated the older children at school, eventually earned for her some *tangible* rewards, including a full athletic scholarship and several first-place trophies.
recommendation [ˌrekəmenˈdeɪʃn]	*n.* 推荐(the act of recommending); 推荐信(sth. that recommends or expresses commendation)
inept [ɪˈnept]	*adj.* 无能的(inefficient); 不适当的(not suitable) 记 联想记忆: in(不) + ept(能干的) → 无能的
reenact [riːˈnækt]	*v.* 再制定(to enact (as a law) again) 例 To have true disciples, a thinker must not be too idiosyncratic: any effective intellectual leader depends on the ability of other people to *reenact* thought processes that did not originate with them.
amalgam [əˈmælgəm]	*n.* 混合物(a combination or mixture) 记 联想记忆: am + alg + am → 前后两个 am 结合 → 混合物 同 admixture, composite, compound, interfusion
credulous [ˈkredʒələs]	*adj.* 轻信的, 易上当的(tending to believe too readily; easily convinced) 记 词根记忆: cred + ulous(多…的) → 太过信任别人的 → 轻信的
recluse [ˈreklus]	*n.* 隐士(a person who leads a secluded or solitary life) *adj.* 隐居的(marked by withdrawal from society) 记 词根记忆: re + clus(关闭) + e → 把门关上 → 隐居的 同 cloistered, seclusive, sequestered
resort [rɪˈzɔːrt]	*v.* 求助, 诉诸(to have recourse) *n.* 度假胜地(a place providing recreation and entertainment) 记 联想记忆: 向上级打报告(report)求助(resort)
hackneyed [ˈhæknɪd]	*adj.* 陈腐的, 老一套的(overfamiliar through overuse; trite) 记 来自 Hackney(*n.* 伦敦近郊城镇), 以养马闻名, hack 的意思是"出租的老马", 引申为"陈腐的"
imprecise [ˌɪmprɪˈsaɪs]	*adj.* 不精确的(not precise) 记 联想记忆: im(不) + precise(精确的) → 不精确的 例 A leading chemist believes that many scientists have difficulty with stereochemistry because much of the relevant nomenclature is *imprecise*, in that it combines concepts that should be kept discrete.
monopolize [məˈnɑːpəlaɪz]	*v.* 垄断, 独占(to assume complete possession or control of) 记 词根记忆: mono(单一) + pol(=poly 出售) + ize → 由一个人出售的 → 垄断, 独占

□ fraught □ tangible □recommendation □ inept □ reenact □ amalgam
□ credulous □ recluse □ resort □ hackneyed □ imprecise □ monopolize

self-procession [ˌselfprəˈseʃn]	*n.* 自行列队
spiny [ˈspaɪni]	*adj.* 针状的(slender and pointed like a spine);多刺的,棘手的(thorny) 记 词根记忆:spin(刺) + y → 多刺的
die [daɪ]	*n.* 金属模子,金属印模(a block of hard metal with a design, etc. cut into it) 记 注意不是"死亡"的意思
ingrate [ɪnˈgreɪt]	*n.* 忘恩负义的人(an ungrateful person) 记 词根记忆:in(不) + grat(感激) + e → 不知感激 → 忘恩负义的人
catalyze [ˈkætəlaɪz]	*v.* 促使(to bring about);激励(to inspire)
intrigue [ɪnˈtriːg]	*v.* 密谋(to plot or scheme secretly);引起…的兴趣(to arouse the interest or curiosity of) 记 词根记忆:in + trig(=tric 小障碍物) + ue → 在里面放入很多小障碍物 → 密谋
propagate [ˈprɑːpəgeɪt]	*v.* 繁殖(to multiply);传播(to cause to spread out; publicize) 记 词根记忆:pro + pag(砍,切) + ate → 把树的旁枝剪掉使主干成长 → 繁殖
underdeveloped [ˌʌndərdɪˈveləpt]	*adj.* 不发达的(not fully grown or developed)
generic [dʒəˈnerɪk]	*adj.* 种类的,类属的(of or characteristic of a genus) 记 来自 genus(*n.* 种类);注意不要和 genetic(*adj.* 遗传的;起源的)相混淆
superficially [ˌsuːpərˈfɪʃəli]	*adv.* 表面上地 同 shallowly
burgeon [ˈbɜːrdʒən]	*v.* 迅速成长,发展(to grow rapidly; proliferate) 记 词根记忆:burg(=bud 花蕾) + eon → 迅速成长;burg 本身是单词,意为"城,镇" → 成长的地方 → 发展 同 blossom, bloom, effloresce, flower, outbloom
invade [ɪnˈveɪd]	*v.* 侵略,侵入(to enter a country or territory with armed forces) 记 词根记忆:in(进入) + vad(走) + e → 走进(其他国家) → 侵略 同 encroach, foray, infringe, raid, trespass
equilibrium [ˌekwɪˈlɪbriəm]	*n.* 平衡(a state of balance or equality between opposing forces) 记 词根记忆:equi(平等的) + libr(平衡) + ium → 平衡
courteous [ˈkɜːrtiəs]	*adj.* 有礼貌的(marked by respect for and consideration of others) 同 complaisant, gallant, polite, mannerly
consort	[kənˈsɔːrt] *v.* 陪伴(to keep company);结交(to associate with) [ˈkɑːnsɔːrt] *n.* 配偶(husband or wife) 记 词根记忆:con(共同) + sort(类型) → 同类相聚 → 结交
dull [dʌl]	*adj.* 不鲜明的(not bright);迟钝的(mentally slow);乏味的 *v.* 变迟钝(to become dull) 记 联想记忆:和充实的(full)相反的是乏味的(dull) 同 blunt, doltish, imbecile, moronic, obtuse

9

□ self-procession	□ spiny	□ die	□ ingrate	□ catalyze	□ intrigue
□ propagate	□ underdeveloped	□ generic	□ superficially	□ burgeon	□ invade
□ equilibrium	□ courteous	□ consort	□ dull		

decadence [ˈdekədəns]	*n.* 衰落，颓废(the process of becoming decadent) 记 词根记忆：de(=down) + cad(落) + ence → 往下落 → 衰落，颓废
validate [ˈvælɪdeɪt]	*v.* 使生效(to make legally valid) 记 联想记忆：valid(有效) + ate → 使生效
revise [rɪˈvaɪz]	*v.* 校订，修正(to change because of new information or more thought) 记 词根记忆：re(一再) + vis(看) + e → 反复看 → 校订，修正 同 redraft, redraw, revamp
aloof [əˈluːf]	*adj.* 远离的(removed or distant either physically or emotionally)；冷淡的，冷漠的 (cool and distant in manner)
blatant [ˈbleɪtnt]	*adj.* 厚颜无耻的 (brazen)；显眼的(completely obvious；conspicuous)；炫耀的(showy) 记 词根记忆：blat (闲聊) + ant → 侃大山 → 喧哗的 → 炫耀的
braid [breɪd]	*v.* 编织(to form into a braid) *n.* 穗子；发辫(plait) 同 plait, twine, weave
fraudulent [ˈfrɔːdʒələnt]	*adj.* 欺骗的，不诚实的(acting with fraud；deceitful) 例 Paradoxically, while it is relatively easy to prove a *fraudulent* work of art is a fraud, it is often virtually impossible to prove that an authentic one is genuine.
elementary [ˌelɪˈmentri]	*adj.* 初级的(in the beginning stages of a course of study) 同 basal, elemental, fundamental, primitive, rudimental
arid [ˈærɪd]	*adj.* 干旱的(dry)；枯燥的(dull；uninteresting) 搭 an arid discussion 枯燥的讨论
clamber [ˈklæmbər]	*v.* 吃力地爬上，攀登(to climb awkwardly)
insignificant [ˌɪnsɪɡˈnɪfɪkənt]	*adj.* 无价值的，无意义的，无用的 (lacking meaning or importance；unimportant) 例 The acts of vandalism that these pranksters had actually perpetrated were *insignificant* compared with those they had contemplated but had not attempted. 同 purposeless, trivial, unmeaning
inexpensive [ˌɪnɪkˈspensɪv]	*adj.* 廉价的，便宜的(reasonable in price) 例 Because many of the minerals found on the ocean floor are still plentiful on land, where mining is relatively *inexpensive*, mining the ocean floor has yet to become a profitable enterprise.
counterpart [ˈkaʊntərpɑːrt]	*n.* 相对应或具有相同功能的人或物(a person or thing that corresponds to or has the same function as) 记 组合词：counter(相反地) + part(部分) → 相对物 → 相对应或具有相同功能的人或物

☐ decadence ☐ validate ☐ revise ☐ aloof ☐ blatant ☐ braid
☐ fraudulent ☐ elementary ☐ arid ☐ clamber ☐ insignificant ☐ inexpensive
☐ counterpart

surrogate [ˈsɜːrəgət]	*n.* 代替品（one that serves as a substitute）；代理人（one appointed to act in place of another, deputy）
narcotic [nɑːrˈkɑːtɪk]	*n.* 麻醉剂 *adj.* 麻醉的，催眠的（having the properties of or yielding a narcotic） 记 词根记忆：narc（麻木；昏迷）+ ot + ic → 麻醉的，催眠的
emphatic [ɪmˈfætɪk]	*adj.* 重视的，强调的（showing or using emphasis） 记 词根记忆：em（表加强）+ pha（说话）+ tic → 用力说话的 → 重视的，强调的
reciprocally [rɪˈsɪprəkli]	*adv.* 相互地；相反地 同 mutually
notoriety [ˌnoʊtəˈraɪəti]	*n.* 臭名昭著（the quality or state of being notorious）；臭名昭著的人（a notorious person）
decry [dɪˈkraɪ]	*v.* 责难（to denounce）；贬低（to depreciate officially；disparage） 记 de + cry（喊）→ 向下喊 → 贬低；注意不要和 descry（看见，望到）相混
transient [ˈtrænʃnt]	*adj.* 短暂的，转瞬即逝的（passing quickly into and out of existence；transitory） 记 词根记忆：trans（穿过）+ ient → 时光穿梭，转瞬即逝 → 短暂的 例 Lexy's joy at finding the perfect Christmas gift for John was *transient*, for she still had to find presents for the cousins and Uncle Bob. 同 ephemeral, evanescent, fleeting, fugacious, fugitive
restore [rɪˈstɔːr]	*v.* 使回复，恢复（to bring sb./sth. back to a former position or condition）；修复，修补（to rebuild or repair sth. so that it is like the original） 记 联想记忆：re（重新）+ store（储存）→ 重新储存能量 → 恢复；修复
phlegmatic [flegˈmætɪk]	*adj.* 冷淡的，不动感情的（of slow and stolid temperature；unemotional） 记 来自 phlegm（痰），西方人认为痰多的人不易动感情 同 apathetic, impassive, stoic, stolid
penetrating [ˈpenɪtreɪtɪŋ]	*adj.*（声音）响亮的，尖锐的；（气味）刺激的；（思想）敏锐的，有洞察力的（acute, discerning）
amicably [ˈæmɪkəbli]	*adv.* 友善地（in an amicable manner）
reparable [rɪˈperəbl]	*adj.* 能补救的，可挽回的（capable of being repaired） 记 来自 repair（*v.* 修补）
pesticide [ˈpestɪsaɪd]	*n.* 杀虫剂（an agent used to kill pests） 记 词根记忆：pest（害虫）+ i + cide（杀）→ 杀虫剂
decelerate [ˌdiːˈseləreɪt]	*v.*（使）减速（to reduce the speed；to decrease the rate of progress） 同 delay, detain, embog
vital [ˈvaɪtl]	*adj.* 极其重要的；充满活力的（full of life and force） 记 词根记忆：vit（生命）+ al → 事关生命的 → 极其重要的 例 The president was noncommittal about farm subsidies, nor did he say much about the even more *vital* topic of unemployment.

9

□ surrogate	□ narcotic	□ emphatic	□ reciprocally	□ notoriety	□ decry
□ transient	□ restore	□ phlegmatic	□ penetrating	□ amicably	□ reparable
□ pesticide	□ decelerate	□ vital			

103

deploy [dɪ'plɔɪ]	*v.* 部署（to place in battle formation or appropriate positions）；拉长（战线），展开（to extend (a military unit) especially in width）
inappropriate [ˌɪnə'proʊpriət]	*adj.* 不恰当的，不适宜的（unsuitable） 例 Because the majority of the evening cable TV programs available dealt with violence and sex, the parents decided that the programs were *inappropriate* for the children to watch. 同 inapt, inept, malapropos, unfitted, unmeet
axiom ['æksiəm]	*n.* 公理（maxim）；定理（an established principle） 记 联想记忆：ax（斧子）+ iom → 斧子之下出公理 → 公理
paean ['piːən]	*n.* 赞美歌，颂歌（a song of joy, praise, triumph） 记 参考：hymn（*n.* 赞美歌）
viable ['vaɪəbl]	*adj.* 切实可行的（capable of working, functioning, or developing adequately）；能活下去的（capable of living） 记 词根记忆：via（道路）+ able → 有路可走 → 切实可行的 例 It is true that the seeds of some plants have germinated after two hundred years of dormancy, but reports that *viable* seeds have been found in ancient tombs such as the pyramids are entirely unfounded.
foible ['fɔɪbl]	*n.* 小缺点，小毛病（a small weakness；fault） 记 与 feeble（*adj.* 虚弱的，衰弱的）一起记
condemnation [ˌkɑːndem'neɪʃn]	*n.* 谴责（censure; blame） 同 conviction, damnation, denunciation
undistorted [ˌʌndɪ'stɔːrtɪd]	*adj.* 未失真的
exploit	[ɪk'splɔɪt] *v.* 剥削（to make use of meanly or unfairly for one's own advantage）；充分利用（to utilize productively） ['eksplɔɪt] *n.* 英勇行为（a notable or heroic act） 记 词根记忆：ex + plo（折）+ it → 向外折 → 充分利用
schism ['skɪzəm]	*n.* 教会分裂（formal division in or separation from a church or religious body）；分裂（division; separation） 例 Unenlightened authoritarian managers rarely recognize a crucial reason for the low levels of serious conflict among members of democratically run work groups: a modicum of tolerance for dissent often prevents *schism*. 同 fissure, fracture, rift
underwater [ˌʌndər'wɔːtər]	*adj.* 在水下的，在水中的（lying or growing below the surface of the water）
duplicity [duː'plɪsəti]	*n.* 欺骗，口是心非（hypocritical cunning or deception） 记 词根记忆：du（二）+ plic（重叠）+ ity → 有两种（态度）→ 口是心非 同 deceit, dissemblance, dissimulation, guile

exploit

collateral [kə'lætərəl]	*adj.* 平行的(side by side; parallel); 附属的(subordinate); 旁系的(having an ancestor in common but descended from a different line) *n.* 担保品 (property pledged by a borrower to protect the interests of the lender) 记 词根记忆：col(共同) + later(边缘) + al → 共同的边 → 平行的
exhilarate [ɪg'zɪləreɪt]	*v.* 使兴奋，使高兴(to make cheerful); 使振作，鼓舞(to animate) 记 词根记忆：ex + hilar(高兴的) + ate → 使高兴
incapacitate [ˌɪnkə'pæsɪteɪt]	*v.* 使无能力，使不适合(disable)
invariable [ɪn'verəriəbl]	*adj.* 恒定的，不变的(not changing or capable of change) 同 changeless, consonant, equable, invariant
ultrasonic [ˌʌltrə'sɑːnɪk]	*adj.* 超音速的，超声(波)的 同 supersonic
permeable ['pɜːrmiəbl]	*adj.* 可渗透的(penetrable) 记 词根记忆：per(贯穿) + mea(通过) + ble → 可通过的 → 可渗透的
touching ['tʌtʃɪŋ]	*adj.* 动人的，感人的(moving); 令人同情的(causing a feeling of pity or sympathy)
overpowering [ˌoʊvər'paʊərɪŋ]	*adj.* 压倒性的，不可抗拒的(overwhelming) 记 来自 overpower(*v.* 压倒) 例 Charlotte Salomon's biography is a reminder that the currents of private life, however diverted, dislodged, or twisted by *overpowering* public events, retain their hold on the individual recording them.
revert [rɪ'vɜːrt]	*v.* 恢复，回复到(to go back to); 重新考虑(to talk about or consider again) 记 词根记忆：re(重新) + vert(转) → 转回去 → 恢复
confidently ['kɑːnfɪdəntli]	*adv.* 确信地；肯定地(certainly) 记 来自 confident(*n.* 信心)
hamper ['hæmpər]	*v.* 妨碍，阻挠(to hinder, impede, encumber) *n.* (有盖的)大篮子(a large basket, especially with a cover)
annex [ə'neks]	*v.* 兼并(to obtain or take for oneself), 附加(to attach as a quality, conse-quence, or condition)

□ collateral　□ exhilarate　□ incapacitate　□ ultrasonic　□ permeable　□ touching
□ overpowering　□ revert　□ confidently　□ hamper　□ annex

105

protest	[prə'test] *v.* 抗议，反对
	['proutest] *n.* 抗议，反对(organized public demonstration of disapproval)
	记 联想记忆：pro(很多) + test(测验) → 考试太多，遭到学生抗议 → 抗议，反对
	例 Black religion was in part a *protest* movement—a *protest* against a system and a society that was deliberately designed to demean the dignity of a segment of God's creation.
aptitude	*n.* 适宜(a natural tendency)；才能，资质(a natural ability to do sth.)
['æptɪtuːd]	记 词根记忆：apt(能力) + itude(状态) → 才能，资质
	搭 aptitude for 有…方面的才能
revoke	*v.* 撤销，废除(to rescind)；召回(to bring or call back)
[rɪ'vouk]	
garish	*adj.* 俗丽的，过于艳丽的(too bright or gaudy; tastelessly showy)
['gerɪʃ]	记 词根记忆：gar(花) + ish → 花哨的 → 俗丽的；注意不要和 garnish (*v.* 装饰)相混
prosecute	*v.* 起诉(to carry on a legal suit)；告发(to carry on a prosecution)
['prɑːsɪkjuːt]	记 词根记忆：pro(提前) + secut(追踪) → 事先追踪行进 → 告发
breach	*v.* 打破，突破(to make a breach in)；违背(to break, violate) *n.* 裂缝，缺
[briːtʃ]	□(a broken or torn place)
	记 来自 break(*v.* 打破)
vitality	*n.* 活力，精力(capacity to live and develop)；生命力(power of enduring)
[vaɪ'tæləti]	
critic	*n.* 批评者(one who expresses a reasoned opinion on any matter especially involving a judgment of its value, truth, etc.)
['krɪtɪk]	
equivocal	*adj.* 模棱两可的(subject to two or more interpretations and usually used to mislead or confuse)；不明确的，不确定的(of uncertain nature or classification, undecided)
[ɪ'kwɪvəkl]	同 ambiguous, obscure
inexorable	*adj.* 不为所动的(incapable of being moved or influenced)；无法改变的 (that cannot be altered)
[ɪn'eksərəbl]	记 词根记忆：in(不) + ex(出) + or(说) + able → 不可被说服的 → 不为所动的
dependable	*adj.* 可靠的，可信赖的(capable of being depended on)
[dɪ'pendəbl]	记 来自 depend(*v.* 依靠；信任)
redeem	*v.* 弥补，赎回，偿还(to atone for; expiate)
[rɪ'diːm]	记 词根记忆：re(重新) + deem(买) → 重新买回 → 赎回
spiritual	*adj.* 精神的(of the spirit rather than the body)
['spɪrɪtʃuəl]	例 Because medieval women's public participation in *spiritual* life was not welcomed by the male establishment, a compensating involvement with religious writings, inoffensive to the members of the establishment because of its privacy, became important for many women.

106

□ protest   □ aptitude   □ revoke   □ garish   □ prosecute   □ breach
□ vitality   □ critic   □ equivocal   □ inexorable   □ dependable   □ redeem
□ spiritual

depict [dɪˈpɪkt]	*v.* 描绘(to represent by or as if by a picture); 描写, 描述(to describe) 记 词根记忆: de(加强) + pict(描画) → 描绘
munificent [mjuːˈnɪfɪsnt]	*adj.* 慷慨的(very liberal in giving or bestowing); 丰厚的(characterized by great liberality or generosity)
advantage [ədˈvæntɪdʒ]	*n.* 利益, 益处(benefit) *v.* 有利于, 有益于 搭 have the advantage of... 有…优势 同 allowance, avail, interest
protective [prəˈtektɪv]	*adj.* 保护的, 防护的 例 Why do some plant stems develop a *protective* bark that enables them to survive the winter, while others shrivel at the first frost?
slimy [ˈslaɪmi]	*adj.* 黏滑的(of, relating to, or resembling slime) 同 glutinous, miry, muddy, viscous
animated [ˈænɪmeɪtɪd]	*adj.* 活生生的, 生动的(full of vigor and spirit) 记 来自 animate(*adj.* 有生气的)
multifaceted [ˌmʌltiˈfæsɪtɪd]	*adj.* 多方面的(having many facets or aspects) 同 protean, various, versatile
coarse [kɔːrs]	*adj.* 粗糙的; 低劣的(of low quality); 粗俗的(not refined) 记 联想记忆: coar(看作 coal, 煤炭) + se → 煤炭是很粗糙的 → 粗糙的
criticize [ˈkrɪtɪsaɪz]	*v.* 评论, 批评; 挑剔(to evaluate; find fault with) 同 blame, censure, condemn, denounce, reprehend, reprobate
ragged [ˈrægɪd]	*adj.* 褴褛的, 破烂的(torn or worn to tatters)
concentric [kənˈsentrɪk]	*adj.* 同心的(having a common center) 记 词根记忆: con + centr(中心) + ic → 共同的中心 → 同心的
piousness [ˈpaɪəsnəs]	*n.* 虔诚 记 来自 pious(*adj.* 虔诚的)
tacit [ˈtæsɪt]	*adj.* 心照不宣的(understood without being put into words) 记 注意和 taciturn(*adj.* 沉默寡言的)区分开, tacit 指"心里明白但嘴上不说" 例 Samuel Johnson gave more than *tacit* cooperation to his biographer, James Boswell; he made himself available to Boswell night after night, furnished Boswell with correspondence, and even read his biographer's notes.
inoffensive [ˌɪnəˈfensɪv]	*adj.* 无害的 (causing no harm or injury); 不讨厌的 (not objectionable to the senses) 例 Because medieval women's public participation in spiritual life was not welcomed by the male establishment, a compensating involvement with religious writings, *inoffensive* to the members of the establishment because of its privacy, became important for many women.
virulence [ˈvɪrələns]	*n.* 恶意, 毒性(the quality or state of being virulent)

interlocking [ˌɪntərˈlɑːkɪŋ]	*adj.* 连锁的；关联的 记 来自 interlock(*v.* 连锁；连结)
affirmation [ˌæfərˈmeɪʃn]	*n.* 肯定；断言(the act of affirming or the state of being affirmed; assertion)
banish [ˈbænɪʃ]	*v.* 放逐(to send sb. out of the country as a punishment) 记 发音记忆："把你死" → 通过放逐把你弄死 → 放逐
pathological [ˌpæθəˈlɑːdʒɪkl]	*adj.* 病态的，不理智的(unreasonable, irrational)；病理学的(of or relating to pathology)
equestrian [ɪˈkwestriən]	*adj.* 骑马的(of horse riding)；骑士阶层的(of, relating to, or composed of knights) *n.* 骑师(one who rides on horseback) 记 词根记忆：equ(古意：马) + estrian(人) → 骑在马上的人 → 骑师
shiftless [ˈʃɪftləs]	*adj.* 没出息的，懒惰的(lacking in ambition or incentive; lazy)；无能的(inefficient)
uncontroversial [ˌʌnkɑːntrəˈvɜːrʃl]	*adj.* 未引起争论的(not causing, or not likely to cause, any disagreement) 同 noncontroversial
repress [rɪˈpres]	*v.* 抑制，压抑(to hold in by self-control)；镇压(to put down by force)
acidic [əˈsɪdɪk]	*adj.* 酸的，酸性的(acid) 记 词根记忆：acid(*n.* 酸) + ic → 酸的
verbose [vɜːrˈboʊs]	*adj.* 冗长的，啰嗦的(containing more words than necessary) 记 词根记忆：verb(词语) + ose(多…的) → 多词的 → 冗长的 例 He is much too *verbose* in his writings: he writes a page when a sentence should suffice. 同 prolix, redundant, wordy
improvise [ˈɪmprəvaɪz]	*v.* 即席创作(to extemporize) 记 词根记忆：im(不) + pro(在…前面) + vis(看) + e → 没有预先看过 → 即席创作
benefactor [ˈbenɪfæktər]	*n.* 行善者，捐助者(a person who has given financial help; patron) 记 词根记忆：bene(好) + fact(做) + or → 做好事的人 → 行善者
stoic [ˈstoʊɪk]	*n.* 坚忍克己之人(a person firmly restraining response to pain or distress) 记 来自希腊哲学流派 Stoic(斯多葛学派)，主张坚忍克己
episodic [ˌepɪˈsɑːdɪk]	*adj.* 偶然发生的(occurring irregularly)；分散性的 记 来自 episode(*n.* 片断)
segment [ˈsegmənt]	*n.* 部分(bit; fragment) 记 词根记忆：seg(=sect 部分) + ment → 部分
friend [frend]	*n.* 赞助者，支持者 (one who supports, sympathizes with, or patronizes a group, cause, or movement) 例 Queen Elizabeth I has quite correctly been called a *friend* of the arts, because many young artists received her patronage.

□ interlocking □ affirmation □ banish □ pathological □ equestrian □ shiftless
□ uncontroversial □ repress □ acidic □ verbose □ improvise □ benefactor
□ stoic □ episodic □ segment □ friend

enviable	*adj.* 令人羡慕的(highly desirable)
[ˈenviəbl]	记 来自 envy(*n./v.* 羡慕)
terrifying	*adj.* 恐怖的(causing terror or apprehension)
[ˈterɪfaɪɪŋ]	同 frightening, intimidating, shocking
contention	*n.* 争论(the act of dispute; discord); 论点(a statement one argues for as
[kənˈtenʃn]	valid)
	记 词根记忆: con + tent(拉) + ion → 你拉我夺 → 争论
withstand	*v.* 反抗(to oppose with force or resolution); 经受(to endure successfully)
[wɪðˈstænd]	记 词根记忆: with(反) + st(站) + and → 反着站 → 反抗
	例 Having billed himself as "Mr. Clean", Hosokawa could not *withstand* the notoriety of a major financial scandal.
desecrate	*v.* 玷辱, 亵渎(to treat as not sacred; profane)
[ˈdesɪkreɪt]	记 词根记忆: de(向下) + secr(神圣) + ate → 玷辱
inconsolable	*adj.* 无法慰藉的(incapable of being consoled), 悲痛欲绝的
[ˌɪnkənˈsoʊləbl]	例 In the poem *Annabel Lee*, the speaker reveals that he is not resigned to the death of his beloved; on the contrary, he is *inconsolable*.
vaulted	*adj.* 拱形的
[ˈvɔːltɪd]	
toxic	*adj.* 有毒的, 中毒的(of a poison or toxin)
[ˈtɑːksɪk]	记 词根记忆: tox(毒) + ic → 有毒的
	例 People who take megadoses of vitamins and minerals should take care: though beneficial in small quantities, in large amounts these substances may have *toxic* effects.
dichotomy	*n.* 两分法; 矛盾对立, 分歧(bifurcation); 具有两分特征的事物(sth. with
[daɪˈkɑːtəmi]	seemingly contradictory qualities)
overbear	*v.* 压倒(to bring down by superior weight or physical force); 镇压(to
[ˌoʊvərˈber]	domineer over); 比…更重要, 超过(to surpass in importance or cogency)
disconsolate	*adj.* 闷闷不乐的, 郁郁寡欢的(cheerless, dejected, downcast)
[dɪsˈkɑːnsələt]	记 词根记忆: dis(不) + con + sol(安慰) + ate → 没有安慰的 → 闷闷不乐的
observant	*adj.* 密切注意的, 警惕的(paying strict attention; watchful; mindful); 遵守
[əbˈzɜːrvənt]	的, 遵从的(careful in observing(as rites, laws, or customs)); 敏锐的 (quick to perceive or apprehend; alert)
outgrowth	*n.* 结果(consequence); 副产品(by-product)
[ˈaʊtɡroʊθ]	记 组合词: out(出来) + growth(生长) → 结果; 副产品
prior	*adj.* 在前的(previous); 优先的(taking precedence)
[ˈpraɪər]	记 词根记忆: pri(=prim 第一, 首先) + or → 在前的; 优先的
	例 Students of the Great Crash of 1929 have never understood why even the most informed observers did not recognize and heed the *prior* economic danger signals that in retrospect seem so apparent.
	同 antecedent, anterior, former, preceding

☐ enviable	☐ terrifying	☐ contention	☑ withstand	☐ desecrate	☐ inconsolable
☐ vaulted	☐ toxic	☐ dichotomy	☐ overbear	☐ disconsolate	☐ observant
☐ outgrowth	☐ prior				

109

rebellious	*adj.* 造反的，反叛的(given to or engaged in rebellion; refractory)；难控制的
[rɪˈbeljəs]	记 词根记忆：re(反) + bell(打斗，战争) + ious → 打回去 → 造反的
mundane	*adj.* 现世的，世俗的 (relating to the world; worldly)；平凡的，普通的 (commonplace)
[mʌnˈdeɪn]	记 词根记忆：mund(世界) + ane → 现世的，世俗的
predatory	*adj.* 掠夺的(of, relating to, or practicing plunder, pillage, or rapine)；食肉的(predaceous)
[ˈpredətɔːri]	例 Aimed at curbing European attempts to seize territory in the Americas, the Monroe Doctrine was a warning to *predatory* foreign powers.
	同 predatorial, rapacious, raptorial
aggrandize	*v.* 增大，扩张(to make greater or more powerful)；吹捧(to praise highly)
[əˈɡrænˌdaɪz]	记 词根记忆：ag + grand(大) + ize → 增大
	搭 aggrandize oneself 妄自尊大
	同 augment, extend, heighten, magnify, multiply
constituent	*n.* 成分(component; element)；选区内的选民(a member of a constituency)
[kənˈstɪtʃuənt]	记 词根记忆：con + stit(=stat 站) + uent → 站在一起投票 → 选区内的选民
slothful	*adj.* 迟钝的，懒惰的(lazy)
[ˈsloʊθfl]	记 联想记忆：sloth(树獭，在树上生活，行动迟缓) + ful → 像树獭一样懒散的 → 懒惰的
	同 sluggish
homemade	*adj.* 自制的，家里做的 (made in the home, on the premises, or by one's own efforts)
[ˌhəʊmˈmeɪd]	
ribaldry	*n.* 下流的语言，粗鄙的幽默(ribald language or humor)
[ˈrɪbldri]	同 obscenity
despondent	*adj.* 失望的，意气消沉的(disheartened; depressed; hopeless)
[dɪˈspɑːndənt]	记 词根记忆：de + spond(允诺) + ent → 没有得到允诺 → 失望的
well-deserved	*adj.* 当之无愧的；罪有应得的
[ˌweldɪˈzɜːrvd]	
tyrannical	*adj.* 暴虐的，残暴的(being or characteristic of a tyrant or tyranny)
[tɪˈrænɪkl]	同 despotic, oppressive, tyrannic
prerequisite	*n.* 先决条件(sth. that is necessary to an end)
[ˌpriːˈrekwəzɪt]	记 词根记忆：pre(预先) + re(一再) + quis(要求) + ite → 预先一再要求 → 先决条件
domain	*n.* 领土(territory; dominion)；领域(field or sphere of activity or influence)
[doʊˈmeɪn]	记 词根记忆：dom(家) + ain → 领土；领域
grating	*adj.* (声音)刺耳的(harsh and rasping)；恼人的(irritating or annoying)
[ˈɡreɪtɪŋ]	同 hoarse, raucous
perspicacious	*adj.* 独具慧眼的，敏锐的(of acute mental vision or discernment)
[ˌpɜːrspɪˈkeɪʃəs]	记 词根记忆：per(全部) + spic(=spect 看) + acious → 全部都看到的 → 独具慧眼的，敏锐的

□ rebellious	□ mundane	□ predatory	□ aggrandize	□ constituent	□ slothful
□ homemade	□ ribaldry	□ despondent	□ well-deserved	□ tyrannical	□ prerequisite
□ domain	□ grating	□ perspicacious			

specter [ˈspektər]	*n.* 鬼怪，幽灵（a ghostly apparition）；缠绕心头的恐惧，凶兆（sth. that haunts or perturbs the mind） 记 词根记忆：spect(看) + er → 看到而摸不着的东西 → 鬼怪 同 eidolon, phantasm, phantom, spirit
ferment	[fərˈment] *v.* 使发酵（to cause fermentation in）；（使）激动，（使）动乱（to excite; agitate） [ˈfɜːrment] *n.* 发酵（a living organism that causes fermentation）；骚动（a state of unrest） 记 词根记忆：ferm(=ferv 热) + ent → 生热 → 发酵
offhand [ˌɔːfˈhænd]	*adj.* 无准备的，即席的（performed or expressed without preparation or forethought）；随便的（casual）*adv.* 无准备地，即席地（without preparation or forethought）；随便地（casually）
solicit [səˈlɪsɪt]	*v.* 恳求（to make petition to）；教唆（to entice into evil） 记 词根记忆：soli(=sole 唯一，全部) + cit(引出) → 引出大家做某事 → 恳求；教唆
pitfall [ˈpɪtfɔːl]	*n.* 陷阱，隐患（a hidden or not easily recognized danger or difficulty） 记 组合词：pit(坑，洞) + fall(落下) → 让人下落的坑 → 陷阱
incise [ɪnˈsaɪz]	*v.* 切入，切割（to cut into） 记 词根记忆：in(进入) + cis(切) + e → 切入 同 gash, pierce, slash, slice, slit
euphonious [juːˈfoʊniəs]	*adj.* 悦耳的（having a pleasant sound; harmonious） 记 词根记忆：eu(好的) + phon(声音) + ious → 声音好听的 → 悦耳的
impressive [ɪmˈpresɪv]	*adj.* 给人印象深刻的，感人的（making or tending to make a marked impression） 例 A born teller of tales, Olsen used her *impressive* narrative skills to advantage in her story *I Stand Here Ironing*. 同 gorgeous, lavish, poignant, splendid, sumptuous
atrophy [ˈætrəfi]	*n.* 萎缩，衰退（decrease in size or wasting away of a body part or tissue） 记 词根记忆：a(无) + troph(营养) + y → 无营养会萎缩 → 萎缩 同 decadence, declination, degeneracy, degeneration, deterioration
omit [əˈmɪt]	*v.* 忽略，遗漏（to leave out）；不做，未能做（to leave undone） 记 联想记忆：om(音似："呕") + it(它) → 把它呕出去 → 忽略 同 disregard, ignore, neglect
mitigate [ˈmɪtɪgeɪt]	*v.* 使缓和，使减轻（to lessen in force or intensity） 记 词根记忆：miti(小的；轻的) + gat(=ag 做) + e → 弄轻 → 使缓和，使减轻
irrefutable [ˌɪrɪˈfjuːtəbl]	*adj.* 无可辩驳的，毋庸置疑的（impossible to refute） 同 inarguable, incontestable, incontrovertible
speculative [ˈspekjələtɪv]	*adj.* 推理的，思索的（based on speculation）；投机的（risky） 同 conjectured, guessed, supposed, surmised

□ specter	□ ferment	□ offhand	□ solicit	□ pitfall	□ incise
□ euphonious	□ impressive	□ atrophy	□ omit	□ mitigate	□ irrefutable
□ speculative					

elapse [ɪˈlæps]	*v.* 消逝，过去(to pass; go by) *n.* 消逝(passage) 记 词根记忆：e(出) + laps(落下) + e → 滑落 → 消逝
allegiance [əˈliːdʒəns]	*n.* 忠诚，拥护(loyalty or devotion to a cause or a person) 记 词根记忆：al(加强) + leg(法律) + iance → 拥护法律 → 拥护
whittle [ˈwɪtl]	*v.* 削(木头)(to pare or cut off chips)；削减(to reduce; pare) 记 联想记忆：wh(看作 whet，磨刀) + ittle(看作 little，小的) → 磨刀把木头削小 → 削(木头)
profile [ˈprəʊfaɪl]	*n.* 轮廓，外形(outline)；(尤指人面部的)侧面 (a human head or face represented or seen in a side view) 记 词根记忆：pro(前面) + fil(线条) + e → 外部的线条 → 轮廓，外形 profile
drone [drəʊn]	*v.* 嗡嗡地响(to make monotonous humming or buzzing sound)；单调地说(to speak in a monotonous tone) *n.* 单调的低音(a bass voice)
divisive [dɪˈvaɪsɪv]	*adj.* 引起分歧的，导致分裂的(creating disunity or dissension) 记 词根记忆：di(分开) + vis(看) + ive → 往不同方向看的 → 引起分歧的
suppress [səˈpres]	*v.* 镇压(to put down by authority or force)；抑制(to inhibit the growth or development of) 例 As serious as she is about the bullfight, she does not allow respect to *suppress* her sense of whimsy when painting it. 同 quell, quench, repress, squash
dissimilar [dɪˈsɪmɪlər]	*adj.* 不同的，不相似的(unlike) 同 different, disparate, distant, divergent, diverse
crooked [ˈkrʊkɪd]	*adj.* 不诚实的(dishonest)；弯曲的(not straight) 记 来自 crook(*v.* 弯曲)
bombastic [bɑːmˈbæstɪk]	*adj.* 夸夸其谈的(full of important-sounding insincere words with little meaning)
indent [ɪnˈdent]	*v.* 切割成锯齿状(to cut tooth-like points; notch) 记 联想记忆：in(进入) + dent(牙齿) → 切割成锯齿状
creed [kriːd]	*n.* 教义(a brief authoritative formula of religious belief)；信条(a set of fundamental beliefs)
durable [ˈdʊrəbl]	*adj.* 持久的(lasting)；耐用的(able to exist for a long time without significant deterioration) 记 词根记忆：dur(持续) + able → 持久的
pretense [prɪˈtens]	*n.* 妄称，自称(a claim made or implied)；假装，伪装，假象(a false show; an affectation; make-believe)；借口，托词(a professed but feigned reason or excuse; a pretext) 例 An example of an illegitimate method of argument is to lump dissimilar cases together deliberately under the *pretense* that the same principles apply to each.

armored [ˈɑːrmərd]	*adj.* 披甲的，装甲的（equipped or protected with armor） 搭 an armored car 装甲车
affection [əˈfekʃn]	*n.* 喜爱（fond or tender feeling） 记 词根记忆：affect（*v.* 影响，感染）+ ion → 喜爱
outstrip [ˌaʊtˈstrɪp]	*v.* 超过，超越（to excel; surpass）；比…跑得快（to run faster） 记 联想记忆：out（出）+ strip（剥去，夺去）→ 比别人夺得多 → 超过 同 exceed, outdo, transcend
ambitious [æmˈbɪʃəs]	*adj.* 有抱负的，雄心勃勃的（having a desire to achieve a particular goal） 同 emulous
chubby [ˈtʃʌbi]	*adj.* 丰满的，圆胖的（plump） 搭 chubby cheeks 胖乎乎的脸
underhanded [ˌʌndərˈhændɪd]	*adj.* 秘密的，狡诈的（marked by secrecy and deception; sly） 记 联想记忆：under（在…下面）+ handed（有手的）→ 在下面做手脚 → 秘密的
paradoxical [ˌpærəˈdɑːksɪkl]	*adj.* 矛盾的（of the nature of a paradox）；不正常的（not being the normal or usual kind） 例 The concept of timelessness is *paradoxical* from the start, for adult consciousness is permeated by the awareness of duration.
tantamount [ˈtæntəmaʊnt]	*adj.* 同等的，相当于（equivalent in value, significance, or effect） 记 词根记忆：tant（相等）+ a + mount（数量）→ 同等的，相当于
shrivel [ˈʃrɪvl]	*v.* （使）枯萎（to draw into wrinkles especially with a loss of moisture） 同 mummify, wilt, wither
containment [kənˈteɪnmənt]	*n.* 阻止，遏制（keeping sth. within limits） 搭 a policy of containment 遏制政策
sparse [spɑːrs]	*adj.* 稀少的，贫乏的（not thickly grown or settled）；稀疏的 记 联想记忆：稀疏的（sparse）火花（spark）
premise [ˈpremɪs]	*n.* 前提（a proposition antecedently supposed or proved as a basis of argument or inference） 记 词根记忆：pre（在前面）+ mis（放）+ e → 放在前面的东西 → 前提
static [ˈstætɪk]	*adj.* 静态的（showing little change; stationary）；呆板的 记 联想记忆：stat（看作 state，处于某种状态）+ ic（…的）→ 静态的 例 That the brain physically changes when stimulated, instead of remaining *static* from infancy to death, as previously thought, was Doctor Marian Diamond's first, and perhaps most far reaching discovery.
attrition [əˈtrɪʃn]	*n.* 摩擦，磨损（the act of wearing or grinding down by friction） 记 词根记忆：at + trit（摩擦）+ ion → 摩擦，磨损

□ armored	□ affection	□ outstrip	□ ambitious	□ chubby	□ underhanded
□ paradoxical	□ tantamount	□ shrivel	□ containment	□ sparse	□ premise
□ static	□ attrition				

accentuate [ək'sentʃueɪt]	*v.* 强调(to emphasize)；重读(to pronounce with an accent or stress) 词根记忆：ac(加强) + cent(=cant 唱，说) + uate → 不断说 → 强调
reversible [rɪ'vɜːrsəbl]	*adj.* 可逆的，可反转的(capable of being reversed or of reversing)
tension ['tenʃn]	*n.* 紧张，焦虑(anxiety)；张力(the amount of a force stretching sth.) 词根记忆：tens(伸展) + ion → 伸展出的状态 → 张力 例 As painted by Constable, the scene is not one of bucolic serenity; rather it shows a striking emotional and intellectual *tension*.
flourish ['flɜːrɪʃ]	*v.* 繁荣，兴旺(to develop well and be successful)；活跃而有影响力(to be very active and influential) 词根记忆：flour(=flor 花) + ish → 花一样开放 → 繁荣，兴旺
fertilizer ['fɜːrtəlaɪzər]	*n.* 肥料，化肥(natural or artificial substance added to soil to make it more productive)
pacifist ['pæsɪfɪst]	*n.* 和平主义者，反战主义者(a person who believes that all wars are wrong and refuses to fight in them) 词根记忆：pac(和平的，宁静的) + if(使) + ist → 和平主义者
consternation [ˌkɑːnstər'neɪʃn]	*n.* 大为吃惊，惊骇(great fear or shock) 词根记忆：con + stern(僵硬) + ation → 吓得全身僵硬 → 惊骇
mitigant ['mɪtəgənt]	*adj.* 缓和的，减轻的 *n.* 缓和物 来自 mitigate(*v.* 使缓和，使减轻)
delineate [dɪ'lɪnieɪt]	*v.* 勾画，描述(to sketch out；draw；describe) 联想记忆：de(加强) + line(线条) + ate → 加强线条 → 勾画
preservative [prɪ'zɜːrvətɪv]	*adj.* 保护的；防腐的(having the power of preserving) *n.* 防腐剂(an additive used to protect against decay) 来自 preserve(*v.* 保护；保存)
dual ['duːəl]	*adj.* 双重的(having or composed of two parts) 词根记忆：du(二，双) + al → 两个的 → 双重的
genial ['dʒiːniəl]	*adj.* 友好的，和蔼的(cheerful, friendly and amiable) 联想记忆：做个和蔼的(genial)天才(genius)
portray [pɔːr'treɪ]	*v.* 描述（ to depict or describe in words)；描绘，描画（ to make a picture of) 联想记忆：por(看作 pour，倒) + tray(碟) → 将(颜料)倒在碟子上 → 描绘，描画
pliable ['plaɪəbl]	*adj.* 易弯曲的，柔软的(supple enough to bend freely；ductile)；易受影响的(easily influenced) 词根记忆：pli(=ply 弯，折) + able → 易弯曲的
symbiosis [ˌsɪmbaɪ'oʊsɪs]	*n.* 共生(关系)(the living together in more or less intimate association or closer union of two dissimilar organisms) 词根记忆：sym(共同) + bio(生命) + sis → 共生(关系)
thousandfold ['θaʊzndfoʊld]	*adj.* 千倍的(a thousand times as much) *adv.* 千倍地 组合词：thousand(一千) + fold(折叠) → 一千个叠起来 → 千倍的

□ accentuate	□ reversible	□ tension	□ flourish	□ fertilizer	□ pacifist
□ consternation	□ mitigant	□ delineate	□ preservative	□ dual	□ genial
□ portray	□ pliable	□ symbiosis	□ thousandfold		

shortsighted [ˌʃɔːrt ˈsaɪtɪd]	*adj.* 缺乏远见的(lacking foresight); 近视的
	同 nearsighted
deride [dɪ ˈraɪd]	*v.* 嘲笑, 愚弄(to laugh at in contempt or scorn; ridicule)
	记 词根记忆: de + rid(笑) + e → 嘲笑
ignominious [ˌɪɡnə ˈmɪniəs]	*adj.* 可耻的(despicable); 耻辱的(dishonorable)
	同 disgraceful, humiliating
synchronous [ˈsɪŋkrənəs]	*adj.* 同时发生的(happening at precisely the same time)
	同 coexistent, concurrent
snippet [ˈsnɪpɪt]	*n.* 小片, 片段(a small part, piece, or thing)
	搭 snippet of information/news 简短的信息/新闻
befriend [bɪ ˈfrend]	*v.* 以朋友态度对待(to become or act as a friend to)
	记 词根记忆: be + friend(朋友) → 当作朋友 → 以朋友态度对待
furtive [ˈfɜːrtɪv]	*adj.* 偷偷的, 秘密的(done or acting in a stealthy manner; sneaky)
	例 The teacher suspected cheating as soon as he noticed the pupil's *furtive* glances at his classmate's paper.
	同 catlike, clandestine, covert, secret, surreptitious
groundless [ˈɡraʊndləs]	*adj.* 无理由的, 无根据的(having no ground or foundation)
	搭 groundless fear 没由来的恐惧

10

When an end is lawful and obligatory, the indispensable means to it are also lawful and obligatory.

如果一个目的是正当而必须做的，则达到这个目的的必要手段也是正当而必须采取的。

——美国政治家 林肯(Abraham Lincoln, American statesman)

Word List 11

音频

assiduous [əˈsɪdʒuəs]	*adj.* 勤勉的（diligent；persevering）；专心的（attentive） 记 词根记忆：as + sid(坐) + uous → 坐得多的 → 勤勉的 搭 be assiduous in... 专心于…
inevitable [ɪnˈevɪtəbl]	*adj.* 不可避免的，必然的（incapable of being avoided or evaded） 记 联想记忆：in(不) + evitable(可避免的) → 不可避免的 例 Because vast organizations are an *inevitable* element in modern life, it is futile to aim at their abolition. 同 ineluctable, ineludible, inescapable, inevasible
characteristic [ˌkærəktəˈrɪstɪk]	*adj.* 有特色的；典型性的 *n.* 与众不同的特征 记 来自 character(*n.* 性格；特征)
multiple [ˈmʌltɪpl]	*adj.* 多样的，多重的（various；including more than one） 记 词根记忆：multi(多的) + ple(折叠) → 多次折叠 → 多样的，多重的
interminable [ɪnˈtɜːrmɪnəbl]	*adj.* 无止境的，没完没了的（without end；lasting） 记 词根记忆：in(不) + termin(尽头) + able → 无尽头的 → 无止境的
demolish [dɪˈmɑːlɪʃ]	*v.* 破坏，摧毁（to destroy；ruin）；拆除（to break to pieces） 记 词根记忆：de(加强) + mol(碾碎) + ish → 摧毁
drastic [ˈdræstɪk]	*adj.* 猛烈的，激烈的（strong；violent and severe） 搭 a drastic change 剧烈的变化
subtract [səbˈtrækt]	*v.* 减去，减掉（to take away by or as if by deducting） 记 词根记忆：sub(下面) + tract(拉) → 拉下去 → 减去
definitive [dɪˈfɪnətɪv]	*adj.* 明确的，有权威的（clear and having final authority）；最终的（conclusive）
huckster [ˈhʌkstə]	*n.* 叫卖小贩，零售商（a peddler or hawker） 记 词根记忆：huck(=back，背) + ster(人) → 背东西卖的人 → 叫卖小贩
orchestrate [ˈɔːrkɪstreɪt]	*v.* 给…配管弦乐（to provide with orchestration）；精心安排，组织（to arrange or combine so as to achieve a desired or maximum effect）
averse [əˈvɜːrs]	*adj.* 反对的，不愿意的（not willing or inclined；opposed） 记 词根记忆：a + verse(转) → 转开 → 反对的，不愿意的

assertion [əˈsɜːrʃn]	*n.* 断言，声明；主张(declaration；affirmation) 记 来自 assert(*v.* 明确肯定，断言)
archaic [ɑːrˈkeɪɪk]	*adj.* 古老的（of, relating to, or characteristic of an earlier or more primitive time)
pretentious [prɪˈtenʃəs]	*adj.* 夸耀的，炫耀的(making or marked by an extravagant outward show；ostentatious)；自命不凡的，狂妄的(making usually unjustified or excessive claims as of value or standing)
impervious [ɪmˈpɜːrviəs]	*adj.* 不能渗透的（not allowing entrance or passage)；不为所动的(not capable of being affected or disturbed) 记 联想记忆：im(不) + pervious(渗透的) → 不能渗透的
unpack [ˌʌnˈpæk]	*v.* 打开包裹(或行李)，卸货(to take packed things out of)
colloquial [kəˈloʊkwiəl]	*adj.* 口语的，口头的(conversational) 记 词根记忆：col(共同) + loqu(说) + ial → 两人一起说 → 口语的
ravage [ˈrævɪdʒ]	*v.* 摧毁，使荒废(to ruin and destroy) 同 desolate, devastate, havoc
arrogant [ˈærəgənt]	*adj.* 傲慢的，自大的(overbearing；haughty；proud)
return [rɪˈtɜːrn]	*v.* 回复(to revert)；归还；回答，反驳(to retort) *n.* 回报(sth. given in repayment or reciprocation) *adj.* 返回的；重现的(taking place for the second time)
coax [koʊks]	*v.* 哄诱，巧言诱哄(to induce；persuade by soothing words；wheedle) 搭 coax sth. out of/from sb. 哄劝；哄诱得到
distribute [dɪˈstrɪbjuːt]	*v.* 分发，分配(to separate sth. into part and give a share to each person) 记 词根记忆：dis(分开) + tribut(给予) + e → 分开给 → 分发
forfeit [ˈfɔːrfət]	*v.* 丧失，被罚没收（to lose, or be deprived of) *n.* 丧失的东西(sth. one loses) 记 词根记忆：for(出去) + feit(=fect，做) → 做出去 → 丧失 forfeit 随地吐痰 罚款十元
voluminous [vəˈluːmɪnəs]	*adj.* 长篇的（filling or capable of filling a large volume or several volumes)；大量的（having or marked by great volume or bulk) 记 联想记忆：volum(=volume 容量) + in + ous → 大量的
exposition [ˌekspəˈzɪʃn]	*n.* 阐释(detailed explanation)；博览会(a public exhibition or show) 记 词根记忆：ex + pos(放) + ition → 放出来(让人看) → 博览会 apex　apogee
antique [ænˈtiːk]	*adj.* 古时的，古老的(existing since or belonging to earlier times) *n.* 古物，古董(a relic or object of ancient times) 记 词根记忆：anti(前) + que → 以前的 → 古时的 antique

11

□ assertion	□ archaic	□ pretentious	□ impervious	□ unpack	□ colloquial
□ ravage	□ arrogant	□ return	□ coax	□ distribute	□ forfeit
□ voluminous	□ exposition	□ antique			

117

untarnished	adj. 未失去光泽的（unblemished）
[ˌʌnˈtɑːrnɪʃt]	同 stainless, unstained, unsullied, untained
stunning	adj. 极富魅力的（strikingly impressive in beauty or excellence）
[ˈstʌnɪŋ]	同 amazing, dazzling, marvellous
generous	adj. 慷慨的（liberal in giving）；大量的（marked by abundance or ample proportions）
[ˈdʒenərəs]	记 词根记忆：gener(产生) + ous → 产生很多的 → 大量的
	例 Famous among job seekers for its largesse, the company, quite apart from *generous* salaries, bestowed on its executives annual bonuses and such perquisites as low-interest home mortgages and company cars.
negate	v. 取消（to nullify or invalidate）；否认（to deny）
[nɪˈgeɪt]	记 词根记忆：neg(否认) + ate → 否认
antagonism	n. 对抗，敌对
[ænˈtægənɪzəm]	同 animosity, animus, antipathy, opposition, rancor
excess	n. 过分，过度（lack of moderation；intemperance）
[ɪkˈses]	记 词根记忆：ex + cess(走) → 走出常规 → 过分
	例 Perhaps because he feels confined by an *excess* of parental restrictions and rules, at adolescence the repressd child may break out dramatically.
herbaceous	adj. 草本的（of, relating to, or having the characteristics of an herb）
[ɜːrˈbeɪʃəs]	记 词根记忆：herb(草) + aceous → 草本的
self-realization	n. 自我实现，自我完成（fulfillment by oneself of the possibilities of one's character or personality）
[ˌselfˌriːələˈzeɪʃn]	
penalize	v. 置…于不利地位（to put at a serious disadvantage）；处罚（to inflict a penalty on）
[ˈpiːnəlaɪz]	记 来自 penal（adj. 惩罚的，刑罚的）
obliterate	v. 涂掉，擦掉（to efface；erase）
[əˈblɪtəreɪt]	记 词根记忆：ob(去掉) + liter(文字) + ate → 去掉(文字等) → 涂掉，擦掉
atonement	n. 弥补（reparation for an offense or injury）
[əˈtoʊnmənt]	记 来自 atone（v. 弥补，赎罪）
extrapolate	v. 预测，推测（to speculate）
[ɪkˈstræpəleɪt]	记 词根记忆：extra(外面) + pol(放) + ate → 放出想法 → 预测，推测
utilize	v. 利用，使用（to make use of）
[ˈjuːtəlaɪz]	记 词根记忆：ut(用) + ilize → 利用
	例 The failure of many psychotherapists to *utilize* the results of pioneering research could be due in part to the specialized nature of such findings: even momentous findings may not be useful.
	同 apply, exercise, exploit, handle

utilize

rush [rʌʃ]	*v.* 急促；匆忙行事（to perform in a short time or at a high speed）*n.* 冲，奔（a violent forward motion） 例 Having just published his fourth novel in an almost 40-year career, Gaddis describes himself, with some understatement, as a writer who has never been in a *rush* to get into print.
sensitive [ˈsensətɪv]	*adj.* 敏感的（highly responsive or susceptible） 记 词根记忆：sens（感觉）+ itive → 敏感的 搭 be sensitive to sth. 对某事敏感 同 susceptive
gain [geɪn]	*n.* 利润，收获（profit, the act or process of gaining） 同 earnings, lucre
itinerant [aɪˈtɪnərənt]	*adj.* 巡回的（peripatetic; nomadic） 记 词根记忆：it（走）+ iner + ant → 巡回的
content	[kənˈtent] *adj.* 知足的，满意的（satisfied）*v.* （使）满意；（使）满足 *n.* 满意（the state of being content） [ˈkɑːntent] *n.* 内容（what is contained） 记 词根记忆：con + tent（拉）→ 全部拉开 → 全身舒展 → 满意的
bibliomania [ˌbɪbliəˈmeɪniə]	*n.* 藏书癖（extreme preoccupation with collecting books）
callous [ˈkæləs]	*adj.* 结硬块的（thick and hardened）；无情的（lacking pity; unfeeling） 记 来自 callus（*n.* 老茧）
subordinate [səˈbɔːrdɪnət]	*adj.* 次要的（inferior）；下级的（submissive to or controlled by authority）*n.* 下级（one that is subordinate） 记 sub（在下面）+ ordin（顺序）+ ate → 顺序在下的 → 次要的；下级的
counterclockwise [ˌkaʊntərˈklɑːkwaɪz]	*adj./adv.* 逆时针方向的（地）(in a direction opposite to that in which the hands of a clock rotate as viewed from in front)
unpremeditated [ˌʌnpriːˈmedɪteɪtɪd]	*adj.* 无预谋的，非故意的 记 联想记忆：un（不）+ premeditated（预谋的）→ 无预谋的
hive [haɪv]	*n.* 蜂房，蜂巢（a container for housing honeybees）；热闹的场所（a place swarming with activity）
premonition [ˌpriːməˈnɪʃn]	*n.* 预感，预兆（a feeling that sth. is going to happen） 记 词根记忆：pre（预先）+ mon（警告）+ it + ion → 预先给出的警告 → 预感，预兆 同 foreboding, prenotion, presage, presentiment
nonchalant [ˌnɑːnʃəˈlɑːnt]	*adj.* 冷淡的，冷漠的（having an air of easy unconcern or indifference; not showing interest） 例 No real life hero of ancient or modern days can surpass James Bond with his *nonchalant* disregard of death and the fortitude with which he bears torture.

subordinate

119

dispassionate [dɪsˈpæʃənət]	*adj.* 平心静气的(free from passion, emotion, or bias) 记 联想记忆：dis(不) + passionate(激情的) → 不表现激情的 → 平心静气的
residential [ˌrezɪˈdenʃl]	*adj.* 住宅的，与居住有关的(of or relating to residence or residences)
provocation [ˌprɑːvəˈkeɪʃn]	*n.* 挑衅，激怒(the act of provoking; incitement) 记 来自 provoke(*v.* 激怒)
shun [ʃʌn]	*v.* 避免，闪避(to avoid deliberately) 同 bilk, duck, elude, eschew, evade
trample [ˈtræmpl]	*v.* 踩坏，践踏(to tread heavily so as to bruise, crush, or injure)；蹂躏 记 联想记忆：tr(看作 tree，树) + ample(大量的) → 大量的树苗被踩坏 → 踩坏，践踏
intuitive [ɪnˈtuːɪtɪv]	*adj.* 直觉的(of, relating to, or arising from intuition) 例 She is an interesting paradox, an infinitely shy person who, in apparent contradiction, possesses an enormously *intuitive* gift for understanding people.
predominate [prɪˈdɑːmɪneɪt]	*v.* 统治(to exert control over; dominate)；(数量上)占优势，以…为主(to hold advantage in numbers or quantity) 例 The author argues for serious treatment of such arts as crochet and needlework, finding in too many art historians a cultural blindness traceable to their prejudice against textiles as a medium in which women artists *predominate*.
urgency [ˈɜːrdʒənsi]	*n.* 紧急(的事)(the quality or state of being urgent) 同 importunity, urging
euphoric [juːˈfɔːrɪk]	*adj.* 欢欣的(feeling very happy and excited) 例 Our mood swings about the economy grow more extreme: when things go well, we become *euphoric*; when things go poorly, gloom descends.
interrelate [ˌɪntərɪˈleɪt]	*v.* 相互关联，相互影响(to bring into mutual relation; have mutual relationship)
packed [pækt]	*adj.* 压紧的，压实的(compressed)；充满人的，拥挤的(crowded; crammed) 记 来自 pack(*v.* 打包，包装)
obsequiousness [əbˈsiːkwiəsnəs]	*n.* 谄媚(abject submissiveness) 同 servility, subservience
immaculate [ɪˈmækjələt]	*adj.* 洁净的，无瑕的(perfectly clean; unsoiled; impeccable) 记 词根记忆：im(不) + macul(斑点) + ate → 无斑点的 → 洁净的，无瑕的
chivalrous [ˈʃɪvlrəs]	*adj.* 骑士精神的(of, relating to, or characteristic of chivalry and knight-errantry)；对女人彬彬有礼的(gallant; courteous) 记 词根记忆：chival(=caval 骑马) + rous → 骑马的 → 骑士的 → 骑士精神的

□ dispassionate	□ residential	□ provocation	□ shun	□ trample	□ intuitive
□ predominate	□ urgency	□ euphoric	□ interrelate	□ packed	□ obsequiousness
□ immaculate	□ chivalrous				

sight [saɪt]	*n.* 景象(spectacle)；视力(the process, power, or function of seeing)；视野(the range of vision) *v.* 看到(to get or catch sight of) 同 eyesight, seeing
overtax [ˌoʊvər'tæks]	*v.* 课税过重
extinction [ɪk'stɪŋkʃn]	*n.* 消灭，废除（the process of eliminating or reducing a conditioned response by not reinforcing it）
intellectual [ˌɪntə'lektʃuəl]	*adj.* 智力的（of or relating to the intellect）；理性的（rational rather than emotional）*n.* 知识分子 记 词根记忆：intel(在…中间) + lect(选择) + ual → 能从中选择的 → 智力的 例 As painted by Constable, the scene is not one of bucolic serenity; rather it shows a striking emotional and *intellectual* tension. 同 cerebral, intellective, intelligent
candid ['kændɪd]	*adj.* 率直的(not hiding one's thoughts) 记 词根记忆：cand(白，发光) + id → 白的 → 坦白的 → 率直的 同 frank, openhearted, plain, straightforward, unconcealed
imposing [ɪm'poʊzɪŋ]	*adj.* 给人深刻印象的(impressive)；壮丽的，雄伟的(grand)
satiated ['seɪʃieɪtɪd]	*adj.* 厌倦的，生腻的(tired of)；充分满足的(fully satisfied) 记 联想记忆：sat(坐) + i + ate(吃) + d → 我可以坐下吃东西了 → 充分满足的
subside [səb'saɪd]	*v.* (建筑物等)下陷(to tend downward, descend)；平息，减退(to become quiet or less) 记 词根记忆：sub(下面) + side(坐) → 坐下去 → 下陷 例 Because he had assumed that the child's first, fierce rush of grief would quickly *subside*, Murdstone was astonished to find him still disconsolate. 同 ebb, lull, moderate, slacken, wane
overestimate [ˌoʊvər'estɪmeɪt]	*v.* 评价过高 记 组合词：over(在…上) + estimate(评估) → 评价过高
retrospective [ˌretrə'spektɪv]	*adj.* 回顾的，追溯的(of, relating to, or given to retrospection) 例 Famous in her time and then forgotten, the 17th century Dutch painter Judith Leyster was rescued from obscurity when, in 1993, the Worcester Art Museum organized the first *retrospective* exhibition of her work.
spectral ['spektrəl]	*adj.* 幽灵的(ghostly)；谱的，光谱的(of, relating to, or produced by a spectrum) 搭 spectral analysis 光谱分析
satirize ['sætəraɪz]	*v.* 讽刺(to use satire against) 同 lampoon, mock, quip, scorch

11

abut [əˈbʌt]	*v.* 邻接，毗邻 (to border upon) 记 联想记忆：about 去掉 o；注意不要和 abet (*v.* 教唆) 相混
nonsensical [nɑːnˈsensɪkl]	*adj.* 无意义的 (having no meaning or conveying no intelligible ideas)；荒谬的 (absurd)
pancreas [ˈpæŋkriəs]	*n.* 胰腺 (a large lobulated gland of vertebrates that secretes digestive enzymes and the hormones insulin and glucagon) 记 词根记忆：pan (全部) + cre (肉) + as → 帮助身体消化养分的器官 → 胰腺
eclipse [ɪˈklɪps]	*n.* 日食，月食；黯然失色，衰退 (a fall into obscurity or disuse; a decline) 记 联想记忆：ec + lipse (看作 lapse，滑走) → 日月的光华滑走 → 日食，月食
outlying [ˈaʊtlaɪɪŋ]	*adj.* 边远的，偏僻的 (remote from a center or main body)
shatter [ˈʃætər]	*v.* 使落下，使散开 (to cause to drop or be dispersed)；砸碎，粉碎 (to break at once into pieces)；破坏，毁坏 (to cause the disruption or annihilation of sth.) 记 发音记忆："筛它" → 使落下，使散开
disciple [dɪˈsaɪpl]	*n.* 信徒，弟子 (a convinced adherent of a school or individual) 记 和 discipline (*n.* 纪律) 一起记；信徒 (disciple) 必须遵守纪律 (discipline)
sedentary [ˈsednteri]	*adj.* 久坐的 (requiring much sitting) 记 词根记忆：sed (坐) + entary → 久坐的 例 Noting the murder victim's flaccid musculature and pearlike figure, she deduced that the unfortunate fellow had earned his living in some *sedentary* occupation.
irresistible [ˌɪrɪˈzɪstəbl]	*adj.* 无法抗拒的；不能压制的 (impossible to resist) 记 联想记忆：ir (不) + resist (抵抗，抵制) + ible (能…的) → 无法抗拒的；不能压制的
ungrateful [ʌnˈɡreɪtfl]	*adj.* 不感激的，不领情的 (showing no gratitude)
survivor [sərˈvaɪvər]	*n.* 幸存者 (someone who continues to live after an accident, war, or illness)
glacial [ˈɡleɪʃl]	*adj.* 冰河期的 (of the Ice Age)；寒冷的 (very cold) 记 词根记忆：glaci (冰) + al → 冰河期的
assertive [əˈsɜːrtɪv]	*adj.* 断言的，肯定的 (expressing or tending to express strong opinions or claims)
sheltered [ˈʃeltərd]	*adj.* 遮蔽的 同 covered, shielded
introvert [ˈɪntrəvɜːrt]	*n.* 性格内向的人 (one whose thoughts and feelings are directed toward onself) 例 Because he was an *introvert* by nature, he preferred reading a book in the privacy of his own study to visiting a night club with friends.

122

□ abut　　□ nonsensical　　□ pancreas　　□ eclipse　　□ outlying　　□ shatter
□ disciple　　□ sedentary　　□ irresistible　　□ ungrateful　　□ survivor　　□ glacial
□ assertive　　□ sheltered　　□ introvert

pedantry [ˈpedntri]	*n.* 迂腐(pedantic presentation or application of knowledge or learning) 例 Learned though she was, her erudition never degenerated into *pedantry*.
ongoing [ˈɑːŋɡoʊɪŋ]	*adj.* 进行中的(being actually in process)；前进的；不间断的 同 ceaseless, continuous, endless, everlasting
subversive [səbˈvɜːrsɪv]	*adj.* 颠覆性的，破坏性的(intended to overthrow or undermine an established government) 记 词根记忆：sub(下面) + vers(转) + ive → 转到下面的 → 颠覆性的
vibrant [ˈvaɪbrənt]	*adj.* 振动的；响亮的；明快的(bright)；充满生气的，精力充沛的(pulsating with life) 记 词根记忆：vibr(振动) + ant → 振动的 例 The attorney's *vibrant* voice and outstanding sense of timing were as useful to him as his prodigious preparation, attention to detail, and mastery of the law.
stalwart [ˈstɔːlwərt]	*adj.* 健壮的(of outstanding strength)；坚定的 记 联想记忆：stal(=support) + wart(=worth) → 值得依靠的 → 坚定的
banter [ˈbæntər]	*n.* 打趣，玩笑(playful, good-humored joking) 记 发音记忆：绊他 → 打趣，玩笑
host [hoʊst]	*n.* 东道主(one that receives or entertains guests socially)；(寄生动植物的)寄主，宿主(a living animal or plant on or in which a parasite lives)
thwart [θwɔːrt]	*v.* 阻挠，使受挫折，挫败(to defeat the hopes or aspirations of) 同 baffle, balk, foil, frustrate
spice [spaɪs]	*n.* 香料(any of various aromatic vegetable products) *v.* 给…调味(to add spice to food in order to give it more flavor)
detection [dɪˈtekʃn]	*n.* 查明，探测(the act of detecting) 记 来自 detect(v. 洞察；查明)
implication [ˌɪmplɪˈkeɪʃn]	*n.* 暗示(something that is not openly stated) 记 来自 imply(v. 暗示，暗指)
elate [iˈleɪt]	*v.* 使高兴，使得意(to fill with joy or pride) 同 commove, exhilarate, intoxicate
superfluous [suːˈpɜːrfluəs]	*adj.* 多余的，累赘的(exceeding what is needed) 记 词根记忆：super(超过) + flu(流) + ous → 流得过多 → 多余的 例 Joe spoke of *superfluous* and vital matters with exactly the same degree of intensity, as though for him serious issues mattered neither more nor less than did trivialities.
fervor [ˈfɜːrvər]	*n.* 热诚，热烈(great warmth of emotion；ardor) 同 enthusiasm, fury, passion

11

spice

□ pedantry	□ ongoing	□ subversive	□ vibrant	□ stalwart	□ banter
□ host	□ thwart	□ spice	□ detection	□ implication	□ elate
□ superfluous	□ fervor				

123

customary [ˈkʌstəmeri]	*adj.* 合乎习俗的（according to custom） 记 来自 custom（*n.* 习俗）
tangle [ˈtæŋgl]	*v.* 缠结（to become a confused mass of disordered and twisted threads） *n.* 纷乱（a confused disordered state） 记 联想记忆：两人缠结（tangle）在一起跳探戈（tango）
subvert [səbˈvɜːrt]	*v.* 颠覆，推翻（to overturn or overthrow from the foundation） 记 词根记忆：sub（下面）+ vert（转）→ 在下面转 → 推翻
settled [ˈsetld]	*adj.* 固定的（fixed） 搭 settled life 稳定的生活
charlatan [ˈʃɑːrlətən]	*n.* 江湖郎中，骗子（fake；mountebank；quack） 记 联想记忆：意大利有个地方叫 Charlat，专卖假药并出江湖郎中（quack），所以叫 charlatan 同 quacksalver, quackster, saltimbanque
disorganize [dɪsˈɔːgənaɪz]	*v.* 扰乱，使混乱（to destroy or interrupt the orderly structure or function of）
sculptural [ˈskʌlptʃərəl]	*adj.* 雕刻的（of or relating to sculpture）；雕刻般的 搭 sculptural arts 雕塑艺术
disparate [ˈdɪspərət]	*adj.* 迥然不同的（essentially not alike；distinct or different in kind） 记 dis（不）+ par（平等）+ ate → 不平等的 → 迥然不同的
bestow [bɪˈstoʊ]	*v.* 给予，赐赠（to give or present） 记 联想记忆：be + stow（收藏）→ 给予以便收藏 → 赐赠
dorsal [ˈdɔːrsl]	*adj.* 背部的，背脊的（of, on, or near the back） 记 词根记忆：dors（背）+ al → 背部的
imminent [ˈɪmɪnənt]	*adj.* 即将发生的，逼近的（about to occur） 记 词根记忆：im（进入）+ min（突出）+ ent → 突进来 → 逼近的 例 Rosa was such a last-minute worker that she could never start writing a paper till the deadline was *imminent*. 同 close, impending, proximate
pharmaceutical [ˌfɑːrməˈsuːtɪkl]	*adj.* 制药的，卖药的（of the manufacture and sale of medicines） 记 来自 pharmacy（*n.* 药房；药剂学）
untamed [ˌʌnˈteɪmd]	*adj.* 未驯服的（not controlled by anyone）
negligibly [ˈneglɪdʒəbli]	*adv.* 无足轻重地，不值一提地 记 来自 negligible（*adj.* 可以忽略的，微不足道的）
foster [ˈfɔːstər]	*v.* 鼓励，促进（to promote the growth or development of sth.）；养育，抚养（to give parental care to） 记 联想记忆：fost（看作 fast，快速的）+ er → 鼓励，促进 例 In attempting to reconcile estranged spouses, counselors try to *foster* a spirit of compromise rather than one of stubborn implacability.

□ customary　　□ tangle　　□ subvert　　□ settled　　□ charlatan　　□ disorganize
□ sculptural　　□ disparate　　□ bestow　　□ dorsal　　□ imminent　　□ pharmaceutical
□ untamed　　□ negligibly　　□ foster

commentator [ˈkɑːmənteɪtər]	*n.* 评论员(one who gives a commentary)
saturate [ˈsætʃəreɪt]	*v.* 浸湿, 浸透(to imbue or impregnate thoroughly); 使大量吸收或充满(to soak, fill, or load to capacity completely) 记 词根记忆: sat(足够) + urate → 使足够 → 使大量吸收或充满
brink [brɪŋk]	*n.* (峭壁的)边沿, 边缘(the edge of a steep place; verge; border) 记 比较记忆: blink(*v.* 眨眼睛)
atrocity [əˈtrɑːsəti]	*n.* 邪恶(state of being atrocious); 暴行(an atrocious act)
unpalatable [ʌnˈpælətəbl]	*adj.* 味道差的, 不好吃的(not palatable; unpleasant to taste); 令人不快的(unpleasant and difficult for the mind to accept) 记 联想记忆: un(不) + palatable(合意的) → 令人不快的 例 Animals that have tasted *unpalatable* plants tend to recognize them afterward on the basis of their most conspicuous features, such as their flowers.
brilliant [ˈbrɪliənt]	*adj.* 卓越的, 出众的(striking distinctive); 辉煌的, 壮丽的(glorious; magnificent) 记 词根记忆: brilli(发光) + ant(…的) → 发光的 → 辉煌的 搭 a brilliant painter 一位杰出的画家
bacterium [bækˈtɪriəm]	*n.* 细菌(any of a domain of prokaryotic round, spiral- or rod-shaped single celled microorganisms)
mortify [ˈmɔːrtɪfaɪ]	*v.* 使丢脸, 侮辱(to cause to experience humiliation and chagrin) 记 词根记忆: mort(死) + ify → 让人想死 → 使丢脸, 侮辱
contentious [kənˈtenʃəs]	*adj.* 好争吵的(argumentative; belligerent); 有争议的(controversial) 搭 a contentious issue 有争议的问题
flexible [ˈfleksəbl]	*adj.* 易弯曲的(easily bent); 灵活的(adjustable to change) 记 词根记忆: flex(弯曲) + ible(能…的) → 易弯曲的
nebulous [ˈnebjələs]	*adj.* 模糊的(hazy; indistinct; vague); 云状的(cloudlike) 记 词根记忆: neb(云, 雾) + bl + ous → 云状的
hale [heɪl]	*adj.* 健壮的, 矍铄的(free from defect, disease, or infirmity sound; healthy) 记 词根记忆: hal(呼吸) + e → 呼吸得很好的 → 精神矍铄的
deliberation [dɪˌlɪbəˈreɪʃn]	*n.* 细想, 考虑(the act of deliberating) 同 cogitation, consideration, speculation
renounce [rɪˈnaʊns]	*v.* 声明放弃(to give up or resign by formal declaration); 拒绝, 否认(to refuse to follow, obey, or recognize any further) 记 词根记忆: re(重新) + nounc(讲话, 通告) + e → 重新宣布 → 声明放弃
reciprocation [rɪˌsɪprəˈkeɪʃn]	*n.* 互换(a mutual exchange); 报答(a return in kind or of like value); 往复运动(an alternating motion) 搭 reciprocation of …的回报

11

□ commentator □ saturate □ brink ■ atrocity □ unpalatable □ brilliant
□ bacterium □ mortify □ contentious ■ flexible □ nebulous □ hale
□ deliberation □ renounce □ reciprocation

125

crimson [ˈkrɪmzn]	*n.* 绯红色（any of several deep purplish reds）*adj.* 绯红色的（of the color crimson）*v.* （使）变得绯红（to make crimson；to become crimson）
reimburse [ˌriːɪmˈbɜːrs]	*v.* 偿还（to pay back to sb.；repay） 记 词根记忆：re + im(进入) + burse(钱包) → 重新进入钱包 → 偿还
conventional [kənˈvenʃənl]	*adj.* 因循守旧的，传统的（based on convention） 记 来自 convention(*n.* 习俗，惯例） 同 orthodox
squander [ˈskwɑːndər]	*v.* 浪费，挥霍（to spend extravagantly） 记 源自方言，因莎士比亚在《威尼斯商人》一剧中使用而广泛流传
billion [ˈbɪljən]	*num.* 十亿（one thousand million）
surmise	[ˈsɜːrmaɪz] *n.* 推测，猜测（conjecture） [sərˈmaɪz] *v.* 推测，猜测（to infer on slight ground） 记 词根记忆：sur(在…下) + mise(放) → 放下想法 → 推测，猜测
jumble [ˈdʒʌmbl]	*v.* 使混乱，混杂（to mix in disorder）*n.* 混杂，杂乱（a disorderly mixture） 记 联想记忆：jum(看作 jump，跳) + ble → 上蹿下跳，群魔乱舞 → 混杂
ascetic [əˈsetɪk]	*adj.* 禁欲的 （self-denying）*n.* 苦行者 （anyone who lives with strict self-discipline） 记 来自希腊文，原意是"刻苦锻炼并隐居的人" 同 astringent, austere, mortified, severe, stern
cabinet [ˈkæbɪnət]	*n.* 橱柜（a case or cupboard usu. having doors and shelves）；内阁（group of the most important government ministers）
revitalize [ˌriːˈvaɪtəlaɪz]	*v.* 使重新充满活力 （to give new life or vigor to；rejuvenate） 记 词根记忆：re(反) + vital(有活力的) + ize(使) → 使重新有活力 复活吧 revitalize
coloration [ˌkʌləˈreɪʃn]	*n.* 着色法，染色法 （the method of dyeing）；颜色，色泽（color） 记 来自 color(*n.* 颜色）

音频

prohibit [proʊˈhɪbɪt]	*v.* 禁止(to forbid by authority)；阻止(to prevent from doing sth.) 记 词根记忆：pro(提前) + hibit(拿住) → 提前拿住 → 禁止；阻止 同 inhibit, interdict
distant [ˈdɪstənt]	*adj.* 疏远的，冷淡的(reserved or aloof in personal relationship) 记 词根记忆：dis(分开) + tant → 分开了的 → 疏远的 同 insociable, unsociable
tyrant [ˈtaɪrənt]	*n.* 暴君(a ruler who exercises absolute power oppressively or brutally) 同 autocrat, despot
terrorize [ˈterəraɪz]	*v.* 恐吓(to fill with terror or anxiety) 同 intimidate, menace, threaten
intentional [ɪnˈtenʃənl]	*adj.* 存心的，故意的(on purpose) 同 deliberate, intended, purposeful, willful
profuse [prəˈfjuːs]	*adj.* 丰富的(bountiful)；浪费的(extravagant) 记 词根记忆：pro(许多) + fus(流) + e → 多得向外流 → 丰富的
tempting [ˈtemptɪŋ]	*adj.* 诱惑人的(having an appeal) 同 alluring, attractive, enticing, inviting, seductive
inadvertent [ˌɪnədˈvɜːrtənt]	*adj.* 疏忽的 (not focusing the mind on a matter)；不经意的，无心的 (unintentional) 例 Professional photographers generally regard *inadvertent* surrealism in a photograph as a curse rather than a blessing; magazine photographers, in particular, consider themselves fortunate to the extent that they can minimize its presence in their photographs.
recount [rɪˈkaʊnt]	*v.* 叙述，描写(to relate in detail; narrate)
theatrical [θiˈætrɪkl]	*adj.* 戏剧的，戏剧性的(of or relating to the theater or the presentation of plays; dramatic) 例 Crowther maintained that the current revival was the most fatuous and inane production of the entire *theatrical* season.
populous [ˈpɑːpjələs]	*adj.* 人口稠密的(densely populated) 记 词根记忆：popul(人) + ous(多…的) → 人口稠密的

□ prohibit	□ distant	□ tyrant	□ terrorize	□ intentional	□ profuse
□ tempting	□ inadvertent	□ recount	□ theatrical	□ populous	

skew [skjuː]	*adj.* 不直的，歪斜的（running obliquely; slanting） 同 crooked
pliant ['plaɪənt]	*adj.* 易受影响的（easily influenced）；易弯的（pliable） 同 malleable
impertinent [ɪm'pɜːrtnənt]	*adj.* 不切题的（irrelevant）；无礼的，莽撞的（exceeding the limits of propriety or good manners）
byproduct ['baɪˌprɑːdʌkt]	*n.* 副产品；副作用（side effect） 记 词根记忆：by（在旁边；副的）+ product（产品）→ 副产品
virtuoso [ˌvɜːrtʃu'oʊsoʊ]	*n.* 艺术大师（a person who has great skill at some endeavor） 例 The sage, by definition, possesses wisdom; the *virtuoso*, by definition, possesses expertise.
dismember [dɪs'membər]	*v.* 肢解（to cut off or disjoin the limbs, members, or parts of）；分割（to break up or tear into pieces）
strive [straɪv]	*v.* 奋斗，努力（to struggle hard; make a great effort） 记 联想记忆：st（看作 stress，压力）+ rive（看作 drive，动力）→ 奋斗的过程需要压力和动力 → 奋斗，努力
rancid ['rænsɪd]	*adj.* 不新鲜的，变味的（rank; stinking） 记 联想记忆：ran（跑）+cid（看作 acid，酸）→ 变酸了 → 不新鲜的，变味的
temporal ['tempərəl]	*adj.* 时间的（relating to time）；世俗的（relating to earthly things） 记 词根记忆：tempor（时间）+ al → 时间的
antiquated ['æntɪkweɪtɪd]	*adj.* 陈旧的，过时的（outmoded or discredited by reason of age）；年老的（advanced in age） 搭 antiquated idea 过时的想法 同 antique, archaic, dated
covet ['kʌvət]	*v.* 贪求，妄想（to want ardently） 记 联想记忆：covert 去掉一个 r 变成 covet，由秘密变成公开的贪求
tenable ['tenəbl]	*adj.* 站得住脚的，合理的（defensible, reasonable） 记 词根记忆：ten（拿住）+ able（能…的）→ 能够拿住的 → 站得住脚的
belittle [bɪ'lɪtl]	*v.* 轻视，贬低（to speak slightingly of） 记 联想记忆：be + little（小）→ 把（人）看小 → 轻视
compassion [kəm'pæʃn]	*n.* 同情，怜悯（sorrow for the sufferings or trouble of others） 记 词根记忆：com + pass（感情）+ ion → 共同的感情 → 同情
fortuitous [fɔːr'tuːɪtəs]	*adj.* 偶然发生的，偶然的（happening by chance; accidental）；幸运的（lucky） 记 词根记忆：fortu（看作 fortune，运气）+ itous → 运气的 → 偶然发生的 例 Although he had spent many hours at the computer trying to solve the problem, he was the first to admit that the final solution was *fortuitous* and not the result of his labor. 同 casual, contingent, incidental

□ skew	□ pliant	□ impertinent	□ byproduct	□ virtuoso	□ dismember
□ strive	□ rancid	□ temporal	□ antiquated	□ covet	□ tenable
□ belittle	□ compassion	□ fortuitous			

glance [glæns]	*v.* 瞥见(to take a quick look at) *n.* 一瞥 搭 at first glance 乍一看
solicitude [sə'lɪsɪtuːd]	*n.* 关怀，牵挂(anxious, kind, or eager care) 搭 solicitude for... 对…的关怀/牵挂
ill-will [ɪl'wɪl]	*n.* 敌意，仇视，恶感(enmity) 同 malice
flamboyant [flæm'bɔɪənt]	*adj.* 艳丽的，显眼的，炫耀的(too showy or ornate; florid; extravagant) 记 联想记忆: flam(火) + boy(男孩) + ant(蚂蚁) → 男孩和蚂蚁高举火把 → 显眼的 例 Thomas Paine, whose political writing was often *flamboyant*, was in private life a surprisingly simple man: he lived in rented rooms, ate little, and wore drab clothes.
cast [kæst]	*n.* 演员阵容；剧团(troupe) *v.* 扔(to throw)；铸造(to give a shape to (a substance) by pouring in liquid into a mold)
obsessed [əb'sest]	*adj.* 着迷的，沉迷的(considering sb. or sth. as so important that you are always thinking about them) 记 来自 obsess(*v.* 迷住；困扰)
whimsical ['wɪmzɪkl]	*adj.* 古怪的，异想天开的(exhibiting whims) 同 capricious, impulsive
gouge [gaʊdʒ]	*v.* 挖出(to scoop out)；敲竹杠(to cheat out of money) *n.* 半圆凿(a semicircular chisel) 记 不要和 gauge(*n.* 准则，规范)相混
jocular ['dʒɑːkjələr]	*adj.* 滑稽的，幽默的(characterized by jesting; humorous)；爱开玩笑的(given to jesting; playful) 记 词根记忆: joc(=joke 笑话) + ular → 爱开玩笑的
reticent ['retɪsnt]	*adj.* 沉默寡言的(inclined to be silent; reserved) 记 词根记忆: re + tic(=silent 安静) + ent → 安静的 → 沉默寡言的 例 Though extremely *reticent* about his own plans, the man allowed his associates no such privacy and was constantly soliciting information about what they intended to do next. 同 taciturn, uncommunicative
doctrine ['dɑːktrɪn]	*n.* 教义，教条，主义，学说(a set of beliefs held by a church, political party, group of scientists, etc.) 记 词根记忆: doc(教导) + trine → 教义
ascent [ə'sent]	*n.* 上升，攀登(the act of rising or mounting upward)；上坡路(an upward slope or rising grade)；提高，提升(an advance in social status or reputation)
discernible [dɪ'sənəbl]	*adj.* 可识别的，可辨的(being recognized or identified) 记 联想记忆: discern(洞悉，辨别) + ible(可…的) → 可识别的，可辨的 例 Many of the earliest colonial houses that are still standing have been so modified and enlarged that the initial design is no longer *discernible*.

12

unwieldy	*adj.* 难控制的; 笨重的(not easily managed or used; cumbersome)
[ʌnˈwiːldi]	记 联想记忆: un(不) + wieldy(支配的, 控制的) → 不可控制的 → 难控制的
coterie	*n.* (有共同兴趣的)小团体(a close circle of friends who share a common
[ˈkoʊtəri]	interest or background; clique)
	记 来自 cote(小屋, 笼) + rie → 一个屋子里的人 → 小团体
optimism	*n.* 乐观主义(a tendency to expect the best possible outcome or dwell on
[ˈɑːptɪmɪzəm]	the most hopeful aspects of a situation)
	记 词根记忆: optim(最好的) + ism → 什么都往最好的一面想 → 乐观主义
	例 While the delegate clearly sought to dampen the *optimism* that has
	emerged recently, she stopped short of suggesting that the conference
	was near collapse and might produce nothing of significance.
formidable	*adj.* 令人畏惧的, 可怕的(causing fear or dread); 难以克服的(hard to
[ˈfɔːrmɪdəbl]	handle or overcome)
	例 Even though *formidable* winters are the norm in the Dakotas, many
	people were unprepared for the ferocity of the blizzard of 1888.
burdensome	*adj.* 繁重的, 劳累的(imposing or constituting a burden)
[ˈbɜːrdnsəm]	记 来自 burden(*n.* 负担, 重担)
decimate	*v.* 毁掉大部分; 大量杀死(to destroy or kill a large part)
[ˈdesɪmeɪt]	记 词根记忆: decim(十分之一) + ate → 杀…的十分之一 → 大量杀死
seriousness	*n.* 认真, 严肃; 严重性, 严峻
[ˈsɪriəsnəs]	例 The *seriousness* of the drought could only be understood by those
	who had seen the wilted crops in the fields.
fascinate	*v.* 迷惑, 迷住(to charm; captivate; attract)
[ˈfæsɪneɪt]	记 词根记忆: fas(说话) + cin + ate → 巫婆通过说话把人迷住 → 迷住
embellish	*v.* 装饰, 美化(to make beautiful with ornamentation; decorate)
[ɪmˈbelɪʃ]	记 词根记忆: em + bell(美的) + ish → 使…美丽 → 装饰, 美化
strip	*v.* 剥去(to remove clothing on covering from) *n.* 狭长的一片(a long
[strɪp]	narrow piece)
	记 联想记忆: s(音似: 死) + trip(旅行) → 死亡剥夺了人在世间的时间之旅
	→ 剥去
	同 denude, disrobe
apropos	*adj./adv.* 适当的(地)(seasonabl(y)); 有关(with reference to; regarding)
[ˌæprəˈpoʊ]	记 联想记忆: a+prop(看作 proper, 适当的) + os → 适当的(地)
taxing	*adj.* 繁重的(burdensome)
[ˈtæksɪŋ]	记 来自 tax(*v.* 向…征税; 使负重担)
perfidious	*adj.* 不忠的, 背信弃义的(faithless)
[pərˈfɪdiəs]	记 词根记忆: per(假装) + fid(相信) + ious → 不相信的 → 不忠的, 背信
	弃义的
eviscerate	*v.* 取出内脏(to remove the viscera from; disembowel); 除去主要部分(to
[ɪˈvɪsəreɪt]	deprive of vital content or force)
	记 联想记忆: e + viscera(内脏) + te → 取出内脏

□ unwieldy	□ coterie	□ optimism	□ formidable	□ burdensome	□ decimate
□ seriousness	□ fascinate	□ embellish	□ strip	□ apropos	□ taxing
□ perfidious	□ eviscerate				

congruent [ˈkɑːŋgruənt]	*adj.* 全等的，一致的(having identical shape and size) 记 词根记忆：con + gru(=gree 一致) + ent → 全等的，一致的
compelling [kəmˈpelɪŋ]	*adj.* 引起兴趣的(keenly interesting；captivating) 搭 a compelling subject 感兴趣的学科
brusqueness [ˈbrʌsknəs]	*n.* 唐突(abruptness)；直率(candor) 记 来自 brusque(*adj.* 寡言而无礼的)
commensurate [kəˈmenʃərət]	*adj.* 同样大小的(equal in measure)；相称的(proportionate) 记 词根记忆：com(共同) + mensur(测量) + ate → 测量结果相同 → 同样大小的 搭 be commensurate with 与…相称
contemplation [ˌkɑːntəmˈpleɪʃn]	*n.* 注视；凝视(an act of considering with attention)；意图；期望(intention；expectation)
insider [ɪnˈsaɪdər]	*n.* 局内人，圈内人(a person inside a given place or group) 例 Though dealers insist that professional art dealers can make money in the art market, even an *insider*'s knowledge is not enough: the art world is so fickle that stock-market prices are predictable by comparison.
eccentric [ɪkˈsentrɪk]	*adj.* 古怪的，反常的(deviating from the norm；unconventional)；(指圆形)没有共同圆心的 *n.* 古怪的人(an eccentric person) 记 词根记忆：ec(出) + centr(中心) + ic → 离开中心 → 古怪的 例 In Germany her startling powers as a novelist are widely admired, but she is almost unknown in the English-speaking world because of the difficulties of translating her *eccentric* prose.
imperative [ɪmˈperətɪv]	*adj.* 紧急的(urgent；pressing) 记 词根记忆：imper(命令) + ative → 命令的，紧急的 → 紧急的 例 Although strong legal remedies for nonpayment of child support are available, the delay and expense associated with these remedies make it *imperative* to develop other options. 同 exigent, importunate
exalted [ɪgˈzɔːltɪd]	*adj.* 崇高的，高贵的(having a very high rank and being highly respected) 记 词根记忆：ex + alt(高的) + ed → 崇高的
exhale [eksˈheɪl]	*v.* 呼出(to breathe out)；呼气；散发 记 词根记忆：ex(出) + hale(呼吸) → 呼出
munificence [mjuːˈnɪfɪsns]	*n.* 慷慨给予，宽宏大量(generosity) 记 词根记忆：muni(公共) + fic(做) + ence → 为公共着想 → 慷慨给予，宽宏大量 同 largess, liberality, magnanimity, openhandedness
delight [dɪˈlaɪt]	*n.* 快乐，高兴，乐事(joy, sth. that gives great pleasure) *v.* 使高兴，使欣喜(to take great pleasure) 记 联想记忆：de(向下) + light(阳光) → 沐浴在阳光下 → 使高兴 同 exult, jubilate

□ congruent □ compelling □ brusqueness □ commensurate □ contemplation □ insider
□ eccentric □ imperative □ exalted □ exhale □ munificence □ delight

131

ascribe [əˈskraɪb]	*v.* 归因于，归咎于（to consider sth. to be caused by） 记 词根记忆：a + scribe(写) → 把(错误原因)写上去 → 归因于，归咎于
inherently [ɪnˈhɪrəntli]	*adv.* 固有地，天性地（intrinsically） 例 Although scientists claim that the seemingly literal language of their reports is more precise than the figurative language of fiction, the language of science, like all language, is *inherently* allusive.
recapitulate [ˌriːkəˈpɪtʃuleɪt]	*v.* 扼要重述（to repeat the principal points; summarize） 记 词根记忆：re(重新) + capit(头) + ulate → 将核心(即"头")重新讲述一遍 → 扼要重述
eulogistic [ˌjuːləˈdʒɪstɪk]	*adj.* 颂扬的，歌功颂德的（praising highly; laudatory） 记 词根记忆：eu(好的) + log(说) + istic → 说好话的 → 颂扬的
thrive [θraɪv]	*v.* 茁壮成长；繁荣，兴旺（to prosper; flourish） 记 联想记忆：th + rive(看作 river, 河) →《清明上河图》描绘了北宋时期汴京的繁荣景象 → 繁荣，兴旺
strenuous [ˈstrenjuəs]	*adj.* 奋发的（vigorously active）；热烈的（fervent, zealous） 同 earnest, energetic, spirited
iconoclastic [aɪˌkɑːnəˈklæstɪk]	*adj.* 偶像破坏的，打破旧习的 搭 iconoclastic ideas 打破旧习的思想
nocturnal [nɑːkˈtɜːrnl]	*adj.* 夜晚的，夜间发生的（of, relating to, or happening in the night） 记 词根记忆：noct(夜) + urnal → 夜晚的
hilarity [hɪˈlærəti]	*n.* 欢闹，狂欢（boisterous and high-spirited merriment or laughter） 同 glee, jocularity, jocundity, jollity, mirth
impermissible [ˌɪmpɜːrˈmɪsəbl]	*adj.* 不容许的（not permissible） 搭 impermissible behavior 越轨行为
buoyant [ˈbuːjənt]	*adj.* 有浮力的（showing buoyancy）；快乐的（cheerful）
synoptic [sɪˈnɑːptɪk]	*adj.* 摘要的（affording a general view of a whole） 例 The sheer bulk of data from the mass media seems to overpower us and drive us to *synoptic* accounts for an easily and readily digestible portion of news.
infiltrate [ˈɪnfɪltreɪt]	*v.* 渗透，渗入（to pass through） 记 词根记忆：in(进入) + filtr(过滤) + ate → 过滤进去 → 渗透，渗入
instantly [ˈɪnstəntli]	*adv.* 立即，即刻（with importunity）*conj.* 一…就（as soon as） 记 directly, forthwith, immediately
misapprehension [ˌmɪsæprɪˈhenʃn]	*n.* 误会，误解（misunderstanding） 同 misconception, misinterpretation
prescient [ˈpresiənt]	*adj.* 有先见的，预知的（knowing or appearing to know about things before they happen） 例 Famed athlete Bobby Orr was given his first pair of skates by a *prescient* Canadian woman who somehow "knew" he would use them to attain sporting greatness.

shortrange [ˌʃɔːrt ˈreɪndʒ]	*adj.* 近程的(relating to or fit for short distances) 搭 shortrange missles 短程导弹
spectrum [ˈspektrəm]	*n.* 光谱；范围(a continuous sequence or range) 记 词根记忆：spectr(看) + um → 看到颜色的范围 → 光谱
incoherent [ˌɪnkoʊ ˈhɪrənt]	*adj.* 不连贯的(lacking coherence)；语无伦次的
unbridgeable [ʌn ˈbrɪdʒəbl]	*adj.* 不能架桥的，不能逾越的(impossible to span)
imperturbable [ˌɪmpər ˈtɜːrbəbl]	*adj.* 冷静的，沉着的(unshakably calm and collected) 记 联想记忆：im(不) + perturb(打扰) + able → 不能被打扰的 → 冷静的，沉着的 例 During the Battle of Trafalgar, Admiral Nelson remained *imperturbable* and in full command of the situation in spite of the hysteria and panic all around him. 同 cool, disimpassioned, unflappable, unruffled
eventual [ɪ ˈventʃuəl]	*adj.* 最终的(ultimately resulting) 同 final, last, terminal
cacophonous [kə ˈkɑːfənəs]	*adj.* 发音不和谐的，不协调的(marked by cacophony) 记 词根记忆：caco(不好的) + phon(声音) + ous → 发音不和谐的
shoal [ʃoʊl]	*n.* 浅滩，浅水处(a sandbank where the water is shallow)；一群(鱼等) *adj.* 浅的，薄的(shallow) 记 联想记忆：形似拼音 shao，水少的地方 → 浅滩，浅水处
hostility [hɑː ˈstɪləti]	*n.* 敌意，敌对状态(enmity) 例 He had expected gratitude for his disclosure, but instead he encountered indifference bordering on *hostility*.
evanescent [ˌevə ˈnesnt]	*adj.* 易消失的，短暂的(vanishing；ephemeral；transient) 记 词根记忆：e + van(空) + escent(开始…的) → 一出现就空了的 → 短暂的
reinstate [ˌriːɪn ˈsteɪt]	*v.* (使)恢复(原来的地位或职位)(to restore to a previous effective state or position) 记 词根记忆：re(重新) + in(进入) + state(状态) → 重新进入原来的状态 → 恢复
quaint [kweɪnt]	*adj.* 离奇有趣的(unusual and attractive)；古色古香的 记 联想记忆：和 paint(*n.* 油漆)一起记；paint to become quaint(漆上油漆变得离奇有趣)
artless [ˈɑːrtləs]	*adj.* 朴实的，自然的(without artificiality；natural)；粗俗的(uncultured；ignorant)
vogue [voʊɡ]	*n.* 时尚，流行(popular acceptation or favor)

12

identifiable [aɪˌdentɪ ˈfaɪəbl]	*adj.* 可辨认的(acknowledgeable)
	例 Longdale and Stern discovered that mitochondria and chloroplasts share a long, *identifiable* sequence of DNA; such a coincidence could be explained only by the transfer of DNA between the two systems.
underrepresented [ˌʌndəˌreprɪ ˈzentɪd]	*adj.* 未被充分代表的(inadequately represented)
	例 Despite the growing prominence of Hispanic actors in the American theater, many Hispanic experts feel that the Spanish-speaking population is *underrepresented* on the stage.
apply [ə ˈplaɪ]	*v.* 应用(to put to use);适用(to have relevance or a valid connection)
	记 和supply(*v.* 提供)一起记
	搭 apply to 适用于
	同 bestow, employ, exploit, handle, utilize
cite [saɪt]	*v.* 引用,引述(to speak or write words taken from a passage)
	记 词根记忆:cit(引用;唤起) + e → 引用,引述
fast [fæst]	*n.* 禁食,斋戒(the practice of very) *adv.* 很快地;紧紧地;深沉地
discourage [dɪs ˈkɜːrɪdʒ]	*v.* 使气馁,使沮丧(to deprive of courage or confidence);阻碍(to dissuade or attempt to dissuade from doing sth.)
	记 联想记忆:dis(消失) + courage(精神) → 使精神消失 → 使沮丧
somber [ˈsɑːmbər]	*adj.* 忧郁的(melancholy);阴暗的(dark and gloomy)
	同 dim, grave, shadowy, shady
bootless [ˈbuːtlɪs]	*adj.* 无益处的(without advantage or benefit);无用的(useless)
	同 futile, otiose, unavailing
bastion [ˈbæstiən]	*n.* 堡垒,防御工事(a projecting part of a fortification)
politically [pə ˈlɪtɪkli]	*adv.* 政治上
	记 来自political(*adj.* 政治的;政治性的)
resign [rɪ ˈzaɪn]	*v.* 委托(to consign);放弃(to give up deliberately);辞职(to quit)
	记 联想记忆:re(不) + sign(签名) → 不签名 → 放弃
	同 abandon, cede, relinquish, surrender
rarefy [ˈrerəfaɪ]	*v.* 使稀少,使稀薄(to make rare, thin, porous, or less dense)
	同 attenuate, dilute
flaunt [flɔːnt]	*v.* 炫耀,夸耀(to display or obtrude oneself to public notice)
	记 联想记忆:fl(看作fly,飞) + aunt(姑姑) → 姑姑到处飞 → 炫耀
	例 Fortunately, she was deprecatory about her accomplishments, properly unwilling to *flaunt* them before her friends.
	同 flash, parade, show off

134
□ identifiable □ underrepresented □ apply □ cite □ fast □ discourage
□ somber □ bootless □ bastion □ politically □ resign □ rarefy
□ flaunt

hover [ˈhʌvər]	*v.* 翱翔(to remain fluttering in the air); (人)徘徊 (to linger near a place) 记 联想记忆：爱人（lover）在自己身边徘徊 （hover）
defy [dɪˈfaɪ]	*v.* 违抗，藐视(to refuse to respect sb. as an authority) 例 Hundreds of people today *defied* the ban on political gatherings.
diehard [ˈdaɪhɑːrd]	*n.* 顽固分子(a fanatically determined person) 记 组合词：die(死) + hard(硬的) → 死硬（分子）→ 顽固分子
perception [pərˈsepʃn]	*n.* 感知，知觉(the process, act, or faculty of perceiving); 洞察力(quick, acute, and intuitive cognition) 记 来自percept(*n.* 感知；感知对象)
sanguine [ˈsæŋgwɪn]	*adj.* 乐观的 (cheerful and confident; optimistic); 红润的 (of a healthy reddish color) 记 词根记忆：sangui(血) + ne → 有血色的 → 红润的
blithe [blaɪð]	*adj.* 快乐的, 无忧无虑的(cheerful; carefree)
credible [ˈkredəbl]	*adj.* 可信的, 可靠的(offering reasonable grounds for being believed) 记 词根记忆：cred(相信) + ible(能…的) → 可靠的 同 authentic, convincing, creditable, trustworthy, trusty
congruity [kənˈgruɪti]	*n.* 一致性, 适合性(the quality or state of being congruent or congruous); 共同点(a point of agreement)
negligible [ˈneglɪdʒəbl]	*adj.* 可以忽略的, 微不足道的(so small or unimportant or of so little consequence as to warrant little or no attention; trifling) 例 Because the damage to his car had been *negligible*, Michael decided he wouldn't bother to report the matter to his insurance company.
absurd [əbˈsɜːrd]	*adj.* 荒谬的, 可笑的 (ridiculously unreasonable; ludicrous) 记 词根记忆：ab + surd (不合理的) → 不合理的 → 荒谬的 搭 absurd assumptions 荒谬的推断
criss-cross [ˈkrɪs krɔːs]	*v.* 交叉往来(to go or pass back and forth) 例 The city is *criss-crossed* with canals.
frequency [ˈfriːkwənsi]	*n.* 频率(rate of occurrence or repetition of sth.) 记 来自frequent(*adj.* 频繁的)
morose [məˈroʊs]	*adj.* 郁闷的(sullen or gloomy) 记 联想记忆：mo(音似"没") + rose(玫瑰) → 情人节没收到玫瑰，不高兴 了 → 郁闷的
persuasive [pərˈsweɪsɪv]	*adj.* 易使人信服的, 有说服力的(tending or having the power to persuade)

□ hover	□ defy	□ diehard	□ perception	□ sanguine	□ blithe
□ credible	□ congruity	□ negligible	□ absurd	□ criss-cross	□ frequency
□ morose	□ persuasive				

spurious [ˈspjʊriəs]	*adj.* 假的(false)；伪造的(falsified; forged) 记 来自 spuria(*n.* 伪造的作品) 例 Lovejoy, the hero of Jonathan Gash's mystery novels, is an antique dealer who gives the reader advice on how to tell *spurious* antiques from the real thing. 同 artificial, counterfeit, dummy, ersatz, pseudo
prudent [ˈpruːdnt]	*adj.* 审慎的(acting with or showing care and foresight)，精明的(showing good judgement)；节俭的，精打细算的(frugal) 记 词根记忆：prud(小心的) + ent → 审慎的 例 It was a war the queen and her more *prudent* counselors wished to avoid if they could and were determined in any event to postpone as long as possible. 同 judicious, sage, sane
empiricism [ɪmˈpɪrɪsɪzəm]	*n.* 经验主义(the practice of relying on observation and experiment) 记 来自 empiric(*n.* 经验主义者)
soothe [suːð]	*v.* 抚慰(to comfort or calm)；减轻(to make less painful) 记 来自 sooth(*adj.* 抚慰的) 同 allay, becalm, lull, tranquilize
sedative [ˈsedətɪv]	*adj.* (药物)镇静的(tending to calm excitement) *n.* 镇静剂 同 calming, relaxing, soothing; tranquillizer
pronounced [prəˈnaʊnst]	*adj.* 显著的，明确的(strongly marked) 记 来自 pronounce(*v.* 宣称，宣布)
irrational [ɪˈræʃənl]	*adj.* 不理智的(not endowed with reason or understanding)；失去理性的，不合理的(not governed by or according to reason) 例 In the seventeenth century, direct flouting of a generally accepted system of values was regarded as *irrational*, even as a sign of madness. 同 fallacious, illogical, unreasoned
sanctimonious [ˌsæŋktɪˈmoʊniəs]	*adj.* 假装虔诚的(hypocritically pious or devout) 搭 sanctimonious preaching 伪善的讲道
bland [blænd]	*adj.* (人)情绪平稳的(pleasantly smooth)；(食物)无味的(insipid) 记 发音记忆："布蓝的" → 布是清淡的蓝色的 → 无味的
span [spæn]	*n.* 跨度；两个界限间的距离(a stretch between two limits) 同 extent, length, reach, spread
plethora [ˈpleθərə]	*n.* 过多，过剩(excess; superfluity) 记 词根记忆：plet(满的) + hora → 满满的 → 过多，过剩 例 At the present time, we are suffering from a *plethora* of stories about the war. 同 overabundance, overflow, overmuch, overplus
prospect [ˈprɑːspekt]	*v.* 勘探(to explore) *n.* 期望(reasonable hope that sth. will happen)；前景(sth. which is possible or likely for the future)

ruin [ˈruːɪn]	n. 废墟；祸根（a cause of destruction）；毁坏 v. 毁坏（to devastate）；毁灭（to damage irreparably）；使破产（to bankrupt） 记 联想记忆：大雨（rain）毁坏了（ruin）庄稼 例 According to poet John Berryman, there were so many ways to *ruin* a poem that it was quite amazing good ones ever got written. 同 demolish, dilapidate, wreck
petulant [ˈpetʃələnt]	adj. 暴躁的，易怒的（insolent；peevish） 记 来自 pet（n. 不高兴，不悦）
spinal [ˈspaɪnl]	adj. 脊骨的，脊髓的（of, relating to, or situated near the spinal column）
intent [ɪnˈtent]	adj. 专心的，专注的（having the attention applied; engrossed）；热切的，渴望的（directed with strained or eager attention; full of eager interest） n. 目的，意向（purpose） 记 来自 intend（v. 打算） 例 The idea that people are basically economic creatures, *intent* only upon their own material advantage, induces disbelief in the integrity of any unselfish motive.
tangential [tænˈdʒenʃl]	adj. 切线的（of the nature of a tangent）；离题的（divergent; digressive） 同 discursive, excursive, rambling
dossier [ˈdɔːsieɪ]	n. 卷宗，档案（a collection of documents and reports） 记 发音记忆："东西压" → 被东西压着的东西 → 堆在一起的档案 → 档案
ulterior [ʌlˈtɪriər]	adj. 较远的，将来的（more distant; further）；隐秘的，别有用心的（going beyond what is openly said or shown and especially what is proper） 记 词根记忆：ult（高，远）+ erior → 较远的 例 He was so convinced that people were driven by *ulterior* motives that he believed there was no such thing as a purely unselfish act.
resurge [rɪˈsɜːrdʒ]	v. 复活（to rise again into life） 记 词根记忆：re（再）+ surg（起来）→ 再次站起来 → 复活
antiseptic [ˌæntiˈseptɪk]	n. 杀菌剂（any substance that inhibit the action of microorganisms） adj. 防腐的（preventing infection or decay） 记 词根记忆：anti（反）+ sept（菌）+ ic → 杀菌剂
squirt [skwɜːrt]	v. 喷出，溅进（to spurt） 搭 squirt...with... 用…喷…
steadiness [ˈstedinəs]	n. 稳健，坚定 同 firmness, stability

12

□ ruin	□ petulant	□ spinal	□ intent	□ tangential	□ dossier
□ ulterior	□ resurge	□ antiseptic	□ squirt	□ steadiness	

137

Word List 13

音频

improvised [ˈɪmprəvaɪzd]	*adj.* 临时准备的，即席而作的(making offhand) 例 The villagers fortified the town hall, hoping this *improvised* bastion could protect them from the guerrilla raids.
photosynthesis [ˌfoʊtoʊˈsɪnθəsɪs]	*n.* 光合作用(synthesis of chemical compounds with the aid of radiant energy and especially light) 记 联想记忆: photo(光) + synthesis(合成) → 光合作用
inflamed [ɪnˈfleɪmd]	*adj.* 发炎的，红肿的(red and swollen because of infection) 记 联想记忆: in(在…里面) + flame(火焰) + d → 像有火焰在里面烧 → 发炎的，红肿的
conciliatory [kənˈsɪliətɔːri]	*adj.* 抚慰的，调和的(intended or likely to conciliate) 记 来自 conciliate(*v.* 调和，安慰)
inedible [ɪnˈedəbl]	*adj.* 不能吃的，不可食的(not fit to be eaten)
smother [ˈsmʌðər]	*v.* 熄灭；覆盖(to cover thickly)；使窒息(to make sb. unable to breathe) 记 联想记忆: s(看作 she) + mother(母亲) → 母亲的爱使她快要窒息 → 使窒息
chip [tʃɪp]	*n.* 薄片，碎片(shard; fragment)；集成电路片
segregate [ˈsegrɪgeɪt]	*v.* 分离，隔离(to separate or set apart from others or from the general mass) 记 词根记忆: seg(切割) + reg + ate → 隔离
universal [ˌjuːnɪˈvɜːrsl]	*adj.* 全体的(including or covering all or a whole collectively or distributively without limit or exception)；普遍的(present or occurring everywhere) 例 If Amelia Earhart's acceptance was by no means *universal*, her fame was unusually widespread and her popularity long-lived. 同 cosmic, cosmopolitan, omnipresent, ubiquitous

□ improvised   □ photosynthesis   □ inflamed   □ conciliatory   □ inedible   □ smother
□ chip   □ segregate   □ universal

igneous [ˈɪgnɪəs]	*adj.* 火的，似火的（having the nature of fire；fiery） 记 词根记忆：ign(点燃) + eous → 火的
nonentity [nɑːˈnentəti]	*n.* 无足轻重的人或事（a person or thing of no importance） 记 联想记忆：non(不) + entity(存在) → 不存在 → 无足轻重的人或事
opposed [əˈpoʊzd]	*adj.* 反对的（set or placed in opposition） 搭 be opposed to 反对…
reportorial [ˌrepərˈtɔːriəl]	*adj.* 记者的；报道的
self-sacrifice [ˌselfˈsækrɪfaɪs]	*n.* 自我牺牲（sacrifice of oneself or one's interest for others or for a cause or ideal）
perpendicular [ˌpɜːrpənˈdɪkjələr]	*adj.* 垂直的，竖直的（exactly upright；vertical） 记 词根记忆：per(彻底) + pend(挂) + icular → 彻底挂着的 → 垂直的
prodigal [ˈprɑːdɪgl]	*adj.* 挥霍的（lavish）*n.* 挥霍者（one who spends lavishly） 记 词根记忆：prodig(巨大，浪费) + al(…的) → 挥霍的 例 Left to endure a penniless old age, the improvident man lived to regret his *prodigal* youth.
potential [pəˈtenʃl]	*adj.* 潜在的，可能的（capable of development into actuality） 记 词根记忆：pot(有力的) + ent + ial → 潜在的，可能的 例 A major goal of law, to deter *potential* criminals by punishing wrongdoers, is not served when the penalty is so seldom invoked that it ceases to be a credible threat. 同 hidden, latent, lurking
ill-paying [ˌɪlˈpeɪɪŋ]	*adj.* 工资低廉的
multicellular [ˌmʌltiˈseljələr]	*adj.* 多细胞的 记 联想记忆：multi(多的) + cellular(细胞的；由细胞组成的) → 多细胞的
cynical [ˈsɪnɪkl]	*adj.* 愤世嫉俗的（captious, peevish, having or showing the attitude or temper of a cynic）
warranted [ˈwɔːrəntɪd]	*adj.* 保证的；担保的 例 Despite many decades of research on the gasification of coal, the data accumulated are not directly applicable to environmental questions; thus a new program of research specifically addressing such questions is *warranted*.
particularity [pərˌtɪkjuˈlærəti]	*n.* 独特性（the quality or state of being particular as distinguished from universal）
circulation [ˌsɜːrkjəˈleɪʃn]	*n.* 循环，流通（going around continuously）；发行量（the average number of copies of a publication sold over a given period）
arboreal [ɑːrˈbɔːriəl]	*adj.* 树木的（of or like a tree） 记 词根记忆：arbor(树) + eal → 树木的

13

resignation [ˌrezɪgˈneɪʃn]	*n.* 听从，顺从（submissiveness）；辞职（a formal notification of resigning） 记 来自 resign（*v.* 放弃；辞职）
mischievous [ˈmɪstʃɪvəs]	*adj.* 淘气的（playfully annoying）；有害的（harmful） 记 联想记忆：mis（坏）+ chiev（看作 achieve，完成，达到）+ ous → 带来坏结果的 → 有害的
recital [rɪˈsaɪtl]	*n.* 独奏会，独唱会，小型舞蹈表演会（a concert given by an individual musician or dancer）；吟诵（the act or process or an instance of reciting） 记 来自 recite（*v.* 背诵）；re + cit（唤起）+ e → 重新引出 → 背诵 例 Halls and audiences for lieder *recitals* tend to be smaller than for opera and thus more conducive to the intimacy and sense of close involvement, which is the *recital's* particular charm.
quiescence [kwiˈesns]	*n.* 静止，沉寂（the quality or state of being quiescent） 同 quietness, stillness, tranquillity
dynamic [daɪˈnæmɪk]	*adj.* 动态的（opposed to static）；有活力的（energetic; vigorous） 记 词根记忆：dynam（力量）+ ic → 有活力的
deficient [dɪˈfɪʃnt]	*adj.* 有缺点的（lacking in some necessary quality or element）；缺少的；不足的（not up to a normal standard or complement） 记 词根记忆：de（变坏）+ fic（做）+ ient → 做得不好的 → 有缺点的；不足的 同 defective, inadequate, insufficient, scant, scarce
dormant [ˈdɔːrmənt]	*adj.* 冬眠的（torpid in winter）；静止的（quiet; still） 记 词根记忆：dorm（睡眠）+ ant → 冬眠的
prerogative [prɪˈrɑːgətɪv]	*n.* 特权（privilege; the discretionary power） 记 词根记忆：pre（预先）+ rog（要求）+ ative → 预先要求的权力 → 特权 例 Wearing the latest fashions was exclusively the *prerogative* of the wealthy until the 1850's, when mass production, aggressive entrepreneurs, and the availability of the sewing machine made them accessible to the middle class. 同 birthright, perquisite
tasteless [ˈteɪstləs]	*adj.* 没味道的（having no taste） 同 bland, flat, flavorless, insipid, unsavory
balm [bɑːm]	*n.* 香油，药膏（any fragrant ointment or aromatic oil）；镇痛剂，安慰物 记 来自 balsam（*n.* 凤仙花；香脂）
aspen [ˈæspən]	*n.* 白杨 记 联想记忆：as + pen（笔）→ 像笔一样直的树木 → 白杨
plumb [plʌm]	*n.* 测深锤，铅锤 *adj.* 垂直的（exactly vertical）*adv.* 精确地（exactly）*v.* 深入了解（to examine minutely and critically）；测量深度（to measure the depth with a plumb）
farce [fɑːrs]	*n.* 闹剧，滑稽剧（an exaggerated comedy）；可笑的行为，荒唐的事情（sth. ridiculous or absurd）
unwitting [ʌnˈwɪtɪŋ]	*adj.* 无意的，不知不觉的（not intended; inadvertent; unaware） 记 联想记忆：un（不）+ witting（知道的，有意的）→ 无意的，不知不觉的

□ resignation	□ mischievous	□ recital	□ quiescence	□ dynamic	□ deficient
□ dormant	□ prerogative	□ tasteless	□ balm	□ aspen	□ plumb
□ farce	□ unwitting				

arbitrary [ˈɑːrbətreri]	*adj.* 专横的，武断的(discretionary; despotic; dictatorial) 记 词根记忆：arbitr(判断) + ary(…的) → 自己作判断 → 武断的 同 autarchic, autocratic, monolithic
audacious [ɔːˈdeɪʃəs]	*adj.* 大胆的(daring; fearless; brave) 记 词根记忆：aud(大胆) + acious(多…的) → 大胆的
efficacious [ˌefɪˈkeɪʃəs]	*adj.* 有效的(producing the desired result) 例 If *efficacious* new medicines have side effects that are commonly observed and unremarkable, such medicines are too often considered safe, even when laboratory tests suggest caution.
infant [ˈɪnfənt]	*n.* 婴儿(a child in the first period of life) 记 联想记忆：in + fant(看作 faint, 虚弱的) → 尚处于无力虚弱的状态 → 婴儿
monolith [ˈmɑːnəlɪθ]	*n.* 单块巨石(a single great stone often in the form of an obelisk or column)；单一的庞大组织(an organized whole that acts as a single unified powerful or influential force) 例 Publishers have discovered that black America is not a *monolith* of attitudes and opinions but a rich mixture lending itself to numerous expressions in print.
applicability [əˌplɪkəˈbɪləti]	*n.* 适用性，适应性 记 来自 apply(*v.* 应用，适用)
disjunctive [dɪsˈdʒʌŋktɪv]	*adj.* 分离的；转折的，反意的(showing opposition or contrast between two ideas) 记 词根记忆：dis(分离) + junct(捆绑) + ive → 分开绑的 → 分离的；转折的
foodstuff [ˈfuːdstʌf]	*n.* 食料，食品(any substance used as food) 记 组合词：food(食物) + stuff(东西) → 食品
exemplar [ɪgˈzemplɑːr]	*n.* 模范，榜样(one that serves as a model or example) 同 ideal
fractious [ˈfrækʃəs]	*adj.* (脾气)易怒的，好争吵的(peevish; irritable) 记 词根记忆：fract(碎裂) + ious(易…的) → 脾气易碎 → (脾气)易怒的
sedimentary [ˌsedɪˈmentri]	*adj.* 沉积的，沉淀性的(of, relating to, or containing sediment) 搭 sedimentary rock 沉积岩
condescending [ˌkɑːndɪˈsendɪŋ]	*adj.* 谦逊的，故意屈尊的(behaving as though one is better or more important than others)
fetid [ˈfetɪd]	*adj.* 有恶臭的(having a heavy offensive smell) 同 foul, noisome, smelly
aggravate [ˈægrəveɪt]	*v.* 加重，恶化(to make worse; intensify)；激怒，使恼火 记 词根记忆：ag + grav(重) + ate → 加重 同 exasperate, irritate, peeve, pique, provoke
cognitive [ˈkɑːgnətɪv]	*adj.* 认知的；感知的(of, relating to, being, or involving conscious intellectual activity) 记 词根记忆：cognit(看作 cognis, 知道) + ive → 认知的

13

idealism [aɪˈdiːəlɪzəm]	*n.* 理想主义(the act or practice of envisioning things in an ideal form); 唯心主义(a theory that only the perceptible is real) 例 In sharp contrast to the intense *idealism* of the young republic, with its utopian faith in democracy and hopes for eternal human progress, recent developments suggest a mood of almost unrelieved cynicism.
devastate [ˈdevəsteɪt]	*v.* 摧毁, 破坏(to ravage; destroy) 记 联想记忆: de(变坏) + vast(大量的) + ate → 大量弄坏 → 破坏 同 depredate, wreck
self-deprecating [ˌself ˈdeprəkeɪtɪŋ]	*adj.* 自贬的(conscious of one's own shortcomings) 例 Egocentric, at times vindictive when he believed his authority was being questioned, White could also be kind, gracious, and even *self-deprecating* when the circumstances seemed to require it.
inexhaustible [ˌɪnɪɡˈzɔːstəbl]	*adj.* 用不完的, 无穷无尽的(incapable of being used up or emptied) 记 联想记忆: in(不) + exhaust(耗尽) + ible → 用不完的 例 The sheer diversity of tropical plants represents a seemingly *inexhaustible* source of raw materials, of which only a few have been utilized.
protozoan [ˌproʊtəˈzoʊən]	*n.* 原生动物 记 词根记忆: proto(起初) + zo(动物) + an → 原生动物
assail [əˈseɪl]	*v.* 质问(to attack with arguments); 攻击(to assault) 记 词根记忆: as + sail(跳上去) → 跳上去打 → 攻击 同 aggress, beset, storm, strike
inviolate [ɪnˈvaɪələt]	*adj.* 不受侵犯的, 未受损害的(not violated or profaned) 记 联想记忆: in(不) + violate(侵犯, 妨碍) → 不受侵犯的
periphery [pəˈrɪfəri]	*n.* 次要部分(the less important part of sth.); 外围, 周围(the outer edge of a particular area); 外表面(the external boundary or surface of a body) 记 词根记忆: peri(周围) + pher(带) + y → 带到周围 → 外围, 周围
recompose [ˌriːkəmˈpoʊz]	*v.* 重写(to compose again); 重新安排
court [kɔːrt]	*n.* 法庭; 宫廷 *v.* 献殷勤(to seek the affections of); 追求(to seek to gain or achieve)
replenish [rɪˈplenɪʃ]	*v.* 补充, 把…再备足(to fill or build up again) 记 词根记忆: re(重新) + plen(满) + ish → 重新填满 → 补充
jubilant [ˈdʒuːbɪlənt]	*adj.* 欢呼的, 喜气洋洋的(elated; exultant) 记 词根记忆: jubil(大叫) + ant → 高兴得大叫的 → 欢呼的
appreciative [əˈpriːʃətɪv]	*adj.* 赞赏的; 感激的(having or showing appreciation) 记 来自 appreciate(*v.* 欣赏, 感激)
dramatic [drəˈmætɪk]	*adj.* 戏剧的 (of or relating to the drama); 引人注目的 (striking in appearance or effect); 戏剧般的(of an opera singer) 记 来自 drama(*n.* 戏剧) 同 dramaturgic, histrionic, theatric, theatrical, thespian

□ idealism	□ devastate	□ self-deprecating	□ inexhaustible	□ protozoan	□ assail
□ inviolate	□ periphery	□ recompose	□ court	□ replenish	□ jubilant
□ appreciative	□ dramatic				

perfume [pər'fjuːm]	*n.* 香味(the scent of sth. sweet-smelling); 香水(a substance that emits a pleasant odor) 记 联想记忆: per(贯穿) + fume(气体) → 缭绕在身上的气体 → 香味 例 His olfactory sense was so highly developed that he was often called in to judge *perfume*. 同 aroma, balm, fragrance, redolence
irascible [ɪ'ræsəbl]	*adj.* 易怒的(easily angered) 记 词根记忆: ira(愤怒) + sc + ible → 易怒的
caustic ['kɔːstɪk]	*adj.* 腐蚀性的(corrosive); 刻薄的(biting; sarcastic) *n.* 腐蚀剂 记 词根记忆: caus(烧灼) + tic → 腐蚀性的 搭 caustic responses 刻薄的反应
abrasive [ə'breɪsɪv]	*adj.* 研磨的(tending to abrade) 记 来自 abrade(*v.* 磨损)
intricacy ['ɪntrɪkəsi]	*n.* 错综复杂(the quality of being intricate) 记 词根记忆: in(在里面) + tric(小障碍物) + acy → 在里面放入很多小障碍物 → 错综复杂
recurrent [rɪ'kɜːrənt]	*adj.* 循环的(running or turning back in a direction opposite to a former course); 一再发生的(returning or happening time after time)
unwarranted [ʌn'wɑːrəntɪd]	*adj.* 没有根据的(unwelcome and done without good reason) 记 联想记忆: un(不) + warranted(有根据的) → 没有根据的
traceable ['treɪsəbl]	*adj.* 可追踪的(capable of being trailed) 记 来自 trace(*v.* 追踪)
acerbic [ə'sɜːrbɪk]	*adj.* 尖酸的; 刻薄的(bitter; sharp; harsh) 记 词根记忆: acerb(尖, 酸) + ic → 尖酸的; 刻薄的
inadvisable [ˌɪnəd'vaɪzəbl]	*adj.* 不明智的, 不妥当的(not wise or prudent) 例 It would be beneficial if someone so radical could be brought to believe that old customs need not necessarily be worthless and that change may possibly be *inadvisable*. 同 impolitic, inexpedient, unadvisable
untenable [ʌn'tenəbl]	*adj.* 难以防守的(not able to be defended); 不能租赁的(not able to be occupied) 例 Upon realizing that his position was *untenable*, the general ordered his men to retreat to a neighboring hill.
convince [kən'vɪns]	*v.* 使某人确信(to make sb. feel certain); 说服(to persuade) 记 词根记忆: con(全部) + vinc(征服, 克服) + e → 彻底征服对方 → 使某人确信
cognizant ['kɑːgnɪzənt]	*adj.* 知道的, 认识的(having knowledge of sth.) 记 词根记忆: co + gn(知道) + izant → 知道的
dissect [dɪ'sekt]	*v.* 解剖(to cut up a dead body); 剖析(to analyze and interpret minutely) 记 词根记忆: dis(分开) + sect(切) → 切开 → 解剖 同 dichotomize, disjoin, disjoint, dissever, separate

13

□ perfume	□ irascible	□ caustic	□ abrasive	□ intricacy	□ recurrent
□ unwarranted	□ traceable	□ acerbic	□ inadvisable	□ untenable	□ convince
□ cognizant	□ dissect				

ranching ['ræntʃɪŋ]	*n.* 大牧场（a large farm for raising horses, beef cattle, or sheep）
harsh [hɑːrʃ]	*adj.* 严厉的（stern）；粗糙的（rough）；刺耳的（sharp） 记 联想记忆：har（看作 hard，坚硬的）+ sh → 态度强硬 → 严厉的 同 rugged, scabrous
exaggerate [ɪɡ'zædʒəreɪt]	*v.* 夸大，夸张（to overstate）；过分强调（to overemphasize；intensify） 记 词根记忆：ex（出）+ ag（表加强）+ ger（搬运）+ ate → 全部运出 → 夸张 同 magnify
poignant ['pɔɪnjənt]	*adj.* 令人痛苦的，伤心的（painfully affecting the feelings）；尖锐的，尖刻的（cutting） 记 词根记忆：poign（刺）+ ant → 用针刺的 → 尖锐的
convex ['kɑːnveks]	*adj.* 凸出的（curving outward） 记 对比：concave（*adj.* 凹的）
unfailing [ʌn'feɪlɪŋ]	*adj.* 无尽的，无穷的（everlasting；inexhaustible）
complacency [kəm'pleɪsnsi]	*n.* 满足，安心（self-satisfaction） 记 词根记忆：com + plac（平静，满足）+ ency → 满足，安心
discriminatory [dɪ'skrɪmɪnətɔːri]	*adj.* 歧视的，差别对待的，偏见的（showing prejudice） 记 来自 discriminate（*v.* 歧视，差别对待）
paraphrase ['pærəfreɪz]	*n.* 释义，解释，改写（a restatement of a text, passage, or work giving the meaning in another form）*v.* 释义，解释，改写（to restate in a paraphrase） 记 词根记忆：para（旁边）+ phras（告诉）+ e → 在旁边说 → 释义，解释
reconcile ['rekənsaɪl]	*v.* 和解，调和（to restore to friendship or harmony） 记 联想记忆：re（再次）+ con（共同）+ cile → 重新回到原来的关系 → 和解 例 In attempting to *reconcile* estranged spouses, counselors try to foster a spirit of compromise rather than one of stubborn implacability. 同 attune, harmonize, reconciliate
unsurpassed [ˌʌnsər'pæst]	*adj.* 未被超越的（unrivalled） 同 unexceeded, unexcelled
climax ['klaɪmæks]	*n.* 顶点，高潮（most significant event or point in time；summit） 记 联想记忆：cli(m)（看作 climb）+ max（最大）→ 爬到最大值 → 顶点
potable ['poʊtəbl]	*adj.* 适于饮用的（suitable for drinking） 记 词根记忆：pot（喝）+ able → 可以喝的 → 适于饮用的
disprove [ˌdɪs'pruːv]	*v.* 证明…有误（to show that sth. is wrong） 记 词根记忆：dis（分离）+ prov（试验）+ e → 经试验后被否定 → 证明…有误

□ ranching	□ harsh	□ exaggerate	□ poignant	□ convex	□ unfailing
□ complacency	□ discriminatory	□ paraphrase	□ reconcile	□ unsurpassed	□ climax
□ potable	□ disprove				

veer	v. 转向，改变(话题等)(to change direction or course)
[vɪr]	同 curve, sheer, slew, slue, swerve
autonomous	adj. 自治的 (marked by autonomy)；自主的 (having the right or power of
[ɔːˈtɑːnəməs]	self-government)
stymie	v. 妨碍，阻挠(to present an obstacle to)
[ˈstaɪmi]	记 原指高尔夫球中的妨碍球
timorous	adj. 胆小的，胆怯的(of timid disposition, fearful)
[ˈtɪmərəs]	记 词根记忆：tim(胆怯) + orous → 胆怯的
conflict	[kənˈflɪkt] v. 斗争，冲突，抵触
	[ˈkɑːnflɪkt] n. 冲突 (a clash between ideas；
	opposition)
	记 词根记忆：con(共同) + flict(打击) → 共同打
	击 → 冲突
	搭 conflict with sb./sth. 与某人/某事有冲突
supercilious	adj. 目中无人的(coolly or patronizingly haughty)
[ˌsuːpərˈsɪliəs]	记 词根记忆：super(超过) + cili(眉毛) + ous → 超过眉毛 → 目中无人的
idiosyncracy	n. 特质
[ˌɪdiːəʊˈsɪŋkrəsi]	搭 innate idiosyncracy 内在特质
florid	adj. 华丽的(highly decorated；showy)；(脸)红润的(rosy；ruddy)
[ˈflɑːrɪd]	记 词根记忆：flor(花) + id → 像花一样的 → 华丽的
slipperiness	n. 滑溜；防滑性
[ˈslɪpərinəs]	
exasperation	n. 激怒，恼怒(the state of being exasperated；the act or an instance of
[ɪɡˌzæspəˈreɪʃn]	exasperating)
promptness	n. 敏捷，迅速；机敏
[ˈprɑːmptnəs]	
salutary	adj. 有益的，有益健康的(promoting or conducive to health)
[ˈsæljəteri]	记 词根记忆：sal(健康) + utary → 有益的，有益健康的
myriad	adj. 许多的，无数的(innumerable)
[ˈmɪriəd]	同 legion, multitudinous, numerous
distinctive	adj. 出众的，有特色的(distinguishing；characteristic or typical)
[dɪˈstɪŋktɪv]	
introspective	adj. 内省的，自省的(characteristic of sb. who is inclined to introspect)
[ˌɪntrəˈspektɪv]	记 来自 introspect(v. 内省，反省)
	例 Unlike many recent interpretations of Beethoven's piano sonatas, the
	recitalist's performance was a delightfully free and *introspective* one；
	nevertheless, it was also, seemingly paradoxically, quite controlled.
incorruptible	adj. 廉洁的，不腐败的(unable to be corrupted morally)
[ˌɪnkəˈrʌptəbl]	记 联想记忆：in(不) + corrupt(变腐败) + ible → 不会腐败的 → 廉洁的

13

agony [ˈægəni]	*n.* 极大的痛苦(very great mental or physical pain) 记 词根记忆: agon(挣扎) + y → 拼命挣扎 → 极大的痛苦; 谐音: "爱过你"
considerable [kənˈsɪdərəbl]	*adj.* 相当多的 (great in amount or size); 重要的; 值得考虑的(worth consideration) 记 来自 consider(*v.* 考虑) 同 respectable, sensible, sizable, consequential, momentous
skimp [skɪmp]	*v.* 节省花费(to give barely sufficient funds for sth.) 搭 be skimp on... 对···吝惜
enthral [ɪnˈθrɔːl]	*v.* 迷惑(to hold spellbound) 记 词根记忆: en(使) + thral(奴隶) → 使成为奴隶 → 迷惑
receptive [rɪˈseptɪv]	*adj.* 善于接受的, 能接纳的(able or inclined to receive) 例 The newborn human infant is not a passive figure, nor an active one, but what might be called an actively *receptive* one, eagerly attentive as it is to sights and sounds.
blindness [ˈblaɪndnəs]	*n.* 失明(loss of sight) 搭 cultural blindness 文化盲目性
constitute [ˈkɑːnstətuːt]	*v.* 组成, 构成(to form a whole); 建立(to establish) 记 词根记忆: con + stitut(建立, 放) + e → 建立 同 compose, comprise, institute
religion [rɪˈlɪdʒən]	*n.* 宗教; 宗教信仰 记 联想记忆: reli(=rely 依赖)+gi(看作 giant, 巨大的) + on → 可以依赖的巨大的力量 → 宗教
dogged [ˈdɔːɡɪd]	*adj.* 顽强的(stubborn; tenacious) 记 联想记忆: dog(狗) + ged → 像狗一样顽强 → 顽强的
reclaim [rɪˈkleɪm]	*v.* 纠正, 改造(to rescue from an undesirable state); 开垦(土地)(to make available for human use by changing natural conditions) 记 词根记忆: re + claim(喊) → 喊回来 → 纠正, 改造
dialect [ˈdaɪəlekt]	*n.* 方言(a form of a language used in a part of a country) 记 词根记忆: dia(对面) + lect(讲) → 对面讲话 → 方言
demobilize [diːˈmoʊbəlaɪz]	*v.* 遣散, 使复员(to discharge from military service) 同 disband
avocational [ˌævoʊˈkeɪʃənl]	*adj.* 副业的, 嗜好的(of or relating to an avocation)
rhapsodic [ræpˈsɑːdɪk]	*adj.* 狂热的, 狂喜的(extravagantly emotional); 狂想曲的(resembling or characteristic of a rhapsody)
definite [ˈdefɪnət]	*adj.* 清楚的, 明确的(clear; not doubtful) 记 来自 define(*v.* 下定义)
vindictive [vɪnˈdɪktɪv]	*adj.* 报复的(vengeful) 例 The Muses are *vindictive* deities: they avenge themselves without mercy on those who weary of their charms.

equitable [ˈekwɪtəbl]	*adj.* 公正的，合理的(dealing fairly) 例 I am seeking an *equitable* solution to this dispute, one that will be fair and acceptable to both sides. 同 dispassionate, impartial, impersonal, nondiscriminatory, objective
discharge [dɪsˈtʃɑːrdʒ]	*v.* 排出，流出(to emit)；释放(to officially allow sb. to leave)；解雇(to dismiss from employment)；履行义务(to carry out duty)；放电(to release electrical energy) 记 联想记忆：dis(离开) + charge(充电) → 放电
hedonist [ˈhiːdənɪst]	*n.* 享乐主义者(believer in hedonism) 记 联想记忆：he(他) + don(看作 done，做) + ist → 他做了自己想做的一切 → 享乐主义者
justify [ˈdʒʌstɪfaɪ]	*v.* 证明…是正当或合理的(to show that sb./sth. is reasonable or just) 记 词根记忆：just(正确的) + ify(使…) → 证明…是正当或合理的 例 The accusations we bring against others should be warnings to ourselves; they should not *justify* complacency and easy judgments on our part concerning our own moral conduct. 同 confirm, corroborate, substantiate, validate, verify
ironic [aɪˈrɑːnɪk]	*adj.* 挖苦的，讽刺的(sarcastic)；出乎意料的(directly opposite to what might be expected) 例 It is *ironic* that a critic of such overwhelming vanity now suffers from a measure of the oblivion to which he was forever consigning others, in the end, all his self-adulation has only worked against him.
domineer [ˌdɑːmɪˈnɪə]	*v.* 压制(to exercise arbitrary or overbearing control; tyrannize over) 同 dominate, predominate, preponderate, prevail, reign
reluctance [rɪˈlʌktəns]	*n.* 勉强，不情愿(the quality or state of being reluctant)
terse [tɜːrs]	*adj.* 简洁的，简明的(concise) 记 联想记忆：诗歌(verse)力求简洁明了(terse)
purchase [ˈpɜːrtʃəs]	*n.* 支点(阻止东西下滑)(a mechanical hold) 记 purchase 作为"购买"之意大家都很熟悉
glossy [ˈɡlɔːsi]	*adj.* 有光泽的，光滑的(having a smooth, shiny appearance) 同 glassy, glistening, lustrous, polished
unlikely [ʌnˈlaɪkli]	*adj.* 不太可能的(not likely)；没有希望的(unpromising) 同 improbable, unbelievable, unconvincing
transcendent [trænˈsendənt]	*adj.* 超越的，卓越的，出众的(extremely great; supreme) 同 ultimate, unsurpassable, utmost, uttermost

13

feign	*v.* 假装，装作(to make a false show of; pretend)
[feɪn]	同 counterfeit, fake, sham, simulate
	例 Although Johnson *feigned* great enthusiasm for his employees' project, in reality his interest in the project was so perfunctory as to be almost non-existent.
blissful	*adj.* 极幸福的(extremely happy)
[ˈblɪsfl]	记 来自 bliss(*n.* 天赐之福)
recondite	*adj.* 深奥的，晦涩的(difficult or impossible for understanding)
[ˈrekəndaɪt]	记 词根记忆：re(反) + con(共同) + dit(说) + e → 不是对所有人都能说明白 → 深奥的
culpable	*adj.* 有罪的，该受谴责的(deserving blame; blameworthy)
[ˈkʌlpəbl]	记 词根记忆：culp(罪行) + able → 有罪的
tactile	*adj.* 有触觉的(relating to the sense of touch)
[ˈtæktl]	记 词根记忆：tact(接触) + ile → 有触觉的
unpretentious	*adj.* 不炫耀的(not attempting to seem special, important or wealthy)
[ˌʌnprɪˈtenʃəs]	记 联想记忆：un(不) + pretentious(自命不凡的) → 不炫耀的
prig	*n.* 自命清高者，道学先生(a person who demonstrates an exaggerated conformity or propriety, especially in an irritatingly arrogant or smug manner)
[prɪg]	
pomposity	*n.* 自大的行为或言论(pompous behavior, demeanor, or speech)
[pɑːmˈpɑːsəti]	记 来自 pomp(*n.* 炫耀；盛况)
vigorous	*adj.* 精力充沛的，有力的(strong, healthy, and full of energy)
[ˈvɪgərəs]	记 联想记忆：vigor(活力) + ous → 精力充沛的
	例 One of Detroit's great success stories tells of Lee Lacocca's revitalization of the moribund Chrysler Corporation, turning it into a *vigorous* competitor.
	同 energetic, lusty, strenuous
foul	*adj.* 污秽的，肮脏的(full of dirt or mud); 恶臭的(stinking; loathsome); 邪恶的(very wicked) *v.* 弄脏(to soil; defile) *n.* (体育等)犯规(an infraction of the rules, as of a game or sport)
[faʊl]	
amateur	*n.* 业余爱好者 (one who engages in sth. as a pastime rather than as a profession)
[ˈæmətər]	记 词根记忆：amat(=amor 爱) + cur(人) → 爱好的人 → 业余爱好者

| □ feign | □ blissful | □ recondite | □ culpable | □ tactile | □ unpretentious |
| □ prig | □ pomposity | □ vigorous | □ foul | □ amateur | |

Word List 14

音频

overpower [ˌoʊvərˈpaʊər]	*v.* 压倒(to affect with overwhelming intensity) 例 The sheer bulk of data from the mass media seems to *overpower* us and drive us to synoptic accounts for an easily and readily digestible portion of news.
viscous [ˈvɪskəs]	*adj.* 黏滞的，黏性的，黏的(glutinous)
horrific [həˈrɪfɪk]	*adj.* 可怕的(causing horror) 同 terrifying
venerate [ˈvenəreɪt]	*v.* 崇敬，敬仰(to regard with reverential respect) 记 词根记忆：vener(尊敬) + ate → 崇敬 同 adore, revere, worship
ethos [ˈiːθɑːs]	*n.* (个人、团体或民族)风貌，气质(the characteristic and distinguishing attitudes, habits, beliefs of an individual or of a group) 记 词根记忆：eth(=ethn 民族，种族) + os → 风貌
flounder [ˈflaʊndər]	*v.* 挣扎(to plunge about in a stumbling manner)；艰苦地移动(to struggle awkwardly to move) *n.* 比目鱼(flatfish) 记 联想记忆：flo(看作 flow, 流) + under(在…下面) → 在下面流动 → 挣扎
slash [slæʃ]	*v.* 大量削减(to reduce sharply) 同 cut
clarification [ˌklærəfɪˈkeɪʃn]	*n.* 解释，澄清(an interpretation that removes obstacles to understanding) 记 来自 clarify(*v.* 澄清)
capricious [kəˈprɪʃəs]	*adj.* 变化无常的，任性的(erratic; flighty) 同 inconstant, lubricious, mercurial, whimsical, whimsied
tentative [ˈtentətɪv]	*adj.* 试探性的，尝试性的(not fully worked out or developed) 记 词根记忆：tent(测试) + ative → 尝试性的 例 Science is always *tentative*, expecting that modifications of its present theories will sooner or later be found necessary.
sculpt [skʌlpt]	*v.* 雕刻 (to carve; sculpture)；造型 (to shape, mold, or fashion especially with artistry or precise)

□ overpower	□ viscous	□ horrific	□ venerate	□ ethos	□ flounder
□ slash	□ clarification	□ capricious	□ tentative	□ sculpt	

epic	*n.* 叙事诗，史诗（a long narrative poem）*adj.* 史诗的，叙事诗的；英雄的；大规模的（of great size）
['epɪk]	例 Telling gripping tales about a central character engaged in a mighty struggle with events, modern biographies satisfy the American appetite for *epic* narratives.
remorselessly	*adv.* 冷酷地，无悔意地（mercilessly）
[rɪˈmɔːrsləsli]	
verify	*v.* 证明，证实（to establish the accuracy of）
[ˈverɪfaɪ]	记 词根记忆：ver(真实的) + ify(使…) → 使…真实 → 证明，证实
	同 confirm, corroborate, justify, substantiate, validate
automated	*adj.* 自动的（using computers and machines to do a job, rather than people）
[ˈɔːtəmeɪtɪd]	
insolent	*adj.* 粗野的，无礼的（boldly disrespectful in speech or behavior; impudent）
[ˈɪnsələnt]	
deplete	*v.* 大量减少；耗尽，使枯竭（to exhaust）
[dɪˈpliːt]	记 词根记忆：de + plet(满) + e → 不满 → 倒空 → 使枯竭
	同 drain, impoverish
offspring	*n.* 〈总称〉后代（the progeny or descendants of a person, an animal, or a plant considered as a group）；儿女（children from particular parents）
[ˈɔːfsprɪŋ]	
empty	*adj.* 空的，缺乏的（containing nothing; null; hollow）*v.*（使）变空，把…弄空（to make empty; become empty）
[ˈempti]	同 idle, vacant, vacuous, void
prevalent	*adj.* 流行的，盛行的（widespread）
[ˈprevələnt]	记 词根记忆：pre(在前面) + val(力量) + ent → 有走在前面的力量的 → 流行的
	同 prevailing, rampant, regnant, rife
oust	*v.* 驱逐，把…赶走（to expel; force out）
[aʊst]	记 联想记忆：out(出去)中加上 s → 死也要让他出去 → 驱逐
caterpillar	*n.* 毛毛虫，蝴蝶的幼虫（the elongated wormlike larva of a butterfly or moth）
[ˈkætərpɪlər]	记 来自中古英语：cater(猫) + pillar(毛) → 原意为有毛的猫 → 毛毛虫
overawe	*v.* 威慑（to restrain or subdue by awe）
[ˌoʊvərˈɔː]	记 联想记忆：over(过度) + awe(敬畏) → 过度敬畏 → 威慑
constant	*adj.* 稳定的，不变的（unchanging）*n.* 常数（a figure, quality, or measurement that stays the same）
[ˈkɑːnstənt]	记 词根记忆：con(始终) + stant(站，立) → 始终站立 → 不变的
	同 inflexible, immovable, immutable, inalterable, invariable
fecund	*adj.* 肥沃的，多产的（fruitful in offspring or vegetation）；创造力旺盛的（intellectually productive or inventive to a marked degree）
[ˈfekənd]	记 发音记忆："翻垦" → 可翻垦的土地 → 肥沃的
	同 fertile, prolific

prevalent

□ epic	□ remorselessly	□ verify	□ automated	□ insolent	□ deplete
□ offspring	□ empty	□ prevalent	□ oust	□ caterpillar	□ overawe
□ constant	□ fecund				

rift [rɪft]	*n.* 裂口，断裂(fissure；crevasse)；矛盾(a separation between people) 例 With the *rift* between the two sides apparently widening, analysts said they considered the likelihood of a merger between the two corporations to be deteriorating.
recuperate [rɪ'ku:pəreɪt]	*v.* 恢复(健康、体力)，复原(to regain；to recover) 记 词根记忆：re(再次) + cuper(=gain 获得) + ate → 再次获得原来的状态 → 复原
dissolve [dɪ'zɑːlv]	*v.* (使)溶解(to make a solid become liquid) 记 词根记忆：dis(分开) + solv(松开) + e → 松开 → (使)溶解
defensive [dɪ'fensɪv]	*adj.* 自卫的 (devoted to resisting or preventing aggression or attack) *n.* 戒备；防御 搭 on/onto the defensive 处于防御姿态；采取守势
irrelevant [ɪ'reləvənt]	*adj.* 不相关的；不切题的 搭 be irrelevant to 与…不相关
vulnerable ['vʌlnərəbl]	*adj.* 易受伤的，脆弱的(capable of being physically wounded；assailable) 记 词根记忆：vulner(伤) + able → 总是受伤 → 易受伤的
renowned [rɪ'naʊnd]	*adj.* 有名的(having renown) 同 celebrated, famous
proscribe [proʊ'skraɪb]	*v.* 禁止(to forbid as harmful or unlawful；prohibit) 记 词根记忆：pro(前面) + scrib(写) + e → 写在前面 → 禁止
audible ['ɔːdəbl]	*adj.* 听得见的(capable of being heard clearly) 记 词根记忆：audi(听) + ble → 能听的 → 听得见的
prudish ['pruːdɪʃ]	*adj.* 过分守礼的，假道学的(marked by prudery；priggish)
specialization [ˌspeʃələ'zeɪʃn]	*n.* 特殊化(making sth. become specialized) 例 The new *specialization* of knowledge has created barriers between people: everyone believes that his or her subject cannot and possibly should not be understood by others.
inspire [ɪn'spaɪər]	*v.* 鼓舞，激励(to impel；motivate) 记 词根记忆：in(使) + spir(呼吸) + e → 使…呼吸澎湃 → 鼓舞 同 animate, elate, exalt, exhilarate
defecate ['defəkeɪt]	*v.* 澄清(to clarify)；净化
anarchy ['ænərki]	*n.* 无政府(absence of government)；政治混乱(political disorder) 记 词根记忆：an(不，无) + archy(统治) → 无统治 → 无政府
detriment ['detrɪmənt]	*n.* 损害，伤害(injury, damage) 记 词根记忆：de(加强) + tri(擦) + ment → 用力擦 → 损害
integrate ['ɪntɪɡreɪt]	*v.* 使成整体，使一体化(to make whole or complete) 记 词根记忆：in(不) + tegr(触摸) + ate → 未被触摸 → 使成整体

dissolve

14

□ rift	□ recuperate	□ dissolve	□ defensive	□ irrelevant	□ vulnerable
□ renowned	□ proscribe	□ audible	□ prudish	□ specialization	□ inspire
□ defecate	□ anarchy	□ detriment	□ integrate		

insubordinate	*adj.* 不服从的，违抗的（disobedient）
[ˌɪnsə'bɔːrdɪnət]	记 联想记忆：in(不) + subordinate(服从的) → 不服从的
	例 By idiosyncratically refusing to dismiss an *insubordinate* member of his staff, the manager not only contravened established policy, but he also jeopardized his heretofore good chances for promotion.
disinterest	*v.* 使失去兴趣（to cause to regard sth. with no interest or concern）*n.* 无兴趣（lack of interest）
[dɪs'ɪntrəst]	搭 disinterest in... 对…无兴趣
raze	*v.* 夷为平地（to destroy to the ground）；彻底破坏（to destroy completely）
[reɪz]	
assessment	*n.* 估价，评价（the action or an instance of assessing）
[ə'sesmənt]	记 来自 assess(*v.* 评价，评定)
belligerent	*adj.* 发动战争的（waging war）；好斗的，好挑衅的（inclined to or exhibiting assertiveness, hostility, or combativeness）
[bə'lɪdʒərənt]	
fearsome	*adj.* 吓人的，可怕的（causing fear）
['fɪrsəm]	记 来自 fear(*n./v.* 害怕)
fallacious	*adj.* 欺骗性的，误导的（misleading or deceptive）；谬误的（erroneous）
[fə'leɪʃəs]	记 词根记忆：fall(错误) + aci + ous(多…的) → 谬误的
diplomatic	*adj.* 外交的；圆滑的（tactful and adroit; suave）
[ˌdɪplə'mætɪk]	记 词根记忆：di(双，两) + plo(折叠) + matic → 有着双重手段的 → 外交的
novice	*n.* 生手，新手（apprentice; beginner）
['nɑːvɪs]	记 联想记忆：no(不) + vice(副的) → 连副的都不是 → 新手
sentimentalize	*v.* (使)感伤（to indulge in sentiment; to look upon or imbue with sentiment）
[ˌsentɪ'mentəlaɪz]	
bolster	*n.* 枕垫（cushion or pillow）*v.* 支持，鼓励（to support, strengthen, or reinforce）
['boʊlstər]	记 联想记忆：bol（倒着看 lob） + ster → lobster（龙虾），拿龙虾当枕垫 → 枕垫
uninitiated	*adj.* 外行的，缺乏经验的（not knowledgeable or skilled; inexperienced）
[ˌʌnɪ'nɪʃieɪtɪd]	记 联想记忆：un(不) + initiate(传授) + d → 没有被传授过相关知识的 → 外行的
	例 The systems analyst hesitated to talk to strangers about her highly specialized work, fearing it was too esoteric for people *uninitiated* in the computer field to understand.
opprobrious	*adj.* 辱骂的，侮辱的（expressing scorn; abusive）
[ə'proʊbriəs]	记 词根记忆：op(反) + pro(向前) + br(=fer 搬运) + ious → 以相反的方向往前搬运 → 辱骂的
consummate	*adj.* 完全的，完善的（complete or perfect）*v.* 完成（to finish; accomplish）
['kɑːnsəmət]	记 词根记忆：con + sum(总数) + mate → 总数的，全数的 → 完全的

flickering ['flɪkərɪŋ]	*adj.* 闪烁的，摇曳的，忽隐忽现的(glittery, twinkling) 记 来自 flicker(*v.* 闪烁，摇曳)
exhilaration [ɪɡˌzɪlə'reɪʃn]	*n.* 高兴，兴奋(the feeling or the state of being exhilarated) 搭 the exhilaration of …的兴奋之情
fuse [fju:z]	*v.* 熔化；融合(to reduce to a liquid or plastic state by heat; combine; become blended or joined)
rescind [rɪ'sɪnd]	*v.* 废除，取消(to make void) 记 词根记忆：re + scind(=cut 砍) → 砍掉 → 废除
neolithic [ni:ə'lɪθɪk]	*adj.* 新石器时代的 记 词根记忆：neo(新的) + lith(石头) + ic → 新石头的 → 新石器时代的
blueprint ['blu:prɪnt]	*n.* 蓝图(photographic print of building plans)；方案(detailed plan) 记 组合词：blue(蓝) + print(印刷的图) → 蓝图
rivet ['rɪvɪt]	*n.* 铆钉 *v.* 吸引(注意力)(to attract completely) 搭 be riveted to the spot/ground 呆若木鸡
facile ['fæsl]	*adj.* 易做到的(easily accomplished or attained)；肤浅的(superficial) 记 词根记忆：fac(做) + ile(能…的) → 能做的 → 易做到的
off-key [ˌɔːf'kiː]	*adj.* 走调的，不和谐的(out of tune)
insoluble [ɪn'sɑːljəbl]	*adj.* 不能溶解的(incapable of being dissolved)；不能解决的(incapable of being solved) 记 词根记忆：in(不) + solu(溶解；解决) + ble → 不能溶解的；不能解决的
unbroken [ʌn'brəʊkən]	*adj.* 完整的；连续的(not interrupted or disturbed) 同 unplowed, unploughed
underrate [ˌʌndə'reɪt]	*v.* 低估，轻视(to rate too low) 记 联想记忆：under(不足，少于) + rate(估价) → 低估 例 The discovery that, friction excluded, all bodies fall at the same rate is so simple to state and to grasp that there is a tendency to *underrate* its significance.
possess [pə'zes]	*v.* 拥有(to have as an attribute, knowledge, or skill; own)；支配，主宰(to gain or exert influence or control over; dominate)；受摆布，缠住，迷住(to bring or cause to fall under the influence, possession, or control of some emotional or intellectual response or reaction) 记 联想记忆：poss(看作 boss, 老板) + ess → 老板拥有很多财产 → 拥有 例 The architects of New York's early skyscrapers, hinting here at a twelfth-century cathedral, there at a fifteenth-century palace, sought to legitimize the city's social strivings by evoking a history the city did not truly *possess*.

possess

14

turmoil ['tɜːrmɔɪl]	*n.* 混乱，骚乱（a state of extreme confusion or agitation） 记 词根记忆：tur(=turbulent 混乱的) + moil(喧闹) → 混乱，骚乱 例 Many of her followers remain loyal to her, and even those who have rejected her leadership are unconvinced of the wisdom of replacing her during the current *turmoil*. 同 tumult, turbulence
trend [trend]	*v.* 趋向，倾向（to show a tendency）*n.* 趋势，倾向（a prevailing tendency or inclination）
impunity [ɪm'pjuːnəti]	*n.* 免受惩罚（exemption from punishment） 记 词根记忆：im(不) + pun(惩罚) + ity → 免受惩罚 例 Because outlaws were denied protection under medieval law, anyone could raise a hand against them with legal *impunity*.
unimpassioned [ˌʌnɪm'pæʃnd]	*adj.* 没有激情的（without passion or zeal） 记 联想记忆：un(不) + impassioned(充满激情的) → 没有激情的
insinuate [ɪn'sɪnjueɪt]	*v.* 暗指，暗示（to hint or suggest indirectly；imply） 记 词根记忆：in(进入) + sinu(弯曲) + ate → 绕弯说出来 → 暗指
grim [ɡrɪm]	*adj.* 冷酷的，可怕的（appearing stern；forbidding） 同 ghastly
unobtrusive [ˌʌnəb'truːsɪv]	*adj.* 不引人注目的（not very noticeable or easily seen） 记 联想记忆：un(不) + obtrusive(突出的) → 不引人注目的
synchronization [ˌsɪŋkrənə'zeɪʃn]	*n.* 同步（the act or result of synchronizing, the state of being synchronous）
momentous [moʊ'mentəs]	*adj.* 极为重要的，重大的（of great importance or consequence） 例 The failure of many psychotherapists to utilize the results of pioneering research could be due in part to the specialized nature of such findings: even *momentous* findings may not be useful. 同 consequential, considerable, significant, substantial
unsound [ˌʌn'saʊnd]	*adj.* 不健康的，不健全的（not healthy or whole）；不结实的，不坚固的（not firmly made, placed, or fixed）；无根据的（not valid or true） 记 联想记忆：un(不) + sound(健康的) → 不健康的
reprehensible [ˌreprɪ'hensəbl]	*adj.* 应受谴责的（deserving reprehension；culpable） 例 When such *reprehensible* remarks are circulated, we can only blame and despise those who produce them. 同 blameworthy, blamable, blameful, censurable
potted ['pɑːtɪd]	*adj.* 盆栽的（planted or grown in a pot）；瓶装的，罐装的，壶装的（preserved in a pot, jar, or can）
provident ['prɑːvɪdənt]	*adj.* 深谋远虑的（prudent）；节俭的（frugal；thrifty） 记 词根记忆：pro(向前) + vid(看) + ent(…的) → 向前看的 → 深谋远虑的

154

□ turmoil　　□ trend　　□ impunity　　□ unimpassioned　□ insinuate　　□ grim
□ unobtrusive　□ synchronization　□ momentous　　□ unsound　　□ reprehensible　□ potted
□ provident

investigative [ɪnˈvestɪɡeɪtɪv]	*adj.* 调查的 记 来自 investigate(*v.* 调查)
concoction [kənˈkɑːkʃn]	*n.* (古怪或少见的)混合(物)(a strange or unusual mixture of things)
moderately [ˈmɑːdərətli]	*adv.* 适度地,有节制地 记 来自 moderate(*adj.* 适当的,有节制的)
anomaly [əˈnɑːməli]	*n.* 异常,反常(deviation from common rule);异常事物(sth. anomalous) 记 词根记忆:a + nomal(看作 normal, 正常的) + y → 异常
omnipotent [ɑːmˈnɪpətənt]	*adj.* 全能的,万能的(almighty; all-powerful) 记 词根记忆:omni(全) + pot(有力的) + ent → 全能的
verifiable [ˈverɪfaɪəbl]	*adj.* 能作证的(capable of being verified) 同 confirmable, falsifiable
countenance [ˈkaʊntənəns]	*v.* 支持,赞成(to sanction) *n.* 表情(the look on a person's face) 同 advocate, approbate, approve, encourage, favor
detour [ˈdiːtʊr]	*v.* 绕道,迂回 *n.* 弯路(a roundabout way);绕行之路(a route used when the direct or regular route is not available) 记 联想记忆:de + tour(旅行,走) → 绕着走 → 绕道 搭 detour around 绕行
security [səˈkjʊrəti]	*n.* 安全(safety);保证(surety);保护(protection) 例 Having sufficient income of her own constituted for Alice a material independence that made possible a degree of *security* in her emotional life as well.
motif [moʊˈtiːf]	*n.* (文艺作品等的)主题,主旨(a main theme or idea) 记 词根记忆:mot(动) + if → 促成移动的原因 → 主题,主旨 例 If you listen carefully, you can hear this simple *motif* throughout the entire score. 同 leitmotiv, subject
protract [prəˈtrækt]	*v.* 延长,拖长(prolong) 记 词根记忆:pro(向前) + tract(拉) → 向前拉 → 延长,拖长 同 elongate, extend, lengthen, prolongate
impartiality [ˌɪmˌpɑːrʃiˈæləti]	*n.* 公平,公正(the quality or state of being just and unbiased) 同 fair
adulatory [ˈædʒələtɔːri]	*adj.* 奉承的(having excessive or slavish admiration or flattery)
sanctum [ˈsæŋktəm]	*n.* (寺庙或教堂的)圣所(a sacred place) 搭 inner sanctum 私室,密室
flagging [ˈflæɡɪŋ]	*adj.* 下垂的;衰弱的(drooping; weakening) 同 languid, languorous, limp, listless, lymphatic, spiritless
fertilize [ˈfɜːrtəlaɪz]	*v.* 使受精;使肥沃(to make soil productive) 记 词根记忆:fer(带来) + til + ize → 带来果实 → 使受精

14

□ investigative	□ concoction	□ moderately	□ anomaly	□ omnipotent	□ verifiable
□ countenance	□ detour	□ security	□ motif	□ protract	□ impartiality
□ adulatory	□ sanctum	□ flagging	□ fertilize		

permissive [pərˈmɪsɪv]	*adj.* 许可的，容许的（granting or inclined to grant permission; tolerant or lenient）；过分纵容的（indulgent）
uneventful [ˌʌnɪˈventfl]	*adj.* 平凡的；平安无事的（marked by no noteworthy or untoward incidents） 例 The biographer of Tennyson is confronted with the problem, rarely solved, of how to make a basically *uneventful* life interesting.
counterbalance [ˌkaʊntərˈbæləns]	*v.* 起平衡作用（to act as a balance to sb./sth.） 记 组合词：counter(反对，相反) + balance(平衡) → 相反的两边保持平衡 → 起平衡作用
aspiration [ˌæspəˈreɪʃn]	*n.* 抱负，渴望（strong desire or ambition） 记 词根记忆：a + spir(呼吸) + ation → 屏住呼吸下决心 → 抱负
detest [dɪˈtest]	*v.* 厌恶，憎恨（to dislike intensely; hate; abhor） 记 联想记忆：de + test(测试) → 有的学生十分憎恶测试 → 厌恶
indubitably [ɪnˈduːbɪtəbli]	*adv.* 无疑地，确实地（certainly or without doubt） 例 Before the inflation spiral, one could have had a complete meal in a restaurant for a dollar, including the tip, whereas today a hot dog, coffee, and dessert would *indubitably* add up to two or three times that much.
indefatigable [ˌɪndɪˈfætɪɡəbl]	*adj.* 不知疲倦的（not yielding to fatigue; untiring） 记 联想记忆：in(不) + de(表强调) + fatigable(易疲倦的) → 不知疲倦的
overrule [ˌoʊvərˈruːl]	*v.* 驳回，否决（to decide against by exercising one's higher authority） 记 组合词：over(在…上) + rule(统治) → 凌驾于他人之上 → 驳回，否决
sloping [ˈsloʊpɪŋ]	*adj.* 倾斜的，有坡度的 搭 sloping line 斜线
choreographic [ˌkɔːriəˈɡræfɪk]	*adj.* 舞蹈术的，舞台舞蹈的 记 来自 choreography(*n.* 编舞设计，舞蹈设计)
archive [ˈɑːrkaɪv]	*n.* 档案室（a place where public record or document are kept）
irradicable [ɪˈrædɪkəbl]	*adj.* 无法根除的，根深蒂固的（impossible to eradicate） 同 confirmed, entrenched, ineradicable, inveterate
represent [ˌreprɪˈzent]	*v.* 呈现（to present）；代表（to typify）；体现（to describe as having a specified character or quality） 记 联想记忆：re + present(出席) → 代表 例 Although the discovery of antibiotics led to great advances in clinical practice, it did not *represent* a panacea for bacterial illness, for there are some bacteria that cannot be effectively treated with antibiotics.
spectator [ˈspekteɪtər]	*n.* 目击者（an observer of an event）；观众，观看者 记 词根记忆：spect(看) + ator → 旁观者 → 观众 同 beholder, bystander, eyewitness

---

| **foresight** | *n.* 远见，深谋远虑(an act or the power of foreseeing) |
| [ˈfɔːrsaɪt] | 记 组合词：fore(预先) + sight(看见) → 远见 |

| **misconstrue** | *v.* 误解，曲解 |
| [ˌmɪskənˈstruː] | 同 misapprehend, misconceive, misinterpret, misunderstand |

| **devious** | *adj.* 不坦诚的(not straightforward or frank)；弯曲的，迂回的(roundabout; winding) |
| [ˈdiːviəs] | 记 词根记忆：de(偏离) + vi(道路) + ous → 偏离正常道路的 → 弯曲的 |

| **invulnerable** | *adj.* 不会受伤害的，刀枪不入的(incapable of being wounded or injured) |
| [ɪnˈvʌlnərəbl] | 记 词根记忆：in(不) + vuln(伤害) + erable → 不易被伤害的 → 不会受伤害的 |

| **impulse** | *n.* 动力，刺激(an impelling or motivating force) |
| [ˈɪmpʌls] | 记 词根记忆：im(在内) + puls(推) + e → 在内推 → 动力 |

| **polite** | *adj.* 文雅的，有教养的(of, relating to, or having the characteristics of advanced culture) |
| [pəˈlaɪt] | 同 courteous, genteel, mannerly |

| **coercive** | *adj.* 强制的，强迫性的(serving or intended to coerce) |
| [koʊˈɜːrsɪv] | |

| **well-intentioned** | *adj.* 出于善意的 |
| [ˌwelɪnˈtenʃnd] | |

| **coherent** | *adj.* 连贯的，一致的(consistent; clearly articulated) |
| [koʊˈhɪrənt] | 记 词根记忆：co + her(粘连) + ent → 粘连在一起 → 连贯的，一致的 |

eclectic	*adj.* 折衷的；兼容并蓄的(selecting the best from various systems, doctrines, or sources)
[ɪˈklektɪk]	记 词根记忆：ec(出) + lect(选) + ic → 选出的 → 折衷的
	例 Although *eclectic* in her own responses to the plays she reviewed, the theatre critic was, paradoxically, suspicious of those who would deny that a reviewer must have a single method of interpretation.

| **asymmetric** | *adj.* 不对称的(having sides that are not alike) |
| [ˌeɪsɪˈmetrɪk] | 记 词根记忆：a(不) + sym(相同) + metr(测量) + ic → 测量不同 → 不对称的 |

| **forte** | *n.* 长处，特长(special accomplishment or strong point) *adj.* (音乐)强音的(used as a direction in music) |
| [fɔːrt] | |

| **flock** | *n.* 羊群；鸟群(a group of certain animals, as goats or sheep, or of birds) |
| [flɑːk] | 同 crowd, drove, horde, host, legion, mass |

| **embroider** | *v.* 刺绣，镶边(to ornament with needlework)；装饰(to provide embellishments) |
| [ɪmˈbrɔɪdər] | 记 联想记忆：em + broider(刺绣) → 刺绣 |

| **preempt** | *v.* 以优先权获得(to gain possession of by prior right or opportunity, especially to settle on (public land) so as to obtain the right to buy before others)；取代(to replace with) |
| [priˈempt] | 记 词根记忆：pre(预先) + empt(拿到) → 预先拿到 → 以优先权取得 |

14

□ foresight	□ misconstrue	□ devious	■ invulnerable	□ impulse	□ polite
□ coercive	□ well-intentioned	□ coherent	■ eclectic	□ asymmetric	□ forte
□ flock	□ embroider	□ preempt			

compel [kəm'pel]	*v.* 强迫 (to force or constrain) 记 词根记忆：com + pel(推) → 一起推 → 强迫 同 coerce, concuss, oblige
ingrain [ɪn'ɡreɪn]	*adj.* 根深蒂固的 (thoroughly worked in) *n.* 本质 (innate quality or character) 记 联想记忆：in(进入) + grain(木头的纹理) → 进入纹理 → 根深蒂固的
optimal ['ɑːptɪməl]	*adj.* 最佳的，最理想的 (most desirable or satisfactory) 同 optimum
morbid ['mɔːrbɪd]	*adj.* 病态的，不健康的 (diseased; unhealthy) 记 词根记忆：morb(病) + id → 病态的
veracious [və'reɪʃəs]	*adj.* 诚实的，说真话的 (truthful; honest) 例 I can vouch for his honesty, because I have always found him *veracious* and carefully observant of the truth. 同 faithful, veridical
recourse ['riːkɔːrs]	*n.* 求助，依靠 (a turning to sb. or sth. for help or protection) 例 Any population increase beyond a certain level necessitates greater *recourse* to vegetable foods; thus, the ability of a society to choose meat over cereals always arises, in part, from limiting the number of people.
worthwhile [ˌwɜːrθ'waɪl]	*adj.* 值得做的 (being worth the time or effort spent) 记 组合词：worth(值得) + while(时间) → 值得花时间的 → 值得做的 例 Although most *worthwhile* criticism concentrates on the positive, one should not indiscriminately praise everything.
hesitant ['hezɪtənt]	*adj.* 犹豫的 (tending to hesitate) 搭 be hesitant to 犹豫，不愿意 同 faltering, halting, irresolute, vacillating
poise [pɔɪz]	*v.* 使平衡 (to hold in equilibrium) *n.* 泰然自若，沉着自信 (easy self-possessed assurance of manner)
jaded ['dʒeɪdɪd]	*adj.* 疲惫的 (wearied)；厌倦的 (dull or satiated) 搭 be jaded by 厌倦…
salubrious [sə'luːbriəs]	*adj.* 有益健康的 (promoting health; healthful) 记 词根记忆：sal(健康) + ubrious → 健康的 → 有益健康的
dampen ['dæmpən]	*v.* (使)潮湿 (to make damp; moisten)；使沮丧，泼凉水 (to deaden; depress) 记 来自 damp(*adj.* 潮湿的)
notoriously [noʊ'tɔːriəsli]	*adv.* 臭名昭著地 (in a notorious manner) 例 The testimony of eyewitnesses is *notoriously* unreliable; emotion and excitement all too often cause our minds to distort what we see.
evoke [ɪ'voʊk]	*v.* 引起 (to draw forth or elicit)；唤起 (to call forth or summon a spirit) 记 词根记忆：e + vok(喊) + e → 喊出来 → 唤起 同 educe, induce

□ compel	□ ingrain	□ optimal	□ morbid	□ veracious	□ recourse
□ worthwhile	□ hesitant	□ poise	□ jaded	□ salubrious	□ dampen
□ notoriously	□ evoke				

stylize [ˈstaɪlaɪz]	*v.* 使…风格化(to conform to a conventional style)
pervasive [pərˈveɪsɪv]	*adj.* 弥漫的，遍布的(pervading or tending to pervade) 记 来自 pervade(*v.* 弥漫，遍及) 例 The influence of the Timaeus among early philosophical thinkers was *pervasive*, if only because it was the sole dialogue available in Europe for almost 1,000 years.
reparation [ˌrepəˈreɪʃn]	*n.* 赔偿，补偿(repairing; restoration; compensation)
purposiveness [ˈpɜːrpəsɪvnəs]	*n.* 目的性 记 来自 purpose(*n.* 目的)
circumscribe [ˈsɜːrkəmskraɪb]	*v.* 划界限；限制(to restrict; restrain; limit) 记 词根记忆：circum(绕圈) + scribe(画) → 画地为牢 → 限制
impediment [ɪmˈpedɪmənt]	*n.* 妨碍，阻碍物(obstacle) 搭 an impediment to reform 改革的障碍
indolent [ˈɪndələnt]	*adj.* 懒惰的(idle; lazy) 记 词根记忆：in(不) + dol(悲痛) + ent → 不悲痛的 → 不因时间的流逝而悲痛的 → 懒惰的 同 faineant, slothful, slowgoing, work-shy
slanderous [ˈslændərəs]	*adj.* 诽谤的(false and defamatory) 同 abusive
undermine [ˌʌndərˈmaɪn]	*v.* 破坏，削弱(to subvert or weaken insidiously) 记 组合词：under(在…下面) + mine(挖) → 在下面挖 → 破坏 例 It is no accident that most people find Davis' book disturbing, for it is calculated to *undermine* a number of beliefs they have long cherished. 同 attenuate, cripple, debilitate, sap, unbrace

14

Word List 15

音频

genre [ˈʒɑːnrə]	*n.* (文学、艺术等的)类型，体裁(a kind of works of literature, art, etc.) 记 词根记忆：gen(种属) + re → 类型，体裁
superstructure [ˈsuːpərstrʌktʃər]	*n.* 上层建筑(an entity, concept, or complex based on a more fundamental one)；上层构造(a structure built as a vertical extension of sth. else) 例 Ultimately, the book's credibility is strained; the slender, though far from nonexistent, web of evidence presented on one salient point is expected to support a vast *superstructure* of implications.
fluorescent [ˌfluːˈresnt]	*adj.* 荧光的, 发亮的(producing light) 记 词根记忆：fluor(荧光) + escent(发生⋯的) → 荧光的, 发亮的
recalcitrant [rɪˈkælsɪtrənt]	*adj.* 顽抗的(obstinately defiant of authority or restraint; unruly) 记 词根记忆：re(反)+calcitr(=calc 石头)+ant → 像石头一样坚硬顽强地反抗 → 顽抗的
succumb [səˈkʌm]	*v.* 屈从, 屈服(to yield to superior strength)；因⋯死亡(to die) 记 词根记忆：suc(下面) + cumb(躺) → 躺下去 → 因⋯死亡
sunlit [ˈsʌnlɪt]	*adj.* 阳光照射的(lighted by or as if by the sun) 记 联想记忆：sun(太阳) + lit(light 的过去式，照亮) → 阳光照射的
noisome [ˈnɔɪsəm]	*adj.* 有恶臭的(offensive to the senses and especially to the sense of smell)；令人作呕的, 令人讨厌的(highly obnoxious or objectionable) 记 词根记忆：noi(=annoy 讨厌) + some → 讨厌的 → 令人讨厌的
tie [taɪ]	*n.* 平局, 不分胜负(an equality in number) *v.* 系, 拴, 绑(to fasten, attach, or close by means of a tie)
consecutive [kənˈsekjətɪv]	*adj.* 连续的(following one after the other in order) 例 She was absent for nine *consecutive* days.
autonomy [ɔːˈtɑːnəmi]	*n.* 自治, 自主(self-government; independent function) 记 词根记忆：auto(自己) + nomy(治理) → 自治
inaugurate [ɪˈnɔːɡjəreɪt]	*v.* 举行就职典礼(to induct into an office with suitable ceremonies)；创始, 开创(to initiate; commence) 记 联想记忆：in(进入) + augur(预示) + ate → 通过预示创新 → 开创 同 instate, institute, launch, originate

□ genre　　□ superstructure　□ fluorescent　　□ recalcitrant　　□ succumb　　□ sunlit
□ noisome　□ tie　　□ consecutive　□ autonomy　□ inaugurate

dietary [ˈdaɪətɪri]	*adj.* 饮食的（of or relating to a diet or to the rules of a diet） 记 来自 diet（ *n.* 饮食）
component [kəmˈpoʊnənt]	*n.* 成分，零部件（any of the parts of which sth. is made） 记 词根记忆：com（共同）+ pon（放）+ ent → 放到一起（的东西）→ 成分
trendsetter [ˈtrendsetər]	*n.* 引领新潮的人（a person or institution that starts a new fashion or trend）
storage [ˈstɔːrɪdʒ]	*n.* 仓库（space or a place for storing）；贮存（the act of storing） 例 Created to serve as perfectly as possible their workaday function, the wooden *storage* boxes made in America's Shaker communities are now valued for their beauty.
extend [ɪkˈstend]	*v.* 延伸，扩大（to make sth. longer or larger）；舒展（肢体）（to stretch out the body or a limb at full length）；宽延，延缓（to stretch out in time） 记 词根记忆：ex（出）+ tend（伸展）→ 伸出去 → 延伸 例 The primary criterion for judging a school is its recent performance: critics are reluctant to *extend* credit for earlier victories. 同 expand, outspread, outstretch, unfold
rhetorical [rɪˈtɔːrɪkl]	*adj.* 修辞的，修辞学的（of, relating to, or concerned with rhetoric）；虚夸的，辞藻华丽的（characterized by overelaborate or bombastic rhetoric）
involvement [ɪnˈvɑːlvmənt]	*n.* 参与（participation）；连累；投入（the feeling of excitement and satisfaction that you get from an activity） 例 Halls and audiences for lieder recitals tend to be smaller than for opera and thus more conducive to the intimacy and sense of close *involvement*, which is the recital's particular charm.
sensitivity [ˌsensəˈtɪvəti]	*n.* 敏感，敏感性（the quality or state of being sensitive） 例 The successful reconstruction of an archaeological site requires scientific knowledge as well as cultural *sensitivity*.
unalterable [ʌnˈɔːltərəbl]	*adj.* 不能改变的（not capable of being altered or changed） 同 changeable, inalterable
propitiate [prəˈpɪʃieɪt]	*v.* 讨好（to gain or regain the favor or goodwill of）；抚慰（to appease） 记 词根记忆：pro（向前）+ piti（=pet 寻求）+ ate → 主动寻求和解 → 讨好 例 At the height of the storm, the savages tried to *propitiate* the angry gods by offering sacrifices. 同 assuage, conciliate, mollify, pacify, placate
extensive [ɪkˈstensɪv]	*adj.* 广大的，广阔的；多方面的，广泛的（having wide or considerable extent） 例 The development of containers, possibly made from bark or the skins of animals, although this is a matter of conjecture, allowed the *extensive* sharing of forage foods in prehistoric human societies.
erode [ɪˈroʊd]	*v.* 侵蚀（to eat into or away by slow destruction of substance）；受到侵蚀（to undergo erosion） 记 词根记忆：e + rod（咬）+ e → 咬掉 → 侵蚀

15

□ dietary	□ component	□ trendsetter	□ storage	□ extend	□ rhetorical
□ involvement	□ sensitivity	□ unalterable	□ propitiate	□ extensive	□ erode

161

ignoble [ɪgˈnoʊbl]	*adj.* 卑鄙的(dishonorable; base; mean) 记 词根记忆: ig(不) + noble(高贵) → 不高贵的 → 卑鄙的
generate [ˈdʒenəreɪt]	*v.* 造成(to bring into being); 产生(to originate or produce) 记 词根记忆: gener(种属; 产生) + ate → 产生
painstakingly [ˈpeɪnzteɪkɪŋli]	*adv.* 细心地, 专注地(fastidiously); 辛苦地 例 The President reached a decision only after lengthy deliberation, *painstakingly* weighing the divergent opinions expressed by cabinet members. 同 assiduously, exhaustively, meticulously
flaw [flɔː]	*n.* 瑕疵(imperfection; defect) *v.* 生裂缝; 变得有缺陷(to become defective) 同 blemish, bug, fault, shortcoming
precarious [prɪˈkeriəs]	*adj.* 根据不足的, 未证实的(dependent on uncertain premises); 不稳固的, 危险的(characterized by a lack of security or stability that threatens with danger; unsafe) 记 联想记忆: pre(在前面) + car(汽车) + ious → 在汽车前面 → 危险的 例 Although his broker had told him that the stock was a *precarious* investment, he insisted on buying 100 shares.
gymnastic [dʒɪmˈnæstɪk]	*adj.* 体操的, 体育的(of or relating to gymnastics) 同 athletic
conflagration [ˌkɑːnfləˈgreɪʃn]	*n.* (建筑物或森林)大火(a big, destructive fire) 记 词根记忆: con + flagr(烧) + ation → 大火
dwindle [ˈdwɪndl]	*v.* 变小, 减少(to diminish; shrink; decrease) 记 联想记忆: d + wind(风) + le → 随风而去, 越来越小 → 变小; 注意不要和 swindle(*n./v.* 欺骗, 诈骗)相混 同 abate, bate, wane
teem [tiːm]	*v.* 充满(to abound); 到处都是(to be present in large quantity); (雨、水等)暴降, 倾注
indenture [ɪnˈdentʃər]	*n.* 契约, 合同 (a written contract or agreement) *v.* 以契约约束(to bind (as an apprentice) by or as if by indentures) 记 来自 indent(*v.* 切割成锯齿状), 原指古代师徒间分割成锯齿状的契约
distort [dɪˈstɔːrt]	*v.* 扭曲, 弄歪(to twist sth. out of its usual shape) 记 词根记忆: dis(坏) + tort(扭曲) → 扭坏了 → 弄歪 同 contort, deform, misshape, torture, warp
roam [roʊm]	*v.* 漫游, 漫步(to go from place to place without purpose or direction) 记 联想记忆: 他的思绪漫游(roam)在广阔的空间(room)里
overtire [ˌoʊvərˈtaɪər]	*v.* 使过度疲劳

teem

□ ignoble	□ generate	□ painstakingly	□ flaw	□ precarious	□ gymnastic
□ conflagration	□ dwindle	□ teem	□ indenture	□ distort	□ roam
□ overtire					

raciness [ˈreɪsɪnəs]	*n.* 生动活泼
adhere [ədˈhɪr]	*v.* 粘着，坚持(to stick fast; stay attached) 记 词根记忆：ad + here(粘连) → 粘着 搭 adhere to 坚持
retribution [ˌretrɪˈbjuːʃn]	*n.* 报应，惩罚(sth. given as punishment) 记 词根记忆：re(反) + tribut(给予) + ion → 反过来给予 → 报应 搭 retribution for 因…而受到的报应
ungainly [ʌnˈgeɪnli]	*adj.* 笨拙的(lacking in smooth or dexterity; clumsy) 记 联想记忆：un(不) + gainly(优雅的) → 笨拙的
calculable [ˈkælkjələbl]	*adj.* 可计算的(subject to or ascertainable by calculation)；可信赖的(that may be counted on)
natty [ˈnæti]	*adj.* 整洁的(trimly neat and tidy)；敏捷的，灵巧的(neatly or trimly smart) 同 dapper, dashing, jaunty, spruce
irreproachable [ˌɪrɪˈproʊtʃəbl]	*adj.* 无可指责的，无瑕疵的(blameless; impeccable) 例 One might dispute the author's handling of particular points of Kandinsky's interaction with his artistic environment, but her main theses are *irreproachable*.
futile [ˈfjuːtl]	*adj.* 无效的，无用的 (completely ineffective)；（人）没出息的；琐细的 (occupied with trifles) 记 联想记忆：f (看作 fail, 失败) + uti (用) + le → 无法利用的 → 无效的，无用的 同 abortive, bootless, ineffectual, unavailing, vain
reveal [rɪˈviːl]	*v.* (神)启示；揭露(to make sth. secret or hidden publicly or generally known)；显示 (to open up to view) 记 联想记忆：re (相反) + veal (看作 veil, 面纱) → 除去面纱 → 显示 例 Hampshire's assertions, far from showing that we can dismiss the ancient puzzles about objectivity, *reveal* the issue to be even more relevant than we had thought. 同 disclose, divulge
renown [rɪˈnaʊn]	*n.* 名望，声誉(fame) 记 词根记忆：re(反复) + nown(=nomen 名字) → 名字反复出现 → 名望 例 For many years an unheralded researcher, Barbara McClintock gained international *renown* when she won the Nobel Prize in Physiology and Medicine.
psyche [ˈsaɪki]	*n.* 心智，精神(mind; soul)

15

festive ['festɪv]	*adj.* 欢宴的，节日的（of, relating to, or suitable for a feast or festival） 记 词根记忆：fest（=feast 盛宴）+ ive → 欢宴的
unimpeachable [ˌʌnɪm'piːtʃəbl]	*adj.* 无可指责的，无可怀疑的（irreproachable; blameless） 记 联想记忆：un（不）+ impeachable（可指责的）→ 无可指责的
outweigh [ˌaʊt'weɪ]	*v.* 比…重，比…更重要（to exceed in weight, value, or importance）
fervid ['fɜːrvɪd]	*adj.* 炽热的（extremely hot）；热情的（marked by great passion） 记 词根记忆：ferv（沸腾）+ id → 炽热的；热情的
steadfast ['stedfæst]	*adj.* 忠实的（faithful）；不动的，不变的（fixed or unchanging） 记 联想记忆：stead（=stand 站）+ fast（稳固的）→ 不变的
prostrate ['prɑːstreɪt]	*adj.* 俯卧的（prone）；沮丧的（powerless; helpless）*v.* 使下跪鞠躬，使拜服（to make oneself bow or kneel down in humility or adoration）
undesirable [ˌʌndɪ'zaɪərəbl]	*adj.* 不受欢迎的，讨厌的（not desirable; unwanted） 记 联想记忆：un（不）+ desirable（可取的）→ 不可取的 → 不受欢迎的
graze [greɪz]	*v.* （让动物）吃草（to feed on growing grass）；放牧（to put livestock to eat grass） 记 来自 grass（*n.* 草）；和 glaze（*v.* 装玻璃，上釉于）一起记
seclude [sɪ'kluːd]	*v.* 使隔离，使孤立（to isolate） 记 词根记忆：se（分开）+ clude（关闭）→ 分开关闭 → 使隔离，使孤立
appropriate [ə'proʊpriət]	*v.* 拨款（to set money aside for a specific use）；盗用（to take improperly） *adj.* 恰当的（fitting） 记 词根记忆：ap + propr（拥有）+ iate → 自己拥有 → 盗用
antidote ['æntidoʊt]	*n.* 解药（a remedy to counteract a poison） 记 词根记忆：anti（反）+ dote（药剂）→ 反毒的药 → 解药
plunge [plʌndʒ]	*v.* 跳进，陷入（to thrust or cast oneself into or as if into water）；俯冲（to move suddenly forwards and downwards） 记 发音记忆："扑浪急" → 掉入水里，着急地扑打着浪花 → 跳进
embezzlement [ɪm'bezlmənt]	*n.* 贪污，盗用（act of using money that is placed in one's care in a wrong way to benefit oneself） 记 联想记忆：em + bozzle（看作 bezzant，金银币）+ ment → 将金钱据为己有 → 贪污，盗用 例 The bank teller's *embezzlement* of the funds was not discovered until the auditors examined the accounts.
threat [θret]	*n.* 威胁，恐吓（expression of intention to inflict evil, injury, or damage）；凶兆，征兆（indication of future danger）
predecessor ['predəsesər]	*n.* 前任，前辈（the person who held an office or position before sb. else）；原有事物，前身（sth. that has been replaced by another） 记 词根记忆：pre（在前面）+ de + cess（走）+ or → 在前面走的人 → 前任，前辈

implement	[ˈɪmplɪmənt] *n.* 工具，器具
	[ˈɪmplɪment] *v.* 实现，实施（fulfill；accomplish）
	记 词根记忆：im(进入) + ple(满的) + ment → 进入圆满 → 实现
	例 The political success of any government depends on its ability to *implement* both foreign and domestic policies.
cone [koʊn]	*n.* 松果；圆锥体（solid body that narrows to a point from a circular flat base）
gene [dʒiːn]	*n.* 基因（unit in a chromosome which controls heredity）
renegade [ˈrenɪɡeɪd]	*n.* 叛教者，叛徒（a deserter from a faith, cause, or allegiance）
	记 词根记忆：re(反) + neg(否定) +ade → 回头否定的人 → 叛教者，叛徒
	例 Because he had abandoned his post and joined forces with the Indians, his fellow officers considered the hero of *Dances with Wolves* a *renegade*.
	同 apostate, defector
intruding [ɪnˈtruːdɪŋ]	*adj.* 入侵的，入侵性的（intrusive）
	记 来自 intrude（*v.* 侵入，侵扰）
impiety [ɪmˈpaɪəti]	*n.* 不虔诚，无信仰（the quality or state of being impious）
irrepressible [ˌɪrɪˈpresəbl]	*adj.* 抑制不住的，压抑不住的（incapable of being controlled）
	记 联想记忆：ir(不) + repress(抑制) + ible → 抑制不住的
untasted [ˌʌnˈteɪstɪd]	*adj.* 未尝过的，未体验过的
	例 Either the Polynesian banquets at Waikiki are *untasted*, or the one I visited was a poor example.
continental [ˌkɑːntɪˈnentl]	*adj.* 大陆的，大陆性的（of, relating to, or characteristic of a continent）
	搭 continental drift 大陆漂移（说）
ostentatious [ˌɑːstenˈteɪʃəs]	*adj.* 华美的；炫耀的（marked by or fond of conspicuous or vainglorious and sometimes pretentious display）
	例 Compared with the *ostentatious* glamour of opera, classical song is a more subdued tradition.
	同 flamboyant, peacockish, splashy, swank
immense [ɪˈmens]	*adj.* 极大的（very large）；无限的（limitless；infinite）
	记 词根记忆：im(不) + mense(=measure 测量) → 不能测量的 → 极大的
	搭 have an immense influence on... 对…有极大的影响
	同 colossal, monstrous, prodigious, titanic
presumptuous [prɪˈzʌmptʃuəs]	*adj.* 放肆的，过分的（going beyond what is right or proper；excessively forward）
	例 Not wishing to appear *presumptuous*, the junior member of the research group refrained from venturing any criticism of the senior members' plan for dividing up responsibility for the entire project.
	同 overweening, presuming, uppity

15

□ implement	□ cone	□ gene	▪ renegade	□ intruding	□ impiety
□ irrepressible	□ untasted	□ continental	□ ostentatious	□ immense	□ presumptuous

165

decorum [dɪ'kɔːrəm]	*n.* 礼节，礼貌(propriety and good taste in behavior, dress；etiquette) 记 词根记忆：decor(美，装饰) + um → 美的行为 → 礼节
philanthropic [ˌfɪlænˈθrəpɪk]	*adj.* 慈善(事业)的，博爱的(of, relating to, or characterized by philanthropy；humanitarian) 记 词根记忆：phil(爱) + anthrop(人) + ic → 爱人的 → 博爱的 例 The marketers' motivations in donating the new basketball backboards to the school system are not solely *philanthropic*; they plan to sell advertising space on the backboards.
peculiar [pɪˈkjuːliər]	*adj.* 独特的(distinctive)；古怪的(eccentric；queer) 同 characteristic, idiosyncratic, individual
unenlightened [ˌʌnɪnˈlaɪtnd]	*adj.* 愚昧无知的(without knowledge or understanding)；不文明的(having wrong beliefs because of lack of knowledge) 记 联想记忆：un(不) + enlightened(有知识的，开明的) → 愚昧无知的
efficacy ['efɪkəsi]	*n.* 功效，有效性(the power to produce an effect) 记 词根记忆：ef(出) + fic(做) + acy → 做出了成绩 → 功效，有效性 同 capability, effectiveness, efficiency
floral ['flɔːrəl]	*adj.* 花的，植物的(of or relating to a flora) 搭 a floral arrangement/display 插花，花展
discipline ['dɪsəplɪn]	*n.* 纪律(a rule or system of rules governing conduct or activity)；惩罚，处分(punishment) *v.* 训练，训导(to train or develop by instruction and exercise especially in self-control) 记 联想记忆：dis(不) + cip + line(线) → 不站成一线就要受惩罚 → 惩罚 同 educate
arbiter ['ɑːrbɪtər]	*n.* 权威人士，泰斗(arbitrator；a person fully qualified to judge or decide) 记 词根记忆：arbit(判断，裁决) + er → 判断之人 → 权威人士，泰斗
pervade [pərˈveɪd]	*v.* 弥漫，遍及(to become diffused throughout) 记 词根记忆：per(贯穿) + vad(走) + e → 走遍 → 弥漫，遍及
formulaic [ˌfɔːrmjuˈleɪɪk]	*adj.* 公式的，刻板的 (containing or made from ideas or expressions that have been used many times before and are therefore not very new or interesting)
contemptuous [kənˈtemptʃuəs]	*adj.* 鄙视的，表示轻蔑的(showing contempt) 记 注意 contemptible 和 contemptuous 都来自 contempt；contemptible 是指做的事令人轻视，而 contemptuous 是指人轻视的态度
unheralded [ʌnˈherəldɪd]	*adj.* 未预先通知的，未预先警告过的(not previously mentioned；happening without any warning) 例 For many years an *unheralded* researcher, Barbara McClintock gained international renown when she won the Nobel Prize in Physiology and Medicine.
hardship ['hɑːrdʃɪp]	*n.* 困苦，拮据(privation, suffering) 记 联想记忆：hard(艰苦的) + ship(表状态) → 困苦 同 asperity, difficulty, hardness, rigor

□ decorum　　□ philanthropic　□ peculiar　　□ unenlightened □ efficacy　　□ floral
□ discipline　□ arbiter　　　□ pervade　　□ formulaic　　□ contemptuous □ unheralded
□ hardship

keen [kiːn]	*adj.* 锋利的，锐利的（having a fine edge or point）；敏锐的，灵敏的（pungent to the sense; extremely sensitive in perception）；热心的（enthusiastic） 例 Our young people, whose *keen* sensitivities have not yet become calloused, have a purer and more immediate response than we do to our environment.
sibling ['sɪblɪŋ]	*n.* 兄弟或姊妹 记 词根记忆：sib(同胞) + ling → 兄弟或姊妹
informative [ɪn'fɔːrmətɪv]	*adj.* 提供信息的（imparting knowledge; instructive）；见闻广博的
patriarchal [ˌpeɪtri'ɑːrkl]	*adj.* 家长的，族长的（of, relating to, or being a patriarch）；父权制的（of, or relating to a patriarchy）
blur [blɜːr]	*n.* 模糊不清的事物（anything indistinct or hazy）*v.* 使…模糊（to make or become hazy or indistinct） 记 比较记忆：slur(*v.* 含糊不清地说)
burning ['bɜːrnɪŋ]	*adj.* 燃烧的（being on fire）；强烈的（ardent; intense）
nurture ['nɜːrtʃər]	*v.* 养育，教养（to care for and educate）*n.* 养育（the act of bringing up）；营养物（sth. that nourishes） 记 联想记忆：大自然(nature)像母亲一样养育(nurture)着人类 同 cultivate, foster
rowdy ['raʊdi]	*adj.* 吵闹的；粗暴的 记 联想记忆：row(吵闹) + dy → 吵闹的 例 In the light of Dickens's description of the lively, even *rowdy* dance parties of his time, Sharp's approach to country dancing may seem overly formal, suggesting more decorum than is necessary.
comprehensively [ˌkɑːmprɪ'hensɪvli]	*adv.* 包括地；全面地 记 词根记忆：comprehen（=comprehend 理解）+ sive + ly → 完全理解地 → 全面地
convertible [kən'vɜːrtəbl]	*adj.* 可转换的（capable of being converted）*n.* 敞篷车（an automobile with a canvas top that can be folded back or removed） 记 词根记忆：con + vert(转) + ible → 能够转动的 → 可转换的
docile ['dɑːsl]	*adj.* 驯服的，听话的（(of a person or an animal) easy to control） 记 词根记忆：doc(教导) + ile(能…的) → 能教的 → 听话的 例 He was habitually so *docile* and accommodating that his friends could not understand his sudden outburst against his employers.
hitherto [ˌhɪðər'tuː]	*adv.* 到目前为止（until this or that time） 搭 a hitherto unknown fact 至今无人知道的事实
sedulous ['sedʒələs]	*adj.* 聚精会神的；勤勉的（diligent in application or pursuit） 记 词根记忆：sed(坐) + ulous(多…的) → 坐得多的 → 勤勉的

15

□ keen	□ sibling	□ informative	□ patriarchal	□ blur	□ burning
□ nurture	□ rowdy	□ comprehensively	□ convertible	□ docile	□ hitherto
□ sedulous					

167

informal [ɪn ˈfɔːrml]	*adj.* 随便的，日常的（characteristic of or appropriate to ordinary, casual, or familiar use）; 不拘礼节的，非正式的（marked by the absence of formality or ceremony）
reside [rɪ ˈzaɪd]	*v.* 居住（to dwell permanently or continuously） 搭 reside in sb./sth. 在于; 由…造成
uninspired [ˌʌnɪn ˈspaɪərd]	*adj.* 无灵感的，枯燥的（having no intellectual, emotional, or spiritual excitement; dull） 例 Although Simpson was ingenious at contriving to appear innovative and spontaneous, beneath the ruse he remained *uninspired* and rigid in his approach to problem-solving.
antiquarianism [ˌænti ˈkweəriənizəm]	*n.* 古物研究，好古癖（study, collection or sale of valuable old objects） 记 词根记忆: antiqu(古老的) + arian + ism → 古物研究
symptomatic [ˌsɪmptə ˈmætɪk]	*adj.* 有症状的（being a symptom of a disease） 例 Many artists believe that successful imitation, far from being *symptomatic* of a lack of originality, is the first step in learning to be creative.
contravene [ˌkɑːntrə ˈviːn]	*v.* 违背(法规、习俗等)（to conflict with; violate） 记 词根记忆: contra(反) + ven(走) + e → 反着走 → 违背 同 breach, infract, infringe, offend, transgress
discreet [dɪ ˈskriːt]	*adj.* 小心的，言行谨慎的（prudent; modest） 记 词根记忆: dis + creet(分辨) → 分辨出不同来 → 小心的; 注意不要和 discrete(*adj.* 个别的)相混 同 calculating, cautious, chary, circumspect, gingerly
forebode [fɔː ˈboʊd]	*v.* 预感，预示(灾祸等)，预兆（to foretell; predict） 记 组合词: fore(提前) + bode(兆头) → 预兆
fusion [ˈfjuːʒn]	*n.* 融合（a union by or as if by melting）; 核聚变（union of atomic nuclear） 同 admixture, amalgam, blend, merger, mixture
esoteric [ˌesə ˈterɪk]	*adj.* 秘传的; 机密的，隐秘的（beyond the understanding or knowledge of most people） 记 联想记忆: es(出) + oter(看作 outer, 外面的) + ic → 不出外面的 → 秘传的 同 abstruse, occult, recondite
address [ə ˈdres]	*v.* 处理，对付，设法解决（to tackle sth.）; 致辞（to deliver a formal speech to）
reproach [rɪ ˈproʊtʃ]	*n.* 谴责，责骂（an expression of rebuke or disapproval） 记 联想记忆: re(反) + proach(靠近) → 以反对的方式靠近 → 谴责 同 admonish, chide, monish, reprimand, reprove
insurmountable [ˌɪnsər ˈmaʊntəbl]	*adj.* 不能克服的，不能超越的（incapable of being surmounted） 同 impassable, insuperable

□ informal	□ reside	□ uninspired	□ antiquarianism	□ symptomatic	□ contravene
□ discreet	□ forebode	□ fusion	□ esoteric	□ address	□ reproach
□ insurmountable					

exemplary [ɪgˈzempləri]	*adj.* 模范的，典范的（serving as an example）；可仿效的（deserving imitation） 记 来自 exemplar（*n.* 模范，榜样）
unmatched [ˌʌnˈmætʃt]	*adj.* 无可匹敌的（cannot be matched） 同 matchless, nonpareil, unmatchable, unrivaled
assume [əˈsuːm]	*v.* 假定（to accept sth. as true before there is proof）；承担，担任（to take on duties or responsibilities） 记 联想记忆：as(加强) + sume(拿，取) → 拿住 → 承担
deference [ˈdefərəns]	*n.* 敬意，尊重（courteous regard or respect） 搭 deference to 对…尊重
individual [ˌɪndɪˈvɪdʒuəl]	*adj.* 单独的，单个的（single; separate）；特有的（particular）；个人的，个体的 *n.* 个人，个体（single human being） 记 联想记忆：in + divid(e)(分割) + ual → 分割开的 → 单独的，单个的 例 Unlike a judge, who must act alone, a jury discusses a case and then reaches its decision as a group, thus minimizing the effect of *individual* bias. 同 distinctive, idiosyncratic
exclusive [ɪkˈskluːsɪv]	*adj.* (人)孤僻的（single and sole）；(物)专用的（not shared or divided） 记 词根记忆：ex(出) + clus(关闭) + ive → 关在外面的 → 孤僻的
inexplicable [ˌɪnɪkˈsplɪkəbl]	*adj.* 无法解释的（incapable of being explained or accounted for） 记 联想记忆：in(不) + explicable(可解释的) → 无法解释的 例 There were contradictions in her nature that made her seem an *inexplicable* enigma: she was severe and gentle; she was modest and disdainful; she longed for affection and was cold.
subtle [ˈsʌtl]	*adj.* 微妙的，精巧的（delicate; refined） 例 An obvious style, easily identified by some superficial quirk, is properly decried as a mere mannerism, whereas a complex and *subtle* style resists reduction to a formula.
dilate [daɪˈleɪt]	*v.* 使膨胀，使扩大（to swell; expand） 记 词根记忆：di + lat(搬运) + e → 分开搬运 → 使扩大；注意不要和 dilute (*v.* 冲淡，稀释)相混
infection [ɪnˈfekʃn]	*n.* 传染；感染（an act or process of infecting） 记 词根记忆：in(进入) + fect(做) → 在里面做 → 传染
certainty [ˈsɜːrtnti]	*n.* 确定的事情（thing that is certain） 记 来自 certain(*adj.* 确定的，必然的)
grief [griːf]	*n.* 忧伤，悲伤（deep or violent sorrow） 例 Because he had assumed that the child's first, fierce rush of *grief* would quickly subside, Murdstone was astonished to find him still disconsolate.

学习雷锋好榜样

exemplary

15

□ exemplary □ unmatched □ assume □ deference □ individual □ exclusive
□ inexplicable □ subtle □ dilate □ infection □ certainty □ grief

169

bane	*n.* 祸根(the cause of distress, death, or ruin)
[beɪn]	记 发音记忆: "背运" → 因为有祸根而背运 → 祸根
commiserate	*v.* 同情, 怜悯(to feel or show sorrow or pity for sb.)
[kəˈmɪzəreɪt]	记 词根记忆: com + miser(可怜) + ate → 同情, 怜悯
plastic	*adj.* 创造性的, 塑造的(formative; creative); 易受影响的(easily influenced); 可塑的(capable of being molded or modeled); 塑性的(capable of being deformed continuously and permanently in any direction without rupture)
[ˈplæstɪk]	同 adaptable, ductile, malleable, moldable, pliant, supple
embellishment	*n.* 装饰; 装饰品(ornament)
[ɪmˈbelɪʃmənt]	同 decoration
clause	*n.* 从句; (法律等)条款(a stipulation in a document)
[klɔːz]	记 联想记忆: cause(原因, 事业) 中加 "l", 有事业必有条款加以限制
spruce	*n.* 云杉 *adj.* 整洁的(neat or smart; trim)
[spruːs]	
crawl	*v.* 爬, 爬行(to move slowly in a prone position without or as if without the use of limbs)
[krɔːl]	记 联想记忆: c + raw(生疏的) + l → 对地形生疏, 就要缓慢地行进 → 爬行
category	*n.* 类别, 范畴(a class or division in a scheme of classification)
[ˈkætəgɔːri]	记 联想记忆: cat(猫) + ego(自我) + ry → 猫和我是两类生物 → 类别
genetic	*adj.* 遗传的(having to do with genetic); 起源的(of the genesis)
[dʒəˈnetɪk]	例 Ethologists are convinced that many animals survive through learning—but learning that is dictated by their *genetic* programming, learning as thoroughly stereotyped as the most instinctive of behavioral responses.
oblivious	*adj.* 遗忘的, 忘却的(lacking all memory; forgetful); 疏忽的(lacking conscious awareness; unmindful)
[əˈblɪviəs]	记 词根记忆: ob + liv (使光滑) + ious → 使记忆变得完全光滑 → 遗忘的; 疏忽的
disinclination	*n.* 不愿意, 不情愿(a preference for avoiding sth.)
[ˌdɪsˌɪnklɪˈneɪʃn]	同 aversion, disfavor, dislike, disrelish, dissatisfaction
impartial	*adj.* 公平的, 无私的(without prejudice or bias)
[ɪmˈpɑːrʃl]	记 联想记忆: im(不) + partial(偏见的) → 没有偏见的 → 公平的
	例 New judges often fear that the influence of their own backgrounds will condition their verdicts, no matter how sincere they are in wanting to be *impartial*.
	同 dispassionate, equitable, nondiscriminatory, unbiased, unprejudiced
baroque	*adj.* 过分装饰的(gaudily ornate)
[bəˈroʊk]	记 由 17 世纪 "巴洛克" 艺术而来, 以古怪精巧为特色
topographical	*adj.* 地形学的 (concerned with the artistic representation of a particular locality)
[ˌtɑːpəˈgræfɪkl]	

□ bane	□ commiserate	□ plastic	■ embellishment	□ clause	□ spruce
□ crawl	□ category	□ genetic	□ oblivious	□ disinclination	□ impartial
□ baroque	□ topographical				

dysfunctional [dɪsˈfʌŋkʃənl]	*adj.* 功能失调的（functioning abnormally） 记 联想记忆：dys(坏) + function(功能) + al → 功能坏了的 → 功能失调的
ameliorate [əˈmiːliəreɪt]	*v.* 改善，改良（to improve） 记 词根记忆：a + melior(=better 更好) + ate → 改善，改良
null [nʌl]	*adj.* 无效的（having no legal or binding force）；等于零的（amounting to nothing）
aberration [ˌæbəˈreɪʃn]	*n.* 越轨（being aberrant） 记 词根记忆：ab + err(错误) + ation → 错误的行为 → 越轨
shunt [ʃʌnt]	*v.* 使(火车)转到另一轨道（to switch a train from one track to another）；改变(某物)的方向
transcontinental [ˌtrænzˌkɑːntɪˈnentl]	*adj.* 横贯大陆的（extending or going across a continent）
instructive [ɪnˈstrʌktɪv]	*adj.* 传授知识的（giving much useful information），教育的；有益的（helpful） 记 来自 instruct(*v.* 教导，教授) 例 The parables in the Bible are both entertaining and *instructive*.
unencumbered [ˌʌnɪnˈkʌmbərd]	*adj.* 无阻碍的（free of encumbrance） 例 Isozaki's love for detail is apparent everywhere in the new museum, but fortunately the details are subordinated to the building's larger formal composition, which is *unencumbered* by the busyness of much recent architecture.
edifice [ˈedɪfɪs]	*n.* 宏伟的建筑(如宫殿、教堂等)（a large, imposing building） 记 词根记忆：edi(建筑) + fic(做) + e → 宏伟的建筑
innermost [ˈɪnərmoʊst]	*adj.* 最里面的（farthest inward） 记 组合词：inner(里面的) + most(最) → 最里面的

15

□ dysfunctional □ ameliorate □ null □ aberration □ shunt □ transcontinental
□ instructive □ unencumbered □ edifice □ innermost

171

Word List 16

音频

inimitable [ɪˈnɪmɪtəbl]	*adj.* 无法仿效的（incapable of being imitated or matched） 记 词根记忆：in(不) + imit(模仿) + able → 不可模仿的 → 无法仿效的
toxin [ˈtɑːksɪn]	*n.* 毒素，毒质（a poisonous substance） 同 poison, venom
concomitant [kənˈkɑːmɪtənt]	*adj.* 伴随的（accompanying；attendant） 记 联想记忆：con(共同) + com(看作 come) + itant → 一起来 → 伴随的
irritating [ˈɪrɪteɪtɪŋ]	*adj.* 刺激的（irritative）；使人愤怒的，气人的（annoying） 例 His critical reviews were enjoyed by many of his audience, but the subjects of his analysis dreaded his comments; he was vitriolic, devastating, *irritating* and never constructive.
tined [taɪnd]	*adj.* 尖端的（of a slender pointed projecting part） 记 来自 tine(*n.* 叉尖，尖端)
totalitarian [toʊˌtæləˈteriən]	*adj.* 极权主义的（authoritarian；dictatorial） 同 autocratic, despotic, tyrannic
gush [ɡʌʃ]	*v.* 涌出，迸出（to pour out；spout）；滔滔不绝地说（to talk effusively）*n.* 涌出，迸发（a sudden copious outflow）
compendium [kəmˈpendiəm]	*n.* 简要，概略（summary；abstract） 同 digest, pandect, sketch, syllabus
relieve [rɪˈliːv]	*v.* 减轻，解除（to free from a burden；mitigate） 记 词根记忆：re + liev(=lev 轻) + e → 减轻，解除 同 allay, alleviate, assuage, mollify
triumph [ˈtraɪʌmf]	*n.* 成功，胜利(的喜悦或满足) *v.* 成功，获胜（to obtain victory） 记 联想记忆：胜利(triumph)之后吹喇叭(trump) 同 conquer, overcome, prevail
confront [kənˈfrʌnt]	*v.* 面临（to face）；对抗（to face or oppose defiantly or antagonistically） 记 词根记忆：con + front(面，前面) → 面对面 → 对抗
ambidextrous [ˌæmbiˈdekstrəs]	*adj.* 十分灵巧的（very skillful or versatile） 记 词根记忆：ambi(两个) + dextr(右的) + ous → 两只手都像右手一样灵巧 → 十分灵巧的 同 bimanal

boastfulness [ˈboʊstflnəs]	*n.* 自吹自擂；浮夸（the act or an instance of boasting） 记 来自 boast(*v.* 自夸，自吹自擂)
deliberate	[dɪˈlɪbərət] *adj.* 深思熟虑的（carefully thought out and formed）；故意的（done on purpose） [dɪˈlɪbəreɪt] *v.* 慎重考虑（to think or consider carefully and fully） 记 词根记忆：de(表加强) + liber(权衡) + ate → 反复权衡 → 深思熟虑的
suspension [səˈspenʃn]	*n.* 暂停（the state or period of being suspended）；悬浮 例 To avoid annihilation by parasites, some caterpillars are able to curtail periods of active growth by pre-maturely entering a dormant state, which is characterized by the *suspension* of feeding. 同 abeyance, quiescence
trustworthy [ˈtrʌstwɜːrði]	*adj.* 值得信赖的，可靠的（warranting trust; reliable） 记 组合词：trust(信赖) + worthy(值得的) → 值得信赖的 例 Since she believed him to be both candid and *trustworthy*, she refused to consider the possibility that his statement had been insincere.
infrared [ˌɪnfrəˈred]	*adj.* 红外线的
deprecatory [ˈdeprɪkətɔːri]	*adj.* 不赞成的，反对的（disapproving） 搭 be deprecatory about... 反对…
quantum [ˈkwɑːntəm]	*n.* 量子（any of the small subdivisions of a quantized physical magnitude）；定量 记 词根记忆：quant(数量) + um → 定量
relevance [ˈreləvəns]	*n.* 相关性（the quality of being connected with and important to sth. else） 记 来自 relevant(*adj.* 相关的) 例 Adam Smith's *Wealth of Nations* (1776) is still worth reading, more to appreciate the current *relevance* of Smith's valid contributions to economics than to see those contributions as the precursors of present-day economics.
redistribution [ˌriːdɪˈstrɪbjuːʃn]	*n.* 重新分配（altering the distribution） 记 联想记忆：re(重新) + distribution(分配) → 重新分配
base [beɪs]	*adj.* 卑鄙的（devoid of high values or ethics）
preeminent [priˈemɪnənt]	*adj.* 出类拔萃的，杰出的（supreme; outstanding） 记 联想记忆：pre(在前面) + eminent(著名的) → 比著名的人还著名 → 出类拔萃的 例 Industrialists seized economic power only after industry had supplanted agriculture as the *preeminent* form of production; previously such power had resided in land ownership.

16

□ boastfulness □ deliberate □ suspension □ trustworthy □ infrared □ deprecatory
□ quantum □ relevance □ redistribution □ base □ preeminent

173

haunt [hɔːnt]	*v.* (思想，回忆等)萦绕心头(to remain in one's thoughts)；经常去(某地)(to visit often)；(鬼魂)常出没于(to visit or inhabit as a ghost) *n.* 常去的地方 记 联想记忆：姑妈(aunt)常去的地方(haunt)是商店
faddish ['fædɪʃ]	*adj.* 流行一时的，时尚的(having the nature of a fad) 记 来自 fad(*n.* 时尚)
premature [ˌpriːmə'tʃʊr]	*adj.* 早熟的，过早的(developing or happening before the natural or proper time) 记 联想记忆：pre(预先) + mature(成熟的) → 还没成熟的 → 早熟的，过早的
optical ['ɑːptɪkl]	*adj.* 视觉的(of or relating to vision)；光学的(of or relating to the science of optics) 记 词根记忆：opt(眼睛) + ical → 视觉的
disperse [dɪ'spɜːrs]	*v.* 消散，驱散(to spread or distribute from a fixed or constant source) 记 词根记忆：di(分开) + spers(散开) + e → 分散开 → 驱散 同 dispel, dissipate, scatter
causal ['kɔːzl]	*adj.* 原因的，因果关系的(implying a cause and effect relationship) 记 来自 cause(*n.* 原因)
dispute [dɪ'spjuːt]	*v.* 争论(to argue about; debate) 记 词根记忆：dis + put(思考) + e → 思考相悖 → 争论
unreliable [ˌʌnrɪ'laɪəbl]	*adj.* 不可靠的(that cannot be trusted or depended on) 例 The testimony of eyewitnesses is notoriously *unreliable*; emotion and excitement all too often cause our minds to distort what we see. dispute
approach [ə'proʊtʃ]	*v.* 接近，靠近(to come nearer)；着手处理(to begin to handle) *n.* 方法(method) 记 词根记忆：ap + proach(接近) → 靠近 搭 approach to …的方法 approach
perennial [pə'reniəl]	*adj.* 终年的，全年的(present all the year)；永久的，持久的(perpetual; enduring) 记 词根记忆：per(全部) + enn(年) + ial → 全年的；永久的 例 A *perennial* goal in zoology is to infer function from structure, relating the behavior of an organism to its physical form and cellular organization. 同 continuing, eternal, lifelong, permanent
ebb [eb]	*v.* 退潮(to recede from the flood)；衰退(to decline; wane) 记 发音记忆："二步" → 退后一步 → 衰退

174

□ haunt	□ faddish	□ premature	□ optical	□ disperse	□ causal
□ dispute	□ unreliable	□ approach	□ perennial	□ ebb	

evasive	*adj.* 回避的，逃避的，推脱的（tending or intended to evade）
[ɪ'veɪsɪv]	记 来自 evade（*v.* 躲避，逃避）
	例 In the midst of so many *evasive* comments, this forthright statement, whatever its intrinsic merit, plainly stands out as an anomaly.
descriptive	*adj.* 描述的（serving to describe）
[dɪ'skrɪptɪv]	记 词根记忆：de（加强）+ script（写）+ ive → 描述的
curtail	*v.* 削减，缩短（to make sth. shorter or less）
[kɜːr'teɪl]	记 联想记忆：cur（看作 curt，短）+ tail（尾巴）→ 短尾巴 → 缩短
	同 abridge, diminish, lessen, minify
dominate	*v.* 控制，支配（to control, govern or rule）
['dɑːmɪneɪt]	记 词根记忆：domin（支配）+ ate → 控制，支配
	同 direct, handle, manage, predominate
predispose	*v.* 使预先有倾向（to dispose in advance）；（使）易受感染（to make susceptible；bring about susceptibility）
[ˌpriːdɪ'spoʊz]	
copious	*adj.* 丰富的，多产的（very plentiful；abundant）
['koʊpiəs]	记 联想记忆：copi（看作 copy）+ ous → 能拷贝很多 → 丰富的
monotony	*n.* 单调，千篇一律（tedious sameness）
[mə'nɑːtəni]	同 humdrum, monotone
exhaustiveness	*n.* 全面，详尽，彻底
[ɪɡ'zɔːstɪvnəs]	
passively	*adv.* 被动地，顺从地
['pæsɪvli]	记 来自 passive（*adj.* 被动的）
unique	*adj.* 独一无二的，独特的（being the only one of this type）；无与伦比的（being without a like or equal）
[ju'niːk]	记 词根记忆：uni（单一）+ que → 独一无二的，独特的
	例 The semantic opacity of ancient documents is not *unique*; even in our own time, many documents are difficult to decipher.
	同 singular, sole
supportive	*adj.* 支持的（showing agreement and giving encouragement）
[sə'pɔːrtɪv]	搭 be supportive of 支持…
convoluted	*adj.* 旋绕的（coiled；spiraled）；费解的（extremely involved；intricate；complicated）
['kɑːnvəluːtɪd]	记 词根记忆：con + volut（转）+ ed → 全部转 → 旋绕的
overt	*adj.* 公开的，非秘密的（apparent；manifest）
[oʊ'vɜːrt]	记 词根记忆：o（出）+ vert（转）→ 转出来 → 公开的
	例 Such an *overt* act of hostility can only lead to war.
attribute	[ə'trɪbjuːt] *v.* 把…归于（to assign or ascribe to）
	['ætrɪbjuːt] *n.* 属性，特质（a characteristic or quality）
	记 词根记忆：at + tribute（给与）→ 把…归于
	搭 attribute... to... 把…归于…
	同 trait, virtue

16

huddle [ˈhʌdl]	*v.* 挤成一团(to crowd or nestle close together) *n.* 一堆人(或物) 记 联想记忆：聚集在一起(huddle)处理(handle)问题
ingest [ɪnˈdʒest]	*v.* 咽下，吞下(to take into the body by swallowing) 记 词根记忆：in(进入) + gest(搬运) → 搬进去 → 咽下，吞下
placebo [pləˈsiːbəʊ]	*n.* 安慰剂(a substance containing no medication and prescribed or given to reinforce a patient's expectation to get well)；起安慰作用的东西(sth. tending to soothe) 记 词根记忆：plac(平静的) + ebo → 安慰剂
servile [ˈsɜːrvl]	*adj.* 奴性的，百依百顺的(meanly or cravenly submissive; abject) 记 词根记忆：serv(服务) + ile → 百依百顺的
fragmentary [ˈfrægmənteri]	*adj.* 碎片的，片段的(consisting of fragments) 例 Although the records of colonial New England are sketchy in comparison with those available in France or England, the records of other English colonies in America are even more *fragmentary*.
polar [ˈpoʊlər]	*adj.* 极地的，两极的，近地极的(of or near the North or South Pole)；磁极的(connected with the poles of a magnet) 记 来自 pole(*n.* 地极；磁极)
specified [ˈspesɪfaɪd]	*adj.* 特定的 同 designated, indicated
deprecate [ˈdeprəkeɪt]	*v.* 反对(to express disapproval of)；轻视(to belittle) 记 词根记忆：de(去掉) + prec(价值) + ate → 去掉价值 → 轻视
accommodate [əˈkɑːmədeɪt]	*v.* 与…一致(to make fit, suitable, or congruous)；提供住宿(to make room for)；顺应，使适应 记 联想记忆：ac + commo(看作 common，普通的) + date(日子) → 人们适应了过普通的日子 → 使适应 同 attune, harmonize, reconcile
untainted [ʌnˈteɪntɪd]	*adj.* 无污点的(not damaged or spoiled) 同 stainless, unstained, unsullied, untarnished
simulation [ˌsɪmjuˈleɪʃn]	*n.* 模拟(the act or process of simulating) 搭 simulation training 模拟训练
transform [trænsˈfɔːrm]	*v.* 改变，变化(to change in composition or structure)；变换，转换(to subject to mathematical transformation) 记 词根记忆：trans(改变) + form(形状) → 改变，变化 同 convert, mutate, transfer, transmogrify, transmute
thatch [θætʃ]	*v.* 以茅草覆盖(to cover with or as if with thatch) *n.* 茅草屋顶；茅草(a plant material used as a sheltering cover)
untalented [ʌnˈtæləntɪd]	*adj.* 没有天赋的(without a natural ability to do sth. well)
cliche [kliːˈʃeɪ]	*n.* 陈词滥调(a trite phrase or expression)

unfeigned [ʌnˈfeɪnd]	*adj.* 真实的，真诚的（genuine） 记 联想记忆：un(不) + feigned(假的) → 真实的
infirm [ɪnˈfɜːrm]	*adj.* 虚弱的（physically weak） 记 联想记忆：in(不) + firm(坚定的) → 不坚定的 → 虚弱的
scarlet [ˈskɑːrlət]	*adj.* 猩红的，鲜红的（bright red in colour） 搭 scarlet fever 猩红热
unstinting [ʌnˈstɪntɪŋ]	*adj.* 慷慨的，大方的（very generous） 记 联想记忆：un(不) + stint(吝惜，限制) + ing → 慷慨的
perspective [pərˈspektɪv]	*n.* 思考方法（a way of thinking about sth.）；观点，看法（a point of view）；透视法 记 词根记忆：per(贯穿) + spect(看) + ive → 贯穿看 → 透视法
abysmal [əˈbɪzməl]	*adj.* 极深的（bottomless；unfathomable）；糟透的（wretched；immeasurably bad） 记 来自 abyss(*n.* 深渊，深坑)
approaching [əˈproʊtʃɪŋ]	*adj.* 接近的，逼近的
competence [ˈkɑːmpɪtəns]	*n.* 胜任，能力（the quality or state of being competent） 记 compete(竞争) + nce → 竞争需要能力 → 胜任，能力
subtly [ˈsʌtli]	*adv.* 敏锐地，巧妙地 同 artfully, shrewdly
psychology [saɪˈkɑːlədʒi]	*n.* 心理学（the study or science of the mind and the way it works and influences behavior） 记 词根记忆：psycho(心灵，精神) + logy(…学) → 心理学
adventurous [ədˈventʃərəs]	*adj.* 爱冒险的，大胆的（disposed to seek adventure），充满危险的（characterized by unknown dangers and risks） 同 adventuresome, audacious
rhythmic [ˈrɪðmɪk]	*adj.* 有节奏的（marked by pronounced rhythm） 记 来自 rhythm(*n.* 节奏)
postulate [ˈpɑːstʃəleɪt]	*v.* 要求（to demand；claim）；假定（to assume；presume） 记 词根记忆：post(放) + ul + ate → 放出观点 → 要求；假定
nonviable [nɑːnˈvaɪəbl]	*adj.* 无法生存的，不能成活的（not able to live） 记 联想记忆：non(不) + viable(能存活的) → 无法生存的
coordinate	[koʊˈɔːrdɪneɪt] *v.* 使各部分协调（to cause different parts, limbs to function together efficiently） [koʊˈɔːrdɪnət] *adj.* 同等的（of equal importance, rank, or degree） 记 词根记忆：co + ordin(顺序) + ate → 顺序一样 → 同等的
calumny [ˈkæləmni]	*n.* 诽谤，中伤（a false and malicious statement） 记 词根记忆：calumn(=beguile 欺诈) + y → 欺诈性的话 → 诽谤
underestimate [ˌʌndərˈestɪmeɪt]	*v.* 低估（to estimate as being less than the actual size, quantity, or number）；看轻（to place too low a value on）

16

notable [ˈnoʊtəbl]	*adj.* 值得注意的，显著的(deserving to be noticed; remarkable) 记 词根记忆: not(标示) + able → 能被标示的 → 值得注意的 例 Perhaps predictably, since an ability to communicate effectively is an important trait of any great leader, it has been the exceptional Presidents who have delivered the most *notable* inaugural addresses. 同 distinguished, eminent, famed, memorable, noteworthy
predator [ˈpredətər]	*n.* 食肉动物(an animal that lives by killing and consuming other animals) 记 词根记忆: pred(掠夺) + at + or → 食肉动物
commodious [kəˈmoʊdiəs]	*adj.* 宽敞的(offering plenty of room; spacious; roomy) 记 词根记忆: com + mod(=code 方式，范围) + ious → 大的范围 → 宽敞的
parable [ˈpærəbl]	*n.* 寓言(a short fictitious story that illustrates a moral attitude or a religious principle) 记 词根记忆: para(旁边) + bl(扔) + e → 向旁边扔，能平行比较 → 寓言 例 In certain forms of discourse such as the *parable*, the central point of a message can be effectively communicated even though this point is not explicit.
revere [rɪˈvɪr]	*v.* 尊敬(to have deep respect) 记 联想记忆: 我们都很敬畏(revere)这位严厉(severe)的老师
cosmopolitan [ˌkɑːzməˈpɑːlɪtən]	*adj.* 世界性的，全球的(having worldwide rather than limited or provincial scope or bearing) *n.* 世界主义者，四海为家的人(a person who has traveled widely and feels equally at home everywhere)
grumble [ˈɡrʌmbl]	*v.* 嘟囔，抱怨，发牢骚(to utter or mumble in discontent) 搭 grumble at 抱怨
sterile [ˈsterəl]	*adj.* 贫瘠且无植被的(producing little vegetation); 无细菌的(free from living organisms)
expeditiously [ˌekspəˈdɪʃəsli]	*adv.* 迅速地，敏捷地(promptly and efficiently) 同 rapidly, speedily, swiftly
continuation [kənˌtɪnjuˈeɪʃn]	*n.* 继续，延续(a resumption after an interruption; without stopping) 记 来自 continue(*v.* 继续)
parasite [ˈpærəsaɪt]	*n.* 食客(a person who lives off others and gives nothing in return); 寄生物(an organism that grows, feeds, and is sheltered on or in a different organism while contributing nothing to the survival of its host) 记 词根记忆: para(旁边) + sit(食物) + e → 坐在旁边吃的人或物 → 食客; 寄生物
clutter [ˈklʌtər]	*v.* 弄乱(to run in disorder) *n.* 零乱(a crowded or confused mass or collection)
auspices [ˈɔːspɪsɪz]	*n.* 支持，赞助(approval and support) 记 词根记忆: au + spic(看) + es → 看到(好事) → 赞助
misery [ˈmɪzəri]	*n.* 悲惨的境遇(a state of suffering); 痛苦，苦恼(a state of great unhappiness and emotional distress) 同 agony, dolor, woe

□ notable	□ predator	□ commodious	□ parable	□ revere	□ cosmopolitan
□ grumble	□ sterile	□ expeditiously	□ continuation	□ parasite	□ clutter
□ auspices	□ misery				

respite [ˈrespɪt]	*n.* 休息(an interval of rest or relief)；暂缓(a period of temporary delay) 记 词根记忆：re + spit(=spect 看) + e → 再看一下 → 暂缓
invigorate [ɪnˈvɪɡəreɪt]	*v.* 鼓舞，使精力充沛(to give life and energy to) 记 联想记忆：in(使…) + vigor(活力) + ate → 使有活力 → 鼓舞，使精力充沛
dispel [dɪˈspel]	*v.* 驱散，消除(to scatter and drive away；disperse) 记 词根记忆：dis(分开) + pel(推) → 推开 → 驱散
endorse [ɪnˈdɔːrs]	*v.* 赞同(to approve openly)；背书(to write one's name on the back) 记 词根记忆：en + dors(背) + e → 在背后签字 → 背书
probity [ˈproʊbəti]	*n.* 刚直，正直(uprightness；honesty) 例 Such was Brandon's *probity* that he was at times described as being honest as the day was long.
retrospect [ˈretrəspekt]	*n.* 回顾(a review of or meditation on past events) *v.* 回顾(to refer back)；回想(to go back over in thought) 搭 in retrospect 回顾，回想 同 reconsideration, reexamination, retrospection
terrestrial [təˈrestriəl]	*adj.* 地球的(of the Earth)；陆地的(relating to land) 记 词根记忆：terr(地) + estrial → 地球的
authenticate [ɔːˈθentɪkeɪt]	*v.* 证明…是真实的(to prove or serve to prove the authenticity of)
chromosome [ˈkroʊməsoʊm]	*n.* 染色体 记 词根记忆：chrom(颜色) + o + some(体) → 染色体
plot [plɑːt]	*n.* 情节(the plan or main story of a literary work)；阴谋(a secret plan；intrigue) *v.* 密谋，策划(to form a plot for；prearrange secretly or deviously)
clog [klɑːɡ]	*v.* 阻塞(to obstruct) *n.* 障碍(an obstruction) 记 联想记忆：c + log(木头) → 放上木头 → 阻塞
regressive [rɪˈɡresɪv]	*adj.* 退步的，退化的(moving backward to a primitive state or condition) 同 recessive, retrograde, retrogressive
fastidious [fæˈstɪdiəs]	*adj.* 难取悦的，挑剔的(not easy to please；very critical or discriminating) 记 联想记忆：fast(绝食) + idious(看作 tedious，乏味的) → 因乏味而绝食 → 挑剔的
untapped [ˌʌnˈtæpt]	*adj.* 未开发的，未利用的(not yet put to use) 记 来自 tap(*v.* 开发，利用)
impetuous [ɪmˈpetʃuəs]	*adj.* 冲动的，鲁莽的(impulsive；sudden) 搭 an impetuous decision 草率的决定
antagonize [ænˈtæɡənaɪz]	*v.* 使…敌对；与…对抗(to arouse hostility；show opposition) 记 词根记忆：ant(反) + agon(打斗，比赛) + ize → 对着打 → 与…对抗
accompany [əˈkʌmpəni]	*v.* 伴随，陪伴(to walk with sb. as a companion) 记 词根记忆：ac + company(陪伴) → 伴随，陪伴

16

□ respite　□ invigorate　□ dispel　□ endorse　□ probity　□ retrospect
□ terrestrial　□ authenticate　□ chromosome　□ plot　□ clog　□ regressive
□ fastidious　□ untapped　□ impetuous　□ antagonize　□ accompany

179

pedestrian [pə'destriən]	*adj.* 徒步的 (going or performed on foot)；缺乏想象力的 (unimaginative) *n.* 行人 (a person traveling on foot) 记 词根记忆：ped(脚) + estr + ian(表人) → 用脚走路的人 → 行人 例 We were amazed that a man who had been heretofore the most *pedestrian* of public speakers could, in a single speech, electrify an audience and bring them cheering to their feet.
dilute [daɪ'luːt]	*v.* 稀释，冲淡 (to thin down or weaken by mixing with water or other liquid) 记 词根记忆：di + lut(冲洗) + e → 冲开 → 稀释
enterprise ['entərpraɪz]	*n.* 公司，企业 (business company or firm)；进取心 (willingness to take risks and do difficult or new things)
caricature ['kærɪkətʃər]	*n.* 讽刺画；滑稽模仿 (art that has the qualities of caricature) 记 联想记忆：car(汽车) + i(我) + cat(猫) + ure → 我在汽车和猫之间 → 很滑稽的样子 → 滑稽模仿 同 burlesque, mock, mockery, travesty
self-sufficient [ˌselfsə'fɪʃnt]	*adj.* 自给自足的 (able to maintain oneself or itself without outside aid) 同 independent
abeyance [ə'beɪəns]	*n.* 中止，搁置 (temporary suspension of an activity) 记 发音记忆："又被压死" → (事情)因搁置而死 → 搁置 搭 in abeyance 搁置；暂停使用
permeate ['pɜːrmieɪt]	*v.* 扩散，弥漫 (to spread or diffuse through)；穿透 (to pass through the pores or interstices) 记 词根记忆：per(贯穿) + mea(通过) + te → 通过 → 扩散；穿透 同 impenetrate, penetrate, percolate
novelty ['nɑːvlti]	*n.* 新奇 (the quality of being novel; newness)；新奇的事物 (sth. new and unusual) 记 词根记忆：nov(新的) + el + ty → 新奇
noncommittal [ˌnɑːnkə'mɪtl]	*adj.* 态度暧昧的 (giving no clear indication of attitude or feeling)；不承担义务的 记 联想记忆：non(不) + committal(承担义务) → 不承担义务的 例 The president was *noncommittal* about farm subsidies, nor did he say much about the even more vital topic of unemployment.
expediency [ɪk'spiːdiənsi]	*n.* 方便 (advantageousness)；权宜之计 (a regard for what is politic or advantageous rather than for what is right or just) 记 词根记忆：ex + ped(脚) + iency → 把脚迈出去 → 权宜之计
narrow ['nærəʊ]	*adj.* 狭窄的 (of slender width)；狭隘的 (prejudiced) *v.* 变窄 (to contract) 例 The well-trained engineer must understand fields as diverse as physics, economics, geology, and sociology; thus, an overly *narrow* engineering curriculum should be avoided.

dilute

---

correlated [ˈkɔːrəleɪtɪd]	*adj.* 有相互关系的(mutually or reciprocally related) 同 correlative
beset [bɪˈset]	*v.* 镶嵌(to set or stud with or as if with ornaments); 困扰(to harass from all directions)
asceticism [əˈsetɪsɪzəm]	*n.* 禁欲主义
ineligible [ɪnˈelɪdʒəbl]	*adj.* 不合格的(not legally or morally qualified) 记 联想记忆: in(不) + eligible(合格的) → 不合格的
temptation [tempˈteɪʃn]	*n.* 诱惑, 诱惑物(sth. tempting) 例 In discussing Rothko's art, Breslin is scrupulous in keeping to the facts and resisting the *temptation* of fanciful interpretation. 同 allurement, decoy, enticement, inveiglement, lure
indented [ɪnˈdentɪd]	*adj.* 锯齿状的; 高低不平的
succinctness [səkˈsɪŋktnəs]	*n.* 简明, 简洁 同 conciseness, concision
saturnine [ˈsætərnaɪn]	*adj.* 忧郁的, 阴沉的(sluggish; sullen) 记 来自 Saturn(*n.* 土星)
turbulent [ˈtɜːrbjələnt]	*adj.* 混乱的(causing unrest, violence, or disturbance); 骚乱的(tempestuous) 记 词根记忆: turb(搅动) + ulent → 搅得厉害 → 骚乱的
descry [dɪˈskraɪ]	*v.* 看见, 察觉(to catch sight of; discern) 记 词根记忆: de(向下) + scry(写) → 写下 → 看见; 不要和 decry(*v.* 谴责)或 outcry(*v.* 呐喊)相混
mordant [ˈmɔːrdnt]	*adj.* 讥讽的, 尖酸的(biting or sarcastic in thought, manner, or style) 记 词根记忆: mord(咬) + ant → 咬人的 → 尖酸的
impostor [ɪmˈpɑːstər]	*n.* 冒充者, 骗子(a person who deceives under an assumed name) 记 词根记忆: im(进入) + pos(放) + tor → 把自己放入别人的角色 → 冒充者 例 The "*impostor* syndrome" often afflicts those who fear that true self-disclosure will lower them in others' esteem; rightly handled, however, candor may actually enhance one's standing.
indubitable [ɪnˈduːbɪtəbl]	*adj.* 不容置疑的(unquestionable) 记 词根记忆: in(不) + dub(不确定的) + it + able → 不容置疑的
tribulation [ˌtrɪbjuˈleɪʃn]	*n.* 苦难, 忧患(distress or suffering resulting from oppression or persecution) 记 词根记忆: tribul(给予) + ation → 上天给予的(惩罚) → 苦难
entitle [ɪnˈtaɪtl]	*v.* 使有权(做某事)(to give sb. the right to do sth.) 记 联想记忆: en(使) + title(权力) → 使有权

16

misnomer [ˌmɪsˈnoʊmər]	*n.* 名称的误用（an error in naming a person or place）；误用的名称（a name wrongly or unsuitably applied to a person or an object） 记 词根记忆：mis(错) + nom(名字) + er → 名称的误用 例 The term mole rat is a *misnomer*, for these small, furless rodents are neither moles nor rats.
homogeneous [ˌhoʊməˈdʒiːniəs]	*adj.* 同类的，相似的（of the same or similar kind or nature） 搭 a homogeneous grouping of students 一组同类的学生
angular [ˈæŋgjələr]	*adj.* 生硬的，笨拙的（lacking grace or smoothness；awkward）；有角的（having angles）；(指人)瘦削的(thin and bony)
precede [prɪˈsiːd]	*v.* 在…之前，早于(to be earlier than) 记 词根记忆：pre(在前面) + ced(走) + e → 走在…之前 → 早于
document	[ˈdɑːkjumənt] *n.* 文件(an original or official paper) [ˈdɑːkjument] *v.* 为…提供书面证明(to prove or support with documents) 同 certification, documentation, monument
proficiency [prəˈfɪʃnsi]	*n.* 进步（advancement in knowledge or skill）；熟练，精通（the quality or state of being proficient）
purport [ˈpɜːrpɔːrt]	*n.* 意义，涵义，主旨(meaning conveyed, implied；gist) 记 词根记忆：pur(附近) + port(带) → 带到主要意思附近，领会主旨 → 意义，主旨
altruism [ˈæltruɪzəm]	*n.* 利他主义；无私(selflessness) 记 词根记忆：altru(其他) + ism(主义) → 利他主义
deceptive [dɪˈseptɪv]	*adj.* 欺骗的，导致误解的（tending or having power to deceive） 搭 a deceptive advertisement 虚假广告
feigned [feɪnd]	*adj.* 假装的(pretended；simulated)；假的；不真诚的 记 和 feint(*n.* 佯攻) 一起记；A feint is a feigned attack. 佯攻是假装进攻。
curt [kɜːrt]	*adj.* (言词、行为)简略而草率的（brief, esp. to the point of rudeness；terse）

deceptive

减肥茶
一
天
掉
10
斤

Word List 17

suffragist [ˈsʌfrədʒɪst]	*n.* 参政权扩大论者；妇女政权论者（one who advocates extension of suffrage especially for women） 记 联想记忆：suff + rag（破布）+ ist → 主张让穿破布的人也参政 → 参政权扩大论者
taunt [tɔːnt]	*n.* 嘲笑，讥讽（a sarcastic challenge or insult）*v.* 嘲弄，嘲讽（to reproach or challenge in a mocking or insulting manner）
impeccable [ɪmˈpekəbl]	*adj.* 无瑕疵的（faultless；flawless） 记 词根记忆：im（无）+ pecc（斑点）+ able → 无斑点的 → 无瑕疵的 同 fleckless, immaculate, indefectible, irreproachable, perfect
gospel [ˈɡɑːspl]	*n.* 教义，信条（any doctrine or rule widely or ardently maintained） 记 来自《圣经·新约》中的福音书（Gospel）；Go（看作 God，上帝）+ spel（看作 spell，符咒、咒语）→ 上帝的话 → 教义，信条
rationale [ˌræʃəˈnæl]	*n.* 基本原理（fundamental reasons；the basis）
fortify [ˈfɔːrtɪfaɪ]	*v.* 加强，巩固（to make strong） 记 词根记忆：fort（强大）+ ify → 力量化 → 巩固
emend [iˈmend]	*v.* 订正，校订（to make scholarly corrections） 记 词根记忆：e（出）+ mend（错误）→ 找出错误 → 订正
dispensable [dɪˈspensəbl]	*adj.* 不必要的，可有可无的（capable of being dispensed with） 记 词根记忆：dis（分离）+ pens（重量）+ able → 重量可被分割的 → 不必要的
scenic [ˈsiːnɪk]	*adj.* 风景如画的（of or relating to natural scenery） 搭 scenic lift 观光电梯
ominous [ˈɑːmɪnəs]	*adj.* 恶兆的，不祥的（portentous；of an evil omen） 记 来自 omen（*n.* 预兆，征兆）
pursuit [pərˈsuːt]	*n.* 追赶（the act of pursuing）；职业（occupation） 记 联想记忆：钱包（purse）被小偷偷去，赶忙追赶（pursuit）
viral [ˈvaɪrəl]	*adj.* 病毒性的（caused by a virus） 记 来自 virus（*n.* 病毒）

□ suffragist	□ taunt	□ impeccable	□ gospel	□ rationale	□ fortify
□ emend	□ dispensable	□ scenic	□ ominous	□ pursuit	□ viral

deleterious [ˌdeləˈtɪriəs]	*adj.* 有害的，有毒的(harmful often in a subtle or unexpected way; injurious) 记 词根记忆：delete(删除) + rious → 要删除的东西 → 有害的 同 damaging, detrimental, hurtful, mischievous
particulate [pɑːrˈtɪkjələt]	*adj.* 微粒的(of or relating to minute separate particles) *n.* 微粒(a minute separate particle, as of a granular substance or powder)
posthumous [ˈpɑːstʃəməs]	*adj.* 死后的，身后的(following or occurring after death) 记 词根记忆：post(在…之后) + hum(地面) + ous → 埋到地下以后 → 死后的，身后的
urbane [ɜːrˈbeɪn]	*adj.* 温文尔雅的(notably polite or polished in manner) 同 refined, svelte
designate [ˈdezɪgneɪt]	*v.* 指定，任命(to indicate and set apart for a specific purpose, office, or duty)；指明，指出 *adj.* (已受委派)尚未上任的(appointed to a job but not yet having officially started it) 记 词根记忆：de + sign(标出) + ate → 标出来 → 指定
protrude [proʊˈtruːd]	*v.* 突出，伸出(to jut out) 记 词根记忆：pro(向前) + trud(伸出) +e → 向前伸 → 伸出
hypersensitive [ˌhaɪpərˈsensətɪv]	*adj.* 非常敏感的(excessively or abnormally sensitive) 搭 hypersensitive to pollen 花粉过敏
illustrative [ɪˈlʌstrətɪv]	*adj.* 解说性的，用作说明的(serving, tending, or designed to illustrate) 搭 for illustrative purposes 为了便于说明
potshot [ˈpɑːtʃɑːt]	*n.* 盲目射击(a shot taken from ambush or at a random or easy target)；肆意抨击(a critical remark made in a random or sporadic manner) *v.* 肆意抨击
profound [prəˈfaʊnd]	*adj.* 深的(deep)；深刻的，深远的(very strongly felt)；渊博的；深奥的(difficult to fathom or understand) 记 联想记忆：pro(在…前) + found(创立) → 有超前创见性的 → 深刻的，深远的 例 No one is neutral about Stephens; he inspires either uncritical adulation or *profound* antipathy in those who work for him. 同 abstruse, esoteric, occult, recondite
spherical [ˈsferɪkl]	*adj.* 球的，球状的(having the form of a sphere or of one of its segments) 同 globe-shaped, globular, rotund, round
delude [dɪˈluːd]	*v.* 欺骗，哄骗(to mislead; deceive; trick) 记 词根记忆：de + lud(玩弄) + e → 玩弄别人 → 欺骗 同 beguile, bluff
cogent [ˈkoʊdʒənt]	*adj.* 有说服力的(compelling; convincing; valid) 记 联想记忆：cog(齿轮牙) + ent → 像齿轮牙咬合一样严谨 → 有说服力的 搭 cogent arguments 有说服力的争辩
unproven [ʌnˈpruːvn]	*adj.* 未经证实的(not proved or tested)

184

□ deleterious	□ particulate	□ posthumous	□ urbane	□ designate	□ protrude
□ hypersensitive	□ illustrative	□ potshot	□ profound	□ spherical	□ delude
□ cogent	□ unproven				

connoisseur [ˌkɑːnəˈsɜːr]	*n.* 鉴赏家，行家（a person who has expert knowledge and keen discrimination in some field in the fine arts or in matters of taste） 记 词根记忆：con + nois(知道) + s + eur(人) → 什么都知道的人 → 行家
antagonistic [ænˌtægəˈnɪstɪk]	*adj.* 敌对的，对抗性的（marked by or resulting from antagonism） 同 adverse, antipathetic, opposed, opposing
mite [maɪt]	*n.* 极小量（a very little）；小虫 记 mite 原指"螨虫"
uphold [ʌpˈhoʊld]	*v.* 维护，支持（to give support to） 记 联想记忆：up(向上) + hold(举) → 举起来 → 支持
veil [veɪl]	*n.* 面纱；遮蔽物 *v.* 以面纱掩盖（to cover, obscure, or conceal with a veil）
commodity [kəˈmɑːdəti]	*n.* 商品（any article of commerce） 搭 a drop in commodity prices 商品价格的下跌
pithy [ˈpɪθi]	*adj.* （讲话或文章）简练有力的，言简意赅的（tersely cogent） 同 concise
jolting [ˈdʒoʊltɪŋ]	*adj.* 令人震惊的 同 astonishing, astounding, startling, surprising
confound [kənˈfaʊnd]	*v.* 使迷惑，搞混（to puzzle and surprise sb.） 记 词根记忆：con + found(基础) → 把基础的东西全放到一起了 → 搞混
impute [ɪmˈpjuːt]	*v.* 归咎于（to charge with fault）；归于（to attribute） 记 词根记忆：im(进入) + put(认为) + e → 认为某人有罪 → 归咎于
entrepreneur [ˌɑːntrəprəˈnɜːr]	*n.* 企业家，创业人（a person who organizes and manages a business undertaking） 记 来自法语，等同于 enterpriser
aspect [ˈæspekt]	*n.* （问题等的）方面（a particular status or phase in which sth. appears or may be regarded）；面貌，外表（appearance） 记 词根记忆：a+spect(看) → 看向的地方 → （问题等的）方面
skeptical [ˈskeptɪkl]	*adj.* 怀疑的；多疑的（marked by or given to doubt） 搭 be skeptical of 怀疑…
humanitarian [hjuːˌmænɪˈteriən]	*n.* 人道主义者（a person promoting human welfare and social reform） 同 philanthropist
unremitting [ˌʌnrɪˈmɪtɪŋ]	*adj.* 不间断的，持续的（never stopping） 记 联想记忆：un(不) + remitting(间断的) → 不间断的，持续的 例 In the nineteenth century, novelists and unsympathetic travelers portrayed the American West as a land of *unremitting* adversity, whereas promoters and idealists created a compelling image of a land of infinite promise.
incomprehensible [ɪnˌkɑːmprɪˈhensəbl]	*adj.* 难以理解的，难懂的（impossible to comprehend）

17

□ connoisseur	□ antagonistic	□ mite	□ uphold	□ veil	□ commodity
□ pithy	□ jolting	□ confound	□ impute	□ entrepreneur	□ aspect
□ skeptical	□ humanitarian	□ unremitting	□ incomprehensible		

185

unreasonable [ʌnˈriːznəbl]	*adj.* 不讲道理的 (not governed by or acting according to reason); 非理智的, 过分的 (exceeding the bounds of reason or moderation) 例 Although Tom was aware that it would be impolitic to display annoyance publicly at the sales conference, he could not hide his irritation with the client's *unreasonable* demands.
intact [ɪnˈtækt]	*adj.* 完整的, 完好无缺的 (complete; unimpaired) 记 词根记忆: in(不) + tact(接触) → 未被接触的 → 完整的 例 The hierarchy of medical occupations is in many ways a caste system; its strata remain *intact* and the practitioners in them have very little vertical mobility. 同 flawless, unblemished, unmarred
incipient [ɪnˈsɪpiənt]	*adj.* 初期的, 起初的 (beginning to exist or appear) 记 词根记忆: in + cip(掉) + ient → 掉进来的 → 初期的 例 It is wise to begin to treat a progressive disease while it is still in its *incipient* stage. 同 inceptive, initial, initiatory, introductory, nascent
exert [ɪgˈzɜːrt]	*v.* 运用, 行使, 施加 (to apply with great energy or straining effort) 记 词根记忆: ex(出) + ert(=sert 放置) → 将力量释放出来 → 运用
impudent [ˈɪmpjədənt]	*adj.* 鲁莽的, 无礼的 (marked by contemptuous or cocky boldness or disregard of others)
recur [rɪˈkɜːr]	*v.* 重现, 再发生 (to come up again); 复发 (to occur again after an interval)
platitude [ˈplætɪtuːd]	*n.* 陈词滥调 (a banal, trite, or stale remark) 记 词根记忆: plat(平的) + itude → 平庸之词 → 陈词滥调
obligated [ˈɑːblɪɡeɪtɪd]	*adj.* 有义务的, 有责任的 同 beholden, indebted, obliged
combative [kəmˈbætɪv]	*adj.* 好斗的 (marked by eagerness to fight or contend) 记 来自 combat(*v.* 与…搏斗)
momentarily [ˌmoʊmənˈterəli]	*adv.* 暂时地 (for a moment); 片刻, 立刻 (in a moment) 记 来自 momentary(*adj.* 短暂的, 瞬间的)
addict [ˈædɪkt]	*v.* 沉溺; 上瘾 (to be an addict; devote oneself to sth. habitually) 记 词根记忆: ad(一再) + dict(说, 要求) → 一再要求 → 上瘾
astigmatic [ˌæstɪɡˈmætɪk]	*adj.* 散光的, 乱视的 (affected with, relating to astigmatism) 记 词根记忆: a + stigma(污点) + tic → 看不见污点 → 散光的
guile [ɡaɪl]	*n.* 欺骗, 欺诈 (deceit); 狡猾 (cunning) 记 发音记忆: "贵了" → 东西买贵了 → 被欺骗了 → 欺骗
drudgery [ˈdrʌdʒəri]	*n.* 苦工, 苦活 (dull and fatiguing work) 记 来自 drudge(*v.* 做苦工)

□ unreasonable □ intact □ incipient □ exert □ impudent □ recur
□ platitude □ obligated □ combative □ momentarily □ addict □ astigmatic
□ guile □ drudgery

discredit [dɪsˈkredɪt]	*v.* 怀疑(to reject as untrue; disbelieve) *n.* 丧失名誉(disgrace; dishonor) 记 词根记忆：dis(不) + cred(相信) + it → 不相信 → 怀疑
homogeneity [ˌhɑːmədʒəˈniːəti]	*n.* 同种，同质(quality of being homogeneous) 记 词根记忆：homo(同类的) + gene(基因) + ity(表性质) → 具有同种基因 → 同种，同质
inestimable [ɪnˈestɪməbl]	*adj.* 无法估计的(incapable of being estimated or computed)；无价的，极有价值的(too valuable or excellent to be measured or appreciated)
effervescence [ˌefərˈvesns]	*n.* 冒泡(bubbling, hissing, and foaming as gas escapes)；活泼(liveliness or exhilaration) 同 buoyancy, ebullience, exuberance, exuberancy
heinous [ˈheɪnəs]	*adj.* 十恶不赦的，可憎的(grossly wicked or reprehensible; abominable) 记 联想记忆：he(他) + in + ous(音似：恶死) → 他在恶死中 → 十恶不赦的
profitable [ˈprɑːfɪtəbl]	*adj.* 有利可图的(affording profits) 例 There are simply no incentives for buying stock in certain industries since rapidly changing environmental restrictions will make a *profitable* return on any investment very unlikely. 同 advantageous, gainful, lucrative, remunerative
blazing [ˈbleɪzɪŋ]	*adj.* 炽烧的，闪耀的(of outstanding power, speed, heat, or intensity) 记 来自 blaze(*v.* 燃烧；照耀)
economy [ɪˈkɑːnəmi]	*n.* 节约(thrifty and efficient use of material resources)；经济(the structure or conditions of economic life) *adj.* 经济的(designed to save money) 记 发音记忆："依靠农民" → 中国是农业大国，经济发展离不开农民 → 经济 同 frugality
supernova [ˌsuːpərˈnoʊvə]	*n.* 超新星 记 联想记忆：super(超级) + nova(新星) → 超新星
abhor [əbˈhɔːr]	*v.* 憎恨，厌恶(to detest; hate) 记 词根记忆：ab + hor(恨，怕) → 憎恨，厌恶 同 abominate, execrate, loathe
stem [stem]	*n.* (植物的)茎，叶柄 *v.* 阻止，遏制(水流等)(to stop or dam up) 例 This new government is faced not only with managing its economy but also with implementing new rural development programs to *stem* the flow of farm workers to the city.
underlie [ˌʌndərˈlaɪ]	*v.* 位于…之下(to lie or be situated under)；构成…的基础(to be at the basis of)；【经】(权力、索赔等)优先于(to constitute a prior financial claim over)
ostracize [ˈɑːstrəsaɪz]	*v.* 排斥(to exclude from a group by common consent)；放逐(to exile by ostracism) 记 词根记忆：ostrac (贝壳) + ize → 用投贝壳的方法决定是否放逐某人 → 放逐 例 As news of his indictment spread through the town, the citizens began to *ostracize* him and to avoid meeting him. 同 banish, expatriate, expulse, oust

17

□ discredit	□ homogeneity	□ inestimable	■ effervescence	□ heinous	□ profitable
□ blazing	□ economy	□ supernova	□ abhor	□ stem	□ underlie
□ ostracize					

bravado [brəˈvɑːdoʊ]	*n.* 故作勇敢，虚张声势（pretended courage） 记 来自 bravo（*interj.* 欢呼；好极了）；词根记忆：brav（勇敢）+ ado（状态） → 故作勇敢
exemplify [ɪɡˈzemplɪfaɪ]	*v.* 是…的典型，作为…例子（to be a typical example of sth.） 同 demonstrate, illustrate
extension [ɪkˈstenʃn]	*n.* 延伸，扩展（the action of extending; an enlargement in scope or operation） 同 elongation, prolongation, protraction
colonize [ˈkɑːlənaɪz]	*v.* 建立殖民地，拓殖（to establish a colony in an area）；定居，居于
wistful [ˈwɪstfl]	*adj.* 惆怅的，渴望的（thoughtful and rather sad） 同 pensive, yearning
impermanent [ɪmˈpɜːrmənənt]	*adj.* 暂时的（temporary） 记 联想记忆：im（不）+ permanent（永久的）→ 不能永久的 → 暂时的
anatomical [ˌænəˈtɑːmɪkl]	*adj.* 解剖学的（of, or relating to anatomy） 记 来自 anatomy（*n.* 解剖学，解剖）；ana（分开）+ tomy（切）→ 切开 → 解剖
repugnance [rɪˈpʌɡnəns]	*n.* 嫌恶，反感（strong dislike, distaste, or antagonism） 例 Few of us take the pains to study our cherished convictions; indeed, we almost have a natural *repugnance* to doing so.
redirect [ˌriːdəˈrekt]	*v.* 改寄（信件）（to send in a new direction）；改变方向（to change the course or direction） 记 词根记忆：re（重新）+ direct（指向）→ 改变方向
conscientious [ˌkɑːnʃiˈenʃəs]	*adj.* 尽责的（careful to do what one ought to do）；小心谨慎的（scrupulous） 记 词根记忆：con + sci（知道）+ entious（多…的）→ 所有事情都了解 → 尽责的 搭 be conscientious of... 对…尽责
confusion [kənˈfjuːʒn]	*n.* 困惑，糊涂（an act or instance of confusing）；混乱，骚乱（a confused mass or mixture） 搭 be in confusion about... 对…感到困惑 同 clutter, disarray
reconciliation [ˌrekənsɪliˈeɪʃn]	*n.* 和解（the action of reconciling）；调解 例 Their change of policy brought out a *reconciliation* with Britain.
obliqueness [əˈbliːknəs]	*n.* 斜度；倾斜 记 来自 oblique（*adj.* 斜的，歪的）
fret [fret]	*v.* （使）烦躁，焦虑（to irritate; annoy）*n.* 烦躁，焦虑（an agitation of mind） 同 cark, pother, ruffle, vex
ossify [ˈɑːsɪfaɪ]	*v.* 骨化（to change or develop into bone）；僵化（to become hardened or conventional and opposed to change） 记 词根记忆：oss（骨头）+ ify（…化）→ 骨化；僵化

ridicule [ˈrɪdɪkjuːl]	*n.* 嘲笑，奚落(unkind expression of amusement) 记 词根记忆：rid(笑) + icule → 嘲笑 例 Like many other pioneers, Dr. Elizabeth Blackwell, founder of the New York Infirmary, the first American hospital staffed entirely by women, faced *ridicule* from her contemporaries but has received great honor posthumously.
proselytize [ˈprɑːsəlataɪz]	*v.* (使)皈依(to recruit or convert to a new faith) 记 词根记忆：pros(靠近) + elyt(来到) + ize → 走到(佛祖)面前 → (使)皈依
despicable [dɪˈspɪkəbl]	*adj.* 可鄙的，卑劣的(deserving to be despised; contemptible) 记 词根记忆：de + spic(看) + able → 不值得看的 → 卑劣的
adamant [ˈædəmənt]	*adj.* 坚决的，固执的（unyielding; inflexible）；强硬的（too hard to be broken） 记 联想记忆：adam(亚当) + ant(蚂蚁) → 亚当和蚂蚁都很固执 → 固执的 搭 remain adamant in 对…很固执 同 obdurate, rigid, unbending
debase [dɪˈbeɪs]	*v.* 贬低，贬损(to make lower in value, quality or dignity) 记 词根记忆：de + base(低) → 使低下去 → 贬低
wholesale [ˈhoʊlseɪl]	*adj.* 批发的(of, relating to, or engaged in the sale of commodities in quantity for resale)；大规模的(performed or existing on a large scale)
irredeemable [ˌɪrɪˈdiːməbl]	*adj.* 无法挽回的，不可救药的(incapable of being remedied) 记 联想记忆：ir(不) + redeem(挽回，弥补) + able → 无法挽回的，不可救药的
steady [ˈstedi]	*adj.* 稳定的(direct or sure in movement)；不变的(fixed) 记 联想记忆：st + eady（看作 ready，有准备的）→ 事先有准备，心里就有底 → 稳定的 例 Although some consider forcefulness and persistence to be two traits desirable to the same degree, I think that making a violent effort is much less useful than maintaining a *steady* one. 同 abiding, constant, equable, stabile, steadfast
imperial [ɪmˈpɪriəl]	*adj.* 帝王的，至尊的（of, relating to, or suggestive of an empire or a sovereign） 例 The sale of Alaska was not so much an American coup as a matter of expediency for an *imperial* Russia that was short of cash and unable to defend its own continental coastline.
untreated [ˌʌnˈtriːtɪd]	*adj.* 未治疗的(not receiving medical treatment)；未经处理的(in a natural state)
discursive [dɪsˈkɜːrsɪv]	*adj.* 散漫的，不得要领的（rambling or wandering from topic to topic without order） 记 词根记忆：dis + curs(跑) + ive → 到处乱跑 → 散漫的
exposure [ɪkˈspoʊʒər]	*n.* 暴露，显露，曝光(action of exposing or state of being exposed) 记 词根记忆：ex(出) + pos(放) + ure → 放出来 → 暴露，显露

17

□ ridicule	□ proselytize	□ despicable	□ adamant	□ debase	□ wholesale
□ irredeemable	□ steady	□ imperial	□ untreated	□ discursive	□ exposure

dictate [ˈdɪkteɪt]	*v.* 口述（to speak or read aloud for sb. else to write down）；命令（to prescribe or command forcefully） 记 词根记忆：dict(讲话；命令) + ate → 口述；命令
impropriety [ˌɪmprəˈpraɪəti]	*n.* 不得体的言行举止（an improper or indecorous act or remark）；不合适，不适当（the quality or state of being improper）
secular [ˈsekjələr]	*adj.* 世俗的，尘世的（worldly rather than spiritual） 例 For those Puritans who believed that *secular* obligations were imposed by divine will, the correct course of action was not withdrawal from the world but conscientious discharge of the duties of business.
utility [juːˈtɪləti]	*n.* 实用（fitness for some purpose or worth to some end）；有用（something useful or designed for use） 记 词根记忆：util(使用) + ity → 实用；有用 例 We look with pride at our new bridges and dams, for they are works of art as well as of *utility*.
egoist [ˈiːɡoʊɪst]	*n.* 自我主义者（a believer in egoism） 记 来自 ego(*n.* 自我)
scarcity [ˈskersəti]	*n.* 不足，缺乏（a state of being scarce） 搭 scarcity of... …的短缺
vestige [ˈvestɪdʒ]	*n.* 痕迹，遗迹（the very small slight remains of sth.） 同 relic, trace
innovative [ˈɪnəveɪtɪv]	*adj.* 革新的，创新的（introducing or using new ideas or techniques） 记 来自 innovate(*v.* 革新，创新)
explicitly [ɪkˈsplɪsɪtli]	*adv.* 明白地；明确地 同 definitely, distinctly, expressly
chart [tʃɑːrt]	*n.* 图表（map; a sheet） *v.* 绘制地图，制订计划（to make a map or chart） 同 graph, tabulation
intensification [ɪnˌtensɪfɪˈkeɪʃn]	*n.* 增强，加剧；激烈化 记 来自 intensify(*v.* 增强，加剧)
reciprocate [rɪˈsɪprəkeɪt]	*v.* 回报，答谢（to make a return for sth.） 记 词根记忆：re + cip(收下) + rocate → 再次收下 → 答谢
chronological [ˌkrɑːnəˈlɑːdʒɪkl]	*adj.* 按年代顺序排列的（of, relating to, or arranged in or according to the order of time）
antedate [ˌæntiˈdeɪt]	*v.* （在信、支票等上）填写比实际日期早的日期；早于（to assign to a date prior to that of actual occurrence） 记 词根记忆：ante(前面) + date(日期) → 在现在的日期前面 → 早于 同 antecede, forerun, pace, precede, predate
ratify [ˈrætɪfaɪ]	*v.* 批准（to approve formally; confirm） 记 词根记忆：rat(估算，清点) + ify → 一一地清点 → 批准

□ dictate	□ impropriety	□ secular	□ utility	□ egoist	□ scarcity
□ vestige	□ innovative	□ explicitly	□ chart	□ intensification	□ reciprocate
□ chronological	□ antedate	□ ratify			

pensive [ˈpensɪv]	*adj.* 沉思的（reflective；meditative）；忧心忡忡的 （suggestive of sad thoughtfulness） 记 词根记忆：pens(挂) + ive → 挂在心上 → 沉 思的；忧心忡忡的
motivate [ˈmoʊtɪveɪt]	*v.* 激发，刺激（to provide with a motive） 记 词根记忆：mot(动) + iv + ate(使…) → 激发
accuracy [ˈækjərəsi]	*n.* 精确，准确（precision；exactness） 记 词根记忆：ac + cur(关心) + acy → 不断关心 才能保证精确 → 精确
drizzly [ˈdrɪzli]	*adj.* 毛毛细雨的 记 注意该单词虽以-ly 结尾，但不是副词，而是形容词
bizarre [bɪˈzɑːr]	*adj.* 奇异的，古怪的（grotesque；fantastic） 记 集市(bazaar)上有各种古怪的(bizarre)东西 同 oddball, outlandish, peculiar, queer, weird
architectural [ˌɑːrkɪˈtektʃərəl]	*adj.* 建筑上的；建筑学的（of or relating to architecture） 搭 architectural design 建筑设计
tragic [ˈtrædʒɪk]	*adj.* 悲惨的（of, marked by, or expressive of tragedy） 例 Though set in a mythical South American country, Isabel Allende's novel is rooted in the *tragic* history of Chile.
outgrow [ˌaʊtˈɡroʊ]	*vt.* 生长速度超过…，长得比…快（to grow or increase faster than） 记 组合词：out(向外；超越) + grow(生长) → 生长速度超过…
outspoken [aʊtˈspoʊkən]	*adj.* 坦率的，直言不讳的（direct and open in speech or expression） 记 组合词：out(出) + spoken(口头的，说的) → 说出来的 → 直言不讳的 例 While Parker is very *outspoken* on issues she cares about, she is not fanatical; she concedes the strength of opposing arguments when they expose weaknesses inherent in her own.
galaxy [ˈɡæləksi]	*n.* 星系；一群(杰出人物)（an assemblage of brilliant or notable persons）
barren [ˈbærən]	*adj.* 不育的；贫瘠的；不结果实的（sterile；bare） 记 发音记忆："拔了" → 拔了所有植物 → 贫瘠的
ultimately [ˈʌltɪmətli]	*adv.* 最后，终于（in the end, eventually） 例 Just as all roads once led to Rome, all blood vessels in the human body *ultimately* empty into the heart.
glossary [ˈɡlɑːsəri]	*n.* 词汇表；难词表（a list of difficult, technical, or foreign terms with definitions or translations） 记 词根记忆：gloss(舌头；语言) + ary → 词汇表
evade [ɪˈveɪd]	*v.* 躲避，逃避（to avoid or escape by deceit or cleverness；elude）；规避 （to avoid facing up to） 记 词根记忆：e + vad(走) + e → 走出去 → 逃避 同 duck, eschew, shun

□ pensive	□ motivate	□ accuracy	□ drizzly	□ bizarre	□ architectural
□ tragic	□ outgrow	□ outspoken	□ galaxy	□ barren	□ ultimately
□ glossary	□ evade				

salient	*adj.* 显著的，突出的（noticeable; conspicuous; prominent）
[ˈseɪliənt]	记 词根记忆：sal(跳) + ient → 跳起来 → 突出的
	例 Ultimately, the book's credibility is strained; the slender, though far from nonexistent, web of evidence presented on one *salient* point is expected to support a vast superstructure of implications.
remote	*adj.* 遥远的（far removed in space, time, or relation）；偏僻的（secluded）
[rɪˈmoʊt]	记 词根记忆：re(反) + mot(移动) + e → 向相反方向移动，越来越远的 → 遥远的
regale	*v.* 款待，宴请（to feast with delicacies）；使…快乐（to give pleasure or amusement to）
[rɪˈgeɪl]	记 词根记忆：re(使) + gale(高兴) → 使客人高兴 → 款待
emblematic	*adj.* 作为象征的（symbolic; representative）
[ˌembləˈmætɪk]	记 来自emblem(*n.* 象征)
symmetrical	*adj.* 对称的（having, involving, or exhibiting symmetry）
[sɪˈmetrɪkl]	同 balanced, proportional, proportionate
braggart	*n.* 吹牛者（the person who brags）
[ˈbrægərt]	
spiral	*adj.* 螺旋形的；上升的 *v.* 螺旋式上升或下降
[ˈspaɪrəl]	记 来自spire(*n.* 螺旋)
	同 coil, curl, entwine, twist
vainglory	*n.* 自负（excessive or ostentatious pride especially in one's achievements）；虚荣（vanity）
[ˌveɪnˈglɔːri]	同 egoism, egotism, swellheadedness
shuffle	*v.* 洗牌（to rearrange (as playing cards, dominoes, or tiles) to produce a random order）；拖步走；支吾（to act or speak in an evasive manner）
[ˈʃʌfl]	记 参考：reshuffle(*n./v.* 重新改组)
intuition	*n.* 直觉（the act or faculty of knowing or sensing without the use of rational processes; immediate cognition）；直觉知识（knowledge gained by this power）
[ˌɪntuˈɪʃn]	记 来自intuit(*v.* 由直觉知道)
fundamental	*adj.* 根本的，基本的（of or forming the basis or foundation of sth.）；十分重要的（essential）
[ˌfʌndəˈmentl]	记 来自fundament(*n.* 基础)
cellular	*adj.* 细胞的（of, relating to, or consisting of cells）；蜂窝式的（containing cavities）
[ˈseljələr]	搭 cellular organization 细胞组织
eloquent	*adj.* 雄辩的，流利的（marked by forceful and fluent expression）
[ˈeləkwənt]	记 词根记忆：e + loqu(说) + ent(…的) → 能说会道的 → 雄辩的
	同 articulate

eloquent

wordy [ˈwɜːrdi]	*adj.* 冗长的，多言的(using or containing many and usually too many words)
fused [fjuːzd]	*adj.* 熔化的 记 来自 fuse(*v.* 熔化；融合)
inferable [ɪnˈfɜːrəbl]	*adj.* 能推理的，能推论的
nubile [ˈnuːbaɪl]	*adj.* 适婚的(marriageable)；性感的(sexually attractive) 记 词根记忆：nub(结婚) + ile → 适婚的
fraternity [frəˈtɜːrnəti]	*n.* 同行(a group of people with the same beliefs, interests, work, etc.)；友爱(fraternal relationship or spirit)
unrepresentative [ˌʌnˌreprɪˈzentətɪv]	*adj.* 没有代表性的(not exemplifying a class) 例 It would be misleading to use a published play to generalize about fifteenth-century drama: the very fact of publication should serve as a warning of the play's *unrepresentative* character.
unfertilized [ʌnˈfɜːrtəlaɪzd]	*adj.* 未施肥的；未受精的 同 unimpregnated
aggressive [əˈɡresɪv]	*adj.* 好斗的(militant; assertive)；有进取心的(full of enterprise and initiative) 记 词根记忆：ag(加强) + gress(行走) + ive → 到处乱走的 → 好斗的 搭 aggressive entrepreneur 有进取心的企业家 同 assertory, pushful, self-assertive
unadorned [ˌʌnəˈdɔːrnd]	*adj.* 未装饰的，朴素的 例 Rousseau's short discourse, a work that was generally consistent with the cautious, *unadorned* prose of the day, deviated from that prose style in its unrestrained discussion of the physical sciences. outline
outline [ˈaʊtlaɪn]	*n.* 轮廓；概要(the main ideas or facts) 记 组合词：out(出来) + line(线条) → 划出线条 → 轮廓
discomfit [dɪsˈkʌmfɪt]	*v.* 使难堪，使困惑(to make uneasy; disconcert; embarrass) 记 联想记忆：dis(不) + comfit(看作 comfort, 舒适) → 使不舒服 → 使难堪

17

□ wordy　　□ fused　　□ inferable　　□ nubile　　□ fraternity　　□ unrepresentative
 □ unfertilized　　□ aggressive　　□ unadorned　　□ outline　　□ discomfit

193

音频

beleaguer [bɪ'liːgə]	*v.* 围攻 (to besiege by encircling)；骚扰 (to harass) 记 联想记忆：be + leaguer(围攻的部队或兵营) → 围攻 同 beset
participate [pɑːr'tɪsɪpeɪt]	*v.* 分担 (to possess some of the attributes of a person, thing, or quality)；参与 (to take part in sth.)；分享 (to have a part or share in sth.) 记 联想记忆：parti(看作 party, 晚会) + cip(抓, 拿) + ate → 找人参加晚会 → 参与 搭 participate in 参与…
trigger ['trɪgər]	*n.* 扳机 *v.* 引发，引起，触发 (to initiate, actuate, or set off) 同 activate, spark, trip
avaricious [ˌævə'rɪʃəs]	*adj.* 贪婪的，贪心的 (full of avarice; greedy) 记 来自 avarice(*n.* 贪婪，贪心)
irrevocable [ɪ'revəkəbl]	*adj.* 不能撤回的，无法取消的 (not possible to revoke) 记 词根记忆：ir(不) + re(向后) + voc(叫喊) + able → 不能向后叫喊的 → 不能撤回的，无法取消的
consumption [kən'sʌmpʃn]	*n.* 消费，消耗 (the act or process of consuming) 记 来自 consume(*v.* 消耗，耗费)
corrosive [kə'rousɪv]	*adj.* 腐蚀性的，腐蚀的，蚀坏的 (tending or having the power to corrode) 同 caustic, erosive
infertile [ɪn'fɜːrtl]	*adj.* 贫瘠的，不结果实的 (not fertile or productive)
exorcise ['eksɔːrsaɪz]	*v.* 驱除妖魔 (to expel by adjuration; free of an evil spirit)；去除(坏念头等) (to get rid of) 记 词根记忆：ex + or(说) + cise → 通过说话把不好的东西赶出 → 驱除妖魔
iterate ['ɪtəreɪt]	*v.* 重申，重做 (to do or utter repeatedly) 记 词根记忆：iter(=again 再) + ate → 再来一次 → 重申，重做
debilitate [dɪ'bɪlɪteɪt]	*v.* 使衰弱 (to make weak or feeble; weaken) 同 depress, enervate
climactic [klaɪ'mæktɪk]	*adj.* 高潮的 (of, relating to, or constituting a climax) 记 来自 climax(*n.* 高潮)

☐ beleaguer ☐ participate ☐ trigger ☐ avaricious ☐ irrevocable ☐ consumption
☐ corrosive ☐ infertile ☐ exorcise ☐ iterate ☐ debilitate ☐ climactic

sharpen [ˈʃɑːrpən]	*v.* 削尖 (to make sharp or sharper); 使敏锐, 使敏捷 同 hone
intractable [ɪnˈtræktəbl]	*adj.* 倔强的, 难以管理的 (not easily managed; unruly or stubborn); 难以加工的, 难以操作的 (difficult to mold or manipulate) 记 词根记忆: in(不) + tract(拉) + able → 拉不动的 → 倔强的
serenity [səˈrenəti]	*n.* 平静 (the quality or state of being serene) 例 As painted by Constable, the scene is not one of bucolic *serenity*; rather it shows a striking emotional and intellectual tension. 同 placidity, repose, tranquility
sincere [sɪnˈsɪr]	*adj.* 诚实的, 坦率的 (honest; straightforward); 诚挚的 (not pretended; genuine) 记 联想记忆: sin(罪) + cere → 把自己的罪过告诉你 → 诚挚的 例 Einstein's humility was so profound that it might have seemed a pose affected by a great man had it not been so obviously *sincere*.
debauch [dɪˈbɔːtʃ]	*v.* 使堕落, 败坏 (to lead away from virtue or excellence) *n.* 堕落 (an act or occasion of debauchery) 同 corrupt, deprave, pervert
render [ˈrendər]	*v.* 呈递, 提供 (to present or send in); 给予, 归还 (to give sth. in return or exchange) 记 联想记忆: 给予(render)后自然成为出借人(lender)
repel [rɪˈpel]	*v.* 击退 (to fight against; resist); 使反感 (to cause aversion) 记 词根记忆: re(反) + pel(推) → 反推 → 击退 例 Gaddis is a formidably talented writer whose work has been, unhappily, more likely to intimidate or *repel* his readers than to lure them into his fictional world.
boundless [ˈbaʊndləs]	*adj.* 无限的, 无边无际的 (having no boundaries) 记 组合词: bound(边界, 范围) + less(较少的) → 无边无际的
stabilize [ˈsteɪbəlaɪz]	*v.* 使稳定, 使坚固 (to make stable, steadfast, or firm) 记 来自 stable(*adj.* 稳固的)
reflective [rɪˈflektɪv]	*adj.* 反射的, 反照的 (capable of reflecting light, images, or sound waves); 深思熟虑的 (thoughtful) 搭 be reflective of 是…的反映或体现
valve [vælv]	*n.* 活门, 阀门
pop [pɑːp]	*v.* 发出"砰"的一声 (to make or burst with a sharp sound); 突然出现 (to go, come, or appear suddenly)
opinionated [əˈpɪnjəneɪtɪd]	*adj.* 固执己见的 (holding obstinately to one's own opinions) 记 来自 opinion(*n.* 观点)
thematic [θiːˈmætɪk]	*adj.* 主题的 (of, relating to, or constituting a theme) 记 来自 theme(*n.* 主题)

18

□ sharpen	□ intractable	□ serenity	□ sincere	□ debauch	□ render
□ repel	□ boundless	□ stabilize	□ reflective	□ valve	□ pop
□ opinionated	□ thematic				

stingy	*adj.* 吝啬的，小气的(not generous or liberal)
[ˈstɪndʒi]	同 chinchy, miserly, niggard, parsimonious, penurious, pinchpenny
academic	*adj.* 学院的，学术的 (associated with an academy or school)；理论的 (theoretical)
[ˌækəˈdemɪk]	记 来自 academy(*n.* 学院，学术团体)
	搭 academic field 学术领域
exhaust	*v.* 耗尽；使筋疲力尽(to make sb. very tired) *n.* (机器排出的)废气
[ɪgˈzɔːst]	记 词根记忆：ex(出) + haust(抽) → 把水全部抽出 → 耗尽
umbrage	*n.* 不快，愤怒(a feeling of pique, resentment or insult)
[ˈʌmbrɪdʒ]	记 词根记忆：umbra(影子) + ge → 心里的影子 → 不快
scramble	*v.* 攀登(to move or climb hastily)；搅乱，使混杂(to toss or mix together)；争夺(to struggle eagerly for possession of sth.)
[ˈskræmbl]	记 联想记忆：scr(看作 scale，攀登) + amble(行走) → 攀登
nonplussed	*adj.* 不知所措的，陷于困境的
[ˌnɑːnˈplʌst]	记 来自 nonplus(*v.* 使迷惑)
belie	*v.* 掩饰(to disguise or misrepresent)；证明为假(to prove false)
[bɪˈlaɪ]	记 联想记忆：be + lie(谎言) → 使…成谎言 → 证明为假
	同 distort, falsify, garble, misstate
condone	*v.* 宽恕，原谅(to treat an offence as if it were not serious)
[kənˈdoʊn]	记 词根记忆：con(共同) + done(给予) → 全部给予 → 大度，宽容 → 宽恕
inferior	*adj.* 下级的，下属的；低等的，较差的(lower in rank, importance, etc.)
[ɪnˈfɪriər]	搭 to make sb. feel inferior 使某人自惭形秽
unavoidable	*adj.* 不可避免的(not avoidable)
[ˌʌnəˈvɔɪdəbl]	同 ineluctable, inescapable
exacerbate	*v.* 使加重，使恶化(to aggravate disease, pain, annoyance, etc.)
[ɪgˈzæsərbeɪt]	记 词根记忆：ex(表加强) + acerb(苦涩的) + ate → 非常苦涩 → 使恶化
airborne	*adj.* 空运地(transported or carried by the air)，空降的(trained for deployment by air and especially by parachute)；空气传播的
[ˈerbɔːrn]	
propitious	*adj.* 吉利的，顺利的(auspicious；favorable)；有利的(advantageous)
[prəˈpɪʃəs]	记 词根记忆：pro(向前) + piti(=pet 寻求) + ous → 寻求前进的 → 吉利的，顺利的
	例 An experienced politician who knew better than to launch a campaign in troubled political waters, she intended to wait for a more *propitious* occasion before she announced her plans.
partisan	*n.* 党派支持者，党羽(a firm adherent to a party)
[ˈpɑːrtəzn]	记 来自 party(*n.* 党，政党)
irrigate	*v.* 灌溉(to supply land with water)；冲洗(伤口)(to flush (a body part) with a stream of liquid)
[ˈɪrɪgeɪt]	记 词根记忆：ir(进入) + rig(水) + ate → 把水引进 → 灌溉

□ stingy	□ academic	□ exhaust	□ umbrage	□ scramble	□ nonplussed
□ belie	□ condone	□ inferior	□ unavoidable	□ exacerbate	□ airborne
□ propitious	□ partisan	□ irrigate			

rekindle [ˌriːˈkɪndl]	v. 再点火；使重新振作 搭 to rekindle hopes 重新点燃希望
discomfort [dɪsˈkʌmfərt]	v. 使不适(to make uncomfortable or uneasy) n. 不适(mental or physical uneasiness)
squalid [ˈskwɑːlɪd]	adj. 污秽的，肮脏的(filthy and degraded from neglect or poverty) 同 dirty, seedy, slummy, sordid, unclean
temporary [ˈtempəreri]	adj. 暂时的，临时的(lasting for a limited time) 记 词根记忆：tempor(时间) + ary → 时间很短 → 暂时的 例 Only by ignoring decades of mismanagement and inefficiency could investors conclude that a fresh infusion of cash would provide anything more than a *temporary* solution to the company's financial woes.
disarm [dɪsˈɑːrm]	v. 使缴械 (to take weapons away from sb.)；使缓和 (to make sb. less angry, hostile, etc) 记 联想记忆：dis(除去) + arm(武器) → 除去某人的武器 → 使缴械
unfettered [ʌnˈfetərd]	adj. 自由的，不受约束的(free, unrestrained) 例 Liberty is not easy, but far better to be an *unfettered* fox, hungry and threatened on its hill, than a well-fed canary, safe and secure in its cage.
ferromagnetic [ˌferoʊmæɡˈnetɪk]	adj. 铁磁的，铁磁体的 记 联想记忆：ferr(铁) + o + magnetic(磁的) → 铁磁的
criterion [kraɪˈtɪriən]	n. 评判的标准，尺度(standard by which sth. is judged) 记 词根记忆：crit(判断) + er(看作 err，错误) + ion → 判断对错的标准 → 尺度；注意其复数形式为 criteria
assimilate [əˈsɪməleɪt]	v. 同化；吸收(to absorb and incorporate) 记 词根记忆：as + simil (相同) + ate → 使相同 → 同化
antithesis [ænˈtɪθəsɪs]	n. 对立，相对(a contrast or opposition) 记 词根记忆：anti(反) + thesis(放) → 反着放 → 对立
endow [ɪnˈdaʊ]	v. 捐赠(to give money or property to)；赋予(to equip or supply with a talent or quality) 同 bequeath, contribute
erratic [ɪˈrætɪk]	adj. 无规律的，不稳定的(irregular; random; wandering)；古怪的(eccentric; queer) 记 联想记忆：err(出错) + atic → 性格出错 → 古怪的 同 bizarre, idiosyncratic, oddball
impugn [ɪmˈpjuːn]	v. 提出异议，对…表示怀疑(to challenge as false or questionable) 记 词根记忆：im(进入) + pugn(打斗) → 马上就要进入打斗状态 → 提出异议
sequester [sɪˈkwestər]	v. (使)隐退(to seclude; withdraw)；使隔离(to set apart) 记 注意不要和 sequestrate(v. 扣押)相混

assimilate

□ rekindle	□ discomfort	□ squalid	□ temporary	□ disarm	□ unfettered
□ ferromagnetic	□ criterion	□ assimilate	□ antithesis	□ endow	□ erratic
□ impugn	□ sequester				

awe-inspiring [ˌɔːɪn ˈspaɪərɪŋ]	*adj.* 令人敬畏的(inspiring awe from others)
	记 组合词：awe(敬畏) + inspiring(鼓舞人心的) → 令人敬畏的
resurrect [ˌrezə ˈrekt]	*v.* 使复活(to raise from the dead)；复兴(to bring to view)
	记 词根记忆：re + sur(下面) + rect(直) → 再次从下面直立起来 → 使复活
estrange [ɪ ˈstreɪndʒ]	*v.* 使疏远(to alienate the affections)
	记 联想记忆：e + strange(陌生的) → 使…陌生 → 使疏远
glandular [ˈɡlændʒələr]	*adj.* 腺状的，腺的(of, relating to, or involving glands, gland cells, or their products)
capitulate [kə ˈpɪtʃuleɪt]	*v.* (有条件地)投降(to surrender conditionally)
	记 词根记忆：capit(头) + ulate → 低头 → 投降
subjective [səb ˈdʒektɪv]	*adj.* 主观的，想象的(influenced by personal feelings and therefore perhaps unfair)
	记 来自subject(*n.* 主题)
gullible [ˈɡʌləbl]	*adj.* 易受骗的(easily cheated or deceived; credulous)
	记 来自gull(*v.* 欺骗)
demonstrate [ˈdemənstreɪt]	*v.* 证明，论证(to prove or make clear by reasoning or evidence)；示威(to make a demonstration)
	记 词根记忆：de(加强) + monstr(显示) + ate → 加强显示 → 证明
	同 evince, illustrate
parsimony [ˈpɑːrsəmoʊni]	*n.* 过分节俭，吝啬(the quality of being stingy)
	同 thrift
ambiguous [æm ˈbɪɡjuəs]	*adj.* 含糊的(not clear; uncertain; vague)
	记 词根记忆：ambi(二) + guous(做…的) → 两件事都想做的 → 含糊的
shallowness [ˈʃæloʊnəs]	*n.* 浅；浅薄
	同 superficiality
singularity [ˌsɪŋɡju ˈlærəti]	*n.* 独特(unusual or distinctive manner or behavior; peculiarity)；奇点(天文学上密度无穷大、体积无穷小的点)
	记 来自singular(*adj.* 单数的；非凡的)
	例 The Gibsons were little given to conformism in any form; not one of them was afraid of *singularity*, of being and seeming unlike their neighbors.
paramount [ˈpærəmaʊnt]	*adj.* 最重要的(of chief concern or importance)；最高权力的，至高无上的(supreme in rank, power, or authority; dominant)
	记 词根记忆：para(旁边) + mount(山) → 在山坡旁边的 → 最重要的
saline [ˈseɪliːn]	*adj.* 含盐的，咸的(consisting of or containing salt)
	搭 saline water 盐水；海水
eliminate [ɪ ˈlɪmɪneɪt]	*v.* 除去，淘汰(to remove; eradicate)
	记 联想记忆：e(出) + limin(看作limit，界限) + ate → 划到界限之外 → 除去，淘汰
	同 debar, exclude, purge

demonstrate

bellicose	*adj.* 好战的，好斗的(eager to fight; warlike; belligerent)
[ˈbelɪkoʊs]	记 词根记忆：bell(战争) + icose(形容词后缀) → 好斗的
unliterary	*adj.* 不矫揉造作的，不咬文嚼字的
[ʌnˈlɪtəreri]	记 和 nonliterary(*adj.* 不咬文嚼字的)一起记
worthy	*adj.* 值得的(having worth or value)；有价值的(having sufficient worth or
[ˈwɜːrði]	importance) *n.* 知名人士(a worthy or prominent person)
attune	*v.* 使调和(to put into correct and harmonious tune)
[əˈtuːn]	记 联想记忆：at + tune(调子) → 使调子一致 → 使调和
retrieve	*v.* 寻回，取回(to regain)；挽回(错误)(to remedy the evil consequences)
[rɪˈtriːv]	记 词根记忆：re + triev (=find 找到) + e → 重新找到 → 寻回
revile	*v.* 辱骂，恶言相向(to use abusive language; rail)
[rɪˈvaɪl]	记 词根记忆：re + vil(卑鄙的，邪恶的) + e → 辱骂
dense	*adj.* 密集的，浓密的(marked by compactness or crowding together of parts)
[dens]	记 联想记忆：和 sense(*n.* 感觉)一起记
interpret	*v.* 解释，说明(to explain or tell the meaning of)；演绎(to represent by means of art)
[ɪnˈtɜːrprɪt]	记 词根记忆：inter(在…之间) + pret(传播) → 在两种语言中间说 → 解释
	搭 interpret...as... 把…理解为…
	同 construe, explicate, expound
acrimony	*n.* 尖刻，刻薄(asperity)
[ˈækrɪmoʊni]	记 词根记忆：acri(尖，酸) + mony(表示名词) → 尖刻
diversify	*v.* (使)多样化(to give variety to)
[daɪˈvɜːrsɪfaɪ]	记 来自 diverse(*adj.* 多样的)
radiant	*adj.* 发光的(vividly bright and shining)；容光焕发的(marked by or expressive of love, confidence, or happiness)
[ˈreɪdiənt]	记 词根记忆：rad(光线) + i + ant(的) → 发光的
thesis	*n.* 论题，论文(statement of theory put forward and supported by arguments)
[ˈθiːsɪs]	
sprawl	*v.* 散乱地延伸；四肢摊开着坐、卧或倒下(to lie or sit with arms and legs spread out)
[sprɔːl]	
nonchalantly	*adv.* 冷淡地，冷漠地(indifferently)
[ˌnɑːnʃəˈlɑːntli]	例 Instead of taking exaggerated precautions against touching or tipping or jarring the bottle of wine, the waitress handled it quite *nonchalantly*, being careful only to use a napkin to keep her hands from the cool bottle itself.
retire	*v.* 撤退，后退(to withdraw; move back)；退休，退役
[rɪˈtaɪər]	记 联想记忆：re + tire(劳累) → 不再劳累 → 退休，退役
	搭 retire from 退出

interpret

□ bellicose	□ unliterary	□ worthy	■ attune	□ retrieve	□ revile
□ dense	□ interpret	□ acrimony	□ diversify	□ radiant	□ thesis
□ sprawl	□ nonchalantly	□ retire			

199

upstage [ˌʌpˈsteɪdʒ]	*adj.* 高傲的（haughty） 记 联想记忆：up(向上) + stage(舞台) → 在舞台上 → 高高在上的 → 高傲的
fossilized [ˈfɑːsəlaɪzd]	*adj.* 变成化石的 记 来自 fossilize(*v.* 变成化石)
egregious [ɪˈɡriːdʒəs]	*adj.* 极端恶劣的（conspicuously bad; flagrant） 记 词根记忆：e(出) + greg(团体) + ious → 超出一般人 → 极端恶劣的
unscathed [ʌnˈskeɪðd]	*adj.* 未受损伤的，未受伤害的（wholly unharmed） 记 联想记忆：un(不) + scathed(损伤的) → 未受损伤的
converge [kənˈvɜːrdʒ]	*v.* 聚合，集中于一点（to come together at a point）；汇聚（to come together and unite in a common interest or focus） 记 词根记忆：con + verg(转) + e → 转到一起 → 汇聚
defiance [dɪˈfaɪəns]	*n.* 挑战；违抗，反抗（open disobedience） 记 来自 defy(*v.* 公然反抗) 搭 defiance against 对…的反抗或挑战 同 contempt, contumacy, recalcitrance, stubbornness
perceptive [pərˈseptɪv]	*adj.* 感知的，知觉的（responsive to sensory stimuli）；有洞察力的，敏锐的（capable of or exhibiting keen perception）
dissonant [ˈdɪsənənt]	*adj.* 不和谐的，不一致的（opposing in opinion, temperament; discordant） 记 词根记忆：dis(分开) + son(声音) + ant → 声音分散的 → 不和谐的
ideological [ˌaɪdiəˈlɑːdʒɪkl]	*adj.* 意识形态的，思想体系的（of, relating to, or based on ideology）；思想上的（of or concerned with ideas）
amble [ˈæmbl]	*v.* 缓行，漫步（to saunter） 记 词根记忆：amble 本身就是一个词根=ambul(走路)
defect [ˈdiːfekt]	*n.* 缺点，瑕疵（fault; flaw）*v.* 变节，脱党（to forsake a cause or party） 记 词根记忆：de + fect(做) → 没做好 → 缺点 同 blemish
defense [dɪˈfens]	*n.* 防御，防护（the action of fighting against attack） 记 来自 defend(*v.* 防御，防护)
ethereal [iˈθɪriəl]	*adj.* 太空的（of or like the ether）；轻巧的，轻飘飘的（very light; airy） 记 来自 ether(*n.* 太空；苍天)
synthesis [ˈsɪnθəsɪs]	*n.* 综合，合成（the combining of separate things or ideas into a complete whole） 例 Even though the survey was designated as an interdisciplinary course, it involved no real *synthesis* of subject matter.
stipulate [ˈstɪpjuleɪt]	*v.* 要求以…为条件（to demand an express term in an agreement）；约定，规定（to make an agreement） 记 词根记忆：stip(点) + ulate → 点明 → 要求以…为条件

defect

□ upstage　　□ fossilized　　□ egregious　　□ unscathed　　□ converge　　□ defiance
□ perceptive　　□ dissonant　　□ ideological　　□ amble　　□ defect　　□ defense
□ ethereal　　□ synthesis　　□ stipulate

intelligible [ɪnˈtelɪdʒəbl]	*adj.* 可理解的，易于理解的（capable of being understood；comprehensible） 记 词根记忆：intel（在…中间）+ lig（选择）+ ible → 能从中间选择出来的 → 可理解的
proposition [ˌprɑːpəˈzɪʃn]	*n.* 看法，主张（statement that expresses a judgement or an opinion）；提议（proposal） 记 来自 propose（*v.* 建议，提议）
cerebral [səˈriːbrəl]	*adj.* 大脑的（of the brain）；深思的（of the intellect rather than the emotions） 记 词根记忆：cerebr（脑）+ al → 大脑的 搭 cerebral cortex 大脑皮层
stagnate [ˈstæɡneɪt]	*v.* 停滞（to become or remain stagnant）
figment [ˈfɪɡmənt]	*n.* 虚构的事（sth. merely imagined） 记 词根记忆：fig（做）+ ment → 做出来的 → 虚构的事
commingle [kəˈmɪŋɡl]	*v.* 掺和，混合（to mix up） 记 词根记忆：com（共同）+ mingle（结合，混合）→ 掺和，混合 同 commix, compound, immingle, immix, intermingle
trespass [ˈtrespəs]	*v.* 侵犯，闯入私人领地（to make an unwarranted or uninvited incursion） 记 词根记忆：tres（横向）+ pass（经过）→ 横着经过某人的地盘 → 侵犯
extravagance [ɪkˈstrævəɡəns]	*n.* 奢侈，挥霍（the quality or fact of being extravagant） 记 词根记忆：extra（外面）+ vag（走）+ ance → 走到外面，超过限度 → 奢侈
appall [əˈpɔːl]	*v.* 使惊骇，使胆寒（to fill with horror or dismay；shock） 记 词根记忆：ap + pal（=pale 苍白）+ l → 脸色变白 → 使惊骇
appetizing [ˈæpɪtaɪzɪŋ]	*adj.* 美味可口的，促进食欲的（stimulating the appetite） 同 delicious, tasty
reactionary [riˈækʃəneri]	*adj.* 极端保守的，反动的（ultraconservative in politics） 记 联想记忆：re（反）+ action（动）+ ary → 反动的
balmy [ˈbɑːmi]	*adj.* 芳香的；（指空气）温和的（soothing；mild；pleasant）；止痛的
tepid [ˈtepɪd]	*adj.* 微温的（moderately warm）；不热情的（lacking in emotional warmth or enthusiasm） 例 Considering how long she had yearned to see Italy, her first reaction was curiously *tepid*. 同 halfhearted, lukewarm, unenthusiastic
complicate [ˈkɑːmplɪkeɪt]	*v.* 使复杂化（to make sth. more difficult to do） 记 词根记忆：com（全部）+ plic（重叠）+ ate → 全部重叠起来 → 使复杂化 同 entangle, muddle, perplex, ravel, snarl
unobstructed [ˌʌnəbˈstrʌktɪd]	*adj.* 没有阻碍的（free from obstructions）

18

quarrel ['kwɔːrəl]	*n.* 争吵 (a usually verbal conflict between antagonists) *v.* 争吵 (to contend or dispute actively) 例 Read's apology to Heflin was not exactly abject and did little to resolve their decades-long *quarrel*, which had been as acrimonious as the academic etiquette of scholarly journals permitted.
presume [prɪ'zuːm]	*v.* 推测，假定 (to take for granted as being true in the absence of proof to the contrary)；认定 (to give reasonable evidence for assuming) 记 词根记忆：pre(预先) + sum(抓住) + e → 预先抓住 → 推测，假定
primitive ['prɪmətɪv]	*adj.* 原始的，远古的 (of or relating to an earliest or original stage or state)；基本的 (assumed as a basis) 记 词根记忆：prim(第一，首先) + itive(具…性质的) → 第一时间的 → 原始的 例 Tacitus' descriptions of Germanic tribal customs were limited by the *primitive* state of communications in his day, but they match the accounts of other contemporary writers. 同 original, prime, primeval
counterproductive [ˌkaʊntərprə'dʌktɪv]	*adj.* 事与愿违的 (having the opposite effect to that intended) 记 组合词：counter(相反的) + productive(有成效的) → 与想象有相反效果的 → 事与愿违的
obdurate ['ɑːbdərət]	*adj.* 固执的，顽固的 (stubbornly persistent；inflexible) 记 词根记忆：ob(表加强) + dur(持续) + ate → 非常坚持的 → 固执的 例 If you come to the conference table with such an *obdurate* attitude, we cannot expect to reach any harmonious agreement. 同 adamant, dogged
amicable ['æmɪkəbl]	*adj.* 友好的 (friendly in feeling；showing good will) 记 联想记忆：am(是) + i(我) + cable(电缆) → 我是电缆，友好地通向别人 → 友好的
tortuous ['tɔːrtʃuəs]	*adj.* 曲折的，拐弯抹角的 (marked by devious or indirect tactics)；弯弯曲曲的 (winding) 记 词根记忆：tort(弯曲) + uous → 弯弯曲曲的
fray [freɪ]	*n.* 吵架，打斗 (a noisy quarrel or fight) *v.* 磨破 (to become worn, ragged or raveled by rubbing) 记 联想记忆：f + ray(光线) → 时光催人老 → 磨破
pestilential [ˌpestɪ'lenʃl]	*adj.* 引起瘟疫的 (causing or tending to cause pestilence)，致命的；〈口〉极讨厌的 同 deadly；irritating
unfounded [ʌn'faʊndɪd]	*adj.* 无事实根据的 (groundless；unwarranted) 记 联想记忆：un(不) + founded(有根据的) → 无事实根据的 例 The true historian finds the facts about Marlowe and Shakespeare far more interesting than people's *unfounded* conjectures.
unsuspecting [ˌʌnsə'spektɪŋ]	*adj.* 不怀疑的，无猜疑的，可信任的 (feeling no suspicion；trusting)

ramshackle [ˈræmʃækl]	*adj.* 摇摇欲坠的(rickety) 例 Most of the settlements that grew up near the logging camps were *ramshackle* affairs, thrown together in a hurry because people needed to live on the job.
indestructible [ˌɪndɪˈstrʌktəbl]	*adj.* 不能破坏的, 不可毁灭的 (incapable of being destroyed, ruined, or rendered ineffective)
truncate [ˈtrʌŋkeɪt]	*v.* 截短, 缩短(to shorten by cutting off) 记 联想记忆: trun(k)(树干) + cate → 截去树干 → 截短 例 Rather than allowing these dramatic exchanges between her characters to develop fully, Ms. Norman unfortunately tends to *truncate* the discussions involving the two women.
inflict [ɪnˈflɪkt]	*v.* 使遭受(痛苦、损伤等)(to cause sth. unpleasant to be endured) 记 词根记忆: in(进入) + flict(击, 打) → 使进入打斗状态 → 使遭受(痛苦、损伤等)
coincidental [koʊˌɪnsɪˈdentl]	*adj.* 巧合的(resulting from a coincidence); 同时发生的(occurring or existing at the same time)
communal [kəˈmjuːnl]	*adj.* 全体共用的, 共享的(held in common) 记 词根记忆: com + mun(公共) + al → 公共的 → 全体共用的, 共享的
unctuous [ˈʌŋktʃuəs]	*adj.* 油质的(fatty); 油腔滑调的(oily) 例 Far from being *unctuous*, Pat was always loath to appear acquiescent. 同 greasy, oleaginous
espouse [ɪˈspaʊz]	*v.* 支持, 拥护(to take up; support; advocate) 记 词根记忆: e(出) + spous(约定) + e → 给出约定 → 支持
physiological [ˌfɪziəˈlɑːdʒɪkl]	*adj.* 生理(技能)的(of, or concerning the bodily functions); 生理学的(of, or concerning physiology) 记 来自 physiology(*n.* 生理学)
venerable [ˈvenərəbl]	*adj.* 值得尊敬的, 庄严的(deserving to be venerated) 同 august, revered
contemplative [kənˈtemplətɪv]	*adj.* 沉思的(marked by or given to contemplation) *n.* 沉思者(a person who practices contemplation)
brutality [bruːˈtæləti]	*n.* 野蛮(the quality or state of being brutal); 暴行(a brutal act or course of action)
placate [ˈpleɪkeɪt]	*v.* 抚慰, 平息(to soothe or mollify) 记 词根记忆: plac(平静的) + ate → 使平静 → 抚慰, 平息
frivolity [frɪˈvɑːləti]	*n.* 轻浮的行为(a frivolous act or thing) 例 Despite an affected nonchalance which convinced casual observers that he was indifferent about his painting and enjoyed only *frivolity*, Warhol cared deeply about his art and labored at it diligently.
incompatibility [ˈɪnkəmˌpætəˈbɪləti]	*n.* 不相容(性)(the quality or state of being incompatible)

18

threadlike	*adj.* 线状的
[ˈθredlaɪk]	记 组合词：thread（线）+ like（像……一样）→ 像线一样 → 线状的
obvious	*adj.* 明显的，显而易见的（easy to see and understand）
[ˈɑːbviəs]	记 词根记忆：ob + vi(路) + ous → 在路上的，随处可见 → 明显的
	例 While not teeming with the colorfully *obvious* forms of life that are found in a tropical rain forest, the desert is host to a surprisingly large number of species.
	同 apparent, evident, manifest, palpable
encounter	*v.* 遭遇；邂逅（to come upon face-to-face）
[ɪnˈkaʊntər]	记 联想记忆：en（使）+ counter（相反的）→ 使从两个相反的方向而来 → 邂逅
ostentation	*n.* 夸示，炫耀（showy display；pretentiousness）
[ˌɑːstenˈteɪʃn]	记 词根记忆：os(在前面) + tent(伸展) + ation → 在他人面前伸展 → 显现出来 → 夸示，炫耀
indebted	*adj.* 感激的，蒙恩的（owing gratitude）
[ɪnˈdetɪd]	记 联想记忆：in(进入) + debt(债务) + ed → 欠人情债的 → 感激的，蒙恩的
discourteous	*adj.* 失礼的，粗鲁的（lacking courtesy）
[dɪsˈkɜːrtiəs]	记 联想记忆：dis(离开) + court(宫廷) + eous → 远离宫廷的 → 村野匹夫的 → 失礼的，粗鲁的
incorrigible	*adj.* 积习难改的，不可救药的（incapable of being corrected）
[ɪnˈkɔːrɪdʒəbl]	记 联想记忆：in(不) + corrigible(可改正的)→ 积习难改的
committed	*adj.* （对事业，本职工作等）尽忠的（devoted to a cause）
[kəˈmɪtɪd]	记 来自 commit（*v.* 忠于某个人或机构等）

The ideals which have lighted my way, and time after time have given me new courage to face life cheerfully have been kindness, beauty and truth.
有些理想曾为我指引过道路，并不断给我新的勇气以欣然面对人生，那些理想就是———真、善、美。

———美国科学家　爱因斯坦（Albert Einstein, American scientist）

□ threadlike　　□ obvious　　□ encounter　　□ ostentation　　□ indebted　　□ discourteous
□ incorrigible　　□ committed

音频

censure [ˈsenʃər]	*n.* 指责，谴责（a judgment involving condemnation）*v.* 指责，谴责（to find fault with and criticize as blameworthy） 同 denounce, denunciate, reprehend, reprobate
specimen [ˈspesɪmən]	*n.* 范例，样品，标本（a portion or quantity of material for use in testing, or study） 记 词根记忆：speci（种类）+ men → 不同种类的东西 → 样品 例 It is possible to analyze a literary work to death, dissecting what should be a living experience as if it were a laboratory *specimen*.
byzantine [ˈbɪzəntiːn]	*adj.* 错综复杂的（complicated） 记 来自 Byzantine（*adj.* 拜占庭帝国的），拜占庭帝国以政治错综复杂而著名
vanity [ˈvænəti]	*n.* 虚荣，自负（inflated pride in oneself; conceit） 记 词根记忆：van（空）+ ity → 空虚 → 虚荣 例 It is ironic that a critic of such overwhelming *vanity* now suffers from a measure of the oblivion to which he was forever consigning others; in the end, all his self-adulation has only worked against him.
sketch [sketʃ]	*n.* 草图，概略（a brief description or outline）*v.* 画草图，写概略（to make a sketch, rough draft, or outline） 同 compendium, digest, syllabus
impracticability [ɪmˌpræktɪkəˈbɪləti]	*n.* 无法实施；不能实施的事项 例 The *impracticability* of such utopian notions is reflected by the quick disintegration of the idealistic community at Brooke Farm.
schematic [skiːˈmætɪk]	*adj.* 纲要的，图解的（of, relating to, or in the form of a scheme or diagram） 记 来自 schema（*n.* 图表；纲要）
apprise [əˈpraɪz]	*v.* 通知，告知（to inform or notify） 记 联想记忆：app（看作 appear）+ rise → 出现 + 升起 → 通知 同 acquaint, advise, warn
defunct [dɪˈfʌŋkt]	*adj.* 死亡的（dead or extinct） 记 词根记忆：de + funct（功能）→ 无功能的 → 死亡的
compliance [kəmˈplaɪəns]	*n.* 顺从，遵从（obedience to a rule, agreement or demand） 记 来自 comply（*v.* 顺从）

recurring [rɪˈkɜːrɪŋ]	*adj.* 反复的；再次发生的
	例 Because it has no distinct and recognizable typographical form and few *recurring* narrative conventions, the novel is, of all literary genres, the least susceptible to definition.
fruitlessly [ˈfruːtləsli]	*adv.* 徒劳地，无益地(unproductively)
	同 unprofitably
incongruity [ˌɪnkɑːnˈgruːəti]	*n.* 不协调，不相称(the quality or state of being incongruous)
	记 联想记忆：in(不) + congruity(一致，和谐) → 不协调，不相称
fabricate [ˈfæbrɪkeɪt]	*v.* 捏造(to make up for the purpose of deception)；制造(to construct; manufacture)
	记 来自 fabric(*n.* 构造)
	同 frame
unrestricted [ˌʌnrɪˈstrɪktɪd]	*adj.* 无限制的，自由的(not limited by anyone or anything)
folly [ˈfɑːli]	*n.* 愚蠢(lack of wisdom)；愚蠢的想法或做法(a foolish act or idea)
	同 foolery, idiocy, insanity
germinate [ˈdʒɜːrmɪneɪt]	*v.* 发芽(to sprout or cause to sprout)；发展(to start developing or growing)
	记 词根记忆：germ(种子，幼芽) + inate → 发芽
civility [səˈvɪləti]	*n.* 彬彬有礼，斯文(politeness)
	记 词根记忆：civil(文明的，市民的) + ity → 彬彬有礼
undemanding [ˌʌndɪˈmɑːndɪŋ]	*adj.* 不严格的(not demanding)；要求不高的(requiring little if any patience or effort or skill)
multiply [ˈmʌltɪplaɪ]	*v.* 乘；增加(to greatly increase)；繁殖(to breed)
	记 词根记忆：multi(多的) + ply(折叠) → 多次折叠 → 乘；增加
eschew [ɪsˈtʃuː]	*v.* 避开，戒绝(to shun; avoid; abstain from)
	记 联想记忆：es(出) + chew(咀嚼；深思) → 通过深思而去掉 → 戒绝
comprehend [ˌkɑːmprɪˈhend]	*v.* 理解(to understand sth. fully)；包括(to include)
	记 词根记忆：com(全部) + prehend(抓住) → 全部抓住 → 理解；包括
recollect [ˌrekəˈlekt]	*v.* 回忆(to remember)；想起(to remind oneself of sth. temporarily forgotten)
	同 reminisce, retrospect
undeserving [ˌʌndɪˈzɜːrvɪŋ]	*adj.* 不值得的(not deserving to have or receive sth.)
	同 unworthy
translucent [trænsˈluːsnt]	*adj.* (半)透明的(allowing light to pass through but not transparent)
	记 词根记忆：trans(穿过) + luc(明亮) + ent → 光线能穿过 → (半)透明的
serviceable [ˈsɜːrvɪsəbl]	*adj.* 可用的，耐用的(fit for use)
	记 来自 service(*n.* 服务)
besiege [bɪˈsiːdʒ]	*v.* 围攻；困扰(to overwhelm, harass, or beset)
	记 词根记忆：be + siege(围攻, siege 本身是一个单词) → 围攻

□ recurring	□ fruitlessly	□ incongruity	□ fabricate	□ unrestricted	□ folly
□ germinate	□ civility	□ undemanding	□ multiply	□ eschew	□ comprehend
□ recollect	□ undeserving	□ translucent	□ serviceable	□ besiege	

endemic [en'demɪk]	*adj.* 地方性的(restricted to a locality or region; native) 记 词根记忆：en + dem(人民) + ic → 在人民之内 → 地方性的
quote [kwoʊt]	*v.* 引用，引述(to repeat in speech or writing the words of a person or a book)
imposture [ɪm'pɑːstʃər]	*n.* 冒充(being an impostor; fraud) 记 词根记忆：im(进入) + pos(放) + ture → 把别的东西放进去 → 冒充
ordeal [ɔːr'diːl]	*n.* 严峻的考验(any difficult and severe trial) 记 发音记忆："恶地儿" → 险恶之地 → 严峻的考验 例 The senator's reputation, though shaken by false allegations of misconduct, emerged from the *ordeal* unscathed. 同 affliction, tribulation
denote [dɪ'noʊt]	*v.* 指示，表示(to mark, indicate; signify) 记 词根记忆：de + not(知道) + e → 让人知道 → 表示
confide [kən'faɪd]	*v.* 吐露(心事)(to show confidence by imparting secrets)；倾诉(to tell confidentially) 记 词根记忆：con + fid(相信) + e → 相信别人 → 吐露
unyielding [ʌn'jiːldɪŋ]	*adj.* 坚定的，不屈的(characterized by firmness or obduracy)；坚硬的，不能弯曲的(characterized by lack of softness or flexibility)
periodic [ˌpɪri'ɑːdɪk]	*adj.* 周期的，定期的(occurring or recurring at regular intervals) 记 来自period(*n.* 一段时间)
press [pres]	*v.* 挤压(to act upon through steady pushing) 同 squeeze
arresting [ə'restɪŋ]	*adj.* 醒目的，引人注意的(catching the attention) 记 来自arrest(*v.* 吸引，注意)
obviate ['ɑːbvieɪt]	*v.* 排除，消除(困难、危险等)(to remove; get rid of) 记 词根记忆：ob(反) + vi(路) + ate → 使障碍等离开道路 → 排除，消除 同 eliminate, exclude, preclude
hostile ['hɑːstl]	*adj.* 敌对的，敌意的(of or relating to an enemy; antagonistic) 记 联想记忆：host(主人) + ile → 反客为主 → 敌对的 搭 be hostile to/towards... 对…有敌意的 同 inimicable, inimical
rueful ['ruːfl]	*adj.* 抱憾的(feeling or showing pity or sympathy)；后悔的，悔恨的(mournful; regretful)
unskilled [ˌʌn'skɪld]	*adj.* 不熟练的(lacking skill or technical training)；无需技能的(not requiring skill)
precipitous [prɪ'sɪpɪtəs]	*adj.* 陡峭的(very steep, perpendicular, or overhanging in rise or fall)

19

□ endemic	□ quote	□ imposture	□ ordeal	□ denote	□ confide
□ unyielding	□ periodic	□ press	□ arresting	□ obviate	□ hostile
□ rueful	□ unskilled	□ precipitous			

frenetic [frə'netɪk]	*adj.* 狂乱的，发狂的(frantic; frenzied) 记 联想记忆：fren(=phren 心灵) + etic → 心灵承受不了的 → 狂乱的，发狂的
prosaic [prə'zeɪɪk]	*adj.* 散文(体)的；单调的，无趣的(dull; unimaginative) 记 来自 prose(*n.* 散文) 例 He felt that the uninspiring routine of office work was too *prosaic* for someone of his talent and creativity.
excessively [ɪk'sesɪvli]	*adv.* 过度地(overly) 例 Helen valued people who behaved as if they respected themselves; nothing irritated her more than an *excessively* obsequious waiter or a fawning salesclerk.
swift [swɪft]	*adj.* 迅速的(able to move at a great speed)；敏捷的(ready or quick in action) 记 联想记忆：电梯(lift)飞快(swift)上升
iconoclasm [aɪ'kɑːnəklæzəm]	*n.* 破坏偶像的理论，打破旧习(the doctrine, practice, or attitude of an iconoclast)
rip [rɪp]	*v.* 撕，撕裂(to tear or split apart or open) 搭 rip at sth. 猛烈撕扯；用力割
semimolten [ˌsemi'moʊltən]	*adj.* 半熔化的
texture ['tekstʃər]	*n.* 质地(identifying quality)；结构(overall structure) 记 词根记忆：text(编织) + ure → 质地
afflict [ə'flɪkt]	*v.* 折磨；使痛苦(to cause persistent pain or suffering) 记 词根记忆：af + flict(打击) → 一再打击 → 折磨；使痛苦
amiability [ˌeɪmiə'bɪləti]	*n.* 亲切，友善(the state of being friendly) 同 agreeableness, cordiality, geniality, pleasance, pleasantness
chagrin [ʃə'ɡrɪn]	*n.* 失望，懊恼(a feeling of annoyance because one has been disappointed) 记 联想记忆：cha(拼音：茶) + grin(苦笑) → 喝茶苦笑 → 失望，懊恼
chary ['tʃeri]	*adj.* 小心的，审慎的(careful; cautious) 搭 be chary of/about... 对…小心的 同 calculating, circumspect, discreet, gingerly, wary
grandiose ['ɡrændioʊs]	*adj.* 宏伟的(impressive because of uncommon largeness)；浮夸的(characterized by affectation or exaggeration) 记 词根记忆：grandi(大的) + ose(多…的) → 多大(话)的 → 浮夸的
scrupulous ['skruːpjələs]	*adj.* 恪守道德规范的(having moral integrity)；一丝不苟的(punctiliously exact) 搭 be scrupulous in sth./doing sth. 审慎正直的；恪守道德规范的 同 conscientious, meticulous, punctilious
hypocritical ['hɪpəkrɪtɪkl]	*adj.* 虚伪的，伪善的(characterized by hypocrisy or being a hypocrite) 搭 hypocritical affection 虚假的情谊

□ frenetic	□ prosaic	□ excessively	□ swift	□ iconoclasm	□ rip
□ semimolten	□ texture	□ afflict	□ amiability	□ chagrin	□ chary
□ grandiose	□ scrupulous	□ hypocritical			

obsequious [əbˈsiːkwiəs]	*adj.* 逢迎的，谄媚的（showing too great a willingness to serve or obey） 记 词根记忆：ob（在⋯后面）+ sequ（跟随）+ ious → 跟在后面的 → 逢迎的，谄媚的 例 Helen valued people who behaved as if they respected themselves; nothing irritated her more than an excessively *obsequious* waiter or a fawning salesclerk. 同 menial, servile, slavish, subservient
abatement [əˈbeɪtmənt]	*n.* 减少，减轻（the act or process of abating） 记 来自 abate（*v.* 减轻，减弱）
spongy [ˈspʌndʒi]	*adj.* 像海绵的（resembling a sponge）；不坚实的（not firm or solid） 搭 spongy topsoil 松软的表土
harass [ˈhærəs]	*v.* 侵扰，烦扰（to annoy persistently） 搭 harass the border area 窜扰边境
vexation [vekˈseɪʃn]	*n.* 恼怒，苦恼（the act of harassing；irritation） 记 联想记忆：vex（烦恼，恼怒）+ ation → 恼怒，苦恼
circumvent [ˌsɜːrkəmˈvent]	*v.* 回避（to bypass）；用计谋战胜或回避（to get the better of or prevent from happening by craft or ingenuity） 记 词根记忆：circum（绕圈）+ vent（来）→ 绕着圈过来 → 回避
escapism [ɪˈskeɪpɪzəm]	*n.* 逃避现实（的习气）（the tendency to escape from daily realities by means of entertainment）
passionate [ˈpæʃənət]	*adj.* 充满激情的（showing or filled with passion） 记 来自 passion（*n.* 激情） 例 Though science is often imagined as a disinterested exploration of external reality, scientists are no different from anyone else: they are *passionate* human beings enmeshed in a web of personal and social circumstances. 同 ardent, fervid, impassioned
underutilized [ˌʌndərˈjuːtəlaɪzd]	*adj.* 未充分利用的 记 联想记忆：under（不足，少于）+ utilize（利用）+ d → 未充分利用的
radicalism [ˈrædɪkəlɪzəm]	*n.* 激进主义（the quality or state of being radical） 记 来自 radical（*adj.* 激进的；彻底的）
inventive [ɪnˈventɪv]	*adj.* 善于发明的，有创造力的（adept or prolific at producing inventions）；发明的（characterized by invention） 例 The reader has the happy impression of watching an extraordinarily *inventive* and intellectually fecund novelist working at the height of her powers.
deluge [ˈdeljuːdʒ]	*n.* 大洪水（a great flood）；暴雨（heavy rainfall） 记 词根记忆：de + lug（=luv 冲洗）+ e → 冲掉 → 大洪水
acolyte [ˈækəlaɪt]	*n.*（教士的）助手，侍僧（one who assists the celebrant in the performance of liturgical rites） 记 发音记忆："爱过来的" → 爱过来帮忙的人 → 助手

19

□ obsequious	□ abatement	□ spongy	□ harass	□ vexation	□ circumvent
□ escapism	□ passionate	□ underutilized	□ radicalism	□ inventive	□ deluge
□ acolyte					

prod [prɑːd]	*v.* 戳，刺(to poke)；刺激，激励(to stir up；urge) 搭 prod sb. into doing sth. 促使或推动某人做某事
inane [ɪˈneɪn]	*adj.* 无意义的，空洞的(empty；lacking sense；void)；愚蠢的(silly) 例 Just as an insipid dish lacks flavor, an *inane* remark lacks sense. 同 innocuous, insipid, jejune, sapless, vapid
compass [ˈkʌmpəs]	*n.* 指南针，罗盘；界限，范围(scope；range) 记 词根记忆：com(共同) + pass(通过) → 共同通过的地方 → 界限
extricable [ˈekstrɪkəbl]	*adj.* 可解救的，能脱险的(capable of being freed from difficulty) 记 词根记忆：ex(外面) + tric(小障碍物) + able → 能摆脱小障碍物的 →可解救的
assuredness [əˈʃʊrdnəs]	*n.* 确定；自信 记 来自 assure(*v.* 使确信)
enzyme [ˈenzaɪm]	*n.* 酵素，酶(biochemical catalyst) 记 词根记忆：en(在…里) + zym(发酵) + e → 酵素，酶
dogma [ˈdɔːgmə]	*n.* 教条，信条(doctrine；principle)
pinpoint [ˈpɪnpɔɪnt]	*v.* 准确地确定(to locate or aim with great precision or accuracy)；使突出，引起注意(to cause to stand out conspicuously) *adj.* 极精确的(very exact) 记 组合词：pin(针) + point(尖) → 像针尖一样精确 → 极精确的
ignominy [ˈɪgnəmini]	*n.* 羞耻，耻辱(shame and dishonor；infamy) 记 词根记忆：ig(不) + nomin(名声) + y → 名声不好 → 耻辱 同 disgrace, disrepute, opprobrium
heretical [həˈretɪkl]	*adj.* 异端的，异教的(of or relating to heresy or heretics) 同 dissident, heterodox, unorthodox
coerce [koʊˈɜːrs]	*v.* 强迫(to force or compel to do sth.)；压制 (to restrain or constrain by force) 记 发音记忆："可扼死" → 可以扼死 → 压制
enmity [ˈenməti]	*n.* 敌意，仇恨(hostility；antipathy) 记 来自 enemy(*n.* 敌人) 搭 enmity toward 对…的敌意
vindicate [ˈvɪndɪkeɪt]	*v.* 辩白(to free from allegation or blame)；证明…正确(to provide justification or defense for) 记 词根记忆：vin(=force 力量) + dic(说) + ate → 使有力地说 → 证明…正确
inconsequential [ɪnˌkɑːnsɪˈkwenʃl]	*adj.* 不重要的，微不足道的(unimportant；trivial) 记 联想记忆：in(不) + consequential(重要的) → 不重要的 例 While admitting that the risks incurred by use of the insecticide were not *inconsequential*, the manufacturer's spokesperson argued that effective substitutes were simply not available.
agrarian [əˈgreriən]	*adj.* 土地的(of land) 记 词根记忆：agr(田地，农业) + arian(表形容词) → 土地的

210

□ prod　　　　　□ inane　　　　　□ compass　　　　☑ extricable　　　□ assuredness　　□ enzyme
□ dogma　　　　□ pinpoint　　　　□ ignominy　　　　□ heretical　　　□ coerce　　　　　□ enmity
□ vindicate　　　□ inconsequential　□ agrarian

circuitous [sər'kjuːɪtəs]	*adj.* 迂回的，绕圈子的(roundabout; indirect; devious) 记 词根记忆：circu(绕圈) + it(走) + ous → 迂回的；circuit 本身是个单词，意为"圆，电路"
indiscriminate [ˌɪndɪ'skrɪmɪnət]	*adj.* 不加选择的 (not marked by careful distinction)；随意的，任意的 (haphazard; random)
encapsulation [ɪnˌkæpsjuˈleɪʃən]	*n.* 包装(packing) 记 来自 encapsulate(*v.* 封装)
conclusive [kən'kluːsɪv]	*adj.* 最后的，结论的，决定性的(of, relating to, or being a conclusion)；确凿的，消除怀疑的(convincing) 记 来自 conclude(*v.* 作结论)
anomalous [ə'nɑːmələs]	*adj.* 反常的(inconsistent with what is usual, normal, or expected)，不协调的(marked by incongruity or contradiction) 同 aberrant, abnormal, deviant, divergent, irregular
antiquity [æn'tɪkwəti]	*n.* 古老(the quality of being ancient)；古人(the people of ancient times)；古迹(objects, buildings or work of art from the ancient past)
flawed [flɔːd]	*adj.* 有缺点的；错误的(spoiled by having mistakes, weaknesses, or by being damaged)
uncanny [ʌn'kæni]	*adj.* 神秘的，离奇的(weird; supernatural) 记 联想记忆：un(不) + canny(安静的，谨慎的) → 神秘的
radically ['rædɪkli]	*adv.* 根本上(in origin or essence)；以激进方式(in a radical or extreme manner) 例 When trees go dormant in winter, the procedure is anything but sleepy: it is an active metabolic process that changes the plant *radically*.
overdue [ˌoʊvər'duː]	*adj.* 到期未付的(left unpaid too long)；晚来的，延误的(coming or arriving after the scheduled or expected time; later than expected) 记 组合词：over(越过) + due(应付的；约定的) → 过了应付或约定的时间的 → 到期未付的；晚来的 例 The college librarian initiated a new schedule of fines for *overdue* books with the acquiescence, if not the outright encouragement, of the faculty library committee.
uneven [ʌn'iːvn]	*adj.* 不平坦的(not even)；不一致的(not uniform)；不对等的(unequal) 例 All critics have agreed that the opera's score is *uneven*, but, curiously, no two critics have agreed which passages to praise and which to damn.
tedious ['tiːdiəs]	*adj.* 冗长的，乏味的(tiresome because of length or dullness) 例 The pungent verbal give-and-take among the characters makes the novel *tedious* reading, and this very inventiveness suggests to me that some of the opinions voiced may be the author's. 同 boresome, insipid, irksome, wearisome
acrimonious [ˌækrɪ'moʊniəs]	*adj.* 尖酸刻薄的，激烈的(caustic, biting, or rancorous) 同 indignant, irate, ireful, wrathful, wroth

19

audience [ˈɔːdiəns]	*n.* 听众，观众（a group of listeners or spectators）；读者（a reading public） 记 词根记忆：audi（听）+ ence → 听众
repulse [rɪˈpʌls]	*v.* 击退（to repel）；（粗暴无礼地）回绝（to repel by discourtesy, coldness, or denial）*n.* 击退（the act of repulsing or the state of being repulsed）；回绝，拒绝（rebuff; rejection） 记 词根记忆：re（反）+ pulse（推）→ 推回去 → 击退
overload [ˌoʊvərˈloʊd]	*v.* 使超载
expedient [ɪkˈspiːdiənt]	*n.* 权宜之计，临时手段（a temporary means to an end）*adj.* （指行动）有用的（useful, helpful or advisable）
prose [proʊz]	*n.* 散文（written or spoken language that is not in verse form） 记 联想记忆：p + rose（玫瑰）→ 散文如玫瑰花瓣，形散而神聚 → 散文
ally	[əˈlaɪ] *v.* （使）结盟，（使）联合（to associate） [ˈælaɪ] *n.* 同盟者，伙伴（one that is associated with another） 记 联想记忆：all（全部）+ y → 把全部人都聚集在一起 → （使）结盟
venal [ˈviːnl]	*adj.* 腐败的，贪赃枉法的（characterized by or associated with corrupt bribery）
involuntary [ɪnˈvɑːlənteri]	*adj.* 无意的（done without intention） 记 词根记忆：in（无）+ volunt（意识）+ ary → 无意的
insulting [ɪnˈsʌltɪŋ]	*adj.* 侮辱的，污蔑的（abusive） 记 来自 insult（*v.* 侮辱，辱骂）
quiescent [kwiˈesnt]	*adj.* 不动的，静止的（marked by inactivity or repose） 记 词根记忆：qui（=quiet 安静的）+ escent（状态）→ 静止的 例 The astronomer and feminist Maria Mitchell's own prodigious activity and the vigor of the Association for the Advancement of Women during the 1870s belie any assertion that feminism was *quiescent* in that period. 同 abeyant, dormant, latent
equate [iˈkweɪt]	*v.* 认为…相等或相仿（to consider sth. as equal to sth. else） 记 词根记忆：equ（相等的）+ ate（表动作）→ 使相等 → 认为…相等或相仿
acute [əˈkjuːt]	*adj.* 灵敏的，敏锐的（keen; shrewd; sensitive）；剧烈的（characterized by sharpness or severity）；急性的 记 联想记忆：a + cut（切）+ e → 一刀切 → 剧烈的
humidity [hjuːˈmɪdəti]	*n.* 湿度，湿气（moistness, dampness） 记 来自 humid（*adj.* 潮湿的）
aquatic [əˈkwætɪk]	*adj.* 水生的，水中的（growing or living in or upon water） 记 词根记忆：aqua（水）+ tic → 水中的
annotate [ˈænəteɪt]	*v.* 注解（to provide critical or explanatory notes） 记 词根记忆：an + not（标示）+ ate → 注解
amaze [əˈmeɪz]	*v.* 使大为吃惊，使惊奇（to fill with wonder） 记 发音记忆："啊美死" → 使惊奇 同 astound, dumbfound, flabbergast

□ audience	□ repulse	□ overload	□ expedient	□ prose	□ ally
□ venal	□ involuntary	□ insulting	□ quiescent	□ equate	□ acute
□ humidity	□ aquatic	□ annotate	□ amaze		

simplistic [sɪmˈplɪstɪk]	*adj.* 过分简单化的(of, relating to, or characterized by simplism; oversimple) 例 Our new tools of systems analysis, powerful though they may be, lead to *simplistic* theories, especially, and predictably, in economics and political science, where productive approaches have long been highly elusive.
blockbuster [ˈblɑːkbʌstər]	*n.* 巨型炸弹(a very large high-explosive bomb); 一鸣惊人的事物; 非常成功的书或电影
deprecation [ˌdeprɪˈkeɪʃn]	*n.* 反对(disapproval) 记 来自 deprecate(*v.* 反对)
promotion [prəˈmoʊʃn]	*n.* 晋升(the act or fact of being raised in position or rank); 促进(the act of furthering the growth or development of sth.) 例 By idiosyncratically refusing to dismiss an insubordinate member of his staff, the manager not only contravened established policy, but he also jeopardized his heretofore good chances for *promotion*.
tidy [ˈtaɪdi]	*adj.* 整齐的, 整洁的(neat and orderly); 相当好的 记 发音记忆: "泰迪" → 出售的泰迪熊是整洁漂亮的 → 整洁的 例 Regardless of what *tidy* theories of politics may propound, there is nothing that requires daily politics to be clear, thorough, and consistent—nothing, that is, that requires reality to conform to theory. 同 shipshape, trim, uncluttered
influential [ˌɪnfluˈenʃl]	*adj.* 有影响力的(exerting or possessing influence)
culminate [ˈkʌlmɪneɪt]	*v.* 达到顶点(to rise to or form a summit); 使达到最高点(to bring to a head or to the highest point)
unintelligible [ˌʌnɪnˈtelɪdʒəbl]	*adj.* 不可能理解的, 难懂的(being such that understanding or comprehension is difficult or impossible; incomprehensible)
earnest [ˈɜːrnɪst]	*adj.* 诚挚的, 认真的(showing deep sincerity or seriousness) 记 联想记忆: earn(挣钱) + est → 要想挣钱就得认真地干 → 认真的
vessel [ˈvesl]	*n.* 血管; 容器(a container); 船只(a watercraft) 记 注意不要和 vassal(*n.* 陪臣, 诸侯)相混
rectify [ˈrektɪfaɪ]	*v.* 改正, 矫正(to correct by removing errors; adjust); 提纯(to purify by repeated distillation) 记 词根记忆: rect(直) + ify → 使…变直 → 改正, 矫正
provocative [prəˈvɑːkətɪv]	*adj.* 挑衅的, 煽动的(serving or tending to provoke, excite, or stimulate) 例 The results of the experiments performed by Elizabeth Hazen and Rachel Brown were *provocative* not only because these results challenged old assumptions but also because they called the prevailing methodology into question.

vessel

□ simplistic	□ blockbuster	□ deprecation	□ promotion	□ tidy	□ influential
□ culminate	□ unintelligible	□ earnest	□ vessel	□ rectify	□ provocative

censorious	*adj.* 挑剔的(marked by or given to censure)
[sen'sɔːriəs]	记 词根记忆：cens(评价) + orious → 爱评价他人的 → 挑剔的
unearth	*v.* 挖出(to dig up out of the earth; exhume)；发现(to bring to light)
[ʌn'ɜːrθ]	记 联想记忆：un(打开) + earth(地) → 挖出
ecological	*adj.* 生态的；生态学的
[ˌiːkə'lɑːdʒɪkl]	例 With the evolution of wings, insects were able to disperse to the far *ecological* comers, across deserts and bodies of water, to reach new food sources and inhabit a wider variety of promising environmental niches.
epoch	*n.* 新纪元(the beginning of a new and important period in the history)；重大的事件(a noteworthy and characteristic event)
['epək]	
unnoteworthy	*adj.* 不显著的，不值得注意的
[ˌʌn'noʊtwɜːrði]	
circumspect	*adj.* 慎重的(careful to consider all circumstances and possible consequences)
['sɜːrkəmspekt]	
gloat	*v.* 幸灾乐祸地看，心满意足地看(to gaze or think with exultation, or malicious pleasure)
[gloʊt]	搭 gloat over 幸灾乐祸地看
insecure	*adj.* 无保障的，不安全的(not adequately guarded or sustained)
[ˌɪnsɪ'kjʊr]	同 unprotected, unsafe
fanciful	*adj.* 幻想的，奇特的(marked by fancy or unrestrained imagination)
['fænsɪfl]	例 In discussing Rothko's art, Breslin is scrupulous in keeping to the facts and resisting the temptation of *fanciful* interpretation.
brevity	*n.* 短暂(shortness of duration)
['brevəti]	记 词根记忆：brev(短的) + i + ty → 短暂
undemonstrable	*adj.* 无法证明的，难以证明的
[ˌʌndɪ'mɑːnstrəbl]	
enduring	*adj.* 持久的(lasting)；不朽的
[ɪn'dʊrɪŋ]	记 词根记忆：en + dur(持续) + ing → 持久的
pernicious	*adj.* 有害的(noxious)；致命的(deadly)
[pər'nɪʃəs]	记 词根记忆：per(表加强) + nic(伤害) + ious → 带来极大伤害的 → 有害的；致命的
positive	*adj.* 积极的(marked by optimism)；明确的(expressed clearly or peremptorily)；有信心的(confident)；无条件的(independent of changing circumstances; unconditioned) *n.* 正片(a photographic image in which the lights and darks appear as they do in nature)；积极的要素或特点(an affirmative element or characteristic)
['pɑːzətɪv]	记 联想记忆：posit(看作 post, 邮件) + ive → 邮件上的地址要写清楚 → 明确的
	例 Although most worthwhile criticism concentrates on the *positive*, one should not indiscriminately praise everything.

□ censorious	□ unearth	□ ecological	□ epoch	□ unnoteworthy	□ circumspect
□ gloat	□ insecure	□ fanciful	□ brevity	□ undemonstrable	□ enduring
□ pernicious	□ positive				

interactive [ˌɪntərˈæktɪv]	*adj.* 交互式的(mutually or reciprocally active) 记 来自 interact(*v.* 相互作用，相互影响)
walrus [ˈwɔːlrəs]	*n.* 海象(a large gregarious marine mammal)
decipher [dɪˈsaɪfər]	*v.* 破译(to decode)；解开(疑团)(to make out the meaning) 记 词根记忆：de(去掉) + cipher(密码) → 解开密码 → 破译 同 crack, decrypt
variety [vəˈraɪəti]	*n.* 多样性(the quality or state of having different forms or types)；种类(assortment)；变种(subspecies) 记 词根记忆：vari(改变) + ety → 多样性 例 The theory of cosmic evolution states that the universe, having begun in a state of simplicity and homogeneity, has differentiated into great *variety*. 同 diversity, multeity, multiformity, multiplicity
phenomenal [fəˈnɑːmɪnl]	*adj.* 显著的，非凡的(extraordinary；remarkable) 记 来自 phenomenon(*n.* 现象；奇迹)；phen(出现) + omen(征兆) + on → 出现征兆 → 现象；奇迹
impenetrable [ɪmˈpenɪtrəbl]	*adj.* 不能穿透的 (incapable of being penetrated)；不可理解的(unfathomable；inscrutable) 记 联想记忆：im(不) + penetrable(可穿透的) → 不能穿透的 例 The First World War began in a context of jargon and verbal delicacy and continued in a cloud of euphemism as *impenetrable* as language and literature, skillfully used, could make it. 同 impassable, impermeable, imporviable, impervious
optimist [ˈɑːptɪmɪst]	*n.* 乐观主义者(the person who is always hopeful and expects the best in all things) 例 Always trying to look on the bright side of every situation, she is a born *optimist*.
enervate [ˈenərveɪt]	*v.* 使虚弱，使无力(to lessen the vitality or strength of) 记 词根记忆：e + nerv(力量；神经) + ate → 力量出去 → 使无力
cannily [ˈkænɪli]	*adv.* 机灵地
heavenly [ˈhevnli]	*adj.* 天空的，天上的(of or relating to heaven or the heavens) 同 celestial

19

□ interactive	□ walrus	□ decipher	□ variety	□ phenomenal	□ impenetrable
□ optimist	□ enervate	□ cannily	□ heavenly		

215

Word List 20

音频

outlast	*v.* 比…持久
[ˌaʊt ˈlæst]	记 组合词: out(超越) + last(坚持) → 比…持久
preconception	*n.* 先入之见(a preconceived idea); 偏见(prejudice)
[ˌpriːkən ˈsepʃn]	记 联想记忆: pre(在前面) + conception(观念) → 先入之见
balk	*n.* 梁木, 大梁(thick, roughly squared wooden beam) *v.* 妨碍; 畏缩不前 (be reluctant to tackle sth. because it is difficult)
[bɔːk]	同 baffle, bilk, foil, thwart
destine	*v.* 命运注定, 预定(to decree beforehand)
[ˈdestɪn]	同 foreordain, predestine
carnage	*n.* 大屠杀, 残杀(bloody and extensive slaughter)
[ˈkɑːrnɪdʒ]	记 联想记忆: carn(肉) + age → 大堆的肉 → 大屠杀
	同 bloodbath, massacre
devout	*adj.* 虔诚的(seriously concerned with religion); 忠诚的, 忠心的(totally committed to a cause or a belief)
[dɪ ˈvaʊt]	记 可能来自 devote(*v.* 投身于, 献身)
spanking	*adj.* 强烈的(strong); 疾行的(fast)
[ˈspæŋkɪŋ]	搭 at a spanking pace/rate 步伐/速度非常快地
stellar	*adj.* 星的, 星球的(of or relating to the stars)
[ˈstelər]	记 词根记忆: stell(星星) + ar → 星的, 星球的
	例 Although supernovas are among the most luminous of cosmic events, these *stellar* explosions are often hard to detect, either because they are enormously far away or because they are dimmed by intervening dust and gas clouds.
pertinent	*adj.* 有关的, 相关的(having a clear decisive relevance to the matter in hand)
[ˈpɜːrtnənt]	记 词根记忆: per(始终) + tin(拿住) + ent → 始终拿着不放的 → 有关的
	例 Those interested in learning more about how genetics applies to trees will have to resort to the excellent technical journals where most of the *pertinent* material is found.
	同 germane

| □ outlast | □ preconception | □ balk | □ destine | □ carnage | □ devout |
| □ spanking | □ stellar | □ pertinent | | | |

devour [dɪ'vaʊər]	*v.* 狼吞虎咽地吃，吞食（to eat or eat up hungrily）；贪婪地看（或听、读等）（to enjoy avidly） 记 词根记忆：de + vour（吃）→ 吞食
explicate ['eksplɪkeɪt]	*v.* 详细解说（to make clear or explicit; explain fully） 同 elucidate, illustrate, interpret
bleach [bliːtʃ]	*v.* 去色，漂白（to cause sth. to become white）*n.* 漂白剂；漂白的行为 记 联想记忆：b + leach（过滤）→ 将其他颜色滤去 → 去色
baffle ['bæfl]	*v.* 使困惑，难倒（to confuse; puzzle; confound） 记 发音记忆："拜服了" → 被难倒了，所以拜服了 → 难倒
heterodox ['hetərədɑːks]	*adj.* 异端的，非正统的（unorthodox） 记 词根记忆：hetero（其他的；相异的）+ dox（思想）→ 持异端思想的 → 异端的 同 dissident, heretical
tissue ['tɪʃuː]	*n.* （动植物的）组织（animal or plant cells）；薄纸，棉纸（light thin paper）
edify ['edɪfaɪ]	*v.* 陶冶，启发（to enlighten, or uplift morally or spiritually） 记 词根记忆：ed（吃）+ ify（表动作）→ 吃下去 → 陶冶，启发 同 illume, illuminate, illumine
pejorative [pɪ'dʒɔːrətɪv]	*adj.* 轻视的，贬低的（tending to disparage; depreciatory） 记 词根记忆：pejor（坏的）+ ative → 变坏的 → 轻视的，贬低的 例 The campus police who monitored the demonstrations had little respect for the student protesters, generally speaking of them in *pejorative* terms.
ponderous ['pɑːndərəs]	*adj.* 笨重的，（因太重太大而）不便搬运的（unwieldy or clumsy because of weight and size） 记 词根记忆：pond（重量）+ er + ous（多…的）→ 重的 → 笨重的
particular [pər'tɪkjələr]	*n.* 细节，详情（an individual fact or detail; item） 同 fact
pedagogic [ˌpedə'gɑːdʒɪk]	*adj.* 教育学的（of, relating to, or befitting a teacher or education） 记 词根记忆：ped（= child 儿童）+ agog（引导）+ ic → 教育学的
fluid ['fluːɪd]	*adj.* 流体的，流动的（capable of flowing）；易变的，不固定的（subject to change or movement） 记 词根记忆：flu（流动）+ id → 流动的
parody ['pærədi]	*n.* 拙劣的模仿（a feeble or ridiculous imitation）；滑稽模仿作品或表演（a literary or artistic work that imitates the characteristic style of an author or a work for comic effect or ridicule） 记 词根记忆：par（旁边）+ ody（=ode 唱）→ 在旁边唱 → 拙劣的模仿
visible ['vɪzəbl]	*adj.* 可见的，看得见的（capable of being seen）；能注意到的（exposed to view）；明显的，可察觉到的（capable of being discovered or perceived） 记 词根记忆：vis（看）+ ible（可…的）→ 看得见的；明显的

□ devour	□ explicate	□ bleach	□ baffle	□ heterodox	□ tissue
□ edify	□ pejorative	□ ponderous	□ particular	□ pedagogic	□ fluid
□ parody	□ visible				

pungent [ˈpʌndʒənt]	*adj.* 辛辣的，刺激的（piquant）；尖锐的，尖刻的（being sharp and to the point） 记 词根记忆：pung(刺) + ent → 尖锐的，尖刻的 例 The *pungent* verbal give-and-take among the characters makes the novel tedious reading.
eligible [ˈelɪdʒəbl]	*adj.* 合格的，有资格的（qualified to be chosen；suitable） 记 词根记忆：e + lig(=lect 选择) + ible → 能被选出来的 → 合格的
encroach [ɪnˈkroʊtʃ]	*v.* 侵占，蚕食（to enter by gradual steps or by stealth into the possessions or rights of another） 记 词根记忆：en(进入) + croach(钩) → 钩进去 → 侵占
superb [suːˈpɜːrb]	*adj.* 上乘的，出色的（marked to the highest degree by excellence, brilliance, or competence） 记 词根记忆：super(超过) + b → 超群的 → 上乘的，出色的 同 lofty, sublime
assure [əˈʃʊr]	*v.* 保证（to tell sb. positively）；使确信（to convince） 记 词根记忆：as(一再) + sure(肯定) → 一再肯定 → 使确信
supersede [ˌsuːpərˈsiːd]	*v.* 淘汰（to force out of use as inferior）；取代（to take the place, room, or position of） 记 词根记忆：super(在…上面) + sede(坐) → 坐在别人上面 → 取代
ambivalent [æmˈbɪvələnt]	*adj.* (对人或物)有矛盾看法的（having simultaneous and contradictory attitudes or feelings toward sb. or sth.）
archaeological [ˌɑːrkiəˈlɑːdʒɪkl]	*adj.* 考古学的
compliant [kəmˈplaɪənt]	*adj.* 服从的，顺从的（complying；yielding；submissive） 记 词根记忆：com + pliant(柔顺的) → 顺从的
explore [ɪkˈsplɔːr]	*v.* 探究（to investigate, study, or analyze）；勘探（to travel over for adventure or discovery）；考察（to make or conduct a systematic search） 记 联想记忆：ex + pl + ore(矿石) → 把矿石挖出来 → 勘探 例 One reason why pertinent fossils are uncommon is that crucial stages of evolution occurred in the tropics where it is difficult to *explore* for fossils, and so their discovery has lagged.
soliloquy [səˈlɪləkwi]	*n.* 自言自语（the act of talking to oneself）；戏剧独白（a dramatic monologue that represents a series of unspoken reflections）
symmetry [ˈsɪmətri]	*n.* 对称；匀称（balanced proportions） 记 词根记忆：sym(共同) + metry(测量) → 两边所测量的距离相同 → 对称
concentration [ˌkɑːnsnˈtreɪʃn]	*n.* 专心，专注（the act or process of concentrating）；集中（a concentrated mass or thing）；浓度（the amount of a component in a given area or volume） concentration

□ pungent	□ eligible	□ encroach	□ superb	□ assure	□ supersede
□ ambivalent	□ archaeological	□ compliant	□ explore	□ soliloquy	□ symmetry
□ concentration					

unaesthetic [ˌʌnəsˈθetɪk]	*adj.* 无美感的(deficient in tastefulness or beauty) 记 和 inaesthetic(*adj.* 不美的)一起记
heed [hiːd]	*v.* 注意，留心(to give attention to) *n.* 注意，留心(careful attention) 记 和 need(*n.* 需要)一起记；需要(need)的东西格外注意、留心(heed) 例 Students of the Great Crash of 1929 have never understood why even the most informed observers did not recognize and *heed* the prior economic danger signals that in retrospect seem so apparent.
incentive [ɪnˈsentɪv]	*n.* 刺激，诱因，动机(motive)；刺激因素(sth. that incites to determination or action) 记 词根记忆：in(进入) + cent(=cant 唱，说) + ive → 说服他人做某事 → 刺激，诱因 例 Imposing steep fines on employers for on-the-job injuries to workers could be an effective *incentive* to creating a safer workplace, especially in the case of employers with poor safety records. 同 goad, impetus, impulse, stimulus incentive 下次努力!
core [kɔːr]	*n.* 果心(centre of fruits)；核心(the most important part) *v.* 去掉某物的中心部分(to take out the core of sth.)
tapering [ˈteɪpərɪŋ]	*adj.* 尖端细的 记 来自 taper(*v.* 逐渐变细)
reliable [rɪˈlaɪəbl]	*adj.* 可信赖的(suitable or fit to be relied on) *n.* 可信赖的人(one that is reliable) 例 Experienced and proficient, Susan is a good, *reliable* trumpeter; her music is often more satisfying than Carol's brilliant but erratic playing.
gibe [dʒaɪb]	*v.* 嘲弄，讥笑(to jeer or taunt; scoff) *n.* 嘲笑，讥笑 记 联想记忆：也写作 jibe，但 jibe 还有另一个意思 "与…一致"，是 GRE 常考的释义
forsake [fərˈseɪk]	*v.* 遗弃(to leave; abandon)，放弃(to give up; renounce) 记 联想记忆：for(出去) + sake(缘故) → 为了某种缘故而抛出去 → 遗弃
stout [staʊt]	*adj.* 肥胖的(bulky in body)；强壮的(sturdy, vigorous) 记 联想记忆：st + out(出来) → 肌肉都鼓出来了 → 强壮的 stout
flippant [ˈflɪpənt]	*adj.* 无礼的(frivolous and disrespectful)；轻率的(lacking proper respect or seriousness)
incendiary [ɪnˈsendieri]	*adj.* 放火的，纵火的(pertaining to the criminal setting on fire of property) 记 词根记忆：in(进入) + cend(=cand 发光) + iary → 燃烧发光 → 放火的
buttress [ˈbʌtrəs]	*n.* 拱墙，拱壁(a projecting structure built against a wall to support or reinforce it) *v.* 支持(to prop up; bolster)

| □ unaesthetic | □ heed | □ incentive | □ core | □ tapering | □ reliable |
| □ gibe | □ forsake | □ stout | □ flippant | □ incendiary | □ buttress |

219

incandescent [ˌɪnkæn'desnt]	*adj.* 遇热发光的，发白热光的（white, glowing, or luminous with intense heat）
fade [feɪd]	*v.* 变暗，褪色，枯萎，凋谢（to lose brightness, color, vigor or freshness） 同 dim, wither
fussy ['fʌsi]	*adj.* 爱挑剔的，难取悦的（overly exacting and hard to please） 同 dainty, exacting, fastidious, finicky, meticulous
outdated [ˌaʊt'deɪtɪd]	*adj.* 过时的（no longer current） 同 outmoded
imprudent [ɪm'pruːdnt]	*adj.* 轻率的（indiscreet）；不理智的（not wise） 例 It would be *imprudent* to invest all your money in one company.
puncture ['pʌŋktʃər]	*v.* 刺穿，戳破（to pierce with a pointed instrument）*n.* 刺孔，穿孔 记 词根记忆：punct(点) + ure → 点破 → 刺穿，戳破
wearisome ['wɪrisəm]	*adj.* 使人感到疲倦或厌倦的（causing one to feel tired or bored） 记 来自 weary(*v.* 疲倦，厌倦)
paradox ['pærədɑːks]	*n.* 似非而是的理论（a statement that is seemingly contradictory or opposed to common sense and yet is perhaps true）；矛盾的人或物（one exhibiting inexplicable or contradictory aspects）；与通常的见解相反的观点（a statement contrary to received opinion） 记 词根记忆：para(相反的) + dox(观点) → 与一般观点相反的观点 → 与通常见解相反的观点 例 She is an interesting *paradox*, an infinitely shy person who, in apparent contradiction, possesses an enormously intuitive gift for understanding people.
spontaneity [ˌspɑːntə'neɪti]	*n.* 自然，自发（the quality or state of being spontaneous） 例 Unfortunately, excessive care in choosing one's words often results in a loss of *spontaneity*.
truce [truːs]	*n.* 停战，休战（协定）（agreement between enemies to stop fighting for a certain period）
persist [pər'sɪst]	*v.* 坚持不懈，执意（to go on resolutely or stubbornly in spite of opposition, importunity, or warning）；坚持问，不停地说（to be insistent in the repetition or pressing of an utterance）；继续存在，长存（to continue in existence; last） 记 词根记忆：per(始终) + sist(坐) → 始终坐着 → 坚持不懈 例 The chances that a species will *persist* are reduced if any vital function is restricted to a single kind of organ; redundancy by itself possesses an enormous survival advantage. 同 abide, endure, perdure, persevere

carve [kɑːrv]	*v.* 雕刻（to shape by cutting, chipping and hewing）；（把肉等）切成片（to slice）
	同 cleave, dissect, dissever, sever, split
demean [dɪˈmiːn]	*v.* 贬抑，降低（to degrade；humble）
	记 联想记忆：de(加强) + mean(低下的) → 使低下 → 贬抑
weather [ˈweðər]	*v.* 风化，侵蚀；经受住风雨；平安度过危难（to come through (sth.) safely；survive）
publicize [ˈpʌblɪsaɪz]	*v.* （公开）宣传，宣扬；引人注意
	记 联想记忆：public(公开的) + ize(使) → 使公开 → 宣传，宣扬
	例 Though the ad writers had come up with a highly creative campaign to *publicize* the company's newest product, the head office rejected it for a more prosaic, down-to-earth approach.
nominally [ˈnɑːmɪnəli]	*adv.* 名义上地；有名无实地
	记 来自 nominal(*adj.* 名义上的；有名无实的)
desultory [ˈdesəltɔːri]	*adj.* 不连贯的（disconnected）；散漫的（not methodical；random）
	记 词根记忆：de + sult(跳) + ory → 跳来跳去 → 散漫的
profundity [prəˈfʌndəti]	*n.* 深奥的事物（something profound or abstruse）；深刻，深厚（the quality or state of being profound or deep）
clarify [ˈklærəfaɪ]	*v.* 澄清（to cause sth. to become clear to understand）
	记 词根记忆：clar(清楚，明白) + ify(…化) → 澄清
	同 elucidate, illuminate, illustrate
cantankerous [kænˈtæŋkərəs]	*adj.* 脾气坏的（bad-tempered）；好争吵的（quarrelsome）
	记 联想记忆：cant(黑话) + anker(看作 anger，愤怒) + ous → 用黑话愤怒地争吵 → 脾气坏的
	搭 a cantankerous man 脾气坏的人
	同 bearish, cranky, irascible, irritable, ornery
proverb [ˈprɑːvɜːrb]	*n.* 谚语（a brief popular epigram or maxim）
	记 词根记忆：pro(起初) + verb(话) → 早期人们说的话 → 谚语
quash [kwɔːʃ]	*v.* 镇压（to suppress）；（依法）取消（to nullify by judicial action）
	同 abrogate, repeal, rescind
crystalline [ˈkrɪstəlaɪn]	*adj.* 水晶的（resembling crystal）；透明的（strikingly clear or sparkling）
	记 来自 crystal(*n.* 水晶)
incisive [ɪnˈsaɪsɪv]	*adj.* 尖锐的，深刻的（keen；penetrating；sharp）
	搭 incisive comments 深刻的评论
elude [iˈluːd]	*v.* 逃避（to avoid adroitly）；搞不清，理解不了（to escape the perception or understanding）
	记 词根记忆：e + lud(玩弄) + e → 通过玩弄的方式出去 → 逃避
	同 eschew, evade, shun
tenacity [təˈnæsəti]	*n.* 坚持，固执（the quality or state of being tenacious）
	同 doggedness, persistence, perverseness, stubbornness

□ carve	□ demean	□ weather	□ publicize	□ nominally	□ desultory
□ profundity	□ clarify	□ cantankerous	□ proverb	□ quash	□ crystalline
□ incisive	□ elude	□ tenacity			

interchangeably	*adv.* 可互换地
[ˌɪntərˈtʃeɪndʒəbli]	例 Although newscasters often use the terms Chicano and Latino *interchangeably*, students of Hispanic-American culture are profoundly aware of the dissimilarities between the two.
refrain	*v.* 抑制(to curb; restrain) *n.* (歌曲或诗歌中的)叠句(a regular recurring phrase or verse)
[rɪˈfreɪn]	记 词根记忆:re + frain(笼头) → 上笼头 → 抑制
draft	*n.* 草稿, 草案(preliminary written version of sth.); 汇票(written order to a bank to pay money to sb.)
[dræft]	
fluctuation	*n.* 波动, 起伏, 涨落(undulation, waving)
[ˌflʌktʃuˈeɪʃn]	记 来自fluctuate(*v.* 波动; 变动)
pack	*n.* 兽群(a number of wild animals living and hunting together)
[pæk]	记 该词的"包裹"一义大家应该比较熟悉
wary	*adj.* 谨慎的, 小心翼翼的(marked by keen caution, cunning, and watchfulness especially in detecting and escaping danger)
[ˈweri]	
humdrum	*adj.* 单调的, 乏味的(dull; monotonous; boring)
[ˈhʌmdrʌm]	记 组合词:hum(嗡嗡声) + drum(鼓声) → 单调的
nuance	*n.* 细微差异(a subtle difference)
[ˈnuːɑːns]	同 nicety, shade, subtlety, refinement
sprout	*v.* 长出, 萌芽(to grow; spring up) *n.* 嫩芽(a young shoot)
[spraʊt]	记 联想记忆:spr(看作spring) + out(出) → 春天来了, 嫩芽长出来了 → 长出, 萌芽
philistine	*n.* 庸俗的人, 对文化艺术无知的人(a smug, ignorant, especially middle-class person who is regarded as being indifferent or antagonistic to artistic and cultural values)
[ˈfɪlɪstiːn]	记 来自腓力斯人(Philistia), 是庸俗的市侩阶层
toed	*adj.* 有趾的(having a toe or toes)
[toʊd]	记 来自toe(*n.* 脚趾)
sabotage	*n.* 阴谋破坏, 颠覆活动(deliberate subversion)
[ˈsæbətɑːʒ]	搭 an act of military sabotage 军事破坏活动
divergent	*adj.* 分叉的, 叉开的(diverging from each other); 发散的, 扩散的; 不同的
[daɪˈvɜːrdʒənt]	记 词根记忆:di(二) + verg(倾斜) + ent → 向两边倾斜的 → 发散的
	同 disparate, dissimilar, distant, diverse
derivative	*adj.* 派生的(derived); 无创意的(not original)
[dɪˈrɪvətɪv]	同 derivate, derivational
anathema	*n.* 被诅咒的人(one that is cursed); (天主教的)革出教门, 诅咒(a formal ecclesiastical ban; curse)
[əˈnæθəmə]	记 联想记忆:ana(错误) + them(他们) + a → 他们做错了所以被诅咒 → 被诅咒的人
chastisement	*n.* 惩罚(punishment)
[tʃæˈstaɪzmənt]	同 castigation, penalty

indulgent [ɪnˈdʌldʒənt]	*adj.* 放纵的，纵容的 (indulging or characterized by indulgence) 搭 indulgent parents 纵容子女的父母
monetary [ˈmʌnɪteri]	*adj.* 金钱的 (about money)；货币的 (of or relating to a nation's currency or coinage) 记 来自 money (*n.* 金钱；货币) 例 He was indifferent to success, painting not for the sake of fame or *monetary* reward, but for the sheer love of art. 同 financial, fiscal, pecuniary
equivocator [ɪˈkwɪvəkeɪtər]	*n.* 说模棱话的人，说话支吾的人 记 词根记忆：equi (相同的) + voc (叫喊) + at + or → 发出相同声音的人 → 说模棱话的人
enormous [ɪˈnɔːrməs]	*adj.* 极大的，巨大的 (shockingly large) 记 词根记忆：e(出) + norm(规范) + ous(…的) → 超出规范的 → 巨大的 同 colossal, gargantuan, immense, titanic, tremendous
humility [hjuːˈmɪləti]	*n.* 谦逊，谦恭 (the quality or state of being humble) 同 modesty
expand [ɪkˈspænd]	*v.* 扩大，膨胀 (to increase in extent, scope, or volume) 记 词根记忆：ex + pand(分散) → 分散出去 → 扩大
wane [weɪn]	*v.* 减少，衰落 (to decrease in size, extent, or degree; dwindle) 记 联想记忆：天鹅 (swan) 的数量在减少 (wane) 同 abate, ebb, shrink, slacken, subside
ingeniousness [ɪnˈdʒiːniəsnəs]	*n.* 独创性 (ingenuity)
indignation [ˌɪndɪɡˈneɪʃn]	*n.* 愤慨，义愤 (anger or scorn; righteous anger) 搭 to be full of righteous indignation 义愤填膺
irritable [ˈɪrɪtəbl]	*adj.* 易怒的，急躁的 (easily annoyed; choleric; fretful; irascible)；易受刺激的 (responsive to stimuli) 记 词根记忆：irrit(痒) + able → 易怒的，急躁的
misdirect [ˌmɪsdəˈrekt]	*v.* 误导 (to give a wrong direction to) 记 联想记忆：mis(坏) + direct(指导) → 坏的指导 → 误导
explicit [ɪkˈsplɪsɪt]	*adj.* 明白的，清楚的 (distinctly expressed; definite)；不含糊的，明确的 (fully developed and formulated) 记 词根记忆：ex + plic(重叠) + it → 把重叠在一起的弄清楚 → 清楚的
repressive [rɪˈpresɪv]	*adj.* 抑制的 (inhibitory)；镇压的，残暴的 同 oppressive
supplementary [ˌsʌplɪˈmentri]	*adj.* 增补的，补充的 (added or serving as a supplement) 例 Because its average annual rainfall is only about four inches, one of the major tasks faced by the country has been to find *supplementary* sources of water.
sonorous [ˈsɑːnərəs]	*adj.* (声音)洪亮的 (full or loud in sound) 记 词根记忆：son(声音)+orous → (声音)洪亮的

20

□ indulgent	□ monetary	□ equivocator	□ enormous	□ humility	□ expand
□ wane	□ ingeniousness	□ indignation	□ irritable	□ misdirect	□ explicit
□ repressive	□ supplementary	□ sonorous			

woolly [ˈwʊli]	*adj.* 羊毛的；模糊的（lacking sharp detail or clarity）
seismic [ˈsaɪzmɪk]	*adj.* 地震的，由地震引起的（of or caused by an earthquake） 记 词根记忆：seism（地震）+ ic → 地震的
paucity [ˈpɔːsəti]	*n.* 少量（fewness）；缺乏（dearth） 记 词根记忆：pauc（少的）+ ity → 少量；缺乏
sustain [səˈsteɪn]	*v.* 承受（困难）（undergo）；支撑（重量或压力）（to carry or withstand a weight or pressure） 记 词根记忆：sus + tain（拿住）→ 在下面支撑住 → 支撑 同 bolster, prop, underprop
modernize [ˈmɑːdərnaɪz]	*v.* 使现代化（to make modern（as in taste, style, or usage）） 同 update
actuate [ˈæktʃueɪt]	*v.* 开动，促使（to motivate; activate） 记 词根记忆：act（行动）+ uate（动词后缀）→ 使行动起来 → 促使
counterfeit [ˈkaʊntərfɪt]	*v.* 伪造，仿造（to make an imitation of money, picture, etc. usually in order to deceive or defraud）*adj.* 伪造的，假冒的（made in imitation of sth. else with intent to deceive） 记 词根记忆：counter（反）+ feit（=fact 做）→ 和真的对着干 → 伪造
adaptive [əˈdæptɪv]	*adj.* 适应的（showing or having a capacity for or tendency toward adaptation）
impulsive [ɪmˈpʌlsɪv]	*adj.* 冲动的，由冲动引起的（arising from an impulse）；易冲动的（prone to act on impulse） 例 Though *impulsive* in her personal life, Edna St. Vincent Millay was nonetheless disciplined about her work, usually producing several pages of complicated rhyme in a day. 同 automatic, instinctive, involuntary, spontaneous
symbolize [ˈsɪmbəlaɪz]	*v.* 象征（to represent, express, or identify by a symbol） 同 denote, signify
strait [streɪt]	*n.* 海峡 *adj.* 狭窄的（narrow） 参 isthmus（*n.* 地峡）
frugality [fruˈgæləti]	*n.* 朴素；节俭（prudence in avoiding waste） 例 Her *frugality* should not be confused with miserliness; as long as I have known her, she has always been willing to assist those who are in need. 同 economy, thriftiness
drab [dræb]	*adj.* 黄褐色的（of a dull yellowish brown）；单调的，乏味的（not bright or lively; monotonous） 例 Thomas Paine, whose political writing was often flamboyant, was in private life a surprisingly simple man: he lived in rented rooms, ate little, and wore *drab* clothes.

□ woolly	□ seismic	□ paucity	□ sustain	□ modernize	□ actuate
□ counterfeit	□ adaptive	□ impulsive	□ symbolize	□ strait	□ frugality
□ drab					

subdue [səbˈduː]	v. 征服 (to conquer, vanquish); 压制 (to bring under control); 减轻(to reduce the intensity or degree of)
	记 词根记忆: sub(在下面) + due(=duce 引导) → 引到下面 → 征服
	同 crush, overpower, subjugate
unsure [ˌʌnˈʃʊr]	adj. 缺乏自信的(having little self-confidence); 不确定的(not having certain knowledge)
disinterested [dɪsˈɪntrəstɪd]	adj. 公正的, 客观的(impartial; unbiased)
	记 注意区别 uninterested(adj. 不感兴趣的)
	搭 be disinterested in... 对…客观的、公正的; disinterested attitude 公正的态度
	同 detached, dispassionate, neutral
vitiate [ˈvɪʃieɪt]	v. 削弱, 损害(to make faulty or defective; impair)
	记 联想记忆: viti(=vice 恶的) + ate → 损害
dissipate [ˈdɪsɪpeɪt]	v. (使)消失, (使)消散(to break up and scatter or vanish); 浪费(to waste or squander)
	记 联想记忆: dis (表加强) + sip (喝, 饮) + ate → 到处吃喝 → 浪费; sip 本身是一个常考单词
excavate [ˈekskəveɪt]	v. 开洞, 凿洞(to make a hole or cavity in); 挖掘, 发掘(to uncover or expose)
	记 词根记忆: ex + cav(洞) + ate → 挖出洞 → 凿洞
	同 scoop, shovel, unearth
discretion [dɪˈskreʃn]	n. 谨慎, 审慎
	同 circumspection, prudence
instantaneous [ˌɪnstənˈteɪniəs]	adj. 立即的, 即刻的(immediate); 瞬间的(occurring, or acting without any perceptible duration of time)
	记 来自instant(adj. 立即的, 即刻的 n. 瞬间, 顷刻)
sully [ˈsʌli]	v. 玷污, 污染(to make soiled or tarnished; defile)
	同 stain, tarnish
extol [ɪkˈstoʊl]	v. 赞美(to praise highly; laud)
	记 词根记忆: ex + tol(举起) → 举起来 → 赞美
congruous [ˈkɒŋgruəs]	adj. 一致的, 符合的(being in agreement, harmony, or correspondence); [数] 全等的
ceramic [səˈræmɪk]	adj. 陶器的(made of clay and permanently hardened by heat) n. 陶瓷制品(the making of pots or tiles by shaping pieces of clay and baking them)
	记 词根记忆: ceram(陶瓷) + ic → 陶器的
birthright [ˈbɜːrθraɪt]	n. 与生俱来的权利(a right, privilege, or possession to which a person is entitled by birth)
previous [ˈpriːviəs]	adj. 在先的, 以前的(prior; preceding)
	记 词根记忆: pre(在前面) + vi(道路) + ous → 走在前面的 → 在先的, 以前的

□ subdue	□ unsure	□ disinterested	□ vitiate	□ dissipate	□ excavate
□ discretion	□ instantaneous	□ sully	□ extol	□ congruous	□ ceramic
□ birthright	□ previous				

sentient ['sentiənt]	*adj.* 有知觉的(responsive to or conscious of sense impressions); 知悉的(aware)
strategic [strə'tiːdʒɪk]	*adj.* 战略上的(of, relating to, or marked by strategy); 关键的, 重要的(necessary to or important in the initiation, conduct, or completion of a strategic plan)
unregulated [ˌʌn'reɡjuleɪtɪd]	*adj.* 未受控制的, 未受约束的(not controlled by a government or law) 记 联想记忆: un(不) + regulat(e)(管制) + ed → 未受控制的, 未受约束的
approximate [ə'prɑːksɪmət]	*adj.* 近似的, 大约的(much like; nearly correct or exact) 记 词根记忆: ap + proxim(接近) + ate → 近似的, 大约的
unconfirmed [ˌʌnkən'fɜːrmd]	*adj.* 未经证实的(not proved to be true; not confirmed)
inducement [ɪn'duːsmənt]	*n.* 引诱; 引诱物, 诱因, 动机 记 来自induce(*v.* 引诱)
debatable [dɪ'beɪtəbl]	*adj.* 未决定的, 有争执的(open to dispute) 记 来自debate(*v.* 辩论)
odorless ['oʊdərləs]	*adj.* 无嗅的, 没有气味的 记 来自odor(*n.* 气味, 香气)
overrate [ˌoʊvər'reɪt]	*v.* 对…估价过高, 对…评价过高(to rate, value, or estimate too highly) 同 overesteem, overestimate, overprize, overvalue
specious ['spiːʃəs]	*adj.* 似是而非的(having a false look of truth or genuineness); 华而不实的(having deceptive attraction or allure) 记 词根记忆: spec(看) + ious → 用来看的 → 华而不实的
contempt [kən'tempt]	*n./v.* 轻视, 鄙视 记 联想记忆: con + tempt(尝试) → 大家都敢尝试 → 小意思 → 轻视 搭 contempt for... 轻视… 同 defiance, disdain, disparagement
ballad ['bæləd]	*n.* 歌谣, 小曲(a song or poem that tells a story in short stanzas) 记 联想记忆: ball(球) + ad → 像球一样一代代传下来 → 歌谣
gall [ɡɔːl]	*n.* 胆汁(bile); 怨恨(hatred; bitter feeling) 记 和wall(*n.* 墙)一起记
newsworthy ['nuːzwɜːrði]	*adj.* 有新闻价值的, 有报道价值的(interesting enough to the general public to warrant reporting)
proliferate [prə'lɪfəreɪt]	*v.* 激增(to increase rapidly; multiply); (迅速)繁殖, 增生(to grow by rapid production) 记 词根记忆: pro(许多) + lifer(生命) + ate → 产生许多生命 → 繁殖, 增生
rigidity [rɪ'dʒɪdəti]	*n.* 严格; 坚硬, 僵硬(the quality or state of being rigid) 例 The child needed physical therapy to counteract the *rigidity* that had tragically immobilized his legs.

adaptable [əˈdæptəbl]	*adj.* 有适应能力的（able to adjust oneself to new circumstances）；可改编的（capable of being adapted） 记 词根记忆：adapt(适应) + able(能…的) → 有适应能力的
ragtime [ˈræɡtaɪm]	*n.* 雷格泰姆音乐（a type of music of black US origin）*adj.* 使人发笑的，滑稽的（funny） 记 联想记忆：rag(破衣服) + time(节拍) → 黑人穿破衣服打拍子 → 使人发笑的

If you put out your hands, you are a laborer; if you put out your hands and mind, you are a craftsperson; if you put out your hands, mind, heart and soul, you are an artist.

如果你用双手工作,你是一个劳力;如果你用双手和头脑工作,你是一个工匠;如果你用双手和头脑工作,并且全身心投入,你就是一个艺术家。

——美国电影 *American Heart and Soul*

Word List 21

音频

chantey	*n.* 船歌(a song sung by sailors in rhythm with their work)
[ˈʃæntɪ]	
envision	*v.* 想象，预想(to picture to oneself)
[ɪnˈvɪʒn]	记 词根记忆：en + vis(看) + ion → 想象，预想
intersect	*v.* 相交 (to meet and cross at a point)；贯穿，横穿 (to divide into two
[ˌɪntərˈsekt]	parts; cut across)
amendment	*n.* 改正，修正(a correction of errors, faults)；修正案(a revision made in a
[əˈmendmənt]	bill, law, constitution, etc.)
aphorism	*n.* 格言(maxim; adage)
[ˈæfərɪzəm]	记 词根记忆：a + phor(带来) + ism → 带来智慧的话 → 格言
frail	*adj.* 脆弱的(fragile; delicate)；不坚实的(slender and delicate)
[freɪl]	记 可能是 fragile(*adj.* 易碎的)的变体
	例 A human being is quite a *frail* creature, for the gloss of rationality that
	covers his or her fears and insecurity is thin and often easily breached.
	同 feeble, flimsy
prohibitive	*adj.* 禁止的，抑制的(tending to prohibit or restrain)；贵得买不起的(so
[prəˈhɪbətɪv]	high or burdensome as to discourage purchase or use)
	记 词根记忆：pro(提前) + hibit(拿住) + ive(…的) → 提前拿住的 → 禁止
	的，抑制的
decompose	*v.* (使)腐烂(to rot; decay)
[ˌdiːkəmˈpoʊz]	记 词根记忆：de(否定) + compose(组成) → 腐烂
instigate	*v.* 怂恿，鼓动，煽动(to urge on; foment; incite)
[ˈɪnstɪɡeɪt]	记 词根记忆：in(进入) + stig(=sting 刺激) + ate → 刺激起来 → 怂恿，鼓
	动，煽动
	同 abet, provoke, stir
resent	*v.* 憎恶，怨恨(to feel or express annoyance or ill will)
[rɪˈzent]	记 词根记忆：re(反) + sent(感情) → 反感 → 憎恶
	例 Was he so thin-skinned, then, to *resent* any small jest at his expense?
vulgar	*adj.* 无教养的，庸俗的(morally crude, undeveloped)
[ˈvʌlɡər]	记 词根记忆：vulg(庸俗) + ar → 庸俗的

□ chantey	□ envision	□ intersect	□ amendment	□ aphorism	□ frail
□ prohibitive	□ decompose	□ instigate	□ resent	□ vulgar	

justifiable [ˈdʒʌstɪfaɪəbl]	*adj.* 有理由的，无可非议的（capable of being justified or defended as correct） 记 来自 justify（*v.* 证明…是正当或合理的）
formidably [ˈfɔːrmɪdəbli]	*adv.* 可怕地，难对付地，强大地（strongly） 记 来自 formidable（*adj.* 可怕的，难对付的）
diffusion [dɪˈfjuːʒn]	*n.* 扩散，弥漫（diffuseness）；冗长（prolixity）；反射（reflection of light by a rough reflecting surface）；漫射（transmission of light through a translucent material; scattering）
candor [ˈkændər]	*n.* 坦白，率直（frankness） 记 词根记忆：cand（白）+ or（表状态）→ 坦白 例 *Candor* may actually enhance one's standing.
conflate [kənˈfleɪt]	*v.* 合并（to combine or mix） 记 联想记忆：con（共同）+ flat（吹气）+ e → 吹到一起 → 合并
formalized [ˈfɔːrməlaɪzd]	*adj.* 形式化的，正式的 记 来自 formalize（*v.* 使形式化，使正式）
misanthrope [ˈmɪsənθroʊp]	*n.* 厌恶人类者（a person who hates humankind） 记 词根记忆：mis（恨）+ anthrop（人类）+ e → 恨人类的人 → 厌恶人类者 例 Because he was a *misanthrope*, he shunned human society.
subsidize [ˈsʌbsɪdaɪz]	*v.* 津贴，资助（to furnish with a subsidy） 同 finance, fund, sponsor
purified [ˈpjʊrɪfaɪd]	*adj.* 纯净的 记 来自 purify（*v.* 使洁净；净化）
antibiotic [ˌæntibaɪˈɑːtɪk]	*adj.* 抗菌的（of, or relating to antibiotics）*n.* 抗生素（substance that can destroy or prevent the growth of bacteria） 记 词根记忆：anti（反）+ bio（生命）+ tic → 抗生素
caste [kæst]	*n.* 社会等级，等级（class distinction） 记 原指印度教的种姓制度；发音记忆："卡死他" → 在一个等级上卡死他，不让他上来 → 社会等级 搭 a caste system 等级体系
tact [tækt]	*n.* 机智；圆滑（a keen sense of what to do or say） 例 She has sufficient *tact* to handle the ordinary crises of diplomatic life; however, even her diplomacy is insufficient to enable her to weather the current emergency.
cautious [ˈkɔːʃəs]	*adj.* 小心的，谨慎的（marked by or given to caution） 记 联想记忆：caut（看作 cat）+ ious（…的）→ 像猫一样的 → 小心的，谨慎的 同 chary, circumspect, discreet, gingerly, wary
impersonal [ɪmˈpɜːrsənl]	*adj.* 不受个人感情影响的（having no personal reference or connection） 记 联想记忆：im（不）+ personal（个人的）→ 不投入个人感情的 → 不受个人感情影响的
beaded [ˈbiːdɪd]	*adj.* 以珠装饰的（decorated with beads），珠状的 搭 beaded with sth. 带着…，缀着…

responsive [rɪˈspɑːnsɪv]	*adj.* 响应的，做出反应的(giving response)；敏感的，反应快的 同 respondent; sensitive
rage [reɪdʒ]	*n.* 盛怒(violent and uncontrolled anger) *v.* 狂怒，大发雷霆(to be in a rage) 搭 be all the rage 十分流行，成为时尚
unconscious [ʌnˈkɑːnʃəs]	*adj.* 不省人事的(having lost consciousness)；未发觉的，无意识的(not knowing about sth.)
convivial [kənˈvɪviəl]	*adj.* 欢乐的，快乐的 (having sth. to do with a feast or festive activity) 记 词根记忆：con + viv(活) + ial → 一起活跃 → 欢乐的
decisive [dɪˈsaɪsɪv]	*adj.* 决定性的(having the power or quality of deciding)；坚定的，果断的(resolute; unquestionable) 同 bent, decided, determined, resolved
overshadow [ˌoʊvərˈʃædoʊ]	*v.* 使蒙上阴影(to cast a shadow over)；使黯然失色 记 组合词：over(在…上) + shadow(阴影) → 蒙上一层阴影 → 使蒙上阴影；使黯然失色
adverse [ˈædvɜːrs]	*adj.* 有害的，不利的(not favorable)；敌对的(hostile)，相反的(contrary) 记 词根记忆：ad(坏) + verse(转) → 不利的；敌对的
incidence [ˈɪnsɪdəns]	*n.* 发生，出现(an instance of happening)；发生率(rate of occurrence or influence) 记 词根记忆：in + cid(落下) + ence → 落下来的事 → 发生，出现
self-assured [ˌselfəˈʃʊrd]	*adj.* 有自信的(sure of oneself) 同 confident
decrepit [dɪˈkrepɪt]	*adj.* 衰老的，破旧的(broken down or worn out by old age, illness, or long use) 记 词根记忆：de + crepit(破裂声) → 破旧的
contrary [ˈkɑːntreri]	*adj.* 相反的(being so different as to be at opposite extremes)；对抗的(being opposite to or in conflict with each other) 记 词根记忆：contra(相反) + ry → 相反的 搭 be contrary to 与…相反
precipitate	[prɪˈsɪpɪteɪt] *v.* 使突然降临，加速，促成(to bring about abruptly; hasten) [prɪˈsɪpɪtət] *adj.* 鲁莽的，轻率的(impetuous) 记 词根记忆：pre(预先) + cip(落下) + it + ate → 预先落下 → 使突然降临，加速 搭 precipitate sb./sth. into sth. 使…突然陷入(某种状态)
applaud [əˈplɔːd]	*v.* 鼓掌；称赞(to show approval by clapping the hands) 记 词根记忆：ap(加强) + plaud(鼓掌) → 鼓掌 同 acclaim, commend, compliment
astound [əˈstaʊnd]	*v.* 使震惊(to overcome sb. with surprise) 记 联想记忆：as + tound(看作 sound) → 像被大声吓倒 → 使震惊

chafe [tʃeɪf]	*v.* (将皮肤等)擦热, 擦破(to warm by rubbing); 激怒(to annoy) 记 联想记忆: 在 cafe 中加了一个 h(看作 hot) → 热咖啡 → 擦热
ridiculous [rɪ'dɪkjələs]	*adj.* 荒谬的, 可笑的(absurd, preposterous) 记 词根记忆: rid(笑) + icul + ous(…的) → 被人嘲笑的 → 荒谬的, 可笑的 同 comical, droll, farcical, laughable, ludicrous
scheme [ski:m]	*n.* 阴谋(a crafty or secret plan); (作品等)体系, 结构(a systematic or organized framework; design) 记 注意不要和 schema(*n.* 图表)相混
overlap [ˌoʊvər'læp]	*v.* 部分重叠(to coincide in part with) 记 组合词: over(在…上) + lap(大腿) → 把一条腿放在另一条腿上 → 部分重叠 同 lap, overlie, override
impede [ɪm'pi:d]	*v.* 妨碍 (to bar or hinder the progress of; obstruct) 记 词根记忆: im(进入) + ped(脚) + e → 把脚放入 → 妨碍
verdant ['vɜːrdnt]	*adj.* 葱郁的, 翠绿的(green in tint or color) 记 词根记忆: verd(绿色) + ant → 翠绿的
exigency ['eksɪdʒənsi]	*n.* 紧急要求, 迫切需要(that which is required in a particular situation) 记 词根记忆: ex(外) + ig(驱赶) + ency → 赶到外边 → 紧急要求
incumbent [ɪn'kʌmbənt]	*n.* 在职者, 现任者 (the holder of an office or benefice) *adj.* 义不容辞的(obligatory) 记 词根记忆: in + cumb(躺) + ent → 躺在(职位)上的人 → 在职者
voluntary ['vɑːlənteri]	*adj.* 自愿的, 志愿的(of, relating to, subject to, or regulated by the will) 记 词根记忆: volunt(自动) + ary(…的) → 自己选择的 → 自愿的
recast [ˌriː'kæst]	*v.* 重铸(to mold again); 更换演员(to change the cast of (a theatrical production)) 记 词根记忆: re(重新) + cast(铸) → 重铸
certitude ['sɜːrtɪtuːd]	*n.* 确定无疑(certainty of act or event) 记 词根记忆: cert(确定) + itude(状态) → 确定的状态 → 确定无疑
stocky ['stɑːki]	*adj.* (人或动物)矮而结实的, 粗壮的(compact, sturdy, and relatively thick in build) 记 来自 stock(*n.* 树桩)
circumstantial [ˌsɜːrkəm'stænʃl]	*adj.* 不重要的, 偶然的(incidental); 描述详细的(marked by careful attention to detail) 记 词根记忆: circum(绕圈) + stant(站, 立) + ial → 处于周围 → 不重要的
euphemistic [ˌjuːfə'mɪstɪk]	*adj.* 委婉的 同 inoffensive

21

ridiculous

overlap

irreconcilable [ɪˈrekənsaɪləbl]	*adj.* 无法调和的，矛盾的(incompatible; conflicting) 记 联想记忆：ir(不) + reconcilable(可调和的) → 无法调和的 例 The faculty senate warned that, if its recommendations were to go unheeded, the differences between the administration and the teaching staff would be exacerbated and eventually rendered *irreconcilable*.
appreciate [əˈpriːʃieɪt]	*v.* 欣赏(to understand and enjoy)；感激(to recognize with gratitude) 记 词根记忆：ap + preci(价值) + ate → 给以价值 → 欣赏
modify [ˈmɑːdɪfaɪ]	*v.* 修改，更改(to alter partially; amend) 记 词根记忆：mod(方式) + ify → 使改变方式 → 修改，更改
impermeable [ɪmˈpɜːrmiəbl]	*adj.* 不可渗透的，不透水的(not allowing a liquid to pass through) 记 联想记忆：im(不) + permeable(可渗透的) → 不可渗透的
recreational [ˌrekriˈeɪʃnl]	*adj.* 娱乐的，休闲的(of, relating to, or characteristic of recreation)
self-conscious [ˌself ˈkɑːnʃəs]	*adj.* 自觉的；害羞的，不自然的 同 awkward, bashful, embarrassed
exorbitant [ɪgˈzɔːrbɪtənt]	*adj.* 过分的，过度的 (exceeding the bounds of custom, propriety, or reason) 记 联想记忆：ex + orbit(轨道，常规) + ant → 走出常规 → 过分的 搭 exorbitant fees 过度收费 同 excessive, extravagant, extreme, immoderate, inordinate
thrifty [ˈθrɪfti]	*adj.* 节俭的(marked by economy and good management) 记 来自 thrift(*n.* 节约)
overstate [ˌoʊvərˈsteɪt]	*v.* 夸张，对…言过其实(to exaggerate) 记 组合词：over(过分) + state(陈述) → 夸张
auspicious [ɔːˈspɪʃəs]	*adj.* 幸运的(favored by future; successful)；吉兆的(propitious) 记 联想记忆：au + spic(看) + ious → 看到(好事)的 → 吉兆的
irritate [ˈɪrɪteɪt]	*v.* 激怒(to provoke anger)；刺激(to induce irritability in or of) 记 词根记忆：irrit(痒) + ate → 激怒；刺激 同 exasperate, peeve, pique, roil
grave [greɪv]	*adj.* 严肃的，庄重的(serious) *n.* 墓穴 记 词根记忆：grav(重)+e → 庄重的
structure [ˈstrʌktʃər]	*n.* 结构(makeup) *v.* 建造(to construct) 例 Even though the basic organization of the brain does not change after birth, details of its *structure* and function remain plastic for some time, particularly in the cerebral cortex.
inelastic [ˌɪnɪˈlæstɪk]	*adj.* 无弹性的(inflexible) 记 联想记忆：in(不) + elastic(有弹性的) → 无弹性的
embrace [ɪmˈbreɪs]	*v.* 拥抱 (to take a person into one's arms as a sign of affection)；包含(to take in or include as a part) 记 词根记忆：em(进入) + brac(胳膊) + e → 进入怀抱 → 拥抱

□ irreconcilable	□ appreciate	□ modify	■ impermeable	□ recreational	□ self-conscious
□ exorbitant	□ thrifty	□ overstate	■ auspicious	□ irritate	■ grave
□ structure	□ inelastic	□ embrace			

transgress [trænzˈgres]	*v.* 冒犯，违背 (to go beyond limits prescribed by; violate) 记 词根记忆：trans(横向) + gress(走) → 横着走 → 冒犯
gregarious [grɪˈgeriəs]	*adj.* 群居的 (living in herds or flocks)；爱社交的 (sociable) 记 词根记忆：greg(群体) + arious → 群居的 例 Contrary to her customary *gregarious* behavior, Susan began leaving parties early to seek the solitude of her room.
dupe [duːp]	*n.* 易上当者 (a person easily tricked or fooled) 记 发音记忆："丢谱" → 瞎摆谱，结果上了当，丢了面子 → 易上当者
impatience [ɪmˈpeɪʃns]	*n.* 不耐烦，焦躁 (the quality or state of being impatient) 记 来自 patient (*adj.* 有耐心的)
headstrong [ˈhedstrɔːŋ]	*adj.* 刚愎自用的 (determined to have one's own way; obstinate; unruly) 记 组合词：head(头) + strong(强的) → 头很强 → 刚愎自用的
insincere [ˌɪnsɪnˈsɪr]	*adj.* 不诚恳的，虚伪的 (hypocritical) 例 Since she believed him to be both candid and trustworthy, she refused to consider the possibility that his statement had been *insincere*.
fumigate [ˈfjuːmɪgeɪt]	*v.* 用烟熏消毒 (to expose to the action of fumes in order to disinfect or kill the vermin) 记 词根记忆：fum(=fume 烟) + igate(用…的) → 用烟熏消毒
ruthless [ˈruːθləs]	*adj.* 无情的 (merciless)；残忍的 (cruel) 例 Wemmick, the soul of kindness in private, is obliged in public to be uncompassionate and even *ruthless* on behalf of his employer, the harsh lawyer Jaggers.
perspire [pərˈspaɪər]	*v.* 出汗 (to sweat) 记 词根记忆：per + spir(呼吸) + e → 全身都呼吸 → 出汗
facilitate [fəˈsɪlɪteɪt]	*v.* 使容易，促进 (to make easy or easier) 同 assist, ease, speed
impair [ɪmˈper]	*v.* 损害，削弱 (to damage; reduce; injure) 记 词根记忆：im(进入) + pair(坏) → 使…变坏 → 损害 例 Exposure to sustained noise has been claimed to *impair* blood pressure regulation in human beings and, particularly, to increase hypertension, even though some researchers have obtained inconclusive results that obscure the relationship. 同 blemish, mar, prejudice, tarnish, vitiate
obstinateness [ˈɑːbstɪnətnəs]	*n.* 固执，顽固 记 来自 obstinate (*adj.* 顽固的，固执的)
ancestor [ˈænsestər]	*n.* 祖先，祖宗 (one from whom a person is descended) 记 词根记忆：ance (看作 ante，先) + stor → 祖先，祖宗

☐ transgress ☐ gregarious ☐ dupe ■ impatience ☐ headstrong ☐ insincere
☐ fumigate ☐ ruthless ☐ perspire ■ facilitate ☐ impair ☐ obstinateness
☐ ancestor

233

closet [ˈklɑːzət]	*adj.* 秘密的 (closely private) *n.* 壁橱 (a small room where clothing and personal objects are kept)
cringe [krɪndʒ]	*v.* 畏缩 (to shrink from sth. dangerous or painful); 谄媚 (to act in a timid, servile manner; fawn) 记 联想记忆：c + ring (响铃) + e → 一响铃就退缩 → 畏缩 搭 cringe from 因…畏缩
unequivocal [ˌʌnɪˈkwɪvəkl]	*adj.* 毫无疑问的 (leaving no doubt; unquestionable) 例 Dr. Smith cautioned that the data so far are not sufficiently *unequivocal* to warrant dogmatic assertions by either side in the debate.
negotiate [nɪˈɡoʊʃieɪt]	*v.* 协商，商定，议定 (to arrange for or bring about through conference, discussion, and compromise) 例 The actual rigidity of Wilson's position was always betrayed by his refusal to compromise after having initially agreed to *negotiate* a settlement.
adversity [ədˈvɜːrsəti]	*n.* 逆境，不幸 (a state, condition, or instance of serious or continued difficulty or adverse fortune)
affective [əˈfektɪv]	*adj.* 感情的 (relating to, arising from, or influencing feelings or emotions), 表达感情的 (expressing emotion)
countless [ˈkaʊntləs]	*adj.* 无数的 (too numerous to be counted) 同 incalculable, innumerable, numberless, uncountable
plump [plʌmp]	*adj.* 丰满的 (having a full rounded usually pleasing form) *v.* 使丰满，使变圆 (to make well-rounded or full in form)
elongate [ɪˈlɔːŋɡeɪt]	*v.* 延长，伸长 (to extend the length of) 记 词根记忆：e + long (长的) + ate → 向外变长 → 伸长
irreparable [ɪˈrepərəbl]	*adj.* 不能挽回的，无法弥补的 (irremediable) 搭 irreparable damage 不可弥补的损害
unjustifiable [ʌnˈdʒʌstɪfaɪəbl]	*adj.* 不合道理的 (incapable of being justified or explained) 例 The commission of inquiry censured the senator for his lavish expenditure of public funds, which they found to be *unjustifiable*.
remiss [rɪˈmɪs]	*adj.* 疏忽的，不留心的 (negligent in the performance of work or duty) 记 词根记忆：re (一再) + miss (放) → 一再放掉 → 疏忽的
revival [rɪˈvaɪvl]	*n.* 苏醒；恢复；复兴 (renewed attention to or interest in sth.) 记 词根记忆：re (又) + viv (生命) + al → 生命重现 → 恢复 例 Crowther maintained that the current *revival* was the most fatuous and inane production of the entire theatrical season. 同 reanimation, renaissance, renascence, resuscitation, revivification
patience [ˈpeɪʃns]	*n.* 耐性 (the capacity, habit, or fact of being patient) 例 The diplomat, selected for her demonstrated *patience* and skill in conducting such delicate negotiations, declined to make a decision during the talks because any sudden commitment at that time would have been inopportune.

□ closet	□ cringe	□ unequivocal	□ negotiate	□ adversity	□ affective
234 □ countless	□ plump	□ elongate	□ irreparable	□ unjustifiable	□ remiss
□ revival	□ patience				

chorus [ˈkɔːrəs]	*n.* 合唱队，歌舞团（a group of dancers and singers） 记 词根记忆：chor（跳舞）+ us → 跳舞的人 → 歌舞团
grudge [grʌdʒ]	*v.* 吝惜，勉强给或承认（to be reluctant to give or admit）；不满，怨恨（to feel resentful about sth.） 记 联想记忆：去做苦工（drudge）肯定会怨恨（grudge）
concede [kənˈsiːd]	*v.* 承认（to admit）；让步（to make a concession） 记 词根记忆：con + ced（割让）+ e → 让出去 → 让步
beneficiary [ˌbenɪˈfɪʃieri]	*n.* 受益人（one that benefits from sth.） 记 来自 benefit（*n.* 益处，好处）
vigilance [ˈvɪdʒɪləns]	*n.* 警惕，警觉（the quality or state of being vigilant） 同 alertness, watchfulness
initiate [ɪˈnɪʃieɪt]	*v.* 发起，开始（to set going by taking the first step; begin）；接纳（to admit into membership, as with ceremonies or ritual） 记 词根记忆：in（朝内）+ it（走）+ ial → 朝内走 → 发起，开始 同 commence, inaugurate, institute, originate
verbosity [vɜːrˈbɑːsəti]	*n.* 冗长（an expressive style that uses excessive words） 例 Her *verbosity* is always a source of irritation: she never uses a single word when she can substitute a long clause or phrase in its place.
venturesome [ˈventʃərsəm]	*adj.* 好冒险的（inclined to court or incur risk or danger）；（行为）冒险的（involving risk）
self-determination [ˌselfdɪˌtɜːrmɪˈneɪʃn]	*n.* 自主，自决（free choice of one's own acts or states without external compulsion）
haphazardly [hæpˈhæzərdli]	*adv.* 偶然地（accidentally）；随意地（randomly）；杂乱地（in a jumble） 记 联想记忆：hap（机会，运气）+ hazard（危险；意外）+ ly → 偶然地；随意地
naivete [naɪˈiːvəti]	*n.* 天真的言行举止（a naive remark or action）；天真无邪（the quality or state of being naive） 例 We realized that John was still young and impressionable, but were nevertheless surprised at his *naivete*.
extraneous [ɪkˈstreɪniəs]	*adj.* 外来的（coming from outside）；无关的（not pertinent） 记 词根记忆：extra（外面）+ neous → 外来的
analogous [əˈnæləgəs]	*adj.* 相似的，可比拟的 搭 be analogous to... 与…相似 同 akin, comparable, corresponding, parallel, undifferentiated
deft [deft]	*adj.* 灵巧的，熟练的（skillful in a quick, sure, and easy way; dexterous） 同 adroit, handy, nimble
animosity [ˌænɪˈmɑːsəti]	*n.* 憎恶，仇恨（a feeling of strong dislike or hatred） 记 词根记忆：anim（生命）+ osity → 用整个生命去恨 → 仇恨 同 animus, antagonism, enmity, hostility, ranco

grudge

21

supple [ˈsʌpl]	*adj.* 柔软的，灵活的（readily adaptable or responsive to new situations）；柔顺的，顺从的 同 flexible, limber, pliable
expressly [ɪkˈspresli]	*adv.* 清楚地（explicitly）；特意地（particularly） 记 来自 express（*v.* 表达 *adj.* 特别的；清楚的）
sympathetic [ˌsɪmpəˈθetɪk]	*adj.* 有同情心的（given to, marked by, or arising from sympathy） 同 commiserative, compassionate, condolatory, pitying
emancipate [ɪˈmænsɪpeɪt]	*v.* 解放，释放（to free from restraint） 记 词根记忆：e + man(手) + cip(落下) + ate → 使从手中落下 → 解放
incessant [ɪnˈsesnt]	*adj.* 不停的，不断的（continuing without interruption） 记 词根记忆：in(不) + cess(走) + ant → 不停的
volcanic [vɑːlˈkænɪk]	*adj.* 火山的（of, relating to, or produced by a volcano）
verification [ˌverɪfɪˈkeɪʃn]	*n.* 确认，查证（the act or process of verifying）
therapy [ˈθerəpi]	*n.* 治疗（therapeutic treatment especially of bodily, mental, or behavioral disorder） 例 The child needed physical *therapy* to counteract the rigidity that had tragically immobilized his legs.
inflate [ɪnˈfleɪt]	*v.* 使充气，使膨胀（to fill with air） 记 词根记忆：in(朝内) + flat(吹气) + e → 朝内吹气 → 使充气
charitable [ˈtʃærətəbl]	*adj.* 行善的（full of love for and goodwill toward others）；仁爱的（liberal in benefactions to the needy） 同 benevolent, clement, humanitarian, lenient, philanthropic
virtue [ˈvɜːrtʃuː]	*n.* 美德（conformity to a standard of right）；优点（merit）；潜能（potency） 例 People should not be praised for their *virtue* if they lack the energy to be wicked; in such cases, goodness is merely the effect of indolence. 同 morality, probity, rectitude, righteousness
stronghold [ˈstrɔːŋhoʊld]	*n.* 要塞（a fortified place）；堡垒，根据地（a place of security or survival） 同 fortress
venomous [ˈvenəməs]	*adj.* 有毒的（full of venom; poisonous） 同 deadly, vicious, virulent
mysticism [ˈmɪstɪsɪzəm]	*n.* 神秘主义（immediate consciousness of the transcendent or ultimate reality） 例 No longer sustained by the belief that the world around us was expressly designed for humanity, many people try to find intellectual substitutes for that lost certainty in astrology and in *mysticism*.
alloy [ˈælɔɪ]	*n.* 合金（a substance composed of two or more metals） 记 联想记忆：all(所有的) + oy → 把所有金属混在一起 → 合金 同 admixture, amalgam, composite, fusion, interfusion

□ supple　　　□ expressly　　　□ sympathetic　　□ emancipate　　□ incessant　　□ volcanic
□ verification　□ therapy　　　□ inflate　　　　□ charitable　　□ virtue　　　□ stronghold
□ venomous　　□ mysticism　　□ alloy

hospitable [hɑːˈspɪtəbl]	*adj.* 热情好客的（disposed to treat guests with warmth and generosity）；易接受的（having an open mind；receptive） 记 联想记忆：hospita(l)（医院）+ (a)ble（能…的）→ 在医院治疗要接受医生的安排 → 易接受的 例 Our times seem especially *hospitable* to bad ideas, probably because in throwing off the shackles of tradition, we have ended up being quite vulnerable to untested theories and untried remedies.
dumbfound [dʌmˈfaʊnd]	*v.* 使…惊讶（to astonish） 记 组合词：dumb（哑）+ found（被发现）→ 惊讶得说不出话来 → 使…惊讶 同 amaze, astound
outgoing [ˈaʊtɡoʊɪŋ]	*adj.* 友善的（openly friendly；sociable）；即将离去的（going out；leaving） 例 Rebuffed by his colleagues, the initially *outgoing* young researcher became increasingly withdrawn.
taut [tɔːt]	*adj.* 绷紧的，拉紧的（having no slack；tightly drawn） 同 stiff, tense
infantile [ˈɪnfəntaɪl]	*adj.* 幼稚的，孩子气的（like or typical of a small child） 记 来自 infant（*n.* 婴儿）
surveillance [sɜːrˈveɪləns]	*n.* 监视，盯梢（close observation of a person） 同 inspection, supervision
incompatible [ˌɪnkəmˈpætəbl]	*adj.* 无法和谐共存的，不相容的（not able to exist in harmony or agreement） 记 联想记忆：in（不）+ compatible（和谐共存的）→ 无法和谐共存的，不相容的 搭 be incompatible with 与…不相容 同 disconsonant, dissonant, incongruent, incongruous, inconsonant
nonporous [ˌnɑːnˈpɔːrəs]	*adj.* 无孔的；不渗透的 记 联想记忆：non（不）+ porous（多孔的；能渗透的）→ 无孔的；不渗透的
obligatory [əˈblɪɡətɔːri]	*adj.* 强制性的，义不容辞的（binding in law or conscience） 同 compulsory, imperative, mandatory
robust [roʊˈbʌst]	*adj.* 健壮的（having or exhibiting strength） 记 联想记忆：中国的矿泉水品牌"乐百氏"就来自这个单词
unarticulated [ˌʌnɑːrˈtɪkjəleɪtɪd]	*adj.* 表达不清的（not articulated）
bonanza [bəˈnænzə]	*n.* 富矿脉，贵金属矿（an exceptionally large and rich mineral deposit） 同 eldorado, golconda
transitoriness [ˈtrænsətɔːrinəs]	*n.* 暂时，短暂（the state of being not persistent） 例 Parts of seventeenth-century Chinese pleasure gardens were not necessarily intended to look cheerful; they were designed expressly to evoke the agreeable melancholy resulting from a sense of the *transitoriness* of natural beauty and human glory.

21

□ hospitable	□ dumbfound	□ outgoing	□ taut	□ infantile	□ surveillance
□ incompatible	□ nonporous	□ obligatory	□ robust	□ unarticulated	□ bonanza
□ transitoriness					

237

preternatural [ˌpriːtərˈnætʃrəl]	*adj.* 异常的(extraordinary); 超自然的(existing outside of nature) 记 联想记忆: preter(超越) + natural(自然的) → 超自然的
understate [ˌʌndərˈsteɪt]	*v.* 保守地说，轻描淡写地说(to state with less completeness or truth than seems warranted by the facts) 记 联想记忆: under(在…下面) + state(说话) → 在衣服下面说 → 保守地说 例 Because of its inclination to *understate*, most Indian art is reminiscent of Japanese art, where symbols have been minimized and meaning has been conveyed by the merest suggestion.
reverse [rɪˈvɜːrs]	*n.* 反面(the back part of sth.); 相反的事物(opposite) *v.* 倒车(to perform action in the opposite direction); 反转 (to turn backward); 彻底转变(to change to the opposite) 记 词根记忆: re + vers(转) + e → 反转 同 invert, revert, transplace, transpose
pious [ˈpaɪəs]	*adj.* 虔诚的(showing and feeling deep respect for God and religion) 同 devout, pietistic, prayerful, religious
provincial [prəˈvɪnʃl]	*adj.* 省的，地方的; 偏狭的，粗俗的(limited in outlook) 记 来自province(*n.* 省) 例 This poetry is not *provincial*; it is more likely to appeal to an international audience than is poetry with strictly regional themes. 同 agrestic, bucolic, countrified, rustic
coalesce [ˌkoʊəˈles]	*v.* 联合，合并(to unite or merge into a single body; mix) 记 词根记忆: co + al(=ally 联盟) + esce → 一起联盟 → 联合 同 associate, bracket, combine, conjoin
restatement [ˌriːˈsteɪtmənt]	*n.* 再声明，重述
pugnacious [pʌɡˈneɪʃəs]	*adj.* 好斗的(having a quarrelsome or combative nature) 记 词根记忆: pugn(打斗) + acious(…的) → 好斗的
spurn [spɜːrn]	*n.* 拒绝，摈弃(disdainful rejection) 记 联想记忆: spur (刺激) + n (看作 no) → 不再刺激，不再鼓励 → 拒绝，摈弃
dilatory [ˈdɪlətɔːri]	*adj.* 慢吞吞的，磨蹭的(inclined to delay; slow or late in doing things) 记 词根记忆: di + lat(搬运) + ory → 分开搬运 → 慢吞吞的
narrative [ˈnærətɪv]	*adj.* 叙述性的(of, or in the form of story-telling) 记 来自narrate(*v.* 叙述) 例 Because it has no distinct and recognizable typographical form and few recurring *narrative* conventions, the novel is, of all literary genres, the least susceptible to definition.

infest [ɪnˈfest]	*v.* 大批出没于，骚扰(to spread or swarm in or over in a troublesome manner)；寄生于(to live in or on as a parasite)
	记 联想记忆：in(进入) + fest(集会) → 全部来参加集会 → 大批出没于，骚扰
hunch [hʌntʃ]	*n.* 直觉，预感(an intuitive feeling or a premonition)
	搭 have a hunch (that) 有预感(将发生…)
regulatory [ˈreɡjələtɔːri]	*adj.* 按规矩来的，依照规章的；调整的
plausible [ˈplɔːzəbl]	*adj.* 看似有理的，似是而非的(superficially fair, reasonable, or valuable but often specious)；有道理的，可信的(appearing worthy of belief)
	记 词根记忆：plaus(鼓掌) + ible → 值得鼓掌的 → 看似有理的，似是而非的
	例 Eric was frustrated because, although he was adept at making lies sound *plausible*, when telling the truth, he lacked the power to make himself believed.
	同 believable, colorable, credible, creditable
audit [ˈɔːdɪt]	*v.* 旁听(to attend (a course) without working for or expecting to receive formal credit)；审计，查账(to examine and check account)
nomadic [noʊˈmædɪk]	*adj.* 游牧的(of nomad)；流浪的
	同 itinerant, peripatetic, vagabond, vagrant
diurnal [daɪˈɜːrnl]	*adj.* 白昼的，白天的(of daytime)
	记 词根记忆：di(白天) + urnal(…的) → 白天的
sanctuary [ˈsæŋktʃueri]	*n.* 圣地；庇护所，避难所；庇护
	搭 wildlife sanctuary 野生动物保护区
contrive [kənˈtraɪv]	*v.* 计划，设计(to think up; devise; scheme)
	记 词根记忆：contri(反) + ve(=ven 走) → (和普通人)反着走 → 设计(新东西) → 计划，设计
	同 connive, intrigue, machinate, plot
cardinal [ˈkɑːrdɪnl]	*adj.* 首要的，主要的(of basic importance) *n.* 红衣主教
	记 词根记忆：card(心) + inal → 心一样的 → 首要的，主要的

sanctuary

禁猎区

□ infest	□ hunch	□ regulatory	□ plausible	□ audit	□ nomadic
□ diurnal	□ sanctuary	□ contrive	□ cardinal		

239

vicious [ˈvɪʃəs]	*adj.* 邪恶的，堕落的（having the nature or quality of vice or immorality）；恶意的，恶毒的（spiteful；malicious）；凶猛的，危险的（dangerously aggressive） 记 联想记忆：vic(e)(邪恶) + ious → 邪恶的；恶毒的
authentic [ɔːˈθentɪk]	*adj.* 真正的，真实的（genuine；real）；可信的（legally attested） 记 词根记忆：authent(=author 作家) + ic → 自己就是作家 → 真正的
unbecoming [ˌʌnbɪˈkʌmɪŋ]	*adj.* 不合身的（not suited to the wearer）；不得体的（improper） 记 联想记忆：un(不) + becoming(合适的) → 不合身的
approbation [ˌæprəˈbeɪʃn]	*n.* 赞许（commendation）；认可（official approval） 记 词根记忆：ap + prob(=prove 证实) + ation → 证实是好的 → 赞许
slavish [ˈsleɪvɪʃ]	*adj.* 卑屈的；效仿的，无创造性的（copying obsequiously or without originality） 记 词根记忆：slav(e)(奴隶) + ish(形容词后缀，表属性) → 奴性的 → 卑屈的
sage [seɪdʒ]	*adj.* 智慧的（wise；discerning）*n.* 智者（a very wise person） 例 The *sage*, by definition, possesses wisdom; the virtuoso, by definition, possesses expertise.
aghast [əˈɡæst]	*adj.* 惊骇的，吓呆的（feeling great horror or dismay；terrified） 记 联想记忆：a(…的) + ghast(=ghost 鬼) → 像看到鬼似的 → 吓呆的 同 frightened, scared, scary
flaggy [ˈflæɡi]	*adj.* 枯萎的；松软无力的（lacking vigor or force）
construction [kənˈstrʌkʃn]	*n.* 结构，句法关系（syntactical arrangement）；解释，理解 同 construal, explanation, explication, exposition, interpretation
earthiness [ˈɜːrθinəs]	*n.* 土质，土性（the state of earth） 记 来自 earthy(*adj.* 泥土的，土的)
intimate	[ˈɪntɪmət] *adj.* 亲密的（closely acquainted）*n.* 密友（an intimate friend or companion） [ˈɪntɪmeɪt] *v.* 暗示（to hint or imply；suggest） 记 词根记忆：intim(最深入的) + ate → 亲密的 例 Even those siblings whose childhood was dominated by familial feuding and intense rivalry for their parents' affection can nevertheless develop congenial and even *intimate* relationships with each other in their adult lives.
foreshadow [fɔːrˈʃædoʊ]	*v.* 成为先兆，预示（to represent, indicate, or typify beforehand） 记 组合词：fore(预先) + shadow(影子) → 影子先来 → 预示
institutionalized [ˌɪnstɪˈtuːʃənəlaɪzd]	*adj.* 制度化的（making into an institution） 例 As the creation of new knowledge through science has become *institutionalized* resistance to innovation has become less aggressive taking the form of inertia rather than direct attack.

□ vicious	□ authentic	□ unbecoming	□ approbation	□ slavish	□ sage
□ aghast	□ flaggy	□ construction	□ earthiness	□ intimate	□ foreshadow
□ institutionalized					

invalidate [ɪnˈvælɪdeɪt]	*v.* 使无效，使作废(to make invalid) 例 Strindberg's plays are marked by his extreme misogyny; he felt modern woman needed to dominate man and by subordinating him *invalidate* his masculinity.
privacy [ˈpraɪvəsi]	*n.* 隐居，隐退(the quality or state of being apart from company or observation)；隐私(freedom from unauthorized intrusion)；秘密(secrecy) 例 Though extremely reticent about his own plans, the man allowed his associates no such *privacy* and was constantly soliciting information about what they intended to do next. 同 concealment, privateness
underscore [ˌʌndərˈskɔːr]	*v.* 在…下面画线(to draw a line under)；强调(to make evident) 记 组合词：under(在…下面) + score(画线) → 在…下面画线
paragon [ˈpærəɡɑːn]	*n.* 模范，典范(a model of excellence or perfection) 记 词根记忆：para(旁边) + gon(比较) → 放在旁边作为比较的对象 → 模范，典范
pitcher [ˈpɪtʃər]	*n.* 有柄水罐(a container for liquids that usually has a handle) 同 jug
rudimentary [ˌruːdɪˈmentri]	*adj.* 初步的(fundamental; elementary)；未充分发展的 记 词根记忆：rudi(无知的，粗鲁的) + ment + ary → 无知状态 → 初步的
reaffirm [ˌriːəˈfɜːrm]	*v.* 再次确定(confirm again)；重申(to state again positively) 记 分析记忆：re(再次) + affirm(确定) → 再次确定
transformation [ˌtrænsfərˈmeɪʃn]	*n.* 转化，转变(an act, process, or instance of transforming or being transformed) 例 Doreen justifiably felt she deserved recognition for the fact that the research institute had been returned to a position of preeminence, since it was she who had directed the *transformation*.
infinitesimal [ˌɪnfɪnɪˈtesɪml]	*adj.* 极微小的(infinitely small) *n.* 极小量 记 词根记忆：in(不) + fin(边界) + ite + sim(百分之一) + al → 无穷小的 → 极微小的
discontent [ˌdɪskənˈtent]	*n.* 不满(lack of contentment) *v.* 使不满(to make discontented) *adj.* 不满的(discontented)
hieroglyph [ˈhaɪərəɡlɪf]	*n.* 象形文字，神秘符号(a picture or symbol used in hieroglyphic writing) 记 词根记忆：hier(神圣的) + o + glyph(写，刻) → 神写的字 → 神秘符号 hieroglyph
reciprocity [ˌresɪˈprɑːsəti]	*n.* 相互性(the quality or state of being reciprocal)；互惠(a mutual exchange of privileges) 例 The state is a network of exchanged benefits and beliefs, a *reciprocity* between rulers and citizens based on those laws and procedures that are conducive to the maintenance of community.

22

□ invalidate	□ privacy	□ underscore	□ paragon	□ pitcher	□ rudimentary
□ reaffirm	□ transformation	□ infinitesimal	□ discontent	□ hieroglyph	□ reciprocity

disdain [dɪs'deɪn]	*v.* 轻视，鄙视（to refuse or reject with aloof contempt or scorn）*n.* 轻视，鄙视（contempt） 记 词根记忆：dis(不) + dain(=dign 高贵) → 把人弄得不高贵 → 轻视 搭 disdain for 轻视 同 contemn, despise
transcribe [træn'skraɪb]	*v.* 抄写，转录（to make a written copy） 记 词根记忆：trans(交换) + (s)cribe(写) → 交换着写 → 抄写
grandiloquence [græn'dɪləkwəns]	*n.* 豪言壮语，夸张之言（a lofty, extravagantly colorful, pompous, or bombastic style, manner, or quality especially in language）
picturesque [ˌpɪktʃə'resk]	*adj.* 如画的（resembling a picture）；独特的，别具风格的（charming or quaint in appearance）
unspoiled [ˌʌn'spɔɪld]	*adj.* 未损坏的，未宠坏的 记 联想记忆：un(不) + spoil(损坏) + ed → 未损坏的
problematic [ˌprɑːblə'mætɪk]	*adj.* 成问题的（posing a problem）；有疑问的，值得怀疑的（open to doubt; debatable）；未知的，未解决的（not definite or settled） 例 As early as the seventeenth century, philosophers called attention to the *problematic* character of the issue, and their twentieth-century counterparts still approach it with uneasiness.
nonradioactive [ˌnɑːn'reɪdioʊ'æktɪv]	*adj.* 非放射性的 记 联想记忆：non(不) + radioactive(放射性的) → 非放射性的 搭 nonradioactive labeling 非放射性标记
recklessness ['rekləsnəs]	*n.* 鲁莽，轻率 记 来自 reckless（*adj.* 鲁莽的；不计后果的）
snub [snʌb]	*v.* 冷落，不理睬（to treat with contempt or neglect） 同 cold-shoulder, rebuff
obstacle ['ɑːbstəkl]	*n.* 障碍，妨碍物 记 词根记忆：ob(反) + sta(站) + (a)cle(表东西) → 反着站，挡住了去路 → 障碍 搭 obstacle to (doing) sth. (做)某事的障碍 同 hurdle, impediment, obstruction, snag
rag [ræg]	*n.* 旧布，碎布（old cloth）；破旧衣服（an old worn-out garment） 搭 lose one's rag 发怒，生气
modifier ['mɑːdɪfaɪər]	*n.* 修改者（one that modifies）；修饰语（a word or phrase that makes specific the meaning of another word or phrase）
prototype ['proʊtətaɪp]	*n.* 原型（an original model; archetype）；典型（a standard or typical example） 记 词根记忆：proto(起初) + type(形状) → 起初的形状 → 原型 例 This project is the first step in a long-range plan of research whose ultimate goal, still many years off, is the creation of a new *prototype*.
interdependent [ˌɪntərdɪ'pendənt]	*adj.* 相互依赖的，互助的（mutually dependent） 记 联想记忆：inter(在…中间) + dependent(依赖的) → 在中间依赖的 → 相互依赖的

entertain [ˌentərˈteɪn]	*v.* 款待，招待(to show hospitality to)；使欢乐，娱乐(to provide entertainment for) 记 联想记忆：enter(进入) + tain(拿住) → 拿着东西进去 → 款待，招待
optimistic [ˌɑːptɪˈmɪstɪk]	*adj.* 乐观的(believing that good things will happen in the future) 记 词根记忆：optim(最好的) + istic → 最好的 → 乐观的 搭 be optimistic about 对…持乐观的心态
paleolithic [ˌpæliəˈlɪθɪk]	*adj.* 旧石器时代的(of or relating to the earliest period of the Stone Age characterized by rough or chipped stone implements) 记 词根记忆：paleo(古老的) + lith(石头) + ic → 旧石器的 → 旧石器时代的
undercut [ˌʌndərˈkʌt]	*v.* 削价(与竞争者)抢生意(to sell goods or services more cheaply than a competitor) 记 联想记忆：under(在…下面) + cut(砍) → 偷偷把价格砍掉 → 削价(与竞争者)抢生意
dehydrate [diːˈhaɪdreɪt]	*v.* 使脱水(to remove water from) 记 词根记忆：de(去除) + hydr(水) + ate → 使脱水
recoil [rɪˈkɔɪl]	*v.* 弹回，反冲(to fall back under pressure)；退却，退缩(to shrink back physically or emotionally) 记 词根记忆：re(反) + coil(卷，盘绕) → 卷回去 → 退缩
evocative [ɪˈvɑːkətɪv]	*adj.* 唤起的，激起的(tending to evoke) 例 The documentary film about high school life was so realistic and *evocative* that feelings of nostalgia flooded over the college-age audience.
kidney [ˈkɪdni]	*n.* 肾 记 联想记忆：kid(孩子) + ney → 这个孩子爱吃腰花 → 肾
distraught [dɪˈstrɔːt]	*adj.* 心神狂乱的，发狂的(mentally confused)；心烦意乱的(distressed) 记 由 distract(*v.* 分散注意力；使不安)变化而来
digressive [daɪˈgresɪv]	*adj.* 离题的，枝节的(characterized by digressions) 搭 digressive remarks 离题的言论
blackmail [ˈblækmeɪl]	*v./n.* 敲诈，勒索(payment extorted by threatening) 记 组合词：black(黑) + mail(寄信) → 寄黑信 → 敲诈
defrost [ˌdiːˈfrɔːst]	*v.* 解冻(to release from a frozen state)；将…除霜(to free from ice) 记 分拆记忆：de + frost(霜冻) → 将霜除去 → 解冻
replicate [ˈreplɪkeɪt]	*v.* 复制(to produce a replica of itself) 记 词根记忆：re(再次) + plic(折叠) + ate → 再次折叠 → 复制
venture [ˈventʃər]	*v.* 敢于(to expose to hazard)；冒险(to undertake the risks and dangers of) *n.* 冒险(an undertaking involving chance, risk, or danger) 记 发音记忆："玩车" → 玩车一族追求的就是冒险 → 冒险 同 adventure

optimistic

22

snug [snʌg]	*adj.* 温暖舒适的(warm and comfortable; cozy) 搭 snug harbor 避风港
murderous ['mɜːrdərəs]	*adj.* 蓄意谋杀的，凶残的(having the purpose or capability of murder)；极厉害的，要命的(having the ability or power to overwhelm)
odious ['oʊdiəs]	*adj.* 可憎的，令人作呕的(disgusting; offensive) 记 发音记忆："呕得要死" → 可憎的，令人作呕的
irony ['aɪrəni]	*n.* 反话(the use of words to express something other than and especially the opposite of the literal meaning)；讽刺意味(incongruity between what might be expected and what actually occurs)；出乎意料的结果(the opposite of what is expected) 记 联想记忆：iron（铁）+ y → 像铁一样冷冰冰的话 → 反话 例 This final essay, its prevailing kindliness marred by occasional flashes of savage *irony*, bespeaks the dichotomous character of the author.
function ['fʌŋkʃn]	*v.* 运行(to serve; operate) *n.* 功能；职责(professional or official position) 记 发音记忆："放颗心" → 公务员的职责就是让人民放心 → 职责
untold [ˌʌn'toʊld]	*adj.* 无数的，数不清的(too great or numerous to count)
stereotype ['steriətaɪp]	*n.* 固定形式，老套(sth. conforming to a fixed or general pattern) 记 联想记忆：stereo(立体) + type(形状) → 固定形式
dubious ['duːbiəs]	*adj.* 可疑的(slightly suspicious about)；有问题的，靠不住的(questionable or suspect as to true nature or quality) 记 词根记忆：dub（二，双）+ ious → 两种状态 → 不肯定的，怀疑的 → 可疑的 同 disputable, dubitable, equivocal, problematic
tricky ['trɪki]	*adj.* 狡猾的(inclined to or marked by trickery) 同 crafty, cunning
astute [ə'stuːt]	*adj.* 机敏的，精明的(showing clever or shrewd mind; cunning; crafty) 记 来自拉丁文 astus(灵活)
divulge [daɪ'vʌldʒ]	*v.* 泄露，透露(to make known; disclose) 记 词根记忆：di(分离) + vulg(人们) → 使从秘密状态中脱离并被人们知道 → 透露 同 betray, reveal
repudiation [rɪˌpjuːdi'eɪʃn]	*n.* 拒绝接受，否认(the act of repudiating) 例 The *repudiation* of Puritanism in seventeenth-century England expressed itself not only in retaliatory laws to restrict Puritans, but also in a general attitude of contempt for Puritans.

□ snug	□ murderous	□ odious	□ irony	□ function	□ untold
□ stereotype	□ dubious	□ tricky	□ astute	□ divulge	□ repudiation

perpetuate [pərˈpetʃueɪt]	*v.* 使永存(to make perpetual) 记 词根记忆：per(贯穿) + pet(追求) + uate → 永远追求 → 使永存
architect [ˈɑːrkɪtekt]	*n.* 建筑师 (person who designs buildings and supervises their construction) 记 联想记忆：archi(统治者，主要的) + tect(做) → 统治造房的人 → 建筑师
vent [vent]	*v.* 发泄(感情，尤指愤怒)(to discharge; expel)；开孔(to provide with a vent) *n.* 孔，口(an opening)
solemnity [səˈlemnəti]	*n.* 庄严，肃穆(formal or ceremonious observance) 记 来自 solemn(*adj.* 严肃的) 同 sedateness, solemnness, staidness
onerous [ˈɑːnərəs]	*adj.* 繁重的，费力的(burdensome) 记 词根记忆：oner(负担) + ous → 负担重的 → 繁重的
sap [sæp]	*n.* 树液(the watery fluid that circulates through a plant)；活力(vigor; vitality) *v.* 削弱，耗尽(to weaken; exhaust) 同 attenuate, cripple, debilitate, enfeeble, unbrace, undermine
raisin [ˈreɪzn]	*n.* 葡萄干(a grape that has been dried)
sincerity [sɪnˈserəti]	*n.* 诚挚(the quality or state of being sincere) 同 candour, frankness, genuineness, honesty
impressionable [ɪmˈpreʃənəbl]	*adj.* 易受影响的(easily affected by impressions) 例 We realized that John was still young and *impressionable*, but were nevertheless surprised at his naivete.
invention [ɪnˈvenʃn]	*n.* 发明，创造 (the act or process of inventing)；发明才能，创造力(skill in inventing; inventiveness)；发现，找到(discovery; finding)
atomic [əˈtɑːmɪk]	*adj.* 原子的(of, relating to, or concerned with atoms)；微小的(minute) 记 来自 atom(*v.* 原子)
primordial [praɪˈmɔːrdiəl]	*adj.* 原始的，最初的(first created or developed) 同 primeval, primitive
voluptuous [vəˈlʌptʃuəs]	*adj.* 撩人的(suggesting sensual pleasure)；沉溺酒色的(abandoned to enjoyments of luxury, pleasure, or sensual gratification) 记 词根记忆：volupt(享乐，快感) + uous → 沉溺酒色的
intemperance [ɪnˈtempərəns]	*n.* 放纵，不节制，过度(lack of temperance) 同 excess, overindulgence, surfeit
inert [ɪˈnɜːrt]	*adj.* 惰性的(having few or no active chemical or other properties)；呆滞的，迟缓的(dull; slow) 记 词根记忆：in(不) + ert(动) → 不动的 → 惰性的
indict [ɪnˈdaɪt]	*v.* 控诉，起诉(to make a formal accusation against; accuse) 记 词根记忆：in(进入) + dict(说) → (在法庭上)把…说出来 → 控诉 同 criminate, impeach, incriminate, inculpate
untutored [ˌʌnˈtuːtərd]	*adj.* 未受教育的(having no formal learning or training)

□ perpetuate	□ architect	□ vent	□ solemnity	□ onerous	□ sap
□ raisin	□ sincerity	□ impressionable	□ invention	□ atomic	□ primordial
□ voluptuous	□ intemperance	□ inert	□ indict	□ untutored	

unpredictable [ˌʌnprɪˈdɪktəbl]	*adj.* 不可预知的
discourse [ˈdɪskɔːrs]	*n.* 演讲，论述 (a long and formal treatment of a subject, in speech or writing; dissertation) 记 联想记忆: dis + course (课程) → 进行课堂演讲 → 演讲
undertake [ˌʌndərˈteɪk]	*v.* 承担 (to take upon oneself); 担保，保证 (to guarantee, promise) 记 联想记忆: under (在…下面) + take (拿) → 在下面拿 → 承担
contact [ˈkɑːntækt]	*v.* 接触 (to touch); 互通信息 (to get in communication with) 记 词根记忆: con + tact (接触) → 接触 同 contingence, commerce, communion, intercourse
ductile [ˈdʌktaɪl]	*adj.* 易延展的 (capable of being stretched); 可塑的 (easily molded; pliable) 记 词根记忆: duct (引导) + ile → 易引导的 → 可塑的
crestfallen [ˈkrestfɔːlən]	*adj.* 挫败的，失望的 (dejected, disheartened, or humbled) 记 联想记忆: crest (鸡冠) + fallen → 鸡冠下垂 → 斗败了的 → 挫败的
affordable [əˈfɔːrdəbl]	*adj.* 负担得起的 (being able to buy sth.) 记 词根记忆: afford (*v.* 买得起) + able (*adj.* 能) → 负担得起的
restitution [ˌrestɪˈtuːʃn]	*n.* 归还 (a restoration to its rightful owner); 赔偿 (giving an equivalent for some injury) 记 词根记忆: re (重新) + stitut (站立) + ion → 重新站过去 → 归还
unquestionable [ʌnˈkwestʃənəbl]	*adj.* 毫无疑问的，无懈可击的 (not questionable) 同 authentic, veritable
opportune [ˌɑːpərˈtuːn]	*adj.* 合适的，适当的 (right for a particular purpose) 记 词根记忆: op (向) + port (搬运) + une → 向着某物搬 → 合适的，适当的
modulate [ˈmɑːdʒəleɪt]	*v.* 调整，调节 (to adjust to or keep in proper measure or proportion; regulate by or adjust to); 调音 (to tune to a key or pitch)
conversant [kənˈvɜːrsnt]	*adj.* 精通的，熟悉的 (familiar or acquainted; versed) 记 词根记忆: con + vers (转) + ant → 全方位转 → 精通的
dental [ˈdentl]	*adj.* 牙齿的，牙科的 (of or relating to the teeth or dentistry) 记 词根记忆: dent (牙齿) + al (…的) → 牙齿的
essentially [ɪˈsenʃəli]	*adv.* 本质上；基本上 (basically) 记 来自 essential (*adj.* 本质的；基本的)
porous [ˈpɔːrəs]	*adj.* 可渗透的 (capable of being penetrated); 多孔的 (full of pores) 记 来自 pore (*n.* 孔)
disposable [dɪˈspoʊzəbl]	*adj.* 一次性的 (made to be thrown away after use); 可自由使用的 (available for use)
conserve [kənˈsɜːrv]	*v.* 保存，保藏 (to keep in a safe or sound state) 记 词根记忆: con (全部) + serv (服务，保持) + e → 全都保持下去，保存

incongruous [ɪn'kɑːŋɡruəs]	*adj.* 不协调的，不一致的（incompatible, disagreeing, inconsistent within itself; unsuitable）
detrimental [ˌdetrɪ'mentl]	*adj.* 损害的，造成伤害的(causing detriment; harmful) 记 来自 detriment(*n.* 损害，伤害) 同 damaging, deleterious, injurious, mischievous, nocuous
cyclical ['saɪklɪkl]	*adj.* 循环的(recurring in cycles) 记 来自 cycle(*n.* 循环)
misogyny [mɪ'sɑːdʒɪni]	*n.* 厌恶女人(hatred of women) 例 Strindberg's plays are marked by his extreme *misogyny*; he felt modern woman needed to dominate man and by subordinating him invalidate his masculinity.
alternative [ɔːl'tɜːrnətɪv]	*adj.* 轮流的，交替的（alternate）；两者择一的（offering or expressing a choice） 记 词根记忆：alter（改变状态，其他的）+ native（⋯的）→ 改变状态的 → 轮流的，交替的 同 backup, substitute, surrogate
immutability [ɪˌmjuːtə'bɪləti]	*n.* 不变，不变性(the quality of being incapable of mutation)
stratagem ['strætədʒəm]	*n.* 谋略，策略(a cleverly contrived trick or scheme) 记 词根记忆：strata(层次) + gem → 有层次的计划 → 谋略 例 That the Third Battalion's fifty-percent casualty rate transformed its assault on Hill 306 from a brilliant *stratagem* into a debacle does not gainsay eyewitness reports of its commander's extraordinary cleverness in deploying his forces.
brownish ['braʊnɪʃ]	*adj.* 成褐色的 记 来自 brown(*n.* 褐色)
significant [sɪɡ'nɪfɪkənt]	*adj.* 相当数量的(considerable)；意义重大的(having an important meaning) 记 联想记忆：sign(标记) + i + fic(做)+ant → 做了很多标记的 → 相当数量的；意义重大的 同 substantial; momentous
coercion [koʊ'ɜːrʒn]	*n.* 强制，高压统治(the act, process, or power of coercing) 同 compulsion, constraint, enforcement
tribal ['traɪbl]	*adj.* 部落的，部族的(of, relating to, or characteristic of a tribe)
immobile [ɪ'moʊbl]	*adj.* 稳定的，不动的，静止的(fixed, motionless)
unbridled [ʌn'braɪdld]	*adj.* 放纵的，不受约束的(unrestrained) 同 unchecked, uncurbed, ungoverned

22

economize [ɪ'kɑːnəmaɪz]	*v.* 节约，节省(to save) 记 来自 economy(*adj.* 经济的 *n.* 节约)
bereave [bɪ'riːv]	*v.* 夺去，丧亲(to deprive; dispossess) 记 词根记忆：be + reave(抢夺) → 抢夺掉 → 丧亲；reave 本身是一个单词 同 disinherit, divest, oust
propaganda [ˌprɑːpə'ɡændə]	*n.* 宣传(the spreading of ideas, information)
yearn [jɜːrn]	*v.* 盼望，渴望(to long persistently) 记 联想记忆：year(年) + n → 一年到头盼望 → 盼望，渴望 同 crave, hanker, lust, pine
informality [ˌɪnfɔːr'mæləti]	*n.* 非正式，不拘礼节
intrinsic [ɪn'trɪnsɪk]	*adj.* 固有的，内在的，本质的(belonging to the essential nature) 例 In his address, the superintendent exhorted the teachers to discover and develop each student's *intrinsic* talents. 同 congenital, connate, elemental, inherent, innate
trait [treɪt]	*n.* (人的)显著特性(a distinguishing feature, as of a person's character) 同 attribute, characteristic, peculiarity
downfall ['daʊnfɔːl]	*n.* 垮台(a sudden fall) 同 overthrow, upset
adequate ['ædɪkwət]	*adj.* 足够的(sufficient) 记 词根记忆：ad(加强) + equ(平等) + ate(…的) → 比平等多的 → 足够的 同 competent, satisfactory
thoughtful ['θɔːtfl]	*adj.* 深思的(absorbed in thought) 例 Even those who disagreed with Carmen's views rarely faulted her for expressing them, for the positions she took were as *thoughtful* as they were controversial. 同 cogitative, contemplative, meditative, pensive
trace [treɪs]	*n.* 痕迹 *v.* 追踪 例 As delicate and fragile as insect bodies are, it is remarkable that over the ages enough of them have survived, preserved in amber, for scientists to *trace* insect evolution. 同 engram, relic
reward [rɪ'wɔːrd]	*n.* 报酬，奖赏 *v.* 酬谢，奖赏(to give a reward to) 记 联想记忆：re + ward(看作 word, 话语) → 再次发话给予奖赏 → 奖赏 例 He was indifferent to success, painting not for the sake of fame or monetary *reward*, but for the sheer love of art.
exoneration [ɪɡˌzɑːnə'reɪʃn]	*n.* 免除(责任、义务、苦难等)(a freeing or clearing from a responsibility, obligation, or hardship)

institution [ˌɪnstɪˈtuːʃn]	*n.* 机构(an established organization or corporation); 制度 记 来自 institute(*v.* 设立，创立；制定) 例 During the 1960's assessments of the family shifted remarkably, from general endorsement of it as a worthwhile, stable *institution* to wide spread censure of it as an oppressive and bankrupt one whose dissolution was both imminent and welcome.
warrantable [ˈwɔːrəntəbl]	*adj.* 可保证的，可承认的(capable of being warranted)
resonant [ˈrezənənt]	*adj.* (声音)洪亮的(enriched by resonance)；回响的，共鸣的(echoing) 记 词根记忆：re(反) + son(声音) + ant → 回声 → 回响的
crash [kræʃ]	*v.* 猛撞(to break violently and noisily)；猛冲直闯(to enter or attend without invitation or paying)；撞碎(to break or go to pieces with or as if with violence and noise) 记 象声词：破裂声 → 撞碎
trauma [ˈtraʊmə]	*n.* 创伤，外伤(an injury to living tissue caused by an extrinsic agent) 例 Because of the *trauma* they have experienced, survivors of a major catastrophe are likely to exhibit aberrations of behavior and may require the aid of competent therapists.
sophomoric [ˌsɑːfəˈmɔːrɪk]	*adj.* 一知半解的(conceited and overconfident of knowledge but poorly informed and immature)
formation [fɔːrˈmeɪʃn]	*n.* 组成，形成(thing that is formed)；编队，排列(an arrangement of a group of persons in some prescribed manner or for a particular purpose) 记 词根记忆：form(形状) + ation → 形成形状 → 形成
talented [ˈtæləntɪd]	*adj.* 天才的(showing a natural aptitude for sth.) 例 Gaddis is a formidably *talented* writer whose work has been, unhappily, more likely to intimidate or repel his readers than to lure them into his fictional world.
pilgrim [ˈpɪlgrɪm]	*n.* 朝圣者(one who travels to a shrine as a devotee)；(在国外的)旅行者 同 wayfarer
reverential [ˌrevəˈrenʃl]	*adj.* 表示尊敬的，恭敬的(expressing or having a quality of reverence) 例 The columnist was almost *reverential* when he mentioned his friends, but he was unpleasant and even acrimonious when he discussed people who irritated him.
unreserved [ˌʌnrɪˈzɜːrvd]	*adj.* 无限制的(without limit)；未被预订的(not reserved) 记 联想记忆：un(不) + reserved(预订的) → 未被预订的
captious [ˈkæpʃəs]	*adj.* 吹毛求疵的(quick to find fault; carping) 记 联想记忆：capt(拿) + ious → 拿(别人的缺点) → 吹毛求疵的
sordid [ˈsɔːrdɪd]	*adj.* 卑鄙的；肮脏的(dirty, filthy) 同 foul, mean, seedy
negotiable [nɪˈɡoʊʃiəbl]	*adj.* 可协商的(capable of being negotiated)；可通行的 同 navigable, passable

22

□ institution	□ warrantable	□ resonant	□ crash	□ trauma	□ sophomoric
□ formation	□ talented	□ pilgrim	□ reverential	□ unreserved	□ captious
□ sordid	□ negotiable				

monumental [ˌmɑːnjuˈmentl]	*adj.* 极大的（massive；impressively large）；纪念碑的（built as a monument） 记 来自 monument（*n.* 纪念碑）	**monumental**
awe [ɔː]	*n./v.* 敬畏（to cause a mixed feeling of reverence and fear） 记 发音记忆：发音像"噢"→ 表示敬畏的声音 → 敬畏 搭 be in awe of... 对…望而生畏；对…感到害怕	
cryptic [ˈkrɪptɪk]	*adj.* 秘密的，神秘的（mysterious；baffling） 记 词根记忆：crypt（秘密）+ ic → 秘密的	
intransigent [ɪnˈtrænzɪdʒənt]	*adj.* 不妥协的（uncompromising） 记 联想记忆：in（不）+ transigent（妥协的）→ 不妥协的 例 Always circumspect, she was reluctant to make judgments, but once arriving at a conclusion, she was *intransigent* in its defense. 同 incompliant, intractable, obstinate, pertinacious	

Genius only means hard-working all one's life.

天才只意味着终身不懈地努力。

——俄国化学家 门捷列夫（Mendeleyev, Russian chemist）

gusher ['gʌʃər]	*n.* 滔滔不绝的说话者(a person who gushes);喷油井(an oil well) 记 来自gush(*v.* 喷出,涌出;滔滔不绝地说话)
bemused [bɪ'mjuːzd]	*adj.* 茫然的,困惑的(confused) 记 联想记忆:be + muse(沉思) + d → 进入沉思 → 困惑的
levy ['levi]	*v.* 征税(to impose a tax);征兵(to draft into military service) 记 词根记忆:lev(升起) + y → 把税收升起来 → 征税
harness ['hɑːrnɪs]	*n.* 马具,挽具 *v.* 束以马具;利用,控制(to control so as to use the power) 记 联想记忆:har(看作 hard,结实的) + ness(表名词) → 马具通常都很结实 → 马具
pledge [pledʒ]	*n.* 誓言,保证(a solemn promise) *v.* 发誓(to vow to do sth.) 同 commitment, swear
cumber ['kʌmbər]	*v.* 拖累,妨碍(to hinder by obstruction or interference; hamper) 记 词根记忆:cumb(睡) + er → 睡在(路上) → 拖累,妨碍
sublimate ['sʌblɪmeɪt]	*v.* (使)升华,净化(to sublime) 记 来自sublime(*v.* 使崇高)
myopic [maɪ'oʊpɪk]	*adj.* 近视眼的;目光短浅的,缺乏远见的(lacking of foresight or discernment) 搭 a myopic child 近视的孩子
serpentine ['sɜːrpəntiːn]	*adj.* 像蛇般蟠曲的,蜿蜒的(winding or turning one way or another) 记 联想记忆:serpent(蛇) + ine → 像蛇般蜷曲的
lump [lʌmp]	*n.* 块;肿块 *v.* 形成块状(to become lumpy) 搭 lump...together 将…合在一起
labile ['leɪbaɪl]	*adj.* 易变化的,不稳定的(open to change; unstable) 同 fickle, unsteady
retort [rɪ'tɔːrt]	*v.* 反驳(to answer by a counter argument) 记 词根记忆:re(反) + tort(扭) → 反着扭 → 反驳
stultify ['stʌltɪfaɪ]	*v.* 使显得愚蠢(to make stupid);使变得无用或无效(to render useless) 同 impair, invalidate, negate

serpentine

□ gusher	□ bemused	□ levy	□ harness	□ pledge	□ cumber
□ sublimate	□ myopic	□ serpentine	□ lump	□ labile	□ retort
□ stultify					

abstinent	*adj.* 饮食有度的，有节制的，禁欲的（constraining from indulgence of an
[ˈæbstɪnənt]	appetite or craving or from eating some foods）
	记 词根记忆：abs（脱离）+ tin（拿住）+ ent → 把握自己脱离某物 → 禁欲的
reel	*n.* 卷轴；旋转 *v.* 卷⋯于轴上（to wind on a reel）
[riːl]	搭 a reel of film 一盘影片
upheaval	*n.* 动乱，剧变（extreme agitation or disorder）
[ʌpˈhiːvl]	记 来自 upheave（*v.* （使）发生混乱）
despotic	*adj.* 专横的，暴虐的（autocratic；tyrannical）
[dɪˈspɑːtɪk]	记 来自 despot（*n.* 暴君）
lank	*adj.* 细长的（long and thin；slender）；长、直且柔软的（long, straight and
[læŋk]	limp）
outmaneuver	*v.* 以策略制胜（to overcome an opponent by artful, clever maneuvering）
[ˌaʊtməˈnuːvər]	记 组合词：out（超出）+ maneuver（策略）→ 以策略制胜
epidermis	*n.* 表皮，外皮（the outmost layer of the skin）
[ˌepɪˈdɜːrmɪs]	记 词根记忆：epi（在⋯外）+ derm（皮肤）+ is → 外皮
subscribe	*v.* 捐助（to give sth. in accordance with a promise）；订购（to enter one's
[səbˈskraɪb]	name for a publication or service）
	记 词根记忆：sub（下面）+ scribe（写）→ 写下订单 → 订购
felon	*n.* 重罪犯（a person guilty of a major crime）
[ˈfelən]	记 联想记忆：fel（=fell 倒下）+ on → 倒在罪恶之上 → 重罪犯
ventriloquist	*n.* 口技表演者，腹语表演者（one who uses or is skilled in ventriloquism）
[venˈtrɪləkwɪst]	记 词根记忆：ventr（腹部）+ i + loqu（说话）+ ist（人）→ 会说腹语的人 →
	口技表演者，腹语表演者
maraud	*v.* 抢劫，掠夺（to rove in search of plunder；pillage）
[məˈrɔːd]	同 loot, rob
synopsis	*n.* 摘要，概要（a condensed statement or outline）
[sɪˈnɑːpsɪs]	记 词根记忆：syn（一起）+ op（看）+ sis → 让大家一起看 → 摘要
stouthearted	*adj.* 刚毅的，大胆的（brave or resolute）
[ˌstaʊtˈhɑːrtɪd]	记 组合词：stout（勇敢的，坚决的）+ heart（心）+ ed → 刚毅的，大胆的
picayunish	*adj.* 微不足道的，不值钱的（of little value）
[ˌpɪkəˈjuːnɪʃ]	同 petty, small-minded
rapids	*n.* 急流，湍流（a part of a river where the current is fast and the surface is
[ˈræpɪdz]	broken by obstructions）
	记 联想记忆：rapid（快速）+ s → 急流，湍流
airtight	*adj.* 密闭的，不透气的（too tight for air or gas to enter or escape）
[ˈertaɪt]	记 组合词：air（空气）+ tight（紧的，不透气的）→ 密闭的，不透气的
crimp	*v.* 使起皱，使（头发）卷曲（to cause to become wavy, bent, or pinched）；
[krɪmp]	抵制，束缚（to be an inhibiting or restraining influence on）

magenta [mə'dʒentə]	*adj.* 紫红色的(of deep purple red) *n.* 紫红色(purplish red) 记 源自意大利城市 Magenta
pacify ['pæsɪfaɪ]	*v.* 使安静，抚慰(to make calm, quiet, and satisfied) 记 词根记忆：pac(和平，平静) + ify → 使变得平和 → 使安静，抚慰
ciliate ['sɪlɪɪt]	*adj.* 有纤毛的(having minute hairs)；有睫毛的 记 词根记忆：cili(毛) + ate → 有纤毛的
pretence ['priːtens]	*n.* 假装(mere ostentation)；借口(pretext) 记 词根记忆：pre(预先) + tenc(=tens 伸展) + e → 预先伸展开来 → 假装
recollection [ˌrekə'lekʃn]	*n.* 记忆力(the power or action of remembering the past)；往事(sth. in one's memory of the past) 记 来自 recollect(*v.* 回想)；re + col(一起) + lect(收集) → 回想
liquefy ['lɪkwɪfaɪ]	*v.* (使)液化，(使)溶解(to make or become liquid; melt) 记 词根记忆：liqu(液体) + efy → (使)液化
rebuff [rɪ'bʌf]	*v.* 断然拒绝(to reject or criticize sharply; snub) 记 词根记忆：re(反) + buff(=puff 喷，吹) → 反过喷气 → 断然拒绝
demoralize [dɪ'mɔːrəlaɪz]	*v.* 使士气低落(to dispirit) 记 词根记忆：de(去掉) + moral(e)(士气) + ize → 去掉士气 → 使士气低落
sacrament ['sækrəmənt]	*n.* 圣礼，圣事(any of certain rites instituted by Jesus) 记 词根记忆：sacra(神圣) + ment → 圣事
hoist [hɔɪst]	*v.* 提起，升起(to raise or haul up) *n.* 起重机 同 elevate, lift
oscillate ['ɑːsɪleɪt]	*v.* 摆动(to swing regularly)；犹豫(to vacillate) 记 词根记忆：oscill(摆动) + ate → 摆动
podiatrist [pə'daɪətrɪst]	*n.* 足病医生(chiropodist) 记 词根记忆：pod(足，脚) + iatr(治疗) + ist → 足病医生
whet [wet]	*v.* 磨快(to sharpen)；刺激(to excite; stimulate) 同 acuminate, edge, hone
concord ['kɑːŋkɔːrd]	*n.* 一致(agreement)；和睦(friendly and peaceful relations) 记 词根记忆：con(一起) + cord(心) → 心在一起 → 一致；和睦
befuddle [bɪ'fʌdl]	*v.* 使迷惑不解；使酒醉昏迷(to confuse; muddle or stupefy with or as if with drink) 记 联想记忆：be + fuddle(迷糊) → 使迷惑不解
cuddle ['kʌdl]	*v.* 搂抱，拥抱(to hold lovingly and gently; embrace and fondle) *n.* 搂抱，拥抱 记 注意不要和 puddle(*n.* 水坑)相混
swindle ['swɪndl]	*v.* 诈骗(to obtain money or property by fraud or deceit) 记 联想记忆：s + wind(风) + le → 四处吹风，搞诈骗 → 诈骗
environ [ɪn'vaɪrən]	*v.* 包围，围绕(to encircle, surround) 记 词根记忆：en(进入) + viron(圆) → 进入圆 → 包围，围绕

23

□ magenta	□ pacify	□ ciliate	□ pretence	□ recollection	□ liquefy
□ rebuff	□ demoralize	□ sacrament	□ hoist	□ oscillate	□ podiatrist
□ whet	□ concord	□ befuddle	□ cuddle	□ swindle	□ environ

dissociation	*n.* 分离，脱离关系
[dɪˌsoʊʃiˈeɪʃn]	记 词根记忆：dis(分开) + soci(社会) + ation → 和社会分开 → 分离
pan	*v.* 〈口〉严厉批评(to criticize severely)
[pæn]	
annul	*v.* 宣告无效(to invalidate)；取消(to cancel; abolish)
[əˈnʌl]	记 词根记忆：an(来) + nul(消除) → 取消
ordinance	*n.* 法令，条例(a governmental statute of regulation)
[ˈɔːrdɪnəns]	记 词根记忆：ordin(命令) + ance → 法令，条例
sentiment	*n.* 多愁善感(a tender feeling or emotion)；思想感情
[ˈsentɪmənt]	记 词根记忆：sent(感觉) + iment → 感情丰富 → 多愁善感
decentralize	*v.* 分散，权力下放(to transfer (power, authority) from central government to regional government)
[ˌdiːˈsentrəlaɪz]	记 词根记忆：de(离开) + centr(中心) + alize → 离开中心 → 分散
salve	*n.* 药膏(oily substance used on wounds) *v.* 减轻，缓和(to soothe; assuage)
[sælv]	记 词根记忆：salv(救) + e → 解救的东西 → 药膏
canyon	*n.* 峡谷(a long, narrow valley between cliffs)
[ˈkænjən]	记 联想记忆：can(能) + y(像峡谷的形状) + on(在…上) → 能站在峡谷上 → 峡谷
	参 gorge(*n.* 山谷，峡谷)；gully(*n.* 溪谷，冲沟)；ravine(*n.* 峡谷，溪谷)；valley(*n.* 山谷)
pollster	*n.* 民意调查员(one that conducts a poll)
[ˈpoʊlstər]	记 联想记忆：poll(民意调查) + st + er(人) → 民意调查员
lurk	*v.* 潜伏，埋伏(to stay hidden; lie in wait)
[lɜːrk]	记 联想记忆：为捉一只云雀(lark)埋伏(lurk)在小树林里
expunge	*v.* 删除(to erase or remove completely; delete; cancel)
[ɪkˈspʌndʒ]	记 词根记忆：ex(出) + pung(刺) + e → 把刺挑出 → 删除
excerpt	*n.* 摘录，选录，节录(passage, extract from a book, film, piece of music, etc.)
[ˈeksɜːrpt]	参 except(*prep.* 除…之外)；expert(*n.* 专家)
insouciance	*n.* 漠不关心，漫不经心(lighthearted unconcern)
[ɪnˈsuːsiəns]	记 词根记忆：in(不) + souc(担心) + iance → 不担心 → 漠不关心
bouffant	*adj.* 蓬松的；鼓胀的(puffed out)
[buːˈfɑːnt]	同 puffy
salute	*v.* 行礼致敬(to make a salute)；致意(to greet with polite words or with a sign) *n.* 行军礼(a military sign of recognition)
[səˈluːt]	
bearing	*n.* 关系，意义(connection with or influence on sth.)；方位(the situation or horizontal direction of one point with respect to another)
[ˈberɪŋ]	
waddle	*v.* 摇摇摆摆地走(to walk with short steps from side to side)
[ˈwɑːdl]	记 发音记忆："歪倒" → 走路走得歪歪斜斜，像要倒下去 → 摇摇摆摆地走

lacerate [ˈlæsəreɪt]	*v.* 撕裂(to tear jaggedly)；深深伤害(to cause sharp mental or emotional pain to) 记 词根记忆：lac(撕破) + er + ate → 撕裂
mean [miːn]	*adj.* 吝啬的(selfish in a petty way；stingy) 同 close-fisted, niggardly, miserly, ungenerous
candidacy [ˈkændɪdəsi]	*n.* 候选人资格(the state of being a candidate) 记 联想记忆：经过公正的(candid)选拔，他获得了候选人资格(candidacy)
defile [dɪˈfaɪl]	*v.* 弄污，弄脏(to make filthy or dirty；pollute) *n.* (山间)峡谷，隘路(any narrow valley or mountain pass) 记 词根记忆：de + file(=vile 卑鄙的) → 使…卑下 → 弄污
jaundiced [ˈdʒɔːndɪst]	*adj.* 有偏见的(prejudiced) 记 来自 jaundice(*n.* 偏见)
tinder [ˈtɪndər]	*n.* 火绒，火种(sth. that serves to incite or inflame) 记 词根记忆：tind(点燃) + er → 用于点火的东西 → 火绒
nefarious [nɪˈferiəs]	*adj.* 极恶毒的，邪恶的(extremely wicked；evil) 记 词根记忆：ne(=not) + far(公正) + ious → 不公正的 → 邪恶的
stench [stentʃ]	*n.* 臭气，恶臭(stink) 记 注意不要和 stanch(*v.* 止住)相混
icon [ˈaɪkɑːn]	*n.* 圣像(an image or picture of Jesus, Mary, a saint, etc)；偶像 记 icon 本身可作构词成分，如：iconize(*v.* 盲目崇拜)，iconoclasm(*n.* 打破圣像的行动)
petitioner [pəˈtɪʃənər]	*n.* 请愿人(the person who makes a request) 记 来自 petition(*v./n.* 请愿)
defuse [ˌdiːˈfjuːz]	*v.* 拆除(爆破物的)引信，使除去危险性(to remove the fuse from a mine)；平息(to remove the tension from a potentially dangerous situation) 记 词根记忆：de + fuse(导火线) → 拆除(爆破物的)引信
quota [ˈkwoʊtə]	*n.* 定额，配额(a number or amount that has been officially fixed as someone's share)
bouncing [ˈbaʊnsɪŋ]	*adj.* 活泼的；健康的(lively, animated；enjoying good health)
excursive [ɪksˈkɜːrsɪv]	*adj.* 离题的(digressive) 记 词根记忆：ex(出) + curs(跑) + ive → 跑出去 → 离题的
potentiate [pəˈtenʃieɪt]	*v.* 加强，强化(to make effective or active)
mien [miːn]	*n.* 风采，态度(air；bearing；demeanor) 记 发音记忆："迷你" → 迷人的风采 → 风采
obtuse [əbˈtuːs]	*adj.* 愚笨的(dull or insensitive)；钝的(blunt) 记 词根记忆：ob(向) + tus(敲击) + e → 用钝器敲击 → 钝的

☐ lacerate	☐ mean	☐ candidacy	☐ defile	☐ jaundiced	☐ tinder
☐ nefarious	☐ stench	☐ icon	☐ petitioner	☐ defuse	☐ quota
☐ bouncing	☐ excursive	☐ potentiate	☐ mien	☐ obtuse	

255

gaff [gæf]	*n.* 大鱼钩，鱼叉；【海】斜桁 例 A stay for racing or cruising vessels is used to steady the mast against the strain of the *gaff*.
bumble ['bʌmbl]	*v.* 说话含糊(to stumble)；拙劣地做(to proceed clumsily) 同 burr, buzz, hum
expulsion [ɪk'spʌlʃn]	*n.* 驱逐，逐出(the act of expelling) 记 词根记忆：ex + puls(推) + ion → 推出去 → 驱逐，逐出
emaciate [ɪ'meɪʃieɪt]	*v.* 使瘦弱(to become very thin) 记 词根记忆：e + maci(瘦) + ate → 使瘦弱
autocracy [ɔː'tɑːkrəsi]	*n.* 独裁政府(government by one person that with unlimited power) 记 词根记忆：auto(自己) + cracy(统治) → 自己一个人统治 → 独裁政府
wigwag ['wɪgwæg]	*v.* 摇动，摇摆，摆动(to move back and forth steadily or rhythmically) 同 sway, teeter, totter, waver, weave
cherubic [tʃə'ruːbɪk]	*adj.* 天使的，无邪的，可爱的(angelic; innocent looking) 记 来自 cherub(*n.* 小天使)
svelte [svelt]	*adj.* (女人)体态苗条的(slender; lithe) 同 slim, willowy
apron ['eɪprən]	*n.* 围裙(a protective skirt worn over one's clothing) 记 联想记忆：在四月(April)穿上围裙(apron)去干活
wretched ['retʃɪd]	*adj.* 可怜的，不幸的，悲惨的((of a person) in a very unhappy or unfortunate state)
hew [hjuː]	*v.* 砍伐(to chop or cut with an ax)；遵守(to conform; adhere) 记 联想记忆：早上去砍伐(hew)树木，露珠(dew)被震下来
lopsided [ˌlɑːp'saɪdɪd]	*adj.* 倾向一方的，不平衡的(lacking in symmetry or balance or proportion) 记 组合词：lop(低垂) + side(侧面，边) + (e)d → 垂向一边的 → 倾向一方的
agape [ə'geɪp]	*adj./adv.* (嘴)大张着的(地)(open-mouthed) 记 词根记忆：a(…的) + gape(张开，张大) → 大张着的(地)
plain [pleɪn]	*adj.* 简单的(simple)；清楚的(clear)；不漂亮的，不好看的(lacking beauty or distinction) *n.* 平原(a large stretch of flat land) 例 According to the Senator, it was not hypocrisy for a politician in search of votes to compliment a mother on the beauty of her *plain* child; it was merely sound political common sense.
swoop [swuːp]	*v.* 猛扑(to move in a sudden sweep)；攫取(to seize or snatch in or as if in a sudden sweeping movement)
mesmerism ['mezmərɪzəm]	*n.* 催眠术，催眠引导法(hypnotic induction held to involve animal magnetism) 记 来自奥地利医生 Mesmer，其始创了催眠术
pushy ['pʊʃi]	*adj.* 有进取心的，爱出风头的，固执己见的(aggressive often to an objectionable degree)

plunder	v. 抢劫，掠夺(to take the goods by force; pillage)
[ˈplʌndər]	记 联想记忆：pl(看作 place，放) + under(在…下面) → 放在自己下面 → 抢劫
nullify	v. 使无效(to invalidate)；抵消(to cancel out)
[ˈnʌlɪfaɪ]	记 联想记忆：null(无) + ify → 使无效
epilogue	n. 收场白；尾声(a closing section)
[ˈepɪlɔːg]	记 词根记忆：epi(在…后) + logue(说话) → 在后面说话 → 尾声
ensue	v. 接着发生(to happen afterwards)
[ɪnˈsuː]	记 词根记忆：en(进入) + sue(跟从；起诉) → 接着发生
unbidden	adj. 未经邀请的(unasked; uninvited)
[ʌnˈbɪdn]	记 联想记忆：un(不) + bid(邀请) + den → 未经邀请的
soggy	adj. 湿透的(saturated or heavy with water or moisture)
[ˈsɑːgi]	同 clammy, dank, sopping, waterlogged
repartee	n. 机敏的应答(a quick and witty reply)
[ˌrepɑːrˈtiː]	记 词根记忆：re(反) + part(部分) + ee → 拿出部分作为回答 → 机敏的应答
convene	v. 集合(to come together; assemble)；召集(to call to meet)
[kənˈviːn]	记 词根记忆：con(共同) + ven(来) + e → 共同来 → 集合
presage	[ˈpresɪdʒ] n. 预感(an intuition or feeling of the future)
	[prɪˈseɪdʒ] v. 预示(to foreshadow; foretell)
	记 联想记忆：pre(预先) + sage(智者；智慧) → 预感
warranty	n. 保证，担保；根据，理由；授权，批准
[ˈwɔːrənti]	搭 under warranty 在保修期内
guzzle	v. 大吃大喝(to drink greedily or immoderately)；大量消耗
[ˈgʌzl]	搭 guzzle beer 狂饮啤酒
pall	v. 令人发腻，失去吸引力(to become boring)
[pɔːl]	
severe	adj. 严厉的(very serious)；剧烈的(extremely violent)
[sɪˈvɪr]	记 联想记忆：曾经(ever)艰难(severe)的日子，一去不复返了
	例 There were contradictions in her nature that made her seem an inexplicable enigma: she was *severe* and gentle; she was modest and disdainful; she longed for affection and was cold.
emaciation	n. 消瘦，憔悴，衰弱(the state of being weaker)
[ɪˌmeɪsiˈeɪʃn]	同 boniness, gauntness, maceration
riot	v. 暴动，闹事(to create or engage in a riot)
[ˈraɪət]	同 carouse, frolic, revel
aboveboard	adj./adv. 光明正大的(地)(honest(ly) and open(ly))
[əˌbʌvˈbɔːrd]	记 联想记忆：above（ 在…上 ） + board（ 会议桌 ） → 可以放到桌面上谈 → 光明正大的(地)
artifice	n. 巧妙办法(skill or ingenuity)；诡计(a sly trick)
[ˈɑːrtɪfɪs]	记 词根记忆：arti(技巧) + fice(做) → 做的技巧 → 巧妙办法

23

waver [ˈweɪvər]	*v.* 摇摆 (to move unsteadily back and forth); 踌躇 (to fluctuate in opinion, allegiance, or direction)
chameleon [kəˈmiːliən]	*n.* 变色龙，蜥蜴; 善变之人 (someone who is very changeable)
muck [mʌk]	*n.* 堆肥，粪肥 (soft moist farmyard manure) *v.* 施肥 (to dress (as soil) with muck); 捣乱 (to interfere; meddle)
lackluster [ˈlæklʌstər]	*adj.* 无光泽的 (lacking brightness); 呆滞的 (dull) 记 组合词: lack(缺少) + luster(光泽) → 缺少光泽的 → 无光泽的
capacious [kəˈpeɪʃəs]	*adj.* 容量大的，宽敞的 (containing a great deal; spacious) 记 词根记忆: cap(抓) + acious → 能抓住东西 → 宽敞的
dispatch [dɪˈspætʃ]	*v.* 派遣 (to send off or out promptly); 迅速处理 (to dispose of rapidly or efficiently); 匆匆吃完 (to eat up quickly) *n.* 迅速 (promptness; haste) 记 词根记忆: dis(除去) + patch(妨碍) → 去掉妨碍，迅速完成 → 迅速处理
knit [nɪt]	*v.* 编织 (to make by joining woolen threads into a close network with needles); 密接，紧密相联 (to connect closely)
harp [hɑːrp]	*n.* 竖琴 *v.* 弹竖琴; 喋喋不休地说或写 (to talk or write about to an excessive and tedious degree) 记 联想记忆: 要学会弹竖琴(harp)就需要努力(hard)练习
gutter [ˈɡʌtər]	*n.* 水槽; 街沟 (a channel at the edge of a street) 记 词根记忆: gut(肠胃，引申为"沟") + ter → 街沟
revenge [rɪˈvendʒ]	*n.* 报复，报仇 (retaliation) 记 词根记忆: re(反) + veng(惩罚) + e → 反惩罚 → 报复
gangling [ˈɡæŋɡlɪŋ]	*adj.* 瘦长得难看的 (tall, thin and awkward-looking) 记 发音记忆: "杠铃" → 像杠铃一样瘦而难看 → 瘦长得难看的
wispy [ˈwɪspi]	*adj.* 纤细的; 脆弱的; 一缕缕的 搭 wispy hair 一缕缕头发
toll [toʊl]	*n.* 通行费 (money paid for the use of a road, bridge, etc.); 代价，损失 (loss or damage caused by sth.) *v.* (缓慢而有规律地)敲 (to sound with slow measured strokes) 记 发音记忆: "痛" → 受伤了，很痛 → 代价，损失 例 In a nation where the economic reversals of the past few years have taken a psychological as well as a financial *toll* on many regions, what most distinguishes the South may be the degree of optimism throughout the region.
chirp [tʃɜːrp]	*v.* (鸟或虫)唧唧叫 (to utter in a sharp, shrill tone) 记 动物的不同叫声: 狗-bark(吠); 狼-howl(嗥); 牛、羊-blat(咩咩叫，哞哞叫); 狮、虎-roar(吼)
peer [pɪr]	*n.* 同等之人、同辈 (one belonging to the same societal group especially based on age, grade, or status)

| **inveigle** | *v.* 诱骗，诱使 (to win with deception; lure) |
| [ɪn'veɪɡl] | 记 联想记忆：in + veigle (看作 veil, 面纱) → 盖上面纱 → 诱骗 |

| **aspersion** | *n.* 诽谤，中伤 (disparaging remark; slander) |
| [ə'spɜːrʒn] | 记 词根记忆：a + spers (散开) + ion → 散布坏东西 → 诽谤 |

| **scamper** | *v.* 奔跑，蹦蹦跳跳 (to run nimbly and playfully about) |
| ['skæmpər] | 记 联想记忆：s (音似：死) + camper (露营者) → 露营者死 (跑) → 奔跑 |

| **mumble** | *v.* 咕哝，含糊不清地说 (to speak or say unclearly) |
| ['mʌmbl] | 同 grumble, murmur, mutter |

| **thrust** | *v.* 猛力推 (to push or drive with force)；刺，戳 (to stab; pierce) |
| [θrʌst] | 搭 thrust sth./sb. on/upon sb. 把…强加于；强迫…接受 |

| **kindle** | *v.* 着火，点燃 (to set on fire; ignite) |
| ['kɪndl] | 记 联想记忆：和candle (*n.* 蜡烛) 一起记 |

| **reproof** | *n.* 责备，斥责 (criticism for a fault; rebuke) |
| [rɪ'pruːf] | 同 admonishment, reprimand, reproach, scolding |

| **trapeze** | *n.* 高空秋千，吊架 (a short bar hung high above the ground from two ropes used by gymnasts and acrobats) |
| [træ'piːz] | |

| **commemorate** | *v.* 纪念 (伟人、大事件等) (to call to remembrance)；庆祝 |
| [kə'meməreɪt] | 记 词根记忆：com (共同) + memor (记住) + ate → 大家一起记住 → 纪念 |

| **offish** | *adj.* 冷淡的 (distant and reserved) |
| ['ɔːfɪʃ] | 记 联想记忆：off (离开) + (f)ish (鱼) → 鱼离开了，池塘冷清 → 冷淡的 |

mature	*adj.* 成熟的 (fully developed)；深思熟虑的 (carefully decided)
[mə'tʃʊr]	记 联想记忆：当自然 (nature) 中的 n 变成 m，万物变得成熟 (mature)
	例 In television programming, a later viewing time often implies a more *mature* audience and, therefore, more challenging subjects and themes.

23

| **siege** | *n.* 包围，围攻 (a military blockade of a city or fortified place to compel it to surrender) |
| [siːdʒ] | 记 参见 besiege (*v.* 围攻) |

| **contaminate** | *v.* 弄脏，污染 (to make impure; pollute; smudge) |
| [kən'tæmɪneɪt] | 记 词根记忆：con + tamin (接触) + ate → 接触脏东西 → 弄脏，污染 |

contaminate

| **tamp** | *v.* 捣实，夯实 (to drive in or down by a succession of blows) |
| [tæmp] | 记 发音记忆："踏" → 用力踏 → 夯实 |

| **vindication** | *n.* 证明无罪，辩护 (justification against denial or censure; defense) |
| [ˌvɪndɪ'keɪʃn] | 同 apology, exculpation |

| **gaiety** | *n.* 欢乐，快活 (cheerfulness) |
| ['ɡeɪəti] | 记 来自 gay (*adj.* 欢乐的) |

□ inveigle	□ aspersion	□ aspersion	□ scamper	□ mumble	□ thrust
□ kindle	□ reproof	□ trapeze	□ commemorate	□ offish	□ mature
□ siege	□ contaminate	□ tamp	□ vindication	□ gaiety	

259

unregenerate [ˌʌnrɪˈdʒenərət]	*adj.* 不悔改的(making no attempt to change one's bad practices) 同 hardened, impenitent, remorseless
impenitent [ɪmˈpenɪtənt]	*adj.* 不知悔悟的(without regret; unrepentant) 记 联想记忆：im(不) + penitent(悔过的) → 死不悔改的 → 不知悔悟的
ken [ken]	*n.* 视野(perception); 知识范围 搭 beyond one's ken 为某人所不理解，在某人的知识范围外
resplendent [rɪˈsplendənt]	*adj.* 华丽的，光辉的(shining brilliantly) 记 词根记忆：re(反复) + splend(发光) + ent → 不断发光的 → 光辉的
hearken [ˈhɑːrkən]	*v.* 倾听(to listen attentively) 记 来自 hear(v. 听)

Jovons saw the kettle boil and cried out with the delighted voice of a child; Marshal too had seen the kettle boil and sat down silently to build an engine.

杰文斯看见壶开了，高兴得像孩子似地叫了起来；马歇尔也看见壶开了，却悄悄地坐下来造了一部蒸气机。

——英国经济学家 凯恩斯(John Maynard Keynes, British economist)

agile [ˈædʒl]	*adj.* 敏捷的，灵活的（able to move quickly and easily） 记 词根记忆：ag(做) + ile(易…的) → 动作容易的 → 敏捷的
voracity [vəˈræsəti]	*n.* 贪食；贪婪（the quality or state of being voracious） 同 greed, rapacity
avert [əˈvɜːrt]	*v.* 避免，防止（to ward off; prevent）；转移（to turn away） 记 词根记忆：a(向) + vert(转) → 转开 → 避免
chide [tʃaɪd]	*v.* 斥责，责骂（to scold; reprove mildly） 记 联想记忆：斥责(chide)孩子(child)
smarmy [ˈsmɑːrmi]	*adj.* 虚情假意的（revealing or marked by a false earnestness） 同 oily, smooth, sleek, unctuous
earthshaking [ˈɜːrθˌʃeɪkɪŋ]	*adj.* 极其重大或重要的（very important） 记 组合词：earth(地球) + shaking(震动) → 使地球震动的 → 极其重大或重要的
abate [əˈbeɪt]	*v.* 减轻，减少（to make less in amount; wane） 记 词根记忆：a(加强) + bate(减弱，减少) → 减轻
indelible [ɪnˈdeləbl]	*adj.* 擦拭不掉的，不可磨灭的（incapable of being erased） 记 词根记忆：in(不) + de(消失) + li(=liv 石灰) + ble → 用石灰无法去掉的 → 擦拭不掉的
spatter [ˈspætər]	*v.* 洒，溅（to splash with or as if with a liquid） 同 slop, spray, swash
stationary [ˈsteɪʃəneri]	*adj.* 静止的，不动的（fixed in a station; immobile） 记 词根记忆：sta(站，立) + tion + ary → 总在一个地方的 → 静止的，不动的
dexterity [dekˈsterəti]	*n.* 纯熟，灵巧（skill in using one's hands or body; adroitness） 记 词根记忆：dexter(右) + ity → 像右手一样 → 纯熟，灵巧
apprentice [əˈprentɪs]	*n.* 学徒（one who is learning by practical experience under skilled workers） 记 词根记忆：ap(接近) + prent(=prehend 抓住) + ice → 为了抓住技术的人 → 学徒
induct [ɪnˈdʌkt]	*v.* 使就职（to install）；使入伍（to enroll in the armed forces） 记 词根记忆：in(进去) + duct(拉) → 拉进 → 使入伍

□ agile	□ voracity	□ avert	□ chide	□ smarmy	□ earthshaking
□ abate	□ indelible	□ spatter	□ stationary	□ dexterity	□ apprentice
□ induct					

confidant [ˈkɑːnfɪdænt]	*n.* 心腹朋友，知己，密友（one to whom secrets are entrusted） 记 词根记忆：con(加强) + fid(相信) + ant → 非常信任的人 → 知己，密友
snide [snaɪd]	*adj.* 挖苦的，讽刺的（slyly disparaging；insinuating） 记 联想记忆：把 n 藏在一边(side) → 含沙射影的 → 讽刺的
prophecy [ˈprɑːfəsi]	*n.* 预言（a statement telling sth. that will happen in the future）
sport [spɔːrt]	*v.* 炫耀，卖弄（to display or wear ostentatiously） 搭 sport a beard 故意蓄着大胡子
verbiage [ˈvɜːrbiɪdʒ]	*n.* 冗词，废话（a profusion of words of little content） 记 词根记忆：verb(字，词) + i + age → 冗词，废话
foreword [ˈfɔːrwɜːrd]	*n.* 前言，序（prefatory comments） 记 联想记忆：fore(前面的) + word(话) → 写在前面的话 → 前言
disgust [dɪsˈɡʌst]	*n.* 反感，厌恶（strong dislike） 记 词根记忆：dis(不) + gust(胃口) → 没有胃口 → 反感 例 For many young people during the Roaring Twenties, a *disgust* with the excesses of American culture combined with a wanderlust to provoke an exodus abroad.
ingress [ˈɪngres]	*n.* 进入（the act of entering） 记 词根记忆：in(进去) + gress(走) → 走进去 → 进入
entwine [ɪnˈtwaɪn]	*v.* 使缠绕，交织（to twine, weave, or twist together） 记 词根记忆：en(使) + twine(缠绕) → 使缠绕
reckon [ˈrekən]	*v.* 推断，估计（to count；calculate）；猜想，设想（to think；suppose） 同 estimate
abound [əˈbaʊnd]	*v.* 大量存在（to be great in number or amount）；充满，富于（to be fully supplied or filled of；teem with） 记 联想记忆：a + bound(边界) → 没有边界 → 充满
linger [ˈlɪŋɡər]	*v.* 逗留，继续存留（to continue to stay）；徘徊 记 联想记忆：那位歌手(singer)徘徊(linger)于曾经的舞台
ripple [ˈrɪpl]	*v.* (使)泛起涟漪（to move in small waves） *n.* 波痕，涟漪 搭 a ripple of applause/laughter 一阵阵的掌声/笑声
lope [loʊp]	*n.* 轻快的步伐（an easy, swinging stride） *v.* 大步跑（to run with a steady, easy gait） 记 注意不要和 lobe(n. 耳垂)相混
disclaim [dɪsˈkleɪm]	*v.* 放弃权利（to give up or renounce）；拒绝承认（to refuse to acknowledge；deny） 记 词根记忆：dis(不) + claim(要求) → 不再要求 → 放弃权利

recline [rɪˈklaɪn]	*v.* 斜倚，躺卧(to lie down) 记 词根记忆：re(回) + clin(倾斜) + e → 斜回去 → 斜倚，躺卧
recess [ˈriːses]	*n.* 壁凹(alcove; cleft)；休假(a suspension of business for rest and relaxation) 记 词根记忆：re(反) + cess(走) → 向内反着走 → 壁凹
enjoin [ɪnˈdʒɔɪn]	*v.* 命令，吩咐(to direct or impose by authoritative order; command) 记 联想记忆：en(使) + join(参加) → 使(别人)参加 → 命令
expire [ɪkˈspaɪər]	*v.* 期满；断气，去世(to breathe one's last breath; die) 记 词根记忆：ex + pir(呼吸) + e → 没有了呼吸 → 去世
brew [bruː]	*v.* 酿酒(to brew beer or ale)；沏(茶)，煮(咖啡) (to make a hot drink of tea or coffee)；酝酿，即 将发生(to be in the process of forming)
earthy [ˈɜːrθi]	*adj.* 粗俗的，土气的(rough, plain in taste) 记 词根记忆：earth(土地) + y → 土气的
falsehood [ˈfɔːlshʊd]	*n.* 谎言(an untrue statement) 记 联想记忆：false(虚伪的) + hood(名词后缀) → 谎言
filibuster [ˈfɪlɪbʌstər]	*v.* 妨碍议事，阻挠议案通过(to obstruct the passage of) *n.* 阻挠议事的人 或行动 记 发音记忆："费力拍死它" → 阻碍法案或议事的通过 → 阻挠议案通过
condemn [kənˈdem]	*v.* 谴责(to disapprove of strongly)；判刑(to inflict a penalty upon) 记 词根记忆：con + demn(=damn 诅咒) → 一再诅咒 → 谴责
boast [boʊst]	*v.* 自夸(to speak of or assert with excessive pride) *n.* 自夸 记 和 roast(*v.* 烤，烘)一起记
ventilate [ˈventɪleɪt]	*v.* 使通风(to cause fresh air to circulate through) 记 来自 vent(*n.* 通风口)
prescience [ˈpresiəns]	*n.* 预知，先见(foreknowledge of events) 记 词根记忆：pre(预先) + sci(知道) + ence → 预知，先见
upswing [ˈʌpswɪŋ]	*n.* 上升，增长(a marked increase)；进步，改进(a marked improvement) 记 组合词：up(向上) + swing(摆动) → 向上摆动 → 上升
miserly [ˈmaɪzərli]	*adj.* 吝啬的(penurious) 记 来自 miser(*n.* 吝啬鬼)
garnish [ˈgɑːrnɪʃ]	*v.* 装饰(to decorate; embellish) 记 词根记忆：gar(花) + nish → 布满花 → 装饰
analogy [əˈnælədʒi]	*n.* 相似(partial resemblance)；类比(the likening of one thing to another) 记 词根记忆：ana(并列) + log(说话) + y → 放在一起说 → 类比
gargantuan [gɑːrˈgæntʃuən]	*adj.* 巨大的，庞大的(of tremendous size or volume) 记 来自法国作家拉伯雷的著作《巨人传》中的巨人 Gargantua 同 colossal, enormous, gigantic

24

□ recline	□ recess	□ enjoin	□ expire	□ brew	□ earthy
□ falsehood	□ filibuster	□ condemn	□ boast	□ ventilate	□ prescience
□ upswing	□ miserly	□ garnish	□ analogy	□ gargantuan	

263

attach [əˈtætʃ]	*v.* 系上，贴上，附上（to fasten sth. to sth.） 记 词根记忆：at(向) + tach(接触) → 将某物系在(另一物)上 → 系上，贴上，附上
tauten [ˈtɔːtn]	*v.* (使)拉紧，(使)绷紧（to make or become taut） 记 来自 taut(*adj.* 绷紧的)
distrait [dɪˈstre]	*adj.* 心不在焉的（absent-minded; distracted）
slay [sleɪ]	*v.* 杀戮，杀死（to kill violently or in great numbers） 记 和 stay(*v.* 停留)一起记
chic [ʃiːk]	*adj.* 漂亮的，时髦的（cleverly stylish; currently fashionable） 同 modish, posh, swanky
iconoclast [aɪˈkɑːnəklæst]	*n.* 攻击传统观念或风俗的人（one who attacks and seeks to destroy widely accepted ideas, beliefs） 记 词根记忆：icon(圣像) + o + clas(打破) + t → 打破圣像的人 → 攻击传统观念或风俗的人
flay [fleɪ]	*v.* 剥皮（to strip off the skin or hide）；抢夺，掠夺（to rob; pillage）；严厉指责（to criticize or scold mercilessly） 记 和 fray(*v.* 吵架，冲突)一起记
retch [retʃ]	*v.* 作呕，恶心（to vomit）
prosecution [ˌprɑːsɪˈkjuːʃn]	*n.* 起诉，检举（the act or process of prosecuting）；进行，经营（carrying out or being occupied with sth.） 记 来自 prosecute(*v.* 起诉，检举)
occlude [əˈkluːd]	*v.* 使闭塞（to prevent the passage of） 记 词根记忆：oc + clud(关闭) + e → 一再关起来 → 使闭塞
traipse [treɪps]	*v.* 漫步，闲荡（to walk or travel about without apparent plan but with or without a purpose）
squeamish [ˈskwiːmɪʃ]	*adj.* 易受惊的；易恶心的（easily shocked or sickened） 记 the squeamish 神经脆弱的人
camouflage [ˈkæməflɑːʒ]	*v.* 掩饰，伪装（to disguise in order to conceal） *n.* 伪装 记 联想记忆：cam(看作 came) + ou(看作 out) + flag(旗帜) + e → 扛着旗帜出来 → 伪装成革命战士 → 伪装
unsettling [ʌnˈsetlɪŋ]	*adj.* 使人不安的，扰乱的（having the effect of upsetting, disturbing, or discomposing） 记 来自 unsettle(*v.* 使不安宁，扰乱)
overhaul [ˈoʊvərhɔːl]	*v.* 彻底检查（to check thoroughly）；大修（to repair thoroughly） 记 组合词：over(全部) + haul(拉，拖) → 全部拉上来修理 → 大修
prognosis [prɑːɡˈnoʊsɪs]	*n.* 【医】(对病情的)预断，预后（forecast of the likely course of a disease or an illness） 记 词根记忆：pro(前) + gno(知道) + sis → 先知道 → 预后

收件人： 123@123.com
抄送：
主题： Hello
附件： file.doc

attach

intangibility [ɪnˌtændʒəˈbɪləti]	*n.* 无形 记 词根记忆：in(不) + tang(触摸) + ibility → 触摸不到的 → 无形
certification [ˌsɜːrtɪfɪˈkeɪʃn]	*n.* 证明(action of certifying) 记 来自 certify(*v.* 证明)；cert(搞清) + ify(…化) → 搞清楚 → 证明
extrovert [ˈekstrəvɜːrt]	*n.* 性格外向者(a person who is active and unreserved) 记 词根记忆：extro(外) + vert(转) → 向外转的人 → 性格外向者
dainty [ˈdeɪnti]	*n.* [常*pl.*] 美味；精美的食品(small tasty piece of food, especially a small cake) *adj.* 娇美的(delicately pretty)；挑剔的(fastidious; particular) 记 词根记忆：dain(=dign 高贵) + ty → 高级食品 → 精美的食品
inoculate [ɪˈnɑːkjuleɪt]	*v.* 注射预防针(to inject a serum, vaccine to create immunity) 记 词根记忆：in(进入) + ocul(萌芽) + ate → 在萌芽时进入 → 注射预防针
rendering [ˈrendərɪŋ]	*n.* 表演(performance)；翻译(translation) 记 来自 render(*v.* 表演；翻译)
procrastinate [proʊˈkræstɪneɪt]	*v.* 耽搁，拖延(to put off intentionally and habitually) 记 词根记忆：pro(向前) + crastin(明天) + ate → 直到明天再干 → 拖延
receipt [rɪˈsiːt]	*n.* 收到，接到(act of receiving or being received)；发票，收据(a writing acknowledging the receiving of goods or money) 记 来自 receive(*v.* 收到)
cozen [ˈkʌzən]	*v.* 欺骗，哄骗(to coax; deceive) 记 联想记忆：编了一打(dozen)的谎话来欺骗(cozen)她
saddle [ˈsædl]	*n.* 鞍，马鞍(a seat of a rider on a horse) 记 联想记忆：sad(非常糟糕的) + dle → 骑马没鞍可就糟了 → 马鞍
scotch [skɑːtʃ]	*v.* 镇压，扑灭(to put an end to) 记 和 Scotch(苏格兰)一起记
corrode [kəˈroʊd]	*v.* 腐蚀，侵蚀(to destroy slowly by chemical action) 记 词根记忆：cor(全部) + rod(咬) + e → 全部咬掉 → 腐蚀，侵蚀
consequential [ˌkɑːnsəˈkwenʃl]	*adj.* 傲慢的，自尊自大的(thinking oneself very important; self-important) 同 arrogant
vertical [ˈvɜːrtɪkl]	*adj.* 垂直的，直立的(perpendicular to the plane of the horizon; upright) 记 来自 vertex(*n.* 顶点)
sequestrate [ˈsiːkwəstreɪt]	*v.* 扣押，没收(to place property in custody) 同 seclude, sequester
scare [sker]	*n./v.* 惊吓，受惊，惊恐(to frighten especially suddenly) 记 联想记忆：s + care(照顾) → 照顾不好，受到惊吓 → 惊吓，受惊
chipper [ˈtʃɪpər]	*adj.* 爽朗的，活泼的(sprightly) 记 联想记忆：她很爽朗(chipper)，将新研发的芯片(chip)拿出来给大家看
loiter [ˈlɔɪtər]	*v.* 闲逛，游荡(to linger)；慢慢前行(to travel or move slowly and indolently)；消磨时光，虚度光阴

24

drub [drʌb]	*v.* 重击(to beat severely); 打败(to defeat decisively)
obsolete [ˌɑːbsəˈliːt]	*adj.* 废弃的(no longer in use); 过时的(out of date; old) 同 old-fashioned
vagrancy [ˈveɪɡrənsi]	*n.* 漂泊, 流浪(the state of being a vagrant) 记 来自 vagrant(*adj.* 流浪的, 漂泊的)
trim [trɪm]	*v.* 修剪(to make neat by cutting or clipping) *adj.* 井井有条的(in good and neat order)
seraphic [səˈræfɪk]	*adj.* 如天使般的, 美丽的(like an angel) 记 来自 seraph(*n.* 守卫上帝宝座的六翼天使)
bully [ˈbʊli]	*v.* 威胁, 以强欺弱(to frighten or tyrannize) *n.* 欺凌弱小者 记 联想记忆: bully 古意为 "情人", 因为在争夺情人的斗争中总是强的打败弱的, 所以演化为"以强欺弱"之意
fasten [ˈfæsn]	*v.* 使固定(to fix sth. firmly) 记 来自 fast(*adj.* 紧的, 牢固的)
charm [tʃɑːrm]	*n.* 魅力(a physical grace or attraction); 咒语, 咒符(incantation; amulet) *v.* 吸引, 迷住(to delight, attract or influence by charm) 记 联想记忆: char(音似: 茶) + m(看作 man) → 被男士约出去喝茶, 因为很有魅力 → 魅力 搭 particular charm 独特的魅力
blunt [blʌnt]	*adj.* 钝的(without a sharp edge); 直率的(frank and straightforward) *v.* 使迟钝
complaisance [kəmˈpleɪzəns]	*n.* 彬彬有礼; 殷勤; 柔顺(willingness to do what pleases others) 记 联想记忆: com(共同) + plais(看作 please, 使喜欢) + ance → 彬彬有礼才能使大家喜欢 → 彬彬有礼
amplify [ˈæmplɪfaɪ]	*v.* 放大(to make larger; extend); 详述(to develop with details) 记 词根记忆: ampl(大) + ify → 放大
bust [bʌst]	*n.* 半身(雕)像 记 联想记忆: 灌木丛(bush)中发现了一尊佛的半身像(bust)
devise [dɪˈvaɪz]	*v.* 发明, 设计(to invent); 图谋(to plan to obtain or bring about); 遗赠给(to give estate by will) 记 联想记忆: 发明(devise)设备(device)
stimulant [ˈstɪmjələnt]	*n.* 兴奋剂, 刺激物(an agent that produces a temporary increase of the functional activity) 记 词根记忆: stimul(刺激) + ant → 刺激物
brisk [brɪsk]	*adj.* 敏捷的, 活泼的(quick, lively); 清新健康的(giving a healthy feeling) 记 联想记忆: b + risk(冒险) → 喜欢冒险的人 → 敏捷的, 活泼的
impermeability [ɪmˌpɜːrmiəˈbɪləti]	*n.* 不渗透性 记 联想记忆: im(不) + permeability(可渗透性) → 不渗透性

□ drub	□ obsolete	□ vagrancy	□ trim	□ seraphic	□ bully
□ fasten	□ charm	□ blunt	□ complaisance	□ amplify	□ bust
□ devise	□ stimulant	□ brisk	□ impermeability		

furor	*n.* 喧闹，轰动(a fashionable craze)；盛怒(frenzy; great anger)
[ˈfjʊrɔːr]	记 来自 fury(*n.* 狂怒)
	同 rage, uproar
enfetter	*v.* 给…上脚镣(to bind in fetters)；束缚，使受制于(to enchain)
[ɪnˈfetər]	记 词根记忆：en(进入) + fetter(镣铐) → 给…上脚镣
asinine	*adj.* 愚笨的(of asses; stupid; silly)
[ˈæsɪnaɪn]	记 联想记忆：as(看作 ass, 驴子) + in + in + e → 笨得像驴 → 愚笨的
abash	*v.* 使羞愧，使尴尬(to make embarrassed)
[əˈbæʃ]	记 联想记忆：ab + ash(灰) → 中间有灰，灰头灰脸 → 使尴尬
moody	*adj.* 喜怒无常的(given to changeable moods)；抑郁的(gloomy)
[ˈmuːdi]	记 来自 mood(*n.* 情绪)
cacophony	*n.* 刺耳的声音(harsh, jarring sound)
[kəˈkɑːfəni]	记 词根记忆：caco(坏) + phony(声音) → 声音不好 → 刺耳的声音
subterfuge	*n.* 诡计，托辞(a deceptive device or stratagem)
[ˈsʌbtərfjuːdʒ]	记 词根记忆：subter(私下) + fuge(逃跑) → 诡计，托辞
hardihood	*n.* 大胆，刚毅(boldness; fortitude)；厚颜
[ˈhɑːrdihʊd]	记 来自 hardy(*adj.* 强壮的；大胆的，勇敢的)
douse	*v.* 把…浸入水中(to plunge into water)；熄灭(to extinguish)
[daʊs]	记 联想记忆：do + use → 又做又用 → 在水中做 → 把…浸入水中
dispense	*v.* 分配，分发(to distribute in portions)
[dɪˈspens]	记 词根记忆：dis(分开) + pens(花费) + e → 分开花费 → 分配，分发
uproarious	*adj.* 骚动的(marked by uproar)；喧嚣的(loud and full; boisterous)；令人
[ʌpˈrɔːriəs]	捧腹大笑的(very funny)
medal	*n.* 奖牌，勋章(an award for winning a championship or commemorating
[ˈmedl]	some other event)
	记 联想记忆：奖牌(medal)是金属(metal)做的
zoom	*v.* 急速上升，猛增(to increase sharply)
[zuːm]	同 hike, skyrocket, surge
aftermath	*n.* 后果，余波(an unpleasant result or consequence)
[ˈæftərmæθ]	记 联想记忆：after(在…之后) + math(数学) → 做完数学后一塌糊涂的结
	果 → 后果
mandate	*n.* 命令，训令(an authoritative order or command)
[ˈmændeɪt]	记 词根记忆：mand(命令) + ate → 命令
incriminate	*v.* 连累，牵连(to involve in)
[ɪnˈkrɪmɪneɪt]	记 词根记忆：in(进入) + crimin(罪行) + ate → 被牵连在罪行中 → 连累
affected	*adj.* 不自然的(behaving in an artificial way)；假装的(assumed)
[əˈfektɪd]	记 factitious, fictitious, unnatural
elephantine	*adj.* 笨拙的(clumsy)；巨大的(having enormous size; massive)
[ˌelɪˈfæntiːn]	记 来自 elephant(*n.* 大象)

24

churl [tʃɜːrl]	*n.* 粗鄙之人（a surly, ill-bred person）
	记 联想记忆：粗鄙之人（churl）不宜进教堂（church）
forecast [ˈfɔːrkæst]	*v.* 预报，预测（to tell in advance）*n.* 预测（statement that predicts）
	记 词根记忆：fore(预先) + cast(扔) → 预先扔下 → 预测
collage [kəˈlɑːʒ]	*n.* 拼贴画（an artistic composition made of various materials）
	记 和 college(*n.* 学院)一起记
ulcerate [ˈʌlsəreɪt]	*v.* 溃烂（to affect with an ulcer）
	记 来自 ulcer(*n.* 溃疡)
burlesque [bɜːrˈlesk]	*n.* 讽刺或滑稽的戏剧，滑稽剧（derisive caricature; parody）
	记 发音记忆："不如乐死去" → 玩笑话 → 滑稽剧
recombine [ˌriːkəmˈbaɪn]	*v.* 重组，再结合（to combine again or anew）
	记 联想记忆：re(重新) + combine(组合) → 重组
blooming [ˈbluːmɪŋ]	*adj.* 开着花的（having flowers）；旺盛的
	记 来自 bloom(*v.* 开花)
solitude [ˈsɑːlətuːd]	*n.* 孤独（the quality or state of being alone or remote from society）
	例 Contrary to her customary gregarious behavior, Susan began leaving parties early to seek the *solitude* of her room.
flimflam [ˈflɪmflæm]	*n.* 欺骗（deception）；胡言乱语（deceptive nonsense）
	同 poppycock, swindle
martial [ˈmɑːrʃl]	*adj.* 战争的，军事的（of or suitable to war and soldiers）
	记 联想记忆：mar(毁坏) + tial → 战争常常意味着毁灭 → 战争的
	搭 martial law 戒严令
wheeze [wiːz]	*v.* 喘息（to breathe with difficulty, producing a hoarse whistling sound）；发出呼哧呼哧的声音（to make a sound resembling laborious breathing）
wince [wɪns]	*v.* 畏缩，退缩（to shrink back involuntarily；flinch）
	同 cringe, quail
gobble [ˈgɑːbl]	*v.* 贪婪地吃，狼吞虎咽（to eat quickly and greedily）；吞没
	记 来自 gob(*n.* 一块，大量)
	同 gulp, swallow
dint [dɪnt]	*v.* 击出凹痕（to make a dent in）
	搭 by dint of 凭借…
simmer [ˈsɪmər]	*v.* 炖，慢煮（to stew gently below or just at the boiling point）*n.* 即将沸腾的状态，即将发作
	记 联想记忆：在夏天（summer），人往往处于（怒火）即将发作（simmer）的状态

evacuate [ɪˈvækjueɪt]	*v.* 撤离(to withdraw from); 疏散(to remove inhabitants from a place for protective purposes) 记 词根记忆：e + vacu(空) + ate → 空出去 → 撤离
germicide [ˈdʒɜːrmɪsaɪd]	*n.* 杀菌剂(substance used for killing germs) 记 词根记忆：germ(细菌) + i + cid(切) + e → 杀菌剂
utopia [juːˈtoʊpiə]	*n.* 乌托邦(an imagined place or state of things in which everything is perfect) 记 发音记忆："乌托邦" → 乌托邦
plateau [plæˈtoʊ]	*n.* 高原(tableland); 平稳时期(a relatively stable period) 记 词根记忆：plat(平的) + eau → 平稳时期
snobbish [ˈsnɑːbɪʃ]	*adj.* 势利眼的(being, characteristic of, or befitting a snob); 假充绅士的 记 来自 snob(*n.* 势利小人)
nil [nɪl]	*n.* 无，零(nothing; zero) 记 词根记忆：ni(=ne 无，没有) + l → 无，零
feline [ˈfiːlaɪn]	*adj.* 猫的，猫科的(of, relating to, or affecting cats or the cat family) 记 词根记忆：fel(猫) + ine → 猫的，猫科的
bruise [bruːz]	*v.* 受伤，擦伤(to injure the skin) 记 联想记忆：和 cruise(*v.* 乘船巡游)一起记
lymphatic [lɪmˈfætɪk]	*adj.* 无力的(lacking in physical or mental energy); 迟缓的; 淋巴的 记 来自 lymph(*n.* 淋巴)
abase [əˈbeɪs]	*v.* 降低…的地位，贬抑，使卑下 (to lower oneself/sb. in dignity; degrade oneself/sb.) 记 词根记忆：a(到) + base(降低) → 降低…的地位
ban [bæn]	*n.* 禁令(an order banning sth.) *v.* 禁止，取缔(to officially forbid) 记 发音记忆："颁" → (颁布)禁令 → 禁止
accomplished [əˈkɑːmplɪʃt]	*adj.* 完成了的(being achieved); 有技巧的(skilled) 搭 accomplished performer 有技巧的表演者
leach [liːtʃ]	*v.* 过滤(to draw out or remove as if by percolation) 记 和 beach(*n.* 海滩)一起记
infatuate [ɪnˈfætʃueɪt]	*v.* 使迷恋(to inspire with a foolish or extravagant love or admiration); 使糊涂(to cause to deprive of sound judgment) 记 词根记忆：in(进入) + fatu(愚蠢的) + ate → 因迷恋而变得愚蠢 → 使迷恋
repressed [rɪˈprest]	*adj.* 被抑制的，被压抑的(suffering from suppression of the emotions)
eulogy [ˈjuːlədʒi]	*n.* 颂词，颂文(high speech or commendation) 同 acclaim, applause, celebration, compliment
pecan [pɪˈkɑːn]	*n.* 山核桃(a nut with a long thin reddish shell) 记 发音记忆："皮啃" → 皮很难啃动的坚果 → 山核桃
limp [lɪmp]	*v.* 跛行(to walk lamely) *adj.* 软弱的，无力的(flaccid; drooping); 柔软的 同 floppy, loose

24

□ evacuate	□ germicide	□ utopia	□ plateau	□ snobbish	□ nil
□ feline	□ bruise	□ lymphatic	□ abase	□ ban	□ accomplished
□ leach	□ infatuate	□ repressed	□ eulogy	□ pecan	□ limp

nomad [ˈnoʊmæd]	*n.* 流浪者(any wanderer)；游牧部落的人 记 联想记忆：no + mad(疯狂的) → 流浪者不疯也狂 → 流浪者
vitalize [ˈvaɪtəlaɪz]	*v.* 赋予生命，使有生气(to endow with life) 同 energize, exhilarate, invigorate, stimulate
execrable [ˈeksɪkrəbl]	*adj.* 可憎的，讨厌的(deserving to be execrated; abominable; detestable) 搭 execrable poetry 拙劣的诗
harpsichord [ˈhɑːrpsɪkɔːrd]	*n.* 键琴(钢琴的前身) 记 组合词：harp(竖琴) + si + chord(琴弦) → 键琴
inmate [ˈɪnmeɪt]	*n.* 同住者，同居者(any of a group occupying a single place of residence) 记 联想记忆：in + mate(配偶) → 配偶住在一起 → 同住者
molest [məˈlest]	*v.* 骚扰，困扰(to bother or annoy) 记 词根记忆：mol(磨) + est → 摩擦 → 骚扰
lattice [ˈlætɪs]	*n.* (用木片或金属片叠成的)格子架(a frame of crossed strips of wood or iron) 记 联想记忆：l + attic(阁楼) + e → 阁楼边上搭着一个格子架 → 格子架
secure [səˈkjʊr]	*adj.* 安全的(safe)；稳固的(steady) *v.* 握紧，关牢(to hold or close tightly)；使安全(to make safe) 记 联想记忆：se(看作 see，看) + cure(治愈) → 亲眼看到治愈，确定其是安全的 → 安全的 例 Liberty is not easy, but far better to be an unfettered fox, hungry and threatened on its hill, than a well-fed canary, safe and *secure* in its cage.

Man errs so long as he strives.
人只要奋斗就会犯错误。

——德国诗人、剧作家 歌德
(Johann Wolfgang Goethe, German poet and dramatist)

□ nomad　　□ vitalize　　□ execrable　　□ harpsichord　　□ inmate　　□ molest
□ lattice　　□ secure

traverse [trəˈvɜːrs]	*v.* 横穿，横跨(to go or travel across or over) 记 词根记忆：tra(穿过)+vers(转向)+e → 横穿，横跨	traverse
gist [dʒɪst]	*n.* 要点，要旨(the essence or main point) 记 联想记忆：和 list(*v.* 列出)一起记：list(列出) the gists(要点) 例 Peter has a bad habit of making digressive remarks that cause us to forget the *gist* of what he is saying.	
noxious [ˈnɑːkʃəs]	*adj.* 有害的，有毒的(injurious；pernicious) 记 词根记忆：nox(伤害) + ious → 有毒的	
insuperable [ɪnˈsuːpərəbl]	*adj.* 难以克服的(impossible to overcome) 记 词根记忆：in(不) + super(在…之上) + able → 不可超越的 → 难以克服的	
limousine [ˈlɪməziːn]	*n.* 大型轿车，(常指)大型豪华轿车(a large and usually luxurious car) 记 常简写为 limo	
implore [ɪmˈplɔːr]	*v.* 哀求，恳求(to beg) 记 词根记忆：im(进入) + plor(哭泣) + e → 哭泣 → 哀求	
mattress [ˈmætrəs]	*n.* 床垫(a large rectangular pad that is used to sleep on)	
nifty [ˈnɪfti]	*adj.* 极好的，极妙的(very good；very attractive) 同 great	
furbish [ˈfɜːrbɪʃ]	*v.* 磨光，刷新(to brighten by rubbing or scouring；polish) 记 注意不要和 furnish(*v.* 装饰；提供)相混 同 renovate	
privilege [ˈprɪvəlɪdʒ]	*n.* 特权，特殊利益(a right granted as a peculiar benefit, advantage, or favor) 记 词根记忆：priv(分开；个人) + i + leg(法律) + e → 在法律上将人分等级 → 特权	

□ traverse	□ gist	□ noxious	□ insuperable	□ limousine	□ implore
□ mattress	□ nifty	□ furbish	□ privilege		

sprint	*v.* 短距离全速奔跑(to run at top speed for a short distance)
[sprɪnt]	记 联想记忆：s + print（印刷）→ 像印刷机印钞票一样快地奔跑 → 短距离全速奔跑
persnickety	*adj.* 势利的(of a snob)；爱挑剔的(fussy；fastidious)
[pərˈsnɪkəti]	搭 a persnickety job 难以应付的工作
spark	*n.* 火花，火星(a small particle of a burning substance)
[spɑːrk]	记 联想记忆：s+park（公园）→ 公园是情侣们约会擦出感情火花的地方 → 火花
digestion	*n.* 消化，吸收(the action, process, or power of digesting)
[daɪˈdʒestʃən]	记 来自digest(*v.* 消化)
crass	*adj.* 愚钝的；粗糙的(crude and unrefined)
[kræs]	记 和class(*n.* 班级；课)一起记
confess	*v.* 承认，供认(to admit that one has done wrong)
[kənˈfes]	记 词根记忆：con(全部) + fess(说) → 全部说出 → 供认
abrogate	*v.* 废止，废除(to repeal by authority; abolish)
[ˈæbrəgeɪt]	记 词根记忆：ab(脱离) + rog(要求) + ate → 要求离开 → 废除
dissimulate	*v.* 隐藏，掩饰（感情、动机等）(to hide one's feelings or motives by pretense; dissemble)
[dɪˈsɪmjuleɪt]	记 词根记忆：dis(不) + simul(相同) + ate → 不和(本来面目)相同 → 掩饰
duress	*n.* 胁迫(the use of force or threats；compulsion)
[duˈres]	记 和dress(*v.* 穿衣)一起记
simile	*n.* 明喻((use of) comparison of one thing with another)
[ˈsɪməli]	记 词根记忆：simil(相类似的)+e → 把相类似的事物进行比较 → 明喻
aplomb	*n.* 沉着，镇静(complete and confident composure)
[əˈplɑːm]	记 联想记忆：apl（看作apple） + omb（看作tomb） → 坟墓中的苹果，很静 → 镇静
iridescence	*n.* 彩虹色(colors of rainbow)
[ˌɪrɪˈdesns]	记 词根记忆：irid(=iris 虹光) + escence → 彩虹色
idle	*adj.* (指人)无所事事的(avoiding work)；无效的(useless) *v.* 懒散，无所事事(to do nothing)
[ˈaɪdl]	记 发音记忆："爱斗" → 无所事事的人才爱斗 → 无所事事
lactic	*adj.* 乳汁的(of or relating to milk)
[ˈlæktɪk]	记 词根记忆：lact(乳) + ic → 乳汁的
byline	*n.* (报刊等的文章开头或结尾)标出作者名字的一行(a line identifying the writer)
[ˈbaɪlaɪn]	记 联想记忆：by + line（字行）→ 第二行 → 大标题下面写着作家姓名的一行 → 标出作者名字的一行
myopia	*n.* 近视；缺乏远见(lack of foresight or discernment)
[maɪˈoʊpiə]	记 词根记忆：my(闭上) + op(眼睛) + ia(表病) → 近视

idle

□ sprint	□ persnickety	□ spark	□ digestion	□ crass	□ confess
□ abrogate	□ dissimulate	□ duress	□ simile	□ aplomb	□ iridescence
□ idle	□ lactic	□ byline	□ myopia		

episode [ˈepɪsoʊd]	*n.* 一段情节（one event in a chain of events）；插曲，片断 同 circumstance, development, happening, incident
adolescent [ˌædəˈlesnt]	*adj.* 青春期的（of or typical of adolescence）*n.* 青少年（young person between childhood and adulthood） 记 联想记忆：ado（看作 adult，成人）+ lescent（看作 licence，许可证）→ 青少年即将拿到成年的许可证 → 青春期的
convoy [ˈkɑːnvɔɪ]	*v.* 护航，护送（to escort；accompany） 记 词根记忆：con + voy（路；看）→ 一路（照看）→ 护送
jab [dʒæb]	*v.* 猛刺（to make quick or abrupt thrusts with a sharp object） 记 联想记忆：和 job（*n.* 工作）一起记
restrain [rɪˈstreɪn]	*v.* 克制，抑制（to keep under control） 记 词根记忆：re（重新）+ strain（拉紧）→ 重新拉紧 → 克制，抑制
canopy [ˈkænəpi]	*n.* 蚊帐（a cloth covering suspended over a bed）；华盖（a drapery, awning, or other rooflike covering）
lubricant [ˈluːbrɪkənt]	*n.* 润滑剂（a substance for reducing friction） 记 词根记忆：lubric（光滑）+ ant → 润滑剂
boreal [ˈbɔːriəl]	*adj.* 北方的，北风的（of, relating to, or located in northern regions）
compunction [kəmˈpʌŋkʃn]	*n.* 懊悔；良心不安（a sense of guilt；remorse；penitence） 记 词根记忆：com+punct（刺，点）+ion → （心）不断被刺 → 良心不安
blasé [blɑːˈzeɪ]	*adj.* 厌倦享乐的，玩厌了的（bored with pleasure or dissipation） 记 联想记忆：对责骂（blame）已经厌倦（blasé）
enclosure [ɪnˈkloʊʒər]	*n.* 圈地，围场（the act or action of enclosing） 记 词根记忆：en + clos（=close）+ ure → 进入围绕状态 → 圈地 例 From the outset, the concept of freedom of the seas from the proprietary claims of nations was challenged by a contrary notion—that of the *enclosure* of the oceans for reasons of national security and profit.
comatose [ˈkoʊmətoʊs]	*adj.* 昏迷的（unconscious；torpid） 记 来自 coma（*n.* 昏迷）
vanquish [ˈvæŋkwɪʃ]	*v.* 征服，击溃（to defeat in a conflict or contest；subdue） 同 conquer, crush, rout, subjugate
ravish [ˈrævɪʃ]	*v.* 使着迷（to overcome with emotion）；强夺（to take away by force） 记 词根记忆：rav（抓，抢夺）+ ish → 夺去注意力 → 使着迷；注意不要和 lavish（*v.* 浪费）相混
spout [spaʊt]	*v.* 喷出（to eject in a stream）；滔滔不绝地讲（to speak readily） 记 联想记忆：sp（看作 speak，说）+out（出）→ 一直不停地说话 → 滔滔不绝地讲
lasting [ˈlæstɪŋ]	*adj.* 持久的，永久的（continuing for a long time） 同 enduring

25

□ episode	□ adolescent	□ convoy	□ jab	□ restrain	□ canopy
□ lubricant	□ boreal	□ compunction	□ blasé	□ enclosure	□ comatose
□ vanquish	□ ravish	□ spout	□ lasting		

273

exculpate [ˈekskʌlpeɪt]	*v.* 开脱（to free from blame）；申明无罪，证明无罪（to declare or prove guiltless） 记 词根记忆：ex(出) + culp(指责) + ate → 使不受指责 → 开脱
boulder [ˈboʊldər]	*n.* 巨砾（large rock worn by water or the weather） 记 联想记忆：用肩膀（shoulder）扛着巨砾（boulder）
deputy [ˈdepjuti]	*n.* 代表（a person appointed to act for another）；副手 记 联想记忆：de + puty（看作 duty，责任）→ 代理人应负责 → 代表
illustrious [ɪˈlʌstriəs]	*adj.* 著名的，显赫的（very distinguished；outstanding） 记 词根记忆：il(进入) + lus(光) + tr + ious → 进入光中 → 著名的
mellifluous [meˈlɪfluəs]	*adj.* （音乐等）柔美流畅的（sweetly or smoothly flowing） 记 词根记忆：melli(蜂蜜) + flu(流) + ous → 像蜂蜜一样流出来的 → 柔美流畅的 例 The combination of elegance and earthiness in Edmund's speech can be startling, especially when he slyly slips in some juicy vulgarity amid the *mellifluous* circumlocutions of a gentleman of the old school.
depose [dɪˈpoʊz]	*v.* 免职（to remove from office or a position of power）；宣誓作证（to state by affidavit） 记 词根记忆：de + pose(放) → 放下去 → 免职
grotesque [groʊˈtesk]	*adj.* （外形或方式）怪诞的，古怪的（bizarre；fantastic）；（艺术等）风格怪异的 记 来自 grotto(岩洞) + picturesque(图画的)，原意为"岩洞里的图画" → （绘画，雕刻等）怪诞的 → （艺术等）风格怪异的
clement [ˈklemənt]	*adj.* 仁慈的（merciful）；温和的（mild） 搭 clement weather 温和的气候
emasculate [iˈmæskjuleɪt]	*v.* 使柔弱（to weaken）；阉割（to castrate）*adj.* 柔弱的 记 词根记忆：e(不) + mascul(男人) + ate → 不让做男人 → 阉割
jug [dʒʌg]	*v.* 用陶罐等炖（(to stew) in an earthenware vessel）；关押（to jail; imprison）
august [ɔːˈgʌst]	*adj.* 威严的，令人敬畏的（impressive; majestic） 记 联想记忆：八月（August）丰收大地金黄，金黄色是威严的帝王的象征 → 威严的
testify [ˈtestɪfaɪ]	*v.* 见证，证实（to bear witness to） 记 词根记忆：test(看到)+ify → 见证，证实
embolden [ɪmˈboʊldən]	*v.* 鼓励（to give confidence to sb.） 记 词根记忆：em + bold(大胆) + en → 使人大胆 → 鼓励
fermentation [ˌfɜːrmenˈteɪʃn]	*n.* 发酵（a chemical change with effervescence；ferment） 记 来自 ferment（*v.* 使发酵）

□ exculpate □ boulder □ deputy □ illustrious □ mellifluous □ depose
□ grotesque □ clement □ emasculate □ jug □ august □ testify
□ embolden □ fermentation

buoy [ˈbuːi]	*n.* 浮标(a floating object); 救生圈 *v.* 支持，鼓励(to encourage) 同 animate, elate, exhilarate, flush, inspirit
apologize [əˈpɑːlədʒaɪz]	*v.* 道歉(to say one is sorry); 辩解(to make a formal defence) 记 词根记忆：apo(远) + log(说话) + ize → 离(别人)远一点说话，不面对面骂 → 道歉
rumple [ˈrʌmpl]	*v.* 弄皱，弄乱(to make or become disheveled or tousled) 记 联想记忆：rum(看作 room，房间)+ple(看作 people，人) → 房间里面来了好多人，把房间弄乱了 → 弄乱
whoop [huːp]	*n.* 高喊，欢呼(a loud yell expressive of eagerness, exuberance, or jubilation)
unification [ˌjuːnɪfɪˈkeɪʃn]	*n.* 统一，一致(the result of unifying) 记 来自 unify(*v.* 统一)
enunciate [ɪˈnʌnsieɪt]	*v.* 发音(to pronounce clearly and distinctly; utter); (清楚地)表达(to state definitely; express in a systematic way) 记 词根记忆：e(出) + nunci(=nounce 报告，说) + ate → 说出来 → 发音，表达
char [tʃɑːr]	*v.* 烧焦(to make or become black by burning); 把…烧成炭 记 联想记忆：椅子(chair)的一个腿(i)儿被烧焦(char)了
frisk [frɪsk]	*n.* 欢跃，蹦跳(a lively, playful movement) *v.* 欢跃，嬉戏 记 联想记忆：f(看作 for) + risk(冒险) → 欢跃不是冒险 → 欢跃
fleece [fliːs]	*n.* 生羊皮，羊毛(the wool covering a sheep; wool) *v.* 骗取，欺诈(to strip of money or property by fraud or extortion) 记 联想记忆：flee(逃跑) + ce → 骗完钱就跑 → 骗取
impasse [ˈɪmpæs]	*n.* 僵局(deadlock); 死路(blind alley) 记 联想记忆：im(不) + pass(通过) + e → 通不过 → 僵局；死路
dismay [dɪsˈmeɪ]	*n.* 沮丧，气馁(feeling of shock and discouragement) *v.* 使气馁 记 词根记忆：dis(不) + may(可能) → 不可能做 → 沮丧 搭 to one's dismay 令…沮丧
even-tempered [ˌiːvn ˈtempərd]	*adj.* 性情平和的(placid; calm); 不易生气的(not easily angered or excited)
pullet [ˈpʊlɪt]	*n.* 小母鸡(a young hen during its first year of laying eggs) 记 联想记忆：子弹(bullet)打中了小母鸡(pullet)
allergic [əˈlɜːrdʒɪk]	*adj.* 过敏的(of allergy); 对…讨厌的(averse or disinclined)
martyr [ˈmɑːrtər]	*n.* 烈士，殉道者(any of those persons who choose to suffer or die rather than give up their faith or principles) 记 词根记忆：本身为词根，指"目击者"

25

□ buoy	□ apologize	□ rumple	□ whoop	□ unification	□ enunciate
□ char	□ frisk	□ fleece	□ impasse	□ dismay	□ even-tempered
□ pullet	□ allergic	□ martyr			

daub	*v.* 涂抹(to cover or smear with sticky, soft matter); 乱画(to paint coarsely or unskillfully)
[dɔːb]	
interlace	*v.* 编织(to weave together); 交错(to connect intricately)
[ˌɪntərˈleɪs]	记 词根记忆: inter(在…中间) + lac(线) + e → 使线在中间交叉 → 编织
intensify	*v.* 使加剧(to cause to become more intense)
[ɪnˈtensɪfaɪ]	记 来自 intense(*adj.* 强烈的)
confidential	*adj.* 机密的(kept secret)
[ˌkɑːnfɪˈdenʃl]	记 联想记忆: confident(相信) + ial → 亲信才知道 → 机密的
ennoble	*v.* 授予爵位, 使高贵(to make noble)
[ɪˈnoʊbl]	记 词根记忆: en(使) + noble(贵族; 高贵的) → 使高贵
wiry	*adj.* 瘦而结实的(being lean, supple, and vigorous)
[ˈwaɪəri]	
consent	*v.* 同意, 允许(to give agreement)
[kənˈsent]	记 词根记忆: con(共同) + sent(感觉) → 有共同的感觉 → 同意
woo	*v.* 求爱, 求婚(to sue for the affection of and usually marriage with; court); 恳求, 争取(to solicit or entreat especially with importunity)
[wuː]	
accrue	*v.* (利息等)增加(to increase the interest on money); 积累(to accumulate)
[əˈkruː]	记 词根记忆: ac(加强) + cru(增长)+te → 更加增长 → 增加; 积累
sullen	*adj.* 忧郁的(dismal; gloomy)
[ˈsʌlən]	同 brooding, morose, sulky
annoy	*v.* 惹恼(to cause slight anger); 打搅, 骚扰(to cause trouble to sb.)
[əˈnɔɪ]	同 bother, chafe, irritate, nettle, rile, vex
manifesto	*n.* 宣言, 声明(a public declaration)
[ˌmænɪˈfestoʊ]	记 来自 manifest(*vt.* 表明)
oxidize	*v.* 氧化, 生锈(to combine with oxygen)
[ˈɑːksɪdaɪz]	记 联想记忆: oxid(e)(氧化物) + ize → 氧化
spite	*n.* 怨恨, 恶意(petty ill will or hatred)
[spaɪt]	搭 in spite of 尽管, 不管, 不顾
enthralling	*adj.* 迷人的, 吸引人的(holding the complete attention and interest of as if by magic)
[ɪnˈθrɔːlɪŋ]	记 联想记忆: en(使) + thrall(奴隶) + ing → 成为(爱的)奴隶的 → 迷人的
incogitant	*adj.* 未经思考的, 考虑不周的(thoughtless; inconsiderate)
[ɪnˈkɑːdʒɪtənt]	记 词根记忆: in(不) + co(共同) + g(=ag 开动) + it + ant → 不开动脑筋的 → 未经思考的
unassuming	*adj.* 不摆架子的, 不装腔作势的, 谦逊的 (not arrogant or presuming; modest)
[ˌʌnəˈsuːmɪŋ]	记 联想记忆: un(不) + assuming(傲慢的) → 谦逊的
anneal	*v.* 使(金属、玻璃等)退火; 使加强, 使变硬(to strengthen or harden)
[əˈniːl]	

□ daub	□ interlace	□ intensify	□ confidential	□ ennoble	□ wiry
□ consent	□ woo	□ accrue	□ sullen	□ annoy	□ manifesto
□ oxidize	□ spite	□ enthralling	□ incogitant	□ unassuming	□ anneal

disinter	*v.* 挖出，掘出(to unearth; remove from a grave, tomb)
[ˌdɪsɪnˈtɜːr]	记 词根记忆：dis(除去) + inter(埋葬) → 把埋葬的(东西)掘出 → 挖出
debark	*v.* 下船，下飞机，下车；卸载(客、货)
[dɪˈbɑːrk]	记 词根记忆：de(下) + bark(船) → 下船
celerity	*n.* 快速，迅速(swiftness in acting or moving; speed)
[sɪˈlerəti]	记 词根记忆：celer(速度) + ity → 快速，迅速
forfeiture	*n.* (名誉等)丧失(the act of forfeiting)
[ˈfɔːrfətʃər]	记 来自forfeit(*v.* 被没收)
malfeasance	*n.* 不法行为，渎职(misconduct by a public official)
[ˌmælˈfiːzəns]	记 词根记忆：mal(坏的) + feas(做，行为) + ance → 坏的行为 → 不法行为
corrupt	*adj.* 腐败的，堕落的(venal; immoral)；(语言、版本等)讹误的，走样的((of language, text, etc.) containing errors or changes) *v.* 使腐败，使堕落
[kəˈrʌpt]	记 词根记忆：cor(全部) + rupt(断) → 全断了 → 腐败的
	搭 corrupt the morals of 败坏…的道德
scurvy	*adj.* 卑鄙的，下流的(despicable)
[ˈskɜːrvi]	记 不要和scurry(*v.* 急跑，疾行)相混
ogle	*v.* 送秋波(to eye amorously or provocatively) *n.* 媚眼(an amorous or coquettish glance)
[ˈoʊɡl]	
weld	*v.* 焊接，熔接，锻接(to unite or reunite)
[weld]	搭 weld leg 焊脚
pharmacology	*n.* 药理学，药物学；药理
[ˌfɑːrməˈkɑːlədʒi]	
vouch	*v.* 担保，保证(to guarantee the reliability of)
[vaʊtʃ]	例 I can *vouch* for his honesty; I have always found him veracious and carefully observant of the truth.
cringing	*n./adj.* 谄媚(的)，奉承(的)
[ˈkrɪndʒɪŋ]	记 联想记忆：cring(= cringe 畏缩) + ing → 一直向后退缩 → 谄媚的
wheedle	*v.* 哄骗，诱骗(to influence or entice by soft words or flattery)
[ˈwiːdl]	同 cajole, coax, seduce
careen	*v.* (船)倾斜(to lean sideways)；使倾斜(to cause a ship to lean)
[kəˈriːn]	记 联想记忆：船倾斜(careen)了，但船家并不在意(care)
peculate	*v.* 挪用(公款)(to embezzle)
[ˈpekjuleɪt]	记 词根记忆：pecu(原义为"牛"，引申为"钱财") + lat(搬运) + e → 把公有钱财搬回家里 → 挪用(公款)
vandalism	*n.* (对公物等的)恶意破坏(willful or malicious destruction or defacement of public or private property)
[ˈvændəlɪzəm]	例 The acts of *vandalism* that these pranksters had actually perpetrated were insignificant compared with those they had contemplated but had not attempted.

□ disinter	□ debark	□ celerity	□ forfeiture	□ malfeasance	□ corrupt
□ scurvy	□ ogle	□ weld	□ pharmacology	□ vouch	□ cringing
□ wheedle	□ careen	□ peculate	□ vandalism		

anguish [ˈæŋɡwɪʃ]	*n.* 极大的痛苦(great suffering; distress) 记 词根记忆: angu(痛苦) + ish → 极大的痛苦
entreaty [ɪnˈtriːti]	*n.* 恳求, 哀求(an act of entreating; plea) 记 来自 entreat (v. 恳求)
oratory [ˈɔːrətɔːri]	*n.* 演讲术(the art of making good speeches) 记 来自 orate (v. 演讲)
entrance [ˈentrəns]	*v.* 使出神, 使入迷(to fill with great wonder and delight as if by magic) 记 来自 enter (v. 进入)
desert [dɪˈzɜːrt]	*v.* 遗弃, 离弃(to abandon) 记 词根记忆: de(分开) + sert(加入) → 不再加入 → 离弃
effulgent [ɪˈfʌldʒənt]	*adj.* 灿烂的, 光辉的(of great brightness) 记 词根记忆: ef + fulg(闪亮) + ent → 闪亮的 → 灿烂的
abolish [əˈbɑːlɪʃ]	*v.* 废止, 废除(法律、制度、习俗等)(to end the observance or effect of) 记 联想记忆: ab(脱离) + (p)olish(抛光, 优雅) → 不优雅的东西就应该废除 → 废除
compatible [kəmˈpætəbl]	*adj.* 能和谐共处的, 相容的(capable of living together harmoniously) 记 词根记忆: com(一起) + pat(=path 感情) + ible → 有共同感情的 → 相容的 搭 be compatible with 与…和谐相处
thermal [ˈθɜːrml]	*adj.* 热的, 热量的(pertaining to heat); 温暖的(warm) *n.* 上升的暖气流(a rising current of warm air)
bribe [braɪb]	*v.* 贿赂(to induce or influence by bribery)
amass [əˈmæs]	*v.* 积聚(to collect; gather; accumulate) 记 联想记忆: a + mass(一团) → 变成一团 → 积聚
encomiast [enˈkoʊmiæst]	*n.* 赞美者(a person who delivers or writes an encomium; a eulogist) 记 联想记忆: en + com(看作 come) + iast → 有目的而来的人 → 赞美者
carouse [kəˈraʊz]	*n.* 狂饮寻乐(a noisy, merry drinking party) 记 联想记忆: car + (r)ouse(唤起) → 开着汽车欢闹 → 狂饮寻乐
dally [ˈdæli]	*v.* 闲荡, 嬉戏(to waste time; loiter; trifle) 记 和 daily(*adj.* 每日的)一起记
cephalic [sɪˈfælɪk]	*adj.* 头的, 头部的(of the head or skull) 记 词根记忆: cephal(头) + ic → 头的
pellucid [pəˈluːsɪd]	*adj.* 清晰的, 清澈的(transparent; clear) 记 词根记忆: pel(=per 全部) + luc(光) + id → 光线充足的 → 清晰的
wan [wɑːn]	*adj.* 虚弱的(feeble); 病态的(sickly pallid) 同 ghastly, haggard, sallow
preponderate [prɪˈpɑːndəreɪt]	*v.* 超过, 胜过(to exceed) 记 词根记忆: pre(在…之前) + pond(重量) + er + ate → 重量超过前面 → 超过, 胜过

□ anguish	□ entreaty	□ oratory	□ entrance	□ desert	□ effulgent
□ abolish	□ compatible	□ thermal	□ bribe	□ amass	□ encomiast
□ carouse	□ dally	□ cephalic	□ pellucid	□ wan	□ preponderate

homely [ˈhoʊmli]	*adj.* 朴素的(simple and unpretentious); 不漂亮的(plain or unattractive)
	记 联想记忆: home(家) + ly → 家庭用的 → 朴素的
snuggle [ˈsnʌɡl]	*v.* 紧靠, 依偎(to draw close for comfort or in affection)
	记 联想记忆: snug(温暖的) + gle → 依偎在一起感觉很温暖 → 依偎
spontaneous [spɑːnˈteɪniəs]	*adj.* 自发的(proceeding from natural feelings); 自然的(natural)
	记 词根记忆: spont(自然)+aneous → 自然产生的 → 自发的
	例 The Battle of Lexington was not, as most of us have been taught, a *spontaneous* rising of individual farmers, but was instead a tightly organized, well-planned event.
disparity [dɪˈspærəti]	*n.* 不同, 差异(inequality or difference)
	搭 the wide disparity between rich and poor 贫富悬殊
offend [əˈfend]	*v.* 得罪, 冒犯(to be displeasing; violate)
	搭 offend against sb. 触犯、冒犯或得罪某人
blackball [ˈblækbɔːl]	*v.* 投票反对(to vote against); 排斥(to ostracize)
	记 组合词: black(黑) + ball(投票) → 投票反对
flush [flʌʃ]	*v.* 脸红(to become red in the face; blush); 奔流(to flow and spread suddenly and rapidly); 冲洗(to pour liquid over or through) *n.* 激动; 脸红
	记 和 blush(*v.* 脸红)一起记
hubris [ˈhjuːbrɪs]	*n.* 傲慢, 目中无人(overbearing pride or presumption; arrogance)
	记 联想记忆: hub(中心) + ris(看作 rise, 升起) → 中心升起 → 以(自我)为中心 → 目中无人
riveting [ˈrɪvɪtɪŋ]	*adj.* 非常精彩的, 引人入胜的(engrossing; fascinating)
	例 The English novelist William Thackeray considered the cult of the criminal so dangerous that he criticized Dickens' *Oliver Twist* for making the characters in the thieves' kitchen so *riveting*.
tutor [ˈtuːtər]	*n.* 助教(an assistant lecturer in a college); 导师, 辅导教师(one that gives additional, special, or remedial instruction); 监护人(the legal guardian of a minor and of the minor's property) *v.* 辅导, 指导(to give instruction to)
encyclopedia [ɪnˌsaɪkləˈpiːdiə]	*n.* 百科全书(books dealing with every branch of knowledge or with one particular branch)
	记 联想记忆: en + cyclo(看作 cycle, 全套) + ped(儿童) + ia → 为儿童提供全套教育 → 百科全书
shabby [ˈʃæbi]	*adj.* 破旧的(dilapidated); 卑鄙的(despicable; contemptible)
	同 scruffy; shoddy
moat [moʊt]	*n.* 壕沟, 护城河(a deep, wide trench around the rampart of a fortified place that is usually filled with water)
deprivation [ˌdeprɪˈveɪʃn]	*n.* 剥夺(removal from an office, dignity, or benefice); 丧失(the state of being deprived)
	记 来自 deprive(*v.* 剥夺)

小学数学咋这么难
tutor

25

□ homely	□ snuggle	□ spontaneous	□ disparity	□ offend	□ blackball
□ flush	□ hubris	□ riveting	□ tutor	□ encyclopedia	□ shabby
□ moat	□ deprivation				

heckle [ˈhekl]	*v.* 诘问，责问（to annoy or harass by interrupting with questions or taunts） 记 联想记忆：he(他) + ckle(看作 buckle，扣上) → 他因无故把人扣住不放受到诘问 → 诘问
compulsion [kəmˈpʌlʃn]	*n.* 强迫（that which compels）；（难以抗拒的）冲动（an irresistible, irrational impulse to perform some act） 记 词根记忆：com(一起) + puls(推，冲) + ion → 一起推 → 强迫
musket [ˈmʌskɪt]	*n.* 旧式步枪，毛瑟枪（a type of gun used in former times） 记 联想记忆：想把毛瑟枪(musket)藏在篮筐(basket)里
evasion [ɪˈveɪʒn]	*n.* 躲避，借口（a means of evading） 记 词根记忆：e(出) + vas(走) + ion → 走出去 → 躲避
habitable [ˈhæbɪtəbl]	*adj.* 可居住的（capable of being lived in; suitable for habitation） 记 词根记忆：habit(居) + able(可…的) → 可居住的
demonstrative [dɪˈmɑːnstrətɪv]	*adj.* 证明的，论证的（demonstrating as real or true）；感情流露的（showing the feelings readily）
snarl [snɑːrl]	*v.* 纠缠，混乱（to intertwine; tangle）；咆哮，怒骂（to growl）*n.* 纠缠，混乱；怒吼声，咆哮声 同 knot
grumpy [ˈɡrʌmpi]	*adj.* 脾气暴躁的（grouchy; peevish） 记 来自 grump(*v.* 发脾气，生气) 例 The *grumpy* man found fault with everything.
compress [kəmˈpres]	*v.* 压缩；压紧（to press together; contract） 记 词根记忆：com(全部) + press(挤压) → 全部挤压 → 压缩
passive [ˈpæsɪv]	*adj.* 被动的，缺乏活力的（not active; submissive） 记 词根记忆：pass(感情) + ive(…的) → 感情用事的 → 被动的 例 The amusements of modern urban people tend more and more to be *passive* and to consist of the observation of the skilled activities of others.
tangy [ˈtæŋi]	*adj.* 气味刺激的，扑鼻的（having a pleasantly sharp flavor）
impeach [ɪmˈpiːtʃ]	*v.* 控告（to accuse）；怀疑（to challenge or discredit; accuse）；弹劾（to charge with a crime or misdemeanor） 记 联想记忆：im(进入) + peach(告发) → 控告；弹劾
snappy [ˈsnæpi]	*adj.* 生气勃勃的（marked by vigor or liveliness）；漂亮的，时髦的（stylish; smart）
applicant [ˈæplɪkənt]	*n.* 申请人（person who applies, especially for a job） 同 applier, proposer
acrid [ˈækrɪd]	*adj.* 辛辣的，刻薄的（bitterly pungent; bitter; sharp）
muster [ˈmʌstər]	*v.* 召集，聚集（to gather or summon） 记 联想记忆：主人(master)有权召集(muster)家丁们

schematize [ˈskiːmətaɪz]	*v.* 扼要表示(to express or depict in an outline)
integral [ˈɪntɪɡrəl]	*adj.* 构成整体所必需的(necessary for completeness); 完整的(whole) 记 词根记忆: in(不) + tegr(触摸) + al → 未被触摸的 → 完整的
cession [ˈseʃn]	*n.* 割让, 转让 记 来自 cede(*v.* 割让)
pittance [ˈpɪtns]	*n.* 微薄的薪俸, 少量的收入(a meager monetary allowance, wage, or remuneration); 少量(a very small amount)
maul [mɔːl]	*v.* 打伤, 伤害(to injure by or as if by beating; lacerate) 记 联想记忆: 和 haul(*n./v.* 用力拖)一起记
leisureliness [ˈliːʒərlinəs]	*n.* 悠然, 从容 记 来自 leisurely(*adj.* 悠然的)
shattered [ˈʃætərd]	*adj.* 破碎的 记 来自 shatter(*v.* 粉碎)
perverse [pərˈvɜːrs]	*adj.* 刚愎自用的, 固执的(obstinate in opposing; wrongheaded) 记 词根记忆: per(始终) + vers(转) + e → 始终和别人反着转 → 固执的
tensile [ˈtensl]	*adj.* 张力的(of, or relating to tension); 可伸展的(capable of being stretched)
nadir [ˈneɪdɪr]	*n.* 最低点(the lowest point) 搭 the nadir of one's career 某人事业上的低谷
lustrous [ˈlʌstrəs]	*adj.* 有光泽的(having luster; bright) 记 来自 luster(*n.* 光辉; 光泽)
ooze [uːz]	*v.* 慢慢地流, 渗出(to leak out slowly); (勇气)逐渐消失 记 联想记忆: oo(像水渗出来时冒的泡泡) + ze → 渗出
maple [ˈmeɪpl]	*n.* 枫树 记 联想记忆: 和 apple(*n.* 苹果)一起记
comeuppance [kʌmˈʌpəns]	*n.* 应得的惩罚, 因果报应(a deserved rebuke or penalty) 记 联想记忆: come up(发生) + p + ance(表名词) → 某些信念认为世上发生(come up)的所有坏事都是有因果报应的 → 因果报应

□ schematize	□ integral	□ cession	□ pittance	□ maul	□ leisureliness
□ shattered	□ perverse	□ tensile	□ nadir	□ lustrous	□ ooze
□ maple	□ comeuppance				

extrude [ɪk'struːd]	v. 挤出，推出，逐出（to force or push out; thrust out）；伸出，突出（to protrude）
	记 词根记忆：ex + trud(刺) + e → 向外刺 → 挤出
motility [moʊ'tɪləti]	n. 运动性
	记 词根记忆：mot(动) + ility → 运动性
forensic [fə'rensɪk]	adj. 公开辩论的，争论的（of public debate or formal argumentation）
	记 来自 forum(n. 讨论会)
contiguous [kən'tɪɡjuəs]	adj. 接壤的；接近的（near, adjacent）
	记 词根记忆：con(共同) + tig(接触) + uous → 共同接触 → 接近的
	搭 be contiguous with 与…接壤
mode [moʊd]	n. 样式（style or fashion in clothes, art, etc.）；模式；方式，形式；时尚，风尚
	例 Irony can, after a fashion, become a *mode* of escape: to laugh at the terrors of life is in some sense to evade them.
abject ['æbdʒekt]	adj. 极可怜的（miserable; wretched）；卑下的（degraded; base）
	记 词根记忆：ab(脱离) + ject(抛，扔) → 被人抛弃的 → 极可怜的
shrewd [ʃruːd]	adj. 机灵的，精明的（marked by clever discerning awareness）
	记 注意不要和 shrew(n. 泼妇)相混
worship ['wɜːrʃɪp]	n. 崇拜，敬仰（strong feelings of love, respect, and admiration） v. 崇拜，敬仰（to regard with great or extravagant respect, honor, or devotion）
arouse [ə'raʊz]	v. 唤醒（to wake up）；激发（to cause to become active）
	同 brace, energize, stimulate, stir
magnitude ['mæɡnɪtuːd]	n. 重要性（greatness）；星球的亮度（the degree of brightness of a celestial body）
	记 词根记忆：magn(大的) + itude(表状态) → 大的状态 → 重要性
pilot ['paɪlət]	n. 飞行员（one who operates the controls of an aircraft）；领航员（the person who is licensed to guide ships through a canal, the entrance to a harbour, etc.）
dawdle ['dɔːdl]	v. 闲荡，虚度光阴（to waste time in trifling; idle; loiter）
	记 联想记忆：daw(n)(黎明) + dle → 漫无目的地游荡到黎明 → 闲荡
malaise [mə'leɪz]	n. 不适，不舒服（a feeling of illness）
	记 发音记忆："没累死" → 差点没累死 → 不适
dismantle [dɪs'mæntl]	v. 拆除（to take a part; disassemble）
	记 词根记忆：dis(除去) + mantle(覆盖物) → 拆掉覆盖物 → 拆除
zigzag ['zɪɡzæɡ]	n. 之字形 adj. 之字形的 v. 弯弯曲曲地行进
	搭 a zigzag path 弯曲的羊肠小道
sneaking ['sniːkɪŋ]	adj. 鬼鬼祟祟的，私下的（furtive; underhanded）
	搭 sneaking suspicion 私下怀疑
protuberant [proʊ'tuːbərənt]	adj. 突出的，隆起的（thrusting out; prominent）
	记 词根记忆：pro(向前) + tuber(块茎) + ant → 像块茎一样突出的 → 突出的

282

☐ extrude ☐ motility ☐ forensic ☐ contiguous ☐ mode ☐ abject
☐ shrewd ☐ worship ☐ arouse ☐ magnitude ☐ pilot ☐ dawdle
☐ malaise ☐ dismantle ☐ zigzag ☐ sneaking ☐ protuberant

lateral [ˈlætərəl]	*adj.* 侧面的(of, at, from, or towards the side) 记 词根记忆：later(侧面) + al → 侧面的
disaster [dɪˈzæstər]	*n.* 灾难，灾祸，不幸(calamity; catastrophe; cataclysm) 记 词根记忆：dis(离开) + aster(星星) → 离开星星，星位不正 → 灾难
twee [twiː]	*adj.* 矫揉造作的，故作多情的(affectedly or excessively dainty, delicate, cute, or quaint)
crafty [ˈkræfti]	*adj.* 狡诈的(subtly deceitful; sly)；灵巧的(proficient) 记 来自 craft(*n.* 手腕，技巧)
stain [steɪn]	*v.* 玷污(to taint with guilt or corruption)；染色(to color by processes) 记 联想记忆：一下雨(rain)，到处都是污点(stain)
doleful [ˈdoʊlfl]	*adj.* 悲哀的，忧郁的(full of sorrow or sadness) 记 词根记忆：dole(悲哀) + ful → 悲哀的
culprit [ˈkʌlprɪt]	*n.* 罪犯(one who is guilty of a crime) 记 联想记忆：犯罪(sin)的人被称为罪犯(culprit)
nettle [ˈnetl]	*n.* 荨麻 *v.* 烦忧，激怒(to irritate; provoke) 记 联想记忆：用 nettle(荨麻)织网(net)
reminisce [ˌremɪˈnɪs]	*v.* 追忆，回想(to indulge in reminiscence) 记 词根记忆：re(重新) + min(=mind 思维) + isce → 重新回到思维中 → 追忆
assuage [əˈsweɪdʒ]	*v.* 缓和，减轻(to lessen; relieve) 记 词根记忆：as + suage(甜) → 变甜 → 缓和
oleaginous [ˌoʊliˈædʒɪnəs]	*adj.* 油腻的(of or relating to oil)；圆滑的，满口恭维的(falsely or smugly earnest; unctuous)
inadvertently [ˌɪnədˈvɜːrtəntli]	*adv.* 不小心地，疏忽地(by accident) 记 来自 inadvertent(*adj.* 疏忽的)
remit [rɪˈmɪt]	*v.* 免除(to refrain from inflicting)；宽恕(to release from the guilt or penalty of)；汇款(to send money)
ruminate [ˈruːmɪneɪt]	*v.* 反刍；深思(to turn sth. over in the mind; meditate) 同 cogitate, contemplate, deliberate, ponder
variegate [ˈveriɡeɪt]	*v.* 使多样化，使色彩斑斓(to exhibit different colors, especially as irregular patches or streaks) 记 词根记忆：vari(变化) + eg(做) + ate → 做出变化 → 使多样化
wallow [ˈwɑːloʊ]	*v.* 打滚(to roll the body about in or as if in water, snow, or mud)；沉迷(to take unrestrained pleasure) *n.* 打滚(the act or an instance of wallowing) 记 联想记忆：wal(看作 wall，墙)+low(地势低的) → 在墙底下打滚 → 打滚
lumber [ˈlʌmbər]	*v.* 跌跌撞撞地走，笨拙地走(to move with heavy clumsiness) *n.* 杂物(miscellaneous discarded household articles)；木材(timber)
menthol [ˈmenθɔːl]	*n.* 薄荷醇(a white substance which smells and tastes of mint)

26

□ lateral	□ disaster	□ twee	□ crafty	□ stain	□ doleful
□ culprit	□ nettle	□ reminisce	□ assuage	□ oleaginous	□ inadvertently
□ remit	□ ruminate	□ variegate	□ wallow	□ lumber	□ menthol

persecute	*v.* 迫害（to oppress or harass with ill treatment）
[ˈpɜːrsɪkjuːt]	记 词根记忆：per（始终）+ secut（跟随）+ e → 坏事一直跟着 → 迫害
stealth	*n.* 秘密行动（the action of moving or acting secretly）
[stelθ]	记 来自 steal（*v.* 偷）
rigor	*n.* 严厉，严格，苛刻（severity；strictness）；严密，精确（strict precision）
[ˈrɪgər]	例 By identifying scientific *rigor* with a quantitative approach, researchers in the social sciences may often have limited their scope to those narrowly circumscribed topics that are well suited to quantitative methods.
stanza	*n.* （诗的）节，段（a division of a poem consisting of a series of lines）
[ˈstænzə]	记 词根记忆：stan（站住）+ za → 诗中停顿的地方 → 节，段
rumpus	*n.* 喧闹，骚乱（a usually noisy commotion）
[ˈrʌmpəs]	同 clamor, tumult, uproar
misshapen	*adj.* 畸形的，奇形怪状的（badly shaped）
[ˌmɪsˈʃeɪpən]	记 联想记忆：mis（坏的）+ shapen（形状的）→ 畸形的
spleen	*n.* 怒气（feelings of anger）
[spliːn]	同 rancor, resentment, wrath
writ	*n.* 令状（a written order issued by a court, commanding the party to whom it is addressed to perform or cease performing a specified act）；书面命令（an order in writing）
[rɪt]	记 联想记忆：write 去掉 e 就变成了 writ
lukewarm	*adj.* 微温的，不冷不热的（not very warm or enthusiastic）
[ˌluːkˈwɔːrm]	记 词根记忆：luke（微温的）+ warm（温暖的）→ 微温的
fold	*n.* 羊栏（a pen in which to keep sheep）*v.* 折叠（to lay one part over another part of）
[foʊld]	记 联想记忆：f + old（旧）→ 旧东西有许多褶 → 折叠
obeisance	*n.* 鞠躬，敬礼（a gesture of respect or reverence）
[oʊˈbiːsns]	记 词根记忆：ob（加强）+ eis（=aud 听话）+ ance → 表示听话 → 鞠躬
mirage	*n.* 海市蜃楼；幻想，幻影（sth. illusory and unattainable）
[məˈrɑːʒ]	记 词根记忆：mir（惊奇）+ age → 使人惊奇之物 → 海市蜃楼
peremptory	*adj.* 不容反抗的；专横的（masterful）
[pəˈremptəri]	记 词根记忆：per（加强）+ empt（抓）+ ory → 采取强硬态度的 → 专横的
beget	*v.* 产生，引起（to bring into being; produce）
[bɪˈget]	记 联想记忆：be + get（得到）→ 确实得到了 → 产生
scatter	*v.* 散开，驱散（to separate or cause to separate widely）
[ˈskætər]	同 dispel, disperse, dissipate
choleric	*adj.* 易怒的，暴躁的（having irascible nature; irritable）
[ˈkɑːlərɪk]	记 词根记忆：choler（胆汁）+ ic → 胆汁质的 → 易怒的，暴躁的
jeer	*v.* 嘲笑（to mock; taunt; scoff at）
[dʒɪr]	搭 jeer at 嘲笑

spate [speɪt]	*n.* 许多，大量（a large number or amount）；（水流）暴涨，发洪水（flood） 搭 a spate of 一连串，接二连三（通常指不愉快的事物）
aspirant [ə'spaɪərənt]	*n.* 有抱负者（a person who aspires after honors or high positions） 同 aspirer
incubation [ˌɪŋkju'beɪʃn]	*n.* 孵卵期，潜伏期（the phase of development of a disease between the infection and the first appearance of symptoms）
merited ['merɪtɪd]	*adj.* 该得的，理所当然的（deserving, worthy of） 记 联想记忆：merit（价值）+ ed → 值得的 → 该得的
invoke [ɪn'voʊk]	*v.* 祈求，恳求（to implore；entreat）；使生效（to put into effect or operation use） 记 词根记忆：in（进入）+ vok（叫喊）+ e → 叫起来 → 祈求
allowance [ə'laʊəns]	*n.* 津贴，补助（amount of money allowed or given regularly）；承认，允许（permission） 记 联想记忆：allow（允许）+ ance → 允许自由支配的钱 → 津贴
predilection [ˌpredl'ekʃn]	*n.* 偏爱，嗜好（a special liking that has become a habit） 记 联想记忆：pre + dilection（看作 direction，趋向）→ 兴趣的趋向 → 偏爱，嗜好
cavalry ['kævlri]	*n.* 骑兵部队，装甲部队 记 联想记忆：骑兵（cavalier）组成了骑兵部队（cavalry）
exiguous [eg'zɪgjuəs]	*adj.* 太少的，不足的（scanty；meager） 同 scarce, skimpy, sparse
acumen ['ækjəmən]	*n.* 敏锐，精明（keenness and depth of perception） 记 词根记忆：acu（尖，酸，锐利）+ men（表名词）→ 敏锐，精明
wade [weɪd]	*v.* 涉水（to walk in water）；跋涉（to make one's way arduously） 同 plod, slog, slop, toil, trudge
spur [spɜːr]	*v.* 刺激，激励；用马刺刺马 记 联想记忆：美国 NBA 中有马刺队 Spurs
provenance ['prɑːvənəns]	*n.* 出处，起源（origin；source） 记 词根记忆：pro（前面）+ ven（来）+ ance → 前面来的东西 → 起源
disfranchise [ˌdɪs'fræntʃaɪz]	*v.* 剥夺…的权利，剥夺…公民权（to deprive of the rights of citizenship） 记 词根记忆：dis（剥夺）+ franchise（选举权，赋予权利）→ 剥夺…的权利
modish ['moʊdɪʃ]	*adj.* 时髦的（fashionable；stylish） 记 来自 mode（*n.* 时尚）
redolent ['redələnt]	*adj.* 芬芳的，芳香的（scented；aromatic） 记 词根记忆：red（=re 加强）+ ol（气味）+ ent → 散发出浓郁的气味 → 芳香的
numismatist [nuː'mɪzmətɪst]	*n.* 钱币学家，钱币收藏家（a person who studies or collects coins, tokens, and paper money）

26

self-assertion [ˌselfə'sɜːrʃən]	*n.* 自作主张 (the act of asserting oneself or one's own rights, claims, or opinions) 记 参考 self-consuming (*adj.* 自耗的), self-contained (*adj.* 自制的), self-content(*adj.* 自满的)
gourmand ['gʊrmɑːnd]	*n.* 嗜食者 (a person who indulges in food and drink, glutton) 记 联想记忆: g (看作 go, 去) + our + man + d → 我们的人都爱去吃各种美食 → 嗜食者
profiteer [ˌprɑːfə'tɪr]	*n.* 奸商, 牟取暴利者 (one who makes an unreasonable profit) 记 联想记忆: profit(利润) + eer(人) → 只顾利益之人 → 奸商
agog [ə'gɑːg]	*adj.* 兴奋的, 有强烈兴趣的 (in a state of eager anticipation or excitement) 记 agog 可以作词根, 意为"引导", 如: demagog (*n.* 煽动者)
dimple ['dɪmpl]	*n.* 酒窝, 笑靥 (a small dent or pucker, especially in the skin of sb.'s cheeks or chin) 记 联想记忆: d + imp(小精灵) + le → 像小精灵一样可爱 → 笑靥
pod [pɑːd]	*n.* 豆荚 *v.* 剥掉(豆荚) (to take peas out of pods) 搭 like as peas in a pod 一模一样, 酷似
toothsome ['tuːθsəm]	*adj.* 可口的, 美味的 (of palatable flavor and pleasing texture) 同 appetizing, delectable, divine, savory, yummy
hurdle ['hɜːrdl]	*n.* 跨栏; 障碍 (obstacle) *v.* 克服(障碍) (to overcome; surmount) 同 barrier, block, obstruction, snag
poll [poʊl]	*n.* 民意调查 (a survey of the public opinion); 投票选举 (voting in an election)
gargoyle ['gɑːrgɔɪl]	*n.* (雕刻成怪兽状的)滴水嘴 (a waterspout usually in the form of a grotesquely carved animal or fantastic creature); 面貌丑恶的人 (a person with grotesque features) 记 来自 gargle (*n./v.* 漱口)
rabid ['ræbɪd]	*adj.* 患狂犬病的 (affected with rabies); 疯狂的, 狂暴的 (going to extreme lengths in expressing or pursuing a feeling, interest or opinion) 记 来自 rabies(*n.* 狂犬病)
particularize [pər'tɪkjələraɪz]	*v.* 详述, 列举 (to give the details of sth. one by one) 记 来自 particular(*adj.* 详细的)
vie [vaɪ]	*v.* 竞争 (to compete) 同 contend, contest, emulate, rival
hinge [hɪndʒ]	*n.* 铰链 (a joint); 关键 (a determining factor)
delusion [dɪ'luːʒn]	*n.* 欺骗; 幻想 (illusion; hallucination) 记 来自 delude (*v.* 欺骗)
gander ['gændər]	*n.* 雄鹅; 笨人, 傻瓜 *v.* 闲逛 记 和 gender(*n.* 性别)一起记: 连性别(gender)都分不清的笨人 (gander)

barn [bɑːrn]	*n.* 谷仓(a farm building for sheltering harvested crops) 记 酒吧(bar)加了个门(n)，就变成了谷仓(barn)
putrid [ˈpjuːtrɪd]	*adj.* 腐臭的(rotten) 同 malodorous
enchant [ɪnˈtʃænt]	*v.* 使陶醉(to rouse to ecstatic admiration)；施魔法于(to bewitch) 记 词根记忆：en + chant(唱歌) → (巫婆)唱歌以施魔法 → 施魔法于
plush [plʌʃ]	*adj.* 豪华的(notably luxurious)
remonstrance [rɪˈmɑːnstrəns]	*n.* 抗议，抱怨(an earnest presentation of reasons for opposition or grievance) 记 词根记忆：re(重新) + monstr(显现) + ance → 一再表示对别人的不满 → 抗议，抱怨
gruff [grʌf]	*adj.* 粗鲁的，板着脸孔的(rough)；(声音)粗哑的(hoarse) 例 Though she tried to be happy living with Clara in the city, Heidi pined for the mountains and for her *gruff* but loving grandfather.
liken [ˈlaɪkən]	*v.* 把…比作(to compare to) 记 来自like(*prep.* 像)
filial [ˈfɪliəl]	*adj.* 子女的(of a son or daughter) 记 词根记忆：fil(儿子) + ial → 子的 → 子女的
abnegate [ˈæbnɪɡeɪt]	*v.* 否认，放弃(to deny; renounce) 记 词根记忆：ab(脱离) + neg(否认) + ate → 否认，放弃
ensconce [ɪnˈskɑːns]	*v.* 安置，安坐(to shelter; establish; settle) 记 联想记忆：en(进入) + sconce(小堡垒，遮蔽) → 进入遮盖 → 安置
hoodoo [ˈhuːduː]	*n.* 厄运；招来不幸的人(sb. that brings bad luck)
vista [ˈvɪstə]	*n.* 远景(a distant view; prospect)；展望(an extensive mental view) 记 词根记忆：vis(看)+ta → 远景；展望
egoism [ˈeɡoʊɪzəm]	*n.* 利己主义(a doctrine that self-interest is the valid end) 记 词根记忆：ego(自我) + ism → 自私自利 → 利己主义
cloy [klɔɪ]	*v.* (吃甜食)生腻，吃腻(to surfeit by too much of sth. sweet) 同 satiate
pitiless [ˈpɪtiləs]	*adj.* 无情的，冷酷的，无同情心的(devoid of pity) 同 cruel, harsh
discern [dɪˈsɜːrn]	*v.* 识别，看出(to recognize as separate or different; distinguish) 记 词根记忆：dis(除去) + cern(=sift 筛) → 筛出来 → 识别
tusk [tʌsk]	*n.* (象等的)长牙(an elongated, greatly enlarged tooth) 记 联想记忆：保护好自己的长牙(tusk)是大象们的重要任务(task)之一
avocation [ˌævoʊˈkeɪʃn]	*n.* 副业；嗜好(hobby; distraction) 记 a(不) + vocation(职业) → 非正规职业 → 副业；注意不要把 vocation(职业)和 vacation(度假)相混

26

□ barn	□ putrid	□ enchant	□ plush	□ remonstrance	□ gruff
□ liken	□ filial	□ abnegate	□ ensconce	□ hoodoo	□ vista
□ egoism	□ cloy	□ pitiless	□ discern	□ tusk	□ avocation

trounce [traʊns]	v. 痛击，严惩 (to thrash or punish severely)
brutal [ˈbruːtl]	adj. 残忍的，野蛮的 (savage; violent); 冷酷的 (very harsh and rigorous) 记 来自 brute (n. 人面兽心的人；残暴的人)
emergency [iˈmɜːrdʒənsi]	n. 紧急情况，不测事件，非常时刻 (exigency) 记 注意不要和 emergence (n. 出现) 相混 例 Dr. Charles Drew's technique for preserving and storing blood plasma for *emergency* use proved so effective that it became the model for the present blood bank system used by the American Red Cross.
discriminate [dɪˈskrɪmɪneɪt]	v. 区别，歧视 (to make a clear distinction) 记 联想记忆：dis + crimin (=crime 罪行) + ate → 区别对待有罪的人 → 区别，歧视
winkle [ˈwɪŋkl]	v. 挑出，剔出，取出 (to pry, extract, or force from a place or position)
district [ˈdɪstrɪkt]	n. 地区；行政区；区域 (a fixed division of a country, a city made for various official purposes)
cohesion [koʊˈhiːʒn]	n. 内聚力，凝聚力 (tendency to stick together) 搭 group cohesion 团体凝聚力
leak [liːk]	v. 泄漏 (to enter or escape through an opening usually by a fault or mistake) n. 泄漏；漏出量；裂缝，漏洞 (hole, crack, etc. through which liquid or gas may wrongly get in or out) 记 联想记忆：航行于湖 (lake) 面上的小舟因船底有漏洞 (leak) 沉没了
parturition [ˌpɑːrtjʊˈrɪʃn]	n. 生产，分娩 (the action or process of giving birth to offspring) 记 词根记忆：par (生产) + turi + tion → 分娩
beacon [ˈbiːkən]	n. 烽火，灯塔 (a signal light for warning or guiding) 记 联想记忆：beac (=beach 海岸) + on → 在海岸上的灯塔 → 灯塔
stoop [stuːp]	v. 弯腰，俯身 (to bend the body); 屈尊 (to descend from a superior rank) 记 联想记忆：站 (stood) 直了别弯腰 (stoop)
shriek [ʃriːk]	v. 尖叫 (to utter a sharp shrill sound)
accessory [əkˈsesəri]	adj. 附属的，次要的 (additional; supplementary; subsidiary)
dogmatism [ˈdɔːɡmətɪzəm]	n. 教条主义，武断 ((quality of) being dogmatic) 记 词根记忆：dogma (教条) + t + ism (表主义) → 教条主义
differentiate [ˌdɪfəˈrenʃieɪt]	v. 辨别，区别 (to mark or show a difference in) 记 词根记忆：different (不同的) + iate → 辨别，区别
curdle [ˈkɜːrdl]	v. 使凝结，变稠 (to form into curd; coagulate; congeal) 记 来自 curd (n. 凝乳)

gaffe [gæf]	*n.* (社交上令人不快的)失礼，失态 (a social or diplomatic blunder) 记 联想记忆：gaff(鱼叉) + e → 像用鱼叉刺人 → 失言，失态
wend [wend]	*v.* 行，走，前进 (to proceed on) 搭 wend one's way 朝…走去
traduce [trə'duːs]	*v.* 中伤，诽谤 (to slander or defame) 记 词根记忆：tra(=trans 横)+duc(引导)+e → 引到歪里去 → 诽谤
vicissitudinous [ˌvɪsɪsɪ'tjuːdɪnəs]	*adj.* 有变化的，变迁的 (marked by or filled with vicissitudes) 记 来自 vicissitude(*n.* 人生沉浮，兴衰枯荣)
clarity ['klærəti]	*n.* 清楚，明晰 (condition of being clear; clearness) 记 词根记忆：clar(清楚，明白) + ity → 清楚，明晰
scud [skʌd]	*v.* 疾行，飞奔 (to move or run swiftly)
gutless ['gʌtləs]	*adj.* 没有勇气的，怯懦的 (lacking courage) 记 联想记忆：gut(勇气) + less(无) → 没有勇气的 同 cowardly, spineless
magniloquent [mæg'nɪloʊkwənt]	*adj.* 夸张的 (characterized by a high-flown often bombastic style or manner) 记 词根记忆：magn(i)(大的) + loqu(话) + ent → 说大话 → 夸张的
appoint [ə'pɔɪnt]	*v.* 任命，指定 (to name for an office or position)；约定 记 联想记忆：ap(加强) + point(指向，指出) → 指定某人做某事 → 任命，指定
potboiler ['pɑːtbɔɪlər]	*n.* 粗制滥造的文艺作品 (a literary or artistic work of poor quality, produced quickly for profit) 记 来自 potboil(*v.* 为混饭吃而粗制滥造)
boding ['boʊdɪŋ]	*n.* 凶兆，前兆，预感 (an omen, prediction, etc., especially of coming evil) *adj.* 凶兆的，先兆的
demarcate ['diːmɑːrkeɪt]	*v.* 划分，划界 (to mark the limits; to mark the difference between) 记 词根记忆：de + marc(=mark 标记) + ate → 做标记 → 划分，划界
opulence ['ɑːpjələns]	*n.* 富裕 (wealth; affluence)；丰富 (great abundance; profusion)
smudge [smʌdʒ]	*n.* 污迹，污点 (a blurry spot or streak) *v.* 弄脏 (to smear sth. with dirt, or ink) 记 联想记忆：s + mud(泥) + ge → 污迹，污点
consecrate ['kɑːnsɪkreɪt]	*v.* 奉献，使神圣 (to dedicate; sanctify) 记 词根记忆：con + secr(神圣) + ate → 献给神 → 奉献
flux [flʌks]	*n.* 不断的变动，变迁，动荡不安 (continual change; condition of not being settled) 记 词根记忆：flu(流动) + x → 不断的变动
jeopardy ['dʒepərdi]	*n.* 危险 (great danger; peril) 搭 in jeopardy 处于危险境地，受到威胁

26

resigned	adj. 顺从的，听从的（acquiescent）
[rɪˈzaɪnd]	搭 be resigned to 对…顺从的
everlasting	adj. 永恒的，永久的（lasting a long time）；无休止的
[ˌevərˈlæstɪŋ]	记 组合词：ever（永远）+lasting（持续）→ 永久的

Ordinary people merely think how they shall spend their time; a man of talent tries to use it.

普通人只想到如何度过时间，有才能的人设法利用时间。

——德国哲学家 叔本华（Arthur Schopenhauer, German philosopher）

音频

shove [ʃʌv]	*v.* 推挤，猛推(to move sth. by using force) 记 注意不要和 shovel(*n.* 铁锹)相混
dote [doʊt]	*v.* 溺爱(to be excessively or foolishly fond)；昏聩(to be foolish or weak minded)
sip [sɪp]	*v.* 啜饮(to drink in small quantities) *n.* 小口喝，抿；一小口的量 搭 a sip of wine 一口酒
consolidate [kən'sɑːlɪdeɪt]	*v.* 巩固(to make stable and firmly established)；加强(to strengthen)；合并(to merge; unite; join) 记 词根记忆：con(加强) + solid(结实) + ate → 巩固
corporeal [kɔːr'pɔːriəl]	*adj.* 肉体的，身体的(of the body)；物质的(material, rather than spiritual) 记 词根记忆：corpor(身体) + eal(看作 real，真的) → 真身 → 肉体的
harshly ['hɑːrʃli]	*adv.* 严酷地，无情地 同 severely, toughly
neurosis [nʊ'roʊsɪs]	*n.* 神经官能症 记 词根记忆：neur(神经) + osis(表病) → 神经官能症
queer [kwɪr]	*adj.* 奇怪的，反常的(eccentric; unconventional) 记 和 queen(*n.* 女王)一起记
overriding [ˌoʊvər'raɪdɪŋ]	*adj.* 最主要的，优先的(chief; principal) 例 Numerous historical examples illustrate both the *overriding* influence that scientists' prejudices have on their interpretation of data and the consequent impairment of their intellectual objectivity.
judicial [dʒuː'dɪʃl]	*adj.* 法庭的，法官的(of law, courts, judges; judiciary) 记 词根记忆：jud(判断) + icial → 判案的 → 法庭的 搭 judicial decisions 司法判决
brochure [broʊ'ʃʊr]	*n.* 小册子，说明书(a small thin book with a paper cover)
zealotry ['zelətri]	*n.* 狂热(fanatical devotion) 搭 religious zealotry 宗教狂热行为
pother ['pɒðə]	*n.* 喧扰，骚动(confused or fidgety flurry or activity) *v.* 烦恼(to put into a pother)

□ shove	□ dote	□ sip	□ consolidate	□ corporeal	□ harshly
□ neurosis	□ queer	□ overriding	□ judicial	□ brochure	□ zealotry
□ pother					

stranded	*adj.* 搁浅的, 处于困境的(caught in a difficult situation)
[ˈstrændid]	搭 a stranded ship 搁浅的船
ensign	*n.* 舰旗(船上表示所属国家的旗帜)
[ˈensən]	记 联想记忆: en + sign(标志) → 表示所属国家标志的旗帜 → 舰旗
perish	*v.* 死, 暴卒(to become destroyed or ruined; die)
[ˈperɪʃ]	记 联想记忆: 珍惜(cherish)生命, 不应随意毁灭(perish)
beholden	*adj.* 因受恩惠而心存感激, 感谢; 欠人情 (owing sth. such as gratitude or
[bɪˈhoʊldən]	appreciation to another)
	同 grateful, owing
obtrude	*v.* 突出(to thrust out); 强加(to force or impose)
[əbˈtruːd]	记 词根记忆: ob(向外) + trud(伸出) + e → 向外伸 → 突出
thump	*v.* 重击, 捶击(to pound)
[θʌmp]	同 punch, smack, whack
retard	*v.* 妨碍(to impede); 使减速(to slow down)
[rɪˈtɑːrd]	记 词根记忆: re + tard(慢的) → 使迟缓 → 妨碍
perforate	*v.* 打洞(to make a hole through)
[ˈpɜːrfəreɪt]	记 词根记忆: per(贯穿) + for(门, 开口) + ate → 打穿 → 打洞
dissertation	*n.* 专题论文(long essay on a particular subject)
[dɪsərˈteɪʃn]	记 词根记忆: dis(加强) + sert(断言) + ation → 加强言论, 说明言论的东西 → 专题论文
striking	*adj.* 引人注目的, 显著的(attracting attention or notice)
[ˈstraɪkɪŋ]	记 来自 strike(*v.* 打击)
	例 As painted by Constable, the scene is not one of bucolic serenity; rather it shows a *striking* emotional and intellectual tension.
hone	*n.* 磨刀石 *v.* 磨刀(to sharpen with a hone)
[hoʊn]	记 注意不要和 horn(*n.* 号角)相混
dislocate	*v.* 使脱臼(to displace a bone from its proper position at a joint); 把…弄乱(to disarrange; disrupt)
[ˈdɪsloʊkeɪt]	记 dis(不) + locate(安置) → 不安置 → 使脱臼; 把…弄乱
niggling	*adj.* 琐碎的(petty; trivial)
[ˈnɪɡlɪŋ]	记 词根记忆: nig(小气的) + gling → 琐碎的
interweave	*v.* 交织(to weave together; interlace)
[ˌɪntərˈwiːv]	记 联想记忆: inter(在…中间) + weave(编织) → 交织
ersatz	*adj.* 代用的, 假的(substitute or synthetic; artificial)
[ˈersɑːts]	
shuttle	*v.* (使) 穿梭移动, 往返运送 (to cause to move or travel back and forth frequently)
[ˈʃʌtl]	
surge	*v.* 波涛汹涌(to rise and move in waves or billows)
[sɜːrdʒ]	记 本身为词根, 意为"升起, 立起"

gaseous [ˈɡæsiəs]	*adj.* 气体的，气态的 (like, containing or being gas) 记 来自 gas (*n.* 气体)
fruition [fruˈɪʃn]	*n.* 实现，完成 (fulfillment of hopes, plans, etc.) 记 联想记忆：fruit (水果) + ion → 有果实，有成果 → 实现，完成
cramp [kræmp]	*n.* 铁箍，夹子 *v.* 把…箍紧 (to fasten or hold with a cramp) 搭 cramp one's style 束缚…的手脚，限制…的才华
fabulous [ˈfæbjələs]	*adj.* 难以置信的 (incredible; astounding)；寓言的 (imaginary; fictitious) 记 词根记忆：fab (说) + ulous → 传说中的 → 难以置信的
gum [ɡʌm]	*n.* 树胶，树脂，橡皮糖，口香糖 记 chewing gum 口香糖
extinguish [ɪkˈstɪŋɡwɪʃ]	*v.* 使…熄灭 (to cause to cease burning)；使…不复存在 (to end the existence of) 记 词根记忆：ex(出) + ting(=sting 刺) + uish → 用针刺使没有 → 使…熄灭
fallibility [ˌfæləˈbɪləti]	*n.* 易出错，不可靠 (liability to err) 记 来自 fall (*n.* 失败)
merit [ˈmerɪt]	*v.* 值得 (to be worthy of) *n.* 价值；长处 记 本身为词根，意为"值得" 例 In the midst of so many evasive comments, this forthright statement, whatever its intrinsic *merit*, plainly stands out as an anomaly.
gadget [ˈɡædʒɪt]	*n.* 小工具，小机械 (any small mechanical contrivance or device) 记 联想记忆：gad(尖头棒) + get → 尖头棒是小工具的一种 → 小工具；还可以和 fidget(*n./v.* 坐立不安)一起记，丢了心爱的小工具(gadget)，他坐立不安(fidget)
homage [ˈhɑːmɪdʒ]	*n.* 效忠 (allegiance)；敬意 (honor) 记 词根记忆：hom (=hum 人) + age → 对别人表示敬意 → 敬意
odoriferous [ˌoʊdəˈrɪfərəs]	*adj.* 有气味的 (giving off an odor) 记 词根记忆：odor(气味) + i + fer(带有) + ous → 有气味的
archetype [ˈɑːkitaɪp]	*n.* 原型 (the original pattern; prototype)；典型 (a perfect example) 记 词根记忆：arch(旧的) + e + typ (模型，印象) + e → 原型
jibe [dʒaɪb]	*v.* 与…一致，符合 (to be in harmony, agreement, or accord) 注 jibe 作为"嘲笑"一义大家较为熟悉，但"符合"一义在 GRE 考试中更重要
pulpit [ˈpʊlpɪt]	*n.* 讲道坛 (a raised platform used in preaching)
natal [ˈneɪtl]	*adj.* 出生的，诞生时的 (of, relating to, or present at birth) 记 词根记忆：nat(出生) + al → 出生的，诞生时的
pertain [pərˈteɪn]	*v.* 属于 (to belong as a part)；关于 (to have reference) 记 词根记忆：per(始终) + tain(拿住) → 始终都拿在手里 → 属于
liability [ˌlaɪəˈbɪləti]	*n.* 责任 (the state of being liable)；债务 (obligation; debt) 记 词根记忆：li(=lig 捆) + ability → 将人捆住 → 责任

27

□ gaseous	□ fruition	□ cramp	□ fabulous	□ gum	□ extinguish
□ fallibility	□ merit	□ gadget	□ homage	□ odoriferous	□ archetype
□ jibe	□ pulpit	□ natal	□ pertain	□ liability	

cynic [ˈsɪnɪk]	*n.* 犬儒主义者，愤世嫉俗者（one who believes that human conduct is motivated wholly by self-interest） 记 词根记忆：cyn(狗) + ic → 犬儒主义者
outlet [ˈaʊtlet]	*n.* 出口（a way through which sth. may go out） 记 组合词：out(出来) + let(让) → 让出来 → 出口
cupidity [kjuːˈpɪdəti]	*n.* 贪婪（strong desire for wealth；avarice；greed） 记 联想记忆：Cupid(丘比特)是罗马神话中的爱神，爱神引起人们对爱情的"贪婪" → 贪婪
figurine [ˌfɪɡjəˈriːn]	*n.* 小塑像，小雕像（a small sculptured or molded figure；statuette） 记 联想记忆：figur(雕像) + ine(小的) → 小雕像
aleatory [ˈeɪliətɔːri]	*adj.* 侥幸的，偶然的（depending on an uncertain event or contingency as to both profit and loss）
bungle [ˈbʌŋɡl]	*v.* 笨拙地做（to act or work clumsily and awkwardly） 同 botch, bumble, fumble, muff, stumble
lineal [ˈlɪniəl]	*adj.* 直系的，嫡系的（in the direct line of descent from an ancestor） 记 词根记忆：lim(线) + eal → 直系的
drivel [ˈdrɪvl]	*v.* 胡说（to talk nonsense）*n.* 糊涂话（nonsense） 记 联想记忆：drive(开车) + l → 一边开车一边胡说 → 胡说
sardonic [sɑːrˈdɑːnɪk]	*adj.* 讽刺的，嘲笑的（disdainfully sneering, ironic, or sarcastic） 记 来自 sardinian plant(撒丁岛植物)，据说人食用后会狂笑而死
palaver [pəˈlɑːvər]	*n.* 空谈（idle chatter）*v.* 空谈（to chatter idly）；奉承（to flatter or cajole） 记 联想记忆：pala(ce)(宫殿) + aver(承认, 说话) → 宫殿里的话 → 奉承
jot [dʒɑːt]	*v.* 草草记下（to write briefly or hurriedly） 记 联想记忆：与 lot(*n.* 一堆，许多)一起记
blasphemy [ˈblæsfəmi]	*n.* 亵渎(神明)（profane or contemptuous speech；cursing） 记 词根记忆：blas (=blame 责备) + phem (出现) + y → 受责备的事出现 → 亵渎
dereliction [ˌderəˈlɪkʃn]	*n.* 遗弃（state of being deserted）；玩忽职守的 记 来自 derelict(*adj.* 遗弃的)
waive [weɪv]	*v.* 放弃（to relinquish voluntarily）；推迟（to postpone） 搭 waive one's claim 放弃要求
complicity [kəmˈplɪsəti]	*n.* 合谋，串通（participation；involvement in a crime） 记 词根记忆：com (共同) + plic (重叠) + ity → 共同重叠 → 同谋关系 → 合谋
rote [roʊt]	*n.* 死记硬背（a memorizing process using routine or repetition, often without full attention or comprehension） 记 词根记忆：rot(转) + e → 摇头晃脑地转着背 → 死记硬背
fraternal [frəˈtɜːrnl]	*adj.* 兄弟的，兄弟般的（brotherly） 记 词根记忆：frater(兄弟) + nal → 兄弟的

shirk [ʃɜːrk]	v. 逃避，回避(to avoid; evade) 记 和 shirt(n. 衬衣)一起记
atonal [eɪ'toʊnl]	adj.(音乐)无调的(marked by avoidance of traditional musical tonality) 记 词根记忆：a + ton(声音) + al → 无声的 → 无调的
fang [fæŋ]	n.(蛇的)毒牙 记 联想记忆：和 tang(n. 强烈的气味)一起记
snare [sner]	n. 圈套，陷阱(trap; gin) 记 参考 ensnare(v. 使进入圈套)
archer ['ɑːrtʃər]	n.(运动或战争中的)弓箭手，射手(a person who shoots with a bow and arrows) 记 词根记忆：arch(弓) + er → 弓箭手；arch 本身是一个单词，意为"使…弯成弓形"
deluxe [ˌdə'lʌks]	adj. 豪华的，华丽的(notably luxurious, elegant, or expensive) 搭 a deluxe hotel 豪华宾馆
famine ['fæmɪn]	n. 饥荒(instance of extreme scarcity of food in a region) 记 联想记忆：fa(看作 far, 远的) + mine(我的) → 粮食离我很远 → 饥荒 例 The technical know-how, if not the political commitment, appears already at hand to feed the world's exploding population and so to eradicate at last the ancient scourges of malnutrition and *famine*.
nip [nɪp]	v. 小口啜饮(to sip in a small amount) 记 和 lip(n. 嘴唇)一起记
languor ['læŋɡər]	n. 无精打采，衰弱无力(lack of vigor or vitality; weakness) 记 词根记忆：lang(松弛) + uor → 无精打采
malfunction [ˌmæl'fʌŋkʃn]	v. 发生故障，失灵(to fail to function) n. 故障(failure of this sort) 记 联想记忆：mal(坏的) + function(功能) → 功能不好 → 故障
entreat [ɪn'triːt]	v. 恳求(to make an earnest request; plead) 记 联想记忆：en(进入) + treat(处理) → 要求进入处理 → 恳求
mend [mend]	v. 修改，改进(to put into good shape or working order) 同 amend, correct, improve
endearing [ɪn'dɪrɪŋ]	adj. 讨人喜欢的(resulting in affection) 记 词根记忆：en(进入) + dear(喜爱) + ing → 进入被喜爱的状态 → 讨人喜欢的
renal ['riːnl]	n. 肾脏的，肾的(relating to, involving, or located in the region of the kidneys)
asterisk ['æstərɪsk]	n. 星号(a mark like a star used to draw attention) 记 词根记忆：aster(星星) + isk → 星号
fertile ['fɜːrtl]	adj. 多产的(productive; fecund); 肥沃的 记 词根记忆：fert(=fer 带来) + ile → 带来果实的 → 多产的
serried ['serid]	adj. 密集的(crowded or pressed together; compact) 搭 serried ranks of soldiers 密集排列的士兵

27

□ shirk	□ atonal	□ fang	□ snare	□ archer	□ deluxe
□ famine	□ nip	□ languor	□ malfunction	□ entreat	□ mend
□ endearing	□ renal	□ asterisk	□ fertile	□ serried	

topsy-turvy [ˌtɑ:psi'tɜ:rvi]	*adj.* 颠倒的，相反的(with the top or head downward)；乱七八糟的，混乱的(in utter confusion or disorder)
obsess [əb'ses]	*v.* 迷住；使…困扰，使…烦扰(to haunt or excessively preoccupy the mind of) 记 词根记忆：ob(反) + sess(=sit 坐) → 坐着不动，妨碍前进 → 迷住；使…困扰
slouch [slaʊtʃ]	*n.* 没精打采的样子(a tired-looking way) *v.* 没精打采地坐(站、走) 记 发音记忆："似老去" → 没精打采的样子
vengeful ['vendʒfl]	*adj.* 渴望复仇的，复仇心重的(showing a fierce desire to punish sb. for the harm they have done to oneself)
mendacity [men'dæsəti]	*n.* 不诚实(untruthfulness) 记 来自 mendacious(*adj.* 习惯性说谎的)
rout [raʊt]	*n.* 溃败(an overwhelming defeat) 记 联想记忆：route(道路)去掉 e → 成功的道路上一失误就会溃败 → 溃败
status ['steɪtəs]	*n.* 身份，地位(social standing; present condition) 记 联想记忆：stat(看作 state，声明) + us(我们) → 声明我们是谁 → 身份
recant [rɪ'kænt]	*v.* 撤回(声明)，放弃(信仰)(to withdraw or repudiate (a statement or belief)) 记 词根记忆：re(反) + cant(唱) → 唱反调 → 放弃(信仰)
deception [dɪ'sepʃn]	*n.* 欺骗，诡计(a ruse; trick) 记 词根记忆：de(坏) + cept(拿，抓) + ion → 拿坏的东西来 → 欺骗
mushy ['mʌʃi]	*adj.* 糊状的(having the consistency of mush)；感伤的，多情的(excessively tender or emotional)
modicum ['mɒdɪkəm]	*n.* 少量(a moderate or small amount) 搭 a modicum of 一点，少数
kudos ['ku:dɑ:s]	*n.* 声誉，名声(fame and renown) 同 reputation, prestige
depredation [ˌdeprə'deɪʃn]	*n.* 劫掠，蹂躏(act of robbing, plundering) 记 词根记忆：de + pred(=plunder 掠夺) + ation → 劫掠
wily ['waɪli]	*adj.* 诡计多端的，狡猾的(full of wiles; crafty) 记 来自 wile(*n.* 诡计)
characterization [ˌkærəktəraɪ'zeɪʃn]	*n.* 描绘，刻画(the delineation of character) 记 来自 character(*n.* 性格，角色)
mighty ['maɪti]	*adj.* 强有力的，强大的(very great in power, strength)；巨大的 例 Telling gripping tales about a central character engaged in a *mighty* struggle with events, modern biographies satisfy the American appetite for epic narratives.

convict	[kənˈvɪkt] v. 定罪 (to find guilty of an offence) [ˈkɑːnvɪkt] n. 罪犯 (a person found guilty of a crime and sentenced by a court) 记 词根记忆：con + vict (征服，胜利) → 征服罪犯 → 定罪	 convict 谋杀罪 死刑
motile [ˈmoʊtaɪl]	adj. 能动的 (exhibiting or capable of movement) 记 词根记忆：mot(动) + ile → 能动的	
conscience [ˈkɑːnʃəns]	n. 良心，是非感 (a person's awareness of right and wrong) 记 词根记忆：con(全部) + sci(知道) + ence → 全部知道 → 有良知 → 是非感 搭 the reproaches of conscience 良心上的谴责	
mourn [mɔːrn]	v. 悲痛，哀伤 (to feel or express sorrow or grief)；哀悼 同 bemoan, bewail, grieve, lament	
diffuse [dɪˈfjuːs]	v. 散布，(光等)漫射 (to disperse in every direction) adj. 漫射的，散漫的 (spreading out or dispersed) 记 词根记忆：dif(不同) + fuse(流) → 向不同方向流动 → 漫射	
carp [kɑːrp]	n. 鲤鱼 v. 吹毛求疵 (to complain continually) 记 联想记忆：结婚这么多年还买不起车 (car)，妻子对丈夫总是吹毛求疵 (carp)	
onslaught [ˈɑːnslɔːt]	n. 猛攻，猛袭 (a fierce attack) 记 联想记忆：on + slaught(打击) → 猛攻，猛袭	
austerity [ɔːˈsterəti]	n. 朴素，艰苦 同 asceticism, nonindulgence	
monarch [ˈmɑːnərk]	n. 君主，帝王 (a hereditary sovereign) 记 词根记忆：mon(单个的) + arch(统治者) → 最高统治者 → 君主	
timeworn [ˈtaɪmwɔːrn]	adj. 陈旧的，陈腐的 (hackneyed; stale) 记 组合词：time(时间) + worn(用旧的) → 陈旧的	
crook [krʊk]	v. 使弯曲 (to bend or curve) n. 钩状物 记 注意不要和 creek(n. 小河)相混	
gloomy [ˈgluːmi]	adj. 阴暗的 (dismally and depressingly dark)；没有希望的 (lacking in promise or hopefulness)；阴郁的，忧郁的 (low in spirits) 记 来自 gloom(n. 黑暗，阴暗) 同 pessimistic, sullen	 gloomy 失业 失恋
bustle [ˈbʌsl]	v. 奔忙，忙乱 (to be busily astir) n. 喧闹，熙熙攘攘 (noisy, energetic, and often obtrusive activity)	
caprice [kəˈpriːs]	n. 奇思怪想，反复无常，任性 (sudden change in attitude or behavior) 记 联想记忆：cap(帽子) + rice(米饭) → 戴上帽子才吃米饭 → 任性	

□ convict	□ motile	□ conscience	□ mourn	□ diffuse	□ carp
□ onslaught	□ austerity	□ monarch	□ timeworn	□ crook	□ gloomy
□ bustle	□ caprice				

297

rapprochement	*n.* 友好，友善关系的建立（establishment of cordial relations）
[ˌræprɑːʃˈmɑːn]	记 联想记忆：r + approche（看作 approach，靠近）+ ment → 靠在一起 → 友好
excrete	*v.* 排泄，分泌（to pass out waste matter）
[ɪkˈskriːt]	记 词根记忆：ex + cret(分离) + e → 分离出来 → 排泄
jerk	*v.* 猛拉（to pull with a sudden, sharp movement）*n.* 猛拉
[dʒɜːrk]	搭 jerk off（紧张得）结结巴巴地说
punch	*v.* 以拳猛击（to strike with the fist）；打孔（to make a hole；pierce）
[pʌntʃ]	记 发音记忆："乓哧"（重击的声音）→ 以拳猛击
dyspeptic	*adj.* 消化不良的（indigestible）；不高兴的（morose；grouchy）
[dɪsˈpeptɪk]	
wacky	*adj.*（行为等）古怪的，乖僻的（absurdly or amusingly eccentric or irrational）
[ˈwæki]	
amuse	*v.* 使愉快，逗某人笑（to make sb. smile）
[əˈmjuːz]	记 联想记忆：a + muse(缪斯，古希腊文艺女神) → 使愉快
augmentation	*n.* 增加（increase）
[ˌɔːgmenˈteɪʃn]	记 来自 augment（*v.* 增加，增大）
cultivate	*v.* 种植（to grow from seeds）；培养（友谊）（to seek to develop familiarity with）
[ˈkʌltɪveɪt]	记 词根记忆：cult(培养，种植) + iv + ate(表示动作) → 种植
agnostic	*adj.* 不可知论的(of, relating to, or being an agnostic or the beliefs of agnostics)
[ægˈnɑːstɪk]	*n.* 不可知论者
	记 词根记忆：a(不) + gno(知道) + stic → 认为无法了解神是否存在的人 → 不可知论者
bogus	*adj.* 伪造的，假的（not genuine；spurious）
[ˈboʊgəs]	记 联想记忆：来自一种叫"Bogus"的机器，用于制造伪钞
plait	*n.* 发辫（a braid of hair）*v.* 编成辫
[plæt]	同 pigtail
stigma	*n.* 耻辱的标志，污点（a mark of shame or discredit）
[ˈstɪgmə]	同 stain
delectation	*n.* 享受，愉快（delight；enjoyment；entertainment）
[ˌdiːlekˈteɪʃn]	同 joy, pleasure
adjudicate	*v.* 充当裁判（to serve as a judge in a dispute）；判决（to settle judicially）
[əˈdʒuːdɪkeɪt]	记 词根记忆：ad(来) + jud(判断) + icate → 进行判断 → 充当裁判
foray	*v.* 突袭，偷袭；劫掠，掠夺（to raid for spoils；plunder；pillage）*n.* 突袭
[ˈfɔːreɪ]	记 联想记忆：fo(看作 for，为了) + ray(光线) → 为了光明，偷袭敌人 → 突袭，偷袭
finable	*adj.* 应罚款的（liable to a fine）
[ˈfaɪnəbl]	记 来自 fine（*v.* 罚款）

ceremony [ˈserəmouni]	*n.* 典礼，仪式（formal acts performed on a religious or public occasion） 记 联想记忆：cere（蜡）+ mony（看作 money，钱）→ 古代做典礼时，蜡烛和钱是少不了的 → 典礼
friable [ˈfraɪəbl]	*adj.* 脆的，易碎的（easily broken up or crumbled） 搭 friable soil 松散的土壤
skullduggery [skʌlˈdʌɡəri]	*n.* 欺骗，使诈（underhanded or unscrupulous behavior） 记 联想记忆：skull（头颅，脑袋）+ dug（挖）+ gery → 挖脑袋 → 想方设法作假 → 欺骗，使诈
blemish [ˈblemɪʃ]	*v.* 损害；玷污（to mar; spoil the perfection of）*n.* 瑕疵，缺点（defect） 记 词根记忆：blem（弄伤）+ ish → 把…弄伤 → 损害；玷污
badge [bædʒ]	*n.* 徽章（a distinctive token, emblem, or sign）
lucre [ˈluːkər]	*n.* 〈贬〉钱，利益（money or profits） 记 词根记忆：lucr（获利）+ e → 利益
poignancy [ˈpɔɪnjənsi]	*n.* 辛辣，尖锐（the quality or state of being poignant）
brusque [brʌsk]	*adj.* 唐突的，鲁莽的（rough or abrupt; blunt） 记 发音记忆："不如屁壳（郎）" → 鲁莽的
scar [skɑːr]	*n.* 伤痕，伤疤（a mark remaining on the skin from a wound） 记 联想记忆：s + car（汽车）→ 被汽车撞了一下 → 留下伤痕 → 伤痕，伤疤
piddle [ˈpɪdl]	*v.* 鬼混，浪费（to spend time aimlessly; diddle） 同 dawdle, putter
shear [ʃɪr]	*v.* 剪（羊毛），剪发（to cut off the hair from） 记 联想记忆：sh（看作 she）+ ear（耳朵）→ 她剪了个齐耳的短发 → 剪发
to-do [təˈduː]	*n.* 喧闹，骚乱（fuss） 同 commotion, stir
josh [dʒɑːʃ]	*v.* （无恶意地）戏弄，戏耍（to tease good-naturedly） 同 banter, jest
licit [ˈlɪsɪt]	*adj.* 合法的（permitted by law; lawful; legal） 记 参考：illicit（*adj.* 违法的）
unflappable [ˌʌnˈflæpəbl]	*adj.* 不惊慌的，镇定的（marked by assurance and self-control） 同 composed, imperturbable, self-possessed, unruffled
vendetta [venˈdetə]	*n.* 血仇，世仇（blood feud）；宿怨，深仇（a bitter, destructive feud） 记 词根记忆：vend（=vindic 复仇）+ etta → 血仇，世仇
contented [kənˈtentɪd]	*adj.* 心满意足的（showing content and satisfied） 记 来自 content（*v.* 满意，满足）

scar

27

ritzy	*adj.* 高雅的(elegant)；势利的(snobbish)
[ˈrɪtsi]	同 exclusive, refined, polished
exalt	*v.* 赞扬，歌颂(to praise; glorify; extol)
[ɪɡˈzɔːlt]	记 词根记忆：ex + alt(高) → 评价高 → 赞扬
erase	*v.* 擦掉，抹去(to rub, scrape, or wipe out)
[ɪˈreɪs]	记 词根记忆：e + rase(擦) → 擦掉
rankle	*v.* 怨恨(to cause resentment)；激怒(to cause anger and irritation)
[ˈræŋkl]	记 联想记忆：ran(跑) + kle(看作 ankle, 脚踝) → 跑时扭伤了脚踝 → 怒了 → 激怒
lunatic	*n.* 疯子(an insane person) *adj.* 极蠢的(utterly foolish)
[ˈluːnətɪk]	记 词根记忆：lun(月亮) + atic → 人们认为精神病与月亮的盈亏有关 → 疯子；Luna 原指罗马神话中的月亮女神
gracious	*adj.* 大方的，和善的 (kind, polite and generous)；奢华的 (marked by luxury)；优美的，雅致的
[ˈɡreɪʃəs]	例 Egocentric, at times vindictive when he believed his authority was being questioned, while could also be kind, *gracious*, and even self-deprecating when the circumstances seemed to require it.
rollicking	*adj.* 欢乐的，喧闹的(noisy and jolly)
[ˈrɑːlɪkɪŋ]	记 联想记忆：rol(卷) + lick(舔) + ing → 把好吃的东西卷起来舔，气氛很欢乐 → 欢乐的
ecstatic	*adj.* 狂喜的，心花怒放的(enraptured)
[ɪkˈstætɪk]	记 来自 ecstasy(*n.* 狂喜)
choice	*adj.* 上等的(of high quality)；精选的(selected with care)
[tʃɔɪs]	同 dainty, delicate, elegant, exquisite, superior

lapse [læps]	*n.* 失误（small error；fault）；（时间等）流逝（a gliding or passing away of time） 搭 lapse of time 时间流逝
redemptive [rɪˈdemptɪv]	*adj.* 赎回的，救赎的，挽回的（acting to save someone from error or evil） 同 redeeming
caudal [ˈkɔːdl]	*adj.* 尾部的，像尾部的（of, relating to, or being a tail; situated in or directed toward the hind part of the body）
parochial [pəˈroʊkiəl]	*adj.* 教区的（of or relating to a church parish）；地方性的，狭小的（restricted to a small area or scope; narrow）
automation [ˌɔːtəˈmeɪʃn]	*n.* 自动装置（mechanism that imitates actions of humans） 记 词根记忆：auto(自己) + mat(动) + ion → 自动 → 自动装置
mansion [ˈmænʃn]	*n.* 公寓；大厦（a large imposing house） 记 词根记忆：man(逗留) + sion → 逗留之处 → 居住的地方 → 公寓
lap [læp]	*v.* 舔食（to take in food or drink with the tongue） 记 联想记忆：和 tap(*n.* 水龙头)一起记
simulate [ˈsɪmjuleɪt]	*v.* 假装，模仿（to assume the appearance with the intent to deceive） 记 词根记忆：simul(类似)+ate(使…) → 使某物类似于某物 → 模仿
cardiologist [ˌkɑːrdiˈɑːlədʒɪst]	*n.* 心脏病专家（an expert of the heart disease） 记 词根记忆：cardi(=card 心) + olog(=ology 学科) + ist(人) → 研究心脏的人 → 心脏病专家
ligneous [ˈlɪɡniəs]	*adj.* 木质的，木头般的（having the nature of wood; woody） 记 词根记忆：lign(木头) + eous → 木质的
oracle [ˈɔːrəkl]	*n.* 代神发布神谕的人（a person through whom a deity is believed to speak） 记 词根记忆：ora(说话) + cle → 代神发布神谕的人
phantom [ˈfæntəm]	*n.* 鬼怪，幽灵（a ghost）；幻影，幻象（sth. elusive or visionary） 记 词根记忆：phan(显现) + tom → 显现的东西 → 幽灵

卖拐
卖拐

simulate

□ lapse	□ redemptive	□ caudal	□ parochial	□ automation	□ mansion
□ lap	□ simulate	□ cardiologist	□ ligneous	□ oracle	□ phantom

301

periphrastic [ˌperiˈfræstɪk]	*adj.* 迂回的，冗赘的(of, relating to, or characterized by periphrasis) 记 联想记忆：peri(周围) + phras(=phrase 句子，词语) + tic → 绕圈子说话 → 迂回的
monolithic [ˌmɑːnəˈlɪθɪk]	*adj.* 坚若磐石的；巨大的(huge; massive) 记 词根记忆：mono(单个的) + lith(石头) + ic → 单块大石头的 → 巨大的
vault [vɔːlt]	*n.* 拱顶(an arched structure)；地窖(an underground storage compartment)
fathom [ˈfæðəm]	*n.* 英寻 *v.* 彻底了解，弄清真相(to understand thoroughly)
purported [pərˈpɔːrtɪd]	*adj.* 传言的，据称的(reputed; alleged) 记 词根记忆：pur(向前，向外) + port(带) + ed → 带到外面的 → 传言的
zest [zest]	*n.* 刺激性(an enjoyable exciting quality)；兴趣，热心(keen enjoyment) 记 联想记忆：对考试(test)有兴趣(zest)
onset [ˈɑːnset]	*n.* 开始，发作(beginning; commencement)；攻击，袭击(attack; assault) 例 Although adolescent maturational and developmental states occur in an orderly sequence, their timing varies with regard to *onset* and duration.
decomposition [ˌdiːkɑːmpəˈzɪʃn]	*n.* 分解，腐烂；崩溃 同 breakdown, decay, deterioration, disintegration, rot
feeble [ˈfiːbl]	*adj.* 虚弱的(weak; faint) 同 fragile, frail, powerless
uproar [ˈʌprɔːr]	*n.* 喧嚣，吵闹(a heated controversy)；骚动，骚乱(a condition of noisy excitement and confusion; tumult) 记 联想记忆：up(向上)+roar(吼叫) → 喧嚣；骚动
trinket [ˈtrɪŋkɪt]	*n.* 小装饰品，（尤指）不值钱的珠宝(a small ornament，especially a small, cheap piece of jewelry)；琐事(a trivial thing; trifle)
encompass [ɪnˈkʌmpəs]	*v.* 包围，围绕(to enclose; envelop) 记 词根记忆：en(进入) + compass(罗盘，范围) → 进入范围 → 包围
costume [ˈkɑːstuːm]	*n.* 服装(dress including accessories)；戏装(a set of clothes worn in a play or at a masquerade) 记 联想记忆：cost(花费) + u(你)+me(我) → 你我都免不了花钱买服装 → 服装
dicker [ˈdɪkər]	*v.* 讨价还价(to bargain) 同 haggle, higgle, huckster, negotiate, palter
reciprocal [rɪˈsɪprəkl]	*adj.* 相互的，互惠的(mutual; shared by both sides) 搭 reciprocal banquet 答谢宴会
unscrupulousness [ʌnˈskruːpjələsnəs]	*n.* 狂妄，不择手段 记 来自 unscrupulous(*adj.* 肆无忌惮的，不讲道德的)

encompass

costume

gangly	*adj.* 身材瘦长难看的(tall, thin and awkward-looking)
[ˈgæŋgli]	同 gangling
plagiarize	*v.* 剽窃,抄袭(to take(sb. else's ideas, words. etc) and use them as if they were one's own)
[ˈpleɪdʒəraɪz]	记 词根记忆: plagi(斜的) + ar + ize → 做歪事 → 剽窃,抄袭
clammy	*adj.* 湿冷的,发粘的(being damp, soft, sticky, and usually cool)
[ˈklæmi]	记 联想记忆: clam(蛤蜊) + my → 像蛤蜊一样又冷又湿 → 湿冷的,发粘的
sterilize	*v.* 使不育;杀菌(to make sterile)
[ˈsterəlaɪz]	搭 sterilize surgical instruments 给外科手术器械消毒
temerity	*n.* 鲁莽,大胆(audacity; rashness; recklessness)
[təˈmerəti]	记 词根记忆: tem(黑暗的)+er+ity → 摸黑行动 → 鲁莽,大胆
boor	*n.* 粗野的人(a rude, awkward person);农民(a peasant)
[bʊr]	记 联想记忆: 粗野的人(boor)的人通常比较穷(poor)
swig	*v.* 痛饮(to drink in long drafts)
[swɪg]	同 gulp, guzzle
mollycoddle	*v.* 过分爱惜,娇惯(to overly coddle; pamper) *n.* 娇生惯养的人
[ˈmɑːlikɑːdl]	记 联想记忆: moll(软的) + y + coddle(纵容) → 娇惯
loaf	*n.* 一条(面包) *v.* 虚度光阴(to idle; dawdle)
[loʊf]	同 dillydally, loiter, lounge
hie	*v.* 疾走,快速(to go quickly; hasten)
[haɪ]	同 hurry, speed
ribald	*adj.* 下流的,粗俗的(crude; using coarse indecent humor)
[ˈrɪbld]	记 联想记忆: ri(拼音: 日) + bald(光秃的) → 白天光着身子 → 下流的
bristling	*adj.* 竖立的(be stiffly erect)
[ˈbrɪslɪŋ]	
aquiline	*adj.* 鹰的,似鹰的(of, relating to, or resembling an eagle)
[ˈækwɪlaɪn]	记 词根记忆: aquil(鹰) + ine → 鹰的
derivation	*n.* 发展,起源(development or origin);词源(first form and meaning of a word)
[ˌderɪˈveɪʃn]	记 来自 derive(*v.* 派生,导出)
scamp	*v.* 草率地做(to perform or deal with in a hasty manner) *n.* 流氓(rascal; rogue);顽皮的家伙
[skæmp]	
slit	*v.* 撕裂(to sever) *n.* 裂缝(a long narrow cut or opening)
[slɪt]	记 参考 split(*v./n.* 分裂); slice(*v.* 切开)
steep	*adj.* 陡峭的;过高的(lofty, high) *v.* 浸泡,浸透(to soak in a liquid)
[stiːp]	记 联想记忆: 阶梯(step)中又加一个 e 就更陡峭(steep)
	例 Imposing *steep* fines on employers for on-the-job injuries to workers could be an effective incentive to creat a safer workplace, especially in the case of employers with poor safety records.

28

□ gangly	□ plagiarize	□ clammy	■ sterilize	□ temerity	□ boor
□ swig	□ mollycoddle	□ loaf	□ hie	□ ribald	□ bristling
□ aquiline	□ derivation	□ scamp	□ slit	□ steep	

303

conceit [kən'siːt]	*n.* 自负，自大(an exaggerated opinion of oneself；vanity) 记 词根记忆：con + ceit(=ceive 拿) → 拿架子 → 自负
ineluctable [ˌɪnɪ'lʌktəbl]	*adj.* 不能逃避的(certain；inevitable) 记 词根记忆：in(不) + e(出) + luct(挣扎) + able → 无法挣脱的 → 不能逃避的
auxiliary [ɔːɡ'zɪliəri]	*adj.* 辅助的，附加的，补充的(subordinate；additional；supplementary) 记 词根记忆：aux(=aug 提高) + iliary(形容词后缀) → 提高的 → 辅助的
pavid ['pævɪd]	*adj.* 害怕的，胆小的(exhibiting or experiencing fear；timid)
dishevel [dɪ'ʃevl]	*v.* 使蓬乱，使(头发)凌乱(to throw into disorder or disarray) 记 联想记忆：dish(盘子)+eve(夏娃)+l → 夏娃吃完饭，盘子脏乱 → 使蓬乱
humid ['hjuːmɪd]	*adj.* 湿润的(damp) 记 联想记忆：hum(嗡嗡声) + id → 蚊虫总有嗡嗡的声音，而潮湿的地方多蚊虫 → 湿润的 例 Even as the local climate changed from *humid* to arid and back—a change that caused other animals to become almost extinct—our human ancestors survived by learning how to use the new flora.
grisly ['ɡrɪzli]	*adj.* 恐怖的，可怕的(inspiring horror or greatly frightened) 同 frightening, ghastly, horrible
droop [druːp]	*v.* 低垂(to bend or hang downward)；萎靡(to become weakened) 记 由 drop(*v.* 落下)变化而来
outwit [ˌaʊt'wɪt]	*v.* 以机智胜过(to overcome by cleverness) 记 组合词：out(出) + wit(机智) → 机智超过别人 → 以机智胜过
tease [tiːz]	*v.* 逗乐，戏弄(to make fun of)；强求，强要(to obtain by repeated coaxing) *n.* 逗乐，戏弄(the act of teasing)
flatten ['flætn]	*v.* (使)变平(to become or make sth. flat)；彻底打败，击倒(to defeat sb. completely)
stubborn ['stʌbərn]	*adj.* 固执的(determined)；难以改变的(difficult to change) 记 联想记忆：stub(根)+born(生) → 生根的 → 固执的 例 In attempting to reconcile estranged spouses, counselors try to foster a spirit of compromise rather than one of *stubborn* implacability.
envisage [ɪn'vɪzɪdʒ]	*v.* 正视(to face；confront)；想象(to visualize；imagine) 记 词根记忆：en(进入) + vis(看) + age → 进入看的状态 → 正视
affix	[ə'fɪks] *v.* 黏上，贴上(to stick；attach)；(尤指在末尾)添上(to add sth. in writing) ['æfɪks] *n.* 词缀(prefix or suffix) 记 词根记忆：af + fix(固定) → 固定上去 → 黏上，贴上
indignant [ɪn'dɪɡnənt]	*adj.* 愤慨的，愤愤不平的(feeling or expressing anger) 同 angry

□ conceit	□ ineluctable	□ auxiliary	□ pavid	□ dishevel	□ humid
□ grisly	□ droop	□ outwit	□ tease	□ flatten	□ stubborn
□ envisage	□ affix	□ indignant			

neutralize [ˈnuːtrəlaɪz]	*v.* 使无效(to make ineffective; nullify); 中和, 使中性(to make neutral) 记 词根记忆: ne(不) + utr(= uter 二者中的任一) + alize → 不偏向任何一方 → 中和
overweening [ˌoʊvərˈwiːnɪŋ]	*adj.* 自负的, 过于自信的(arrogant; excessively proud) 记 组合词: over(过分) + ween(想) + ing → 把自己想得过分伟大 → 自负的
crib [krɪb]	*v.* 抄袭, 剽窃(to steal, plagiarize) 记 和 crab(*v.* 发牢骚)一起记
feint [feɪnt]	*n.* 佯攻, 佯击(a pretended attack or blow) *v.* 佯攻; 伪装 记 注意不要和 faint(*adj.* 虚弱的)相混
aroma [əˈroʊmə]	*n.* 芳香, 香气(a pleasant, often spicy odor; fragrance) 记 发音记忆: "爱了吗" → 爱了就有芳香 → 芳香, 香气
ornery [ˈɔːrnəri]	*adj.* 顽固的, 爱争吵的(having an irritable disposition) 同 cantankerous
veritable [ˈverɪtəbl]	*adj.* 名副其实的, 真正的, 确实的(being truly so called; real and genuine) 同 authentic, unquestionable
oasis [oʊˈeɪsɪs]	*n.* 绿洲(a fertile place in desert) 搭 a green oasis in the heart of the city 都市中心的绿茵
caption [ˈkæpʃn]	*n.* 标题(short title of an article) 记 词根记忆: capt(拿, 抓) + ion → 抓住主要内容 → 标题
odometer [oʊˈdɑːmɪtər]	*n.* (汽车)里程表(an instrument for measuring the distance traveled (as by a vehicle)) 记 词根记忆: od(路) + o + meter(测量) → 测量路程的东西 → 里程表
abhorrent [əbˈhɔːrənt]	*adj.* 可恨的, 讨厌的(causing disgust or hatred; detestable, hateful) 同 obscene, repugnant, repulsive
soulful [ˈsoʊlfl]	*adj.* 充满感情的, 深情的(full of or expressing feeling or emotion) 搭 a soulful song 一首凄婉的歌
daredevil [ˈderdevl]	*adj.* 胆大的, 冒失的 (bold and reckless) *n.* 胆大的人, 冒失的人 记 组合词: dare(大胆) + devil(鬼) → 比鬼还大胆 → 胆大的
reliance [rɪˈlaɪəns]	*n.* 信赖, 信任(the state of being dependent on or having confidence in) 记 来自 rely(*v.* 依赖) 例 The success of science is due in great part to its emphasis on objectivity: the *reliance* on evidence rather than preconceptions and the willingness to draw conclusions even when they conflict with traditional beliefs.
formative [ˈfɔːrmətɪv]	*adj.* 形成的; 影响发展的(helping to shape, develop, or mold) 记 来自 form(*v.* 形成)
inelasticity [ˌɪnɪlæˈstɪsəti]	*n.* 无弹性, 无伸缩性 记 联想记忆: in(无) + elastic(有弹性的) + ity(表性质) → 无弹性, 无伸缩性

28

□ neutralize	□ overweening	□ crib	□ feint	□ aroma	□ ornery
□ veritable	□ oasis	□ caption	□ odometer	□ abhorrent	□ soulful
□ daredevil	□ reliance	□ formative	□ inelasticity		

pilfer [ˈpɪlfər]	*v.* 偷窃(to steal in small quantities) 同 filch, pinch
oversee [ˌoʊvərˈsiː]	*v.* 监督(to watch; supervise) 记 组合词: over(全部) + see(看) → 监督
yielding [ˈjiːldɪŋ]	*adj.* 易弯曲的, 柔软的(lacking rigidity or stiffness; flexible); 顺从的, 服从的(disposed to submit or comply)
virtual [ˈvɜːrtʃuəl]	*adj.* 实质上的, 实际上的(being such in essence or effect though not formally recognized or admitted)
negation [nɪˈɡeɪʃn]	*n.* 否定, 否认(action of denying) 记 词根记忆: neg(否认) + ation → 否定, 否认
roughen [ˈrʌfn]	*v.* (使)变粗糙(to make or become rough) 记 来自 rough(*adj.* 粗糙的)
tempestuous [temˈpestʃuəs]	*adj.* 狂暴的(turbulent; stormy) 搭 a tempestuous relationship 冲突不断的关系
downpour [ˈdaʊnpɔːr]	*n.* 倾盆大雨(a heavy fall of rain) 记 组合词: down(向下) + pour(倾倒) → 向下倾倒 → 倾盆大雨
slurp [slɜːrp]	*v.* 出声地吃或喝(to drink with the sound of noisy sucking) *n.* 啜食, 啜食声
superimpose [ˌsuːpərɪmˈpoʊz]	*v.* 重叠, 叠加(to place or lay over or above sth.) 记 词根记忆: super(在…上面) + im + pose(放置) → 放在上面的 → 重叠, 叠加
strife [straɪf]	*n.* 纷争, 冲突(bitter conflict or dissension) 同 fight, struggle
acclaim [əˈkleɪm]	*v.* 欢呼, 称赞(to greet with loud applause; hail) 记 词根记忆: ac(向) + claim(叫喊) → 向某人大声叫喊 → 欢呼, 称赞 搭 universal acclaim 普遍赞誉; 广受好评
funk [fʌŋk]	*n.* 怯懦, 恐惧(a state of paralyzing fear); 懦夫(one that funks) 记 联想记忆: 懦夫(funk)也要真诚坦率(frank)
atrocious [əˈtroʊʃəs]	*adj.* 残忍的, 凶恶的(very cruel, brutal; outrageous) 记 词根记忆: atroc(阴沉, 凶残) + ious → 残忍的
residue [ˈrezɪduː]	*n.* 剩余(remainder; what is left behind)
malice [ˈmælɪs]	*n.* 恶意, 怨恨(desire to do mischief; spite) 记 词根记忆: mal(坏的) + ice → 恶意
correspondent [ˌkɔːrəˈspɑːndənt]	*adj.* 符合的, 一致的(agreeing; matching) *n.* 记者, 通讯员(a person who writes for a magazine or newspaper) 记 联想记忆: cor + respond(反应) + ent(…的) → 有共同反应的 → 符合的, 一致的

despise [dɪˈspaɪz]	v. 鄙视，蔑视(to look down on with contempt or aversion) 同 contemn, disdain, scorn, scout
gnawing [ˈnɔːɪŋ]	n. 啃，咬 adj. 痛苦的，折磨人的(excruciating) 记 来自 gnaw(v. 啃，咬) 搭 gnawing doubts 令人痛苦的疑虑
undulate [ˈʌndʒəleɪt]	v. 波动，起伏(to form or move in waves; fluctuate) 记 词根记忆：und(波浪)+ul+ate → 波动，起伏
cello [ˈtʃeloʊ]	n. 大提琴 记 联想记忆：violin(n. 小提琴)；viola(n. 中提琴)
ague [ˈeɪɡjuː]	n. 冷战，发冷(a fit of shivering)
poach [poʊtʃ]	v. 偷猎，窃取(to catch without permission on sb. else's property) 搭 poach ideas from sb. 将某人的思想窃为己有
oppress [əˈpres]	v. 压迫，压制(to rule in a hard and cruel way) 记 词根记忆：op(向)+press(压)→ 压下去 → 压迫
hilarious [hɪˈleriəs]	adj. 欢闹的(noisily merry)；引起大笑的(producing great merriment) 记 词根记忆：hilar(高兴)+ious → 高兴的 → 欢闹的；引起大笑的
augury [ˈɔːɡjʊri]	n. 占卜术；预兆 记 来自 augur(v. 占卜，预言)
gawky [ˈɡɔːki]	adj. 迟钝的，笨拙的(awkward) 记 来自 gawk(v. 呆头呆脑地盯着)
hoarse [hɔːrs]	adj. 嘶哑的，粗哑的(rough and husky in sound) 记 联想记忆：horse(马)中间加一个 a → 马的叫声很嘶哑 → 嘶哑的
plentitude [ˈplentɪtuːd]	n. 充分(the quality or state of being full) 记 词根记忆：plen(满)+titude → 充分
shamble [ˈʃæmbl]	v. 蹒跚而行，踉跄地走(to walk awkwardly with dragging feet) 同 shuffle
plangent [ˈplændʒənt]	adj. 轰鸣的；凄凉的(having a plaintive quality) 记 来自拉丁文 plangere，意为"拍打胸脯以示哀痛"
sheen [ʃiːn]	n. 光辉，光泽(a bright or shining condition)
chuckle [ˈtʃʌkl]	v. 轻声地笑，咯咯地笑(to laugh softly in a low tone) 同 chortle
muniments [ˈmjuːnɪmənts]	n. 契据 记 词根记忆：mun(保护，加强)+iments → 加强买卖关系的东西 → 契据
loutish [ˈlaʊtɪʃ]	adj. 粗鲁的(rough and rude) 记 来自 lout(n. 蠢人，笨蛋)
sophism [ˈsɒfɪzəm]	n. 诡辩；诡辩法(术)(an argument apparently correct in form but actually invalid)

28

tinkle [ˈtɪŋkl]	*v.* (使)发出叮当声(to make or emit light metallic sounds)
preside [prɪˈzaɪd]	*v.* 担任主席(to act as president or chairman); 负责(to be in charge of); 指挥(to exercise control) 记 词根记忆: pre(在…之前) + sid(坐) + e → 坐在前面 → 指挥
steer [stɪr]	*v.* 掌舵, 驾驶(to control the course) *n.* 公牛, 食用牛 记 联想记忆: 驾驶着(steer)一艘钢铁(steel)打造的大船
rampage	[ræmˈpeɪdʒ] *v.* 乱冲乱跑(to rush wildly about) [ˈræmpeɪdʒ] *n.* 狂暴行为 (violent action or behavior) 记 联想记忆: ram(羊) + page(书页) → 羊翻书, 使人怒 → 狂暴行为
offbeat [ˌɑːfˈbiːt]	*adj.* 不规则的, 不平常的(unconventional) 记 组合词: off(离开) + beat(节奏) → 无节奏 → 不规则的
bid [bɪd]	*v.* 命令(to command); 出价, 投标(to make a bid) 记 发音记忆: "必得" → 出价时抱着必得的态度 → 出价, 投标
promissory [ˈprɑːmɪsəri]	*adj.* 允诺的, 约定的(containing or conveying a promise or assurance) 搭 promissory note 本票, 期票
sly [slaɪ]	*adj.* 狡猾的, 狡诈的(clever in deceiving) 搭 on the sly 偷偷地; 背地里
slue [sluː]	*v.* (使)旋转(to rotate; slew) 记 slew(*v.* 旋转)的变体
analgesia [ˌænəlˈdʒiːʒə]	*n.* 无痛觉, 痛觉丧失(insensibility to pain without loss of consciousness) 记 词根记忆: an(没有) + alg(痛) + esia → 无痛觉
sleight [slaɪt]	*n.* 巧妙手法; 诡计; 灵巧(dexterity; skill) 记 联想记忆: sl(看作 sly, 狡猾) + eight → 八面玲珑 → 灵巧
flighty [ˈflaɪti]	*adj.* 轻浮的(skittish); 反复无常的(capricious) 记 联想记忆: f + light(轻的) + y → 因为轻而飘浮着 → 轻浮的
buxom [ˈbʌksəm]	*adj.* 体态丰满的(having a shapely, full-bosomed figure) 同 curvaceous, curvy
sneer [snɪr]	*v.* 嘲笑, 鄙视(to express scorn or contempt) 同 deride, fleer, scoff, taunt
scabrous [ˈskeɪbrəs]	*adj.* 粗糙的(rough with small points or knobs; scabby) 记 联想记忆: scab(疤) + rous → 多疤的 → 粗糙的
clairvoyant [klerˈvɔɪənt]	*adj.* 透视的, 有洞察力的(having power that can see in the mind either future events or things that exist or are happening out of sight) 记 联想记忆: clair(看作 clear, 清楚的) + voy(看) + ant → 看得清楚的 → 有洞察力的

308

□ tinkle   □ preside   □ steer   □ rampage   □ offbeat   □ bid
□ promissory □ sly   □ slue   □ analgesia   □ sleight   □ flighty
□ buxom   □ sneer   □ scabrous   □ clairvoyant

imprint [ɪmˈprɪnt]	*v.* 盖印，刻印(to mark by pressing or stamping) 记 联想记忆：im(不) + print(印记) → 留下印记 → 盖印
subsidy [ˈsʌbsədi]	*n.* 补助金(a grant or gift of money) 记 联想记忆：sub(下面)+sid(坐)+y → 坐下来领补助金 → 补助金
reconnoiter [ˌrekəˈnɔɪtər]	*v.* 侦察，勘察(to make reconnaissance of) 记 联想记忆：re + connoiter(观察，源自法语) → 侦察，勘察
zesty [ˈzesti]	*adj.* 兴致很高的，热望的(having or characterized by keen enjoyment) 记 来自 zest(*n.* 兴趣，热心)
pierce [pɪrs]	*v.* 刺穿(to run into or through; stab)；穿透(to force through) 记 联想记忆：r 从一片(piece)中穿过 → 刺穿
supine [ˈsuːpaɪn]	*adj.* 仰卧的(lying on the back)；懒散的(mentally or morally slack) 同 prone; inactive
badger [ˈbædʒər]	*n.* 獾 *v.* 烦扰，纠缠不休(to torment; nag) 同 beleaguer, bug, pester, tease
beatific [ˌbiːəˈtɪfɪk]	*adj.* 幸福的，快乐的(blissful or blessed; delightful) 记 词根记忆：beat(幸福) + ific → 幸福的
smirch [smɜːrtʃ]	*v.* 弄脏(to make dirty, stained, or discolored) *n.* 污点 同 blemish, soil, sully, tarnish
enlightening [ɪnˈlaɪtnɪŋ]	*adj.* 有启迪作用的(giving spiritual and intellectual insight)；使人领悟的 例 A family physician is unlikely to be an *enlightening* source of general information about diet.
ostensible [ɑːˈstensəbl]	*adj.* 表面上的(apparent; seeming; professed) 记 词根记忆：os(向上) + tens(拉) + ible → 向上拉长的 → 表面上的
virulent [ˈvɪrələnt]	*adj.* 剧毒的(extremely poisonous or venomous)；恶毒的(full of malice) 记 词根记忆：vir(毒)+ul+ent → 剧毒的
glow [gloʊ]	*v.* 发光，发热(to give out heat or light)；(脸)发红(to show redness) *n.* 发光；兴高采烈 同 blush, flush; incandescence
simultaneous [ˌsaɪmlˈteɪniəs]	*adj.* 同时发生的(exactly coincident) 记 词根记忆：simul(相同)+taneous(…的) → 同时发生的 搭 simultaneous with 与…同时进行
intestate [ɪnˈtesteɪt]	*adj.* 未留遗嘱的(having made no legal will) 记 词根记忆：in(无) + test(看到) + ate → 没有留下可以看的东西 → 未留遗嘱的
rue [ruː]	*n.* 后悔，懊悔(repent or regret) 同 compunction, contrition, penitence, remorse
digress [daɪˈgres]	*v.* 离题(to depart temporarily from the main subject) 记 词根记忆：di(离开) + gress(走) → 走离 → 离题

28

languish [ˈlæŋgwɪʃ]	*v.* 衰弱，憔悴（to lose vigor or vitality） 记 词根记忆：lang(松弛) + uish → 衰弱
wobble [ˈwɑːbl]	*v.* 摇晃，摇摆（to move with a staggering motion）；犹豫（to hesitate） 同 falter, stumble, teeter, tooter
sulky [ˈsʌlki]	*adj.* 生气的（moodily silent） 记 词根记忆：sulk(生气) + y → 生气的
imbroglio [ɪmˈbroʊlioʊ]	*n.* 纠纷，纠葛，纠缠不清（confused misunderstanding or disagreement） 记 词根记忆：im(进入) + bro(混乱) + glio → 纠纷
providential [ˌprɑːvɪˈdenʃl]	*adj.* 幸运的（fortunate）；适时的（happening as if through divine intervention; opportune）
sartorial [sɑːrˈtɔːriəl]	*adj.* 裁缝的，缝制的（of or relating to a tailor or tailored clothes） 记 联想记忆：sartor(裁缝) + ial → 裁缝的
mentor [ˈmentɔːr]	*n.* 导师（a wise and trusted counselor or teacher） 记 词根记忆：ment(精神) + or → 精神上的指导人 → 导师
knotty [ˈnɑːti]	*adj.* 多节的，多瘤的（having or full of knots）；困难的，棘手的（hard to solve or explain; puzzling） 记 来自knot(*n.* 节疤)

The man who has made up his mind to win will never say "impossible".
凡是决心取得胜利的人是从来不说"不可能的"。
——法国皇帝 拿破仑（Bonaparte Napoleon, French emperor）

□ languish   □ wobble   □ sulky   □ imbroglio   □ providential   □ sartorial
□ mentor   □ knotty

inspired [ɪnˈspaɪərd]	*adj.* 有创见的，有灵感的(outstanding or brilliant in a way or to a degree suggestive of divine inspiration) 记 词根记忆：in(进入) + spir(呼吸) + ed → 吸入(灵气) → 有灵感的 例 Her first concert appearance was disappointingly perfunctory and derivative, rather than the *inspired* performance in the innovative style we had anticipated.
familiarity [fəˌmɪliˈærəti]	*n.* 熟悉(close acquaintance)；亲近，亲密(intimacy)；不拘礼仪(an excessively informal act) 记 来自 familiar(*adj.* 熟悉的)
patriotism [ˈpeɪtriətɪzəm]	*n.* 爱国主义，爱国心(love for or devotion to one's country) 记 来自 patriot(*n.* 爱国者)
abstentious [əbˈstenʃəs]	*adj.* 有节制的(temperate)
ordain [ɔːrˈdeɪn]	*v.* 任命(神职)(to make sb. a priest or minister)；颁发命令(to decree; order)
assemble [əˈsembl]	*v.* 集合，聚集(to collect)；装配，组装(to fit together the parts) 记 联想记忆：as(加强) + semble(类似) → 物以类聚 → 集合
rectitude [ˈrektɪtuːd]	*n.* 诚实，正直，公正(moral integrity; righteousness) 记 词根记忆：rect(直的) + itude → 正直
rapt [ræpt]	*adj.* 入迷的，全神贯注的(engrossed; absorbed; enchanted) 记 词根记忆：rap(抓取) + t → 夺去了所有注意力 → 入迷的
exclaim [ɪkˈskleɪm]	*v.* 惊叫，呼喊(to cry out suddenly and loudly) 记 词根记忆：ex(出) + claim(叫喊) → 惊叫，呼喊 搭 exclaim over 对…感叹
sibyl [ˈsɪbl]	*n.* 女预言家，女先知(a female prophet) 同 prophetess
cordial [ˈkɔːrdʒəl]	*adj.* 热诚的(warmly friendly; gracious; heartfelt) *n.* 兴奋剂(a stimulating medicine or drink) 记 词根记忆：cord(心脏；一致) + ial → 发自内心的 → 热诚的

exclaim

安红！
我想你！

□ inspired	□ familiarity	□ patriotism	□ abstentious	□ ordain	□ assemble
□ rectitude	□ rapt	□ exclaim	□ sibyl	□ cordial	

311

mingle [ˈmɪŋgl]	*v.* (使)混合 (to bring or mix together) 同 blend, merge
enthrall [ɪnˈθrɔːl]	*v.* 迷惑, 迷住 (to hold spellbound; charm) 记 联想记忆: en(使) + thrall(奴隶) → 成为(爱的)奴隶 → 迷住
gaze [geɪz]	*v.* 凝视, 注视 (to look intently and steadily; stare) *n.* 凝视, 注视 记 发音记忆: "盖茨" → 比尔·盖茨令世人瞩目 → 凝视, 注视
snatch [snætʃ]	*v.* 强夺, 攫取 (to take or grasp abruptly or hastily without permission) *n.* 强夺, 攫取 记 联想记忆: sna(看作 snap, 迅速的) + tch(看作 catch, 抓) → 迅速地抓 → 强夺, 攫取
zephyr [ˈzefər]	*n.* 和风 (a gentle breeze); 西风 (a breeze from the west) 记 来自希腊神话中的西风之神 Zephyros
spurt [spɜːrt]	*n.* (液体等的)喷出, 迸发 (spout) 同 gush, jet, spew, squirt
preposterous [prɪˈpɑːstərəs]	*adj.* 荒谬的 (contradictory to nature or common sense; absurd) 记 联想记忆: pre(前) + post(后) + erous → "前、后"两个前缀放在一起了 → 荒谬的
quack [kwæk]	*n.* 冒牌医生, 庸医 (a pretender to medical skill) *adj.* 庸医的 记 和 quick (*adj.* 快的)一起记: 庸医骗完钱就很快消失 例 The popularity of pseudoscience and *quack* medicines in the nineteenth century suggests that people were very credulous, but the gullibility of the public today makes citizens of yesterday look like hard-nosed skeptics.
etymology [ˌetɪˈmɑːlədʒi]	*n.* 语源学 (the branch of linguistics dealing with word origin and development) 记 来自 etymon (*n.* 词源, 字根)
embarrass [ɪmˈbærəs]	*v.* 使局促不安, 使窘迫 (to cause sb. to feel self-conscious or ashamed) 记 词根记忆: em(进入) + barrass(套子) → 进入套子 → 使窘迫
industrious [ɪnˈdʌstriəs]	*adj.* 勤劳的, 勤勉的 (hard-working; diligent) 记 词根记忆: in(在里面) + du + str(=struct 建造) + ious → 在里面建造 → 勤劳的
piquant [ˈpiːkənt]	*adj.* 辛辣的, 开胃的 (agreeably stimulating to the palate; spicy); 刺激的 (engagingly provocative)
backset [ˈbækset]	*n.* 倒退, 逆流 (reversal; countercurrent) 同 countermatch, regradation, retrogress, retroversion
typhoon [taɪˈfuːn]	*n.* 台风 (a tropical hurricane or cyclone)

embarrass

scripture [ˈskrɪptʃər]	*n.* 经文，圣典（a body of writing considered sacred or authoritative） 记 词根记忆：script(写) + ure → 写出的东西 → 经文，圣典
fluke [fluːk]	*n.* 侥幸（thing that is accidentally successful）；意想不到的事（a result brought about by accident） 记 和flake(*n.* 雪片)一起记
latent [ˈleɪtnt]	*adj.* 潜在的，潜伏的（present but invisible; dormant; quiescent） 记 联想记忆：late(晚) + nt → 晚到的 → 潜在的，潜伏的
ungrudging [ʌnˈɡrʌdʒɪŋ]	*adj.* 慷慨的；情愿的（being without envy or reluctance） 记 联想记忆：un(不)+grudging(吝啬的；勉强的) → 慷慨的；情愿的
double-cross [ˌdʌblˈkrɔːs]	*v.* 欺骗，出卖（to betray or swindle by an action contrary to an agreed upon course）
elated [iˈleɪtɪd]	*adj.* 得意洋洋的，振奋的（marked by high spirits; exultant） 记 词根记忆：e + lat(放) + ed → 放出(高兴神态) → 得意洋洋的 搭 be elated by 因…而欢欣的
upfront [ˌʌpˈfrʌnt]	*adj.* 坦率的（very direct and making no attempt to hide one's meaning） 记 联想记忆：up(向上)+front(举止) → 在行为举止上毫不掩饰 → 坦率的
toil [tɔɪl]	*v.* 苦干，辛苦劳作（to work hard and long）*n.* 辛苦，辛劳（long strenuous fatiguing labor）
flit [flɪt]	*v.* 掠过，迅速飞过（to fly lightly and quickly） 记 联想记忆：fl(看作fly, 飞) + it → 飞过它 → 掠过，迅速飞过
multiplicity [ˌmʌltɪˈplɪsəti]	*n.* 多样性（a large number or great variety） 记 来自multiple(*adj.* 多种多样的)
behoove [bɪˈhuːv]	*v.* 理应，有必要（to be right or necessary to）
informer [ɪnˈfɔːrmər]	*n.* 告发者，告密者（a person who secretly accuses） 记 联想记忆：inform(通知) + er(人) → 通知的人 → 告发者，告密者
empower [ɪmˈpaʊər]	*v.* 授权，准许（to give lawful power or authority to） 记 联想记忆：em(进入) + power(权力) → 进入权力的状态 → 授权
vicinity [vəˈsɪnəti]	*n.* 附近，邻近（proximity; neighborhood） 记 词根记忆：vicin(邻近的)+ity → 附近，邻近
footle [ˈfuːtl]	*v.* 说胡话，做傻事（to act or talk foolishly）；浪费(时间)（to waste (time)） 记 联想记忆：foot(脚) + le → 走来走去 → 浪费(时间)
damp [dæmp]	*v.* 减弱，抑制（to make sth. less strong）*adj.* 潮湿的（moist） 记 联想记忆：dam(水坝) + p → 水坝上很潮湿 → 潮湿的
deadlock [ˈdedlɑːk]	*n.* 相持不下，僵局（standstill; stalemate） 记 组合词：dead(死) + lock(锁) → 僵局
restorative [rɪˈstɔːrətɪv]	*adj.* 恢复健康的（having power to restore） 记 词根记忆：re(重新) + stor(储存) + ative → 重新储存能量 → 恢复健康的

29

ponder [ˈpɑːndər]	*v.* 仔细考虑，衡量（to weigh in the mind; reflect on） 记 词根记忆：pond（重量）+ er → 掂重量 → 仔细考虑，衡量
striated [ˈstraɪeɪtɪd]	*adj.* 有条纹的（marked with striations） 记 来自 striate（*v.* 加条纹）
canard [kəˈnɑːrd]	*n.* 谣言，假新闻（a false malicious report） 记 联想记忆：金丝雀（canary）在造谣（canard）
morale [məˈræl]	*n.* 士气，民心（a sense of common purpose with respect to a group） 记 联想记忆：和 moral（*adj.* 道德的）一起记 例 Many industries are so beleaguered by the impact of government sanctions, equipment failure, and foreign competition that they are beginning to rely on industrial psychologists to salvage what remains of employee *morale*.
sustained [səˈsteɪnd]	*adj.* 持久的，持续的（prolonged） 记 来自 sustain（*v.* 保持） 例 Exposure to *sustained* noise has been claimed to impair blood pressure regulation in human beings and, particularly, to increase hypertension, even though some researchers have obtained inconclusive results that obscure.
exaltation [ˌegzɔːlˈteɪʃn]	*n.* （成功带来的）得意，高兴（elation; rapture） 记 联想记忆：exalt（提拔）+ ation → 得到提拔后的心情 → 得意、高兴
substance [ˈsʌbstəns]	*n.* 主旨，实质（most important or essential part of sth.）；物质（particular type of matter） 例 One of photography's most basic and powerful traits is its ability to give *substance* to history, to present precise visual details of a time gone by.
slew [sluː]	*v.* （使）旋转（to turn, twist）*n.* 大量（a large number） 记 和 slow（*adj.* 慢的）一起记
lottery [ˈlɑːtəri]	*n.* 抽彩给奖法 记 来自 lot（*n.* 签）
pluralist [ˈplʊrəlɪst]	*n.* 兼任数个宗教职位者，兼职者（a person who holds two or more offices, especially two or more benefices, at the same time）
relent [rɪˈlent]	*v.* 变温和，变宽厚（to become compassionate or forgiving）；减弱（to soften; mollify） 记 词根记忆：re + lent（柔软的）→ 心肠软了下来 → 变温和，变宽厚
sag [sæg]	*v.* 松弛，下垂（to lose firmness, resiliency, or vigor）
welsh [welʃ]	*v.* 欠债不还（to avoid payment）；失信（to break one's word） 记 联想记忆：和威尔士人（Welsh）的拼写一样
invective [ɪnˈvektɪv]	*n.* 谩骂，痛骂（a violent verbal attack; diatribe） 记 词根记忆：in（进入）+ vect（搬运）+ ive → 把不好的东西往人心里运 → 谩骂

deserter [dɪˈzɜːrtər]	*n.* 背弃者；逃兵 记 来自 desert(*v.* 遗弃，离弃)
staid [steɪd]	*adj.* 稳重的，沉着的(self-restraint; sober) 记 联想记忆：sta(看作 stay，坚持) + id(看作 ID，身份) → 坚持自己的身 份 → 稳重的
lean [liːn]	*v.* 倾斜(to incline)；斜靠 *adj.* 瘦的(thin) 搭 lean on 依靠，依赖
jovial [ˈdʒoʊviəl]	*adj.* 愉快的(very cheerful and good-humored) 同 gleeful, jolly, merry
libelous [ˈlaɪbələs]	*adj.* 诽谤的(publishing libels) 同 defamatory
advert [ˈædvɜːrt]	*v.* 注意，留意；提及(to call attention; refer) 记 词根记忆：ad(向) + vert(转) → 一再转到这个话题 → 注意，留意
inveigh [ɪnˈveɪ]	*v.* 痛骂，猛烈抨击(to utter censure or invective) 记 联想记忆：in(进入) + veigh(看作 weigh，重量) → 重重地骂 → 痛骂
lithe [laɪð]	*adj.* 柔软的，易弯曲的(easily bent)；自然优雅的(characterized by easy flexibility and grace) 记 词根记忆：lith(可弯曲的)+e → 柔软的，易弯曲的
forbidding [fərˈbɪdɪŋ]	*adj.* 令人生畏的；(形势)险恶的(looking dangerous, threatening)；令人反 感的，讨厌的(disagreeable) 记 来自 forbid(*v.* 禁止)
amiable [ˈeɪmiəbl]	*adj.* 和蔼的，亲切的(good natured; affable; genial) 记 联想记忆：am(爱，友爱) + i + able → 和蔼的，亲切的
bleary [ˈblɪri]	*adj.* 视线模糊的，朦胧的(dull or dimmed especially from fatigue or sleep; poorly outlined or defined)；精疲力尽的(tired to the point of exhaustion)
clasp [klæsp]	*n.* 钩子，扣子(device for fastening things)；紧握(firm hold) 同 clench, clutch, grasp, grip
tract [trækt]	*n.* 传单(a leaflet of political or religion propaganda)；大片土地(a large stretch or area of land)
spiel [spiːl]	*n.* 滔滔不绝的讲话(pitch)
iota [aɪˈoʊtə]	*n.* 极少量，极少(a very small quantity) 记 来自希腊语第九个字母，相当于英语中的字母 i，因其位置靠后而引申 为"极少量"
insouciant [ɪnˈsuːsiənt]	*adj.* 漫不经心的(unconcerned) 同 indifferent, nonchalant
gulp [gʌlp]	*v.* 吞食，咽下(to swallow hastily or greedily)；抑制，忍住 同 gobble
beam [biːm]	*n.* (房屋等的)大梁；光线(a shaft or stream of light) 记 联想记忆：be + am → 做我自己，成为国家的栋梁 → 大梁

29

stolid [ˈstɑːlɪd]	*adj.* 无动于衷的（expressing little or no sensibility; unemotional） 记 solid(*adj.* 结实的)中间加个 t
piddling [ˈpɪdlɪŋ]	*adj.* 琐碎的，微不足道的（so trifling or trivial as to be beneath one's consideration）
bonny [ˈbɑːni]	*adj.* 健美的，漂亮的（attractive, fair） 同 bonnie, comely
incision [ɪnˈsɪʒn]	*n.* 切口（a cut; gash）；切割 记 词根记忆：in(向内) + cis(切) + ion → 切割
pact [pækt]	*n.* 协定，条约（an agreement; covenant） 同 treaty
glimpse [ɡlɪmps]	*v.* 瞥见，看一眼（to look quickly; glance）*n.* 一瞥，一看 记 联想记忆：glim(灯光) + pse → 像灯光一闪 → 瞥见
polemic [pəˈlemɪk]	*n.* 争论，论战（an aggressive attack or refutation） 记 词根记忆：polem(战争) + ic → 争论，论战
garbled [ˈɡɑːrbld]	*adj.* 引起误解的（misleading）；窜改的（falsifying） 例 He gave a *garbled* account of what had happened.
diversity [daɪˈvɜːrsəti]	*n.* 多样，千变万化（the condition of being diverse） 例 The sheer *diversity* of tropical plants represents a seemingly inexhaustible source of raw materials, of which only a few have been utilized.
jocund [ˈdʒɑːkənd]	*adj.* 快乐的，高兴的（cheerful; genial; gay） 记 词根记忆：joc(=joke 玩笑) + und → 充满玩笑的 → 快乐的
meek [miːk]	*adj.* 温顺的，顺从的（gentle and uncomplaining） 同 mild, patient, subdued, tame
sorcery [ˈsɔːrsəri]	*n.* 巫术，魔术（the use of evil magical power） 记 词根记忆：sorc(巫术) + ery → 巫术，魔术
antic [ˈæntɪk]	*adj.* 古怪的（fantastic and queer） 记 和 antique(*n.* 古董)来自同一词源
crescendo [krəˈʃendoʊ]	*n.* (音乐)渐强（a gradual increase in loudness）；高潮 记 词根记忆：crescend(成长；上升) + o → (音乐)渐强
hobble [ˈhɑːbl]	*v.* 蹒跚（to go unsteadily）；跛行（to walk lamely; limp） 记 联想记忆：和 hobby(*n.* 癖好)一起记
pillage [ˈpɪlɪdʒ]	*n.* 抢劫，掠夺（looting; plundering; ravage）*v.* 抢夺（to plunder ruthlessly） 记 来自 pill(*v.* 抢劫)
unprepossessing [ˌʌnˌpriːpəˈzesɪŋ]	*adj.* 不吸引人的（unattractive） 记 联想记忆：un(不)+prepossessing(引人注意的) → 不吸引人的
chaos [ˈkeɪɑːs]	*n.* 混乱（extreme confusion or disorder） 记 发音记忆："吵死" → 混乱

dank [dæŋk]	*adj.* 阴湿的，透水的(damp; unpleasantly wet) 记 联想记忆：河岸(bank)边一定是阴湿的(dank)
peaky ['pi:ki]	*adj.* 消瘦的，虚弱的(thin; weak) 记 来自peak(*v.* 变得憔悴)
recall [rɪ'kɔ:l]	*v.* 回想，回忆起(to bring back to the mind)；收回(to take back) *n.* 唤回 (call to return) 记 词根记忆：re(反) + call(喊，叫) → 唤回
acarpous [ei'kɑ:pəs]	*adj.* 不结果实的(impotent to bear fruit)
adherent [əd'hɪrənt]	*n.* 拥护者，信徒(one that adheres as a follower or a believer) 记 词根记忆：ad(一再) + her(粘连) + ent → 粘在身后的人 → 拥护者
nag [næg]	*v.* 不断叨扰，指责，抱怨(to find fault incessantly; complain)
escort	[ɪ'skɔ:rt] *v.* 护送(to accompany to protect or show honor or courtesy) ['eskɔ:rt] *n.* 护送者 记 联想记忆：e + scor (看作score，得分) + t → 得到好分数，一路护送你 上大学 → 护送
ruthlessness ['ru:θləsnəs]	*n.* 无情，冷酷，残忍(cruelty) 记 来自ruthless(*adj.* 残忍的，无情的)
gustation [gʌ'steɪʃn]	*n.* 品尝(the act of tasting)；味觉(the sensation of tasting) 记 联想记忆：一阵强风(gust)吹来，他们没办法在露天茶座惬意地进行美食 品尝(gustation)了
swamp [swɑ:mp]	*n.* 沼泽(land which is always full of water) *v.* 使陷入困境(to cause to have a large amount of problems to deal with)；淹没
terminal ['tɜ:rmɪnl]	*adj.* 末端的(of, or relating to an end) *n.* 终点，末端(an end or extremity of sth.) 记 词根记忆：termin(结束)+al → 终点，末端
tilt [tɪlt]	*v.* (使)倾斜(to slant) *n.* 倾斜(the act of tilting or the condition of being tilted)；斜坡(a sloping surface)
secretive ['si:krətɪv]	*adj.* 守口如瓶的(liking to keep one's thoughts) 搭 be secretive about sth. 对…守口如瓶
coddle ['kɑ:dl]	*v.* 溺爱，悉心照料(to treat with great care and tenderness) 同 cater, cosset, pamper, spoil
narcissist [nɑ:r'sɪsɪst]	*n.* 自恋狂，自恋者(a person who has abnormal and excessive love or admiration for oneself)
panic ['pænɪk]	*adj.* 恐慌的 *n.* 恐慌，惊惶(a sudden unreasoning terror) 记 来自希腊神话中的畜牧神潘(Pan)，panic 是指潘的出现所引起的恐惧 例 During the Battle of Trafalgar, Admiral Nelson remained imperturbable and in full command of the situation in spite of the hysteria and *panic* all around him.

29

□ dank	□ peaky	□ recall	□ acarpous	□ adherent	□ nag
□ escort	□ ruthlessness	□ gustation	□ swamp	□ terminal	□ tilt
□ secretive	□ coddle	□ narcissist	□ panic		

slump [slʌmp]	*v.* 大幅度下降；暴跌（to fall or sink suddenly） 同 plunge, plummet, tumble
lissome ['lɪsəm]	*adj.* 柔软的（lithe; supple; limber） 记 词根记忆：liss（可弯曲的）+ ome → 柔软的
excitability [ɪkˌsaɪtə'bɪləti]	*n.* 易兴奋，易激动（quality of being excitable） 记 来自 excite（*v.* 使兴奋，使激动）
damn [dæm]	*v.*（严厉地）批评，谴责（to criticize severely）*adj.* 该死的（expressing disapproval, anger, impatience, etc.） 记 发音记忆："打母" → 殴打母亲应该受到严厉的批评 → 谴责
parch [pɑːrtʃ]	*v.* 烘烤（to toast）；烤焦（to become scorched） 记 联想记忆：用火把（torch）来烘烤（parch）
table ['teɪbl]	*v.* 搁置，不予考虑（to remove from consideration indefinitely） 记 联想记忆：table 原意为"桌子" → 把问题放在桌子上不去看 → 搁置
goldbrick ['gouldbrɪk]	*v.* 逃避责任，偷懒（to shirk one's assigned duties or responsibility） 记 联想记忆：gold（金）+ brick（砖）→ 一边偷懒一边梦想金砖 → 偷懒
mutter ['mʌtər]	*v.* 咕哝，嘀咕（to speak in a low and indistinct voice） 记 联想记忆：m + utter（发出声音）→ 只会发出 m 音 → 咕哝
bombast ['bɑːmbæst]	*n.* 高调，夸大之辞（pompous language） 记 联想记忆：bomb（空洞的声音；炸弹）+ ast → 像炮弹声 → 高调
glower ['glauər]	*v.* 怒目而视（to stare with sullen anger; scowl） 记 联想记忆：glow（发光）+ er → 眼睛发亮看对方 → 怒目而视
muse [mjuːz]	*v.* 沉思，冥想（to think or meditate in silence） 记 来自 Muse（希腊神话中的缪斯女神）
expel [ɪk'spel]	*v.* 排出（to discharge; eject）；开除（to cut off from membership） 记 词根记忆：ex（出）+ pel（推）→ 向外推 → 排出；开除
endue [ɪn'djuː]	*v.* 赋予，授予（to provide; endow）
protocol ['proutəkɔːl]	*n.* 外交礼节（official etiquette）；协议，草案（an original draft of a document or transaction） 记 词根记忆：proto（首要的）+ col（胶水）→ 礼节很重要，把人凝聚到一起 → 外交礼节
parity ['pærəti]	*n.*（水平、地位、数量等的）同等，相等（equality） 记 词根记忆：par（相等）+ ity → 同等，相等
passe [pæ'seɪ]	*adj.* 已过盛年的（past one's prime）；过时的（behind the times） 同 outmoded
monograph ['mɑːnəgræf]	*n.* 专题论文（a learned treatise on a particular subject） 记 词根记忆：mono（单个的）+ graph（写）→ 为一个主题而写 → 专题论文

□ slump	□ lissome	□ excitability	□ damn	□ parch	□ table
□ goldbrick	□ mutter	□ bombast	□ glower	□ muse	□ expel
□ endue	□ protocol	□ parity	□ passe	□ monograph	

impose [ɪmˈpoʊz]	*v.* 征收(to establish or apply by authority)；强加 记 词根记忆：im(进入) + pos(放) + e → 放进去 → 强加
install [ɪnˈstɔːl]	*v.* 安装，装置(to fix equipment, etc.)；使就职(to induct into an office) 记 词根记忆：in (进) + stall (放) → 放进去 → 安装
hymn [hɪm]	*n.* 赞美诗(any song of praise) 同 psalm
senile [ˈsiːnaɪl]	*adj.* 衰老的(of old age) 记 词根记忆：sen(老)+ile → 衰老的
detraction [dɪˈtrækʃn]	*n.* 贬低，诽谤(unfair criticism) 记 词根记忆：de(向下) + tract(拉，拖) + ion → 向下拉 → 贬低
epithet [ˈepɪθet]	*n.* (贬低人的)短语或形容词(an adjective or phrase used to characterize a person or thing in a derogative sense)；绰号，称号 记 词根记忆：epi(在…下) + thet(=put 放) → (人)放到下面的话 → (贬低人的)短语或形容词
captivate [ˈkæptɪveɪt]	*v.* 迷惑，迷住(to fascinate, attract) 记 联想记忆：captiv(e)(俘房) + ate → 使成为漂亮的俘房来迷惑敌人 → 迷惑
prognosticate [prɒɡˈnɒstɪkeɪt]	*v.* 预言，预示(to foretell from signs or symptoms；predict) 记 词根记忆：pro(提前) + gno(知道) + stic + ate → 预示
sloppy [ˈslɑːpi]	*adj.* 邋遢的，粗心的(slovenly；careless) 记 联想记忆：slop(溅出，弄脏)+py → 衣服弄脏后显得很邋遢 → 邋遢的
den [den]	*n.* 兽穴，窝(animal's hidden home) 同 burrow, hole, lair
advocate	[ˈædvəkeɪt] *v.* 提倡，主张，拥护(to speak publicly in favor) [ˈædvəkət] *n.* 支持者，拥护者(person who supports) 记 词根记忆：ad(向) + voc(叫喊，声音) + ate → 为其摇旗呐喊 → 拥护
gauche [ɡoʊʃ]	*adj.* 笨拙的，不会社交的(lacking social polish；tactless) 同 awkward
greenhorn [ˈɡriːnhɔːrn]	*n.* 初学者(beginner；novice)；容易受骗的人(dupe) 记 组合词：green(绿色) + horn(角) → 原指初生牛犊等动物 → 初学者
rewarding [rɪˈwɔːrdɪŋ]	*adj.* 有益的，值得的(worth doing or having) 同 advantageous, lucrative, profitable, remunerative
projectile [prəˈdʒektl]	*n.* 抛射体(a body projected by external force) 记 词根记忆：pro(向前) + ject(扔) + ile → 扔向前的东西 → 抛射体
punctilious [pʌŋkˈtɪliəs]	*adj.* 一丝不苟的(careful) 记 词根记忆：punct(刺) + ilious → 针刺般准确 → 一丝不苟的

29

scintillate ['sɪntɪleɪt]	*v.* 闪烁(to emit sparks; sparkle); (言谈举止中)焕发才智 记 词根记忆: scintill(火花) + ate → 闪烁
skirmish ['skɜːrmɪʃ]	*n.* 小规模战斗, 小冲突(a minor dispute or contest) 记 联想记忆: skir(看作 skirt, 裙子)+mish(看作 famish, 饥饿) → 女人会为了裙子而起冲突, 为了穿漂亮的裙子宁可饿肚子 → 小冲突
scurry ['skɜːri]	*v.* 急跑, 疾行(to move in a brisk pace; scamper) 记 词根记忆: s + cur(跑) + ry → 急跑
deviate ['diːvieɪt]	*v.* 越轨, 偏离(to diverge; digress) 记 词根记忆: de(偏离) + vi(道路) + ate → 偏离道路的 → 偏离 搭 deviate from 偏离…
smirk [smɜːrk]	*v.* 假笑, 得意地笑(to smile in an affected manner) 同 simper
lust [lʌst]	*n.* 强烈的欲望(overmastering desire) 记 参考: wanderlust(*n.* 旅行癖)
wrought [rɔːt]	*adj.* 做成的, 形成的(worked into shape by artistry or effort); 精制的(made delicately or elaborately)
aristocracy [ˌærɪ'stɑːkrəsi]	*n.* 贵族(the people of the highest social class especially from noble families); 贵族政府, 贵族统治(government in which power is held by the nobility) 记 词根记忆: aristo(最好的) + cracy(统治) → 贵族统治
flossy ['flɑːsi]	*adj.* 华丽的, 时髦的(stylish or glamorous especially at first impression); 丝棉般的, 柔软的(of, relating to, or having the characteristics of floss)
grovel ['grɑːvl]	*v.* 摇尾乞怜, 奴颜婢膝(to behave humbly or abjectly; stoop); 匍匐 记 联想记忆: 在小树林(grove)中匍匐(grovel)前进
sift [sɪft]	*v.* 筛选, 过滤(to separate out by a sieve) 搭 sift sth. out 筛选; 剔除

□ scintillate	□ skirmish	□ scurry	□ deviate	□ smirk	□ lust
□ wrought	□ aristocracy	□ flossy	□ grovel	□ sift	

wage [weɪdʒ]	*v.* 开始，进行(to begin and continue) 搭 wage a war 进行战争
straiten [ˈstreitən]	*v.* 使为难(to subject to distress, privation, or deficiency)；使变窄(to make strait or narrow)
encyclopedic [ɪnˌsaɪkləˈpiːdɪk]	*adj.* 广博的，知识渊博的 记 词根记忆: en + cyclo(圆圈) + ped(儿童教育) + ic → 受遍教育 → 广博的，知识渊博的
slippage [ˈslɪpɪdʒ]	*n.* 滑动，下降(slipping) 记 来自 slip(*v.* 滑)
sever [ˈsevər]	*v.* 断绝，分离(to divide) 记 和 severe(*adj.* 严重的)一起记
incertitude [ɪnˈsɜːrtɪtjuːd]	*n.* 不确定(性)(uncertainty)；无把握，怀疑 记 词根记忆: in(不) + cert(确定的) + itude(表状态) → 不确定(性)
treachery [ˈtretʃəri]	*n.* 背叛(violation of allegiance；treason) 记 词根记忆: treach(=trick 诡计)+ery → 在背后耍诡计 → 背叛 例 The heretofore peaceful natives, seeking retribution for the *treachery* of their supposed allies, became, justifiably enough according to their perspective, embittered and vindictive.
levelheaded [ˌlevlˈhedɪd]	*adj.* 头脑冷静的，清醒的(self-composed and sensible) 记 组合词: level(平坦的) + head(头脑) + ed → 大脑平坦的 → 头脑冷静的
coruscate [ˈkɔːrəskeɪt]	*v.* 闪亮(to give off flashes of light；glitter；sparkle) 记 来自拉丁文 coruscate(*v.* 闪亮)
funky [fʌŋki]	*adj.* 有霉臭味的，有恶臭的(having an offensive odor) 记 联想记忆: 身上有恶臭的(funky)懦夫(funk) 同 foul
delirium [dɪˈlɪriəm]	*n.* 精神错乱(a temporary state of extreme mental disorder；insanity；mania)
mope [moʊp]	*v.* 抑郁，闷闷不乐(to be gloomy and dispirited) *n.* 情绪低落 记 联想记忆: 她天天拖地(mop)，很抑郁(mope)

□ wage	□ straiten	□ encyclopedic	□ slippage	□ sever	□ incertitude
□ treachery	□ levelheaded	□ coruscate	□ funky	□ delirium	□ mope

321

juxtapose [ˌdʒʌkstəˈpoʊz]	v. 并列，并置（to put side by side or close together）
	记 词根记忆：juxta(接近) + pos(放) + e → 挨着放 → 并列，并置
inkling [ˈɪŋklɪŋ]	n. 暗示(hint); 略知，模糊概念（a slight knowledge or vague notion）
	记 联想记忆：ink(墨水) + ling(小东西) → 小墨迹 → 暗示
debris [dəˈbriː]	n. 碎片，残骸（the remains of sth. broken down or destroyed）
	记 发音记忆："堆玻璃" → 一堆碎玻璃 → 碎片，残骸
regurgitate [rɪˈɡɜːrdʒɪteɪt]	v. 涌回，流回（to become thrown or poured back）; 反胃，反刍（to cause to pour back, especially to cast up）
glamor [ˈɡlæmər]	v. 迷惑（to attract and confuse）n. 魔法，魔力（a magic spell）; 迷人的美，魅力（an exciting and often illusory and romantic attractiveness）
wallop [ˈwɑːləp]	n. 重击，猛击（a hard or severe blow）v. 重击，猛打（to hit with force）
	记 联想记忆：wall(墙)+op → 在生气时用力打墙 → 重击，猛打
advisable [ədˈvaɪzəbl]	adj. 适当的，可取的（proper to be advised or recommended）
	记 来自 advise（v. 建议）
slattern [ˈslætərn]	adj. 不整洁的(slatternly) n. 邋遢的女人（an untidy slovenly woman）
	同 slut
hoe [hoʊ]	n. 锄头（any of various implements for tilling, mixing or raking）
	记 联想记忆：用锄头(hoe)挖洞(hole)
tart [tɑːrt]	adj. 酸的(acid); 尖酸的（acrimonious; biting）
	搭 a tart reply 尖刻的答复
stupor [ˈstuːpər]	n. 昏迷，恍惚（no sensibility）
	同 swoon, torpor, trance
resentment [rɪˈzentmənt]	n. 愤恨，怨恨（the feeling of resenting sth.）
	例 Despite the team members' *resentment* of the new coach's training rules, they tolerated them as long as he did not apply them too strictly.
mince [mɪns]	v. 切碎（to chop into very small pieces）; 装腔作势地小步走（to move with short, affected steps）
	记 参考：minute(adj. 微小的); minutia(n. 细节)
supreme [suːˈpriːm]	adj. 最高的（having the highest position）; 极度的（highest in degree）
	记 联想记忆：supre(=super 超过)+me → 超越我的 → 最高的
brace [breɪs]	v. 支撑，加固（to strengthen; prop up）n. 支撑物(fastener)
	记 联想记忆：brac(手臂) + e → 用手臂支撑使稳固 → 支撑，加固
murmur [ˈmɜːrmər]	v. 柔声地说; 抱怨（to complain; grumble）
	搭 murmur against（私下）发牢骚
extenuate [ɪkˈstenjueɪt]	v. 掩饰（罪行），减轻（罪行等）（to lessen the seriousness of an offense or guilt by giving excuses）
	记 词根记忆：ex + tenu(细的) + ate → 使…微不足道 → 掩饰（罪行）
fancied [ˈfænsɪd]	adj. 空想的，虚构的（of or relating to fancy）
	记 来自 fancy(n. 想象的事物)

spasmodic [spæz'mɑːdɪk]	adj. 痉挛的(of a spasm); 间歇性的(intermittent) 搭 spasmodic fighting 零星的战斗
refraction [rɪ'frækʃn]	n. 折射(bending of a ray of light) 搭 atmosphere refraction 大气折射
matriculate [mə'trɪkjuleɪt]	v. 录取(to enroll in college or graduate school) 记 词根记忆：matr(母亲) + iculate → 成为母校 → 录取
pell-mell [ˌpel'mel]	adv. 混乱地(in mingled confusion or disorder) 记 组合词：pell(羊皮纸) + mell(使混合) → 羊皮纸揉和在一起 → 混乱地
drench [drentʃ]	v. 使湿透(to wet through; soak) 记 词根记忆：drench(=drink 喝) → 喝饱 → 使湿透；注意不要和 trench (v. 挖战壕)相混
grit [grɪt]	n. 沙粒(rough, hard particles of sand); 决心，勇气(stubborn courage; pluck) v. 下定决心，咬紧牙关(to clench or grind the teeth in anger or determination)
mulish ['mjuːlɪʃ]	adj. 骡一样的，执拗的(stubborn as a mule) 同 adamant, headstrong, obstinate
gesture ['dʒestʃər]	n. 姿势，手势(the movement of the body to express a certain meaning); 姿态，表示 例 As a *gesture* of good will, we have decided to waive the charges on this occasion.
remonstrate [rɪ'mɑːnstreɪt]	v. 抗议(to earnestly present and urge reasons in opposition); 告诫(to expostulate) 记 词根记忆：re(重新) + monstr(显现) + ate → 一再表示对别人的不满 → 抗议
buffet ['bʌfɪt]	v. 反复敲打；连续打击(to strike sharply especially with the hand; to strike repeatedly)
rudder ['rʌdər]	n. 船舵；领导者 记 联想记忆：最前面的奔跑者(runner)是领导者(rudder)
sticky ['stɪki]	adj. 湿热的(humid); 闷热的(muggy) 记 来自 stick(v. 粘住)
carbohydrate [ˌkɑːrbou'haɪdreɪt]	n. 碳水化合物(a natural class of food that provides energy to the body) 记 词根记忆：carbo(碳) + hydr(水) + ate → 碳水化合物
hanker ['hæŋkər]	v. 渴望，追求(to have a strong or persistent desire) 记 hanger(绞刑执行者)渴望(hanker)心灵的平静
membrane ['membreɪn]	n. 薄膜(a thin sheet of synthetic material used as a filter, separator); 膜 (a thin soft pliable sheet or layer especially of animal or plant origin) 记 词根记忆：membr(=member 成员) + ane → 身体的一部分 → 膜
staunch [stɔːntʃ]	adj. 坚定的，忠诚的(steadfast in loyalty or principle) 同 constant, inflexible, stalwart, tried-and-true

30

jar [dʒɑːr]	*v.* 震动，摇晃；冲突，抵触(to clash)；震惊(to give a sudden shock)；发出刺耳声(to make a harsh or discordant sound) *n.* 广口坛子 记 联想记忆：酒吧(bar)里摆满了酒坛子(jar) 例 Instead of taking exaggerated precautions against touching or tipping or *jarring* the bottle of wine, the waitress handled it quite nonchalantly, being careful only to use a napkin to keep her hands from the cool bottle itself.
utter [ˈʌtər]	*adj.* 完全的(complete) *v.* 发出(声音)，说(话)(to make a sound or produce words)
luster [ˈlʌstər]	*n.* 光辉；光泽 *v.* 使有光泽；使有光彩，给…增光；发光 记 词根记忆：lus(光) + ter → 光辉
catharsis [kəˈθɑːrsɪs]	*n.* 宣泄，净化(the purifying of the emotions) 记 词根记忆：cathar(清洁) + sis → 净化
cogitate [ˈkɑːdʒɪteɪt]	*v.* 慎重思考，思索(to think seriously and deeply; ponder) 记 联想记忆：有说服力的(cogent)东西总是经过慎重思考(cogitate)的
chauvinistic [ˌʃoʊvɪˈnɪstɪk]	*adj.* 沙文主义的，盲目爱国的(excessive or blind patriotism) 记 来自人名 Chauvin，因其过分的爱国主义和对拿破仑的忠诚而闻名
penicillin [ˌpenɪˈsɪlɪn]	*n.* 青霉素 记 发音记忆："盘尼西林"
quail [kweɪl]	*v.* 畏缩，发抖，恐惧(to coil in dread or fear; cower) 记 原意为"鹌鹑"，鹌鹑胆子较小，所以就有了"恐惧"的意思
distress [dɪˈstres]	*n.* 痛苦，悲痛(pain; suffering; agony; anguish) 记 词根记忆：di(s)(加强) + stress(压力，紧张) → 压倒 → 悲痛
bullion [ˈbʊliən]	*n.* 金条，银条(gold or silver in the form of ingots) 记 联想记忆：bull(公牛) + (l)ion(狮子) → 卖公牛，狮子得金银 → 金条，银条
rescission [rɪˈsɪʒn]	*n.* 撤销，废除(an act of rescinding) 记 词根记忆：re + sciss(切) + ion → 切除 → 废除
wicked [ˈwɪkɪd]	*adj.* 邪恶的(morally very bad)；讨厌的(disgustingly unpleasant)；有害的(causing or likely to cause harm, distress, or trouble)；淘气的(playful in a rather troublesome way) 例 People should not be praised for their virtue if they lack the energy to be *wicked*; in such cases, goodness is merely the effect of indolence.
satiny [ˈsætni]	*adj.* 光滑的，柔软的(smooth, soft, and glossy) 记 联想记忆：satin(缎子) + y → 像缎子一样光滑的 → 光滑的
crabbed [ˈkræbɪd]	*adj.* 暴躁的(peevish; ill-tempered; cross)
effrontery [ɪˈfrʌntəri]	*n.* 厚颜无耻，放肆(unashamed boldness; impudence) 记 词根记忆：ef + front(脸，面) + ery → 不要脸面 → 厚颜无耻

budget [ˈbʌdʒɪt]	*n.* 预算(plan of how money will be spent over a period of time) *v.* 做预算，安排开支(to plan in advance the expenditure of) 记 联想记忆：bud(花蕾) + get(得到) → 得到花蕾 → 用钱买花 → 做预算 搭 on a (tight) budget 拮据
plumber [ˈplʌmər]	*n.* 管子工，铅管工(a person whose job is to fit and repair water pipes or bathroom apparatus)
unkempt [ˌʌnˈkempt]	*adj.* 蓬乱的，未梳理的(not combed)；不整洁的，乱糟糟的(messy)
vacuous [ˈvækjuəs]	*adj.* 空虚的，发呆的(marked by lack of ideas or intelligence) 同 bare, blank, empty, inane, vacant
consonant [ˈkɑːnsənənt]	*adj.* 协调的，一致的(being in agreement or accord) 记 词根记忆：con(共同) + son(声音) + ant → 同声的 → 一致的
rupture [ˈrʌptʃər]	*n./v.* 破裂，断裂(to break apart or burst) 记 词根记忆：rupt(断) + ure → 断裂
swear [swer]	*v.* 诅咒(to use profane or obscene language) 同 blaspheme, execrate
maleficent [məˈlefɪsənt]	*adj.* 有害的；作恶的，犯罪的(doing evil) 记 词根记忆：male(坏的) + fic(做) + ent → 做坏事的 → 作恶的
tranquility [trænˈkwɪləti]	*n.* 宁静，安静(the quality or state of being tranquil) 记 来自 tranquil(*adj.* 宁静的，安静的)
discombobulated [ˌdɪskəmˈbɑːbjuleitɪd]	*adj.* 扰乱的，打乱的(in a state of confusion)
maunder [ˈmɔːndər]	*v.* 胡扯(to speak indistinctly or disconnectedly)；游荡(to wander slowly and idly)
finagle [fɪˈneɪɡl]	*v.* 骗取，骗得(to obtain by trickery) 同 cheat, defraud, swindle
illusive [ɪˈluːsɪv]	*adj.* 迷惑人的，迷幻的(deceiving and unreal) 记 词根记忆：il + lus(玩耍) + ive → 头脑对某事闹着玩的 → 迷幻的
tatter [ˈtætər]	*n.* 碎片(a part torn and left hanging) *v.* 撕碎(to make ragged) 搭 in tatters 破烂不堪；被毁坏的
vest [vest]	*v.* 授予，赋予(to grant or endow with a particular authority, right, or property)
stroll [stroʊl]	*v.* 漫步，闲逛(to walk in an idle manner; ramble) 记 联想记忆：st(看作 street，街道) + roll(转) → 在大街上转悠 → 闲逛
coma [ˈkoʊmə]	*n.* 昏迷(deep, prolonged unconsciousness) 搭 go into/be in a coma 陷入/处于昏迷状态

30

entirety	*n.* 整体，全面（completeness）
[ɪnˈtaɪərəti]	记 来自 entire（*v.* 完整的）
whisper	*v.* 耳语，低语（to speak softly）
[ˈwɪspər]	记 联想记忆：whi（看作 who，谁）+sper（看作 speaker，说话者）→ 谁在小声说话 → 耳语，低语
lace	*n.* 带子（a cord or leather strip）；网眼织物（a netlike decorative cloth made of fine thread）
[leɪs]	记 发音记忆："蕾丝" → 网眼织物
seasoned	*adj.* 经验丰富的，老练的（experienced）
[ˈsiːznd]	搭 seasoned soldier 老兵
celebrated	*adj.* 有名的，知名的（famous; renowned）
[ˈselɪbreɪtɪd]	记 来自 celebrate（*v.* 庆祝，赞扬）
	搭 be widely celebrated 广泛知名的
brake	*n.* 刹车；阻碍 *v.* 刹车（to slow down or stop with a brake）；阻止（to retard as if by a brake）
[breɪk]	记 是 break（*v.* 打破，违反）的古典形式
forge	*n.* 铁匠铺（smithy）*v.* 使形成，达成（to form or shape）；伪造（to counterfeit）；锻制，打铁
[fɔːrdʒ]	记 发音记忆："仿制" → 伪造
needle	*n.* 针；针叶（a narrow stiff leaf of conifers）
[ˈniːdl]	搭 a needle in a haystack 几乎不可能找到的东西
brackish	*adj.* 微咸的（somewhat saline）；难吃的（distasteful）
[ˈbrækɪʃ]	记 联想记忆：brack（看作 black）+ ish（看作 fish）→ 黑色的咸鱼 → 微咸的
saucy	*adj.* 粗鲁的（rude and impudent）；俏皮的（impertinent in an entertaining way）；漂亮的（pretty）
[ˈsɔːsi]	
kin	*n.* 亲属（the members of one's family）
[kɪn]	例 Their hierarchy of loyalties is first to oneself, next to *kin*, then to fellow tribe members, and finally to compatriots.
masticate	*v.* 咀嚼（to chew food）；把…磨成浆（to grind to a pulp）
[ˈmæstɪkeɪt]	记 词根记忆：mast（乳房）+ icate → 原指小孩吃奶 → 咀嚼
spell	*n.* 连续的一段时间（a continuous period of time）
[spel]	记 spell 还有"拼写"、"咒语"等意思
	例 The breathing *spell* provided by the moratorium on arms shipments should give all the combatants a chance to reevaluate their positions.
bazaar	*n.* 集市，市场（a market or street of shops）
[bəˈzɑːr]	记 外来词，原指"东方国家的大集市"，今天的中国新疆一带仍把集市叫"巴扎"
locus	*n.* 地点，所在地（site；location）
[ˈloʊkəs]	记 词根记忆：loc（地方）+ us → 地点，所在地
	例 She writes across generational lines, making the past so vivid that our belief that the present is the true *locus* of experience is undermined.

□ entirety	□ whisper	□ lace	□ seasoned	□ celebrated	□ brake
□ forge	□ needle	□ brackish	□ saucy	□ kin	□ masticate
□ spell	□ bazaar	□ locus			

epideictic [ˌepɪˈdaɪktɪk]	*adj.* 夸耀的(pretentious)
premium [ˈpriːmɪəm]	*n.* 保险费(the consideration paid for a contract of insurance); 奖金(a reward or recompense) 记 词根记忆: pre(在…之前) + m(=empt 拿; 买) + ium → 提前买下的东西 → 保险费
scrutable [ˈskruːtəbl]	*adj.* 可以了解的, 可解读的(capable of being deciphered)
purgatory [ˈpɜːrɡətɔːri]	*n.* 炼狱(a place of great suffering) 记 联想记忆: purg(清洁的) + at + ory → 使灵魂清洁的地方 → 炼狱
scald [skɔːld]	*v.* 烫伤, 烫洗(to burn with hot liquid or steam) *n.* 烫伤(an injury caused by scalding)
inspiration [ˌɪnspəˈreɪʃn]	*n.* 启示, 灵感(thought or emotion inspired by sth.) 记 词根记忆: in(进入) + spir(呼吸) + ation → 吸入(灵气) → 灵感
slake [sleɪk]	*v.* 满足; 平息(to satisfy; quench) 记 联想联想: s+lake(湖) → 看到湖水很满足 → 满足
scandal [ˈskændl]	*n.* 丑闻; 流言飞语, 诽谤(malicious or defamatory gossip) 记 联想记忆: scan(扫描) + dal → 扫描时事, 揭露丑闻 → 丑闻 例 She was accused of plagiarism in a dispute over a short story, and, though exonerated, she never recovered from the accusation and the *scandal*.
coagulate [koʊˈæɡjuleɪt]	*v.* 使凝结(to curdle; clot) 记 词根记忆: co(一起) + ag(做) + ulate → 做到一起 → 使凝结
thaw [θɔː]	*v.* 解冻, 融化(to go from a frozen to a liquid state; melt) 记 联想记忆: t + haw(看作 hoe, 锄地) → 冰雪融化便可以锄地了 → 解冻, 融化
pastiche [pæˈstiːʃ]	*n.* 混合拼凑的作品(a musical, literary, or artistic composition made up of selections from different works)
pedestal [ˈpedɪstl]	*n.* (柱石或雕像的)基座(base; foundation) 记 词根记忆: ped(脚) + estal → 做脚的东西 → 基座
namby-pamby [ˌnæmbɪˈpæmbɪ]	*adj.* 乏味的(insipid); 懦弱的(infirm) *n.* 懦弱的人
derogate [ˈderəɡeɪt]	*v.* 贬低, 诽谤(to lower in esteem; disparage) 记 词根记忆: de(坏) + rog(问, 说) +·ate → 说坏话 → 贬低
extricate [ˈekstrɪkeɪt]	*v.* 摆脱, 脱离; 拯救, 救出(to set free; release) 记 词根记忆: ex + tric(小障碍物) + ate → 从小障碍物中出来 → 救出
neologism [niˈɑːlədʒɪzəm]	*n.* 新字, 新词(a new word or phrase) 记 词根记忆: neo(新的) + log(说话) + ism → 新的话语 → 新字, 新词
regress [rɪˈɡres]	*v.* 倒退, 复归, 逆行(to return to a former or a less developed state) 记 词根记忆: re(向后) + gress(行走) → 向后走 → 倒退, 复归, 逆行

30

---

externalize	*v.* 使…表面化（to make sth. external）
[ɪk'stɜ:rnəlaɪz]	记 来自 external（*adj.* 外来的，在外的）
lasso	*n.* （捕捉牛、马用的）套索（a long rope used to catch cattle or wild horses）
['læsoʊ]	记 谐音记忆："拉索" → 套索
comma	*n.* 逗号（punctuation mark to indicate a light pause）
['kɑ:mə]	记 和 coma（*n.* 昏迷）一起记
quotidian	*adj.* 每日的（occurring everyday）；平凡的（commonplace）
[kwoʊ'tɪdiən]	记 词根记忆：quoti（每）+ di（日子）+ an → 每日的
	搭 quotidian behavior 日常行为
bonhomie	*n.* 好性情，和蔼（good-natured easy friendliness）
[ˌbɑːnə'miː]	记 联想记忆：bon（好）+ homie（看作 home，家）→ 好好待在家里 → 好性情，和蔼
accost	*v.* 搭话（to approach and speak first to a person boldly）
[ə'kɔːst]	记 联想记忆：ac（靠近）+ cost（花费）→ 和人认识后要花钱 → 搭话
readily	*adv.* 乐意地（without hesitation；willingly）；容易地（without difficulty；easily）
['redɪli]	记 来自 ready（*adj.* 乐意的，情愿的）
	例 The sheer bulk of data from the mass media seems to overpower us and drive us to synoptic accounts for an easily and *readily* digestible portion of news.
chaste	*adj.* 贞洁的（virtuous）；朴实的（restrained and simple）
[tʃeɪst]	记 联想记忆：贞洁的（chaste）姑娘被追逐（chase）
lurch	*n.* 突然的倾斜 *v.* 蹒跚而行（to stagger）
[lɜːrtʃ]	记 联想记忆：和 lunch（*n.* 午餐）一起记
befoul	*v.* 弄脏，诽谤（to make foul as with dirt or waste）
[bɪ'faʊl]	同 defile, maculate
legislature	*n.* 立法机关，立法团体（body of people with the power to make and change laws）
['ledʒɪsleɪtʃər]	记 词根记忆：leg（法律）+ is + lature → 立法机关，立法团体
	例 Sponsors of the bill were relieved because there was no opposition to it within the *legislature* until after the measure had been signed into law.
faze	*v.* 打扰，扰乱（to disconcert；dismay；embarrass）
[feɪz]	记 和 laze（*v.* 懒散）一起记
caulk	*v.* 填塞（缝隙）使不漏水（to stop up the cracks, seams, etc.）
[kɔːk]	
croon	*v.* 低声歌唱（to sing in a soft manner）
[kruːn]	记 联想记忆：cr（看作 cry，哭泣）+ oon（看作 moon，月亮）→ 对着月亮哭泣 → 低声歌唱
eloquence	*n.* 雄辩，口才（the ability to express ideas and opinions readily and well）
['eləkwəns]	记 词根记忆：e + loqu（说）+ ence → 能说 → 雄辩

□ externalize	□ lasso	□ comma	□ quotidian	□ bonhomie	□ accost
□ readily	□ chaste	□ lurch	□ befoul	□ legislature	□ faze
□ caulk	□ croon	□ eloquence			

penury [ˈpenjəri]	n. 贫穷(severe poverty); 吝啬(extreme and often niggardly frugality) 同 destitution
disengage [ˌdɪsɪnˈɡeɪdʒ]	v. 脱离，解开(to release from sth. engaged) 记 词根记忆：dis(不) + engage(与…建立密切关系) → 不与…建立密切关系 → 脱离
deed [diːd]	n. 行为，行动(action); (土地或建筑物的)转让契约、证书(a document which transfers a present interest in property)
raff [ræf]	n. 大量，许多(a great deal, many)
nugatory [ˈnuːɡətɔːri]	adj. 无价值的，琐碎的(trifling; worthless) 记 词根记忆：nug(玩笑) + atory → 让人一笑而过的 → 无价值的
plague [pleɪɡ]	n. 瘟疫(fatal epidemic disease); 讨厌的人(nuisance) v. 烦扰(to disturb or annoy persistently) 例 One of the great killers until barely 50 years ago, tuberculosis ("consumption" as it was then named) seemed a scourge or *plague* rather than the long-term chronic illness it was.
imbecile [ˈɪmbəsl]	n. 低能者，弱智者，极愚蠢的人(a very foolish or stupid person) 记 dolt, fool, idiot
squabble [ˈskwɑːbl]	n. 争吵(a noisy quarrel, usually about a trivial matter) 同 bicker, fuss, row, spat, tiff
wrist [rɪst]	n. 腕，腕关节 (the joint between the hand and the lower part of the arm) 搭 wrist watch 手表
slick [slɪk]	adj. 熟练的 (skillful and effective); 圆滑的 (clever); 光滑的(smooth and slippery)
interrogate [ɪnˈterəɡeɪt]	v. 审问，审讯(to question formally and systematically) 记 词根记忆：inter(在…中间) + rog(问) + ate → 在中间问 → 审问
hoodwink [ˈhʊdwɪŋk]	v. 蒙混，欺骗(to mislead or confuse by trickery; dupe) 记 联想记忆：hood(帽兜) + wink(眨眼) → 眨眼之间从帽兜中变出(像变魔术一样) → 蒙混，欺骗
inappreciable [ˌɪnəˈpriːʃəbl]	adj. 微不足道的(too small to be perceived) 记 词根记忆：in(不) + ap + preci(价值) + able(能…的) → 没有价值的 → 微不足道的
impel [ɪmˈpel]	v. 推进(to push; propel); 驱使(to force, compel, or urge) 记 词根记忆：im(在…里面) + pel(推) → 推进
seamy [ˈsiːmi]	adj. 丑恶的，污秽的(unpleasant; degraded; sordid) 记 联想记忆：seam(缝)+y → 裂缝里的 → 污秽的
fatten [ˈfætn]	v. 长胖，变肥(to become fat); 使…肥沃(to make fertile); 装满 记 来自 fat(adj. 胖的)

30

squabble

□ penury	□ disengage	□ deed	□ raff	□ nugatory	□ plague
□ imbecile	□ squabble	□ wrist	□ slick	□ interrogate	□ hoodwink
□ inappreciable	□ impel	□ seamy	□ fatten		

consul [ˈkɑːnsl]	*n.* 领事(an official appointed by a state to live in a foreign country) 记 联想记忆:领事(consul)常常收到来自各方的咨询(consult)
immunity [ɪˈmjuːnəti]	*n.* 免疫力;豁免(exemption) 搭 immunity to/against 对⋯的免疫力
agitated [ˈædʒɪteɪtɪd]	*adj.* 激动的(excited);不安的(perturbed)
encipher [ɪnˈsaɪfər]	*v.* 译成密码(to convert a message into cipher) 记 词根记忆:en(进入) + cipher(密码) → 译成密码
inclement [ɪnˈklemənt]	*adj.* (天气)严酷的(severe; stormy);严厉的(rough; severe) 记 联想记忆:in(不) + clement(仁慈的) → 不仁慈的 → 严酷的;严厉的
guttle [ˈɡʌtl]	*v.* 狼吞虎咽(to eat quickly and greedily) 记 联想记忆:gut(肠子) + tle → 肠子容量很大,消化快 → 狼吞虎咽 同 gobble, gulp, swallow
cow [kaʊ]	*n.* 母牛 *v.* 威胁(to threat)
slack [slæk]	*adj.* 懈怠的,不活跃的(sluggish; inactive);(绳)松弛的(loose) *v.* 懈怠,偷懒
extemporize [ɪkˈstempəraɪz]	*v.* 即兴演说(to speak extemporaneously) 记 词根记忆:ex + tempor(时间) + ize → 不在(安排的)时间之内 → 即兴演说
philology [fɪˈlɑːlədʒi]	*n.* 语文学,语文研究 记 词根记忆:phil(爱) + o + log(说话) + y → 语文学

Few things are impossible in themselves; and it is often for want of will, rather than of means, that man fails to succeed.

事情很少有根本做不成的;其所以做不成,与其说是条件不够,不如说是由于决心不够。

——法国作家 罗切福考尔德(La Rocheforcauld, French writer)

☐ consul   ☐ immunity   ☐ agitated   ☐ encipher   ☐ inclement   ☐ guttle
☐ cow   ☐ slack   ☐ extemporize   ☐ philology

Word List 31

disproof	*n.* 反证，反驳（the act of refuting or disproving）
[ˌdɪsˈpruːf]	记 词根记忆：dis(相反的) + proof(看作 prov, 证明) → 相反的证明 → 反证
pastoral	*adj.* 田园生活的（idyllic；rural）；宁静的（pleasingly peaceful and innocent）
[ˈpæstərəl]	记 联想记忆：pastor(牧人) + al → 田园生活的
aerate	*v.* 充气，让空气进入（to cause air to circulate through）
[ˈereɪt]	记 词根记忆：aer(空气) + ate(表动作) → 充气
frumpy	*adj.* 邋遢的（dowdy）；老式的，过时的（outdated）
[ˈfrʌmpɪ]	记 来自 frump(*n.* 衣着邋遢或老式的女子)
olfactory	*adj.* 嗅觉的（of the sense of smell）
[ɑːlˈfæktəri]	记 词根记忆：ol(=smell 味) + fact(做) + ory → 做出味道来的 → 嗅觉的
	搭 olfactory sense 嗅觉
stifle	*v.* 感到窒息（to be unable to breathe comfortably）；抑止（to prevent from happening）
[ˈstaɪfl]	
windfall	*n.* 被风吹落的果实（fallen fruit）；意外的收获，意料之外（an unexpected gain or advantage）
[ˈwɪndfɔːl]	
noose	*n.* 绳圈，套索（a loop formed in a rope）
[nuːs]	记 和 loose(*adj.* 松的)一起记
ineffable	*adj.* 不可言喻的，难以表达的（inexpressible）；避讳的
[ɪnˈefəbl]	记 词根记忆：in(不) + ef(出) + fa(说) + ble → 不能说出的 → 不可言喻的
suggestive	*adj.* 暗示的（giving a suggestion；indicative）
[səˈdʒestɪv]	同 evocative, redolent, symbolic
gabble	*v.* 急促而不清楚地说（to talk rapidly and incoherently）
[ˈgæbl]	记 来自 gab(*v.* 空谈，瞎扯)；不要和 gobble(*v.* 贪婪地大口吃)相混
cronyism	*n.* 任人唯亲；对好朋友的偏袒（favoritism shown to cronies as in political appointments to office）
[ˈkrəʊniːɪzəm]	记 来自 crony(*n.* 密友，亲密的伙伴)
chisel	*n.* 凿子 *v.* 凿
[ˈtʃɪzl]	

□ disproof	□ pastoral	□ aerate	□ frumpy	□ olfactory	□ stifle
□ windfall	□ noose	□ ineffable	□ suggestive	□ gabble	□ cronyism
□ chisel					

missive [ˈmɪsɪv]	*n.* 信件，(尤指)公函(letter especially written statement) 记 词根记忆：miss(发送) + ive → 由他处送出的 → 信件
gild [gɪld]	*v.* 镀金(to overlay with a thin covering of gold)；虚饰(to give an attractive but often deceptive appearance to) 搭 a gilded frame 镀金框架
cadge [kædʒ]	*v.* 乞讨(to get sth. from sb. by asking)；占便宜 搭 cadge from/off 乞讨
conspire [kənˈspaɪər]	*v.* 密谋，共谋(to act together secretly in order to commit a crime) 记 词根记忆：con (共同) + spir (呼吸) + e → 一个鼻孔出气 → 搞阴谋 → 密谋
landslide [ˈlændslaɪd]	*n.* 山崩(a slide of a large mass of dirt and rock down a mountain or cliff)；压倒性的胜利(an overwhelming victory) 记 组合词：land(地) + slide(滑行) → 地向下滑 → 山崩
arson [ˈɑːrsn]	*n.* 纵火(罪)，放火(罪)(the crime of purposely setting fire) 记 词根记忆：ars(=ard 热) + on → 火在燃烧 → 纵火(罪)
hunker [ˈhʌŋkər]	*v.* 蹲下(to squat close to the ground)；顽固地坚持(to hold stubbornly to a position)
runic [ˈruːnik]	*adj.* 古北欧文字的；神秘的 记 联想记忆：run(追逐) + ic(…的) → 吸引人不断追逐的 → 神秘的
drain [dreɪn]	*v.* 排水(to flow off gradually or completely)；喝光(to drink the entire contents of) 记 联想记忆：d + rain(雨水) → 排去雨水 → 排水
hardbitten [ˌhɑːrdˈbɪtn]	*adj.* 不屈的，顽强的(stubborn; tough; dogged) 记 组合词：hard(硬) + bitten(咬) → 硬得咬不动 → 顽强的
interlock [ˌɪntərˈlɑːk]	*v.* 互锁，连结(to lock together) 记 联想记忆：inter + lock(锁) → 互相锁 → 互锁
expropriate [eksˈprouprieɪt]	*v.* 充公，没收(to deprive of ownership; dispossess) 记 词根记忆：ex + propr(拥有) + iate → 不再拥有 → 没收
prophet [ˈprɑːfit]	*n.* 先知，预言者(a person who claims to be able to tell the course of future events)
accumulate [əˈkjuːmjəleɪt]	*v.* 积聚，积累(to pile up; collect) 记 词根记忆：ac(加强) + cumul(堆积) + ate → 不断堆积 → 积累 搭 accumulate power to... 为…积攒能量
mobile [ˈmoubl]	*adj.* 易于移动的(easy to move) 记 词根记忆：mob(动) + ile(易…的) → 易于移动的 搭 mobile home 活动房屋
fringe [frɪndʒ]	*n.* (窗帘等)须边；边缘(an outer edge; border; margin) 记 联想记忆：f + ring(一圈) + e → 周围一圈 → 边缘；和 flange(*n.* 凸出的轮缘)一起记

□ missive	□ gild	□ cadge	□ conspire	□ landslide	□ arson
□ hunker	□ runic	□ drain	□ hardbitten	□ interlock	□ expropriate
□ prophet	□ accumulate	□ mobile	□ fringe		

332

chase [tʃeɪs]	v. 雕镂(to make a groove in); 追逐(to follow rapidly);追捕 记 联想记忆: 谁动了我的奶酪(cheese), 我就去追赶(chase)谁
harangue [hə'ræŋ]	n. 长篇攻击性演说(a long, scolding speech; tirade) 记 联想记忆: har(看作 hard) + angue(看作 argue) → 强硬的辩论 → 长篇攻击性演说
repercussion [ˌriːpər'kʌʃn]	n. 反响(a reciprocal action); 反应, 影响(a widespread, indirect effect of an act or event); 回声(reflection; resonance) 记 联想记忆: re(反复) + percussion(震动) → 反复震动 → 回声
temporize ['tempəraɪz]	v. 拖延(to draw out discussions or negotiations so as to gain time); 见风使舵(to act to suit the time or occasion) 记 词根记忆: tempor(时间) + ize → 拖延
presumption [prɪ'zʌmpʃn]	n. 放肆, 傲慢(presumptuous attitude or conduct); 假定(assumption) 记 来自 presume(v. 推测, 认定)
peachy ['piːtʃi]	adj. 极好的, 漂亮的(unusually fine) 同 splendid
tasty ['teɪsti]	adj. 美味的(having a pleasant flavor); 有品位的(having or showing good taste)
verge [vɜːrdʒ]	n. 边缘(border; edge; rim) 搭 be on the verge of 很接近, 濒于
prong [prɔːŋ]	v. 刺, 贯穿(to stab, pierce, or break up with a pronged device) n. 叉子, 尖齿; 齿状物
caucus ['kɔːkəs]	n. 政党高层会议(a private meeting of leaders of a political party)
petal ['petl]	n. 花瓣(a leaf-like division of the corolla of a flower)
discretionary [dɪ'skreʃəneri]	adj. 自由决定的(left to one's own discretion or judgement) 记 词根记忆: discret(互不相连的) + ion + ary → 互不相连的决定 → 自由决定的
poster ['poʊstər]	n. 海报, 招贴画(a large placard displayed in a public place) 记 联想记忆: post(邮寄; 张贴)+er → 海报, 招贴画
appraise [ə'preɪz]	v. 评价, 鉴定(to assess the value or quality) 记 联想记忆: ap(加强) + praise(价值, 赞扬) → 给以价值 → 评价
ramble ['ræmbl]	n. 漫步(a leisurely excursion for pleasure) v. 漫步(to move aimlessly from place to place) 记 联想记忆: r + amble(缓行, 漫步) → 漫步
testy ['testi]	adj. 暴躁的, 易怒的(easily annoyed; irritable) 记 联想记忆: test(考试) + y → 为考试伤脑筋, 很不耐烦 → 易怒的
impuissance [ɪm'pjuːɪsəns]	n. 无力, 虚弱(weakness) 记 联想记忆: im(不) + puissance(力量) → 无力

31

expatriate [ˌeks'peɪtriət]	*v.* 驱逐，流放(to banish; exile)；移居国外(to withdraw from residence in one's native country) 记 词根记忆：ex(出) + patri(国家) + ate → 驱逐；移居国外
distaste [dɪs'teɪst]	*v.* 厌恶 *n.* 厌恶，不喜欢 记 词根记忆：dis(不) + taste(爱好) → 不爱好 → 厌恶
orient ['ɔːriənt]	*adj.* 上升的(rising) *v.* 确定方向(to ascertain the bearings of)；使熟悉情况(to acquaint with a particular situation) 记 词根记忆：ori(升起) + ent → 上升的
cheeky ['tʃiːki]	*adj.* 无礼的，厚颜无耻的(insolently bold; impudent) 同 audacious, brash, brazen, impertinent
lexicographer [ˌleksɪ'kɑːɡrəfər]	*n.* 词典编纂者(a person who writes or compiles a dictionary) 记 词根记忆：lex(词汇) + ico + graph(写) + er → 写词典的人 → 词典编纂者 例 Although the meanings of words may necessarily be liable to change, it does not follow that the *lexicographer* is therefore unable to render spelling, in a great measure, constant.
depute [dɪ'pjuːt]	*v.* 派…为代表或代理(to give authority to someone else as deputy) 记 词根记忆：de + pute(放) → 放某人出去 → 派…为代表或代理
revenue ['revənuː]	*n.* 收入，收益(the total income)；税收 记 词根记忆：re(回) + ven(来) + ue → 回来的东西 → 收入
liberty ['lɪbərti]	*n.* 随意(too much freedom in speech or behavior)；自由 记 词根记忆：liber(自由的) + ty → 随意；自由 例 A war, even if fought for individual *liberty* and democratic rights, usually requires that these principles be suspended, for they are incompatible with the regimentation and discipline necessary for military efficiency.
hedge [hedʒ]	*n.* 树篱；保护手段(a means of defense)；障碍(barrier; limit) 记 联想记忆：边缘(edge)被 h 围成了树篱
desist [dɪ'zɪst]	*v.* 停止，中止(to cease to proceed or act) 同 abandon, discontinue, quit, relinquish, remit
procession [prə'seʃn]	*n.* 行列(a group of individuals moving along in an orderly way)；列队行进(continuous forward movement) 记 词根记忆：pro(向前) + cess(走) + ion → 列队行进
ransom ['rænsəm]	*n.* 赎金；赎身 *v.* 赎回(to free from captivity or punishment by paying a price)
prime [praɪm]	*n.* 全盛时期(the most active, thriving, or satisfying state or period) *adj.* 首先的(original)；主要的；最好的(first in rank, authority, or significance) 记 词根记忆：prim(最早的) + e → 主要的 例 The *Prime* Minister tried to act but the plans were frustrated by her cabinet.

□ expatriate	□ distaste	□ orient	□ cheeky	□ lexicographer	□ depute
□ revenue	□ liberty	□ hedge	□ desist	□ procession	□ ransom
□ prime					

334

viscid [ˈvɪsɪd]	*adj.* 黏性的（thick and adhesive） 同 glutinous, viscose, viscous
pettish [ˈpetɪʃ]	*adj.* 易怒的，闹情绪的（fretful; peevish） 同 petulant
mock [mɑːk]	*v.* 嘲笑（to treat with ridicule; deride）；（为嘲笑而）模仿（to mimic in derision） 记 联想记忆：和尚（monk）没头发常受到嘲笑（mock）
giggle [ˈgɪgl]	*v.* 咯咯笑（to laugh with repeated short catches of the breath） 记 发音记忆："叽咯" → 发出叽咯咯的笑声 → 咯咯笑
terminate [ˈtɜːrmɪneɪt]	*v.* 终止，结束（to bring to an end; close） 记 词根记忆：termin(结束) + ate → 终止，结束
regime [reɪˈʒiːm]	*n.* 政权，政治制度（government in power） 记 词根记忆：reg(统治) + ime → 政权 例 Even though political editorializing was not forbidden under the new *regime*, journalists still experienced discreet, though perceptible, governmental pressure to limit dissent.
jounce [dʒaʊns]	*v.* 颠簸地移动（to move in an up-and-down manner） 同 bounce, bump, jolt
scorching [ˈskɔːrtʃɪŋ]	*adj.* 灼热的 同 ardent, baking, boiling, fiery, sultry, torrid
pestle [ˈpesl]	*n.* 杵，碾槌（a club shaped implementation for pounding or grinding substances in a mortar）
inflame [ɪnˈfleɪm]	*v.* 使燃烧（to set on fire）；激怒(某人)（to excite intensely with anger） 记 词根记忆：in(进入) + flam(火焰) + e → 进入火焰 → 使燃烧
supervise [ˈsuːpərvaɪz]	*v.* 监督，管理（to keep watch over a job or the people doing it） 记 词根记忆：super(在…上面)+vise(看) → 在上面看 → 监督
earring [ˈɪrɪŋ]	*n.* 耳环，耳饰 记 组合词：ear(耳朵) + ring(环) → 耳朵上戴的环 → 耳环，耳饰
clinch [klɪntʃ]	*v.* 钉牢（to secure a nail, bolt, etc.）；彻底解决（to settle an argument definitely） 记 联想记忆：cl + inch(英寸) → 一英寸一英寸地钉 → 钉牢
debar [dɪˈbɑːr]	*v.* 阻止（to bar; forbid; exclude） 记 词根记忆：de(加强) + bar(阻拦) → 阻止
choke [tʃoʊk]	*v.* (使)窒息，阻塞（to have great difficulty in breathing） 记 联想记忆：喝可乐（coke）给呛着（choke）了
hidebound [ˈhaɪdbaʊnd]	*adj.* 思想偏狭且顽固的（obstinately conservative and narrow minded） 记 组合词：hide(兽皮) + bound(包裹) → 被皮包裹起来 → 思想偏狭且顽固的
concise [kənˈsaɪs]	*adj.* 简洁的（brief） 记 词根记忆：con + cis(切掉) + e → 把(多余的)全部切掉 → 简洁的

terminate

31

bin [bɪn]	*n.* 大箱子（a large container）
blockade [blɑːˈkeɪd]	*v./n.* 封锁 记 联想记忆：block（阻碍）+ ade → 阻碍物 → 封锁
contort [kənˈtɔːrt]	*v.* 歪曲（to deform）；扭曲（to twist or wrench into grotesque form） 记 词根记忆：con + tort（弯曲）→ 歪曲；扭曲
privation [praɪˈveɪʃn]	*n.* 匮乏，贫困（lack of what is needed for existence） 记 词根记忆：priv（分开）+ ation → 人财两分 → 贫困
bellow [ˈbeloʊ]	*v.* 咆哮；吼叫 同 bawl, roar
amity [ˈæməti]	*n.* （人们或国家之间的）友好关系（friendly relationship between people or countries） 记 词根记忆：am（爱，友爱）+ ity → 友好关系
hieroglyphic [ˌhaɪərəˈɡlɪfɪk]	*n.* 象形文字（a system of writing which uses hieroglyphs）
wither [ˈwɪðər]	*v.* 干枯，枯萎（to shrivel from loss of bodily moisture） 记 联想记忆：天气（weather）不好植物就会枯萎（wither）
supplicate [ˈsʌplɪkeɪt]	*v.* 恳求，祈求（to make a humble entreaty） 记 词根记忆：sup（下面）+ plic（重叠）+ ate → 双膝跪下 → 恳求
platonic [pləˈtɑːnɪk]	*adj.* 理论的（theoretical）；精神上的，纯友谊的（(of love or a friendship between two people) close and deep but not sexual） 记 来自哲学家柏拉图（Plato）
surplus [ˈsɜːrpləs]	*adj.* 过剩的，剩余的（the amount remained）；盈余的（the excess of a corporation's net worth） 记 词根记忆：sur（超过）+plus（加，多余的）→ 剩余的
catalog [ˈkætəlɔːɡ]	*n.* 目录（complete list of items of a book）；系列（series） 记 词根记忆：cata（下面）+ log（说话）→ 概括在下面要说的话 → 目录
balderdash [ˈbɔːldərdæʃ]	*n.* 胡言乱语，废话（nonsense） 同 fiddle-faddle, piffle
tempest [ˈtempɪst]	*n.* 暴风雨（a violent storm）；骚动（tumult; uproar） 记 联想记忆：temp（看作 temper, 脾气）+est → 老天爷发脾气 → 暴风雨
mote [moʊt]	*n.* 尘埃，微尘（a speck of dust） 记 词根记忆：mot（微尘）+ e → 微尘
gracile [ˈɡræsaɪl]	*adj.* 细弱的，纤细优美的（slender, graceful） 例 这位女子虽然纤弱（gracile）但却十分优雅（graceful） 同 slight
bigot [ˈbɪɡət]	*n.* （宗教、政治等的）顽固盲从者（a person who holds blindly to a particular creed）；偏执者（a narrow-minded person） 记 联想记忆：big + (g)ot → 得到大东西不放的人 → 偏执者

□ bin	□ blockade	□ contort	□ privation	□ bellow	□ amity
□ hieroglyphic	□ wither	□ supplicate	□ platonic	□ surplus	□ catalog
□ balderdash	□ tempest	□ mote	□ gracile	□ bigot	

336

spear [spɪr]	*n.* 矛；嫩枝(a young shoot, or sprout) *v.* 用矛刺(to thrust with a spear) 搭 spear fish 叉鱼
nauseate ['nɔːzieɪt]	*v.* (使)作呕，(使)厌恶(to feel or cause to feel disgust) 同 sicken
microbe ['maɪkroʊb]	*n.* 微生物(tiny living creature) 记 词根记忆：micro(小的) + be(=bio 生命) → 微生物
acquisitive [əˈkwɪzətɪv]	*adj.* 渴望得到的，贪婪的(eager to acquire; greedy) 记 词根记忆：ac(加强) + quisit(要求) + ive → 一再想得到 → 贪婪的
purloin [pɜːrˈlɔɪn]	*v.* 偷窃(to appropriate wrongfully; steal) 记 词根记忆：pur(向前，向外) + loin(=long 远) → 把别人的东西带到远方 → 偷窃；注意不要和 purlieu(*n.* 附近)相混
bile [baɪl]	*n.* 胆汁(gall)；愤怒(bitterness of temper)
lionize ['laɪənaɪz]	*v.* 崇拜，看重(to treat as an object of great interest or importance) 记 联想记忆：lion(狮子；名流) + ize → 视为名流 → 崇拜
forward ['fɔːrwərd]	*adj.* 过激的(extreme)；莽撞的(bold)，冒失的，无礼的 记 词根记忆：for(=fore 前面) + ward(向…的) → 向前的 → 莽撞的
halcyon ['hælsiən]	*adj.* 平静的(tranquil; calm)；愉快的(happy; idyllic)；繁荣的(prosperous) 记 原指传说中一能平息风浪的"神翠鸟(halcyon)"
appeal [əˈpiːl]	*v.* 恳求(to supplicate)；有吸引力(to be attractive or interesting)；上诉(to take a lower court's decision to a higher court for review) 记 词根记忆：ap + peal(=pull 拉) → 拉过去 → 有吸引力 搭 appeal to 吸引；呼吁，恳求
bliss [blɪs]	*n.* 狂喜，极乐(great joy)；福气，天赐的福(complete happiness) 记 联想记忆：得到祝福(bless)是有福气(bliss)的
occult [əˈkʌlt]	*adj.* 秘密的，不公开的(hidden; concealed) 记 联想记忆：oc(外) + cult(教派) → 不在教派外公开的 → 秘密的
void [vɔɪd]	*adj.* 空的(empty)；缺乏的(completely lacking; devoid) *n.* 空隙，裂缝(empty space)；空虚感(a feeling of want or hollowness)
renovate ['renəveɪt]	*v.* 翻新，修复，整修(to put back into good condition) 同 furbish, refresh, rejuvenate, renew, restore
remittance [rɪˈmɪtns]	*n.* 汇款(transmittal of money as to a distant place)
rile [raɪl]	*v.* 惹恼，激怒(to irritate; vex) 同 aggravate, annoy, exasperate, provoke
preview ['priːvjuː]	*n.* 预演，预展(a private showing before shown to the general public) *v.* 预演，预先查看 记 联想记忆：pre(预先) + view(观看) → 预先看到的演出 → 预演

31

□ spear　　　□ nauseate　　□ microbe　　　□ acquisitive　　□ purloin　　□ bile
□ lionize　　□ forward　　　□ halcyon　　　□ appeal　　　　□ bliss　　　□ occult
□ void　　　　□ renovate　　□ remittance　　□ rile　　　　　□ preview

337

superannuated [ˌsuːpərˈænjueɪtɪd]	*adj.* 老迈的(incapable or disqualified for active duty by advanced age) 记 词根记忆：super(超过) + annu(年) + ated → 超过一定年龄的 → 老迈的
gingerly [ˈdʒɪndʒərli]	*adj./adv.* 小心的(地)；谨慎的(地)(very careful or very carefully) 记 联想记忆：切生姜(ginger)的时候要小心(gingerly)，别让生姜汁溅到眼睛里 例 He opened the box *gingerly* and looked inside.
discrepancy [dɪsˈkrepənsi]	*n.* 差异，矛盾(lack of agreement；inconsistency) 记 联想记忆：dis(分开) + crep(破裂) + ancy → 裂开 → 矛盾
anesthetic [ˌænəsˈθetɪk]	*adj.* 麻醉的；麻木的(lacking awareness or sensitivity) *n.* 麻醉剂(a drug that makes people feel unconscious) 记 词根记忆：an(无) + esthet(感觉) + ic 无感觉 → 麻醉的
pique [piːk]	*n.* (因自尊心受伤害而导致的)不悦，愤怒(resentment) *v.* 激怒(to arouse anger or resentment；irritate) 记 词根记忆：piqu(刺激) + e → 因受刺激而不悦 → 不悦，愤怒
barefaced [ˈberfeɪst]	*adj.* 厚颜无耻的，公然的(shameless；blatant) 记 联想记忆：bare(空的，没有的) + face(脸) + d → 不要脸的 → 厚颜无耻的
repulsion [rɪˈpʌlʃn]	*n.* 厌恶，反感(very strong dislike)；排斥力(the force by which one object drives another away from it)
restiveness [ˈrestɪvnəs]	*n.* 倔强，难以驾驭 记 来自 restive(*adj.* 不安静的，不安宁的)
espy [eˈspaɪ]	*v.* 突然看到；望见(to catch sight of；descry) 记 联想记忆：e + spy(间谍，发现) → 突然看到
rant [rænt]	*v.* 大声责骂(to scold vehemently)；咆哮(to talk in a loud excited way) 搭 rant and rave (at sb./sth.) 大声地、狠狠地责备或训斥
tally [ˈtæli]	*v.* (使)一致，符合(to correspond；match) 记 联想记忆：t+ally(联盟) → 目标一致，结成同盟 → (使)一致
putative [ˈpjuːtətɪv]	*adj.* 公认的，推定的(commonly accepted or supposed) 记 词根记忆：put(认为) + ative → 公认的
discord [ˈdɪskɔːrd]	*n.* 不和，纷争(disagreement；dissension) 记 词根记忆：dis(不) + cord(一致) → 不一致 → 不和，纷争
malediction [ˌmælɪˈdɪkʃən]	*n.* 诅咒(curse；execration) 记 词根记忆：male(坏的) + dict(说) + ion → 说坏话 → 诅咒
knead [niːd]	*v.* 揉成，捏制(to mix and work into a uniform mass) 记 联想记忆：捏制(knead)面包(bread)
inundate [ˈɪnʌndeɪt]	*v.* 淹没，泛滥(to cover or engulf with a flood)；压倒(to overwhelm with a great amount)
glorify [ˈɡlɔːrɪfaɪ]	*v.* 吹捧，美化(to make ordinary or bad appear better) 记 词根记忆：glor(光荣) + ify(使) → 使光荣 → 美化

virile [ˈvɪrəl]	*adj.* 有男子气的(characteristic of or associated with men; masculine); 刚健的(energetic; vigorous) 记 词根记忆: vir(力量)+ile → 有力量的 → 刚健的
plod [plɑːd]	*v.* 沉重地走(to walk heavily; trudge); 辛勤工作(to drudge) *n.* 艰难行进(the act of moving or walking heavily and slowly)
perpetual [pərˈpetʃuəl]	*adj.* 持续的, 不间断的(continuing without interruption; uninterrupted); 永久的(lasting forever) 记 词根记忆: per(始终) + pet(追求) + ual → 自始至终的追求 → 永久的 例 Micawber's habit of spending more than he earned left him in a state of *perpetual* indigence, but he persevered in hoping to see a more affluent day.
oppose [əˈpoʊz]	*v.* 反对(to be or act against) 记 词根记忆: op(反) + pos(放) + e → 反着放 → 反对 例 Candidates who *oppose* the present state income tax must be able to propose alternate ways to continue the financing of state operations.
demeanour [dɪˈmiːnər]	*n.* 举止, 行为(outward behavior, conduct, deportment) 记 来自 demean, 古义等于 conduct(*n.* 行为)
crab [kræb]	*n.* 蟹, 螃蟹(ten-legged shellfish) *v.* 抱怨, 发牢骚(to complain; grumble) 记 联想记忆: 总是抱怨(crab)的生活是单调无趣的(drab)
kaleidoscopic [kəˌlaɪdəˈskɑːpɪk]	*adj.* 千变万化的(changing constantly) 记 来自 kaleidoscope(万花筒)
genteel [dʒenˈtiːl]	*adj.* 有教养的, 彬彬有礼的(well bred; elegant); 冒充上流的, 附庸风雅的(striving to convey an appearance of refinement) 记 来自 gentle(*adj.* 文雅的)
deaden [ˈdedn]	*v.* 减弱, 缓和(to lessen the power or intensity of sth.) 记 词根记忆: dead(死) + en → 死掉 → 减弱
flinch [flɪntʃ]	*v.* 畏缩, 退缩(to draw back; wince; cower) 记 联想记忆: fl(看作 fly, 飞) + inch(寸) → 一寸一寸向后飞 → 退缩
split [splɪt]	*v.* 破裂, 裂开(to divide into parts or portions) *n.* 裂开, 裂口 记 发音记忆: "死劈了它" → 破裂, 裂开
anvil [ˈænvɪl]	*n.* 铁砧(a steel block)
butt [bʌt]	*v.* 用头抵撞, 顶撞(to strike with the head) *n.* 粗大的一端; 烟蒂 搭 butt in 插嘴; 插手
foment [foʊˈment]	*v.* 煽动(to incite) 记 注意不要和 ferment(*v.* 使发酵; 酝酿)相混

31

□ virile	□ plod	□ perpetual	□ oppose	□ demeanour	□ crab
□ kaleidoscopic	□ genteel	□ deaden	□ flinch	□ split	□ anvil
□ butt	□ foment				

339

tyro [ˈtaɪroʊ]	*n.* 新手（a beginner in learning；novice） 同 a green hand
bale [beɪl]	*n.* 大包，大捆（a large bundle）；灾祸，不幸（disaster） 记 来自 ball（*n.* 球）
soak [soʊk]	*v.* 浸泡，渗透（to lie immersed in liquid；become saturated by, or as if by immersion） 记 联想记忆：soa（看作 soap，肥皂）+k → 在肥皂水中浸泡 → 浸泡
prologue [ˈproʊlɔːɡ]	*n.* 开场白；序言；序幕 记 词根记忆：pro（在前）+ log（话语）+ ue → 前面说的话 → 开场白
carrion [ˈkæriən]	*n.* 腐肉（the decaying flesh of a dead body） 记 词根记忆：carr（=carn 肉）+ ion → 腐肉
placard [ˈplækɑːrd]	*n.* 招贴，布告 *v.* 张贴布告 同 poster
famish [ˈfæmɪʃ]	*v.* 使饥饿（to make or be very hungry） 记 词根记忆：fam（饿的）+ ish → 使饥饿
canary [kəˈneri]	*n.* 金丝雀；女歌星 记 联想记忆：can（能够）+ ary → 有能耐，能歌善舞的人 → 女歌星
roe [roʊ]	*n.* 鱼卵（the eggs of fish）
gregariousness [ɡrɪˈɡeriəsnəs]	*n.*（动物）群居；合群，爱交友 记 来自 gregarious（*adj.* 交际的，合群的）
extort [ɪkˈstɔːrt]	*v.* 勒索，敲诈（to get money from sb. by violence or threats；extract） 记 词根记忆：ex + tort（扭曲）→ 扭出来 → 勒索

My fellow Americans, ask not what your country can do for you, ask what you can do for your country. My fellow citizens of the world: ask not what American will do for you, but what together we can do for the freedom of man.

美国同胞们，不要问国家能为你们做些什么，而要问你们能为国家做些什么。全世界的公民们，不要问美国将为你们做些什么，而要问我们共同能为人类的自由做些什么。

——美国总统 肯尼迪（John Kennedy, American president）

☐ tyro	☐ bale	☐ soak	☐ prologue	☐ carrion	☐ placard
☐ famish	☐ canary	☐ roe	☐ gregariousness	☐ extort	

stroke [stroʊk]	*v.* 抚摸 (to pass the hand over gently) *n.* 击，打 (a hit)；一笔，一画 (a line made by a single movement of a pen or brush)
dabble [ˈdæbl]	*v.* 涉足，浅尝 (to do sth. superficially, not seriously) 记 注意不要和 babble (*v.* 说蠢话) 相混
inconstancy [ɪnˈkɑːnstənsi]	*n.* (指人) 反复无常 (the state or quality of being eccentrically variable or fickle) 记 联想记忆：in (不) + constancy (恒久不变) → 反复无常
grasping [ˈɡræspɪŋ]	*adj.* 贪心的，贪婪的 (eager for gain; greedy) 记 联想记忆：grasp (*v.* 抓取) + ing → 不停地抓取自己喜爱的东西 → 贪婪的 同 avaricious, covetous
adduce [əˈduːs]	*v.* 给予（理由）(to give as reason or proof)；举出（例证）(to cite as an example) 记 词根记忆：ad (向) + duc (引导) + e → 引导出 → 举出
rove [roʊv]	*v.* 流浪，漂泊 (to wander about; roam) 同 drift, gallivant, meander, ramble
palate [ˈpælət]	*n.* 上腭；口味 (sense of taste)；爱好 (a usually intellectual taste or liking) 记 联想记忆：pal + ate (eat 的过去式) → 与吃有关的 → 口味
corrugated [ˈkɔːrəɡeɪtɪd]	*adj.* 起皱纹的 (folded, wrinkled or furrowed) 记 来自 corrugate (*v.* 起皱纹)
affliction [əˈflɪkʃn]	*n.* 折磨，痛苦；痛苦的原因；灾害
filter [ˈfɪltər]	*n.* 过滤材料，(尤指) 滤纸 (a porous article (as of paper) through which a gas or liquid is passed to separate out matter in suspension) *v.* 过滤 (to remove by means of a filter)
excoriate [ˌeksˈkɔːrieɪt]	*v.* 剥皮 (to strip, scratch, or rub off the skin)；严厉批评 (to denounce harshly) 记 词根记忆：ex + cor (皮) + iate → 把皮弄掉 → 剥皮
rattle [ˈrætl]	*v.* 使发出咯咯声 (to make a rapid succession of short sharp noises)；使慌乱 (to make anxious and cause to lose confidence) 记 参考 rattlesnake (*n.* 响尾蛇)

□ stroke	□ dabble	□ inconstancy	□ grasping	□ adduce	□ rove
□ palate	□ corrugated	□ affliction	□ filter	□ excoriate	□ rattle

341

compulsory [kəm'pʌlsəri]	*adj.* 强制性的，必须做的（compelling；coercive） 搭 compulsory education 义务教育
glean [gli:n]	*v.* 拾（落穗）（to gather grains left by reapers）；收集（材料等）（to gather information or material bit by bit） 同 reap
console [kən'soʊl]	*v.* 安慰，抚慰（to make feel less sad；comfort） 记 词根记忆：con（共同）+ sole（孤单）→ 大家孤单 → 同病相怜 → 安慰
smite [smaɪt]	*v.* 重击，猛打（to attack or afflict suddenly and injuriously） 搭 be smitten with/by sb./sth. 突然爱上，完全迷上
stubby ['stʌbi]	*adj.* 短粗的（being short and thickset） 同 squat, stocky, stumpy
plummet ['plʌmɪt]	*v.* 垂直或突然落下（to fall perpendicularly or abruptly） 记 plummet 原意为"测深锤"
cosy（cozy） ['koʊzi]	*adj.* 温暖而舒适的（warm and comfortable；snug） 搭 a cosy feeling 惬意的感觉
sock [sɑːk]	*v.* 重击，痛打（to strike forcefully） 记 sock 更广为人知的意思是"短袜"
unthreatening [ʌn'θretənɪŋ]	*adj.* 不危险的 记 联想记忆：un（不）+ threatening（危险的）→ 不危险的
crouch [kraʊtʃ]	*v.* 蹲伏，弯腰（to stoop or bend low） 记 注意不要和 couch（*n.* 长沙发）相混
mobility [moʊ'bɪləti]	*n.* 可动性，流动性（the quality of being mobile） 例 The hierarchy of medical occupations is in many ways a caste system; its strata remain intact and the practitioners in them have very little vertical *mobility*.
rebuttal [rɪ'bʌtl]	*n.* 反驳，反证（argument or proof that rebuts） 记 联想记忆：re（反）+ butt（顶撞）+ al → 反过来顶撞 → 反驳
divagate ['daɪvəgeit]	*v.* 离题（to stray from the subject）；漂泊（to wander about） 记 词根记忆：di（离开）+ vag（走）+ ate → 走开 → 离题；漂泊
fossilize ['fɑːsəlaɪz]	*v.* 使成为化石（to cause sth. to become a fossil）；使过时（to make sth. out of date） 记 来自 fossil（*n.* 化石）
materialize [mə'tɪriəlaɪz]	*v.* 赋予形体，使具体化（to represent in material form）；出现（to come into existence） 记 来自 material（*n.* 物质 *adj.* 物质的；具体的）
waspish ['wɑːspɪʃ]	*adj.* 易怒的（irascible；petulant；snappish）；尖刻的 记 来自 wasp（*n.* 黄蜂）
snooze [snuːz]	*v.* 打盹儿，打瞌睡（to take a nap） 同 catnap, doze, siesta

felicitate [fəˈlɪsɪteɪt]	*v.* 祝贺，庆祝(to wish happiness to; congratulate) 记 词根记忆：felic(幸福的) + itate → 使…幸福 → 祝贺
timid [ˈtɪmɪd]	*adj.* 羞怯的(lacking self-confidence; shy)；胆怯的，怯懦的(fearful and hesitant) 记 词根记忆：tim(害怕) + id → 胆怯的
well-groomed [ˌwel ˈɡruːmd]	*adj.* 整齐干净的，衣着入时的 记 联想记忆：well(好) + groom(修饰) + ed → 整齐干净的，衣着入时的
obnoxious [əbˈnɑːkʃəs]	*adj.* 令人极不愉快的，可憎的(disgustingly objectionable) 记 词根记忆：ob(to) + nox(伤害) + ious → 给人带来伤害的 → 令人极不愉快的
offensive [əˈfensɪv]	*adj.* 令人不快的，得罪人的(causing anger or displeasure) 记 来自offend(*v.* 得罪，冒犯)
prefigure [ˌpriː ˈfɪɡjər]	*v.* 预示(to show, suggest, or announce by an antecedent type)；预想(to foresee) 记 联想记忆：pre(提前) + figure(形象) → 提前想好形象 → 预想
palpitate [ˈpælpɪteɪt]	*v.* (心脏)急速跳动(to beat rapidly; throb) 记 词根记忆：palp(摸) + it + ate → 摸得着的心跳 → (心脏)急速跳动
elliptical [ɪˈlɪptɪkl]	*adj.* 椭圆的(of, relating to, or shaped like an ellipse)；晦涩的(ambiguous)；省略的 记 来自ellipse(*n.* 椭圆(形))
desiccate [ˈdesɪkeɪt]	*v.* (使)完全干涸，脱水(to dry completely; preserve by drying) 记 词根记忆：de + sicc(干) + ate → 弄干 → 脱水
convergent [kənˈvɜːrdʒənt]	*adj.* 会聚的 (tending to move toward one point or to approach each other) 记 来自converge(*v.* 汇集，聚集)
stipulation [ˌstɪpjuˈleɪʃn]	*n.* 规定，约定(a condition, requirement, or item in a legal instrument) 记 来自stipulate(*v.* 规定，明确要求)
trifle [ˈtraɪfl]	*n.* 微不足道的事物，琐事(sth. of little value, substance, or importance) 同 diddly, picayune, triviality
crumble [ˈkrʌmbl]	*v.* 弄碎(to break into crumbs or small pieces)；崩溃(to fall to pieces; disintegrate)
nostrum [ˈnɑːstrəm]	*n.* 家传秘方，江湖药(quack medicine)；万灵丹；妙策(a usually questionable remedy or scheme) 记 词根记忆：nost(家) + rum → 家传秘方
governance [ˈɡʌvərnəns]	*n.* 统治，支配(power of government) 记 来自govern(*v.* 统治)
understudy [ˈʌndərstʌdi]	*n.* 预备演员，替角 *v.* 充当…的替角(to act as an understudy to)
knack [næk]	*n.* 特殊能力；窍门(a clever, expedient way of doing sth.) 记 联想记忆：敲开(knock)脑袋，得到窍门(knack)

32

submit [səbˈmɪt]	v. 屈服(to admit defeat); 提交, 呈递(to offer for consideration)
	记 词根记忆: sub(下面的) + mit(送, 放出) → 从下面递上 → 提交, 呈递
	例 Because the report contained much more information than the reviewers needed to see, the author was asked to *submit* a compendium instead.

accrete [əˈkriːt]	v. 逐渐增长(to grow or increase by means of gradual additions); 添加生长; 连生(to grow together)
	记 词根记忆: ac(加强) + cre(增长) + te → 逐渐增长

adjourn [əˈdʒɜːrn]	v. (使)延期, (使)推迟(to suspend indefinitely); (使)休会(to suspend a session indefinitely or to another time or place)
	记 词根记忆: ad(附近) + journ(日期) → 改到近日 → 推迟

delegate	[ˈdelɪɡət] n. 代表(representative)
	[ˈdelɪɡeɪt] v. 委派…为代表, 授权(to appoint as sb's representative)
	记 词根记忆: de + legate(使者) → 出去的使者 → 代表

peck [pek]	v. 啄食; 轻啄(to strike with a beak)
	搭 peck sth. out 啄出某物

doodle [ˈduːdl]	v. 涂鸦(to make meaningless drawings); 混时间(to kill time)
	记 和 noodle(n. 面条)一起记; 吃着面条(noodle)混时间(doodle)

cower [ˈkaʊər]	v. 畏缩, 蜷缩(to crouch or huddle up from fear or cold)
	记 联想记忆: cow(威胁) + er → 受到威胁 → 畏缩, 蜷缩

stale [steɪl]	adj. 不新鲜的, 陈腐的(tasteless or unpalatable from age)
	记 联想记忆: s+tale(传说) → 传说说多了就不新鲜了 → 不新鲜的, 陈腐的

fabric [ˈfæbrɪk]	n. 纺织品; 结构(framework of basic structure)
	记 联想记忆: fab(音似: 帆布) + ric → 纺织品

embargo [ɪmˈbɑːrɡoʊ]	n. 禁港令, 封运令(a legal prohibition on commerce)
	记 联想记忆: em(进入) + bar(阻挡) + go(去) → 阻拦(船等)进入 → 禁港令, 封运令

ready [ˈredi]	adj. 敏捷的, 迅速的(promp in reacting)
	例 Broadway audiences have become inured to mediocrity and so desperate to be pleased as to make their *ready* ovations meaningless as an indicator of the quality of the production before them.

impalpable [ɪmˈpælpəbl]	adj. 无法触及的; 不易理解的(too slight or subtle to be grasped)
	记 联想记忆: im(不) + palpable(可触摸的) → 无法触及的

bloated [ˈbloʊtɪd]	adj. 肿胀的(swelled, as with water or air); 傲慢的(arrogant)
	记 联想记忆: bloat(膨胀) + ed → 肿胀的

condescend [ˌkɑːndɪˈsend]	v. 屈尊, 俯就(to deal with people in a patronizingly superior manner)
	记 词根记忆: con + de + scend(爬) → 向下爬 → 俯就

pretension [prɪˈtenʃn]	n. 自负, 骄傲(pretentiousness); 要求, 主张
	记 联想记忆: pre(预先) + tension(紧张, 压力) → 预先感到了压力 → 要求, 主张

□ submit	□ accrete	□ adjourn	□ delegate	□ peck	□ doodle
□ cower	□ stale	□ fabric	□ embargo	□ ready	□ impalpable
□ bloated	□ condescend	□ pretension			

tempo ['tempoʊ]	*n.* （音乐的）速度（the rate of speed of a musical piece or passage indicated by one of a series of directions （as largo, presto, or allegro) and often by an exact metronome marking）；（动作、生活的）步调，节奏（rate of motion or activity） 记 来自词根 tempor（*n.* 时间） 例 During the opera's most famous aria, the *tempo* chosen by the orchestra's conductor seemed capricious, without necessary relation to what had gone before.
irksome ['ɜːrksəm]	*adj.* 令人苦恼的，讨厌的（tending to irk） 记 来自 irk（*v.* 使苦恼）
hinder ['hɪndər]	*v.* 阻碍，妨碍（to thwart; impede; frustrate） 记 词根记忆：hind（后面）+ er → 落在后面 → 阻碍，妨碍
bar [bɑːr]	*v.* 禁止，阻挡（to prevent, forbid）*n.* 条，棒（a straight piece of material that is longer than it is wide）
vibrancy ['vaɪbrənsi]	*n.* 生机勃勃，活泼（the quality or state of being vibrant） 同 animation, sparkle, vivacity
sash [sæʃ]	*n.* 肩带（an ornamental band, ribbon, or scarf worn over the shoulder）
piebald ['paɪbɔːld]	*adj.* 花斑的，黑白两色的（of different colors, especially spotted or blotched with black and white）
accountability [əˌkaʊntə'bɪləti]	*n.* 有责任（responsibility） 记 联想记忆：account（解释）+ ability → 对事情应做解释 → 有责任
swank [swæŋk]	*v.* 夸耀，炫耀（to show; swagger; boast） 记 联想记忆：swan（天鹅）+k → 像天鹅一样骄傲 → 炫耀
scission ['sɪʒən]	*n.* 切断，分离，断开（an action or process of cutting, dividing, or splitting） 记 词根记忆：sciss（切）+ ion → 分离，断开
decoy ['diːkɔɪ]	*v.* 诱骗（to lure or bait）
obstreperous [əb'strepərəs]	*adj.* 吵闹的（noisy; boisterous）；难管束的（unruly） 同 clamorous, vociferous
whit [wɪt]	*n.* 一点儿，少量（the smallest part imaginable; bit） 搭 not a whit 丝毫不，一点也不
bondage ['bɑːndɪdʒ]	*n.* 奴役，束缚（slavery, captivity） 记 词根记忆：bond（使黏合）+ age → 束缚
proffer ['prɑːfər]	*v.* 奉献，贡献（to present for acceptance; offer）；提议，建议（to offer suggestion）*n.* 赠送，献出 记 联想记忆：pr(o)（向前）+ offer（提供）→ 向前提供 → 奉献
squelch [skweltʃ]	*v.* 压制，镇压（to completely suppress; quell） 搭 squelch a rumour/strike/fire 制止谣言；镇压罢工；控制火势蔓延

32

□ tempo	□ irksome	□ hinder	□ bar	□ vibrancy	□ sash
□ piebald	□ accountability	□ swank	□ scission	□ decoy	□ obstreperous
□ whit	□ bondage	□ proffer	□ squelch		

bowdlerize [ˈbaʊdləraɪz]	*v.* 删除，删改（to expurgate） 记 来自人名 Thomas Bowdler，他删改出版了莎士比亚的戏剧
overture [ˈoʊvərtʃər]	*n.* 前奏曲，序曲（a musical introduction to an opera） 记 词根记忆：o(出) + ver(覆盖) + ture → 去掉覆盖物，打开 → 序曲
assault [əˈsɔːlt]	*n.* 突袭（a sudden attack）；猛袭（a violent attack） 记 联想记忆：ass(驴子) + ault(看作 aunt，姑妈) → 驴子袭击姑妈 → 突袭 搭 victims of assault 袭击事件牺牲者
delicate [ˈdelɪkət]	*adj.* 娇弱的（tender when touched）；雅致的，精美的（very carefully made） 搭 delicate and fragile 娇嫩而脆弱的
slot [slɑːt]	*n.* 狭槽（a long straight narrow opening） 搭 slot machine 投币自动售货机
snicker [ˈsnɪkər]	*v./n.* 窃笑，暗笑（suppressed laugh） 同 titter
list [lɪst]	*v.* 倾斜（to tilt to one side）*n.* 倾斜 记 list 意义很多，常见的有"名单，列表"
luxurious [lʌɡˈʒʊriəs]	*adj.* 奢侈的，豪华的（very fine and expensive） 记 词根记忆：lux(光) + ur + ious → 光彩四溢的 → 奢侈的，豪华的
raspy [ˈræspi]	*adj.* 刺耳的（grating；harsh）；易怒的（irritable）
yen [jen]	*v.* 渴望（to have an intense desire） 同 covet, hanker, long
turncoat [ˈtɜːrnkoʊt]	*n.* 背叛者，变节者（one who switches to an opposing side or party） 同 renegade, traitor
projector [prəˈdʒektər]	*n.* 电影放映机，幻灯机（an apparatus for projecting films or pictures onto a surface）
prosperity [prɑːˈsperəti]	*n.* 繁荣（state of being successful）；幸运（state of good fortune） 记 词根记忆：pro(前面) + sper(希望) + ity → 希望就在前方 → 繁荣 例 Paradoxically, England's colonization of North America was undermined by its success: the increasing *prosperity* of the colonies diminished their dependence upon, and hence their loyalty to, their home country.
exceptionable [ɪkˈsepʃənəbl]	*adj.* 引起反感的（open to objection） 记 联想记忆：except(把…除去) + ion + able → 因为反感而把…除去 → 引起反感的
judiciousness [dʒuˈdɪʃəsnəs]	*n.* 明智 记 来自 judicious(*adj.* 明智的)
immemorial [ˌɪməˈmɔːriəl]	*adj.* 太古的，极古的（extending beyond memory or record；ancient） 记 词根记忆：im(不) + memor(记住) + ial → 在记忆之外的 → 太古的

pirate	*n.* 海盗；剽窃者(one who commits piracy) *v.* 盗印(to reproduce without authorization in infringement of copyright)；掠夺(to take or appropriate by piracy)
[ˈpaɪrət]	记 词根记忆：pir(=per 试验；冒险) + ate → 冒险去拿他人的东西 → 掠夺
deductive	*adj.* 推论的，演绎的(reasoning by deduction)
[dɪˈdʌktɪv]	记 来自 deduce(*v.* 演绎，推断)
exhume	*v.* 掘出，发掘(to dig out of the earth)
[ɪɡˈzuːm]	记 词根记忆：ex + hum(地) + e → 从地下挖出 → 发掘
excogitate	*v.* 认真想出(to think out carefully and fully)
[eksˈkɑːdʒiteɪt]	记 词根记忆：ex + co（共同）+ g（=ag 升动）+ itate → 共同开动脑子 → 认真想出
amnesia	*n.* 健忘症(loss of memory due usually to brain injury, illness, etc.)
[æmˈniːʒə]	记 词根记忆：a(无) + mnes(记忆) + ia(病) → 没有记忆的病 → 健忘症
chastise	*v.* 严惩(to punish by beating)；谴责(to scold or condemn)
[tʃæˈstaɪz]	记 联想记忆：追赶(chase)上小偷进行严惩(chastise)
shelter	*n.* 避难所，遮蔽（place or condition of being protected, kept safe, etc.）*v.* 庇护，保护(to give shelter to sb./sth.; protect sb./sth.)
[ˈʃeltər]	记 联想记忆：shel(看作 shell，壳)+ter → 像壳一样可以躲避的地方 → 避难所
traitor	*n.* 卖国贼，叛徒(one who betrays one's country, a cause, or a trust, especially one who commits treason)
[ˈtreɪtər]	记 参考 traditor(*n.* 叛教者)
epitomize	*v.* 概括，摘要(to be typical of; to be an epitome of)
[ɪˈpɪtəmaɪz]	记 词根记忆：epi(在…后) + tom(看作 tome，一卷书) + ize → 写在一卷书后面的话 → 概括
minutes	*n.* 会议记录
[ˈmɪnɪts]	搭 take the minutes 做会议记录
reap	*v.* 收割，收获(to cut and gather)
[riːp]	同 harvest
yank	*v.* 猛拉，拽(to pull or extract with a quick vigorous movement)
[jæŋk]	同 jerk, lurch, snap, twitch, wrench
genuine	*adj.* 真的(real)；真诚的(sincere)
[ˈdʒenjuɪn]	记 词根记忆：genu(出生，产生) + ine → 产生的来源清楚 → 真的
	例 Paradoxically, while it is relatively easy to prove a fraudulent work of art is a fraud, it is often virtually impossible to prove that an authentic one is *genuine*.
adulate	*v.* 谄媚，奉承(to praise or flatter excessively)
[ˈædjuleɪt]	
torment	*n.* 折磨，痛苦(very great pain in mind or body)
[ˈtɔːrment]	记 词根记忆：tor(=tort 扭曲) + ment → 身体和灵魂被扭曲 → 折磨，痛苦

32

□ pirate	□ deductive	□ exhume	□ excogitate	□ amnesia	□ chastise
□ shelter	□ traitor	□ epitomize	□ minutes	□ reap	□ yank
□ genuine	□ adulate	□ torment			

horn [hɔːrn]	*n.* 角(bony outgrowth usually pointed on head of some animals); 喇叭 (an apparatus which makes a loud warning sound)
goof [ɡuːf]	*v.* 犯错误(to make a usually foolish or careless mistake); 闲逛，消磨时间 (to spend time idly or foolishly) 记 联想记忆：经过仔细调查，找到了他犯错(goof)的证据(proof)
boring ['bɔːrɪŋ]	*adj.* 无趣的，乏味的(uninteresting; dull) 记 来自 bore(*v.* 使厌烦)
slosh [slɑːʃ]	*v.* 溅，泼(to splash about in liquid) *n.* 泥泞(slush) 搭 a slosh on the ear 一记耳光
testimony ['testɪmoʊni]	*n.* 证据，证词(firsthand authentication of a fact; evidence) 记 词根记忆：test(看到)+imony → 所看到的 → 证据 例 The *testimony* of eyewitnesses is notoriously unreliable; emotion and excitement all too often cause our minds to distort what we see.
harrow ['hærʊ]	*n.* 耙 *v.* 耙地；使痛苦(to inflict great distress or torment on) 记 联想记忆：农民把土地视作神圣(hallow) 的，勤勤恳恳地进行耙地 (harrow)
flammable ['flæməbl]	*adj.* 易燃的(easily set on fire) 记 词根记忆：flamm(=flam 火) + able → 易燃的
scads [skædz]	*n.* 许多，巨额(large numbers or amounts) 搭 scads of 大量，许多
etch [etʃ]	*v.* 蚀刻(to make a drawing on metal or glass by the action of an acid); 铭记
peril ['perəl]	*n.* 危险(exposure to the risk; danger) 记 词根记忆：per(冒险) + il → 危险
espionage ['espɪɑːʒ]	*n.* 间谍活动(the act of spying) 记 来自法语：e + spion(=spy 看) + age → 出去看 → 间谍活动
pullulate ['pʌljʊleɪt]	*v.* 繁殖(to breed or produce freely); 充满(to teem) 记 词根记忆：pullul(小动物) + ate → 生小动物 → 繁殖
brat [bræt]	*n.* 孩子；顽童(a badly behaved child) 记 联想记忆：b + rat(耗子) → 像耗子般的小孩 → 顽童
prude [pruːd]	*n.* 拘守礼仪的人(a person who is excessively attentive to propriety or decorum) 记 词根记忆：pr(=pro 向前) + ud(=vid 看) + e → 事先看 → 拘守礼仪的人
liaison [li'eɪzɑːn]	*n.* 密切的联系(a close bond or connection); 暧昧的关系(an illicit love affair) 记 词根记忆：lia(捆) + ison → 捆在一起 → 密切的联系
measured ['meʒərd]	*adj.* 量过的，精确的(determined by measurement); 慎重的，恰如其分的 (careful, restrained) 记 来自 measure(*v.* 测量)

hermetic [hɜːrˈmetɪk]	*adj.* 密封的(completely sealed by fusion; airtight); 神秘的，深奥的 (relating to or characterized by occultism or abstruseness) 记 来自 Hermes(古希腊具有发明才能的神)
phoenix [ˈfiːnɪks]	*n.* 凤凰，长生鸟(an imaginary bird believed to live for 500 years and then burn itself and be born again from the ashes)
glare [gler]	*v.* 发炫光(to shine with dazzling light); 怒目而视 (to stare fiercely or angrily) 记 联想记忆：和 flare(*n./v.* 闪光)一起记
lug [lʌg]	*v.* 拖，费力拉(to drag or carry with great effort) *n.* 拖，拉 同 haul, tow, tug
deduct [dɪˈdʌkt]	*v.* 减去，扣除(to take away an amount or a part); 演绎(to deduce) 同 abate, discount, rebate, subtract
desideratum [dɪˌzɪdəˈreɪtəm]	*n.* 必需品(sth. needed and wanted) 记 词根记忆：desider(=desire 渴望) + atum → 渴望的东西 → 必需品
antecedence [ˌæntɪˈsiːdns]	*n.* 居先，先行(priority; precedence) 记 词根记忆：ante(前面) + ced(走) + ence → 走在前面 → 居先，先行
inexpedient [ˌɪnɪkˈspiːdiənt]	*adj.* 不适当的，不明智的(inadvisable; unwise) 记 联想记忆：in(不) + expedient(有利的) → 不利的 → 不明智的
groom [gruːm]	*n.* 马夫；新郎(bridegroom) 记 联想记忆：g(谐音"哥") + room(房间) → 哥进房间接自己的新娘 → 新郎
apostate [əˈpɑːsteɪt]	*n.* 背教者；变节者(a person guilty of apostasy) 同 flopper, renegade, turnabout, turncoat
strangulation [ˌstræŋɡjuˈleɪʃn]	*n.* 扼杀，勒死(the action or process of strangling or strangulating) 记 来自 strangle(*v.* 扼杀，抑制)
medicate [ˈmedɪkeɪt]	*v.* 用药物医治(to treat with medicine); 加药于 记 词根记忆：med(治疗) + ic + ate → 用药物医治
innuendo [ˌɪnjuˈendoʊ]	*n.* 含沙射影，暗讽(an indirect remark, gesture, or reference, usually implying sth. derogatory; insinuation) 记 词根记忆：in(向) + nuen(摇头) + do → 向某人摇头 → 暗讽 例 Demonstrating a mastery of *innuendo*, he issued several veiled insults in the course of the evening's conversation.
delinquent [dɪˈlɪŋkwənt]	*adj.* 怠忽职守的(failing or neglecting to do what duty or law requires) 记 词根记忆：de + linqu(=linger 闲荡) + ent → 闲荡过去 → 怠忽职守的
puerile [ˈpjʊrəl]	*adj.* 幼稚的(immature); 孩子气的(juvenile) 记 词根记忆：puer(=boy 男孩) + ile → 孩子气的
treaty [ˈtriːti]	*n.* 条约(a formal agreement between two or more states); 协议(a contract or agreement) 记 来自 treat(*v.* 处理；协商)

32

□ hermetic	□ phoenix	□ glare	□ lug	□ deduct	□ desideratum
□ antecedence	□ inexpedient	□ groom	□ apostate	□ strangulation	□ medicate
□ innuendo	□ delinquent	□ puerile	□ treaty		

grin	*v.* 露齿而笑（to smile broadly）；（因痛苦，愤恨等）龇牙咧嘴
[grɪn]	记 联想记忆：老人看着收获的谷物（grain）欣慰地露齿而笑（grin）
announce	*v.* 宣布，发表（to proclaim）；通报…的到来（to give notice of the arrival）
[əˈnaʊns]	记 词根记忆：an（来）+ nounc（讲话，说出）+ e → 讲出来 → 宣布
stygian	*adj.* 阴暗的，阴森森的（gloomy; unpleasantly dark）
[ˈstɪdʒiən]	记 来自 Styx（*n.* 地狱冥河）
petulance	*n.* 易怒，性急，暴躁（the quality or state of being petulant）
[ˈpetʃələns]	同 peevishness
commencement	*n.* 开始；毕业典礼（the ceremony at which degrees or diplomas are conferred at a school or college）
[kəˈmensmənt]	
mute	*adj.* 沉默的（silent）*v.* 减弱…的声音（to muffle the sound of）*n.* 弱音器（a device to soften or alter the tone of a musical instrument）
[mjuːt]	例 One theory about intelligence sees language as the logical structure underlying thinking and insists that since animals are *mute*, they must be mindless as well.
daze	*n.* 迷乱，恍惚 *v.* 使茫然，使眩晕（to stun as with a blow or shock; benumb）
[deɪz]	搭 in a daze 迷茫
diagnose	*v.* 判断，诊断（to find out the nature of an illness by observing its symptoms）
[ˌdaɪəɡˈnoʊs]	记 词根记忆：dia（穿过）+ gnose（知道）→ 穿过（皮肤）知道 → 诊断

diagnose

curator	*n.*（博物馆等）馆长（a person in charge of a museum, library, etc.）
[kjʊˈreɪtər]	记 联想记忆：这个地区的副牧师（curate）和博物馆馆长（curator）是至交好友
subjugate	*v.* 征服，镇压（to bring under control and governance）
[ˈsʌbdʒuɡeɪt]	记 词根记忆：sub（下面）+ jug（=yoke 牛轭）+ate → 置于牛轭之下 → 征服
unfold	*v.* 展开，打开（to open from a folded position）；逐渐呈现
[ʌnˈfoʊld]	记 联想记忆：un（不）+ fold（折叠）→ 展开，打开
	例 For those who admire realism, Louis Malle's recent film succeeds because it consciously shuns the stuff of legend and tells an unembellished story as it might actually *unfold* with fallible people in earthly time.
snitch	*v.* 告密（to tell about the wrongdoings of a friend）；偷（to steal by taking quickly）
[snɪtʃ]	记 联想记忆：sni（看作 sin，罪行）+ tch → 告密和偷都是罪行 → 告密；偷
orchard	*n.* 果园（an area of land devoted to the cultivation of fruit or nut trees）
[ˈɔːrtʃərd]	搭 cherry orchard 樱桃园

□ grin	□ announce	□ stygian	□ petulance	□ commencement	□ mute
□ daze	□ diagnose	□ curator	□ subjugate	□ unfold	□ snitch
□ orchard					

warehouse [ˈwerhaʊs]	*n.* 仓库，货栈（a large building for storing things） 同 depository, repository, storehouse
wax [wæks]	*n.* 蜡 *v.* 给…上蜡；增大（to grow gradually larger after being small）；（月亮）渐满
complaisant [kəmˈpleɪzənt]	*adj.* 顺从的；讨好的（affably agreeable；obliging） 同 accommodating, indulgent
marrow [ˈmærəʊ]	*n.* 骨髓；精华，精髓（the innermost and choicest part；pith） 记 联想记忆：和 narrow（*adj.* 狭窄的）一起记
revolt [rɪˈvoʊlt]	*v.* 反叛，造反（to renounce allegiance or subjection；rebel）；反感，厌恶（to turn away with disgust） 记 词根记忆：re(反) + volt(转) → 反过来转 → 反叛
retouch [ˌriːˈtʌtʃ]	*v.* 修描(照片)（to improve a picture or photograph by adding small strokes）；润色 记 联想记忆：re + touch(用画笔轻画) → 修描(照片)；润色
buffer [ˈbʌfər]	*v.* 缓冲，减轻（to lessen the effect of a blow or collision） 记 联想记忆：buff(软皮) + er → 缓冲
accolade [ˈækəleɪd]	*n.* 推崇（approval；appreciation）；赞扬（words of praise） 记 词根记忆：ac(附近) + col(脖子) + ade → 挂在脖子附近 → 赞扬
parlous [ˈpɑːrləs]	*adj.* 靠不住的，危险的（full of danger；hazardous） 记 和 perilous（*adj.* 危险的）一起记
smooth [smuːð]	*v.* 使平坦，使光滑（to make smooth）；消除 *adj.* 光滑的；平稳的 例 In response to the follies of today's commercial and political worlds, the author does not express inflamed indignation, but rather affects the detachment and *smooth* aphoristic prose of an eighteenth-century wit.
underbid [ˌʌndərˈbɪd]	*v.* 叫价低于；要价过低（to bid too low） 记 组合词：under(低于) + bid(出价) → 叫价低于
donate [ˈdoʊneɪt]	*v.* 捐赠，赠送（to give money, goods to a charity） 记 词根记忆：don(给予) + ate → 捐赠，赠送
mollify [ˈmɑːlɪfaɪ]	*v.* 安慰，安抚（to soften in feeling or temper；appease） 记 词根记忆：moll(柔软的) + ify → 使柔软 → 安抚

□ warehouse	□ wax	□ complaisant	▪ marrow	□ revolt	□ retouch
□ buffer	□ accolade	□ parlous	□ smooth	□ underbid	□ donate
□ mollify					

351

poke	*v.* 刺，戳（to prod；stab；thrust）
[poʊk]	搭 poke fun at 嘲弄，戏弄
inculpate	*v.* 控告；归咎于（to incriminate）
[ˈɪnkʌlpeɪt]	记 词根记忆：in(使) + culp(错，罪) + ate → 使(别人)有罪 → 控告
berate	*v.* 猛烈责骂（to scold or rebuke severely）
[bɪˈreɪt]	记 联想记忆：be + rate(责骂) → 猛烈责骂
unprovoked	*adj.* 无缘无故的（not caused by previous action）
[ˌʌnprəˈvoʊkt]	
indemnify	*v.* 赔偿，偿付（to compensate for a loss；reimburse）
[ɪnˈdemnɪfaɪ]	记 词根记忆：in(不) + demn(损坏) + ify → 使损坏消除 → 赔偿
minutia	*n.* 细枝末节，琐事（small or trifling matters）
[mɪˈnuːʃiə]	记 词根记忆：min(小的) + utia → 细小之处 → 细枝末节
ambush	*n.* 埋伏（the act of lying in wait to attack by surprise）；伏击（a sudden attack made from a concealed position）*v.* 埋伏
[ˈæmbʊʃ]	记 联想记忆：am + bush(矮树丛) → 埋伏在矮树丛里 → 埋伏
repent	*v.* 懊悔，后悔（to feel regret or contrition）
[rɪˈpent]	记 词根记忆：re(重新) + pent(惩罚) + → 心灵再次受到惩罚 → 懊悔
growl	*v.* (动物)咆哮，吼叫（to make a low, rumbling, menacing sound）；(雷电等)轰鸣
[graʊl]	记 联想记忆：gr + owl(猫头鹰) → 猫头鹰叫 → 咆哮，吼叫
debility	*n.* 衰弱，虚弱（weakness or feebleness）
[dɪˈbɪləti]	记 词根记忆：de(去掉) + bility(=ability 能力) → 失去能力 → 衰弱
sufficient	*adj.* 足够的（enough to meet the needs）
[səˈfɪʃnt]	例 Having *sufficient* income of her own constituted for Alice a material independence that made possible a degree of security in her emotional life as well.
subsequent	*adj.* 随后的，后来的，连续的（later；following）
[ˈsʌbsɪkwənt]	记 词根记忆：sub(下面) + sequ(跟随) + ent → 跟随在…后面的 → 随后的
	例 Science progresses by building on what has come before；important findings thus form the basis of *subsequent* experiments.
dissociate	*v.* 分离，游离，分裂（to separate from association or union with another）
[dɪˈsoʊʃieɪt]	记 词根记忆：dis(不)+soci(社会)+ate → 不能进入社会的 → 分离，游离
intersperse	*v.* 散布，点缀（to place sth. at intervals in or among）
[ˌɪntərˈspɜːrs]	记 词根记忆：inter + spers(撒播) + e → 在中间撒播 → 点缀
retreat	*n.* 撤退（withdrawal of troops）；隐居处（a place of privacy or safety；refuge）*v.* 撤退
[rɪˈtriːt]	记 词根记忆：re(后) + treat(=tract 拉) → 向后拉 → 撤退
	例 Upon realizing that his position was untenable, the general ordered his men to *retreat* to a neighboring hill.

poisonous [ˈpɔɪzənəs]	*adj.* 有毒的(containing poison);有害的(harmful) 同 venomous
recusant [rəˈkjuːzənt]	*n.* 拒绝服从的人(one who refuses to accept or obey established authority)
fragrance [ˈfreɪɡrəns]	*n.* 香料;香味(pleasant or sweet smell) 记 来自 fragrant(*adj.* 芳香的)
file [faɪl]	*n.* 锉刀 *v.* 锉平(to smooth with a file) 记 file"文件"之意众所周知
vertex [ˈvɜːrteks]	*n.* (三角形等的)顶角;顶点,最高点(summit; the highest point) 同 apex, crest, crown, height
inventory [ˈɪnvəntɔːri]	*n.* 详细目录(a detailed, itemized list);存货清单(a list of goods on hand) 记 词根记忆:in + vent(来) + ory → 对进来的东西进行清查 → 存货清单
lampoon [læmˈpuːn]	*n.* 讽刺文章(a broad satirical piece of writing) *v.* 讽刺(to ridicule or satirize) 记 联想记忆:lamp(灯) + oon → 用灯照别人的缺点 → 讽刺
wastrel [ˈweɪstrəl]	*n.* 挥霍无度的人(one who spends resources foolishly and self-indulgently; profligate) 记 来自 waste(*n./v.* 浪费)
effeminate [ɪˈfemɪnət]	*adj.* 缺乏勇气的,柔弱的(having the qualities generally attributed to women) 记 词根记忆:ef + femin(女) + ate → 露出女人气 → 柔弱的
panorama [ˌpænəˈræmə]	*n.* 概观,全景(a comprehensive presentation; cyclorama) 记 词根记忆:pan(全部) + orama(看) → 全部看得到 → 全景
revulsion [rɪˈvʌlʃn]	*n.* 厌恶,憎恶(a sense of utter distaste);剧变(a sudden or strong reaction)
feral [ˈferəl]	*adj.* 凶猛的,野性的(wild or savage) 同 fierce, inhumane, untamed
ponderable [ˈpɒndərəbl]	*adj.* 可估量的(able to be assessed; appreciable)
disport [dɪˈspɔːrt]	*v.* 玩耍,嬉戏(to indulge in amusement) 记 词根记忆:dis(加强) + port(带) → 带走(时间) → 玩耍
execrate [ˈeksɪkreɪt]	*v.* 憎恶(to loathe; detest; abhor);咒骂(to call down evil upon; curse) 记 词根记忆:ex(出) + ecr(=secr 神圣的) + ate → 走出了神圣 → 咒骂
dissuade [dɪˈsweɪd]	*v.* 劝阻,阻止(to advise against an action) 记 词根记忆:dis(不) + suade(敦促) → 敦促某人不做 → 劝阻
scrumptious [ˈskrʌmpʃəs]	*adj.* 很可口的,美味的(delightful; delicious) 记 可能来自 scrump(*v.* 偷苹果),偷来的苹果最好吃,所以 scrumptious 有"可口的"的意思
speck [spek]	*n.* 斑点(a small spot from stain or decay);少量(a very small amount) 记 参见 peccadillo(*n.* 小过失)

33

sentry [ˈsentri]	*n.* 哨兵，步兵 (a soldier standing guard) 记 词根记忆：sent (感觉) + ry → 感觉灵敏的人 → 哨兵
rasp [ræsp]	*v.* 发出刺耳的声音 (to make a harsh noise)；锉，刮削 搭 rasp sth. away/off 锉掉某物
track [træk]	*n.* 轨迹，踪迹 (a mark or succession of marks left by sth. that has passed)；道路，路径 (a path, route, or course indicated by such marks)；轨道 (a path along which sth. moves) *v.* 跟踪，追踪 (to follow the tracks or traces of)
fondle [ˈfɑːndl]	*v.* 抚弄，抚摸 (to stroke or handle in a tender and loving way；caress) 记 来自 fond (*adj.* 喜爱的)
impinge [ɪmˈpɪndʒ]	*v.* 侵犯 (to infringe；encroach)；撞击 (to collide with) 记 词根记忆：im (进入) + ping (系紧，强加于) + e → 强行进入 → 侵犯
outshine [ˌaʊtˈʃaɪn]	*v.* 比…光亮 (to shine brighter than)；出色，优异 (to excel in splendor or showiness) 记 联想记忆：out (超越) + shine (闪耀) → 比…光亮；出色，优异
latch [lætʃ]	*n.* 门闩 *v.* 用门闩闩牢 记 和 catch (*v.* 抓住) 一起记
detach [dɪˈtætʃ]	*v.* 使分离，使分开，拆卸 (to separate without violence or damage) 记 词根记忆：de (去掉) + tach (接触) → 去掉接触 → 使分离
disentangle [ˌdɪsɪnˈtæŋgl]	*v.* 解决；解脱，解开 (to make straight and free of knots) 记 词根记忆：dis (不) + entangle (纠缠) → 摆脱纠缠 → 解脱
stigmatize [ˈstɪgmətaɪz]	*v.* 诬蔑，玷污 (to describe opprobrious terms) 同 brand, label, tag
rend [rend]	*v.* 撕碎，分裂 (to split or tear apart)；抢夺 (to remove from place by violence) 记 联想记忆：因为被撕碎 (rend) 了，所以要修补 (mend)
spree [spriː]	*n.* 狂欢 (an unrestrained indulgence in or outburst of an activity) 搭 shopping/spending spree 狂购一气；痛痛快快花一通钱
jagged [ˈdʒægɪd]	*adj.* 锯齿状的，参差不齐的 (notched or ragged) 记 来自 jag (*v.* 使成锯齿状)
slander [ˈslændər]	*v.* 诽谤，诋毁 (to defame) *n.* 诽谤，中伤 记 联想记忆：s+land (地) + er → 把人贬到地上 → 诽谤，诋毁
reprieve [rɪˈpriːv]	*v.* 缓期执行 (to delay the punishment of)；暂时解救 (to give relief for a time) *n.* 缓刑，暂缓 记 词根记忆：re (后) + priev (=prehend 抓住) → 抓住放在后面 → 暂不执行死刑 → 缓刑
premiere [prɪˈmɪr]	*n.* (电影、戏剧等) 首次公演 (a first performance or exhibition) 记 来自 premier (*adj.* 首要的；最早的)
collude [kəˈluːd]	*v.* 串通，共谋 (to act in conspire) 记 词根记忆：col (共同) + lud (玩弄) + e → 共同玩弄 → 串通

□ sentry	□ rasp	□ track	□ fondle	□ impinge	□ outshine
□ latch	□ detach	□ disentangle	□ stigmatize	□ rend	□ spree
□ jagged	□ slander	□ reprieve	□ premiere	□ collude	

majestic [mə'dʒestɪk]	*adj.* 雄伟的，庄严的(showing majesty) 记 词根记忆：maj(大的) + estic → 雄伟的 例 The eradication of pollution is not merely a matter of aesthetics, though the *majestic* beauty of nature is indeed an important consideration.
quaff [kwɑːf]	*v.* 痛饮，畅饮(to drink deeply) 记 发音记忆："夸父" → 夸父追日，渴急痛饮 → 痛饮，畅饮
pervert [pər'vɜːrt]	*v.* 使堕落(to corrupt; debase)；滥用(to divert to a wrong purpose; misuse)；歪曲(to interpret incorrectly) 记 词根记忆：per(远离) + vert(转) → 越转越远离正途 → 使堕落
pendulum ['pendʒələm]	*n.* 摆，钟摆 记 词根记忆：pend(挂) + ulum(东西) → 挂的东西 → 钟摆
plaza ['plæzə]	*n.* 广场(a public square)；集市(shopping center) 记 来自拉丁语 platea，意为"庭院；宽敞的大街"
destitution [ˌdestɪ'tuːʃn]	*n.* 缺乏，穷困(the state of being destitute) 记 来自 destitute(*adj.* 贫困的)
friction ['frɪkʃn]	*n.* 摩擦(the rubbing of one body against another)；矛盾，冲突(disagreement between people with different views) 记 联想记忆：润滑油的功能(function)是减小摩擦(friction)
implicit [ɪm'plɪsɪt]	*adj.* 含蓄的，暗示的(not directly expressed) 记 词根记忆：im(进入) + plic(重叠) + it → (意义)叠在里面 → 含蓄的
potation [pəʊ'teɪʃn]	*n.* 喝，饮(the act of drinking or inhaling)；饮料，酒(an alcoholic drink)
sere [sɪr]	*adj.* 干枯的，枯萎的(being dried and withered) 记 不要和 sear(*v.* 烧灼)相混
dour ['daʊər]	*adj.* 严厉的，阴郁的，倔强的(sullen; gloomy; stubborn) 同 glum, moody, morose, saturnine, sour, sulky
posit ['pɑːzɪt]	*v.* 断定，认定(to assume or affirm the existence of; postulate) 记 通过 position(*n.* 位置，立场)来反推 posit
embody [ɪm'bɑːdi]	*v.* 使具体化，体现(to make concrete and perceptible; incorporate) 记 词根记忆：em(进入) + body(身体) → (思想)进入身体 → 体现
commence [kə'mens]	*v.* 开始，着手(to begin; start; originate) 记 词根记忆：com(共同) + mence(说，做) → 一起说，做 → 开始，着手
prowess ['praʊəs]	*n.* 勇敢(distinguished bravery)；非凡的才能(extraordinary ability) 记 来自 prow(*adj.* 〈古〉英勇的)
droll [drəʊl]	*adj.* 古怪的，好笑的(amusing in an odd or wry way; funny) 记 发音记忆："倔老儿" → 倔老头又古怪又好笑 → 古怪的，好笑的
stretch [stretʃ]	*v.* 延伸(to become wider or longer)；伸展(to reach full length or width) 同 elongate, prolongate, protract, unfold

33

□ majestic	□ quaff	□ pervert	□ pendulum	□ plaza	□ destitution
□ friction	□ implicit	□ potation	□ sere	□ dour	□ posit
□ embody	□ commence	□ prowess	□ droll	□ stretch	

momentum	*n.* 推进力，势头(impetus; force or speed of movement)
[moʊˈmentəm]	记 来自 moment(*n.* 瞬间)
sublime	*adj.* 崇高的(lofty in thought, expression, or manner) *v.* 使崇高
[səˈblaɪm]	搭 sublime in art 艺术的崇高
acrobat	*n.* 特技演员，杂技演员(one that performs gymnastic feats requiring skillful control of the body)
[ˈækrəbæt]	记 词根记忆：acro(高) + bat(走) → 高空走的人 → 杂技演员
coeval	*adj.* 同时代的(existing at the same time)
[koʊˈiːvl]	记 词根记忆：co(共同) + ev(时代) + al → 同时代的
pinch	*v.* 捏，掐(to compress; squeeze) *n.* 一撮，少量(a very small amount)
[pɪntʃ]	记 联想记忆：p + inch(英寸) → 以英寸计量的 → 一撮
wizened	*adj.* 干枯的，干瘪的，干皱的(dry, shrunken, and wrinkled as a result of aging or of failing vitality)
[ˈwɪznd]	记 来自 wizen(*v.* 起皱，干瘪)；发音记忆："未整的" → 干瘪的
nethermost	*adj.* 最低的，最下面的(lowest; the farthest down)
[ˈneðəmoʊst]	记 组合词：nether(下面的) + most(最) → 最下面的
swerve	*v.* 突然改变方向(to turn aside abruptly from a straight line or course; deviate)
[swɜːrv]	记 联想记忆：serve(发球)中间加 w(where) → 发球突然改变方向后都不知道球到哪去了 → 突然改变方向
sententious	*adj.* 说教的(abounding in excessive moralizing)；简要的(terse; pithy)
[senˈtenʃəs]	记 联想记忆：sentence(句子) + tious → 一句话说完 → 简要的
omniscient	*adj.* 无所不知的，博识的(knowing all things)
[ɑːmˈnɪsiənt]	记 词根记忆：omni(全) + sci(知道) + ent → 全知道的 → 无所不知的
requite	*v.* 报答(to repay)；报复(to make retaliation)
[rɪˈkwaɪt]	同 avenge, redress, vindicate
seam	*n.* 缝，接缝(line along which two edges are joined)
[siːm]	参 seamstress(*n.* 女裁缝)
genesis	*n.* 创始，起源(beginning; origin)
[ˈdʒenəsɪs]	记 词根记忆：gene(产生，基因) + sis → 创始；大写 Genesis 专指《圣经》中的《创世纪》
slink	*v.* 溜走，潜逃(to go or move stealthily or furtively)
[slɪŋk]	同 creep
engross	*v.* 全神贯注于(to occupy completely)
[ɪnˈɡroʊs]	记 联想记忆：en(进入) + gross(总的) → 全部进入状态 → 全神贯注于
burial	*n.* 埋葬，埋藏(the act or ceremony of putting a dead body into a grave)
[ˈberiəl]	记 来自 bury(*v.* 埋葬，掩埋)
mnemonics	*n.* 记忆法，记忆术(the technique of developing the memory)
[nɪˈmɑːnɪks]	记 词根记忆：mne(记忆) + mon + ics → 记忆法

query [ˈkwɪri]	*v.* 质疑，疑问，询问(to question; inquiry; doubt) *n.* 问题，疑问 记 词根记忆：que(追求) + ry → 追求答案 → 疑问
entourage [ˈɑːntʊrɑːʒ]	*n.* 随从(group of attendants; retinue)；环境(surroundings) 记 联想记忆：en + tour (旅行) + age (年龄) → 上了年龄旅行必须有随从 → 随从
ultramundane [ˌʌltrəˈmʌndein]	*adj.* 世界之外的；超俗的 记 词根记忆：ultra(超出)+mund(世界)+ane → 超俗的
malefactor [ˈmælɪfæktər]	*n.* 罪犯，作恶者(criminal; evildoer) 记 词根记忆：male(坏的) + fact(做) + or → 做坏事的人 → 作恶者
pendent [ˈpendənt]	*adj.* 吊着的，悬挂的(overhanging) 记 词根记忆：pend(挂) + ent → 挂着的 → 吊着的, 悬挂的
vegetate [ˈvedʒəteɪt]	*v.* 像植物那样生长(to grow in the manner of a plant)；无所事事地生活(to lead a passive existence without exertion of body or mind) 记 词根记忆：veg(生活) + et + ate → 无所事事地生活
emolument [ɪˈmɑːljumənt]	*n.* 报酬，薪水(remuneration) 记 词根记忆：e + molu(碾碎) + ment → 磨坊主加工粮食后所得的钱 → 报酬
subcelestial [ˌsʌbsiˈlestiəl]	*adj.* 世俗的，尘世的(worldly) 记 参考 celestial(*adj.* 天上的，神圣的)
fatidic [fæˈtɪdɪk]	*adj.* 预言的(of or relating to prophecy) 同 prophetic
desolate [ˈdesələt]	*adj.* 荒凉的，被遗弃的(left alone; solitary; deserted) 记 词根记忆：de + sol(孤独) + ate → 变得孤独 → 被遗弃的
tactic [ˈtæktɪk]	*n.* 策略，手段(a device for accomplishing an end)；战术(a method of employing forces in combat) 记 词根记忆：tact(使正确) + ic → 策略，手段
array [əˈreɪ]	*v.* 部署(to place armed forces in battle order) *n.* 陈列(impressive display)；大批
exclamation [ˌekskləˈmeɪʃn]	*n.* 惊叹词；惊呼(a sharp or sudden utterance) 记 词根记忆：ex(出) + clam(叫，喊) + ation → 大声喊出来 → 惊呼
jumpy [ˈdʒʌmpi]	*adj.* 紧张不安的，心惊肉跳的(on edge; nervous) 记 来自 jump(*v.* 跳；惊跳)
superlative [suːˈpɜːrlətɪv]	*adj.* 最好的(surpassing all others; supreme) 记 词根记忆：super(在…上面) + lat(放) + ive → 放在别的上面 → 最好的
easel [ˈiːzl]	*n.* 黑板架，画架(wooden frame for holding a blackboard or a picture) 记 联想记忆：ease(轻松) + l → 有了画架，画起画来轻松多了 → 画架
tenure [ˈtenjər]	*n.* 占有期(the term of holding sth.)，任期；终身职位 记 词根记忆：ten(拿住)+ure → 始终拿住 → 占有期，任期

33

□ query	□ entourage	□ ultramundane	□ malefactor	□ pendent	□ vegetate
□ emolument	□ subcelestial	□ fatidic	□ desolate	□ tactic	□ array
□ exclamation	□ jumpy	□ superlative	□ easel	□ tenure	

syndrome [ˈsɪndroʊm]	*n.* 综合症(a set of medical symptoms which represent a physical or mental disorder) 记 词根记忆：syn(一起)+drom(跑)+e → 跑到一起 → 综合症 例 The "impostor *syndrome*" often afflicts those who fear that true self-disclosure will lower them in others' esteem; rightly handled, however, candor may actually enhance one's standing.
multifarious [ˌmʌltɪˈferiəs]	*adj.* 多种的，各式各样的(numerous and varied) 记 词根记忆：multi(多) + fari(部分) + ous → 含有许多部分的 → 多种多样的
floppy [ˈflɑːpi]	*adj.* 松软的(soft and flexible)；软弱的(flabby；flaccid) 记 联想记忆：f + loppy(下垂的) → 松软的
unfasten [ʌnˈfæsn]	*v.* 解开(to undo) 记 联想记忆：un(不)+fasten(扎牢，扣紧) → 解开
miscellany [ˈmɪsəleɪni]	*n.* 混合物(a collection of various items or parts) 记 词根记忆：misc(混合) + ellany → 混合物
clot [klɑːt]	*n.* 凝块(a thickened lump formed within a liquid) *v.* 使凝结成块(to thicken into a clot)
whim [wɪm]	*n.* 一时的兴致，怪念头(a sudden idea；fancy) 同 caprice, fad, vagary, whimsy
gourmet [ˈɡʊrmeɪ]	*n.* 美食家(a person who is an excellent judge of fine foods and drinks) 记 注意与 gourmand 的不同：gourmand 指贪吃的人，而 gourmet 指品尝食品是否美味的人
engaging [ɪnˈɡeɪdʒɪŋ]	*adj.* 迷人的，美丽动人的(tending to draw favorable attention) 记 来自 engage(*v.* 吸引)
enflame [ɪnˈfleɪm]	*v.* 燃烧 记 联想记忆：en(进入) + flame(燃烧) → 进入燃烧 → 燃烧
felicitous [fəˈlɪsɪtəs]	*adj.* (话语等)适当的，得体的(used or expressed in a way suitable to the occasion；appropriate) 记 词根记忆：felic(幸福的) + itous → (讲话)使人幸福的 → 得体的
podium [ˈpoʊdiəm]	*n.* 讲坛，(乐队的)指挥台(a base especially for an orchestral conductor) 记 词根记忆：pod(脚) + ium → 站脚的地方 → 讲坛
perch [pɜːrtʃ]	*v.* (鸟等)栖息(to alight, settle, or rest on a roost or a height) 记 注意不要和 parch(*v.* 烘，烤)相混
disruptive [dɪsˈrʌptɪv]	*adj.* 制造混乱的(causing disruption) 记 来自 disrupt(*v.* 打乱，扰乱)
arraign [əˈreɪn]	*v.* 传讯(to charge in court；indict)；指责(to accuse) 记 联想记忆：安排(arrange)对犯人传讯 (arraign)
animus [ˈænɪməs]	*n.* 敌意，憎恨(animosity) 同 enmity, hatred, hostility, rancour

□ syndrome	□ multifarious	□ floppy	□ unfasten	□ miscellany	□ clot
□ whim	□ gourmet	□ engaging	□ enflame	□ felicitous	□ podium
□ perch	□ disruptive	□ arraign	□ animus		

358

lease [liːs]	*n.* 租约(a rental contract); 租期 *v.* 出租(to rent a property to sb.) 记 联想记忆：l + ease(安心) → 签了租约终于安心了 → 租约
abominate [əˈbɑːmɪneɪt]	*v.* 痛恨，厌恶(to feel hatred and disgust for; loathe) 记 词根记忆：ab(脱离) + om(=hom=man, 人) + in + ate → 脱离人的模样 → 痛恨；厌恶
jaunty [ˈdʒɔːnti]	*adj.* 轻松活泼的(gay and carefree; sprightly) 记 来自jaunt(*n.* 短途旅行)
corrugate [ˈkɔːrəgeɪt]	*v.* 起波纹，起皱纹(to shape into folds or parallel and alternating ridges and grooves) 记 词根记忆：cor + rug(=wrinkle 皱) + ate → 起波纹，起皱纹
inscrutable [ɪnˈskruːtəbl]	*adj.* 高深莫测的，神秘的(unfathomable; enigmatic; mysterious) 记 词根记忆：in(不) + scrut(调查) + able → 不能调查的 → 高深莫测的
sensible [ˈsensəbl]	*adj.* 明智的(reasonable); 可感觉到的(noticeable) 记 词根记忆：sens(感觉)+ible → 可感觉到的 例 Human reaction to the realm of thought is often as strong as that to *sensible* presences; our higher moral life is based on the fact that material sensations actually present may have a weaker influence on our action than do ideas of remote facts.
pivot [ˈpɪvət]	*n.* 枢轴，中心 *v.* 旋转(to turn on as if on a pivot)
flicker [ˈflɪkər]	*v.* 闪烁，摇曳(to burn or shine unsteadily) 记 和flick(*v.* 轻弹)一起记
burrow [ˈbɜːroʊ]	*v.* 挖掘，钻进，翻寻(to dig a hole; penetrate by means of a burrow) *n.* 地洞 记 联想记忆：用犁(furrow)来翻寻(burrow)
atone [əˈtoʊn]	*v.* 赎罪，补偿(to make amends for a wrongdoing) 记 联想记忆：a + tone(看作stone, 石头) → 女娲用石头补天 → 补偿
troll [troʊl]	*v.* 用曳绳钓(鱼); 拖钓(to fish for by trailing a baited line from behind a slowly moving boat); 兴高采烈地唱(to sing in a jovial manner)
exceptional [ɪkˈsepʃənl]	*adj.* 特别(好)的(not ordinary or average) 例 Perhaps predictably, since an ability to communicate effectively is an important trait of any great leader, it has been the *exceptional* Presidents who have delivered the most notable inaugural addresses.
vague [veɪg]	*adj.* 含糊的，不明确的(not clearly expressed); 模糊的(lacking definite shape, form, or character; indistinct) 记 词根记忆：vag(漫游) + ue → 思路四处漫游 → 含糊的；模糊的
gestate [ˈdʒesteɪt]	*v.* 怀孕，孕育(to carry in the uterus during pregnancy); 构思 记 词根记忆：gest(=carry 带有) + ate → 有了 → 怀孕
umpire [ˈʌmpaɪər]	*n.* 仲裁者(one having authority to decide finally a controversy or question between parties) *v.* 对…进行仲裁(to supervise or decide as umpire)

33

□ lease	□ abominate	□ jaunty	□ corrugate	□ inscrutable	□ sensible
□ pivot	□ flicker	□ burrow	□ atone	□ troll	□ exceptional
□ vague	□ gestate	□ umpire			

359

acclimate ['ækləmeɪt]	*v.* (使)服水土(to adjust to climate)；(使)适应(to adapt) 记 词根记忆：ac(向) + clim (倾斜) + ate → (使)向某物倾斜 → (使)服水土
renascent [rɪ'næsnt]	*adj.* 再生的，复活的，新生的(reborn after being forgotten) 搭 renascent herbs 多年生草本植物
fecundity [fɪ'kʌndəti]	*n.* 多产，丰饶(fruitfulness in offspring or vegetation)；繁殖力，生殖力 例 The Neoplatonists' conception of a deity, in which perfection was measured by abundant *fecundity*, was contradicted by that of the Aristotelians, in which perfection was displayed in the economy of creation.
retrench [rɪ'trentʃ]	*v.* 节省，紧缩开支(to economize; cut down expenses) 记 词根记忆：re(回) + trench(切掉) → 把开支再切掉 → 节省，紧缩开支
underdog ['ʌndərdɔːg]	*n.* 居于下风者(a loser or predicted loser in a struggle or contest)；受欺负者，受欺压者(a victim of injustice or persecution) 记 联想记忆：under(在…下面)+dog(狗) → 受欺负者 例 The plot of the motion picture *Hoosiers* is trite; we have all seen this story, the tale of an *underdog* team going on to win a championship, in one form or another countless times.
insignia [ɪn'sɪgniə]	*n.* 徽章(badge; emblem) 记 词根记忆：in + sign(标志，记号) + ia → 作为标志的东西 → 徽章
abortive [ə'bɔːrtɪv]	*adj.* 无结果的，失败的(fruitless; unsuccessful) 记 词根记忆：ab(脱落) + or(=ori 产生) + tive → 从产生的地方脱落 → 无结果的，失败的

You never know what you can do till you try.

除非你亲自尝试一下，否则你永远不知道你能够做什么。

——英国小说家 马里亚特(Frederick Marryat, British novelist)

□ acclimate □ renascent □ fecundity □ retrench □ underdog □ insignia
□ abortive

inculcate [ɪnˈkʌlkeɪt]	*v.* 谆谆教诲，反复灌输(to impress upon the mind by persistent urging; implant) 记 词根记忆：in(进入) + culc(=cult 培养；种植) + ate → 种进去 → 反复灌输
pathetic [pəˈθetɪk]	*adj.* 引起怜悯的，令人难过的(marked by sorrow or melancholy) 记 词根记忆：path(感情) + etic → 有感情的 → 引起怜悯的
nautical [ˈnɔːtɪkl]	*adj.* 船员的，船舶的，航海的(pertaining to sailors, ships or navigation) 记 词根记忆：naut(船) + ical → 船舶的，航海的
pharisaic [ˌfærɪˈseɪɪk]	*adj.* 伪善的，伪装虔诚的 记 来自公元前后犹太教的法利赛人(Pharisee)，以形式上遵守教义的伪善作风闻名
demagogue [ˈdeməɡɑːɡ]	*n.* 蛊惑民心的政客(political leader who tries to win people's support by using emotional and often unreasonable arguments) 记 来自 demagogy(*n.* 煽动，蛊惑民心)
heal [hiːl]	*v.* 治愈(to restore to health or soundness) 同 cure, remedy
enliven [ɪnˈlaɪvn]	*v.* 使…更活跃或更愉快(to make sb./sth. more lively or cheerful) 记 联想记忆：en + live(充满活动的，令人愉快的) + n → 使…更活跃或更愉快
sate [seɪt]	*v.* 使心满意足，使厌腻(to gratify completely；glut) 记 词根记忆：sat(满的) + e → 使心满意足
extradite [ˈekstrədaɪt]	*v.* 引渡 记 词根记忆：ex + trad(递交) + ite → 把…递交出去 → 引渡
errand [ˈerənd]	*n.* 差使(a trip to do a definite thing)；差事(a mission) 记 词根记忆：err(漫游) + and → 跑来跑去的事情 → 差使
concinnity [kənˈsɪnɪti]	*n.* 优美；雅致；协调(harmony or elegance of design)
caress [kəˈres]	*n.* 爱抚，抚摸(loving touch) *v.* 爱抚或抚摸(to touch or stroke lightly in a loving or endearing manner)

□ inculcate	□ pathetic	□ nautical	□ pharisaic	□ demagogue	□ heal
□ enliven	□ sate	□ extradite	□ errand	□ concinnity	□ caress

361

inanimate	*adj.* 无生命的(not animate; lifeless)
[ɪnˈænɪmət]	记 词根记忆：in(无) + anim(生命) + ate → 无生命的
onus	*n.* 义务，负担(a difficult or disagreeable responsibility or necessity)
[ˈoʊnəs]	记 联想记忆：on + us → 在我们身上的"责任" → 义务，负担
idiom	*n.* 方言，土语；术语；特有用语(the language peculiar to a people or to a
[ˈɪdiəm]	district, community, or class)；风格，特色(manner, style)
miscreant	*n.* 恶棍，歹徒(a vicious or depraved person)
[ˈmɪskriənt]	记 词根记忆：mis（坏的）+ cre(=cred 相信) + ant → 相信坏事物的人 → 恶棍
vituperate	*v.* 谩骂，辱骂(to abuse or censure severely or abusively)
[vɪˈtjuːpəreɪt]	记 词根记忆：vitu(过失) + per(准备) + ate → 因过失而遭受 → 谩骂，辱骂
pang	*n.* 一阵剧痛(a sudden sharp feeling of pain)
[pæŋ]	搭 pangs of remorse 悔恨的痛苦
rive	*v.* 撕开，分裂(to rend or tear apart)
[raɪv]	同 break, fracture, rift, shatter, splinter
chant	*n.* 圣歌 *v.* 歌唱，吟诵(to sing or recite)
[tʃænt]	记 发音记忆："唱" → 歌唱
arbitrate	*v.* 仲裁，公断(to decide (a dispute) as an arbitrator)
[ˈɑːrbɪtreɪt]	同 intercede, intermediate, liaise, mediate
stature	*n.* 身高，身材(natural height of the body in an upright position)
[ˈstætʃər]	记 词根记忆：stat(站) + ure(状态) → 站的状态 → 身高，身材
dowdy	*adj.* 不整洁的，过旧的(not neat or stylish; shabby)
[ˈdaʊdi]	同 antique, archaic, fusty, vintage
long-winded	*adj.* 冗长的
[ˌlɔːŋ ˈwɪndɪd]	记 组合词：long(长) + wind(空谈，废话) + ed → 冗长的
enshrine	*v.* 奉为神圣，珍藏(to preserve or cherish as sacred)
[ɪnˈʃraɪn]	记 词根记忆：en(进入) + shrine(圣地) → 奉为神圣
pressing	*adj.* 紧迫的，迫切的(urgently important)；恳切要求的(asking for sth. strongly)
[ˈpresɪŋ]	
swell	*v.* 肿胀，增强(to expand gradually beyond a normal or original limit)
[swel]	记 联想记忆：s + well(泉) → 像泉水一样冒出来 → 肿胀，增强
pith	*n.* 精髓，要点(the essential part; core)
[pɪθ]	
drool	*v.* 流口水；胡说(to drivel)
[druːl]	同 dribble, salivate, slaver, slobber
dissemble	*v.* 假装，掩饰(感情、意图等)(to conceal; disguise)
[dɪˈsembl]	记 词根记忆：dis(不) + semble(相同) → 不和(本来面目)相同 → 掩饰
jamboree	*n.* 喧闹的集会(a boisterous party or noisy revel)
[ˌdʒæmbəˈriː]	

□ inanimate	□ onus	□ idiom	□ miscreant	□ vituperate	□ pang	□ rive
□ chant	□ arbitrate	□ stature	□ dowdy	□ long-winded	□ enshrine	□ pressing
□ swell	□ pith	□ drool	□ dissemble	□ jamboree		

hoop	*n.* （桶的）箍，铁环（a circular band or ring for holding together the staves
[huːp]	of a barrel）
acerbity	*n.* 涩，酸，刻薄（sourness of taste, character, or tone）
[əˈsɜːrbəti]	记 词根记忆：acerb（酸涩的，刻薄的）+ ity → 涩，酸，刻薄
chipmunk	*n.* 花栗鼠（像松鼠的美洲小动物）
[ˈtʃɪpmʌŋk]	
opine	*v.* 想，以为（to hold or express an opinion）
[oʊˈpaɪn]	记 通过 opinion（*n.* 看法）反推 opine（*v.* 想）
refurbish	*v.* 刷新，擦亮（to brighten or freshen up; renovate）
[ˌriːˈfɜːrbɪʃ]	记 联想记忆：re + furbish（磨光，磨亮）→ 刷新，擦亮
swathe	*v.* 包，绑，裹（to bind, wrap, or swaddle with or as if with a bandage）
[sweɪð]	
incinerate	*v.* 焚化，焚毁（to burn to ashes; cremate）
[ɪnˈsɪnəreɪt]	记 词根记忆：in（进入）+ ciner（灰）+ ate → 变成灰 → 焚化
hike	*v.* 抬高，提高（to increase or raise in amount）*n.* 徒步旅行
[haɪk]	搭 hike...up 拉起，提起
finite	*adj.* 有限的（having an end or limit）
[ˈfaɪnaɪt]	记 词根记忆：fin（范围）+ ite → 有限的
associate	[əˈsoʊʃiət] *adj.* 联合的（joined）*n.* 合伙人（partner; colleague）
	[əˈsoʊʃieɪt] *v.* 使发生联系，使联合（to join people or things together）
	记 词根记忆：as（加强）+ soci（同伴，引申为"社会"）+ ate → 成为社团 → 联合的
strand	*n.* （绳、线等的）股，缕 *v.* 搁浅（to cause sb. or sth. to be held at a location）
[strænd]	
jesting	*adj.* 滑稽的（ridiculous）；爱开玩笑的
[ˈdʒestɪŋ]	同 jocose, jocular
colt	*n.* 小雄马（a young male horse）；新手（a youthful or inexperienced
[koʊlt]	person）
cue	*v.* 暗示，提示（to give a sign to sb.）*n.* 暗示，提示（thing said or done to
[kjuː]	signal sb.'s turn to say or do sth.）
	记 联想记忆：线索（clue）有提示（cue）作用
pithiness	*n.* 简洁（state of being precisely brief）
[ˈpɪθɪnəs]	记 来自 pithy（*adj.* 精练的）
slug	*v.* 猛击，拳击（to strike heavily with or as if with the fist or a bat）
[slʌg]	搭 slug it out 决出胜负，一决雌雄
underwrite	*v.* 同意负担…的费用（to support with money and take responsibility for
[ˌʌndərˈraɪt]	possible failure）；通过保单承担（to take responsibility for fulfilling an
	insurance agreement）
	记 联想记忆：under（在…下面）+ write（写）→ 在下面写上自己的名字表示同意 → 同意承担…的费用

34

□ hoop	□ acerbity	□ chipmunk	□ opine	□ refurbish	□ swathe
□ incinerate	□ hike	□ finite	□ associate	□ strand	□ jesting
□ colt	□ cue	□ pithiness	□ slug	□ underwrite	

sedulity	n. 勤奋，勤勉（diligence）
[siˈdjuːliti]	记 来自 sedulous（adj. 孜孜不倦的）
checkered	adj. 多变的（with many changes of fortune）
[ˈtʃekərd]	记 来自 checker（n. 棋盘花格或棋子）
matte	adj. 无光泽的（lacking or deprived of luster or gloss）
[mæt]	记 为 mat 的变体
limbo	n. 不稳定的状态，中间状态（any intermediate, indeterminate state or
[ˈlɪmboʊ]	condition）
	记 原指"地狱的边境"
ruse	n. 骗术，计策（trick to deceive; stratagem）
[ruːz]	记 联想记忆：送玫瑰（rose）是捕获姑娘的芳心的好计策（ruse）→ 骗术，计策
	例 Although Simpson was ingenious at contriving to appear innovative and spontaneous, beneath the *ruse* he remained uninspired and rigid in his approach to problem-solving.
bough	n. 大树枝（a tree branch, especially a large or main branch）
[baʊ]	
assert	v. 断言，主张（to state positively; declare; affirm）
[əˈsɜːrt]	记 词根记忆：as（加强）+ sert（提出）→ 强烈地提出、表达自己的主张 → 主张
smattering	n. 略知（superficial knowledge）；少数（a small scattered number）
[ˈsmætərɪŋ]	同 elements, modicum, smidgen
askance	adv. 斜视地（with a sideways or indirect look）
[əˈskæns]	记 联想记忆：ask + ance（看作 ounce，盎司，黄金的计量单位）→ 问黄金价格 → 斜着眼问 → 斜视地
torrid	adj. 酷热的（intensely hot）
[ˈtɑːrɪd]	记 词根记忆：torr（使干燥）+ id → 酷热的
disenchant	v. 使不抱幻想，使清醒（to free from illusion）
[ˌdɪsɪnˈtʃænt]	记 词根记忆：dis(不) + enchant(使陶醉) → 使不再陶醉在(幻想中) → 使清醒
affiliate	[əˈfɪlieɪt] v. 使隶属于（to bring or receive into close connection as a member or branch）；追溯…的来源（to trace the origin of）；联合（to connect or associate）
	[əˈfɪliət] n. 成员，附属机构
	记 词根记忆：af(=ad 附近) + fil（儿子）+ iate → 形成近乎和儿子一样的关系 → 使隶属于
integrity	n. 正直，诚实（honesty and sincerity）；完整（entirety）
[ɪnˈtegrəti]	记 词根记忆：in(不) + tegr（触摸）+ ity → 未被触摸 → 正直；完整
	例 In some cultures the essence of magic is its traditional *integrity*; it can be efficient only if it has been transmitted without loss from primeval times to the present practitioners.

resident [ˈrezɪdənt]	*n.* 居民(one who lives or has a home in a place) *adj.* 定居的，常驻的(living in a place for some length of time) 记 来自 reside(*v.* 居住，定居)
abrupt [əˈbrʌpt]	*adj.* 突然的，意外的；唐突的(sudden and unexpected) 记 词根记忆：ab(脱离) + rupt(断) → 突然断掉了 → 突然的，意外的
exuberance [ɪgˈzuːbərəns]	*n.* 愉快(the quality of being cheerful)；茁壮(the quality or state of being exuberant) 记 来自 exuberant(*adj.* 茁壮的，繁茂的)
taking [ˈteɪkɪŋ]	*adj.* 楚楚动人的，迷人的(gaining the liking of) 同 attractive, charming
hush [hʌʃ]	*n.* 肃静，安静(absence of noise; silence) *v.* (使)安静下来 记 联想记忆：不要和 husk(*n.* 种子等的外壳)混淆
accurate [ˈækjərət]	*adj.* 精确的，准确的(free from error) 记 词根记忆：ac(加强) + cur(关心) + ate → 不断关心使之正确无误 → 精确的
abdicate [ˈæbdɪkeɪt]	*v.* 退位(to give up a throne or authority)；放弃(to cast off) 记 词根记忆：ab(脱离) + dic(说话，命令) + ate → 不再命令 → 退位；放弃
resourceful [rɪˈsɔːrsfl]	*adj.* 机智的(good at finding ways to deal with difficult situations) 记 和 resource(*n.* 资源)一起记
swirl [swɜːrl]	*v.* 旋转(to move with an eddying motion) *n.* 旋涡(a whirling motion; eddy) 记 词根记忆：s + wirl(转) → 旋转
eidetic [aɪˈdetɪk]	*adj.* (印象)异常清晰的；极为逼真的(marked by or involving extraordinary accuracy)
celebrity [səˈlebrəti]	*n.* 名声(wide recognition)；名人(a famous or well-publicized person) 记 词根记忆：celebr(著名) + ity → 名人
retrace [rɪˈtreɪs]	*v.* 回顾，追溯(to go over sth. again) 记 联想记忆：re + trace(踪迹) → 找回踪迹 → 回顾，追溯
patch [pætʃ]	*n.* 补丁 (a piece of material used to mend or cover a hole)；一小片(土地)(a small piece of land)
denunciate [dɪˈnʌnsieɪt]	*v.* 公开指责，公然抨击，谴责 (to pronounce especially publicly to be blameworthy or evil) 记 词根记忆：de (变坏) + nunci (讲话，说出) + ate → 公开指责，公然抨击
voucher [ˈvaʊtʃər]	*n.* 证件(a piece of supporting evidence)；收据(a documentary record of a business transaction)；凭证(a form or check indicating a credit against future purchases or expenditures)；代金券(a coupon)
subsistence [səbˈsɪstəns]	*n.* 生存，生计 (the ability to live with little money or food)；存在(existence) 记 来自 subsist(*v.* 生存)

□ resident	□ abrupt	□ exuberance	□ taking	□ hush	□ accurate
□ abdicate	□ resourceful	□ swirl	□ eidetic	□ celebrity	□ retrace
□ patch	□ denunciate	□ voucher	□ subsistence		

tinge [tɪndʒ]	*v.* 给…着色(to apply a trace of color to); 使略带…气息(to affect or modify with a slight odor or taste)
assoil [əˈsɔɪl]	*v.* 赦免，释放，补偿(to absolve; acquit; expiate) 同 clear, discharge, exculpate, exonerate
icicle [ˈaɪsɪkl]	*n.* 冰柱，冰垂(a tapering, pointed, hanging piece of ice) 记 词根记忆：ic(=ice 冰) + icle(小东西) → 冰柱
shipshape [ˈʃɪpʃeɪp]	*adj.* 整洁干净的；井然有序的(trim; tidy) 记 联想记忆：ship(船) + shape(形状) → 船的形状 → 整洁干净的
ruddy [ˈrʌdi]	*adj.* (脸色)红润的，红的(having a healthy red color) 搭 a ruddy complexion 红润的脸色
inadvertence [ˌɪnədˈvɜːrtəns]	*n.* 粗心，疏忽，漫不经心(the fact or action of being inadvertent) 记 词根记忆：in(不) + ad(往) + vert(转) + ence → 不转向某物 → 不加以注意 → 漫不经心
waylay [weɪˈleɪ]	*v.* 埋伏，伏击(to lie in wait for and attack from ambush) 同 ambuscade, lurk
blear [blɪr]	*v.* 使模糊(to dim, blur) *adj.* 模糊的(obscure to the view or imagination) 同 bleary, blear-eyed, bleary-eyed
comely [ˈkʌmli]	*adj.* 动人的，美丽的(pleasant to look at) 记 联想记忆：come(来) + ly → 吸引别人过来 → 动人的
dulcet [ˈdʌlsɪt]	*adj.* 美妙的，悦耳的(soothing or pleasant to hear; melodious) 记 词根记忆：dulc(=sweet 甜) + et → 声音甜的 → 美妙的，悦耳的
implant [ɪmˈplænt]	*v.* 植入，插入(to plant firmly or deeply); 灌输(to instill; inculcate) 记 联想记忆：im(进入) + plant(种植) → 植入；灌输
mash [mæʃ]	*v.* 捣成糊状(to convert into a soft pulpy mixture) 记 联想记忆：m + ash(灰) → 弄成灰 → 捣成糊状
perjury [ˈpɜːrdʒəri]	*n.* 伪证(罪)，假誓(false swearing) 搭 commit perjury 犯伪证罪
throng [θrɑːŋ]	*n.* 一大群(a large number) *v.* 拥挤(to crowd together) 同 concourse, flock, swarm
coda [ˈkoʊdə]	*n.* 乐曲结尾部(final passage of a piece of music)
persistence [pərˈsɪstəns]	*n.* 坚持不懈，执意，持续(the quality or state of being persistent) 记 来自 persist(*v.* 坚持，持续，固执) 例 Contrary to the popular conception that it is powered by conscious objectivity, science often operates through error, happy accidents, hunches and *persistence* in spite of mistakes.
besot [bɪˈsɑːt]	*v.* 使沉醉，使糊涂(to make dull or stupid, especially to muddle with drunkness)

stonewall [ˈstoʊnˈwɔːl]	v. 拖延议事，设置障碍（to intentionally delay in a discussion or argument） 同 filibuster, stall
rack [ræk]	v. 使痛苦不堪，使受折磨（to cause great physical or mental suffering to） 记 长距离赛跑（race）让他痛苦不堪（rack）
precept [ˈpriːsept]	n. 箴言，格言；规则（moral instruction; rule or principle that teaches correct behavior） 记 词根记忆：pre（预先）+ cept（拿住）→ 预先接受的话 → 格言
bifurcate [ˈbaɪfərkeɪt]	v. 分为两支，分叉（to divide into two parts or branches） 记 联想记忆：bi（两个）+ furc（看作 fork, 叉）+ ate → 分为两支
instate [ɪnˈsteɪt]	v. 任命（to put sb. in office） 同 inaugurate, install, place
mull [mʌl]	v. 思考，思索（to consider at length）n. 混乱（disorder） 搭 mull sth. over 认真琢磨，反复思考
jaunt [dʒɔːnt]	v. 短途旅游（to take a short trip for pleasure）n. 短途旅行 同 excursion, outing, tour
piteous [ˈpɪtiəs]	adj. 可怜的（of a kind to move to pity or compassion） 同 pathetic
sanitize [ˈsænɪtaɪz]	v. 使清洁（to make clean） 同 decontaminate, disinfect, sterilize
naive [naɪˈiːv]	adj. 天真的，纯朴的（marked by unaffected simplicity） 记 联想记忆：native（原始的，土著的）减去 t → 比土著人懂得还要少 → 天真的，纯朴的
cleft [kleft]	n. 裂缝（an opening; crack; crevice）adj. 劈开的（partially split or divided） 记 联想记忆：c + left（左）→ 左边的裂缝像 c 的形状 → 裂缝
inter [ɪnˈtɜːr]	v. 埋葬（to put into a grave or tomb; bury） 记 词根记忆：in（进入）+ ter（=terr 泥土）→ 埋进泥土 → 埋葬
massacre [ˈmæsəkər]	n. 大屠杀（the indiscriminate, merciless killing of a number of human beings） 记 联想记忆：mass（大批）+ acre（英亩）→ 把一大批人赶到一英亩宽的地方杀掉 → 大屠杀
plenitude [ˈplenɪtuːd]	n. 完全（completeness）；大量（a great sufficiency） 记 词根记忆：plen（满）+ itude → 大量
artificial [ˌɑːrtɪˈfɪʃl]	adj. 人造的，假的（unnatural） 记 词根记忆：arti（=skill 技巧）+ fic（面）+ ial（…的）→ 在表面使技术的 → 人造的，假的
syncretize [ˈsɪŋkrətaɪz]	v. （使）结合，（使）融和（to attempt to unite and harmonize especially without critical examination or logical unity）
impetus [ˈɪmpɪtəs]	n. 推动力；刺激（incentive; impulse） 记 词根记忆：im（在内）+ pet（追求）+ us → 内心的追求 → 刺激

34

□ stonewall	□ rack	□ precept	□ bifurcate	□ instate	□ mull
□ jaunt	□ piteous	□ sanitize	□ naive	□ cleft	□ inter
□ massacre	□ plenitude	□ artificial	□ syncretize	□ impetus	

concession [kənˈseʃn]	*n.* 让步(the act of conceding) 记 来自 concede(*v.* 让步)
alluring [əˈlʊrɪŋ]	*adj.* 吸引人的, 迷人的(attractive; charming) 记 来自 allure(*v.* 引诱)
interlude [ˈɪntərluːd]	*n.* 间歇(time between two events) 记 词根记忆: inter + lud(玩耍) + e → 在活动与活动中间的玩闹时间 → 间歇
influx [ˈɪnflʌks]	*n.* 注入, 涌入(arrival of people or things in large numbers or quantities) 记 词根记忆: in(进入) + flux(流动) → 注入, 涌入
compile [kəmˈpaɪl]	*v.* 汇集(to gather and put together); 编辑(to compose of materials gathered from various sources) 记 词根记忆: com(一起) + pile(堆) → 堆在一起 → 汇集
presentation [ˌpriːzenˈteɪʃn]	*n.* 介绍, 描述(the way in which sth. is shown to others) 记 来自 present(*v.* 介绍; 提出; 显示)
extirpation [ˌekstərˈpeɪʃn]	*n.* 消灭, 根除(extermination) 记 来自 extirpate(*v.* 消灭, 根除)
sway [sweɪ]	*v.* 摇动, 摇摆(to swing from side to side); 影响(to influence sb. so that they change their opinion) *n.* 摇摆(swaying movement) 记 联想记忆: s + way(路) → 走 S 型的路 → 摇摆
factitious [fækˈtɪʃəs]	*adj.* 人为的, 不真实的(not natural; artificial) 记 词根记忆: fact(做) + itious → 做出来的 → 人为的
disguise [dɪsˈgaɪz]	*v.* 假扮(to furnish with a false appearance or an assumed identity); 掩饰(to obscure real nature of) 记 词根记忆: dis + guise(姿态, 伪装) → 假扮; 掩饰
vocation [voʊˈkeɪʃn]	*n.* 天职, 神召(a summons or strong inclination to a particular state or course of action); 职业, 行业(the work in which a person is regularly employed); (对特定职业的)禀性, 才能(the special function of an individual or group) 记 词根记忆: voc(叫喊) + ation → 受到召唤 → 神召; 职业 例 Despite some allowances for occupational mobility, the normal expectation of seventeenth-century English society was that the child's *vocation* would develop along familial lines; divergence from the career of one's parents was therefore limited.
prop [prɑːp]	*n.* 支撑物, 支柱(support) *v.* 支持(to support) 同 strengthen, sustain
perjure [ˈpɜːrdʒər]	*v.* 使作伪证, 发假誓(to tell a lie under oath) 记 词根记忆: per(假地, 错地) + jur(发誓) + e → 虚假地发誓 → 使作伪证, 发假誓

□ concession □ alluring □ interlude □ influx □ compile □ presentation
□ extirpation □ sway □ factitious □ disguise □ vocation □ prop
□ perjure

dispose [dɪ'spoʊz]	*v.* 使倾向于；处理(to give a tendency to; to settle a matter finally) 搭 dispose of 去掉，清除
perky ['pɜːrki]	*adj.* 得意洋洋的；活泼的(jaunty; lively) 同 sprightly
convalescent [ˌkɑːnvə'lesnt]	*adj./n.* 康复中的(病人)((a person who is) recovering from illness) 记 来自 convalesce(*v.* 康复，复原)
husband ['hʌzbənd]	*v.* 节省，节约(to manage prudently and economically) 记 联想记忆：丈夫(husband)省钱(husband)，老婆花钱
sheaf [ʃiːf]	*n.* 一捆，一束(a bundle) 搭 a sheaf of paper 一沓纸
tamper ['tæmpər]	*v.* 干预，损害(to interfere in a harmful manner)；篡改(to alter improperly) 记 是 temper(*v.* 锻造；调和)的变体
patriot ['peɪtriət]	*n.* 爱国者，爱国主义者(one who loves his/her country and supports its authority and interests) 记 词根记忆：patri(父亲)+ ot → 把祖国当父亲看待的人 → 爱国者
sybaritic [ˌsɪbə'rɪtɪk]	*adj.* 骄奢淫逸的，贪图享乐的(devoted to or marked by pleasure and luxury) 记 联想记忆：sy(看作 see，看)+bar(酒吧)+itic → 看着酒吧里放纵的身影 → 骄奢淫逸的
cluster ['klʌstər]	*n.* 串，簇，群 *v.* 群集，丛生(to gather or grow in a cluster or clusters) 记 词根记忆：clust(=clot，凝成块)+ er → 凝块 → 群集
unanimous [ju'nænɪməs]	*adj.* 全体一致的(being of one mind) 记 词根记忆：un(=uni 一个)+anim(生命，精神)+ous → 全体一致的 例 Although some of her fellow scientists decried the unorthodox laboratory methodology that others found innovative, *unanimous* praise greeted her experimental results: at once pioneering and unexceptionable.
browse [braʊz]	*v.* 吃草(to nibble at leaves or twigs)；浏览(to look through a book casually) *n.* 嫩叶；嫩芽 记 联想记忆：brow(眉毛)+ se → 吃像眉毛一样的草 → 吃草
edgy ['edʒi]	*adj.* 急躁的，易怒的(irritable)；尖利的，(刀口)锐利的(sharp)
instill [ɪn'stɪl]	*v.* 滴注(to put in drop by drop)；逐渐灌输(to impart gradually) 记 词根记忆：in(进入)+ still(水滴) → 像水滴一样进入 → 滴注
intermission [ˌɪntər'mɪʃn]	*n.* 暂停，间歇(an interval of time) 记 联想记忆：inter + mission(发送) → 在发送之间 → 间歇

誓死不降

patriot

34

foist [fɔɪst]	v. 偷偷插入(to introduce or insert surreptitiously or without warrant);(以欺骗的方式)强加(to force another to accept especially by stealth or deceit)
ornate [ɔːrˈneɪt]	adj. 华美的(showy or flowery);充满装饰的(heavily ornamented or adorned) 记 词根记忆:orn(装饰) + ate → 装饰过的 → 华美的
digression [daɪˈgreʃn]	n. 离题,题外话(an act of turning aside from the main subject or talk about sth. else)
con [kɑːn]	n. 反对论(an argument or evidence in opposition) v. 欺骗(to swindle) 搭 pros and cons 有利有弊,正反两方面
belabor [bɪˈleɪbər]	v. 过分冗长地做或说(to spend too much time or effort on);痛打(to beat severely) 记 联想记忆:be + labor(劳动) → 不断劳动 → 过分冗长地做或说
vicarious [vaɪˈkeriəs]	adj. 替代的,代理的(serving in place of sb. or sth. else) 记 来自 vicar(n. 教区牧师)
convulse [kənˈvʌls]	v. 使剧烈震动;震撼(to shake or disturb violently;agitate) 记 词根记忆:con + vuls(拉) + e → 一再拉 → 使剧烈震动
flaccid [ˈflæsɪd]	adj. 松弛的(soft and limply flabby);软弱的(weak;feeble) 记 词根记忆:flac(=flab 松的) + cid → 松弛的
amalgamate [əˈmælgəmeɪt]	v. 合并(to unite;combine);混合(to mix)
misperceive [ˌmɪspərˈsiːv]	v. 误解(to misunderstand) 记 联想记忆:mis(错的) + perceive(理解,领会) → 误解
pelt [pelt]	v. 扔(to hurl;throw) n. 毛皮 搭 pelt sth. at sb. 朝某人扔某物
snob [snɑːb]	n. 势利小人 记 参考 snobbery(n. 势利态度,自命不凡)
incarcerate [ɪnˈkɑːrsəreɪt]	v. 把…关进监狱,监禁,禁闭(to imprison;confine) 记 词根记忆:in(进入) + carcer(监狱) + ate → 把…关进监狱,监禁,禁闭
menace [ˈmenəs]	n./v. 威胁,恐吓(to threat) 记 联想记忆:men(人) + ace(看作 face,面临,面对) → 将在比赛中面对的人 → 威胁
recruit [rɪˈkruːt]	n. 新兵(a newly enlisted or drafted soldier);新成员(a newcomer) v. 征募,招募(to seek to enroll) 记 词根记忆:re(重新) + cruit(=cres 成长) → 重新成长 → 新成员

□ foist	□ ornate	□ digression	□ con	□ belabor	□ vicarious
□ convulse	□ flaccid	□ amalgamate	□ misperceive	□ pelt	□ snob
□ incarcerate	□ menace	□ recruit			

音频

dictator [ˈdɪkteɪtər]	*n.* 独裁者（a ruler with absolute power and authority）
	同 autocrat, despot, totalitarian, tyrant
pretext [ˈpriːtekst]	*n.* 借口（a purpose or motive assumed in order to cloak the real intention）
	记 联想记忆：pre(预先) + text(课文) → 预先想好的文章 → 借口
univocal [juːˈnɪvəkl]	*adj.* 单一意思的（having only one meaning）
	搭 univocal concept 单一概念
upright [ˈʌpraɪt]	*adj.* 垂直的，直立的（straight up）；正直的，诚实的（honest；fair）
	同 erect, perpendicular, plumb, upstanding, vertical
stunt [stʌnt]	*v.* 阻碍（成长）（to hinder the normal growth） *n.* 特技，绝技（an unusual or difficult feat requiring great skill）
toy [tɔɪ]	*v.* 不认真地对待，玩弄（to deal with sth. lightly）
	搭 toy with sth. 把…当儿戏
additive [ˈædətɪv]	*n.* 添加剂（substance added in small amounts to sth. especially to food or medicine）
gabby [ˈɡæbi]	*adj.* 饶舌的，多嘴的（talkative）
	记 来自 gab(*n.* 饶舌，多嘴)
spindly [ˈspɪndli]	*adj.* 细长的，纤弱的（very long and thin）
	记 来自 spindle(*n.* 纺锤)
portentous [pɔːrˈtentəs]	*adj.* 凶兆的（ominous）
	记 来自 portent(*n.* 预兆，凶兆)
fury [ˈfɜːri]	*n.* 狂怒，狂暴（intense, disordered rage）；激烈，猛烈；狂怒的人（one who resembles an avenging spirit）；（希腊神话中的）复仇女神（the Furies goddesses in Greek mythology）
bilk [bɪlk]	*v.* 躲债（to avoid paying money borrowed from others）；骗取（to cheat sb. out of sth.）
ostracism [ˈɑːstrəsɪzəm]	*n.* 放逐，排斥（act of stopping accepting someone as a member of the group）
	记 词根记忆：ostrac(贝壳) + ism → 古希腊人用贝壳投票决定是否应该放逐某人 → 放逐

□ dictator	□ pretext	□ univocal	□ upright	□ stunt	□ toy
□ additive	□ gabby	□ spindly	□ portentous	□ fury	□ bilk
□ ostracism					

libel	*n.* (文字)诽谤，中伤(a false and demanding statement) *v.* 诽谤，中伤(to
['laɪbl]	make or publish a libel against)
	记 词根记忆：lib(文字) + el → (文字)诽谤；注意不要和label(*n.* 标签)
	相混
	例 Satisfied that her name had been cleared, she dropped her *libel* suit
	after the newspaper finally published a retraction of its original
	defamatory statement.
dominant	*adj.* 支配的；占优势的(exercising the most influence or control)
['dɑːmɪnənt]	记 词根记忆：domin(=dom 支配) + ant → 支配的
gavel	*n.* (法官所用的) 槌，小木槌
['gævl]	记 联想记忆：gave(给) + l → 法官敲小木槌，给以注意 → 槌，小木槌
paralyze	*v.* 使瘫痪(to affect with paralysis)；使无效(to make ineffective)
['pærəlaɪz]	记 词根记忆：para(一边) + lyz(松开) + e → 身体的一边松了 → 使瘫痪
intoxicate	*v.* (使)沉醉，(使)欣喜若狂(to excite sb. greatly)；(使)喝醉(to cause sb.
[ɪn'tɑːksɪkeɪt]	to lose self-control as a result of the effects of the alcohol)
	记 联想记忆：in(进入) + toxic(有毒的) + ate → 中毒了 → (使)沉醉
tyranny	*n.* 暴政，专制统治(oppressive power exerted by government)；暴行(a
['tɪrəni]	cruel or unjust act)
stinginess	*n.* 小气
['stɪndʒinəs]	记 来自stingy(*adj.* 吝啬的)
positiveness	*n.* 肯定，确信
['pɑːzətɪvnəs]	记 来自positive(*adj.* 肯定的)
statutory	*adj.* 法定的；依照法令的(regulated by statute)
['stætjutɔːri]	搭 statutory offence 法定罪行
inexpiable	*adj.* 不能补偿的(incapable of being expiated or atoned)
[ˌɪnɪk'spɪəbl]	记 联想记忆：in(不) + expiable(可抵偿的) → 不能补偿的；来自expiate
	(*v.* 补偿)
boo	*v.* 发出嘘声 *int.* (表示不满，轻蔑等)嘘
[buː]	记 发音记忆："不" → 发出嘘声
recipe	*n.* 食谱(a set of instructions for cooking)
['resəpi]	记 词根记忆：re + cip(抓) + e → 为做饭提供抓的要点 → 食谱
winnow	*v.* 扬，簸(谷物)(to remove chaff by a current of air)，除去
['wɪnoʊ]	记 注意不要和minnow(*n.* 小鱼)相混
immanent	*adj.* 内在的，固有的(inherent)；普遍存在的，无所不在的(present through
['ɪmənənt]	the universe)
	记 词根记忆：im(进入) + man(停留) + ent → 停留在内部的 → 内在的
reprobate	*v.* 非难，斥责(to condemn strongly) *adj./n.* 堕落的(人)(a person morally
['reprəbeɪt]	corrupt)
	记 词根记忆：re(反) + prob(赞扬) + ate → 不赞扬 → 斥责

□ libel	□ dominant	□ gavel	□ paralyze	□ intoxicate	□ tyranny
□ stinginess	□ positiveness	□ statutory	□ inexpiable	□ boo	□ recipe
□ winnow	□ immanent	□ reprobate			

ethics [ˈeθɪks]	*n.* 伦理学(science that deals with morals); 道德规范(moral correctness) 记 联想记忆：e(看作 east，东方) + thics(看作 thick，厚的) → 东方有深厚的道德规范 → 伦理学 搭 code of ethics 道德准则
congeal [kənˈdʒiːl]	*v.* 凝结，凝固(to solidify or thicken by cooling or freezing) 记 词根记忆：con(一起) + geal(冻结) → 冻结到一起 → 凝结
vaporize [ˈveɪpəraɪz]	*v.* (使)蒸发(to convert or be converted into vapor) 记 来自 vapor(*n.* 蒸汽) 例 Despite the mixture's volatile nature, we found that by lowering its temperature in the laboratory we could dramatically reduce its tendency to *vaporize*.
oracular [əˈrækjələr]	*adj.* 神谕的(of an oracle); 玄妙难懂的(obscure; enigmatic)
unsettle [ˌʌnˈsetl]	*v.* 使不安宁，扰乱(to discompose; disorder) 同 agitate, bother, disquiet, distract, disturb
throe [θroʊ]	*n.* 剧痛(anguish; pang); [*pl.*]挣扎(a hard or painful struggle) 搭 in the throes of sth./doing sth. 正在做，正忙于(尤其指困难或复杂的活动)
insolvency [ɪnˈsɑːlvənsi]	*n.* 无力偿还(inability to pay debts); 破产(bankruptcy) 记 词根记忆：in(无) + solvency(还债能力) → 无还债能力 → 无力偿还
satanic [səˈtænɪk]	*adj.* 似撒旦的，魔鬼的，邪恶的(like Satan; devilish; infernal) 记 来自 Satan(撒旦，与上帝作对的魔鬼)
abstention [əbˈstenʃn]	*n.* 戒除; 弃权(the act or practice of abstaining) 记 来自 abstain(*v.* 禁绝，放弃)
necessitous [nɪˈsesɪtəs]	*adj.* 贫困的(needy; indigent); 紧迫的(urgent) 记 来自 necessity(*n.* 必要，必然性; 必需品)
taciturn [ˈtæsɪtɜːrn]	*adj.* 沉默寡言的(temperamentally disinclined to talk) 同 mute, reserved, reticent, withdrawn
congregate [ˈkɑːŋɡrɪɡeɪt]	*v.* 聚集，集合(to gather into a crowd; assemble) 记 词根记忆：con + greg(群体) + ate → 聚成群体 → 集合
lavender [ˈlævəndər]	*n.* 薰衣草 *adj.* 淡紫色的 搭 lavender oil 薰衣草油
ignite [ɪɡˈnaɪt]	*v.* 发光(to make glow with heat); 点燃，燃烧(to set fire to) 记 词根记忆：ign(点火) + ite → 点燃
prevision [priˈvɪʒən]	*n.* 预知，先见(foresight; prescience) 记 词根记忆：pre(预先) + vis(看) + ion → 预先看到的 → 先见
slant [slænt]	*v.* 倾斜 *n.* 斜面(a slanting direction); 观点(a peculiar or personal point of view)
blare [bler]	*v.* 高声发出(to sound or utter raucously) 记 联想记忆：和 bleat(*n.* 羊的叫声)来自同一词源

35

□ ethics	□ congeal	□ vaporize	□ oracular	□ unsettle	□ throe
□ insolvency	□ satanic	□ abstention	□ necessitous	□ taciturn	□ congregate
□ lavender	□ ignite	□ prevision	□ slant	□ blare	

rent [rent]	*n.* 裂缝(an opening made by rending); (意见)分歧(a split in a party; schism) 记 rent 的"租金"之意众所周知
gaunt [ɡɔːnt]	*adj.* 憔悴的, 瘦削的(thin and bony; hollowed-eyed and haggard) 记 联想记忆: 和 taunt (*n./v.* 嘲弄) 一起记: 因被嘲弄 (taunt), 所以憔悴 (gaunt)
cynosure [ˈsɪnəʃʊr]	*n.* 注意的焦点(any person or thing that is a center of attention or interest) 记 来自 Cynosure(*n.* 小熊星, 北极星)
visceral [ˈvɪsərəl]	*adj.* 内心深处的(felt in or as if in the viscera); 内脏的(splanchnic) 同 inner, interior, internal, inward
coward [ˈkaʊərd]	*n.* 胆小鬼(a person who lacks courage) 记 联想记忆: cow(威胁) + ward(未成年人) → 从很小的时候就开始经常被威胁, 长大后一直像个胆小鬼 → 胆小鬼
irritation [ˌɪrɪˈteɪʃn]	*n.* 愤怒, 恼怒(the state of being irritated) 例 Her verbosity is always a source of *irritation*: she never uses a single word when she can substitute a long clause or phrase in its place.
riotous [ˈraɪətəs]	*adj.* 暴乱的, 狂乱的(turbulent) 同 disorderly, tumultuous, unruly, uproarious
stray [streɪ]	*v.* 偏离, 迷路(to wander away) *adj.* 迷路的(having strayed or escaped from a proper or intended place); 零落的(occurring at random or sporadically) 搭 stray from 偏离
prosperous [ˈprɑːspərəs]	*adj.* 繁荣的, 兴旺的(marked by success or economic well-being)
proclaim [prəˈkleɪm]	*v.* 宣告, 公布(to declare officially); 显示, 表明(to show clearly) 记 词根记忆: pro(在前) + claim(叫, 喊) → 在前面喊 → 宣告, 公布
inhale [ɪnˈheɪl]	*v.* 吸入, 吸气(to breathe air, smoke, or gas into lungs) 记 词根记忆: in(进) + hale(呼吸) → 吸入
meddle [ˈmedl]	*v.* 干涉, 干预(to interfere) 记 词根记忆: med(混杂) + dle → 混杂其中 → 干涉
teeter [ˈtiːtər]	*v.* 摇摇欲坠, 步履蹒跚(to walk or move unsteadily); 踌躇(to hesitate) 同 totter, wobble
buck [bʌk]	*v.* 反抗, 抵制(to oppose; resist) *n.* 雄鹿; 雄兔(male deer or rabbit); <美俚>元, 钱
immure [ɪˈmjʊr]	*v.* 监禁(to imprison; confine; seclude) 记 词根记忆: im(进入) + mur(墙) + e → 进入墙 → 监禁
bricklayer [ˈbrɪkleɪər]	*n.* 砖匠(a person who lays brick) 记 联想记忆: brick(砖) + lay(铺设) + er → 铺砖的人 → 砖匠
filth [fɪlθ]	*n.* 污物(foul or putrid matter); 猥亵的东西(anything viewed as grossly indecent or obscene) 记 和 filch(*v.* 偷)一起记

illuminate [ɪˈluːmɪneɪt]	*v.* 阐明，解释(to make understandable)；照亮(to brighten with lights) 记 词根记忆：il(向内) + lumin(光) + ate → 投入光 → 照亮 例 Since most if not all learning occurs through comparisons, relating one observation to another, it would be strange indeed if the study of other cultures did not also *illuminate* the study of our own.
bawl [bɔːl]	*v.* 大叫，大喊(to shout or call out noisily) 记 联想记忆：b + awl(尖钻) → 被尖钻戳到而大喊 → 大叫，大喊
subreption [səbˈrepʃən]	*n.* 隐瞒真相，歪曲事实(a deliberate misrepresentation)
bulge [bʌldʒ]	*n.* 凸起，膨胀(a protruding part; an outward curve or swelling) *v.* 膨胀，鼓起(to (cause to) curve outward)
fume [fjuːm]	*v.* 发怒，愤怒(to show anger, annoyance, etc.)；冒烟(to give off smoke) *n.* 烟；愤怒，恼怒 记 联想记忆：有声望(fame)的人不会因为小事发怒(fume)
enormity [ɪˈnɔːrməti]	*n.* 极恶 (great wickedness)；暴行 (an outrageous, improper, or immoral act)；巨大(immensity) 记 词根记忆：e(出) + norm(正常) + ity → 出了正常状态 → 极恶，暴行；巨大
jape [dʒeɪp]	*v.* 开玩笑，戏弄(to joke or quip) 记 联想记忆：j + ape(猿) → 把人当猴耍 → 戏弄
retention [rɪˈtenʃn]	*n.* 保留，保持(the act of keeping in possession or use) 记 词根记忆：re(重新) + tent(拿住) + ion → 重新拿住 → 保留
remand [rɪˈmænd]	*v.* 遣回(to send back)；召回(to order back) 记 词根记忆：re(重新，又) + mand(命令) → 命令回来 → 遣回
neonate [ˈniːouneɪt]	*n.* 新生儿(a new born child) 记 词根记忆：neo(新的) + nat(出生) + e → 新生儿
quondam [ˈkwɔndæm]	*adj.* 原来的，以前的(former)
deracinate [ˌdiːˈræsɪneɪt]	*v.* 根除，灭绝(to pull up by the roots; eradicate) 记 词根记忆：de + rac(=race 种族) + inate → 消灭种族 → 根除
hasty [ˈheɪsti]	*adj.* 急急忙忙的(said, made or done too quickly) 记 来自haste(*n.* 急速)
partition [pɑːrˈtɪʃn]	*n.* 隔开(division)；隔墙(an interior dividing wall) 记 词根记忆：part(部分) + i + tion → 分成部分 → 隔开
liquidate [ˈlɪkwɪdeɪt]	*v.* 清算(to settle the affairs of a business by disposing of its assets and liabilities)；清偿(to pay or settle a debt) 记 联想记忆：liquid(清澈的) + ate → 弄清 → 清算；清偿
shudder [ˈʃʌdər]	*v.* 战栗，发抖(to shake uncontrollably for a moment) *n.* 战栗，发抖 记 发音记忆："吓得" → 吓得肩膀(shoulder)直发抖(shudder)

35

eternal [ɪˈtɜːrnl]	*adj.* 永久的，永恒的（without beginning or end） 记 联想记忆：外部（external）世界是永恒的（eternal）诱惑 例 In sharp contrast to the intense idealism of the young republic, with its utopian faith in democracy and hopes for *eternal* human progress, recent developments suggest a mood of almost unrelieved cynicism.	
stickler [ˈstɪklər]	*n.* 坚持细节之人（one who insists on exactness） 记 来自 stickle（*v.* 坚持己见）	
potentate [ˈpoʊtnteɪt]	*n.* 统治者，君主（ruler; sovereign） 记 词根记忆：pot（有力的）+ ent + ate（人）→ 有力量的人 → 统治者	
engulf [ɪnˈɡʌlf]	*v.* 吞噬（to flow over and enclose; overwhelm） 记 联想记忆：en（进入）+ gulf（大沟）→ 吞噬	**engulf**
grate [ɡreɪt]	*v.* 吱嘎磨碎（to grind into small particles）；使人烦躁，刺激（to irritate; annoy; fret） 记 联想记忆：g + rat（耗子）+ e → 耗子发出吱嘎声 → 使人烦躁	欲望
transience [ˈtrænʃəns]	*n.* 短暂，稍纵即逝（the quality or state of being transient） 搭 the transience of human life 人生的短暂	
moldy [ˈmoʊldi]	*adj.* 发霉的（covered with mold） 记 来自mold（*n.* 真菌）	
whine [waɪn]	*v.* 哀号，号哭（to utter a high pitched plaintive or distressed cry） 同 pule, whimper	
impertinence [ɪmˈpɜːrtnəns]	*n.* 无礼，粗鲁（rudeness） 记 联想记忆：im（不）+ pertinence（恰当，适当）→ 行为不恰当 → 无礼	
stitch [stɪtʃ]	*n.* （缝纫时的）一针 *v.* 缝合（to make, mend, or decorate with or as if with stitches）	
retaliation [rɪˌtæliˈeɪʃn]	*n.* 报复（the action of returning a bad deed to someone who has done a bad deed to oneself）	
stock [stɑːk]	*v.* 储备 *adj.* 常用的（commonly used; standard）*n.* 存货 例 If you need car parts that the dealers no longer *stock*, try scavenging for odd bits and pieces at the auto wreckers' yards.	
parley [ˈpɑːrli]	*n.* 和谈（a conference with an enemy）；会谈（a conference for discussion of points in dispute）*v.* 和谈，会谈（to speak with another） 记 词根记忆：parl（讲话）+ ey → 会谈	
vicar [ˈvɪkər]	*n.* 教区牧师（the priest in charge of an area） 记 联想记忆：vi + car（汽车）→ 开着汽车在一个区域内四处传道 → 教区牧师	
induction [ɪnˈdʌkʃn]	*n.* 就职（installation）；归纳（inference of a generalized conclusion from particular instances）	

simper [ˈsɪmpər]	*v.* 假笑，傻笑(to smile in a silly manner) 同 smirk
feisty [ˈfaɪsti]	*adj.* 活跃的(being frisky and exuberant)；易怒的(being touchy and quarrelsome)
coarsen [ˈkɔːrsn]	*v.* (使)变粗糙(to cause sth. to become coarse) 记 来自 coarse(*adj.* 粗糙的)
irremediable [ˌɪrɪˈmiːdiəbl]	*adj.* 无法治愈的，无法纠正的(incurable; not remediable) 记 联想记忆：ir(不) + remediable(可治疗的) → 无法治愈的
vernal [ˈvɜːrnl]	*adj.* 春季的(of, relating to, or occurring in the spring)；春季般的，青春的(fresh or new like the spring)
prune [pruːn]	*n.* 西梅干(a plum dried without fermentation) *v.* 修剪（树木等)(to cut away what is unwanted)
heady [ˈhedi]	*adj.* 任性的(willful)；鲁莽的(impetuous) 同 unruly, rash
spendthrift [ˈspendθrɪft]	*adj./n.* 挥金如土的(人) 记 组合词：spend(花费) + thrift(节约) → 把节约下来的钱全部花掉 → 挥金如土的 同 wasteful
lard [lɑːrd]	*v.* 使丰富，使充满(to enrich or lace heavily with extra material) 搭 lard...with 大量穿插
febrile [ˈfiːbraɪl]	*adj.* 发烧的，热病的(of fever; feverish) 记 词根记忆：febr(热) + ile → 发热的 → 发烧的
hallucination [həˌluːsɪˈneɪʃn]	*n.* 幻觉(illusion of seeing or hearing) 记 联想记忆：hall(大厅) + uci(发音相当于 you see 你看) + nation(国家) → 在大厅里你看到了一个国家 → 产生了幻觉 → 幻觉
lout [laʊt]	*n.* 蠢人，笨蛋(a clumsy, stupid fellow; boor) 记 联想记忆：把那个笨蛋(lout)赶出去(out)
moment [ˈmoʊmənt]	*n.* 瞬间；重要(importance) 搭 the moment of truth (决策的)关键时刻
flagellate [ˈflædʒəleɪt]	*v.* 鞭打，鞭笞(to whip; flog) 记 词根记忆：flagel(鞭) + late → 鞭打
mint [mɪnt]	*n.* 大量(an abundant amount)；造币厂 记 mint 作“薄荷(糖)”讲大家都较熟悉
garrulity [gəˈruːləti]	*n.* 唠叨，饶舌(the quality or state of being garrulous) 记 来自 garrulous(*adj.* 唠叨的，饶舌的)
interference [ˌɪntərˈfɪrəns]	*n.* 干涉，妨碍(interfering) 搭 interference with 干扰
dire [ˈdaɪər]	*adj.* 可怕的(dreadful; miserable) 同 appalling, fearful, formidable, frightful, ghastly, tremendous

35

□ simper	□ feisty	□ coarsen	□ irremediable	□ vernal	□ prune
□ heady	□ spendthrift	□ lard	□ febrile	□ hallucination	□ lout
□ moment	□ flagellate	□ mint	□ garrulity	□ interference	□ dire

barter [ˈbɑːrtər]	*v.* 易货贸易（to give goods in return for other goods） 记 和 banter(*v.* 打趣)一起记
apt [æpt]	*adj.* 易于…的；恰当的 搭 be apt to... 容易…的；很可能…
crack [kræk]	*n.* 爆裂声；裂缝（line along which sth. has broken） *v.* 裂开；破解 同 bang, clap, explosion, snap
hoax [hoʊks]	*n.* 骗局，恶作剧（a trick or fraud） *v.* 欺骗（to deceive; cheat） 记 联想记忆：不要和 coax(*v.* 哄骗)混淆
swagger [ˈswægər]	*v.* 大摇大摆地走（to walk with an air of overbearing self-confidence） 记 参考 waddle(*v.* (鸭子等)摇摆着走)
stupendous [stuːˈpendəs]	*adj.* 巨大的，惊人的（of amazing size or greatness; tremendous） 记 词根记忆：stup(吃惊) + endous → 惊人的
lesion [ˈliːʒn]	*n.* 损害，损伤（a wound or an injury） 记 联想记忆：大脑受到损伤(lesion)，精神时刻处于紧张(tension)状态
futility [fjuːˈtɪləti]	*n.* 无用，无益（the quality of being futile） 例 The legislators of 1563 realized the *futility* of trying to regulate the flow of labor without securing its reasonable remuneration, and so the second part of the statute dealt with establishing wages.
dedication [ˌdedɪˈkeɪʃn]	*n.* 奉献，献身（devotion to a cause or an aim） 记 来自 dedicate(*v.* 奉献)
wholesome [ˈhoʊlsəm]	*adj.* 有益健康的（good for the body or likely to produce health） 记 联想记忆：whole(完整的) + some → 帮助身体变得完整 → 有益健康的
arrest [əˈrest]	*v.* 逮捕；阻止，制止（to stop or check） 记 联想记忆：ar(加强) + rest(休息) → 强制休息 → 逮捕
locution [ləˈkjuːʃn]	*n.* 语言风格（a particular style of speech）；惯用语 记 词根记忆：locu(说话) + tion → 语言风格
shilly-shally [ˈʃɪliʃæli]	*v.* 犹豫不决（to show hesitation or lack of decisiveness）；虚度时光（to fiddle）
pandemonium [ˌpændəˈmoʊniəm]	*n.* 喧嚣，大混乱（a wild uproar; tumult） 记 联想记忆：pan(全部) + demon(魔鬼) + ium → 全是魔鬼 → 大混乱；来自弥尔顿的著作《失乐园》中的地狱之都(Pandemonium)
ticklish [ˈtɪklɪʃ]	*adj.* 怕痒的（sensitive to being tickled）；易怒的（touchy） 记 来自 tickle(*v.* 发痒)
exhaustive [ɪɡˈzɔːstɪv]	*adj.* 彻底的，无遗漏的（covering every possible detail; thorough） 搭 an exhaustive report 详尽的报告
commonsense [ˈkɑːmənsens]	*adj.* 有常识的（having practical judgment gained from experience of life, not by special study） 记 组合词：common(普通的) + sense(认识) → 具有常识的

arrest

feasible [ˈfiːzəbl]	*adj.* 可行的，可能的(capable of being done or carried out; practicable) 记 词根记忆：feas(=fac 做) + ible → 能做的 → 可行的 例 Although the architect's concept at first sounded too visionary to be practicable, his careful analysis of every aspect of the project convinced the panel that the proposed building was indeed, structurally *feasible*.
profane [prəˈfeɪn]	*v.* 亵渎，玷污(to treat with abuse; desecrate) 记 联想记忆：pro(在前) + fane(神庙) → 在神庙前(做坏事) → 亵渎
disclose [dɪsˈkloʊz]	*v.* 揭露(to allow sth. to be seen; reveal) 记 词根记忆：dis(不) + close(关闭) → 不再关闭 → 揭露
effervesce [ˌefərˈves]	*v.* 冒泡(to bubble; foam)；热情洋溢(to show liveliness or exhilaration) 记 词根记忆：ef(出) + ferv(热) + esce → 释放出热力 → 热情洋溢
pedagogy [ˈpedəgɑːdʒi]	*n.* 教育学，教学法(the art, science of teaching) 记 词根记忆：ped(儿童) + agog(引导) + y → 引导儿童之学 → 教育学
liberality [ˌlɪbəˈræləti]	*n.* 慷慨(generosity)；心胸开阔(the quality of being tolerant and open-minded) 记 来自 liberal(*adj.* 慷慨的；开明的)
imprecation [ˌɪmprɪˈkeɪʃn]	*n.* 诅咒(oath or curse) 记 来自 imprecate(*v.* 诅咒)
leeward [ˈliːwərd]	*adj.* 背风的(in the direction toward which the wind blows) 记 联想记忆：lee(背风处) + ward(向…的) → 向着背风处走 → 背风的
square [skwer]	*v.* 一致，符合(to be or make sth. consistent with sth.; agree with)；结清(to balance) 搭 square up 清算账目
impale [ɪmˈpeɪl]	*v.* 刺入，刺穿(to pierce with a sharp-pointed object) 记 联想记忆：im + pale(苍白的) → 被针刺到，脸色苍白 → 刺入
revive [rɪˈvaɪv]	*v.* 使苏醒(to become conscious again)；使再流行(to come or bring back into use) 例 The corporation expects only modest increases in sales next year despite a yearlong effort to *revive* its retailing business.
glee [gliː]	*n.* 欢喜，高兴(lively joy; gaiety; merriment) 记 联想记忆：和 flee(*v.* 逃跑)一起记：因 flee(逃跑)而 glee(欢喜，高兴)
concatenate [kənˈkætəneɪt]	*v.* 连结，连锁(to link together) 记 词根记忆：con(共同) + caten(铁链) + ate → 在同一根铁链中 → 连锁
boggle [ˈbɑːgl]	*v.* 犹豫(to hesitate)；退缩(to overwhelm with wonder or bewilderment) 记 联想记忆：bog(使…陷入泥沼) + gle → 陷入泥沼，会使人退缩 → 退缩
spank [spæŋk]	*v.* 掌掴，拍打(在屁股上)(to strike on the buttocks with the open hands) 同 smack

leeward

35

□ feasible	□ profane	□ disclose	□ effervesce	□ pedagogy	□ liberality
□ imprecation	□ leeward	□ square	□ impale	□ revive	□ glee
□ concatenate	□ boggle	□ spank			

charade [ʃəˈreɪd]	*n.* 猜字谜游戏 *v.* 凭动作猜字谜
dolorous [ˈdoʊlərəs]	*adj.* 悲哀的，忧伤的(very sorrowful or sad; mournful) 记 词根记忆：dol(悲哀) + orous → 悲哀的
redundancy [rɪˈdʌndənsi]	*n.* 多余，累赘；(因劳动力过剩而造成的)裁员；人浮于事 记 本单词亦作 redundance 例 The chances that a species will persist are reduced if any vital function is restricted to a single kind of organ; *redundancy* by itself possesses an enormous survival advantage.
sweltering [ˈsweltərɪŋ]	*adj.* 酷热的(oppressively hot) 记 来自 swelter(*v.* 汗流浃背)
reek [riːk]	*v.* 发臭味(to give off an unpleasant odor)；冒烟(to give out smoke) 同 emit
expiate [ˈekspieɪt]	*v.* 补偿(to make amends or reparation for) 记 词根记忆：ex(加强) + pi(神圣的) + ate → 使变得非常神圣 → 补偿
sportive [ˈspɔːrtiv]	*adj.* 嬉戏的，欢闹的(playful) 同 frolicsome
fractional [ˈfrækʃənl]	*adj.* 微小的，极少的，微不足道的(very small; unimportant) 记 来自 fraction(*n.* 少量，一点儿)
mete [miːt]	*v.* 给予，分配(to give out by measure)；测量(to measure) *n.* 边界 记 和 meet(*v.* 会面)一起记
specifics [spəˈsɪfɪks]	*n.* 细小问题，细节(details; particulars) 记 来自 specific(*adj.* 具体的)

Victory won't come to me unless I go to it.
胜利是不会向我走来的，我必须自己走向胜利。

——美国女诗人 穆尔(M. Moore, American poetess)

□ charade	□ dolorous	□ redundancy	□ sweltering	□ reek	□ expiate
□ sportive	□ fractional	□ mete	□ specifics		

crackpot [ˈkrækpɑːt]	*n.* 怪人，疯子；狂想家（one given to eccentric or lunatic notions） 记 组合词：crack(砸) + pot(罐子) → 疯狂砸开罐子的人 → 疯子
lancet [ˈlænsɪt]	*n.* 柳叶刀（a sharp-pointed surgical instrument used to make small incisions）
alert [əˈlɜːrt]	*adj.* 警惕的，机警的（watchful and prompt to meet danger or emergency） *n.* 警报（warning） 记 Red Alert"红色警戒"，20世纪90年代风靡全球的电脑游戏
trudge [trʌdʒ]	*v.* 跋涉（to walk or march steadily and laboriously） 同 tramp
tremor [ˈtremər]	*n.* 颤动；颤抖，战栗 记 词根记忆：trem(抖动) + or → 颤动；颤抖
implicate [ˈɪmplɪkeɪt]	*v.* 牵连（于罪行中）（to involve in a crime）；暗示（to imply） 记 词根记忆：im(进入) + plic(重叠) + ate → 重叠进去 → 牵连
penalty [ˈpenəlti]	*n.* 刑罚，处罚（punishment for breaking a law or contract） 例 A major goal of law, to deter potential criminals by punishing wrongdoers, is not served when the *penalty* is so seldom invoked that it ceases to be a credible threat.
poncho [ˈpɑːntʃoʊ]	*n.* 斗篷（a blanket worn as a sleeveless garment）；雨披（a waterproof garment）
projection [prəˈdʒekʃn]	*n.* 突起物，隆起物；设计，规划（the forming of a plan）；发射，投射 同 scheming
sparring [ˈspɑːrɪŋ]	*n.* 拳击，争斗 搭 sparring partner 切磋问题的对手
mania [ˈmeɪniə]	*n.* 癫狂（wild or violent mental disorder）；狂热（an excessive, persistent enthusiasm） 记 参考：kleptomania(*n.* 盗窃狂)；bibliomania(*n.* 藏书癖)

(penalty 配图：penalty 迟到五次 奖金全扣)

pamper [ˈpæmpər]	*v.* 纵容，过分关怀（to treat with excess or extreme care） 同 indulge
jettison [ˈdʒetɪsn]	*v.*（船等）向外抛弃货物（to cast overboard off）*n.* 抛弃的货物（jetsam） *n.* 抛弃（action of throwing） 记 来自 jet（*v.* 喷出）
timely [ˈtaɪmli]	*adj.* 适时的，及时的（appropriate or adapted to the times or the occasion） 记 来自 time（*n.* 时间）
expenditure [ɪkˈspendɪtʃər]	*n.* 花费，支出；支出额（amount expended） 搭 lavish expenditure 过多的开支
ingratiate [ɪnˈɡreɪʃieɪt]	*v.* 逢迎，讨好（to bring oneself into another's favor or good graces by conscious effort） 记 词根记忆：in（使）+ grat（感激）+ iate → 使别人感激自己 → 讨别人欢心 → 讨好
limn [lɪm]	*v.* 描写（to describe）；画（to paint or draw） 同 depict, picture, portray, represent
shoddy [ˈʃɑːdi]	*adj.* 劣质的，假冒的（cheaply imitative） 同 second-rate
bounteous [ˈbaʊntiəs]	*adj.* 慷慨的（giving freely and generously, without restraint）；丰富的（provided in abundance；plentiful） 记 词根记忆：bount（=bon 好）+ eous → 好的 → 慷慨的
authorization [ˌɔːθərəˈzeɪʃn]	*n.* 授权，认可（action of authorizing） 记 来自 authorize（*v.* 授权，认可）
condign [kənˈdaɪn]	*adj.* 罪有应得的（(of punishment) severe and well deserved）；适宜的 记 词根记忆：con + dign（高贵）→ 惩罚罪行，弘扬高贵 → 罪有应得的
transfigure [trænsˈfɪɡjər]	*v.* 美化，改观（to transform outwardly for the better） 记 联想记忆：trans（改变）+ figure（形象）→ 美化，改观
stodgy [ˈstɑːdʒi]	*adj.* 枯燥无味的（boring；dull） 例 For a young person, Winston seems remarkably *stodgy*; you'd expect someone of his age to show a little more life.
seep [siːp]	*v.*（液体等）渗漏（to flow or pass slowly；ooze） 同 trickle
culmination [ˌkʌlmɪˈneɪʃn]	*n.* 顶点；高潮（eventual conclusion or result） 记 来自 culminate（*v.* 达到顶点）
bridle [ˈbraɪdl]	*n.* 马笼头（a head harness）*v.* 抑制，控制（to curb or control） 记 和 bride（*n.* 新娘）一起记
lingual [ˈlɪŋɡwəl]	*adj.* 舌的（of the tongue）；语言的（of language） 记 参考：linguist（*n.* 语言学家）
burnish [ˈbɜːrnɪʃ]	*v.* 擦亮，磨光（to become shining by rubbing；polish） 记 联想记忆：burn（烧）+ ish → 烧得发亮 → 擦亮，磨光

stutter ['stʌtər]	*v.* 口吃, 结巴(to speak with involuntary disruption of speech) *n.* 口吃 搭 stutter(out) an apology 结结巴巴地道歉
beckon ['bekən]	*v.* 召唤, 示意(to make a gesture to sb. to come nearer or follow) 记 联想记忆: beck(听从命令) + on → 召唤, 示意
scrawl [skrɔːl]	*v.* 潦草地写, 乱涂(to write awkwardly or carelessly) 记 联想记忆: s + crawl(爬) → 乱爬 → 乱涂
lusty ['lʌsti]	*adj.* 充满活力的, 精力充沛的(full of vigor) 记 词根记忆: lus(光) + ty → 充满活力的
subsidiary [səb'sɪdieri]	*adj.* 辅助的(furnishing aid or support; auxiliary); 次要的(of second importance) 记 词根记忆: sub(下面) + sid(坐) + iary → 坐在下面的 → 辅助的
spoliation [ˌspəuli'eiʃən]	*n.* 抢劫, 掠夺(the act of plundering) 记 来自spoliate(*v.* 强夺, 抢劫)
patent ['peitnt]	*adj.* 显而易见的(readily visible; obvious) *n.* 专利权(证书) 例 Copyright and *patent* laws attempt to encourage innovation by ensuring that inventors are paid for creative work, so it would be ironic if expanded protection under these laws discouraged entrepreneurial innovation by increasing fears of lawsuits.
subsume [səb'suːm]	*v.* 包含, 包括(to include within) 记 词根记忆: sub(下面) + sume(拿) → 拿在下面 → 包含
spat [spæt]	*n.* 口角, 小争论(a brief petty quarrel or angry outburst) 记 不要和spit(*v.* 吐痰)相混
leer [lɪr]	*v.* 斜视, 送秋波(to have a sly, sidelong look) 搭 leer at sb. 色迷迷地看某人, 斜视某人
wrath [ræθ]	*n.* 愤怒, 愤慨(strong vengeful anger or indignation) 同 exasperation, fury, ire, rage
phony ['fəuni]	*adj.* 假的, 欺骗的(not genuine or real) 同 false, sham
prominent ['prɑːmɪnənt]	*adj.* 显著的(noticeable); 著名的(widely and popularly known) 记 词根记忆: pro(向前) + min(伸出) + ent → 向前伸出 → 显著的; 著名的
tome [toum]	*n.* 册, 卷(a volume forming part of a larger work); 大部头的书(a large or scholarly book)
penetrate ['penətreit]	*v.* 刺穿(to pierce); 渗入(to pass in); 了解(to discover the meaning of) 记 联想记忆: pen(全部) + etr(=enter 进入) + ate → 全部进入 → 刺穿
splice [splais]	*v.* 接合, 拼接(to unite by interweaving the strands) 记 注意不要和split(*v.* 破裂)相混
resilience [ri'zɪliəns]	*n.* 恢复力, 弹力(the capability of a strained body to recover its size and shape after deformation caused by compressive stress) 记 来自resile(*v.* 弹回; 恢复活力); re(向后) + sil(跳) +e → 向后跳起 → 弹回

36

scruffy [ˈskrʌfi]	*adj.* 肮脏的，不洁的（unkempt; slovenly; shaggy）
	同 decaying, dingy, scrubby, tatty
melon [ˈmelən]	*n.* 甜瓜（a large rounded fruit with a hard rind and juicy flesh）
	记 词根记忆：mel（甜的）+ on → 甜的东西 → 甜瓜
detergent [dɪˈtɜːrdʒənt]	*n.* 清洁剂
	记 词根记忆：de + terg（擦）+ ent → 擦掉的东西 → 清洁剂
prate [preɪt]	*v.* 瞎扯，唠叨（to talk long and idly; chatter）
	记 和 prattle（*v.* 闲聊）一起记
finale [fɪˈnæli]	*n.* 最后，最终（end）；终曲（the concluding part of a musical composition）
	记 来自 final（*adj.* 最后的）
forswear [fɔːrˈswer]	*v.* 誓绝，发誓放弃（to renounce on oath）
	记 联想记忆：for（出去）+ swear（发誓）→ 为了改过自新而发誓 → 誓绝
obsessive [əbˈsesɪv]	*adj.* 强迫性的，急迫的（excessive often to an unreasonable degree）；使人着迷的（tending to cause obsession）
emerald [ˈemərəld]	*n.* 翡翠（green gemstones）*adj.* 翠绿色的（brightly or richly green）
wile [waɪl]	*n.* 诡计（a beguiling or playful trick）
	同 artifice, craft, gimmick, ploy, ruse
aggregate [ˈæɡrɪɡeɪt]	*v.* 集合（to gather into a whole）；合计（to total; sum）
	记 词根记忆：ag（做）+ greg（团体）+ ate → 成为团体 → 集合
tantrum [ˈtæntrəm]	*n.* 发脾气，发怒（a fit of bad temper）
	记 发音记忆："太蠢" → 大庭广众之下发脾气，真是蠢 → 发脾气，发怒
inflammation [ˌɪnfləˈmeɪʃn]	*n.* 发炎；炎症
	记 词根记忆：in（进入）+ flam（燃烧）+ mation → 仿似开始燃烧 → 发炎
squat [skwɑːt]	*v.* 蹲下（to crouch on the ground）*adj.* 矮胖的（stout）
	同 dumpy
deputize [ˈdepjutaɪz]	*v.* 代理，代表（to work or appoint as a deputy）
	记 来自 depute（*v.* 派…为代表或代理）
presupposition [ˌpriːsʌpəˈzɪʃn]	*n.* 预想，臆测（the act of supposing beforehand）
	记 联想记忆：pre（预先）+ supposition（假定，推测）→ 预先推测 → 预想，臆测
parallelism [ˈpærəlelɪzəm]	*n.* 平行，类似（the state or quality of being parallel）
	记 联想记忆：parallel（平行的）+ ism → 平行，类似
cauterize [ˈkɔːtəraɪz]	*v.* （用腐蚀性物质或烙铁）烧灼（表皮组织）以消毒或止血（to sear with a cautery or caustic）
bewildering [bɪˈwɪldərɪŋ]	*adj.* 令人困惑的；令人费解的（puzzling）
	搭 the bewildering complexity 令人费解的复杂性
dapper [ˈdæpər]	*adj.* 整洁漂亮的（neat and trim）；动作敏捷的（quick in movements）
	记 联想记忆：那只花斑（dapple）猫动作敏捷（dapper）

obloquy [ˈɑːbləkwi]	*n.* 辱骂，斥责（censure or vituperation） 记 词根记忆：ob（反）+ loqu（说话）+ y → 说坏话 → 辱骂
zone [zoʊn]	*n.* 地区（a section of an area or a territory established for a specific purpose）*v.* 分成区（to divide into or assign to zones）
coterminous [koʊˈtɜːrmɪnəs]	*adj.* 毗连的，有共同边界的（contiguous; having a boundary in common） 记 词根记忆：co(n)（共同）+ termin（边界，结束）+ ous → 有共同边界的
sodden [ˈsɑːdn]	*adj.* 浸透了的（soaked through; very wet） 搭 a rain-sodden jacket 一件雨水淋透的夹克
decency [ˈdiːsnsi]	*n.* 正派，端庄体面（the quality or state of being decent） 记 来自 decent（*adj.* 得体的）
deposit [dɪˈpɑːzɪt]	*v.* 存放，使沉积（to let fall (as sediment)） 记 词根记忆：de + posit（放）→ 存放
palette [ˈpælət]	*n.* 调色板，颜料配置
blanch [blæntʃ]	*v.* 使变白（to make white）；使（脸色）变苍白（to turn pale） 记 词根记忆：blanc（白）+ h → 使变白
backslide [ˈbækslaɪd]	*v.* 故态复萌（to revert to bad habits） 记 组合词：back（向后）+ slide（滑动）→ 往后滑 → 故态复萌
carpenter [ˈkɑːrpəntər]	*n.* 木匠（worker who builds or repairs wooden structures） 记 联想记忆：美国六七十年代风靡一时的乐队 Carpenters
prepossessing [ˌpriːpəˈzesɪŋ]	*adj.* 给人好感的（tending to create a favorable impression; attractive） 记 联想记忆：pre（预先）+ possess（拥有）+ ing → 预先就拥有了情感 → 给人好感的
gruesome [ˈɡruːsəm]	*adj.* 令人毛骨悚然的，阴森的（causing horror or disgust; grisly） 记 联想记忆：grue（发抖）+ some（…的）→ 发抖的 → 令人毛骨悚然的 同 ghastly
jabber [ˈdʒæbər]	*v.* 快而含糊地说（to talk or say quickly and not clearly） 记 发音记忆："结巴" → 快而含糊地说
offset [ˈɑːfset]	*v.* 补偿，抵消（to make up for） 同 balance, compensate
crepuscular [krɪˈpʌskjələr]	*adj.* 朦胧的，微明的（of or like twilight; dim） 记 来自 crepuscle（*n.* 黄昏；黎明）
presentiment [prɪˈzentɪmənt]	*n.* 预感（a feeling that sth. will or is about to happen） 记 词根记忆：pre（预先）+ sent（感觉）+ iment → 预感
purify [ˈpjʊrɪfaɪ]	*v.* 使纯净，净化（to make pure） 记 词根记忆：pur（纯洁的）+ ify → 使纯净，净化
abrade [əˈbreɪd]	*v.* 擦伤，磨损（to scrape or rub off） 记 词根记忆：ab（脱离）+ rade（摩擦）→ 摩擦掉 → 磨损

36

straggle	*v.* 迷路 (to stray)；落伍 (to drop behind)；蔓延 (to grow or spread in a messy way)
[ˈstræɡl]	记 联想记忆：迷路 (straggle) 了所以在苦苦挣扎 (struggle)
animate	[ˈænɪmət] *adj.* 活的，有生命的 (alive; having life)
	[ˈænɪmeɪt] *v.* 赋予生命 (to give life to)
	记 词根记忆：anim (生命，精神) + ate → 有生命的；赋予生命
qualm	*n.* 不安，良心的谴责 (an uncomfortable feeling of uncertainty)
[kwɑːm]	记 联想记忆：捧在手掌 (palms) 怕丢了 → 不安 (qualm)
ire	*n.* 愤怒 (anger) *v.* 激怒 (to make angry)
[ˈaɪər]	记 联想记忆：愤怒 (ire) 之火 (fire)
inchoate	*adj.* 刚开始的 (just begun; incipient)；未充分发展的，不成熟的 (not yet completed or fully developed)
[ɪnˈkoʊət]	记 联想记忆：inch (英寸) + oat (燕麦) + e → 燕麦刚长了一英寸 → 未充分发展的，不成熟的
linguistics	*n.* 语言学 (the science of language)
[lɪŋˈɡwɪstɪks]	例 Gould claimed no technical knowledge of *linguistics*, but only a hobbyist's interest in language.
covert	*adj.* 秘密的，隐蔽的 (concealed; hidden)
[ˈkoʊvɜːrt]	记 联想记忆：cover (遮盖) + t → 盖住的 → 秘密的
spacious	*adj.* 广阔的，宽敞的 (vast or ample in extent)
[ˈspeɪʃəs]	记 词根记忆：spac (=space 地方) + ious (多…的)；注意不要和 specious (*adj.* 似是而非的) 相混
lair	*n.* 窝，巢穴 (a resting place of a wild animal)；躲藏处
[ler]	记 联想记忆：有些动物用毛发 (hair) 做窝 (lair)
wiggle	*v.* 扭动，摆动 (to move to and fro with quick jerky or shaking motions)
[ˈwɪɡl]	记 联想记忆：wig (假发) + gle (看作 giggle，吃吃地笑) → 戴着假发扭动着身子吃吃地笑 → 扭动
gab	*n.* 饶舌，爱说话 (idle talk) *v.* 空谈，瞎扯 (to chatter)；闲逛，游荡
[ɡæb]	记 联想记忆：坐在大门 (gate) 口瞎扯 (gab)
peddle	*v.* 兜售 (to travel about selling wares)
[ˈpedl]	同 sell
impend	*v.* 威胁 (to menace)；即将发生 (to be about to occur)
[ɪmˈpend]	记 词根记忆：im + pend (悬挂) → 事情挂在眼前 → 即将发生
commit	*v.* 托付 (to consign)；承诺 (to bind or obligate)；犯罪 (to perpetrate)
[kəˈmɪt]	记 词根记忆：com (共同) + mit (送) → 一起送给 → 托付
rig	*v.* （用不正当手段）操纵，垄断 (to manipulate by deceptive or dishonest means)
[rɪɡ]	
acedia	*n.* 无精打采的样子 (apathy; boredom)；懒惰
[əˈsiːdiə]	

windy	*adj.* 有风的；冗长的；夸夸其谈的(verbose)
[ˈwɪndi]	搭 a windy speaker 夸夸其谈的人
flair	*n.* 天赋，本领，天资(a natural talent or ability)
[fler]	记 和 fair(*adj.* 公正的；美丽的)一起记
bouquet	*n.* 花束(a bunch of cut flowers)；芳香(fragrance)
[buˈkeɪ]	同 redolence, sweetness
disavow	*v.* 否认，否定，抵赖 (to say one does not know of, is not responsible for, or does not approve of)
[ˌdɪsəˈvaʊ]	记 词根记忆：dis + avow(承认) → 不承认 → 否认，否定
nemesis	*n.* 报应(an agent or act of retribution)
[ˈneməsɪs]	记 来自希腊神话中的复仇女神 Nemesis
gerontocracy	*n.* 老人统治的政府 (a government in which a group of old men dominates)
[ˌdʒerənˈtɑːkrəsi]	记 词根记忆：geront(老人) + o + cracy(统治) → 老人统治的政府
plaudit	*v.* 喝彩，赞扬(to praise; approve enthusiastically)
[ˈplɔːdɪt]	记 词根记忆：plaud(鼓掌) + it → 喝彩，赞扬
drawn	*adj.* 憔悴的(showing the effects of tension, pain, or illness)
[drɔːn]	同 careworn, gaunt, haggard, wan, worn
cosmopolitanism	*n.* 世界性，世界主义
[ˌkɑːzməˈpɑːlɪtənɪzəm]	记 来自 cosmopolis (*n.* 国际都市)
gumption	*n.* 进取心，魄力(boldness of enterprise; initiative)；精明强干
[ˈɡʌmpʃn]	例 He didn't have the *gumption* to quit such a good paying job.
polemical	*adj.* 引起争论的，好辩的(controversial; disputatious)
[pəˈlemɪkl]	
nausea	*n.* 作呕，恶心(a feeling of sickness in the stomach)
[ˈnɔːziə]	记 词根记忆：naus(=naut 船) + ea(病) → 在船上会犯的病 → 晕船 → 恶心
jamb	*n.* 侧柱(an upright piece or surface forming the sides of a door, window frame)
[dʒæm]	记 联想记忆：jam(果酱) + b → 果酱抹在了门框上 → 侧柱
neophyte	*n.* 初学者，新手(a beginner or a novice)
[ˈniːəfaɪt]	记 词根记忆：neo(新的) + phyt(植物) + e → 新植物 → 新手
bracelet	*n.* 手镯，臂镯(an ornamental band or chain worn around the wrist)
[ˈbreɪslət]	记 词根记忆：brac （手臂） + e + let （小东西） → 戴在手上的小东西 → 手镯
subpoena	*n.* 【律】传票(a written order requiring a person to appear in court) *v.* 传讯 (to summon with a writ of subpoena)
[səˈpiːnə]	记 词根记忆：sub(下面) + poena(=penalty 惩罚) → 接下来可能受到惩罚 → 传讯

36

negligence	*n.* 粗心，疏忽(disregard of duty; neglect)
[ˈneɡlɪdʒəns]	记 词根记忆：neg(不) + lig(选择) + ence → 不加选择 → 粗心，疏忽
grievous	*adj.* 痛苦的，悲伤的(causing suffering or sorrow)；极严重的
[ˈɡriːvəs]	记 词根记忆：griev(悲痛) + ous → 痛苦的，悲伤的
grievance	*n.* 委屈，抱怨，牢骚(complaint or resentment)
[ˈɡriːvəns]	记 词根记忆：griev(悲痛) + ance(表名词) → 委屈
insane	*adj.* 疯狂的(deranged; demented; mad)
[ɪnˈseɪn]	记 联想记忆：in(不) + sane(清醒的) → 头脑不清醒的 → 疯狂的
summon	*v.* 传唤(to order officially to come)；召集(to call together; convene)
[ˈsʌmən]	
statuary	*n.* 雕像(a collection of statues)；雕塑艺术(the art of making statues)
[ˈstætʃueri]	记 来自statue(*n.* 雕像)
deficit	*n.* 不足额(insufficiency; shortage)；赤字
[ˈdefɪsɪt]	搭 a trade deficit 贸易逆差
nominate	*v.* 提名；任命，指定(to appoint sb. to a position)
[ˈnɑːmɪneɪt]	记 词根记忆：nomin(名字) + ate → 提名
summation	*n.* 总结，概要(a summary)；总数，合计(a total)
[sʌˈmeɪʃn]	同 summing up
scan	*v.* 审视，细看(to examine by point-by-point observation or checking)；浏览，扫描(to glance from point to point, often hastily)；标出格律(to read or mark so as to show metrical structure)
[skæn]	记 发音记忆："死看" → 四处看 → 扫描
barrister	*n.* 出庭律师；律师(counselor at law or lawyer)
[ˈbærɪstər]	记 词根记忆：barr(阻挡) + ister(人) → 阻挡法官判罪的人 → 律师
scrimp	*v.* 节省，精打细算(to economize severely)
[skrɪmp]	同 pinch, scrape, skimp, stint
transpose	*v.* 颠倒顺序，调换(to reverse the order or position of)
[trænˈspoʊz]	记 词根记忆：trans(穿过) + pos(放) + e → 放到另一边 → 颠倒顺序，调换
bray	*v.* 大声而刺耳地发出(叫唤或声音)(to emit (an utterance or a sound) loudly and harshly)
[breɪ]	记 联想记忆：在海湾(bay)能听到波浪发出很大的声音(bray)
blandishment	*n.* 奉承，讨好
[ˈblændɪʃmənt]	记 来自blandish(*v.* 讨好)
repine	*v.* 不满，抱怨(to feel or express discontent)
[rɪˈpaɪn]	记 联想记忆：re(重新) + pine(憔悴) → 因苦恼、不满而憔悴 → 不满
naysay	*v.* 拒绝，否认，反对(to say no)
[ˈneɪseɪ]	记 联想记忆：nay(=no 不) + say(说) → 不说 → 拒绝

quench [kwentʃ]	*v.* 扑灭，熄灭(to put out; extinguish); 解(渴)，止(渴) 同 slake
aspire [əˈspaɪər]	*v.* 渴望，追求，向往(to direct one's hopes and efforts to some important aims) 记 词根记忆：a + spir(呼吸) + e → 因为太渴望得到，所以不停地呼吸 → 向往
betoken [bɪˈtoukən]	*v.* 预示，表示(to signify; indicate) 记 联想记忆：be(使…成为) + token(记号，标志) → 使…成为标志 → 预示
forger [ˈfɔːrdʒər]	*n.* 伪造者(one who commits forgery); 打铁匠(one who forges metal) 记 来自 forge(*v.* 伪造; 打铁)
ancillary [ˈænsəleri]	*adj.* 辅助的(subordinate; auxiliary) *n.* 助手(aid)
dim [dɪm]	*v.* 使暗淡，使模糊(to make or become not bright) *adj.* 昏暗的，暗淡的 记 联想记忆：没有目标(aim)的生活很昏暗(dim)
star-crossed [ˈstɑːrkrɔst]	*adj.* 时运不济的(ill-fated) 同 cursed, ill-omened, jinxed, luckless
ilk [ɪlk]	*n.* 类型，种类(sort, kind) 记 联想记忆：和 ink(*n.* 墨水)一起记
rambunctious [ræmˈbʌŋkʃəs]	*adj.* 骚乱的，喧闹的(marked by uncontrollable exuberance) 记 联想记忆：ram(羊) + bunctious(看作 bumptious, 傲慢的) → 像傲慢的羊一样乱叫 → 骚乱的，喧闹的
absolve [əbˈzɑːlv]	*v.* 赦免，免除(to set free from guilt or obligation; forgive) 记 词根记忆：ab(脱离) + solv(放开) + e → 放开使脱离罪责 → 赦免，免除
expend [ɪkˈspend]	*v.* 花费(to pay out; spend); 用光(to use up) 记 词根记忆：ex(出) + pend(支付) → 花费
muzzy [ˈmʌzi]	*adj.* 头脑糊涂的(muddled; mentally hazy) 搭 a muzzy head 稀里糊涂的大脑
scrape [skreɪp]	*v.* 刮，擦; 擦掉(to remove from a surface by repeated strokes of an edged instrument) 记 联想记忆：scrap(碎屑) + e → 碎屑是被刮下来的 → 刮，擦
harry [ˈhæri]	*v.* 掠夺; 袭扰; 折磨(to harass; annoy; torment) 记 联想记忆：掠夺(harry)时要搬运(carry); 和人名 Harry 一样拼写
emissary [ˈemɪseri]	*n.* 密使(a secret agent), 特使(representative sent on a specific mission) 记 词根记忆：e(出去) + miss(送) + ary(人) → 送出去的人 → 特使
forgo [fɔːrˈgou]	*v.* 放弃，抛弃(to abstain from; give up; relinquish) 记 联想记忆：for(为了) + go(走) → 为了寻求新事物而出去 → 放弃

forgo

减肥中……

□ quench	□ aspire	□ betoken	□ forger	□ ancillary	□ dim
□ star-crossed	□ ilk	□ rambunctious	□ absolve	□ expend	□ muzzy
□ scrape	□ harry	□ emissary	□ forgo		

389

other-directed [ˌʌðədɪˈrektɪd]	*adj.* 受人支配的(directed in thought and action by others) 记 组合词: other(别人) + direct(指挥) + ed → 受人支配的
prevaricate [prɪˈværɪkeɪt]	*v.* 支吾其词, 搪塞(to deviate from the truth; equivocate) 记 词根记忆: pre(预先) + varic(观望) + ate → 预先观望 → 搪塞
rapacious [rəˈpeɪʃəs]	*adj.* 掠夺的; 贪婪的(excessively grasping or covetous) 记 词根记忆: rap(抓取) + acious → 抓得多 → 贪婪的
gimmick [ˈɡɪmɪk]	*n.* 吸引人的花招, 噱头(a trick or device used to attract business or attention) 例 The pretty girl on the cover of the pictorial is just a sales *gimmick*.
curfew [ˈkɜːrfjuː]	*n.* 宵禁(regulation requiring all people to leave the streets at stated times) 记 发音记忆: "可否" → 可否上街 → 不可上街, 因为有宵禁 → 宵禁
bovine [ˈboʊvaɪn]	*adj.* (似)牛的(of an ox); 迟钝的(slow; stolid) 记 词根记忆: bov(牛) + ine → 牛的

And gladly would learn, and gladly teach.
勤于学习的人才能乐于施教。

——英国诗人 乔叟(Chaucer, British poet)

monopoly [məˈnɑːpəli]	*n.* 垄断(exclusive possession or control); 专利权 记 词根记忆: mono(单个) + poly(出售) → 独享出售权 → 垄断
exude [ɪɡˈzuːd]	*v.* 渗出, 慢慢流出(to pass out in drops through pores; ooze); 洋溢(to diffuse or seem to radiate) 记 词根记忆: ex + ud(=sud 汗) + e → 出汗 → 渗出, 慢慢流出
preponderant [prɪˈpɑːndərənt]	*adj.* 占优势的, 突出的, 压倒性的(having superior weight, force, or influence) 记 词根记忆: pre(在…之前) + pond(重量) + er + ant → 重量超过前面的 → 压倒性的
mawkish [ˈmɔːkɪʃ]	*adj.* 自作多情的, 过度伤感的(sickly or puerilely sentimental); 淡而无味的, (味道上)令人作呕的(insipid or nauseating)
disaffect [ˌdɪsəˈfekt]	*v.* 使不满; 使疏远(to make disloyal) 记 词根记忆: dis(不) + affect(感动) → 不再感动 → 使不满
sequacious [siˈkweɪʃəs]	*adj.* 盲从的(intellectually servile) 记 词根记忆: sequ(跟随)+acious(多…) → 跟随大多数的 → 盲从的
conjoin [kənˈdʒɔɪn]	*v.* 使结合(to cause people or things to join together) 记 词根记忆: con + join(结合, 连接) → 使结合
allay [əˈleɪ]	*v.* 减轻, 缓和(to relieve; reduce the intensity) 同 assuage, ease, quench
yummy [ˈjʌmi]	*adj.* 美味的, 可口的(highly attractive or pleasing to the taste or smell; delicious)
contend [kənˈtend]	*v.* 竞争, 争夺(to struggle in order to overcome a rival); 争论, 争辩(to strive in controversy) 记 词根记忆: con + tend(伸展) → 你拉我夺 → 竞争, 争夺 搭 contend with 与…竞争
sundry [ˈsʌndri]	*adj.* 各式各样, 各种的(miscellaneous; various) 记 组合词: sun(太阳) + dry(干) → 太阳晒干各种东西 → 各种的
hammer [ˈhæmər]	*n.* 锤子, 槌(tool used for breaking things, etc.) *v.* 锤击, 锤打(to pound) 例 She *hammered* the nail into the wall.

□ monopoly	□ exude	□ preponderant	□ mawkish	□ disaffect	□ sequacious
□ conjoin	□ allay	□ yummy	□ contend	□ sundry	□ hammer

391

upsurge	*n.* 高涨，高潮（a rapid or sudden rise）
[ˈʌpsɜːrdʒ]	记 组合词：up（向上）+ surge（浪潮）→ 浪潮向上 → 高涨，高潮
stomach	*v.* 吃得下；容忍（to bear without overt reaction or resentment）
[ˈstʌmək]	同 tolerate
marine	*adj.* 海的（of the sea）；海生的（inhabiting in the sea）
[məˈriːn]	记 词根记忆：mar（海）+ ine → 海的
	搭 marine vertebrate zoology 海洋脊椎动物学
ratification	*n.* 正式批准（formal confirmation）
[ˌrætɪfɪˈkeɪʃn]	记 来自 ratify（*v.* 正式批准）
levee	*n.* 堤岸，防洪堤（an embankment）
[ˈlevi]	记 注意不要和 lever（*n.* 杠杆）相混
ration	*n.* 配给（a share of food allowed to one person for a period）*v.* 定量配给
[ˈræʃn]	（to limit sb. to a fixed ration）
	记 词根记忆：rat（清点）+ ion → 对现有物资进行清点 → 定量配给
adulterate	*v.* 掺杂，掺假（to make food or drink less pure by adding another
[əˈdʌltəreɪt]	substance to it）*adj.* 掺杂的，掺假的
drawl	*v.* 慢吞吞地说（to speak slowly）*n.* 慢吞吞的说话方式
[drɔːl]	记 联想记忆：draw（抽）+ l → 一点点抽出来 → 慢吞吞地说
informed	*adj.* 有学识的（having or showing knowledge）；见多识广的，消息灵通的
[ɪnˈfɔːrmd]	（having or displaying reliable information）
	例 There is some irony in the fact that the author of a book as sensitive
	and *informed* as Indian Artisans did not develop her interest in Native
	American art until adulthood, for she grew up in a region rich in American
	Indian culture.
verboten	*adj.* 禁止的，严禁的（prohibited by dictate）
[vɜːrˈboʊtn]	同 forbidden, impermissible, taboo
consonance	*n.* 一致，调和（harmony or agreement among components）；和音
[ˈkɑːnsənəns]	记 con（共同）+ son（声音）+ ance → 共同的声音 → 一致，调和
superfluity	*n.* 过剩（a larger amount than what is needed）
[ˌsuːpərˈfluːəti]	记 来自 superfluous（*adj.* 多余的）
gyrate	*adj.* 旋转的（spiral；convoluted）*v.* 旋转，回旋
[ˈdʒaɪreɪt]	（to move in a circular or spiral motion）
	记 词根记忆：gyr（转）+ ate → 旋转的
	同 revolve, swirl
fatigue	*n.* 疲乏，劳累（physical or mental exhaustion；
[fəˈtiːg]	weariness）
	记 联想记忆：fat（胖的）+ igue → 胖人容易劳累
	→ 疲乏
striate	*v.* 加条纹（to mark with striation）
[ˈstraɪeɪt]	记 联想记忆：stri（看作 strip，条、带）+ate → 加条纹

392

□ upsurge	□ stomach	□ marine	□ ratification	□ levee	□ ration
□ adulterate	□ drawl	□ informed	□ verboten	□ consonance	□ superfluity
□ gyrate	□ fatigue	□ striate			

collision [kəˈlɪʒn]	*n.* 碰撞，冲突（an act or instance of colliding） 记 来自 collide（ *v.* 冲撞）
restless [ˈrestləs]	*adj.* 焦躁不安的，静不下来的（unable to relax）
naysayer [ˈneɪseɪər]	*n.* 怀疑者，否定者（one who denies or is skeptical or cynical about sth.） 记 来自 naysay（ *v.* 拒绝，否认）+er → 怀疑者，否定者
insolence [ˈɪnsələns]	*n.* 傲慢，无礼（the quality or condition of being rude and not showing respect） 记 词根记忆：in(不) + sol(习惯了的) + ence → 不寻常 → 傲慢，无礼
gustatory [ˈɡʌstətəri]	*adj.* 味觉的，品尝的（relating to or associated with eating or the sense of taste） 记 来自 gustation（ *n.* 味觉；品尝）
limb [lɪm]	*n.* 肢，翼（an arm, leg, or wing） 记 联想记忆：攀爬(climb)时，四肢(limb)要灵活
mutate [ˈmjuːteɪt]	*v.* 变异（to undergo mutation） 记 词根记忆：mut(变化) + ate → 变异
empyreal [ˌempaɪˈriːəl]	*adj.* 天空的（celestial；sublime）
torrent [ˈtɑːrənt]	*n.* 洪流，急流（a violently rushing stream） 同 deluge, gush, inundation
compensate [ˈkɑːmpenseɪt]	*v.* 补偿，赔偿（to make equivalent return to；recompense） 记 词根记忆：com(一起) + pens(挂；花费) + ate → 全部给予花费 → 赔偿 搭 compensate for 补偿，弥补
venom [ˈvenəm]	*n.* 毒液（normally secreted by some animals (as snakes, scorpions, or bees) and transmitted to prey or an enemy chiefly by biting or stinging）；毒物（poisonous matter）；恶意（ill will；malevolence）
contest [ˈkɑːntest]	*v.* 竞争（to compete）；质疑（to claim that sth. is not proper） 记 词根记忆：con(共同) + test(测试) → 共同测试 → 竞争
probe [proʊb]	*v.* 调查，探测（to search into and explore） 记 词根记忆：prob(检查，试验) + e → 调查，探测
quell [kwel]	*v.* 制止，镇压（to thoroughly overwhelm） 同 suppress
emit [iˈmɪt]	*v.* 发出（光、热、声音等）（to send out；eject） 记 词根记忆：e（出）+ mit（送）→ 送出 → 发出（光、热、声音等）
incite [ɪnˈsaɪt]	*v.* 激发，刺激（to stimulate to action；foment） 记 词根记忆：in(进入) + cit(唤起) + e → 唤起情绪 → 激发

这是公司的赔偿！

龟派气功

emit

37

□ collision	□ restless	□ naysayer	■ insolence	□ gustatory	□ limb
□ mutate	□ empyreal	□ torrent	■ compensate	■ venom	□ contest
□ probe	□ quell	□ emit	■ incite		

393

transfer	*v.* 转移，传递（to convey or cause to pass from one place, person, or thing to another）；转让（to make over the possession or legal title of）；调任，调动（to move oneself from one location or job to another）
[træns'fɜːr]	记 词根记忆：trans(穿过)+fer(带来) → 从一个地方带到另一个地方 → 转移，传递
	例 It is a great advantage to be able to *transfer* useful genes with as little extra gene material as possible because the donor's genome may contain, in addition to desirable genes, many genes with deleterious effects.
blockage	*n.* 障碍物（thing that blocks）
['blɑːkɪdʒ]	同 closure, occlusion, stop, stoppage
gnaw	*v.* 啃，咬（to bite bit by bit with the teeth）；腐蚀，侵蚀
[nɔː]	例 The dog was *gnawing* a bone. // The waves are *gnawing* the rocky shore.
albeit	*conj.* 虽然，尽管（although）
[ˌɔːl'biːɪt]	
atheism	*n.* 无神论，不信神（the belief that there is no god）
['eɪθiɪzəm]	记 词根记忆：a(无) + the(神) + ism → 无神论
torrential	*adj.* 奔流的，洪流的，湍急的（resembling or forming torrents）
[tə'renʃl]	搭 torrential rain 大雨如注
skirt	*v.* 绕过，回避（to evade）
[skɜːrt]	搭 skirt around / round sth. 避而不提
lassitude	*n.* 疲倦无力，没精打采（listlessness; weariness）
['læsɪtuːd]	记 词根记忆：lass(疲倦的) + itude → 没精打采
decree	*n.* 命令，法令（an official order, edict, or decision）*v.* 颁布命令
[dɪ'kriː]	记 发音记忆："敌克令" → 克服敌人的命令 → 命令
vandalize	*v.* 肆意破坏（to subject to vandalism; damage）
['vændəlaɪz]	记 来自 Vandal(*n.* 汪达尔人)，为日耳曼民族的一支，以故意毁坏文物而闻名
swing	*v.* 摇摆（to move backwards and forwards）；旋转（to move in a smooth curve）*n.* 秋千
[swɪŋ]	记 联想记忆：s+wing(翅膀) → 摇摆翅膀，在风中转向 → 旋转
pauper	*n.* 贫民（a very poor person）；乞丐
['pɔːpər]	记 词根记忆：paup(少) + er → 财富少的人 → 贫民
splashy	*adj.* 容易溅开的，炫耀显眼的（exhibiting ostentatious display）
['splæʃi]	记 来自 splash(*n.* 溅水；卖弄)
piscatorial	*adj.* 捕鱼的，渔业的（dependent on fishing; piscatory）
[ˌpɪskə'tɔːriəl]	记 来自 piscator(*n.* 捕鱼人)
slumber	*v.* 睡眠，安睡（to sleep）*n.* 睡眠（a light sleep）
['slʌmbər]	搭 slumber party 睡衣晚会

assent [əˈsent]	*v.* 同意，赞成（to express acceptance; concur; consent） 记 词根记忆：as（接近）+ sent（感觉）→ 感觉一致 → 同意
gleam [gliːm]	*n.* 微光，闪光（a flash or beam of light）*v.* 发微光，闪烁（to flash） 记 联想记忆：拾起（glean）的金色落穗闪闪发光（gleam）
marsupial [mɑːrˈsuːpiəl]	*n./adj.* 有袋动物（的） 搭 marsupial mammal 有袋类哺乳动物
ejaculate [ɪˈdʒækjuleɪt]	*v.* 突然叫出或说出（to utter suddenly and vehemently）；射出（to eject from a living body; discharge） 记 词根记忆：e + jacul（喷射）+ ate → 喷发 → 突然叫出或说出
remains [rɪˈmeɪnz]	*n.* 残余，遗迹（a remaining part or trace） 记 来自 remain（*v.* 保持）
idolatrize [aɪˈdɒlətraɪz]	*v.* 奉为偶像，盲目崇拜（to admire intensely and often blindly） 记 来自 idol（*n.* 偶像）
smear [smɪr]	*v.* 弄脏，玷污（to overspread sth. adhesive）*n.* 污迹，污点（a spot） 搭 smeared windows 脏了的窗户
groan [groʊn]	*v.* 呻吟，叹息（to make a deep sad sound）*n.* 呻吟，叹息 记 联想记忆：长大后（grown）比小孩更爱叹息（groan）
jolly [ˈdʒɑːli]	*adj.* 欢乐的，快乐的（merry; gay; convivial） 记 词根记忆：jol（冬季节日）+ ly → 有关节日的 → 快乐的
intermingle [ˌɪntərˈmɪŋgl]	*v.* 混合，掺杂（to mix together） 记 联想记忆：inter + mingle（混合）→ 混合
maze [meɪz]	*n.* 迷宫（a confusing, intricate network of winding pathways; labyrinth） 记 联想记忆：这个迷宫（maze）让人吃惊（amaze）
defame [dɪˈfeɪm]	*v.* 诽谤，中伤（to malign, slander, or libel） 记 词根记忆：de（变坏）+ fame（名声）→ 使名声变坏 → 诽谤
gambol [ˈgæmbl]	*n.* 雀跃，嬉戏（a jumping and skipping about in play; frolic）*v.* 雀跃，耍闹 记 来自 gamb（腿，胫）+ ol → 用腿跳跃 → 雀跃；注意不要和 gamble（*n./v.* 赌博）相混
sadden [ˈsædn]	*v.* 使悲伤，使难过（to make sad） 同 deject, depress, dispirit, oppress
rakish [ˈreɪkɪʃ]	*adj.* 潇洒的（jaunty）；放荡的（dissolute） 搭 rakish in manner 不拘小节的风格
gangway [ˈgæŋweɪ]	*n.* （上下船的）跳板（gangplank）；样板；舷梯 记 词根记忆：gang（路）+ way（路）→ 通向路的路 → 跳板
vestment [ˈvestmənt]	*n.* 官服，礼服（an outer garment, especially a robe of ceremony or office）；法衣，祭袍（any of the ritual robes worn by members of the clergy, acolytes, or other assistants at services or rites） 记 词根记忆：vest（穿衣服）+ ment → 礼服

37

□ assent	□ gleam	□ marsupial	□ ejaculate	□ remains	□ idolatrize
□ smear	□ groan	□ jolly	□ intermingle	□ maze	□ defame
□ gambol	□ sadden	□ rakish	□ gangway	□ vestment	

bump [bʌmp]	*v.* 碰撞(to hit or knock against) *n.* 碰撞声(dull sound of a blow) 同 collision, crash, impact, jolt, smash
sideshow [ˈsaɪdʃoʊ]	*n.* 杂耍, 穿插表演(a separate small show at a circus)
peek [piːk]	*v.* 偷看(to look furtively; glance)
garment [ˈɡɑːrmənt]	*n.* 衣服(any article of clothing) 搭 wollen garments 毛衣
commonplace [ˈkɑːmənpleɪs]	*adj.* 普通的, 平庸的(ordinary) 记 组合词: common(普通的) + place(地方) → 普通的地方 → 普通的
inch [ɪntʃ]	*v.* 慢慢前进, 慢慢移动(to move by small degrees) 记 联想记忆: 一寸一寸(inch)地移动, 引申为"慢慢前进"
waggish [ˈwæɡɪʃ]	*adj.* 诙谐的, 滑稽的(humorous) 例 There is perhaps some truth in that *waggish* old definition of a scholar — a siren that calls attention to a fog without doing anything to dispel it.
firearm [ˈfaɪərɑːrm]	*n.* (便携式)枪支(portable gun of any sort) 记 组合词: fire(火) + arm(武器) → 枪支
lumen [ˈluːmen]	*n.* 流明(光通量单位) 记 词根记忆: lum(光) + en → 流明
duplicitous [duːˈplɪsɪtəs]	*adj.* 两面派的, 奸诈的(marked by duplicity); 双重的 记 词根记忆: dup(双的) + licit + ous → 双重的
cadence [ˈkeɪdns]	*n.* 抑扬顿挫(rhythmic rise and fall); 节奏, 韵律(rhythm) 记 词根记忆: cad(落下) + ence → 声音的落下上升 → 抑扬顿挫
interstice [ɪnˈtɜːrstɪs]	*n.* 裂缝, 空隙(a small or narrow space; crevice) 记 词根记忆: inter(在⋯中间) + sti(站) + ice → 站在二者之间 → 空隙
virility [vəˈrɪləti]	*n.* 男子气概; 刚强有力 搭 masculinity virility 男子气
ail [eɪl]	*v.* 生病(to have physical or emotional pain, discomfort, or trouble, especially to suffer ill health) 记 联想记忆: 和 air(*n.* 空气)一起记, 多呼吸空气(air)就会少生病(ail)
chandelier [ˌʃændəˈlɪr]	*n.* 枝形吊灯(烛台)(a lighting fixture)
credence [ˈkriːdns]	*n.* 相信, 信任(belief in the reports or testimony of another) 记 词根记忆: cred(相信) + ence → 相信
buffoon [bəˈfuːn]	*n.* 丑角(clown); 愚蠢的人(fool) 记 联想记忆: buf(看作 but) + foon(看作 fool) → but a fool → 只是个笨蛋 → 愚蠢的人
cinder [ˈsɪndər]	*n.* 余烬, 煤渣(slag from the reduction of metallicores) 记 联想记忆: 灰姑娘(cinderella)每天必须掏煤渣(cinder)

obstinate [ˈɑːbstɪnət]	*adj.* 固执的，倔强的（unreasonably determined；stubborn；dogged） 记 词根记忆：ob(向) + st(站) + inate → 就站在那里 → 固执的
compact [ˈkɑːmpækt]	*adj.* 坚实的（dense；solid）；简洁的（not diffuse or wordy）*n.* 合同，协议 （an agreement or covenant between two or more parties） 记 词根记忆：com(一起) + pact(打包，压紧) → 一起压紧 → 坚实的
pulverize [ˈpʌlvəraɪz]	*v.* 使成粉末，粉碎（to reduce to very small particles）；彻底击败（to annihilate） 记 词根记忆：pulver(粉) + ize → 使成粉末
embitter [ɪmˈbɪtər]	*v.* 使痛苦，使难受（to make bitter） 记 词根记忆：em + bitter(苦) → 使痛苦
rejuvenate [rɪˈdʒuːvəneɪt]	*v.* 使变得年轻（to make young or youthful again） 记 词根记忆：re + juven(年轻的) + ate → 使变得年轻
cloudburst [ˈklaʊdbɜːrst]	*n.* 大暴雨（a sudden, very heavy rain） 记 组合词：cloud(云) + burst(爆裂) → 乌云爆裂，要下暴雨 → 大暴雨
desuetude [dɪˈsjuːɪtjuːd]	*n.* 废止，不用（discontinuance from use or exercise） 记 词根记忆：de + suet(=suit 适合) + ude → 不再适合 → 废止
imputation [ˌɪmpjuˈteɪʃn]	*n.* 归咎，归罪（an attribution of fault or crime；accusation） 记 词根记忆：im(进入) + put(计算) + ation → 算计别人 → 归罪
diligence [ˈdɪlɪdʒəns]	*n.* 勤勉，勤奋（steady effort） 记 联想记忆：dili(音似：地里) + gence → 每天在地里劳作 → 勤勉
snappish [ˈsnæpɪʃ]	*adj.* 脾气暴躁的（arising from annoyance or irascibility） 记 联想记忆：snap(劈啪声，折断) + pish → 脾气暴躁的
demented [dɪˈmentɪd]	*adj.* 疯狂的（insane） 记 词根记忆：de(去掉) + ment(神智) + ed → 没有理智 → 疯狂的
substantial [səbˈstænʃl]	*adj.* 坚固的，结实的（strongly made）；实质的（concerning the important part or meaning） 例 In contrast to the *substantial* muscular activity required for inhalation, exhalation is usually a passive process.
omnipresent [ˌɑːmnɪˈpreznt]	*adj.* 无处不在的（present in all places at all times） 记 词根记忆：omni(全) + present(存在) → 无处不在的
sprain [spreɪn]	*v.* 扭伤（to injure by a sudden twist） 记 联想记忆：sp + rain(雨) → 雨天路滑，扭伤了脚 → 扭伤
delve [delv]	*v.* 深入探究，钻研（to investigate for information；search） 搭 delve into 探索，探究
acquit [əˈkwɪt]	*v.* 宣告无罪（to declare sb. to be not guilty）；脱卸义务和责任（to free or clear sb. of blame, responsibility, etc.）；还清(债务)（to pay off） 记 词根记忆：ac(向) + qui(安静) + t → 让某人心境平和 → 宣告无罪
flak [flæk]	*n.* 高射炮（antiaircraft guns）；抨击（strong and clamorous criticism） 记 和 flake(*n.* 薄片；雪片)一起记

37

tirade [ˈtaɪreɪd]	*n.* 长篇的攻击性演说(a long and angry speech) 记 词根记忆：tir(拉) + ade → 拉长的话 → 长篇的攻击性演说
hortative [ˈhɔːrtətɪv]	*adj.* 劝告的；激励的(serving to encourage or urge) 记 词根记忆：hort(敦促) + ative → 激励的
hoary [ˈhɔːri]	*adj.* (头发)灰白的(gray)；古老的(very old) 记 发音记忆："好理" → 头发灰白，该好好整理了 → 灰白的
propulsion [prəˈpʌlʃn]	*n.* 推进力(power or force to propel) 记 词根记忆：pro(向前) + puls(跳动，推动) + ion → 向前推 → 推进力
temper [ˈtempər]	*v.* 锻炼(to toughen)；调和，使缓和(to dilute, or soften) *n.* 脾气，性情(disposition) 记 联想记忆：用锤子(hammer)锤炼(temper)
nonplus [ˌnɑːnˈplʌs]	*v.* 使困惑(to put in perplexity, bewilder) *n.* 迷惑，困惑 记 联想记忆：non + plus(有利的因素) → 不利 → 迷惑
mutinous [ˈmjuːtənəs]	*adj.* 叛变的(engaged in revolt)；反抗的(rebellious) 搭 a mutinous expression 反抗的神色
vilify [ˈvɪlɪfaɪ]	*v.* 辱骂，诽谤(to utter slanderous and abusive statements) 同 defame, malign, revile
drought [draʊt]	*n.* 干旱，旱灾；干旱期(period of continuous dry weather) 记 联想记忆：dr(看作 dry, 干的) + ought(应该) → 应该干 → 干旱 例 The seriousness of the *drought* could only be understood by those who had seen the wilted crops in the fields.
chicanery [ʃɪˈkeɪnəri]	*n.* 欺骗，欺诈(deception by artful sophistry; trickery) 记 词根记忆：chic(聪明) + anery → 耍聪明 → 欺诈
totter [ˈtɑːtər]	*v.* 摇摇欲坠(to tremble or rock as if about to fall)；步履蹒跚(to stagger; wobble)
fiscal [ˈfɪskl]	*adj.* 国库的(relating to public treasury or revenues)；财政的(financial) 记 词根记忆：fisc(金库) + al → 国库的；财政的
insufficient [ˌɪnsəˈfɪʃnt]	*adj.* 不足的(not enough; inadequate) 记 联想记忆：in(不) + sufficient(足够的) → 不足的 例 She has sufficient tact to survive the ordinary crises of diplomatic life; however, even her diplomacy is *insufficient* to enable her to exaggerate the current emergency.
medieval [ˌmedɪˈiːvl]	*adj.* 中世纪的，中古的(of the Middle Ages) 记 词根记忆：medi(中间) + ev(时间) + al → 中世纪的 搭 the medieval period 中世纪时期
muddy [ˈmʌdi]	*adj.* 多泥的，泥泞的(full of or covered with mud)；浑浊的，不清的(lacking in clarity or brightness) 记 来自 mud(*n.* 泥)
palatial [pəˈleɪʃl]	*adj.* 宫殿般的(like a palace)；宏伟的(magnificent; stately) 记 来自 palace(*n.* 宫殿)，注意不要和 palatable(*adj.* 美味的)相混

□ tirade	□ hortative	□ hoary	□ propulsion	□ temper	□ nonplus
□ mutinous	□ vilify	□ drought	□ chicanery	□ totter	□ fiscal
□ insufficient	□ medieval	□ muddy	□ palatial		

398

spectacular	*adj.* 壮观的，引人入胜的(striking; sensational)
[spek'tækjələr]	记 来自 spectacle(*n.* 奇观，壮观); spect(看)+acle(东西) → 看的东西 → 奇观，壮观
slur	*v.* 含糊不清地讲(to pronounce words in an indistinct way so that they run into each other)
[slɜːr]	记 和 blur(*v.* 弄脏，变模糊)一起记
disheveled	*adj.* (头发、服装等)不整的，凌乱的(untidy of hair or clothing)
[dɪ'ʃevld]	记 来自 dishevel(*v.* 使蓬乱)
inebriate	*v.* 使…醉(to intoxicate) *n.* 酒鬼，酒徒(a drunkard)
[ɪ'niːbrɪeɪt]	记 词根记忆: in(进入) + ebri(醉的) + ate → 使…醉
bare	*v.* 暴露(to make or lay bare; uncover) *adj.* 赤裸的(without clothing)
[ber]	记 和 bear(*n.* 熊)一起记
wreak	*v.* 发泄，报复(to inflict vengeance upon); 发泄怒火(to express anger)
[riːk]	同 avenge, redress, requite, vindicate
puny	*adj.* 弱小的，孱弱的(slight or inferior in power)
['pjuːni]	同 feeble
askew	*adj./adv.* 歪斜的(地)(to one side; awry)
[ə'skjuː]	记 联想记忆: a + skew(歪斜的) → 歪斜的(地)
spin	*v.* 旋转(to move round and round); 纺纱(to draw out and twist fiber into yarn or thread) *n.* 旋转(turning or spinning movement)
[spɪn]	
expeditious	*adj.* 迅速的，敏捷的(prompt; quick)
[ˌekspə'dɪʃəs]	记 来自 expedite(*v.* 使加速，促进)
peak	*v.* 变得憔悴，消瘦(to become thin or sick; emaciate)
[piːk]	搭 peak and pine 憔悴
colloquy	*n.* (非正式的)交谈，会谈(informal discussion; conversation)
['kɑːləkwi]	同 chat, dialogue, discourse
rifle	*n.* 步枪 *v.* 抢夺，偷走(to ransack with the intent to steal)
['raɪfl]	记 发音记忆: "来福" → 来福步枪 → 步枪
erect	*adj.* 竖立的，笔直的(vertical in position)
[ɪ'rekt]	记 词根记忆: e + rect(竖，直) → 竖立的，笔直的
vapid	*adj.* 索然无味的，无生气的(lacking liveliness; flat; dull)
['væpɪd]	记 词根记忆: vap(蒸汽) + id → 蒸汽般的 → 索然无味的
profligate	*adj.* 挥霍的，浪费的(wildly extravagant) *n.* 恣意挥霍者
['prɑːflɪɡət]	记 词根记忆: pro(向前) + flig(拉) + ate → 使向前拉了许多 → 挥霍的
militia	*n.* 民兵(an army composed of ordinary citizens)
[mə'lɪʃə]	记 词根记忆: milit(军事，战斗) + ia → 参与战争的人民 → 民兵
belligerence	*n.* 交战(the state of being at war); 好战性，斗争性(an aggressive attitude, atmosphere, etc.)
[bə'lɪdʒərəns]	记 词根记忆: bell(战斗) + iger + ence → 交战; 好战性

37

despotism [ˈdespətɪzəm]	*n.* 专政；暴政
dingy [ˈdɪndʒi]	*adj.* 肮脏的，昏暗的(dirty colored; grimy; shabby)
ambience [ˈæmbiəns]	*n.* 环境，气氛(environment; atmosphere) 记 词根记忆：ambi(在…周围) + ence → 环境，气氛
mortgage [ˈmɔːrɡɪdʒ]	*n.* 抵押；抵押证书 *v.* 用…作抵押 记 词根记忆：mort(死亡) + gage(抵押品) → 用抵押品使债务死亡 → 抵押
azure [ˈæʒər]	*n.* 天蓝色(sky blue) *adj.* 蔚蓝的 同 cerulean, lazuline, sapphire
laxative [ˈlæksətɪv]	*adj.* (药)通便的 *n.* 轻泻药(any laxative medicine) 记 词根记忆：lax(松的) + ative → 放松的 → 轻泻药
riven [ˈrɪvn]	*adj.* 撕开的，分裂的(split violently apart)
devotee [ˌdevəˈtiː]	*n.* 爱好者，献身者(people who devote to sth.) 同 fanatic, sectary, votary, zealot
cement [sɪˈment]	*n.* 水泥；黏合剂 *v.* 黏合，巩固(to unite or make firm by or as if by cement) 记 联想记忆：ce + ment(看作 mend, 修补) → 修补材料 → 水泥；黏合剂

You have to believe in yourself. That's the secret of success.
人必须相信自己，这是成功的秘诀。

——美国演员 卓别林(Charles Chaplin, American actor)

☐ despotism	☐ dingy	☐ ambience	☐ mortgage	☐ azure	☐ laxative
☐ riven	☐ devotee	☐ cement			

somnolent [ˈsɑːmnələnt]	*adj.* 想睡的(drowsy); 催眠的(likely to induce sleep) 记 词根记忆: somn(睡) + olent → 想睡的
bamboozle [bæmˈbuːzl]	*v.* 欺骗, 隐瞒(to deceive by underhanded methods) 记 联想记忆: bamboo(竹子)+zle → 把东西装在竹筒里 → 欺骗, 隐瞒
assess [əˈses]	*v.* 评定, 核定(to evaluate); 估计, 估价(to estimate the quality)
attenuate [əˈtenjueɪt]	*v.* 变薄(to make slender); 变弱(to lessen; weaken) *adj.* 减弱的 记 词根记忆: at(加强) + ten(薄) + uate → 变薄
queue [kjuː]	*v.* 排队(to arrange or form in a queue) *n.* 长队(a line of persons waiting to be processed) 记 联想记忆: q 站在前面, 后面跟着 ue + ue → 长队
surfeit [ˈsɜːrfɪt]	*n.* 饮食过量, 过度(an overabundant supply) *v.* 使过量 记 词根记忆: sur(过分)+feit(做) → 做过了头 → 过度
garner [ˈgɑːrnər]	*v.* 把…储入谷仓; 收藏, 积累(to collect or gather); 获得 记 发音记忆: "家纳" → 家里收纳下来 → 收藏 同 accumulate, earn, reap
mendicant [ˈmendɪkənt]	*adj.* 行乞的(practicing beggary) *n.* 乞丐(beggar) 记 联想记忆: mend(修补, 改善) + icant → 生活需要改善的人 → 乞丐
valedictory [ˌvælɪˈdɪktəri]	*adj.* 告别的, 离别的(used in saying goodbye) 记 词根记忆: val(值得的) + e + dict(说) + ory → 告别的 例 The *valedictory* address, as it has developed in American colleges and universities over the years, has become a very strict form, a literary genre that permits very little deviation.
ratiocination [ˌreɪʃioʊsɪˈneɪʃn]	*n.* 推理, 推论(reasoning) 记 词根记忆: rat(清点) + iocination → 推理
stagy [ˈsteɪdʒi]	*adj.* 不自然的, 做作的(marked by pretense or artificiality) 同 hokey, sensational, theatrical
resound [rɪˈzaʊnd]	*v.* 回响(to produce a sonorous or echoing sound); 鸣响(to be loudly and clearly heard)

snip [snɪp]	*v.* 剪断 (to cut with scissors) *n.* 剪；碎片 同 fragment
mores [ˈmɔːreɪz]	*n.* 习俗，惯例 (the fixed morally binding customs of a particular group) 记 词根记忆：mor (风俗) + es → 习俗，惯例
pestilent [ˈpestɪlənt]	*adj.* 致命的 (deadly)；有害的 (pernicious) 记 联想记忆：pest (害虫) + il + ent → 有害的
disposed [dɪˈspəʊzd]	*adj.* 愿意的，想干的 (inclined) 记 来自 dispose (*v.* 使倾向于；处理) 例 It is said that the custom of shaking hands originated when primitive men held out empty hands to indicate that they had no concealed weapons and were thus amicably *disposed*.
itinerary [aɪˈtɪnəreri]	*n.* 旅行路线 (proposed route of a journey) 记 词根记忆：it (走) + in + er + ary → 旅行路线
somatic [səʊˈmætɪk]	*adj.* 肉体的，躯体的 (relating to the body) 记 词根记忆：somat (躯体) + ic → 躯体的
gripe [ɡraɪp]	*v.* 抱怨 (to complain naggingly)；惹恼，激怒 记 联想记忆：g (看作 go) + ripe (成熟的) → 成年人容易抱怨 → 抱怨 同 irritate, vex
huffish [ˈhʌfɪʃ]	*adj.* 不高兴的，发怒的 (peevish; sulky)；傲慢的 记 来自 huff (*v./n.* 生气)
killjoy [ˈkɪldʒɔɪ]	*n.* 令人扫兴的人 (a person who intentionally spoils the pleasure of other people) 记 组合词：kill (杀) + joy (欢乐) → 杀欢乐的人 → 令人扫兴的人
mistral [ˈmɪstrəl]	*n.* 寒冷且干燥的强风 (a cold, dry wind) 记 联想记忆：mist (雾) + ral → 风起雾散 → 寒冷且干燥的强风
emigrate [ˈemɪɡreɪt]	*v.* 移居国外 (或外地) (to leave one's place of residence or country to live elsewhere) 记 注意：emigrate 表示"移出"，immigrate 表示"移入"，migrate 指"动物或人来回迁移"，它们都来自词根 migr (移动)
stir [stɜːr]	*v.* 刺激 (to rouse to activity; to call forth) 记 stir 本身是词根，有"刺激"之意
sideline [ˈsaɪdlaɪn]	*n.* 副业，兼职 (a business or activity pursued in addition to one's regular occupation)
sermon [ˈsɜːrmən]	*n.* 布道；说教，训诫 记 联想记忆：布道 (sermon) 时说阿门 (Amen)
pane [peɪn]	*n.* 窗格玻璃 (a single sheet of glass in a frame of a window) 搭 a window pane 窗玻璃
cranky [ˈkræŋki]	*adj.* 怪癖的 (queer; eccentric)；不稳的 (unsteady) 记 来自 crank (*n.* 怪人)

□ snip	□ mores	□ pestilent	□ disposed	□ itinerary	□ somatic
□ gripe	□ huffish	□ killjoy	□ mistral	□ emigrate	□ stir
□ sideline	□ sermon	□ pane	□ cranky		

nucleate	*v.* (使)成核(to form a nucleus) *adj.* 有核的
[ˈnuːklɪeɪt]	记 词根记忆：nucle(核) + ate → (使)成核
yacht	*n.* 帆船，游艇(any of various recreational watercraft)
[jɑːt]	搭 a yacht club/race 帆船俱乐部/比赛
berserk	*adj.* 狂怒的，狂暴的(frenzied, crazed)
[bərˈzɜːrk]	同 amok, demoniac, demoniacal
cargo	*n.* (船、飞机等装载的)货物(load of goods carried in a ship or aircraft)
[ˈkɑːrgoʊ]	记 联想记忆：car(汽车) + go(走) → 汽车运走的东西 → 货物
anticipate	*v.* 预先处理(to foresee and deal with in advance)；预期，期望(to look forward to; expect)
[ænˈtɪsɪpeɪt]	记 词根记忆：anti(前) + cip(落下) + ate → 提前落下 → 预期，期望
indifferent	*adj.* 不感兴趣的，漠不关心的(having or showing no particular interest in or concern for; disinterested)
[ɪnˈdɪfrənt]	记 联想记忆：in(不) + different(不同的) → 对任何事的态度都没什么不同 → 漠不关心的
	搭 be indifferent to 对…冷漠
vivacious	*adj.* 活泼的，有生气的，快活的(lively in temper, conduct, or spirit; sprightly)
[vɪˈveɪʃəs]	记 词根记忆：viv(生命) + aci + ous → 活泼的
grill	*v.* 烤(to broil)；拷问(to question relentlessly) *n.* 烤架
[grɪl]	记 联想记忆：gr + ill(生病) → 严刑拷打会打出病的 → 拷问
contumely	*n.* 无礼，傲慢(haughty and contemptuous rudeness)´
[ˈkɑːntumɪli]	记 词根记忆：con + tume(骄傲) + ly → 傲慢
elixir	*n.* 万能药，长生不老药(cure-all; panacea)
[ɪˈlɪksər]	记 源自阿拉伯人卖药时的叫卖："阿里可舍"，意思是：这个药好啊
osmosis	*n.* 渗透(the diffusion of fluids)；潜移默化(gradual, and often hardly noticeable acceptance of ideas, etc.)
[ɑːzˈmoʊsɪs]	
embroil	*v.* 使混乱，使卷入纠纷(to involve in conflict or difficulties)
[ɪmˈbrɔɪl]	记 词根记忆：em(进入) + broil(争吵) → 进入争吵 → 使混乱，使卷入纠纷
quandary	*n.* 困惑，进退两难，窘境(a state of perplexity or doubt; predicament)
[ˈkwɑːndəri]	记 发音记忆："渴望得力" → 处于进退两难的境地，渴望得到力量 → 进退两难
pulp	*n.* 果肉(a soft mass of vegetable matter)；纸浆(a material prepared in making paper)
[pʌlp]	
induce	*v.* 诱导(to lead into some action)；引起(to bring out)
[ɪnˈduːs]	记 词根记忆：in(进入) + duc(拉) + e → 拉进去 → 诱导
craven	*adj.* 懦弱的，畏缩的(lacking the least bit of courage; cowardly)
[ˈkreɪvn]	记 联想记忆：c + raven(乌鸦) → 像乌鸦一样胆小 → 畏缩的
fracture	*n.* 骨折(a break in the body part)；折断，裂口(a break; crack)
[ˈfræktʃər]	记 词根记忆：fract(碎裂) + ure → 骨头碎了 → 骨折

38

□ nucleate	□ yacht	□ berserk	□ cargo	□ anticipate	□ indifferent
□ vivacious	□ grill	□ contumely	□ elixir	□ osmosis	□ embroil
□ quandary	□ pulp	□ induce	□ craven	□ fracture	

403

fructify [ˈfrʌktɪfaɪ]	*v.* (使)结果实(to bear fruit); (使)成功(to cause to be or become fruitful) 记 词根记忆: fruct(=fruit 果实) + ify(使) → (使)结果实
swarthy [ˈswɔːrði]	*adj.* (皮肤等)黝黑的(of a dark color, complexion) 同 brunet, swart, tan
clandestine [klænˈdestɪn]	*adj.* 秘密的, 偷偷摸摸的(surreptitious; furtive; secret) 记 联想记忆: clan(宗派) + destine(命中注定) → "宗派"和"命中注定"都有一些"秘密"色彩 → 秘密的
pool [puːl]	*n.* 资源的集合(a grouping of resources for the common advantage of the participants); 可共享的物资(a readily available supply)
signify [ˈsɪɡnɪfaɪ]	*v.* 表示(to be a sign of); 有重要性(to have significance) 记 词根记忆: sign(做记号) + ify → 表示
ruckus [ˈrʌkəs]	*n.* 喧闹, 骚动(row; disturbance) 同 commotion
objection [əbˈdʒekʃn]	*n.* 厌恶, 反对(dislike or disapproval) 记 词根记忆: ob(反) + ject(扔) + ion → 反过来扔 → 厌恶, 反对 例 Since the author frequently attacks other scholars, his *objection* to disputes is not only irrelevant but also surprising.
unrepentant [ˌʌnrɪˈpentənt]	*adj.* 顽固不化的, 不后悔的(not penitent) 记 词根记忆: un(不) + re(再, 又) + pen(惩罚) + tant → 不再让心灵受惩罚的 → 顽固不化的, 不后悔的
vengeance [ˈvendʒəns]	*n.* 报仇, 报复(punishment inflicted in retaliation; retribution) 记 词根记忆: veng(复仇) + eance → 报仇, 报复
immensity [ɪˈmensəti]	*n.* 巨大的事物(sth. immense); 巨大, 广大, 无限(the quality or state of being immense)
stammer [ˈstæmər]	*v.* 口吃, 结巴地说(to make involuntary stops and repetitions in speaking) 同 falter, stumble, stutter
cede [siːd]	*v.* 割让(领土), 放弃(to transfer the title or ownership of) 同 abandon, abdicate, demit, relinquish, surrender
cosset [ˈkɑːsɪt]	*v.* 宠爱, 溺爱(to protect too carefully) 记 联想记忆: cos(看作 cost, 花费) + set(固定) → 固定将一笔花费给孩子 → 宠爱, 溺爱
progeny [ˈprɑːdʒəni]	*n.* 后代, 子孙(descendants) 记 词根记忆: pro(前) + gen(产生) + y → 前人所生下的 → 后代
collapse [kəˈlæps]	*v.* 坍塌, 塌陷(to break into pieces and fall down suddenly); 虚脱, 晕倒(to become unconscious) 记 词根记忆: col(共同) + lapse(滑倒) → 全部滑倒 → 坍塌
trek [trek]	*v.* 艰苦跋涉(to make one's way arduously) 同 traipse, trudge
vantage [ˈvæntɪdʒ]	*n.* 优势, 有利地位(superiority in a contest) 搭 vantage point (观察事物的)有利地点

□ fructify	□ swarthy	□ clandestine	□ pool	□ signify	□ ruckus
□ objection	□ unrepentant	□ vengeance	□ immensity	□ stammer	□ cede
□ cosset	□ progeny	□ collapse	□ trek	□ vantage	

dither	*v.* 慌张；犹豫不决(to act nervously or indecisively) *n.* 紧张；慌乱
[ˈdɪðər]	搭 to be in a dither about 对某事犹豫不决
languid	*adj.* 没精打采的，倦怠的(listless; without vigor)
[ˈlæŋgwɪd]	记 词根记忆：lang(松弛) + uid → 精神懈怠的 → 没精打采的
log	*n.* 日志，记录；一段木头 *v.* 记录
[lɔːg]	搭 log in/on 登录，注册
stoke	*v.* 给…添加燃料(to fill with coal or other fuel)
[stoʊk]	记 联想记忆：给火炉(stove)添加燃料(stoke)
depravity	*n.* 堕落，恶习(a morally bad condition; corruption; wickedness)
[dɪˈprævəti]	记 词根记忆：de + prav(坏) + ity → 变坏 → 堕落
irk	*v.* 使苦恼，使厌烦(to annoy; disgust)
[ɜːrk]	记 发音记忆："饿渴" → 又饿又渴，当然很苦恼 → 使苦恼
hazy	*adj.* 朦胧的，不清楚的(made dim or cloudy by or as if by haze)
[ˈheɪzi]	同 foggy, misty, smoky
lot	*n.* 签(an object used as a counter)；命运(a person's destiny) *v.* 抽签；划分(to divide into lots)
[lɑːt]	
conciliate	*v.* 安抚；安慰(to soothe the anger of; placate)；调和(to reconcile; pacify)
[kənˈsɪlieɪt]	记 词根记忆：concil(=council 协商) + iate → 协商(解决) → 调和
wrest	*v.* 扭，拧(to pull, force, or move by violent wringing or twisting movements)；夺取，费力取得(to gain with difficulty by or as if by force, violence, or determined labor)
[rest]	
dilapidate	*v.* (使)荒废，(使)毁坏(to bring into a condition of decay or partial ruin)
[dɪˈlæpɪdeɪt]	记 词根记忆：di(二) + lapid(石头) + ate → 石基倒塌成为两半 → (使)荒废，(使)毁坏
insurrection	*n.* 造反，叛乱(rebellion; revolt)
[ˌɪnsəˈrekʃn]	记 词根记忆：in(反) + surrect(升起) + ion → 反对活动出现 → 造反
metrical	*adj.* 测量的(metric)；韵律的(written in poetic meter)
[ˈmetrɪkl]	记 来自 meter(*n.* 米；韵律)
debunk	*v.* 揭穿真相，暴露(to expose the false or exaggerated claims)
[ˌdiːˈbʌŋk]	记 联想记忆：de + bunk(看作 bank，岸) → 去掉河岸 → 暴露
unbosom	*v.* 倾诉，吐露(to disclose the thoughts or feelings of)
[ʌnˈbʊzəm]	同 reveal
underlying	*adj.* 在下面的；根本的；潜在的
[ˌʌndərˈlaɪɪŋ]	记 联想记忆：under(在…下面) + lying(躺着的) → 在下面躺着的 → 在下面的；根本的；潜在的
	例 Despite the apparently bewildering complexity of this procedure, the *underlying* principle is quite elementary.
hull	*n.* 外壳(the outer covering)；船身 *v.* 剥去外壳(to remove the hulls of)
[hʌl]	记 联想记忆：空有外壳(hull)的东西是没有价值的(null)

38

detonate	*v.* (使)爆炸, 引爆 (to cause a bomb or dynamite to explode)
[ˈdetəneɪt]	记 词根记忆: de + ton(声音, 雷声) + ate → 雷声四散 → (使)爆炸
bicker	*v.* 争吵, 口角 (to quarrel about unimportant things)
[ˈbɪkər]	同 brabble, niggle, pettifog, quibble, squabble
canorous	*adj.* 音调优美的, 有旋律的 (pleasant sounding; melodious)
[kəˈnoʊrəs]	
puissant	*adj.* 强大的, 有权力的 (having strength; powerful)
[ˈpjuːsənt]	同 influential
variance	*n.* 分歧, 不和 (dissension; dispute); 不同, 变化 (difference; variation)
[ˈveriəns]	例 The notion that cultural and biological influences equally determine cross-cultural diversity is discredited by the fact that, in countless aspects of human existence, it is cultural programming that overwhelmingly accounts for cross-population *variance*.
exactitude	*n.* 正确, 精确, 严格 (over-correctness)
[ɪgˈzæktɪtuːd]	同 accuracy, accurateness, exactness, precision
omelet	*n.* 煎蛋卷 (eggs beaten together and cooked in hot fat)
[ˈɑːmlət]	记 联想记忆: o(看作一个蛋) + me(我) + let(让) → 让我吃煎蛋 → 煎蛋卷
fallacy	*n.* 错误, 谬论 (a false or mistaken idea)
[ˈfæləsi]	记 词根记忆: fall(犯错) + acy → 错误
disjunction	*n.* 分离, 分裂 (a sharp cleavage)
[dɪsˈdʒʌŋkʃn]	记 词根记忆: dis(不) + junction(连接) → 不再连接 → 分离
	例 The *disjunction* between educational objectives that stress independence and individuality and those that emphasize obedience to rules and cooperation with others reflects a conflict that arises from the values on which these objectives are based.
virtuosity	*n.* 精湛技巧 (great technical skill)
[ˌvɜːrtʃuˈɑːsəti]	例 Winsor McCay, the cartoonist, could draw with incredible *virtuosity*: his comic strip about Little Nemo was characterized by marvelous draftsmanship and sequencing.
goblet	*n.* 高脚酒杯 (a drinking glass with a base and stem)
[ˈgɑːblət]	同 wineglass
fuss	*n.* 大惊小怪 (a flurry of nervous, needless bustle or excitement)
[ˈfʌs]	记 发音记忆: "发丝" → 男朋友的外套上有别的女孩子的发丝, 于是禁不住发怒, 但被男朋友认为是大惊小怪 → 大惊小怪
intercede	*v.* 说好话, 代为求情 (to plead or make a request on behalf of another)
[ˌɪntərˈsiːd]	记 词根记忆: inter(在…中间) + ced(走) + e → 走到中间 → 代为求情

intercede

他不是故意的

□ detonate	□ bicker	□ canorous	□ puissant	□ variance	□ exactitude
□ omelet	□ fallacy	□ disjunction	□ virtuosity	□ goblet	□ fuss
□ intercede					

nascent [ˈnæsnt]	*adj.* 初生的，萌芽的(beginning to exist or develop) 记 词根记忆：nasc (出生) + ent → 刚出生的 → 初生的	
lunge [lʌndʒ]	*n.* 冲，扑(a sudden forward movement or plunge) 记 联想记忆：向长沙发(lounge)直扑(lunge)过去	
meld [meld]	*v.* (使)混合，(使)合并(to blend; mix) 同 fuse, merge, mingle	
covenant [ˈkʌvənənt]	*n.* 契约(a binding and solemn agreement) *v.* 立书保证(to promise by a covenant) 记 词根记忆：co + ven(来) + ant → 来到一起立约 → 契约	
immolate [ˈɪməleɪt]	*v.* 牺牲，献祭(to offer or kill as a sacrifice) 记 词根记忆：im(在…之上) + mola(用作祭品的肉) + te → 放上祭品 → 牺牲	
foolproof [ˈfuːlpruːf]	*adj.* 极易懂的，十分简单的(so simple, well designed as not to be mishandled) 记 组合词：fool(笨蛋) + proof(防…的) → 以防受限于人的无能而做得尤其简单好用 → 人人都会操作的 → 极易懂的	
hash [hæʃ]	*n.* 杂乱，混乱 (a jumble; a hodgepodge)；杂烩菜 (chopped food, specifically: chopped meat mixed with potatoes and browned)	
behold [bɪˈhoʊld]	*v.* 注视，看见(to hold in view; look at) 记 联想记忆：be + hold(拿住) → 被拿住 → 注视，看见	
recompense [ˈrekəmpens]	*v.* 报酬，赔偿(to give by way of compensation) 记 联想记忆：re(重新) + compense(补偿) → 重新补偿 → 赔偿	
interrupt [ˌɪntəˈrʌpt]	*v.* 暂时中止(to break the continuity of sth. temporarily)；打断，打扰(to stop sb. speaking or causing some other sort of disturbance) 记 词根记忆：inter (在…之间) + rupt (断裂) → 在中间断裂 → 暂时中止；打断	
obverse [ˈɑːbvɜːrs]	*n./adj.* 正面(的)(the front or main surface) 记 词根记忆：ob(外) + vers(转) + e → 转向外的 → 正面的	
ravel [ˈrævl]	*v.* 使纠缠，纠结(to become twisted and knotted)；拆开，拆散(to unravel) 同 entangle	
bumptious [ˈbʌmpʃəs]	*adj.* 傲慢的，自夸的(crudely or loudly assertive) 记 联想记忆：bump(碰撞) + tious → 顶撞人 → 傲慢的	
affiliation [əˌfɪliˈeɪʃn]	*n.* 联系，联合(link or connection made by affiliating)	
artifact [ˈɑːrtɪfækt]	*n.* 人工制品(object made by human beings) 记 词根记忆：arti(技巧) + fact(制作) → 用技巧制作出来的东西 → 人工制品	
cameo [ˈkæmioʊ]	*n.* 刻有浮雕的宝石(jewel carved in relief)；生动刻画；(演员)出演 记 联想记忆：came(来) + o → 来哦 → 演员来哦 → 出演	
ensnare [ɪnˈsner]	*v.* 诱入陷阱，进入罗网(to take in a snare; catch; trap) 记 词根记忆：en(进入) + snare(罗网，陷阱) → 诱入陷阱，进入罗网	

38

□ nascent	□ lunge	□ meld	□ covenant	□ immolate	□ foolproof
□ hash	□ behold	□ recompense	□ interrupt	□ obverse	□ ravel
□ bumptious	□ affiliation	□ artifact	□ cameo	□ ensnare	

407

guffaw	*n.* 哄笑，粗声大笑（a loud, coarse burst of laughter）*v.* 哄笑
[gə'fɔː]	记 联想记忆：guff（胡言，废话）+ aw → 听了他的一番胡言，大家一阵哄笑 → 哄笑
vile	*adj.* 恶劣的，卑鄙的，道德败坏的（morally despicable or abhorrent）
[vaɪl]	同 abject, contemptible, filthy, loathsome
swallow	*v.* 吞下，咽下；忍受（to accept patiently or without question）
['swɑːloʊ]	搭 swallow a bite（鱼）吞饵上钩
impoverish	*v.* 使贫穷（to make poor；reduce to poverty）
[ɪm'pɑːvərɪʃ]	记 词根记忆：im（进入）+ pover（贫困）+ ish → 进入贫困 → 使贫穷
guise	*n.* 外观，装束（outward manner or appearance）；伪装，假装
[gaɪz]	记 发音记忆："盖子" → 外观，装束
bracing	*adj.* 令人振奋的（invigorating）
['breɪsɪŋ]	同 brisk, energizing, fresh, refreshful, refreshing, tonic
justification	*n.* 正当的理由（an acceptable reason）；辩护（the act of justifying）
[ˌdʒʌstɪfɪ'keɪʃn]	记 来自 justify（*v.* 证明…是正当的）
incur	*v.* 招惹（to bring upon oneself）
[ɪn'kɜːr]	记 词根记忆：in（进入）+ cur（跑）→ 跑进来 → 招惹
	例 Lizzie was a brave woman who could dare to *incur* a great danger for an adequate object.
acquiesce	*v.* 勉强同意，默许（to agree or consent quietly without protest; consent）
[ˌækwɪ'es]	记 词根记忆：ac（加强）+ qui（安静）+ esce → 面对某事变得安静 → 默许
flunk	*v.* （考试）不及格（to fail in schoolwork）
[flʌŋk]	搭 flunk out (of sth.)（因不及格而）退学
suavity	*n.* 柔和，愉快（gentleness；jolliness）
['swɑːvəti]	记 来自 suave（*adj.* 温和文雅的）
bide	*v.* 等待，逗留（to wait for; continue in a place）
[baɪd]	同 abide, stay
demolition	*n.* 破坏，毁坏（destruction by explosives）
[ˌdeməˈlɪʃn]	记 来自 demolish（*v.* 拆毁）
wanton	*adj.* 无节制的，肆无忌惮的（being without check or limitation）；嬉戏的，淘气的（mischievous）
['wɑːntən]	记 发音记忆："顽童" → 淘气的
	例 Abandoning the moral principles of his youth, the aging emperor Tiberius led a debauched, *wanton* life.
lathe	*n.* 车床 *v.* 用车床加工
[leɪð]	记 联想记忆：用车床加工（lathe）板条（lath）
deface	*v.* 损坏（to mar the appearance of；destroy）
[dɪ'feɪs]	记 词根记忆：de（变坏）+ face（脸面）→ 把脸面弄坏 → 损坏
violet	*adj.* 紫罗兰色的 *n.* 紫罗兰
['vaɪələt]	记 联想记忆：vio+let（让）→ 让紫罗兰花尽情开放吧 → 紫罗兰

choosy [ˈtʃuːzi]	*adj.* 挑三拣四的，挑剔的(fastidiously selective; particular) 同 finical, fussy, meticulous
advent [ˈædvent]	*n.* 到来，来临(coming or arrival) 记 词根记忆：ad(来) + vent(到来) → 到来
jejune [dʒɪˈdʒuːn]	*adj.* 空洞的(devoid of significance)；不成熟的(not mature) 记 词根记忆：jejun(空肠) + e → 空洞的
infraction [ɪnˈfrækʃn]	*n.* 违犯，违反(violation; infringement) 记 词根记忆：in(使) + fract(破裂) + ion → 使(法律)破裂 → 违反
versatile [ˈvɜːrsətl]	*adj.* 多才多艺的(having many different kinds of skills)；多用途的(having many different uses) 记 词根记忆：vers(转)+atile → 可向多个方向转的 → 多才多艺的
whiff [wɪf]	*n.* (风、烟等的)一阵(a slight, gentle gust of air)*v.* 轻吹 搭 a whiff of perfume 一股香水味
peckish [ˈpekɪʃ]	*adj.* 饿的(hungry)；急躁的(crotchety) 同 ill-tempered, irritable
crumb [krʌm]	*n.* 糕饼屑，面包屑(small particles of bread or cake)；少许，点滴(any bit or scrap) 记 和 crumble(*v.* 弄碎)一起记；crumble the bread into crumbs(把面包弄碎)
repose [rɪˈpoʊz]	*n./v.* 休息，安眠(to lie at rest) 记 词根记忆：re(重新) + pos(放) + e → 重新(将身体)放下去 → 躺下去(睡觉) → 休息
decamp [dɪˈkæmp]	*v.* (士兵)离营(to leave camp)；匆忙秘密地离开(to go away suddenly and secretly) 记 词根记忆：de(离开) + camp(营地) → 离营
serenade [ˌserəˈneɪd]	*n.* 夜曲(a complimentary vocal or instrumental performance) 记 词根记忆：seren(安静) + ade → 夜曲
contain [kənˈteɪn]	*v.* 包含，含有(to hold sth. within itself)；控制(to keep sth. under control)；阻止，遏制(to restrain, check) 记 词根记忆：con + tain(拿住) → 全部拿住 → 包含，含有
enfeeble [ɪnˈfiːbl]	*v.* 使衰弱(to deprive of strength) 记 词根记忆：en(使) + feeble(虚弱的) → 使衰弱
perambulate [pəˈræmbjuleɪt]	*v.* 巡视(to make an official inspection on foot)；漫步(to stroll) 记 词根记忆：per(贯穿) + ambul(行走) + ate → 到处走 → 巡视
sanity [ˈsænəti]	*n.* 头脑清楚，精神健全(soundness of mind and judgement)
moribund [ˈmɔːrɪbʌnd]	*adj.* 即将结束的(coming to an end)；垂死的(dying) 记 词根记忆：mori(=mort 死) + bund(接近的) → 垂死的 例 One of Detroit's great success stories tells of Lee lacocca's revitalization of the *moribund* Chrysler Corporation, turning it into a vigorous competitor.

38

foyer [ˈfɔɪər]	*n.* 门厅，休息室（an entrance hall or lobby） 记 和 foy（*n.* 临别礼物）一起记
voracious [vəˈreɪʃəs]	*adj.* 狼吞虎咽的，贪吃的（having a huge appetite）；贪婪的，贪得无厌的（excessively eager；insatiable） 记 词根记忆：vor（吃）+ aci + ous（多…的）→ 吃得多的 → 狼吞虎咽的；贪婪的
singe [sɪndʒ]	*v.*（轻微地）烧焦，烤焦（to burn superficially or lightly；scorch） 记 联想记忆：sing（唱，唱歌）+ e → 烧焦了还唱 → 烧焦
luminary [ˈluːmɪneri]	*n.* 杰出人物，名人（a person of prominence or brilliant achievement） 记 词根记忆：lumin（光）+ ary → 发光的人 → 名人
refulgent [rɪˈfʌldʒənt]	*adj.* 辉煌的，灿烂的（shining radiantly） 记 词根记忆：re + fulg（发光）+ ent → 辉煌的，灿烂的
mechanism [ˈmekənɪzəm]	*n.* 结构，机制 搭 mechanism for resolving the conflict 解决冲突的机制
cavort [kəˈvɔːrt]	*v.* 腾跃，欢跃（to prance；gambol） 记 发音记忆："渴望他" → 兴奋得跳跃 → 欢跃
pirouette [ˌpɪruˈet]	*n.*（舞蹈）脚尖着地的旋转（a full turn on the toe in ballet） 记 词根记忆：pirou（转）+ ette（小动作）→ 小转 → 脚尖着地的旋转
stun [stʌn]	*v.* 使震惊，打晕（to make senseless, groggy, or dizzy by or as if by a blow） 记 发音记忆：发音像敲击声"当" → 把人打晕 → 打晕
outfox [ˌaʊtˈfɑːks]	*v.* 以机智胜过（to outwit；outsmart） 记 组合词：out（出）+ fox（狐狸）→ 胜过狐狸 → 以机智胜过
recumbent [rɪˈkʌmbənt]	*adj.* 斜靠的（lying down；prone）；休息的（resting） 记 词根记忆：re + cumb（躺）+ ent → 斜靠的

音频

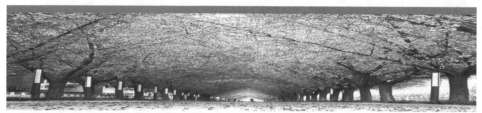

suspicion [sə'spɪʃn]	*n.* 怀疑，嫌疑(doubt) 记 来自 suspect(*v.* 怀疑) 例 She worked for recognition and fame, yet she felt a deep *suspicion* and respect for the world in which recognition and fame are granted, the world of money and opinion and power.
insanity [ɪn'sænəti]	*n.* 疯狂(derangement)；愚昧(great folly) 同 madness
frigidity [frɪ'dʒɪdəti]	*n.* 寒冷；冷淡(the quality or state of being frigid) 记 来自 frigid(*adj.* 寒冷的)
pundit ['pʌndɪt]	*n.* 权威人士，专家(one who gives opinions in an authoritative manner) 记 pandit(*n.* 学者，专家)变体
sentinel ['sentɪnl]	*n.* 哨兵，岗哨(sentry；lookout) 搭 stand sentinel 站岗，守卫
overthrow [ˌoʊvər'θroʊ]	*v.* 推翻；终止(to throw over; overturn) *n.* 推翻；终止(an instance of overthrow-ing)
dejected [dɪ'dʒektɪd]	*adj.* 沮丧的，失望的，灰心的(in low spirits; depressed; disheartened) 记 词根记忆：de + ject(扔) + ed → 被扔掉的 → 沮丧的，失望的，灰心的
mortification [ˌmɔːrtɪfɪ'keɪʃn]	*n.* 耻辱，屈辱(shame；humiliation) 记 来自 mortify(*v.* 使难堪)
marshal ['mɑːrʃl]	*v.* 整理，安排，排列(to arrange in good or effective order) 记 联想记忆：为行军(march)而作安排(marshal)
fitful ['fɪtfl]	*adj.* 间歇的，不规则的 记 联想记忆：fit(一阵) + ful(充满…的) → 一阵阵的 → 间歇的
relic ['relɪk]	*n.* 遗物，遗迹，遗风(a survivor or remnant left after decay, disintegration, or disappearance)
sear [sɪr]	*v.* 烧焦(to burn or scorch with intense heat)
vaporous ['veɪpərəs]	*adj.* 空想的(unsubstantial)；多蒸汽的 记 来自 vapor(*n.* 蒸汽)

□ suspicion	□ insanity	□ frigidity	□ pundit	□ sentinel	□ overthrow
□ dejected	□ mortification	□ marshal	□ fitful	□ relic	□ sear
□ vaporous					

411

comedienne [kəˌmiːdɪˈen]	*n.* 喜剧女演员（a woman who is a comedian）；滑稽人物 记 来自 comedy（*n.* 喜剧）
gorge [ɡɔːrdʒ]	*n.* 峡谷（a narrow steep-walled canyon or part of a canyon） 搭 the Rhine Gorge 莱茵峡谷
dalliance [ˈdælɪəns]	*n.* 虚度光阴；调情（an act of dallying） 记 来自 dally（*v.* 闲荡，嬉戏）
munch [mʌntʃ]	*v.* 用力咀嚼，出声咀嚼（to eat with a chewing action） 记 和 lunch（*n.* 午餐）一起记
luscious [ˈlʌʃəs]	*adj.* 美味的（delicious）；肉感的（voluptuous）
condole [kənˈdoʊl]	*v.* 同情，哀悼（to express sympathy; commiserate） 记 词根记忆：con（一起）+ dole（痛苦）→ 一起痛苦 → 哀悼
ignorant [ˈɪɡnərənt]	*adj.* 无知的，愚昧的（knowing little or nothing） 记 词根记忆：ig（不）+ nor（=gnor 知道）+ ant → 不知道的 → 无知的 搭 be ignorant of 对…无知
overflow [ˌoʊvərˈfloʊ]	*v.* 溢出（to flow over the edges）；充满（to be very full） 记 组合词：over（出）+ flow（流）→ 溢出
percolate [ˈpɜːrkəleɪt]	*v.* 过滤出（to cause to pass through a permeable substance）；渗透（to penetrate; seep） 记 词根记忆：per（贯穿）+ col（过滤）+ ate → 过滤出
emote [ɪˈmoʊt]	*v.* 激动地表达感情（to act in an emotional or theatrical manner） 记 词根记忆：e（出）+ mote（动）→ 感动地说出来 → 激动地表达感情
tramp [træmp]	*v.* 重步走（to walk, tread, or step heavily） 同 plod, stomp, tromp
lamentable [ləˈmentəbl]	*adj.* 令人惋惜的，悔恨的（expressing grief） 记 来自 lament（*n./v.* 悔恨；悲叹）
prelude [ˈpreljuːd]	*n.* 序幕，前奏（an introductory performance, action, or event） 记 词根记忆：pre（在…之前）+ lud（表演）+ e → 表演之前 → 序幕，前奏
excruciate [ɪkˈskruːʃieɪt]	*v.* 施酷刑；折磨（to subject to intense mental distress） 记 联想记忆：ex + cruci（看作 crude，残忍的）+ ate → 给人施酷刑是很残忍的 → 施酷刑
depressed [dɪˈprest]	*adj.* 消沉的（sad and without enthusiasm）；凹陷的（flattened downward） 记 来自 depress（*v.* 消沉，沮丧）
alleviate [əˈliːvieɪt]	*v.* 减轻，缓和（to lighten or relieve） 记 词根记忆：al（加强）+ lev（轻）+ iate（使…）→ 使…轻 → 减轻，缓和
contumacious [ˌkɑːntuˈmeɪʃəs]	*adj.* 违抗的，不服从的（unreasonably disobedient, esp. to an order made by a court） 记 词根记忆：con + tum（肿胀；骄傲）+ acious（…的）→ 坚持自己的骄傲，不受欺压 → 违抗的，不服从的

□ comedienne	□ gorge	□ dalliance	□ munch	□ luscious	□ condole
□ ignorant	□ overflow	□ percolate	□ emote	□ tramp	□ lamentable
□ prelude	□ excruciate	□ depressed	□ alleviate	□ contumacious	

frolic [ˈfrɑːlɪk]	*n.* 嬉戏(a lively party or game);雀跃(gaiety;fun) *v.* 嬉戏 例 The young lambs were *frolicing* in the field.
intrude [ɪnˈtruːd]	*v.* 把(思想等)强加于;闯入(to thrust or force in or upon someone or sth. especially without permission or fitness) 记 词根记忆:in(进入) + trud(推;刺) + e → 推进去 → 闯入
morsel [ˈmɔːrsl]	*n.* (食物的)一小口,一小块(a small bite or portion of food);小量,一点(a small piece or amount) 记 词根记忆:mors(咬) + el → 咬一口 → 一小口
verbal [ˈvɜːrbl]	*adj.* 口头的(spoken);言语的 记 词根记忆:verb(字,词)+al → 口头的,言语的 例 Many philosophers agree that the *verbal* aggression of profanity in certain radical newspapers is not trivial or childish, but an assault on decorum essential to the revolutionaries purpose.
glisten [ˈɡlɪsn]	*v.* 闪烁,闪耀(to shine or sparkle with reflected light) 记 来自 glist(*n.* 闪光);联想记忆:g + listen(听) → 因为善于倾听,所以智慧闪耀 → 闪烁,闪耀
tarry [ˈtæri]	*v.* 耽搁(to delay in starting or going;dawdle;linger) 同 dally, procrastinate, temporize
swipe [swaɪp]	*n.* 猛击(a sweeping blow or stroke) *v.* 猛击(to hit with a sweeping motion) 记 联想记忆:s+wipe(擦) → 起了摩擦后大打出手 → 猛击
cult [kʌlt]	*n.* 异教,教派(a system of religious beliefs and ritual);狂热的崇拜(worship) 记 联想记忆:culture(文化)去掉 ure → 没文化,搞崇拜 → 狂热的崇拜
oath [oʊθ]	*n.* 誓言(a formal promise to fulfill a pledge, especially one made in a court of law);咒骂,诅咒(swearword)
wean [wiːn]	*v.* (孩子)断奶;戒掉(to free from an unwholesome habit or interest) 搭 wean sb. off/from 逐渐戒除恶习(或避免依赖)
stooge [stuːdʒ]	*n.* 配角,陪衬(one who plays a subordinate or compliant role to a principal);傀儡(puppet)
blade [bleɪd]	*n.* 刀刃,刀口(the cutting part of a tool)
scutter [ˈskʌtər]	*v.* 疾走,急跑(to move in or as if in a brisk pace)
measly [ˈmiːzli]	*adj.* 患麻疹的;少得可怜的,微不足道的(contemptibly small;meager) 记 来自 measles(*n.* 麻疹)

39

□ frolic	□ intrude	□ morsel	□ verbal	□ glisten	□ tarry
□ swipe	□ cult	□ oath	□ wean	□ stooge	□ blade
□ scutter	□ measly				

skyrocket [ˈskaɪrɑːkɪt]	*v.* 突升，猛涨（to shoot up abruptly） 记 组合词：sky(天空) + rocket(火箭) → 火箭冲向天空，突然升高 → 突升
gratuity [grəˈtuːəti]	*n.* 赏钱，小费（sth. given voluntarily or beyond obligation usually for some service；tip） 记 词根记忆：grat(感激) + uity → 表示感激的小费 → 小费
forum [ˈfɔːrəm]	*n.* 辩论的场所，论坛（a public meeting place for open discussion） 记 词根记忆：for(门) + um → 门外 → 广场 → 论坛
demote [ˌdiːˈmoʊt]	*v.* 降级，降职（to reduce to a lower grade） 记 词根记忆：de + mote(动) → 动下去 → 降级
suborn [səˈbɔːrn]	*v.* 收买，贿赂（to induce secretly to do an unlawful thing） 记 词根记忆：sub(下面)+orn(装饰) → 在下面给人好处 → 贿赂
wroth [rɔːθ]	*adj.* 暴怒的，非常愤怒的（intensely angry） 搭 be wroth with 非常生气
countrified [ˈkʌntrifaɪd]	*adj.* 乡村的（rural）；粗俗的 记 词根记忆：countri(=country 乡下) + fied → 来自乡下的 → 乡村的
kangaroo [ˌkæŋgəˈruː]	*n.* 袋鼠 记 发音记忆："看加入" → 看着袋鼠宝宝进入妈妈的口袋 → 袋鼠
interjection [ˌɪntərˈdʒekʃn]	*n.* 插入语（sth. that is interjected）；感叹词（words used as an exclamation） 记 来自interject(*v.* 插入)
aerial [ˈeriəl]	*adj.* 空中的，空气的（of, relating to, or occurring in the air or atmosphere） 记 词根记忆：aer(空气) + ial(…的) → 空中的
croak [kroʊk]	*n.* 蛙鸣声（a croaking sound）*v.* 发牢骚，抱怨（to grumble） 记 联想记忆：童话故事里，披着斗篷(cloak)的一群青蛙发出一阵蛙鸣声(croak)
incubus [ˈɪŋkjʊbəs]	*n.* 梦魇（a nightmare）；沉重的负担（an oppressive burden） 记 词根记忆：in + cub(躺) + us → 躺在某物内 → 梦魇
abstemious [əbˈstiːmiəs]	*adj.* 有节制的，节俭的（moderate in eating and drinking; temperate） 记 词根记忆：abs(脱离) + tem(酒) + ious → 不喝酒 → 有节制的
charity [ˈtʃærəti]	*n.* 慈善（benevolence）；施舍（a voluntary giving of money） 记 联想记忆：cha(音似：茶) + rity → 请喝茶 → 施舍
peel [piːl]	*v.* 削去…的皮（to strip off an outer layer of）；剥落（to come off in sheets or scales, as bark, skin, or paint）*n.* 外皮
simonize [ˈsaɪmənaɪz]	*v.* 给…打蜡，把…擦亮（to polish with or as if with wax）
vertigo [ˈvɜːrtɪgoʊ]	*n.* 眩晕，晕头转向（a dizzy, confused state of mind） 记 词根记忆：vert(转)+igo → 眩晕，晕头转向
expatiate [ɪkˈspeɪʃieɪt]	*v.* 细说，详述（to speak or write in detail） 记 词根记忆：ex(出) + pat(走) + iate → 走出去 → 细说，详述

vertigo

□ skyrocket	□ gratuity	□ forum	□ demote	□ suborn	□ wroth
□ countrified	□ kangaroo	□ interjection	□ aerial	□ croak	□ incubus
□ abstemious	□ charity	□ peel	□ simonize	□ vertigo	□ expatiate

howler [ˈhaʊlər]	*n.* 嚎叫的人或动物；滑稽可笑的错误(a ludicrous blunder) 记 来自 howl(*v.* 嚎叫)
roundabout [ˈraʊndəbaʊt]	*adj.* 绕道的，迂回的(indirect; circuitous) 记 组合词：round(迂回地，围绕地) + about(各处，附近) → 迂回的
limnetic [lɪmˈnetɪk]	*adj.* 淡水的，湖泊的(of, relating to, or inhabiting the open water of a body of freshwater)
reversion [rɪˈvɜːrʒn]	*n.* 恢复，复原(an act of returning)；逆转(an act of turning the opposite way) 记 词根记忆：re(回) + vers(转) + ion → 转回去，返回 → 逆转
monsoon [ˌmɑːnˈsuːn]	*n.* 季风(a wind system that influences large climatic regions and reverses direction seasonally)；雨季
terminus [ˈtɜːrmɪnəs]	*n.* (火车、汽车的)终点站(terminal) 记 词根记忆：termin(结束)+us → 结束地 → 终点站
callow [ˈkæloʊ]	*adj.* (鸟)未生羽毛的(unfledged)；(人)未成熟的(immature) 记 联想记忆：call + (l)ow → 叫做低的东西 → 未成熟的
anthem [ˈænθəm]	*n.* 圣歌(a religious choral song)；赞美诗(a song of praise)；国歌 记 联想记忆：an + them → 一首他们一起唱的歌 → 圣歌
interlard [ˌɪntərˈlɑːrd]	*v.* 使混杂，混入(to vary by intermixture; intersperse) 同 interlace, intertwine
suffocate [ˈsʌfəkeɪt]	*v.* (使)窒息，把…闷死(to die from being unable to breathe) 记 词根记忆：suf + foc(喉咙) + ate → 在喉咙下面 → (使)窒息
bruit [bruːt]	*v.* 散布(谣言)(to spread a rumor) 记 联想记忆：br(看作 bring) + u(看作 you) + it → 把它带给你 → 散布(谣言)
implode [ɪmˈploʊd]	*v.* 内爆(to burst inward)；剧减(to undergo violent compression) 记 词根记忆：im(向内) + plod(打击；撞击) + e → 在内部横冲直撞 → 内爆
drenched [drentʃd]	*adj.* 湿透的(soaked or saturated in liquid)
boom [buːm]	*n.* 繁荣(prosperity) *v.* 发出隆隆声(to make a deep hollow sound) 记 联想记忆：原来是象声词："嘣"的一声
misrepresentation [ˌmɪsˌreprɪzenˈteɪʃn]	*n.* 误传，不实的陈述 记 联想记忆：mis(错的) + represent(表达) + ation → 错误的表达 → 误传
nimble [ˈnɪmbl]	*adj.* 敏捷的，灵活的(moving quickly and lightly) 记 联想记忆：偷窃(nim)需要手脚灵活(nimble)
peep [piːp]	*n./v.* 瞥见，偷看(to look cautiously or slyly)；初现(to show slightly) 记 联想记忆：偷看颠倒过来(peep → peep)还是偷看
settle [ˈsetl]	*v.* 安排(to place)；决定(to decide on)；栖息(to come to rest) 记 联想记忆：set(放置) + tle → 安放，放置 → 安排

39

□ howler	□ roundabout	□ limnetic	□ reversion	□ monsoon	□ terminus
□ callow	□ anthem	□ interlard	□ suffocate	□ bruit	□ implode
□ drenched	□ boom	□ misrepresentation	□ nimble	□ peep	□ settle

415

ballyhoo ['bælihuː]	*n.* 喧闹，呐喊（noisy shouting or uproar）*v.* 大肆宣传，大吹大擂（to publicize by sensational methods）
slice [slaɪs]	*n.* 薄片 *v.* 切成片（to cut into pieces）
calibrate ['kælɪbreɪt]	*v.* 量…口径（to determine the calibre of）；校准（to adjust precisely） 记 来自 calibre（*n.* 口径）
sunder ['sʌndər]	*v.* 分裂，分离（to separate by violence or by intervening time or space） 记 发音记忆："散的" → 分离
anonymity [ˌænə'nɪməti]	*n.* 无名，匿名（the quality or state of being anonymous） 记 词根记忆：an（没有）+ onym（名称）+ ity → 无名，匿名
proceeds ['proʊsiːdz]	*n.* 收入（the total amount brought in）；实收款项（the net amount received after deduction of any discount or charges）
arrant ['ærənt]	*adj.* 完全的，彻底的（thoroughgoing）；极坏的，臭名昭著的（being notoriously without moderation）
prehensile [prɪ'hensl]	*adj.* 能抓住东西的，缠绕的（capable of grasping or holding） 记 词根记忆：prehens（=prehend 抓住）+ ile（能…的）→ 能抓住东西的
rustle ['rʌsl]	*v.* 发出沙沙声（to make slight sounds like silk moving or being rubbed together） 记 联想记忆：可能来自 rush（*n.* 匆促）
orthodox ['ɔːrθədɑːks]	*adj.* 正统的（conforming to the usual beliefs of established doctrines） 记 词根记忆：ortho（正的，直的）+ dox（观点）→ 正统观点 → 正统的
belongings [bɪ'lɔːŋɪŋz]	*n.* 所有物，财产（possessions; property） 同 estate, holding
horticulture ['hɔːrtɪkʌltʃər]	*n.* 园艺学 记 词根记忆：horti（花园）+ cult（种植；培养）+ ure → 园艺学
scraggly ['skrægli]	*adj.* 凹凸不平的（irregular in form or growth）；散乱的（unkempt）
crusade [kruː'seɪd]	*n.* 为维护理想、原则而进行的运动或斗争（vigorous, concerted action for some cause or idea, or against some abuse） 记 词根记忆：crus（十字）+ ade → 十字军东征 → 为维护理想、原则而进行的运动或斗争
jolt [dʒoʊlt]	*v.* (使)颠簸（to cause jerky movements）*n.* 震动，摇晃（jerk） 记 联想记忆：防止颠簸（jolt）用门闩（bolt）固定
tweak [twiːk]	*v.* 扭，拧，揪（to pinch and pull with a sudden jerk and twist）；调节，微调（to make usually small adjustments in or to）
lore [lɔːr]	*n.* 知识（knowledge）；特定的知识或传说（a particular body of knowledge or tradition） 记 参考：folklore（*n.* 民间传说）

cartoon [kɑːrˈtuːn]	*n.* 漫画(amusing drawing that comments satirically on current events) 记 发音记忆："卡通" → 漫画
plank [plæŋk]	*n.* 厚木板(a heavy thick board);要点(a principal item of a policy or program) *v.* 铺板(to cover, build, or floor with planks)
rehearse [rɪˈhɜːrs]	*v.* 排练,预演(to practice in order to prepare for a public performance);详述(to tell fully)
forgery [ˈfɔːrdʒəri]	*n.* 伪造(物)(something forged) 记 来自 forge(v. 伪造)
ashen [ˈæʃn]	*adj.* 灰色的,苍白的(resembling ashes(as in color), especially deadly pale)
brattish [ˈbrætɪʃ]	*adj.*(指小孩)讨厌的,被宠坏的,无礼的((of a child) ill-mannered; annoying) 记 联想记忆:brat(小孩)+ tish → 小孩有时候有点讨厌 → 讨厌的
ardent [ˈɑːrdnt]	*adj.* 热心的,热烈的(intensely enthusiastic or devoted; passionate) 记 词根记忆:ard(热)+ ent → 热心的,热烈的
flutter [ˈflʌtər]	*v.* 拍翅((of the wings) to move lightly and quickly) 同 flap
nasal [ˈneɪzl]	*adj.* 鼻的(pertaining to the nose);有鼻音的 记 词根记忆:nas(鼻)+ al → 鼻的
ravening [ˈrævənɪŋ]	*adj.* 狼吞虎咽的(to devour greedily);贪婪的 同 rapacious
equable [ˈekwəbl]	*adj.* 稳定的,不变的(not varying or fluctuating; steady);(脾气)温和的(tranquil; serene) 记 词根记忆:equ(平等)+ able → 能够平等的 → 稳定的
coagulation [kouˌægjuˈleɪʃn]	*n.* 凝结 记 来自 coagulate(v. 使凝结)
heave [hiːv]	*v.* 用力举(to raise or lift with an effort) 记 联想记忆:heaven(天堂)去掉 n → 想把天堂举起,却掉了个 n → 用力举
perishing [ˈperɪʃɪŋ]	*adj.* 严寒的(very cold)
spew [spjuː]	*v.* 呕吐(to vomit);大量喷出(to come forth in a flood or gush)
narcissism [ˈnɑːrsɪsɪzəm]	*n.* 自恋,自爱(inordinate fascination with oneself) 记 来自 Narcissus,希腊神话中的美少年,因过于爱恋自己水中的影子而溺水身亡,化为水仙花(narcissus)
chaffing [ˈtʃæfɪŋ]	*adj.* 玩笑的,嘲弄的(of, relating to jest, banter) 记 来自 chaff(v. 开玩笑)

39

illiberal	*adj.* 偏执的，思想狭隘的(intolerant; bigoted)
[ɪˈlɪbərəl]	记 联想记忆：il(不) + liberal(开明的) → 不开明的 → 偏执的
sour	*adj.* 酸的(having the acid taste or smell of or as if of fermentation)
[ˈsaʊər]	记 发音记忆："馊啊" → 酸的
blather	*v.* 喋喋不休胡说，唠叨(to talk foolishly at length)
[ˈblæðər]	同 babble, blether, blither, smatter
refectory	*n.* (学院等的)餐厅，食堂(a large room in a school or college in which meals are served)
[rɪˈfektri]	记 来自 refection(*n.* 食品，小吃)
peruse	*v.* 细读，精读(to read sth. in a careful way)
[pəˈruːz]	记 词根记忆：per(始终) + us(用) + e → 反复用 → 细读，精读
seafaring	*adj.* 航海的，跟航海有关的(of or relating to the use of the sea for travel or transportation)
[ˈsiːferɪŋ]	记 来自 seafarer(*n.* 水手，海员)；sea(海) + fare(过日子) + (e)r(人) → 靠海生活的人 → 水手，海员
civilian	*n.* 百姓，平民(any person not an active member of the armed forces or police)
[səˈvɪliən]	记 词根记忆：civil(市民的) + ian → 百姓，平民
daft	*adj.* 傻的，愚蠢的(silly; foolish)
[dæft]	
prank	*n.* 恶作剧，玩笑(a trick)
[præŋk]	记 注意不要和 plank(*n.* 厚木板)相混
hearsay	*n.* 谣传，道听途说(rumor; gossip)
[ˈhɪrseɪ]	记 组合词：hear(听到) + say(说) → 道听途说
observance	*n.* (对法律、习俗等的)遵守，奉行
[əbˈzɜːrvəns]	记 词根记忆：ob(加强) + serv(保持) + ance → 遵守
collate	*v.* 对照，核对(to compare critically in order to consolidate)
[kəˈleɪt]	记 词根记忆：col(共同) + late(放) → 放到一起 → 核对
quirk	*n.* 奇事(accident; vagary)；怪癖(a strange habit)
[kwɜːrk]	例 An obvious style, easily identified by some superficial *quirk*, is properly decried as a mere mannerism, whereas a complex and subtle style resists reduction to a formula.
ballot	*n./v.* 投票
[ˈbælət]	记 联想记忆：ball(球) + (l)ot(签) → 用球抽签 → 投票
scissor	*n.* 剪刀
[ˈsɪzər]	记 词根记忆：sciss(切) + or → 切开时所借助的工具 → 剪刀
incorrigibility	*n.* 无可救药(incapability of being corrected or amended)
[ɪnˌkɔrɪdʒəˈbɪləti]	记 词根记忆：in(不) + cor(=com 一起) + rig(直的) + ibility → 无法一起拉直 → 无可救药

redoubtable	*adj.* 令人敬畏的，可怕的（causing fear or alarm; formidable）
[rɪˈdaʊtəbl]	记 联想记忆：re(反复) + doubt(怀疑，疑虑) + able → 行动时产生疑虑，说明对手是可怕的，可敬畏的 → 令人敬畏的，可怕的
ennui	*n.* 倦怠（weariness of mind）；无聊 *v.* 使无聊
[ɑːnˈwiː]	同 boredom
impregnable	*adj.* 固若金汤的，无法攻破的（not capable of being captured or entered by force）
[ɪmˈpregnəbl]	记 词根记忆：im(不) + pregn(拿住) + able(能…的) → 拿不住的 → 无法攻破的
junction	*n.* 交叉路口（an intersection of roads）；连接（an act of joining）
[ˈdʒʌŋkʃn]	记 词根记忆：junct(连接) + ion → 连接；交叉路口
mast	*n.* 船桅，桅杆（a vertical spar for supporting sails）
[mæst]	记 联想记忆：与 mat(*n.* 垫子)一起记
jarring	*adj.* 声音刺耳的（of sounds that have a harsh or an unpleasant effect）
[ˈdʒɑːrɪŋ]	记 来自 jar(*v.* 发出刺耳声)
foppish	*adj.* (似)纨绔子弟的（of or like a fop）；浮华的，俗丽的
[ˈfɑːpɪʃ]	记 来自 fop(*n.* 纨绔子弟)
construct	*v.* 建造，构造（to build sth.）
[kənˈstrʌkt]	记 词根记忆：con(加强) + struct(建立) → 建造，构造
yowl	*v.* 嚎叫，恸哭（to utter a loud long cry of grief, pain, or distress）
[jaʊl]	同 howl, wail
alter	*v.* 改变，更改（to change）
[ˈɔːltər]	记 altor 本身就是词根，意为"改变"
ample	*adj.* 富足的（abundant）；充足的（enough; adequate）
[ˈæmpl]	记 联想记忆：apple(苹果)很 ample(充足)
precocious	*adj.* 早熟的（premature）
[prɪˈkoʊʃəs]	记 词根记忆：pre(预先) + coc(煮) + ious → 提前煮好的 → 早熟的
plenary	*adj.* 全体出席的；完全的，绝对的，无限的
[ˈpliːnəri]	记 词根记忆：plen(满) + ary → 满的 → 完全的
denude	*v.* 脱去（to make bare or naked）；剥蚀（to lay bare by erosion）；剥夺（to deprive of sth. important）
[dɪˈnuːd]	记 词根记忆：de + nude(赤裸的) → 完全赤裸 → 脱去
empirical	*adj.* 经验的，实证的（based on observation or experience）
[ɪmˈpɪrɪkl]	记 来自 empiric(*n.* 经济主义者)
flatulent	*adj.* 自负的，浮夸的（pompously overblow; bloated）
[ˈflætʃələnt]	记 词根记忆：fla(吹) + tul + ent → 吹嘘的 → 自负的
aver	*v.* 极力声明；断言；证实（to state positively; affirm）
[əˈvɜːr]	记 词根记忆：a(向) + ver(真实的) → 向人们说出真相 → 证实

alter

39

□ redoubtable	□ ennui	□ impregnable	□ junction	□ mast	□ jarring
□ foppish	□ construct	□ yowl	□ alter	□ ample	□ precocious
□ plenary	□ denude	□ empirical	□ flatulent	□ aver	

convoke [kən'voʊk]	*v.* 召集；召开(会议)(to summon to assemble; convene) 记 词根记忆：con(一起) + vok(喊) + e → 喊到一起 → 召集
loosen ['luːsn]	*v.* 变松，松开(to become less firmed or fixed) 记 来自 loose(*adj.* 宽松的)
plead [pliːd]	*v.* 辩护(to offer as a plea in defense)；恳求(to appeal) 记 来自 plea(*n.* 恳求；辩护) 例 In their preface, the collection's editors *plead* that certain of the important articles they omitted were published too recently for inclusion, but in the case of many such articles, this excuse is not valid.
lethargy ['leθərdʒi]	*n.* 昏睡(abnormal drowsiness)；呆滞，懒散(the state of being lazy, sluggish) 记 词根记忆：leth(死) + a(不) + rg(=erg 工作) + y → 像死了一样不动的状态 → 昏睡
abscond [əb'skɑːnd]	*v.* 潜逃，逃亡(to run away and hide in order to escape the law) 记 词根记忆：abs(脱离) + cond(藏起来) → 潜逃

Trouble is only opportunity in work clothes.
困难只是穿上工作服的机遇。

——美国实业家 凯泽(H.J. Kaiser, American businessman)

jingoism [ˈdʒɪŋgoʊɪzəm]	*n.* 沙文主义，侵略主义（extreme chauvinism or nationalism marked especially by a belligerent foreign policy） 记 来自 jingo（ *n.* 沙文主义者）
indignity [ɪnˈdɪgnəti]	*n.* 侮辱，轻蔑（insult）；侮辱性的行为（an act that offends against a person's dignity or self-respect） 记 联想记忆：in(不) + dignity(高贵) → 不高贵的行为 → 侮辱性的行为
threadbare [ˈθredber]	*adj.* 磨破的（worn off; shabby）；陈腐的（exhausted of interest or freshness） 记 组合词：thread(线) + bare(露出) → 露出线头 → 磨破的
prey [preɪ]	*n.* 被捕食的动物（an animal taken by a predator as food）；受害者 记 联想记忆：心中暗自祈祷（pray）不要成为受害者（prey） 例 The natural balance between *prey* and predator has been increasingly disturbed, most frequently by human intervention.
destructible [dɪˈstrʌktəbl]	*adj.* 可破坏的（capable of being destroyed） 记 词根记忆：de(坏) + struct(建立) + ible → 把建造的东西弄坏 → 可破坏的
grouch [graʊtʃ]	*n.* 牢骚，不满（a complaint）；好抱怨的人 同 grudge, grumble
verdure [ˈvɜːrdjər]	*n.* 葱郁，青翠（the greenness of growing vegetation）；生机勃勃（a condition of health and vigor）
goad [goʊd]	*n.* 赶牛棒；刺激，激励（any driving impulse; spur）*v.* 刺激，激励 搭 goad sb. toward a goal 激励某人走向目标
hallowed [ˈhæloʊd]	*adj.* 神圣的（holy） 记 来自 hallow（ *vt.* 使神圣，把…视作神圣） 搭 to be buried in hallowed ground 被安葬在神圣的土地上
retiring [rɪˈtaɪərɪŋ]	*adj.* 过隐居生活的，不善社交的（reserved; shy） 记 来自 retire（ *v.* 退休；隐居）；re(后) + tir(拉) + e → 向后拉 → 隐居 例 Although *retiring*, almost self-effacing in his private life, he displays in his plays and essays a strong penchant for publicity and controversy.

□ jingoism	□ indignity	□ threadbare	□ prey	□ destructible	□ grouch
□ verdure	□ goad	□ hallowed	□ retiring		

421

plebeian [pləˈbiːən]	*n.* 平民 *adj.* 平民的(of the common people)；平庸的，粗俗的(common or vulgar) 搭 plebeian tastes 庸俗的趣味
unison [ˈjuːnɪsn]	*n.* 齐奏，齐唱；一致，协调(a harmonious agreement or union; complete accord)
constellation [ˌkɑːnstəˈleɪʃn]	*n.* 星座；星群(an arbitrary configuration of stars) 记 词根记忆：con(一起) + stell(星星) + ation → 星星在一起 → 星群
putrefy [ˈpjuːtrɪfaɪ]	*v.* 使腐烂(to make putrid) 记 词根记忆：putr(腐烂的) + efy → 使腐烂；注意不要和 petrify(*v.* 石化)相混
eaglet [ˈiːglət]	*n.* 小鹰(a young eagle) 记 来自 eagle(*n.* 鹰)
refute [rɪˈfjuːt]	*v.* 反驳，驳斥(to prove wrong by argument or evidence; disprove) 记 词根记忆：re(向后) + fut(倾泻) + e → (观点等)向后倒 → 反驳，驳斥
eugenic [juːˈdʒenɪk]	*adj.* 优生(学)的(relating to, or improved by eugenics) 记 词根记忆：eu(优，好) + gen(产生) + ic → 优生的
tame [teɪm]	*adj.* 驯服的(submissive; docile)；沉闷的，平淡的(unexciting and uninteresting) 同 domesticated
sloven [ˈslʌvən]	*n.* 不修边幅的人(one habitually negligent of neatness or cleanliness)
soil [sɔɪl]	*v.* 弄脏，污辱(to become dirty) 记 soil 更广为人知的意思是"土壤"
pusillanimous [ˌpjuːsɪˈlænɪməs]	*adj.* 胆小的(lacking courage; cowardly) 记 词根记忆：pusill(虚弱的) + anim(生命，精神) + ous → 胆小的
combat [ˈkɑːmbæt]	*n./v.* 搏斗，战斗((to) fight between two people, armies) 记 词根记忆：com(共同) + bat(打，击) → 共同打 → 战斗
hasten [ˈheɪsn]	*v.* 加速，加快，促进(to speed up; accelerate) 同 hurry, quicken
confiscate [ˈkɑːnfɪskeɪt]	*v.* 没收；充公(to seize private property for the public treasury) 记 词根记忆：con(共同) + fisc(钱财) + ate → 钱财归大家 → 充公
dodge [dɑːdʒ]	*v.* 闪开，躲避(to shift suddenly to avoid a blow) 记 联想记忆：do + dge(看作 edge，边缘) → 在边上躲避 → 躲避
salutation [ˌsæljuˈteɪʃn]	*n.* 招呼，致意，致敬(expression of greeting by words or action) 同 salute, welcome
misgiving [ˌmɪsˈgɪvɪŋ]	*n.* 疑虑(doubt, distrust, or suspicion) 记 联想记忆：mis(错的) + giving(给) → 给出错误的解释 → 疑虑
saunter [ˈsɔːntər]	*n./v.* 闲逛，漫步(to walk about idly; stroll) 记 联想记忆：s(看作 see) + aunt(姑姑) + er → 看姑姑去 → 闲逛而去 → 闲逛，漫步

begrudge [bɪˈɡrʌdʒ]	*v.* 吝啬，勉强给（to give with ill-will or reluctance） 记 联想记忆：be + grudge（吝啬）→ 吝啬
inscribe [ɪnˈskraɪb]	*v.*（在某物上）写、题写（to write words on sth. as a formal or permanent record） 记 词根记忆：in（进入）+ scrib（写）+ e → 刻写进去 → 题写
marvel [ˈmɑːrvl]	*v.* 对…感到惊异（to be very surprised）*n.* 奇迹（one that is wonderful or miraculous） 记 联想记忆：mar（毁坏）+ vel（音似：well 好）→ 遭到毁坏再重建好，真是奇迹 → 奇迹
draconian [drəˈkoʊniən]	*adj.* 严厉的，严酷的（extremely severe） 记 来自 Draco（德拉古），Draco 是雅典政治家，制定了雅典的法典，该法典因其公平受到赞扬，但因其严酷而不受欢迎
fusty [ˈfʌsti]	*adj.* 霉臭的（smelling of mildew or decay）；陈腐的，过时的（old-fashioned；musty） 搭 a dark fusty room 阴暗霉湿的房间
skittish [ˈskɪtɪʃ]	*adj.* 轻浮的，活泼的（capricious；frivolous；not serious） 搭 skittish financial market 变幻莫测的金融市场
tatty [ˈtæti]	*adj.* 破旧的，褴褛的；破败的（shabby or dilapidated） 同 decrepit, deteriorated, ragged, shabby
chasten [ˈtʃeɪsn]	*v.*（通过惩罚而使坏习惯等）改正（to punish in order to correct or make better）；磨炼 记 联想记忆：chaste（纯洁的）+ n → 变纯洁 → 改正
full-blown [ˌfʊlˈbloʊn]	*adj.* 成熟的；（花）盛开的；全面的，完善的 记 组合词：full（完全的）+ blown（开花的）→ 盛开的
tractability [ˌtræktəˈbɪləti]	*n.* 温顺 记 来自 tractable（*adj.* 易处理的；易驾驭的）
clairvoyance [klerˈvɔɪəns]	*n.* 超人的洞察力（keen perception or insight） 记 联想记忆：clair（看作 clear，清楚）+ voy（看）+ ance → 看得很清楚 → 超人的洞察力
ocular [ˈɑːkjələr]	*adj.* 眼睛的（of the eye）；视觉的（based on what has been seen） 记 词根记忆：ocul（眼）+ ar → 眼睛的
truant [ˈtruːənt]	*adj.* 逃避责任的（shirking responsibility）*n.* 逃学者（one who is absent without permission, especially from school）；逃避者，玩忽职守者（one who shirks duty）
rhubarb [ˈruːbɑːrb]	*n.*【植物】大黄；热烈的讨论，激烈的争论（a heated dispute or controversy）
depraved [dɪˈpreɪvd]	*adj.* 堕落的，腐化的（morally bad；corrupt） 记 来自 deprave（*v.* 使堕落）
glitter [ˈɡlɪtər]	*v.* 闪烁，闪耀（to shine brightly）*n.* 灿烂的光华（sparkling light）；诱惑力，魅力（attractiveness） 同 flash

40

shield [ʃiːld]	*n.* 盾 *v.* 掩护，保护（to protect from harm） 同 defend
remainder [rɪˈmeɪndər]	*n.* 剩余物（the part of sth. that is left over） 记 来自 remain（*v.* 保留） 例 Because we have completed our analysis of the major components of the proposed project, we are free to devote the *remainder* of this session to a study of the project's incidental details.
husbandry [ˈhʌzbəndri]	*n.*（广义上的）农业（the cultivation or production of plants or animals） 记 联想记忆：husband（丈夫）+ ry → 丈夫所干的活 → 农业
animation [ˌænɪˈmeɪʃn]	*n.* 兴奋，活跃 同 brio, invigoration, spiritedness, vivification
cull [kʌl]	*v.* 挑选，精选（to select from a group）*n.* 剔除的东西（sth. rejected especially as being inferior or worthless）
lexicon [ˈleksɪkən]	*n.* 词典（a dictionary, especially of an ancient language） 记 词根记忆：lex（词汇）+ icon → 词典
exigent [ˈeksɪdʒənt]	*adj.* 迫切的，紧急的（requiring immediate action） 记 词根记忆：ex（出）+ ig（赶）+ ent → 赶到外面 → 迫切的
fumble [ˈfʌmbl]	*v.* 摸索，笨拙地搜寻（to search by feeling about awkwardly；grope clumsily）；弄乱，搞糟
glimmer [ˈɡlɪmər]	*v.* 发微光（to give faint, flickering light）*n.* 摇曳的微光 记 联想记忆：glim（*n.* 灯，灯光）+ mer → 灯光摇曳 → 发微光
granule [ˈɡrænjuːl]	*n.* 小粒，微粒（a small grain） 记 词根记忆：gran（=grain 颗粒）+ ule → 小粒，微粒 同 particle
clench [klentʃ]	*v.* 握紧（to grip tightly）；咬紧（牙关等）（to close the teeth firmly） 同 clasp, clutch, grab, grapple, grasp, seize
sliver [ˈslɪvər]	*n.* 薄长条（a long slender piece）*v.* 裂成细片（to cut into sliver） 记 注意不要和 silver（*n.* 银）相混
distain [dɪsˈteɪn]	*v.* 贬损，伤害名誉（to dispraise；derogate） 记 词根记忆：dis（不）+ tain（拿住）→ 不再拿住好好珍惜 → 贬损，伤害名誉
domesticate [dəˈmestɪkeɪt]	*v.* 驯养，驯化（to tame wild animals and breed for human use） 记 来自 domestic（*adj.* 家庭的）
defraud [dɪˈfrɔːd]	*v.* 欺骗，诈骗（to cheat） 记 词根记忆：de（变坏）+ fraud（欺骗）→ 欺骗，诈骗
harbinger [ˈhɑːrbɪndʒər]	*n.* 先驱，先兆（herald） 同 forerunner, precursor
numinous [ˈnuːmɪnəs]	*adj.* 超自然的，神的（supernatural；divine） 记 联想记忆：numin（看作 numen，守护神）+ ous → 守护神的 → 神的

manure [məˈnʊr]	*n.* 粪肥(waste matter from animals) *v.* 给…施肥(to put manure on) 记 词根记忆:man(手) + ure → 用手施肥 → 给…施肥
suckle [ˈsʌkl]	*v.* 给…哺乳;吮吸 搭 a cow suckling her calves 给小牛吃奶的母牛
cajole [kəˈdʒoʊl]	*v.* (以甜言蜜语)哄骗(to coax with flattery; wheedle) 记 联想记忆:caj(=cage 笼子) + ole → 把(鸟)诱入笼子 → 哄骗
coy [kɔɪ]	*adj.* 腼腆的,忸怩作态的(shy; shrinking from contact with others) 记 和 boy 及 toy 一起记; a coy boy plays toys(害羞男孩玩玩具)
cosmos [ˈkɑːzmoʊs]	*n.* 宇宙(the universe considered as a harmonious and orderly system) 记 词根记忆:cosm(宇宙) + os → 宇宙
gravel [ˈɡrævl]	*n.* 碎石,砂砾(a loose mixture of pebbles and rock fragments) 记 联想记忆:和 gavel(*n.* 小木槌)一起记; 词根记忆:grav(重) + el → 堆在一起很重的东西 → 碎石
weird [wɪrd]	*adj.* 古怪的,怪诞的,离奇的(odd; fantastic) 记 联想记忆:we(我们) + ird(看作 bird,鸟) → 如果我们都变成鸟该多怪异 → 古怪的,怪诞的
emanate [ˈeməneɪt]	*v.* 散发,发出;发源(to come out from a source) 记 词根记忆:e(出) + man(手) + ate → 用手发出(指令) → 发出
braise [breɪz]	*v.* 炖,蒸(to cook slowly in fat and little moisture in a closed pot)
interdisciplinary [ˌɪntərˈdɪsəplɪneri]	*adj.* 跨学科的(covering more than one area of study) 记 联想记忆:inter(在…中间) + disciplinary(学科的) → 跨学科的 搭 interdisciplinary course 跨学科课程
stuffy [ˈstʌfi]	*adj.* 通风不好的,闷热的(oppressive to the breathing) 记 联想记忆:stuff(填满) + y → 填满的 → 通风不好的
jubilation [ˌdʒuːbɪˈleɪʃn]	*n.* 欢腾,欢庆(great joy) 记 词根记忆:jubil(大叫) + ation → 高兴得大叫 → 欢腾,欢庆
niggle [ˈnɪɡl]	*v.* 拘泥小节(to spend too much effort on minor details);小气地给(to give stingily or in tiny portions)
declaim [dɪˈkleɪm]	*v.* 高谈阔论(to speak in a pompous way) 记 词根记忆:de(向下) + claim(喊) → 向下喊 → 高谈阔论
opaque [oʊˈpeɪk]	*adj.* 不透明的(not transparent);难懂的(hard to understand; obscure) 记 联想记忆:opa(cus)(蔽光的) + que → 不透明的
motto [ˈmɑːtoʊ]	*n.* 座右铭,格言,箴言(a maxim) 同 adage, proverb, saying
mariner [ˈmærɪnər]	*n.* 水手,海员(sailor; seaman) 记 词根记忆:mar(海) + in + er(表人) → 海员
hauteur [hɔːˈtɜːr]	*n.* 傲慢(haughtiness; snobbery) 记 来自 haut(*adj.* 高级的;上流社会的)

40

□ manure	□ suckle	□ cajole	□ coy	□ cosmos	□ gravel
□ weird	□ emanate	□ braise	□ interdisciplinary	□ stuffy	□ jubilation
□ niggle	□ declaim	□ opaque	□ motto	□ mariner	□ hauteur

versant [ˈvɜːrsənt]	*adj.* 精通的（conversant） *n.* 山坡（the slope of a side of a mountain or mountain range）；斜坡（the general slope of a region）
tattle [ˈtætl]	*v.* 闲聊（to chatter）；泄露秘密（to tell secrets） 同 leak, snitch, spill, squeal
aversion [əˈvɜːrʒn]	*n.* 厌恶，反感（an intense dislike; loathing） 搭 aversion toward sb./sth. 对…的厌恶
adroit [əˈdrɔɪt]	*adj.* 熟练的，灵巧的（skillful; expert; dexterous） 记 词根记忆：a(…的) + droit(灵巧) → 灵巧的
havoc [ˈhævək]	*n.* 大破坏，混乱（great destruction and devastation） 记 联想记忆：hav(看作 have, 有) + oc(看作 occur, 发生) → 有事发生 → 混乱
fulminate [ˈfʊlmɪneɪt]	*v.* 猛烈抨击，严厉谴责（to shout forth denunciations） 记 词根记忆：fulmin(闪电，雷声) + ate → 像雷电一样 → 严厉谴责
twinge [twɪndʒ]	*n.* （生理、心理上的）剧痛（a sharp, sudden physical pain; a moral or emotional pang） 记 联想记忆：twin(双胞胎)+ge → 据说双胞胎有心理感应，能感知对方的疼痛 →（生理、心理上的）剧痛
villainous [ˈvɪlənəs]	*adj.* 邪恶的，恶毒的（having the character of a villain） 记 来自 villain(*n.* 恶棍)
rotate [ˈroʊteɪt]	*v.* （使）旋转，（使）转动（to turn round a fixed point or axis）；轮流，循环 记 词根记忆：rot(旋转) + ate(使…) → （使）旋转，（使）转动
pagan [ˈpeɪɡən]	*n.* 没有宗教信仰的人（a person who has little or no religion）；异教徒 同 heathen
subvention [səbˈvenʃn]	*n.* 补助金，津贴（the provision of assistance or financial support） 记 词根记忆：sub(下面) + vent(来) + ion → 来到下面作为帮助 → 补助金
redress [rɪˈdres]	*n.* 矫正，修正（correction; remedy） 记 联想记忆：re(重新) + dress(穿衣；整理) → 重新整理 → 矫正，修正
tambourine [ˌtæmbəˈriːn]	*n.* 铃鼓，小手鼓（a small drum played by shaking or striking with the hand） 记 来自 tambour(*n.* 鼓)
poohed [puːd]	*adj.* 疲倦的（worn; tired）
chortle [ˈtʃɔːrtl]	*v.* 开心地笑，咯咯地笑（to utter with a gleeful chuckling sound） *n.* 得意的笑 记 各种笑：chuckle(*v./n.* 轻声笑)；giggle(*v./n.* 咯咯笑)；grin(*v./n.* 咧嘴笑)；guffaw(*v./n.* 哄笑)；simper(*v./n.* 傻笑)；smirk(*v./n.* 假笑)
bucolic [bjuːˈkɑːlɪk]	*adj.* 乡村的（of country life; rural）；牧羊的（pastoral） 记 词根记忆：buc(牛) + olic(养…的) → 养牛的 → 乡村的 搭 bucolic serenity 乡村的宁静
ravishing [ˈrævɪʃɪŋ]	*adj.* 令人陶醉的（unusually attractive or striking） 记 来自 ravish(*v.* 使着迷)

426

□ versant	□ tattle	□ aversion	□ adroit	□ havoc	□ fulminate
□ twinge	□ villainous	□ rotate	□ pagan	□ subvention	□ redress
□ tambourine	□ poohed	□ chortle	□ bucolic	□ ravishing	

mettle [ˈmetl]	*n.* 勇气，斗志（courage and fortitude）
obsession [əbˈseʃn]	*n.* 入迷，着迷（excessive preoccupation with an often unreasonable idea or feeling）；固执的念头（a persistent idea, desire or emotion） 记 来自 obsess（*v.* 迷住）
lambaste [læmˈbeɪst]	*v.* 痛打（to beat soundly）；痛骂（to scold or denounce severely） 记 组合词：lam（鞭打）+ baste（棒打）→ 痛打
detonation [ˌdetəˈneɪʃn]	*n.* 爆炸，爆炸声（explosion） 记 来自 detonate（*v.* 引爆）
centripetal [senˈtrɪpɪtl]	*adj.* 向心的（moving or tending to move toward a center） 记 词根记忆：centri（中心）+ pet（追求）+ al → 追求中心 → 向心的
inveterate [ɪnˈvetərət]	*adj.* 积习已深的，根深蒂固的（habitual; chronic） 记 词根记忆：in（进入）+ vet（老的）+ erate → 长时间占据于内的 → 积习已深的
moan [moʊn]	*n.* 呻吟（a low prolonged sound of pain or of grief）；抱怨（a complaint） *v.* 呻吟；抱怨（to complain）
obedient [əˈbiːdiənt]	*adj.* 服从的，顺从的（submissive; docile） 记 来自 obey（*v.* 服从）
coup [kuː]	*n.* 妙计，成功之举（surprising and successful action） 记 发音记忆："酷" → 一夜暴富得挺酷 → 成功之举
licentious [laɪˈsenʃəs]	*adj.* 放荡的，纵欲的（lascivious）；放肆的（marked by disregard for strict rules of correctness） 记 词根记忆：lic（允许）+ ent + ious → 过度允许的 → 纵欲的
rind [raɪnd]	*n.* （瓜、果等的）外皮（hard or tough outer layer） 记 和 find（*v.* 找到）一起记
dillydally [ˈdɪlidæli]	*v.* 磨蹭，浪费时间（to waste time by loitering or delaying）
logistics [ləˈdʒɪstɪks]	*n.* 后勤学，后勤（the management of the details of an operation） 记 词根记忆：log（树阴，遮蔽处）+ istics → 提供庇护 → 后勤
stiff [stɪf]	*adj.* 僵硬的，呆板的，严厉的（not easily bent or changed in shape） 记 联想记忆：still（静止的）的 ll 变为 ff 就成僵硬的（stiff）
astrology [əˈstrɑːlədʒi]	*n.* 占星术，占星学（primitive astronomy） 记 词根记忆：astro（星）+ (o)logy（学）→ 占星学
interrogative [ˌɪntəˈrɑːɡətɪv]	*adj.* 疑问的（having the form or force of a question）；质疑的 搭 an interrogative gesture 疑问的手势
pester [ˈpestər]	*v.* 纠缠，烦扰（to harass with petty irritations） 记 联想记忆：pest（害虫）+ er → 像害虫一样骚扰 → 纠缠

40

□ mettle	□ obsession	■ lambaste	□ detonation	□ centripetal	□ inveterate
□ moan	□ obedient	□ coup	■ licentious	□ rind	□ dillydally
□ logistics	□ stiff	□ astrology	■ interrogative	□ pester	

pound [paʊnd]	v. 猛击，连续重击 (to strike heavily or repeatedly); (心脏)狂跳，怦怦地跳 (to pulsate rapidly and heavily)
scuff [skʌf]	v. 拖着脚走 (to scrape the feet while walking; shuffle) 同 scuffle, shamble
unaffected [ˌʌnəˈfektɪd]	adj. 自然的，不矫揉造作的 (free from affectation; genuine) 记 联想记忆：un(不) + affected(做作的) → 自然的，不矫揉造作的
remission [rɪˈmɪʃn]	n. 宽恕，豁免 (the act or process of remitting) 记 词根记忆：re(向后) + miss(送) + ion → 送回去，宽恕
consensus [kənˈsensəs]	n. 意见一致 (agreement in opinion) 记 词根记忆：con(共同) + sens(感觉) + us → 感觉相同 → 意见一致 搭 develop a consensus on 在…上达成一致
tremendous [trəˈmendəs]	adj. 恐慌的，可怕的 (being such as may excite trembling or arouse dread); 巨大的，惊人的 (notable by extreme power, greatness or excellence) 记 来自 tremble(v. 颤抖) 例 As an outstanding publisher, Alfred Knopf was able to make occasional mistakes, but his bad judgment was tolerated in view of his *tremendous* success.
heresy [ˈherəsi]	n. 异端邪说 (a religious belief opposed to the orthodox doctrines) 记 联想记忆：here(这里) + sy(看作 say, 说) → 非熟悉的本地人所说的 → 异端邪说
minnow [ˈmɪnoʊ]	n. 鲤科，小鱼 记 注意不要和 winnow(v. 簸；筛选)相混
unilateral [ˌjuːnɪˈlætrəl]	adj. 单方面的 (one sided; affecting only one side) 搭 unilateral nuclear disarmament 单方面裁减核武器
pry [praɪ]	v. 刺探 (to make inquiry curiously); 撬开 (to pull apart with a lever) n. 撬杠，杠杆 同 leverage
cunning [ˈkʌnɪŋ]	adj. 狡猾的，奸诈的 (clever at deceiving people); 灵巧的，精巧的 (ingenious) n. 狡猾，奸诈 (cunning behavior or quality)
wry [raɪ]	adj. 扭曲的，歪曲的 (twisted or bent to one side); 嘲弄的，讽刺的 (cleverly and often ironically or grimly humorous)
parry [ˈpæri]	v. 挡开，避开 (武器、问题等)(to ward off; evade) 搭 parry a question 回避问题
frothy [ˈfrɔːθi]	adj. 起泡的 (foamy); 空洞的 (frivolous in character and content) 搭 frothy coffee 泡沫咖啡
jealousy [ˈdʒeləsi]	n. 嫉妒 (the state of being jealous) 记 来自 jealous(adj. 嫉妒的)
cadet [kəˈdet]	n. 军校或警官学校的学生 (a student at a military school) 搭 army cadets 军校学员

428

□ pound □ scuff □ unaffected □ remission □ consensus □ tremendous
□ heresy □ minnow □ unilateral □ pry □ cunning □ wry
□ parry □ frothy □ jealousy □ cadet

reminder	*n.* 提醒物，纪念品(sth. that makes one remember)
[rɪˈmaɪndər]	记 来自动词 remind(*v.* 提醒)；注意不要与 remainder(*n.* 剩余物)相混
	例 Charlotte Salomon's biography is a *reminder* that the currents of private life, however diverted, dislodged, or twisted by overpowering public events, retain their hold on the individual recording them.
sangfroid	*n.* 沉着，冷静(cool self-possession or composure)
[sɑːŋˈfrwɑː]	记 来自法语，原意为"冷血的"；sang(血) + froid(冷的) → 冷血的
evict	*v.* (依法)驱逐(to force out, expel)
[ɪˈvɪkt]	记 词根记忆：e + vict(征服) → 把…征服出去 → 驱逐
tumult	*n.* 喧哗，吵闹(disorderly agitation or milling about of a crowd usually with uproar and confusion of voices)；骚动，骚乱(a disorderly commotion or disturbance)
[ˈtuːmʌlt]	
startle	*v.* 使吃惊(to give an unexpected slight shock)
[ˈstɑːrtl]	同 astound, consternate, terrorize
realign	*v.* 重新排列(to form into new types of organization, etc.)
[ˌriːəˈlaɪn]	记 联想记忆：re(重新) + align(排列) → 重新排列
eerie	*adj.* 可怕的，怪异的(causing fear; weird)
[ˈɪri]	同 uncanny, unearthly
mendacious	*adj.* 不真实的，虚假的(false or untrue)；习惯性说谎的(telling lies habitually)
[menˈdeɪʃəs]	记 联想记忆：mend(修改) + acious → 过度修改 → 不真实的
debrief	*v.* 盘问，听取报告(to question someone who has returned from a mission)
[ˌdiːˈbriːf]	记 词根记忆：de + brief(简述) → 听取报告
inherit	*v.* 继承(to receive property)
[ɪnˈherɪt]	记 词根记忆：in + her(继承人) + it → 继承
ointment	*n.* 油膏，软膏(salve; unguent)
[ˈɔɪntmənt]	记 词根记忆：oint(=oil 油) + ment → 油膏
illustrate	*v.* 举例说明，用图表等说明(to explain by examples, diagrams, pictures)；阐明(to make clear)
[ˈɪləstreɪt]	记 词根记忆：il(向内) + lus(照亮，光) + trate → 向内给光明 → 阐明
	例 Numerous historical examples *illustrate* both the overriding influence that scientists' prejudices have on their interpretation of data and the consequent impairment of their intellectual objectivity.
canonical	*adj.* 符合规定的(according to, or ordered by church canon)；经典的
[kəˈnɑːnɪkl]	同 orthodox

40

trivia ['trɪviə]	*n.* 琐事，小事（trivial facts or details） 记 词根记忆：tri（三）+ via（路）→ 古罗马时的妇女们常在三岔路口谈论一些琐事，引申为"琐事"→ 琐事
miff [mɪf]	*n.* 小争吵（a trivial quarrel） 记 联想记忆：爱人在一起时常有小争吵（miff），分开时又彼此想念（miss）
verbatim [vɜːr'beɪtɪm]	*adj.* 逐字的，（完全）照字面的（being in or following exact words；word-for-word） 记 词根记忆：verb（字，词）+ atim → 逐字的，（完全）照字面的
purse [pɜːrs]	*v.* 缩拢，皱起（to pucker；contract）*n.* 钱包（wallet） 搭 a deplenished purse 囊空如洗
pendulous ['pendʒələs]	*adj.* 下垂的（inclined or hanging downward）
gape [geɪp]	*v.* 裂开（to come apart）；目瞪口呆地凝视（to look hard in surprise or wonder） 记 联想记忆：地面上裂开（gape）一个大裂口（gap）
extremist [ɪk'striːmɪst]	*n.* 极端主义者（a person who holds extreme views） 记 来自 extreme（*n.* 极端，极度）
thrash [θræʃ]	*v.* 鞭打（to beat soundly with a stick or whip） 记 联想记忆：th+rash（鲁莽的）→ 一时气急，鞭打别人 → 鞭打
tiff [tɪf]	*n.* 口角，小争吵（a petty quarrel） 同 altercation, falling-out, miff
pander ['pændər]	*v.* 怂恿，迎合（不良欲望）（to cater to the low desires of others） 记 联想记忆：pa（音似：拍）+ nder（看作 under，下面）→ 拍低级马屁 → 迎合
creep [kriːp]	*v.* 匍匐前进（to move with body close to the ground）；悄悄地移动，蹑手蹑脚地走（to move stealthily or slowly） 记 联想记忆：兔子偷懒睡觉（sleep）时乌龟缓慢地行进（creep）

音频

infantry [ˈɪnfəntri]	*n.* 步兵（soldiers who fight on foot） 记 联想记忆：infant（婴儿）+（t）ry（尝试）→ 婴儿在尝试走路时很慢，相对其他兵种而言，步兵的行军速度也较慢 → 步兵
importune [ˌɪmpɔːrˈtuːn]	*v.* 强求，胡搅蛮缠（to entreat persistently or repeatedly） 记 词根记忆：im（进入）+ port（搬运）+ une → 向内搬 → 强求
squalor [ˈskwɑːlər]	*n.* 肮脏，污秽（state of being squalid） 记 发音记忆："四筐烂儿" → 四筐破烂儿 → 污秽
horizontal [ˌhɔːrəˈzɑːntl]	*adj.* 水平的（level） 记 来自 horizon（*n.* 地平线）
grimace [ɡrɪˈmeɪs]	*n.* 鬼脸，面部扭曲（a twisting or distortion of the face）*v.* 扮鬼脸 记 联想记忆：grim（可怕的）+ ace（看作 face）→ 可怕的脸 → 鬼脸
brag [bræɡ]	*v.* 吹嘘（to boast） 记 联想记忆：bag（口袋）中间加个 r，"r"像一个嘴巴在吹
muggy [ˈmʌɡi]	*adj.* （天气）闷热而潮湿的（oppressively humid and damp） 搭 a muggy August day 八月里闷热的一天
saturated [ˈsætʃəreɪtɪd]	*adj.* 渗透的；饱和的（having high saturation）；深颜色的 同 soaked
uncouth [ʌnˈkuːθ]	*adj.* 粗野的，笨拙的（boorish; clumsy in speech or behavior） 同 barbaric, coarse, gross, rustic
skim [skɪm]	*v.* 从液体表面撇去（to remove floating fat or solids from the surface of a liquid）；浏览，略读（to read quickly to get the main ideas）
smuggle [ˈsmʌɡl]	*v.* 走私，私运（to import or export sth. in violation of customs laws） 记 联想记忆：不断进行反对走私（smuggle）的斗争（struggle）
fluvial [ˈfluːviəl]	*adj.* 河流的，生长在河中的（of, or living in a stream or river） 记 词根记忆：fluv（=flu 流）+ ial → 河流的
substratum [ˈsʌbˌstreɪtəm]	*n.* 基础；地基（an underlying support; foundation） 记 词根记忆：sub（下面）+ stratum（层次）→ 下面一层 → 基础
tear [ter]	*v.* 撕裂（to pull into pieces by force） 搭 tear sb./sth. to shreds 彻底毁灭

□ infantry	□ importune	□ squalor	□ horizontal	□ grimace	□ brag
□ muggy	□ saturated	□ uncouth	□ skim	□ smuggle	□ fluvial
□ substratum	□ tear				

erupt [ɪˈrʌpt]	*v.* 爆发(to burst out)；喷出(to force out or release suddenly) 记 词根记忆：e(出) + rupt(断) → 断裂后喷出 → 爆发
dignity [ˈdɪɡnəti]	*n.* 尊严，尊贵(quality that deserves respect) 记 词根记忆：dign(高贵) + ity → 尊贵 搭 insult/demean to one's dignity 伤害/贬低…的尊严
interloper [ˈɪntərloupər]	*n.* 闯入者(intruder; one who interferes) 记 联想记忆：inter(在…中间) + lope(大步跑) + (e)r → 大步跑进某地的人 → 闯入者
madrigal [ˈmædrɪɡl]	*n.* 抒情短诗(a short poem, often about love, suitable for being set to music)；合唱曲(a part-song) 记 联想记忆：madri（看作 Madrid, 马德里) + gal → 马德里是个浪漫的城市 → 抒情短诗
fealty [ˈfiːəlti]	*n.* 效忠，忠诚(duty and loyalty; allegiance) 记 发音记忆："肺而铁" → 掏心掏肺的铁哥们 → 忠诚
pleonastic [ˌpliːəˈnæstɪk]	*adj.* 冗言的(using more words than necessary) 记 词根记忆：pleon(太多) + astic → 太多的话 → 冗言的
peeve [piːv]	*v.* 使气恼，怨恨(to cause to be annoyed or resentful) 同 irritate
salmon [ˈsæmən]	*n.* 大马哈鱼；鲜肉色(yellowish-pink)
explicable [ɪkˈsplɪkəbl]	*adj.* 可解释的(capable of being explained; explainable) 记 词根记忆：ex + plic(重叠) + able → 能从多重状态中出来 → 可解释的
lucubrate [ˈluːkjuːbreɪt]	*v.* 刻苦攻读，埋头苦干，专心著作(to work, study, or write laboriously) 记 词根记忆：luc(灯光) + ubrate → 在灯光下工作 → 刻苦攻读
drip [drɪp]	*v.* (使)滴下(to let fall in drops) 记 和 drop(*v.* 落下)一起记
inspissate [ɪnˈspɪseɪt]	*v.* (使)浓缩(to make thick or thicker) 记 词根记忆：in + spiss(厚的；密集的) + ate → 使变密集 → (使)浓缩
bargain [ˈbɑːrɡən]	*n.* 交易 (an agreement made between two people or groups to do sth. in return for sth. else)；特价商品 *v.* 讨价还价 (to negotiate the terms and conditions of a transaction) 记 联想记忆：bar(看作 barter, 交易) + gain(获得) → 交易获得好价钱 → 讨价还价
showy [ˈʃoʊi]	*adj.* 俗艳的(gaudy)；炫耀的(flashy) 同 ostentatious
bromide [ˈbroʊmaɪd]	*n.* 庸俗的人；陈词滥调(a commonplace or tiresome person; a trite saying)；镇静剂，安眠药(medicine as a sedative)
agreeable [əˈɡriːəbl]	*adj.* 令人愉快的(pleasing)；欣然同意的(ready to agree) 记 来自 agree(*v.* 同意)

□ erupt	□ dignity	□ interloper	□ madrigal	□ fealty	□ pleonastic
□ peeve	□ salmon	□ explicable	□ lucubrate	□ drip	□ inspissate
□ bargain	□ showy	□ bromide	□ agreeable		

turgid [ˈtɜːrdʒɪd]	*adj.* 肿胀的（swollen; bloated）; 浮夸的（bombastic; pompous） 搭 a turgid style of writing 浮夸的文体
strew [struː]	*v.* 撒满，散播（to spread randomly; scatter） 同 disseminate
pervious [ˈpɜːrviəs]	*adj.* 可渗透的，可通过的（permeable; accessible） 记 词根记忆：per（始终）+ vi（路）+ ous → 始终都有路走的 → 可通过的
volition [voʊˈlɪʃn]	*n.* 意志，决断力（will; the power of choosing or determining） 记 词根记忆：vol（意志）+ ition → 意志，决断力
pertinacious [ˌpɜːrtnˈeɪʃəs]	*adj.* 固执的，坚决的（stubbornly or perversely persistent）; 坚持的（holding tenaciously to a purpose belief, opinion, or course of action） 记 词根记忆：per（始终）+ tin（拿住）+ acious → 始终拿住不放 → 固执的
habitat [ˈhæbɪtæt]	*n.* 自然环境，栖息地（native environment） 记 词根记忆：habit（住）+ at → 住的地方 → 栖息地 例 The moth's *habitat* is being destroyed and it has nearly died out.
badinage [ˌbædənˈɑːʒ]	*n.* 玩笑，打趣（playful teasing） 记 联想记忆：bad + inage（看作 image, 形象）→ 破坏形象 → 打趣
wield [wiːld]	*v.* 行使（权力）（to exert one's authority by means of）; 支配，控制（to have at one's command or disposal） 参 unwieldy（ *adj.* 笨重的；笨拙的）
infelicitous [ˌɪnfɪˈlɪsɪtəs]	*adj.* 不幸的（unfortunate）; 不妥当的（unsuitable） 记 词根记忆：in（不）+ felic（幸运的）+ it + ous → 不幸的
draggy [ˈdræɡi]	*adj.* 拖拉的，极为讨厌的 记 联想记忆：drag（乏味无聊的事）+ gy → 做乏味无聊的事 → 极为讨厌的
fake [feɪk]	*v.* 伪造（to make seem real by any sort of deception or tampering）; 佯装（to practice deception by simulating）*adj.* 假的 记 联想记忆：严惩造（make）假（fake） fake 李逵 魏
cutlery [ˈkʌtləri]	*n.* （刀、叉、匙等）餐具（knives, forks and spoons used for eating and serving food） 记 联想记忆：cut（割）+ lery（看作 celery, 芹菜） → 割芹菜的东西 → 刀具 →（刀、叉、匙等）餐具
outset [ˈaʊtset]	*n.* 开始，开头（start; beginning） 记 来自词组 set out（出发） 搭 from the outset 从一开始
headlong [ˈhedlɔːŋ]	*adj./adv.* 轻率的/地，迅猛的/地 记 组合词：head + long → 头很长 → 做事长驱直入不假思索 → 轻率的/地
jurisdiction [ˌdʒʊrɪsˈdɪkʃn]	*n.* 司法权，审判权，裁判权（right to exercise legal authority） 记 词根记忆：jur（法律）+ is + dict（说话）+ ion → 在法律上说话 → 司法 权，审判权

41

faculty [ˈfæklti]	*n.* 全体教员 (all the lecturers in a department or group of related departments in a university); 能力，技能 (any of the powers of the body or mind)
unravel [ʌnˈrævl]	*v.* 拆开，拆散 (to disengage or separate the threads of); 解开 (to resolve the complexity of) 记 联想记忆: un(不) + ravel(纠缠) → 拆开，拆散; 解开
slog [slɑːg]	*v.* 猛击 (to hit hard); 苦干 (to work hard and steadily) 搭 slog through sth./slog away(at sth.) 埋头苦干; 坚持不懈地做
enrapture [ɪnˈræptʃər]	*v.* 使狂喜，使高兴 (to fill with delight; elate) 记 词根记忆: en + rapture(狂喜) → 使狂喜
overbearing [ˌoʊvərˈberɪŋ]	*adj.* 专横的，独断的 (arrogant; domineering) 记 组合词: over(过分) + bearing(忍受) → 使别人过分忍受 → 专横的
muffle [ˈmʌfl]	*v.* 消音 (to deaden the sound of); 裹住 (to envelop) 记 来自 muff(*n.* 手笼)
lowbred [ˈloʊbred]	*adj.* 粗野的，粗俗的 (ill-mannered; vulgar; crude) 记 组合词: low(低下) + bred(=breed 养育) → 教养不好 → 粗野的
expostulate [ɪkˈspɑːstʃuleɪt]	*v.* (对人或行为的)抗议 (to object to a person's actions or intentions); 告诫 记 词根记忆: ex(出) + post(放) + ulate → 放出意见 → 抗议
toss [tɑːs]	*v.* 投，掷 (to throw in a careless or aimless way); 使摇动，使颠簸 (to cause to move from side to side or back and forth)
spoilsport [ˈspɔɪlspɔːrt]	*n.* 使人扫兴的人 (one who spoils the pleasure of others) 同 damper, downer, killjoy
hue [hjuː]	*n.* 色彩，色泽 (color); 信仰 搭 hue and cry 公众的强烈抗议
folksy [ˈfoʊksi]	*adj.* 亲切的，友好的 (friendly) 记 来自 folks(*n.* 亲属)
controvert [ˈkɑːntrəvɜːrt]	*v.* 反驳，驳斥 (to argue or reason against; contradict; disprove) 记 词根记忆: contro(反) + vert(转) → 反转 → 反驳，驳斥
conundrum [kəˈnʌndrəm]	*n.* 谜语 (a riddle whose answer is or involves a pun); 难题 记 联想记忆: con + un(d)(看作 under) + drum(鼓) → 全部蒙在鼓里 → 谜语
mirth [mɜːrθ]	*n.* 欢乐，欢笑 (gaiety or jollity) 记 发音记忆: "没事" → 没事当然很欢乐 → 欢乐
crucial [ˈkruːʃl]	*adj.* 决定性的 (very important; decisive) 记 词根记忆: cruc(十字形) + ial → 十字路口 → 决定性的 搭 the crucial stage 关键的阶段; the crucial reason 决定性原因
credo [ˈkriːdoʊ]	*n.* 信条 (creed) 记 词根记忆: cred(相信，信任) + o → 信条

□ faculty	□ unravel	□ slog	□ enrapture	□ overbearing	□ muffle
□ lowbred	□ expostulate	□ toss	□ spoilsport	□ hue	□ folksy
□ controvert	□ conundrum	□ mirth	□ crucial	□ credo	

reputation [ˌrepjuˈteɪʃn]	*n.* 名声(good name) 例 Although he had the numerous films to his credit and a *reputation* for technical expertise, the moviemaker lacked originality; all his films were sadly derivative of the work of others.
divine [dɪˈvaɪn]	*v.* 推测，预言(to discover or guess by or as if by magic) 例 For those Puritans who believed that secular obligations were imposed by *divine* will, the correct course of action was not withdrawal from the world but conscientious discharge of the duties of business.
ebullience [ɪˈbʌliəns]	*n.* (感情等的)奔放，兴高采烈(high spirits; exuberance)；沸腾 记 联想记忆：e + bull(公牛) + ience → 像公牛一样出来 → 兴高采烈
exult [ɪgˈzʌlt]	*v.* 欢腾，喜悦(to rejoice greatly; be jubilant) 记 词根记忆：ex + ult(=sult 跳) → 欢腾
elevate [ˈelɪveɪt]	*v.* 举起；提升 记 词根记忆：e(出) + lev(举起) + ate(使…) → 举起
timbre [ˈtæmbər]	*n.* 音色，音质(the quality given to a sound by its overtones) 记 联想记忆：要想乐器音色(timbre)好，必须用好木材(timber)
persiflage [ˈpɜːrsɪflɑːʒ]	*n.* 挖苦，嘲弄(frivolous bantering talk; raillery) 记 词根记忆：per(始终) + sifl(吹哨) + age → 一直吹哨 → 嘲弄
rumble [ˈrʌmbl]	*v.* 发出低沉的隆隆声(to make a low heavy rolling sound)
abjure [əbˈdʒʊr]	*v.* 发誓放弃(to give up on oath; renounce) 记 词根记忆：ab(脱离) + jur(发誓) + e → 发誓去掉 → 发誓放弃
relapse [rɪˈlæps]	*n.* 旧病复发(a recurrence of symptoms of a disease)；再度恶化(the act or an instance of backsliding, worsening) *v.* 旧病复发；再度恶化(to slip or fall into a former worse state) 记 词根记忆：re + laps(滑) + e → (身体状况)再次下滑 → 再度恶化
confederacy [kənˈfedərəsi]	*n.* 联盟，同盟(alliance) 记 词根记忆：con(加强) + feder(联盟) + acy → 联盟
imbibe [ɪmˈbaɪb]	*v.* 喝(to drink)；吸入(to absorb) 记 词根记忆：im(进入) + bib(喝) + e → 喝入 → 吸入
orotund [ˈɔːrətʌnd]	*adj.* (声音)洪亮的((of sound) strong and deep; resonant)；夸张的(bombastic or pompous) 记 联想记忆：oro + tund(=round，圆的) → 把嘴张圆了(说) → 洪亮的
slippery [ˈslɪpəri]	*adj.* 滑的；狡猾的(not to be trusted) 记 来自 slip(*v.* 滑)
hurtle [ˈhɜːrtl]	*v.* 呼啸而过，快速通过(to move rapidly or forcefully)；猛投，用力投掷(to hurl; fling) 记 和 turtle(*n.* 海龟)一起记
polymath [ˈpɑːlimæθ]	*n.* 博学者(a person of encyclopedic learning) 记 词根记忆：poly(多) + math(学习) → 学得多 → 博学者

41

□ reputation	□ divine	□ ebullience	□ exult	□ elevate	□ timbre
□ persiflage	□ rumble	□ abjure	□ relapse	□ confederacy	□ imbibe
□ orotund	□ slippery	□ hurtle	□ polymath		

prance [præns]	*v.* 昂首阔步(to move about proudly and confidently) 记 联想记忆：那个法国(France)人昂首阔步(prance)地走在大街上
browbeat ['braʊbiːt]	*v.* 欺辱；吓唬(to bully) 记 组合词：brow(眉毛) + beat(打) → 用眉毛来打人 → 吓唬
glib [glɪb]	*adj.* 圆滑的，能言善道的，善辩的(speaking or spoken in a smooth, fluent, easy manner)
protuberance [prəʊ'tjuːbərəns]	*n.* 突起，突出 记 词根记忆：pro(向前) + tuber(块茎) + ance → 像块茎一样突出 → 突起，突出
strident ['straɪdnt]	*adj.* 尖锐的，刺耳的(characterized by harsh sound) 记 联想记忆：stri(看作 stride, 大步走) + dent(凹痕) → 大步走进凹坑传来尖声大叫 → 尖锐的
tackle ['tækl]	*v.* 处理(to take action in order to deal with) *n.* 滑车(a mechanism for lifting weights)
wrench [rentʃ]	*v.* 猛扭(to move with a violent twist) *n.* 扳钳，扳手 同 jerk, wrest, yank
verisimilar [ˌverɪ'sɪmɪlə]	*adj.* 好像真实的，逼真的(appearing to be true)；可能的(probable) 记 词根记忆：veri(=ver 真实的) + simil(相同的) +ar → 逼真的
abuse	[ə'bjuːz] *v.* 辱骂(to use insulting language; revile)；滥用(to use wrongly; misuse) [ə'bjuːs] *n.* 辱骂；滥用 记 词根记忆：ab(脱离) + us(用) + e → 用到不能再用 → 滥用
feat [fiːt]	*n.* 功绩，壮举(remarkable deed) 记 联想记忆：f + eat(吃) → 取得功绩，要大吃一顿，犒劳自己 → 功绩 例 The art critic Vasari saw the painting entitled the *Mona Lisa* as an original and wonderful technical *feat*.
bait [beɪt]	*n.* 诱饵(lure; enticement) *v.* 逗弄(to tease)；激怒(to provoke a reaction) 同 decoy, hook, sweetener
intertwine [ˌɪntər'twaɪn]	*v.* 纠缠，缠绕(to twine together) 记 联想记忆：inter + twine(细绳) → 多股绳交织在一起 → 纠缠
pied [paɪd]	*adj.* 杂色的(of two or more colors in blotches) 记 联想记忆：pie(馅饼) + d → 馅饼中放各种颜色的菜 → 杂色的
swill [swɪl]	*v.* 冲洗(to wash; drench)；痛饮(to guzzle) 记 联想记忆：sw(看作 swim, 游泳) +ill(有病的) → 游泳之后冲个热水澡才不会生病 → 冲洗
meditation [ˌmedɪ'teɪʃn]	*n.* 沉思，冥想 记 词根记忆：med(注意) + it + ation → 加以注意 → 沉思

obstruction [əbˈstrʌkʃn]	*n.* 阻碍(物), 妨碍(action of obstructing)
	记 联想记忆: obstruct(阻隔, 阻碍)+ion → 阻碍(物), 妨碍
equivocate [ɪˈkwɪvəkeɪt]	*v.* 模棱两可地说, 支吾其词, 推诿(to use equivocal terms in order to deceive, mislead or hedge)
sidestep [ˈsaɪdstep]	*v.* 横跨一步躲避(to take a step to the side to avoid); 回避(to avoid)
	同 bypass, evade
elocution [ˌeləˈkjuːʃn]	*n.* 演说术(the art of effective public speaking)
	记 词根记忆: e + locu(说) + tion → 说出去 → 演说术

jog [dʒɑːg]	*v.* 慢跑(to run in a slow, steady manner)
	记 联想记忆: 一边慢跑(jog)一边遛狗(dog)
	例 Fitness experts claim that jogging is addictive; once you begin to *jog* regularly, you may be unable to stop, because you are sure to love it more and more all the time.

jog

disburse [dɪsˈbɜːrs]	*v.* 支付, 支出(to pay out; expend)
	记 词根记忆: dis(除去) + burse(=purse 钱包) → 从钱包里拿(钱) → 支出
infelicity [ˌɪnfɪˈlɪsɪti]	*n.* 不幸(the quality or state of being infelicitous); 不恰当的事物(sth. that is infelicitous)
concave [kɑːnˈkeɪv]	*adj.* 凹的(hollow and curved like the inside of a bowl)
	记 词根记忆: con + cave(洞) → 洞是凹进去的 → 凹的
purvey [pərˈveɪ]	*v.* (大量)供给, 供应(to supply as provisions)
	记 和 survey(*v.* 测量, 调查)一起记
procrustean [ˌprəʊˈkrʌstiən]	*adj.* 强求一致的(marked by arbitrary often ruthless disregard of individual differences or special circumstances)
	记 源自 Procrustes(希腊神话中的巨人), 抓到人后, 缚之床榻, 体长者截下肢, 体短者拔之使与床齐长
solidify [səˈlɪdɪfaɪ]	*v.* 巩固, (使)凝固, (使)团结(to become solid, hard or firm)
	记 词根记忆: solid(固定的) + ify(使…) → 巩固

ruffle [ˈrʌfl]	*v.* 弄皱(to become uneven or wrinkled); 激怒(to become disturbed or irritated) *n.* 褶皱
humor [ˈhjuːmər]	*v.* 纵容, 迁就(to comply with the mood or whim; indulge)
	记 humor 最常见的是作"幽默"讲
leniency [ˈliːniənsi]	*n.* 宽厚, 仁慈
	记 词根记忆: len(软的) + i + ency → 宽厚

ruffle

tumid [ˈtjuːmɪd]	*adj.* 肿起的, 肿胀的(swollen; enlarged)
	记 词根记忆: tum(肿) + id → 肿起的, 肿胀的
immortal [ɪˈmɔːrtl]	*adj.* 不朽的, 流芳百世的(deathless)
	记 词根记忆: im(不) + mort(死) + al → 不死的 → 不朽的

41

□ obstruction	□ equivocate	□ sidestep	□ elocution	□ jog	□ disburse
□ infelicity	□ concave	□ purvey	□ procrustean	□ solidify	□ ruffle
□ humor	□ leniency	□ tumid	□ immortal		

horrendous [hɔ:ˈrendəs]	*adj.* 可怕的，令人恐惧的（horrible; frightful） 记 词根记忆：horr（发抖）+ endous → 令人发抖的 → 可怕的
impact [ˈɪmpækt]	*n.* 冲击，影响（the effect and impression of one thing on another） 例 The *impact* of a recently published collection of essays, written during and about the last presidential campaign, is lessened by its timing; it comes too late to affect us with its immediacy and too soon for us to read it out of historical curiosity.
rife [raɪf]	*adj.* 流行的，普遍的（prevalent to an increasing degree） 记 和 life（*n.* 生命）一起记
expound [ɪkˈspaʊnd]	*v.* 解释（to explain or interpret）；阐述（to state in detail） 记 词根记忆：ex + pound（放）→ 把（道理）放出来 → 解释
intercept [ˌɪntərˈsept]	*v.* 拦截，阻止（to seize or stop on the way） 记 词根记忆：inter（在…中间）+ cept（拿）→ 从中间拿 → 拦截
underling [ˈʌndərlɪŋ]	*n.* 部下，下属，手下（subordinate; inferior） 记 联想记忆：under（在…下面）+ ling → 部下，下属
confer [kənˈfɜ:r]	*v.* 商议，商谈（to have discussions）；授予，赋予（to reward to） 记 词根记忆：con（共同）+ fer（带来，拿来）→ 共同带来观点 → 商谈
tragedy [ˈtrædʒədi]	*n.* 惨剧，惨事，灾难（a terrible event that causes great sadness） 同 affliction, calamity, catastrophe, woe
thespian [ˈθespiən]	*adj.* 戏剧的（relating to drama; dramatic） 记 来自古希腊悲剧创始者 Thespis
petrify [ˈpetrɪfaɪ]	*v.* （使）石化（to convert into stone）；（使）吓呆（to confound with fear or awe） 记 词根记忆：petr（石头）+ ify → （使）石化
veto [ˈvi:toʊ]	*n.* 否决，禁止（an authoritative prohibition; interdiction）；否决权 记 在拉丁文中，veto 的意思是我不准（I forbid），在英语里则表示"否决"或"否决权"
vagrant [ˈveɪɡrənt]	*adj.* 流浪的，漂泊的；*n.* 流浪者，漂泊者（a person who has no home or regular work） 记 词根记忆：vag（漫游）+ rant → 流浪的
heartrending [ˈhɑ:rtrendɪŋ]	*adj.* 令人心碎的（heartbreaking） 记 组合词：heart（心）+ rending（撕碎）→ 令人心碎的
inroad [ˈɪnroʊd]	*n.* 袭击（a hostile invasion）；（以牺牲他人者为代价而取得的）进展（advance often at the expense of sb. or sth.） 记 联想记忆：in（进）+ road（路）→ 进了别人的路 → 袭击
pigment [ˈpɪɡmənt]	*n.* 天然色素（a coloring matter in animals and plants）；粉状颜料（a powdered substance that imparts colors to other materials）
whistle [ˈwɪsl]	*n.* 口哨声；汽笛声 *v.* 吹口哨，鸣笛（to make a whistle） 记 发音记忆："猥琐" → 随随便便对女孩子吹口哨很猥琐 → 吹口哨

diagram [ˈdaɪəɡræm]	*n.* 图解，图表（drawing that uses simple lines to illustrate a machine, structure, or process） 记 词根记忆：dia（穿过，二者之间）+ gram（写，图）→ 交叉对着画 → 图表
ode [oʊd]	*n.* 长诗，颂歌（a lyric poem usually marked by exaltation of feeling and style, varying length of line, and complexity of stanza forms）
pedal [ˈpedl]	*n.* 踏板，脚蹬 *v.* 骑自行车（to ride a bicycle） 记 词根记忆：ped（脚）+ al（东西）→ 踏板
postiche [pɔˈstiːʃ]	*adj.* 伪造的，假的（false; sham）*n.* 伪造品（sth. false; a sham）；假发（a small hairpiece; a toupee）
rebarbative [rɪˈbɑːrbətɪv]	*adj.* 令人讨厌的，冒犯人的（repellent; irritating） 记 词根记忆：re（相对）+ barb（钩子）+ ative → 钩子对着别人 → 冒犯人的
adventitious [ˌædvenˈtɪʃəs]	*adj.* 偶然的（accidental; casual） 记 联想记忆：advent（到来）+ itious → （突然）到来的 → 偶然的
pastry [ˈpeɪstri]	*n.* 糕点，点心（sweet baked goods） 记 联想记忆：past（看作 paste，面团）+ ry → 面团做成的糕点 → 糕点
gratification [ˌɡrætɪfɪˈkeɪʃn]	*n.* 满足，喜悦（the state of being gratified） 记 来自 gratify（*v.* 使高兴，使满意）
pallid [ˈpælɪd]	*adj.* 苍白的，没血色的（wan; lacking sparkle or liveliness） 记 词根记忆：pall（=pale 苍白的）+ id → 苍白的
superiority [suːˌpɪriˈɔːrəti]	*n.* 优越（感）（the quality or state of being superior） 记 来自 superior（*adj.* 优越的）
plaster [ˈplæstər]	*n.* 灰泥，石膏（a pasty composition）*v.* 抹灰泥 记 词根记忆：plas（形式）+ ter → 塑造成墙的东西 → 灰泥
tend [tend]	*v.* 照料，照看（to act as an attendant; serve） 搭 tend the sick 护理病人
invidious [ɪnˈvɪdiəs]	*adj.* 惹人反感的，导致伤害和仇恨的，招人嫉妒的（tending to cause discontent, harm, animosity, or envy） 记 词根记忆：in（不）+ vid（看）+ ious → 不看的 → 惹人反感的
transgression [trænzˈɡreʃn]	*n.* 违法，犯罪（a violation of a law） 记 来自 transgress（*v.* 越轨；违背）
blossom [ˈblɑːsəm]	*n.* 花（flower）*v.*（植物）开花（to produce blossom） 记 联想记忆：bloom 中间开出两个 s 形的花
prompt [prɑːmpt]	*v.* 促进，激起（to move to action; incite）*adj.* 敏捷的，迅速的（quick） 记 词根记忆：pro（向前）+ mpt（=empt 拿，抓）→ 提前拿 → 促进，激起
pawn [pɔːn]	*v.* 典当，抵押（to deposit in pledge）*n.* 典当，抵押；被利用的小人物 记 和 pawnbroker（*n.* 典当商，当铺老板）一起记

41

reprehend [ˌreprɪˈhend]	*v.* 谴责, 责难(to voice disapproval of; censure) 记 词根记忆: re(反) + prehend(抓住) → 反过来抓住(缺点) → 谴责
prolix [ˈprəʊlɪks]	*adj.* 说话啰嗦的, 冗长的(unduly prolonged) 同 wordy
squint [skwɪnt]	*v.* 斜视(to look or peer with eyes partly closed)
diaphanous [daɪˈæfənəs]	*adj.* (布)精致的; 半透明的(characterized by such fineness of texture as to permit seeing through) 记 词根记忆: dia + phan(呈现) + ous → 对面显现 → 半透明的
hardy [ˈhɑːrdi]	*adj.* 耐寒的 (able to endure cold); 强壮的 (robust; vigorous); 大胆的, 勇敢的 记 联想记忆: hard(硬的) + y(…的) → 强壮的; 耐寒的 例 Quick-breeding and immune to most pesticides, cockroaches are so *hardy* that even a professional exterminator may fail to eliminate them.
guileless [ˈɡaɪlləs]	*adj.* 厚道的, 老实的(innocent, naive) 记 组合词: guile(狡诈, 诡计) + less(没有) → 没有诡计 → 老实的
depression [dɪˈpreʃn]	*n.* 抑郁, 消沉(low spirits) 搭 clinical depression 临床抑郁症
reincarnate [ˌriːɪnˈkɑːrneɪt]	*v.* 使转世(to incarnate again) 记 联想记忆: re(重新) + incarnate(化身) → 精神重新进入肉体 → 使转世
protagonist [prəˈtæɡənɪst]	*n.* 倡导者, 拥护者(proponent) 记 词根记忆: prot(首先) + agon(打, 行动) + ist → 首先行动者 → 倡导者
omnivorous [ɑːmˈnɪvərəs]	*adj.* 杂食的 (eating both meat and vegetables or plants); 兴趣杂的 (having wide interests in a particular area or activity) 记 词根记忆: omni(全) + vor(吃) + ous → 全部吃的 → 杂食的
overreach [ˌoʊvərˈriːtʃ]	*v.* 做事过头(to go to excess) 记 组合词: over(过分) + reach(伸出) → 做过了 → 做事过头

stab [stæb]	*v.* 刺伤，戳(to thrust with a pointed weapon) 搭 stab sb. in the back 在某人背后捅刀子
nominal ['nɑːmɪnl]	*adj.* 名义上的，有名无实的(in name only) 记 词根记忆：nomin(名字) + al → 名义上的
disembodied [ˌdɪsɪm'bɑːdid]	*adj.* 无实体的，空洞的(free from bodily existence; incorporeal) 记 词根记忆：dis(不) + embodied(实体的) → 无实体的
devotional [dɪ'voʊʃənl]	*adj.* 献身的，虔诚的(used in religious worship) 记 来自 devotion(*n.* 献身)
brittle ['brɪtl]	*adj.* 易碎的，脆弱的(hard but easily broken) 记 联想记忆：br(看作 break) + ittle(看作 little) → 易碎的，脆弱的
canon ['kænən]	*n.* 经典，真作(the works that are genuine) 记 联想记忆：can(能) + on(在…上) → 能放在桌面上的真家伙 → 经典，真作
abusive [ə'bjuːsɪv]	*adj.* 谩骂的，毁谤的(using harsh insulting language)；虐待的(physically injurious)
sacrilege ['sækrəlɪdʒ]	*n.* 亵渎，冒犯神灵(outrageous violation of what is sacred) 同 blasphemy, desecration, profanation
puffery ['pʌfəri]	*n.* 极力称赞，夸大广告，吹捧(exaggerated commendation especially for promotional purposes) 记 联想记忆：puff(吹嘘) + ery → 极力称赞
frenzy ['frenzi]	*n.* 狂乱，狂暴(the state of extreme excitement)；暂时性疯狂(temporary madness) 记 词根记忆：fren(=phren 心灵) + zy → 有关心灵状态的 → 狂暴
catholic ['kæθlɪk]	*adj.* 普遍的；广泛的(all inclusive; universal)；宽容的(broad in understanding; liberal) 记 联想记忆：和天主教"Catholic"的拼写一致，但第一个字母不大写
autocrat ['ɔːtəkræt]	*n.* 独裁者(a ruler with absolute power; dictator) 记 词根记忆：auto(自己) + crat(统治者) → 独裁者
awry [ə'raɪ]	*adj.* 扭曲的，走样的(not straight; askew) 记 词根记忆：a(加强) + wry(歪的) → 扭曲的

□ stab	□ nominal	□ disembodied	□ devotional	□ brittle	□ canon
□ abusive	□ sacrilege	□ puffery	□ frenzy	□ catholic	□ autocrat
□ awry					

clash [klæʃ]	*v.* 冲突，撞击（to collide or strike together with a loud, harsh and metallic noise） 同 bump
dangle ['dæŋgl]	*v.* 悬荡，悬摆（to hang loosely so as to swing back and forth）；吊胃口 记 发音记忆："荡够" → 悬荡，悬摆
refresh [rɪ'freʃ]	*v.* 消除…的疲劳，使精神振作（to bring back strength and freshness to） 记 联想记忆：re(重新) + fresh(新鲜的) → 使精神振作
unconscionable [ʌn'kɑːnʃənəbl]	*adj.* 无节制的，过度的，不合理的（excessive; unreasonable） 记 联想记忆：un(不) + conscionable(公正的，凭良心的) → 无节制的
rendition [ren'dɪʃn]	*n.* 表演，演绎（the act or result of rendering） 同 execution, interpretation, performance
allocate ['æləkeɪt]	*v.* 配给，分配（to assign sth. for a special purpose; distribute） 记 词根记忆：al + loc(地方) + ate → 不断送给地方 → 配给，分配
quibble ['kwɪbl]	*n.* 遁词（an evasion of the point）；吹毛求疵的反对意见或批评（a minor objection or criticism） 记 quip(*n.* 妙语；借口)的变体
monologue ['mɑːnəlɔːg]	*n.* 独白（soliloquy）；长篇演说，长篇大论（a prolonged discourse） 记 词根记忆：mono(单个) + log(说话) + ue → 一个人说话 → 独白
farewell [ˌfer'wel]	*interj.* 再会，再见 *n.* 辞行，告别（saying goodbye） 记 联想记忆：fare(看作 far，远的) + well(好) → 朋友去远方，说些好听的话 → 告别
rapport [ræ'pɔːr]	*n.* 融洽，和谐（relation marked by harmony, conformity） 记 和 support(*n.* 支持)一起记
hype [haɪp]	*n.* 夸大的广告宣传（promotional publicity of an extravagant or contrived kind）
disfigure [dɪs'fɪgjər]	*v.* 损毁…的外形；使变丑（to mar the appearance of; spoil） 记 词根记忆：dis(除去) + figure(形体) → 去掉形体 → 损毁…的外形
hankering ['hæŋkərɪŋ]	*n.* 渴望，向往（craving; yearning） 记 来自 hanker(*v.* 渴望，追求)
upbraid [ʌp'breɪd]	*v.* 斥责，责骂（to criticize severely; scold vehemently） 记 联想记忆：up(向上) + braid(辫子) → 被揪辫子 → 责骂
crudity ['kruːdəti]	*n.* 粗糙，生硬（the quality or state of being crude） 记 来自 crude(*adj.* 粗糙的)
milk [mɪlk]	*v.* 榨取（to coerce profit or advantage to an extreme degree）
outlandish [aʊt'lændɪʃ]	*adj.* 古怪的（very odd, fantastic; bizarre） 记 联想记忆：out(出) + land(国家) + ish → 从外国来的 → 古怪的
dictum ['dɪktəm]	*n.* 格言，声明（a formal statement of fact, principle or judgement）

□ clash	□ dangle	□ refresh	□ unconscionable	□ rendition	□ allocate
□ quibble	□ monologue	□ farewell	□ rapport	□ hype	□ disfigure
□ hankering	□ upbraid	□ crudity	□ milk	□ outlandish	□ dictum

straightforward [ˌstreɪt ˈfɔːrwərd]	*adj.* 诚实的，坦率的(honest and frank)；易懂的(not difficult to understand)；直接的(direct) 例 At first endorsements were simply that: *straightforward* firsthand testimonials about the virtues of a product.
promenade [ˌprɑːmə ˈneɪd]	*n.* 散步，开车兜风(a leisurely walk or ride for pleasure or display) *v.* 散步，开车兜风 记 词根记忆：pro(向前) + men(to lead) + ade → 引着自己向前 → 散步，开车兜风
vain [veɪn]	*adj.* 自负的(full of self-admiration)；徒劳的(without result) 记 联想记忆：他很自负(vain)，到头来一无所获(gain)
remunerate [rɪ ˈmjuːnəreɪt]	*v.* 酬劳，赔偿(to pay or compensate a person for; reward) 记 词根记忆：re(重新) + muner(礼物) + ate → 回报人礼物 → 酬劳
squeeze [skwiːz]	*v.* 压，挤(to press firmly together) *n.* 压榨，紧握 记 联想记忆：s + quee(看作 queen，女王) + ze → 很想挤进去与女王握手 → 挤
restored [rɪ ˈstɔːrd]	*adj.* 恢复的(returned to an original or regular condition)
highbrow [ˈhaɪbraʊ]	*n.* 自以为文化修养很高的人(a person pretending highly cultivated, or having intellectual tastes) 记 组合词：high(高) + brow(额头，眉毛) → 眉毛挑得很高的人 → 自以为文化修养很高的人
leakage [ˈliːkɪdʒ]	*n.* 渗漏，漏出(leaking) 记 来自 leak(*v.* 泄漏)
full-bodied [ˌfʊl ˈbɑːdid]	*adj.* 魁梧的；(味道)浓烈的；重要的 记 联想记忆：full(完全的) + bodi(=body 身体) + ed(…的) → 全身都有的 → (味道)浓烈的
incongruent [ɪn ˈkɑːŋɡruənt]	*adj.* 不协调的，不和谐的，不合适的(not congruent) 记 联想记忆：in(不) + congruent(协调的，合适的) → 不协调的，不合适的
whirlpool [ˈwɜːrlpuːl]	*n.* 旋涡(a rapidly rotating current of water; vortex) 记 组合词：whirl(旋转，回旋) + pool(水池) → 旋涡
massive [ˈmæsɪv]	*adj.* 巨大的，厚重的(very big and heavy) 记 来自 mass(*n.* 大量，大多数) 例 Unlike other creatures, who are shaped largely by their immediate environment, human beings are products of a culture accumulated over centuries, yet one that is constantly being transformed by *massive* infusions of new information from everywhere.
monocle [ˈmɑːnəkl]	*n.* 单片眼镜(an eye glass for one eye only) 记 词根记忆：mon(单个的) + oc(眼睛) + le → 单片眼镜
undergird [ˌʌndər ˈɡɜːrd]	*v.* 从底层支持，加固…的底部(to strengthen from the bottom) 记 联想记忆：under(在…下面) + gird(束紧) → 在下面束紧 → 从底层支持

42

palliative	*n.* 缓释剂 *adj.* 减轻的，缓和的 (serving to palliate)
[ˈpæliətɪv]	搭 a palliative measure 消极措施
volley	*n.* 齐发，群射 (a number of shots fired at the same time) *v.* 齐发，群射 (to be fired altogether)；截击
[ˈvɑːli]	参 volleyball (*n.* 排球)
meander	*v.* 蜿蜒而流 (to take a winding or tortuous course)；漫步 (to wander aimlessly; ramble)
[miˈændər]	记 来自 the Meander，一条以蜿蜒曲折而著名的河流
huffy	*adj.* 愤怒的，恼怒的 (irritated or annoyed; indignant)
[ˈhʌfi]	同 angry, irate
herbivorous	*adj.* 食草的 (feeding on plants)
[ɜːrˈbɪvərəs]	记 词根记忆：herb(草) + i + vor(吃) + ous → 食草的
vagary	*n.* 奇想，异想天开 (an erratic, unpredictable, or extravagant manifestation)
[ˈveɪɡəri]	记 词根记忆：vag (漫游) + ary → 游移的思想 → 奇想；发音记忆："无规律" → 奇想
snipe	*v.* 狙击 (to shoot at exposed individuals from a usually concealed point of vantage)
[snaɪp]	
idolize	*v.* 将…当作偶像崇拜 (to treat as an idol)；极度仰慕，崇拜 (to admire very much)
[ˈaɪdəlaɪz]	
cub	*n.* 幼兽 (one of the young of certain animals)；笨手笨脚的年轻人 (an inexperienced and awkward youth)
[kʌb]	记 和 cube(*n.* 立方体) 一起记
equine	*adj.* 马的，似马的 (characteristic of a horse)
[ˈiːkwaɪn]	参 equitation(*n.* 骑马术)
petty	*adj.* 琐碎的，次要的 (trivial; unimportant)；小气的 (marked by or reflective of narrow interests and sympathies)
[ˈpeti]	同 minor, subordinate; small-minded
mat	*n.* 垫子，席子 *v.* (使)缠结；铺席于…上
[mæt]	记 联想记忆：猫(cat)在垫子(mat)上睡觉
demure	*adj.* 严肃的，矜持的 (reserved; affectedly modest or shy)
[dɪˈmjʊr]	记 词根记忆：de + mure(墙) → 脸板得像墙一样 → 严肃的
perk	*v.* 恢复，振作 (to gain vigor or cheerfulness especially after a period of weakness or depression)；打扮 (to make smart or spruce in appearance)；竖起 (to stick up)
[pɜːrk]	
rejoin	*v.* 回答，答辩 (to say sharply or critically in response)
[ˌriːˈdʒɔɪn]	记 词根记忆：re(重新) + join(加入) → 重新加入讨论 → 答辩
pontifical	*adj.* 教皇的 (of or relating to a pontiff or pontifex)；自负的 (pretentious; pompous)；武断的 (dogmatic)
[pɑːnˈtɪfɪkl]	
haggard	*adj.* 憔悴的，消瘦的 (gaunt; drawn)
[ˈhæɡərd]	记 联想记忆：hag(巫婆) + gard → 像巫婆一样 → 形容枯槁的 → 消瘦的

comestible [kəˈmestɪbl]	*n.* 食物，食品(sth. fit to be eaten) *adj.* 可吃的(edible) 记 联想记忆：come(来) + s + tible(看作 table，桌子) → 来到桌上 → 食品
munition [mjuːˈnɪʃn]	*n.* 军火，军需品(weapons and ammunition) 记 词根记忆：mun(保护，加强) + ition → 用于保家卫国的东西 → 军火
votary [ˈvoʊtəri]	*n.* 崇拜者，热心支持者(a devoted admirer) 记 词根记忆：vot(宣誓) + ary → 发誓追随 → 崇拜者，热心支持者
neurology [nʊˈrɑːlədʒi]	*n.* 神经学(the scientific study of the nervous system) 记 词根记忆：neur(神经) + ology(学科) → 神经学
hector [ˈhektər]	*v.* 欺凌，威吓(to browbeat; bully) 同 intimidate, threaten
ecstasy [ˈekstəsi]	*n.* 狂喜(great delight; rapture)；出神，入迷 记 词根记忆：ec(出) + stasy(站住) → (高兴得)出群 → 狂喜
strut [strʌt]	*v.* 趾高气扬地走(to walk proudly and stiffly) *n.* 支柱(support) 同 stalk, stride, swagger
kidnap [ˈkɪdnæp]	*v.* 绑架(to seize and detain unlawfully and usually for ransom) 记 联想记忆：kid(小孩) + nap(打盹) → 趁着大人打盹将小孩诱拐走 → 绑架
gladiator [ˈɡlædieɪtər]	*n.* 角斗士，与野兽搏斗者 (a person engaged in a fight to the death as public entertainment for ancient Romans) 记 来自 gladius(*n.* 古罗马军队之短剑)
osseous [ˈɑːsiəs]	*adj.* 骨的，多骨的(composed of bone; bony) 记 词根记忆：oss(骨) + e + ous → 骨的
ulcer [ˈʌlsər]	*n.* 溃疡(a break in skin or mucous membrane with loss of surface tissue, disintegration and necrosis of epithelial tissue, and often pus)；腐烂物 (sth. that festers and corrupts like an open sore)
oven [ˈʌvn]	*n.* 烤箱，烤炉，灶(a chamber used for baking, heating, or drying) 记 发音记忆："爱闻" → 爱闻烤箱里的香味 → 烤箱，烤炉
intervene [ˌɪntərˈviːn]	*v.* 干涉，介入(to interfere with the outcome or course) 记 词根记忆：inter + ven(来) + e → 来到中间 → 干涉，介入
bob [bɑːb]	*v.* 轻拍，轻扣(to strike with a quick light blow)；使上下快速摆动(to move up and down in a short quick movement)
vibrate [ˈvaɪbreɪt]	*v.* 振动，摇摆(to move back and forth or to and fro, especially rhythmically and rapidly)；颤动，震动(to shake or move with or as if with a slight quivering or trembling motion) 记 词根记忆：vibr(振动) + ate → 振动；颤动
squall [skwɔːl]	*n.* 短暂、突然且猛烈的风暴(a brief, sudden, violent windstorm)；短暂的骚动(a brief violent commotion)
tightfisted [ˈtaɪtfɪstɪd]	*adj.* 吝啬的(stingy) 记 联想记忆：tight(紧的) + fist(拳头) + ed → 抓住不松手 → 吝啬的

42

rejoice	v. 欣喜，高兴（to feel joy or great delight）
[rɪˈdʒɔɪs]	记 词根记忆：re + joic(=joy 高兴) + e → 欣喜，高兴
potpourri	n. 混杂物，杂烩（a miscellaneous collection; medley）
[ˌpoʊpʊˈriː]	记 联想记忆：pot(锅) + pour(倾倒) + ri → 倒在一个锅里 → 混杂物
vanilla	n. 香草，香子兰（any of a genus of tropical American climbing orchids）
[vəˈnɪlə]	搭 vanilla ice-cream 香草冰淇淋
resurgence	n. 再起，复活，再现（the return of ideas, beliefs to a state of being active）
[rɪˈsɜːrdʒəns]	记 词根记忆：re(重新) + surg(升起) + ence → 再起
jockey	n. 骑师 v. 谋取（to maneuver to gain an advantage）
[ˈdʒɑːki]	搭 jockey for 耍手腕获取
agenda	n. 议程（program of things to be done）
[əˈdʒendə]	记 词根记忆：ag(做) + enda(表示名词) → 要做的事情 → 议程
fissile	adj. 易分裂的（capable of being split; fissionable）
[ˈfɪsl]	记 词根记忆：fiss(裂开) + ile(易…的) → 易分裂的
dissolute	adj. 放荡的，无节制的（dissipated and immoral; profligate）
[ˈdɪsəluːt]	记 词根记忆：dis(分开) + solute(溶解) → (精力)溶解掉 → 放荡的
gulch	n. 深谷，峡谷（a steep walled valley; narrow ravine）
[gʌltʃ]	记 联想记忆：峡谷(gulch)是大地上的深沟，海湾(gulf)是海中的深沟
unearthly	adj. 奇异的（very strange and unnatural）
[ʌnˈɜːrθli]	记 联想记忆：un(不) + earthly(尘世的) → 不属于这个世间的 → 奇异的
ploy	n. 花招，策略（a tactic; stratagem）
[plɔɪ]	
kernel	n. 果仁；核心（the central; most important part; essence）
[ˈkɜːrnl]	记 词根记忆：kern(=corn 种子) + el → 核心
slight	adj. 轻微的，微小的（small in degree）v. 怠慢，冷落（to treat rudely without respect）n. 冒犯他人的行为、言语等
[slaɪt]	记 联想记忆：s + light(轻的) → 轻微的
	例 In today's world, manufacturers' innovations are easily copied and thus differences between products are usually *slight*.
progenitor	n. 祖先（an ancestor in the direct line; forefather）
[proʊˈdʒenɪtər]	记 词根记忆：pro(前) + gen(产生) + itor → 生在前面的人 → 祖先
unbend	v. 变直（to become straight）；轻松行事，放松（to behave in a less formal and severe manner）
[ˌʌnˈbend]	记 联想记忆：un(不) + bend(弯曲) → 变直
recherche	adj. 精心挑选的；异国风味的（exotic, rare）
[ˌrəʃerˈʃeɪ]	
philately	n. 集邮（stamp-collecting）
[fɪˈlætəli]	记 词根记忆：phil(爱) + ately(邮票) → 集邮

□ rejoice	□ potpourri	□ vanilla	□ resurgence	□ jockey	□ agenda
□ fissile	□ dissolute	□ gulch	□ unearthly	□ ploy	□ kernel
□ slight	□ progenitor	□ unbend	□ recherche	□ philately	

446

deflect [dɪˈflekt]	*v.* 偏离，转向(to turn to aside; deviate) 记 词根记忆：de + flect(弯曲) → 弯到旁边 → 偏离
grove [ɡroʊv]	*n.* 小树林，树丛(a small wood or group of trees) 记 联想记忆：gro(看作 grow) + ve(看作 five) → 五棵树长在一起 → 小树林
destitute [ˈdestɪtuːt]	*adj.* 缺乏的(being without; lacking)；穷困的(living in complete poverty) 记 词根记忆：de + stitute(建立) → 没有建立 → 穷困的
panoramic [ˌpænəˈræmɪk]	*adj.* 全景的，全貌的，概论的(of or relating to a panorama) 记 来自 panorama(*n.* 概观，全景)
ugly [ˈʌɡli]	*adj.* 难看的(unpleasant to look at)；令人不快的(offensive or unpleasant to any sense) 例 The mayor and school superintendent let their dispute over budget cuts escalate to *ugly* and destructive proportions.
gesticulate [dʒeˈstɪkjuleɪt]	*v.* 做手势表达(to make or use gestures) 记 来自 gesture(*n.* 手势，姿势)
adjunct [ˈædʒʌŋkt]	*n.* 附加物，附件(sth. joined or added to another thing but not essentially a part of it) 记 词根记忆：ad(附近) + junct(结合，连接) → 连在上面的东西 → 附加物
iniquity [ɪˈnɪkwəti]	*n.* 邪恶，不公正，不道德(lack of righteousness or justice; wickedness) 记 联想记忆：in(不) + iqu(相同的) + ity → 不相同 → 不公正
teetotal [ˌtiːˈtoʊtl]	*adj.* 滴酒不沾的(completely abstinent from alcoholic drinks)；完全的，全部的(complete, total) 记 来自英国戒酒运动拥护者 Turner 在某次戒酒演讲中的一个口误，total 一词因口吃讹音为 teetotal
fatal [ˈfeɪtl]	*adj.* 致命的(causing death)；灾难性的(causing disaster) 记 来自 fate(*n.* 命运)
cyclone [ˈsaɪkloʊn]	*n.* 气旋，飓风(a windstorm with violent, whirling movement; tornado or hurricane) 记 词根记忆：cycl(圆；转) + one → 转的东西 → 气旋
hangdog [ˈhæŋdɑːɡ]	*adj.* 忧愁的(downcast)；低贱的(shamefaced) 记 组合词：hang(吊) + dog(狗) → 吊起来的狗 → 低贱的 同 dejected, despicable
preach [priːtʃ]	*v.* 布道，讲道(to deliver a sermon) 记 联想记忆：p(看作 priest, 牧师) + reach(到达) → 牧师到达 → 布道，讲道
mangle [ˈmæŋɡl]	*v.* 毁坏，毁损(to ruin or spoil)；(通过切、压等)损坏(to mutilate or disfigure by hacking or crushing; maim)
ecumenical [ˌiːkjuːˈmenɪkl]	*adj.* 世界范围的，普遍的(of worldwide scope or applicability; universal) 记 发音记忆："一口闷" → 把世界一口闷下 → 世界范围的
wink [wɪŋk]	*v.* 使眼色，眨眼示意(to close and open one eye quickly as a signal) *n.* 眨眼，眼色(a winking movement of the eye)

42

gravitate	*v.* 被强烈地吸引 (to be drawn or attracted especially by natural inclination); 受重力/引力作用而运动
[ˈɡrævɪteɪt]	记 词根记忆: grav(重) + it(走) + ate → 受重力作用而运动
epigram	*n.* 讽刺短诗, 警句 (terse, witty statement)
[ˈepɪɡræm]	记 词根记忆: epi(在…旁边) + gram(写) → 旁敲侧击写的东西 → 讽刺短诗
savvy	*adj.* 有见识的, 精明的 (well informed and perceptive; shrewd)
[ˈsævi]	同 astute, canny, perspicacious, slick
opalescence	*n.* 乳白光 (reflecting on iridescent light)
[ˌoʊpəˈlesns]	
decant	*v.* 轻轻倒出 (to pour off gently)
[dɪˈkænt]	记 词根记忆: de(离开) + cant(瓶口) → 轻轻倒出
purge	*v.* 清洗, 洗涤 (to make free of sth. unwanted)
[pɜːrdʒ]	记 词根记忆: purg(清洁的) + e → 清洗, 洗涤
renunciate	*v.* 放弃 (to give up; abandon)
[rɪˈnʌnsieɪt]	记 词根记忆: re (相反) + nunci (讲话, 说出) + ate → 表达相反的意见 → 放弃
smut	*n.* 污迹 (matter that soils or blackens); 黑穗病 *v.* 弄脏
[smʌt]	
renege	*v.* 食言, 违约 (to go back on a promise or commitment)
[rɪˈniːɡ]	记 词根记忆: re(反) + neg(否认) + e → 反过来不承认 → 食言, 违约
conducive	*adj.* 有助于…的, 有益的 (that contributes or leading to)
[kənˈduːsɪv]	搭 be conducive to 对…有帮助
conspicuous	*adj.* 显著的, 显而易见的 (obvious; easy to perceive)
[kənˈspɪkjuəs]	记 词根记忆: con(全部) + spic(看) + uous → 全部人都能看到的 → 显而易见的
	搭 conspicuous feature 显著的特征
debonair	*adj.* 美丽的 (charming); 温雅的 (friendly)
[ˌdebəˈner]	记 联想记忆: deb(看作 debutante, 初进社交界的女孩) + on + air → 在空气中的女孩 → 美丽的
lachrymose	*adj.* 爱哭的 (inclined to shed a lot of tears); 引人落泪的 (causing tears)
[ˈlækrɪmoʊs]	记 词根记忆: lachrym(眼泪) + ose → 爱哭的
dormancy	*n.* 休眠状态 (state of being temporarily inactive)
[ˈdɔːrmənsi]	记 词根记忆: dorm(睡眠) + ancy → 在睡眠状态 → 休眠状态
	例 It is true that the seeds of some plants have germinated after two hundred years of *dormancy*, but reports that viable seeds have been found in ancient tombs such as the pyramids are entirely unfounded.

rinse [rɪns]	*v.* 冲洗掉，漂净（to cleanse by clear water）
pictorial [pɪkˈtɔːriəl]	*adj.* 绘画的（of or relating to the painting or drawing of pictures）；用图片的（having or expressed in pictures） 记 词根记忆：pict（描绘）+ orial → 起描绘作用的 → 用图片的 例 Although Irish literature continued to flourish after the sixteenth century, a comparable tradition is absent in the visual arts: we think about Irish culture in terms of the word, not in terms of *pictorial* images.
annihilate [əˈnaɪəleɪt]	*v.* 消灭（to destroy completely; demolish） 记 词根记忆：an（接近）+ nihil（无）+ ate → 使接近没有 → 消灭
guarantee [ˌɡærənˈtiː]	*v.* 保证，担保（to undertake to do or secure） 记 联想记忆：guar（看作 guard，保卫）+ antee → 保证，担保 他可以做担保人！ guarantee
rural [ˈrʊrəl]	*adj.* 乡村的（characteristic of the country） 记 词根记忆：rur（乡村）+ al（…的）→ 乡村的 例 This new government is faced not only with managing its economy but also with implementing new *rural* development programs to stem the flow of farm workers to the city.
immerse [ɪˈmɜːrs]	*v.* 浸入（to plunge, drop, or dip into liquid）；沉浸于（to engross） 记 词根记忆：im（进入）+ mers（浸入）+ e → 浸入
besmirch [bɪˈsmɜːrtʃ]	*v.* 诽谤（to defile; make dirty） 记 联想记忆：be + smirch（污点，弄脏）→ 诽谤
intermittent [ˌɪntərˈmɪtənt]	*adj.* 断断续续的（periodic; recurrent）；间歇的（alternate） 记 来自 intermit（*v.* 暂停，中断）
tremulous [ˈtremjələs]	*adj.* 颤动的（characterized by or affected with trembling or tremors; quivering）；胆怯的，怯懦的（affected with timidity）
goggle [ˈɡɑːɡl]	*n.* 护目镜（goggles）*v.* 瞪大眼睛看（to stare with wide and bulging eyes） 例 They were *goggling* at us as if we were freaks.
aggrieve [əˈɡriːv]	*v.* 使受委屈，使痛苦（to give pain or trouble to） 记 词根记忆：ag（做）+ griev（悲伤）+ e → 使受委屈，使痛苦
ravenous [ˈrævənəs]	*adj.* 饥饿的（hungry）；贪婪的（rapacious） 记 来自 raven（*n.* 大乌鸦，掠夺）
lark [lɑːrk]	*v.* 玩乐，嬉耍（to play or frolic; have a merry time）*n.* 玩乐 记 联想记忆：在公园（park）玩乐（lark）

42

□ rinse	□ pictorial	□ annihilate	□ guarantee	□ rural	□ immerse
□ besmirch	□ intermittent	□ tremulous	□ goggle	□ aggrieve	□ ravenous
□ lark					

sheer [ʃɪr]	*adj.* 完全的（complete；utter）；陡峭的（very steep）；极薄的（extremely thin） 记 联想记忆：绵羊（sheep）在陡峭的（sheer）山坡上吃草 例 He was indifferent to success, painting not for the sake of fame or monetary reward, but for the *sheer* love of art.
asteroid [ˈæstərɔɪd]	*n.* 小行星（a small planet） 记 词根记忆：aster（星星）+ oid（像…一样）→ 小行星
preamble [priˈæmbl]	*n.* 前言，序言（an introductory statement）；先兆（an introductory factor or circumstance indicating what is to follow） 记 联想记忆：pre（在…之前）+ amble（缓行，漫步）→ 走在前面 → 前言
equity [ˈekwəti]	*n.* 公平，公正（fairness；impartiality；justice） 记 词根记忆：equ（=equal 相同的）+ ity → 公平，公正
animadvert [ˌænəmædˈvət]	*v.* 苛责，非难（to remark or comment critically, usually with strong disapproval or censure）
despoil [dɪˈspɔɪl]	*v.* 夺取，抢夺（to rob；plunder；ravage） 记 词根记忆：de + spoil（夺取，宠坏）→ 夺取，抢夺
amnesty [ˈæmnəsti]	*n.* 大赦，特赦（the act of an authority by which pardon is granted to a large group of individuals） 记 词根记忆：a（无）+ mnes（记忆）+ ty → 不再记仇 → 大赦，特赦
prestige [preˈstiːʒ]	*n.* 威信，威望（respect based on good reputation, past achievements, etc）；影响力 记 联想记忆：pres（看作 president，总统）+ tige（看作 tiger，老虎）→ 总统和老虎两者都是有威信、威望的 → 威信，威望
piecemeal [ˈpiːsmiːl]	*adj.* 一件一件的，零碎的（done, or made piece by piece or in a fragmentary way）
lexical [ˈleksɪkl]	*adj.* 词汇的（of a vocabulary）；词典的 记 词根记忆：lex（词汇）+ ical → 词汇的
escalation [ˌeskəˈleɪʃn]	*n.* 逐步上升，逐步扩大（state of being more intense） 记 来自 escalate（*v.* 使逐步扩大）
frowzy [ˈfraʊzi]	*adj.* 不整洁的，污秽的（dirty and untidy；slovenly；unkempt） 记 联想记忆：和 frown（*v.* 皱眉）一起记：看到 frowzy 就 frown
foreclose [fɔːrˈkloʊz]	*v.* 排除（to shut out；exclude）；取消（抵押品的）赎回权（to extinguish the right to redeem a mortgage） 记 词根记忆：fore（预先）+ clos（关闭）+ e → 预先关闭 → 排除
jostle [ˈdʒɑːsl]	*v.* 推挤（to push and shove）；挤开通路（to make one's way by pushing） 搭 jostle for 争夺，争抢

egotist [ˈegətɪst]	*n.* 自私自利者 (selfish person) ; 自我主义者 记 词根记忆：ego(我，自己) + t + ist → 以自我为中心的人 → 自私自利者
cliché [kliːˈʃeɪ]	*adj.* 陈腐的 ((of phrase or idea) used so often that it has become stale or meaningless) *n.* 陈词滥调
caper [ˈkeɪpər]	*n.* 雀跃，跳跃 (a gay, playful jump or leap) *v.* 雀跃 记 联想记忆：cape(披风) + r → 第一次穿披风走路的人 → 雀跃
disgruntle [dɪsˈɡrʌntl]	*v.* 使不高兴 (to make discontented) 同 disappoint, dissatisfy
stricture [ˈstrɪktʃər]	*n.* 严厉谴责 (an adverse criticism) ; 束缚 (restrictions) 记 来自 strict(*adj.* 严格的)
fleet [fliːt]	*adj.* 快速的 (fast) *v.* 消磨，疾驰 (to pass or run light and quickly) ; 飞逝，掠过 (to fly swiftly) 记 和 flee(*v.* 逃跑) 一起记
hectic [ˈhektɪk]	*adj.* 兴奋的，繁忙的，忙乱的 (characterized by confusion, rush or excitement) 同 busy, exciting
peery [ˈpɪri]	*adj.* 窥视的；好奇的 (curious) ；怀疑的 (suspicious) 记 联想记忆：peer(窥视) + y → 窥视的；好奇的
ingestion [ɪnˈdʒestʃən]	*n.* 摄取，吸收 (the act of taking food or drink into the body) 记 词根记忆：in(进入) + gest(搬运) + ion → 运入体内 → 摄取
kipper [ˈkɪpər]	*v.* 腌制，熏制 (to cure (split dressed fish) by salting and smoking) 记 联想记忆：和 copper(*n.* 铜) 一起记
harrowing [ˈhæroʊɪŋ]	*adj.* 悲痛的，难受的 (mentally distressful) 记 来自 harrow(*v.* 使痛苦) 搭 a harrowing experience 痛苦的经历
taboo [təˈbuː]	*adj.* 忌讳的 (banned on grounds of morality) *n.* 禁忌 (a prohibition imposed by social custom)
vintage [ˈvɪntɪdʒ]	*adj.* 经典的 (of old, recognized, and enduring interest, importance, or quality) ；最好的 (of the best)

□ egotist	□ cliché	□ caper	□ disgruntle	□ stricture	□ fleet
□ hectic	□ peery	□ ingestion	□ kipper	□ harrowing	□ taboo
□ vintage					

451

signature [ˈsɪɡnətʃər]	*n.* 签名，署名(person's name written by himself) 记 词根记忆：sign(做记号) + ature → 用名字做记号 → 签名，署名
weary [ˈwɪri]	*adj.* 疲劳的，疲倦的 (physically or mentally fatigued)；令人厌烦的，令人厌倦的(having one's interest, forbearance, or indulgence worn out) *v.* (使)厌烦，(使)疲倦(to make or become weary) 例 The Muses are vindictive deities: they avenge themselves without mercy on those who are *weary* of their charms.
pouch [paʊtʃ]	*n.* 小袋 *v.* 使成袋状；将(某物)装入袋内
trumpery [ˈtrʌmpəri]	*adj.* 中看不中用的(showy but of little value) 记 来自 trump(*n.* 王牌)
infringe [ɪnˈfrɪndʒ]	*v.* 违反，侵害(to break a law; violate; trespass) 记 词根记忆：in + fring(破坏) + e → 违反
interpose [ˌɪntərˈpoʊz]	*v.* 置于…之间(to place or put between)；使介入(to introduce by way of intervention) 记 词根记忆：inter + pos(放) + e → 放入中间 → 置于…之间 例 Literature is inevitably a distorting rather than a neutral medium for the simple reason that writers *interpose* their own vision between the reader and reality.
oblige [əˈblaɪdʒ]	*v.* 强迫，强制(to constrain)；施恩惠于…(to do sth. as a favor) 记 词根记忆：ob(加强) + lig(绑住) + e → 用力绑住 → 强迫
illuminati [ɪˌluːmɪˈnɑːti]	*n.* 先觉者，先知(persons who are or who claim to be unusually enlightened) 记 词根记忆：il + lumin(光) + ati → 给人带来光明的人 → 先知
plough [plaʊ]	(= plow) *n.* 犁 *v.* 犁地 搭 snow plough 铲雪机
mutineer [ˌmjuːtəˈnɪr]	*n.* 反叛者，背叛者(a person who mutinies) 记 来自 mutiny(*n./v.* 叛变)
verdict [ˈvɜːrdɪkt]	*n.* 裁定，裁决(the finding or decision of a jury) 记 词根记忆：ver(真实的)+dict(说) → 说出真话 → 裁定，裁决 例 The widespread public shock at the news of the guilty *verdict* was caused partly by biased news stories that had predicted acquittal.
addle [ˈædl]	*v.* 使腐坏(to make rotten)；使昏乱(to become muddled or confused) 记 联想记忆：add(增加) + le → 事情增加容易混乱 → 使昏乱
rarefaction [ˌreriˈfækʃn]	*n.* 稀薄(the quality or state of being rarefied) 记 来自 rarefy(*v.* 稀薄)
macerate [ˈmæsəreɪt]	*v.* 浸软(to soften by soaking in liquid)；使消瘦(to cause to grow thin) 记 形近词：lacerate(*v.* 划破，割裂；伤害)
chronic [ˈkrɑːnɪk]	*adj.* 慢性的，长期的(marked by long duration or frequent recurrence) 记 词根记忆：chron(时间) + ic(…的) → 长时间的 → 慢性的 搭 chronic illness 慢性病

□ signature	□ weary	□ pouch	□ trumpery	□ infringe	□ interpose
□ oblige	□ illuminati	□ plough	□ mutineer	□ verdict	□ addle
□ rarefaction	□ macerate	□ chronic			

fad [fæd]	*n.* 时尚(a custom, style in a short time; fashion) 记 和 fade(*v.* 褪色)一起记
minuet [ˌmɪnjuˈet]	*n.* 小步舞(a slow, stately dance in 3/4 time characterized by forward balancing, bowing, and toe pointing) 记 词根记忆：min(小的) + uet → 小步舞 例 Although the *minuet* appeared simple, its intricate steps had to be studied very carefully before they could be gracefully executed in public.
fiat [ˈfiːæt]	*n.* 法令，政令(an order issued by legal authority; decree) 记 联想记忆：fi(看作 fire) + at → 对…开火 → 政令
invoice [ˈɪnvɔɪs]	*n.* 发票，发货清单(bill) *v.* 给开发票(to send an invoice for or to) 记 联想记忆：in + voice(声音) → 大声把人叫进来开发票 → 发票
adapt [əˈdæpt]	*v.* 使适应(to make fit)；修改(to modify) 记 词根记忆：ad(向) + apt(适应) → 使适应
imperil [ɪmˈperəl]	*v.* 使陷于危险，危及(to put in peril; endanger) 记 联想记忆：im(进入) + peril(危险) → 使陷于危险
careworn [ˈkerwɔːrn]	*adj.* 忧心忡忡的，饱经忧患的(showing the effects of worry, anxiety, or burdensome responsibility)
velvety [ˈvelvəti]	*adj.* 天鹅绒般柔软光滑的(having the character of velvet as in being soft, smooth)；醇和的，可口的(smooth to the taste)
dash [dæʃ]	*v.* 猛撞，猛砸，击碎(to ruin)；使受挫，挫败(to depress)；使羞愧，使窘迫(to make ashamed) 搭 dash one's hopes 使某人的希望化为泡影
diatribe [ˈdaɪətraɪb]	*n.* (口头或书面猛烈的)抨击(a bitter, abusive criticism or denunciation) 记 词根记忆：dia(两者之间) + tribe(摩擦) → 两方摩擦 → 抨击
capsule [ˈkæpsjuːl]	*n.* 荚膜，蒴果(seed case of a plant)；胶囊(small soluble case containing a dose of medicine)
manipulate [məˈnɪpjuleɪt]	*v.* (熟练地)操作，处理(to operate or control; handle) 记 词根记忆：mani(手) + pul(拉) + ate → 用手拉 → (熟练地)操作，处理 例 By dint of much practice in the laboratory, the anatomy student became ambidextrous and was able to *manipulate* her dissecting tools with either hand. manipulate
cultivated [ˈkʌltɪveɪtɪd]	*adj.* 耕种的，栽培的(planted)；有教养的((of people, manner, etc.) having or showing good taste and refinement) 搭 a cultivated environment 有修养的环境
nerve [nɜːrv]	*n.* 勇气 *v.* 给予力量(to give strength to) 记 联想记忆：军人为人民服务(serve)首先要有勇气(nerve)

□ fad	□ minuet	□ fiat	□ invoice	□ adapt	□ imperil
□ careworn	□ velvety	□ dash	□ diatribe	□ capsule	□ manipulate
□ cultivated	□ nerve				

pare	*v.* 削(to peel); 修剪(to trim); 削减，缩减(to diminish or reduce by or as
[per]	if by paring)
scoff	*v.* 嘲笑(to sneer; mock); 狼吞虎咽(to eat greedily) *n.* 嘲笑；笑柄
[skɔːf]	同 gibe, insult, jeer, taunt, twit
jaundice	*n.* 偏见(the state of mind in which one is jealous or suspicious); 黄疸
[ˈdʒɔːndɪs]	同 bias, prejudgment, prejudice
euphoria	*n.* 愉快的心情(a feeling of well-being or elation)
[juːˈfɔːriə]	记 词根记忆：eu(好) + phor(带来) + ia(病) → 带来好处的病 → 幸福感 → 愉快的心情
contumacy	*n.* 抗命，不服从(insubordination; disobedience)
[ˈkɑːntuməsi]	记 词根记忆：con + tum(肿胀；骄傲) + acy(表名词) → 坚持自己的骄傲，不受欺压 → 抗命，不服从
penance	*n.* 自我惩罚(an act of self-abatement)
[ˈpenəns]	记 词根记忆：pen(惩罚) + ance → 惩罚 → 自我惩罚
fatuity	*n.* 愚蠢，愚昧(stupidity; foolishness)
[fəˈtjuiti]	记 词根记忆：fatu(愚蠢的) + ity → 愚蠢
fragrant	*adj.* 芳香的(having a pleasant odor)
[ˈfreɪgrənt]	记 和 flagrant(*adj.* 恶名昭著的)一起记
scowl	*n.* 怒容 *v.* 生气地皱眉(to frown angrily); 怒视(to make a scowl)
[skaʊl]	同 glower, lower
stampede	*v.* 惊跑，逃窜(to cause to run away in headlong panic)
[stæmˈpiːd]	搭 a herd of stampeding elephants 一群狂奔的大象
pleat	*n.* (衣服上的)褶(a fold in cloth)
[pliːt]	记 来自plait(*v.* 打褶；编辫子)
velocity	*n.* 速率，速度(quickness of motion; speed); 迅速，快速(rapidity of movement)
[vəˈlɑːsəti]	记 词根记忆：veloc(快速的)+ity → 速度；迅速
proverbially	*adv.* 人皆尽知地
[prəˈvɜːrbiəli]	记 来自 proverb(*n.* 谚语)
oblique	*adj.* 不直接的，不坦率的(not straightforward); 斜的(inclined)
[əˈbliːk]	记 词根记忆：ob(反) + liqu(向上弯) + e → 不向上弯的 → 斜的
drainage	*n.* 排水，排水系统(the act or method of drawing off); 污水
[ˈdreɪnɪdʒ]	记 来自 drain(*v.* 排水)
glide	*v.* 滑行，滑动(to flow or move smoothly and easily); 悄悄地溜走；渐变
[glaɪd]	例 Youth *glided* past without our awareness.
pulchritude	*n.* 美丽，标致(physical comeliness)
[ˈpʌlkrɪtjuːd]	记 词根记忆：pulchr(美丽的) + itude(状态) → 美丽，标致
vying	*adj.* 竞争的(contending; competing)
[ˈvaɪɪŋ]	记 vie(*v.* 竞争)的现在分词也是 vying

454

□ pare □ scoff □ jaundice □ euphoria □ contumacy □ penance
□ fatuity □ fragrant □ scowl □ stampede □ pleat □ velocity
□ proverbially □ oblique □ drainage □ glide □ pulchritude □ vying

scorch [skɔːrtʃ]	*v.* 烤焦，烧焦(to dry or shrivel with intense heat) 同 burn, char, sear, singe
oversight [ˈoʊvərsaɪt]	*n.* 疏忽，失察，勘漏(unintentional failure to notice sth.) 记 组合词：over(在…上) + sight(视线) → 错误在视线之上 → 疏忽
ripen [ˈraɪpən]	*v.* 使成熟(to become or make ripe) 记 来自ripe(*adj.* 成熟的)
headway [ˈhedweɪ]	*n.* 进步，进展(progress) 搭 make headway 取得进展
satire [ˈsætaɪər]	*n.* 讽刺(the use of irony to expose vices) 记 源自拉丁语，意为"讽刺杂咏"，现在在英语中多指"讽刺"或"讽刺文学"
prowl [praʊl]	*v.* 潜行，悄悄踱步(to roam through stealthily) *n.* 四处觅食，徘徊 搭 on the prowl 徘徊；寻找
scalding [ˈskɔːldɪŋ]	*adj./adv.* 滚烫的(hot enough to scald) 搭 scalding hot 灼热
canvass [ˈkænvəs]	*v.* 细查 (to scrutinize)；拉选票(to go around an area asking people for political support) 记 联想记忆：can(能) + v(胜利的标志) + ass(驴子) → 能让驴子得胜 → 拉选票
dilemma [dɪˈlemə]	*n.* 困境，左右为难(predicament；any situation between unpleasant alternatives) 记 发音记忆："地雷嘛" → 陷入雷区 → 进退两难的局面 → 困境
dock [dɑːk]	*v.* 剪短(尾巴等)(to shorten the tail by cutting)；扣去(薪水，津贴等)(to deduct apart from wages) 记 和lock(*v.* 锁上，锁住)一起记
dreary [ˈdrɪri]	*adj.* 沉闷的，乏味的(cheerless；dull) 记 和dream(*n.* 梦想)一起记；A dream is not dreary.(梦想不会乏味。)
entrust [ɪnˈtrʌst]	*v.* 委托(to invest with a trust or duty)；托付(to assign the care of) 记 联想记忆：en(使) + trust(相信) → 给予信任 → 委托
palliate [ˈpælieɪt]	*v.* 减轻(痛苦)(to reduce；abate)；掩饰(罪行)(to extenuate) 记 词根记忆：pall(罩子) + itate → 盖上(罪行) → 掩饰(罪行)
leery [ˈlɪri]	*adj.* 谨防的，怀疑的(wary；cautious；suspicious) 记 联想记忆：你送秋波(leer)，我怀疑(leery)你的动机
sober [ˈsoʊbər]	*adj.* 清醒的(sedate or thoughtful)；严肃的，认真的(marked by temperance, moderation, or seriousness)
centrifugal [ˌsentrɪˈfjuːgl]	*adj.* 离心的(moving or tending to move away from a center) 记 词根记忆：centri(中心) + fug(逃跑) + al → 逃离中心的 → 离心的
immunize [ˈɪmjunaɪz]	*v.* (通过接种)使免疫(to give immunity by inoculation) 记 来自immune(*adj.* 免疫的)

43

□ scorch	□ oversight	□ ripen	□ headway	□ satire	□ prowl
□ scalding	□ canvass	□ dilemma	□ dock	□ dreary	□ entrust
□ palliate	□ leery	□ sober	□ centrifugal	□ immunize	

prorogue [prəʊˈrəʊg]	*v.* 休会(to suspend a legislative session); 延期(to postpone; adjourn) 记 词根记忆: pro(前面) + rog(问) + ue → 在前面通知下次开会(的日期) → 休会
cling [klɪŋ]	*v.* 紧紧抓住(to hold on tightly); 坚持(to be unwilling to abandon) 搭 cling to 紧握不放; 坚持
immune [ɪˈmjuːn]	*adj.* 免疫的(not susceptible to some specified disease); 免除的, 豁免的 记 词根记忆: im(没有) + mun(服务) + e → 不提供服务的 → 免疫的 例 No computer system is *immune* to a virus, a particularly malicious program that is designed to infect and electronically damage the disks on which data are stored.
exultant [ɪgˈzʌltənt]	*adj.* 非常高兴的, 欢跃的, 狂喜的(filled with or expressing great joy or triumph) 记 来自 exult(*v.* 欢腾, 喜悦)
backdrop [ˈbækdrɑːp]	*n.* (事情的)背景; 背景幕布(printed cloth hung at the back of a theatre) 记 组合词: back + drop(后面挂下的幕布) → 背景幕布
rejoinder [rɪˈdʒɔɪndər]	*n.* 回答(an answer to a reply) 同 retort
deceit [dɪˈsiːt]	*n.* 欺骗, 欺诈, 诡计(a dishonest action or trick; fraud or lie) 记 词根记忆: de + ceit(拿) → 在(底下)拿 → 欺骗
hypocrite [ˈhɪpəkrɪt]	*n.* 伪善者, 伪君子(a person who pretends to have opinions or to be what he is not) 记 词根记忆: hypo(在下面) + crit(判断) + e → 在背后下判断 → 伪君子 例 The *hypocrite* simulates feelings which he does not possess but which he feels he should display.
perfidy [ˈpɜːrfədi]	*n.* 不忠, 背叛(the quality of being faithless) 同 disloyalty, treachery
defray [dɪˈfreɪ]	*v.* 支付, 支出(to provide for the payment of) 记 联想记忆: def(看作 deaf, 聋) + ray(光线) → 聋人得到光线 → 有人帮助付款 → 支付
municipality [mjuːˌnɪsɪˈpæləti]	*n.* 自治市; 市政当局(指城市行政区及管理者) 记 来自 municipal(*adj.* 市政的)
monstrous [ˈmɑːnstrəs]	*adj.* 巨大的(huge; immense); 丑陋的, 外表可怕(frightful or hideous in appearance) 记 来自 monster(*n.* 妖怪)
pathology [pəˈθɑːlədʒi]	*n.* 病理学(the study of the essential nature of diseases) 记 词根记忆: path(病) + ology(学科) → 病理学
gross [groʊs]	*adj.* 总的(total; entire); 粗野的(vulgar; coarse) *n.* 全部, 总额 记 联想记忆: 青草(grass)地占了这个公园总的(gross)面积的三分之一
supererogatory [ˌsjuːprəˈrɒgətɔːri]	*adj.* 职责以外的; 多余的 同 superfluous, unnecessary

odium	*n.* 憎恶，反感（hatred）
[ˈoʊdiəm]	同 detestation
elegy	*n.* 哀歌，挽歌（a song or poem expressing sorrow or lamentation）
[ˈelədʒi]	记 联想记忆：e(出) + leg(腿) + y → 悲伤得迈不动步 → 哀歌
suspect	*v.* 怀疑（to doubt the truth or value of） *n.* 嫌疑犯 *adj.* 可疑的（of uncertain truth, quality, legality, etc.）
[səˈspekt]	记 词根记忆：sus + pect(=spect 看) → 从上到下地 → 怀疑
studied	*adj.* 深思熟虑的（carefully thought about or considered）；认真习得的
[ˈstʌdid]	例 The prospects of discovering new aspects of the life of a painter as thoroughly *studied* as Vermeer are not, on the surface, encouraging.
attire	*v.* 使穿衣；打扮（to dress in fine garments） *n.* 盛装，服装（rich apparel; finery）
[əˈtaɪr]	记 词根记忆：at(加强) + tire(梳理) → 梳洗打扮 → 使穿衣；打扮
avow	*v.* 承认（to acknowledge or claim）；公开宣称（to declare openly）
[əˈvaʊ]	记 词根记忆：a(来) + vow(誓言) → 发誓 → 承认
sampler	*n.* 刺绣样品（decorative piece of needlework typically used as an example of skill）；样品检查员（a person who prepares or selects samples for inspection）
[ˈsæmplər]	
tribute	*n.* 赞词，颂词（eulogy）；贡物（a payment by one ruler or nation to another in acknowledgement of submission）
[ˈtrɪbjuːt]	记 词根记忆：tribut(给予) + e → 贡物
calumniate	*v.* 诽谤，中伤（to make maliciously false statements）
[kəˈlʌmnieɪt]	同 defame, malign, slander, slur, vilify
scribble	*v.* 乱写，乱涂（to write and draw hastily and carelessly）
[ˈskrɪbl]	记 词根记忆：scrib(写) + ble → 乱写，乱涂
fissure	*n.* 裂缝，裂隙（a long, narrow and deep cleft or crack）
[ˈfɪʃər]	记 词根记忆：fiss(裂开) + ure → 裂缝
sting	*v.* 刺痛；叮螫（to prick or wound） *n.* 螫刺
[stɪŋ]	记 发音记忆："死叮" → 刺痛；英国有个著名歌手叫斯汀 Sting
protean	*adj.* 变化多端的，多变的（continually changing）
[ˈproʊtiən]	同 versatile
coronation	*n.* 加冕礼（a ceremony at which a person is made king or queen）
[ˌkɔːrəˈneɪʃn]	记 词根记忆：corona(王冠) + tion → 加冕礼
glowing	*adj.* 热情赞扬的（giving enthusiastic praise）
[ˈgloʊɪŋ]	例 The critics were distressed that an essayist of such *glowing* promise could descend to writing such dull, uninteresting prose.
masquerade	*n.* 化装舞会（a gathering of persons wearing masks and fantastic costumes）；*v.* 伪装（to live or act as if in disguise）
[ˌmæskəˈreɪd]	记 来自 masque(=mask *n.* 面具)

43

preen	v. (鸟用嘴)整理羽毛((of a bird) to clean or smooth its feathers (with its beak)); (人)打扮修饰(to dress up; primp)
[pri:n]	记 和 green(n. 绿色)一起记
increment	n. 增加(increase; gain; growth)
[ˈɪŋkrəmənt]	记 词根记忆: in(进入) + cre(生长) + ment → 使生长 → 增加
travesty	v. 滑稽地模仿
[ˈtrævəsti]	记 词根记忆: tra(横) + vest(穿衣) + y → 横过来穿衣 → 滑稽地模仿
largess	n. 赠送, 赏赐(generous giving of money or gifts); 赠款, 赏赐物(money or gifts given in this way)
[lɑːrˈdʒes]	记 联想记忆: large(大的) + ss → 大方 → 赠送; 赠款
citation	n. 引证; 引文; 传票(an official summons to appear, as before a court)
[saɪˈteɪʃn]	记 来自 cite(v. 引证, 引用)
bedraggled	adj. (衣服、头发等)弄湿的; 凌乱不堪的(made wet and dirty)
[bɪˈdrægld]	记 联想记忆: be + draggled(拖湿的; 凌乱的) → 弄湿的; 凌乱不堪的
rotten	adj. 腐烂的(having rotted); 极坏的(very bad, wretched)
[ˈrɑːtn]	记 来自 rot(n./v. 腐烂)
muted	adj. (声音)减弱的, 变得轻柔的
[ˈmjuːtɪd]	记 来自 mute(v. 减弱…的声音)
grant	v. 同意给予(to agree to give what is asked for); 授予
[grænt]	记 联想记忆: 授予(grant)显赫的(grand)贵族爵位
	同 award, grant, vouchsafe
circular	adj. 圆形的; 循环的(shaped like a circle)
[ˈsɜːrkjələr]	记 词根记忆: circ(圆) + ular → 圆形的; 循环的
infernal	adj. 地狱的(of hell); 可恶的(hateful; outrageous)
[ɪnˈfɜːrnl]	记 词根记忆: infern(更低的) + al → 更低的地方 → 地狱的
victimize	v. 使受害, 欺骗(to cause sb. to suffer unfairly)
[ˈvɪktɪmaɪz]	记 来自 victim(n. 受害者)
deduce	v. 演绎, 推断(to arrive at a conclusion by reasoning)
[dɪˈduːs]	记 词根记忆: de(向下) + duce(引导) → 向下引导 → 推断
machination	n. 阴谋(an artful or secret plot or scheme)
[ˌmæʃɪˈneɪʃn]	记 词根记忆: machin(机械; 制造) + ation → 阴谋
painstaking	adj. 煞费苦心的 (involving diligent care and effort)
[ˈpeɪnzteɪkɪŋ]	记 联想记忆: pains (痛苦) + taking (花费…的) → 煞费苦心的
whimper	v. 啜泣, 呜咽(to make a low whining plaintive or broken sound)
[ˈwɪmpər]	同 blubber, pule, sob

charisma [kə'rɪzmə]	*n.* (大众爱戴的)领袖气质(a special quality of leadership);魅力(a special charm or allure that inspires devotion) 记 联想记忆:cha(看作 China) + ris(看作 rise) + ma(看作 mao,引申为毛泽东) → 中国升起毛(泽东) → 领袖气质
beseech [bɪ'siːtʃ]	*v.* 恳求 记 词根记忆:be + seech(=seek 寻求) → 寻求 → 恳求
jargon ['dʒɑːrgən]	*n.* 胡言乱语(confused language);行话(the technical terminology) 例 The First World War began in a context of *jargon* and verbal delicacy and continued in a cloud of euphemism as impenetrable as language and literature, skillfully used, could make it.
stipple ['stɪpl]	*v.* 点画,点描(to apply paint by repeated small touches) 记 词根记忆:stip(点)+ple → 用点画 → 点画
doff [dɑːf]	*v.* 脱掉(外衣、帽子)(to take off) 记 联想记忆:d + off(脱掉) → 把衣服脱掉 → 脱掉(外衣、帽子)
stupefy ['stuːpɪfaɪ]	*v.* 使茫然,使惊讶(to astonish; astound) 记 词根记忆:stup(笨,呆) + efy → 吓呆 → 使惊讶
conscript [kən'skrɪpt]	*v.* 征兵,征召(某人)入伍(to enroll for compulsory service in the armed forces) 记 词根记忆:con + script(写) → 把(名字)写入名单 → 征召(某人)入伍
coffer ['kɔːfər]	*n.* 保险柜,保险箱(a strongbox) 记 联想记忆:保险柜(coffer)里珍藏了一种颇有价值的咖啡(coffee)
calorie ['kæləri]	*n.* 卡路里;卡(热量单位) 记 发音记忆:"卡路里" → 卡
otiose ['oʊʃioʊs]	*adj.* 不必要的,多余的(useless; superfluous) 同 unnecessary
slobber ['slɑːbər]	*n.* 口水(saliva drooled from the mouth) *v.* 流口水;情不自禁地说 搭 slobber over sb./sth. 对…垂涎欲滴;毫不掩饰表示喜爱
vaunting ['vɔːltɪŋ]	*adj.* 吹嘘的,傲慢的 记 来自 vaunt(*v.* 吹嘘,自夸)
stentorian [sten'tɔːriən]	*adj.* 声音洪亮的(extremely loud) 记 来自希腊神话特洛伊战争中的传令官 Stentor,其声音极其洪亮
bleak [bliːk]	*adj.* 寒冷的,阴沉的(cold; frigid);阴郁的,暗淡的(depressing) 同 black, cutting, dim, raw
sturdy ['stɜːrdi]	*adj.* (身体)强健的(strong);结实的(firmly built or constituted) 记 联想记忆:要想学习(study)好需要身体好(sturdy)
apocryphal [ə'pɑːkrɪfl]	*adj.* 假冒的,虚假的(of doubtful authenticity) 同 inveracious, mendacious, ostensible
valediction [ˌvælɪ'dɪkʃn]	*n.* 告别演说,告别词(an address or statement of farewell) 记 词根记忆:val(值得的) + e + dict(说) + ion → 告别演说,告别词

43

tumble [ˈtʌmbl]	*v.* 突然跌倒，突然下跌（to fall suddenly and helplessly）；倒塌（to fall into ruin）
groove [gruːv]	*n.* 沟，槽，辙（a long, narrow furrow）；（刻出的）字沟；习惯（habitual way; rut） 记 联想记忆：戴手套（glove）是一种习惯（groove）；注意：不要和 grove（*n.* 树丛）相混
razor [ˈreɪzər]	*n.* 剃刀，刮胡刀（a keen cutting instrument for shaving） 记 来自 raze（*v.* 夷平，抹掉）
kennel [ˈkenl]	*n.* 狗舍，狗窝（a doghouse） 记 词根记忆：ken（=can 犬）+ nel → 狗窝；注意：不要和 kernel（*n.* 核心）相混
woe [woʊ]	*n.* 悲痛，悲哀（a condition of deep suffering from misfortune, affliction, or grief）；不幸，灾难（calamity; misfortune）
expurgate [ˈekspərgeɪt]	*v.* 删除，删节（to remove passages considered obscene or objectionable） 记 词根记忆：ex + purg（清洗）+ ate → 清洗掉不好的东西 → 删除
hyperactivity [ˌhaɪpərækˈtɪvəti]	*n.* 活动过度，极度活跃（the state or condition of being excessively or pathologically active） 记 词根记忆：hyper（过分）+ activity（活动）→ 活动过度
chimera [kaɪˈmɪrə]	*n.* 神话怪物（fabulous monster）；梦幻（an impossible or foolish fancy） 记 联想记忆：原指"希腊神话中一种狮头羊身蛇尾的会喷火的女妖怪" → 神话怪物
casual [ˈkæʒuəl]	*adj.* 偶然的（occurring by chance）；非正式的，随便的 记 联想记忆：平常的（usual）时候可以穿非正式的（casual）服装 搭 casual conversations 闲谈
hawk [hɔːk]	*n.* 隼，鹰（a kind of eagle）
acuity [əˈkjuːəti]	*n.*（尤指思想或感官）敏锐（sharpness; acuteness） 记 词根记忆：acu（尖，酸，锐利）+ ity（表性质）→ 锐利 → 敏锐
swine [swaɪn]	*n.* 猪（pig） 记 联想记忆：s + wine（酒）→ 喝酒喝多了，就胖得像只猪一样 → 猪

□ tumble	□ groove	□ razor	□ kennel	□ woe	□ expurgate
□ hyperactivity	□ chimera	□ casual	□ hawk	□ acuity	□ swine

附录：数学词汇

算数-整数

integer *n.* 整数
consecutive integer 连续的整数
positive whole number 正整数
negative whole number 负整数
even/even integer 偶数
odd/odd integer 奇数
real number 实数
divisor *n.* 除数，约数；因子
multiple *n.* 倍数
remainder *n.* 余数
composite number 合数
quotient *n.* 商
prime number 质数，素数
prime factor 质因子，质因数
successive *adj.* 连续的
spread *n.* 范围
score *n.* 二十
consecutive *adj.* 连续的
constant *adj.* 恒定的，不变的

算数-分数

numerator *n.* 分子
denominator *n.* 分母
greatest common divisor/greatest common
　factor 最大公约数
least common multiple 最小公倍数
common multiple 公倍数
common factor 公因子

reciprocal/inverse *n.* 倒数
mixed number 带分数(带分数就是将一个分数
　写成整数部分 + 一个真分数)
improper fraction 假分数
proper fraction 真分数
vulgar fraction/common fraction 普通分数
simple fraction 简分数
complex fraction 繁分数
reversible *adj.* 可逆的，可倒转的
nearest whole percent 最接近的百分数

算数-小数

decimal place 小数位
decimal point 小数点
decimal fraction 纯小数
infinite decimal 无穷小数
recurring decimal 循环小数
digit *n.* 位
decimal system 十进制
units digit 个位数
tens digit 十位数
tenths unit 十分位
3-digit number 三位数
quartile *n.* 四分位数
percentile *n.* 百分位数
interquartile range 四分位差
negligible *adj.* 可忽略不计的
closest approximation 最相近似的
calculate to three decimal places
　结果保留3位小数

approximately *adv.* 大约，近似
estimation *n.* 估算，近似

算数-实数

absolute value 绝对值
nonzero number 非零数
natural number 自然数
positive number 正数
negative number 负数
nonnegative *adj.* 非负的
rational *n.* 有理数
irrational（number）无理数

算数-比例

common ratio 公比
direct proportion 正比
percent *n.* 百分比
account for 占（比例）
scatterplot *n.* 点阵图
scale *n.* 比例；刻度

算数-幂和根

cardinal *n.* 基数
ordinal *n.* 序数
exponent *n.* 指数，幂
base/power *n.* 底数/指数，幂
radical sign/root sign 根号
radical *n.* 根式
square root 平方根
cube root 立方根
product *n.* 乘积
common logarithm 常用对数

算数-集合

subset *n.* 子集
proper subset 真子集
union *n.* 合集，并集
intersection *n.* 交集

empty set 空集
solution set 解集（满足一个方程或方程组的所有解的集合叫做该方程或方程组的解集）
set of data/data set 数据集
set *n.* 集合
nonempty *adj.* 非空的
mutually exclusive 互斥的
juxtaposition *n.* 并列
disjoint *adj.* 不相交的
element *n.* 元素
event *n.* 事件
compound event 复合事件
independent event 相互独立事件
sufficient *adj.* 充分的
the sum of A and B/the total of A and B A与B的和
the union of A and B A与B的并集
the intersection of A and B A与B的交集
Venn diagram 韦恩图

算数-统计

average *n.* 平均数
mean *n.* 平均值；平均数；中数
maximum *n.* 最大值
minimum *n.* 最小值
median *n.* 中数，中点，中线，中值
mode *n.* 众数（在一系列数中出现最多的数）
arithmetic mean 算术平均数
weighted average 加权平均值
weighted mean 加权平均数
（是不同比重数据的平均数）
geometric mean 几何平均数
（是指n个观察值连乘积的n次方根）
range *n.* 值域（一系列数中最大值减最小值）
dispersion *n.* 差量，离差
standard deviation 标准方差
to the nearest/round to 四舍五入
round *v.* 保留整数，使成为整数；四舍五入
value *n.* 值，数值
probability *n.* 概率
distribution *n.*（频数或频率）分布

probability distribution 概率分布
frequency distribution 频数分布
normal distribution 正态分布
relative frequency distribution 相关频率分布
standard normal distribution 标准正态分布
factorial notation 阶乘
permutation *n.* 排列；置换
combination *n.* 组合
grid lines 坐标线，网格线
circle graph 饼图
boxplot *n.* 箱型图
bar graph/histogram 柱状图；直方图
at random 随机
random variable 随机变量
discrete random variable 离散随机变量
continuous random variable 连续随机变量
equally likely event 等可能事件
roll a fair die 掷骰子
heads up 正面朝上，头朝上
tails up 背面朝上，数字朝上
toss up 掷硬币；（胜败）机会相等

算数-数学运算

add/plus *v.* 加
subtract/minus *v.* 减
multiplication *n.* 乘
multiply/times *v.* 乘
divide *v.* 除
difference *n.* 差
sum *n.* 和
is equal to 等于
total *n.* 总数（用在加法中，相当于＋）；
　　总计（用于减法中，相当于－）
divisible *adj.* 可被整除的
division *n.* 除；部分
divided evenly 被整除
dividend *n.* 被除数
the difference of A and B A与B的差
the product of A and B A与B的乘积
prime factorization 质因数分解
less than 小于

greater than 大于
no less than 大于等于
no more than 小于等于
no solution 无解
interval *n.* 区间；间隔
invert *v.* 倒置，颠倒
inverse *n.* 倒数
invert a fraction 求分数的倒数
from...subtract 从…减…
be equivalent to 与…相等
increase by 增加了
increase to 增加到
decrease by 减少了
decrease to 减少到
identical *adj.* 相等的
divisibility *n.* 可约性，可除性

代数、方程、不等式

coefficient *n.* 系数
literal coefficient 字母系数
numerical coefficient 数字系数
term *n.* 项
constant term 常数项
quadratic *n.* 二次方程
equivalent equation 同解方程，等价方程
linear equation 线性方程
solution *n.*（方程的）解
inequality *n.* 不等式
expression *n.* 表达式
equation *n.* 方程式，等式
linear *adj.* 一次的，线性的
factorization *n.* 因数分解
function *n.* 函数
inverse function 反函数
trigonometric function 三角函数
complementary function 余函数
variable/variation *n.* 变量
domain *n.* 定义域
sequence *n.* 数列
sequence of numbers 数列
geometric progression 等比数列

arithmetic procession 等差数列
parentheses *n.* 括号
satify *v.* 使…成立
equivalent *adj.* 相等的

几何–直线、垂线

a line segment 线段
midpoint *n.* 中点
endpoint *n.* 端点
right angle 直角
perpendicular *n.* 垂线
perpendicular line 垂直线
perpendicular bisector 垂直平分线
parallel line 平行线
bisect *v.* 平分
partition *v.* 分割，分开
intercept *n.* 截距

几何–相交线和角

acute angle 锐角
obtuse angle 钝角
opposite angles 对角
vertical angle 对顶角
vertex angle 顶角
round angle 周角
straight angle 平角
included angle 夹角
alternate angle 内错角
interior angle 内角
central angle 圆心角
exterior angle 外角
supplementary angles 补角
complementary angles 余角
adjacent angle 邻角
a straight line 直线
angle bisector 角平分线
diagonal *n.* 对角线
intersect *v.* 相交
angle measurement in degrees 角度计算

几何–三角形

altitude *n.* （三角形的）高
arm *n.* 直角三角形的股
equilateral triangle 等边三角形
hypotenuse *n.* 斜边，直角三角形的斜边，弦
inscribed triangle 内接三角形
vertex *n.*（三角形等）顶角，顶点
isosceles triangle 等腰三角形
median of a triangle 三角形的中线
oblique *n.* 斜三角形
opposite *n.* 直角三角形中的对边
right triangle 直角三角形
scalene triangle 不等边三角形
similar triangles 相似三角形
leg *n.* 直角边
included side 夹边
Pythagorean theorem 勾股定理
congruent angles 全等角
congruent line segments 等长线段

几何–四边形和多边形

quadrilateral *n.* 四边形
pentagon *n.* 五边形
hexagon *n.* 六边形
heptagon *n.* 七边形
octagon *n.* 八边形
nonagon *n.* 九边形
decagon *n.* 十边形
polygon *n.* 多边形
multilateral *adj.* 多边的
regular polygon 正多边形
parallelogram *n.* 平行四边形
square *n.* 正方形
rectangle *n.* 长方形，矩形
rhombus *n.* 菱形
equilateral *adj.* 等边形的
trapezoid *n.* 梯形
congruent *adj.* 全等的
symmetric *adj.* 对称的

symmetry *n.* 对称，对称性
perimeter *n.* 周长
overlap *v.* 重叠
coordinate geometry 解析几何
corresponding side 对应边
area of a rectangle 长方形的面积
fold *n.* 对折

几何-圆

center of a circle 圆心
circle *n.* 圆形
concentric circles 同心圆
semicircle *n.* 半圆
circumference *n.* 圆周长，周长
chord *n.* 弦
radius *n.* 半径
diameter *n.* 直径
tangent *n.* 正切
inscribe *v.* 内切，内接
circumscribe *v.* 外切，外接
point of tangency 切点
tangent line 切线
circumscribed *adj.* 外接的
radian *n.* 弧度（弧长/半径）
arc *n.* 弧
segment of a circle 弧形
be parallel to 平行
be perpendicular to 垂直
be tangent to 与…相切

几何-立体几何

edge *n.* 边，棱
length *n.* 长
width *n.* 宽
depth *n.* 深度
volume *n.* 体积
surface area 表面积
cube *n.* 立方体
rectangular solid 长方体
regular solid/regular polyhedron 正多面体

cylinder *n.* 圆柱体
cone *n.* 圆锥
pyramid *n.* 角锥
sphere *n.* 球体
face *n.* 面
cross section 横截面
solid line 实线
dimension *n.* 维数
three-dimensional figure 三维图形
as illustrated 如图所示

几何-几何坐标

coordinate plane 坐标平面
coordinate system 坐标系
rectangular coordinate 直角坐标系
abscissa/x-coordinate *n.* 横坐标
ordinate *n.* 纵坐标
xy-planes *n.* xy平面坐标轴
number line 数轴
origin *n.* 原点
origin O 坐标起点O
axis *n.* 轴
x-axis *n.* X轴
y-axis *n.* y轴
intercept *n.* 截距
x-intercept *n.* x轴截距
quadrant *n.* 象限
four quadrants 四个象限
slope *n.* 斜率
a unique solution 唯一解
parabola *n.* 抛物线
linear function 线性函数

公式和换算

feet *n.* 英尺
1 billion = 10^9 十亿 = 10^9
1 dozen = 12 1打 = 12个
1 feet = 12 inches 1英尺 = 12英寸
1 gallon = 4 quarts 1加仑 = 4夸脱
1 hour = 3,600 seconds 1小时 = 3600秒

1 mile = 5,280 feet 1英里 = 5280英尺

1 million = 10^6 1百万 = 10^6

1 yard = 3 feet = 36 inches 1码
   = 3英尺 = 36英寸

0! = 1! = 1 0的阶乘为1

多边形内角和 = (n – 2) × 180°

$S_\triangle$ = 1/2底 × 高

$S_梯$ = (上底 + 下底) × h/2

圆周长 = 2 π r(r = radius半径)

$S_圆$ = π r^2

弧长 = (X°/360°) × 圆周长

$S_{立方体}$ = 6 a^2

$S_{圆柱}$ = 2 π r (r + h)

$V_长$ = 长 × 宽 × 高

$V_{圆柱}$ = π r^2 h

$V_{圆锥}$ = 1/3π r^2 · h

等差数列 $a_n = a_1 + (n – 1) d$ (d为常数)

等差求和 $S_n = \dfrac{n(a_1 + a_n)}{2} = na_1 + \dfrac{n(n-1)}{2}d$

等比数列 $a_n = a^1 q^{n-1}$

等比求和 $S_n = \dfrac{a_1(1 - q^n)}{1 - q}$ ($q \neq 1$)

利息 = principle(本金) × interest rate(利率)
   × time

句型

be fewer than 小于

be less than 小于

Twice as many A as B A是B的两倍

The ratio of A to B is … A比B(A/B)

A diminished by B / A minus B /
   from A subtract B A减去B

A multiplied by B A乘以B

A divided by B A/B

A divided into B B/A

A is 20% less than B (B–A)/B = 20%

A is 20% more than B (A–B)/B = 20%

A is a divisor of B A是B的除数(约数)(B/A)

be direct/inverse proportion at/to 成正/反比

A is subset of B A是B的子集

be more than twice as many X in A as in B

A里面的X是B里面X的2倍以上

l⊥m line/ l and m are perpendicular
   线l与线m垂直

be proportional to 与…成比例的

be drawn to scale 按比例绘制

实际应用

balance n. 余额

cost of production 产品成本

approximate cost 估算成本，约计成本

down payment 预付定金，首付款

installment n. 分期付款

discount rate 折扣率

charter v. 租赁，包租

charge v. 收费

principal n. 本金

simple interest 单利

compound interest 复利

gross profit 毛利

retail price 零售价

sales revenue 销售额

sales tax 营业税，销售税

property tax 财产税

list price 标价

margin n. 利润；付定金

mark up 涨价

purchase n. 销售数量

rebate n. 退还款，折扣

pointer n. 指针

project v. 预测，估计

corresponding value 对应值

mutual fund 共同基金

expected value 期望值，预期值

intensity n. 强度

intercalary year/leap year 闰年

lifetime n. 寿命

reflection n. 镜射

simplification n. 简化

simplified adj. 简化的

sketch n. 草图，示意图

survey n. 调查

466

solid color 纯色
concentration *n.* 浓度
weight *v.* 加重量于…，使变重
yield *n.* 产量
central tendency 集中趋势
tie *v.* 打平

其他

blot out 涂掉，删掉
buck *n.* 一美元；一澳元
dime *n.* 一角，十分
clockwise *adj.* 顺时针
constant rate 匀速的
cumulative *adj.* 累积的，附加的
defined *adj.* 已定义的

category *n.* 种类
in excess of 超过
in terms of 用…的话，用…来表示
in turn 依次，轮流
distinct point 不同点
nearest 0.1 percent 最接近0.1%
inclusive *adj.* 包括在内的
alongside *prep.* 和…一起
preceding *adj.* 在…前的，先前的
simultaneously *adv.* 同时
respectively *adv.* 各自地，分别地
per capita 按照人数分配的，每人
wall *n.* (容器的)壁
truckload *n.* 一卡车的容量
denote *v.* 表示

索　引

bleak / 459
blear / 366
bleary / 315
blemish / 299
blighted / 94
blindness / 146
bliss / 337
blissful / 148
blithe / 135
bloated / 344
blockade / 336
blockage / 394
blockbuster / 213
blooming / 268
blossom / 439
blueprint / 153
bluff / 75
blunt / 266
blur / 167
boast / 263
boastfulness / 173
bob / 445
boding / 289
boggle / 379
bogus / 298
boisterous / 73
bolster / 152
bombast / 318
bombastic / 112
bonanza / 237
bondage / 345
bonhomie / 328
bonny / 316
boo / 372
boom / 415
boon / 6
boor / 303
boost / 58
bootless / 134
boreal / 273
boredom / 39
boring / 348
bouffant / 254
bough / 364
boulder / 274
bouncing / 255
boundless / 195
bounteous / 382
bouquet / 387
bovine / 390
bowdlerize / 346
bowlegged / 92
brace / 322

bracelet / 387
bracing / 408
brackish / 326
brag / 431
braggart / 192
braid / 102
braise / 425
brake / 326
brassy / 69
brat / 348
brattish / 417
bravado / 188
bray / 388
brazen / 99
breach / 106
breed / 74
brevity / 214
brew / 263
bribe / 278
bricklayer / 374
bridle / 382
brilliant / 125
brink / 125
briny / 37
brisk / 266
bristling / 303
brittle / 441
brochure / 291
bromide / 432
brook / 57
browbeat / 436
brownish / 247
browse / 369
bruise / 269
bruit / 415
brusque / 299
brusqueness / 131
brutal / 288
brutality / 203
brute / 83
buck / 374
buckle / 3
bucolic / 426
budget / 325
buffer / 351
buffet / 323
buffoon / 396
bulge / 375
bulky / 46
bullion / 324
bully / 266
bumble / 256
bump / 396

bumper / 18
bumptious / 407
bungle / 294
buoy / 275
buoyant / 132
burdensome / 130
burgeon / 101
burial / 356
burlesque / 268
burning / 167
burnish / 382
burrow / 359
burst / 63
bust / 266
bustle / 297
butt / 339
buttress / 219
buxom / 308
bygone / 65
byline / 272
byproduct / 128
byzantine / 205
cabinet / 126
cacophonous / 133
cacophony / 267
cadence / 396
cadet / 428
cadge / 332
cajole / 425
calamity / 37
calculable / 163
calibrate / 416
callous / 119
callow / 415
calorie / 459
calumniate / 457
calumny / 177
camaraderie / 55
cameo / 407
camouflage / 264
canard / 314
canary / 340
candid / 121
candidacy / 255
candor / 229
cannily / 215
canny / 66
canon / 441
canonical / 429
canopy / 273
canorous / 406
cantankerous / 221
canvass / 455

canyon / 254
capacious / 258
caper / 451
capitulate / 198
caprice / 297
capricious / 149
capsule / 453
caption / 305
captious / 249
captivate / 319
captivating / 44
capture / 70
carbohydrate / 323
cardiac / 2
cardinal / 239
cardiologist / 301
careen / 277
caress / 361
careworn / 453
cargo / 403
caricature / 180
carnage / 216
carnivorous / 71
carouse / 278
carp / 297
carpenter / 385
carrion / 340
cartoon / 417
carve / 221
cast / 129
caste / 229
castigate / 44
casual / 460
catalog / 336
catalyze / 101
catastrophe / 42
category / 170
cater / 98
caterpillar / 150
catharsis / 324
catholic / 441
caucus / 333
caudal / 301
caulk / 328
causal / 174
caustic / 143
cauterize / 384
cautionary / 42
cautious / 229
cavalry / 285
cavil / 41
cavity / 85
cavort / 410

menthol / 283
mentor / 310
merit / 293
merited / 285
mesmerism / 256
mete / 380
metrical / 405
mettle / 427
microbe / 337
mien / 255
miff / 430
mighty / 296
militia / 399
milk / 442
mince / 322
mingle / 312
minnow / 428
mint / 377
minuet / 453
minutes / 347
minutia / 352
mirage / 284
mirth / 434
misalliance / 25
misanthrope / 229
misapprehension / 132
miscellany / 358
mischievous / 140
misconstrue / 157
miscreant / 362
misdirect / 223
miserable / 25
miserly / 263
misery / 178
misgiving / 422
misnomer / 182
misogyny / 247
misperceive / 370
misrepresentation / 415
misshapen / 284
missive / 332
mistral / 402
mite / 185
mitigant / 114
mitigate / 111
mnemonics / 356
moan / 427
moat / 279
mobile / 332
mobility / 342
mock / 335
mode / 282
moderately / 155

modernize / 224
modest / 9
modestly / 34
modicum / 296
modifier / 242
modify / 232
modish / 285
modulate / 246
moisten / 91
moldy / 376
molecular / 63
molest / 270
mollify / 351
mollycoddle / 303
molten / 10
moment / 377
momentarily / 186
momentous / 154
momentum / 356
monarch / 297
monetary / 223
monochromatic / 71
monocle / 443
monograph / 318
monolith / 141
monolithic / 302
monologue / 442
monopolize / 100
monopoly / 391
monotony / 175
monsoon / 415
monstrous / 456
monumental / 250
moody / 267
mope / 321
morale / 314
moralistic / 37
moratorium / 88
morbid / 158
mordant / 181
mores / 402
moribund / 409
morose / 135
morsel / 413
mortality / 7
mortgage / 400
mortification / 411
mortify / 125
mote / 336
motif / 155
motile / 297
motility / 282
motivate / 191

motley / 51
motto / 425
mourn / 297
mournful / 28
movement / 63
muck / 258
muddle / 63
muddy / 398
muffle / 434
muggy / 431
mulish / 323
mull / 367
multicellular / 139
multifaceted / 107
multifarious / 358
multiple / 116
multiplicity / 313
multiply / 206
mumble / 259
munch / 412
mundane / 110
municipality / 456
munificence / 131
munificent / 107
muniments / 307
munition / 445
mural / 6
murderous / 244
murky / 17
murmur / 322
muse / 318
mushy / 296
musket / 280
muster / 280
mutable / 78
mutate / 393
mute / 350
muted / 458
mutineer / 452
mutinous / 398
mutter / 318
muzzy / 389
myopia / 272
myopic / 251
myriad / 145
mystic / 95
mysticism / 236
mythic / 91
nadir / 281
nag / 317
naive / 367
naivete / 235
namby-pamby / 327

narcissism / 417
narcissist / 317
narcotic / 103
narrative / 238
narrow / 180
nasal / 417
nascent / 407
natal / 293
natty / 163
naturalistic / 33
nausea / 387
nauseate / 337
nautical / 361
navigate / 74
naysay / 388
naysayer / 393
nebulous / 125
necessitous / 373
needle / 326
nefarious / 255
negate / 118
negation / 306
negligence / 388
negligent / 52
negligible / 135
negligibly / 124
negotiable / 249
negotiate / 234
nemesis / 387
neolithic / 153
neologism / 327
neonate / 375
neophyte / 387
nerve / 453
nethermost / 356
nettle / 283
neurology / 445
neurosis / 291
neutralize / 305
neutron / 85
newsworthy / 226
nibble / 90
nifty / 271
niggle / 425
niggling / 292
nil / 269
nimble / 415
nip / 295
nocturnal / 132
noisome / 160
nomad / 270
nomadic / 239
nominal / 441

overlap / 231
overload / 212
overlook / 26
overpower / 149
overpowering / 105
overrate / 226
overreach / 440
override / 83
overriding / 291
overrule / 156
oversee / 306
overshadow / 230
oversight / 455
overstate / 232
overt / 175
overtax / 121
overthrow / 411
overtire / 162
overture / 346
overturn / 40
overweening / 305
overwhelm / 1
overwrought / 34
oxidize / 276
pacifist / 114
pacify / 253
pack / 222
packed / 120
pact / 316
paean / 104
pagan / 426
painstaking / 458
painstakingly / 162
palatable / 11
palate / 341
palatial / 398
palaver / 294
paleolithic / 243
palette / 385
pall / 257
palliate / 455
palliative / 444
pallid / 439
palpable / 20
palpitate / 343
paltry / 60
pamper / 382
pan / 254
panacea / 97
pancreas / 122
pandemonium / 378
pander / 430
pane / 402

pang / 362
panic / 317
panorama / 353
panoramic / 447
pantomime / 75
parable / 178
paradigm / 86
paradox / 220
 paradoxical / 113
paragon / 241
parallelism / 384
paralyze / 372
paramount / 198
paraphrase / 144
parasite / 178
parasitic / 44
parch / 318
pare / 454
parity / 318
parley / 376
parlous / 351
parochial / 301
parody / 217
parry / 428
parsimony / 198
partiality / 8
participate / 194
participation / 62
particular / 217
particularity / 139
particularize / 286
particulate / 184
partisan / 196
partition / 375
parturition / 288
passe / 318
passionate / 209
passive / 280
passively / 175
pastiche / 327
pastoral / 331
pastry / 439
patch / 365
patent / 383
pathetic / 361
pathological / 108
pathology / 456
patience / 234
patriarchal / 167
patriot / 369
patriotism / 311
patronage / 19
patronize / 83

patronizing / 26
paucity / 224
pauper / 394
pavid / 304
pawn / 439
peachy / 333
peak / 399
peaky / 317
pecan / 269
peck / 344
peckish / 409
peculate / 277
peculiar / 166
pedagogic / 217
pedagogy / 379
pedal / 439
pedant / 77
pedantry / 123
peddle / 386
pedestal / 327
pedestrian / 180
peek / 396
peel / 414
peep / 415
peer / 258
peerless / 41
peery / 451
peeve / 432
peevish / 98
pejorative / 217
pellucid / 278
pell-mell / 323
pelt / 370
penal / 92
penalize / 118
penalty / 381
penance / 454
penchant / 36
pendent / 357
pending / 29
pendulous / 430
pendulum / 355
penetrate / 383
penetrating / 103
penicillin / 324
penitent / 40
pensive / 191
penury / 329
perambulate / 409
perception / 135
perceptive / 200
perch / 358
percolate / 412

peremptory / 284
perennial / 174
perfervid / 90
perfidious / 130
perfidy / 456
perforate / 292
perfume / 143
perfunctory / 63
peril / 348
perilous / 9
periodic / 207
peripatetic / 96
peripheral / 27
periphery / 142
periphrastic / 302
perish / 292
perishable / 46
perishing / 417
perjure / 368
perjury / 366
perk / 444
perky / 369
permeable / 105
permeate / 180
permissive / 156
pernicious / 214
perpendicular / 139
perpetrate / 41
perpetual / 339
perpetuate / 245
perquisite / 96
persecute / 284
persevere / 95
persiflage / 435
persist / 220
persistence / 366
persnickety / 272
personally / 71
perspective / 177
perspicacious / 110
perspicuous / 20
perspire / 233
persuasive / 135
pertain / 293
pertinacious / 433
pertinent / 216
peruse / 418
pervade / 166
pervasive / 159
perverse / 281
pervert / 355
pervious / 433
pester / 427

487

pesticide / 103
pestilent / 402
pestilential / 202
pestle / 335
petal / 333
petitioner / 255
petrify / 438
petroleum / 51
pettish / 335
petty / 444
petulance / 350
petulant / 137
phantom / 301
pharisaic / 361
pharmaceutical / 124
pharmacology / 277
phenomenal / 215
philanthropic / 166
philately / 446
philistine / 222
philology / 330
philosophic / 70
phlegmatic / 103
phobia / 49
phoenix / 349
phonetic / 29
phony / 383
photosensitive / 28
photosynthesis / 138
physiological / 203
picayunish / 252
pictorial / 449
picturesque / 242
piddle / 299
piddling / 316
piebald / 345
piecemeal / 450
pied / 436
pierce / 309
piercing / 42
piety / 3
pigment / 438
pilfer / 306
pilgrim / 249
pillage / 316
pilot / 282
pinch / 356
pine / 29
pinpoint / 210
pious / 238
piousness / 107
piquant / 312
pique / 338

pirate / 347
pirouette / 410
piscatorial / 394
pitcher / 241
piteous / 367
pitfall / 111
pith / 362
pithiness / 363
pithy / 185
pitiful / 34
pitiless / 287
pittance / 281
pivot / 359
pivotal / 59
placard / 340
placate / 203
placebo / 176
placid / 53
plagiarize / 303
plague / 329
plain / 256
plainspoken / 25
plaintive / 40
plait / 298
plangent / 307
plank / 417
plaster / 439
plastic / 170
plateau / 269
platitude / 186
platitudinous / 2
platonic / 336
plaudit / 387
plausible / 239
plaza / 355
plead / 420
pleat / 454
plebeian / 422
pledge / 251
plenary / 419
plenitude / 367
plentitude / 307
pleonastic / 432
plethora / 136
pliable / 114
pliant / 128
plod / 339
plot / 179
plough / 452
ploy / 446
plumb / 140
plumber / 325
plummet / 342

plump / 234
plunder / 257
plunge / 164
pluralist / 314
plush / 287
poach / 307
pod / 286
podiatrist / 253
podium / 358
poignancy / 299
poignant / 144
poise / 158
poisonous / 353
poke / 352
polar / 176
polarize / 44
polemic / 316
polemical / 387
polish / 54
polite / 157
politically / 134
poll / 286
pollen / 27
pollinate / 5
pollster / 254
polymath / 435
pomposity / 148
pompous / 26
poncho / 381
ponder / 314
ponderable / 353
ponderous / 217
pontifical / 444
poohed / 426
pool / 404
pop / 195
populous / 127
porous / 246
portend / 45
portentous / 371
portray / 114
posit / 355
positive / 214
positiveness / 372
possess / 153
possessed / 9
postdate / 96
poster / 333
posthumous / 184
posthumously / 51
postiche / 439
postoperative / 10
postulate / 177

postwar / 75
potable / 144
potation / 355
potboiler / 289
potent / 67
potentate / 376
potential / 139
potentiate / 255
pother / 291
potpourri / 446
potshot / 184
potted / 154
pottery / 89
pouch / 452
pounce / 68
pound / 428
pragmatic / 93
prance / 436
prank / 418
prate / 384
preach / 447
preamble / 450
precarious / 162
precede / 182
precedent / 45
precept / 367
precipitate / 230
precipitous / 207
precise / 76
preclude / 31
precocious / 419
preconception / 216
precursor / 50
predator / 178
predatory / 110
predecessor / 164
predestine / 57
predetermine / 42
predictable / 51
predilection / 285
predispose / 175
predominant / 92
predominate / 120
preeminent / 173
preempt / 157
preen / 458
prefabricated / 33
preferably / 86
prefigure / 343
pregnant / 66
prehensile / 416
prehistoric / 71
preliminary / 59

renal / 295
renascent / 360
rend / 354
render / 195
rendering / 265
rendition / 442
renegade / 165
renege / 448
renewal / 45
renounce / 125
renovate / 337
renown / 163
renowned / 151
rent / 374
renunciate / 448
reparable / 103
reparation / 159
repartee / 257
repeal / 30
repel / 195
repellent / 20
repent / 352
repercussion / 333
repertoire / 26
repetition / 37
repetitious / 22
repetitive / 2
repine / 388
replenish / 142
replete / 50
replicate / 243
reportorial / 139
repose / 409
reprehend / 440
reprehensible / 154
represent / 156
repress / 108
repressed / 269
repressive / 223
reprieve / 354
reprimand / 75
reprisal / 60
reproach / 168
reprobate / 372
reproof / 259
repudiate / 9
repudiation / 244
repugnance / 188
repugnant / 69
repulse / 212
repulsion / 338
reputation / 435
repute / 79

requisite / 21
requite / 356
rescind / 153
rescission / 324
rescue / 58
resemble / 13
resent / 228
resentful / 95
resentment / 322
reside / 168
resident / 365
residential / 120
residue / 306
resign / 134
resignation / 140
resigned / 290
resilience / 383
resilient / 14
resonant / 249
resort / 100
resound / 401
resourceful / 365
respect / 58
respiratory / 4
respite / 179
resplendent / 260
responsive / 230
restatement / 238
restitution / 246
restive / 98
restiveness / 338
restless / 393
restoration / 64
restorative / 313
restore / 103
restored / 443
restrain / 273
restrict / 30
resume / 4
resurge / 137
resurgence / 446
resurrect / 198
resuscitate / 8
retain / 80
retaliate / 6
retaliation / 376
retard / 292
retch / 264
retention / 375
retentive / 1
reticent / 129
retire / 199
retiring / 421

retort / 251
retouch / 351
retrace / 365
retract / 38
retreat / 352
retrench / 360
retribution / 163
retrieve / 199
retrospect / 179
retrospective / 121
return / 117
reveal / 163
revelation / 14
revenge / 258
revenue / 334
reverberate / 48
revere / 178
reverential / 249
reverse / 238
reversible / 114
reversion / 415
revert / 105
revile / 199
revise / 102
revitalize / 126
revival / 234
revive / 379
revoke / 106
revolt / 351
revulsion / 353
reward / 248
rewarding / 319
rhapsodic / 146
rhetoric / 40
rhetorical / 161
rhubarb / 423
rhythmic / 177
ribald / 303
ribaldry / 110
ridge / 3
ridicule / 189
ridiculous / 231
rife / 438
rifle / 399
rift / 151
rig / 386
righteousness / 93
rigid / 7
rigidity / 226
rigor / 284
rigorous / 27
rile / 337
rind / 427

rinse / 449
riot / 257
riotous / 374
rip / 208
ripen / 455
ripple / 262
ritual / 56
ritzy / 300
rival / 8
rivalry / 40
rive / 362
riven / 400
rivet / 153
riveting / 279
roam / 162
robust / 237
rocky / 87
roe / 340
rollicking / 300
romance / 63
roseate / 23
rotate / 426
rote / 294
rotten / 458
roughen / 306
roundabout / 415
rout / 296
routine / 65
rove / 341
rowdy / 167
rubbery / 5
ruckus / 404
rudder / 323
ruddy / 366
rudimentary / 241
rue / 309
rueful / 207
ruffle / 437
rugged / 92
ruin / 137
rumble / 435
ruminant / 28
ruminate / 283
rumple / 275
rumpus / 284
runic / 332
rupture / 325
rural / 449
ruse / 364
rush / 119
rustic / 45
rustle / 416
ruthless / 233

496